Selected Works of
JOSEPH CONRAD

Selected Works of
JOSEPH CONRAD

SIX MAJOR STORIES

THREE COMPLETE NOVELS

AUTOBIOGRAPHICAL WRITINGS

EDITED BY STEVEN J. KASDIN

BARNES
&NOBLE
BOOKS
NEW YORK

This edition published by Barnes & Noble, Inc.

1994 Barnes & Noble Books

ISBN 1-56619-535-7

Book design by James Sarfati

Printed and bound in the United States of America

M 9 8 7 6 5 4 3 2 I

CONTENTS

INTRODUCTION

ne of England's greatest novelists, Joseph Conrad was that rare artist whose life is as fascinating as his work.

Everything about his life seemed improbable. That a native of a virtually landlocked region became a sailor was unlikely enough; that he switched careers to become a successful novelist was even more unusual. That he achieved greatness as a master prose stylist in a language he had never spoken before the age of twenty was nothing less than astonishing.

Josef Teodor Konrad Korzeniowski was born on December 3, 1857, in Berdichev, near Kiev, in what was then Russian Poland, now the Ukraine. His father, Apollo Nalecz Korzeniowski, was a poet and intellectual as well as an ardent Polish patriot and revolutionary. A leader in the insurrection againt Russian rule, he was arrested in 1861 by Russian Secret Police in Warsaw, where his family had moved the year before. Condemned to exile, he was sent to Vologda, in northern Russia. His wife, Evelina, voluntarily followed, bringing five-year-old Josef.

Both the weather and living conditions there were brutal: Conrad's mother died of tuberculosis after only four years. During this solitary period Conrad's father made a meager living translating Shakespeare, Hugo, and others into Polish. Young Josef became a voracious reader, escaping from his harsh reality into the world of literature. In 1868, with Apollo's health deteriorating, the Czarist government paroled him, and he brought Josef to Cracow.

But his health had been broken, and when he died the following year Josef went to live with his uncle, Tadeusz Bobrowsky, a lawyer who became Conrad's surrogate father. A warm and cultivated man, Bobrowsky provided the boy with love and a Catholic upbringing. He sent Conrad to the finest schools, first in Cracow, and later in Switzerland, and sponsored the youth's travel around the continent. On one of these trips, at the age of fourteen, while studying in Venice with a private tutor, Conrad first saw the ocean. It was to change his life.

For the next two years Conrad waged a battle with his uncle for the chance to go to sea. Bobrowsky early on had recognized his nephew's academic brilliance, and had hoped the boy would choose a profession such as law or medicine. But Conrad's persistence finally won out. In 1874 he joined the French merchant service and shipped out from Marseilles as an apprentice on the *Mont Blanc*, bound for Martinique.

For the first part of his sea career he sailed on French boats, learning basic seamanship. On some of these voyages he was involved in running contraband, probably guns, to Spain on at least one occasion, and along the coast of Venezuela on another. The latter experience was later fictionalized in his novel *Nostromo*.

After four years Conrad returned to Marseilles. Heavily in debt, he made at least one attempt at suicide. His uncle tried again to convince him to give up his life at sea, but Conrad refused. He did, however, make one change. As a sailor in the French merchant navy he was liable to conscription into the military, so he signed on as a seaman on a British freighter bound for Constantinople with a cargo of coal. After the long journey he landed at Lowestoft, England, in June 1878, speaking only a few words of the language he would eventually adopt. Twenty-one years old, Conrad began taking English lessons from a boat builder, and practicing his pronunciation by reading a newspaper out loud. Though he later became an acknowledged master of the language, he always spoke it with a decided foreign accent.

Overcoming disadvantages of nationality and language, Conrad worked for the next sixteen years as a seaman, rising through the ranks of the British merchant navy and obtaining his master's certificate in 1886. In the same year he became a British subject.

Two periods of Conrad's maritime career were of special significance to his later work as a writer. During the first, between 1882 and 1889, he sailed on the *Palestine*, the *Vidar*, and the *Otago*. As second mate of the *Palestine*, he first visited East Asia. It was to prove an ill-fated voyage, though one that gave him invaluable experience. Beset by gale winds, accidentally rammed by a steamer, and deserted by much of the crew, the ship was approaching the East Indies when the cargo of coal caught fire and the crew had to abandon ship for lifeboats. Conrad's first landfall in the East occurred only after two days in an open boat. Much of this adventure he later recounted, with only slight alterations, in his classic story "Youth." In 1888 he obtained his first and only command, the *Otago*, which he joined at Bangkok and sailed on a difficult, fever-ridden passage to Singapore and Australia.

During the second period, in 1890, Conrad traveled on the Congo River in West Africa. Before this trip, however, Conrad returned to England from the Far East and, while waiting for a ship, began writing his first novel, *Almayer's Folly*, about a half-caste he had met in Dutch Borneo. "If I had not got to know Almayer pretty well," he later wrote, " it is almost certain there would never have been a line of mine in print." He completed seven chapters before returning to sea on what was arguably his most important voyage.

In 1890 the Congo Free State was only five years old, and already notorious as a major site of colonial exploitation. The country was filled with adventurers and merce- naries seeking the rich bounty of its natural resources. What Conrad saw, did, and felt there are largely recorded in his most famous and important work, "Heart of Dark- ness." The title signifies not just the heart of Africa, then called the dark continent, but also the potential for evil and corruption that Conrad perceived in the hearts of all men. This vision is central not just to this story, but to his entire body of work and to his view of mankind in particular. His four months in the Congo affected his life in many ways. He suffered spiritual, psychological, and physical illness there, and for the rest of his life was afflicted with depression, recurring fevers, and gout.

Conrad returned to England in 1891. After a few more voyages he finally ended his twenty-year career at sea. This decision was prompted by the death of his uncle in 1894 and the small inheritance he received as a result. He finished *Almayer's Folly* later that year, and saw it published the following spring. It was the first time he used the name Conrad; he knew from experience that the name Korzeniowski was too difficult for the British to pronounce.

The novel was a commercial failure, but Conrad was determined nonetheless to be a full-time writer. His next novel, *An Outcast of the Islands*, followed a year later, and repeated the themes of the first: a foolish and superficial European character meeting the tragic consequences of his weaknesses in an exotic setting, this time the Malayan archipelago.

Conrad was upset by the public reaction to these two novels; not so much their disappointing sales, but the fact that critics labeled him as merely a writer of sea adventures. This was a frustration that was to dog him through his entire writing career. The works that followed in this period—*The Nigger of the "Narcissus"* (1897), *Lord Jim* (1900), *Youth* (1902), and *Typhoon* (1903)—seemed to confirm this opinion to his slowly growing public.

But to call Conrad merely a teller of adventure tales is to do him, and English literature, a great disservice. True, he set most of his stories either on the high seas or in exotic ports of call from Latin America to Asia. But Conrad used these settings, far from the constraints of "civilized" society, to examine both the great moral and political issues of the day—colonialism and racism, for example—and the core of the human soul. He had a dark view of human nature and its inherent capacity for folly and evil, and this view permeates all of his major fiction. Most of his lead characters have a tragic flaw, and in Conrad's works they either succumb to it, like Nostromo, or overcome it, like Lord Jim. Either way the depth of Conrad's thinking allowed his work to rise well above simple adventure fare.

In 1896 Conrad married the twenty-two-year-old Jessie George despite her family's opposition to the foreigner. They had two sons, Borys and John Alexander. Thereaf- ter, the family resided mainly in the southeast area of England, where Conrad's life was plagued by poor health, near poverty, and depression. The following year he published *The Nigger of the "Narcissus,"* and though it brought him little money, it established him as one of the preeminent writers of his generation. It was at this time that he also began solid friendships with Henry James, Stephen Crane, and F. N. Doubleday among other literary lights, allowing these few to see past the nervous and crusty exterior he maintained for most.

It was not until around 1910 that he began to reap some financial rewards from his writing; at this time, ironically, his best work had already been written. His novel *Chance* was successfully serialized in the *New York Herald* in 1912, and his next, *Victory*, was his most successful to date. Though the quality of his work in this later period was not up to his earlier efforts, he was, later in life, considered a "grand old man" of English letters. In April 1924 he refused an offer of knighthood from Prime Minister Ramsay MacDonald. On August 3 of that year he died of a heart attack and was buried at Canterbury.

In his own lifetime, Conrad went from obscurity to the peak of literary fame. He was praised for his power to depict the struggles between man and nature, civilization and savagery, and the good and evil within each individual. His reputation diminished somewhat just after his death, but enjoyed a revival in the 1930s. This renewed interest and appreciation will certainly continue far into the future. Conrad is now recognized as much more than a great teller of adventure tales. He will be long remembered as one of the greatest prose stylists of the English language.

Steven J. Kasdin
1994

JOSEPH CONRAD

CHRONOLOGY

1857	Born Josef Teodor Konrad Korzeniowski in Berdichev, Polish Ukraine, to Apollo and Evelina Korzeniowski.
1861	Family moves to Warsaw. Apollo arrested for anti-Russian conspiracy.
1862	Father sent into exile to Vologda, in northern Russia. Wife and son Josef follow.
1865	Evelina dies April 5, from tuberculosis due to brutal living conditions.
1869	Apollo Korzeniowski dies; Josef becomes the ward of his uncle, Tadeusz Bobrowsky, a lawyer.
1874	Leaves Poland for Marseilles to join French Merchant Navy.
1878	Attempts suicide, recovers, and joins British ship *Mavis*.
1881	First voyage to East Indies aboard *Palestine*.
1883	Shipwrecked when *Palestine* sinks.
1886	Naturalized as British citizen.
1888	First and only command, aboard the *Otago*.
1889	Returns to London, begins first novel, *Almayer's Folly*.
1890	Journeys to Congo; ill with dysentery, fever, and gout.

1895   *Almayer's Folly* published to poor sales.

1896   *An Outcast of the Islands.* Marries Jessie George, March 24.

1897   *The Nigger of the "Narcissus."*

1899   *Heart of Darkness* serialized.

1900   *Lord Jim.*

1902   *Youth,* a collection of stories.

1904   *Nostromo.*

1907   *The Secret Agent.*

1912   *A Personal Record* (autobiography).

1914   *Chance,* his first best-seller; finally enjoys some prosperity.

1923   Tours United States to great acclaim. Last sea voyage.

1924   Declines knighthood. Dies of sudden heart attack on August 3. Buried at Canterbury.

STORIES

Most of Conrad's stories were written in the middle part of his career, after the failures of his early novels and before the successes of his later ones. Like the novels, the majority of the stories arose from his experiences at sea or from tales he heard from other sailors during those years.

His stories are generally considerably longer than average for the genre; "Heart of Darkness" and "Typhoon" might be considered novellas. Like many of Conrad's other short stories, they are full of action and exotic ports of call, but they have a moral resonance usually found only in much longer works. Their appearance in English magazines in the first decade of this century began to establish Conrad as a literary and commercial success.

"Heart of Darkness" was originally intended to be a quickly written adventure story for the magazine market, which offered proportionately better pay than the market for full-length novels. It was first serialized in *Blackwood's* magazine beginning in February 1899. Arguably his most perfectly realized work, Conrad himself was initially disappointed with it, believing he had made the character of Kurtz "too symbolic."

"The Secret Sharer" contains some memories and impressions from Conrad's first command of a ship—the *Otago*, which sailed throughout southeast Asia—but the dramatic situation is imaginary. Written in 1909, it was published in book form in 1912 and became one of his most popular stories with both critics and readers.

Also based on his experiences aboard the *Otago*, "Typhoon" was written just after *Lord Jim*, in 1900, but was uniformly rejected by magazine publishers because of its then-shocking themes of barbarism and sexual desire. Published in book form in 1903, it stands as one of the most viscerally exciting stories he ever wrote.

Written in 1911, "Prince Roman" deals with the Polish revolutions of his youth and before. It is based on the career of Polish patriot and Siberian exile Prince Roman Sanguszk, a friend and revolutionary comrade of Conrad's paternal grandfather. The story did not appear in book form until 1925, the year after Conrad's death.

One of his earliest stories, "The Lagoon," was also one of his most poetic. Published in 1898, it is perhaps most unique for its religious imagery and emotion, though Conrad considered himself an atheist.

"Freya of the Seven Isles" was based on a story told him by Charles Marris, a seaman who married a Maori tribeswoman. Written in 1911 and published in 1912, it was Conrad's most successful story after "Typhoon," published a decade earlier.

HEART OF DARKNESS

The *Nellie*, a cruising yawl, swung to her anchor without a flutter of the sails, and was at rest. The flood had made, the wind was nearly calm, and being bound down the river, the only thing for it was to come to and wait for the turn of the tide.

The sea-reach of the Thames stretched before us like the beginning of an interminable waterway. In the offing the sea and the sky were welded together without a joint, and in the luminous space the tanned sails of the barges drifting up with the tide seemed to stand still in red clusters of canvas sharply peaked, with gleams of varnished spirits. A haze rested on the low shores that ran out to sea in vanishing flatness. The air was dark above Gravesend, and farther back still seemed condensed into a mournful gloom, brooding motionless over the biggest, and the greatest, town on earth.

The Director of Companies was our captain and our host. We four affectionately watched his back as he stood in the bows looking to seaward. On the whole river there was nothing that looked half so nautical. He resembled a pilot, which to a seaman is trustworthiness personified. It was difficult to realize his work was not out there in the luminous estuary, but behind him, within the brooding gloom.

Between us there was, as I have already said somewhere, the bond of the sea. Besides holding our hearts together through long periods of separation, it had the effect of making us tolerant of each other's yarns—and even convictions. The lawyer—the best of old fellows—had, because of his many years and many virtues, the only cushion on deck, and was lying on the only rug. The accountant had brought out already a box of dominoes, and was toying architecturally with the bones. Marlow sat cross-legged right aft, leaning against the mizzenmast. He had sunken cheeks, a yellow complexion, a straight back, an ascetic aspect, and, with his arms dropped, the palms of hands outwards, resembled an idol. The director, satisfied the anchor had good hold, made

5

his way aft and sat down amongst us. We exchanged a few words lazily. Afterwards there was silence on board the yacht. For some reason or other we did not begin that game of dominoes. We felt meditative, and fit for nothing but placid staring. The day was ending in a serenity of still and exquisite brilliance. The water shone pacifically; the sky, without a speck, was a benign immensity of unstained light; the very mist on the Essex marshes was like a gauzy and radiant fabric, hung from the wooded rises inland, and draping the low shores in diaphanous folds. Only the gloom to the west, brooding over the upper reaches, became more somber every minute, as if angered by the approach of the sun.

And at last, in its curved and imperceptible fall, the sun sank low, and from glowing white changed to a dull red without rays and without heat, as if about to go out suddenly, stricken to death by the touch of that gloom brooding over a crowd of men.

Forthwith a change came over the waters, and the serenity became less brilliant but more profound. The old river in its broad reach rested unruffled at the decline of day, after ages of good service done to the race that peopled its banks, spread out in the tranquil dignity of a waterway leading to the uttermost ends of the earth. We looked at the venerable stream not in the vivid flush of a short day that comes and departs forever, but in the august light of abiding memories. And indeed nothing is easier for a man who has, as the phrase goes, "followed the sea" with reverence and affection, than to evoke the great spirit of the past upon the lower reaches of the Thames. The tidal current runs to and fro in its unceasing service, crowded with memories of men and ships it had borne to the rest of home or to the battles of the sea. It had known and served all the men of whom the nation is proud, from Sir Francis Drake to Sir John Franklin, knights all, titled and untitled—the great knights-errant of the sea. It had borne all the ships whose names are like jewels flashing in the night of time, from the *Golden Hind* returning with her round flanks full of treasure, to be visited by the Queen's Highness and thus pass out of the gigantic tale, to the *Erebus* and *Terror*, bound on other conquests—and that never returned. It had known the ships and the men. They had sailed from Deptford, from Greenwich, from Erith—the adventurers and the settlers; kings' ships and the ships of men on 'Change; captains, admirals, the dark "interlopers" of the Eastern trade, and the commissioned "generals" of East India fleets. Hunters for gold or pursuers of fame, they all had gone out on that stream, bearing the sword, and often the torch, messengers of the might within the land, bearers of a spark from the sacred fire. What greatness had not floated on the ebb of that river into the mystery of an unknown earth! . . . The dreams of men, the seed of commonwealths, the germs of empires.

The sun set; the dusk fell on the stream, and lights began to appear along the shore. The Chapman lighthouse, a three-legged thing erect on a mud-flat, shone strongly. Lights of ships moved in the fairway—a great stir of lights going up and going down. And farther west on the upper reaches the place of the monstrous town was still marked ominously on the sky, a brooding gloom in sunshine, a lurid glare under the stars.

"And this also," said Marlow suddenly, "has been one of the dark places of the earth."

He was the only man of us who still "followed the sea." The worst that could be said of him was that he did not represent his class. He was a seaman, but he was a wanderer, too, while most seamen lead, if one may so express it, a sedentary life. Their minds are of the stay-at-home order, and their home is always with them—the ship; and so is their country—the sea. One ship is very much like another, and the sea is always the same. In the immutability of their surroundings the foreign shores, the foreign faces, the changing immensity of life, glide past, veiled not by a sense of mystery but by a slightly disdainful ignorance; for there is nothing mysterious to a seaman unless it be the sea itself, which is the mistress of his existence and as inscrutable as destiny. For the rest, after his hours of work, a casual stroll or a casual spree on shore suffices to unfold for him the secret of a whole continent, and generally he finds the secret not worth knowing. The yarns of seamen have a direct simplicity, the whole meaning of which lies within the shell of a cracked nut. But Marlow was not typical (if his propensity to spin yarns be excepted), and to him the meaning of an episode was not inside like a kernel but outside, enveloping the tale which brought it out only as a glow brings out a haze, in the likeness of one of these misty halos that sometimes are made visible by the spectral illumination of moonshine.

His remark did not seem at all surprising. It was just like Marlow. It was accepted in silence. No one took the trouble to grunt even; and presently he said, very slow:

"I was thinking of very old times, when the Romans first came here, nineteen hundred years ago—the other day. . . . Light came out of this river since—you say knights? Yes; but it is like a running blaze on a plain, like a flash of lightning in the clouds. We live in the flicker—may it last as long as the old earth keeps rolling! But darkness was here yesterday. Imagine the feelings of a commander of a fine—what d'ye call 'em?—trireme in the Mediterranean, ordered suddenly to the north; run overland across the Gauls in a hurry; put in charge of one of these craft the legionaries—a wonderful lot of handy men they must have been, too—used to build, apparently by the hundred, in a month or two, if we may believe what we read. Imagine him here—the very end of the world, a sea the color of lead, a sky the color of smoke, a kind of ship about as rigid as a concertina—and going up this river with stores, or orders, or what you like. Sandbanks, marshes, forests, savages—precious little to eat fit for a civilized man, nothing but Thames water to drink. No Falernian wine here, no going ashore. Here and there a military camp lost in a wilderness, like a needle in a bundle of hay—cold, fog, tempests, disease, exile, and death—death skulking in the air, in the water, in the bush. They must have been dying like flies here. Oh, yes—he did it. Did it very well, too, no doubt, and without thinking much about it either, except afterwards to brag of what he had gone through in his time, perhaps. They were men enough to face the darkness. And perhaps he was cheered by keeping his eye on a chance of promotion to the fleet at Ravenna by and by, if he had good friends in Rome and survived the awful climate. Or think of a decent young citizen in a toga—perhaps too much dice, you know—coming out here in the train of some prefect, or tax-gatherer, or trader even, to mend his fortunes. Land in a swamp, march through the woods, and in some inland post feel the savagery, the utter savagery, had closed round him—all that mysterious life of the wilderness that stirs in the forest, in the jungles, in the hearts of wild men. There's no initiation either into such mysteries. He has to live in the midst of the incomprehensible, which is also detestable. And it has a fascination, too, that goes to work upon him. The fascination of the abomination— you know, imagine the growing regrets, the longing to escape, the powerless disgust, the surrender, the hate."

He paused.

"Mind," he began again, lifting one arm from the elbow, the palm of the hand outwards, so that, with his legs folded before him, he had the pose of a Buddha preaching in European clothes and without a lotus flower—"Mind, none of us would feel exactly like this. What saves us is efficiency—the devotion to efficiency. But these chaps were not much account, really. They were no colonists; their administration was merely a squeeze, and nothing more, I suspect. They were conquerors, and for that you want only brute force—nothing to boast of, when you have it, since your strength is just an accident arising from the weakness of others. They grabbed what they could get for the sake of what was to be got. It was just robbery with violence, aggravated murder on a great scale, and men going at it blind—as is very proper for those who tackle a darkness. The conquest of the earth, which mostly means the taking it away from those who have a different complexion or slightly flatter noses than ourselves, is not a pretty thing when you look into it too much. What redeems it is the idea only. An idea at the back of it; not a sentimental pretence but an idea; and an unselfish belief in the idea—something you can set up, and bow down before, and offer a sacrifice to. . . ."

He broke off. Flames glided in the river, small green flames, red flames, white flames, pursuing, overtaking, joining, crossing each other—then separating slowly or hastily. The traffic of the great city went on in the deepening night upon the sleepless river. We looked on, waiting patiently—there was nothing else to do till the end of the flood; but it was only after a long silence, when he said, in a hesitating voice, "I suppose you fellows remember I did once turn fresh-water sailor for a bit," that we knew we were fated, before the ebb began to run, to hear about one of Marlow's inconclusive experiences.

"I don't want to bother you much with what happened to me personally," he began, showing in this remark the weakness of many tellers of tales who seem so often unaware of what their audience would best like to hear; "yet to understand the effect of it on me you ought to know how I got out there, what I saw, how I went up that river to the place where I first met the poor chap. It was the farthest point of navigation and the culminating point of my experience. It seemed somehow to throw a kind of light on everything about me—and into my thoughts. It was somber enough, too—and pitiful—not extraordinary in any way—not very clear either. No, not very clear. And yet it seemed to throw a kind of light.

"I had then, as you remember, just returned to London after a lot of Indian Ocean,

Pacific, China Seas—a regular dose of the East—six years or so, and I was loafing about, hindering you fellows in your work and invading your homes, just as though I had got a heavenly mission to civilize you. It was very fine for a time, but after a bit I did get tired of resting. Then I began to look for a ship—I should think the hardest work on earth. But the ships wouldn't even look at me. And I got tired of that game, too.

"Now when I was a little chap I had a passion for maps. I would look for hours at South America, or Africa, or Australia, and lose myself in all the glories of exploration. At that time there were many blank spaces on the earth, and when I saw one that looked particularly inviting on a map (but they all look that) I would put my finger on it and say, 'When I grow up I will go there.' The North Pole was one of these places, I remember. Well, I haven't been there yet, and shall not try now. The glamor's off. Other places were scattered about the Equator, and in every sort of latitude all over the two hemispheres. I have been in some of them, and . . . well, we won't talk about that. But there was one yet—the biggest, the most blank, so to speak—that I had a hankering after.

"True, by this time it was not a blank space any more. It had got filled since my boyhood with rivers and lakes and names. It had ceased to be a blank space of delightful mystery—a white patch for a boy to dream gloriously over. It had become a place of darkness. But there was in it one river especially, a mighty big river, that you could see on the map, resembling an immense snake uncoiled, with its head in the sea, its body at rest curving afar over a vast country, and its tail lost in the depths of the land. And as I looked at the map of it in a shop window, it fascinated me as a snake would a bird—a silly little bird. Then I remembered there was a big concern, a company for trade on that river. Dash it all! I thought to myself, they can't trade without using some kind of craft on that lot of fresh water—steamboats! Why shouldn't I try to get charge of one? I went on along Fleet Street, but could not shake off the idea. The snake had charmed me.

"You understand it was a continental concern, that trading society; but I have a lot of relations living on the continent, because it's cheap and not so nasty as it looks, they say.

"I am sorry to own I began to worry them. This was already a fresh departure for me. I was not used to get things that way, you know. I always went my own road and on my own legs where I had a mind to go. I wouldn't have believed it of myself; but, then—you see—I felt somehow I must get there by hook or by crook. So I worried them. The men said 'My dear fellow,' and did nothing. Then—would you believe it? —I tried the women. I, Charlie Marlow, set the women to work—to get a job. Heavens! Well, you see, the notion drove me. I had an aunt, a dear enthusiastic soul. She wrote: 'It will be delightful. I am ready to do anything, anything for you. It is a glorious idea. I know the wife of a very high personage in the administration, and also a man who has lots of influence with,' etc., etc. She was determined to make no end of fuss to get me appointed skipper of a river steamboat, if such was my fancy.

"I got my appointment—of course; and got it very quick. It appears the company

had received news that one of their captains had been killed in a scuffle with the
natives. This was my chance, and it made me the more anxious to go. It was only
months and months afterwards, when I made the attempt to recover what was left of
the body, that I heard the original quarrel arose from a misunderstanding about some
hens. Yes, two black hens. Fresleven—that was the fellow's name, a Dane—thought
himself wronged somehow in the bargain, so he went ashore and started to hammer
the chief of the village with a stick. Oh, it didn't surprise me in the least to hear this,
and at the same time to be told that Fresleven was the gentlest, quietest creature that
ever walked on two legs. No doubt he was; but he had been a couple of years already
out there engaged in the noble cause, you know, and he probably felt the need at last
of asserting his self-respect in some way. Therefore he whacked the old nigger mercilessly, while a big crowd of his people watched him, thunderstruck, till some man—I
was told the chief's son—in desperation at hearing the old chap yell, made a tentative
jab with a spear at the white man—and of course it went quite easy between the
shoulder blades. Then the whole population cleared into the forest, expecting all kinds
of calamities to happen, while, on the other hand, the steamer Fresleven commanded
left also in a bad panic, in charge of the engineer, I believe. Afterwards nobody seemed
to trouble much about Fresleven's remains, till I got out and stepped into his shoes. I
couldn't let it rest, though; but when an opportunity offered at last to meet my
predecessor, the grass growing through his ribs was tall enough to hide his bones.
They were all there. The supernatural being had not been touched after he fell. And
the village was deserted, the huts gaped black, rotting, all askew within the fallen
enclosures. A calamity had come to it, sure enough. The people had vanished. Mad
terror had scattered them, men, women, and children, through the bush, and they had
never returned. What became of the hens I don't know either. I should think the cause
of progress got them, anyhow. However, through this glorious affair I got my appointment, before I had fairly begun to hope for it.

"I flew around like mad to get ready, and before forty-eight hours I was crossing
the Channel to show myself to my employers, and sign the contract. In a very few
hours I arrived in a city that always makes me think of a whited sepulcher. Prejudice
no doubt. I had no difficulty in finding the company's offices. It was the biggest thing
in the town, and everybody I met was full of it. They were going to run an oversea
empire, and make no end of coin by trade.

"A narrow and deserted street in deep shadow, high houses, innumerable windows
with venetian blinds, a dead silence, grass sprouting between the stones, imposing
carriage archways right and left, immense double doors standing ponderously ajar. I
slipped through one of these cracks, went up a swept and ungarnished staircase, as arid
as a desert, and opened the first door I came to. Two women, one fat and the other
slim, sat on straw-bottomed chairs, knitting black wool. The slim one got up and
walked straight at me—still knitting with downcast eyes—and only just as I began to
think of getting out of her way, as you would for a somnambulist, stood still, and
looked up. Her dress was as plain as an umbrella-cover, and she turned round without
a word and preceded me into a waiting room. I gave my name, and looked about. Deal

table in the middle, plain chairs all round the walls, on one end a large shining map, marked with all the colors of a rainbow. There was a vast amount of red—good to see at any time, because one knows that some real work is done in there, a deuce of a lot of blue, a little green, smears of orange, and, on the East Coast, a purple patch, to show where the jolly pioneers of progress drink the jolly lager beer. However, I wasn't going into any of these. I was going into the yellow. Dead in the center. And the river was there—fascinating—deadly—like a snake. Ough! A door opened, a white-haired secretarial head, but wearing a compassionate expression, appeared, and a skinny fore-finger beckoned me into the sanctuary. Its light was dim, and a heavy writing desk squatted in the middle. From behind that structure came out an impression of pale plumpness in a frock coat. The great man himself. He was five feet six, I should judge, and had his grip on the handle-end of ever so many millions. He shook hands, I fancy, murmured vaguely, was satisfied with my French. *Bon voyage.*

"In about forty-five seconds I found myself again in the waiting room with the compassionate secretary, who, full of desolation and sympathy, made me sign some document. I believe I undertook amongst other things not to disclose any trade secrets. Well, I am not going to.

"I began to feel slightly uneasy. You know I am not used to such ceremonies, and there was something ominous in the atmosphere. It was just as though I had been let into some conspiracy—I don't know—something not quite right; and I was glad to get out. In the outer room the two women knitted black wool feverishly. People were arriving, and the younger one was walking back and forth introducing them. The old one sat on her chair. Her flat cloth slippers were propped up on a foot-warmer, and a cat reposed on her lap. She wore a starched white affair on her head, had a wart on one cheek, and silver-rimmed spectacles hung on the tip of her nose. She glanced at me above the glasses. The swift and indifferent placidity of that look troubled me. Two youths with foolish and cheery countenances were being piloted over, and she threw at them the same quick glance of unconcerned wisdom. She seemed to know all about them and about me, too. An eerie feeling came over me. She seemed uncanny and fateful. Often far away there I thought of these two, guarding the door of darkness, knitting black wool as for a warm pall, one introducing, introducing continuously to the unknown, the other scrutinizing the cheery and foolish faces with unconcerned old eyes. *Ave!* Old knitter of black wool. *Morituri te salutant.* Not many of those she looked at ever saw her again—not half, by a long way.

"There was yet a visit to the doctor. 'A simple formality,' assured me the secretary, with an air of taking an immense part in all my sorrows. Accordingly a young chap wearing his hat over the left eyebrow, some clerk I suppose—there must have been clerks in the business, though the house was as still as a house in a city of the dead—came from somewhere upstairs, and led me forth. He was shabby and careless, with ink-stains on the sleeves of his jacket, and his cravat was large and billowy, under a chin shaped like the toe of an old boot. It was a little too early for the doctor, so I proposed a drink, and thereupon he developed a vein of joviality. As we sat over our vermouths he glorified the company's business, and by and by I expressed casually my surprise at him not going out there. He became very cool and collected all at once. 'I am not such a fool as I look, quoth Plato to his disciples,' he said sententiously, emptied his glass with great resolution, and we rose.

"The old doctor felt my pulse, evidently thinking of something else the while. 'Good, good for there,' he mumbled, and then with a certain eagerness asked me whether I would let him measure my head. Rather surprised, I said 'yes,' when he produced a thing like calipers and got the dimensions back and front and every way, taking notes carefully. He was an unshaven little man in a threadbare coat like a gaberdine, with his feet in slippers, and I thought him a harmless fool. 'I always ask leave, in the interests of science, to measure the crania of those going out there,' he said. 'And when they come back, too?' I asked. 'Oh, I never see them,' he remarked; 'and, moreover, the changes take place inside, you know.' He smiled, as if at some quiet joke. 'So you are going out there. Famous. Interesting, too.' He gave me a searching glance, and made another note. 'Ever any madness in your family?' he asked, in a matter-of-fact tone. I felt very annoyed. 'Is that question in the interests of science, too?' 'It would be,' he said, without taking notice of my irritation, 'interesting for science to watch the mental changes of individuals, on the spot, but . . .' 'Are you an alienist?' I interrupted. 'Every doctor should be—a little,' answered that original, imperturbably. 'I have a little theory which you messieurs who go out there must help me to prove. This is my share in the advantages my country shall reap from the possession of such a magnificent dependency. The mere wealth I leave to others. Pardon my questions, but you are the first Englishman coming under my observation. . . .' I hastened to assure him I was not in the least typical. 'If I were,' said I, 'I wouldn't be talking like this with you.' 'What you say is rather profound, and probably erroneous,' he said, with a laugh. 'Avoid irritation more than exposure to the sun. Adieu. How do you English say, eh? Good-by. Ah! Good-by. Adieu. In the tropics one must before everything keep calm.' . . . He lifted a warning forefinger. . . . '*Du calme, du calme. Adieu.*'

"One thing more remained to do—say good-by to my excellent aunt. I found her triumphant. I had a cup of tea—the last decent cup of tea for many days—and in a room that most soothingly looked just as you would expect a lady's drawing room to look, we had a long quiet chat by the fireside. In the course of these confidences it became quite plain to me I had been represented to the wife of the high dignitary, and goodness knows to how many more people besides, as an exceptional and gifted creature—a piece of good fortune for the company—a man you don't get hold of every day. Good heavens! and I was going to take charge of a two-penny-half-penny river steamboat with a penny whistle attached! It appeared, however, I was also one of the Workers, with a capital—you know. Something like an emissary of light, something like a lower sort of apostle. There had been a lot of such rot let loose in print and talk just about that time, and the excellent woman, living right in the rush of all that humbug, got carried off her feet. She talked about 'weaning those ignorant millions from their horrid ways,' till, upon my word, she made me quite uncomfortable. I ventured to hint that the company was run for profit.

" 'You forget, dear Charlie, that the laborer is worthy of his hire,' she said, brightly. It's queer how out of touch with truth women are. They live in a world of their own, and there had never been anything like it, and never can be. It is too beautiful altogether, and if they were to set it up it would go to pieces before the first sunset. Some confounded fact we men have been living contentedly with ever since the day of creation would start up and knock the whole thing over.

"After this I got embraced, told to wear flannel, be sure to write often, and so on— and I left. In the street—I don't know why—a queer feeling came to me that I was an impostor. Odd thing that I, who used to clear out for any part of the world at twenty-four hours' notice, with less thought than most men give to the crossing of a street, had a moment—I won't say of hesitation, but of startled pause, before this common-place affair. The best way I can explain it to you is by saying that, for a second or two, I felt as though, instead of going to the center of a continent, I were about to set off for the center of the earth.

"I left in a French steamer, and she called in every blamed port they have out there, for, as far as I could see, the sole purpose of landing soldiers and customhouse officers. I watched the coast. Watching a coast as it slips by the ship is like thinking about an enigma. There it is before you—smiling, frowning, inviting, grand, mean, insipid, or savage, and always mute with an air of whispering, Come and find out. This one was almost featureless, as if still in the making, with an aspect of monotonous grimness. The edge of a colossal jungle, so dark-green as to be almost black, fringed with white surf, ran straight, like a ruled line, far, far away along a blue sea whose glitter was blurred by a creeping mist. The sun was fierce, the land seemed to glisten and drip with steam. Here and there grayish-whitish specks showed up clustered inside the white surf, with a flag flying above them perhaps. Settlements some centuries old, and still no bigger than pinheads on the untouched expanse of their background. We pounded along, stopped, landed soldiers; went on, landed customhouse clerks to levy toll in what looked like a God-forsaken wilderness, with a tin shed and a flagpole lost in it; landed more soldiers—to take care of the customhouse clerks, presumably. Some, I heard, got drowned in the surf; but whether they did or not, nobody seemed particularly to care. They were just flung out there, and on we went. Every day the coast looked the same, as though we had not moved; but we passed various places— trading places—with names like Gran' Bassam, Little Popo; names that seemed to belong to some sordid farce acted in front of a sinister back-cloth. The idleness of a passenger, my isolation amongst all these men with whom I had no point of contact, the oily and languid sea, the uniform somberness of the coast, seemed to keep me away from the truth of things, within the toil of a mournful and senseless delusion. The voice of the surf heard now and then was a positive pleasure, like the speech of a brother. It was something natural, that had its reason, that had a meaning. Now and then a boat from the shore gave one a momentary contact with reality. It was paddled by black fellows. You could see from afar the white of their eyeballs glistening. They shouted, sang; their bodies streamed with perspiration; they had faces like grotesque masks—these chaps; but they had bone, muscle, a wild vitality, an intense energy of movement, that was as natural and true as the surf along their coast. They wanted no excuse for being there. They were a great comfort to look at. For a time I would feel I belonged still to a world of straightforward facts; but the feeling would not last long. Something would turn up to scare it away. Once, I remember, we came upon a man-of-war anchored off the coast. There wasn't even a shed there, and she was shelling the bush. It appears the French had one of their wars going on thereabouts. Her ensign dropped limp like a rag; the muzzles of the long six-inch guns stuck out all over the low hull; the greasy, slimy swell swung her up lazily and let her down, swaying her thin masts. In the empty immensity of earth, sky, and water, there she was, incomprehensible, firing into a continent. Pop, would go one of the six-inch guns; a small flame would dart and vanish, a little white smoke would disappear, a tiny projectile would give a feeble screech—and nothing happened. Nothing could happen. There was a touch of insanity in the proceeding, a sense of lugubrious drollery in the sight; and it was not dissipated by somebody on board assuring me earnestly there was a camp of natives—he called them enemies!—hidden out of sight somewhere.

"We gave her her letters (I heard the men in that lonely ship were dying of fever at the rate of three a day) and went on. We called at some more places with farcical names, where the merry dance of death and trade goes on in a still and earthly atmosphere as of an overheated catacomb, all along the formless coast bordered by dangerous surf, as if Nature herself had tried to ward off intruders; in and out of rivers, streams of death in life, whose banks were rotting into mud, whose waters, thickened into slime, invaded the contorted mangroves, that seemed to writhe at us in the extremity of an impotent despair. Nowhere did we stop long enough to get a particularized impression, but the general sense of vague and oppressive wonder grew upon me. It was like a weary pilgrimage amongst hints for nightmares.

"It was upward of thirty days before I saw the mouth of the big river. We anchored off the seat of the government. But my work would not begin till some two hundred miles farther on. So as soon as I could I made a start for a place thirty miles higher up.

"I had my passage on a little seagoing steamer. Her captain was a Swede, and knowing me for a seaman, invited me on the bridge. He was a young man, lean, fair, and morose, with lanky hair and a shuffling gait. As we left the miserable little wharf, he tossed his head contemptuously at the shore. 'Been living there?' he asked. I said, 'Yes.' 'Fine lot these government chaps—are they not?' he went on, speaking English with great precision and considerable bitterness. 'It is funny what some people will do for a few francs a month. I wonder what becomes of that kind when it goes up country?' I said to him I expected to see that soon. 'So-o-o!' he exclaimed. He shuffled athwart, keeping one eye ahead vigilantly. 'Don't be too sure,' he continued. 'The other day I took up a man who hanged himself on the road. He was a Swede, too.' 'Hanged himself! Why, in God's name?' I cried. He kept on looking out watchfully. 'Who knows? The sun too much for him, or the country perhaps.'

"At last we opened a reach. A rocky cliff appeared, mounds of turned-up earth by the shore, houses on a hill, others with iron roofs, amongst a waste of excavations, or hanging to the declivity. A continuous noise of the rapids above hovered over this scene of inhabited devastation. A lot of people, mostly black and naked, moved about like ants. A jetty projected into the river. A blinding sunlight drowned all this at times in a sudden recrudescence of glare. 'There's your company's station,' said the Swede, pointing to three wooden barrack-like structures on the rocky slope. 'I will send your things up. Four boxes did you say? So. Farewell.'

"I came upon a boiler wallowing in the grass, then found a path leading up the hill. It turned aside for the boulders, and also for an undersized railway truck lying there on its back with its wheels in the air. One was off. The thing looked as dead as the carcass of some animal. I came upon more pieces of decaying machinery, a stack of rusty rails. To the left a clump of trees made a shady spot, where dark things seemed to stir feebly. I blinked, the path was steep. A horn tooted to the right, and I saw the black people run. A heavy and dull detonation shook the ground, a puff of smoke came out of the cliff, and that was all. No change appeared on the face of the rock. They were building a railway. The cliff was not in the way or anything; but this objectless blasting was all the work going on.

"A slight clinking behind me made me turn my head. Six black men advanced in a file, toiling up the path. They walked erect and slow, balancing small baskets full of earth on their heads, and the clink kept time with their footsteps. Black rags were wound round their loins, and the short ends behind waggled to and fro like tails. I could see every rib, the joints of their limbs were like knots in a rope; each had an iron collar on his neck, and all were connected together with a chain whose bights swung between them, rhythmically clinking. Another report from the cliff made me think suddenly of that ship of war I had seen firing into a continent. It was the same kind of ominous voice; but these men could by no stretch of imagination be called enemies. They were called criminals, and the outraged law, like the bursting shells, had come to them, an insoluble mystery from the sea. All their meager breasts panted together, the violently dilated nostrils quivered, the eyes stared stonily uphill. They passed me within six inches, without a glance, with that complete, deathlike indifference of unhappy savages. Behind this raw matter one of the reclaimed, the product of the new forces at work, strolled despondently, carrying a rifle by its middle. He had a uniform jacket with one button off, and seeing a white man on the path, hoisted his weapon to his shoulder with alacrity. This was simple prudence, white men being so much alike at a distance that he could not tell who I might be. He was speedily reassured, and with a large, white, rascally grin, and a glance at his charge, seemed to take me into partnership in his exalted trust. After all, I also was a part of the great cause of these high and just proceedings.

"Instead of going up, I turned and descended to the left. My idea was to let that chain gang get out of sight before I climbed the hill. You know I am not particularly tender; I've had to strike and to fend off. I've had to resist and to attack sometimes— that's only one way of resisting—without counting the exact cost, according to the demands of such sort of life as I had blundered into. I've seen the devil of violence, and the devil of greed, and the devil of hot desire; but, by all the stars! these were strong, lusty, red-eyed devils, that swayed and drove men—men, I tell you. But as I stood on this hillside, I foresaw that in the blinding sunshine of that land I would become acquainted with a flabby, pretending, weak-eyed devil of a rapacious and pitiless folly. How insidious he could be, too, I was only to find out several months later and a thousand miles farther. For a moment I stood appalled, as though by a warning. Finally I descended the hill, obliquely, towards the trees I had seen.

"I avoided a vast artificial hole somebody had been digging on the slope, the purpose of which I found it impossible to divine. It wasn't a quarry or a sandpit, anyhow. It was just a hole. It might have been connected with the philanthropic desire of giving the criminals something to do. I don't know. Then I nearly fell into a very narrow ravine, almost no more than a scar in the hillside. I discovered that a lot of imported drainage pipes for the settlement had been tumbled in there. There wasn't one that was not broken. It was a wanton smash-up. At last I got under the trees. My purpose was to stroll into the shade for a moment; but no sooner within than it seemed to me I had stepped into the gloomy circle of some inferno. The rapids were near, and an uninterrupted, uniform, headlong, rushing noise filled the mournful stillness of the grove, where not a breath stirred, not a leaf moved, with a mysterious sound—as though the tearing pace of the launched earth had suddenly become audible.

"Black shapes crouched, lay, sat between the trees leaning against the trunks, cling-ing to the earth, half coming out, half effaced within the dim light, in all the attitudes of pain, abandonment, and despair. Another mine on the cliff went off, followed by a slight shudder of the soil under my feet. The work was going on. The work! And this the place where some of the helpers had withdrawn to die.

"They were dying slowly—it was very clear. They were not enemies, they were not criminals, they were nothing earthly now, nothing but black shadows of disease and starvation, lying confusedly in the greenish gloom. Brought from all the recesses of the coast in all the legality of time contracts, lost in uncongenial surroundings, fed on unfamiliar food, they sickened, became inefficient, and were then allowed to crawl away and rest. These moribund shapes were free as air—and nearly as thin. I began to distinguish the gleam of the eyes under the trees. Then, glancing down, I saw a face near my hand. The black bones reclined at full length with one shoulder against the tree, and slowly the eyelids rose and the sunken eyes looked up at me, enormous and vacant, a kind of blind, white flicker in the depths of the orbs, which died out slowly. The man seemed young—almost a boy—but you know with them it's hard to tell. I found nothing else to do but to offer him one of my good Swede's ship's biscuits I had in my pocket. The fingers closed slowly on it and held—there was no other movement and no other glance. He had tied a bit of white worsted round his neck— Why? Where did he get it? Was it a badge—an ornament—a charm—a propitiatory act? Was there any idea at all connected with it? It looked startling round his black neck, this bit of white thread from beyond the seas.

"Near the same tree two more bundles of acute angles sat with their legs drawn up. One, with his chin propped on his knees, stared at nothing, in an intolerable and appalling manner; his brother phantom rested its forehead, as if overcome with a great weariness; and all about others were scattered in every pose of contorted collapse, as in some picture of a massacre or a pestilence. While I stood horror-struck, one of these creatures rose to his hands and knees, and went off on all fours towards the river to drink. He lapped out of his hand, then sat up in the sunlight, crossing his shins in front of him, and after a time let his wooly head fall on his breastbone.

"I didn't want any more loitering in the shade, and I made haste towards the station. When near the buildings I met a white man, in such an unexpected elegance of getup that in the first moment I took him for a sort of vision. I saw a high starched collar, white cuffs, a light alpaca jacket, snowy trousers, a clear necktie, and varnished boots. No hat. Hair parted, brushed, oiled, under a green-lined parasol held in a big white hand. He was amazing, and had a penholder behind his ear.

"I shook hands with this miracle, and I learned he was the company's chief accountant, and that all the bookkeeping was done at this station. He had come out for a moment, he said, 'to get a breath of fresh air.' The expression sounded wonderfully odd, with its suggestion of sedentary desk life. I wouldn't have mentioned the fellow to you at all, only it was from his lips that I first heard the name of the man who is so indissolubly connected with the memories of that time. Moreover, I respected the fellow. Yes; I respected his collars, his vast cuffs, his brushed hair. His appearance was certainly that of a hairdresser's dummy; but in the great demoralization of the land he kept up his appearance. That's backbone. His starched collars and got-up shirt fronts were achievements of character. He had been out nearly three years; and, later, I could not help asking him how he managed to sport such linen. He had just the faintest blush, and said modestly, 'I've been teaching one of the native women about the station. It was difficult. She had a distaste for the work.' Thus this man had truly accomplished something. And he was devoted to his books, which were in apple-pie order.

"Everything else in the station was in a muddle—heads, things, buildings. Strings of dusty niggers with splay feet arrived and departed; a stream of manufactured goods, rubbishy cottons, beads, and brass wire set into the depths of darkness, and in return came a precious trickle of ivory.

"I had to wait in the station for ten days—an eternity. I lived in a hut in the yard, but to be out of the chaos I would sometimes get into the accountant's office. It was built of horizontal planks, and so badly put together that, as he bent over his high desk, he was barred from the neck to heels with narrow strips of sunlight. There was no need to open the big shutter to see. It was hot there, too; big flies buzzed fiendishly, and did not sting, but stabbed. I sat generally on the floor, while, of faultless appearance (and even slightly scented), perching on a high stool, he wrote, he wrote. Sometimes he stood up for exercise. When a truckle bed with a sick man (some invalid agent from upcountry) was put in there, he exhibited a gentle annoyance. 'The groans of this sick person,' he said, 'distract my attention. And without that it is extremely difficult to guard against clerical errors in this climate.'

"One day he remarked, without lifting his head, 'In the interior you will no doubt meet Mr. Kurtz.' On my asking who Mr. Kurtz was, he said he was a first-class agent; and seeing my disappointment at this information, he added slowly, laying down his pen, 'He is a very remarkable person.' Further questions elicited from him that Mr. Kurtz was at present in charge of a trading post, a very important one, in the true ivory-country, at 'the very bottom of there. Sends in as much ivory as all the others put together. . . .' He began to write again. The sick man was too ill to groan. The flies buzzed in a great peace.

"Suddenly there was a growing murmur of voices and a great tramping of feet. A caravan had come in. A violent babble of uncouth sounds burst out on the other side of the planks. All the carriers were speaking together, and in the midst of the uproar the lamentable voice of the chief agent was heard 'giving it up' tearfully for the twentieth time that day. . . . He rose slowly. 'What a frightful row,' he said. He crossed the room gently to look at the sick man, and returning, said to me, 'He does not hear.' 'What! Dead?' I asked, startled. 'No, not yet,' he answered, with great composure. Then, alluding with a toss of the head to the tumult in the station yard, 'When one has got to make correct entries, one comes to hate those savages—hate them to the death.' He remained thoughtful for a moment. 'When you see Mr. Kurtz,' he went on, 'tell him from me that everything here'—he glanced at the desk—'is very satisfactory. I don't like to write to him—with those messengers of ours you never know who may get hold of your letter—at that Central Station.' He stared at me for a moment with his mild, bulging eyes. 'Oh, he will go far, very far,' he began again. 'He will be a somebody in the administration before long. They, above—the council in Europe, you know—mean him to be.'

"He turned to his work. The noise outside had ceased, and presently in going out I stopped at the door. In the steady buzz of flies the homeward-bound agent was lying flushed and insensible; the other, bent over his books, was making correct entries of perfectly correct transactions; and fifty feet below the doorstep I could see the still treetops of the grove of death.

"Next day I left that station at last, with a caravan of sixty men, for a two-hundred-mile tramp.

"No use telling you much about that. Paths, paths, everywhere; a stamped-in network of paths spreading over the empty land, through long grass, through burnt grass, through thickets, down and up chilly ravines, up and down stony hills ablaze with heat; and a solitude, a solitude, nobody, not a hut. The population had cleared out a long time ago. Well, if a lot of mysterious niggers armed with all kinds of fearful weapons suddenly took to traveling on the road between Deal and Gravesend, catching the yokels right and left to carry heavy loads for them, I fancy every farm and cottage thereabouts would get empty very soon. Only here the dwellings were gone, too. Still I passed through several abandoned villages. There's something pathetically childish in the ruins of grass walls. Day after day, with the stamp and shuffle of sixty pair of bare feet behind me, each pair under a sixty-lb. load. Camp, cook, sleep, strike camp, march. Now and then a carrier dead in harness, at rest in the long grass near the path, with an empty water gourd and his long staff lying by his side. A great silence around and above. Perhaps on some quiet night the tremor of far-off drums, sinking, swelling, a tremor vast, faint; a sound weird, appealing, suggestive, and wild—and perhaps with as profound a meaning as the sound of bells in a Christian country. Once a white man in an unbuttoned uniform, camping on the path with an armed escort of lank Zanzibaris, very hospitable and festive—not to say drunk. Was looking after the upkeep of the road he declared. Can't say I saw any road or any upkeep, unless the body of a middle-aged Negro, with a bullet-hole in the forehead, upon which I absolutely stumbled three miles farther on, may be considered as a permanent improvement. I had a white companion, too, not a bad chap, but rather too fleshy and with the exasperating habit of fainting on the hot hillsides, miles away from the least bit of shade and water. Annoying, you know, to hold your own coat like a parasol over a man's head while he is coming to. I couldn't help asking him once what he meant by coming there at all. 'To make money, of course. What do you think?' he said, scornfully. Then he got fever, and had to be carried in a hammock slung under a pole. As he weighed 224 pounds I had no ends of rows with the carriers. They jibbed, ran away, sneaked off with their loads in the night—quite a mutiny. So, one evening, I made a speech in English with gestures, not one of which was lost to the sixty pairs of eyes before me, and the next morning I started the hammock off in front all right. An hour afterwards I came upon the whole concern wrecked in a bush—man, hammock, groans, blankets, horrors. The heavy pole had skinned his poor nose. He was very anxious for me to kill somebody, but there wasn't the shadow of a carrier near. I remember the old doctor, 'It would be interesting for science to watch the mental changes of individuals, on the spot.' I felt I was becoming scientifically interesting. However, all that is to no purpose. On the fifteenth day I came in sight of the big river again, and hobbled into the Central Station. It was on a back water surrounded by scrub and forest, with a pretty border of smelly mud on one side, and on the three others enclosed by a crazy fence of rushes. A neglected gap was all the gate it had, and the first glance at the place was enough to let you see the flabby devil was running that show. White men with long staves in their hands appeared languidly from amongst the buildings, strolling up to take a look at me, and then retired out of sight somewhere. One of them, a stout, excitable chap with black mustaches, informed me with great volubility and many digressions, as soon as I told him who I was, that my steamer was at the bottom of the river. I was thunderstruck. What, how, why? Oh, it was 'all right.' The 'manager himself' was there. All quite correct. 'Everybody had behaved splendidly! splendidly!'—'you must,' he said in agitation, 'go and see the general manager at once. He is waiting!'

"I did not see the real significance of that wreck at once. I fancy I see it now, but I am not sure—not at all. Certainly the affair was too stupid—when I think of it—to be altogether natural. Still . . . But at the moment it presented itself simply as a confounded nuisance. The steamer was sunk. They had started two days before in a sudden hurry up the river with the manager on board, in charge of some volunteer skipper, and before they had been out three hours they tore the bottom out of her on stones, and she sank near the south bank. I asked myself what I was to do there, now my boat was lost. As a matter of fact, I had plenty to do in fishing my command out of the river. I had to set about it the very next day. That, and the repairs when I brought the pieces to the station, took some months.

"My first interview with the manager was curious. He did not ask me to sit down after my twenty-mile walk that morning. He was commonplace in complexion, in feature, in manners, and in voice. He was of middle size and of ordinary build. His eyes, of the usual blue, were perhaps remarkably cold, and he certainly could make his glance fall on one as trenchant and heavy as an axe. But even at these times the rest of his person seemed to disclaim the intention. Otherwise there was only an indefinable, faint expression of his lips, something stealthy—a smile—not a smile—I remember it, but I can't explain. It was unconscious, this smile was, though just after he had said something it got intensified for an instant. It came at the end of his speeches like a seal applied on the words to make the meaning of the commonest phrase appear absolutely inscrutable. He was a common trader, from his youth up employed in these parts— nothing more. He was obeyed, yet he inspired neither love nor fear, nor even respect. He inspired uneasiness. That was it! Uneasiness. Not a definite mistrust—just uneasiness—nothing more. You have no idea how effective such a . . . a . . . faculty can be. He had no genius for organizing, for initiative, or for order even. That was evident in such things as the deplorable state of the station. He had no learning, and no intelligence. His position had come to him—why? Perhaps because he was never ill . . . He had served three terms of three years out there. . . . Because triumphant health in the general rout of constitutions is a kind of power in itself. When he went home on leave he rioted on a large scale—pompously. Jack ashore—with a difference —in externals only. This one could gather from his casual talk. He originated nothing, he could keep the routine going—that's all. But he was great. He was great by this little thing that it was impossible to tell what could control such a man. He never gave that secret away. Perhaps there was nothing within him. Such a suspicion made one pause—for out there there were no external checks. Once when various tropical diseases had laid low almost every 'agent' in the station, he was heard to say, 'Men who come out here should have no entrails.' He sealed the utterance with that smile of his, as though it had been a door opening into a darkness he had in his keeping. You fancied you had seen things—but the seal was on. When annoyed at mealtimes by the constant quarrels of the white men about precedence, he ordered an immense round table to be made, for which a special house had to be built. This was the station's messroom. Where he sat was the first place—the rest were nowhere. One felt this to be his unalterable conviction. He was neither civil nor uncivil. He was quiet. He allowed his 'boy'—an overfed young Negro from the coast—to treat the white men, under his very eyes, with provoking insolence.

"He began to speak as soon as he saw me. I had been very long on the road. He could not wait. Had to start without me. The up-river stations had to be relieved. There had been so many delays already that he did not know who was dead and who was alive, and how they got on—and so on, and so on. He paid no attention to my explanations, and, playing with a stick of sealing wax, repeated several times that the situation was 'very grave, very grave.' There were rumors that a very important station was in jeopardy, and its chief, Mr. Kurtz, was ill. Hoped it was not true, Mr. Kurtz was . . . I felt weary and irritable. Hang Kurtz, I thought. I interrupted him by saying I had heard of Mr. Kurtz on the coast. 'Ah! So they talk of him down there,' he murmured to himself. Then he began again, assuring me Mr. Kurtz was the best agent he had, an exceptional man, of the greatest importance to the company; therefore I could understand his anxiety. He was, he said, 'very, very uneasy.' Certainly he fidgeted on his chair a good deal, exclaimed, 'Ah, Mr. Kurtz!' broke the stick of sealing wax and seemed dumfounded by the accident. Next thing he wanted to know 'how long it would take to' . . . I interrupted him again. Being hungry, you know, and kept on my feet, too, I was getting savage. 'How could I tell?' I said. 'I hadn't even seen the wreck yet—some months, no doubt.' All this talk seemed to me so futile. 'Some months,' he said. 'Well, let us say three months before we can make a start. Yes. That ought to do the affair.' I flung out of his hut (he lived all alone in a clay hut with a sort of veranda) muttering to myself my opinion of him. He was a chattering idiot. Afterwards I took it back when it was borne in upon me startlingly with what extreme nicety he had estimated the time requisite for the 'affair.'

"I went to work the next day, turning, so to speak, my back on that station. In that way only it seemed to me I could keep my hold on the redeeming facts of life. Still, one must look about sometimes; and then I saw this station, these men strolling aimlessly about in the sunshine of the yard. I asked myself sometimes what it all meant. They wandered here and there with their absurd long staves in their hands, like a lot of faithless pilgrims bewitched inside a rotten fence. The word 'ivory' rang in the air, was whispered, was sighed. You would think they were praying to it. A taint of imbecile rapacity blew through it all, like a whiff from some corpse. By Jove! I've never seen anything so unreal in my life. And outside, the silent wilderness surrounding this cleared speck on the earth struck me as something great and invincible, like evil or truth, waiting patiently for the passing away of this fantastic invasion.

"Oh, these months! Well, never mind. Various things happened. One evening a grass shed full of calico, cotton prints, beads, and I don't know what else, burst into a blaze so suddenly that you would have thought the earth had opened to let an avenging fire consume all that trash. I was smoking my pipe quietly by my dismantled steamer, and saw them all cutting capers in the light, with their arms lifted high, when the stout man with mustaches came tearing down to the river, a tin pail in his hand, assured me that everybody was 'behaving splendidly, splendidly,' dipped about a quart of water and tore back again. I noticed there was a hole in the bottom of his pail.

"I strolled up. There was no hurry. You see the thing had gone off like a box of matches. It had been hopeless from the very first. The flame had leaped high, driven everybody back, lighted up everything—and collapsed. The shed was already a heap of embers glowing fiercely. A nigger was being beaten near by. They said he had caused the fire in some way; be that as it may, he was screeching most horribly. I saw him, later, for several days, sitting in a bit of shade looking very sick and trying to recover himself: afterwards he arose and went out—and the wilderness without a sound took him into its bosom again. As I approached the glow from the dark I found myself at the back of two men, talking. I heard the name of Kurtz pronounced, then the words, 'take advantage of this unfortunate accident.' One of the men was the manager. I wished him a good evening. 'Did you ever see anything like it—eh? It is incredible,' he said, and walked off. The other man remained. He was a first-class agent, young, gentlemanly, a bit reserved, with a forked little beard and a hooked nose. He was standoffish with the other agents, and they on their side said he was the manager's spy upon them. As to me, I had hardly ever spoken to him before. We got into talk, and by and by we strolled away from the hissing ruins. Then he asked me to his room, which was in the main building of the station. He struck a match, and I perceived that this young aristocrat had not only a silver-mounted dressing case but also a whole candle all to himself. Just at that time the manager was the only man supposed to have any right to candles. Native mats covered the clay walls; a collection of spears, assagais, shields, knives was hung up in trophies. The business intrusted to this fellow was the making of bricks—so I had been informed; but there wasn't a fragment of a brick anywhere in the station, and he had been there more than a year—waiting. It seems he could not make bricks without something, I don't know what—straw maybe. Anyways, it could not be found there, and as it was not likely to be sent from Europe, it did not appear clear to me what he was waiting for. An act of special creation perhaps. However, they were all waiting—all the sixteen or twenty pilgrims of them—for something; and upon my word it did not seem an uncongenial occupation, from the way they took it, though the only thing that ever came to them was disease—as far as I could see. They beguiled the time by backbiting and intriguing against each other in a foolish kind of way. There was an air of plotting about that station, but nothing came of it, of course. It was as unreal as everything else—as the philanthropic pretense of the whole concern, as their talk, as their government, as their show of work. The only real feeling was a desire to get appointed to a trading post where ivory was to be had, so that they could earn percentages. They intrigued and slandered and hated each other only on that account, but as to effectually lifting a little finger—oh, no. By heavens! There is something after all in the world allowing one man to steal a horse while another must not look at a halter. Steal a horse straight out. Very well. He has done it. Perhaps he can ride. But there is a way of looking at a halter that would provoke the most charitable of saints into a kick.

"I had no idea why he wanted to be sociable, but as we chatted in there it suddenly occurred to me the fellow was trying to get at something—in fact, pumping me. He alluded constantly to Europe, to the people I was supposed to know there—putting leading questions as to my acquaintances in the sepulchral city, and so on. His little eyes glittered like mica discs—with curiosity—though he tried to keep up a bit of superciliousness. At first I was astonished, but very soon I became awfully curious to see what he would find out from me. I couldn't possibly imagine what I had in me to make it worth his while. It was very pretty to see how he baffled himself, for in truth my body was full only of chills, and my head had nothing in it but that wretched steamboat business. It was evident he took me for a perfectly shameless prevaricator.

At last he got angry, and, to conceal a movement of furious annoyance, he yawned. I rose. Then I noticed a small sketch in oils, on a panel, representing a woman, draped and blindfolded, carrying a lighted torch. The background was somber—almost black. The movement of the woman was stately, and the effect of the torchlight on the face was sinister.

"It arrested me, and he stood by civilly, holding an empty half-pint champagne bottle (medical comforts) with the candle stuck in it. To my question he said Mr. Kurtz had painted this—in this very station more than a year ago—while waiting for means to go to his trading post. 'Tell me, pray,' said I, 'who is this Mr. Kurtz?'

" 'The chief of the Inner Station,' he answered in a short tone, looking away. 'Much obliged,' I said, laughing. 'And you are the brickmaker of the Central Station. Everyone knows that.' He was silent for a while. 'He is a prodigy,' he said at last. 'He is an emissary of pity, and science, and progress, and devil knows what else. We want,' he began to declaim suddenly, 'for the guidance of the cause intrusted to us by Europe, so to speak, higher intelligence, wide sympathies, a singleness of purpose.' 'Who says that?' I asked. 'Lots of them,' he replied. 'Some even write that; and so *he* comes here, a special being, as you ought to know.' 'Why ought I to know?' I interrupted, really surprised. He paid no attention. 'Yes. Today he is chief of the best station, next year he will be assistant manager, two years more and . . . but I daresay you know what he will be in two years' time. You are of the new gang—the gang of virtue. The same people who sent him specially also recommended you. Oh, don't say no. I've my own eyes to trust.' Light dawned upon me. My dear aunt's influential acquaintances were producing an unexpected effect upon that young man. I nearly burst into a laugh. 'Do you read the company's confidential correspondence?' I asked. He hadn't a word to say. It was great fun. 'When Mr. Kurtz,' I continued, severely, 'is general manager, you won't have the opportunity.'

"He blew the candle out suddenly, and we went outside. The moon had risen. Black figures strolled about listlessly, pouring water on the glow, whence proceeded a sound of hissing; steam ascended in the moonlight, the beaten nigger groaned some-where. 'What a row the brute makes!' said the indefatigable man with the mustaches, appearing near us. 'Serve him right. Transgression—punishment—bang! Pitiless, piti-less. That's the only way. This will prevent all conflagrations for the future. I was just telling the manager . . .' He noticed my companion, and became crestfallen all at once. 'Not in bed yet,' he said, with a kind of servile heartiness; 'it's so natural. Ha! Danger—agitation.' He vanished. I went on to the river side, and the other followed me. I heard a scathing murmur at my ear, 'Heap of muffs—go to.' The pilgrims could be seen in knots gesticulating, discussing. Several had still their staves in their hands. I truly believe they took these sticks to bed with them. Beyond the fence the forest stood up spectrally in the moonlight, and through the dim stir, through the faint sounds of that lamentable courtyard, the silence of the land went home to one's very heart—its mystery, its greatness, the amazing reality of its concealed life. The hurt nigger moaned feebly somewhere near by, and then fetched a deep sigh that made me mend my pace away from there. I felt a hand introducing itself under my arm. 'My dear sir,' said the fellow, 'I don't want to be misunderstood, and especially by you, who will see Mr. Kurtz long before I can have that pleasure. I wouldn't like him to get a false idea of my disposition. . . .'

"I let him run on, this papier-mâché Mephistopheles, and it seemed to me that if I tried I could poke my forefinger through him, and would find nothing inside but a little loose dirt, maybe. He, don't you see, had been planning to be assistant manager by and by under the present man, and I could see that the coming of that Kurtz had upset them both not a little. He talked precipitately, and I did not try to stop him. I had my shoulders against the wreck of my steamer, hauled up on the slope like a carcass of some big river animal. The smell of mud, of primeval mud, by Jove! was in my nostrils, the high stillness of primeval forest was before my eyes; there were shiny patches on the black creek. The moon had spread over everything a thin layer of silver —over the rank grass, over the mud, upon the wall of matted vegetation standing higher than the wall of a temple, over the great river I could see through a somber gap glittering, glittering, as it flowed broadly by without a murmur. All this was great, expectant, mute, while the man jabbered about himself. I wondered whether the stillness on the face of the immensity looking at us two were meant as an appeal or as a menace. What were we who had strayed in here? Could we handle that dumb thing, or would it handle us? I felt how big, how confoundedly big, was that thing that couldn't talk, and perhaps was deaf as well. What was in there? I could see a little ivory coming out from there, and I had heard Mr. Kurtz was in there. I had heard enough about it, too—God knows! Yet somehow it didn't bring any image with it— no more than if I had been told an angel or a fiend was in there. I believed it in the same way one of you might believe there are inhabitants in the planet Mars. I knew once a Scotch sailmaker who was certain, dead sure, there were people in Mars. If you asked him for some idea how they looked and behaved, he would get shy and mutter something about 'walking on all fours.' If you as much as smiled, he would—though a man of sixty—offer to fight you. I would not have gone so far as to fight for Kurtz, but I went for him near enough to a lie. You know I hate, detest, and can't bear a lie, not because I am straighter than the rest of us, but simply because it appalls me. There is a taint of death, a flavor of mortality in lies—which is exactly what I hate and detest in the world—what I want to forget. It makes me miserable and sick, like biting something rotten would do. Temperament, I suppose. Well, I went near enough to it by letting the young fool there believe anything he liked to imagine as to my influence in Europe. I became in an instant as much of a pretense as the rest of the bewitched pilgrims. This simply because I had a notion it somehow would be of help to that Kurtz whom at the time I did not see—you understand. He was just a word for me. I did not see the man in the name any more than you do. Do you see him? Do you see the story? Do you see anything? It seems to me I am trying to tell you a dream— making a vain attempt, because no relation of a dream can convey the dream-sensation, that commingling of absurdity, surprise, and bewilderment in a tremor of struggling revolt, that notion of being captured by the incredible which is of the very essence of dreams. . . ."

He was silent for a while.

". . . No, it is impossible; it is impossible to convey the life-sensation of any given epoch of one's existence—that which makes its truth, its meaning—its subtle and penetrating essence. It is impossible. We live, as we dream—alone. . . ."

He paused again as if reflecting, then added:

"Of course in this you fellows see more than I could then. You see me, whom you know. . . ."

It had become so pitch dark that we listeners could hardly see one another. For a long time already he, sitting apart, had been no more to us than a voice. There was not a word from anybody. The others might have been asleep, but I was awake. I listened, I listened on the watch for the sentence, for the word, that would give me the clue to the faint uneasiness inspired by this narrative that seemed to shape itself without human lips in the heavy night air of the river.

". . . Yes—I let him run on," Marlow began again, "and think what he pleased about the powers that were behind me. I did! And there was nothing behind me! There was nothing but that wretched, old, mangled steamboat I was leaning against, while he talked fluently about 'the necessity for every man to get on.' 'And when one comes out here, you conceive, it is not to gaze at the moon.' Mr. Kurtz was a 'universal genius,' but even a genius would find it easier to work with 'adequate tools—intelligent men.' He did not make bricks—why, there was a physical impossibility in the way—as I was well aware; and if he did secretarial work for the manager, it was because 'no sensible man rejects wantonly the confidence of his superiors.' Did I see it? I saw it. What more did I want? What I really wanted was rivets, by heaven! Rivets. To get on with the work—to stop the hole. Rivets I wanted. There were cases of them down at the coast—cases—piled up—burst—split! You kicked a loose rivet at every second step in that station yard on the hillside. Rivets had rolled into the grove of death. You could fill your pockets with rivets for the trouble of stooping down—and there wasn't one rivet to be found where it was wanted. We had plates that would do, but nothing to fasten them with. And every week the messenger, a lone Negro, letter bag on shoulder and staff in hand, left our station for the coast. And several times a week a coast caravan came in with trade goods—ghastly glazed calico that made you shudder only to look at it, glass beads, value about a penny a quart, confounded spotted cotton handkerchiefs. And no rivets. Three carriers could have brought all that was wanted to set that steamboat afloat.

"He was becoming confidential now, but I fancy my unresponsive attitude must have exasperated him at last, for he judged it necessary to inform me he feared neither God nor devil, let alone any mere man. I said I could see that very well, but what I wanted was a certain quantity of rivets—and rivets were what really Mr. Kurtz wanted, if he had only known it. Now letters went to the coast every week. . . . 'My dear sir,' he cried, 'I write from dictation.' I demanded rivets. There was a way—for an intelligent man. He changed his manner; became very cold, and suddenly began to talk about a hippopotamus; wondered whether sleeping on board the steamer (I stuck to my salvage night and day) I wasn't disturbed. There was an old hippo that had the bad habit of getting out on the bank and roaming at night over the station grounds. The pilgrims used to turn out in a body and empty every rifle they could lay hands on at him. Some even had sat up o' nights for him. All this energy was wasted, though. 'That animal has a charmed life,' he said; 'but you can say this only of brutes in this country. No man—you apprehend me?—no man here bears a charmed life.' He stood there for a moment in the moonlight with his delicate hooked nose set a little askew, and his mica eyes glittering without a wink, then, with a curt good night, he strode off. I could see he was disturbed and considerably puzzled, which made me feel more hopeful than I had been for days. It was a great comfort to turn from that chap to my influential friend, the battered, twisted, ruined, tinpot steamboat. I clambered on board. She rang under my feet like an empty Huntley and Palmer biscuit tin kicked along a gutter; she was nothing so solid in make, and rather less pretty in shape, but I had expended enough hard work on her to make me love her. No influential friend would have served me better. She had given me a chance to come out a bit—to find out what I could do. No, I don't like work. I had rather laze about and think of the fine things that can be done. I don't like work—no man does—but I like what is in the work, the chance to find yourself. Your own reality—for yourself, not for others— what no other man can ever know. They can only see the mere show, and never can tell what it really means.

"I was not surprised to see somebody sitting aft, on the deck, with his legs dangling over the mud. You see I rather chummed with the few mechanics there were in that station, whom the other pilgrims naturally despised—on account of their imperfect manners, I suppose. This was the foreman—a boilermaker by trade—a good worker. He was a lank, bony, yellow-faced man, with big intense eyes. His aspect was worried, and his head was as bald as the palm of my hand; but his hair in falling seemed to have stuck to his chin, and had prospered in the new locality, for his beard hung down to his waist. He was a widower with six young children (he had left them in charge of a sister of his to come out there), and the passion of his life was pigeon flying. He was an enthusiast and a connoisseur. He would rave about pigeons. After work hours he used sometimes to come over from his hut for a talk about his children and his pigeons; at work, when he had to crawl in the mud under the bottom of the steamboat, he would tie up that beard of his in a kind of white serviette he brought for the purpose. It had loops to go over his ears. In the evening he could be seen squatted on the bank rinsing that wrapper in the creek with great care, then spreading it solemnly on a bush to dry.

"I slapped him on the back and shouted 'We shall have rivets!' He scrambled to his feet exclaiming 'No! Rivets!' as though he couldn't believe his ears. Then in a low voice, 'You . . . eh?' I don't know why we behaved like lunatics. I put my finger to the side of my nose and nodded mysteriously. 'Good for you!' he cried, snapped his fingers above his head, lifting one foot. I tried a jig. We capered on the iron deck. A frightful clatter came out of that hulk, and the virgin forest on the other bank of the creek sent it back in a thundering roll upon the sleeping station. It must have made some of the pilgrims sit up in their hovels. A dark figure obscured the lighted doorway of the manager's hut, vanished, then, a second or so after, the doorway itself vanished, too. We stopped, and the silence driven away by the stamping of our feet flowed back again from the recesses of the land. The great wall of vegetation, an exuberant and entangled mass of trunks, branches, leaves, boughs, festoons, motionless in the moonlight, was like a rioting invasion of soundless life, a rolling wave of plants, piled up, crested, ready to topple over the creek, to sweep every little man of us out of his little existence. And it moved not. A deadened burst of mighty splashes and snorts reached us from afar, as though an ichthyosaurus had been taking a bath of glitter in the great river. 'After all,' said the boilermaker in a reasonable tone, 'why shouldn't we get the rivets?' Why not, indeed! I did not know of any reason why we shouldn't. 'They'll come in three weeks,' I said, confidently.

"But they didn't. Instead of rivets there came an invasion, an infliction, a visitation. It came in sections during the next three weeks, each section headed by a donkey carrying a white man in new clothes and tan shoes, bowing from that elevation right and left to the impressed pilgrims. A quarrelsome band of footsore sulky niggers trod on the heels of the donkey; a lot of tents, campstools, tin boxes, white cases, brown bales would be shot down in the courtyard, and the air of mystery would deepen a little over the muddle of the station. Five such instalments came, with their absurd air of disorderly flight with the loot of innumerable outfit shops and provision stores, that, one would think, they were lugging, after a raid, into the wilderness for equitable division. It was an inextricable mess of things decent in themselves but that human folly made look like spoils of thieving.

"This devoted band called itself the Eldorado Exploring Expedition, and I believe they were sworn to secrecy. Their talk, however, was the talk of sordid buccaneers: it was reckless without hardihood, greedy without audacity, and cruel without courage; there was not an atom of foresight or of serious intention in the whole batch of them, and they did not seem aware these things are wanted for the work of the world. To tear treasure out of the bowels of the land was their desire, with no more moral purpose at the back of it than there is in burglars breaking into a safe. Who paid the expenses of the noble enterprise I don't know; but the uncle of our manager was leader of that lot.

"In exterior he resembled a butcher in a poor neighborhood, and his eyes had a look of sleepy cunning. He carried his fat paunch with ostentation on his short legs, and during the time his gang infested the station spoke to no one but his nephew. You could see these two roaming about all day long with their heads close together in an everlasting confab.

"I had given up worrying myself about the rivets. One's capacity for that kind of folly is more limited than you would suppose. I said Hang!—and let things slide. I had plenty of time for meditation, and now and then I would give some thought to Kurtz. I wasn't very interested in him. No. Still, I was curious to see whether this man, who had come out equipped with moral ideas of some sort, would climb to the top after all and how he would set about his work when there."

II

One evening as I was lying flat on the deck of my steamboat, I heard voices approaching—and there were the nephew and the uncle strolling along the bank. I laid my head on my arm again, and had nearly lost myself in a doze, when somebody said in my ear, as it were: 'I am as harmless as a little child, but I don't like to be dictated to. Am I the manager—or am I not? I was ordered to send him there. It's incredible.' . . . I became aware that the two were standing on the shore alongside the forepart of the steamboat, just below my head. I did not move; it did not occur to me to move: I was sleepy. 'It *is* unpleasant,' grunted the uncle. 'He has asked the administration to be sent there,' said the other, 'with the idea of showing what he could do; and I was instructed accordingly. Look at the influence that man must have. Is it not frightful?' They both agreed it was frightful, then made several bizarre remarks: 'Make rain and fine weather —one man—the council—by the nose'—bits of absurd sentences that got the better of my drowsiness, so that I had pretty near the whole of my wits about me when the uncle said, 'The climate may do away with this difficulty for you. Is he alone there?' 'Yes,' answered the manager; 'he sent his assistant down the river with a note to me in these terms: "Clear this poor devil out of the country, and don't bother sending more of that sort. I had rather be alone than have the kind of men you can dispose of with me." It was more than a year ago. Can you imagine such impudence!' 'Anything since then?' asked the other, hoarsely. 'Ivory,' jerked the nephew; 'lots of it—prime sort— lots—most annoying, from him.' 'And with that?' questioned the heavy rumble. 'Invoice,' was the reply fired out, so to speak. Then silence. They had been talking about Kurtz.

"I was broad awake by this time, but, lying perfectly at ease, remained still, having no inducement to change my position. 'How did that ivory come all this way?' growled the elder man, who seemed very vexed. The other explained that it had come with a fleet of canoes in charge of an English half-caste clerk Kurtz had with him; that Kurtz had apparently intended to return himself, the station being by that time bare of goods and stores, but after coming three hundred miles, had suddenly decided to go back, which he started to do alone in a small dugout with four paddlers, leaving the half-caste to continue down the river with the ivory. The two fellows there seemed astounded at anybody attempting such a thing. They were at a loss for an adequate motive. As to me, I seemed to see Kurtz for the first time. It was a distinct glimpse: the dugout, four paddling savages, and the lone white man turning his back suddenly on the headquarters, on relief, on thoughts of home—perhaps; setting his face towards the depths of the wilderness, towards his empty and desolate station. I did not know the motive. Perhaps he was just simply a fine fellow who stuck to his work for its own sake. His name, you understand, had not been pronounced once. He was 'that man.' The half-caste, who, as far as I could see, had conducted a difficult trip with great prudence and pluck, was invariably alluded to as 'that scoundrel.' The 'scoundrel' had reported that the 'man' had been very ill—had recovered imperfectly. . . . The two below me moved away then a few paces, and strolled back and forth at some little distance. I heard: 'Military post—doctor—two hundred miles—quite alone now—

unavoidable delays—nine months—no news—strange rumors.' They approached again, just as the manager was saying, 'No one, as far as I know, unless a species of wandering trader—a pestilential fellow, snapping ivory from the natives.' Who was it they were talking about now? I gathered in snatches that this was some man supposed to be in Kurtz's district, and of whom the manager did not approve. 'We will not be free from unfair competition till one of these fellows is hanged for an example,' he said. 'Certainly,' grunted the other; 'get him hanged! Why not? Anything—anything can be done in this country. That's what I say; nobody here, you understand, *here,* can endanger your position. And why? You stand the climate—you outlast them all. The danger is in Europe; but there before I left I took care to—' They moved off and whispered, then their voices rose again. 'The extraordinary series of delays is not my fault. I did my best.' The fat man sighed. 'Very sad.' 'And the pestiferous absurdity of his talk,' continued the other; 'he bothered me enough when he was here. "Each station should be like a beacon on the road towards better things, a center for trade of course, but also for humanizing, improving, instructing." Conceive you—that ass! And he wants to be manager! No, it's—' Here he got choked by excessive indignation, and I lifted my head the least bit. I was surprised to see how near they were—right under me. I could have spat upon their hats. They were looking on the ground, absorbed in thought. The manager was switching his leg with a slender twig; his sagacious relative lifted his head. 'You have been well since you came out this time?' he asked. The other gave a start. 'Who? I? Oh! Like a charm—like a charm. But the rest—oh, my goodness! All sick. They die so quick, too, that I haven't the time to send them out of the country—it's incredible!' 'H'm. Just so,' grunted the uncle. 'Ah! my boy, trust to this —I say, trust to this.' I saw him extend his short flipper of an arm for a gesture that took in the forest, the creek, the mud, the river—seemed to beckon with a dishonoring flourish before the sunlit face of the land a treacherous appeal to the lurking death, to the hidden evil, to the profound darkness of its heart. It was so startling that I leaped to my feet and looked back at the edge of the forest, as though I had expected an answer of some sort to that black display of confidence. You know the foolish notions that come to one sometimes. The high stillness confronted these two figures with its ominous patience, waiting for the passing away of a fantastic invasion.

"They swore aloud together—out of sheer fright, I believe—then pretending not to know anything of my existence, turned back to the station. The sun was low; and leaning forward side by side, they seemed to be tugging painfully uphill their two ridiculous shadows of unequal length, that trailed behind them slowly over the tall grass without bending a single blade.

"In a few days the Eldorado Expedition went into the patient wilderness, that closed upon it as the sea closes over a diver. Long afterwards the news came that all the donkeys were dead. I know nothing as to the fate of the less valuable animals. They, no doubt, like the rest of us, found what they deserved. I did not inquire. I was then rather excited at the prospect of meeting Kurtz very soon. When I say very soon I mean it comparatively. It was just two months from the day we left the creek when we came to the bank below Kurtz's station.

"Going up that river was like traveling back to the earliest beginnings of the world, when vegetation rioted on the earth and the big trees were kings. An empty stream, a great silence, an impenetrable forest. The air was warm, thick, heavy, sluggish. There was no joy in the brilliance of sunshine. The long stretches of the waterway ran on, deserted, into the gloom of overshadowed distances. On silvery sandbanks hippos and alligators sunned themselves side by side. The broadening waters flowed through a mob of wooded islands; you lost your way on that river as you would in a desert, and butted all day long against shoals, trying to find the channel, till you thought yourself bewitched and cut off forever from everything you had known once—somewhere—far away—in another existence perhaps. There were moments when one's past came back to one, as it will sometimes when you have not a moment to spare to yourself; but it came in the shape of an unrestful and noisy dream, remembered with wonder amongst the overwhelming realities of this strange world of plants, and water, and silence. And this stillness of life did not in the least resemble a peace. It was the stillness of an implacable force brooding over an inscrutable intention. It looked at you with a vengeful aspect. I got used to it afterwards; I did not see it any more; I had no time. I had to keep guessing at the channel; I had to discern, mostly by inspiration, the signs of hidden banks; I watched for sunken stones; I was learning to clap my teeth smartly before my heart flew out, when I shaved by a fluke some infernal sly old snag that would have ripped the life out of the tin-pot steamboat and drowned all the pilgrims; I had to keep a lookout for the signs of dead wood we could cut up in the night for next day's steaming. When you have to attend to things of that sort, to the mere incidents of the surface, the reality—the reality, I tell you—fades. The inner truth is hidden—luckily, luckily. But I felt it all the same; I felt often its mysterious stillness watching me at my monkey tricks, just as it watches you fellows performing on your respective tightropes for—what is it? a half crown a tumble—"

"Try to be civil, Marlow," growled a voice, and I knew there was at least one listener awake besides myself.

"I beg your pardon. I forgot the heartache which makes up the rest of the price. And indeed what does the price matter, if the trick be well done? You do your tricks very well. And I didn't do badly either, since I managed not to sink that steamboat on my first trip. It's a wonder to me yet. Imagine a blindfolded man set to drive a van over a bad road. I sweated and shivered over that business considerably, I can tell you. After all, for a seaman, to scrape the bottom of the thing that's supposed to float all the time under his care is the unpardonable sin. No one may know of it, but you never forget the thump—eh? A blow on the very heart. You remember it, you dream of it, you wake up at night and think of it—years after—and go hot and cold all over. I don't pretend to say that steamboat floated all the time. More than once she had to wade for a bit, with twenty cannibals splashing around and pushing. We had enlisted some of these chaps on the way for a crew. Fine fellows—cannibals—in their place. They were men one could work with, and I am grateful to them. And, after all, they did not eat each other before my face: they had brought along a provision of hippo meat which went rotten, and made the mystery of the wilderness stink in my nostrils.

Phoo! I can sniff it now. I had the manager on board and three or four pilgrims with their staves—all complete. Sometimes we came upon a station close by the bank, clinging to the skirts of the unknown, and the white men rushing out of a tumble-down hovel, with great gestures of joy and surprise and welcome, seemed very strange —had the appearance of being held there captive by a spell. The word "ivory" would ring in the air for a while—and on we went again into the silence, along empty reaches, round the still bends, between the high walls of our winding way, reverber-ating in hollow claps the ponderous beat of the stern wheel. Trees, trees, millions of trees, massive, immense, running up high; and at their foot, hugging the bank against the stream, crept the little begrimed steamboat, like a sluggish beetle crawling on the floor of a lofty portico. It made you feel very small, very lost, and yet it was not altogether depressing, that feeling. After all, if you were small, the grimy beetle crawled on—which was just what you wanted it to do. Where the pilgrims imagined it crawled to I don't know. To some place where they expected to get something, I bet! For me it crawled towards Kurtz—exclusively; but when the steam pipes started leaking we crawled very slow. The reaches opened before us and closed behind, as if the forest had stepped leisurely across the water to bar the way for our return. We penetrated deeper and deeper into the heart of darkness. It was very quiet there. At night sometimes the roll of drums behind the curtain of trees would run up the river and remain sustained faintly, as if hovering in the air high over our heads, till the first break of day. Whether it meant war, peace, or prayer we could not tell. The dawns were heralded by the descent of a chill stillness; the woodcutters slept, their fires burned low; the snapping of a twig would make you start. We were wanderers on prehistoric earth, on an earth that wore the aspect of an unknown planet. We could have fancied ourselves the first of men taking possession of an accursed inheritance, to be subdued at the cost of profound anguish and of excessive toil. But suddenly, as we struggled round a bend, there would be a glimpse of rush walls, of peaked grass roofs, a burst of yells, a whirl of black limbs, a mass of hands clapping, of feet stamping, of bodies swaying, of eyes rolling, under the droop of heavy and motionless foliage. The steamer toiled along slowly on the edge of a black and incomprehensible frenzy. The prehis-toric man was cursing us, praying to us, welcoming us—who could tell? We were cut off from the comprehension of our surroundings; we glided past like phantoms, wondering and secretly appalled, as sane men would be before an enthusiastic outbreak in a madhouse. We could not understand because we were too far and could not remember, because we were traveling in the night of first ages, of those ages that are gone, leaving hardly a sign—and no memories.

"The earth seemed unearthly. We are accustomed to look upon the shackled form of a conquered monster, but there—there you could look at a thing monstrous and free. It was unearthly, and the men were— No, they were not inhuman. Well, you know, that was the worst of it—this suspicion of their not being inhuman. It would come slowly to one. They howled and leaped, and spun, and made horrid faces; but what thrilled you was just the thought of their humanity—like yours—the thought of your remote kinship with this wild and passionate uproar. Ugly. Yes, it was ugly enough; but if you were man enough you would admit to yourself that there was in you just the faintest trace of a response to the terrible frankness of that noise, a dim suspicion of there being a meaning in it which you—you so remote from the night of first ages—could comprehend. And why not? The mind of man is capable of anything —because everything is in it, all the past as well as all the future. What was there after all? Joy, fear, sorrow, devotion, valor, rage—who can tell?—but truth—truth stripped of its cloak of time. Let the fool gape and shudder—the man knows, and can look on without a wink. But he must at least be as much of a man as these on the shore. He must meet that truth with his own true stuff—with his own inborn strength. Principles won't do. Acquisitions, clothes, pretty rags—rags that would fly off at the first good shake. No; you want a deliberate belief. An appeal to me in this fiendish row—is there? Very well; I hear; I admit, but I have a voice, too, and for good or evil mine is the speech that cannot be silenced. Of course, a fool, what with sheer fright and fine sentiments, is always safe. Who's that grunting? You wonder I didn't go ashore for a howl and a dance? Well, no—I didn't. Fine sentiments, you say? Fine sentiments, be hanged! I had no time. I had to mess about with white lead and strips of woolen blanket helping to put bandages on those leaky steam pipes—I tell you. I had to watch the steering, and circumvent those snags, and get the tin-pot along by hook or by crook. There was surface truth enough in these things to save a wiser man. And between whiles I had to look after the savage who was fireman. He was an improved specimen; he could fire up a vertical boiler. He was there below me, and, upon my word, to look at him was as edifying as seeing a dog in a parody of breeches and a feather hat, walking on his hind legs. A few months of training had done for that really fine chap. He squinted at the steam gauge and at the water gauge with an evident effort of intrepidity—and he had filed teeth, too, the poor devil, and the wool of his pate shaved into queer patterns, and three ornamental scars on each of his cheeks. He ought to have been clapping his hands and stamping his feet on the bank, instead of which he was hard at work, a thrall to strange witchcraft, full of improving knowledge. He was useful because he had been instructed; and what he knew was this—that should the water in that transparent thing disappear, the evil spirit inside the boiler would get angry through the greatness of his thirst, and take a terrible vengeance. So he sweated and fired up and watched the glass fearfully (with an impromptu charm, made of rags, tied to his arm, and a piece of polished bone, as big as a watch, stuck flatways through his lower lip), while the wooded banks slipped past us slowly, the short noise was left behind, the interminable miles of silence—and we crept on, towards Kurtz. But the snags were thick, the water was treacherous and shallow, the boiler seemed indeed to have a sulky devil in it, and thus neither that fireman nor I had any time to peer into our creepy thoughts.

"Some fifty miles below the Inner Station we came upon a hut of reeds, an inclined and melancholy pole, with the unrecognizable tatters of what had been a flag of some sort flying from it, and a neatly stacked wood pile. This was unexpected. We came to the bank, and on the stack of firewood found a flat piece of board with some faded pencil writing on it. When deciphered it said: 'Wood for you. Hurry up. Approach cautiously.' There was a signature, but it was illegible—not Kurtz—a much longer word. Hurry up. Where? Up the river? 'Approach cautiously.' We had not done so. But the warning could not have been meant for the place where it could be only found after approach. Something was wrong above. But what—and how much? That was the question. We commented adversely upon the imbecility of that telegraphic style. The bush around said nothing, and would not let us look very far, either. A torn curtain of red twill hung in the doorway of the hut, and flapped sadly in our faces. The dwelling was dismantled; but we could see a white man had lived there not very long ago. There remained a rude table—a plank on two posts; a heap of rubbish reposed in a dark corner, and by the door I picked up a book. It had lost its covers, and the pages had been thumbed into a state of extremely dirty softness; but the back had been lovingly stitched afresh with white cotton thread, which looked clean yet. It was an extraordinary find. Its title was, *An Inquiry into Some Points of Seamanship*, by a man Tower, Towson —some such name—Master in his Majesty's Navy. The matter looked dreary reading enough, with illustrative diagrams and repulsive tables of figures, and the copy was sixty years old. I handled this amazing antiquity with the greatest possible tenderness, lest it should dissolve in my hands. Within, Towson or Towser was inquiring earnestly into the breaking strain of ships' chains and tackle, and other such matters. Not a very enthralling book; but at the first glance you could see there a singleness of intention, an honest concern for the right way of going to work, which made these humble pages, thought out so many years ago, luminous with another than a professional light. The simple old sailor, with his talk of chains and purchases, made me forget the jungle and the pilgrims in a delicious sensation of having come upon something unmistakably real. Such a book being there was wonderful enough; but still more astounding were the notes penciled in the margin, and plainly referring to the text. I couldn't believe my eyes! They were in cipher! Yes, it looked like cipher. Fancy a man lugging with him a book of that description into this nowhere and studying it—and making notes—in cipher at that! It was an extravagant mystery.

"I had been dimly aware for some time of a worrying noise, and when I lifted my eyes I saw the wood pile was gone, and the manager, aided by all the pilgrims, was shouting at me from the river side. I slipped the book into my pocket. I assure you to leave off reading was like tearing myself away from the shelter of an old and solid friendship.

"I started the lame engine ahead. 'It must be this miserable trader—this intruder,' exclaimed the manager, looking back malevolently at the place we had left. 'He must be English,' I said. 'It will not save him from getting into trouble if he is not careful,' muttered the manager darkly. I observed with assumed innocence that no man was safe from trouble in this world.

"The current was more rapid now, the steamer seemed at her last gasp, the stern wheel flopped languidly, and I caught myself listening on tiptoe for the next beat of the boat, for in sober truth I expected the wretched thing to give up every moment. It was like watching the last flickers of a life. But still we crawled. Sometimes I would pick out a tree a little way ahead to measure our progress towards Kurtz by, but I lost it invariably before we got abreast. To keep the eyes so long on one thing was too much for human patience. The manager displayed a beautiful resignation. I fretted and fumed and took to arguing with myself whether or no I would talk openly with Kurtz; but before I could come to any conclusion it occurred to me that my speech or my silence, indeed any action of mine, would be a mere futility. What did it matter what anyone knew or ignored? What did it matter who was manager? One gets sometimes such a flash of insight. The essentials of this affair lay deep under the surface, beyond my reach, and beyond my power of meddling.

"Towards the evening of the second day we judged ourselves about eight miles from Kurtz's station. I wanted to push on; but the manager looked grave, and told me the navigation up there was so dangerous that it would be advisable, the sun being very low already, to wait where we were till next morning. Moreover, he pointed out that if the warning to approach cautiously were to be followed, we must approach in daylight— not at dusk, or in the dark. This was sensible enough. Eight miles meant nearly three hours' steaming for us, and I could also see suspicious ripples at the upper end of the reach. Nevertheless, I was annoyed beyond expression at the delay, and most unreasonably, too, since one night more could not matter much after so many months. As we had plenty of wood, and caution was the word, I brought up in the middle of the stream. The reach was narrow, straight, with high sides like a railway cutting. The dusk came gliding into it long before the sun had set. The current ran smooth and swift, but a dumb immobility sat on the banks. The living trees, lashed together by the creepers and every living bush of the undergrowth, might have been changed into stone, even to the slenderest twig, to the lightest leaf. It was not sleep—it seemed unnatural, like a state of trance. Not the faintest sound of any kind could be heard. You looked on amazed, and began to suspect yourself of being deaf—then the night came suddenly, and struck you blind as well. About three in the morning some large fish leaped, and the loud splash made me jump as though a gun had been fired. When the sun rose there was a white fog, very warm and clammy, and more blinding than the night. It did not shift or drive; it was just there, standing all round you like something solid. At eight or nine, perhaps, it lifted as a shutter lifts. We had a glimpse of the towering multitude of trees, of the immense matted jungle, with the blazing little ball of the sun hanging over it—all perfectly still—and then the white shutter came down again, smoothly, as if sliding in greased grooves. I ordered the chain, which we had begun to heave in, to be paid out again. Before it stopped running with a muffled rattle, a cry, a very loud cry, as of infinite desolation, soared slowly in the opaque air. It ceased. A complaining clamor, modulated in savage discords, filled our ears. The sheer unexpectedness of it made my hair stir under my cap. I don't know how it struck the others: to me it seemed as though the mist itself had screamed, so suddenly, and apparently from all sides at once, did this tumultuous and mournful uproar arise. It culminated in a hurried outbreak of almost intolerably excessive shrieking, which stopped short, leaving us stiffened in a variety of silly attitudes, and obstinately listening to the nearly as appalling and excessive silence. 'Good God! What is the meaning—' stammered at my elbow one of the pilgrims, a little fat man, with sandy hair and red whiskers, who wore sidespring boots, and pink pajamas tucked into his socks. Two others remained open-mouthed a whole minute, then dashed into the little cabin, to rush out incontinently and stand darting scared glances, with Winchesters at 'ready' in their hands. What we could see was just the steamer we were on, her outlines blurred as though she had been on the point of dissolving, and a misty strip of water, perhaps two feet broad, around her—and that was all. The rest of the world was nowhere, as far as our eyes and ears were concerned. Just nowhere. Gone, disappeared; swept off without leaving a whisper or a shadow behind.

"I went forward, and ordered the chain to be hauled in short, so as to be ready to trip the anchor and move the steamboat at once if necessary. 'Will they attack?' whispered an awed voice. 'We will be all butchered in this fog,' murmured another. The faces twitched with the strain, the hands trembled slightly, the eyes forgot to wink. It was very curious to see the contrast of expressions of the white men and of the black fellows of our crew, who were as much strangers to that part of the river as we, though their homes were only eight hundred miles away. The whites, of course greatly discomposed, had besides a curious look of being painfully shocked by such an outrageous row. The others had an alert, naturally interested expression; but their faces were essentially quiet, even those of the one or two who grinned as they hauled at the chain. Several exchanged short, grunting phrases, which seemed to settle the matter to their satisfaction. Their headman, a young, broadchested black, severely draped in dark-blue fringed cloths, with fierce nostrils and his hair all done up artfully in oily ringlets, stood near me. 'Aha!' I said, just for good fellowship's sake. 'Catch 'im,' he snapped, with a bloodshot widening of his eyes and a flash of sharp teeth—'catch 'im. Give 'im to us.' 'To you, eh?' I asked; 'what would you do with them?' 'Eat 'im!' he said, curtly, and, leaning his elbow on the rail, looked out into the fog in a dignified and profoundly pensive attitude. I would no doubt have been properly horrified, had it not occurred to me that he and his chaps must be very hungry: that they must have been growing increasingly hungry for at least this month past. They had been engaged for six months (I don't think a single one of them had any clear idea of time, as we at the end of countless ages have. They still belonged to the beginnings of time—had no inherited experience to teach them as it were), and of course, as long as there was a piece of paper written over in accordance with some farcical law or other made down the river, it didn't enter anybody's head to trouble how they would live. Certainly they had brought with them some rotten hippo meat, which couldn't have lasted very long, anyway, even if the pilgrims hadn't, in the midst of a shocking hullabaloo, thrown a considerable quantity of it overboard. It looked like a high-handed proceeding; but it was really a case of legitimate self-defense. You can't breathe dead hippo waking, sleeping, and eating, and at the same time keep your precarious grip on existence. Besides that, they had given them every week three pieces of brass wire, each about nine inches long; and the theory was they were to buy their provisions with that currency in river-side villages. You can see how *that* worked. There were either no villages, or the people were hostile, or the director, who like the rest of us fed out of tins, with an occasional old he-goat thrown in, didn't want to stop the steamer for some more or less recondite reasons. So, unless they swallowed the wire itself, or made loops of it to snare the fishes with, I don't see what good their extravagant salary could be to them. I must say it was paid with a regularity worthy of a large and honorable trading company. For the rest, the only thing to eat—though it didn't look eatable in the least—I saw in their possession was a few lumps of some stuff like half-cooked dough, of a dirty lavender color, they kept wrapped in leaves, and now and then swallowed a piece of, but so small that it seemed done more for the looks of the thing than for any serious purpose of sustenance. Why in the name of all the gnawing devils of hunger they didn't go for us—they were thirty to five—and have a good tuck in for once, amazes me now when I think of it. They were big powerful men, with not much capacity to weigh the consequences, with courage, with strength, even yet, though their skins were no longer glossy and their muscles no longer hard. And I saw that some- thing restraining, one of those human secrets that baffle probability, had come into play there. I looked at them with a swift quickening of interest—not because it occurred to me I might be eaten by them before very long, though I own to you that just then I perceived—in a new light, as it were—how unwholesome the pilgrims looked, and I hoped, yes, I positively hoped, that my aspect was not so—what shall I say?—so—unappetizing: a touch of fantastic vanity which fitted well with the dream- sensation that pervaded all my days at that time. Perhaps I had a little fever, too. One can't live with one's finger everlastingly on one's pulse. I had often 'a little fever,' or a little touch of other things—the playful pawstrokes of the wilderness, the preliminary trifling before the more serious onslaught which came in due course. Yes; I looked at them as you would on any human being, with a curiosity of their impulses, motives, capacities, weaknesses, when brought to the test of an inexorable physical necessity. Restraint! What possible restraint? Was it superstition, disgust, patience, fear—or some kind of primitive honor? No fear can stand up to hunger, no patience can wear it out, disgust simply does not exist where hunger is; and as to superstition, beliefs, and what you may call principles, they are less than chaff in a breeze. Don't you know the devilry of lingering starvation, its exasperating torment, its black thoughts, its somber and brooding ferocity? Well, I do. It takes a man all his inborn strength to fight hunger properly. It's really easier to face bereavement, dishonor, and the perdition of one's soul—than this kind of prolonged hunger. Sad, but true. And these chaps, too, had no earthly reason for any kind of scruple. Restraint! I would just as soon have expected restraint from a hyena prowling amongst the corpses of a battlefield. But there was the fact facing me—the fact dazzling, to be seen, like the foam on the depths of the sea, like a ripple on an unfathomable enigma, a mystery greater—when I thought of it—than the curious, inexplicable note of desperate grief in this savage clamor that had swept by us on the river bank, behind the blind whiteness of the fog.

"Two pilgrims were quarreling in hurried whispers as to which bank. 'Left.' 'No, no; how can you? Right, right, of course.' 'It is very serious,' said the manager's voice behind me; 'I would be desolated if anything should happen to Mr. Kurtz before we came up.' I looked at him, and had not the slightest doubt he was sincere. He was just the kind of man who would wish to preserve appearances. That was his restraint. But when he muttered something about going on at once, I did not even take the trouble to answer him. I knew, and he knew, that it was impossible. Were we to let go our hold of the bottom, we would be absolutely in the air—in space. We wouldn't be able to tell where we were going to—whether up- or down-stream, or across—till we fetched against one bank or the other, and then we wouldn't know at first which it was. Of course I made no move. I had no mind for a smashup. You couldn't imagine a more deadly place for a shipwreck. Whether drowned at once or not, we were sure to perish speedily in one way or another. 'I authorize you to take all the risks,' he said, after a short silence. 'I refuse to take any,' I said, shortly; which was just the answer he expected, though its tone might have surprised him. 'Well, I must defer to your judgment. You are captain,' he said, with marked civility. I turned my shoulder to him in sign of my appreciation, and looked into the fog. How long would it last? It was the most hopeless lookout. The approach to this Kurtz grubbing for ivory in the wretched bush was beset by as many dangers as though he had been an enchanted princess sleeping in a fabulous castle. 'Will they attack, do you think?' asked the manager, in a confidential tone.

"I did not think they would attack, for several obvious reasons. The thick fog was one. If they left the bank in their canoes they would get lost in it, as we would be if we attempted to move. Still, I had also judged the jungle of both banks quite impenetrable—and yet eyes were in it, eyes that had seen us. The river-side bushes were certainly very thick; but the undergrowth behind was evidently penetrable. However, during the short lift I had seen no canoes anywhere in the reach—certainly not abreast of the steamer. But what made the idea of attack inconceivable to me was the nature of the noise—of the cries we had heard. They had not the fierce character boding of immediate hostile intention. Unexpected, wild, and violent as they had been, they had given me an irresistible impression of sorrow. The glimpse of the steamboat had for some reason filled those savages with unrestrained grief. The danger, if any, I expounded, was from our proximity to a great human passion let loose. Even extreme grief may ultimately vent itself in violence—but more generally takes the form of apathy. . . .

"You should have seen the pilgrims stare! They had no heart to grin, or even to revile me: but I believe they thought me gone mad—with fright, maybe. I delivered a regular lecture. My dear boys, it was no good bothering. Keep a lookout? Well, you may guess I watched the fog for the signs of lifting as a cat watches a mouse; but for anything else our eyes were of no more use to us than if we had been buried miles deep in a heap of cotton-wool. It felt like it, too—choking, warm, stifling. Besides, all I said, though it sounded extravagant, was absolutely true to fact. What we afterwards alluded to as an attack was really an attempt at repulse. The action was very far from being aggressive—it was not even defensive, in the usual sense: it was undertaken under the stress of desperation, and in its essence was purely protective.

"It developed itself, I should say, two hours after the fog lifted, and its commencement was at a spot, roughly speaking, about a mile and a half below Kurtz's station. We had just floundered and flopped round a bend, when I saw an islet, a mere grassy hummock of bright green, in the middle of the stream. It was the only thing of the kind; but as we opened the reach more, I perceived it was the head of a long sandbank, or rather of a chain of shallow patches stretching down the middle of the river. They were discolored, just awash, and the whole lot was seen just under the water, exactly as a man's backbone is seen running down the middle of his back under the skin. Now, as far as I did see, I could go to the right or to the left of this. I didn't know either channel, of course. The banks looked pretty well alike, the depth appeared the same; but as I had been informed the station was on the west side, I naturally headed for the western passage.

"No sooner had we fairly entered it than I became aware it was much narrower than I had supposed. To the left of us there was the long uninterrupted shoal, and to the right a high, steep bank heavily overgrown with bushes. Above the bush the trees stood in serried ranks. The twigs overhung the current thickly, and from distance to distance a large limb of some tree projected rigidly over the stream. It was then well on in the afternoon, the face of the forest was gloomy, and a broad strip of shadow had already fallen on the water. In this shadow we steamed up—very slowly, as you may imagine. I sheered her well inshore—the water being deepest near the bank, as the sounding pole informed me.

"One of my hungry and forbearing friends was sounding in the bows just below me. This steamboat was exactly like a decked scow. On the deck, there were two little teakwood houses, with doors and windows. The boiler was in the fore-end, and the machinery right astern. Over the whole there was a light roof, supported on stanchions. The funnel projected through that roof, and in front of the funnel a small cabin built of light planks served for a pilot house. It contained a couch, two camp-stools, a loaded Martini-Henry leaning in one corner, a tiny table, and the steering wheel. It had a wide door in front and a broad shutter at each side. All these were always thrown open, of course. I spent my days perched up there on the extreme fore-end of that roof, before the door. At night I slept, or tried to, on the couch. An athletic black belonging to some coast tribe, and educated by my poor predecessor, was the helmsman. He sported a pair of brass earrings, wore a blue cloth wrapper from the waist to the ankles, and thought all the world of himself. He was the most unstable kind of fool I had ever seen. He steered with no end of a swagger while you were by; but if he lost sight of you, he became instantly the prey of an abject funk, and would let that cripple of a steamboat get the upper hand of him in a minute.

"I was looking down at the sounding pole, and feeling much annoyed to see at each try a little more of it stick out of that river, when I saw my poleman give up the business suddenly, and stretch himself flat on the deck, without even taking the trouble to haul his pole in. He kept hold on it though, and it trailed in the water. At the same time the fireman, whom I could also see below me, sat down abruptly before his furnace and ducked his head. I was amazed. Then I had to look at the river mighty quick, because there was a snag in the fairway. Sticks, little sticks, were flying about—thick: they were whizzing before my nose, dropping below me, striking behind me against my pilot house. All this time the river, the shore, the woods, were very quiet—perfectly quiet. I could only hear the heavy splashing thump of the stern wheel and the patter of these things. We cleared the snag clumsily. Arrows, by Jove! We were being shot at! I stepped in quickly to close the shutter on the land side. That fool helmsman, his hands on the spokes, was lifting his knees high, stamping his feet, champing his mouth, like a reined-in horse. Confound him! And we were staggering within ten feet of the bank. I had to lean right out to swing the heavy shutter, and I saw a face amongst the leaves on the level with my own, looking at me very fierce and steady; and then suddenly, as though a veil had been removed from my eyes, I made out, deep in the tangled gloom, naked breasts, arms, legs, glaring eyes—the bush was swarming with human limbs in movement, glistening, of bronze color. The twigs shook, swayed, and rustled, the arrows flew out of them, and then the shutter came to. 'Steer her straight,' I said to the helmsman. He held his head rigid, face forward; but his eyes rolled, he kept on, lifting and setting down his feet gently, his mouth foamed a little. 'Keep quiet!' I said in a fury. I might just as well have ordered a tree not to sway in the wind. I darted out. Below me there was a great scuffle of feet on the iron deck; confused exclamations; a voice screamed, 'Can you turn back?' I caught sight of a V-shaped ripple on the water ahead. What? Another snag! A fusillade burst out under my feet. The pilgrims had opened with their Winchesters, and were simply squirting lead into that bush. A deuce of a lot of smoke came up and drove slowly forward. I swore at it. Now I couldn't see the ripple or the snag either. I stood in the doorway, peering, and the arrows came in swarms. They might have been poisoned, but they looked as though they wouldn't kill a cat. The bush began to howl. Our woodcutters raised a warlike whoop; the report of a rifle just at my back deafened me. I glanced over my shoulder, and the pilot house was yet full of noise and smoke when I made a dash at the wheel. The fool nigger had dropped everything, to throw the shutter open and let off that Martini-Henry. He stood before the wide opening, glaring, and I yelled at him to come back, while I straightened the sudden twist out of that steam-boat. There was no room to turn even if I had wanted to, the snag was somewhere very near ahead in that confounded smoke, there was no time to lose, so I just crowded her into the bank—right into the bank, where I knew the water was deep.

"We tore slowly along the overhanging bushes in a whirl of broken twigs and flying leaves. The fusillade below stopped short, as I had foreseen it would when the squirts got empty. I threw my head back to a glinting whizz that traversed the pilot house, in at one shutter-hole and out at the other. Looking past that mad helmsman, who was shaking the empty rifle and yelling at the shore, I saw vague forms of men running bent double, leaping, gliding, distinct, incomplete, evanescent. Something big appeared in the air before the shutter, the rifle went overboard, and the man stepped back swiftly, looked at me over his shoulder in an extraordinary, profound, familiar manner, and fell upon my feet. The side of his head hit the wheel twice, and the end of what appeared a long cane clattered round and knocked over a little campstool. It looked as though after wrenching that thing from somebody ashore he had lost his balance in the effort. The thin smoke had blown away, we were clear of the snag, and looking ahead I could see that in another hundred yards or so I would be free to sheer off, away from the bank; but my feet felt so very warm and wet that I had to look down.

The man had rolled on his back and stared straight up at me; both his hands clutched that cane. It was the shaft of a spear that, either thrown or lunged through the opening, had caught him in the side just below the ribs; the blade had gone in out of sight, after making a frightful gash; my shoes were full; a pool of blood lay very still, gleaming dark-red under the wheel; his eyes shone with an amazing luster. The fusillade burst out again. He looked at me anxiously, gripping the spear like something precious, with an air of being afraid I would try to take it away from him. I had to make an effort to free my eyes from his gaze and attend to the steering. With one hand I felt above my head for the line of the steam whistle, and jerked out screech after screech hurriedly. The tumult of angry and warlike yells was checked instantly, and then from the depths of the woods went out such a tremulous and prolonged wail of mournful fear and utter despair as may be imagined to follow the flight of the last hope from the earth. There was a great commotion in the bush; the shower of arrows stopped, a few dropping shots rang out sharply—then silence, in which the languid beat of the stern wheel came plainly to my ears. I put the helm hard a-starboard at the moment when the pilgrim in pink pajamas, very hot and agitated, appeared in the doorway. 'The manager sends me—' he began in an official tone, and stopped short. 'Good God!' he said, glaring at the wounded man.

"We two whites stood over him, and his lustrous and inquiring glance enveloped us both. I declare it looked as though he would presently put to us some question in an understandable language; but he died without uttering a sound, without moving a limb, without twitching a muscle. Only in the very last moment, as though in response to some sign we could not see, to some whisper we could not hear, he frowned heavily, and that frown gave to his black death mask an inconceivably somber, brooding, and menacing expression. The luster of inquiring glance faded swiftly into vacant glassiness. 'Can you steer?' I asked the agent eagerly. He looked very dubious; but I made a grab at his arm, and he understood at once I meant him to steer whether or no. To tell you the truth, I was morbidly anxious to change my shoes and socks. 'He is dead,' murmured the fellow, immensely impressed. 'No doubt about it,' said I, tugging like mad at the shoelaces. 'And by the way, I suppose Mr. Kurtz is dead as well by this time.'

"For the moment that was the dominant thought. There was a sense of extreme disappointment, as though I had found out I had been striving after something altogether without a substance. I couldn't have been more disgusted if I had traveled all this way for the sole purpose of talking with Mr. Kurtz. Talking with . . . I flung one shoe overboard, and became aware that that was exactly what I had been looking forward to—a talk with Kurtz. I made the strange discovery that I had never imagined him as doing, you know, but as discoursing. I didn't say to myself, 'Now I will never see him,' or 'Now I will never shake him by the hand,' but, 'now I will never hear him.' The man presented himself as a voice. Not of course that I did not connect him with some sort of action. Hadn't I been told in all the tones of jealousy and admiration that he had collected, bartered, swindled, or stolen more ivory than all the other agents together? That was not the point. The point was in his being a gifted creature, and that of all his gifts the one that stood out pre-eminently, that carried with it a sense of real presence, was his ability to talk, his words—the gift of expression, the bewildering, the illuminating, the most exalted and the most contemptible, the pulsating stream of light, or the deceitful flow from the heart of an impenetrable darkness.

"The other shoe went flying unto the devil-god of that river. I thought, by Jove! it's all over. We are too late; he has vanished—the gift has vanished, by means of some spear, arrow, or club. I will never hear that chap speak after all, and my sorrow had a startling extravagance of emotion, even such as I had noticed in the howling sorrow of these savages in the bush. I couldn't have felt more of lonely desolation somehow, had I been robbed of a belief or had missed my destiny in life. . . . Why do you sigh in this beastly way, somebody? Absurd? Well, absurd. Good Lord! mustn't a man ever— Here, give me some tobacco." . . .

There was a pause of profound stillness, then a match flared, and Marlow's lean face appeared, worn, hollow, with downward folds and dropped eyelids, with an aspect of concentrated attention; and as he took vigorous draws at his pipe, it seemed to retreat and advance out of the night in the regular flicker of the tiny flame. The match went out.

"Absurd!" he cried. "This is the worst of trying to tell. . . . Here you all are, each moored with two good addresses, like a hulk with two anchors, a butcher round one corner, a policeman round another, excellent appetites, and temperature normal—you hear—normal from year's end to year's end. And you say, Absurd! Absurd be— exploded! Absurd! My dear boys, what can you expect from a man who out of sheer nervousness had just flung overboard a pair of new shoes! Now I think of it, it is amazing I did not shed tears. I am, upon the whole, proud of my fortitude. I was cut to the quick at the idea of having lost the inestimable privilege of listening to the gifted Kurtz. Of course I was wrong. The privilege was waiting for me. Oh, yes, I heard more than enough. And I was right, too. A voice. He was very little more than a voice. And I heard—him—it—this voice—other voices—all of them were so little more than voices—and the memory of that time itself lingers around me, impalpable, like a dying vibration of one immense jabber, silly, atrocious, sordid, savage, or simply mean, without any kind of sense. Voices, voices—even the girl herself—now—"

He was silent for a long time.

"I laid the ghost of his gifts at last with a lie," he began, suddenly. "Girl! What! Did I mention a girl? Oh, she is out of it—completely. They—the women I mean— are out of it—should be out of it. We must help them to stay in that beautiful world of their own, lest ours gets worse. Oh, she had to be out of it. You should have heard the disinterred body of Mr. Kurtz saying, 'My Intended.' You would have perceived directly then how completely she was out of it. And the lofty frontal bone of Mr. Kurtz! They say the hair goes on growing sometimes, but this—ah—specimen, was impressively bald. The wilderness had patted him on the head, and, behold, it was like a ball—an ivory ball; it had caressed him, and—lo!—he had withered; it had taken him, loved him, embraced him, got into his veins, consumed his flesh, and sealed his soul to its own by the inconceivable ceremonies of some devilish initiation. He was its spoiled and pampered favorite. Ivory? I should think so. Heaps of it, stacks of it. The old mud shanty was bursting with it. You would think there was not a single tusk left either above or below the ground in the whole country. 'Mostly fossil,' the manager had remarked, disparagingly. It was no more fossil than I am; but they call it fossil when it is dug up. It appears these niggers do bury the tusks sometimes—but evidently they couldn't bury this parcel deep enough to save the gifted Mr. Kurtz from his fate. We filled the steamboat with it, and had to pile a lot on the deck. Thus he could see and enjoy as long as he could see, because the appreciation of his favor had remained with him to the last. You should have heard him say, 'My ivory.' Oh yes, I heard him. 'My Intended, my ivory, my station, my river, my—' everything belonged to him. It made me hold my breath in expectation of hearing the wilderness burst into a prodigious peal of laughter that would shake the fixed stars in their places. Everything belonged to him—but that was a trifle. The thing was to know what he belonged to, how many powers of darkness claimed him for their own. That was the reflection that made you creepy all over. It was impossible—it was not good for one either—trying to imagine. He had taken a high seat amongst the devils of the land—I mean literally. You can't understand. How could you?—with solid pavement under your feet, surrounded by kind neighbors ready to cheer you or to fall on you, stepping delicately between the butcher and the policeman, in the holy terror of scandal and gallows and lunatic asylums—how can you imagine what particular region of the first ages a man's untrammeled feet may take him into by the way of solitude—utter solitude without a policeman—by the way of silence—utter silence, where no warning voice of a kind neighbor can be heard whispering of public opinion? These little things make all the great difference. When they are gone you must fall back upon your own innate strength, upon your own capacity for faithfulness. Of course you may be too much of a fool to go wrong—too dull even to know you are being assaulted by the powers of darkness. I take it, no fool ever made a bargain for his soul with the devil: the fool is too much of a fool, or the devil too much of a devil—I don't know which. Or you may be such a thunderingly exalted creature as to be altogether deaf and blind to anything but heavenly sights and sounds. Then the earth for you is only a standing place—and whether to be like this is your loss or your gain I won't pretend to say. But most of us are neither one nor the other. The earth for us is a place to live in, where we must put up with sights, with sounds, with smells, too, by Jove!—breathe dead hippo, so to speak, and not be contaminated. And there, don't you see? Your strength comes in, the faith in your ability for the digging of unostentatious holes to bury the stuff in—your power of devotion, not to yourself, but to an obscure, back-breaking business. And that's difficult enough. Mind, I am not trying to excuse or even explain —I am trying to account to myself for—for—Mr. Kurtz—for the shade of Mr. Kurtz. This initiated wraith from the back of Nowhere honored me with its amazing confidence before it vanished altogether. This was because it could speak English to me. The original Kurtz had been educated partly in England, and—as he was good enough to say himself—his sympathies were in the right place. His mother was half-English, his father was half-French. All Europe contributed to the making of Kurtz;

and by and by I learned that, most appropriately, the International Society for the Suppression of Savage Customs had intrusted him with the making of a report, for its future guidance. And he had written it, too. I've seen it. I've read it. It was eloquent, vibrating with eloquence, but too high-strung, I think. Seventeen pages of close writing he had found time for! But this must have been before his—let us say—nerves, went wrong, and caused him to preside at certain midnight dances ending with unspeakable rites, which—as far as I reluctantly gathered from what I heard at various times—were offered up to him—do you understand?—to Mr. Kurtz himself. But it was a beautiful piece of writing. The opening paragraph, however, in the light of later information, strikes me now as ominous. He began with the argument that we whites, from the point of development we had arrived at, 'must necessarily appear to them [savages] in the nature of supernatural beings—we approach them with the might as of a deity,' and so on, and so on. 'By the simple exercise of our will we can exert a power for good practically unbounded,' etc., etc. From that point he soared and took me with him. The peroration was magnificent, though difficult to remember, you know. It gave me the notion of an exotic Immensity ruled by an august Benevolence. It made me tingle with enthusiasm. This was the unbounded power of eloquence—of words—of burning noble words. There were no practical hints to interrupt the magic current of phrases, unless a kind of note at the foot of the last page, scrawled evidently much later, in an unsteady hand, may be regarded as the exposition of a method. It was very simple, and at the end of that moving appeal to every altruistic sentiment it blazed at you, luminous and terrifying, like a flash of lightning in a serene sky: 'Exterminate all the brutes!' The curious part was that he had apparently forgotten all about that valuable postscriptum, because, later on, when he in a sense came to himself, he repeatedly entreated me to take good care of 'my pamphlet' (he called it), as it was sure to have in the future a good influence upon his career. I had full information about all these things, and, besides, as it turned out, I was to have the care of his memory. I've done enough for it to give me the indisputable right to lay it, if I choose, for an everlasting rest in the dust bin of progress, amongst all the sweepings and, figuratively speaking, all the dead cats of civilization. But then, you see, I can't choose. He won't be forgotten. Whatever he was, he was not common. He had the power to charm or frighten rudimentary souls into an aggravated witch dance in his honor; he could also fill the small souls of the pilgrims with bitter misgivings: he had one devoted friend at least, and he had conquered one soul in the world that was neither rudimentary nor tainted with self-seeking. No; I can't forget him, though I am not prepared to affirm the fellow was exactly worth the life we lost in getting to him. I missed my late helmsman awfully—I missed him even while his body was still lying in the pilot house. Perhaps you will think it passing strange this regret for a savage who was no more account than a grain of sand in a black Sahara. Well, don't you see, he had done something, he had steered; for months I had him at my back—a help—an instrument. It was a kind of partnership. He steered for me—I had to look after him, I worried about his deficiencies, and thus a subtle bond had been created, of which I only became aware when it was suddenly broken. And the intimate profundity of that look he gave me when he received his hurt remains to this day in my memory—like a claim of distant kinship affirmed in a supreme moment.

"Poor fool! If he had only left that shutter alone. He had no restraint, no restraint —just like Kurtz—a tree swayed by the wind. As soon as I had put on a dry pair of slippers, I dragged him out, after first jerking the spear out of his side, which operation I confess I performed with my eyes shut tight. His heels leaped together over the little doorstep; his shoulders were pressed to my breast; I hugged him from behind desperately. Oh! he was heavy, heavy; heavier than any man on earth, I should imagine. Then without more ado I tipped him overboard. The current snatched him as though he had been a wisp of grass, and I saw the body roll over twice before I lost sight of it forever. All the pilgrims and the manager were then congregated on the awning deck about the pilot house, chattering at each other like a flock of excited magpies, and there was a scandalized murmur at my heartless promptitude. What they wanted to keep that body hanging about for I can't guess. Embalm it, maybe. But I had also heard another, and a very ominous, murmur on the deck below. My friends the woodcutters were likewise scandalized, and with a better show of reason—though I admit that the reason itself was quite inadmissible. Oh, quite! I had made up my mind that if my late helmsman was to be eaten, the fishes alone should have him. He had been a very second-rate helmsman while alive, but now he was dead he might have become a first-class temptation, and possibly cause some startling trouble. Besides, I was anxious to take the wheel, the man in pink pajamas showing himself a hopeless duffer at the business.

"This I did directly the simple funeral was over. We were going half-speed, keeping right in the middle of the stream, and I listened to the talk about me. They had given up Kurtz, they had given up the station; Kurtz was dead, and the station had been burnt—and so on—and so on. The red-haired pilgrim was beside himself with the thought that at least this poor Kurtz had been properly avenged. 'Say! We must have made a glorious slaughter of them in the bush. Eh? What do you think? Say?' He positively danced, the bloodthirsty little gingery beggar. And he had nearly fainted when he saw the wounded man! I could not help saying, 'You made a glorious lot of smoke, anyhow.' I had seen, from the way the tops of the bushes rustled and flew, that almost all the shots had gone too high. You can't hit anything unless you take aim and fire from the shoulder; but these chaps fired from the hip with their eyes shut. The retreat, I maintained—and I was right—was caused by the screeching of the steam whistle. Upon this they forgot Kurtz, and began to howl at me with indignant protests.

"The manager stood by the wheel murmuring confidentially about the necessity of getting well away down the river before dark at all events, when I saw in the distance a clearing on the river side and the outlines of some sort of building. 'What's this?' I asked. He clapped his hands in wonder. 'That station!' he cried. I edged in at once, still going half-speed.

"Through my glasses I saw the slope of a hill interspersed with rare trees and perfectly free from undergrowth. A long decaying building on the summit was half buried in the high grass; the large holes in the peaked roof gaped black from afar; the jungle and the woods made a background. There was no enclosure or fence of any kind; but there had been one apparently, for near the house half-a-dozen slim posts remained in a row, roughly trimmed, and with their upper ends ornamented with round carved balls. The rails, or whatever there had been between, had disappeared. Of course the forest surrounded all that. The river bank was clear, and on the water side I saw a white man under a hat like a cart wheel beckoning persistently with his whole arm. Examining the edge of the forest above and below, I was almost certain I could see movements—human forms gliding here and there. I steamed past prudently, then stopped the engines and let her drift down. The man on the shore began to shout, urging us to land. 'We have been attacked,' screamed the manager. 'I know—I know. It's all right,' yelled back the other, as cheerful as you please. 'Come along. It's all right. I am glad.'

"His aspect reminded me of something I had seen—something funny I had seen somewhere. As I maneuvered to get alongside, I was asking myself, 'What does this fellow look like?' Suddenly I got it. He looked like a harlequin. His clothes had been made of some stuff that was brown holland probably, but it was covered with patches all over, with bright patches, blue, red, and yellow—patches on the back, patches on the front, patches on elbows, on knees; colored binding around his jacket, scarlet edging at the bottom of his trousers; and the sunshine made him look extremely gay and wonderfully neat withal, because you could see how beautifully all this patching had been done. A beardless, boyish face, very fair, no features to speak of, nose peeling, little blue eyes, smiles and frowns chasing each other over that open countenance like sunshine and shadow on a wind-swept plain. 'Look out, captain!' he cried; 'there's a snag lodged in here last night.' What! Another snag? I confess I swore shamefully. I had nearly holed my cripple, to finish off that charming trip. The harlequin on the bank turned his little pug nose up to me. 'You English?' he asked, all smiles. 'Are you?' I shouted from the wheel. The smiles vanished, and he shook his head as if sorry for my disappointment. Then he brightened up. 'Never mind!' he cried, encouragingly. 'Are we in time?' I asked. 'He is up there,' he replied, with a toss of the head up the hill, and becoming gloomy all of a sudden. His face was like the autumn sky, overcast one moment and bright the next.

"When the manager, escorted by the pilgrims, all of them armed to the teeth, had gone to the house this chap came on board. 'I say, I don't like this. These natives are in the bush,' I said. He assured me earnestly it was all right. 'They are simple people,' he added; 'well, I am glad you came. It took me all my time to keep them off.' 'But you said it was all right,' I cried. 'Oh, they meant no harm,' he said; and as I stared he corrected himself, 'Not exactly.' Then vivaciously, 'My faith, your pilot house wants a clean-up!' In the next breath he advised me to keep enough steam on the boiler to blow the whistle in case of any trouble. 'One good screech will do more for you than all your rifles. They are simple people,' he repeated. He rattled away at such a rate he quite overwhelmed me. He seemed to be trying to make up for lots of silence, and actually hinted, laughing, that such was the case. 'Don't you talk with Mr. Kurtz?' I said. 'You don't talk with that man—you listen to him,' he exclaimed with severe exaltation. 'But now—' He waved his arm, and in the twinkling of an eye was in the uttermost depths of despondency. In a moment he came up again with a jump, possessed himself of both my hands, shook them continuously, while he gabbled: 'Brother sailor . . . honor . . . pleasure . . . delight . . . introduce myself . . . Russian . . . son of an arch-priest . . . Government of Tambov. . . . What? Tobacco! English tobacco; the excellent English tobacco! Now, that's brotherly. Smoke? Where's a sailor that does not smoke?'

"The pipe soothed him, and gradually I made out he had run away from school, had gone to sea in a Russian ship; ran away again; served some time in English ships; was now reconciled with the arch-priest. He made a point of that. 'But when one is young one must see things, gather experience, ideas; enlarge the mind.' 'Here!' I interrupted. 'You can never tell! Here I met Mr. Kurtz,' he said, youthfully solemn and reproachful. I held my tongue after that. It appears he had persuaded a Dutch trading house on the coast to fit him out with stores and goods, and had started for the interior with a light heart, and no more idea of what would happen to him than a baby. He had been wandering about that river for nearly two years alone, cut off from everybody and everything. 'I am not so young as I look. I am twenty-five,' he said. 'At first old Van Shuyten would tell me to go to the devil,' he narrated with keen enjoyment; 'but I stuck to him, and talked and talked, till at last he got afraid I would talk the hind leg off his favorite dog, so he gave me some cheap things and a few guns, and told me he hoped he would never see my face again. Good old Dutchman, Van Shuyten. I've sent him one small lot of ivory a year ago, so that he can't call me a little thief when I get back. I hope he got it. And for the rest I don't care. I had some wood stacked for you. That was my old house. Did you see?'

"I gave him Towson's book. He made as though he would kiss me, but restrained himself. 'The only book I had left, and I thought I had lost it,' he said, looking at it ecstatically. 'So many accidents happen to a man going about alone, you know. Canoes get upset sometimes—and sometimes you've got to clear out so quick when the people get angry.' He thumbed the pages. 'You made notes in Russian?' I asked. He nodded. 'I thought they were written in cipher,' I said. He laughed, then became serious. 'I had lots of trouble to keep these people off,' he said. 'Did they want to kill you?' I asked. 'Oh, no!' he cried, and checked himself. 'Why did they attack us?' I pursued. He hesitated, then said shamefacedly, 'They don't want him to go.' 'Don't they?' I said, curiously. He nodded a nod full of mystery and wisdom. 'I tell you,' he cried, 'this man has enlarged my mind.' He opened his arms wide, staring at me with his little blue eyes that were perfectly round."

III

I looked at him, lost in astonishment. There he was before me, in motley, as though he had absconded from a troupe of mimes, enthusiastic, fabulous. His very existence was improbable, inexplicable, and altogether bewildering. He was an insoluble problem. It was inconceivable how he had existed, how he had succeeded in getting so far, how he had managed to remain—why he did not instantly disappear. 'I went a little farther,' he said, 'then still a little farther—till I had gone so far that I don't know how I'll ever get back. Never mind. Plenty time. I can manage. You take Kurtz away quick—quick —I tell you.' The glamor of youth enveloped his parti-colored rags, his destitution, his loneliness, the essential desolation of his futile wanderings. For months—for years— his life hadn't been worth a day's purchase; and there he was gallantly, thoughtlessly alive, to all appearance indestructible solely by the virtue of his few years and of his unreflecting audacity. I was seduced into something like admiration—like envy. Glamor urged him on, glamor kept him unscathed. He surely wanted nothing from the wilderness but space to breathe in and to push on through. His need was to exist, and to move onwards at the greatest possible risk, and with a maximum of privation. If the absolutely pure, uncalculating, unpractical spirit of adventure had ever ruled a human being, it ruled this bepatched youth. I almost envied him the possession of this modest and clear flame. It seemed to have consumed all thought of self so completely, that even while he was talking to you, you forgot that it was he—the man before your eyes —who had gone through these things. I did not envy him his devotion to Kurtz, though. He had not meditated over it. It came to him, and he accepted it with a sort of eager fatalism. I must say that to me it appeared about the most dangerous thing in every way he had come upon so far.

"They had come together unavoidably, like two ships becalmed near each other, and lay rubbing sides at last. I suppose Kurtz wanted an audience, because on a certain occasion, when encamped in the forest, they had talked all night, or more probably Kurtz had talked. 'We talked of everything,' he said, quite transported at the recollec- tion. 'I forgot there was such a thing as sleep. The night did not seem to last an hour. Everything! Everything! . . . Of love, too.' 'Ah, he talked to you of love!' I said, much amused. 'It isn't what you think,' he cried, almost passionately. 'It was in general. He made me see things—things.'

"He threw his arms up. We were on deck at the time, and the headman of my woodcutters, lounging near by, turned upon him his heavy and glittering eyes. I looked around, and I don't know why, but I assure you that never, never before, did this land, this river, this jungle, the very arch of this blazing sky, appear to me so hopeless and so dark, so impenetrable to human thought, so pitiless to human weakness. 'And, ever since, you have been with him, of course?' I said.

"On the contrary. It appears their intercourse had been very much broken by various causes. He had, as he informed me proudly, managed to nurse Kurtz through two illnesses (he alluded to it as you would to some risky feat), but as a rule Kurtz wandered alone, far in the depths of the forest. 'Very often coming to this station, I had to wait days and days before he would turn up,' he said. 'Ah, it was worth waiting for!—sometimes.' 'What was he doing? Exploring or what?' I asked. 'Oh, yes, of course'; he had discovered lots of villages, a lake, too—he did not know exactly in what direction; it was dangerous to inquire too much—but mostly his expeditions had been for ivory. 'But he had no goods to trade with by that time,' I objected. 'There's a good lot of cartridges left even yet,' he answered, looking away. 'To speak plainly, he raided the country,' I said. He nodded. 'Not alone, surely!' He muttered something about the villages round that lake. 'Kurtz got the tribe to follow him, did he?' I suggested. He fidgeted a little. 'They adored him,' he said. The tone of these words was so extraordinary that I looked at him searchingly. It was curious to see his mingled eagerness and reluctance to speak of Kurtz. The man filled his life, occupied his thoughts, swayed his emotions. 'What can you expect?' he burst out; 'he came to them with thunder and lightning, you know—and they had never seen anything like it—and very terrible. He could be very terrible. You can't judge Mr. Kurtz as you would an ordinary man. No, no, no! Now—just to give you an idea—I don't mind telling you, he wanted to shoot me, too, one day—but I don't judge him.' 'Shoot you!' I cried. 'What for?' 'Well, I had a small lot of ivory the chief of that village near my house gave me. You see I used to shoot game for them. Well, he wanted it, and wouldn't hear reason. He declared he would shoot me unless I gave him the ivory and then cleared out of the country, because he would do so, and had a fancy for it, and there was nothing on earth to prevent him killing whom he jolly well pleased. And it was true, too. I gave him the ivory. What did I care! But I didn't clear out. No, no. I couldn't leave him. I had to be careful, of course, till we got friendly again for a time. He had his second illness then. Afterwards I had to keep out of the way; but I didn't mind. He was living for the most part in those villages on the lake. When he came down to the river, sometimes he would take to me, and sometimes it was better for me to be careful. This man suffered too much. He hated all this, and somehow he couldn't get away. When I had a chance I begged him to try and leave while there was time; I offered to go back with him. And he would say yes, and then he would remain; go off on another ivory hunt; disappear for weeks; forget himself amongst these people— forget himself—you know.' 'Why! he's mad,' I said. He protested indignantly. Mr. Kurtz couldn't be mad. If I had heard him talk, only two days ago, I wouldn't dare hint at such a thing. . . . I had taken up my binoculars while we talked, and was looking at the shore, sweeping the limit of the forest at each side and at the back of the house. The consciousness of there being people in that bush, so silent, so quiet— as silent and quiet as the ruined house on the hill—made me uneasy. There was no sign on the face of nature of this amazing tale that was not so much told as suggested to me in desolate exclamations, completed by shrugs, in interrupted phrases, in hints ending in deep sighs. The woods were unmoved, like a mask—heavy, like the closed door of a prison—they looked with their air of hidden knowledge, of patient expecta- tion, of unapproachable silence. The Russian was explaining to me that it was only lately that Mr. Kurtz had come down to the river, bringing along with him all the fighting men of that lake tribe. He had been absent for several months—getting himself adored, I suppose—and had come down unexpectedly, with the intention to all appearances of making a raid either across the river or downstream. Evidently the appetite for more ivory had got the better of the—what shall I say?—less material aspirations. However he had got much worse suddenly. 'I heard he was lying helpless, and so I came up—took my chance,' said the Russian. 'Oh, he is bad, very bad.' I directed my glass to the house. There were no signs of life, but there was the ruined roof, the long mud wall peeping above the grass, with three little square window holes, no two of the same size; all this brought within reach of my hand, as it were. And then I made a brusque movement, and one of the remaining posts of that vanished fence leaped up in the field of my glass. You remember I told you I had been struck at the distance by certain attempts at ornamentation, rather remarkable in the ruinous aspect of the place. Now I had suddenly a nearer view, and its first result was to make me throw my head back as if before a blow. Then I went carefully from post to post with my glass, and I saw my mistake. These round knobs were not ornamental but symbolic; they were expressive and puzzling, striking and disturbing—food for thought and also for the vultures if there had been any looking down from the sky; but at all events for such ants as were industrious enough to ascend the pole. They would have been even more impressive, those heads on the stakes, if their faces had not been turned to the house. Only one, the first I had made out, was facing my way. I was not so shocked as you may think. The start back I had given was really nothing but a movement of surprise. I had expected to see a knob of wood there, you know. I returned deliberately to the first I had seen—and there it was, black, dried, sunken, with closed eyelids, a head that seemed to sleep at the top of that pole, and, with the shrunken dry lips showing a narrow white line of the teeth, was smiling, too, smiling continuously at some endless and jocose dream of that eternal slumber.

"I am not disclosing any trade secrets. In fact, the manager said afterwards that Mr. Kurtz's methods had ruined the district. I have no opinion on that point, but I want you clearly to understand that there was nothing exactly profitable in these heads being there. They only showed that Mr. Kurtz lacked restraint in the gratification of his various lusts, that there was something wanting in him—some small matter which, when the pressing need arose, could not be found under his magnificent eloquence. Whether he knew of this deficiency himself I can't say. I think the knowledge came to him at last—only at the very last. But the wilderness had found him out early, and had taken on him a terrible vengeance for the fantastic invasion. I think it had whispered to him things about himself which he did not know, things of which he had no conception till he took counsel with this great solitude—and the whisper had proved irresistibly fascinating. It echoed loudly within him because he was hollow at the core. . . . I put down the glass, and the head that had appeared near enough to be spoken to seemed at once to have leaped away from me into inaccessible distance.

"The admirer of Mr. Kurtz was a bit crestfallen. In a hurried, indistinct voice he began to assure me he had not dared to take these—say, symbols—down. He was not afraid of the natives; they would not stir till Mr. Kurtz gave the word. His ascendancy was extraordinary. The camps of these people surrounded the place, and the chiefs came every day to see him. They would crawl. . . . 'I don't want to know anything of the ceremonies used when approaching Mr. Kurtz,' I shouted. Curious, this feeling that came over me that such details would be more intolerable than those heads drying on the stakes under Mr. Kurtz's windows. After all, that was only a savage sight, while I seemed at one bound to have been transported into some lightless region of subtle horrors, where pure, uncomplicated savagery was a positive relief, being something that had a right to exist—obviously—in the sunshine. The young man looked at me with surprise. I suppose it did not occur to him that Mr. Kurtz was no idol of mine. He forgot I hadn't heard any of these splendid monologues on, what was it? On love, justice, conduct of life—or whatnot. If it had come to crawling before Mr. Kurtz, he crawled as much as the veriest savage of them all. I had no idea of the conditions, he said: these heads were the heads of rebels. I shocked him excessively by laughing. Rebels! What would be the next definition I was to hear? There had been enemies, criminals, workers—and these were rebels. Those rebellious heads looked very subdued to me on their sticks. 'You don't know how such a life tries a man like Kurtz,' cried Kurtz's last disciple. 'Well, and you?' I said. 'I! I! I am a simple man. I have no great thoughts. I want nothing from anybody. How can you compare me to? . . .' His feelings were too much for speech, and suddenly he broke down. 'I don't understand,' he groaned. 'I've been doing my best to keep him alive, and that's enough. I had no hand in all this. I have no abilities. There hasn't been a drop of medicine or a mouthful of invalid food for months here. He was shamefully abandoned. A man like this, with such ideas. Shamefully! Shamefully! I—I—haven't slept for the last ten nights. . . .'

"His voice lost itself in the calm of the evening. The long shadows of the forest had slipped downhill while we talked, had gone far beyond the ruined hovel, beyond the symbolic row of stakes. All this was in the gloom, while we down there were yet in the sunshine, and the stretch of the river abreast of the clearing glittered in a still and dazzling splendor, with a murky and overshadowed bend above and below. Not a living soul was seen on the shore. The bushes did not rustle.

"Suddenly round the corner of the house a group of men appeared, as though they had come up from the ground. They waded waist-deep in the grass, in a compact body, bearing an improvised stretcher in their midst. Instantly, in the emptiness of the landscape, a cry arose whose shrillness pierced the still air like a sharp arrow flying straight to the very heart of the land; and as if by enchantment, streams of human beings—of naked human beings—with spears in their hands, with bows, with shields, with wild glances and savage movements, were poured into the clearing by the dark-faced and pensive forest. The bushes shook, the grass swayed for a time, and then everything stood still in attentive immobility.

" 'Now, if he does not say the right thing to them we are all done for,' said the Russian at my elbow. The knot of men with the stretcher had stopped, too, halfway to the steamer, as if petrified. I saw the man on the stretcher sit up, lank and with an uplifted arm, above the shoulders of the bearers. 'Let us hope that the man who can talk so well of love in general will find some particular reason to spare us this time,' I said. I resented bitterly the absurd danger of our situation, as if to be at the mercy of that atrocious phantom had been a dishonoring necessity. I could not hear a sound, but through my glasses I saw the thin arm extended commandingly, the lower jaw moving, the eyes of that apparition shining darkly far in its bony head that nodded with grotesque jerks. Kurtz—Kurtz—that means "short" in German—don't it? Well, the name was as true as everything else in his life—and death. He looked at least seven feet long. His covering had fallen off, and his body emerged from it pitiful and appalling as from a winding sheet. I could see the cage of his ribs all astir, the bones of his arm waving. It was as though an animated image of death carved out of old ivory had been shaking its hand with menaces at a motionless crowd of men made of dark and glittering bronze. I saw him open his mouth wide—it gave him a weirdly voracious aspect, as though he had wanted to swallow all the air, all the earth, all the men before him. A deep voice reached me faintly. He must have been shouting. He fell back suddenly. The stretcher shook as the bearers staggered forward again, and almost at the same time I noticed that the crowd of savages was vanishing without any perceptible movement of retreat, as if the forest that had ejected these beings so suddenly had drawn them in again as the breath is drawn in a long aspiration.

"Some of the pilgrims behind the stretcher carried his arms—two shotguns, a heavy rifle, and a light revolver carbine—the thunderbolts of that pitiful Jupiter. The manager bent over him murmuring as he walked beside his head. They laid him down in one of the little cabins—just a room for a bedplace and a campstool or two, you know. We had brought his belated correspondence, and a lot of torn envelopes and open letters littered his bed. His hand roamed feebly amongst these papers. I was struck by the fire of his eyes and the composed languor of his expression. It was not so much the exhaustion of disease. He did not seem in pain. This shadow looked satiated and calm, as though for the moment it had had its fill of all the emotions.

"He rustled one of the letters, and looking straight in my face said, 'I am glad.' Somebody had been writing to him about me. These special recommendations were turning up again. The volume of tone he emitted without effort, almost without the trouble of moving his lips, amazed me. A voice! a voice! It was grave, profound, vibrating, while the man did not seem capable of a whisper. However, he had enough strength in him—factitious no doubt—to very nearly make an end of us, as you shall hear directly.

"The manager appeared silently in the doorway; I stepped out at once and he drew the curtain after me. The Russian, eyed curiously by the pilgrims, was staring at the shore. I followed the direction of his glance.

"Dark human shapes could be made out in the distance, flitting indistinctly against the gloomy border of the forest, and near the river two bronze figures, leaning on tall spears, stood in the sunlight under fantastic headdresses of spotted skins, warlike and still in statuesque repose. And from right to left along the lighted shore moved a wild and gorgeous apparition of a woman.

"She walked with measured steps, draped in striped and fringed cloths, treading the earth proudly, with a slight jingle and flash of barbarous ornaments. She carried her head high; her hair was done in the shape of a helmet; she had brass leggings to the knee, brass wire gauntlets to the elbow, a crimson spot on her tawny cheek, innumerable necklaces of glass beads on her neck; bizarre things, charms, gifts of witch men, that hung about her, glittered and trembled at every step. She must have had the value of several elephant tusks upon her. She was savage and superb, wild-eyed and magnificent; there was something ominous and stately in her deliberate progress. And in the hush that had fallen suddenly upon the whole sorrowful land, the immense wilderness, the colossal body of the fecund and mysterious life seemed to look at her, pensive, as though it had been looking at the image of its own tenebrous and passionate soul.

"She came abreast of the steamer, stood still, and faced us. Her long shadow fell to the water's edge. Her face had a tragic and fierce aspect of wild sorrow and of dumb pain mingled with the fear of some struggling, half-shaped resolve. She stood looking at us without a stir, and like the wilderness itself, with an air of brooding over an inscrutable purpose. A whole minute passed, and then she made a step forward. There was a low jingle, a glint of yellow metal, a sway of fringed draperies, and she stopped as if her heart had failed her. The young fellow by my side growled. The pilgrims murmured at my back. She looked at us all as if her life had depended upon the unswerving steadiness of her glance. Suddenly she opened her bared arms and threw them up rigid above her head, as though in an uncontrollable desire to touch the sky, and at the same time the swift shadows darted out on the earth, swept around on the river, gathering the steamer into a shadowy embrace. A formidable silence hung over the scene.

"She turned away slowly, walked on, following the bank, and passed into the bushes to the left. Once only her eyes gleamed back at us in the dusk of the thickets before she disappeared.

" 'If she had offered to come aboard I really think I would have tried to shoot her,' said the man of patches, nervously. 'I had been risking my life every day for the last fortnight to keep her out of the house. She got in one day and kicked up a row about those miserable rags I picked up in the storeroom to mend my clothes with. I wasn't decent. At least it must have been that, for she talked like a fury to Kurtz for an hour, pointing at me now and then. I don't understand the dialect of this tribe. Luckily for me, I fancy Kurtz felt too ill that day to care, or there would have been mischief. I don't understand. . . . No—it's too much for me. Ah, well, it's all over now.'

"At this moment I heard Kurtz's deep voice behind the curtain: 'Save me!—save the ivory, you mean. Don't tell me. Save *me!* Why, I've had to save you. You are interrupting my plans now. Sick! Sick! Not so sick as you would like to believe. Never mind. I'll carry my ideas out yet—I will return. I'll show you what can be done. You with your little peddling notions—you are interfering with me. I will return. I . . .'

"The manager came out. He did me the honor to take me under the arm and lead me aside. 'He is very low, very low,' he said. He considered it necessary to sigh, but neglected to be consistently sorrowful. 'We have done all we could for him—haven't we? But there is no disguising the fact, Mr. Kurtz has done more harm than good to the Company. He did not see the time was not ripe for vigorous action. Cautiously, cautiously—that's my principle. We must be cautious yet. The district is closed to us for a time. Deplorable! Upon the whole, the trade will suffer. I don't deny there is a remarkable quantity of ivory—mostly fossil. We must save it, at all events—but look how precarious the position is—and why? Because the method is unsound.' 'Do you,' said I, looking at the shore, 'call it "unsound method"?' 'Without doubt,' he exclaimed, hotly. 'Don't you?' . . .

" 'No method at all,' I murmured after a while. 'Exactly,' he exulted. 'I anticipated this. Shows a complete want of judgment. It is my duty to point it out in the proper quarter.' 'Oh,' said I, 'that fellow—what's his name?—the brickmaker, will make a readable report for you.' He appeared confounded for a moment. It seemed to me I had never breathed an atmosphere so vile, and I turned mentally to Kurtz for relief—positively for relief. 'Nevertheless I think Mr. Kurtz is a remarkable man,' I said with emphasis. He started, dropped on me a cold heavy glance, said very quietly, 'he *was*,' and turned his back on me. My hour of favor was over; I found myself lumped along with Kurtz as a partisan of methods for which the time was not ripe: I was unsound! Ah! but it was something to have at least a choice of nightmares.

"I had turned to the wilderness really, not to Mr. Kurtz, who, I was ready to admit, was as good as buried. And for a moment it seemed to me as if I also were buried in a vast grave full of unspeakable secrets. I felt an intolerable weight oppressing my breast, the smell of the damp earth, the unseen presence of victorious corruption, the darkness of an impenetrable night. . . . The Russian tapped me on the shoulder. I heard him mumbling and stammering something about 'brother seaman—couldn't conceal—knowledge of matters that would affect Mr. Kurtz's reputation.' I waited. For him evidently Mr. Kurtz was not in his grave; I suspect that for him Mr. Kurtz was one of the immortals. 'Well!' said I at last, 'speak out. As it happens, I am Mr. Kurtz's friend—in a way.'

"He stated with a good deal of formality that had we not been 'of the same profession,' he would have kept the matter to himself without regard to consequences. 'He suspected there was an active ill will towards him on the part of these white men that—' 'You are right,' I said, remembering a certain conversation I had overheard. 'The manager thinks you ought to be hanged.' He showed a concern at this intelligence which amused me at first. 'I had better get out of the way quietly,' he said, earnestly. 'I can do no more for Kurtz now, and they would soon find some excuse. What's to stop them? There's a military post three hundred miles from here.' 'Well, upon my word,' said I, 'perhaps you had better go if you have any friends amongst the savages near by.' 'Plenty,' he said. 'They are simple people—and I want nothing, you know.' He stood biting his lip, then: 'I don't want any harm to happen to these whites here, but of course I was thinking of Mr. Kurtz's reputation—but you are a brother seaman and—' 'All right,' said I, after a time. 'Mr. Kurtz's reputation is safe with me.' I did not know how truly I spoke.

"He informed me, lowering his voice, that it was Kurtz who had ordered the attack to be made on the steamer. 'He hated sometimes the idea of being taken away—and then again . . . But I don't understand these matters. I am a simple man. He thought it would scare you away—that you would give it up, thinking him dead. I could not stop him. Oh, I had an awful time of it this last month.' 'Very well,' I said. 'He is all right now.' 'Ye-e-es,' he muttered, not very convinced apparently. 'Thanks,' said I; 'I shall keep my eyes open.' 'But quiet—eh?' he urged, anxiously. 'It would be awful for his reputation if anybody here—' I promised a complete discretion with great gravity. 'I have a canoe and three black fellows waiting not very far. I am off. Could you give me a few Martini-Henry cartridges?' I could, and did, with proper secrecy. He helped himself, with a wink at me, to a handful of my tobacco. 'Between sailors—you know —good English tobacco.' At the door of the pilot house he turned round—'I say, haven't you a pair of shoes you could spare?' He raised one leg. 'Look.' The soles were tied with knotted strings sandalwise under his bare feet. I rooted out an old pair, at which he looked with admiration before tucking it under his left arm. One of his pockets (bright red) was bulging with cartridges, from the other (dark blue) peeped 'Towson's Inquiry,' etc., etc. He seemed to think himself excellently well equipped for a renewed encounter with the wilderness. 'Ah! I'll never, never meet such a man again. You ought to have heard him recite poetry—his own, too, it was, he told me. Poetry!' He rolled his eyes at the recollection of these delights. 'Oh, he enlarged my mind!' 'Good-by,' said I. He shook hands and vanished in the night. Sometimes I ask myself whether I had ever really seen him—whether it was possible to meet such a phenomenon! . . .

"When I woke up shortly after midnight his warning came to my mind with its hint of danger that seemed, in the starred darkness, real enough to make me get up for the purpose of having a look round. On the hill a big fire burned, illuminating fitfully a crooked corner of the station house. One of the agents with a picket of a few of our blacks, armed for the purpose, was keeping guard over the ivory; but deep within the forest, red gleams that wavered, that seemed to sink and rise from the ground amongst confused columnar shapes of intense blackness, showed the exact position of the camp where Mr. Kurtz's adorers were keeping their uneasy vigil. The monotonous beating of a big drum filled the air with muffled shocks and a lingering vibration. A steady droning sound of many men chanting each to himself some weird incantation came out from the black, flat wall of the woods as the humming of bees comes out of a hive, and had a strange narcotic effect upon my half-awake senses. I believe I dozed off leaning over the rail, till an abrupt burst of yells, an overwhelming outbreak of a pent-up and mysterious frenzy, woke me up in a bewildered wonder. It was cut short all at once, and the low droning went on with an effect of audible and soothing silence. I glanced casually into the little cabin. A light was burning within, but Mr. Kurtz was not there.

"I think I would have raised an outcry if I had believed my eyes. But I didn't believe them at first—the thing seemed so impossible. The fact is I was completely unnerved by a sheer blank fright, pure abstract terror, unconnected with any distinct shape of physical danger. What made this emotion so overpowering was—how shall I define it? —the moral shock I received, as if something altogether monstrous, intolerable to thought and odious to the soul, had been thrust upon me unexpectedly. This lasted of course the merest fraction of a second, and then the usual sense of commonplace, deadly danger, the possibility of a sudden onslaught and massacre, or something of the kind, which I saw impending, was positively welcome and composing. It pacified me, in fact, so much, that I did not raise an alarm.

"There was an agent buttoned up inside an ulster and sleeping on a chair on deck within three feet of me. The yells had not awakened him; he snored very slightly; I left him to his slumbers and leaped ashore. I did not betray Mr. Kurtz—it was ordered I should never betray him—it was written I should be loyal to the nightmare of my choice. I was anxious to deal with this shadow by myself alone—and to this day I don't know why I was so jealous of sharing with anyone the peculiar blackness of that experience.

"As soon as I got on the bank I saw a trail—a broad trail through the grass. I remember the exultation with which I said to myself, 'He can't walk—he is crawling on all fours—I've got him.' The grass was wet with dew. I strode rapidly with clenched fists. I fancy I had some vague notion of falling upon him and giving him a drubbing. I don't know. I had some imbecile thoughts. The knitting old woman with the cat obtruded herself upon my memory as a most improper person to be sitting at the other end of such an affair. I saw a row of pilgrims squirting lead in the air out of Winchesters held to the hip. I thought I would never get back to the steamer, and imagined myself living alone and unarmed in the woods to an advanced age. Such silly things—you know. And I remember I confounded the beat of the drum with the beating of my heart, and was pleased at its calm regularity.

"I kept to the track though—then stopped to listen. The night was very clear; a dark blue space, sparkling with dew and starlight, in which black things stood very still. I thought I could see a kind of motion ahead of me. I was strangely cocksure of everything that night. I actually left the track and ran in a wide semicircle (I truly believe chuckling to myself) so as to get in front of that stir, of that motion I had seen —if indeed I had seen anything. I was circumventing Kurtz as though it had been a boyish game.

"I came upon him, and, if he had not heard me coming, I would have fallen over him, too, but he got up in time. He rose, unsteady, long, pale, indistinct, like a vapor exhaled by the earth, and swayed slightly, misty and silent before me; while at my back the fires loomed between the trees, and the murmur of many voices issued from the forest. I had cut him off cleverly; but when actually confronting him I seemed to come to my senses, I saw the danger in its right proportion. It was by no means over yet. Suppose he began to shout? Though he could hardly stand, there was still plenty of vigor in his voice. 'Go away—hide yourself,' he said, in that profound tone. It was very awful. I glanced back. We were within thirty yards from the nearest fire. A black figure stood up, strode on long black legs, waving long black arms, across the glow. It had horns—antelope horns, I think—on its head. Some sorcerer, some witch man, no doubt: it looked fiend-like enough. 'Do you know what you are doing?' I whispered. 'Perfectly,' he answered, raising his voice for that single word: it sounded to me far off and yet loud, like a hail through a speaking trumpet. If he makes a row we are lost, I thought to myself. This clearly was not a case for fisticuffs, even apart from the very natural aversion I had to beat that Shadow—this wandering and tormented thing. 'You will be lost,' I said—'utterly lost.' One gets sometimes such a flash of inspiration, you know. I did say the right thing, though indeed he could not have been more irretrievably lost than he was at this very moment, when the foundations of our intimacy were being laid—to endure—to endure—even to the end—even beyond.

" 'I had immense plans,' he muttered irresolutely. 'Yes,' said I; 'but if you try to shout I'll smash your head with—' There was not a stick or a stone near. 'I will throttle you for good,' I corrected myself. 'I was on the threshold of great things,' he pleaded, in a voice of longing, with a wistfulness of tone that made my blood run cold. 'And now for this stupid scoundrel—' 'Your success in Europe is assured in any case,' I affirmed, steadily. I did not want to have the throttling of him, you understand —and indeed it would have been very little use for any practical purpose. I tried to break the spell—the heavy, mute spell of the wilderness—that seemed to draw him to its pitiless breast by the awakening of forgotten and brutal instincts, by the memory of gratified and monstrous passions. This alone, I was convinced, had driven him out to the edge of the forest, to the bush, towards the gleam of fires, the throb of drums, the drone of weird incantations; this alone had beguiled his unlawful soul beyond the bounds of permitted aspirations. And, don't you see, the terror of the position was not in being knocked on the head—though I had a very lively sense of that danger, too —but in this, that I had to deal with a being to whom I could not appeal in the name of anything high or low. I had, even like the niggers, to invoke him—himself—his own exalted and incredible degradation. There was nothing either above or below him, and I knew it. He had kicked himself loose of the earth. Confound the man! he had kicked the very earth to pieces. He was alone, and I before him did not know whether I stood on the ground or floated in the air. I've been telling you what we said— repeating the phrases we pronounced—but what's the good? They were common everyday words—the familiar, vague sounds exchanged on every waking day of life. But what of that? They had behind them, to my mind, the terrific suggestiveness of words heard in dreams, of phrases spoken in nightmares. Soul! If anybody had ever struggled with a soul, I am the man. And I wasn't arguing with a lunatic either. Believe me or not, his intelligence was perfectly clear—concentrated, it is true, upon himself with horrible intensity, yet clear; and therein was my only chance—barring, of course, the killing him there and then, which wasn't so good, on account of unavoidable noise. But his soul was mad. Being alone in the wilderness, it had looked within itself, and, by heavens! I tell you, it had gone mad. I had—for my sin, I suppose—to go through the ordeal of looking into it myself. No eloquence could have been so withering to one's belief in mankind as his final burst of sincerity. He struggled with himself, too. I saw it, I heard it. I saw the inconceivable mystery of a soul that knew no restraint, no faith, and no fear, yet struggling blindly with itself. I kept my head pretty well; but when I had him at last stretched on the couch, I wiped my forehead, while my legs shook under me as though I had carried half a ton on my back down that hill. And yet I had only supported him, his bony arm clasped round my neck—and he was not much heavier than a child.

"When next day we left at noon, the crowd, of whose presence behind the curtain of trees I had been acutely conscious all the time, flowed out of the woods again, filled the clearing, covered the slope with a mass of naked, breathing, quivering, bronze bodies. I steamed up a bit, then swung downstream, and two thousand eyes followed the evolutions of the splashing, thumping, fierce river-demon beating the water with its terrible tail and breathing black smoke into the air. In front of the first rank, along the river, three men, plastered with bright red earth from head to foot, strutted to and fro restlessly. When we came abreast again, they faced the river, stamped their feet, nodded their horned heads, swayed their scarlet bodies; they shook towards the fierce river-demon a bunch of black feathers, a mangy skin with a pendent tail—something that looked like a dried gourd; they shouted periodically together strings of amazing words that resembled no sounds of human language; and the deep murmurs of the crowd, interrupted suddenly, were like the responses of some satanic litany.

"We had carried Kurtz into the pilot house: there was more air there. Lying on the couch, he stared through the open shutter. There was an eddy in the mass of human bodies, and the woman with helmeted head and tawny cheeks rushed out to the very brink of the stream. She put out her hands, shouted something, and all that wild mob took up the shout in a roaring chorus of articulated, rapid, breathless utterance.

" 'Do you understand this?' I asked.

"He kept on looking out past me with fiery, longing eyes, with a mingled expression of wistfulness and hate. He made no answer, but I saw a smile, a smile of indefinable meaning, appear on his colorless lips that a moment after twitched convulsively. 'Do I not?' he said slowly, gasping, as if the words had been torn out of him by a supernatural power.

"I pulled the string of the whistle, and I did this because I saw the pilgrims on deck getting out their rifles with an air of anticipating a jolly lark. At the sudden screech there was a movement of abject terror through that wedged mass of bodies. 'Don't! Don't you frighten them away,' cried someone on deck disconsolately. I pulled the string time after time. They broke and ran, they leaped, they crouched, they swerved, they dodged the flying terror of the sound. The three red chaps had fallen flat, face down on the shore, as though they had been shot dead. Only the barbarous and superb woman did not so much as flinch, and stretched tragically her bare arms after us over the somber and glittering river.

"And then that imbecile crowd down on the deck started their little fun, and I could see nothing more for smoke.

"The brown current ran swiftly out of the heart of darkness, bearing us down towards the sea with twice the speed of our upward progress; and Kurtz's life was running swiftly, too, ebbing, ebbing out of his heart into the sea of inexorable time. The manager was very placid, he had no vital anxieties now, he took us both in with a comprehensive and satisfied glance: the 'affair' had come off as well as could be wished. I saw the time approaching when I would be left alone of the party of 'unsound method.' The pilgrims looked upon me with disfavor. I was, so to speak, numbered with the dead. It is strange how I accepted this unforeseen partnership, this choice of nightmares forced upon me in the tenebrous land invaded by these mean and greedy phantoms.

"Kurtz discoursed. A voice! a voice! It rang deep to the very last. It survived his strength to hide in the magnificent folds of eloquence the barren darkness of his heart. Oh, he struggled! he struggled! The wastes of his weary brain were haunted by shadowy images now—images of wealth and fame revolving obsequiously round his unextinguishable gift of noble and lofty expression. My Intended, my station, my career, my ideas—these were the subjects for the occasional utterances of elevated sentiments. The shade of the original Kurtz frequented the bedside of the hollow sham, whose fate it was to be buried presently in the mold of primeval earth. But both the diabolic love and the unearthly hate of the mysteries it had penetrated fought for the possession of that soul satiated with primitive emotions, avid of lying fame, of sham distinction, of all the appearances of success and power.

"Sometimes he was contemptibly childish. He desired to have kings meet him at railway stations on his return from some ghastly Nowhere, where he intended to accomplish great things. 'You show them you have in you something that is really profitable, and then there will be no limits to the recognition of your ability,' he would say. 'Of course you must take care of the motives—right motives—always.' The long reaches that were like one and the same reach, monotonous bends that were exactly alike, slipped past the steamer with their multitude of secular trees looking patiently after this grimy fragment of another world, the forerunner of change, of conquest, of trade, of massacres, of blessings. I looked ahead—piloting. 'Close the shutter,' said Kurtz suddenly one day; 'I can't bear to look at this.' I did so. There was a silence. 'Oh, but I will wring your heart yet!' he cried at the invisible wilderness.

"We broke down—as I had expected—and had to lie-up for repairs at the head of an island. This delay was the first thing that shook Kurtz's confidence. One morning he gave me a packet of papers and a photograph—the lot tied together with a shoestring. 'Keep this for me,' he said. 'This noxious fool' (meaning the manager) 'is capable of prying into my boxes when I am not looking.' In the afternoon I saw him. He was lying on his back with closed eyes, and I withdrew quietly, but I heard him mutter, 'Live rightly, die, die. . . .' I listened. There was nothing more. Was he rehearsing some speech in his sleep, or was it a fragment of a phrase from some newspaper article? He had been writing for the papers and meant to do so again, 'for the furthering of my ideas. It's a duty.'

"His was an impenetrable darkness. I looked at him as you peer down at a man who is lying at the bottom of a precipice where the sun never shines. But I had not much time to give him, because I was helping the engine driver to take to pieces the leaky cylinders, to straighten a bent connecting rod, and in other such matters. I lived in an infernal mess of rust, filings, nuts, bolts, spanners, hammers, ratchet drills— things I abominate, because I don't get on with them. I tended the little forge we fortunately had aboard; I toiled wearily in a wretched scrapheap—unless I had the shakes too bad to stand.

"One evening coming in with a candle I was startled to hear him say a little tremulously, 'I am lying here in the dark waiting for death.' The light was within a foot of his eyes. I forced myself to murmur, "Oh, nonsense!' and stood over him as if transfixed.

"Anything approaching the change that came over his features I have never seen before, and hope never to see again. Oh, I wasn't touched. I was fascinated. It was as though a veil had been rent. I saw on that ivory face the expression of somber pride, of ruthless power, of craven terror—of an intense and hopeless despair. Did he live his life again in every detail of desire, temptation, and surrender during that supreme moment of complete knowledge? He cried in a whisper at some image, at some vision —he cried out twice, a cry that was no more than a breath: 'The horror! The horror!'

"I blew the candle out and left the cabin. The pilgrims were dining in the mess-room, and I took my place opposite the manager, who lifted his eyes to give me a questioning glance, which I successfully ignored. He leaned back, serene, with that peculiar smile of his sealing the unexpressed depths of his meanness. A continuous shower of small flies streamed upon the lamp, upon the cloth, upon our hands and faces. Suddenly the manager's boy put his insolent black head in the doorway, and said in a tone of scathing contempt—

" 'Mistah Kurtz—he dead.'

"All the pilgrims rushed out to see. I remained, and went on with my dinner. I believe I was considered brutally callous. However, I did not eat much. There was a lamp in there—light, don't you know—and outside it was so beastly, beastly dark. I went no more near the remarkable man who had pronounced a judgment upon the adventures of his soul on this earth. The voice was gone. What else had been there? But I am of course aware that next day the pilgrims buried something in a muddy hole.

"And then they very nearly buried me.

"However, as you see, I did not go to join Kurtz there and then. I did not. I remained to dream the nightmare out to the end, and to show my loyalty to Kurtz once more. Destiny. My destiny! Droll thing life is—that mysterious arrangement of merciless logic for a futile purpose. The most you can hope from it is some knowledge of yourself—that comes too late—a crop of unextinguishable regrets. I have wrestled with death. It is the most unexciting contest you can imagine. It takes place in an impalpable grayness, with nothing underfoot, with nothing around, without specta-tors, without clamor, without glory, without the great desire of victory, without the great fear of defeat, in a sickly atmosphere of tepid skepticism, without much belief in your own right, and still less in that of your adversary. If such is the form of ultimate wisdom, then life is a greater riddle than some of us think it to be. I was within a hair's-breadth of the last opportunity for pronouncement, and I found with humilia-tion that probably I would have nothing to say. This is the reason why I affirm that Kurtz was a remarkable man. He had something to say. He said it. Since I had peeped over the edge myself, I understand better the meaning of his stare, that could not see the flame of the candle, but was wide enough to embrace the whole universe, piercing enough to penetrate all the hearts that beat in the darkness. He had summed up—he had judged. 'The horror!' He was a remarkable man. After all, this was the expression of some sort of belief; it had candor, it had conviction, it had a vibrating note of revolt in its whisper, it had the appalling face of a glimpsed truth—the strange commingling of desire and hate. And it is not my own extremity I remember best—a vision of grayness without form filled with physical pain, and a careless contempt for the evanescence of all things—even of this pain itself. No! It is his extremity that I seem to have lived through. True, he had made that last stride, he had stepped over the edge, while I had been permitted to draw back my hesitating foot. And perhaps in this is the whole difference; perhaps all the wisdom, and all truth, and all sincerity, are just compressed into that inappreciable moment of time in which we step over the threshold of the invisible. Perhaps! I like to think my summing-up would not have been a word of careless contempt. Better his cry—much better. It was an affirmation, a moral victory paid for by innumerable satisfactions. But it was a victory! That is why I have remained loyal to Kurtz to the last, and even beyond, when a long time after I heard once more, not his own voice, but the echo of his magnificent eloquence thrown to me from a soul as translucently pure as a cliff of crystal.

"No, they did not bury me, though there is a period of time which I remember mistily, with a shuddering wonder, like a passage through some inconceivable world that had no hope in it and no desire. I found myself back in the sepulchral city resenting the sight of people hurrying through the streets to filch a little money from each other, to devour their infamous cookery, to gulp their unwholesome beer, to dream their insignificant and silly dreams. They trespassed upon my thoughts. They were intruders whose knowledge of life was to me an irritating pretense, because I felt so sure they could not possibly know the things I knew. Their bearing, which was simply the bearing of commonplace individuals going about their business in the assurance of perfect safety, was offensive to me like the outrageous flauntings of folly in the face of a danger it is unable to comprehend. I had no particular desire to enlighten them, but I had some difficulty in restraining myself from laughing in their faces, so full of stupid importance. I daresay I was not very well at that time. I tottered about the streets—there were various affairs to settle—grinning bitterly at perfectly respectable persons. I admit my behavior was inexcusable, but then my temperature was seldom normal in these days. My dear aunt's endeavors to 'nurse up my strength' seemed altogether beside the mark. It was not my strength that wanted nursing, it was my imagination that wanted soothing. I kept the bundle of papers given me by Kurtz, not knowing exactly what to do with it. His mother had died lately, watched over, as I was told, by his Intended. A clean-shaved man, with an official manner and wearing gold-rimmed spectacles, called on me one day and made inquiries, at first circuitous, afterwards suavely pressing, about what he was pleased to denominate certain 'documents.' I was not surprised, because I had had two rows with the manager on the subject out there. I had refused to give up the smallest scrap out of that package, and I took the same attitude with the spectacled man. He became darkly menacing at last, and with much heat argued that the company had the right to every bit of information about its 'territories.' And said he, 'Mr. Kurtz's knowledge of unexplored regions must have been necessarily extensive and peculiar—owing to his great abilities and to the deplorable circumstances in which he had been placed: therefore—' I assured him Mr. Kurtz's knowledge, however extensive, did not bear upon the problems of commerce or administration. He invoked then the name of science. 'It would be an incalculable loss if,' etc., etc. I offered him the report on the 'Suppression of Savage Customs,' with the postscriptum torn off. He took it up eagerly, but ended by sniffing at it with an air of contempt. 'This is not what we had a right to expect,' he remarked. 'Expect nothing else,' I said. 'There are only private letters.' He withdrew upon some threat of legal proceedings, and I saw him no more; but another fellow, calling himself Kurtz's cousin, appeared two days later, and was anxious to hear all the details about his dear relative's last moments. Incidentally he gave me to understand that Kurtz had been essentially a great musician. 'There was the making of an immense success,' said the man, who was an organist, I believe, with lank gray hair flowing over a greasy coat collar. I had no reason to doubt his statement; and to this day I am unable to say what was Kurtz's profession, whether he ever had any—which was the greatest of his talents. I had taken him for a painter who wrote for the papers, or else for a journalist who could paint—but even the cousin (who took snuff during the interview) could not tell me what he had been—exactly. He was a universal genius—on that point I agreed with the old chap, who thereupon blew his nose noisily into a large cotton handkerchief and withdrew in senile agitation, bearing off some family letters and memoranda without importance. Ultimately a journalist anxious to know something of the fate of his 'dear colleague' turned up. This visitor informed me Kurtz's proper sphere ought to have been politics 'on the popular side.' He had furry straight eyebrows, bristly hair cropped short, an eye-glass on a broad ribbon, and, becoming expansive, confessed his opinion that Kurtz really couldn't write a bit—'but heavens! how that man could talk. He electrified large meetings. He had faith—don't you see?—he had the faith. He could get himself to believe anything—anything. He would have been a splendid leader of an extreme party.' 'What party?' I asked. 'Any party,' answered the other. 'He was an—an—extremist.' Did I not think so? I assented. Did I know, he asked, with a sudden flash of curiosity, 'what it was that had induced him to go out there?' 'Yes,' said I, and forthwith handed him the famous report for publication, if he thought fit. He glanced through it hurriedly, mumbling all the time, judged 'it would do,' and took himself off with this plunder.

"Thus I was left at last with a slim packet of letters and the girl's portrait. She struck me as beautiful—I mean she had a beautiful expression. I know that the sunlight can be made to lie, too, yet one felt that no manipulation of light and pose could have conveyed the delicate shade of truthfulness upon those features. She seemed ready to listen without mental reservation, without suspicion, without a thought for herself. I concluded I would go and give her back her portrait and those letters myself. Curiosity? Yes; and also some other feeling perhaps. All that had been Kurtz's had passed out of my hands: his soul, his body, his station, his plans, his ivory, his career. There remained only his memory and his Intended—and I wanted to give that up, too, to the past, in a way—to surrender personally all that remained of him with me to that oblivion which is the last word of our common fate. I don't defend myself. I had no clear perception of what it was I really wanted. Perhaps it was an impulse of unconscious loyalty, or the fulfilment of one of these ironic necessities that lurk in the facts of human existence. I don't know. I can't tell. But I went.

"I thought his memory was like the other memories of the dead that accumulate in every man's life—a vague impress on the brain of shadows that had fallen on it in their swift and final passage; but before the high and ponderous door, between the tall houses of a street as still and decorous as a well-kept alley in a cemetery, I had a vision of him on the stretcher, opening his mouth voraciously, as if to devour all the earth with all its mankind. He lived then before me; he lived as much as he had ever lived—a shadow insatiable of splendid appearances, of frightful realities; a shadow darker than the shadow of the night, and draped nobly in the folds of a gorgeous eloquence. The vision seemed to enter the house with me—the stretcher, the phantom-bearers, the wild crowd of obedient worshipers, the gloom of the forests, the glitter of the reach between the murky bends, the beat of the drum, regular and muffled like the beating of a heart—the heart of a conquering darkness. It was a moment of triumph for the wilderness, an invading and vengeful rush which, it seemed to me, I would have to keep back alone for the salvation of another soul. And the memory of what I had heard him say afar there, with the horned shapes stirring at my back, in the glow of fires, within the patient woods, those broken phrases came back to me, were heard again in their ominous and terrifying simplicity. I remembered his abject pleading, his abject threats, the colossal scale of his vile desires, the meanness, the torment, the tempestuous anguish of his soul. And later on I seemed to see his collected languid manner, when he said one day, "This lot of ivory now is really mine. The company did not pay for it. I collected it myself at a very great personal risk. I am afraid they will try to claim it as theirs though. H'm. It is a difficult case. What do you think I ought to do—resist? Eh? I want no more than justice.' . . . He wanted no more than justice —no more than justice. I rang the bell before a mahogany door on the first floor, and while I waited he seemed to stare at me out of the glassy panel—stare with that wide and immense stare embracing, condemning, loathing all the universe. I seemed to hear the whispered cry, 'The horror! The horror!'

"The dusk was falling. I had to wait in a lofty drawing room with three long windows from floor to ceiling that were like three luminous and bedraped columns. The bent gilt legs and backs of the furniture shone in indistinct curves. The tall marble fireplace had a cold and monumental whiteness. A grand piano stood massively in a corner; with dark gleams on the flat surfaces like a somber and polished sarcophagus. A high door opened—closed. I rose.

"She came forward, all in black, with a pale head, floating towards me in the dusk. She was in mourning. It was more than a year since his death, more than a year since the news came; she seemed as though she would remember and mourn forever. She took both my hands in hers and murmured, 'I had heard you were coming.' I noticed she was not very young—I mean not girlish. She had a mature capacity for fidelity, for belief, for suffering. The room seemed to have grown darker, as if all the sad light of the cloudy evening had taken refuge on her forehead. This fair hair, this pale visage, this pure brow, seemed surrounded by an ashy halo from which the dark eyes looked out at me. Their glance was guileless, profound, confident, and trustful. She carried her sorrowful head as though she were proud of that sorrow, as though she would say, I—I alone know how to mourn for him as he deserves. But while we were still shaking hands, such a look of awful desolation came upon her face that I perceived she was one of those creatures that are not the playthings of Time. For her he had died only yesterday. And, by Jove! the impression was so powerful that for me, too, he seemed to have died only yesterday—nay, this very minute. I saw her and him in the same instant of time—his death and her sorrow—I saw her sorrow in the very moment of his death. Do you understand? I saw them together—I heard them together. She had said, with a deep catch of the breath, 'I have survived' while my strained ears seemed to hear distinctly, mingled with her tone of despairing regret, the summing-up whisper of his eternal condemnation. I asked myself what I was doing there, with a sensation of panic in my heart as though I had blundered into a place of cruel and absurd mysteries not fit for a human being to behold. She motioned me to a chair. We sat down. I laid the packet gently on the little table, and she put her hand over it. . . . 'You knew him well,' she murmured, after a moment of mourning silence.

" 'Intimacy grows quickly out there,' I said. 'I knew him as well as it is possible for one man to know another.'

" 'And you admired him,' she said. 'It was impossible to know him and not to admire him. Was it?'

" 'He was a remarkable man,' I said, unsteadily. Then before the appealing fixity of her gaze, that seemed to watch for more words on my lips, I went on, 'It was impossible not to—'

" 'Love him,' she finished eagerly, silencing me into an appalled dumbness. 'How true! how true! But when you think that no one knew him so well as I! I had all his noble confidence. I knew him best.'

" 'You knew him best,' I repeated. And perhaps she did. But with every word spoken the room was growing darker, and only her forehead, smooth and white, remained illumined by the unextinguishable light of belief and love.

" 'You were his friend,' she went on. 'His friend,' she repeated, a little louder. 'You must have been, if he had given you this, and sent you to me. I feel I can speak to you —and oh! I must speak. I want you—you who have heard his last words—to know I have been worthy of him. . . . It is not pride. . . . Yes! I am proud to know I understood him better than anyone on earth—he told me so himself. And since his mother died I have had no one—no one—to—to—'

"I listened. The darkness deepened. I was not even sure whether he had given me the right bundle. I rather suspect he wanted me to take care of another batch of his papers which, after his death, I saw the manager examining under the lamp. And the girl talked, easing her pain in the certitude of my sympathy; she talked as thirsty men drink. I had heard that her engagement with Kurtz had been disapproved by her people. He wasn't rich enough or something. And indeed I don't know whether he had not been a pauper all his life. He had given me some reason to infer that it was his impatience of comparative poverty that drove him out there.

" '. . . Who was not his friend who had heard him speak once?' she was saying. 'He drew men towards him by what was best in them.' She looked at me with intensity. 'It is the gift of the great,' she went on, and the sound of her low voice seemed to have the accompaniment of all the other sounds, full of mystery, desolation, and sorrow, I had ever heard—the ripple of the river, the soughing of the trees swayed by the wind, the murmurs of the crowds, the faint ring of incomprehensible words cried from afar, the whisper of a voice speaking from beyond the threshold of an eternal darkness. 'But you have heard him! You know!' she cried.

" 'Yes, I know,' I said with something like despair in my heart, but bowing my head before the faith that was in her, before that great and saving illusion that shone with an unearthly glow in the darkness, in the triumphant darkness from which I could not have defended her—from which I could not even defend myself.

" 'What a loss to me—to us!'—she corrected herself with beautiful generosity; then added in a murmur, 'To the world.' By the last gleams of twilight I could see the glitter of her eyes, full of tears—of tears that would not fall.

" 'I have been very happy—very fortunate—very proud,' she went on. 'Too fortunate. Too happy for a little while. And now I am unhappy for—for life.'

"She stood up; her fair hair seemed to catch all the remaining light in a glimmer of gold. I rose, too.

" 'And of all this,' she went on, mournfully, 'of all his promise, and of all his greatness, of his generous mind, of his noble heart, nothing remains—nothing but a memory. You and I—'

" 'We shall always remember him,' I said, hastily.

" 'No!' she cried. 'It is impossible that all this should be lost—that such a life should be sacrificed to leave nothing—but sorrow. You know what vast plans he had. I knew of them, too—I could not perhaps understand—but others knew of them. Something must remain. His words, at least, have not died.'

" 'His words will remain,' I said.

" 'And his example,' she whispered to herself. 'Men looked up to him—his goodness shone in every act. His example—'

" 'True,' I said; 'his example, too. Yes, his example. I forgot that.'

" 'But I do not. I cannot—I cannot believe—not yet. I cannot believe that I shall never see him again, that nobody will see him again, never, never, never.'

"She put her arms as if after a retreating figure, stretching them back and with clasped pale hands across the fading and narrow sheen of the window. Never see him! I saw him clearly enough then. I shall see this eloquent phantom as long as I live, and I shall see her, too, a tragic and familiar Shade, resembling in this gesture another one, tragic also, and bedecked with powerless charms, stretching bare brown arms over the glitter of the infernal stream, the stream of darkness. She said suddenly very low, 'He died as he lived.'

" 'His end,' said I, with dull anger stirring in me, 'was in every way worthy of his life.'

" 'And I was not with him,' she murmured. My anger subsided before a feeling of infinite pity.

" 'Everything that could be done—' I mumbled.

" 'Ah, but I believed in him more than anyone on earth—more than his own mother, more than—himself. He needed me! Me! I would have treasured every sigh, every word, every sign, every glance.'

"I felt like a chill grip on my chest. 'Don't,' I said, in a muffled voice.

" 'Forgive me. I—I—have mourned so long in silence—in silence. . . . You were with him—to the last? I think of his loneliness. Nobody near to understand him as I would have understood. Perhaps no one to hear. . . .'

" 'To the very end,' I said, shakily. 'I heard his very last words. . . .' I stopped in a fright.

" 'Repeat them,' she murmured in a heartbroken tone. 'I want—I want—something—something—to—to live with.'

"I was on the point of crying at her, 'Don't you hear them?' The dusk was repeating them in a persistent whisper all around us, in a whisper that seemed to swell menacingly like the first whisper of a rising wind. 'The horror! the horror!'

" 'His last word—to live with,' she insisted. 'Don't you understand I loved him—I loved him—I loved him!'

"I pulled myself together and spoke slowly.

" 'The last word he pronounced was—your name.'

"I heard a light sigh and then my heart stood still, stopped dead short by an exulting and terrible cry, by the cry of inconceivable triumph and of unspeakable pain. 'I knew it—I was sure!' . . . She knew. She was sure. I heard her weeping; she had hidden her face in her hands. It seemed to me that the house would collapse before I could escape, that the heavens would fall upon my head. But nothing happened. The heavens do not fall for such a trifle. Would they have fallen, I wonder, if I had rendered Kurtz that justice which was his due? Hadn't he said he wanted only justice? But I couldn't. I could not tell her. It would have been too dark—too dark altogether. . . ."

Marlow ceased, and sat apart, indistinct and silent, in the pose of a meditating Buddha. Nobody moved for a time. "We have lost the first of the ebb," said the director, suddenly. I raised my head. The offing was barred by a black bank of clouds, and the tranquil waterway leading to the uttermost ends of the earth flowed somber under an overcast sky—seemed to lead into the heart of an immense darkness.

THE SECRET SHARER

AN EPISODE FROM THE COAST

I

On my right hand there were lines of fishing stakes resembling a mysterious system of half-submerged bamboo fences, incomprehensible in its division of the domain of tropical fishes, and crazy of aspect as if abandoned forever by some nomad tribe of fishermen now gone to the other end of the ocean; for there was no sign of human habitation as far as the eye could reach. To the left a group of barren islets, suggesting ruins of stone walls, towers, and blockhouses, had its foundations set in a blue sea that itself looked solid, so still and stable did it lie below my feet; even the track of light from the westering sun shone smoothly, without that animated glitter which tells of an imperceptible ripple. And when I turned my head to take a parting glance at the tug which had just left us anchored outside the bar, I saw the straight line of the flat shore joined to the stable sea, edge to edge, with a perfect and unmarked closeness, in one leveled floor half brown, half blue under the enormous dome of the sky. Corresponding in their insignificance to the islets of the sea, two small clumps of trees, one on each side of the only fault in the impeccable joint, marked the mouth of the river Meinam we had just left on the first preparatory stage of our homeward journey; and, far back on the inland level, a larger and loftier mass, the grove surrounding the great Paknam pagoda, was the only thing on which the eye could rest from the vain task of exploring the monotonous sweep of the horizon. Here and there gleams as of a few scattered pieces of silver marked the windings of the great river; and on the nearest of them, just within the bar, the tug steaming right into the land became lost to my sight, hull and funnel and masts, as though the impassive earth had swallowed her up without an effort, without a tremor. My eye followed the light cloud of her smoke, now here, now there, above the plain, according to the devious curves of the stream, but always fainter and farther away, till I lost it at last behind the miter-shaped hill of the great pagoda. And then I was left alone with my ship, anchored at the head of the Gulf of Siam.

She floated at the starting point of a long journey, very still in an immense stillness, the shadows of her spars flung far to the eastward by the setting sun. At that moment I was alone on her decks. There was not a sound in her—and around us nothing moved, nothing lived, not a canoe on the water, not a bird in the air, not a cloud in the sky. In this breathless pause at the threshold of a long passage we seemed to be measuring our fitness for a long and arduous enterprise, the appointed task of both our existences to be carried out, far from all human eyes, with only sky and sea for spectators and for judges.

There must have been some glare in the air to interfere with one's sight, because it was only just before the sun left us that my roaming eyes made out beyond the highest ridge of the principal islet of the group something which did away with the solemnity of perfect solitude. The tide of darkness flowed on swiftly; and with tropical sudden-ness a swarm of stars came out above the shadowy earth, while I lingered yet, my hand resting lightly on my ship's rail as if on the shoulder of a trusted friend. But, with all that multitude of celestial bodies staring down at one, the comfort of quiet commu-nion with her was gone for good. And there were also disturbing sounds by this time —voices, footsteps forward; the steward flitted along the main deck, a busily minister-ing spirit; a hand bell tinkled urgently under the poop deck. . . .

I found my two officers waiting for me near the supper table, in the lighted cuddy. We sat down at once, and as I helped the chief mate, I said:

"Are you aware that there is a ship anchored inside the islands? I saw her mastheads above the ridge as the sun went down."

He raised sharply his simple face, overcharged by a terrible growth of whisker, and emitted his usual ejaculations: "Bless my soul, sir! You don't say so!"

My second mate was a round-cheeked, silent young man, grave beyond his years, I thought; but as our eyes happened to meet I detected a slight quiver on his lips. I looked down at once. It was not my part to encourage sneering on board my ship. It must be said, too, that I knew very little of my officers. In consequence of certain events of no particular significance, except to myself, I had been appointed to the command only a fortnight before. Neither did I know much of the hands forward. All these people had been together for eighteen months or so, and my position was that of the only stranger on board. I mention this because it has some bearing on what is to follow. But what I felt most was my being a stranger to the ship; and if all the truth must be told, I was somewhat of a stranger to myself. The youngest man on board (barring the second mate), and untried as yet by a position of the fullest responsibility, I was willing to take the adequacy of the others for granted. They had simply to be equal to their tasks; but I wondered how far I should turn out faithful to that ideal conception of one's own personality every man sets up for himself secretly.

Meantime the chief mate, with an almost visible effect of collaboration on the part of his round eyes and frightful whiskers, was trying to evolve a theory of the anchored ship. His dominant trait was to take all things into earnest consideration. He was of a painstaking turn of mind. As he used to say, he "liked to account to himself" for practically everything that came in his way, down to a miserable scorpion he had found in his cabin a week before. The why and the wherefore of that scorpion—how it got on board and came to select his room rather than the pantry (which was a dark place and more what a scorpion would be partial to), and how on earth it managed to drown itself in the inkwell of his writing desk—had exercised him infinitely. The ship within the islands was much more easily accounted for; and just as we were about to rise from the table he made his pronouncement. She was, he doubted not, a ship from home lately arrived. Probably she drew too much water to cross the bar except at the top of spring tides. Therefore she went into that natural harbor to wait for a few days in preference to remaining in an open roadstead.

"That's so," confirmed the second mate, suddenly, in his slightly hoarse voice. "She draws over twenty feet. She's the Liverpool ship *Sephora* with a cargo of coal. Hundred and twenty-three days from Cardiff."

We looked at him in surprise.

"The tugboat skipper told me when he came on board for your letters, sir," explained the young man. "He expects to take her up the river the day after tomorrow."

After thus overwhelming us with the extent of his information he slipped out of the cabin. The mate observed regretfully that he "could not account for that young fellow's whims." What prevented him telling us all about it at once, he wanted to know.

I detained him as he was making a move. For the last two days the crew had had plenty of hard work, and the night before they had very little sleep. I felt painfully that I—a stranger—was doing something unusual when I directed him to let all hands turn in without setting an anchor watch. I proposed to keep on deck myself till one o'clock or thereabouts. I would get the second mate to relieve me at that hour.

"He will turn out the cook and the steward at four," I concluded, "and then give you a call. Of course at the slightest sign of any sort of wind we'll have the hands up and make a start at once."

He concealed his astonishment. "Very well, sir." Outside the cuddy he put his head in the second mate's door to inform him of my unheard-of caprice to take a five hours' anchor watch on myself. I heard the other raise his voice incredulously: "What? The captain himself?" Then a few more murmurs, a door closed, then another. A few moments later I went on deck.

My strangeness, which had made me sleepless, had prompted that unconventional arrangement, as if I had expected in those solitary hours of the night to get on terms with the ship of which I knew nothing, manned by men of whom I knew very little more. Fast alongside a wharf, littered like any ship in port with a tangle of unrelated things, invaded by unrelated shore people, I had hardly seen her yet properly. Now, as she lay cleared for sea, the stretch of her main deck seemed to me very fine under the stars. Very fine, very roomy for her size, and very inviting. I descended the poop and paced the waist, my mind picturing to myself the coming passage through the Malay

Archipelago, down the Indian Ocean, and up the Atlantic. All its phases were familiar enough to me, every characteristic, all the alternatives which were likely to face me on the high seas—everything! . . . except the novel responsibility of command. But I took heart from the reasonable thought that the ship was like other ships, the men like other men, and that the sea was not likely to keep any special surprises expressly for my discomfiture.

Arrived at that comforting conclusion, I bethought myself of a cigar and went below to get it. All was still down there. Everybody at the after end of the ship was sleeping profoundly. I came out again on the quarterdeck, agreeably at ease in my sleeping suit on that warm breathless night, barefooted, a glowing cigar in my teeth, and, going forward, I was met by the profound silence of the fore end of the ship. Only as I passed the door of the forecastle I heard a deep, quiet, trustful sigh of some sleeper inside. And suddenly I rejoiced in the great security of the sea as compared with the unrest of the land, in my choice of that untempted life presenting no disquieting problems, invested with an elementary moral beauty by the absolute straightforwardness of its appeal and by the singleness of its purpose.

The riding light in the fore-rigging burned with a clear, untroubled, as if symbolic, flame, confident and bright in the mysterious shades of the night. Passing on my way aft along the other side of the ship, I observed that the rope side ladder, put over, no doubt, for the master of the tug when he came to fetch away our letters, had not been hauled in as it should have been. I became annoyed at this, for exactitude in small matters is the very soul of discipline. Then I reflected that I had myself peremptorily dismissed my officers from duty, and by my own act had prevented the anchor watch being formally set and things properly attended to. I asked myself whether it was wise ever to interfere with the established routine of duties even from the kindest of motives. My action might have made me appear eccentric. Goodness only knew how that absurdly whiskered mate would "account" for my conduct, and what the whole ship thought of that informality of their new captain. I was vexed with myself.

Not from compunction certainly, but, as it were mechanically, I proceeded to get the ladder in myself. Now a side ladder of that sort is a light affair and comes in easily, yet my vigorous tug, which should have brought it flying on board, merely recoiled upon my body in a totally unexpected jerk. What the devil! . . . I was so astounded by the immovableness of that ladder that I remained stock-still, trying to account for it to myself like that imbecile mate of mine. In the end, of course, I put my head over the rail.

The side of the ship made an opaque belt of shadow on the darkling glassy shimmer of the sea. But I saw at once something elongated and pale floating very close to the ladder. Before I could form a guess a faint flash of phosphorescent light, which seemed to issue suddenly from the naked body of a man, flicked in the sleeping water with the elusive, silent play of summer lightning in a night sky. With a gasp I saw revealed to my stare a pair of feet, the long legs, a broad livid back immersed right up to the neck in a greenish cadaverous glow. One hand, awash, clutched the bottom rung of the ladder. He was complete but for the head. A headless corpse! The cigar dropped out of my gaping mouth with a tiny plop and a short hiss quite audible in the absolute stillness of all things under heaven. At that I suppose he raised up his face, a dimly pale oval in the shadow of the ship's side. But even then I could only barely make out down there the shape of his black-haired head. However, it was enough for the horrid, frost-bound sensation which had gripped me about the chest to pass off. The movement of vain exclamations was past, too. I only climbed on the spare spar and leaned over the rail as far as I could, to bring my eyes nearer to that mystery floating alongside.

As he hung by the ladder, like a resting swimmer, the sea lightning played about his limbs at every stir; and he appeared in it ghastly, silvery, fishlike. He remained as mute as a fish, too. He made no motion to get out of the water, either. It was inconceivable that he should not attempt to come on board, and strangely troubling to suspect that perhaps he did not want to. And my first words were prompted by just that troubled incertitude.

"What's the matter?" I asked in my ordinary tone, speaking down to the face upturned exactly under mine.

"Cramp," it answered, no louder. Then slightly anxious, "I say, no need to call anyone."

"I was not going to," I said.

"Are you alone on deck?"

"Yes"

I had somehow the impression that he was on the point of letting go the ladder to swim away beyond my ken—mysterious as he came. But, for the moment, this being appearing as if he had risen from the bottom of the sea (it was certainly the nearest land to the ship) wanted only to know the time. I told him. And he, down there, tentatively:

"I suppose your captain's turned in?"

"I am sure he isn't," I said.

He seemed to struggle with himself, for I heard something like the low, bitter murmur of doubt. "What's the good?" His next words came out with a hesitating effort.

"Look here, my man. Could you call him out quietly?"

I thought the time had come to declare myself.

"I am the captain."

I heard a "By Jove!" whispered at the level of the water. The phosphorescence flashed in the swirl of the water all about his limbs, his other hand seized the ladder.

"My name's Leggatt."

The voice was calm and resolute. A good voice. The self-possession of that man had somehow induced a corresponding state in myself. It was very quietly that I remarked:

"You must be a good swimmer."

"Yes. I've been in the water practically since nine o'clock. The question for me now is whether I am to let go this ladder and go on swimming till I sink from exhaustion, or—to come on board here."

I felt this was no mere formula of desperate speech, but a real alternative in the view of a strong soul. I should have gathered from this that he was young; indeed, it is only the young who are ever confronted by such clear issues. But at the time it was pure intuition on my part. A mysterious communication was established already between us two—in the face of that silent, darkened tropical sea. I was young, too; young enough to make no comment. The man in the water began suddenly to climb up the ladder, and I hastened away from the rail to fetch some clothes.

Before entering the cabin I stood still, listening in the lobby at the foot of the stairs. A faint snore came through the closed door of the chief mate's room. The second mate's door was on the hook, but the darkness in there was absolutely soundless. He, too, was young and could sleep like a stone. Remained the steward, but he was not likely to wake up before he was called. I got a sleeping suit out of my room and, coming back on deck, saw the naked man from the sea sitting on the main hatch, glimmering white in the darkness, his elbows on his knees and his head in his hands. In a moment he had concealed his damp body in a sleeping suit of the same gray-stripe pattern as the one I was wearing and followed me like my double on the poop. Together we moved right aft, barefooted, silent.

"What is it?" I asked in a deadened voice, taking the lighted lamp out of the binnacle, and raising it to his face.

"An ugly business."

He had rather regular features; a good mouth; light eyes under somewhat heavy, dark eyebrows; a smooth, square forehead; no growth on his cheeks; a small, brown mustache, and a well-shaped, round chin. His expression was concentrated, meditative, under the inspecting light of the lamp I held up to his face; such as a man thinking hard in solitude might wear. My sleeping suit was just right for his size. A well-knit young fellow of twenty-five at most. He caught his lower lip with the edge of white, even teeth.

"Yes," I said, replacing the lamp in the binnacle. The warm, heavy tropical night closed upon his head again.

"There's a ship over there," he murmured.

"Yes, I know. The Sephora. Did you know of us?"

"Hadn't the slightest idea. I am the mate of her—" He paused and corrected himself. "I should say I was."

"Aha! Something wrong?"

"Yes. Very wrong indeed. I've killed a man."

"What do you mean? Just now?"

"No, on the passage. Weeks ago. Thirty-nine south. When I say a man—"

"Fit of temper," I suggested, confidently.

The shadowy, dark head, like mine, seemed to nod imperceptibly above the ghostly gray of my sleeping suit. It was, in the night, as though I had been faced by my own reflection in the depths of a somber and immense mirror.

"A pretty thing to have to own up to for a Conway boy," murmured my double, distinctly.

"You're a Conway boy?"

"I am," he said, as if startled. Then, slowly . . . "Perhaps you too—"

It was so; but being a couple of years older I had left before he joined. After a quick interchange of dates a silence fell; and I thought suddenly of my absurd mate with his terrific whiskers and the "Bless my soul—you don't say so" type of intellect. My double gave me an inkling of his thoughts by saying:

"My father's a parson in Norfolk. Do you see me before a judge and jury on that charge? For myself I can't see the necessity. There are fellows that an angel from heaven ——And I am not that. He was one of those creatures that are just simmering all the time with a silly sort of wickedness. Miserable devils that have no business to live at all. He wouldn't do his duty and wouldn't let anybody else do theirs. But what's the good of talking! You know well enough the sort of ill-conditioned snarling cur—"

He appealed to me as if our experiences had been as identical as our clothes. And I knew well enough the pestiferous danger of such a character where there are no means of legal repression. And I knew well enough also that my double there was no homicidal ruffian. I did not think of asking him for details, and he told me the story roughly in brusque, disconnected sentences. I needed no more. I saw it all going on as though I were myself inside that other sleeping suit.

"It happened while we were setting a reefed foresail, at dusk. Reefed foresail! You understand the sort of weather. The only sail we had left to keep the ship running; so you may guess what it had been like for days. Anxious sort of job, that. He gave me some of his cursed insolence at the sheet. I tell you I was overdone with this terrific weather that seemed to have no end to it. Terrific, I tell you—and a deep ship. I believe the fellow himself was half crazed with funk. It was no time for gentlemanly reproof, so I turned round and felled him like an ox. He up and at me. We closed just as an awful sea made for the ship. All hands saw it coming and took to the rigging, but I had him by the throat, and went on shaking him like a rat, the men above us yelling, 'Look out! look out!' Then a crash as if the sky had fallen on my head. They say that for over ten minutes hardly anything was to be seen of the ship—just the three masts and a bit of the forecastle head and of the poop all awash driving along in a smother of foam. It was a miracle that they found us, jammed together behind the forebits. It's clear that I meant business, because I was holding him by the throat still when they picked us up. He was black in the face. It was too much for them. It seems they rushed us aft together, gripped as we were, screaming 'Murder!' like a lot of lunatics, and broke into the cuddy. And the ship running for her life, touch and go all the time, any minute her last in a sea fit to turn your hair gray only a-looking at it. I understand that the skipper, too, started raving like the rest of them. The man had been deprived of sleep for more than a week, and to have this sprung on him at the height of a furious gale nearly drove him out of his mind. I wonder they didn't fling me overboard after getting the carcass of their precious shipmate out of my fingers. They had rather a job to separate us, I've been told. A sufficiently fierce story to make an old judge and a respectable jury sit up a bit. The first thing I heard when I came to myself was the maddening howling of that endless gale, and on that the voice of the old man. He was hanging on to my bunk, staring into my face out of his sou'wester.

"'Mr. Leggatt, you have killed a man. You can act no longer as chief mate of this ship.'"

His care to subdue his voice made it sound monotonous. He rested a hand on the end of the skylight to steady himself with, and all that time did not stir a limb, so far as I could see. "Nice little tale for a quiet tea party," he concluded in the same tone.

One of my hands, too, rested on the end of the skylight; neither did I stir a limb, so far as I knew. We stood less than a foot from each other. It occurred to me that if old "Bless my soul—you don't say so" were to put his head up the companion and catch sight of us, he would think he was seeing double, or imagine himself come upon a scene of weird witchcraft; the strange captain having a quiet confabulation by the wheel with his own gray ghost. I became very much concerned to prevent anything of the sort. I heard the other's soothing undertone.

"My father's a parson in Norfolk," it said. Evidently he had forgotten he had told me this important fact before. Truly a nice little tale.

"You had better slip down into my stateroom now," I said, moving off stealthily. My double followed my movements; our bare feet made no sound; I let him in, closed the door with care, and, after giving a call to the second mate, returned on deck for my relief.

"Not much sign of any wind yet," I remarked when he approached.

"No, sir. Not much," he assented, sleepily, in his hoarse voice, with just enough deference, no more, and barely suppressing a yawn.

"Well, that's all you have to look out for. You have got your orders."

"Yes, sir."

I paced a turn or two on the poop and saw him take up his position face forward with his elbow in the ratlines of the mizzen-rigging before I went below. The mate's faint snoring was still going on peacefully. The cuddy lamp was burning over the table on which stood a vase with flowers, a polite attention from the ship's provision merchant—the last flowers we should see for the next three months at the very least. Two bunches of bananas hung from the beam symmetrically, one on each side of the rudder casing. Everything was as before in the ship—except that two of her captain's sleeping suits were simultaneously in use, one motionless in the cuddy, the other keeping very still in the captain's stateroom.

It must be explained here that my cabin had the form of the capital letter L, the door being within the angle and opening into the short part of the letter. A couch was to the left, the bed-place to the right; my writing desk and the chronometers' table faced the door. But anyone opening it, unless he stepped right inside, had no view of what I call the long (or vertical) part of the letter. It contained some lockers sur-mounted by a bookcase; and a few clothes, a thick jacket or two, caps, oilskin coat, and such like, hung on hooks. There was at the bottom of that part a door opening into my bathroom, which could be entered also directly from the saloon. But that way was never used.

The mysterious arrival had discovered the advantage of this particular shape. Entering my room, lighted strongly by a big bulkhead lamp swung on gimbals above my writing desk, I did not see him anywhere till he stepped out quietly from behind the coats hung in the recessed part.

"I heard somebody moving about, and went in there at once," he whispered.

I, too, spoke under my breath.

"Nobody is likely to come in here without knocking and getting permission."

He nodded. His face was thin and the sunburn faded, as though he had been ill. And no wonder. He had been, I heard presently, kept under arrest in his cabin for nearly seven weeks. But there was nothing sickly in his eyes or in his expression. He was not a bit like me, really; yet, as we stood leaning over my bed-place, whispering side by side, with our dark heads together and our backs to the door, anybody bold enough to open it stealthily would have been treated to the uncanny sight of a double captain busy talking in whispers with his other self.

"But all this doesn't tell me how you came to hang on to our side ladder," I inquired, in the hardly audible murmurs we used, after he had told me something more of the proceedings on board the *Sephora* once the bad weather was over.

"When we sighted Java Head I had had time to think all those matters out several times over. I had six weeks of doing nothing else, and with only an hour or so every evening for a tramp on the quarter-deck."

He whispered, his arms folded on the side of my bedplace, staring through the open port. And I could imagine perfectly the manner of this thinking out—a stubborn if not a steadfast operation; something of which I should have been perfectly incapable.

"I reckoned it would be dark before we closed with the land," he continued, so low that I had to strain my hearing, near as we were to each other, shoulder touching shoulder almost. "So I asked to speak to the old man. He always seemed very sick when he came to see me—as if he could not look me in the face. You know, that foresail saved the ship. She was too deep to have run long under the bare poles. And it was I that managed to set it for him. Anyway, he came. When I had him in my cabin —he stood by the door looking at me as if I had the halter around my neck already— I asked him right away to leave my cabin door unlocked at night while the ship was going through Sunda Straits. There would be the Java coast within two or three miles, off Angier Point. I wanted nothing more. I've had a prize for swimming my second year in the Conway."

"I can believe it," I breathed out.

"God only knows why they locked me in every night. To see some of their faces you'd have thought they were afraid I'd go about at night strangling people. Am I a murdering brute? Do I look it? By Jove! if I had been he wouldn't have trusted himself like that into my room. You'll say I might have chucked him aside and bolted out, there and then—it was dark already. Well, no. And for the same reason I wouldn't think of trying to smash the door. There would have been a rush to stop me at the noise, and I did not mean to get into a confounded scrimmage. Somebody else might have got killed—for I would not have broken out only to get chucked back, and I did not want any more of that work. He refused, looking more sick than ever. He was afraid of the men, and also of that old second mate of his who had been sailing with him for years—a gray-headed old humbug; and his steward, too, had been with him devil knows how long—seventeen years or more—a dogmatic sort of loafer who hated me like poison, just because I was the chief mate. No chief mate ever made more than one voyage in the *Sephora*, you know. Those two old chaps ran the ship. Devil only knows what the skipper wasn't afraid of (all his nerve went to pieces altogether in that hellish spell of bad weather we had)—of what the law would do to him—of his wife, perhaps. Oh, yes! she's on board. Though I don't think she would have meddled. She would have been only too glad to have me out of the ship in any way. The 'brand of Cain' business, don't you see. That's all right. I was ready enough to go off wandering on the face of the earth—and that was price enough to pay for an Abel of that sort. Anyhow, he wouldn't listen to me. 'This thing must take its course. I represent the law here.' He was shaking like a leaf. 'So you won't?' 'No!' 'Then I hope you will be able to sleep on that,' I said, and turned my back on him. 'I wonder that *you* can,' cries he, and locks the door.

"Well, after that, I couldn't. Not very well. That was three weeks ago. We have had a slow passage through the Java Sea; drifted about Carimata for ten days. When we anchored here they thought, I suppose, it was all right. The nearest land (and that's five miles) is the ship's destination; the consul would soon set about catching me; and there would have been no object in bolting to these islets there. I don't suppose there's a drop of water on them. I don't know how it was, but tonight that steward, after bringing me my supper, went out to let me eat it, and left the door unlocked. And I ate it—all there was, too. After I had finished I strolled out on the quarter-deck. I don't know that I meant to do anything. A breath of fresh air was all I wanted, I believe. Then a sudden temptation came over me. I kicked off my slippers and was in the water before I had made up my mind fairly. Somebody heard the splash and they raised an awful hullabaloo. 'He's gone! Lower the boats! He's committed suicide! No, he's swimming.' Certainly I was swimming. It's not so easy for a swimmer like me to commit suicide by drowning. I landed on the nearest islet before the boat left the ship's side. I heard them pulling about in the dark, hailing, and so on, but after a bit they gave up. Everything quieted down and the anchorage became as still as death. I sat down on a stone and began to think. I felt certain they would start searching for me at daylight. There was no place to hide on those stony things—and if there had been, what would have been the good? But now I was clear of that ship, I was not going back. So after a while I took off all my clothes, tied them up in a bundle with a stone inside, and dropped them in the deep water on the outer side of that islet. That was suicide enough for me. Let them think what they liked, but I didn't mean to drown myself. I meant to swim till I sank—but that's not the same thing. I struck out for another of these little islands, and it was from that one that I first saw your riding light. Something to swim for. I went on easily, and on the way I came upon a flat rock a foot or two above water. In the daytime, I dare say, you might make it out with a glass from your poop. I scrambled up on it and rested myself for a bit. Then I made another start. That last spell must have been over a mile."

His whisper was getting fainter and fainter, and all the time he stared straight out through the porthole, in which there was not even a star to be seen. I had not interrupted him. There was something that made comment impossible in his narrative, or perhaps in himself; a sort of feeling, a quality, which I can't find a name for. And when he ceased, all I found was a futile whisper: "So you swam for our light?"

"Yes—straight for it. It was something to swim for. I couldn't see any stars low down because the coast was in the way, and I couldn't see the land, either. The water was like glass. One might have been swimming in a confounded thousand-feet deep cistern with no place for scrambling out anywhere; but what I didn't like was the notion of swimming round and round like a crazed bullock before I gave out; and as I didn't mean to go back . . . No. Do you see me being hauled back, stark naked, off one of these little islands by the scruff of the neck and fighting like a wild beast? Somebody would have got killed for certain, and I did not want any of that. So I went on. Then your ladder—"

"Why didn't you hail the ship?" I asked, a little louder.

He touched my shoulder lightly. Lazy footsteps came right over our heads and stopped. The second mate had crossed from the other side of the poop and might have been hanging over the rail, for all we knew.

"He couldn't hear us talking—could he?" My double breathed into my very ear, anxiously.

His anxiety was an answer, a sufficient answer, to the question I had put to him. An answer containing all the difficulty of that situation. I closed the porthole quietly, to make sure. A louder word might have been overheard.

"Who's that?" he whispered then.

"My second mate. But I don't know much more of the fellow than you do."

And I told him a little about myself. I had been appointed to take charge while I least expected anything of the sort, not quite a fortnight ago. I didn't know either the ship or the people. Hadn't had the time in port to look about me or size anybody up. And as to the crew, all they knew was that I was appointed to take the ship home. For the rest, I was almost as much of a stranger on board as himself, I said. And at the moment I felt it most acutely. I felt that it would take very little to make me a suspect person in the eyes of the ship's company.

He had turned about meantime; and we, the two strangers in the ship, faced each other in identical attitudes.

"Your ladder—" he murmured, after a silence. "Who'd have thought of finding a ladder hanging over at night in a ship anchored out here! I felt just then a very unpleasant faintness. After the life I've been leading for nine weeks, anybody would have got out of condition. I wasn't capable of swimming round as far as your rudder chains. And, lo and behold! there was a ladder to get hold of. After I gripped it I said to myself, 'What's the good?' When I saw a man's head looking over I thought I would swim away presently and leave him shouting—in whatever language it was. I didn't mind being looked at. I—I liked it. And then you speaking to me so quietly— as if you had expected me—made me hold on a little longer. It had been a confounded lonely time—I don't mean while swimming. I was glad to talk a little to somebody that didn't belong to the *Sephora.* As to asking for the captain, that was a mere impulse. It could have been no use, with all the ship knowing about me and the other people pretty certain to be round here in the morning. I don't know—I wanted to be seen, to talk with somebody, before I went on. I don't know what I would have said. . . . 'Fine night, isn't it?' or something of the sort."

"Do you think they will be round here presently?" I asked with some incredulity.

"Quite likely," he said, faintly.

He looked extremely haggard all of a sudden. His head rolled on his shoulders.

"H'm. We shall see then. Meantime get into that bed," I whispered. "Want help? There."

It was a rather high bed-place with a set of drawers underneath. This amazing swimmer really needed the lift I gave him by seizing his leg. He tumbled in, rolled over on his back, and flung one arm across his eyes. And then, with his face nearly hidden, he must have looked exactly as I used to look in that bed. I gazed upon my other self for a while before drawing across carefully the two green serge curtains which ran on a brass rod. I thought for a moment of pinning them together for greater safety, but I sat down on the couch, and once there I felt unwilling to rise and hunt for a pin. I would do it in a moment. I was extremely tired, in a peculiarly intimate way, by the strain of stealthiness, by the effort of whispering and the general secrecy of this excitement. It was three o'clock by now and I had been on my feet since nine, but I was not sleepy; I could not have gone to sleep. I sat there, fagged out, looking at the curtains, trying to clear my mind of the confused sensation of being in two places at once, and greatly bothered by an exasperating knocking in my head. It was a relief to discover suddenly that it was not in my head at all, but on the outside of the door. Before I could collect myself the words "Come in" were out of my mouth, and the steward entered with a tray, bringing in my morning coffee. I had slept, after all, and I was so frightened that I shouted, "This way! I am here, steward," as though he had been miles away. He put down the tray on the table next to the couch and only then said, very quietly, "I can see you are here, sir." I felt him give me a keen look, but I dared not meet his eyes just then. He must have wondered why I had drawn the curtains of my bed before going to sleep on the couch. He went out, hooking the door open as usual.

I heard the crew washing decks above me. I knew I would have been told at once if there had been any wind. Calm, I thought, and I was doubly vexed. Indeed, I felt dual more than ever. The steward reappeared suddenly in the doorway. I jumped up from the couch so quickly that he gave a start.

"What do you want here?"

"Close your port, sir—they are washing decks."

"It is closed," I said, reddening.

"Very well, sir." But he did not move from the doorway and returned my stare in an extraordinary, equivocal manner for a time. Then his eyes wavered, all his expression changed, and in a voice unusually gentle, almost coaxingly:

"May I come in to take the empty cup away, sir?"

"Of course!" I turned my back on him while he popped in and out. Then I unhooked and closed the door and even pushed the bolt. This sort of thing could not go on very long. The cabin was as hot as an oven, too. I took a peep at my double, and discovered that he had not moved, his arm was still over his eyes; but his chest heaved; his hair was wet; his chin glistened with perspiration. I reached over him and opened the port.

"I must show myself on deck," I reflected.

Of course, theoretically, I could do what I liked, with no one to say nay to me within the whole circle of the horizon; but to lock my cabin door and take the key away I did not dare. Directly I put my head out of the companion I saw the group of my two officers, the second mate barefooted, the chief mate in long india-rubber boots, near the break of the poop, and the steward halfway down the poop ladder talking to them eagerly. He happened to catch sight of me and dived, the second ran down on the main deck shouting some order or other, and the chief mate came to meet me, touching his cap.

There was a sort of curiosity in his eye that I did not like. I don't know whether the steward had told them that I was "queer" only, or downright drunk, but I know the man meant to have a good look at me. I watched him coming with a smile which, as he got into point-blank range, took effect and froze his very whiskers. I did not give him time to open his lips.

"Square the yards by lifts and braces before the hands go to breakfast."

It was the first particular order I had given on board that ship; and I stayed on deck to see it executed, too. I had felt the need of asserting myself without loss of time. That sneering young cub got taken down a peg or two on that occasion, and I also seized the opportunity of having a good look at the face of every foremast man as they filed past me to go to the after braces. At breakfast time, eating nothing myself, I presided with such frigid dignity that the two mates were only too glad to escape from the cabin as soon as decency permitted; and all the time the dual working of my mind distracted me almost to the point of insanity. I was constantly watching myself, my secret self, as dependent on my actions as my own personality, sleeping in that bed, behind that door which faced me as I sat at the head of the table. It was very much like being mad, only it was worse because one was aware of it.

I had to shake him for a solid minute, but when at last he opened his eyes it was in the full possession of his senses, with an inquiring look.

"All's well so far," I whispered. "Now you must vanish into the bathroom."

He did so, as noiseless as a ghost, and I then rang for the steward, and facing him boldly, directed him to tidy up my stateroom while I was having my bath—"and be quick about it." As my tone admitted of no excuses, he said, "Yes, sir," and ran off to fetch his dustpan and brushes. I took a bath and did most of my dressing, splashing, and whistling softly for the steward's edification, while the secret sharer of my life stood drawn up bolt upright in that little space, his face looking very sunken in daylight, his eyelids lowered under the stern, dark line of his eyebrows drawn together by a slight frown.

When I left him there to go back to my room the steward was finishing dusting. I sent for the mate and engaged him in some insignificant conversation. It was, as it were, trifling with the terrific character of his whiskers; but my object was to give him an opportunity for a good look at my cabin. And then I could at last shut, with a clear conscience, the door of my stateroom and get my double back into the recessed part. There was nothing else for it. He had to sit still on a small folding stool, half smothered by the heavy coats hanging there. We listened to the steward going into the bathroom out of the saloon, filling the water bottles there, scrubbing the bath, setting things to rights, whisk, bang, clatter—out again into the saloon—turn the key—click. Such was my scheme for keeping my second self invisible. Nothing better could be contrived under the circumstances. And there we sat; I at my writing desk ready to appear busy with some papers, he behind me, out of sight of the door. It would not have been prudent to talk in daytime; and I could not have stood the excitement of that queer sense of whispering to myself. Now and then, glancing over my shoulder, I saw him far back there, sitting rigidly on the low stool, his bare feet close together, his arms folded, his head hanging on his breast—and perfectly still. Anybody would have taken him for me.

I was fascinated by it myself. Every moment I had to glance over my shoulder. I was looking at him when a voice outside the door said:

"Beg pardon, sir."

"Well!" . . . I kept my eyes on him, and so, when the voice outside the door announced, "There's a ship's boat coming our way, sir," I saw him give a start—the first movement he had made for hours. But he did not raise his bowed head.

"All right. Get the ladder over."

I hesitated. Should I whisper something to him? But what? His immobility seemed to have been never disturbed. What could I tell him he did not know already? . . . Finally I went on deck.

II

The skipper of the *Sephora* had a thin red whisker all round his face, and the sort of complexion that goes with hair of that color; also the particular, rather smeary shade of blue in the eyes. He was not exactly a showy figure; his shoulders were high, his stature but middling—one leg slightly more bandy than the other. He shook hands, looking vaguely around. A spiritless tenacity was his main characteristic, I judged. I behaved with a politeness which seemed to disconcert him. Perhaps he was shy. He mumbled to me as if he were ashamed of what he was saying; gave his name (it was something like Archbold—but at this distance of years I hardly am sure), his ship's name, and a few other particulars of that sort, in the manner of a criminal making a reluctant and doleful confession. He had had terrible weather on the passage out—terrible—terrible—wife aboard, too.

By this time we were seated in the cabin and the steward brought in a tray with a bottle and glasses. "Thanks! No." Never took liquor. Would have some water, though. He drank two tumblerfuls. Terrible thirsty work. Ever since daylight had been exploring the islands round his ship.

"What was that for—fun?" I asked, with an appearance of polite interest.

"No!" He sighed. "Painful duty."

As he persisted in his mumbling and I wanted my double to hear every word, I hit upon the notion of informing him that I regretted to say I was hard of hearing.

"Such a young man, too!" he nodded, keeping his smeary blue, unintelligent eyes fastened upon me. What was the cause of it—some disease? he inquired, without the least sympathy and as if he thought that, if so, I'd got no more than I deserved.

"Yes; disease," I admitted in a cheerful tone which seemed to shock him. But my point was gained, because he had to raise his voice to give me his tale. It is not worth while to record that version. It was just over two months since all this had happened, and he had thought so much about it that he seemed completely muddled as to its bearings, but still immensely impressed.

"What would you think of such a thing happening on board your own ship? I've had the *Sephora* for these fifteen years. I am a well-known shipmaster."

He was densely distressed—and perhaps I should have sympathized with him if I had been able to detach my mental vision from the unsuspected sharer of my cabin as though he were my second self. There he was on the other side of the bulkhead, four or five feet from us, no more, as we sat in the saloon. I looked politely at Captain Archbold (if that was his name), but it was the other I saw, in a gray sleeping suit, seated on a low stool, his bare feet close together, his arms folded, and every word said between us falling into the ears of his dark head bowed on his chest.

"I have been at sea now, man and boy, for seven-and-thirty years, and I've never heard of such a thing happening in an English ship. And that it should be my ship. Wife on board, too."

I was hardly listening to him.

"Don't you think," I said, "that the heavy sea which, you told me, came aboard just then might have killed the man? I have seen the sheer weight of a sea kill a man very neatly, by simply breaking his neck."

"Good God!" he uttered impressively, fixing his smeary blue eyes on me. "The sea! No man killed by the sea ever looked like that." He seemed positively scandalized at my suggestion. And as I gazed at him, certainly not prepared for anything original on his part, he advanced his head close to mine and thrust his tongue out at me so suddenly that I couldn't help starting back.

After scoring over my calmness in this graphic way he nodded wisely. If I had seen the sight, he assured me, I would never forget it as long as I lived. The weather was too bad to give the corpse a proper sea burial. So next day at dawn they took it up on the poop, covering its face with a bit of bunting; he read a short prayer, and then, just as it was, in its oilskins and long boots, they launched it amongst those mountainous seas that seemed ready every moment to swallow up the ship herself and the terrified lives on board of her.

"That reefed foresail saved you," I threw in.

"Under God—it did," he exclaimed fervently. "It was by a special mercy, I firmly believe, that it stood some of those hurricane squalls."

"It was the setting of that sail which—" I began.

"God's own hand in it," he interrupted me. "Nothing less could have done it. I don't mind telling you that I hardly dared give the order. It seemed impossible that we could touch anything without losing it, and then our last hope would have been gone."

The terror of that gale was on him yet. I let him go on for a bit, then said, casually —as if returning to a minor subject:

"You were very anxious to give up your mate to the shore people, I believe?"

He was. To the law. His obscure tenacity on that point had in it something incomprehensible and a little awful; something, as it were, mystical, quite apart from his anxiety that he should not be suspected of "countenancing any doings of that sort." Seven-and-thirty virtuous years at sea, of which over twenty of immaculate command, and the last fifteen in the *Sephora*, seemed to have laid him under some pitiless obligation.

"And you know," he went on, groping shamefacedly amongst his feelings, "I did not engage that young fellow. His people had some interest with my owners. I was in a way forced to take him on. He looked very smart, very gentlemanly, and all that. But do you know—I never liked him, somehow. I am a plain man. You see, he wasn't exactly the sort for the chief mate of a ship like the *Sephora*."

I had become so connected in thoughts and impressions with the secret sharer of my cabin that I felt as if I, personally, were being given to understand that I, too, was not the sort that would have done for the chief mate of a ship like the *Sephora*. I had no doubt of it in my mind.

"Not at all the style of man. You understand," he insisted, superfluously, looking hard at me.

I smiled urbanely. He seemed at a loss for a while.

"I suppose I must report a suicide."

"Beg pardon?"

"Sui-cide! That's what I'll have to write to my owners directly I get in."

"Unless you manage to recover him before tomorrow," I assented, dispassionately. . . . "I mean, alive."

He mumbled something which I really did not catch, and I turned my ear to him in a puzzled manner. He fairly bawled:

"The land—I say, the mainland is at least seven miles off my anchorage."

"About that."

My lack of excitement, of curiosity, of surprise, of any sort of pronounced interest, began to arouse his distrust. But except for the felicitous pretense of deafness I had not tried to pretend anything. I had felt utterly incapable of playing the part of ignorance

properly, and therefore was afraid to try. It is also certain that he had brought some
ready-made suspicions with him, and that he viewed my politeness as a strange and
unnatural phenomenon. And yet how else could I have received him? Not heartily!
That was impossible for psychological reasons, which I need not state here. My only
object was to keep off his inquiries. Surlily? Yes, but surliness might have provoked a
point-blank question. From its novelty to him and from its nature, punctilious courtesy was the manner best calculated to restrain the man. But there was the danger of
his breaking through my defense bluntly. I could not, I think, have met him by a direct
lie, also for psychological (not moral) reasons. If he had only known how afraid I was
of his putting my feeling of identity with the other to the test! But, strangely enough
—(I thought of it only afterward)—I believe that he was not a little disconcerted by
the reverse side of that weird situation, by something in me that reminded him of the
man he was seeking—suggested a mysterious similitude to the young fellow he had
distrusted and disliked from the first.

However that might have been, the silence was not very prolonged. He took
another oblique step.

"I reckon I had no more than a two-mile pull to your ship. Not a bit more."

"And quite enough, too, in this awful heat," I said.

Another pause full of mistrust followed. Necessity, they say, is mother of invention,
but fear, too, is not barren of ingenious suggestions. And I was afraid he would ask me
point-blank for news of my other self.

"Nice little saloon, isn't it?" I remarked, as if noticing for the first time the way his
eyes roamed from one closed door to the other. "And very well fitted out, too. Here,
for instance," I continued, reaching over the back of my seat negligently and flinging
the door open, "is my bathroom."

He made an eager movement, but hardly gave it a glance. I got up, shut the door of
the bathroom, and invited him to have a look round, as if I were very proud of my
accommodation. He had to rise and be shown round, but he went through the
business without any raptures whatever.

"And now we'll have a look at my stateroom," I declared, in a voice as loud as I
dared to make it, crossing the cabin to the starboard side with purposely heavy steps.

He followed me in and gazed around. My intelligent double had vanished. I played
my part.

"Very convenient—isn't it?"

"Very nice. Very comf . . ." He didn't finish, and went out brusquely as if to
escape from some unrighteous wiles of mine. But it was not to be. I had been too
frightened not to feel vengeful; I felt I had him on the run, and I meant to keep him
on the run. My polite insistence must have had something menacing in it, because he
gave in suddenly. And I did not let him off a single item; mate's room, pantry,
storerooms, the very sail locker which was also under the poop—he had to look into
them all. When at last I showed him out on the quarter-deck he drew a long, spiritless
sigh, and mumbled dismally that he must really be going back to his ship now. I
desired my mate, who had joined us, to see to the captain's boat.

The man of whiskers gave a blast on the whistle which he used to wear hanging round his neck, and yelled, *"Sephora's* away!" My double down there in my cabin must have heard, and certainly could not feel more relieved than I. Four fellows came running out from somewhere forward and went over the side, while my own men, appearing on deck too, lined the rail. I escorted my visitor to the gangway ceremoniously, and nearly overdid it. He was a tenacious beast. On the very ladder he lingered, and in that unique, guiltily conscientious manner of sticking to the point:

"I say . . . you . . . you don't think that—"

I covered his voice loudly:

"Certainly not. . . . I am delighted. Good-by."

I had an idea of what he meant to say, and just saved myself by the privilege of defective hearing. He was too shaken generally to insist, but my mate, close witness of that parting, looked mystified and his face took on a thoughtful cast. As I did not want to appear as if I wished to avoid all communication with my officers, he had the opportunity to address me.

"Seems a very nice man. His boat's crew told our chaps a very extraordinary story, if what I am told by the steward is true. I suppose you had it from the captain, sir?"

"Yes. I had a story from the captain."

"A very horrible affair—isn't it, sir?"

"It is."

"Beats all these tales we hear about murders in Yankee ships."

"I don't think it beats them. I don't think it resembles them in the least."

"Bless my soul—you don't say so! But of course I've no acquaintance whatever with American ships, not I, so I couldn't go against your knowledge. It's horrible enough for me. . . . But the queerest part is that those fellows seemed to have some idea the man was hidden aboard here. They had really. Did you ever hear of such a thing?"

"Preposterous—isn't it?"

We were walking to and fro athwart the quarter-deck. No one of the crew forward could be seen (the day was Sunday), and the mate pursued:

"There was some little dispute about it. Our chaps took offense. 'As if we would harbor a thing like that,' they said. 'Wouldn't you like to look for him in our coal hole?' Quite a tiff. But they made it up in the end. I suppose he did drown himself. Don't you, sir?"

"I don't suppose anything."

"You have no doubt in the matter, sir?"

"None whatever."

I left him suddenly. I felt I was producing a bad impression, but with my double down there it was most trying to be on deck. And it was almost as trying to be below. Altogether a nerve-trying situation. But on the whole I felt less torn in two when I was with him. There was no one in the whole ship whom I dared take into my confidence. Since the hands had got to know his story, it would have been impossible to pass him off for anyone else, and an accidental discovery was to be dreaded now more than ever. . . .

The steward being engaged in laying the table for dinner, we could talk only with our eyes when I first went down. Later in the afternoon we had a cautious try at whispering. The Sunday quietness of the ship was against us; the stillness of air and water around her was against us; the elements, the men were against us—everything was against us in our secret partnership; time itself—for this could not go on forever. The very trust in Providence was, I suppose, denied to his guilt. Shall I confess that this thought cast me down very much? And as to the chapter of accidents which counts for so much in the book of success, I could only hope that it was closed. For what favorable accident could be expected?

"Did you hear everything?" were my first words as soon as we took up our position side by side, leaning over my bed-place.

He had. And the proof of it was his earnest whisper, "The man told you he hardly dared to give the order."

I understood the reference to be to that saving foresail.

"Yes. He was afraid of it being lost in the setting."

"I assure you he never gave the order. He may think he did, but he never gave it. He stood there with me on the break of the poop after the maintopsail blew away, and whimpered about our last hope—positively whimpered about it and nothing else— and the night coming on! To hear one's skipper go on like that in such weather was enough to drive any fellow out of his mind. It worked me up into a sort of desperation. I just took it into my own hands and went away from him, boiling, and—. But what's the use telling you? *You* know! . . . Do you think that if I had not been pretty fierce with them I should have got the men to do anything? Not it! The bosun perhaps? Perhaps! It wasn't a heavy sea—it was a sea gone mad! I suppose the end of the world will be something like that; and a man may have the heart to see it coming once and be done with it—but to have to face it day after day—I don't blame anybody. I was precious little better than the rest. Only—I was an officer of that old coal-wagon, anyhow—"

"I quite understand," I conveyed that sincere assurance into his ear. He was out of breath with whispering; I could hear him pant slightly. It was all very simple. The same strung-up force which had given twenty-four men a chance, at least, for their lives, had, in a sort of recoil, crushed an unworthy mutinous existence.

But I had no leisure to weigh the merits of the matter—footsteps in the saloon, a heavy knock. "There's enough wind to get under way with, sir." Here was the call of a new claim upon my thoughts and even upon my feelings.

"Turn the hands up," I cried through the door. "I'll be on deck directly."

I was going out to make the acquaintance of my ship. Before I left the cabin our eyes met—the eyes of the only two strangers on board. I pointed to the recessed part where the little campstool awaited him and laid my finger on my lips. He made a gesture—somewhat vague—a little mysterious, accompanied by a faint smile, as if of regret.

This is not the place to enlarge upon the sensations of a man who feels for the first time a ship move under his feet to his own independent word. In my case they were not unalloyed. I was not wholly alone with my command; for there was that stranger in my cabin. Or rather, I was not completely and wholly with her. Part of me was absent. That mental feeling of being in two places at once affected me physically as if the mood of secrecy had penetrated my very soul. Before an hour had elapsed since the ship had begun to move, having occasion to ask the mate (he stood by my side) to take a compass bearing of the Pagoda, I caught myself reaching up to his ear in whispers. I say I caught myself, but enough had escaped to startle the man. I can't describe it otherwise than by saying that he shied. A grave, preoccupied manner, as though he were in possession of some perplexing intelligence, did not leave him henceforth. A little later I moved away from the rail to look at the compass with such a stealthy gait that the helmsman noticed it—and I could not help noticing the unusual roundness of his eyes. These are trifling instances, though it's to no commander's advantage to be suspected of ludicrous eccentricities. But I was also more seriously affected. There are to a seaman certain words, gestures, that should in given conditions come as naturally, as instinctively as the winking of a menaced eye. A certain order should spring on to his lips without thinking; a certain sign should get itself made, so to speak, without reflection. But all unconscious alertness had abandoned me. I had to make an effort of will to recall myself back (from the cabin) to the conditions of the moment. I felt that I was appearing an irresolute commander to those people who were watching me more or less critically.

And, besides, there were the scares. On the second day out, for instance, coming off the deck in the afternoon (I had straw slippers on my bare feet) I stopped at the open pantry door and spoke to the steward. He was doing something there with his back to me. At the sound of my voice he nearly jumped out of his skin, as the saying is, and incidentally broke a cup.

"What on earth's the matter with you?" I asked, astonished.

He was extremely confused. "Beg your pardon, sir. I made sure you were in your cabin."

"You see I wasn't."

"No, sir. I could have sworn I had heard you moving in there not a moment ago. It's most extraordinary . . . very sorry, sir."

I passed on with an inward shudder. I was so identified with my secret double that I did not even mention the fact in those scanty, fearful whispers we exchanged. I suppose he had made some slight noise of some kind or other. It would have been miraculous if he hadn't at one time or another. And yet, haggard as he appeared, he looked always perfectly self-controlled, more than calm—almost invulnerable. On my suggestion he remained almost entirely in the bathroom, which, upon the whole, was the safest place. There could be really no shadow of an excuse for anyone ever wanting to go in there, once the steward had done with it. It was a very tiny place. Sometimes he reclined on the floor, his legs bent, his head sustained on one elbow. At others I would find him on the campstool, sitting in his gray sleeping suit and with his cropped dark hair like a patient, unmoved convict. At night I would smuggle him into my bed-place, and we would whisper together, with the regular footfalls of the officer of the watch passing and repassing over our heads. It was an infinitely miserable time. It was lucky that some tins of fine preserves were stowed in a locker in my stateroom; hard bread I could always get hold of; and so he lived on stewed chicken, paté de foie gras, asparagus, cooked oysters, sardines—on all sorts of abominable sham delicacies out of tins. My early morning coffee he always drank; and it was all I dared do for him in that respect.

Every day there was the horrible maneuvering to go through so that my room and then the bathroom should be done in the usual way. I came to hate the sight of the steward, to abhor the voice of that harmless man. I felt that it was he who would bring on the disaster of discovery. It hung like a sword over our heads.

The fourth day out, I think (we were then working down the east side of the Gulf of Siam, tack for tack, in light winds and smooth water)—the fourth day, I say, of this miserable juggling with the unavoidable, as we sat at our evening meal, that man, whose slightest movement I dreaded, after putting down the dishes ran up on deck busily. This could not be dangerous. Presently he came down again; and then it appeared that he had remembered a coat of mine which I had thrown over a rail to dry after having been wetted in a shower which had passed over the ship in the afternoon. Sitting stolidly at the head of the table I became terrified at the sight of the garment on his arm. Of course he made for my door. There was no time to lose.

"Steward," I thundered. My nerves were so shaken that I could not govern my voice and conceal my agitation. This was the sort of thing that made my terrifically whisk-ered mate tap his forehead with his forefinger. I had detected him using that gesture while talking on deck with a confidential air to the carpenter. It was too far to hear a word, but I had no doubt that this pantomime could only refer to the strange new captain.

"Yes, sir," the pale-faced steward turned resignedly to me. It was this maddening course of being shouted at, checked without rhyme or reason, arbitrarily chased out of my cabin, suddenly called into it, sent flying out of his pantry on incomprehensible errands, that accounted for the growing wretchedness of his expression.

"Where are you going with that coat?"

"To your room, sir."

"Is there another shower coming?"

"I'm sure I don't know, sir. Shall I go up again and see, sir?"

"No! never mind."

My object was attained, as of course my other self in there would have heard everything that passed. During this interlude my two officers never raised their eyes off their respective plates; but the lip of that confounded cub, the second mate, quivered visibly.

I expected the steward to hook my coat on and come out at once. He was very slow about it; but I dominated my nervousness sufficiently not to shout after him. Suddenly I became aware (it could be heard plainly enough) that the fellow for some reason or other was opening the door of the bathroom. It was the end. The place was literally not big enough to swing a cat in. My voice died in my throat and I went stony all over.

I expected to hear a yell of surprise and terror, and made a movement, but had not the strength to get on my legs. Everything remained still. Had my second self taken the poor wretch by the throat? I don't know what I would have done next moment if I had not seen the steward come out of my room, close the door, and then stand quietly by the sideboard.

Saved, I thought. But, no! Lost! Gone! He was gone!

I laid my knife and fork down and leaned back in my chair. My head swam. After a while, when sufficiently recovered to speak in a steady voice, I instructed my mate to put the ship round at eight o'clock himself.

"I won't come on deck," I went on. "I think I'll turn in, and unless the wind shifts I don't want to be disturbed before midnight. I feel a bit seedy."

"You did look middling bad a little while ago," the chief mate remarked without showing any great concern.

They both went out, and I stared at the steward clearing the table. There was nothing to be read on that wretched man's face. But why did he avoid my eyes I asked myself. Then I thought I should like to hear the sound of his voice.

"Steward!"

"Sir!" Startled as usual.

"Where did you hang up that coat?"

"In the bathroom, sir." The usual anxious tone. "It's not quite dry yet, sir."

For some time longer I sat in the cuddy. Had my double vanished as he had come? But of his coming there was an explanation, whereas his disappearance would be inexplicable. . . . I went slowly into my dark room, shut the door, lighted the lamp, and for a time dared not turn round. When at last I did I saw him standing bolt upright in the narrow recessed part. It would not be true to say I had a shock, but an irresistible doubt of his bodily existence flitted through my mind. Can it be, I asked myself, that he is not visible to other eyes than mine? It was like being haunted. Motionless, with a grave face, he raised his hands slightly at me in a gesture which meant clearly, "Heavens! what a narrow escape!" Narrow indeed. I think I had come creeping quietly as near insanity as any man who has not actually gone over the border. That gesture restrained me, so to speak.

The mate with the terrific whiskers was now putting the ship on the other tack. In the moment of profound silence which follows upon the hands going to their stations I heard on the poop his raised voice: "Hard alee!" and the distant shout of the order repeated on the maindeck. The sails, in that light breeze, made but a faint fluttering noise. It ceased. The ship was coming round slowly; I held my breath in the renewed stillness of expectation; one wouldn't have thought that there was a single living soul on her decks. A sudden brisk shout, "Mainsail haul!" broke the spell, and in the noisy cries and rush overhead of the men running away with the main brace we two, down in my cabin, came together in our usual position by the bed-place.

He did not wait for my question. "I heard him fumbling here and just managed to squat myself down in the bath," he whispered to me. "The fellow only opened the door and put his arm in to hang the coat up. All the same—"

"I never thought of that," I whispered back, even more appalled than before at the closeness of the shave, and marveling at that something unyielding in his character which was carrying him through so finely. There was no agitation in his whisper. Whoever was being driven distracted, it was not he. He was sane. And the proof of his sanity was continued when he took up the whispering again.

"It would never do for me to come to life again."

It was something that a ghost might have said. But what he was alluding to was his old captain's reluctant admission of the theory of suicide. It would obviously serve his turn—if I had understood at all the view which seemed to govern the unalterable purpose of his action.

"You must maroon me as soon as ever you can get amongst these islands off the Cambodje shore," he went on.

"Maroon you! We are not living in a boy's adventure tale," I protested. His scornful whispering took me up.

"We aren't indeed! There's nothing of a boy's tale in this. But there's nothing else for it. I want no more. You don't suppose I am afraid of what can be done to me? Prison or gallows or whatever they may please. But you don't see me coming back to explain such things to an old fellow in a wig and twelve respectable tradesmen, do you? What can they know whether I am guilty or not—or of *what* I am guilty, either? That's my affair. What does the Bible say? 'Driven off the face of the earth.' Very well. I am off the face of the earth now. As I came at night so I shall go."

"Impossible!" I murmured. "You can't."

"Can't? . . . Not naked like a soul on the Day of Judgment. I shall freeze on to this sleeping suit. The Last Day is not yet—and . . . you have understood thoroughly. Didn't you?"

I felt suddenly ashamed of myself. I may say truly that I understood—and my hesitation in letting that man swim away from my ship's side had been a mere sham sentiment, a sort of cowardice.

"It can't be done now till next night," I breathed out. "The ship is on the offshore tack and the wind may fail us."

"As long as I know that you understand," he whispered. "But of course you do. It's a great satisfaction to have got somebody to understand. You seem to have been there on purpose." And in the same whisper, as if we two whenever we talked had to say things to each other which were not fit for the world to hear, he added, "It's very wonderful."

We remained side by side talking in our secret way—but sometimes silent or just exchanging a whispered word or two at long intervals. And as usual he stared through the port. A breath of wind came now and again into our faces. The ship might have been moored in dock, so gently and on an even keel she slipped through the water, that did not murmur even at our passage, shadowy and silent like a phantom sea.

At midnight I went on deck, and to my mate's great surprise put the ship round on the other tack. His terrible whiskers flitted round me in silent criticism. I certainly should not have done it if it had been only a question of getting out of that sleepy gulf as quickly as possible. I believe he told the second mate, who relieved him, that it was a great want of judgment. The other only yawned. That intolerable cub shuffled about so sleepily and lolled against the rails in such a slack, improper fashion that I came down on him sharply.

"Aren't you properly awake yet?"

"Yes, sir! I am awake."

"Well, then, be good enough to hold yourself as if you were. And keep a lookout. If there's any current we'll be closing with some islands before daylight."

The east side of the gulf is fringed with islands, some solitary, others in groups. On the blue background of the high coast they seem to float on silvery patches of calm water, arid and gray, or dark green and rounded like clumps of evergreen bushes, with the larger ones, a mile or two long, showing the outlines of ridges, ribs of gray rock under the dark mantle of matted leafage. Unknown to trade, to travel, almost to geography, the manner of life they harbor is an unsolved secret. There must be villages —settlements of fishermen at least—on the largest of them, and some communication with the world is probably kept up by native craft. But all that forenoon, as we headed for them, fanned along by the faintest of breezes, I saw no sign of man or canoe in the field of the telescope I kept on pointing at the scattered group.

At noon I gave no orders for a change of course, and the mate's whiskers became much concerned and seemed to be offering themselves unduly to my notice. At last I said:

"I am going to stand right in. Quite in—as far as I can take her."

The stare of extreme surprise imparted an air of ferocity also to his eyes, and he looked truly terrific for a moment.

"We're not doing well in the middle of the gulf," I continued, casually. "I am going to look for the land breezes tonight."

"Bless my soul! Do you mean, sir, in the dark amongst the lot of all them islands and reefs and shoals?"

"Well—if there are any regular land breezes at all on this coast one must get close inshore to find them, mustn't one?"

"Bless my soul!" he exclaimed again under his breath. All that afternoon he wore a dreamy, contemplative appearance which in him was a mark of perplexity. After dinner I went into my stateroom as if I meant to take some rest. There we two bent our dark heads over a half-unrolled chart lying on my bed.

"There," I said. "It's got to be Koh-ring. I've been looking at it ever since sunrise. It has got two hills and a low point. It must be inhabited. And on the coast opposite there is what looks like the mouth of a biggish river—with some town, no doubt, not far up. It's the best chance for you that I can see."

"Anything. Koh-ring let it be."

He looked thoughtfully at the chart as if surveying chances and distances from a lofty height—and following with his eyes his own figure wandering on the blank land of Cochin-China, and then passing off that piece of paper clean out of sight into uncharted regions. And it was as if the ship had two captains to plan her course for her. I had been so worried and restless running up and down that I had not had the patience to dress that day. I had remained in my sleeping suit, with straw slippers and a soft floppy hat. The closeness of the heat in the gulf had been most oppressive, and the crew were used to seeing me wandering in that airy attire.

"She will clear the south point as she heads now," I whispered into his ear. "Goodness only knows when, though, but certainly after dark. I'll edge her in to half a mile, as far as I may be able to judge in the dark—"

"Be careful," he murmured, warningly—and I realized suddenly that all my future, the only future for which I was fit, would perhaps go irretrievably to pieces in any mishap to my first command.

I could not stop a moment longer in the room. I motioned him to get out of sight and made my way on the poop. That unplayful cub had the watch. I walked up and down for a while thinking things out, then beckoned him over.

"Send a couple of hands to open the two quarter-deck ports," I said, mildly.

He actually had the impudence, or else so forgot himself in his wonder at such an incomprehensible order, as to repeat:

"Open the quarter-deck ports! What for, sir?"

"The only reason you need concern yourself about is because I tell you to do so. Have them open wide and fastened properly."

He reddened and went off, but I believe made some jeering remark to the carpenter as to the sensible practice of ventilating a ship's quarter-deck. I know he popped into the mate's cabin to impart the fact to him because the whiskers came on deck, as it were by chance, and stole glances at me from below—for signs of lunacy or drunkenness, I suppose.

A little before supper, feeling more restless than ever, I rejoined, for a moment, my second self. And to find him sitting so quietly was surprising, like something against nature, inhuman.

I developed my plan in a hurried whisper.

"I shall stand in as close as I dare and then put her round. I shall presently find means to smuggle you out of here into the sail locker, which communicates with the lobby. But there is an opening, a sort of square for hauling the sails out, which gives straight on the quarter-deck and which is never closed in fine weather, so as to give air to the sails. When the ship's way is deadened in stays and all the hands are aft at the main braces you shall have a clear road to slip out and get overboard through the open quarter-deck port. I've had them both fastened up. Use a rope's end to lower yourself into the water so as to avoid a splash—you know. It could be heard and cause some beastly complication."

He kept silent for a while, then whispered, "I understand."

"I won't be there to see you go," I began with an effort. "The rest . . . I only hope I have understood, too."

"You have. From first to last," and for the first time there seemed to be a faltering, something strained in his whisper. He caught hold of my arm, but the ringing of the supper bell made me start. He didn't, though; he only released his grip.

After supper I didn't come below again till well past eight o'clock. The faint, steady breeze was loaded with dew; and the wet, darkened sails held all there was of propelling power in it. The night, clear and starry, sparkled darkly, and the opaque, lightless patches shifting slowly against the low stars were the drifting islets. On the port bow there was a big one more distant and shadowily imposing by the great space of sky it eclipsed.

On opening the door I had a back view of my very own self looking at a chart. He had come out of the recess and was standing near the table.

"Quite dark enough," I whispered.

He stepped back and leaned against my bed with a level, quiet glance. I sat on the couch. We had nothing to say to each other. Over our heads the officer of the watch moved here and there. Then I heard him move quickly. I knew what that meant. He was making for the companion; and presently his voice was outside my door.

"We are drawing in pretty fast, sir. Land looks rather close."

"Very well," I answered. "I am coming on deck directly."

I waited till he was gone out of the cuddy, then rose. My double moved too. The time had come to exchange our last whispers, for neither of us was ever to hear each other's natural voice.

"Look here!" I opened a drawer and took out three sovereigns. "Take this, anyhow. I've got six and I'd give you the lot, only I must keep a little money to buy some fruit and vegetables for the crew from native boats as we go through Sunda Straits."

He shook his head.

"Take it," I urged him, whispering desperately. "No one can tell what—"

He smiled and slapped meaningly the only pocket of the sleeping jacket. It was not safe, certainly. But I produced a large old silk handkerchief of mine, and tying the three pieces of gold in a corner, pressed it on him. He was touched, I suppose, because he took it at last and tied it quickly round his waist under the jacket, on his bare skin.

Our eyes met; several seconds elapsed, till, our glances still mingled, I extended my hand and turned the lamp out. Then I passed through the cuddy, leaving the door of my room wide open. . . . . "Steward!"

He was still lingering in the pantry in the greatness of his zeal, giving a rub-up to a plated cruet stand the last thing before going to bed. Being careful not to wake up the mate, whose room was opposite, I spoke in an undertone.

He looked round anxiously. "Sir!"

"Can you get me a little hot water from the galley?"

"I am afraid, sir, the galley fire's been out for some time now."

"Go and see."

He fled up the stairs.

"Now," I whispered, loudly, into the saloon—too loudly, perhaps, but I was afraid I couldn't make a sound. He was by my side in an instant—the double captain slipped past the stairs—through the tiny dark passage . . . a sliding door. We were in the sail locker, scrambling on our knees over the sails. A sudden thought struck me. I saw myself wandering barefooted, bareheaded, the sun beating on my dark poll. I snatched off my floppy hat and tried hurriedly in the dark to ram it on my other self. He dodged and fended off silently. I wonder what he thought had come to me before he understood and suddenly desisted. Our hands met gropingly, lingered united in a steady, motionless clasp for a second. . . . No word was breathed by either of us when they separated.

I was standing quietly by the pantry door when the steward returned.

"Sorry, sir. Kettle barely warm. Shall I light the spirit lamp?"

"Never mind."

I came out on deck slowly. It was now a matter of conscience to shave the land as close as possible—for now he must go overboard whenever the ship was put in stays. Must! There could be no going back for him. After a moment I walked over to leeward and my heart flew into my mouth at the nearness of the land on the bow. Under any other circumstances I would not have held on a minute longer. The second mate had followed me anxiously.

I looked on till I felt I could command my voice.

"She will weather," I said then in a quiet tone.

"Are you going to try that, sir?" he stammered out incredulously.

I took no notice of him and raised my tone just enough to be heard by the helmsman.

"Keep her good full."

"Good full, sir."

The wind fanned my cheek, the sails slept, the world was silent. The strain of watching the dark loom of the land grow bigger and denser was too much for me. I had shut my eyes—because the ship must go closer. She must! The stillness was intolerable. Were we standing still?

When I opened my eyes the second view started my heart with a thump. The black southern hill of Koh-ring seemed to hang right over the ship like a towering fragment of the everlasting night. On that enormous mass of blackness there was not a gleam to be seen, not a sound to be heard. It was gliding irresistibly toward us and yet seemed already within reach of the hand. I saw the vague figures of the watch grouped in the waist, gazing in awed silence.

"Are you going on, sir?" inquired an unsteady voice at my elbow.

I ignored it. I had to go on.

"Keep her full. Don't check her way. That won't do now," I said warningly.

"I can't see the sails very well," the helmsman answered me, in strange, quavering tones.

Was she close enough? Already she was, I won't say in the shadow of the land, but in the very blackness of it, already swallowed up as it were, gone too close to be recalled, gone from me altogether.

"Give the mate a call," I said to the young man who stood at my elbow as still as death. "And turn all hands up."

My tone had a borrowed loudness reverberated from the height of the land. Several voices cried out together: "We are all on deck, sir."

Then stillness again, with the great shadow gliding closer, towering higher, without a light, without a sound. Such a hush had fallen on the ship that she might have been a bark of the dead floating in slowly under the very gate of Erebus.

"My God! Where are we?"

It was the mate moaning at my elbow. He was thunderstruck, and as it were deprived of the moral support of his whiskers. He clapped his hands and absolutely cried out, "Lost!"

"Be quiet," I said sternly.

He lowered his tone, but I saw the shadowy gesture of his despair. "What are we doing here?"

"Looking for the land wind."

He made as if to tear his hair, and addressed me recklessly.

"She will never get out. You have done it, sir. I knew it'd end in something like this. She will never weather, and you are too close now to stay. She'll drift ashore before she's round. O my God!"

I caught his arm as he was raising it to batter his poor devoted head, and shook it violently.

"She's ashore already," he wailed, trying to tear himself away.

"Is she? . . . Keep good full there!"

"Good full, sir," cried the helmsman in a frightened, thin, childlike voice.

I hadn't let go the mate's arm and went on shaking it. "Ready about, do you hear? You go forward"—shake—"and stop there"—shake—"and hold your noise"—shake —"and see these head sheets properly overhauled"—shake, shake—shake.

And all the time I dared not look toward the land lest my heart should fail me. I released my grip at last and he ran forward as if fleeing for dear life.

I wondered what my double there in the sail locker thought of this commotion. He was able to hear everything—and perhaps he was able to understand why, on my conscience, it had to be thus close—no less. My first order "Hard alee!" re-echoed ominously under the towering shadow of Koh-ring as if I had shouted in a mountain gorge. And then I watched the land intently. In that smooth water and light wind it was impossible to feel the ship coming-to. No! I could not feel her. And my second self was making now ready to slip out and lower himself overboard. Perhaps he was gone already . . . ?

The great black mass brooding over our very mastheads began to pivot away from the ship's side silently. And now I forgot the secret stranger ready to depart, and remembered only that I was a total stranger to the ship. I did not know her. Would she do it? How was she to be handled?

I swung the mainyard and waited helplessly. She was perhaps stopped, and her very fate hung in the balance, with the black mass of Koh-ring like the gate of the everlasting night towering over her taffrail. What would she do now? Had she way on her yet? I stepped to the side swiftly, and on the shadowy water I could see nothing except a faint phosphorescent flash revealing the glassy smoothness of the sleeping surface. It was impossible to tell—and I had not learned yet the feel of my ship. Was she moving? What I needed was something easily seen, a piece of paper, which I could throw overboard and watch. I had nothing on me. To run down for it I didn't dare. There was no time. All at once my strained, yearning stare distinguished a white object floating within a yard of the ship's side. White on the black water. A phosphorescent flash passed under it. What was that thing? . . . I recognized my own floppy hat. It must have fallen off his head . . . and he didn't bother. Now I had what I wanted—the saving mark for my eyes. But I hardly thought of my other self, now gone from the ship, to be hidden forever from all friendly faces, to be a fugitive and a vagabond on the earth, with no brand of the curse on his sane forehead to stay a slaying hand . . . too proud to explain.

And I watched the hat—the expression of my sudden pity for his mere flesh. It had been meant to save his homeless head from the dangers of the sun. And now—behold —it was saving the ship, by serving me for a mark to help out the ignorance of my strangeness. Ha! It was drifting forward, warning me just in time that the ship had gathered sternway.

"Shift the helm," I said in a low voice to the seaman standing still like a statue.

The man's eyes glistened wildly in the binnacle light as he jumped round to the other side and spun round the wheel.

I walked to the break of the poop. On the overshadowed deck all hands stood by the forebraces waiting for my order. The stars ahead seemed to be gliding from right to left. And all was so still in the world that I heard the quiet remark "She's round," passed in a tone of intense relief between two seamen.

"Let go and haul."

The foreyards ran round with a great noise, amidst cheery cries. And now the frightful whiskers made themselves heard giving various orders. Already the ship was drawing ahead. And I was alone with her. Nothing! no one in the world should stand now between us, throwing a shadow on the way of silent knowledge and mute affection, the perfect communion of a seaman with his first command.

Walking to the taffrail, I was in time to make out, on the very edge of a darkness thrown by a towering black mass like the very gateway of Erebus—yes, I was in time to catch an evanescent glimpse of my white hat left behind to mark the spot where the secret sharer of my cabin and of my thoughts, as though he were my second self, had lowered himself into the water to take his punishment; a free man, a proud swimmer striking out for a new destiny.

TYPHOON

aptain MacWhirr, of the steamer *Nan-Shan*, had a physiognomy that, in the order of material appearances, was the exact counterpart of his mind: it presented no marked characteristics of firmness or stupidity; it had no pronounced characteristics whatever; it was simply ordinary, irresponsive, and unruffled.

The only thing his aspect might have been said to suggest, at times, was bashfulness; because he would sit, in business offices ashore, sunburnt and smiling faintly, with downcast eyes. When he raised them, they were perceived to be direct in their glance and of blue color. His hair was fair and extremely fine, clasping from temple to temple the bald dome of his skull in a clamp as of fluffy silk. The hair of his face, on the contrary, carroty and flaming, resembled a growth of copper wire clipped short to the line of the lip; while, no matter how close he shaved, fiery metallic gleams passed, when he moved his head, over the surface of his cheeks. He was rather below the medium height, a bit round-shouldered, and so sturdy of limb that his clothes always looked a shade too tight for his arms and legs. As if unable to grasp what is due to the difference of latitudes, he wore a brown bowler hat, a complete suit of a brownish hue, and clumsy black boots. These harbor togs gave to his thick figure an air of stiff and uncouth smartness. A thin silver watchchain looped his waistcoat, and he never left his ship for the shore without clutching in his powerful, hairy fist an elegant umbrella of the very best quality, but generally unrolled. Young Jukes, the chief mate, attending his commander to the gangway, would sometimes venture to say, with the greatest gentleness, "Allow me, sir"—and possessing himself of the umbrella deferentially, would elevate the ferule, shake the folds, twirl a neat furl in a jiffy, and hand it back; going through the performance with a face of such portentous gravity, that Mr. Solomon Rout, the chief engineer, smoking his morning cigar over the skylight, would turn away his head in order to hide a smile. "Oh! aye! The blessed gamp. . . . Thank 'ee, Jukes, thank 'ee," would mutter Captain MacWhirr, heartily, without looking up.

Having just enough imagination to carry him through each successive day, and no more, he was tranquilly sure of himself; and from the very same cause he was not in the least conceited. It is your imaginative superior who is touchy, overbearing, and difficult to please; but every ship Captain MacWhirr commanded was the floating abode of harmony and peace. It was, in truth, as impossible for him to take a flight of fancy as it would be for a watchmaker to put together a chronometer with nothing except a two-pound hammer and a whipsaw in the way of tools. Yet the uninteresting lives of men so entirely given to the actuality of the bare existence have their mysterious side. It was impossible in Captain MacWhirr's case, for instance, to understand what under heaven could have induced that perfectly satisfactory son of a petty grocer in Belfast to run away to sea. And yet he had done that very thing at the age of fifteen. It was enough, when you thought it over, to give you the idea of an immense, potent, and invisible hand thrust into the ant-heap of the earth, laying hold of shoulders, knocking heads together, and setting the unconscious faces of the multitude towards inconceivable goals and in undreamt-of directions.

His father never really forgave him for this undutiful stupidity. "We could have got on without him," he used to say later on, "but there's the business. And he an only son, too!" His mother wept very much after his disappearance. As it had never occurred to him to leave word behind, he was mourned over for dead till, after eight months, his first letter arrived from Talcahuano. It was short, and contained the statement: "We had very fine weather on our passage out." But evidently, in the writer's mind, the only important intelligence was to the effect that his captain had, on the very day of writing, entered him regularly on the ship's articles as Ordinary Seaman. "Because I can do the work," he explained. The mother again wept copiously, while the remark, "Tom's an ass," expressed the emotions of the father. He was a corpulent man, with a gift for sly chaffing, which to the end of his life he exercised in his intercourse with his son, a little pityingly, as if upon a half-witted person.

MacWhirr's visits to his home were necessarily rare, and in the course of years he dispatched other letters to his parents, informing them of his successive promotions and of his movements upon the vast earth. In these missives could be found sentences like this: "The heat here is very great." Or: "On Christmas day at 4 P.M. we fell in with some icebergs." The old people ultimately became acquainted with a good many names of ships, and with the names of the skippers who commanded them—with the names of Scots and English shipowners—with the names of seas, oceans, straits, promontories—with outlandish names of lumber ports, of rice ports, of cotton ports —with the names of islands—with the name of their son's young woman. She was called Lucy. It did not suggest itself to him to mention whether he thought the name pretty. And then they died.

The great day of MacWhirr's marriage came in due course, following shortly upon the great day when he got his first command.

All these events had taken place many years before the morning when, in the chart room of the steamer *Nan-Shan,* he stood confronted by the fall of a barometer he had no reason to distrust. The fall—taking into account the excellence of the instrument, the time of the year, and the ship's position on the terrestrial globe—was of a nature ominously prophetic; but the red face of the man betrayed no sort of inward disturbance. Omens were as nothing to him, and he was unable to discover the message of a prophecy till the fulfillment had brought it home to his very door. "That's a fall, and no mistake," he thought. "There must be some uncommonly dirty weather knocking about."

The *Nan-Shan* was on her way from the southward to the treaty port of Fu-chau, with some cargo in her lower holds, and two hundred Chinese coolies returning to their village homes in the province of Fo-kien, after a few years of work in various tropical colonies. The morning was fine, the oily sea heaved without a sparkle, and there was a queer white misty patch in the sky like a halo of the sun. The foredeck, packed with Chinamen, was full of somber clothing, yellow faces, and pigtails, sprinkled over with a good many naked shoulders, for there was no wind, and the heat was close. The coolies lounged, talked, smoked, or stared over the rail; some, drawing water over the side, sluiced each other; a few slept on hatches, while several small parties of six sat on their heels surrounding iron trays with plates of rice and tiny teacups; and every single Celestial of them was carrying with him all he had in the world—a wooden chest with a ringing lock and brass on the corners, containing the savings of his labors: some clothes of ceremony, sticks of incense, a little opium maybe, bits of nameless rubbish of conventional value, and a small hoard of silver dollars, toiled for in coal lighters, won in gambling houses or in petty trading, grubbed out of earth, sweated out in mines, on railway lines, in deadly jungle, under heavy burdens— amassed patiently, guarded with care, cherished fiercely.

A cross swell had set in from the direction of Formosa Channel about ten o'clock, without disturbing these passengers much, because the *Nan-Shan,* with her flat bottom, rolling chocks on bilges, and great breadth of beam, had the reputation of an exceptionally steady ship in a seaway. Mr. Jukes, in moments of expansion on shore, would proclaim loudly that the "old girl was as good as she was pretty." It would never have occurred to Captain MacWhirr to express his favorable opinion so loud or in terms so fanciful.

She was a good ship, undoubtedly, and not old either. She had been built in Dumbarton less than three years before, to the order of a firm of merchants in Siam— Messrs. Sigg and Son. When she lay afloat, finished in every detail and ready to take up the work of her life, the builders contemplated her with pride.

"Sigg has asked us for a reliable skipper to take her out," remarked one of the partners; and the other, after reflecting for a while, said: "I think MacWhirr is ashore just at present." "Is he? Then wire him at once. He's the very man," declared the senior, without a moment's hesitation.

Next morning MacWhirr stood before them unperturbed, having traveled from London by the midnight express after a sudden but undemonstrative parting with his wife. She was the daughter of a superior couple who had seen better days.

"We had better be going together over the ship, Captain," said the senior partner; and the three men started to view the perfections of the *Nan-Shan* from stem to stern, and from her keelson to the trucks of her two stumpy pole-masts.

Captain MacWhirr had begun by taking off his coat, which he hung on the end of a steam windlass embodying all the latest improvements.

"My uncle wrote of you favorably by yesterday's mail to our good friends—Messrs. Sigg, you know—and doubtless they'll continue you out there in command," said the junior partner. "You'll be able to boast of being in charge of the handiest boat of her size on the coast of China, Captain," he added.

"Have you? Thank 'ee," mumbled vaguely MacWhirr, to whom the view of a distant eventuality could appeal no more than the beauty of a wide landscape to a purblind tourist; and his eyes happening at the moment to be at rest upon the lock of the cabin door, he walked up to it, full of purpose, and began to rattle the handle vigorously, while he observed, in his low, earnest voice, "You can't trust the workmen nowadays. A brand-new lock, and it won't act at all. Stuck fast. See? See?"

As soon as they found themselves alone in their office across the yard: "You praised that fellow up to Sigg. What is it you see in him?" asked the nephew, with faint contempt.

"I admit he has nothing of your fancy skipper about him, if that's what you mean," said the elder man, curtly. "Is the foreman of the joiners on the *Nan-Shan* outside? . . . Come in, Bates. How is it that you let Tait's people put us off with a defective lock on the cabin door? The captain could see directly he set eyes on it. Have it replaced at once. The little straws, Bates . . . the little straws. . . ."

The lock was replaced accordingly, and a few days afterwards the *Nan-Shan* steamed out to the East, without MacWhirr having offered any further remark as to her fittings, or having been heard to utter a single word hinting at pride in his ship, gratitude for his appointment, or satisfaction at his prospects.

With a temperament neither loquacious nor taciturn he found very little occasion to talk. There were matters of duty, of course—directions, orders, and so on; but the past being to his mind done with, and the future not there yet, the more general actualities of the day required no comment—because facts can speak for themselves with overwhelming precision.

Old Mr. Sigg liked a man of few words, and one that "you could be sure would not try to improve upon his instructions." MacWhirr satisfying these requirements, was continued in command of the *Nan-Shan*, and applied himself to the careful navigation of his ship in the China seas. She had come out on a British register, but after some time Messrs. Sigg judged it expedient to transfer her to the Siamese flag.

At the news of the contemplated transfer Jukes grew restless, as if under a sense of personal affront. He went about grumbling to himself, and uttering short scornful laughs. "Fancy having a ridiculous Noah's Ark elephant in the ensign of one's ship," he said once at the engine-room door. "Dash me if I can stand it; I'll throw up the billet. Don't it make *you* sick, Mr. Rout?" The chief engineer only cleared his throat with the air of a man who knows the value of a good billet.

The first morning the new flag floated over the stern of the *Nan-Shan* Jukes stood looking at it bitterly from the bridge. He struggled with his feelings for a while, and then remarked, "Queer flag for a man to sail under, sir."

"What's the matter with the flag?" inquired Captain MacWhirr. "Seems all right to me." And he walked across to the end of the bridge to have a good look.

"Well, it looks queer to me," burst out Jukes, greatly exasperated, and flung off the bridge.

Captain MacWhirr was amazed at these manners. After a while he stepped quietly into the chart room, and opened his International Signal Code Book at the plate where the flags of all the nations are correctly figured in gaudy rows. He ran his finger over them, and when he came to Siam he contemplated with great attention the red field and the white elephant. Nothing could be more simple; but to make sure he brought the book out on the bridge for the purpose of comparing the colored drawing with the real thing at the flagstaff astern. When next Jukes, who was carrying on the duty that day with a sort of suppressed fierceness, happened on the bridge, his commander observed:

"There's nothing amiss with that flag."

"Isn't there?" mumbled Jukes, falling on his knees before a deck locker and perking therefrom viciously a spare lead line.

"No. I looked up the book. Length twice the breadth and the elephant exactly in the middle. I thought the people ashore would know how to make the local flag. Stands to reason. You were wrong, Jukes. . . ."

"Well, sir," began Jukes, getting up excitedly, "all I can say—" He fumbled for the end of the coil of line with trembling hands.

"That's all right." Captain MacWhirr soothed him, sitting heavily on a little canvas folding stool he greatly affected. "All you have to do is to take care they don't hoist the elephant upside-down before they get quite used to it."

Jukes flung the new lead line over on the foredeck with a loud "Here you are, bosun —don't forget to wet it thoroughly," and turned with immense resolution towards his commander; but Captain MacWhirr spread his elbows on the bridge rail comfortably.

"Because it would be, I suppose, understood as a signal of distress," he went on. "What do you think? That elephant there, I take it, stands for something in the nature of the Union Jack in the flag. . . ."

"Does it!" yelled Jukes, so that every head on the *Nan-Shan's* decks looked towards the bridge. Then he sighed, and with sudden resignation: "It would certainly be a dam' distressful sight," he said, meekly.

Later in the day he accosted the chief engineer with a confidential, "Here, let me tell you the old man's latest."

Mr. Solomon Rout (frequently alluded to as Long Sol, Old Sol, or Father Rout), from finding himself almost invariably the tallest man on board every ship he joined, had acquired the habit of a stooping, leisurely condescension. His hair was scant and sandy, his flat cheeks were pale, his bony wrists and long scholarly hands were pale, too, as though he had lived all his life in the shade.

He smiled from on high at Jukes, and went on smoking and glancing about quietly, in the manner of a kind uncle lending an ear to the tale of an excited schoolboy. Then, greatly amused but impassive, he asked:

"And did you throw up the billet?"

"No," cried Jukes, raising a weary, discouraged voice above the harsh buzz of the *Nan-Shan's* friction winches. All of them were hard at work, snatching slings of cargo, high up, to the end of long derricks, only, as it seemed, to let them rip down recklessly by the run. The cargo chains groaned in the gins, clinked on coamings, rattled over the side; and the whole ship quivered, with her long gray flanks smoking in wreaths of steam. "No," cried Jukes, "I didn't. What's the good? I might just as well fling my resignation at this bulkhead. I don't believe you can make a man like that understand anything. He simply knocks me over."

At that moment Captain MacWhirr, back from the shore, crossed the deck, umbrella in hand, escorted by a mournful, self-possessed Chinaman, walking behind in paper-soled silk shoes, and who also carried an umbrella.

The master of the *Nan-Shan*, speaking just audibly and gazing at his boots as his manner was, remarked that it would be necessary to call at Fu-chau this trip, and desired Mr. Rout to have steam up tomorrow afternoon at one o'clock sharp. He pushed back his hat to wipe his forehead, observing at the same time that he hated going ashore anyhow; while overtopping him Mr. Rout, without deigning a word, smoked austerely, nursing his right elbow in the palm of his left hand. Then Jukes was directed in the same subdued voice to keep the forward 'tween-deck clear of cargo. Two hundred coolies were going to be put down there. The Bun Hin Company were sending that lot home. Twenty-five bags of rice would be coming off in a sampan directly, for stores. All seven-years'-men they were, said Captain MacWhirr, with a camphor-wood chest to every man. The carpenter should be set to work nailing three-inch battens along the deck below, fore and aft, to keep these boxes from shifting in a seaway. Jukes had better look to it at once. "D'ye hear, Jukes?" This Chinaman here was coming with the ship as far as Fu-chau—a sort of interpreter he would be. Bun Hin's clerk he was, and wanted to have a look at the space. Jukes had better take him forward. "D'ye hear, Jukes?"

Jukes took care to punctuate these instructions in proper places with the obligatory "Yes, sir," ejaculated without enthusiasm. His brusque "Come along, John; make look see" set the Chinaman in motion at his heels.

"Wanchee look see, all same look see can do," said Jukes, who having no talent for foreign languages mangled the very pidgin-English cruelly. He pointed at the open hatch. "Catchee number one piecie place to sleep in. Eh?"

He was gruff, as became his racial superiority, but not unfriendly. The Chinaman, gazing sad and speechless into the darkness of the hatchway, seemed to stand at the head of a yawning grave.

"No catchee rain down there—savee?" pointed out Jukes. "Suppose all'ee same fine weather, one piecie coolie-man come topside," he pursued, warming up imaginatively. "Make so—Phooooo!" He expanded his chest and blew out his cheeks. "Savee, John?

Breathe—fresh air. Good. Eh? Washee him piecie pants, chow-chow topside—see, John?"

With his mouth and hands he made exuberant motions of eating rice and washing clothes; and the Chinaman, who concealed his distrust of this pantomime under a collected demeanor tinged by a gentle and refined melancholy, glanced out of his almond eyes from Jukes to the hatch and back again. "Velly good," he murmured, in a disconsolate undertone, and hastened smoothly along the decks, dodging obstacles in his course. He disappeared, ducking low under a sling of ten dirty gunny bags full of some costly merchandise and exhaling a repulsive smell.

Captain MacWhirr meantime had gone on the bridge, and into the chart room, where a letter, commenced two days before, awaited termination. These long letters began with the words, "My darling wife," and the steward, between the scrubbing of the floors and the dusting of chronometer boxes, snatched at every opportunity to read them. They interested him much more than they possibly could the woman for whose eye they were intended; and this for the reason that they related in minute detail each successive trip of the *Nan-Shan*.

Her master, faithful to facts, which alone his consciousness reflected, would set them down with painstaking care upon many pages. The house in a northern suburb to which these pages were addressed had a bit of garden before the bow-windows, a deep porch of good appearance, colored glass with imitation lead frame in the front door. He paid five-and-forty pounds a year for it, and did not think the rent too high, because Mrs. MacWhirr (a pretentious person with a scraggy neck and a disdainful manner) was admittedly ladylike, and in the neighborhood considered as "quite superior." The only secret of her life was her abject terror of the time when her husband would come home to stay for good. Under the same roof there dwelt also a daughter called Lydia and a son, Tom. These two were but slightly acquainted with their father. Mainly, they knew him as a rare but privileged visitor, who of an evening smoked his pipe in the dining room and slept in the house. The lanky girl, upon the whole, was rather ashamed of him; the boy was frankly and utterly indifferent in a straightforward, delightful, unaffected way manly boys have.

And Captain MacWhirr wrote home from the coast of China twelve times every year, desiring quaintly to be "remembered to the children," and subscribing himself "your loving husband," as calmly as if the words so long used by so many men were, apart from their shape, worn-out things, and of a faded meaning.

The China seas north and south are narrow seas. They are seas full of everyday, eloquent facts, such as islands, sand banks, reefs, swift and changeable currents—tangled facts that nevertheless speak to a seaman in clear and definite language. Their speech appealed to Captain MacWhirr's sense of realities so forcibly that he had given up his stateroom below and practically lived all his days on the bridge of his ship, often having his meals sent up, and sleeping at night in the chart room. And he indited there his home letters. Each of them, without exception, contained the phrase, "The weather has been very fine this trip," or some other form of a statement to that effect. And this statement, too, in its wonderful persistence, was of the same perfect accuracy as all the others they contained.

Mr. Rout likewise wrote letters; only no one on board knew how chatty he could be pen in hand, because the chief engineer had enough imagination to keep his desk locked. His wife relished his style greatly. They were a childless couple, and Mrs. Rout, a big, high-bosomed, jolly woman of forty, shared with Mr. Rout's toothless and venerable mother a little cottage near Teddington. She would run over her correspondence, at breakfast, with lively eyes, and scream out interesting passages in a joyous voice at the deaf old lady, prefacing each extract by the warning shout, "Solomon says!" She had the trick of firing off Solomon's utterances also upon strangers, astonishing them easily by the unfamiliar text and the unexpectedly jocular vein of these quotations. On the day the new curate called for the first time at the cottage, she found occasion to remark, "As Solomon says: 'the engineers that go down to the sea in ships behold the wonders of sailor nature' "; when a change in the visitor's countenance made her stop and stare.

"Solomon. . . . Oh! . . . Mrs. Rout," stuttered the young man, very red in the face, "I must say . . . I don't. . . ."

"He's my husband," she announced in a great shout, throwing herself back in the chair. Perceiving the joke, she laughed immoderately with a handkerchief to her eyes, while he sat wearing a forced smile, and, from his inexperience of jolly women, fully persuaded that she must be deplorably insane. They were excellent friends afterwards; for, absolving her from irreverent intention, he came to think she was a very worthy person indeed; and he learned in time to receive without flinching other scraps of Solomon's wisdom.

"For my part," Solomon was reported by his wife to have said once, "give me the dullest ass for a skipper before a rogue. There is a way to take a fool; but a rogue is smart and slippery." This was an airy generalization drawn from the particular case of Captain MacWhirr's honesty, which, in itself, had the heavy obviousness of a lump of clay. On the other hand, Mr. Jukes, unable to generalize, unmarried, and unengaged, was in the habit of opening his heart after another fashion to an old chum and former shipmate, actually serving as second officer on board an Atlantic liner.

First of all he would insist upon the advantages of the Eastern trade, hinting at its superiority to the Western ocean service. He extolled the sky, the seas, the ships, and the easy life of the Far East. The *Nan-Shan*, he affirmed, was second to none as a sea boat.

"We have no brass-bound uniforms, but then we are like brothers here," he wrote. "We all mess together and live like fighting cocks. . . . All the chaps of the black-squad are as decent as they make that kind, and old Sol, the Chief, is a dry stick. We are good friends. As to our old man, you could not find a quieter skipper. Sometimes you would think he hadn't sense enough to see anything wrong. And yet it isn't that. Can't be. He has been in command for a good few years now. He doesn't do anything actually foolish, and gets his ship along all right without worrying anybody. I believe he hasn't brains enough to enjoy kicking up a row. I don't take advantage of him. I would scorn it. Outside the routine of duty he doesn't seem to understand more than half of what you tell him. We get a laugh out of this at times; but it is dull, too, to be with a man like this—in the long run. Old Sol says he hasn't much conversation. Conversation! O Lord! He never talks. The other day I had been yarning under the bridge with one of the engineers, and he must have heard us. When I came up to take my watch, he steps out of the chart room and has a good look all round, peeps over at the sidelights, glances at the compass, squints upwards at the stars. That's his regular performance. By and by he says: 'Was that you talking just now in the port alleyway?' 'Yes, sir.' 'With the third engineer?' 'Yes, sir.' He walks off to starboard, and sits under the dodger on a little campstool of his, and for half an hour perhaps he makes no sound, except that I heard him sneeze once. Then after a while I hear him getting up over there, and he strolls across to port, where I was. 'I can't understand what you can find to talk about,' says he. 'Two solid hours. I am not blaming you. I see people ashore at it all day long, and then in the evening they sit down and keep at it over the drinks. Must be saying the same things over and over again. I can't understand.'

"Did you ever hear anything like that? And he was so patient about it. It made me quite sorry for him. But he is exasperating, too, sometimes. Of course one would not do anything to vex him even if it were worth while. But it isn't. He's so jolly innocent that if you were to put your thumb to your nose and wave your fingers at him he would only wonder gravely to himself what got into you. He told me once quite simply that he found it very difficult to make out what made people always act so queerly. He's too dense to trouble about, and that's the truth."

Thus wrote Mr. Jukes to his chum in the Western ocean trade, out of the fullness of his heart and the liveliness of his fancy.

He had expressed his honest opinion. It was not worth while trying to impress a man of that sort. If the world had been full of such men, life would have probably appeared to Jukes an unentertaining and unprofitable business. He was not alone in his opinion. The sea itself, as if sharing Mr. Jukes' good-natured forbearance, had never put itself out to startle the silent man, who seldom looked up, and wandered innocently over the waters with the only visible purpose of getting food, raiment, and house-room for three people ashore. Dirty weather he had known, of course. He had been made wet, uncomfortable, tired in the usual way, felt at the time and presently forgotten. So that upon the whole he had been justified in reporting fine weather at home. But he had never been given a glimpse of immeasurable strength and of immoderate wrath, the wrath that passes exhausted but never appeased—the wrath and fury of the passionate sea. He knew it existed, as we know that crime and abominations exist; he had heard of it as a peaceable citizen in a town that hears of battles, famines, and floods, and yet knows nothing of what these things mean—though, indeed, he may have been mixed up in a street row, have gone without his dinner once, or been soaked to the skin in a shower. Captain MacWhirr had sailed over the surface of the oceans as some men go skimming over the years of existence to sink gently into a placid grave, ignorant of life to the last, without ever having been made to see all it may contain of perfidy, of violence, and of terror. There are on sea and land such men thus fortunate—or thus disdained by destiny or by the sea.

II

Observing the steady fall of the barometer, Captain MacWhirr thought, "There's some dirty weather knocking about." This is precisely what he thought. He had had an experience of moderately dirty weather—the term dirty as applied to the weather implying only moderate discomfort to the seaman. Had he been informed by an indisputable authority that the end of the world was to be finally accomplished by a catastrophic disturbance of the atmosphere, he would have assimilated the information under the simple idea of dirty weather, and no other, because he had no experience of cataclysms, and belief does not necessarily imply comprehension. The wisdom of his country had pronounced by means of an Act of Parliament that before he could be considered as fit to take charge of a ship he should be able to answer certain simple questions on the subject of circular storms such as hurricanes, cyclones, typhoons; and apparently he had answered them, since he was now in command of the *Nan-Shan* in the China seas during the season of typhoons. But if he had answered he remembered nothing of it. He was, however, conscious of being made uncomfortable by the clammy heat. He came out on the bridge, and found no relief to this oppression. The air seemed thick. He gasped like a fish, and began to believe himself greatly out of sorts.

The *Nan-Shan* was plowing a vanishing furrow upon the circle of the sea that had the surface and the shimmer of an undulating piece of gray silk. The sun, pale and without rays, poured down leaden heat in a strangely indecisive light, and the China-men were lying prostrate about the decks. Their bloodless, pinched, yellow faces were like the faces of bilious invalids. Captain MacWhirr noticed two of them especially, stretched out on their backs below the bridge. As soon as they had closed their eyes they seemed dead. Three others, however, were quarreling barbarously away forward; and one big fellow, half naked, with herculean shoulders, was hanging limply over a winch; another, sitting on the deck, his knees up and his head drooping sideways in a girlish attitude, was plaiting his pigtail with infinite languor depicted in his whole person and in the very movement of his fingers. The smoke struggled with difficulty out of the funnel, and instead of streaming away spread itself out like an infernal sort of cloud, smelling of sulphur and raining soot all over the decks.

"What the devil are you doing there, Mr. Jukes?" asked Captain MacWhirr.

This unusual form of address, though mumbled rather than spoken, caused the body of Mr. Jukes to start as though it had been prodded under the fifth rib. He had had a low bench brought on the bridge, and sitting on it, with a length of rope curled about his feet and a piece of canvas stretched over his knees, was pushing a sail-needle vigorously. He looked up, and his surprise gave to his eyes an expression of innocence and candor.

"I am only roping some of that new set of bags we made last trip for whipping up coals," he remonstrated, gently. "We shall want them for the next coaling, sir."

"What became of the others?"

"Why, worn out of course, sir."

Captain MacWhirr, after glaring down irresolutely at his chief mate, disclosed the gloomy and cynical conviction that more than half of them had been lost overboard, "if only the truth was known," and retired to the other end of the bridge. Jukes, exasperated by this unprovoked attack, broke the needle at the second stitch, and dropping his work got up and cursed the heat in a violent undertone.

The propeller thumped, the three Chinamen forward had given up squabbling very suddenly, and the one who had been plaiting his tail clasped his legs and stared dejectedly over his knees. The lurid sunshine cast faint and sickly shadows. The swell ran higher and swifter every moment, and the ship lurched heavily in the smooth, deep hollows of the sea.

"I wonder where that beastly swell comes from," said Jukes aloud, recovering himself after a stagger.

"Northeast," grunted the literal MacWhirr, from his side of the bridge. "There's some dirty weather knocking about. Go and look at the glass."

When Jukes came out of the chart room, the cast of his countenance had changed to thoughtfulness and concern. He caught hold of the bridge rail and stared ahead.

The temperature in the engine room had gone up to a hundred and seventeen degrees. Irritated voices were ascending through the skylight and through the fiddle of the stokehold in a harsh and resonant uproar, mingled with angry clangs and scrapes of metal, as if men with limbs of iron and throats of bronze had been quarreling down there. The second engineer was falling foul of the stokers for letting the steam go down. He was a man with arms like a blacksmith, and generally feared; but that afternoon the stokers were answering him back recklessly, and slammed the furnace doors with the fury of despair. Then the noise ceased suddenly, and the second engineer appeared, emerging out of the stokehold streaked with grime and soaking wet like a chimney sweep coming out of a well. As soon as his head was clear of the fiddle he began to scold Jukes for not trimming properly the stokehold ventilators; and in answer Jukes made with his hands deprecatory soothing signs meaning: "No wind—can't be helped—you can see for yourself." But the other wouldn't hear reason. His teeth flashed angrily in his dirty face. He didn't mind, he said, the trouble of punching their blanked heads down there, blank his soul, but did the condemned sailors think you could keep steam up in the God-forsaken boilers simply by knocking the blanked stokers about? No, by George! You had to get some draught, too—may he be everlastingly blanked for a swab-headed deck hand if you didn't! And the chief, too, rampaging before the steam gauge and carrying on like a lunatic up and down the engine room ever since noon. What did Jukes think he was stuck up there for, if he couldn't get one of his decayed, good-for-nothing deck-cripples to turn the ventilators to the wind?

The relations of the "engine room" and the "deck" of the *Nan-Shan* were, as is known, of a brotherly nature; therefore Jukes leaned over and begged the other in a restrained tone not to make a disgusting ass of himself; the skipper was on the other side of the bridge. But the second declared mutinously that he didn't care a rap who was on the other side of the bridge, and Jukes, passing in a flash from lofty disapproval into a state of exaltation, invited him in unflattering terms to come up and twist the beastly things to please himself, and catch such wind as a donkey of his sort could find. The second rushed up to the fray. He flung himself at the port ventilator as though he meant to tear it out bodily and toss it overboard. All he did was to move the cowl round a few inches, with an enormous expenditure of force, and seemed spent in the effort. He leaned against the back of the wheelhouse, and Jukes walked up to him.

"Oh, Heavens!" ejaculated the engineer in a feeble voice. He lifted his eyes to the sky, and then let his glassy stare descend to meet the horizon that, tilting up to an angle of forty degrees, seemed to hang on a slant for a while and settled down slowly. "Heavens! Phew! What's up, anyhow?"

Jukes, straddling his long legs like a pair of compasses, put on an air of superiority. "We're going to catch it this time," he said. "The barometer is tumbling down like anything, Harry. And you trying to kick up that silly row. . . ."

The word "barometer" seemed to revive the second engineer's mad animosity. Collecting afresh all his energies, he directed Jukes in a low and brutal tone to shove the unmentionable instrument down his gory throat. Who cared for his crimson barometer? It was the steam—the steam—that was going down; and what between the firemen going faint and the chief going silly, it was worse than a dog's life for him; he didn't care a tinker's curse how soon the whole show was blown out of the water. He seemed on the point of having a cry, but after regaining his breath he muttered darkly, "I'll faint them," and dashed off. He stopped upon the fiddle long enough to shake his fist at the unnatural daylight, and dropped into the dark hole with a whoop.

When Jukes turned, his eyes fell upon the rounded back and the big red ears of Captain MacWhirr, who had come across. He did not look at his chief officer, but said at once, "That's a very violent man, that second engineer."

"Jolly good second, anyhow," grunted Jukes. "They can't keep up steam," he added, rapidly, and made a grab at the rail against the coming lurch.

Captain MacWhirr, unprepared, took a run and brought himself up with a jerk by an awning stanchion.

"A profane man," he said, obstinately. "If this goes on, I'll have to get rid of him the first chance."

"It's the heat," said Jukes. "The weather's awful. It would make a saint swear. Even up here I feel exactly as if I had my head tied up in a woolen blanket."

Captain MacWhirr looked up. "D'ye mean to say, Mr. Jukes, you ever had your head tied up in a blanket? What was that for?"

"It's a manner of speaking, sir," said Jukes, stolidly.

"Some of you fellows do go on! What's that about saints swearing? I wish you wouldn't talk so wild. What sort of saint would that be that would swear? No more saint than yourself, I expect. And what's a blanket got to do with it—or the weather either. . . . The heat does not make me swear—does it? It's filthy bad temper. That's what it is. And what's the good of your talking like this?"

Thus Captain MacWhirr expostulated against the use of images in speech, and at the end electrified Jukes by a contemptuous snort, followed by words of passion and resentment: "Damme! I'll fire him out of the ship if he don't look out."

And Jukes, incorrigible, thought: "Goodness me! Somebody's put a new inside to my old man. Here's temper, if you like. Of course it's the weather; what else? It would make an angel quarrelsome—let alone a saint."

All the Chinamen on deck appeared at their last gasp.

At its setting the sun had a diminished diameter and an expiring brown, rayless glow, as if millions of centuries elapsing since the morning had brought it near its end. A dense bank of cloud became visible to the northward; it had a sinister dark-olive tint, and lay low and motionless upon the sea, resembling a solid obstacle in the path of the ship. She went floundering towards it like an exhausted creature driven to its death. The coppery twilight retired slowly, and the darkness brought out overhead a swarm of unsteady, big stars, that, as if blown upon, flickered exceedingly and seemed to hang very near the earth. At eight o'clock Jukes went into the chart room to write up the ship's log.

He copied neatly out of the rough-book the number of miles, the course of the ship, and in the column for "wind" scrawled the word "calm" from top to bottom of the eight hours since noon. He was exasperated by the continuous, monotonous rolling of the ship. The heavy inkstand would slide away in a manner that suggested perverse intelligence in dodging the pen. Having written in the large space under the head of "Remarks" "Heat very oppressive," he stuck the end of the penholder in his teeth, pipe fashion, and mopped his face carefully.

"Ship rolling heavily in a high cross swell," he began again, and commented to himself, "Heavily is no word for it." Then he wrote: "Sunset threatening, with a low bank of clouds to N. and E. Sky clear overhead."

Sprawling over the table with arrested pen, he glanced out of the door, and in that frame of his vision he saw all the stars flying upwards between the teakwood jambs on a black sky. The whole lot took flight together and disappeared, leaving only a blackness flecked with white flashes, for the sea was as black as the sky and speckled with foam afar. The stars that had flown to the roll came back on the return swing of the ship, rushing downwards in their glittering multitude, not of fiery points, but enlarged to tiny discs brilliant with a clear wet sheen.

Jukes watched the flying big stars for a moment, and then wrote: "8 P.M. Swell increasing. Ship laboring and taking water on her decks. Battened down the coolies for the night. Barometer still falling." He paused, and thought to himself, "Perhaps nothing whatever'll come of it." And then he closed resolutely his entries: "Every appearance of a typhoon coming on."

On going out he had to stand aside, and Captain MacWhirr strode over the doorstep without saying a word or making a sign.

"Shut the door, Mr. Jukes, will you?" he cried from within.

Jukes turned back to do so, muttering ironically: "Afraid to catch cold, I suppose." It was his watch below, but he yearned for communion with his kind; and he remarked cheerily to the second mate: "Doesn't look so bad, after all—does it?"

The second mate was marching to and fro on the bridge, tripping down with small steps one moment, and the next climbing with difficulty the shifting slope of the deck. At the sound of Jukes' voice he stood still, facing forward, but made no reply.

"Hallo! That's a heavy one," said Jukes, swaying to meet the long roll till his lowered hand touched the planks. This time the second mate made in his throat a noise of an unfriendly nature.

He was an oldish, shabby little fellow, with bad teeth and no hair on his face. He had been shipped in a hurry in Shanghai, that trip when the second officer brought from home had delayed the ship three hours in port by contriving (in some manner Captain MacWhirr could never understand) to fall overboard into an empty coal lighter lying alongside, and had to be sent ashore to the hospital with concussion of the brain and a broken limb or two.

Jukes was not discouraged by the unsympathetic sound. "The Chinamen must be having a lovely time of it down there," he said. "It's lucky for them the old girl has the easiest roll of any ship I've ever been in. There now! This one wasn't so bad."

"You wait," snarled the second mate.

With his sharp nose, red at the tip, and his thin pinched lips, he always looked as though he were raging inwardly; and he was concise in his speech to the point of rudeness. All his time off duty he spent in his cabin with the door shut, keeping so still in there that he was supposed to fall asleep as soon as he had disappeared; but the man who came in to wake him for his watch on deck would invariably find him with his eyes wide open, flat on his back in the bunk, and glaring irritably from a soiled pillow. He never wrote any letters, did not seem to hope for news from anywhere; and though he had been heard once to mention West Hartlepool, it was with extreme bitterness, and only in connection with the extortionate charges of a boardinghouse. He was one of those men who are picked up at need in the ports of the world. They are competent enough, appear hopelessly hard up, show no evidence of any sort of vice, and carry about them all the signs of manifest failure. They come aboard on an emergency, care for no ship afloat, live in their own atmosphere of casual connection amongst their shipmates who know nothing of them, and make up their minds to leave at inconvenient times. They clear out with no words of leave-taking in some God-forsaken port other men would fear to be stranded in, and go ashore in company of a shabby sea chest, corded like a treasure box, and with an air of shaking the ship's dust off their feet.

"You wait," he repeated, balanced in great swings with his back to Jukes, motionless and implacable.

"Do you mean to say we are going to catch it hot?" asked Jukes with boyish interest.

"Say? . . . I say nothing. You don't catch me," snapped the little second mate, with a mixture of pride, scorn, and cunning, as if Jukes' question had been a trap cleverly detected. "Oh, no! None of you here shall make a fool of me if I know it," he mumbled to himself.

Jukes reflected rapidly that this second mate was a mean little beast, and in his heart he wished poor Jack Allen had never smashed himself up in the coal lighter. The far-off blackness ahead of the ship was like another night seen through the starry night of the earth—the starless night of the immensities beyond the created universe, revealed in its appalling stillness through a low fissure in the glittering sphere of which the earth is the kernel.

"Whatever there might be about," said Jukes, "we are steaming straight into it."

"*You've* said it," caught up the second mate, always with his back to Jukes. "You've said it, mind—not I."

"Oh, go to Jericho!" said Jukes, frankly; and the other emitted a triumphant little chuckle.

"You've said it," he repeated.

"And what of that?"

"I've known some real good men get into trouble with their skippers for saying a dam' sight less," answered the second mate feverishly. "Oh, no! You don't catch me."

"You seem deucedly anxious not to give yourself away," said Jukes, completely soured by such absurdity. "I wouldn't be afraid to say what I think."

"Aye, to me! That's no great trick. I am nobody, and well I know it."

The ship, after a pause of comparative steadiness, started upon a series of rolls, one worse than the other, and for a time Jukes, preserving his equilibrium, was too busy to open his mouth. As soon as the violent swinging had quieted down somewhat, he said: "This is a bit too much of a good thing. Whether anything is coming or not I think she ought to be put head on to that swell. The old man is just gone in to lie down. Hang me if I don't speak to him."

But when he opened the door of the chart room he saw his captain reading a book. Captain MacWhirr was not lying down: he was standing up with one hand grasping the edge of the bookshelf and the other holding open before his face a thick volume. The lamp wriggled in the gimbals, the loosened books toppled from side to side on the shelf, the long barometer swung in jerky circles, the table altered its slant every moment. In the midst of all this stir and movement Captain MacWhirr, holding on, showed his eyes above the upper edge, and asked, "What's the matter?"

"Swell getting worse, sir."

"Noticed that in here," muttered Captain MacWhirr. "Anything wrong?"

Jukes, inwardly disconcerted by the seriousness of the eyes looking at him over the top of the book, produced an embarrassed grin.

"Rolling like old boots," he said, sheepishly.

"Aye! Very heavy—very heavy. What do you want?"

At this Jukes lost his footing and began to flounder.

"I was thinking of our passengers," he said, in the manner of a man clutching at a straw.

"Passengers?" wondered the Captain, gravely. "What passengers?"

"Why, the Chinamen, sir," explained Jukes, very sick of this conversation.

"The Chinamen! Why don't you speak plainly? Couldn't tell what you meant. Never heard a lot of coolies spoken of as passengers before. Passengers, indeed! What's come to you?"

Captain MacWhirr, closing the book on his forefinger, lowered his arm and looked completely mystified. "Why are you thinking of the Chinamen, Mr. Jukes?" he inquired.

Jukes took a plunge, like a man driven to it. "She's rolling her decks full of water, sir. Thought you might put her head on perhaps—for a while. Till this goes down a bit—very soon, I dare say. Head to the eastward. I never knew a ship roll like this."

He held on in the doorway, and Captain MacWhirr, feeling his grip on the shelf inadequate, made up his mind to let go in a hurry, and fell heavily on the couch.

"Head to the eastward?" he said, struggling to sit up. "That's more than four points off her course."

"Yes, sir. Fifty degrees. . . . Would just bring her head far enough round to meet this. . . ."

Captain MacWhirr was now sitting up. He had not dropped the book, and he had not lost his place.

"To the eastward?" he repeated, with dawning astonishment. "To the . . . Where do you think we are bound to? You want me to haul a full-powered steamship four points off her course to make the Chinamen comfortable! Now, I've heard more than enough of mad things done in the world—but this. . . . If I didn't know you, Jukes, I would think you were in liquor. Steer four points off. . . . And what afterwards? Steer four points over the other way, I suppose, to make the course good. What put it into your head that I would start to tack a steamer as if she were a sailing ship?"

"Jolly good thing she isn't," threw in Jukes, with bitter readiness. "She would have rolled every blessed stick out of her this afternoon."

"Aye! And you just would have had to stand and see them go," said Captain MacWhirr, showing a certain animation. "It's a dead calm, isn't it?"

"It is, sir. But there's something out of the common coming, for sure."

"Maybe. I suppose you have a notion I should be getting out of the way of that dirt," said Captain MacWhirr, speaking with the utmost simplicity of manner and tone, and fixing the oilcloth on the floor with a heavy stare. Thus he noticed neither Jukes' discomfiture nor the mixture of vexation and astonished respect on his face.

"Now, here's this book," he continued with deliberation, slapping his thigh with the closed volume. "I've been reading the chapter on the storms there."

This was true. He had been reading the chapter on the storms. When he had entered the chart room, it was with no intention of taking the book down. Some influence in the air—the same influence, probably, that caused the steward to bring without orders the Captain's sea boots and oilskin coat up to the chart room—had as it were guided his hand to the shelf; and without taking the time to sit down he had waded with a conscious effort into the terminology of the subject. He lost himself amongst advancing semicircles, left- and right-hand quadrants, the curves of the tracks, the probable bearing of the center, the shifts of wind and the readings of barometer. He tried to bring all these things into a definite relation to himself, and ended by becoming contemptuously angry with such a lot of words and with so much advice, all headwork and supposition, without a glimmer of certitude.

"It's the damnedest thing, Jukes," he said. "If a fellow was to believe all that's in there, he would be running most of his time all over the sea trying to get behind the weather."

Again he slapped his leg with the book; and Jukes opened his mouth, but said nothing.

"Running to get behind the weather! Do you understand that, Mr. Jukes? It's the maddest thing!" ejaculated Captain MacWhirr, with pauses, gazing at the floor profoundly. "You would think an old woman had been writing this. It passes me. If that thing means anything useful, then it means that I should at once alter the course away, away to the devil somewhere, and come booming down on Fu-chau from the northward at the tail of this dirty weather that's supposed to be knocking about in our way. From the north! Do you understand, Mr. Jukes? Three hundred extra miles to the distance, and a pretty coal bill to show. I couldn't bring myself to do that if every word in there was gospel truth, Mr. Jukes. Don't you expect me. . . ."

And Jukes, silent, marveled at this display of feeling and loquacity.

"But the truth is that you don't know if the fellow is right, anyhow. How can you tell what a gale is made of till you get it? He isn't aboard here, is he? Very well. Here he says that the center of them things bears eight points off the wind; but we haven't got any wind, for all the barometer falling. Where's his center now?"

"We will get the wind presently," mumbled Jukes.

"Let it come, then," said Captain MacWhirr, with dignified indignation. "It's only to let you see, Mr. Jukes, that you don't find everything in books. All these rules for dodging breezes and circumventing the winds of heaven, Mr. Jukes, seem to me the maddest thing, when you come to look at it sensibly."

He raised his eyes, saw Jukes gazing at him dubiously, and tried to illustrate his meaning.

"About as queer as your extraordinary notion of dodging the ship head to sea, for I don't know how long, to make the Chinamen comfortable; whereas all we've got to do is to take them to Fu-chau, being timed to get there before noon on Friday. If the weather delays me—very well. There's your logbook to talk straight about the weather. But suppose I went swinging off my course and came in two days late, and they asked me: 'Where have you been all that time, Captain?' What could I say to that? 'Went around to dodge the bad weather,' I would say. 'It must've been dam' bad,' they would say. 'Don't know,' I would have to say; 'I've dodged clear of it.' See that, Jukes? I have been thinking it all out this afternoon."

He looked up again in his unseeing, unimaginative way. No one had ever heard him say so much at one time. Jukes, with his arms open in the doorway, was like a man invited to behold a miracle. Unbounded wonder was the intellectual meaning of his eye, while incredulity was seated in his whole countenance.

"A gale is a gale, Mr. Jukes," resumed the Captain, "and a full-powered steamship has got to face it. There's just so much dirty weather knocking about the world, and the proper thing is to go through it with none of what old Captain Wilson of the *Melita* calls 'storm strategy.' The other day ashore I heard him hold forth about it to a lot of shipmasters who came in and sat at a table next to mine. It seemed to me the greatest nonsense. He was telling them how he outmaneuvered, I think he said, a terrific gale, so that it never came nearer than fifty miles to him. A neat piece of headwork he called it. How he knew there was a terrific gale fifty miles off beats me altogether. It was like listening to a crazy man. I would have thought Captain Wilson was old enough to know better."

Captain MacWhirr ceased for a moment, then said, "It's your watch below, Mr. Jukes?"

Jukes came to himself with a start. "Yes, sir."

"Leave orders to call me at the slightest change," said the Captain. He reached up to put the book away, and tucked his legs upon the couch. "Shut the door so that it don't fly open, will you? I can't stand a door banging. They've put a lot of rubbishy locks into this ship, I must say."

Captain MacWhirr closed his eyes.

He did so to rest himself. He was tired, and he experienced that state of mental vacuity which comes at the end of an exhaustive discussion that has liberated some belief matured in the course of meditative years. He had indeed been making his confession of faith, had he only known it; and its effect was to make Jukes, on the other side of the door, stand scratching his head for a good while.

Captain MacWhirr opened his eyes.

He thought he must have been asleep. What was that loud noise? Wind? Why had he not been called? The lamp wriggled in its gimbals, the barometer swung in circles, the table altered its slant every moment; a pair of limp sea boots with collapsed tops went sliding past the couch. He put out his hand instantly, and captured one.

Jukes' face appeared in a crack of the door; only his face, very red, with staring eyes. The flame of the lamp leaped, a piece of paper flew up, a rush of air enveloped Captain MacWhirr. Beginning to draw on the boot, he directed an expectant gaze at Jukes' swollen, excited features.

"Came on like this," shouted Jukes, "five minutes ago . . . all of a sudden."

The head disappeared with a bang, and a heavy splash and patter of drops swept past the closed door as if a pailful of melted lead had been flung against the house. A whistling could be heard now upon the deep vibrating noise outside. The stuffy chart room seemed as full of drafts as a shed. Captain MacWhirr collared the other sea boot on its violent passage along the floor. He was not flustered, but he could not find at once the opening for inserting his foot. The shoes he had flung off were scurrying from end to end of the cabin, gamboling playfully over each other like puppies. As soon as he stood up he kicked at them viciously, but without effect.

He threw himself into the attitude of a lunging fencer, to reach after his oilskin coat; and afterwards he staggered all over the confined space while he jerked himself into it. Very grave, straddling his legs far apart, and stretching his neck, he started to tie deliberately the strings of his sou-wester under his chin, with thick fingers that trembled slightly. He went through all the movements of a woman putting on her bonnet before a glass, with a strained, listening attention, as though he had expected every moment to hear the shout of his name in the confused clamor that had suddenly beset his ship. Its increase filled his ears while he was getting ready to go out and confront whatever it might mean. It was tumultuous and very loud—made up of the rush of the wind, the crashes of the sea, with that prolonged deep vibration of the air, like the roll of an immense and remote drum beating the charge of the gale.

He stood for a moment in the light of the lamp, thick, clumsy, shapeless in his panoply of combat, vigilant and red-faced.

"There's a lot of weight in this," he muttered.

As soon as he attempted to open the door the wind caught it. Clinging to the handle, he was dragged out over the doorstep, and at once found himself engaged with the wind in a sort of personal scuffle whose object was the shutting of that door. At the last moment a tongue of air scurried in and licked out the flame of the lamp.

Ahead of the ship he perceived a great darkness lying upon a multitude of white flashes; on the starboard beam a few amazing stars drooped, dim and fitful, above an immense waste of broken seas, as if seen through a mad drift of smoke.

On the bridge a knot of men, indistinct and toiling, were making great efforts in the light of the wheelhouse windows that shone mistily on their heads and backs. Suddenly darkness closed upon one pane, then on another. The voices of the lost group reached him after the manner of men's voices in a gale, in shreds and fragments of forlorn shouting snatched past the ear. All at once Jukes appeared at his side, yelling, with his head down.

"Watch—put—in—wheelhouse—shutters—glass—afraid—blow in."

Jukes heard his commander upbraiding.

"This—come—anything—warning—call me."

He tried to explain, with the uproar pressing on his lips.

"Light air—remained—bridge—sudden—northeast—could turn—thought—you —sure—hear."

They had gained the shelter of the weather cloth, and could converse with raised voices, as people quarrel.

"I got the hands along to cover up all the ventilators. Good job I had remained on deck. I didn't think you would be asleep, and so . . . What did you say, sir? What?"

"Nothing," cried Captain MacWhirr. "I said—all right."

"By all the powers! We've got it this time," observed Jukes in a howl.

"You haven't altered her course?" inquired Captain MacWhirr, straining his voice.

"No, sir. Certainly not. Wind came out right ahead. And here comes the head sea."

A plunge of the ship ended in a shock as if she had landed her forefoot upon something solid. After a moment of stillness a lofty flight of sprays drove hard with the wind upon their faces.

"Keep her at it as long as we can," shouted Captain MacWhirr.

Before Jukes had squeezed the salt water out of his eyes all the stars had disappeared.

III

Jukes was as ready a man as any half-dozen young mates that may be caught by casting a net upon the waters; and though he had been somewhat taken aback by the startling viciousness of the first squall, he had pulled himself together on the instant, had called out the hands and had rushed them along to secure such openings about the deck as had not been already battened down earlier in the evening. Shouting in his fresh, stentorian voice, "Jump, boys, and bear a hand!" he led in the work, telling himself the while that he had "just expected this."

But at the same time he was growing aware that this was rather more than he had expected. From the first stir of the air felt on his cheek the gale seemed to take upon itself the accumulated impetus of an avalanche. Heavy sprays enveloped the *Nan-Shan* from stem to stern, and instantly in the midst of her regular rolling she began to jerk and plunge as though she had gone mad with fright.

Jukes thought, "This is no joke." While he was exchanging explanatory yells with his captain, a sudden lowering of the darkness came upon the night, falling before their vision like something palpable. It was as if the masked lights of the world had been turned down. Jukes was uncritically glad to have his captain at hand. It relieved him as though that man had, by simply coming on deck, taken most of the gale's weight upon his shoulders. Such is the prestige, the privilege, and the burden of command.

Captain MacWhirr could expect no relief of that sort from anyone on earth. Such is the loneliness of command. He was trying to see, with that watchful manner of a seaman who stares into the wind's eye as if into the eye of an adversary, to penetrate the hidden intention and guess the aim and force of the thrust. The strong wind swept at him out of a vast obscurity; he felt under his feet the uneasiness of his ship, and he could not even discern the shadow of her shape. He wished it were not so; and very still he waited, feeling stricken by a blind man's helplessness.

To be silent was natural to him, dark or shine. Jukes, at his elbow, made himself heard yelling cheerily in the gusts, "We must have got the worst of it at once, sir." A faint burst of lightning quivered all round, as if flashed into a cavern—into a black and secret chamber of the sea, with a floor of foaming crests.

It unveiled for a sinister, fluttering moment a ragged mass of clouds hanging low, the lurch of the long outlines of the ship, the black figures of men caught on the bridge, heads forward, as if petrified in the act of butting. The darkness palpitated down upon all this, and then the real thing came at last.

It was something formidable and swift, like the sudden smashing of a vial of wrath. It seemed to explode all round the ship with an overpowering concussion and a rush of great waters, as if an immense dam had been blown up to windward. In an instant the men lost touch of each other. This is the disintegrating power of a great wind: it isolates one from one's kind. An earthquake, a landslip, an avalanche, overtake a man incidentally, as it were—without passion. A furious gale attacks him like a personal enemy, tries to grasp his limbs, fastens upon his mind, seeks to rout his very spirit out of him.

Jukes was driven away from his commander. He fancied himself whirled a great distance through the air. Everything disappeared—even, for a moment, his power of thinking; but his hand had found one of the rail stanchions. His distress was by no means alleviated by an inclination to disbelieve the reality of this experience. Though young, he had seen some bad weather, and had never doubted his ability to imagine the worst; but this was so much beyond his powers of fancy that it appeared incompatible with the existence of any ship whatever. He would have been incredulous about himself in the same way, perhaps, had he not been so harassed by the necessity of exerting a wrestling effort against a force trying to tear him away from his hold. Moreover, the conviction of not being utterly destroyed returned to him through the sensations of being half-drowned, bestially shaken, and partly choked.

It seemed to him he remained there precariously alone with the stanchion for a long, long time. The rain poured on him, flowed, drove in sheets. He breathed in gasps; and sometimes the water he swallowed was fresh and sometimes it was salt. For the most part he kept his eyes shut tight, as if suspecting his sight might be destroyed in the immense flurry of the elements. When he ventured to blink hastily, he derived some moral support from the green gleam of the starboard light shining feebly upon the flight of rain and sprays. He was actually looking at it when its ray fell upon the uprearing sea which put it out. He saw the head of the wave topple over, adding the mite of its crash to the tremendous uproar raging around him, and almost at the same instant the stanchion was wrenched away from his embracing arms. After a crushing thump on his back he found himself suddenly afloat and borne upwards. His first irresistible notion was that the whole China Sea had climbed on the bridge. Then, more sanely, he concluded himself gone overboard. All the time he was being tossed, flung, and rolled in great volumes of water, he kept on repeating mentally, with the utmost precipitation, the words: "My God! My God! My God! My God!"

All at once, in a revolt of misery and despair, he formed the crazy resolution to get out of that. And he began to thrash about with his arms and legs. But as soon as he commenced his wretched struggles he discovered that he had become somehow mixed up with a face, an oilskin coat, somebody's boots. He clawed ferociously all these things in turn, lost them, found them again, lost them once more, and finally was himself caught in the firm clasp of a pair of stout arms. He returned the embrace closely round a thick solid body. He had found his captain.

They tumbled over and over, tightening their hug. Suddenly the water let them down with a brutal bang; and, stranded against the side of the wheelhouse, out of breath and bruised, they were left to stagger up in the wind and hold on where they could.

Jukes came out of it rather horrified, as though he had escaped some unparalleled outrage directed at his feelings. It weakened his faith in himself. He started shouting aimlessly to the man he could feel near him in that fiendish blackness, "Is it you, sir? Is it you, sir?" till his temples seemed ready to burst. And he heard in answer a voice, as if crying far away, as if screaming to him fretfully from a very great distance, the one word "Yes!" Other seas swept again over the bridge. He received them defenselessly right over his bare head, with both his hands engaged in holding.

The motion of the ship was extravagant. Her lurches had an appalling helplessness: she pitched as if taking a header into a void, and seemed to find a wall to hit every time. When she rolled she fell on her side headlong, and she would be righted back by such a demolishing blow that Jukes felt her reeling as a clubbed man reels before he collapses. The gale howled and scuffled about gigantically in the darkness, as though the entire world were one black gully. At certain moments the air streamed against the ship as if sucked through a tunnel with a concentrated solid force of impact that seemed to lift her clean out of the water and keep her up for an instant with only a quiver running through her from end to end. And then she would begin her tumbling again as if dropped back into a boiling caldron. Jukes tried hard to compose his mind and judge things coolly.

The sea, flattened down in the heavier gusts, would uprise and overwhelm both ends of the *Nan-Shan* in snowy rushes of foam, expanding wide, beyond both rails, into the night. And on this dazzling sheet, spread under the blackness of the clouds and emitting a bluish glow, Captain MacWhirr could catch a desolate glimpse of a few tiny specks black as ebony, the tops of the hatches, the battened companions, the heads of the covered winches, the foot of a mast. This was all he could see of his ship. Her middle structure, covered by the bridge which bore him, his mate, the closed wheelhouse where a man was steering shut up with the fear of being swept overboard together with the whole thing in one great crash—her middle structure was like a half-tide rock awash upon a coast. It was like an outlying rock with the water boiling up, streaming over, pouring off, beating round—like a rock in the surf to which ship-wrecked people cling before they let go—only it rose, it sank, it rolled continuously, without respite and rest, like a rock that should have miraculously struck adrift from a coast and gone wallowing upon the sea.

The *Nan-Shan* was being looted by the storm with a senseless, destructive fury: trysails torn out of the extra gaskets, double-lashed awnings blown away, bridge swept clean, weather cloths burst, rails twisted, lightscreens smashed—and two of the boats had gone already. They had gone unheard and unseen, melting, as it were, in the shock and smother of the wave. It was only later, when upon the white flash of another high sea hurling itself amidships, Jukes had a vision of two pairs of davits leaping black and empty out of the solid blackness, with one overhauled fall flying and an ironbound block capering in the air, that he became aware of what had happened within about three yards of his back.

He poked his head forward, groping for the ear of his commander. His lips touched it—big, fleshy, very wet. He cried in an agitated tone, "Our boats are going now, sir."

And again he heard that voice, forced and ringing feebly, but with a penetrating effect of quietness in the enormous discord of noises, as if sent out from some remote spot of peace beyond the black wastes of the gale; again he heard a man's voice—the frail and indomitable sound that can be made to carry an infinity of thought, resolution and purpose, that shall be pronouncing confident words on the last day, when heavens fall, and justice is done—again he heard it, and it was crying to him, as if from very, very far—"All right."

He thought he had not managed to make himself understood. "Our boats—I say boats—the boats, sir! Two gone!"

The same voice, within a foot of him and yet so remote, yelled sensibly, "Can't be helped."

Captain MacWhirr had never turned his face, but Jukes caught some more words on the wind.

"What can—expect—when hammering through—such—— Bound to leave—something behind—stands to reason."

Watchfully Jukes listened for more. No more came. This was all Captain MacWhirr had to say; and Jukes could picture to himself rather than see the broad squat back before him. An impenetrable obscurity pressed down upon the ghostly glimmers of the sea. A dull conviction seized upon Jukes that there was nothing to be done.

If the steering gear did not give way, if the immense volumes of water did not burst the deck in or smash one of the hatches, if the engines did not give up, if way could be kept on the ship against this terrific wind, and she did not bury herself in one of these awful seas, of whose white crests alone, topping high above her bows, he could now and then get a sickening glimpse—then there was a chance of her coming out of it. Something within him seemed to turn over, bringing uppermost the feeling that the *Nan-Shan* was lost.

"She's done for," he said to himself, with a surprising mental agitation, as though he had discovered an unexpected meaning in this thought. One of these things was bound to happen. Nothing could be prevented now, and nothing could be remedied. The men on board did not count, and the ship could not last. This weather was too impossible.

Jukes felt an arm thrown heavily over his shoulders; and to this overture he responded with great intelligence by catching hold of his captain round the waist.

They stood clasped thus in the blind night, bracing each other against the wind, cheek to cheek and lip to ear, in the manner of two hulks lashed stem to stern together.

And Jukes heard the voice of his commander hardly any louder than before, but nearer, as though, starting to march athwart the prodigious rush of the hurricane, it had approached him, bearing that strange effect of quietness like the serene glow of a halo.

"D'ye know where the hands got to?" it asked, vigorous and evanescent at the same time, overcoming the strength of the wind, and swept away from Jukes instantly.

Jukes didn't know. They were all on the bridge when the real force of the hurricane struck the ship. He had no idea where they had crawled to. Under the circumstances they were nowhere, for all the use that could be made of them. Somehow the Captain's wish to know distressed Jukes.

"Want the hands, sir?" he cried, apprehensively.

"Ought to know," asserted Captain MacWhirr. "Hold hard."

They held hard. An outburst of unchained fury, a vicious rush of the wind absolutely steadied the ship; she rocked only, quick and light like a child's cradle, for a terrific moment of suspense, while the whole atmosphere, as it seemed, streamed furiously past her, roaring away from the tenebrous earth.

It suffocated them, and with eyes shut they tightened their grasp. What from the magnitude of the shock might have been a column of water running upright in the dark, butted against the ship, broke short, and fell on her bridge, crushingly, from on high, with a dead burying weight.

A flying fragment of that collapse, a mere splash, enveloped them in one swirl from their feet over their heads, filling violently their ears, mouths and nostrils with salt water. It knocked out their legs, wrenched in haste at their arms, seethed away swiftly under their chins; and opening their eyes, they saw the piled-up masses of foam dashing to and fro amongst what looked like the fragments of a ship. She had given way as if driven straight in. Their panting hearts yielded, too, before the tremendous blow; and all at once she sprang up again to her desperate plunging, as if trying to scramble out from under the ruins.

The seas in the dark seemed to rush from all sides to keep her back where she might perish. There was hate in the way she was handled, and a ferocity in the blows that fell. She was like a living creature thrown to the rage of a mob: hustled terribly, struck at, borne up, flung down, leaped upon. Captain MacWhirr and Jukes kept hold of each other, deafened by the noise, gagged by the wind; and the great physical tumult beating about their bodies, brought, like an unbridled display of passion, a profound trouble to their souls. One of those wild and appalling shrieks that are heard at times passing mysteriously overhead in the steady roar of a hurricane, swooped, as if borne on wings, upon the ship, and Jukes tried to outscream it.

"Will she live through this?"

The cry was wrenched out of his breast. It was as unintentional as the birth of a thought in the head, and he heard nothing of it himself. It all became extinct at once —thought, intention, effort—and of his cry the inaudible vibration added to the tempest waves of the air.

He expected nothing from it. Nothing at all. For indeed what answer could be made? But after a while he heard with amazement the frail and resisting voice in his ear, the dwarf sound, unconquered in the giant tumult.

"She may!"

It was a dull yell, more difficult to seize than a whisper. And presently the voice returned again, half submerged in the vast crashes, like a ship battling against the waves of an ocean.

"Let's hope so!" it cried—small, lonely and unmoved, a stranger to the visions of hope or fear; and it flickered into disconnected words: "Ship. . . . This. . . . Never —Anyhow . . . for the best." Jukes gave it up.

Then, as if it had come suddenly upon the one thing fit to withstand the power of a storm, it seemed to gain force and firmness for the last broken shouts:

"Keep on hammering . . . builders . . . good men. . . . And chance it . . . engines. . . . Rout . . . good man."

Captain MacWhirr removed his arm from Jukes' shoulders, and thereby ceased to exist for his mate, so dark it was; Jukes, after a tense stiffening of every muscle, would let himself go limp all over. The gnawing of profound discomfort existed side by side with an incredible disposition to somnolence, as though he had been buffeted and worried into drowsiness. The wind would get hold of his head and try to shake it off his shoulders; his clothes, full of water, were as heavy as lead, cold and dripping like an armor of melting ice: he shivered—it lasted a long time; and with his hands closed hard on his hold, he was letting himself sink slowly into the depths of bodily misery. His mind became concentrated upon himself in an aimless, idle way, and when something pushed lightly at the back of his knees he nearly, as the saying is, jumped out of his skin.

In the start forward he bumped the back of Captain MacWhirr, who didn't move; and then a hand gripped his thigh. A lull had come, a menacing lull of the wind, the holding of a stormy breath—and he felt himself pawed all over. It was the boatswain. Jukes recognized these hands, so thick and enormous that they seemed to belong to some new species of man.

The boatswain had arrived on the bridge, crawling on all fours against the wind, and had found the chief mate's legs with the top of his head. Immediately he crouched and began to explore Jukes' person upwards with prudent, apologetic touches, as became an inferior.

He was an ill-favored, undersized, gruff sailor of fifty, coarsely hairy, short-legged, long-armed, resembling an elderly ape. His strength was immense; and in his great lumpy paws, bulging like brown boxing gloves on the end of furry forearms, the heaviest objects were handled like playthings. Apart from the grizzled pelt on his chest, the menacing demeanor and the hoarse voice, he had none of the classical attributes of his rating. His good nature almost amounted to imbecility: the men did what they liked with him, and he had not an ounce of initiative in his character, which was easygoing and talkative. For these reasons Jukes disliked him; but Captain MacWhirr, to Jukes' scornful disgust, seemed to regard him as a first-rate petty officer.

He pulled himself up by Jukes' coat, taking that liberty with the greatest moderation, and only so far as it was forced upon him by the hurricane.

"What is it, bosun, what is it?" yelled Jukes, impatiently. What could that fraud of a bosun want on the bridge? The typhoon had got on Jukes' nerves. The husky bellowings of the other, though unintelligible, seemed to suggest a state of lively satisfaction. There could be no mistake. The old fool was pleased with something.

The boatswain's other hand had found some other body, for in a changed tone he began to inquire: "Is it you, sir? Is it you, sir?" The wind strangled his howls.

"Yes!" cried Captain MacWhirr.

I V

All that the boatswain, out of a superabundance of yells, could make clear to Captain MacWhirr was the bizarre intelligence that "All them Chinamen in the fore 'tween-deck have fetched away, sir."

Jukes to leeward could hear these two shouting within six inches of his face, as you may hear on a still night half a mile away two men conversing across a field. He heard Captain MacWhirr's exasperated "What? What?" and the strained pitch of the other's hoarseness. "In a lump . . . seen them myself. . . . Awful sight, sir . . . thought . . . tell you."

Jukes remained indifferent, as if rendered irresponsible by the force of the hurricane, which made the very thought of action utterly vain. Besides, being very young, he had found the occupation of keeping his heart completely steeled against the worst so engrossing that he had come to feel an overpowering dislike towards any other form of activity whatever. He was not scared; he knew this because, firmly believing he would never see another sunrise, he remained calm in that belief.

These are the moments of do-nothing heroics to which even good men surrender at times. Many officers of ships can no doubt recall a case in their experience when just such a trance of confounded stoicism would come all at once over a whole ship's company. Jukes, however, had no wide experience of men or storms. He conceived himself to be calm—inexorably calm; but as a matter of fact he was daunted; not abjectly, but only so far as a decent man may, without becoming loathsome to himself.

It was rather like a forced-on numbness of spirit. The long, long stress of a gale does it; the suspense of the interminably culminating catastrophe; and there is a bodily fatigue in the mere holding on to existence within the excessive tumult; a searching and insidious fatigue that penetrates deep into a man's breast to cast down and sadden his heart, which is incorrigible, and of all the gifts of the earth—even before life itself— aspires to peace.

Jukes was benumbed much more than he supposed. He held on—very wet, very cold, stiff in every limb; and in a momentary hallucination of swift visions (it is said that a drowning man thus reviews all his life) he beheld all sorts of memories alto-gether unconnected with his present situation. He remembered his father, for instance: a worthy businessman, who at an unfortunate crisis in his affairs went quietly to bed and died forthwith in a state of resignation. Jukes did not recall these circumstances, of course, but remaining otherwise unconcerned he seemed to see distinctly the poor man's face; a certain game of nap played when quite a boy in Table Bay on board a ship, since lost with all hands; the thick eyebrows of his first skipper; and without any emotion, as he might years ago have walked listlessly into her room and found her sitting there with a book, he remembered his mother—dead, too, now—the resolute woman, left badly off, who had been very firm in his bringing up.

It could not have lasted more than a second, perhaps not so much. A heavy arm had fallen about his shoulders; Captain MacWhirr's voice was speaking his name into his ear.

"Jukes! Jukes!"

He detected the tone of deep concern. The wind had thrown its weight on the ship, trying to pin her down amongst the seas. They made a clean breach over her, as over a deep-swimming log; and the gathered weight of crashes menaced monstrously from afar. The breakers flung out of the night with a ghostly light on their crests—the light of sea foam that in a ferocious, boiling-up pale flash showed upon the slender body of the ship the toppling rush, the downfall, and the seething mad scurry of each wave. Never for a moment could she shake herself clear of the water; Jukes, rigid, perceived in her motion the ominous sign of haphazard floundering. She was no longer struggling intelligently. It was the beginning of the end; and the note of busy concern in Captain MacWhirr's voice sickened him like an exhibition of blind and pernicious folly.

The spell of the storm had fallen upon Jukes. He was penetrated by it, absorbed by it; he was rooted in it with a rigor of dumb attention. Captain MacWhirr persisted in his cries, but the wind got between them like a solid wedge. He hung round Jukes' neck as heavy as a millstone, and suddenly the sides of their heads knocked together.

"Jukes! Mr. Jukes, I say!"

He had to answer that voice that would not be silenced. He answered in the customary manner: ". . . Yes, sir."

And directly, his heart, corrupted by the storm that breeds a craving for peace, rebelled against the tyranny of training and command.

Captain MacWhirr had his mate's head fixed firm in the crook of his elbow, and pressed it to his yelling lips mysteriously. Sometimes Jukes would break in, admonishing hastily: "Look out, sir!" or Captain MacWhirr would bawl an earnest exhortation to "Hold hard, there!" and the whole black universe seemed to reel together with the ship. They paused. She floated yet. And Captain MacWhirr would resume his shouts. ". . . Says . . . whole lot . . . fetched away. . . . Ought to see . . . what's the matter."

Directly the full force of the hurricane had struck the ship, every part of her deck became untenable; and the sailors, dazed and dismayed, took shelter in the port alleyway under the bridge. It had a door aft, which they shut; it was very black, cold, and dismal. At each heavy fling of the ship they would groan all together in the dark, and tons of water could be heard scuttling about as if trying to get at them from above. The boatswain had been keeping up a gruff talk, but a more unreasonable lot of men, he said afterwards, he had never been with. They were snug enough there, out of harm's way, and not wanted to do anything, either; and yet they did nothing but grumble and complain peevishly like so many sick kids. Finally, one of them said that if there had been at least some light to see each other's noses by, it wouldn't be so bad.

It was making him crazy, he declared, to lie there in the dark waiting for the blamed hooker to sink.

"Why don't you step outside, then, and be done with it at once?" the boatswain turned on him.

This called up a shout of execration. The boatswain found himself overwhelmed with reproaches of all sorts. They seemed to take it ill that a lamp was not instantly created for them out of nothing. They would whine after a light to get drowned by—anyhow! And though the unreason of their revilings was patent—since no one could hope to reach the lamp room, which was forward—he became greatly distressed. He did not think it was decent of them to be nagging at him like this. He told them so, and was met by general contumely. He sought refuge, therefore, in an embittered silence. At the same time their grumbling and sighing and muttering worried him greatly, but by and by it occurred to him that there were six globe lamps hung in the 'tween-deck, and that there could be no harm in depriving the coolies of one of them.

The *Nan-Shan* had an athwartship coal bunker, which, being at times used as cargo space, communicated by an iron door with the fore 'tween-deck. It was empty then, and its manhole was the foremost one in the alleyway. The boatswain could get in, therefore, without coming out on deck at all; but to his great surprise he found he could induce no one to help him in taking off the manhole cover. He groped for it all the same, but one of the crew lying in his way refused to budge.

"Why, I only want to get you that blamed light you are crying for," he expostulated, almost pitifully.

Somebody told him to go and put his head in a bag. He regretted he could not recognize the voice, and that it was too dark to see, otherwise, as he said, he would have put a head on *that* son of a sea cook, anyway, sink or swim. Nevertheless, he had made up his mind to show them he could get a light, if he were to die for it.

Through the violence of the ship's rolling, every movement was dangerous. To be lying down seemed labor enough. He nearly broke his neck dropping into the bunker. He fell on his back, and was sent shooting helplessly from side to side in the dangerous company of a heavy iron bar—a coal-trimmer's slice probably—left down there by somebody. This thing made him as nervous as though it had been a wild beast. He could not see it, the inside of the bunker coated with coaldust being perfectly and impenetrably black; but he heard it sliding and clattering, and striking here and there, always in the neighborhood of his head. It seemed to make an extraordinary noise, too—to give heavy thumps as though it had been as big as a bridge girder. This was remarkable enough for him to notice while he was flung from port to starboard and back again, and clawing desperately the smooth sides of the bunker in the endeavor to stop himself. The door into the 'tween-deck not fitting quite true, he saw a thread of dim light at the bottom.

Being a sailor, and a still active man, he did not want much of a chance to regain his feet; and as luck would have it, in scrambling up he put his hand on the iron slice, picking it up as he rose. Otherwise he would have been afraid of the thing breaking his legs, or at least knocking him down again. At first he stood still. He felt unsafe in this darkness that seemed to make the ship's motion unfamiliar, unforeseen, and difficult to counteract. He felt so much shaken for a moment that he dared not move for fear of "taking charge again." He had no mind to get battered to pieces in that bunker.

He had struck his head twice; he was dazed a little. He seemed to hear yet so plainly the clatter and bangs of the iron slice flying about his ears that he tightened his grip to prove to himself he had it there safely in his hand. He was vaguely amazed at the plainness with which down there he could hear the gale raging. Its howls and shrieks seemed to take on, in the emptiness of the bunker, something of the human character, of human rage and pain—being not vast but infinitely poignant. And there were, with every roll, thumps, too—profound, ponderous thumps, as if a bulky object of five-ton weight or so had got play in the hold. But there was no such thing in the cargo. Something on deck? Impossible. Or alongside? Couldn't be.

He thought all this quickly, clearly, competently, like a seaman, and in the end remained puzzled. This noise, though, came deadened from outside, together with the washing and pouring of water on deck above his head. Was it the wind? Must be. It made down there a row like the shouting of a big lot of crazed men. And he discovered in himself a desire for a light, too—if only to get drowned by—and a nervous anxiety to get out of that bunker as quickly as possible.

He pulled back the bolt: the heavy iron plate turned on its hinges; and it was as though he had opened the door to the sounds of the tempest. A gust of hoarse yelling met him: the air was still; and the rushing of water overhead was covered by a tumult of strangled, throaty shrieks that produced an effect of desperate confusion. He straddled his legs the whole width of the doorway and stretched his neck. And at first he perceived only what he had come to seek: six small yellow flames swinging violently on the great body of the dusk.

It was stayed like the gallery of a mine, with a row of stanchions in the middle, and crossbeams overhead, penetrating into the gloom ahead—indefinitely. And to port there loomed, like the caving in of one of the sides, a bulky mass with a slanting outline. The whole place, with the shadows and the shapes, moved all the time. The boatswain glared: the ship lurched to starboard, and a great howl came from that mass that had the slant of fallen earth.

Pieces of wood whizzed past. Planks, he thought, inexpressibly startled, and fling-ing back his head. At his feet a man went sliding over, open-eyed, on his back, straining with uplifted arms for nothing: and another came bounding like a detached stone with his head between his legs and his hands clenched. His pigtail whipped in the air; he made a grab at the boatswain's legs, and from his opened hand a bright white disc rolled against the boatswain's foot. He recognized a silver dollar, and yelled at it with astonishment. With a precipitated sound of trampling and shuffling of bare feet, and with guttural cries, the mound of writhing bodies piled up to port detached itself from the ship's side and sliding, inert and struggling, shifted to starboard, with a dull, brutal thump. The cries ceased. The boatswain heard a long moan through the roar and whistling of the wind; he saw an inextricable confusion of heads and shoul-ders, naked soles kicking upwards, fists raised, tumbling backs, legs, pigtails, faces.

"Good Lord!" he cried, horrified, and banged-to the iron door upon this vision.

This was what he had come on the bridge to tell. He could not keep it to himself; and on board ship there is only one man to whom it is worth while to unburden yourself. On his passage back the hands in the alleyway swore at him for a fool. Why didn't he bring that lamp? What the devil did the coolies matter to anybody? And when he came out, the extremity of the ship made what went on inside of her appear of little moment.

At first he thought he had left the alleyway in the very moment of her sinking. The bridge ladders had been washed away, but an enormous sea filling the afterdeck floated him up. After that he had to lie on his stomach for some time, holding to a ring bolt, getting his breath now and then, and swallowing salt water. He struggled farther on his hands and knees, too frightened and distracted to turn back. In this way he reached the after-part of the wheelhouse. In that comparatively sheltered spot he found the second mate. The boatswain was pleasantly surprised—his impression being that everybody on deck must have been washed away a long time ago. He asked eagerly where the Captain was.

The second mate was lying low, like a malignant little animal under a hedge.

"Captain? Gone overboard, after getting us into this mess." The mate, too, for all he knew or cared. Another fool. Didn't matter. Everybody was going by and by.

The boatswain crawled out again into the strength of the wind; not because he much expected to find anybody, he said, but just to get away from "that man." He crawled out as outcasts go to face an inclement world. Hence his great joy at finding Jukes and the Captain. But what was going on in the 'tween-deck was to him a minor matter by that time. Besides, it was difficult to make yourself heard. But he managed to convey the idea that the Chinamen had broken adrift together with their boxes, and that he had come up on purpose to report this. As to the hands, they were all right. Then, appeased, he subsided on the deck in a sitting posture, hugging with his arms and legs the stand of the engine-room telegraph—an iron casting as thick as a post. When that went, why, he expected he would go, too. He gave no more thought to the coolies.

Captain MacWhirr had made Jukes understand that he wanted him to go down below—to see.

"What am I to do then, sir?" And the trembling of his whole wet body caused Jukes' voice to sound like bleating.

"See first . . . Bosun . . . says . . . adrift."

"That bosun is a confounded fool," howled Jukes, shakily.

The absurdity of the demand made upon him revolted Jukes. He was as unwilling to go as if the moment he had left the deck the ship were sure to sink.

"I must know . . . can't leave. . . ."

"They'll settle, sir."

"Fight . . . bosun says they fight. . . . Why? Can't have . . . fighting . . . board ship. . . . Much rather keep you here . . . case . . . I should . . . washed overboard myself. . . . Stop it . . . some way. You see and tell me . . . through engine-room tube. Don't want you . . . come up here . . . too often. Dangerous . . . moving about . . . deck."

Jukes, held with his head in chancery, had to listen to what seemed horrible suggestions.

"Don't want . . . you get lost . . . so long . . . ship isn't. . . . Rout . . . Good man. . . . Ship . . . may . . . through this . . . all right yet."

All at once Jukes understood he would have to go.

"Do you think she may?" he screamed.

But the wind devoured the reply, out of which Jukes heard only the one word, pronounced with great energy ". . . Always. . . ."

Captain MacWhirr released Jukes, and bending over the boatswain, yelled, "Get back with the mate." Jukes only knew that the arm was gone off his shoulders. He was dismissed with his orders—to do what? He was exasperated into letting go his hold carelessly, and on the instant was blown away. It seemed to him that nothing could stop him from being blown right over the stern. He flung himself down hastily, and the boatswain, who was following, fell on him.

"Don't you get up yet, sir," cried the boatswain. "No hurry!"

A sea swept over. Jukes understood the boatswain to splutter that the bridge ladders were gone. "I'll lower you down, sir, by your hands," he screamed. He shouted also something about the smokestack being as likely to go overboard as not. Jukes thought it very possible, and imagined the fires out, the ship helpless. . . . The boatswain by his side kept on yelling. "What? What is it?" Jukes cried distressfully; and the other repeated, "What would my old woman say if she saw me now?"

In the alleyway, where a lot of water had got in and splashed in the dark, the men were still as death, till Jukes stumbled against one of them and cursed him savagely for being in the way. Two or three voices then asked, eager and weak, "Any chance for us, sir?"

"What's the matter with you fools?" he said brutally. He felt as though he could throw himself down amongst them and never move any more. But they seemed cheered; and in the midst of obsequious warnings, "Look out! Mind that manhole lid, sir," they lowered him into the bunker. The boatswain tumbled down after him, and as soon as he had picked himself up he remarked, "She would say, 'Serve you right, you old fool, for going to sea.'"

The boatswain had some means, and made a point of alluding to them frequently. His wife—a fat woman —and two grown-up daughters kept a greengrocer's shop in the East End of London.

In the dark, Jukes, unsteady on his legs, listened to a faint thunderous patter. A deadened screaming went on steadily at his elbow, as it were; and from above the louder tumult of the storm descended upon these near sounds. His head swam. To him, too, in that bunker, the motion of the ship seemed novel and menacing, sapping his resolution as though he had never been afloat before.

He had half a mind to scramble out again; but the remembrance of Captain

MacWhirr's voice made this impossible. His orders were to go and see. What was the good of it, he wanted to know. Enraged, he told himself he would see—of course. But the boatswain, staggering clumsily, warned him to be careful how he opened that door; there was a blamed fight going on. And Jukes, as if in great bodily pain, desired irritably to know what the devil they were fighting for.

"Dollars! Dollars, sir. All their rotten chests got burst open. Blamed money skipping all over the place, and they are tumbling after it head over heels—tearing and biting like anything. A regular little hell in there."

Jukes convulsively opened the door. The short boatswain peered under his arm.

One of the lamps had gone out, broken perhaps. Rancorous, guttural cries burst out loudly on their ears, and a strange panting sound, the working of all these straining breasts. A hard blow hit the side of the ship: water fell above with a stunning shock, and in the forefront of the gloom, where the air was reddish and thick, Jukes saw a head bang the deck violently, two thick calves waving on high, muscular arms twined round a naked body, a yellow face, openmouthed and with a set wild stare, look up and slide away. An empty chest clattered turning over; a man fell headfirst with a jump, as if lifted by a kick; and farther off, indistinct, others streamed like a mass of rolling stones down a bank, thumping the deck with their feet and flourishing their arms wildly. The hatchway ladder was loaded with coolies swarming on it like bees on a branch. They hung on the steps in a crawling, stirring cluster, beating madly with their fists the underside of the battened hatch, and the headlong rush of the water above was heard in the intervals of their yelling. The ship heeled over once more, and they began to drop off: first one, then two, then all the rest went away together, falling straight off with a great cry.

Jukes was confounded. The boatswain, with gruff anxiety, begged him, "Don't you go in there, sir."

The whole place seemed to twist upon itself, jumping incessantly the while; and when the ship rose to a sea Jukes fancied that all these men would be shot upon him in a body. He backed out, swung the door to, and with trembling hands pushed at the bolt. . . .

As soon as his mate had gone Captain MacWhirr, left alone on the bridge, sidled and staggered as far as the wheelhouse. Its door being hinged forward, he had to fight the gale for admittance, and when at last he managed to enter, it was with an instantaneous clatter and a bang, as though he had been fired through the wood. He stood within, holding on to the handle.

The steering gear leaked steam, and in the confined space the glass of the binnacle made a shiny oval of light in a thin white fog. The wind howled, hummed, whistled, with sudden booming gusts that rattled the doors and shutters in the vicious patter of sprays. Two coils of lead line and a small canvas bag hung on a long lanyard, swung wide off, and came back clinging to the bulkheads. The gratings underfoot were nearly afloat; with every sweeping blow of a sea, water squirted violently through the cracks all round the door, and the man at the helm had flung down his cap, his coat, and stood propped against the gear casing in a striped cotton shirt open on his breast. The little brass wheel in his hands had the appearance of a bright and fragile toy. The cords of his neck stood hard and lean, a dark patch lay in the hollow of his throat, and his face was still and sunken as in death.

Captain MacWhirr wiped his eyes. The sea that had nearly taken him overboard had, to his great annoyance, washed his sou'wester hat off his bald head. The fluffy, fair hair, soaked and darkened, resembled a mean skein of cotton threads festooned round his bare skull. His face, glistening with sea water, had been made crimson with the wind, with the sting of sprays. He looked as though he had come off sweating from before a furnace.

"You here?" he muttered, heavily.

The second mate had found his way into the wheelhouse some time before. He had fixed himself in a corner with his knees up, a fist pressed against each temple; and this attitude suggested rage, sorrow, resignation, surrender, with a sort of concentrated unforgiveness. He said mournfully and defiantly, "Well, it's my watch below now; ain't it?"

The steam gear clattered, stopped, clattered again; and the helmsman's eyeballs seemed to project out of a hungry face as if the compass card behind the binnacle glass had been meat. God knows how long he had been left there to steer, as if forgotten by all his shipmates. The bells had not been struck; there had been no reliefs; the ship's routine had gone down wind; but he was trying to keep her head north-northeast. The rudder might have been gone for all he knew, the fires out, the engines broken down, the ship ready to roll over like a corpse. He was anxious not to get muddled and lose control of her head, because the compass card swung far both ways, wriggling on the pivot, and sometimes seemed to whirl right round. He suffered from mental stress. He was horribly afraid, also, of the wheelhouse going. Mountains of water kept on tumbling against it. When the ship took one of her desperate dives the corners of his lips twitched.

Captain MacWhirr looked up at the wheelhouse clock. Screwed to the bulkhead, it had a white face on which the black hands appeared to stand quite still. It was half-past one in the morning.

"Another day," he muttered to himself.

The second mate heard him, and lifting his head as one grieving amongst ruins, "You won't see it break," he exclaimed. His wrists and his knees could be seen to shake violently. "No, by God! You won't. . . ."

He took his face again between his fists.

The body of the helmsman had moved slightly, but his head didn't budge on his neck—like a stone head fixed to look one way from a column. During a roll that all but took his booted legs from under him, and in the very stagger to save himself, Captain MacWhirr said austerely, "Don't you pay any attention to what that man says." And then, with an indefinable change of tone, very grave, he added, "He isn't on duty."

The sailor said nothing.

The hurricane boomed, shaking the little place, which seemed air-tight; and the light of the binnacle flickered all the time.

"You haven't been relieved," Captain MacWhirr went on, looking down. "I want you to stick to the helm, though, as long as you can. You've got the hang of her. Another man coming here might make a mess of it. Wouldn't do. No child's play. And the hands are probably busy with a job down below. . . . Think you can?"

The steering gear leaped into an abrupt short clatter, stopped smoldering like an ember; and the still man, with a motionless gaze, burst out, as if all the passion in him had gone into his lips: "By Heavens, sir! I can steer forever if nobody talks to me."

"Oh! aye! All right. . . ." The Captain lifted his eyes for the first time to the man, ". . . Hackett."

And he seemed to dismiss this matter from his mind. He stooped to the engine-room speaking tube, blew in, and bent his head. Mr. Rout below answered, and at once Captain MacWhirr put his lips to the mouthpiece.

With the uproar of the gale around him he applied alternately his lips and his ear, and the engineer's voice mounted to him, harsh and as if out of the heat of an engagement. One of the stokers was disabled, the others had given in, the second engineer and the donkeyman were firing-up. The third engineer was standing by the steam valve. The engines were being tended by hand. How was it above?

"Bad enough. It mostly rests with you," said Captain MacWhirr. Was the mate down there yet? No? Well, he would be presently. Would Mr. Rout let him talk through the speaking tube?—through the deck speaking tube, because he—the Captain—was going out again on the bridge directly. There was some trouble amongst the Chinamen. They were fighting, it seemed. Couldn't allow fighting anyhow. . . .

Mr. Rout had gone away, and Captain MacWhirr could feel against his ear the pulsation of the engines, like the beat of the ship's heart. Mr. Rout's voice down there shouted something distantly. The ship pitched headlong, the pulsation leaped with a hissing tumult, and stopped dead. Captain MacWhirr's face was impassive, and his eyes were fixed aimlessly on the crouching shape of the second mate. Again Mr. Rout's voice cried out in the depths, and the pulsating beats recommenced, with slow strokes —growing swifter.

Mr. Rout had returned to the tube. "It don't matter much what they do," he said, hastily; and then, with irritation, "She takes these dives as if she never meant to come up again."

"Awful sea," said the Captain's voice from above.

"Don't let me drive her under," barked Solomon Rout up the pipe.

"Dark and rain. Can't see what's coming," uttered the voice. "Must—keep—her—moving—enough to steer—and chance it," it went on to state distinctly.

"I am doing as much as I dare."

"We are—getting—smashed up—a good deal up here," proceeded the voice mildly. "Doing—fairly well—though. Of course, if the wheelhouse should go. . . ."

Mr. Rout, bending an attentive ear, muttered peevishly something under his breath.

But the deliberate voice up there became animated to ask: "Jukes turned up yet?"

Then, after a short wait, "I wish he would bear a hand. I want him to be done and come up here in case of anything. To look after the ship. I am all alone. The second mate's lost. . . ."

"What?" shouted Mr. Rout into the engine room, taking his head away. Then up the tube he cried, "Gone overboard?" and clapped his ear to.

"Lost his nerve," the voice from above continued in a matter-of-fact tone. "Damned awkward circumstance."

Mr. Rout, listening with bowed neck, opened his eyes wide at this. However, he heard something like the sounds of a scuffle and broken exclamations coming down to him. He strained his hearing; and all the time Beale, the third engineer, with his arms uplifted, held between the palms of his hands the rim of a little black wheel projecting at the side of a big copper pipe. He seemed to be poising it above his head, as though it were a correct attitude in some sort of game.

To steady himself, he pressed his shoulder against the white bulkhead, one knee bent, and a sweat-rag tucked in his belt hanging on his hip. His smooth cheek was begrimed and flushed, and the coaldust on his eyelids, like the black penciling of a make-up, enhanced the liquid brilliance of the whites, giving to his youthful face something of a feminine, exotic and fascinating aspect. When the ship pitched he would with hasty movements of his hands screw hard at the little wheel.

"Gone crazy," began the Captain's voice suddenly in the tube. "Rushed at me. . . . Just now. Had to knock him down. . . . This minute. You heard, Mr. Rout?"

"The devil!" muttered Mr. Rout. "Look out, Beale!"

His shout rang out like the blast of a warning trumpet, between the iron walls of the engine room. Painted white, they rose high into the dusk of the skylight, sloping like a roof; and the whole lofty space resembled the interior of a monument, divided by floors of iron grating, with lights flickering at different levels, and a mass of gloom lingering in the middle, within the columnar stir of machinery under the motionless swelling of the cylinders. A loud and wild resonance, made up of all the noises of the hurricane, dwelt in the still warmth of the air. There was in it the smell of hot metal, of oil, and a slight mist of steam. The blows of the sea seemed to traverse it in an unringing, stunning shock, from side to side.

Gleams, like pale long flames, trembled upon the polish of metal; from the flooring below the enormous crank-heads emerged in their turns with a flash of brass and steel —going over; while the connecting rods, big-jointed, like skeleton limbs, seemed to thrust them down and pull them up again with an irresistible precision. And deep in the half-light other rods dodged deliberately to and fro, crossheads nodded, discs of metal rubbed smoothly against each other, slow and gentle, in a commingling of shadows and gleams.

Sometimes all those powerful and unerring movements would slow down simultaneously, as if they had been the functions of a living organism, stricken suddenly by the blight of languor; and Mr. Rout's eyes would blaze darker in his long sallow face. He was fighting this fight in a pair of carpet slippers. A short shiny jacket barely covered his loins, and his white wrists protruded far out of the tight sleeves, as though the emergency had added to his stature, had lengthened his limbs, augmented his pallor, hollowed his eyes.

He moved, climbing high up, disappearing low down, with a restless, purposeful industry, and when he stood still, holding the guard rail in front of the starting gear, he would keep glancing to the right at the steam gauge, at the water gauge, fixed upon the white wall in the light of a swaying lamp. The mouths of two speaking tubes gaped stupidly at his elbow, and the dial of the engine-room telegraph resembled a clock of large diameter, bearing on its face curt words instead of figures. The grouped letters stood out heavily black, around the pivot-head of the indicator, emphatically symbolic of loud exclamations: AHEAD, ASTERN, SLOW, HALF, STAND BY; and the fat black hand pointed downwards to the word FULL, which, thus singled out, captured the eye as a sharp cry secures attention.

The wood-encased bulk of the low-pressure cylinder, frowning portly from above, emitted a faint wheeze at every thrust, and except for that low hiss the engines worked their steel limbs headlong or slow with a silent, determined smoothness. And all this, the white walls, the moving steel, the floor plates under Solomon Rout's feet, the floors of iron grating above his head, the dusk and the gleams, uprose and sank continuously, with one accord, upon the harsh wash of the waves against the ship's side. The whole loftiness of the place, booming hollow to the great voice of the wind, swayed at the top like a tree, would go over bodily, as if borne down this way and that by the tremendous blasts.

"You've got to hurry up," shouted Mr. Rout, as soon as he saw Jukes appear in the stokehold doorway.

Jukes' glance was wandering and tipsy; his red face was puffy, as though he had overslept himself. He had had an arduous road, and had traveled over it with immense vivacity, the agitation of his mind corresponding to the exertions of his body. He had rushed up out of the bunker, stumbling in the dark alleyway amongst a lot of bewildered men who, trod upon, asked "What's up, sir?" in awed mutters all round him; down the stokehold ladder, missing many iron rungs in his hurry, down into a place deep as a well, black as Tophet, tipping over back and forth like a seesaw. The water in the bilges thundered at each roll, and lumps of coal skipped to and fro, from end to end, rattling like an avalanche of pebbles on a slope of iron.

Somebody in there moaned with pain, and somebody else could be seen crouching over what seemed the prone body of a dead man; a lusty voice blasphemed; and the glow under each fire door was like a pool of flaming blood radiating quietly in a velvety blackness.

A gust of wind struck upon the nape of Jukes' neck and next moment he felt it streaming about his wet ankles. The stokehold ventilators hummed; in front of the six fire doors two wild figures, stripped to the waist, staggered and stooped, wrestling with two shovels.

"Hallo! Plenty of draft now," yelled the second engineer at once, as though he had been all the time looking out for Jukes. The donkeyman, a dapper little chap with a dazzling fair skin and a tiny, gingery mustache, worked in a sort of mute transport.

They were keeping a full head of steam, and a profound rumbling, as of an empty furniture van trotting over a bridge, made a sustained bass to all the other noises of the place.

"Blowing off all the time," went on yelling the second. With a sound as of a hundred scoured saucepans, the orifice of a ventilator spat upon his shoulder a sudden gush of salt water, and he volleyed a stream of curses upon all things on earth including his own soul, ripping and raving, and all the time attending to his business. With a sharp clash of metal the ardent pale glare of the fire opened upon his bullet head, showing his spluttering lips, his insolent face, and with another clang closed like the white-hot wink of an iron eye.

"Where's the blooming ship? Can you tell me? Blast my eyes! Under water—or what? It's coming down here in tons. Are the condemned cowls gone to Hades? Hey? Don't you know anything—you jolly sailor-man you . . . ?"

Jukes, after a bewildered moment, had been helped by a roll to dart through; and as soon as his eyes took in the comparative vastness, peace and brilliance of the engine room, the ship, setting her stern heavily in the water, sent him charging head down upon Mr. Rout.

The chief's arm, long like a tentacle, and straightening as if worked by a spring, went out to meet him, and deflected his rush into a spin towards the speaking tubes. At the same time Mr. Rout repeated earnestly:

"You've got to hurry up, whatever it is."

Jukes yelled "Are you there, sir?" and listened. Nothing. Suddenly the roar of the wind fell straight into his ear, but presently a small voice shoved aside the shouting hurricane quietly.

"You, Jukes?—Well?"

Jukes was ready to talk: it was only time that seemed to be wanting. It was easy enough to account for everything. He could perfectly imagine the coolies battened down in the reeking 'tween-deck, lying sick and scared between the rows of chests. Then one of these chests—or perhaps several at once—breaking loose in a roll, knocking out others, sides splitting, lids flying open, and all these clumsy Chinamen rising up in a body to save their property. Afterwards every fling of the ship would hurl that tramping, yelling mob here and there, from side to side, in a whirl of smashed wood, torn clothing, rolling dollars. A struggle once started, they would be unable to stop themselves. Nothing could stop them now except main force. It was a disaster. He had seen it, and that was all he could say. Some of them must be dead, he believed. The rest would go on fighting. . . .

He sent up his words, tripping over each other, crowding the narrow tube. They mounted as if into a silence of an enlightened comprehension dwelling alone up there with a storm. And Jukes wanted to be dismissed from the face of that odious trouble intruding on the great need of the ship.

V

He waited. Before his eyes the engines turned with slow labor, that in the moment of going off into a mad fling would stop dead at Mr. Rout's shout, "Look out, Beale!" They paused in an intelligent immobility, stilled in mid-stroke, a heavy crank arrested on the cant, as if conscious of danger and the passage of time. Then, with a "Now, then!" from the chief, and the sound of a breath expelled through clenched teeth, they would accomplish the interrupted revolution and begin another.

There was the prudent sagacity of wisdom and the deliberation of enormous strength in their movements. This was their work—this patient coaxing of a distracted ship over the fury of the waves and into the very eye of the wind. At times Mr. Rout's chin would sink on his breast, and he watched them with knitted eyebrows as if lost in thought.

The voice that kept the hurricane out of Jukes' ear began: "Take the hands with you . . . ," and left off unexpectedly.

"What could I do with them, sir?"

A harsh, abrupt, imperious clang exploded suddenly. The three pairs of eyes flew up to the telegraph dial to see the hand jump from FULL to STOP, as if snatched by a devil. And then these three men in the engine room had the intimate sensation of a check upon the ship, of a strange shrinking, as if she had gathered herself for a desperate leap.

"Stop her!" bellowed Mr. Rout.

Nobody—not even Captain MacWhirr, who alone on deck had caught sight of a white line of foam coming on at such a height that he couldn't believe his eyes—nobody was to know the steepness of that sea and the awful depth of the hollow the hurricane had scooped out behind the running wall of water.

It raced to meet the ship, and, with a pause, as of girding the loins, the *Nan-Shan* lifted her bows and leaped. The flames in all the lamps sank, darkening the engine room. One went out. With a tearing crash and a swirling, raving tumult, tons of water fell upon the deck, as though the ship had darted under the foot of a cataract.

Down there they looked at each other, stunned.

"Swept from end to end, by God!" bawled Jukes.

She dipped into the hollow straight down, as if going over the edge of the world. The engine room toppled forward menacingly, like the inside of a tower nodding in an earthquake. An awful racket, of iron things falling, came from the stokehold. She hung on this appalling slant long enough for Beale to drop on his hands and knees and begin to crawl as if he meant to fly on all fours out of the engine room, and for Mr. Rout to turn his head slowly, rigid, cavernous, with the lower jaw dropping. Jukes had shut his eyes, and his face in a moment became hopelessly blank and gentle, like the face of a blind man.

At last she rose slowly, staggering, as if she had to lift a mountain with her bows. Mr. Rout shut his mouth; Jukes blinked; and little Beale stood up hastily.

"Another one like this, and that's the last of her," cried the chief.

He and Jukes looked at each other, and the same thought came into their heads.

The Captain! Everything must have been swept away. Steering gear gone—ship like a log. All over directly.

"Rush!" ejaculated Mr. Rout thickly, glaring with enlarged, doubtful eyes at Jukes, who answered him by an irresolute glance.

The clang of the telegraph gong soothed them instantly. The black hand dropped in a flash from STOP to FULL.

"Now then, Beale!" cried Mr. Rout.

The steam hissed low. The piston rods slid in and out. Jukes put his ear to the tube. The voice was ready for him. It said: "Pick up all the money. Bear a hand now. I'll want you up here." And that was all.

"Sir?" called up Jukes. There was no answer.

He staggered away like a defeated man from the field of battle. He had got, in some way or other, a cut above his left eyebrow—a cut to the bone. He was not aware of it in the least: quantities of the China Sea, large enough to break his neck for him, had gone over his head, had cleaned, washed, and salted that wound. It did not bleed, but only gaped red; and this gash over the eye, his disheveled hair, the disorder of his clothes, gave him the aspect of a man worsted in a fight with fists.

"Got to pick up the dollars." He appealed to Mr. Rout, smiling pitifully at random.

"What's that?" asked Mr. Rout, wildly. "Pick up . . . ? I don't care. . . ." Then, quivering in every muscle, but with an exaggeration of paternal tone, "Go away now, for God's sake. You deck people'll drive me silly. There's that second mate been going for the old man. Don't you know? You fellows are going wrong for want of something to do. . . ."

At these words Jukes discovered in himself the beginnings of anger. Want of something to do—indeed. . . . Full of hot scorn against the chief, he turned to go the way he had come. In the stokehold the plump donkeyman toiled with his shovel mutely, as if his tongue had been cut out; but the second was carrying on like a noisy, undaunted maniac, who had preserved his skill in the art of stoking under a marine boiler.

"Hallo, you wandering officer? Hey! Can't you get some of your slush-slingers to wind up a few of them ashes? I am getting choked with them here. Curse it! Hallo! Hey! Remember the articles: *Sailors and firemen to assist each other.* Hey! D'ye hear?"

Jukes was climbing out frantically, and the other, lifting up his face after him, howled, "Can't you speak? What are you poking about here for? What's your game, anyhow?"

A frenzy possessed Jukes. By the time he was back amongst the men in the darkness of the alleyway, he felt ready to wring all their necks at the slightest sign of hanging back. The very thought of it exasperated him. *He* couldn't hang back. They shouldn't.

The impetuosity with which he came amongst them carried them along. They had already been excited and startled at all his comings and goings—by the fierceness and rapidity of his movements; and more felt than seen in his rushes, he appeared formidable—busied with matters of life and death that brooked no delay. At his first word he heard them drop into the bunker one after another obediently, with heavy thumps.

They were not clear as to what would have to be done. "What is it? What is it?" they were asking each other. The boatswain tried to explain; the sounds of a great scuffle surprised them; and the mighty shocks, reverberating awfully in the black bunker, kept them in mind of their danger. When the boatswain threw open the door it seemed that an eddy of the hurricane, stealing through the iron sides of the ship, had set all these bodies whirling like dust: there came to them a confused uproar, a tempestuous tumult, a fierce mutter, gusts of screams dying away, and the tramping of feet mingling with the blows of the sea.

For a moment they glared amazed, blocking the doorway. Jukes pushed through them brutally. He said nothing, and simply darted in. Another lot of coolies on the ladder, struggling suicidally to break through the battened hatch to a swamped deck, fell off as before, and he disappeared under them like a man overtaken by a landslide.

The boatswain yelled excitedly: "Come along. Get the mate out. He'll be trampled to death. Come on."

They charged in, stamping on breasts, on fingers, on faces, catching their feet in heaps of clothing, kicking broken wood; but before they could get hold of him Jukes emerged waist deep in a multitude of clawing hands. In the instant he had been lost to view, all the buttons of his jacket had gone, its back had got split up to the collar, his waistcoat had been torn open. The central struggling mass of Chinamen went over to the roll, dark, indistinct, helpless, with a wild gleam of many eyes in the dim light of the lamps.

"Leave me alone—damn you. I am all right," screeched Jukes. "Drive them forward. Watch your chance when she pitches. Forward with 'em. Drive them against the bulkhead. Jam 'em up."

The rush of the sailors into the seething 'tween-deck was like a splash of cold water into a boiling caldron. The commotion sank for a moment.

The bulk of Chinamen were locked in such a compact scrimmage that, linking their arms and aided by an appalling dive of the ship, the seamen sent it forward in one great shove, like a solid block. Behind their backs small clusters and loose bodies tumbled from side to side.

The boatswain performed prodigious feats of strength. With his long arms open, and each great paw clutching at a stanchion, he stopped the rush of seven entwined Chinamen rolling like a boulder. His joints cracked; he said, "Ha!" and they flew apart. But the carpenter showed the greater intelligence. Without saying a word to anybody he went back into the alleyway, to fetch several coils of cargo gear he had seen there—chain and rope. With these life lines were rigged.

There was really no resistance. The struggle, however it began, had turned into a scramble of blind panic. If the coolies had started up after their scattered dollars they were by that time fighting only for their footing. They took each other by the throat merely to save themselves from being hurled about. Whoever got a hold anywhere would kick at the others who caught at his legs and hung on, till a roll sent them flying together across the deck.

The coming of the white devils was a terror. Had they come to kill? The individuals torn out of the ruck became very limp in the seamen's hands: some, dragged aside by the heels, were passive, like dead bodies, with open, fixed eyes. Here and there a coolie would fall on his knees as if begging for mercy; several, whom the excess of fear made unruly, were hit with hard fists between the eyes, and cowered; while those who were hurt submitted to rough handling, blinking rapidly without a plaint. Faces streamed with blood; there were raw places on the shaven heads, scratches, bruises, torn wounds, gashes. The broken porcelain out of the chests was mostly responsible for the latter. Here and there a Chinaman, wild-eyed, with his tail unplaited, nursed a bleeding sole.

They had been ranged closely, after having been shaken into submission, cuffed a little to allay excitement, addressed in gruff words of encouragement that sounded like promises of evil. They sat on the deck in ghastly, drooping rows, and at the end the carpenter, with two hands to help him, moved busily from place to place, setting taut and hitching the life lines. The boatswain, with one leg and one arm embracing a stanchion, struggled with a lamp pressed to his breast, trying to get a light, and growling all the time like an industrious gorilla. The figures of seamen stooped repeatedly, with the movements of gleaners, and everything was being flung into the bunker: clothing, smashed wood, broken china, and the dollars, too, gathered up in men's jackets. Now and then a sailor would stagger towards the doorway with his arms full of rubbish; and dolorous, slanting eyes followed his movements.

With every roll of the ship the long rows of sitting Celestials would sway forward brokenly, and her headlong dives knocked together the line of shaven polls from end to end. When the wash of water rolling on the deck died away for a moment, it seemed to Jukes, yet quivering from his exertions, that in his mad struggle down there he had overcome the wind somehow: that a silence had fallen upon the ship, a silence in which the sea struck thunderously at her sides.

Everything had been cleared out of the 'tween-deck—all the wreckage, as the men said. They stood erect and tottering above the level of heads and drooping shoulders. Here and there a coolie sobbed for his breath. Where the high light fell, Jukes could see the salient ribs of one, the yellow, wistful face of another; bowed necks; or would meet a dull stare directed at his face. He was amazed that there had been no corpses; but the lot of them seemed at their last gasp, and they appeared to him more pitiful than if they had been all dead.

Suddenly one of the coolies began to speak. The light came and went on his lean, straining face; he threw his head up like a baying hound. From the bunker came the sounds of knocking and the tinkle of some dollars rolling loose; he stretched out his arm, his mouth yawned black, and the incomprehensible guttural hooting sounds, that did not seem to belong to a human language, penetrated Jukes with a strange emotion as if a brute had tried to be eloquent.

Two more started mouthing what seemed to Jukes fierce denunciations; the others stirred with grunts and growls. Jukes ordered the hands out of the 'tween-decks hurriedly. He left last himself, backing through the door, while the grunts rose to a loud murmur and hands were extended after him as after a malefactor. The boatswain shot the bolt, and remarked uneasily, "Seems as if the wind had dropped, sir."

The seamen were glad to get back into the alleyway. Secretly each of them thought that at the last moment he could rush out on deck—and that was a comfort. There is something horribly repugnant in the idea of being drowned under a deck. Now they had done with the Chinamen, they again became conscious of the ship's position.

Jukes on coming out of the alleyway found himself up to the neck in the noisy water. He gained the bridge, and discovered he could detect obscure shapes as if his sight had become preternaturally acute. He saw faint outlines. They recalled not the familiar aspect of the *Nan-Shan*, but something remembered—an old dismantled steamer he had seen years ago rotting on a mudbank. She recalled that wreck.

There was no wind, not a breath, except the faint currents created by the lurches of the ship. The smoke tossed out of the funnel was settling down upon her deck. He breathed it as he passed forward. He felt the deliberate throb of the engines, and heard small sounds that seemed to have survived the great uproar: the knocking of broken fittings, the rapid tumbling of some piece of wreckage on the bridge. He perceived dimly the squat shape of his captain holding on to a twisted bridge rail, motionless and swaying as if rooted to the planks. The unexpected stillness of the air oppressed Jukes.

"We have done it, sir," he gasped.

"Thought you would," said Captain MacWhirr.

"Did you?" murmured Jukes to himself.

"Wind fell all at once," went on the Captain.

Jukes burst out: "If you think it was an easy job—"

But his captain, clinging to the rail, paid no attention. "According to the books the worst is not over yet."

"If most of them hadn't been half dead with seasickness and fright, not one of us would have come out of that 'tween-deck alive," said Jukes.

"Had to do what's fair by them," mumbled MacWhirr, stolidly. "You don't find everything in books."

"Why, I believe they would have risen on us if I hadn't ordered the hands out of that pretty quick," continued Jukes with warmth.

After the whisper of their shouts, their ordinary tones, so distinct, rang out very loud to their ears in the amazing stillness of the air. It seemed to them they were talking in a dark and echoing vault.

Through a jagged aperture in the dome of clouds the light of a few stars fell upon the black sea, rising and falling confusedly. Sometimes the head of a watery cone would topple on board and mingle with the rolling flurry of foam on the swamped deck; and the *Nan-Shan* wallowed heavily at the bottom of a circular cistern of clouds. This ring of dense vapors, gyrating madly round the calm of the center, encompassed the ship like a motionless and unbroken wall of an aspect inconceivably sinister.

Within, the sea, as if agitated by an internal commotion, leaped in peaked mounds that jostled each other, slapping heavily against her sides; and a low moaning sound, the infinite plaint of the storm's fury, came from beyond the limits of the menacing calm. Captain MacWhirr remained silent, and Jukes' ready ear caught suddenly the faint, long-drawn roar of some immense wave rushing unseen under that thick blackness, which made the appalling boundary of his vision.

"Of course," he started resentfully, "they thought we had caught at the chance to plunder them. Of course! You said—pick up the money. Easier said than done. They couldn't tell what was in our heads. We came in, smash—right into the middle of them. Had to do it by a rush."

"As long as it's done . . . ," mumbled the Captain, without attempting to look at Jukes. "Had to do what's fair."

"We shall find yet there's the devil to pay when this is over," said Jukes, feeling very sore. "Let them only recover a bit, and you'll see. They will fly at our throats, sir. Don't forget, sir, she isn't a British ship now. These brutes know it well, too. The damned Siamese flag."

"We are on board, all the same," remarked Captain MacWhirr.

"The trouble's not over yet," insisted Jukes, prophetically, reeling and catching on. "She's a wreck," he added, faintly.

"The trouble's not over yet," assented Captain MacWhirr, half aloud. . . . "Look out for her a minute."

"Are you going off the deck, sir?" asked Jukes, hurriedly, as if the storm were sure to pounce upon him as soon as he had been left alone with the ship.

He watched her, battered and solitary, laboring heavily in a wild scene of mountainous black waters lit by the gleams of distant worlds. She moved slowly, breathing into the still core of the hurricane the excess of her strength in a white cloud of steam —and the deep-toned vibration of the escape was like the defiant trumpeting of a living creature of the sea impatient for the renewal of the contest. It ceased suddenly. The still air moaned. Above Jukes' head a few stars shone into a pit of black vapors. The inky edge of the cloud-disc frowned upon the ship under the patch of glittering sky. The stars, too, seemed to look at her intently, as if for the last time, and the cluster of their splendor sat like a diadem on a lowering brow.

Captain MacWhirr had gone into the chart room. There was no light there; but he could feel the disorder of that place where he used to live tidily. His armchair was upset. The books had tumbled out on the floor: he scrunched a piece of glass under his boot. He groped for the matches, and found a box on a shelf with a deep ledge. He struck one, and puckering the corners of his eyes, held out the little flame towards the barometer whose glittering top of glass and metals nodded at him continuously.

It stood very low—incredibly low, so low that Captain MacWhirr grunted. The match went out, and hurriedly he extracted another, with thick, stiff fingers.

Again a little flame flared up before the nodding glass and metal of the top. His eyes looked at it, narrowed with attention, as if expecting an imperceptible sign. With his grave face he resembled a booted and misshapen pagan burning incense before the oracle of a joss. There was no mistake. It was the lowest reading he had ever seen in his life.

Captain MacWhirr emitted a low whistle. He forgot himself till the flame diminished to a blue spark, burnt his fingers and vanished. Perhaps something had gone wrong with the thing!

There was an aneroid glass screwed above the couch. He turned that way, struck another match, and discovered the white face of the other instrument looking at him from the bulkhead, meaningly, not to be gainsaid, as though the wisdom of men were made unerring by the indifference of matter. There was no room for doubt now. Captain MacWhirr pshawed at it, and threw the match down.

The worst was to come, then—and if the books were right this worst would be very bad. The experience of the last six hours had enlarged his conception of what heavy weather could be like. "It'll be terrific," he pronounced, mentally. He had not consciously looked at anything by the light of the matches except at the barometer; and yet somehow he had seen that his water bottle and the two tumblers had been flung out of their stand. It seemed to give him a more intimate knowledge of the tossing the ship had gone through. "I wouldn't have believed it," he thought. And his table had been cleared, too; his rulers, his pencils, the inkstand—all the things that had their safe appointed places—they were gone, as if a mischievous hand had plucked them out one by one and flung them on the wet floor. The hurricane had broken in upon the orderly arrangements of his privacy. This had never happened before, and the feeling of dismay reached the very seat of his composure. And the worst was to come yet! He was glad the trouble in the 'tween-deck had been discovered in time. If the ship had to go after all, then, at least, she wouldn't be going to the bottom with a lot of people in her fighting teeth and claw. That would have been odious. And in that feeling there was a humane intention and a vague sense of the fitness of things.

These instantaneous thoughts were yet in their essence heavy and slow, partaking of the nature of the man. He extended his hand to put back the matchbox in its corner of the shelf. There were always matches there—by his order. The steward had his instructions impressed upon him long before. "A box . . . just there, see? Not so very full . . . where I can put my hand on it, steward. Might want a light in a hurry. Can't tell on board ship *what* you might want in a hurry. Mind, now."

And of course on his side he would be careful to put it back in its place scrupulously. He did so now, but before he removed his hand it occurred to him that perhaps he would never have occasion to use that box anymore. The vividness of the thought checked him and for an infinitesimal fraction of a second his fingers closed again on the small object as though it had been the symbol of all these little habits that chain us to the weary round of life. He released it at last, and letting himself fall on the settee, listened for the first sounds of returning wind.

Not yet. He heard only the wash of water, the heavy splashes, the dull shocks of the confused seas boarding his ship from all sides. She would never have a chance to clear her decks.

But the quietude of the air was startlingly tense and unsafe, like a slender hair holding a sword suspended over his head. By this awful pause the storm penetrated the defenses of the man and unsealed his lips. He spoke out in the solitude and the pitch darkness of the cabin, as if addressing another being awakened within his breast.

"I shouldn't like to lose her," he said half aloud.

He sat unseen, apart from the sea, from his ship, isolated, as if withdrawn from the very current of his own existence, where such freaks as talking to himself surely had no place. His palms reposed on his knees, he bowed his short neck and puffed heavily, surrendering to a strange sensation of weariness he was not enlightened enough to recognize for the fatigue of mental stress.

From where he sat he could reach the door of a washstand locker. There should have been a towel there. There was. Good. . . . He took it out, wiped his face, and afterwards went on rubbing his wet head. He toweled himself with energy in the dark, and then remained motionless with the towel on his knees. A moment passed, of a stillness so profound that no one could have guessed there was a man sitting in that cabin. Then a murmur arose.

"She may come out of it yet."

When Captain MacWhirr came out on deck, which he did brusquely, as though he had suddenly become conscious of having stayed away too long, the calm had lasted already more than fifteen minutes—long enough to make itself intolerable even to his imagination. Jukes, motionless on the forepart of the bridge, began to speak at once. His voice, blank and forced as though he were talking through hard-set teeth, seemed to flow away on all sides into the darkness, deepening again upon the sea.

"I had the wheel relieved. Hackett began to sing out that he was done. He's lying in there alongside the steering gear with a face like death. At first I couldn't get anybody to crawl out and relieve the poor devil. That bosun's worse than no good, I always said. Thought I would have had to go myself and haul out one of them by the neck."

"Ah, well," muttered the Captain. He stood watchful by Jukes' side.

"The second mate's in there, too, holding his head. Is he hurt, sir?"

"No—crazy," said Captain MacWhirr, curtly.

"Looks as if he had a tumble, though."

"I had to give him a push," explained the Captain.

Jukes gave an impatient sigh.

"It will come very sudden," said Captain MacWhirr, "and from over there, I fancy. God only knows though. These books are only good to muddle your head and make you jumpy. It will be bad, and there's an end. If we only can steam her round in time to meet it. . . ."

A minute passed. Some of the stars winked rapidly and vanished.

"You left them pretty safe?" began the Captain abruptly, as though the silence were unbearable.

"Are you thinking of the coolies, sir? I rigged life lines all ways across that 'tween-deck."

"Did you? Good idea, Mr. Jukes."

"I didn't . . . think you cared to . . . know," said Jukes—the lurching of the ship cut his speech as though somebody had been jerking him around while he talked —"how I got on with . . . that infernal job. We did it. And it may not matter in the end."

"Had to do what's fair, for all—they are only Chinamen. Give them the same chance with ourselves—hang it all. She isn't lost yet. Bad enough to be shut up below in a gale—"

"That's what I thought when you gave me the job, sir," interjected Jukes, moodily.

"—without being battered to pieces," pursued Captain MacWhirr with rising vehemence. "Couldn't let that go on in my ship, if I knew she hadn't five minutes to live. Couldn't bear it, Mr. Jukes."

A hollow echoing noise, like that of a shout rolling in a rocky chasm, approached the ship and went away again. The last star, blurred, enlarged, as if returning to the fiery mist of its beginning, struggled with the colossal depth of blackness hanging over the ship—and went out.

"Now for it!" muttered Captain MacWhirr. "Mr. Jukes."

"Here, sir."

The two men were growing indistinct to each other.

"We must trust her to go through it and come out on the other side. That's plain and straight. There's no room for Captain Wilson's storm-strategy here."

"No, sir."

"She will be smothered and swept again for hours," mumbled the Captain. "There's not much left by this time above deck for the sea to take away—unless you or me."

"Both, sir," whispered Jukes, breathlessly.

"You are always meeting trouble halfway, Jukes," Captain MacWhirr remonstrated quaintly. "Though it's a fact that the second mate is no good. D'ye hear, Mr. Jukes? You would be left alone if . . ."

Captain MacWhirr interrupted himself, and Jukes, glancing on all sides, remained silent.

"Don't you be put out by anything," the Captain continued, mumbling rather fast. "Keep her facing it. They may say what they like, but the heaviest seas run with the wind. Facing it—always facing it—that's the way to get through. You are a young sailor. Face it. That's enough for any man. Keep a cool head."

"Yes, sir," said Jukes, with a flutter of the heart.

In the next few seconds the Captain spoke to the engine room and got an answer.

For some reason Jukes experienced an access of confidence, a sensation that came from outside like a warm breath, and made him feel equal to every demand. The distant muttering of the darkness stole into his ears. He noted it unmoved, out of that sudden belief in himself, as a man safe in a shirt of mail would watch a point.

The ship labored without intermission amongst the black hills of water, paying with this hard tumbling the price of her life. She rumbled in her depths, shaking a white plummet of steam into the night, and Jukes' thought skimmed like a bird through the engine room, where Mr. Rout—good man—was ready. When the rumbling ceased it seemed to him that there was a pause of every sound, a dead pause in which Captain MacWhirr's voice rang out startlingly.

"What's that? A puff of wind?"—it spoke much louder than Jukes had ever heard it before—"On the bow. That's right. She may come out of it yet."

The mutter of the winds drew near apace. In the forefront could be distinguished a drowsy waking plaint passing on, and far off the growth of a multiple clamor, marching and expanding. There was the throb as of many drums in it, a vicious rushing note, and like the chant of a tramping multitude.

Jukes could no longer see his captain distinctly. The darkness was absolutely piling itself upon the ship. At most he made out movements, a hint of elbows spread out, of a head thrown up.

Captain MacWhirr was trying to do up the top button of his oilskin coat with unwonted haste. The hurricane, with its power to madden the seas, to sink ships, to uproot trees, to overturn strong walls and dash the very birds of the air to the ground, had found this taciturn man in its path, and, doing its utmost, had managed to wring out a few words. Before the renewed wrath of winds swooped on his ship, Captain MacWhirr was moved to declare, in a tone of vexation, as it were: "I wouldn't like to lose her."

He was spared that annoyance.

VI

On a bright sunshiny day, with the breeze chasing her smoke far ahead, the *Nan-Shan* came into Fu-chau. Her arrival was at once noticed on shore, and the seamen in harbor said: "Look! Look at that steamer. What's that? Siamese—isn't she? Just look at her!"

She seemed, indeed, to have been used as a running target for the secondary batteries of a cruiser. A hail of minor shells could not have given her upper works a more broken, torn, and devastated aspect; and she had about her the worn, weary air of ships coming from the far ends of the world—and indeed with truth, for in her short passage she had been very far; sighting, truly, even the coast of the Great Beyond, whence no ship ever returns to give up her crew to the dust of the earth. She was incrusted and gray with salt to the trucks of her masts and to the top of her funnel; as though (as some facetious seaman said) "the crowd on board had fished her out somewhere from the bottom of the sea and brought her in here for salvage." And further, excited by the felicity of his own wit, he offered to give five pounds for her— "as she stands."

Before she had been quite an hour at rest, a meager little man, with a red-tipped nose and a face cast in an angry mold, landed from a sampan on the quay of the Foreign Concession, and incontinently turned to shake his fist at her.

A tall individual, with legs much too thin for a rotund stomach, and with watery eyes, strolled up and remarked, "Just left her—eh? Quick work."

He wore a soiled suit of blue flannel with a pair of dirty cricketing shoes; a dingy gray mustache drooped from his lip, and daylight could be seen in two places between the rim and the crown of his hat.

"Hallo! what are you doing here?" asked the ex-second mate of the *Nan-Shan*, shaking hands hurriedly.

"Standing by for a job—chance worth taking—got a quiet hint," explained the man with the broken hat, in jerky, apathetic wheezes.

The second shook his fist again at the *Nan-Shan*. "There's a fellow there that ain't fit to have the command of a scow," he declared, quivering with passion, while the other looked about listlessly.

"Is there?"

But he caught sight on the quay of a heavy seaman's chest, painted brown under a fringed sailcloth cover, and lashed with new manila line. He eyed it with awakened interest.

"I would talk and raise trouble if it wasn't for that damned Siamese flag. Nobody to go to—or I would make it hot for him. The fraud! Told his chief engineer—that's another fraud for you—I had lost my nerve. The greatest lot of ignorant fools that ever sailed the seas. No! You can't think. . . ."

"Got your money all right?" inquired his seedy acquaintance suddenly.

"Yes. Paid me off on board," raged the second mate. " 'Get your breakfast on shore,' says he."

"Mean skunk!" commented the tall man, vaguely, and passed his tongue on his lips. "What about having a drink of some sort?"

"He struck me," hissed the second mate.

"No! Struck! You don't say?" The man in blue began to bustle about sympathetically. "Can't possibly talk here. I want to know all about it. Struck—eh? Let's get a fellow to carry your chest. I know a quiet place where they have some bottled beer. . . ."

Mr. Jukes, who had been scanning the shore through a pair of glasses, informed the chief engineer afterwards that "our late second mate hasn't been long in finding a friend. A chap looking uncommonly like a bummer. I saw them walk away together from the quay."

The hammering and banging of the needful repairs did not disturb Captain MacWhirr. The steward found in the letter he wrote, in a tidy chart room, passages of such absorbing interest that twice he was nearly caught in the act. But Mrs. MacWhirr, in the drawing room of the forty-pound house, stifled a yawn—perhaps out of self-respect—for she was alone.

She reclined in a plush-bottomed and gilt hammock-chair near a tiled fireplace, with Japanese fans on the mantel and a glow of coals in the grate. Lifting her hands, she glanced wearily here and there into the many pages. It was not her fault they were so prosy, so completely uninteresting—from "My darling wife" at the beginning, to "Your loving husband" at the end. She couldn't be really expected to understand all these ship affairs. She was glad, of course, to hear from him, but she had never asked herself why, precisely.

". . . They are called typhoons. . . . The mate did not seem to like it. . . . Not in books. . . . Couldn't think of letting it go on. . . ."

The paper rustled sharply. ". . . A calm that lasted more than twenty minutes," she read perfunctorily; and the next words her thoughtless eyes caught, on the top of another page, were: "see you and the children again. . . ." She had a movement of impatience. He was always thinking of coming home. He had never had such a good salary before. What was the matter now?

It did not occur to her to turn back overleaf to look. She would have found it recorded there that between 4 and 6 A.M. on December 25th, Captain MacWhirr did actually think that his ship could not possibly live another hour in such a sea, and that he would never see his wife and children again. Nobody was to know this (his letters got mislaid so quickly)—nobody whatever but the steward, who had been greatly impressed by that disclosure. So much so, that he tried to give the cook some idea of the "narrow squeak we all had" by saying solemnly, "The old man himself had a dam' poor opinion of our chance."

"How do you know?" asked, contemptuously, the cook, an old soldier. "He hasn't told you, maybe?"

"Well, he did give me a hint to that effect," the steward brazened it out.

"Get along with you! He will be coming to tell _me_ next," jeered the old cook, over his shoulder.

Mrs. MacWhirr glanced farther, on the alert. ". . . Do what's fair. . . . Miserable objects. . . . Only three, with a broken leg each, and one. . . . Thought had better keep the matter quiet . . . hope to have done the fair thing. . . ."

She let fall her hands. No: there was nothing more about coming home. Must have been merely expressing a pious wish. Mrs. MacWhirr's mind was set at ease, and a black marble clock, priced by the local jeweler at £3 18_s._ 6_d._, had a discreet stealthy tick.

The door flew open, and a girl in the long-legged, short-frocked period of existence, flung into the room. A lot of colorless, rather lanky hair was scattered over her shoulders. Seeing her mother, she stood still, and directed her pale prying eyes upon the letter.

"From father," murmured Mrs. MacWhirr. "What have you done with your ribbon?"

The girl put her hands up to her head and pouted.

"He's well," continued Mrs. MacWhirr, languidly. "At least I think so. He never says." She had a little laugh. The girl's face expressed a wandering indifference, and Mrs. MacWhirr surveyed her with fond pride.

"Go and get your hat," she said after a while. "I am going out to do some shopping. There is a sale at Linom's."

"Oh, how jolly!" uttered the child, impressively, in unexpectedly grave vibrating tones, and bounded out of the room.

It was a fine afternoon, with a gray sky and dry sidewalks. Outside the draper's Mrs. MacWhirr smiled upon a woman in a black mantle of generous proportions armored in jet and crowned with flowers blooming falsely above a bilious matronly countenance. They broke into a swift little babble of greetings and exclamations both together, very hurried, as if the street were ready to yawn open and swallow all that pleasure before it could be expressed.

Behind them the high glass doors were kept on the swing. People couldn't pass, men stood aside waiting patiently, and Lydia was absorbed in poking the end of her parasol between the stone flags. Mrs. MacWhirr talked rapidly.

"Thank you very much. He's not coming home yet. Of course it's very sad to have him away, but it's such a comfort to know he keeps so well." Mrs. MacWhirr drew breath. "The climate there agrees with him," she added, beamingly, as if poor MacWhirr had been away touring in China for the sake of his health.

Neither was the chief engineer coming home yet. Mr. Rout knew too well the value of a good billet.

"Solomon says wonders will never cease," cried Mrs. Rout joyously at the old lady in her armchair by the fire. Mr. Rout's mother moved slightly, her withered hands lying in black half-mittens on her lap.

The eyes of the engineer's wife fairly danced on the paper. "That captain of the ship he is in—a rather simple man, you remember, mother?—has done something rather clever, Solomon says."

"Yes, my dear," said the old woman meekly, sitting with bowed silvery head, and that air of inward stillness characteristic of very old people who seem lost in watching the last flickers of life. "I think I remember."

Solomon Rout, Old Sol, Father Sol, the Chief, "Rout, good man"—Mr. Rout, the condescending and paternal friend of youth, had been the baby of her many children —all dead by this time. And she remembered him best as a boy of ten—long before he went away to serve his apprenticeship in some great engineering works in the North. She had seen so little of him since, she had gone through so many years, that she had now to retrace her steps very far back to recognize him plainly in the mist of time. Sometimes it seemed that her daughter-in-law was talking of some strange man.

Mrs. Rout, junior, was disappointed. "H'm. H'm." She turned the page. "How provoking! He doesn't say what it is. Says I couldn't understand how much there was in it. Fancy! What could it be so very clever? What a wretched man not to tell us!"

She read on without further remark soberly, and at last sat looking into the fire. The chief wrote just a word or two of the typhoon; but something had moved him to express an increased longing for the companionship of the jolly woman. "If it hadn't been that mother must be looked after, I would send you your passage money today. You could set up a small house out here. I would have a chance to see you sometimes then. We are not growing younger. . . ."

"He's well, mother," sighed Mrs. Rout, rousing herself.

"He always was a strong healthy boy," said the old woman, placidly.

But Mr. Jukes' account was really animated and very full. His friend in the Western Ocean trade imparted it freely to the other officers of his liner. "A chap I know writes to me about an extraordinary affair that happened on board his ship in that typhoon —you know—that we read of in the papers two months ago. It's the funniest thing! Just see for yourself what he says. I'll show you his letter."

There were phrases in it calculated to give the impression of lighthearted, indomitable resolution. Jukes had written them in good faith, for he felt thus when he wrote. He described with lurid effect the scenes in the 'tween-deck. ". . . It struck me in a flash that those confounded Chinamen couldn't tell we weren't a desperate kind of robbers. 'T isn't good to part the Chinaman from his money if he is the stronger party. We need have been desperate indeed to go thieving in such weather, but what could these beggars know of us? So, without thinking of it twice, I got the hands away in a jiffy. Our work was done—that the old man had set his heart on. We cleared out without staying to inquire how they felt. I am convinced that if they had not been so unmercifully shaken, and afraid—each individual one of them—to stand up, we would have been torn to pieces. Oh! It was pretty complete, I can tell you; and you may run to and fro across the Pond to the end of time before you find yourself with such a job on your hands."

After this he alluded professionally to the damage done to the ship, and went on thus:

"It was when the weather quieted down that the situation became confoundedly delicate. It wasn't made any better by us having been lately transferred to the Siamese flag; though the skipper can't see that it makes any difference—'as long as *we* are on board'—he says. There are feelings that this man simply hasn't got—and there's an end of it. You might just as well try to make a bedpost understand. But apart from this it is an infernally lonely state for a ship to be going about the China seas with no proper consuls, not even a gunboat of her own anywhere, nor a body to go to in case of some trouble.

"My notion was to keep these Johnnies under hatches for another fifteen hours or so; as we weren't much farther than that from Fu-chau. We would find there, most likely, some sort of a man-of-war, and once under her guns we were safe enough; for surely any skipper of a man-of-war—English, French, or Dutch—would see white men through as far as row on board goes. We could get rid of them and their money afterwards by delivering them to their Mandarin or Taotai, or whatever they call these chaps in goggles you see being carried about in sedan chairs through their stinking streets.

"The old man wouldn't see it somehow. He wanted to keep the matter quiet. He got that notion into his head, and a steam windlass couldn't drag it out of him. He wanted as little fuss made as possible, for the sake of the ship's name and for the sake of the owners—'for the sake of all concerned,' says he, looking at me very hard. It made me angry hot. Of course you couldn't keep a thing like that quiet; but the chests had been secured in the usual manner and were safe enough for any earthly gale, while this had been an altogether fiendish business I couldn't give you even an idea of.

"Meantime, I could hardly keep on my feet. None of us had a spell of any sort for nearly thirty hours, and there the old man sat rubbing his chin, rubbing the top of his head, and so bothered he didn't even think of pulling his long boots off.

" 'I hope, sir,' says I, 'you won't be letting them out on deck before we make ready for them in some shape or other.' Not, mind you, that I felt very sanguine about controlling these beggars if they meant to take charge. A trouble with a cargo of Chinamen is no child's play. I was dam' tired, too. 'I wish,' said I, 'you would let us throw the whole lot of these dollars down to them and leave them to fight it out amongst themselves, while we get a rest.'

" 'Now you talk wild, Jukes,' says he, looking up in his slow way that makes you ache all over, somehow. 'We must plan out something that would be fair to all parties.'

"I had no end of work on hand, as you may imagine, so I set the hands going, and then I thought I would turn in a bit. I hadn't been asleep in my bunk ten minutes when in rushes the steward and begins to pull at my leg.

" 'For God's sake, Mr. Jukes, come out! Come on deck quick, sir. Oh, do come out!'

"The fellow scared all the sense out of me. I didn't know what had happened: another hurricane—or what. Could hear no wind.

" 'The Captain's letting them out. Oh, he is letting them out! Jump on deck, sir, and save us. The chief engineer has just run below for his revolver.'

"That's what I understood the fool to say. However, Father Rout swears he went in there only to get a clean pocket handkerchief. Anyhow, I made one jump into my trousers and flew on deck aft. There was certainly a good deal of noise going on forward of the bridge. Four of the hands with the bosun were at work abaft. I passed up to them some of the rifles all the ships on the China coast carry in the cabin, and led them on the bridge. On the way I ran against Old Sol, looking startled and sucking at an unlighted cigar.

" 'Come along,' I shouted to him.

"We charged, the seven of us, up to the chart room. All was over. There stood the old man with his sea boots still drawn up to the hips and in shirtsleeves—got warm thinking it out, I suppose. Bun Hin's dandy clerk at his elbow, as dirty as a sweep, was still green in the face. I could see directly I was in for something.

" 'What the devil are these monkey tricks, Mr. Jukes?' asks the old man, as angry as ever he could be. I tell you frankly it made me lose my tongue. 'For God's sake, Mr. Jukes,' says he, 'do take away these rifles from the men. Somebody's sure to get hurt before long if you don't. Damme, if this ship isn't worse than Bedlam! Look sharp now. I want you up here to help me and Bun Hin's Chinaman to count that money. You wouldn't mind lending a hand, too, Mr. Rout, now you are here. The more of us the better.'

"He had settled it all in his mind while I was having a snooze. Had we been an English ship, or only going to land our cargo of coolies in an English port, like Hong Kong, for instance, there would have been no end of inquiries and bother, claims for damages and so on. But these Chinamen know their officials better than we do.

"The hatches had been taken off already, and they were all on deck after a night and a day down below. It made you feel queer to see so many gaunt, wild faces together. The beggars stared about at the sky, at the sea, at the ship, as though they had expected the whole thing to have been blown to pieces. And no wonder! They had had a doing that would have shaken the soul out of a white man. But then they say a

Chinaman has no soul. He has, though, something about him that is deuced tough. There was a fellow (amongst others of the badly hurt) who had had his eye all but knocked out. It stood out of his head the size of half a hen's egg. This would have laid out a white man on his back for a month; and yet there was that chap elbowing here and there in the crowd and talking to the others as if nothing had been the matter. They made a great hubbub amongst themselves, and whenever the old man showed his bald head on the foreside of the bridge, they would all leave off jawing and look at him from below.

"It seems that after he had done his thinking he made that Bun Hin's fellow go down and explain to them the only way they could get their money back. He told me afterwards that, all the coolies having worked in the same place and for the same length of time, he reckoned he would be doing the fair thing by them as near as possible if he shared all the cash we had picked up equally among the lot. You couldn't tell one man's dollars from another's, he said, and if you asked each man how much money he brought on board he was afraid they would lie, and he would find himself a long way short. I think he was right there. As to giving up the money to any Chinese official he could scare up in Fu-chau, he said he might just as well put the lot in his own pocket at once for all the good it would be to them. I suppose they thought so, too.

"We finished the distribution before dark. It was rather a sight: the sea running high, the ship a wreck to look at, these Chinamen staggering up on the bridge one by one for their share, and the old man still booted, and in his shirtsleeves, busy paying out at the chartroom door, perspiring like anything, and now and then coming down sharp on myself or Father Rout about one thing or another not quite to his mind. He took the share of those who were disabled himself to them on the No. 2 hatch. There were three dollars left over, and these went to the three most damaged coolies, one to each. We turned-to afterwards, and shoveled out on deck heaps of wet rags, all sorts of fragments of things without shape, and that you couldn't give a name to, and let them settle the ownership themselves.

"This certainly is coming as near as can be to keeping the thing quiet for the benefit of all concerned. What's your opinion, you pampered mailboat swell? The old chief says that this was plainly the only thing that could be done. The skipper remarked to me the other day, 'There are things you find nothing about in books.' I think that he got out of it very well for such a stupid man."

PRINCE ROMAN

vents which happened seventy years ago are perhaps rather too far off to be dragged aptly into a mere conversation. Of course the year 1831 is for us an historical date, one of these fatal years when in the presence of the world's passive indignation and eloquent sympathies we had once more to murmur '*Væ Victis*' and count the cost in sorrow. Not that we were ever very good at calculating, either, in prosperity or in adversity. That's a lesson we could never learn, to the great exasperation of our enemies who have bestowed upon us the epithet of Incorrigible. . . ."

The speaker was of Polish nationality, that nationality not so much alive as surviving, which persists in thinking, breathing, speaking, hoping, and suffering in its grave, railed in by a million bayonets and triple-sealed with the seals of three great empires.

The conversation was about aristocracy. How did this, nowadays discredited, subject come up? It is some years ago now and the precise recollection has faded. But I remember that it was not considered practically as an ingredient in the social mixture; and I truly believed that we arrived at that subject through some exchange of ideas about patriotism—a somewhat discredited sentiment, because the delicacy of our humanitarians regards it as a relic of barbarism. Yet neither the great Florentine painter who closed his eyes in death thinking of his city, nor St. Francis blessing with his last breath the town of Assisi, were barbarians. It requires a certain greatness of soul to interpret patriotism worthily—or else a sincerity of feeling denied to the vulgar refinement of modern thought which cannot understand the august simplicity of a sentiment proceeding from the very nature of things and men.

The aristocracy we were talking about was the very highest, the great families of Europe, not impoverished, not converted, not liberalized, the most distinctive and specialized class of all classes, for which even ambition itself does not exist among the usual incentives to activity and regulators of conduct.

The undisputed right of leadership having passed away from them, we judged that their great fortunes, their cosmopolitanism brought about by wide alliances, their elevated station, in which there is so little to gain and so much to lose, must make their position difficult in times of political commotion or national upheaval. No longer born to command—which is the very essence of aristocracy—it becomes difficult for them to do anything else but hold aloof from the great movements of popular passion.

We had reached that conclusion when the remark about far-off events was made and the date of 1831 mentioned. And the speaker continued:

"I don't mean to say that I knew Prince Roman at that remote time. I begin to feel pretty ancient, but I am not so ancient as that. In fact Prince Roman was married the very year my father was born. It was in 1828; the nineteenth century was young yet and the Prince was even younger than the century, but I don't know exactly by how much. In any case his was an early marriage. It was an ideal alliance from every point of view. The girl was young and beautiful, an orphan heiress of a great name and of a great fortune. The Prince, then an officer in the Guards and distinguished amongst his fellows by something reserved and reflective in his character, had fallen headlong in love with her beauty, her charm, and the serious qualities of her mind and heart. He was a rather silent young man; but his glances, his bearing, his whole person expressed his absolute devotion to the woman of his choice, a devotion which she returned in her own frank and fascinating manner.

"The flame of this pure young passion promised to burn for ever; and for a season it lit up the dry, cynical atmosphere of the great world of St. Petersburg. The Emperor Nicholas himself, the grandfather of the present man, the one who died from the Crimean War, the last perhaps of the autocrats with a mystical belief in the divine character of his mission, showed some interest in this pair of married lovers. It is true that Nicholas kept a watchful eye on all the doings of the great Polish nobles. The young people leading a life appropriate to their station were obviously wrapped up in each other; and society, fascinated by the sincerity of a feeling moving serenely among the artificialities of its anxious and fastidious agitation, watched them with benevolent indulgence and an amused tenderness.

"The marriage was the social event of 1828, in the capital. Just forty years afterwards I was staying in the country house of my mother's brother in our southern provinces.

"It was the dead of winter. The great lawn in front was as pure and smooth as an alpine snowfield, a white and feathery level sparkling under the sun as if sprinkled with diamond-dust, declining gently to the lake—a long, sinuous piece of frozen water looking bluish and more solid than the earth. A cold brilliant sun glided low above an undulating horizon of great folds of snow in which the villages of Ukrainian peasants remained out of sight, like clusters of boats hidden in the hollows of a running sea. And everything was very still.

"I don't know now how I had managed to escape at eleven o'clock in the morning from the schoolroom. I was a boy of eight, the little girl, my cousin, a few months younger than myself, though hereditarily more quick-tempered, was less adventurous.

So I had escaped alone; and presently I found myself in the great stone-paved hall, warmed by a monumental stove of white tiles, a much more pleasant locality than the schoolroom, which for some reason or other, perhaps hygienic, was always kept at a low temperature.

"We children were aware that there was a guest staying in the house. He had arrived the night before just as we were being driven off to bed. We broke back through the line of beaters to rush and flatten our noses against the dark windowpanes; but we were too late to see him alight. We had only watched in a ruddy glare the big traveling carriage on sleigh-runners harnessed with six horses, a black mass against the snow, going off to the stables, preceded by a horseman carrying a blazing ball of tow and resin in an iron basket at the end of a long stick swung from his saddle bow. Two stable boys had been sent out early in the afternoon along the snow-tracks to meet the expected guest at dusk and light his way with these road torches. At that time, you must remember, there was not a single mile of railways in our southern provinces. My little cousin and I had no knowledge of trains and engines, except from picture books, as of things rather vague, extremely remote, and not particularly interesting unless to grownups who traveled abroad.

"Our notion of princes, perhaps a little more precise, was mainly literary and had a glamor reflected from the light of fairy tales, in which princes always appear young, charming, heroic, and fortunate. Yet, as well as any other children, we could draw a firm line between the real and the ideal. We knew that princes were historical personages. And there was some glamor in that fact, too. But what had driven me to roam cautiously over the house like an escaped prisoner was the hope of snatching an interview with a special friend of mine, the head forester, who generally came to make his report at that time of the day. I yearned for news of a certain wolf. You know, in a country where wolves are to be found, every winter almost brings forward an individual eminent by the audacity of his misdeeds, by his more perfect wolfishness—so to speak. I wanted to hear some new thrilling tale of that wolf—perhaps the dramatic story of his death. . . .

"But there was no one in the hall.

"Deceived in my hopes, I became suddenly very much depressed. Unable to slip back in triumph to my studies I elected to stroll spiritlessly into the billiard room where certainly I had no business. There was no one there either, and I felt very lost and desolate under its high ceiling, all alone with the massive English billiard table which seemed, in heavy, rectilinear silence, to disapprove of that small boy's intrusion.

"As I began to think of retreat I heard footsteps in the adjoining drawing room; and, before I could turn tail and flee, my uncle and his guest appeared in the doorway. To run away after having been seen would have been highly improper, so I stood my ground. My uncle looked surprised to see me; the guest by his side was a spare man, of average stature, buttoned up in a black frock coat and holding himself very erect with a stiffly soldier-like carriage. From the folds of a soft white cambric neck-cloth peeped the points of a collar close against each shaven cheek. A few wisps of thin gray hair were brushed smoothly across the top of his bald head. His face, which must have been beautiful in its day, had preserved in age the harmonious simplicity of its lines. What amazed me was its even, almost deathlike pallor. He seemed to me to be prodigiously old. A faint smile, a mere momentary alteration in the set of his thin lips acknowledged my blushing confusion; and I became greatly interested to see him reach into the inside breastpocket of his coat. He extracted therefrom a lead pencil and a block of detachable pages, which he handed to my uncle with an almost imperceptible bow.

"I was very much astonished, but my uncle received it as a matter of course. He wrote something at which the other glanced and nodded slightly. A thin wrinkled hand—the hand was older than the face—patted my cheek and then rested on my head lightly. An unringing voice, a voice as colorless as the face itself, issued from his sunken lips, while the eyes, dark and still, looked down at me kindly.

" 'And how old is this shy little boy?' "

"Before I could answer my uncle wrote down my age on the pad. I was deeply impressed. What was this ceremony? Was this personage too great to be spoken to? Again he glanced at the pad, and again gave a nod, and again that impersonal, mechanical voice was heard: 'He resembles his grandfather.'

"I remembered my paternal grandfather. He had died not long before. He, too, was prodigiously old. And to me it seemed perfectly natural that two such ancient and venerable persons should have known each other in the dim ages of creation before my birth. But my uncle obviously had not been aware of the fact. So obviously that the mechanical voice explained: 'Yes, yes. Comrades in '31. He was one of those who knew. Old times, my dear sir, old times. . . .

"He made a gesture as if to put aside an importunate ghost. And now they were both looking down at me. I wondered whether anything was expected from me. To my round, questioning eyes my uncle remarked: 'He's completely deaf.' And the unrelated, inexpressive voice said: 'Give me your hand.'

"Acutely conscious of inky fingers I put it out timidly. I had never seen a deaf person before and was rather startled. He pressed it firmly and then gave me a final pat on the head.

"My uncle addressed me weightily: 'You have shaken hands with Prince Roman S——. It's something for you to remember when you grow up.'

"I was impressed by his tone. I had enough historical information to know vaguely that the Princes S—— counted amongst the sovereign Princes of Ruthenia till the union of all Ruthenian lands to the kingdom of Poland, when they became great Polish magnates, some time at the beginning of the fifteenth century. But what concerned me most was the failure of the fairy-tale glamour. It was shocking to discover a prince who was deaf, bald, meager, and so prodigiously old. It never occurred to me that this imposing and disappointing man had been young, rich, beautiful; I could not know that he had been happy in the felicity of an ideal marriage uniting two young hearts, two great names and two great fortunes; happy with a happiness which, as in fairy tales, seemed destined to last forever. . . .

*   *   *

"But it did not last forever. It was fated not to last very long even by the measure of the days allotted to men's passage on this earth where enduring happiness is only found in the conclusion of fairy tales. A daughter was born to them and shortly afterwards, the health of the young princess began to fail. For a time she bore up with smiling intrepidity, sustained by the feeling that now her existence was necessary for the happiness of two lives. But at last the husband, thoroughly alarmed by the rapid changes in her appearance, obtained an unlimited leave and took her away from the capital to his parents in the country.

"The old prince and princess were extremely frightened at the state of their beloved daughter-in-law. Preparations were at once made for a journey abroad. But it seemed as if it were already too late; and the invalid herself opposed the project with gentle obstinacy. Thin and pale in the great armchair, where the insidious and obscure nervous malady made her appear smaller and more frail every day without effacing the smile of her eyes or the charming grace of her wasted face, she clung to her native land and wished to breathe her native air. Nowhere else could she expect to get well so quickly, nowhere else would it be so easy for her to die.

"She died before her little girl was two years old. The grief of the husband was terrible and the more alarming to his parents because perfectly silent and dry-eyed. After the funeral, while the immense bareheaded crowd of peasants surrounding the private chapel on the grounds was dispersing, the Prince, waving away his friends and relations, remained alone to watch the masons of the estate closing the family vault. When the last stone was in position he uttered a groan, the first sound of pain which had escaped from him for days, and walking away with lowered head shut himself up again in his apartments.

"His father and mother feared for his reason. His outward tranquility was appalling to them. They had nothing to trust to but that very youth which made his despair so self-absorbed and so intense. Old Prince John, fretful and anxious, repeated: 'Poor Roman should be roused somehow. He's so young.' But they could find nothing to rouse him with. And the old princess, wiping her eyes, wished in her heart he were young enough to come and cry at her knee.

"In time Prince Roman, making an effort, would join now and again the family circle. But it was as if his heart and his mind had been buried in the family vault with the wife he had lost. He took to wandering in the woods with a gun, watched over secretly by one of the keepers, who would report in the evening that 'His Serenity has never fired a shot all day.' Sometimes walking to the stables in the morning he would order in subdued tones a horse to be saddled, wait switching his boot till it was led up to him, then mount without a word and ride out of the gates at a walking pace. He would be gone all day. People saw him on the roads looking neither to the right nor to the left, white-faced, sitting rigidly in the saddle like a horseman on stone on a living mount.

"The peasants working in the fields, the great unhedged fields, looked after him from the distance; and sometimes some sympathetic old woman on the threshold of a low, thatched hut was moved to make the sign of the cross in the air behind his back; as though he were one of themselves, a simple village soul struck by a sore affliction.

"He rode looking straight ahead, seeing no one, as if the earth were empty and all mankind buried in that grave which had opened so suddenly in his path to swallow up his happiness. What were men to him with their sorrows, joys, labors and passions from which she who had been all the world to him had been cut off so early?

"They did not exist; and he would have felt as completely lonely and abandoned as a man in the toils of a cruel nightmare if it had not been for this countryside where he had been born and had spent his happy boyish years. He knew it well—every slight rise crowned with trees amongst the plowed fields, every dell concealing a village. The dammed streams made a chain of lakes set in the green meadows. Far away to the north the great Lithuanian forest faced the sun, no higher than a hedge; and to the south, the way to the plains, the vast brown spaces of the earth touched the blue sky.

"And this familiar landscape associated with the days without thought and without sorrow, this land the charm of which he felt without even looking at it soothed his pain, like the presence of an old friend who sits silent and disregarded by one in some dark hour of life.

"One afternoon, it happened that the Prince after turning his horse's head for home remarked a low dense cloud of dark dust cutting off slantwise a part of the view. He reined in on a knoll and peered. There were slender gleams of steel here and there in that cloud, and it contained moving forms which revealed themselves at last as a long line of peasant carts full of soldiers, moving slowly in double file under the escort of mounted Cossacks.

"It was like an immense reptile creeping over the fields; its head dipped out of sight in a slight hollow and its tail went on writhing and growing shorter as though the monster were eating its way slowly into the very heart of the land.

"The Prince directed his way through a village lying a little off the track. The roadside inn with its stable, byre, and barn under one enormous thatched roof resembled a deformed, hunchbacked, ragged giant, sprawling amongst the small huts of the peasants. The innkeeper, a portly, dignified Jew, clad in a black satin coat reaching down to his heels and girt with a red sash, stood at the door stroking his long silvery beard.

"He watched the Prince approach and bowed gravely from the waist, not expecting to be noticed even, since it was well known that their young lord had no eyes for anything or anybody in his grief. It was quite a shock for him when the Prince pulled up and asked:

" 'What's all this, Yankel?'

" 'That is, please your Serenity, that is a convoy of foot soldiers. They are hurrying down to the south.'

"He glanced right and left cautiously, but as there was no one near but some children playing in the dust of the village street, he came up close to the stirrup.

" 'Doesn't your Serenity know? It has begun already down there. All the landowners great and small are out in arms and even the common people have risen. Only yesterday the saddler from Grodek (it was a tiny market town near by) went through here with his two apprentices on his way to join. He left even his cart with me. I gave him a guide through our neighborhood. You know, your Serenity, our people they travel a lot and they see all that's going on, and they know all the roads.'

"He tried to keep down his excitement, for the Jew Yankel, innkeeper and tenant of all the mills on the estate, was a Polish patriot. And in a still lower voice:

"'I was already a married man when the French and all the other nations passed this way with Napoleon. Tse! Tse! That was a great harvest for death, *nu!* Perhaps this time God will help.'

"The Prince nodded. 'Perhaps'—and falling into deep meditation he let his horse take him home.

"That night he wrote a letter, and early in the morning sent a mounted express to the post town. During the day he came out of his taciturnity, to the great joy of the family circle, and conversed with his father of recent events—the revolt in Warsaw, the flight of the Grand Duke Constantine, the first slight successes of the Polish army (at that time there was a Polish army); the risings in the provinces. Old Prince John, moved and uneasy, speaking from a purely aristocratic point of view, mistrusted the popular origins of the movement, regretted its democratic tendencies, and did not believe in the possibility of success. He was sad, inwardly agitated.

"'I am judging all this calmly. There are secular principles of legitimity and order which have been violated in this reckless enterprise for the sake of most subversive illusions. Though of course the patriotic impulses of the heart. . . .'

"Prince Roman had listened in a thoughtful attitude. He took advantage of the pause to tell his father quietly that he had sent that morning a letter to St. Petersburg resigning his commission in the Guards.

"The old prince remained silent. He thought that he ought to have been consulted. His son was also ordnance officer to the Emperor and he knew that the Tsar would never forget this appearance of defection in a Polish noble. In a discontented tone he pointed out to his son that as it was he had an unlimited leave. The right thing would have been to keep quiet. They had too much tact at Court to recall a man of his name. Or at worst some distant mission might have been asked for—to the Caucasus for instance—away from this unhappy struggle which was wrong in principle and therefore destined to fail.

"'Presently you shall find yourself without any interest in life and with no occupation. And you shall need something to occupy you, my poor boy. You have acted rashly, I fear.'

"Prince Roman murmured.

"'I thought it better.'

"His father faltered under his steady gaze.

"'Well, well—perhaps! But as ordnance officer to the Emperor and in favor with all the Imperial family. . . .'

" 'Those people had never been heard of when our house was already illustrious,' the young man let fall disdainfully.

"This was the sort of remark to which the old prince was sensible.

" 'Well—perhaps it is better,' he conceded at last.

"The father and son parted affectionately for the night. The next day Prince Roman seemed to have fallen back into the depths of his indifference. He rode out as usual. He remembered that the day before he had seen a reptile-like convoy of soldiery, bristling with bayonets, crawling over the face of that land which was his. The woman he loved had been his, too. Death had robbed him of her. Her loss had been to him a moral shock. It had opened his heart to a greater sorrow, his mind to a vaster thought, his eyes to all the past and to the existence of another love fraught with pain but as mysteriously imperative as that lost one to which he had entrusted his happiness.

"That evening he retired earlier than usual and rang for his personal servant.

" 'Go and see if there is light yet in the quarters of the Master-of-the-Horse. If he is still up ask him to come and speak to me.'

"While the servant was absent on this errand the Prince tore up hastily some papers, locked the drawers of his desk, and hung a medallion, containing the miniature of his wife, round his neck against his breast.

"The man the Prince was expecting belonged to that past which the death of his love had called to life. He was of a family of small nobles who for generations had been adherents, servants, and friends of the Princes S——. He remembered the times before the last partition and had taken part in the struggles of the last hour. He was a typical old Pole of that class, with a great capacity for emotion, for blind enthusiasm; with martial instincts and simple beliefs; and even with the old-time habit of larding his speech with Latin words. And his kindly shrewd eyes, his ruddy face, his lofty brow and his thick, gray, pendent mustache were also very typical of his kind.

" 'Listen, Master Francis,' the Prince said familiarly and without preliminaries. 'Listen, old friend. I am going to vanish from here quietly. I go where something louder than my grief and yet something with a voice very like it calls me. I confide in you alone. You will say what's necessary when the time comes.'

"The old man understood. His extended hands trembled exceedingly. But as soon as he found his voice he thanked God aloud for letting him live long enough to see the descendant of the illustrious family in its youngest generation give an example *coram Gentibus* of the love of his country and of valor in the field. He doubted not of his dear Prince attaining a place in council and in war worthy of his high birth; he saw already that *in fulgore* of family glory *affulget patride serenitas*. At the end of the speech he burst into tears and fell into the Prince's arms.

"The Prince quieted the old man and when he had him seated in an armchair and comparatively composed he said:

" 'Don't misunderstand me, Master Francis. You know how I loved my wife. A loss like that opens one's eyes to unsuspected truths. There is no question here of leadership and glory. I mean to go alone and to fight obscurely in the ranks. I am going to offer my country what is mine to offer, that is my life, as simply as the saddler from Grodek who went through yesterday with his apprentices.'

"The old man cried out at this. That could never be. He could not allow it. But he had to give way before the arguments and the express will of the Prince.

" 'Ha! If you say that it is a matter of feeling and conscience—so be it. But you cannot go utterly alone. Alas! that I am too old to be of any use. *Cripit verba dolor*, my dear Prince, at the thought that I am over seventy and of no more account in the world than a cripple in the church porch. It seems that to sit at home and pray to God for the nation and for you is all I am fit for. But there is my son, my youngest son, Peter. He will make a worthy companion for you. And as it happens he's staying with me here. There has not been for ages a Prince S—— hazarding his life without a companion of our name to ride by his side. You must have by you somebody who knows who you are if only to let your parents and your old servant hear what is happening to you. And when does your Princely Mightiness mean to start?'

" 'In an hour,' said the Prince; and the old man hurried off to warn his son.

"Prince Roman took up a candlestick and walked quietly along a dark corridor in the silent house. The head nurse said afterwards that waking up suddenly she saw the Prince looking at his child, one hand shading the light from its eyes. He stood and gazed at her for some time, and then putting the candlestick on the floor bent over the cot and kissed lightly the little girl who did not wake. He went out noiselessly, taking the light away with him. She saw his face perfectly well, but she could read nothing of his purpose in it. It was pale but perfectly calm and after he turned away from the cot he never looked back at it once.

"The only other trusted person, besides the old man and his son Peter, was the Jew Yankel. When he asked the Prince where precisely he wanted to be guided the Prince answered: 'To the nearest party.' A grandson of the Jew, a lanky youth, conducted the two young men by little-known paths across woods and morasses, and led them in sight of the few fires of a small detachment camped in a hollow. Some invisible horses neighed, a voice in the dark cried: 'Who goes there?' . . . and the young Jew departed hurriedly, explaining that he must make haste home to be in time for keeping the Sabbath.

"Thus humbly and in accord with the simplicity of the vision of duty he saw when death had removed the brilliant bandage of happiness from his eyes, did Prince Roman bring his offering to his country. His companion made himself known as the son of the Master-of-the-Horse to the Princes S—— and declared him to be a relation, a distant cousin from the same parts as himself and, as people presumed, of the same name. In truth no one inquired much. Two more young men clearly of the right sort had joined. Nothing more natural.

"Prince Roman did not remain long in the south. One day while scouting with several others, they were ambushed near the entrance of a village by some Russian infantry. The first discharge laid low a good many and the rest scattered in all directions. The Russians, too, did not stay, being afraid of a return in force. After some time, the peasants coming to view the scene extricated Prince Roman from under his dead horse. He was unhurt but his faithful companion had been one of the first to fall. The Prince helped the peasants to bury him and the other dead.

"Then alone, not certain where to find the body of partisans which was constantly moving about in all directions, he resolved to try and join the main Polish army facing the Russians on the borders of Lithuania. Disguised in peasant clothes, in case of meeting some marauding Cossacks, he wandered a couple of weeks before he came upon a village occupied by a regiment of Polish cavalry on outpost duty.

"On a bench, before a peasant hut of a better sort, sat an elderly officer whom he took for the colonel. The Prince approached respectfully, told his story shortly and stated his desire to enlist; and when asked his name by the officer, who had been looking him over carefully, he gave on the spur of the moment the name of his dead companion.

"The elderly officer thought to himself: Here's the son of some peasant proprietor of the liberated class. He liked his appearance.

" 'And can you read and write, my good fellow?' he asked.

" 'Yes, your honor, I can,' said the Prince.

" 'Good. Come along inside the hut; the regimental adjutant is there. He will enter your name and administer the oath to you.'

"The adjutant stared very hard at the newcomer but said nothing. When all the forms had been gone through and the recruit gone out, he turned to his superior officer.

" 'Do you know who that is?'

" 'Who? That Peter? A likely chap.'

" 'That's Prince Roman S——.'

" 'Nonsense.'

"But the adjutant was positive. He had seen the Prince several times, about two years before, in the Castle in Warsaw. He had even spoken to him once at a reception of officers held by the Grand Duke.

" 'He's changed. He seems much older, but I am certain of my man. I have a good memory for faces.'

"The two officers looked at each other in silence.

" 'He's sure to be recognized sooner or later,' murmured the adjutant. The colonel shrugged his shoulders.

" 'It's no affair of ours—if he has a fancy to serve in the ranks. As to being recognized it's not so likely. All our officers and men come from the other end of Poland.'

"He meditated gravely for a while, then smiled. 'He told me he could read and write. There's nothing to prevent me making him a sergeant at the first opportunity. He's sure to shape all right.'

"Prince Roman as a noncommissioned officer surpassed the colonel's expectations. Before long Sergeant Peter became famous for his resourcefulness and courage. It was not the reckless courage of a desperate man; it was a self-possessed, as if conscientious, valor which nothing could dismay; a boundless but equable devotion, unaffected by time, by reverses, by the discouragement of endless retreats, by the bitterness of waning hopes and the horrors of pestilence added to the toils and perils of war. It was in this year that the cholera made its first appearance in Europe. It devastated the camps of both armies, affecting the firmest minds with the terror of a mysterious death stalking silently between the piled-up arms and around the bivouac fires.

"A sudden shriek would wake up the harassed soldiers and they would see in the glow of embers one of themselves writhe on the ground like a worm trodden on by an invisible foot. And before the dawn broke he would be stiff and cold. Parties so visited have been known to rise like one man, abandon the fire and run off into the night in mute panic. Or a comrade talking to you on the march would stammer suddenly in the middle of a sentence, roll affrighted eyes, and fall down with distorted face and blue lips, breaking the ranks with the convulsions of his agony. Men were struck in the saddle, on sentry duty, in the firing line, carrying orders, serving the guns. I have been told that in a battalion forming under fire with perfect steadiness for the assault of a village, three cases occurred within five minutes at the head of the column; and the attack could not be delivered because the leading companies scattered all over the fields like chaff before the wind.

"Sergeant Peter, young as he was, had a great influence over his men. It was said that the number of desertions in the squadron in which he served was less than in any other in the whole of that cavalry division. Such was supposed to be the compelling example of one man's quiet intrepidity in facing every form of danger and terror.

"However that may be, he was liked and trusted generally. When the end came and the remnants of that army corps, hard pressed on all sides, were preparing to cross the Prussian frontier, Sergeant Peter had enough influence to rally round him a score of troopers. He managed to escape with them at night, from the hemmed-in army. He led this band through two hundred miles of country covered by numerous Russian detachments and ravaged by the cholera. But this was not to avoid captivity, to go into hiding and try to save themselves. No. He led them into a fortress which was still occupied by the Poles, and where the last stand of the vanquished revolution was to be made.

"This looks like mere fanaticism. But fanaticism is human. Man has adored ferocious divinities. There is ferocity in every passion, even in love itself. The religion of undying hope resembles the mad cult of despair, of death, of annihilation. The difference lies in the moral motive springing from the secret needs and the unexpressed aspiration of the believers. It is only to vain men that all is vanity; and all is deception only to those who have never been sincere with themselves.

"It was in the fortress that my grandfather found himself together with Sergeant Peter. My grandfather was a neighbor of the S——— family in the country but he did not know Prince Roman, who however knew his name perfectly well. The Prince introduced himself one night as they both sat on the ramparts, leaning against a gun carriage.

"The service he wished to ask for was, in case of his being killed, to have the intelligence conveyed to his parents.

"They talked in low tones, the other servants of the piece lying about near them. My grandfather gave the required promise, and then asked frankly—for he was greatly interested by the disclosure so unexpectedly made:

" 'But tell me, Prince, why this request? Have you any evil forebodings as to yourself?'

" 'Not in the least; I was thinking of my people. They have no idea where I am,' answered Prince Roman. 'I'll engage to do as much for you, if you like. It's certain that half of us at least shall be killed before the end, so there's an even chance of one of us surviving the other.'

"My grandfather told him where, as he supposed, his wife and children were then. From that moment till the end of the siege the two were much together. On the day of the great assault my grandfather received a severe wound. The town was taken. Next day the citadel itself, its hospital full of dead and dying, its magazines empty, its defenders having burnt their last cartridge, opened its gates.

"During all the campaign the Prince, exposing his person conscientiously on every occasion, had not received a scratch. No one had recognized him or at any rate had betrayed his identity. Till then, as long as he did his duty, it had mattered nothing who he was.

"Now, however, the position was changed. As ex-guardsman and as late ordnance officer to the Emperor, this rebel ran a serious risk of being given special attention in the shape of a firing squad at ten paces. For more than a month he remained lost in the miserable crowd of prisoners packed in the casemates of the citadel, with just enough food to keep body and soul together but otherwise allowed to die from wounds, privation, and disease at the rate of forty or so a day.

"The position of the fortress being central, new parties, captured in the open in the course of a thorough pacification, were being sent in frequently. Amongst such newcomers there happened to be a young man, a personal friend of the Prince from his school days. He recognized him, and in the extremity of his dismay cried aloud: 'My God! Roman, you here!'

"It is said that years of life embittered by remorse paid for this momentary lack of self-control. All this happened in the main quadrangle of the citadel. The warning gesture of the Prince came too late. An officer of the gendarmes on guard had heard the exclamation. The incident appeared to him worth inquiring into. The investigation which followed was not very arduous because the Prince, asked categorically for his real name, owned up at once.

"The intelligence of the Prince S—— being found amongst the prisoners was sent to St. Petersburg. His parents were already there living in sorrow, incertitude, and apprehension. The capital of the Empire was the safest place to reside in for a noble whose son had disappeared so mysteriously from home in a time of rebellion. The old people had not heard from him, or of him, for months. They took care not to contradict the rumors of suicide from despair circulating in the great world, which remembered the interesting love-match, the charming and frank happiness brought to an end by death. But they hoped secretly that their son survived, and that he had been able to cross the frontier with that part of the army which had surrendered to the Prussians.

"The news of his captivity was a crushing blow. Directly, nothing could be done for him. But the greatness of their name, of their position, their wide relations and connections in the highest spheres, enabled his parents to act indirectly and they moved heaven and earth, as the saying is, to save their son from the 'consequences of his madness,' as poor Prince John did not hesitate to express himself. Great personages were approached by society leaders, high dignitaries were interviewed, powerful officials were induced to take an interest in that affair. The help of every possible secret influence was enlisted. Some private secretaries got heavy bribes. The mistress of a certain senator obtained a large sum of money.

"But, as I have said, in such a glaring case no direct appeal could be made and no open steps taken. All that could be done was to incline by private representation the mind of the President of the Military Commission to the side of clemency. He ended by being impressed by the hints and suggestions, some of them from very high quarters, which he received from St. Petersburg. And, after all, the gratitude of such great nobles as the Princes S—— was something worth having from a worldly point of view. He was a good Russian but he was also a good-natured man. Moreover, the hate of Poles was not at that time a cardinal article of patriotic creed as it became some thirty years later. He felt well disposed at first sight towards that young man, bronzed, thin-faced, worn out by months of hard campaigning, the hardships of the siege and the rigors of captivity.

"The Commission was composed of three officers. It sat in the citadel in a bare vaulted room behind a long black table. Some clerks occupied the two ends, and besides the gendarmes who brought in the Prince there was no one else there.

"Within those four sinister walls shutting out from him all the sights and sounds of liberty, all hopes of the future, all consoling illusions—alone in the face of his enemies erected for judges, who can tell how much love of life there was in Prince Roman? How much remained in that sense of duty, revealed to him in sorrow? How much of his awakened love for his native country? That country which demands to be loved as no other country has ever been loved, with the mournful affection one bears to the unforgotten dead and with the unextinguishable fire of a hopeless passion which only a living, breathing, warm ideal can kindle in our breasts for our pride, for our weariness, for our exultation, for our undoing.

"There is something monstrous in the thought of such an exaction till it stands before us embodied in the shape of a fidelity without fear and without reproach. Nearing the supreme moment of his life the Prince could only have had the feeling that it was about to end. He answered the questions put to him clearly, concisely— with the most profound indifference. After all those tense months of action, to talk was a weariness to him. But he concealed it, lest his foes should suspect in his manner the apathy of discouragement or the numbness of a crushed spirit. The details of his conduct could have no importance one way or another; with his thoughts these men had nothing to do. He preserved a scrupulously courteous tone. He had refused the permission to sit down.

"What happened at this preliminary examination is only known from the presiding officer. Pursuing the only possible course in that glaringly bad case he tried from the first to bring to the Prince's mind the line of defense he wished him to take. He absolutely framed his questions so as to put the right answers in the culprit's mouth, going so far as to suggest the very words: how, distracted by excessive grief after his young wife's death, rendered irresponsible for his conduct by his despair, in a moment of blind recklessness, without realizing the highly reprehensible nature of the act, nor yet its danger and its dishonor, he went off to join the nearest rebels on a sudden impulse. And that now, penitently. . . .

"But Prince Roman was silent. The military judges looked at him hopefully. In silence he reached for a pen and wrote on a sheet of paper he found under his hand: 'I joined the national rising from conviction.'

"He pushed the paper across the table. The president took it up, showed it in turn to his two colleagues sitting to the right and left, then looking fixedly at Prince Roman let it fall from his hand. And the silence remained unbroken till he spoke to the gendarmes ordering them to remove the prisoner.

"Such was the written testimony of Prince Roman in the supreme moment of his life. I have heard that the Princes of the S—— family, in all its branches, adopted the last two words: 'From conviction' for the device under the armorial bearings of their house. I don't know whether the report is true. My uncle could not tell me. He remarked only, that naturally, it was not to be seen on Prince Roman's own seal.

"He was condemned for life to Siberian mines. Emperor Nicholas, who always took personal cognizance of all sentences on Polish nobility, wrote with his own hand in the margin: 'The authorities are severely warned to take care that this convict walks in chains like any other criminal every step of the way.'

"It was a sentence of deferred death. Very few survived entombment in these mines for more than three years. Yet as he was reported as still alive at the end of that time he was allowed, on a petition of his parents and by way of exceptional grace, to serve as common soldier in the Caucasus. All communication with him was forbidden. He had no civil rights. For all practical purposes except that of suffering he was a dead man. The little child he had been so careful not to wake up when he kissed her in her cot, inherited all the fortune after Prince John's death. Her existence saved those immense estates from confiscation.

"It was twenty-five years before Prince Roman, stone deaf, his health broken, was permitted to return to Poland. His daughter married splendidly to a Polish-Austrian grand seigneur and, moving in the cosmopolitan sphere of the highest European aristocracy, lived mostly abroad in Nice and Vienna. He, settling down on one of her estates, not the one with the palatial residence but another where there was a modest little house, saw very little of her.

"But Prince Roman did not shut himself up as if his work were done. There was hardly anything done in the private and public life of the neighborhood, in which

Prince Roman's advice and assistance were not called upon, and never in vain. It was well said that his days did not belong to himself but to his fellow citizens. And especially he was the particular friend of all returned exiles, helping them with purse and advice, arranging their affairs and finding them means of livelihood.

"I heard from my uncle many tales of his devoted activity, in which he was always guided by a simple wisdom, a high sense of honor, and the most scrupulous conception of private and public probity. He remains a living figure for me because of that meeting in a billiard room, when, in my anxiety to hear about a particularly wolfish wolf, I came in momentary contact with a man who was pre-eminently a man amongst all men capable of feeling deeply, of believing steadily, of loving ardently.

"I remember to this day the grasp of Prince Roman's bony, wrinkled hand closing on my small inky paw, and my uncle's half-serious, half-amused way of looking down at his trespassing nephew.

"They moved on and forgot that little boy. But I did not move; I gazed after them, not so much disappointed as disconcerted by this prince so utterly unlike a prince in a fairy tale. They moved very slowly across the room. Before reaching the other door the Prince stopped, and I heard him—I seem to hear him now—saying: 'I wish you would write to Vienna about filling up that post. He's a most deserving fellow—and your recommendation would be decisive.'

"My uncle's face turned to him expressed genuine wonder. It said as plainly as any speech could say: What better recommendation than a father's can be needed? The Prince was quick at reading expressions. Again he spoke with the toneless accent of a man who has not heard his own voice for years, for whom the soundless world is like an abode of silent shades.

"And to this day I remember the very words: 'I ask you because, you see, my daughter and my son-in-law don't believe me to be a good judge of men. They think that I let myself be guided too much by mere sentiment.'"

THE LAGOON

he white man, leaning with both arms over the roof of the little house in the stern of the boat, said to the steersman:

"We will pass the night in Arsat's clearing. It is late."

The Malay only grunted, and went on looking fixedly at the river. The white man rested his chin on his crossed arms and gazed at the wake of the boat. At the end of the straight avenue of forests cut by the intense glitter of the river, the sun appeared unclouded and dazzling, poised low over the water that shone smoothly like a band of metal. The forests, somber and dull, stood motionless and silent on each side of the broad stream. At the foot of big, towering trees, trunkless nipa palms rose from the mud of the bank, in bunches of leaves enormous and heavy, that hung unstirring over the brown swirl of eddies. In the stillness of the air every tree, every leaf, every bough, every tendril of creeper and every petal of minute blossoms seemed to have been bewitched into an immobility perfect and final. Nothing moved on the river but the eight paddles that rose flashing regularly, dipped together with a single splash; while the steersman swept right and left with a periodic and sudden flourish of his blade describing a glinting semicircle above his head. The churned-up water frothed alongside with a confused murmur. And the white man's canoe, advancing upstream in the short-lived disturbance of its own making, seemed to enter the portals of a land from which the very memory of motion had forever departed.

The white man, turning his back upon the setting sun, looked along the empty and broad expanse of the sea-reach. For the last three miles of its course the wandering, hesitating river, as if enticed irresistibly by the freedom of an open horizon, flows straight into the sea, flows straight to the east—to the east that harbors both light and darkness. Astern of the boat the repeated call of some bird, a cry discordant and feeble, skipped along over the smooth water and lost itself, before it could reach the other shore, in the breathless silence of the world.

The steersman dug his paddle into the stream, and held hard with stiffened arms, his body thrown forward. The water gurgled aloud; and suddenly the long straight reach seemed to pivot on its center, the forests swung in a semicircle, and the slanting beams of sunset touched the broadside of the canoe with a fiery glow, throwing the slender and distorted shadows of its crew upon the streaked glitter of the river. The white man turned to look ahead. The course of the boat had been altered at right angles to the stream, and the carved dragon head of its prow was pointing now at a gap in the fringing bushes of the bank. It glided through, brushing the overhanging twigs, and disappeared from the river like some slim and amphibious creature leaving the water for its lair in the forests.

The narrow creek was like a ditch: tortuous, fabulously deep; filled with gloom under the thin strip of pure and shining blue of the heaven. Immense trees soared up, invisible behind the festooned draperies of creepers. Here and there, near the glistening blackness of the water, a twisted root of some tall tree showed amongst the tracery of small ferns, black and dull, writhing and motionless, like an arrested snake. The short words of the paddlers reverberated loudly between the thick and somber walls of vegetation. Darkness oozed out from between the trees, through the tangled maze of the creepers, from behind the great fantastic and unstirring leaves; the darkness, mysterious and invincible; the darkness scented and poisonous of impenetrable forests.

The men poled in the shoaling water. The creek broadened, opening out into a wide sweep of a stagnant lagoon. The forests receded from the marshy bank, leaving a level strip of bright green, reedy grass to frame the reflected blueness of the sky. A fleecy pink cloud drifted high above, trailing the delicate coloring of its image under the floating leaves and the silvery blossoms of the lotus. A little house, perched on high piles, appeared black in the distance. Near it, two tall nibong palms, that seemed to have come out of the forests in the background, leaned slightly over the ragged roof, with a suggestion of sad tenderness and care in the droop of their leafy and soaring heads.

The steersman, pointing with his paddle, said, "Arsat is there. I see his canoe fast between the piles."

The polers ran along the sides of the boat glancing over their shoulders at the end of the day's journey. They would have preferred to spend the night somewhere else than on this lagoon of weird aspect and ghostly reputation. Moreover, they disliked Arsat, first as a stranger, and also because he who repairs a ruined house, and dwells in it, proclaims that he is not afraid to live amongst the spirits that haunt the places abandoned by mankind. Such a man can disturb the course of fate by glances or words; while his familiar ghosts are not easy to propitiate by casual wayfarers upon whom they long to wreak the malice of their human master. White men care not for such things, being unbelievers and in league with the Father of Evil, who leads them unharmed through the invisible dangers of this world. To the warnings of the righteous they oppose an offensive pretense of disbelief. What is there to be done?

So they thought, throwing their weight on the end of their long poles. The big canoe glided on swiftly, noiselessly, and smoothly, towards Arsat's clearing, till, in a great rattling of poles thrown down, and the loud murmurs of "Allah be praised!" it came with a gentle knock against the crooked piles below the house.

The boatmen with uplifted faces shouted discordantly, "Arsat! O Arsat!" Nobody came. The white man began to climb the rude ladder giving access to the bamboo platform before the house. The juragan of the boat said sulkily, "We will cook in the sampan, and sleep on the water."

"Pass my blankets and the basket," said the white man, curtly.

He knelt on the edge of the platform to receive the bundle. Then the boat shoved off, and the white man, standing up, confronted Arsat, who had come out through the low door of his hut. He was a man young, powerful, with broad chest and muscular arms. He had nothing on but his sarong. His head was bare. His big, soft eyes stared eagerly at the white man, but his voice and demeanor were composed as he asked, without any words of greeting:

"Have you medicine, Tuan?"

"No," said the visitor in a startled tone. "No. Why? Is there sickness in the house?"

"Enter and see," replied Arsat, in the same calm manner, and turning short round, passed again through the small doorway. The white man, dropping his bundles, followed.

In the dim light of the dwelling he made out on a couch of bamboos a woman stretched on her back under a broad sheet of red cotton cloth. She lay still, as if dead; but her big eyes, wide open, glittered in the gloom, staring upwards at the slender rafters, motionless and unseeing. She was in a high fever, and evidently unconscious. Her cheeks were sunk slightly, her lips were partly open, and on the young face there was the ominous and fixed expression—the absorbed, contemplating expression of the unconscious who are going to die. The two men stood looking down at her in silence.

"Has she been long ill?" asked the traveler.

"I have not slept for five nights," answered the Malay, in a deliberate tone. "At first she heard voices calling her from the water and struggled against me who held her. But since the sun of today rose she hears nothing—she hears not me. She sees nothing. She sees not me—me!"

He remained silent for a minute, then asked softly:

"Tuan, will she die?"

"I fear so," said the white man, sorrowfully. He had known Arsat years ago, in a far country in times of trouble and danger, when no friendship is to be despised. And since his Malay friend had come unexpectedly to dwell in the hut on the lagoon with a strange woman, he had slept many times there, in his journeys up and down the river. He liked the man who knew how to keep faith in council and how to fight without fear by the side of his white friend. He liked him—not so much perhaps as a man likes his favorite dog—but still he liked him well enough to help and ask no questions, to think sometimes vaguely and hazily in the midst of his own pursuits, about the lonely man and the long-haired woman with audacious face and triumphant eyes, who lived together hidden by the forests—alone and feared.

The white man came out of the hut in time to see the enormous conflagration of sunset put out by the swift and stealthy shadows that, rising like a black and impalpable vapor above the treetops, spread over the heaven, extinguishing the crimson glow of floating clouds and the red brilliance of departing daylight. In a few moments all the stars came out above the intense blackness of the earth and the great lagoon gleaming suddenly with reflected lights resembled an oval patch of night sky flung down into the hopeless and abysmal night of the wilderness. The white man had some supper out of the basket, then collecting a few sticks that lay about the platform, made up a small fire, not for warmth, but for the sake of the smoke, which would keep off the mosquitoes. He wrapped himself in the blankets and sat with his back against the reed wall of the house, smoking thoughtfully.

Arsat came through the doorway with noiseless steps and squatted down by the fire. The white man moved his outstretched legs a little.

"She breathes," said Arsat in a low voice, anticipating the expected question. "She breathes and burns as if with a great fire. She speaks not; she hears not—and burns!"

He paused for a moment, then asked in a quiet, incurious tone:

"Tuan . . . will she die?"

The white man moved his shoulders uneasily and muttered in a hesitating manner: "If such is her fate."

"No, Tuan," said Arsat, calmly. "If such is my fate. I hear, I see, I wait. I remember. . . . Tuan, do you remember the old days? Do you remember my brother?"

"Yes," said the white man. The Malay rose suddenly and went in. The other, sitting still outside, could hear the voice in the hut. Arsat said: "Hear me! Speak!" His words were succeeded by a complete silence. "O Diamelen!" he cried, suddenly. After that cry there was a deep sigh. Arsat came out and sank down again in his old place.

They sat in silence before the fire. There was no sound within the house, there was no sound near them; but far away on the lagoon they could hear the voices of the boatmen ringing fitful and distinct on the calm water. The fire in the bows of the sampan shone faintly in the distance with a hazy red glow. Then it died out. The voices ceased. The land and the water slept invisible, unstirring and mute. It was as though there had been nothing left in the world but the glitter of stars streaming, ceaseless and vain, through the black stillness of the night.

The white man gazed straight before him into the darkness with wide-open eyes. The fear and fascination, the inspiration and the wonder of death—of death near, unavoidable, and unseen, soothed the unrest of his race and stirred the most indistinct, the most intimate of his thoughts. The ever-ready suspicion of evil, the gnawing suspicion that lurks in our hearts, flowed out into the stillness round him—into the stillness profound and dumb, and made it appear untrustworthy and infamous, like the placid and impenetrable mask of an unjustifiable violence. In that fleeting and powerful disturbance of his being the earth enfolded in the starlight peace became a shadowy country of inhuman strife, a battlefield of phantoms terrible and charming, august or ignoble, struggling ardently for the possession of our helpless hearts. An unquiet and mysterious country of inextinguishable desires and fears.

A plaintive murmur rose in the night; a murmur saddening and startling, as if the great solitudes of surrounding woods had tried to whisper into his ear the wisdom of their immense and lofty indifference. Sounds hesitating and vague floated in the air round him, shaped themselves slowly into words; and at last flowed on gently in a murmuring stream of soft and monotonous sentences. He stirred like a man waking up and changed his position slightly. Arsat, motionless and shadowy, sitting with bowed head under the stars, was speaking in a low and dreamy tone:

". . . for where can we lay down the heaviness of our trouble but in a friend's heart? A man must speak of war and of love. You, Tuan, know what war is, and you have seen me in time of danger seek death as other men seek life! A writing may be lost; a lie may be written; but what the eye has seen is truth and remains in the mind!"

"I remember," said the white man, quietly. Arsat went on with mournful composure:

"Therefore I shall speak to you of love. Speak in the night. Speak before both night and love are gone—and the eye of day looks upon my sorrow and my shame; upon my blackened face; upon my burnt-up heart."

A sigh, short and faint, marked an almost imperceptible pause, and then his words flowed on, without a stir, without a gesture.

"After the time of trouble and war was over and you went away from my country in the pursuit of your desires, which we, men of the islands, cannot understand, I and my brother became again, as we had been before, the sword bearers of the Ruler. You know we were men of family, belonging to a ruling race, and more fit than any to carry on our right shoulder the emblem of power. And in the time of prosperity Si Dendring showed us favor, as we, in time of sorrow, had showed to him the faithfulness of our courage. It was a time of peace. A time of deer hunts and cock fights; of idle talks and foolish squabbles between men whose bellies are full and weapons are rusty. But the sower watched the young rice shoots grow up without fear, and the traders came and went, departed lean and returned fat into the river of peace. They brought news, too. Brought lies and truth mixed together, so that no man knew when to rejoice and when to be sorry. We heard from them about you also. They had seen you here and had seen you there. And I was glad to hear, for I remembered the stirring times, and I always remembered you, Tuan, till the time came when my eyes could see nothing in the past, because they had looked upon the one who is dying there—in the house."

He stopped to exclaim in an intense whisper, "O Mara bahia! O Calamity!" then went on speaking a little louder:

"There's no worse enemy and no better friend than a brother, Tuan, for one brother knows another, and in perfect knowledge is strength for good or evil. I loved my brother. I went to him and told him that I could see nothing but one face, hear nothing but one voice. He told me: 'Open your heart so that she can see what is in it —and wait. Patience is wisdom. Inchi Midah may die or our Ruler may throw off his fear of a woman!' . . . I waited! . . . You remember the lady with the veiled face,

Tuan, and the fear of our Ruler before her cunning and temper. And if she wanted her servant, what could I do? But I fed the hunger of my heart on short glances and stealthy words. I loitered on the path to the bathhouses in the daytime, and when the sun had fallen behind the forest I crept along the jasmine hedges of the women's courtyard. Unseeing, we spoke to one another through the scent of flowers, through the veil of leaves, through the blades of long grass that stood still before our lips; so great was our prudence, so faint was the murmur of our great longing. The time passed swiftly . . . and there were whispers amongst women—and our enemies watched—my brother was gloomy, and I began to think of killing and of a fierce death. . . . We are of a people who take what they want—like you whites. There is a time when a man should forget loyalty and respect. Might and authority are given to rulers, but to all men is given love and strength and courage. My brother said, 'You shall take her from their midst. We are two who are like one.' And I answered, 'Let it be soon, for I find no warmth in sunlight that does not shine upon her.' Our time came when the Ruler and all the great people went to the mouth of the river to fish by torchlight. There were hundreds of boats, and on the white sand, between the water and the forests, dwellings of leaves were built for the households of the Rajahs. The smoke of cooking fires was like a blue mist of the evening, and many voices rang in it joyfully. While they were making the boats ready to beat up the fish, my brother came to me and said, 'Tonight!' I looked to my weapons, and when the time came our canoe took its place in the circle of boats carrying the torches. The lights blazed on the water, but behind the boats there was darkness. When the shouting began and the excitement made them like mad we dropped out. The water swallowed our fire, and we floated back to the shore that was dark with only here and there the glimmer of embers. We could hear the talk of slave girls amongst the sheds. Then we found a place deserted and silent. We waited there. She came. She came running along the shore, rapid and leaving no trace, like a leaf driven by the wind into the sea. My brother said gloomily, 'Go and take her; carry her into our boat.' I lifted her in my arms. She panted. Her heart was beating against my breast. I said, 'I take you from those people. You came to the cry of my heart, but my arms take you into my boat against the will of the great!' 'It is right,' said my brother. 'We are men who take what we want and can hold it against many. We should have taken her in daylight.' I said, 'Let us be off'; for since she was in my boat I began to think of our Ruler's many men. 'Yes. Let us be off,' said my brother. 'We are cast out and this boat is our country now —and the sea is our refuge.' He lingered with his foot on the shore, and I entreated him to hasten, for I remembered the strokes of her heart against my breast and thought that two men cannot withstand a hundred. We left, paddling downstream close to the bank; and as we passed by the creek where they were fishing, the great shouting had ceased, but the murmur of voices was loud like the humming of insects flying at noonday. The boats floated, clustered together, in the red light of torches, under a black roof of smoke; and men talked of their sport. Men that boasted, and praised, and jeered—men that would have been our friends in the morning, but on that night were already our enemies. We paddled swiftly past. We had no more friends in the country of our birth. She sat in the middle of the canoe with covered face; silent as she is now; unseeing as she is now—and I had no regret at what I was leaving because I could hear her breathing close to me—as I can hear her now."

He paused, listened with his ear turned to the doorway, then shook his head and went on:

"My brother wanted to shout the cry of challenge—one cry only—to let the people know we were freeborn robbers who trusted our arms and the great sea. And again I begged him in the name of our love to be silent. Could I not hear her breathing close to me? I knew the pursuit would come quick enough. My brother loved me. He dipped his paddle without a splash. He only said, 'There is half a man in you now— the other half is in that woman. I can wait. When you are a whole man again, you will come back with me here to shout defiance. We are sons of the same mother.' I made no answer. All my strength and all my spirit were in my hands that held the paddle— for I longed to be with her in a safe place beyond the reach of men's anger and of women's spite. My love was so great, that I thought it could guide me to a country where death was unknown, if I could only escape from Inchi Midah's fury and from our Ruler's sword. We paddled with haste, breathing through our teeth. The blades bit deep into the smooth water. We passed out of the river; we flew in clear channels amongst the shallows. We skirted the black coast; we skirted the sand beaches where the sea speaks in whispers to the land; and the gleam of white sand flashed back past our boat, so swiftly she ran upon the water. We spoke not. Only once I said, 'Sleep, Diamelen, for soon you may want all your strength.' I heard the sweetness of her voice, but I never turned my head. The sun rose and still we went on. Water fell from my face like rain from a cloud. We flew in the light and heat. I never looked back, but I knew that my brother's eyes, behind me, were looking steadily ahead, for the boat went as straight as a bushman's dart, when it leaves the end of the sumpitan. There was no better paddler, no better steersman than my brother. Many times, together, we had won races in that canoe. But we never had put out our strength as we did then—then, when for the last time we paddled together! There was no braver or stronger man in our country than my brother. I could not spare the strength to turn my head and look at him, but every moment I heard the hiss of his breath getting louder behind me. Still he did not speak. The sun was high. The heat clung to my back like a flame of fire. My ribs were ready to burst, but I could no longer get enough air into my chest. And then I felt I must cry out with my last breath, 'Let us rest!' . . . 'Good!' he answered; and his voice was firm. He was strong. He was brave. He knew not fear and no fatigue . . . My brother!"

A murmur powerful and gentle, a murmur vast and faint; the murmur of trembling leaves, of stirring boughs, ran through the tangled depths of the forests, ran over the starry smoothness of the lagoon, and the water between the piles lapped the slimy timber once with a sudden splash. A breath of warm air touched the two men's faces and passed on with a mournful sound—a breath loud and short like an uneasy sigh of the dreaming earth.

Arsat went on in an even, low voice.

"We ran our canoe on the white beach of a little bay close to a long tongue of land that seemed to bar our road; a long wooded cape going far into the sea. My brother knew that place. Beyond the cape a river has its entrance, and through the jungle of that land there is a narrow path. We made a fire and cooked rice. Then we lay down to sleep on the soft sand in the shade of our canoe, while she watched. No sooner had I closed my eyes than I heard her cry of alarm. We leaped up. The sun was halfway down the sky already, and coming in sight in the opening of the bay we saw a prau manned by many paddlers. We knew it at once; it was one of our Rajah's praus. They were watching the shore, and saw us. They beat the gong, and turned the head of the prau into the bay. I felt my heart become weak within my breast. Diamelen sat on the sand and covered her face. There was no escape by sea. My brother laughed. He had the gun you had given him, Tuan, before you went away, but there was only a handful of powder. He spoke to me quickly: 'Run with her along the path. I shall keep them back, for they have no firearms, and landing in the face of a man with a gun is certain death for some. Run with her. On the other side of that wood there is a fisherman's house—and a canoe. When I have fired all the shots I will follow. I am a great runner, and before they can come up we shall be gone. I will hold out as long as I can, for she is but a woman—that can neither run nor fight, but she has your heart in her weak hands.' He dropped behind the canoe. The prau was coming. She and I ran, and as we rushed along the path I heard shots. My brother fired—once—twice—and the boom-ing of the gong ceased. There was silence behind us. That neck of land is narrow. Before I heard my brother fire the third shot I saw the shelving shore, and I saw the water again; the mouth of a broad river. We crossed a grassy glade. We ran down to the water. I saw a low hut above the black mud, and a small canoe hauled up. I heard another shot behind me. I thought, 'That is his last charge.' We rushed down to the canoe; a man came running from the hut, but I leaped on him, and we rolled together in the mud. Then I got up, and he lay still at my feet. I don't know whether I had killed him or not. I and Diamelen pushed the canoe afloat. I heard yells behind me, and I saw my brother run across the glade. Many men were bounding after him. I took her in my arms and threw her into the boat, then leaped in myself. When I looked back I saw that my brother had fallen. He fell and was up again, but the men were closing round him. He shouted, 'I am coming!' The men were close to him. I looked. Many men. Then I looked at her. Tuan, I pushed the canoe! I pushed it into deep water. She was kneeling forward looking at me, and I said, 'Take your paddle,' while I struck the water with mine. Tuan, I heard him cry. I heard him cry my name twice; and I heard voices shouting, 'Kill! Strike!' I never turned back. I heard him calling my name again with a great shriek, as when life is going out together with the voice—and I never turned my head. My own name! . . . My brother! Three times he called—but I was not afraid of life. Was she not there in that canoe? And could I not with her find a country where death is forgotten—where death is unknown!"

The white man sat up. Arsat rose and stood, an indistinct and silent figure above the dying embers of the fire. Over the lagoon a mist drifting and low had crept, erasing slowly the glittering images of the stars. And now a great expanse of white vapor covered the land: it flowed cold and gray in the darkness, eddied in noiseless whirls round the tree trunks and about the platform of the house, which seemed to float upon a restless and impalpable illusion of a sea. Only far away the tops of the trees stood outlined on the twinkle of heaven, like a somber and forbidding shore—a coast deceptive, pitiless and black.

Arsat's voice vibrated loudly in the profound peace.

"I had her there! I had her! To get her I would have faced all mankind. But I had her—and—"

His words went out ringing into the empty distances. He paused, and seemed to listen to them dying away very far—beyond help and beyond recall. Then he said quietly:

"Tuan, I loved my brother."

A breath of wind made him shiver. High above his head, high above the silent sea of mist the drooping leaves of the palms rattled together with a mournful and expiring sound. The white man stretched his legs. His chin rested on his chest, and he murmured sadly without lifting his head:

"We all love our brothers."

Arsat burst out with an intense whispering violence:

"What did I care who died? I wanted peace in my own heart."

He seemed to hear a stir in the house—listened—then stepped in noiselessly. The white man stood up. A breeze was coming in fitful puffs. The stars shone paler as if they had retreated into the frozen depths of immense space. After a chill gust of wind there were a few seconds of perfect calm and absolute silence. Then from behind the black and wavy line of the forests a column of golden light shot up into the heavens and spread over the semicircle of the eastern horizon. The sun had risen. The mist lifted, broke into drifting patches, vanished into thin flying wreaths; and the unveiled lagoon lay, polished and black, in the heavy shadows at the foot of the wall of trees. A white eagle rose over it with a slanting and ponderous flight, reached the clear sunshine and appeared dazzlingly brilliant for a moment, then soaring higher, became a dark and motionless speck before it vanished into the blue as if it had left the earth forever. The white man, standing gazing upwards before the doorway, heard in the hut a confused and broken murmur of distracted words ending with a loud groan. Suddenly Arsat stumbled out with outstretched hands, shivered, and stood still for some time with fixed eyes. Then he said:

"She burns no more."

Before his face the sun showed its edge above the treetops rising steadily. The breeze freshened; a great brilliance burst upon the lagoon, sparkled on the rippling water. The forests came out of the clear shadows of the morning, became distinct, as if they had rushed nearer—to stop short in a great stir of leaves, of nodding boughs, of swaying branches. In the merciless sunshine the whisper of unconscious life grew louder, speaking in an incomprehensible voice round the dumb darkness of that human sorrow. Arsat's eyes wandered slowly, then stared at the rising sun.

"I can see nothing," he said half aloud to himself.

"There is nothing," said the white man, moving to the edge of the platform and waving his hand to his boat. A shout came faintly over the lagoon and the sampan began to glide towards the abode of the friend of ghosts.

"If you want to come with me, I will wait all the morning," said the white man, looking away upon the water.

"No, Tuan," said Arsat, softly. "I shall not eat or sleep in this house, but I must first see my road. Now I can see nothing—see nothing! There is no light and no peace in the world; but there is death—death for many. We are sons of the same mother—and I left him in the midst of enemies; but I am going back now."

He drew a long breath and went on in a dreamy tone:

"In a little while I shall see clear enough to strike—to strike. But she has died, and . . . now . . . darkness."

He flung his arms wide open, let them fall along his body, then stood still with unmoved face and stony eyes, staring at the sun. The white man got down into his canoe. The polers ran smartly along the sides of the boat, looking over their shoulders at the beginning of a weary journey. High in the stern, his head muffled up in white rags, the juragan sat moody, letting his paddle trail in the water. The white man, leaning with both arms over the grass roof of the little cabin, looked back at the shining ripple of the boat's wake. Before the sampan passed out of the lagoon into the creek he lifted his eyes. Arsat had not moved. He stood lonely in the searching sunshine; and he looked beyond the great light of a cloudless day into the darkness of a world of illusions.

FREYA OF THE SEVEN ISLES

A STORY OF SHALLOW WATERS

I

O ne day—and that day was many years ago now—I received a long, chatty letter from one of my old chums and fellow-wanderers in Eastern waters. He was still out there, but settled down, and middle-aged; I imagined him grown portly in figure and domestic in his habits; in short, overtaken by the fate common to all except to those who, being specially beloved by the gods, get knocked on the head early. The letter was of the reminiscent "do you remember" kind—a wistful letter of backward glances. And, among other things, "surely you remember old Nelson," he wrote.

Remember old Nelson! Certainly. And to begin with, his name was not Nelson. The Englishmen in the Archipelago called him Nelson because it was more convenient, I suppose, and he never protested. It would have been mere pedantry. The true form of his name was Nielsen. He had come out East long before the advent of telegraph cables, had served English firms, had married an English girl, had been one of us for years, trading and sailing in all directions through the Eastern Archipelago, across and around, transversely, diagonally, perpendicularly, in semicircles, and zigzags, and figures of eights, for years and years.

There was no nook or cranny of these tropical waters that the enterprise of old Nelson (or Nielsen) had not penetrated in an eminently pacific way. His tracks, if plotted out, would have covered the map of the Archipelago like a cobweb—all of it, with the sole exception of the Philippines. He would never approach that part, from a strange dread of Spaniards, or, to be exact, of the Spanish authorities. What he imagined they could do to him it is impossible to say. Perhaps at some time in his life he had read some stories of the Inquisition.

But he was in general afraid of what he called "authorities"; not the English authorities, which he trusted and respected, but the other two of that part of the world. He was not so horrified at the Dutch as he was at the Spaniards, but he was

173

even more mistrustful of them. Very mistrustful indeed. The Dutch, in his view, were capable of "playing any ugly trick on a man" who had the misfortune to displease them. There were their laws and regulations, but they had no notion of fair play in applying them. It was really pitiable to see the anxious circumspection of his dealings with some official or other, and remember that this man had been known to stroll up to a village of cannibals in New Guinea in a quiet, fearless manner (and note that he was always fleshy all his life, and, if I may say so, an appetizing morsel) on some matter of barter that did not amount perhaps to fifty pounds in the end.

Remember old Nelson! Rather! Truly, none of us in my generation had known him in his active days. He was "retired" in our time. He had bought, or else leased, part of a small island from the sultan of a little group called the Seven Isles, not far north from Banka. It was, I suppose, a legitimate transaction, but I have no doubt that had he been an Englishman the Dutch would have discovered a reason to fire him out without ceremony. In this connection the real form of his name stood him in good stead. In the character of an unassuming Dane whose conduct was most correct, they let him be. With all his money engaged in cultivation he was naturally careful not to give even the shadow of offense, and it was mostly for prudential reasons of that sort that he did not look with a favorable eye on Jasper Allen. But of that later. Yes! One remembered well enough old Nelson's big, hospitable bungalow erected on a shelving point of land, his portly form, costumed generally in a white shirt and trousers (he had a confirmed habit of taking off his alpaca jacket on the slightest provocation), his round blue eyes, his straggly, sandy-white moustache sticking out all ways like the quills of the fretful porcupine, his propensity to sit down suddenly and fan himself with his hat. But there's no use concealing the fact that what one remembered really was his daughter, who at that time came out to live with him—and be a sort of Lady of the Isles.

Freya Nelson (or Nielsen) was the kind of a girl one remembers. The oval of her face was perfect; and within that fascinating frame the most happy disposition of line and feature, with an admirable complexion, gave an impression of health, strength, and what I might call unconscious self-confidence—a most pleasant and, as it were, whimsical determination. I will not compare her eyes to violets, because the real shade of their color was peculiar, not so dark and more lustrous. They were of the wide-open kind, and looked at one frankly in every mood. I never did see the long, dark eyelashes lowered—I dare say Jasper Allen did, being a privileged person—but I have no doubt that the expression must have been charming in a complex way. She could—Jasper told me once with a touchingly imbecile exultation—sit on her hair. I dare say, I dare say. It was not for me to behold these wonders; I was content to admire the neat and becoming way she used to do it up so as not to conceal the good shape of her head. And this wealth of hair was so glossy that when the screens of the west veranda were down, making a pleasant twilight there, or in the shade of the grove of fruit-trees near the house, it seemed to give out a golden light of its own.

She dressed generally in a white frock, with a skirt of walking length, showing her neat, laced, brown boots. If there was any color about her costume it was just a bit of blue perhaps. No exertion seemed to distress her. I have seen her land from the dinghy after a long pull in the sun (she rowed herself about a good deal) with no quickened breath and not a single hair out of its place. In the morning when she came out on the veranda for the first look westward, Sumatra way; over the sea, she seemed as fresh and sparkling as a dewdrop. But a dewdrop is evanescent, and there was nothing evanescent about Freya. I remember her round, solid arms with the fine wrists, and her broad, capable hands with tapering fingers.

I don't know whether she was actually born at sea, but I do know that up to twelve years of age she sailed about with her parents in various ships. After old Nelson lost his wife it became a matter of serious concern for him what to do with the girl. A kind lady in Singapore, touched by his dumb grief and deplorable perplexity, offered to take charge of Freya. This arrangement lasted some six years, during which old Nelson (or Nielsen) "retired" and established himself on his island and then it was settled (the kind lady going away to Europe) that his daughter should join him.

As the first and most important preparation for that event the old fellow ordered from his Singapore agent a Steyn and Ebhart's "upright grand." I was then command-ing a little steamer in the island trade, and it fell to my lot to take it out to him, so I know something of Freya's "upright grand." We landed the enormous packing-case with difficulty on a flat piece of rock among some bushes, nearly knocking the bottom out of one of my boats in the course of that nautical operation. Then, all my crew assisting, engineers and firemen included, by the exercise of much anxious ingenuity, and by means of rollers, levers, tackles, and inclined planes of soaped planks, toiling in the sun like ancient Egyptians at the building of a pyramid, we got it as far as the house and up on to the edge of the west veranda—which was the actual drawing room of the bungalow. There, the case being ripped off cautiously, the beautiful rosewood monster stood revealed at last. In reverent excitement we coaxed it against the wall and drew the first free breath of the day. It was certainly the heaviest movable object on that islet since the creation of the world. The volume of sound it gave out in that bungalow (which acted as a sounding-board) was really astonishing. It thundered sweetly right over the sea. Jasper Allen told me that early of a morning on the deck of the *Bonito* (his wonderfully fast and pretty brig) he could hear Freya playing her scales quite distinctly. But the fellow always anchored foolishly close to the point, as I told him more than once. Of course, these seas are almost uniformly serene, and the Seven Isles is a particularly calm and cloudless spot as a rule. But still, now and again, an afternoon thunderstorm over Banka, or even one of these vicious thick squalls, from the distant Sumatra coast, would make a sudden sally upon the group, enveloping it for a couple of hours in whirlwinds and bluish-black murk of a particularly sinister aspect. Then, with the lowered rattan-screens rattling desperately in the wind and the bungalow shaking all over, Freya would sit down to the piano and play fierce Wagner music in the flicker of blinding flashes, with thunderbolts falling all round, enough to make your hair stand on end; and Jasper would remain stock still on the veranda, adoring the back view of her supple, swaying figure, the miraculous sheen of her fair head, the rapid hands on the keys, the white nape of her neck—while the brig, down at the point there, surged at her cables within a hundred yards of nasty, shiny, black rock-heads. Ugh!

And this, if you please, for no reason but that, when he went on board at night and laid his head on the pillow, he should feel that he was as near as he could conveniently get to his Freya slumbering in the bungalow. Did you ever! And, mind, this brig was the home to be—their home—the floating paradise which he was gradually fitting out like a yacht to sail his life blissfully away in with Freya. Imbecile! But the fellow was always taking chances.

One day, I remember I watched with Freya on the verandah the brig approaching the point from the northward. I suppose Jasper made the girl out with his long glass. What does he do? Instead of standing on for another mile and a half along the shoals and then tacking for the anchorage in a proper and seaman-like manner, he spies a gap between two disgusting old jagged reefs, puts the helm down suddenly, and shoots the brig through, with all her sails shaking and rattling, so that we could hear the racket on the verandah. I drew my breath through my teeth, I can tell you, and Freya swore. Yes! She clenched her capable fists and stamped with her pretty brown boot and said "Damn!" Then, looking at me with a little heightened color—not much—she remarked, "I forgot you were there," and laughed. To be sure, to be sure. When Jasper was in sight she was not likely to remember that anybody else in the world was there. In my concern at this mad trick I couldn't help appealing to her sympathetic common sense.

"Isn't he a fool!" I said with feeling.

"Perfect idiot," she agreed warmly, looking at me straight with her wide-open, earnest eyes and the dimple of a smile on her cheek.

"And that," I pointed out to her, "just to save twenty minutes or so in meeting you."

We heard the anchor go down, and then she became very resolute and threatening. "Wait a bit. I'll teach him."

She went into her own room and shut the door, leaving me alone on the verandah with my instructions. Long before the brig's sails were furled, Jasper came up three steps at a time, forgetting to say how d'ye do, and looking right and left eagerly.

"Where's Freya? Wasn't she here just now?"

When I explained to him that he was to be deprived of Miss Freya's presence for a whole hour, "just to teach him," he said I had put her up to it, no doubt, and that he feared he would have yet to shoot me some day. She and I were getting too thick together. Then he flung himself into a chair, and tried to talk to me about his trip. But the funny thing was that the fellow actually suffered. I could see it. His voice failed him, and he sat there dumb, looking at the door with the face of a man in pain. Fact . . . And the next still funnier thing was that the girl calmly walked out of her room in less than ten minutes. And then I left. I mean to say that I went away to seek old Nelson (or Nielsen) on the back verandah, which was his own special nook in the distribution of that house, with the kind purpose of engaging him in conversation lest he should start roaming about and intrude unwittingly where he was not wanted just then.

He knew that the brig had arrived, though he did not know that Jasper was already with his daughter. I suppose he didn't think it was possible in the time. A father naturally wouldn't. He suspected that Allen was sweet on his girl; the fowls of the air and the fishes of the sea, most of the traders in the Archipelago, and all sorts and conditions of men in the town of Singapore were aware of it. But he was not capable of appreciating how far the girl was gone on the fellow. He had an idea that Freya was too sensible to ever be gone on anybody—I mean to an unmanageable extent. No; it was not that which made him sit on the back verandah and worry himself in his unassuming manner during Jasper's visits. What he worried about were the Dutch "authorities." For it is a fact that the Dutch looked askance at the doings of Jasper Allen, owner and master of the brig *Bonito*. They considered him much too enterprising in his trading. I don't know that he ever did anything illegal; but it seems to me that his immense activity was repulsive to their stolid character and slow-going methods. Anyway, in old Nelson's opinion, the captain of the *Bonito* was a smart sailor, and a nice young man, but not a desirable acquaintance upon the whole. Somewhat compromising, you understand. On the other hand, he did not like to tell Jasper in so many words to keep away. Poor old Nelson himself was a nice fellow. I believe he would have shrunk from hurting the feelings even of a mop-headed cannibal, unless, perhaps, under very strong provocation. I mean the feelings, not the bodies. As against spears, knives, hatchets, clubs, or arrows, old Nelson had proved himself capable of taking his own part. In every other respect he had a timorous soul. So he sat on the back verandah with a concerned expression, and whenever the voices of his daughter and Jasper Allen reached him, he would blow out his cheeks and let the air escape with a dismal sound, like a much tried man.

Naturally I derided his fears which he, more or less, confided to me. He had a certain regard for my judgment, and a certain respect, not for my moral qualities, however, but for the good terms I was supposed to be on with the Dutch "authorities." I knew for a fact that his greatest bugbear, the Governor of Banka—a charming, peppery, hearty, retired rear-admiral—had a distinct liking for him. This consoling assurance, which I used always to put forward, made old Nelson (or Nielsen) brighten up for a moment; but in the end he would shake his head doubtfully, as much as to say that this was all very well, but that there were depths in the Dutch official nature which no one but himself had ever fathomed. Perfectly ridiculous.

On this occasion I am speaking of, old Nelson was even fretty; for while I was trying to entertain him with a very funny and somewhat scandalous adventure which happened to a certain acquaintance of ours in Saigon, he exclaimed suddenly:

"What the devil he wants to turn up here for!"

Clearly he had not heard a word of the anecdote. And this annoyed me, because the anecdote was really good. I stared at him.

"Come, come!" I cried. "Don't you know what Jasper Allen is turning up here for?"

This was the first open allusion I had ever made to the true state of affairs between Jasper and his daughter. He took it very calmly.

"Oh, Freya is a sensible girl!" he murmured absently, his mind's eye obviously fixed on the "authorities." No; Freya was no fool. He was not concerned about that. He didn't mind it in the least. The fellow was just company for her; he amused the girl; nothing more.

When the perspicacious old chap left off mumbling, all was still in the house. The other two were amusing themselves very quietly, and no doubt very heartily. What more absorbing and less noisy amusement could they have found than to plan their future? Side by side on the verandah they must have been looking at the brig, the third party in that fascinating game. Without her there would have been no future. She was the fortune and the home, and the great free world for them. Who was it that likened a ship to a prison? May I be ignominiously hanged at a yardarm if that's true. The white sails of that craft were the white wings—pinions, I believe, would be the more poetical style—well, the white pinions, of their soaring love. Soaring as regards Jasper. Freya, being a woman, kept a better hold of the mundane connections of this affair.

But Jasper was elevated in the true sense of the word ever since the day when, after they had been gazing at the brig in one of those decisive silences that alone establish a perfect communion between creatures gifted with speech, he proposed that she should share the ownership of that treasure with him. Indeed, he presented the brig to her altogether. But then his heart was in the brig since the day he bought her in Manila from a certain middle-aged Peruvian, in a sober suit of black broadcloth, enigmatic and sententious, who, for all I know, might have stolen her on the South American coast, whence he said he had come over to the Philippines "for family reasons." This "for family reasons" was distinctly good. No true *caballero* would care to push on inquiries after such a statement.

Indeed, Jasper was quite the *caballero*. The brig herself was then all black and enigmatical, and very dirty; a tarnished gem of the sea, or, rather, a neglected work of art. For he must have been an artist, the obscure builder who had put her body together on lovely lines out of the hardest tropical timber fastened with the purest copper. Goodness only knows in what part of the world she was built. Jasper himself had not been able to ascertain much of her history from his sententious, saturnine Peruvian—if the fellow was a Peruvian, and not the devil himself in disguise, as Jasper jocularly pretended to believe. My opinion is that she was old enough to have been one of the last pirates, a slaver perhaps, or else an opium clipper of the early days, if not an opium smuggler.

However that may be, she was as sound as on the day she first took the water, sailed like a witch, steered like a little boat, and, like some fair women of adventurous life famous in history, seemed to have the secret of perpetual youth; so that there was nothing unnatural in Jasper Allen treating her like a lover. And that treatment restored the luster of her beauty. He clothed her in many coats of the very best white paint so skillfully, carefully, artistically put on and kept clean by his badgered crew of picked Malays, that no costly enamel such as jewelers use for their work could have looked better and felt smoother to the touch. A narrow gilt molding defined her elegant sheer as she sat on the water, eclipsing easily the professional good looks of any pleasure yacht that ever came to the East in those days. For myself, I must say I prefer a molding of deep crimson color on a white hull. It gives a stronger relief besides being less expensive; and I told Jasper so. But no, nothing less than the best gold-leaf would do, because no decoration could be gorgeous enough for the future abode of his Freya.

His feelings for the brig and for the girl were as indissolubly united in his heart as you may fuse two precious metals together in one crucible. And the flame was pretty hot, I can assure you. It induced in him a fierce inward restlessness both of activity and desire. Too fine in face, with a lateral wave in his chestnut hair, spare, long-limbed, with an eager glint in his steely eyes and quick, brusque movements, he made me think sometimes of a flashing sword-blade perpetually leaping out of the scabbard. It was only when he was near the girl, when he had her there to look at, that this peculiarly tense attitude was replaced by a grave devout watchfulness of her slightest movements and utterances. Her cool, resolute, capable, good-humored self-possession seemed to steady his heart. Was it the magic of her face, of her voice, of her glances which calmed him so? Yet these were the very things one must believe which had set his imagination ablaze—if love begins in imagination. But I am no man to discuss such mysteries, and it strikes me that we have neglected poor old Nelson inflating his cheeks in a state of worry on the back verandah.

I pointed out to him that, after all, Jasper was not a very frequent visitor. He and his brig worked hard all over the Archipelago. But all old Nelson said, and he said it uneasily, was:

"I hope Heemskirk won't turn up here while the brig's about."

Getting up a scare about Heemskirk now! Heemskirk! . . . Really, one hadn't the patience—

II

For, pray, who was Heemskirk? You shall see at once how unreasonable this dread of Heemskirk . . . Certainly, his nature was malevolent enough. That was obvious, directly you heard him laugh. Nothing gives away more a man's secret disposition than the unguarded ring of his laugh. But, bless my soul! if we were to start at every evil guffaw like a hare at every sound, we shouldn't be fit for anything but the solitude of a desert, or the seclusion of a hermitage. And even there we should have to put up with the unavoidable company of the devil.

However, the devil is a considerable personage, who has known better days and has moved high up in the hierarchy of Celestial Host; but in the hierarchy of mere earthly Dutchmen, Heemskirk, whose early days could not have been very splendid, was merely a naval officer forty years of age, of no particular connections or ability to boast of. He was commanding the *Neptun,* a little gunboat employed on dreary patrol duty up and down the Archipelago, to look after the traders. Not a very exalted position truly. I tell you, just a common middle-aged lieutenant of some twenty-five years' service and sure to be retired before long—that's all.

He never bothered his head very much as to what was going on in the Seven Isles group till he learned from some talk in Mintok or Palembang, I suppose, that there was a pretty girl living there. Curiosity, I presume, caused him to go poking around that way and then, after he had once seen Freya, he made a practice of calling at the group whenever he found himself within half a day's steaming from it.

I don't mean to say that Heemskirk was a typical Dutch naval officer. I have seen enough of them not to fall into that absurd mistake. He had a big, clean-shaven face; great flat, brown cheeks, with a thin, hooked nose and a small, pursy mouth squeezed in between. There were a few silver threads in his black hair, and his unpleasant eyes were nearly black, too. He had a surly way of casting side glances without moving his head, which was set low on a short, round neck. A thick, round trunk in a dark undress jacket with gold shoulder-straps was sustained by a straddly pair of thick, round legs, in white drill trousers. His round skull under a white cap looked as if it were immensely thick too, but there were brains enough in it to discover and take advantage maliciously of poor old Nelson's nervousness before everything that was invested with the merest shred of authority.

Heemskirk would land on the point and perambulate silently every part of the plantation as if the whole place belonged to him, before he went to the house. On the verandah he would take the best chair, and would stay for tiffin or dinner, just simply stay on, without taking the trouble to invite himself by so much as a word.

He ought to have been kicked, if only for his manner to Miss Freya. Had he been a naked savage, armed with spears and poisoned arrows, old Nelson (or Nielsen) would have gone for him with his bare fists. But these gold shoulder-straps—Dutch shoulder-straps at that—were enough to terrify the old fellow; so he let the beggar treat him with heavy contempt, devour his daughter with his eyes, and drink the best part of his little stock of wine.

I saw something of this, and on one occasion I tried to pass a remark on the subject. It was pitiable to see the trouble in old Nelson's round eyes. At first he cried out that the lieutenant was a good friend of his; a very good fellow. I went on staring at him pretty hard, so that at last he faltered, and had to own that, of course, Heemskirk was not a very genial person outwardly, but all the same at bottom . . .

"I haven't yet met a genial Dutchman out here," I interrupted. "Geniality, after all, is not of much consequence, but don't you see—"

Nelson looked suddenly so frightened at what I was going to say that I hadn't the heart to go on. Of course, I was going to tell him that the fellow was after his girl. That just describes it exactly. What Heemskirk might have expected or what he thought he could do, I don't know. For all I can tell, he might have imagined himself irresistible, or have taken Freya for what she was not, on account of her lively, assured, unconstrained manner. But there it is. He was after that girl. Nelson could see it well enough. Only he preferred to ignore it. He did not want to be told of it.

"All I want is to live in peace and quietness with the Dutch authorities," he mumbled shamefacedly.

He was incurable. I was sorry for him, and I really think Miss Freya was sorry for her father, too. She restrained herself for his sake, and like everything she did she did it simply, unaffectedly, and even good humoredly. No small effort that, because in Heemskirk's attentions there was an insolent touch of scorn, hard to put up with. Dutchmen of that sort are overbearing to their inferiors, and that officer of the king looked upon old Nelson and Freya as quite beneath him in every way.

I can't say I felt sorry for Freya. She was not the sort of girl to take anything tragically. One could feel for her and sympathize with her difficulty, but she seemed equal to any situation. It was rather admiration she extorted by her competent serenity. It was only when Jasper and Heemskirk were together at the bungalow, as it happened now and then, that she felt the strain, and even then it was not for everybody to see. My eyes alone could detect a faint shadow on the radiance of her personality. Once I could not help saying to her appreciatively:

"Upon my word you are wonderful."

She let it pass with a faint smile.

"The great thing is to prevent Jasper becoming unreasonable," she said; and I could see real concern lurking in the quiet depths of her frank eyes gazing straight at me. "You will help to keep him quiet, won't you?"

"Of course, we must keep him quiet," I declared, understanding very well the nature of her anxiety.

"He's such a lunatic, too, when he's roused."

"He is!" she assented, in a soft tone; for it was our joke to speak of Jasper abusively. "But I have tamed him a bit. He's quite a good boy now."

"He would squash Heemskirk like a blackbeetle all the same," I remarked.

"Rather!" she murmured. "And that wouldn't do," she added quickly. "Imagine the state poor papa would get into. Besides, I mean to be mistress of the dear brig and sail about these seas, not go off wandering ten thousand miles away from here."

"The sooner you are on board to look after the man and the brig the better," I said seriously. "They need you to steady them both a bit. I don't think Jasper will ever get sobered down till he has carried you off from this island. You don't see him when he is away from you, as I do. He's in a state of perpetual elation which almost frightens me."

At this she smiled again, and then looked serious. For it could not be unpleasant to her to be told of her power, and she had some sense of her responsibility. She slipped away from me suddenly, because Heemskirk, with old Nelson in attendance at his elbow, was coming up the steps of the verandah. Directly his head came above the level of the floor his ill-natured black eyes shot glances here and there.

"Where's your girl, Nelson?" he asked, in a tone as if every soul in the world belonged to him. And then to me: "The goddess has flown, eh?"

Nelson's Cove—as we used to call it—was crowded with shipping that day. There was first my steamer, then the *Neptun* gunboat further out, and the *Bonito* brig, anchored as usual so close inshore that it looked as if, with a little skill and judgment, one could shy a hat from the verandah on to her scrupulously holystoned quarter-deck. Her brasses flashed like gold, her white body-paint had a sheen like a satin robe. The rake of her varnished spars and the big yards, squared to a hair, gave her a sort of martial elegance. She was a beauty. No wonder that in possession of a craft like that and the promise of a girl like Freya, Jasper lived in a state of perpetual elation fit, perhaps, for the seventh heaven, but not exactly safe in a world like ours.

I remarked politely to Heemskirk that, with three guests in the house, Miss Freya had no doubt domestic matters to attend to. I knew, of course, that she had gone to meet Jasper at a certain cleared spot on the banks of the only stream on Nelson's little island. The commander of the *Neptun* gave me a dubious black look, and began to make himself at home, flinging his thick, cylindrical carcass into a rocking-chair, and unbuttoning his coat. Old Nelson sat down opposite him in a most unassuming manner, staring anxiously with his round eyes and fanning himself with his hat. I tried to make conversation to while the time away; not an easy task with a morose, enamored Dutchman constantly looking from one door to another and answering one's advances either with a jeer or a grunt.

However, the evening passed off all right. Luckily there is a degree of bliss too intense for elation. Jasper was quiet and concentrated silently in watching Freya. As we went on board our respective ships I offered to give his brig a tow out next morning. I did it on purpose to get him away at the earliest possible moment. So in the first cold light of the dawn we passed by the gunboat lying black and still without a sound in her at the mouth of the glassy cove. But with tropical swiftness the sun had climbed twice its diameter above the horizon before we had rounded the reef and got abreast of the point. On the biggest boulder there stood Freya, all in white and, in her helmet, like a feminine and martial statue with a rosy face, as I could see very well with my glasses. She fluttered an expressive handkerchief, and Jasper, running up the main rigging of the white and warlike brig, waved his hat in response. Shortly afterwards we parted, I to the northward, and Jasper heading east with a light wind on the quarter, for Banjermassin and two other ports, I believe it was, that trip.

This peaceful occasion was the last on which I saw all these people assembled together; the charmingly fresh and resolute Freya, the innocently round-eyed old Nelson, Jasper, keen, long limbed, lean faced, admirably self-contained in his manner, because inconceivably happy under the eyes of his Freya; all three tall, fair, and blue-eyed in varied shades, and among them the swarthy, arrogant, black-haired Dutchman, shorter nearly by a head, and so much thicker than any of them that he seemed to be a creature capable of inflating itself, a grotesque specimen of mankind from some other planet.

The contrast struck me all at once as we stood in the lighted verandah, after rising from the dinner-table. I was fascinated by it for the rest of the evening, and I remember the impression of something funny and ill-omened at the same time in it to this day.

III

A few weeks later, coming early one morning into Singapore, from a journey to the southward, I saw the brig lying at anchor in all her usual symmetry and splendor of aspect as though she had been taken out of a glass case and put delicately into the water that very moment.

She was well out in the roadstead, but I steamed in and took up my habitual berth close in front of the town. Before we had finished breakfast a quartermaster came to tell me that Captain Allen's boat was coming our way.

His smart gig dashed alongside, and in two bounds he was up our accommodation-ladder and shaking me by the hand with his nervous grip, his eyes snapping inquisitively, for he supposed I had called at the Seven Isles group on my way. I reached into my pocket for a nicely folded little note, which he grabbed out of my hand without ceremony and carried off on the bridge to read by himself. After a decent interval I followed him up there, and found him pacing to and fro; for the nature of his emotions made him restless even in his most thoughtful moments.

He shook his head at me triumphantly.

"Well, my dear boy," he said, "I shall be counting the days now."

I understood what he meant. I knew that those young people had settled already on a runaway match without official preliminaries. This was really a logical decision. Old Nelson (or Nielsen) would never have agreed to give up Freya peaceably to this compromising Jasper. Heavens! What would the Dutch authorities say to such a match! It sounds too ridiculous for words. But there's nothing in the world more selfishly hard than a timorous man in a fright about his "little estate," as old Nelson used to call it in apologetic accents. A heart permeated by a particular sort of funk is proof against sense, feeling, and ridicule. It's a flint.

Jasper would have made his request all the same and then taken his own way; but it was Freya who decided that nothing should be said, on the ground that, "Papa would only worry himself to distraction." He was capable of making himself ill, and then she wouldn't have the heart to leave him. Here you have the sanity of feminine outlook and the frankness of feminine reasoning. And for the rest, Miss Freya could read "poor dear papa" in the way a woman reads a man—like an open book. His daughter once gone, old Nelson would not worry himself. He would raise a great outcry, and make no end of lamentable fuss, but that's not the same thing. The real agonies of indecision, the anguish of conflicting feelings would be spared to him. And as he was too unassuming to rage, he would, after a period of lamentation, devote himself to his "little estate," and to keeping on good terms with the authorities.

Time would do the rest. And Freya thought she could afford to wait, while ruling over her own home in the beautiful brig and over the man who loved her. This was the life for her who had learned to walk on a ship's deck. She was a ship-child, a sea-girl if ever there was one. And of course she loved Jasper and trusted him; but there was a shade of anxiety in her pride. It is very fine and romantic to possess for your very own a finely tempered and trusty sword-blade, but whether it is the best weapon to counter with the common cudgel-play of Fate—that's another question.

She knew that she had the more substance of the two—you needn't try any cheap jokes, I am not talking of their weights. She was just a little anxious while he was away, and she had me who, being a tried confidant, took the liberty to whisper frequently "The sooner the better." But there was a peculiar vein of obstinacy in Miss Freya, and her reason for delay was characteristic. "Not before my twenty-first birthday; so that there shall be no mistake in people's minds as to me being old enough to know what I am doing."

Jasper's feelings were in such subjection that he had never even remonstrated against the decree. She was just splendid, whatever she did or said, and there was an end of it for him. I believe that he was subtle enough to be even flattered at bottom—at times. And then to console him he had the brig, which seemed pervaded by the spirit of Freya, since whatever he did on board was always done under the supreme sanction of his love.

"Yes. I'll soon begin to count the days," he repeated. "Eleven months more. I'll have to crowd three trips into that."

"Mind you don't come to grief trying to do too much," I admonished him. But he dismissed my caution with a laugh and an elated gesture. Pooh! Nothing, nothing could happen to the brig, he cried, as if the flame of his heart could light up the dark nights of uncharted seas, and the image of Freya serve for an unerring beacon among hidden shoals; as if the winds had to wait on his future, the stars fight for it in their courses; as if the magic of his passion had the power to float a ship on a drop of dew or sail her through the eye of a needle—simply because it was her magnificent lot to be the servant of a love so full of grace as to make all the ways of the earth safe, resplendent, and easy.

"I suppose," I said, after he had finished laughing at my innocent enough remark, "I suppose you will be off today."

That was what he meant to do. He had not gone at daylight only because he expected me to come in.

"And only fancy what has happened yesterday," he went on. "My mate left me suddenly. Had to. And as there's nobody to be found at a short notice I am going to take Schultz with me. The notorious Schultz! Why don't you jump out of your skin? I tell you I went and unearthed Schultz late last evening, after no end of trouble. 'I am your man, Captain,' he says, in that wonderful voice of his, 'but I am sorry to confess I have practically no clothes to my back. I have had to sell all my wardrobe to get a little food from day to day.' What a voice that man has got. Talk about moving stones! But people seem to get used to it. I had never seen him before, and, upon my word, I felt suddenly tears rising to my eyes. Luckily it was dusk. He was sitting very quiet under a tree in a native compound as thin as a lath, and when I peered down at him all he had on was an old cotton singlet and a pair of ragged pajamas. I bought him six white suits and two pairs of canvas shoes. Can't clear the ship without a mate. Must have somebody. I am going on shore presently to sign him on, and I shall take him with me as I go back on board to get under way. Now, I am a lunatic—am I not? Mad, of course. Come on! Lay it on thick. Let yourself go. I like to see you get excited."

He so evidently expected me to scold that I took especial pleasure in exaggerating the calmness of my attitude.

"The worst that can be brought up against Schultz," I began, folding my arms and speaking dispassionately, "is an awkward habit of stealing the stores of every ship he has ever been in. He will do it. That's really all that's wrong. I don't credit absolutely that story Captain Robinson tells of Schultz conspiring in Chantabun with some ruffians in a Chinese junk to steal the anchor off the starboard bow of the *Bohemian Girl* schooner. Robinson's story is too ingenious altogether. That other tale of the engineers of the *Nan-Shan* finding Schultz at midnight in the engine-room busy hammering at the brass bearings to carry them off for sale on shore seems to me more authentic. Apart from this little weakness, let me tell you that Schultz is a smarter sailor than many who never took a drop of drink in their lives, and perhaps no worse morally than some men you and I know who have never stolen the value of a penny. He may not be a desirable person to have on board one's ship, but since you have no choice he may be made to do, I believe. The important thing is to understand his psychology. Don't give him any money till you have done with him. Not a cent, if he begs you ever so. For as sure as Fate the moment you give him any money he will begin to steal. Just remember that."

I enjoyed Jasper's incredulous surprise.

"The devil he will!" he cried. "What on earth for? Aren't you trying to pull my leg, old boy?"

"No. I'm not. You must understand Schultz's psychology. He's neither a loafer nor a cadger. He's not likely to wander about looking for somebody to stand him drinks. But suppose he goes on shore with five dollars, or fifty for that matter, in his pocket? After the third or fourth glass he becomes fuddled and charitable. He either drops his money all over the place, or else distributes the lot around; gives it to anyone who will take it. Then it occurs to him that the night is young yet, and that he may require a good many more drinks for himself and his friends before morning. So he starts off cheerfully for his ship. His legs never get affected nor his head either in the usual way. He gets aboard and simply grabs the first thing that seems to him suitable—the cabin lamp, a coil of rope, a bag of biscuits, a drum of oil—and converts it into money without thinking twice about it. This is the process and no other. You have only to look out that he doesn't get a start. That's all."

"Confound his psychology," muttered Jasper. "But a man with a voice like his is fit to talk to the angels. Is he incurable do you think?"

I said that I thought so. Nobody had prosecuted him yet, but no one would employ him any longer. His end would be, I feared, to starve in some hole or other.

"Ah, well," reflected Jasper. "The *Bonito* isn't trading to any ports of civilization. That'll make it easier for him to keep straight."

That was true. The brig's business was on uncivilized coasts, with obscure rajahs dwelling in nearly unknown bays; with native settlements up mysterious rivers opening their somber, forest-lined estuaries among a welter of pale green reefs and dazzling sandbanks, in lonely straits of calm blue water all aglitter with sunshine. Alone, far from the beaten tracks, she glided, all white, round dark, frowning headlands, stole out, silent like a ghost, from behind points of land stretching out all black in the moonlight; or lay hove-to, like a sleeping sea-bird, under the shadow of some nameless mountain waiting for a signal. She would be glimpsed suddenly on misty, squally days dashing disdainfully aside the short aggressive waves of the Java Sea; or be seen far, far away, a tiny dazzling white speck flying across the brooding purple masses of thunder-clouds piled up on the horizon. Sometimes, on the rare mail tracks, where civilization brushes against wild mystery, when the naïve passengers crowding along the rail ex-claimed, pointing at her with interest: "Oh, here's a yacht!" the Dutch captain, with a hostile glance, would grunt contemptuously: "Yacht! No! That's only English Jasper. A pedlar—"

"A good seaman you say," ejaculated Jasper, still in the matter of the hopeless Schultz with the wonderfully touching voice.

"First rate. Ask any one. Quite worth having—only impossible," I declared.

"He shall have his chance to reform in the brig," said Jasper, with a laugh. "There will be no temptations either to drink or steal where I am going to this time."

I didn't press him for anything more definite on that point. In fact, intimate as we were, I had a pretty clear notion of the general run of his business.

But as we are going ashore in his gig he asked suddenly: "By the way, do you know where Heemskirk is?"

I eyed him covertly, and was reassured. He had asked the question, not as a lover, but as a trader. I told him that I had heard in Palembang that the *Neptun* was on duty down about Flores and Sumbawa. Quite out of his way. He expressed his satisfaction.

"You know," he went on, "that fellow, when he gets on the Borneo coast, amuses himself by knocking down my beacons. I have had to put up a few to help me in and out of the rivers. Early this year a Celebes trader becalmed in a prau was watching him at it. He steamed the gunboat full tilt at two of them, one after another, smashing them to pieces, and then lowered a boat on purpose to pull out a third, which I had a lot of trouble six months ago to stick up in the middle of a mudflat for a tide mark. Did you ever hear of anything more provoking—eh?"

"I wouldn't quarrel with the beggar," I observed casually, yet disliking that piece of news strongly. "It isn't worth while."

"I quarrel?" cried Jasper. "I don't want to quarrel. I don't want to hurt a single hair of his ugly head. My dear fellow, when I think of Freya's twenty-first birthday, all the world's my friend, Heemskirk included. It's a nasty, spiteful amusement, all the same."

We parted rather hurriedly on the quay, each of us having his own pressing business to attend to. I would have been very much cut up had I known that this hurried grasp of the hand with "So long, old boy. Good luck to you!" was the last of our partings.

On his return to the Straits I was away, and he was gone again before I got back. He was trying to achieve three trips before Freya's twenty-first birthday. At Nelson's Cove I missed him again by only a couple of days. Freya and I talked of "that lunatic" and "perfect idiot" with great delight and infinite appreciation. She was very radiant, with a more pronounced gaiety, notwithstanding that she had just parted from Jasper. But this was to be their last separation.

"Do get aboard as soon as you can, Miss Freya," I entreated.

She looked me straight in the face, her color a little heightened and with a sort of solemn ardour—if there was a little catch in her voice.

"The very next day."

Ah, yes! The very next day after her twenty-first birthday. I was pleased at this hint of deep feeling. It was as if she had grown impatient at last of the self-imposed delay. I supposed that Jasper's recent visit had told heavily.

"That's right," I said approvingly. "I shall be much easier in my mind when I know you have taken charge of that lunatic. Don't you lose a minute. He, of course, will be on time—unless heavens fall."

"Yes. Unless—" she repeated in a thoughtful whisper, raising her eyes to the evening sky without a speck of cloud anywhere. Silent for a time, we let our eyes wander over the waters below, looking mysteriously still in the twilight, as if trustfully composed for a long, long dream in the warm, tropical night. And the peace all round us seemed without limits and without end.

And then we began to talk Jasper over in our usual strain. We agreed that he was too reckless in many ways. Luckily, the brig was equal to the situation. Nothing apparently was too much for her. A perfect darling of a ship, said Miss Freya. She and her father had spent an afternoon on board. Jasper had given them some tea. Papa was grumpy . . . I had a vision of old Nelson under the brig's snowy awnings, nursing his unassuming vexation, and fanning himself with his hat. A comedy father . . . As a new instance of Jasper's lunacy, I was told that he was distressed at his inability to have solid silver handles fitted to all the cabin doors. "As if I would have let him!" commented Miss Freya, with amused indignation. Incidentally, I learned also that Schultz, the nautical kleptomaniac with the pathetic voice, was still hanging on to his job, with Miss Freya's approval. Jasper had confided to the lady of his heart his purpose of straightening out the fellow's psychology. Yes, indeed. All the world was his friend because it breathed the same air with Freya.

Somehow or other, I brought Heemskirk's name into conversation, and, to my great surprise, startled Miss Freya. Her eyes expressed something like distress, while she bit her lip as if to contain an explosion of laughter. Oh! Yes. Heemskirk was at the bungalow at the same time with Jasper, but he arrived the day after. He left the same day as the brig, but a few hours later.

"What a nuisance he must have been to you two," I said feelingly.

Her eyes flashed at me a sort of frightened merriment, and suddenly she exploded into a clear burst of laughter. "Ha, ha, ha!"

I echoed it heartily, but not with the same charming tone: "Ha, ha, ha! . . . Isn't he grotesque? Ha, ha ha!" And the ludicrousness of old Nelson's inanely fierce round eyes in association with his conciliatory manner to the lieutenant presenting itself to my mind brought on another fit.

"He looks," I spluttered, "he looks—Ha, ha, ha!—among you three . . . like an unhappy blackbeetle. Ha, ha ha!"

She gave out another ringing peal, ran off into her own room, and slammed the door behind her, leaving me profoundly astounded. I stopped laughing at once.

"What's the joke?" asked old Nelson's voice, half way down the steps.

He came up, sat down, and blew out his cheeks, looking inexpressibly fatuous. But I didn't want to laugh any more. And what on earth, I asked myself, have we been laughing at in this uncontrollable fashion. I felt suddenly depressed.

Oh, yes. Freya had started it. The girl's overwrought, I thought. And really one couldn't wonder at it.

I had no answer to old Nelson's question, but he was too aggrieved at Jasper's visit to think of anything else. He as good as asked me whether I wouldn't undertake to hint to Jasper that he was not wanted at the Seven Isles group. I declared that it was not necessary. From certain circumstances which had come to my knowledge lately, I had reason to think that he would not be much troubled by Jasper Allen in the future.

He emitted an earnest "Thank God!" which nearly set me laughing again, but he did not brighten up proportionately. It seemed Heemskirk had taken special pains to make himself disagreeable. The lieutenant had frightened old Nelson very much by expressing a sinister wonder at the Government permitting a white man to settle down in that part at all. "It is against our declared policy," he had remarked. He had also charged him with being in reality no better than an Englishman. He had even tried to pick a quarrel with him for not learning to speak Dutch.

"I told him I was too old to learn now," sighed out old Nelson (or Nielsen) dismally. "He said I ought to have learned Dutch long before. I had been making my living in Dutch dependencies. It was disgraceful of me not to speak Dutch, he said. He was as savage with me as if I had been a Chinaman."

It was plain he had been viciously badgered. He did not mention how many bottles of his best claret he had offered up on the altar of conciliation. It must have been a generous libation. But old Nelson (or Nielsen) was really hospitable. He didn't mind that; and I only regretted that this virtue should be lavished on the lieutenant-commander of the *Neptun.* I longed to tell him that in all probability he would be relieved from Heemskirk's visitations also. I did not do so only from the fear (absurd, I admit) of arousing some sort of suspicion in his mind. As if with this guileless comedy father such a thing were possible!

Strangely enough, the last words on the subject of Heemskirk were spoken by Freya, and in that very sense. The lieutenant was turning up persistently in old Nelson's conversation at dinner. At last I muttered a half audible "Damn the lieutenant." I could see that the girl was getting exasperated, too.

"And he wasn't well at all—was he, Freya?" old Nelson went on moaning. "Perhaps it was that which made him so snappish, hey, Freya? He looked very bad when he left us so suddenly. His liver must be in a bad state, too."

"Oh, he will end by getting over it," said Freya impatiently. "And do leave off worrying about him, papa. Very likely you won't see much of him for a long time to come."

The look she gave me in exchange for my discreet smile had no hidden mirth in it. Her eyes seemed hollowed, her face gone wan in a couple of hours. We had been laughing too much. Overwrought! Overwrought by the approach of the decisive moment. After all, sincere, courageous, and self-reliant as she was, she must have felt both the passion and the compunction of her resolve. The very strength of love which had carried her up to that point must have put her under a great moral strain, in which there might have been a little simple remorse, too. For she was honest—and there, across the table, sat poor old Nelson (or Nielsen) staring at her, round-eyed and so pathetically comic in his fierce aspect as to touch the most lightsome heart.

He retired early to his room to soothe himself for a night's rest by perusing his account-books. We two remained on the verandah for another hour or so, but we exchanged only languid phrases on things without importance, as though we had been emotionally jaded by our long day's talk on the only momentous subject. And yet there was something she might have told a friend. But she didn't. We parted silently. She distrusted my masculine lack of common sense, perhaps . . . O! Freya!

Going down the precipitous path to the landing-stage, I was confronted in the shadows of boulders and bushes by a draped feminine figure whose appearance startled me at first. It glided into my way suddenly from behind a piece of rock. But in a moment it occurred to me that it could be no one else but Freya's maid, a half-caste Malacca Portuguese. One caught fleeting glimpses of her olive face and dazzling white teeth about the house. I had also observed her at times from a distance, as she sat within call under the shade of some fruit-trees, brushing and plaiting her long raven locks. It seemed to be the principal occupation of her leisure hours. We had often exchanged nods and smiles—and a few words, too. She was a pretty creature. And once I had watched her approvingly make funny and expressive grimaces behind Heemskirk's back. I understood (from Jasper) that she was in the secret, like a comedy camerista. She was to accompany Freya on her irregular way to matrimony and "ever after" happiness. Why should she be roaming by night near the cove—unless on some love affair of her own—I asked myself. But there was nobody suitable within the Seven Isles group, as far as I knew. It flashed upon me that it was myself she had been lying in wait for.

She hesitated, muffled from head to foot, shadowy and bashful. I advanced another pace, and how I felt is nobody's business.

"What is it?" I asked, very low.

"Nobody knows I am here," she whispered.

"And nobody can see us," I whispered back.

The murmur of words "I've been so frightened" reached me. Just then forty feet above our head, from the yet lighted verandah, unexpected and startling, Freya's voice rang out in a clear, imperious call:

"Antonia!"

With a stifled exclamation, the hesitating girl vanished out of the path. A bush near by rustled; then silence. I waited wondering. The lights on the verandah went out. I waited a while longer then continued down the path to my boat, wondering more than ever.

I remember the occurrences of that visit especially, because this was the last time I saw the Nelson bungalow. On arriving at the Straits I found cable messages which made it necessary for me to throw up my employment at a moment's notice and go home at once. I had a desperate scramble to catch the mailboat which was due to leave next day, but I found time to write two short notes, one to Freya, the other to Jasper. Later on I wrote at length, this time to Allen alone. I got no answer. I hunted up then his brother, or, rather, half-brother, a solicitor in the city, a sallow, calm, little man who looked at me over his spectacles thoughtfully.

Jasper was the only child of his father's second marriage, a transaction which had failed to commend itself to the first grown-up family.

"You haven't heard for ages," I repeated, with secret annoyance. "May I ask what 'for ages' means in this connection?"

"It means that I don't care whether I ever hear from him or not," retorted the little man of law, turning nasty suddenly.

I could not blame Jasper for not wasting his time in correspondence with such an outrageous relative. But why didn't he write to me—a decent sort of friend, after all; enough of a friend to find for his silence the excuse of forgetfulness natural to a state of transcendental bliss? I waited indulgently, but nothing ever came. And the East seemed to drop out of my life without an echo, like a stone falling into a well of prodigious depth.

I V

I suppose praiseworthy motives are a sufficient justification almost for anything. What could be more commendable in the abstract than a girl's determination that "poor papa" should not be worried, and her anxiety that the man of her choice should be kept by any means from every occasion of doing something rash, something which might endanger the whole scheme of their happiness?

Nothing could be more tender and more prudent. We must also remember the girl's self-reliant temperament, and the general unwillingness of women—I mean women of sense—to make a fuss over matters of that sort.

As has been said already, Heemskirk turned up some time after Jasper's arrival at Nelson's Cove. The sight of the brig lying right under the bungalow was very offensive to him. He did not fly ashore before his anchor touched the ground as Jasper used to do. On the contrary, he hung about his quarter-deck mumbling to himself; and when he ordered his boat to be manned it was in an angry voice. Freya's existence, which lifted Jasper out of himself into a blissful elation, was for Heemskirk a cause of secret torment, of hours of exasperated brooding.

While passing the brig he hailed her harshly and asked if the master was on board. Schultz, smart and neat in a spotless white suit, leaned over the taffrail, finding the question somewhat amusing. He looked humorously down into Heemskirk's boat, and answered, in the most amiable modulations of his beautiful voice: "Captain Allen is up at the house, sir." But his expression changed suddenly at the savage growl: "What the devil are you grinning at?" which acknowledged that information.

He watched Heemskirk land and, instead of going to the house, stride away by another path into the grounds.

The desire-tormented Dutchman found old Nelson (or Nielsen) at his drying-sheds, very busy superintending the manipulation of his tobacco crop, which, though small, was of excellent quality, and enjoying himself thoroughly. But Heemskirk soon put a stop to this simple happiness. He sat down by the old chap, and by the sort of talk which he knew was best calculated for the purpose, reduced him before long to a state of concealed and perspiring nervousness. It was a horrid talk of "authorities," and old Nelson tried to defend himself. If he dealt with English traders it was because he had to dispose of his produce somehow. He was as conciliatory as he knew how to be, and this very thing seemed to excite Heemskirk, who had worked himself up into a heavily breathing state of passion.

"And the worst of them all is that Allen," he growled. "Your particular friend—eh? You have let in a lot of these Englishmen into this part. You ought never to have been allowed to settle here. Never. What's he doing here now?"

Old Nelson (or Nielsen), becoming very agitated, declared that Jasper Allen was no particular friend of his. No friend at all—at all. He had bought three tons of rice from him to feed his workpeople on. What sort of evidence of friendship was that? Heemskirk burst out at last with the thought that had been gnawing at his vitals:

"Yes. Sell three tons of rice and flirt three days with that girl of yours. I am speaking to you as a friend, Nielsen. This won't do. You are only on sufferance here."

Old Nelson was taken aback at first, but recovered pretty quickly. Won't do! Certainly! Of course, it wouldn't do! The last man in the world. But his girl didn't care for the fellow, and was too sensible to fall in love with anyone. He was very earnest in impressing on Heemskirk his own feeling of absolute security. And the lieutenant, casting doubting glances sideways, was yet willing to believe him.

"Much you know about it," he grunted nevertheless.

"But I do know," insisted old Nelson, with the greater desperation because he wanted to resist the doubts arising in his own mind. "My own daughter! In my own house, and I not to know! Come! It would be a good joke, lieutenant."

"They seem to be carrying on considerably," remarked Heemskirk moodily. "I suppose they are together now," he added, feeling a pang which changed what he meant for a mocking smile into a strange grimace.

The harassed Nelson shook his hand at him. He was at bottom shocked at this insistence, and was even beginning to feel annoyed at the absurdity of it.

"Pooh! Pooh! I'll tell you what, lieutenant: you go to the house and have a drop of gin-and-bitters before dinner. Ask for Freya. I must see the last of this tobacco put away for the night, but I'll be along presently."

Heemskirk was not insensible to this suggestion. It answered to his secret longing, which was not a longing for drink, however. Old Nelson shouted solicitously after his broad back a recommendation to make himself comfortable, and that there was a box of cheroots on the verandah.

It was the west verandah that old Nelson meant, the one which was the living-room of the house, and had split-rattan screens of the very finest quality. The east verandah, sacred to his own privacy, puffing out of cheeks, and other signs of perplexed thinking, was fitted with stout blinds of sailcloth. The north verandah was not a verandah at all, really. It was more like a long balcony. It did not communicate with the other two, and could only be approached by a passage inside the house. Thus it had a privacy which made it a convenient place for a maiden's meditations without words, and also for the discourses, apparently without sense, which, passing between a young man and a maid, become pregnant with a diversity of transcendental meanings.

This north verandah was embowered with climbing plants. Freya, whose room opened out on it, had furnished it as a sort of boudoir for herself, with a few cane chairs and a sofa of the same kind. On this sofa she and Jasper sat as close together as is possible in this imperfect world where neither can a body be in two places at once nor yet two bodies can be in one place at the same time. They had been sitting together all the afternoon, and I won't say that their talk had been without sense. Loving him with a little judicious anxiety lest in his elation he should break his heart over some mishap, Freya naturally would talk to him soberly. He, nervous and brusque when away from her, appeared always as if overcome by her visibility, by the great wonder of being palpably loved. An old man's child, having lost his mother early, thrown out to sea out of the way while very young, he had not much experience of tenderness of any kind.

In this private, foliage-embowered verandah, and at this late hour of the afternoon, he bent down a little, and, possessing himself of Freya's hands, was kissing them one after another, while she smiled and looked down at his head with the eyes of approving compassion. At that same moment Heemskirk was approaching the house from the north.

Antonia was on the watch on that side. But she did not keep a very good watch. The sun was setting; she knew that her young mistress and the captain of the *Bonito* were about to separate. She was walking to and fro in the dusky grove with a flower in her hair, and singing softly to herself, when suddenly, within a foot of her, the lieutenant appeared from behind a tree. She bounded aside like a startled fawn, but Heemskirk, with a lucid comprehension of what she was there for, pounced upon her, and, catching her arm, clapped his other thick hand over her mouth.

"If you try to make a noise I'll twist your neck!"

This ferocious figure of speech terrified the girl sufficiently. Heemskirk had seen plainly enough on the verandah Freya's golden head with another head very close to it. He dragged the unresisting maid with him by a circuitous way into the compound, where he dismissed her with a vicious push in the direction of the cluster of bamboo huts for the servants.

She was very much like the faithful camerista of Italian comedy, but in her terror she bolted away without a sound from that thick, short, black-eyed man with a cruel grip of fingers like a vice. Quaking all over at a distance, extremely scared and half inclined to laugh, she saw him enter the house at the back.

The interior of the bungalow was divided by two passages crossing each other in the middle. At that point Heemskirk, by turning his head slightly to the left as he passed, secured the evidence of "carrying on" so irreconcilable with old Nelson's assurances that it made him stagger, with a rush of blood to his head. Two white figures, distinct against the light, stood in an unmistakable attitude. Freya's arms were round Jasper's neck. Their faces were characteristically superimposed on each other, and Heemskirk went on, his throat choked with a sudden rising of curses, till on the west verandah he stumbled blindly against a chair and then dropped into another as though his legs had been swept from under him. He had indulged too long in the habit of appropriating Freya to himself in his thoughts. "Is that how you entertain your visitors—you . . ." he thought, so outraged that he could not find a sufficiently degrading epithet.

Freya struggled a little and threw her head back.

"Somebody has come in," she whispered. Jasper, holding her clasped closely to his breast, and looking down into her face, suggested casually:

"Your father."

Freya tried to disengage herself, but she had not the heart absolutely to push him away with her hands.

"I believe it's Heemskirk," she breathed out at him.

He, plunging into her eyes in a quiet rapture, was provoked to a vague smile by the sound of the name.

"The ass is always knocking down my beacons outside the river," he murmured. He attached no other meaning to Heemskirk's existence; but Freya was asking herself whether the lieutenant had seen them.

"Let me go, kid," she ordered in a peremptory whisper. Jasper obeyed, and, stepping back at once, continued his contemplation of her face under another angle. "I must go and see," she said to herself anxiously.

She instructed him hurriedly to wait a moment after she was gone and then to slip on to the back verandah and get a quiet smoke before he showed himself.

"Don't stay late this evening," was her last recommendation before she left him.

Then Freya came out on the west verandah with her light, rapid step. While going through the doorway she managed to shake down the folds of the looped-up curtains at the end of the passage so as to cover Jasper's retreat from the bower. Directly she appeared Heemskirk jumped up as if to fly at her. She paused and he made her an exaggerated low bow.

It irritated Freya.

"Oh! It's you, Mr. Heemskirk. How do you do?"

She spoke in her usual tone. Her face was not plainly visible to him in the dusk of the deep verandah. He dared not trust himself to speak, his rage at what he had seen was so great. And when she added with serenity: "Papa will be coming in before long," he called her horrid names silently, to himself, before he spoke with contorted lips.

"I have seen your father already. We had a talk in the sheds. He told me some very interesting things. Oh, very—"

Freya sat down. She thought: "He has seen us, for certain." She was not ashamed. What she was afraid of was some foolish or awkward complication. But she could not conceive how much her person had been appropriated by Heemskirk (in his thoughts). She tried to be conversational.

"You are coming now from Palembang, I suppose?"

"Eh? What? Oh, yes! I come from Palembang. Ha, ha, ha! You know what your father said? He said he was afraid you were having a very dull time of it here."

"And I suppose you are going to cruise in the Moluccas," continued Freya, who wanted to impart some useful information to Jasper if possible. At the same time she was always glad to know that those two men were a few hundred miles apart when not under her eye.

Heemskirk growled angrily.

"Yes. Moluccas," glaring in the direction of her shadowy figure. "Your father thinks it's very quiet for you here. I tell you what, Miss Freya. There isn't such a quiet spot on earth that a woman can't find an opportunity of making a fool of somebody."

Freya thought: "I mustn't let him provoke me." Presently the Tamil boy, who was Nelson's head servant, came in with the lights. She addressed him at once with voluble directions where to put the lamps, told him to bring the tray with the gin-and-bitters, and to send Antonia into the house.

"I will have to leave you to yourself, Mr. Heemskirk, for a while," she said.

And she went to her room to put on another frock. She made a quick change of it because she wished to be on the verandah before her father and the lieutenant met again. She relied on herself to regulate that evening's intercourse between these two. But Antonia, still scared and hysterical, exhibited a bruise on her arm which roused Freya's indignation.

"He jumped on me out of the bush like a tiger," said the girl, laughing nervously with frightened eyes.

"The brute!" thought Freya. "He meant to spy on us, then." She was enraged, but the recollection of the thick Dutchman in white trousers wide at the hips and narrow at the ankles, with his shoulder-straps and black bullet head, glaring at her in the light of the lamps, was so repulsively comical that she could not help a smiling grimace. Then she became anxious. The absurdities of three men were forcing this anxiety upon her: Jasper's impetuosity, her father's fears, Heemskirk's infatuation. She was very tender to the first two, and she made up her mind to display all her feminine diplomacy. All this, she said to herself, will be over and done with before very long now.

Heemskirk on the verandah, lolling in a chair, his legs extended and his white cap reposing on his stomach, was lashing himself into a fury of an atrocious character altogether incomprehensible to a girl like Freya. His chin was resting on his chest, his eyes gazed stonily at his shoes. Freya examined him from behind the curtain. He didn't stir. He was ridiculous. But this absolute stillness was impressive. She stole back along the passage to the east verandah, where Jasper was sitting quietly in the dark, doing what he was told, like a good boy.

"Psst," she hissed. He was by her side in a moment.

"Yes. What is it?" he murmured.

"It's that beetle," she whispered uneasily. Under the impression of Heemskirk's sinister immobility she had half a mind to let Jasper know that they had been seen. But she was by no means certain that Heemskirk would tell her father—and at any rate not that evening. She concluded rapidly that the safest thing would be to get Jasper out of the way as soon as possible.

"What has he been doing?" asked Jasper in a calm undertone.

"Oh, nothing! Nothing. He sits there looking cross. But you know how he's always worrying papa."

"Your father's quite unreasonable," pronounced Jasper judicially.

"I don't know," she said in a doubtful tone. Something of old Nelson's dread of the authorities had rubbed off on the girl since she had to live with it day after day. "I don't know. Papa's afraid of being reduced to beggary, as he says, in his old days. Look here, kid, you had better clear out tomorrow, first thing."

Jasper had hoped for another afternoon with Freya, an afternoon of quiet felicity with the girl by his side and his eyes on his brig, anticipating a blissful future. His silence was eloquent with disappointment, and Freya understood it very well. She, too, was disappointed. But it was her business to be sensible.

"We shan't have a moment to ourselves with that beetle creeping round the house," she argued in a low, hurried voice. "So what's the good of your staying? And he won't go while the brig's here. You know he won't."

"He ought to be reported for loitering," murmured Jasper with a vexed little laugh.

"Mind you get under way at daylight," recommended Freya under her breath.

He detained her after the manner of lovers. She expostulated without struggling because it was hard for her to repulse him. He whispered into her ear while he put his arms round her.

"Next time we two meet, next time I hold you like this, it shall be on board. You and I, in the brig—all the world, all the life—" And then he flashed out: "I wonder I can wait! I feel as if I must carry you off now, at once. I could run with you in my hands—down the path—without stumbling—without touching the earth—"

She was still. She listened to the passion in his voice. She was saying to herself that if she were to whisper the faintest yes, if she were but to sigh lightly her consent, he would do it. He was capable of doing it—without touching the earth. She closed her eyes and smiled in the dark, abandoning herself in a delightful giddiness, for an instant, to his encircling arm. But before he could be tempted to tighten his grasp she was out of it, a foot away from him and in full possession of herself.

That was the steady Freya. She was touched by the deep sigh which floated up to her from the white figure of Jasper, who did not stir.

"You are a mad kid," she said tremulously. Then with a change of tone: "No one could carry me off. Not even you. I am not the sort of girl that gets carried off." His

white form seemed to shrink a little before the force of that assertion and she relented.
"Isn't it enough for you to know that you have—that you have carried me away?" she
added in a tender tone.

He murmured an endearing word, and she continued:

"I've promised you—I've said I would come—and I shall come of my own free
will. You shall wait for me on board. I shall get up the side—by myself, and walk up
to you on the deck and say: "Here I am, kid." And then—and then I shall be carried
off. But it will be no man who will carry me off—it will be the brig, your brig—our
brig . . . I love the beauty!"

She heard an inarticulate sound, something like a moan wrung out by pain or
delight, and glided away. There was that other man on the other verandah, that dark,
surly Dutchman who could make trouble between Jasper and her father, bring about a
quarrel, ugly words, and perhaps a physical collision. What a horrible situation! But,
even putting aside that awful extremity, she shrank from having to live for some three
months with a wretched, tormented, angry, distracted, absurd man. And when the day
came, the day and the hour, what should she do if her father tried to detain her by
main force—as was, after all, possible? Could she actually struggle with him hand to
hand? But it was of lamentations and entreaties that she was really afraid. Could she
withstand them? What an odious, cruel, ridiculous position would that be!

"But it won't be. He'll say nothing," she thought as she came out quickly on the
west verandah, and, seeing that Heemskirk did not move, sat down on a chair near the
doorway and kept her eyes on him. The outraged lieutenant had not changed his
attitude; only his cap had fallen off his stomach and was lying on the floor. His thick
black eyebrows were knitted by a frown, while he looked at her out of the corners of
his eyes. And their sideways glance in conjunction with the hooked nose, the whole
bulky, ungainly, sprawling person, struck Freya as so comically moody that, inwardly
discomposed as she was, she could not help smiling. She did her best to give that smile
a conciliatory character. She did not want to provoke Heemskirk needlessly.

And the lieutenant, perceiving that smile, was mollified. It never entered his head
that his outward appearance, a naval officer, in uniform, could appear ridiculous to
that girl of no position—the daughter of old Nielsen. The recollection of her arms
round Jasper's neck still irritated and excited him. "The hussy!" he thought. "Smiling
—eh? That's how you are amusing yourself. Fooling your father finely, aren't you? You
have a taste for that sort of fun—have you? Well, we shall see—" He did not alter his
position, but on his pursed-up lips there also appeared a smile of surly and ill-omened
amusement, while his eyes returned to the contemplation of his boots.

Freya felt hot with indignation. She sat radiantly fair in the lamplight, her strong,
well-shaped hands lying one on top of the other in her lap . . . "Odious creature,"
she thought. Her face colored with sudden anger. "You have scared my maid out of
her senses," she said aloud. "What possessed you?"

He was thinking so deeply of her that the sound of her voice, pronouncing these
unexpected words, startled him extremely. He jerked up his head and looked so
bewildered that Freya insisted impatiently:

"I mean Antonia. You have bruised her arm. What did you do it for?"

"Do you want to quarrel with me?" he asked thickly, with a sort of amazement. He blinked like an owl. He was funny. Freya, like all women, had a keen sense of the ridiculous in outward appearance.

"Well, no; I don't think I do." She could not help herself. She laughed outright, a clear, nervous laugh in which Heemskirk joined suddenly with a harsh "Ha, ha, ha!"

Voices and footsteps were heard in the passage, and Jasper, with old Nelson, came out. Old Nelson looked at his daughter approvingly, for he liked the lieutenant to be kept in good humor. And he also joined sympathetically in the laugh. "Now, lieutenant, we shall have some dinner," he said, rubbing his hands cheerily. Jasper had gone straight to the balustrade. The sky was full of stars, and in the blue velvety night the cove below had a denser blackness, in which the riding-lights of the brig and of the gunboat glimmered redly, like suspended sparks. "Next time this riding-light glimmers down there, I'll be waiting for her on the quarter-deck to come and say 'Here I am,' " Jasper thought; and his heart seemed to grow bigger in his chest, dilated by an oppressive happiness that nearly wrung out a cry from him. There was no wind. Not a leaf below him stirred, and even the sea was but a still uncomplaining shadow. Far away on the unclouded sky the pale lightning, the heat-lightning of the tropics, played tremulously among the low stars in short, faint, mysteriously consecutive flashes, like incomprehensible signals from some distant planet.

The dinner passed off quietly. Freya sat facing her father, calm but pale. Heemskirk affected to talk only to old Nelson. Jasper's behavior was exemplary. He kept his eyes under control, basking in the sense of Freya's nearness, as people bask in the sun without looking up to heaven. And very soon after dinner was over, mindful of his instructions, he declared that it was time for him to go on board his ship.

Heemskirk did not look up. Ensconced in the rocking-chair, and puffing at a cheroot, he had the air of meditating surlily over some odious outbreak. So at least it seemed to Freya. Old Nelson said at once, "I'll stroll down with you." He had begun a professional conversation about the dangers of the New Guinea coast, and wanted to relate to Jasper some experience of his own "over there." Jasper was such a good listener! Freya made as if to accompany them but her father frowned, shook his head, and nodded significantly towards the immovable Heemskirk blowing out smoke with half-closed eyes and protruded lips. The lieutenant must not be left alone. Take offense, perhaps.

Freya obeyed these signs. "Perhaps it is better for me to stay," she thought. Women are not generally prone to review their own conduct, still less to condemn it. The embarrassing masculine absurdities are in the main responsible for its ethics. But, looking at Heemskirk, Freya felt regret and even remorse. His thick bulk in repose suggested the idea of repletion, but as a matter of fact he had eaten very little. He had drunk a great deal, however. The fleshy lobes of his unpleasant big ears with deeply folded rims were crimson. They quite flamed in the neighborhood of the flat, sallow cheeks. For a considerable time he did not raise his heavy brown eyelids. To be at the mercy of such a creature was humiliating; and Freya, who always ended by being frank with herself, thought regretfully: "If only I had been open with papa from the first! But then what an impossible life he would have led me!" Yes. Men were absurd in many ways; lovably like Jasper, impractically like her father, odiously like that grotesquely supine creature in the chair. Was it possible to talk him over? Perhaps it was not necessary? "Oh! I can't talk to him," she thought. And when Heemskirk, still without looking at her, began resolutely to crush his half-smoked cheroot on the coffee-tray, she took alarm, glided towards the piano, opened it in tremendous haste, and struck the keys before she sat down.

In an instant the verandah, the whole carpetless wooden bungalow raised on piles, became filled with an uproarious, confused resonance. But through it all she heard, she felt on the floor the heavy, prowling footsteps of the lieutenant moving to and fro at her back. He was not exactly drunk, but he was sufficiently primed to make the suggestions of his excited imagination seem perfectly feasible and even clever; beautifully, unscrupulously clever. Freya, aware that he had stopped just behind her, went on playing without turning her head. She played with spirit, brilliantly, a fierce piece of music, but when his voice reached her she went cold all over. It was the voice, not the words. The insolent familiarity of tone dismayed her to such an extent that she could not understand at first what he was saying. His utterance was thick, too.

"I suspected . . . Of course I suspected something of your little goings on. I am not a child. But from suspecting to seeing—seeing, you understand—there's an enormous difference. That sort of thing . . . Come! One isn't made of stone. And when a man has been worried by a girl as I have been worried by you, Miss Freya—sleeping and waking, then, of course . . . But I am a man of the world. It must be dull for you here . . . I say, won't you leave off this confounded playing . . . ?"

This last was the only sentence really which she made out. She shook her head negatively, and in desperation put on the loud pedal, but she could not make the sound of the piano cover his raised voice.

"Only, I am surprised that you should . . . An English trading skipper, a common fellow. Low, cheeky lot, infesting these islands. I would make short work of such trash! While you have here a good friend, a gentleman ready to worship at your feet—your pretty feet—an officer, a man of family. Strange, isn't it? But what of that! You are fit for a prince."

Freya did not turn her head. Her face went stiff with horror and indignation. This adventure was altogether beyond her conception of what was possible. It was not in her character to jump up and run away. It seemed to her, too, that if she did move there was no saying what might happen. Presently her father would be back, and then the other would have to leave off. It was best to ignore—to ignore. She went on playing loudly and correctly as though she were alone, as if Heemskirk did not exist. That proceeding irritated him.

"Come! You may deceive your father," he bawled angrily, "but I am not to be made a fool of! Stop this infernal noise . . . Freya . . . Hey! You Scandinavian Goddess of Love! Stop! Do you hear? That's what you are—of love. But the heathen gods are only devils in disguise, and that's what you are, too—a deep little devil. Stop it, I say, or I will lift you off that stool!"

Standing behind her, he devoured her with his eyes, from the golden crown of her rigidly motionless head to the heels of her shoes, the line of her shapely shoulders, the curves of her fine figure swaying a little before the keyboard. She had on a light dress; the sleeves stopped short at the elbows in an edging of lace. A satin ribbon encircled her waist. In an access of irresistible, reckless hopefulness he clapped both his hands on that waist—and then the irritating music stopped at last. But, quick as she was in springing away from the contact (the round music-stool going over with a crash), Heemskirk's lips, aiming at her neck, landed a hungry, smacking kiss just under her ear. A deep silence reigned for a time. And then he laughed rather feebly.

He was disconcerted somewhat by her white, still face, the big light violet eyes resting on him stonily. She had not uttered a sound. She faced him, steadying herself on the corner of the piano with one extended hand. The other went on rubbing with mechanical persistency the place his lips had touched.

"What's the trouble?" he said, offended. "Startled you? Look here: don't let us have any of that nonsense. You don't mean to say a kiss frightens you so much as all that . . . I know better . . . I don't mean to be left out in the cold."

He had been gazing into her face with such strained intentness that he could no longer see it distinctly. Everything round him was rather misty. He forgot the overturned stool, caught his foot against it, and lurched forward slightly, saying in an ingratiating tone:

"I'm not bad fun, really. You try a few kisses to begin with—"

He said no more, because his head received a terrific concussion, accompanied by an explosive sound. Freya had swung her round, strong arm with such force that the impact of her open palm on his flat cheek turned him half round. Uttering a faint, hoarse yell, the lieutenant clapped both his hands to the left side of his face, which had taken on suddenly a dusky brick-red tinge. Freya, very erect, her violet eyes darkened, her palm still tingling from the blow, a sort of restrained, determined smile showing a tiny gleam of her white teeth, heard her father's rapid, heavy tread on the path below the verandah. Her expression lost its pugnacity and became sincerely concerned. She was sorry for her father. She stooped quickly to pick up the music-stool, as if anxious to obliterate the traces . . . But that was no good. She had resumed her attitude, one hand resting lightly on the piano, before old Nelson got up to the top of the stairs.

Poor father! How furious he will be—how upset! And afterwards, what tremors, what unhappiness! Why had she not been open with him from the first? His round, innocent stare of amazement cut her to the quick. But he was not looking at her. His stare was directed to Heemskirk, who, with his back to him and with his hands still up to his face, was hissing curses through his teeth, and (she saw him in profile) glaring at her balefully with one black, evil eye.

"What's the matter?" asked old Nelson, very much bewildered.

She did not answer him. She thought of Jasper on the deck of the brig, gazing up at the lighted bungalow, and she felt frightened. It was a mercy that one of them at least was on board out of the way. She only wished he were a hundred miles off. And yet she was not certain that she did. Had Jasper been mysteriously moved that moment to reappear on the verandah she would have thrown her consistency, her firmness, her self-possession, to the winds, and flown into his arms.

"What is it? What is it?" insisted the unsuspecting Nelson, getting quite excited. "Only this minute you were playing a tune, and—"

Freya, unable to speak in her apprehension of what was coming (she was also fascinated by that black, evil, glaring eye), only nodded slightly at the lieutenant, as much as to say: "Just look at him!"

"Why, yes!" exclaimed old Nelson. "I see. What on earth—"

Meantime he had cautiously approached Heemskirk, who, bursting into incoherent imprecations, was stamping with both feet where he stood. The indignity of the blow, the rage of baffled purpose, the ridicule of the exposure, and the impossibility of revenge maddened him to a point when he simply felt he must howl with fury.

"Oh, oh, oh!" he howled, stamping across the verandah as though he meant to drive his foot through the floor at every step.

"Why, is his face hurt?" asked the astounded old Nelson. The truth dawned suddenly upon his innocent mind. "Dear me!" he cried, enlightened. "Get some brandy, quick, Freya . . . You are subject to it, lieutenant? Fiendish, eh? I know, I know! Used to go crazy all of a sudden myself at the time . . . And the little bottle of laudanum from the medicine-chest, too, Freya. Look sharp . . . Don't you see he's got a toothache?"

And, indeed, what other explanation could have presented itself to the guileless old Nelson, beholding this cheek nursed with both hands, these wild glances, these stampings, this distracted swaying of the body? It would have demanded a preternatural acuteness to hit upon the true cause. Freya had not moved. She watched Heemskirk's savagely inquiring, black stare directed stealthily upon herself. "Aha, you would like to be let off!" she said to herself. She looked at him unflinchingly, thinking it out. The temptation of making an end of it all without further trouble was irresistible. She gave an almost imperceptible nod of assent, and glided away.

"Hurry up that brandy!" old Nelson shouted, as she disappeared in the passage.

Heemskirk relieved his deeper feelings by a sudden string of curses in Dutch and English which he sent after her. He raved to his heart's content, flinging to and fro the verandah and kicking chairs out of his way; while Nelson (or Nielsen), whose sympathy was profoundly stirred by these evidences of agonizing pain, hovered round this dear (and dreaded) lieutenant, fussing like an old hen.

"Dear me, dear me! Is it so bad? I know well what it is. I used to frighten my poor wife sometimes. Do you get it often like this, lieutenant?"

Heemskirk shouldered him viciously out of his way, with a short, insane laugh. But his staggering host took it in good part; a man beside himself with excruciating toothache is not responsible.

"Go into my room, lieutenant," he suggested urgently. "Throw yourself on my bed. We will get something to ease you in a minute."

He seized the poor sufferer by the arm and forced him gently onwards to the very bed, on which Heemskirk, in a renewed access of rage, flung himself down with such force that he rebounded from the mattress to the height of quite a foot.

"Dear me!" exclaimed the scared Nelson, and incontinently ran off to hurry up the brandy and the laudanum, very angry that so little alacrity was shown in relieving the tortures of his precious guest. In the end he got these things himself.

Half an hour later he stood in the inner passage of the house, surprised by faint, spasmodic sounds of a mysterious nature, between laughter and sobs. He frowned; then went straight towards his daughter's room and knocked at the door.

Freya, her glorious fair hair framing her white face and rippling down a dark-blue dressing-gown, opened it partly.

The light in the room was dim. Antonia, crouching in a corner, rocked herself backwards and forwards, uttering feeble moans. Old Nelson had not much experience in various kinds of feminine laughter, but he was certain there had been laughter there.

"Very unfeeling, very unfeeling!" he said, with weighty displeasure. "What is there so amusing in a man being in pain? I should have thought a woman—a young girl—"

"He was so funny," murmured Freya, whose eyes glistened strangely in the semi-obscurity of the passage. "And then, you know, I don't like him," she added, in an unsteady voice.

"Funny!" repeated old Nelson, amazed at this evidence of callousness in one so young. "You don't like him! Do you mean to say that, because you don't like him, you —Why, it's simply cruel! Don't you know it's about the worst sort of pain there is? Dogs have been known to go mad with it."

"He certainly seemed to have gone mad," Freya said with an effort, as if she were struggling with some hidden feeling.

But her father was launched.

"And you know how he is. He notices everything. He is a fellow to take offense for the least little thing—regular Dutchman—and I want to keep friendly with him. It's like this, my girl: if that rajah of ours were to do something silly—and you know he is a sulky, rebellious beggar—and the authorities took into their heads that my influence over him wasn't good, you would find yourself without a roof over your head—"

She cried: "What nonsense, father!" in a not very assured tone, and discovered that he was angry, angry enough to achieve irony; yes, old Nelson (or Nielsen), irony! Just a gleam of it.

"Oh, of course, if you have means of your own—a mansion, a plantation that I know nothing of—" But he was not capable of sustained irony. "I tell you they would bundle me out of here," he whispered forcibly; "without compensation, of course. I know these Dutch. And the lieutenant's just the fellow to start the trouble going. He has the ear of influential officials. I wouldn't offend him for anything—for anything— on no consideration whatever . . . What did you say?"

It was only an inarticulate exclamation. If she ever had a half-formed intention of telling him everything she had given it up now. It was impossible, both out of regard for his dignity and for the peace of his poor mind.

"I don't care for him myself very much," old Nelson's subdued undertone confessed in a sigh. "He's easier now," he went on, after a silence. "I've given him up my bed for the night. I shall sleep on my verandah, in the hammock. No; I can't say I like him either, but from that to laugh at a man because he's driven crazy with pain is a long way. You've surprised me, Freya. That side of his face is quite flushed."

Her shoulders shook convulsively under his hands, which he laid on her paternally. His straggly, wiry moustache brushed her forehead in a good-night kiss. She closed the door, and went away from it to the middle of the room before she allowed herself a tired-out sort of laugh, without buoyancy.

"Flushed! A little flushed!" she repeated to herself. "I hope so, indeed! A little—"

Her eyelashes were wet. Antonia, in her corner, moaned and giggled, and it was impossible to tell where the moans ended and the giggles began.

The mistress and the maid had been somewhat hysterical, for Freya, on fleeing into her room, had found Antonia there, and had told her everything.

"I have avenged you, my girl," she exclaimed.

And then they had laughingly cried and cryingly laughed with admonitions—"Ssh, not so loud! Be quiet!" on one part, and interludes of "I am so frightened . . . He's an evil man," on the other.

Antonia was very much afraid of Heemskirk. She was afraid of him because of his personal appearance: because of his eyes and his eyebrows, and his mouth and his nose and his limbs. Nothing could be more rational. And she thought him an evil man, because, to her eyes, he looked evil. No ground for an opinion could be sounder. In the dimness of the room, with only a nightlight burning at the head of Freya's bed, the camerista crept out of her corner to crouch at the feet of her mistress, supplicating in whispers:

"There's the brig. Captain Allen. Let us run away at once—oh, let us run away! I am so frightened. Let us! Let us!"

"I! Run away!" thought Freya to herself, without looking down at the scared girl. "Never."

Both the resolute mistress under the mosquito-net and the frightened maid lying curled up on a mat at the foot of the bed did not sleep very well that night. The person that did not sleep at all was Lieutenant Heemskirk. He lay on his back staring vindictively in the darkness. Inflaming images and humiliating reflections succeeded each other in his mind, keeping up, augmenting his anger. A pretty tale this to get about! But it must not be allowed to get about. The outrage had to be swallowed in silence. A pretty affair! Fooled, led on, and struck by the girl—and probably fooled by the father, too. But no. Nielsen was but another victim of that shameless hussy, that brazen minx, that sly, laughing, kissing, lying . . .

"No; he did not deceive me on purpose," thought the tormented lieutenant. "But I should like to pay him off, all the same, for being such an imbecile—"

Well, some day, perhaps. One thing he was firmly resolved on: he had made up his mind to steal early out of the house. He did not think he could face the girl without going out of his mind with fury.

"Fire and perdition! Ten thousand devils! I shall choke here before the morning!" he muttered to himself, lying rigid on his back on old Nelson's bed, his breast heaving for air.

He arose at daylight and started cautiously to open the door. Faint sounds in the passage alarmed him, and remaining concealed he saw Freya coming out. This unexpected sight deprived him of all power to move away from the crack of the door. It was the narrowest crack possible, but commanding the view of the end of the verandah. Freya made for that end hastily to watch the brig passing the point. She wore her dark dressing-gown; her feet were bare, because, having fallen asleep towards the morning, she ran out headlong in her fear of being too late. Heemskirk had never seen her looking like this, with her hair drawn back smoothly to the shape of her head, and hanging in one heavy, fair tress down her back, and with that air of extreme youth, intensity, and eagerness. And at first he was amazed, and then he gnashed his teeth. He could not face her at all. He muttered a curse, and kept still behind the door.

With a low, deep-breathed "Ah!" when she first saw the brig already under way, she reached for Nelson's long glass reposing on brackets high up the wall. The wide sleeve of the dressing-gown slipped back, uncovering her white arm as far as the shoulder. Heemskirk, gripping the door-handle, as if to crush it, felt like a man just risen to his feet from a drinking bout.

And Freya knew that he was watching her. She knew. She had seen the door move as she came out of the passage. She was aware of his eyes being on her, with scornful bitterness, with triumphant contempt.

"You are there," she thought, leveling the long glass. "Oh, well, look on, then!"

The green islets appeared like black shadows, the ashen sea was smooth as glass, the clear robe of the colorless dawn, in which even the brig appeared shadowy, had a hem of light in the east. Directly Freya had made out Jasper on deck with his own long glass directed to the bungalow, she laid hers down and raised both her beautiful white arms above her head. In that attitude of supreme cry she stood still, glowing with the consciousness of Jasper's adoration going out to her figure held in the field of his glass away there, and warmed too, by the feeling of evil passion, the burning, covetous eyes of the other, fastened on her back. In the fervor of her love, in the caprice of her mind, and with that mysterious knowledge of masculine nature women seem to be born to, she thought:

"You are looking on—you will—you must! Then you shall see something."

She brought both her hands to her lips, then flung them out, sending a kiss over the sea, as if she wanted to throw her heart along with it on the deck of the brig. Her face was rosy, her eyes shone. Her repeated, passionate gesture seemed to fling kisses by the hundred again and again and again, while the slowly ascending sun brought the glory of color to the world, turning the islets green, the sea blue, the brig below her white—dazzlingly white in the spread of her wings—with the red ensign streaming like a tiny flame from the peak. And each time she murmured with a rising inflexion: "Take this—and this—and this—" till suddenly her arms fell. She had seen the ensign dipped in response, and next moment the point below hid the hull of the brig from her view.

Then she turned away from the balustrade, and, passing slowly before the door of her father's room with her eyelids lowered, and an enigmatic expression on her face, she disappeared behind the curtain.

But instead of going along the passage, she remained concealed and very still on the other side to watch what would happen. For some time the broad, furnished verandah remained empty. Then the door of old Nelson's room came open suddenly, and Heemskirk staggered out. His hair was rumpled, his eyes bloodshot, his unshaven face looked very dark. He gazed wildly about, saw his cap on a table, snatched it up, and made for the stairs quietly, but with a strange, tottering gait, like the last effort of waning strength.

Shortly after his head had sunk below the level of the floor, Freya came out from behind the curtain, with compressed, scheming lips, and no softness at all in her luminous eyes. He could not be allowed to sneak off scot free. Never—never! She was excited, she tingled all over, she had tasted blood! He must be made to understand that she had been aware of having been watched; he must know that he had been seen slinking off shamefully. But to run to the front rail and shout after him would have been childish, crude—undignified. And to shout—what? What word? What phrase? No; it was impossible. Then how? . . . She frowned, discovered it, dashed at the piano, which had stood open all night, and made the rosewood monster growl savagely in an irritated bass. She struck chords as if firing shots after that straddling, broad figure in ample white trousers and a dark uniform jacket with gold shoulder-straps, and then she pursued him with the same thing she had played the evening before—a modern, fierce piece of love music which had been tried more than once against the thunderstorms of the group. She accentuated its rhythm with triumphant malice, so absorbed in her purpose that she did not notice the presence of her father, who, wearing an old threadbare ulster of a check pattern over his sleeping-suit, had run out from the back verandah to inquire the reason of this untimely performance. He stared at her.

"What on earth? . . . Freya!" . . . His voice was nearly drowned by the piano. "What's become of the lieutenant?" he shouted.

She looked up at him as if her soul were lost in her music, with unseeing eyes.

"Gone."

"Wha-a-t? . . . Where?"

She shook her head slightly, and went on playing louder than before. Old Nelson's innocently anxious gaze, starting from the open door of his room, explored the whole place high and low, as if the lieutenant were something small which might have been crawling on the floor or clinging to a wall. But a shrill whistle coming somewhere from below pierced the ample volume of sound rolling out of the piano in great, vibrating waves. The lieutenant was down at the cove, whistling for the boat to come and take him off to his ship. And he seemed to be in a terrific hurry, too, for he whistled again almost directly, waited for a moment, and then sent out a long, interminable, shrill call as distressful to hear as though he had shrieked without drawing breath. Freya ceased playing suddenly.

"Going on board," said old Nelson, perturbed by the event. "What could have made him clear out so early? Queer chap. Devilishly touchy, too! I shouldn't wonder if it was your conduct last night that hurt his feelings? I noticed you, Freya. You as well as laughed in his face, while he was suffering agonies from neuralgia. It isn't the way to get yourself liked. He's offended with you."

Freya's hands now reposed passive on the keys; she bowed her fair head, feeling a sudden discontent, a nervous lassitude, as though she had passed through some exhausting crisis. Old Nelson (or Nielsen), looking aggrieved, was resolving matters of policy in his bald head.

"I think it would be right for me to go on board just to inquire, some time this morning," he declared fussily. "Why don't they bring me my morning tea? Do you hear, Freya? You have astonished me, I must say. I didn't think a young girl could be so unfeeling. And the lieutenant thinks himself a friend of ours, too! What? No? Well, he calls himself a friend, and that's something to a person in my position. Certainly! Oh, yes, I must go on board."

"Must you?" murmured Freya listlessly; then added in her thought: "Poor man!"

V

In respect of the next seven weeks, all that is necessary to say is, first, that old Nelson (or Nielsen) failed in paying his politic call. The *Neptun* gunboat of H.M. the King of the Netherlands, commanded by an outraged and infuriated lieutenant, left the cove at an unexpectedly early hour. When Freya's father came down to the shore, after seeing his precious crop of tobacco spread out properly in the sun, she was already steaming round the point. Old Nelson regretted the circumstance for many days.

"Now, I don't know in what disposition the man went away," he lamented to his hard daughter. He was amazed at her hardness. He was almost frightened by her indifference.

Next, it must be recorded that the same day the gunboat *Neptun*, steering east, passed the brig *Bonito* becalmed in sight of Carimata, with her head to the eastward, too. Her captain, Jasper Allen, giving himself up consciously to a tender, possessive reverie of his Freya, did not get out of his long chair on the poop to look at the *Neptun*, which passed so close that the smoke belching out suddenly from her short black funnel rolled between the masts of the *Bonito*, obscuring for a moment the sunlit whiteness of her sails, consecrated to the service of love. Jasper did not even turn his head for a glance. But Heemskirk, on the bridge, had gazed long and earnestly at the brig from the distance, gripping hard the brass rail in front of him, till, the two ships closing, he lost all confidence in himself, and retreating to the chartroom, pulled the door to with a crash. There, his brows knitted, his mouth drawn on one side in sardonic meditation, he sat through many still hours—a sort of Prometheus in the bonds of unholy desire, having his very vitals torn by the beak and claws of humiliated passion.

That species of fowl is not to be shooed off as easily as a chicken. Fooled, cheated, deceived, led on, outraged, mocked at—beak and claws! A sinister bird! The lieutenant had no mind to become the talk of the Archipelago, as the naval officer who had had his face slapped by a girl. Was it possible that she really loved that rascally trader? He tried not to think, but worse than thoughts, definite impressions beset him in his retreat. He saw her—a vision plain, close to, detailed, plastic, colored, lighted up—he saw her hanging round the neck of that fellow. And he shut his eyes, only to discover that this was no remedy. Then a piano began to play near by, very plainly; and he put his fingers to his ears with no better effect. It was not to be borne—not in solitude. He bolted out of the chartroom, and talked of indifferent things somewhat wildly with the officer of the watch on the bridge, to the mocking accompaniment of a ghostly piano.

The last thing to be recorded is that Lieutenant Heemskirk, instead of pursuing his course towards Ternate, where he was expected, went out of his way to call at Makasser, where no one was looking for his arrival. Once there, he gave certain explanations and laid a certain proposal before the governor, or some other authority, and obtained permission to do what he thought fit in these matters. Thereupon the *Neptun*, giving up Ternate altogether, steamed north in view of the mountainous coast of Celebes, and then crossing the broad straits took up her station on the low coast of virgin forests, inviolate and mute, in waters phosphorescent at night, deep blue in daytime with gleaming green patches over the submerged reefs. For days the *Neptun* could be seen moving smoothly up and down the somber face of the shore, or hanging about with a watchful air near the silver breaks of broad estuaries, under the great luminous sky never softened, never veiled, and flooding the earth with the everlasting sunshine of the tropics—that sunshine which, in its unbroken splendor, oppresses the soul with an inexpressible melancholy more intimate, more penetrating, more profound than the grey sadness of the northern mists.

The trading brig *Bonito* appeared gliding round a somber forest-clad point of land on the silvery estuary of a great river. The breath of air that gave her motion would not have fluttered the flame of a torch. She stole out into the open from behind a veil of unstirring leaves, mysteriously silent, ghostly white, and solemnly stealthy in her imperceptible progress; and Jasper, his elbow in the main rigging, and his head leaning against his hand, thought of Freya. Everything in the world reminded him of her. The beauty of the loved woman exists in the beauties of Nature. The swelling outlines of the hills, the curves of a coast, the free sinuosities of a river are less suave than the harmonious lines of her body, and when she moves, gliding lightly, the grace of her progress suggests the power of occult forces which rule the fascinating aspects of the visible world.

Dependent on things as all men are, Jasper loved his vessel—the house of his dreams. He lent to her something of Freya's soul. Her deck was the foothold of their love. The possession of his brig appeased his passion in a soothing certitude of happiness already conquered.

The full moon was some way up, perfect and serene, floating in air as calm and limpid as the glance of Freya's eyes. There was not a sound in the brig.

"Here she will stand, by my side, on evenings like this," he thought, with rapture.

And it was at that moment, in this peace, in this serenity, under the full, benign gaze of the moon propitious to lovers, on a sea without a wrinkle, under a sky without a cloud, as if all Nature had assumed its most clement mood in a spirit of mockery, that the gunboat *Neptun*, detaching herself from the dark coast under which she had been lying invisible, steamed out to intercept the trading brig *Bonito* standing out to sea.

Directly the gunboat had been made out emerging from her ambush, Schultz, of the fascinating voice, had given signs of strange agitation. All that day, ever since leaving the Malay town up the river, he had shown a haggard face, going about his duties like a man with something weighing on his mind. Jasper had noticed it, but the mate, turning away, as though he had not liked being looked at, had muttered shame-facedly of a headache and a touch of fever. He must have had it very badly when, dodging behind his captain, he wondered aloud: "What can that fellow want with us?" . . . A naked man standing in a freezing blast and trying not to shiver could not have spoken with a more harshly uncertain intonation. But it might have been fever—a cold fit.

"He wants to make himself disagreeable, simply," said Jasper, with perfect good humor. "He has tried it on me before. However, we shall soon see."

And, indeed, before long the two vessels lay abreast within easy hail. The brig, with her fine lines and her white sails, looked vaporous and sylph-like in the moonlight. The gunboat, short, squat, with her stumpy dark spars naked like dead trees, raised against the luminous sky of that resplendent night, threw a heavy shadow on the lane of water between the two ships.

Freya haunted them both like an ubiquitous spirit, and as if she were the only woman in the world. Jasper remembered her earnest recommendation to be guarded and cautious in all his acts and words while he was away from her. In this quite unforeseen encounter he felt on his ear the very breath of these hurried admonitions customary to the last moment of their partings, heard the half-jesting final whisper of the "Mind, kid, I'd never forgive you!" with a quick pressure on his arm, which he answered by a quiet, confident smile. Heemskirk was haunted in another fashion. There were no whispers in it; it was more like visions. He saw that girl hanging round the neck of a low vagabond—*that* vagabond, the vagabond who had just answered his hail. He saw her stealing barefooted across a verandah with great, clear, wide-open, eager eyes to look at a brig—*that* brig. If she had shrieked, scolded, called names! . . . But she had simply triumphed over him. That was all. Led on (he firmly believed it), fooled, deceived, outraged, struck, mocked at . . . Beak and claws! The two men, so differently haunted by Freya of the Seven Isles, were not equally matched.

In the intense stillness, as of sleep, which had fallen upon the two vessels, in a world that itself seemed but a delicate dream, a boat pulled by Javanese sailors crossing the dark lane of water came alongside the brig. The white warrant officer in her, perhaps the gunner, climbed abroad. He was a short man, with a rotund stomach and a wheezy voice. His immovable fat face looked lifeless in the moonlight, and he walked with his thick arms hanging away from his body as though he had been stuffed. His cunning little eyes glittered like bits of mica. He conveyed to Jasper, in broken English, a request to come on board the *Neptun*.

Jasper had not expected anything so unusual. But after a short reflection he decided to show neither annoyance, nor even surprise. The river from which he had come had been politically disturbed for a couple of years, and he was aware that his visits there were looked upon with some suspicion. But he did not mind much the displeasure of the authorities, so terrifying to old Nelson. He prepared to leave the brig, and Schultz followed him to the rail as if to say something, but in the end stood by in silence. Jasper, getting over the side, noticed his ghastly face. The eyes of the man who had found salvation in the brig from the effects of his peculiar psychology looked at him with a dumb, beseeching expression.

"What's the matter?" Jasper asked.

"I wonder how this will end?" said he of the beautiful voice, which had even fascinated the steady Freya herself. But where was its charming timbre now? These words had sounded like a raven's croak.

"You are ill," said Jasper positively.

"I wish I were dead!" was the startling statement uttered by Schultz talking to himself in the extremity of some mysterious trouble. Jasper gave him a keen glance, but this was not the time to investigate the morbid outbreak of a feverish man. He did not look as though he were actually delirious, and that for the moment must suffice. Schultz made a dart forward.

"That fellow means harm!" he said desperately. "He means harm to you, Captain Allen. I feel it, and I—"

He choked with inexplicable emotion.

"All right, Schultz. I won't give him an opening." Jasper cut him short and swung himself into the boat.

On board the *Neptun* Heemskirk, standing straddle-legs in the flood of moonlight, his inky shadow falling right across the quarter-deck, made no sign at his approach, but secretly he felt something like the heave of the sea in his chest at the sight of that man. Jasper waited before him in silence.

Brought face to face in direct personal contact, they fell at once into the manner of their casual meetings in old Nelson's bungalow. They ignored each other's existence— Heemskirk moodily; Jasper, with a perfectly colorless quietness.

"What's going on in that river you've just come out of?" asked the lieutenant straight away.

"I know nothing of the troubles, if you mean that," Jasper answered. "I've landed there half a cargo of rice, for which I got nothing in exchange, and went away. There's no trade there now, but they would have been starving in another week if I hadn't turned up."

"Meddling! English meddling! And suppose the rascals don't deserve anything better than to starve, eh?"

"There are women and children there, you know," observed Jasper, in his even tone.

"Oh, yes! When an Englishman talks of women and children, you may be sure there's something fishy about the business. Your doings will have to be investigated."

They spoke in turn, as though they had been disembodied spirits—mere voices in empty air; for they looked at each other as if there had been nothing there, or, at most, with as much recognition as one gives to an inanimate object, and no more. But now a silence fell. Heemskirk had thought, all at once: "She will tell him all about it. She will tell him while she hangs round his neck laughing." And the sudden desire to annihilate Jasper on the spot almost deprived him of his senses by its vehemence. He lost the power of speech, of vision. For a moment he absolutely couldn't see Jasper. But he heard him inquiring, as of the world at large:

"Am I, then, to conclude that the brig is detained?"

Heemskirk made a recovery in a flush of malignant satisfaction.

"She is. I am going to take her to Makassar in tow."

"The courts will have to decide on the legality of this," said Jasper, aware that the matter was becoming serious, but with assumed indifference.

"Oh, yes, the courts! Certainly. And as to you, I shall keep you on board here."

Jasper's dismay at being parted from his ship was betrayed by a stony immobility. It lasted but an instant. Then he turned away and hailed the brig. Mr. Schultz answered:

"Yes, sir."

"Get ready to receive a tow-rope from the gunboat! We are going to be taken to Makassar."

"Good God! What's that for, sir?" came an anxious cry faintly.

"Kindness, I suppose," Jasper, ironical, shouted with great deliberation. "We might have been—becalmed in here—for days. And hospitality. I am invited to stay—on board here."

The answer to this information was a loud ejaculation of distress. Jasper thought anxiously: "Why, the fellow's nerve's gone to pieces"; and with an awkward uneasiness of a new sort, looked intently at the brig. The thought that he was parted from her— for the first time since they came together—shook the apparently careless fortitude of his character to its very foundations, which were deep. All that time neither Heemskirk nor even his inky shadow had stirred in the least.

"I am going to send a boat's crew and an officer on board your vessel," he announced to no one in particular. Jasper, tearing himself away from the absorbed contemplation of the brig, turned round, and, without passion, almost without expression in his voice, entered his protest against the whole of the proceedings. What he was thinking of was the delay. He counted the days. Makassar was actually on his way; and to be towed there really saved time. On the other hand, there would be some vexing formalities to go through. But the thing was too absurd. "The beetle's gone mad," he thought. "I'll be released at once. And if not, Mesman must enter into a bond for me." Mesman was a Dutch merchant with whom Jasper had had many dealings, a considerable person in Makassar.

"You protest? H'm!" Heemskirk muttered, and for a little longer remained motionless, his legs planted well apart, and his head lowered as though he were studying his own comical, deeply split shadow. Then he made a sign to the rotund gunner, who had kept at hand, motionless, like a vilely stuffed specimen of a fat man, with a lifeless face and glittering little eyes. The fellow approached, and stood at attention.

"You will board the brig with a boat's crew!"

"Ya, mynherr!"

"You will have one of your men to steer her all the time," went on Heemskirk, giving his orders in English, apparently for Jasper's edification. "You hear?"

"Ya, mynherr."

"You will remain on deck and in charge all the time."

"Ya, mynherr."

Jasper felt as if, together with the command of the brig, his very heart were being taken out of his breast. Heemskirk asked, with a change of tone:

"What weapons have you on board?"

At one time all the ships trading in the China Seas had a license to carry a certain quantity of firearms for purposes of defense. Jasper answered:

"Eighteen rifles with their bayonets, which were on board when I bought her, four years ago. They have been declared."

"Where are they kept?"

"Fore-cabin. Mate has the key."

"You will take possession of them," said Heemskirk to the gunner.

"Ya, mynherr."

"What is this for? What do you mean to imply?" cried out Jasper; then bit his lip. "It's monstrous!" he muttered.

Heemskirk raised for a moment a heavy, as if suffering, glance.

"You may go," he said to his gunner. The fat man saluted, and departed.

During the next thirty hours the steady towing was interrupted once. At a signal from the brig, made by waving a flag on the forecastle, the gunboat was stopped. The badly stuffed specimen of a warrant-officer, getting into his boat, arrived on board the *Neptun* and hurried straight into his commander's cabin, his excitement at something he had to communicate being betrayed by the blinking of his small eyes. These two were closeted together for some time, while Jasper at the taffrail tried to make out if anything out of the common had occurred on board the brig. But nothing seemed to be amiss on board. However, he kept a look-out for the gunner; and, though he had avoided speaking to anybody since he had finished with Heemskirk, he stopped that man when he came out on deck again to ask how his mate was.

"He was feeling not very well when I left," he explained.

The fat warrant-officer, holding himself as though the effort of carrying his big stomach in front of him demanded a rigid carriage, understood with difficulty. Not a single one of his features showed the slightest animation, but his little eyes blinked rapidly at last.

"Oh, ya! The mate. Ya, ya! He is very well. But, mein Gott, he is one very funny man!"

Jasper could get no explanation of that remark, because the Dutchman got into the boat hurriedly, and went back on board the brig. But he consoled himself with the thought that very soon all this unpleasant and rather absurd experience would be over. The roadstead of Makassar was in sight already. Heemskirk passed by him going on the bridge. For the first time the lieutenant looked at Jasper with marked intention; and the strange roll of his eyes was so funny—it had been long agreed by Jasper and Freya that the lieutenant was funny—so ecstatically gratified, as though he were rolling a tasty morsel on his tongue, that Jasper could not help a broad smile. And then he turned to his brig again.

To see her, his cherished possession, animated by something of his Freya's soul, the only foothold of two lives on the wide earth, the security of his passion, the companion of adventure, the power to snatch the calm, adorable Freya to his breast, and carry her off to the end of the world; to see this beautiful thing embodying worthily his pride and his love, to see her captive at the end of a tow-rope was not indeed a pleasant experience. It had something nightmarish in it, as, for instance, the dream of a wild sea-bird loaded with chains.

Yet what else could he want to look at? Her beauty would sometimes come to his heart with the force of a spell, so that he would forget where he was. And, besides, that sense of superiority which the certitude of being loved gives to a young man, that illusion of being set above the Fates by a tender look in a woman's eyes, helped him, the first shock over, to go through these experiences with an amused self-confidence. For what evil could touch the elect of Freya?

It was now afternoon, the sun being behind the two vessels as they headed for the harbor. "The beetle's little joke will soon be over," thought Jasper, without any great animosity. As a seaman well acquainted with that part of the world, a casual glance was enough to tell him what was being done. "Hallo," he thought, "he is going through Spermonde Passage. We shall be rounding Tamissa reef presently." And again he returned to the contemplation of his brig, that mainstay of his material and emotional existence which would be soon in his hands again. On a sea, calm as a millpond, a heavy smooth ripple undulated and streamed away from her bows, for the powerful *Neptun* was towing at great speed, as if for a wager. The Dutch gunner appeared on the forecastle of the *Bonito*, and with him a couple of men. They stood looking at the coast, and Jasper lost himself in a loverlike trance.

The deep-toned blast of the gunboat's steam-whistle made him shudder by its unexpectedness. Slowly he looked about. Swift as lightning he leaped from where he stood, bounding forward along the deck.

"You will be on Tamissa reef!" he yelled.

High up on the bridge Heemskirk looked back over his shoulder heavily; two seamen were spinning the wheel round, and the *Neptun* was already swinging rapidly away from the edge of the pale water over the danger. Ha! Just in time. Jasper turned about instantly to watch his brig; and, even before he realized that—in obedience, it appears, to Heemskirk's orders given beforehand to the gunner—the tow-rope had been let go at the blast of the whistle, before he had time to cry out or to move a limb, he saw her cast adrift and shooting across the gunboat's stern with the impetus of her speed. He followed her fine, gliding form with eyes growing big with incredulity, wild with horror. The cries on board of her came to him only as a dreadful and confused murmur through the loud thumping of blood in his ears, while she held on. She ran upright in a terrible display of her gift of speed, with an incomparable air of life and grace. She ran on till the smooth level of water in front of her bows seemed to sink down suddenly as if sucked away; and, with a strange, violent tremor of her mastheads she stopped, inclined her lofty spars a little, and lay still. She lay still on the reef, while the *Neptun,* fetching a wide circle, continued at full speed up Spermonde Passage, heading for the town. She lay still, perfectly still, with something ill-omened and unnatural in her attitude. In an instant the subtle melancholy of things touched by decay had fallen on her in the sunshine; she was but a speck in the brilliant emptiness of space, already lonely, already desolate.

"Hold him!" yelled a voice from the bridge.

Jasper had started to run to his brig with a headlong impulse, as a man dashes forward to pull away with his hands a living, breathing, loved creature from the brink of destruction. "Hold him! Stick to him!" vociferated the lieutenant at the top of the bridge-ladder, while Jasper struggled madly without a word, only his head emerging from the heaving crowd of the *Neptun's* seamen, who had flung themselves upon him obediently. "Hold—I would not have that fellow drown himself for anything now!"

Jasper ceased struggling.

One by one they let go of him; they fell back gradually farther and farther, in attentive silence, leaving him standing unsupported in a widened, clear space, as if to give him plenty of room to fall after the struggle. He did not even sway perceptibly. Half an hour later, when the *Neptun* anchored in front of the town, he had not stirred yet, had moved neither head nor limb as much as a hair's breadth. Directly the rumble of the gunboat's cable had ceased, Heemskirk came down heavily from the bridge.

"Call a sampan," he said, in a gloomy tone, as he passed the sentry at the gangway, and then moved on slowly towards the spot where Jasper, the object of many awed glances, stood looking at the deck, as if lost in a brown study. Heemskirk came up close, and stared at him thoughtfully, with his fingers over his lips. Here he was, the favored vagabond, the only man to whom that infernal girl was likely to tell the story. But he would not find it funny. The story how Lieutenant Heemskirk—No, he would not laugh at it. He looked as though he would never laugh at anything in his life.

Suddenly Jasper looked up. His eyes, without any other expression but bewilderment, met those of Heemskirk, observant and sombre.

"Gone on the reef!" he said, in a low, astounded tone. "On—the—reef!" he repeated still lower and as if attending inwardly to the birth of some awful and amazing sensation.

"On the very top of high-water, spring tides," Heemskirk struck in, with a vindictive, exulting violence which flashed and expired. He paused, as if weary, fixing upon Jasper his arrogant eyes, over which secret disenchantment, the unavoidable shadow of all passion, seemed to pass like a saddening cloud. "On the very top," he repeated, rousing himself in fierce reaction to snatch his laced cap off his head with a horizontal, derisive flourish towards the gangway. "And now you may go ashore to the courts, you damned Englishman!" he said.

VI

The affair of the brig *Bonito* was bound to cause a sensation in Makassar, the prettiest, and perhaps the cleanest-looking of all the towns in the Islands; which however knows few occasions for excitement. The "front," with its special population, was soon aware that something had happened. A steamer towing a sailing vessel had been observed far out to sea for some time, and when the steamer came in alone, leaving the other outside, attention was aroused. Why was that? Her masts only could be seen—with furled sails—remaining in the same place to the southward. And soon the rumor ran all along the crowded seashore street that there was a ship on Tamissa reef. That crowd interpreted the appearance correctly. Its cause was beyond their penetration, for who could associate a girl nine hundred miles away with the stranding of a ship on Tamissa reef, or look for the remote filiation of that event in the psychology of at least three people, even if one of them, Lieutenant Heemskirk, was at that very moment passing among them on his way to make his verbal report?

No; the minds on the "front" were not competent for that sort of investigation, but many hands there—brown hands, yellow hands, white hands—were raised to shade the eyes gazing out to sea. The rumor spread quickly. Chinese shopkeepers came to their doors, more than one white merchant, even, rose from his desk to go to the window. After all, a ship on Tamissa was not an everyday occurrence. And presently the rumor took a more definite shape. An English trader—detained on suspicion at sea by the *Neptun*—Heemskirk was towing him in to test a case, and by some strange accident—

Later on the name came out. "The *Bonito*—what! Impossible! Yes—yes, the *Bonito*. Look! You can see from here; only two masts. It's a brig. Didn't think that man would ever let himself be caught. Heemskirk's pretty smart, too. They say she's fitted out in her cabin like a gentleman's yacht. That Allen is a sort of gentleman too. An extravagant beggar."

A young man entered smartly Messrs. Mesman Brothers' office on the "front," bubbling with some further information.

"Oh, yes; that's the *Bonito* for certain! But you don't know the story I've heard just now. The fellow must have been feeding that river with firearms for the last year or two. Well, it seems he has grown so reckless from long impunity that he has actually dared to sell the very ship's rifles this time. It's a fact. The rifles are not on board. What impudence! Only, he didn't know that there was one of our warships on the coast. But those Englishmen are so impudent that perhaps he thought that nothing would be done to him for it. Our courts do let off these fellows too often, on some miserable excuse or other. But, at any rate, there's an end of the famous *Bonito*. I have just heard in the harbor-office that she must have gone on at the very top of high-water; and she is in ballast, too. No human power, they think, can move her from where she is. I only hope it is so. It would be fine to have the notorious *Bonito* stuck up there as a warning to others."

Mr. J. Mesman, a colonial-born Dutchman, a kind, paternal old fellow, with a clean-shaven, quiet, handsome face, and a head of fine iron-grey hair curling a little on his collar, did not say a word in defense of Jasper and the *Bonito*. He rose from his arm-chair suddenly. His face was visibly troubled. It had so happened that once, from a business talk of ways and means, island trade, money matters, and so on, Jasper had been led to open himself to him on the subject of Freya; and the excellent man, who had known old Nelson years before and even remembered something of Freya, was much astonished and amused by the unfolding of the tale.

"Well, well, well! Nelson! Yes; of course. A very honest sort of man. And a little child with very fair hair. Oh, yes! I have a distinct recollection. And so she has grown into such a fine girl, so very determined, so very—" And he laughed almost boisterously. "Mind, when you have happily eloped with your future wife, Captain Allen, you must come along this way, and we shall welcome her here. A little fair-headed child! I remember. I remember."

It was that knowledge which brought trouble to his face at the first news of the wreck. He took up his hat.

"Where are you going, Mr. Mesman?"

"I am going to look for Allen. I think he must be ashore. Does anybody know?"

No one of those present knew. And Mr. Mesman went out on the "front" to make inquiries.

The other part of the town, the part near the church and the fort, got its information in another way. The first thing disclosed to it was Jasper himself walking rapidly, as though he were pursued. And, as a matter of fact, a Chinaman, obviously a sampan man, was following him at the same headlong pace. Suddenly, while passing Orange House, Jasper swerved and went in, or, rather, rushed in, startling Gomez, the hotel clerk, very much. But a Chinaman beginning to make an unseemly noise at the door claimed the immediate attention of Gomez. His grievance was that the white man whom he had brought on shore from the gunboat had not paid him his boat-fare. He had pursued him so far, asking for it all the way. But the white man had taken no notice whatever of his just claim. Gomez satisfied the coolie with a few coppers, and then went to look for Jasper, whom he knew very well. He found him standing stiffly by a little round table. At the other end of the verandah a few men sitting there had stopped talking, and were looking at him in silence. Two billiard-players, with cues in their hands, had come to the door of the billiard-room and stared, too.

On Gomez coming up to him, Jasper raised one hand to point at his own throat. Gomez noted the somewhat soiled state of his white clothes, then took one look at his face, and fled away to order the drink for which Jasper seemed to be asking.

Where he wanted to go—for what purpose—where he, perhaps, only imagined himself to be going, when a sudden impulse or the sight of a familiar place had made him turn into Orange House—it is impossible to say. He was steadying himself lightly with the tips of his fingers on the little table. There were on that verandah two men whom he knew well personally, but his gaze, roaming incessantly as though he were looking for a way of escape, passed and repassed over them without a sign of recognition. They, on their side, looking at him, doubted the evidence of their own eyes. It was not that his face was distorted. On the contrary, it was still, it was set. But its expression, somehow, was unrecognizable. Can that be him? they wondered with awe.

In his head there was a wild chaos of clear thoughts. Perfectly clear. It was this clearness which was so terrible in conjunction with the utter inability to lay hold of any single one of them all. He was saying to himself, or to them: "Steady, steady." A China boy appeared before him with a glass on a tray. He poured the drink down his throat, and rushed out. His disappearance removed the spell of wonder from the beholders. One of the men jumped up and moved quickly to that side of the verandah from which almost the whole of the roadstead could be seen. At the very moment when Jasper, issuing from the door of the Orange House, was passing under him in the street below, he cried to the others excitedly:

"That was Allen right enough! But where is his brig?"

Jasper heard these words with extraordinary loudness. The heavens rang with them as if calling him to account; for those were the very words Freya would have to use. It was an annihilating question; it struck his consciousness like a thunderbolt and brought a sudden night upon the chaos of his thoughts even as he walked. He did not check his pace. He went on in the darkness for another three strides, and then fell.

The good Mesman had to push on as far as the hospital before he found him. The doctor there talked of a slight heatstroke. Nothing very much. Out in three days . . . It must be admitted that the doctor was right. In three days, Jasper Allen came out of the hospital and became visible to the town—very visible indeed—and remained so for quite a long time; long enough to become almost one of the sights of the place; long enough to become disregarded at last; long enough for the tale of his haunting visibility to be remembered in the islands to this day.

The talk on the "front" and Jasper's appearance in the Orange House stand at the beginning of the famous *Bonito* case, and give a view of its two aspects—the practical and the psychological. The case for the courts and the case for compassion; that last terribly evident and yet obscure.

It has, you must understand, remained obscure even for that friend of mine who wrote me the letter mentioned in the very first lines of this narrative. He was one of those in Mr. Mesman's office, and accompanied that gentleman in his search for Jasper. His letter described to me the two aspects and some of the episodes of the case. Heemskirk's attitude was that of deep thankfulness for not having lost his own ship, and that was all. Haze over the land was his explanation of having got so close to Tamissa reef. He saved his ship, and for the rest he did not care. As to the fat gunner, he deposed simply that he thought at the time that he was acting for the best by letting go the tow-rope, but admitted that he was greatly confused by the suddenness of the emergency.

As a matter of fact, he had acted on very precise instructions from Heemskirk, to whom through several years' service together in the East he had become a sort of devoted henchman. What was most amazing in the detention of the *Bonito* was his story how, proceeding to take possession of the firearms as ordered, he discovered that there were no firearms on board. All he found in the fore-cabin was an empty rack for the proper number of eighteen rifles, but of the rifles themselves never a single one anywhere in the ship. The mate of the brig, who looked rather ill and behaved excitedly, as though he were perhaps a lunatic, wanted him to believe that Captain Allen knew nothing of this; that it was he, the mate, who had recently sold these rifles in the dead of night to a certain person up the river. In proof of this story he produced a bag of silver dollars and pressed it on his, the gunner's, acceptance. Then, suddenly flinging it down on the deck, he beat his own head with both his fists and started heaping shocking curses upon his own soul for an ungrateful wretch not fit to live.

All this the gunner reported at once to his commanding officer.

What Heemskirk intended by taking upon himself to detain the *Bonito* it is difficult to say, except that he meant to bring some trouble into the life of the man favored by Freya. He had been looking at Jasper with a desire to strike that man of kisses and embraces to the earth. The question was: How could he do it without giving himself away? But the report of the gunner created a serious case enough. Yet Allen had friends —and who could tell whether he wouldn't somehow succeed in wriggling out of it? The idea of simply towing the brig so much compromised on to the reef came to him while he was listening to the fat gunner in his cabin. There was but little risk of being disapproved now. And it should be made to appear an accident.

Going out on deck he had gloated upon his unconscious victim with such a sinister roll of his eyes, such a queerly pursed mouth, that Jasper could not help smiling. And the lieutenant had gone on the bridge, saying to himself:

"You wait! I shall spoil the taste of those sweet kisses for you. When you hear of Lieutenant Heemskirk in the future that name won't bring a smile on your lips, I swear. You are delivered into my hands."

And this possibility had come about without any planning, one could almost say naturally, as if events had mysteriously shaped themselves to fit the purposes of a dark passion. The most astute scheming could not have served Heemskirk better. It was given to him to taste a transcendental, an incredible perfection of vengeance; to strike a deadly blow into that hated person's heart, and to watch him afterwards walking about with the dagger in his breast.

For that is what the state of Jasper amounted to. He moved, acted, weary-eyed, keen-faced, lank and restless, with brusque movements and fierce gestures; he talked incessantly in a frenzied and fatigued voice, but within himself he knew that nothing would ever give him back the brig, just as nothing can heal a pierced heart. His soul, kept quiet in the stress of love by the unflinching Freya's influence, was like a still but overwound string. The shock had started it vibrating, and the string had snapped. He had waited for two years in a perfectly intoxicated confidence for a day that now would never come to a man disarmed for life by the loss of the brig, and, it seemed to him, made unfit for love to which he had no foothold to offer.

Day after day he would traverse the length of the town, follow the coast, and, reaching the point of land opposite that part of the reef on which his brig lay stranded, look steadily across the water at her beloved form, once the home of an exulting hope, and now, in her inclined, desolated immobility, towering above the lonely sea-horizon, a symbol of despair.

The crew had left her in due course in her own boats, which directly they reached the town were sequestrated by the harbor authorities. The vessel, too, was sequestrated pending proceedings; but these same authorities did not take the trouble to set a guard on board. For, indeed, what could move her from there? Nothing, unless a miracle; nothing, unless Jasper's eyes, fastened on her tensely for hours together, as though he hoped by the mere power of vision to draw her to his breast.

All this story, read in my friend's very chatty letter, dismayed me not a little. But it was really appalling to read his relation of how Schultz, the mate, went about everywhere affirming with desperate pertinacity that it was he alone who had sold the rifles. "I stole them," he protested. Of course, no one would believe him. My friend himself did not believe him, though he, of course, admired this self-sacrifice. But a good many people thought it was going too far to make oneself out a thief for the sake of a friend. Only, it was such an obvious lie, too, that it did not matter, perhaps.

I, who, in view of Schultz's psychology, knew how true that must be, admit that I was appalled. So this was how a perfidious destiny took advantage of a generous impulse! And I felt as though I were an accomplice in this perfidy, since I did to a certain extent encourage Jasper. Yet I had warned him as well.

"The man seemed to have gone crazy on this point," wrote my friend. "He went to Mesman with his story. He says that some rascally white man living among the natives up that river made him drunk with some gin one evening, and then jeered at him for never having any money. Then he, protesting to us that he was an honest man and must be believed, described himself as being a thief whenever he took a drop too much, and told us that he went on board and passed the rifles one by one without the slightest compunction to a canoe which came alongside that night, receiving ten dollars apiece for them.

"Next day he was ill with shame and grief, but had not the courage to confess his lapse to his benefactor. When the gunboat stopped the brig he felt ready to die with the apprehension of the consequences, and would have died happily, if he could have been able to bring the rifles back by the sacrifice of his life. He said nothing to Jasper, hoping that the brig would be released presently. When it turned out otherwise and his captain was detained on board the gunboat, he was ready to commit suicide from despair; only he thought it his duty to live in order to let the truth be known. "I am an honest man! I am an honest man!" he repeated, in a voice that brought tears to our eyes. "You must believe me when I tell you that I am a thief—a vile, low, cunning, sneaking thief as soon as I've had a glass or two. Take me somewhere where I may tell the truth on oath.""

"When we had at last convinced him that his story could be of no use to Jasper—for what Dutch court, having once got hold of an English trader, would accept such an explanation; and, indeed, how, when, where could one hope to find proofs of such a tale?—he made as if to tear his hair in handfuls, but, calming down, said: "Good-bye, then, gentlemen," and went out of the room so crushed that he seemed hardly able to put one foot before the other. That very night he committed suicide by cutting his throat in the house of a half-caste with whom he had been lodging since he came ashore from the wreck."

That throat, I thought with a shudder, which could produce the tender, persuasive, manly, but fascinating voice which had aroused Jasper's ready compassion and had secured Freya's sympathy! Who could ever have supposed such an end in store for the impossible, gentle Schultz, with his idiosyncrasy of naïve pilfering, so absurdly straightforward that, even in the people who had suffered from it, it aroused nothing more than a sort of amused exasperation? He was really impossible. His lot evidently should have been a half-starved, mysterious, but by no means tragic existence as a mild-eyed, inoffensive beachcomber on the fringe of native life. There are occasions when the irony of fate, which some people profess to discover in the working out of our lives, wears the aspect of crude and savage jesting.

I shook my head over the manes of Schultz, and went on with my friend's letter. It told me how the brig on the reef, looted by the natives from the coast villages, acquired gradually the lamentable aspect, the grey ghostliness of a wreck; while Jasper, fading daily into a mere shadow of a man, strode brusquely all along the "front" with horribly lively eyes and a faint, fixed smile on his lips, to spend the day on a lonely spit of sand looking eagerly at her, as though he had expected some shape on board to rise up and make some sort of sign to him over the decaying bulwarks. The Mesmans were taking care of him as far as it was possible. The *Bonito* case had been referred to Batavia, where no doubt it would fade away in a fog of official papers . . . It was heart-rending to read all this. That active and zealous officer, Lieutenant Heemskirk, his air of sullen, darkly pained self-importance not lightened by the approval of his action conveyed to him unofficially, had gone on to take up his station in the Molucas . . .

Then, at the end of the bulky, kindly meant epistle, dealing with the island news of half a year at least, my friend wrote: "A couple of months ago old Nelson turned up here, arriving by the mail-boat from Java. Came to see Mesman, it seems. A rather mysterious visit, and extraordinarily short, after coming all that way. He stayed just four days at the Orange House with apparently nothing in particular to do, and then caught the south-going steamer for the Straits. I remember people saying at one time that Allen was rather sweet on old Nelson's daughter, the girl that was brought up by Mrs. Harley and then went to live with him at the Seven Isles group. Surely you remember old Nelson—"

Remember old Nelson! Rather!

The letter went on to inform me further that old Nelson, at least, remembered me, since some time after his flying visit to Makassar he had written to the Mesmans asking for my address in London.

That old Nelson (or Nielsen), the note of whose personality was a profound, echoless irresponsiveness to everything around him, should wish to write, or find anything to write about to anybody, was in itself a cause for no small wonder. And to me, of all people? I waited with uneasy impatience for whatever disclosure could come from that naturally benighted intelligence, but my impatience had time to wear out before my eyes beheld old Nelson's trembling, painfully formed handwriting, senile and childish at the same time, on an envelope bearing a penny stamp and the postal mark of the Notting Hill office. I delayed opening it in order to pay the tribute of astonishment due to the event by flinging my hands above my head. So he had come home to England, to be definitely Nelson; or else was on his way home to Denmark, where he would revert for ever to his original Nielsen! But old Nelson (or Nielsen) out of the tropics seemed unthinkable. And yet he was there, asking me to call.

His address was at a boarding-house in one of those Bayswater squares, once of leisure, which nowadays are reduced to earning their living. Somebody had recommended him there. I started to call on him on one of those January days in London, one of those wintry days composed of the four devilish elements, cold, wet, mud, and grime, combined with a particular stickiness of atmosphere that clings like an unclean garment to one's very soul. Yet on approaching his abode I saw, like a flicker far behind the soiled veil of the four elements, the wearisome and splendid glitter of a blue sea with the Seven Islets like minute specks swimming in my eye, the high red roof of the bungalow crowning the very smallest of them all. This visual reminiscence was profoundly disturbing. I knocked at the door with a faltering hand.

Old Nelson (or Nielsen) got up from the table at which he was sitting with a shabby pocket-book full of papers before him. He took off his spectacles before shaking hands. For a moment neither of us said a word; then, noticing me looking round somewhat expectantly, he murmured some words, of which I caught only "daughter" and "Hong Kong," cast his eyes down and sighed.

His mustache, sticking all ways out, as of yore, was quite white now. His old cheeks were softly rounded, with some color in them; strangely enough, that something childlike always noticeable in the general contour of his physiognomy had become much more marked. Like his handwriting, he looked childish and senile. He showed his age most in his unintelligently furrowed, anxious forehead and in his round, innocent eyes, which appeared to me weak and blinking and watery; or was it that they were full of tears? . . .

To discover old Nelson fully informed upon any matter whatever was a new experience. And after the first awkwardness had worn off he talked freely, with, now and then, a question to start him going whenever he lapsed into silence, which he would do suddenly, clasping his hands on his waistcoat in an attitude which would recall to me the east verandah, where he used to sit talking quietly and puffing out his cheeks in what seemed now old, very old days. He talked in a reasonable, somewhat anxious tone.

"No, no. We did not know anything for weeks. Out of the way like that, we couldn't, of course. No mail service to the Seven Isles. But one day I ran over to Banka in my big sailing-boat to see whether there were any letters, and saw a Dutch paper. But it looked only like a bit of marine news: English brig *Bonito* gone ashore outside Makassar roads. That was all. I took the paper home with me and showed it to her. "I will never forgive him!" she cries with her old spirit. "My dear," I said, "you are a sensible girl. The best man may lose a ship. But what about your health?" I was beginning to be frightened at her looks. She would not let me talk even of going to Singapore before. But, really, such a sensible girl couldn't keep on objecting for ever. 'Do what you like, papa,' she says. Rather a job, that. Had to catch a steamer at sea, but I got her over all right. There, doctors, of course. Fever. Anaemia. Put her to bed. Two or three women very kind to her. Naturally in our papers the whole story came out before long. She reads it to the end, lying on the couch; then hands the newspaper back to me, whispers 'Heemskirk,' and goes off into a faint."

He blinked at me for quite a long time, his eyes running full of tears again.

"Next day," he began, without any emotion in his voice, "she felt stronger, and we had a long talk. She told me everything."

Here old Nelson, with his eyes cast down, gave me the whole story of the Heemskirk episode in Freya's words; then went on in his rather jerky utterance, and looking up innocently:

" 'My dear,' I said, 'you have behaved in the main like a sensible girl.' 'I have been horrid,' she cries, 'and he is breaking his heart over there.' Well, she was too sensible not to see she wasn't in a state to travel. But I went. She told me to go. She was being looked after very well. Anaemia. Getting better, they said."

He paused.

"You did see him?" I murmured.

"Oh, yes; I did see him," he started again, talking in that reasonable voice as though he were arguing a point. "I did see him. I came upon him. Eyes sunk an inch into his head; nothing but skin on the bones of his face, a skeleton in dirty white clothes. That's what he looked like. How Freya . . . But she never did—not really. He was sitting there, the only live thing for miles along the coast, on a drift-log washed up on the shore. They had clipped his hair in the hospital, and it had not grown again. He stared, holding his chin in his hand, and with nothing on the sea between him and the sky but that wreck. When I came up to him he just moved his head a bit. 'Is that you, old man?' says he—like that.

"If you had seen him you would have understood at once how impossible it was for Freya to have ever loved that man. Well, well. I don't say. She might have—something. She was lonely, you know. But really to go away with him! Never! Madness. She was too sensible . . . I began to reproach him gently. And by and by he turns on me. 'Write to you! What about? Come to her! What with? If I had been a man I would have carried her off, but she made a child, a happy child, of me. Tell her that the day the only thing I had belonging to me in the world perished on this reef I discovered that I had no power over her . . . Has she come here with you?' he shouts, blazing at me suddenly with his hollow eyes. I shook my head. Come with me, indeed! Anaemia! 'Aha! You see? Go away, then, old man, and leave me alone here with that ghost,' he says, jerking his head at the wreck of his brig.

"Mad! It was getting dusk. I did not care to stop any longer all by myself with that man in that lonely place. I was not going to tell him of Freya's illness. Anaemia! What was the good? Mad! And what sort of husband would he have made, anyhow, for a sensible girl like Freya? Why, even my little property I could not have left them. The Dutch authorities would never have allowed an Englishman to settle there. It was not sold then. My man Mahmat, you know, was looking after it for me. Later on I let it go for a tenth of its value to a Dutch half-caste. But never mind. It was nothing to me then. Yes; I went away from him. I caught the return mail-boat. I told everything to Freya. 'He's mad,' I said; 'and, my dear, the only thing he loved was his brig.'

" 'Perhaps,' she says to herself, looking straight away—her eyes were nearly as hollow as his—'perhaps it is true. Yes! I would never allow him any power over me.' "

Old Nelson paused. I sat fascinated, and feeling a little cold in that room with a blazing fire.

"So you see," he continued, "she never really cared for him. Much too sensible. I took her away to Hong Kong. Change of climate, they said. Oh, these doctors! My God! Winter time! There came ten days of cold mists and wind and rain. Pneumonia. But look here! We talked a lot together. Days and evenings. Who else had she? . . . She talked a lot to me, my own girl. Sometimes she would laugh a little. Look at me and laugh a little—"

I shuddered. He looked up vaguely, with a childish, puzzled moodiness.

"She would say: 'I did not really mean to be a bad daughter to you, papa.' And I would say: 'Of course, my dear. You could not have meant it.' She would lie quiet and then say: 'I wonder?' And sometimes, 'I've been really a coward,' she would tell me. You know, sick people they say things. And so she would say too: 'I've been conceited, headstrong, capricious. I sought my own gratification. I was selfish or afraid.' . . . But sick people, you know, they say anything. And once, after lying silent almost all day, she said: 'Yes; perhaps, when the day came I would not have gone. Perhaps! I don't know,' she cried. 'Draw the curtain, papa. Shut the sea out. It reproaches me with my folly.' " He gasped and paused.

"So you see," he went on in a murmur. "Very ill, very ill indeed. Pneumonia. Very sudden." He pointed his finger at the carpet, while the thought of the poor girl, vanquished in her struggle with three men's absurdities, and coming at last to doubt her own self, held me in a very anguish of pity.

"You see yourself," he began again in a downcast manner. "She could not have really . . . She mentioned you several times. Good friend. Sensible man. So I wanted to tell you myself—let you know the truth. A fellow like that! How could it be? She was lonely. And perhaps for a while . . . Mere nothing. There could never have been a question of love for my Freya—such a sensible girl—"

"Man!" I cried, rising upon him wrathfully, "don't you see that she died of it?"

He got up too. "No! no!" he stammered, as if angry. "The doctors! Pneumonia. Low state. The inflammation of the . . . They told me. Pneu—"

He did not finish the word. It ended in a sob. He flung his arms out in a gesture of despair, giving up his ghastly pretense with a low, heartrending cry:

"And I thought that she was so sensible!"

Novels

f the dozen novels Conrad wrote, the three printed here in their entirety represent the full scope and power of his writing, as well as the range of his interests.

The Nigger of the "Narcissus" (1897) deals with his years at sea and the cultural clash between the Western powers and the lands they colonized. It was initially serialized in *Blackwood's* magazine and, though it had only a modest critical and popular reception, was widely admired by writers from H. G. Wells to Stephen Crane.

Lord Jim (1900), probably his best and best-loved work, examines the nature of courage and cowardice in an exotic Asian setting. Also serialized in *Blackwood's*, it was his most successful work to that date, and still stands as his finest long work.

Nostromo (1904), a thriller set in Latin America, is a masterpiece of adventure and political insight. Initially dismissed by critics as facile and gratuitous, it was also ignored by the public. Conrad was bitterly disappointed by its reception, but by the end of his life, *Nostromo* had come to be recognized as a classic work of political and adventure literature.

THE NIGGER OF THE "NARCISSUS"

To My Readers in America

rom that evening when James Wait joined the ship—late for the muster of the crew—to the moment when he left us in the open sea, shrouded in sailcloth, through the open port, I had much to do with him. He was in my watch. A negro in a British forecastle is a lonely being. He has no chums. Yet James Wait, afraid of death and making her his accomplice, was an impostor of some character—mastering our compassion, scornful of our sentimentalism, triumphing over our suspicions.

But in the book he is nothing; he is merely the center of the ship's collective psychology and the pivot of the action. Yet he, who in the family circle and amongst my friends is familiarly referred to as the Nigger, remains very precious to me. For the book written round him is not the sort of thing that can be attempted more than once in a lifetime. It is the book by which, not as a novelist perhaps, but as an artist striving for the utmost sincerity of expression, I am willing to stand or fall. Its pages are the tribute of my unalterable and profound affection for the ships, the seamen, the winds and the great sea—the moulders of my youth, the companions of the best years of my life.

After writing the last words of that book, in the revulsion of feeling before the accomplished task, I understood that I had done with the sea, and that henceforth I had to be a writer. And almost without laying down the pen I wrote a preface, trying to express the spirit in which I was entering on the task of my new life. That preface on advice (which I now think was wrong) was never published with the book. But the late W. E. Henley, who had the courage at that time (1897) to serialize my "Nigger" in the *New Review* judged it worthy to be printed as an afterword at the end of the last installment of the tale.

I am glad that this book which means so much to me is coming out again, under its proper title of "The Nigger of the *Narcissus*" and under the auspices of my good friends and publishers Doubleday & Co., into the light of publicity.

Half the span of a generation has passed since W. E. Henley, after reading two chapters, sent me a verbal message: "Tell Conrad that if the rest is up to the sample it shall certainly come out in the *New Review*." The most gratifying recollection of my writer's life!

And here is the Suppressed Preface.

J. C.
1914

To Edward Garnett,

This Tale About My Friends of the Sea

. . . My Lord in his discourse discovered

a great deal of love to this ship.

Diary of Samuel Pepys

Mr. Baker, chief mate of the ship *Narcissus,* stepped in one stride out of his lighted cabin into the darkness of the quarter-deck. Above his head, on the break of the poop, the night-watchman rang a double stroke. It was nine o'clock. Mr. Baker, speaking up to the man above him, asked:—"Are all the hands aboard, Knowles?"

The man limped down the ladder, then said reflectively:—"I think so, sir. All our old chaps are there, and a lot of new men has come. . . . They must be all there."

"Tell the boatswain to send all hands aft," went on Mr. Baker; "and tell one of the youngsters to bring a good lamp here. I want to muster our crowd."

The main deck was dark aft, but halfway from forward, through the open doors of the forecastle, two streaks of brilliant light cut the shadow of the quiet night that lay upon the ship. A hum of voices was heard there, while port and starboard, in the illuminated doorways, silhouettes of moving men appeared for a moment, very black, without relief, like figures cut out of sheet tin. The ship was ready for sea. The carpenter had driven in the last wedge of the main-hatch battens, and, throwing down his maul, had wiped his face with great deliberation, just on the stroke of five. The decks had been swept, the windlass oiled and made ready to heave up the anchor; the big tow-rope lay in long bights along one side of the main deck, with one end carried up and hung over the bows, in readiness for the tug that would come paddling and hissing noisily, hot and smoky, in the limpid, cool quietness of the early morning. The captain was ashore, where he had been engaging some new hands to make up his full crew; and, the work of the day over, the ship's officers had kept out of the way, glad of a little breathing-time. Soon after dark the few liberty-men and the new hands began to arrive in shore-boats rowed by white-clad Asiatics, who clamored fiercely for payment before coming alongside the gangway-ladder. The feverish and shrill babble of Eastern language struggled against the masterful tones of tipsy seamen, who argued

233

against brazen claims and dishonest hopes by profane shouts. The resplendent and bestarred peace of the East was torn into squalid tatters by howls of rage and shrieks of lament raised over sums ranging from five annas to half a rupee; and every soul afloat in Bombay Harbor became aware that the new hands were joining the *Narcissus.*

Gradually the distracting noise had subsided. The boats came no longer in splashing clusters of three or four together, but dropped alongside singly, in a subdued buzz of expostulation cut short by a "Not a pice more! You go to the devil!" from some man staggering up the accommodation-ladder—a dark figure, with a long bag poised on the shoulder. In the forecastle the newcomers, upright and swaying amongst corded boxes and bundles of bedding, made friends with the old hands, who sat one above another in the two tiers of bunks, gazing at their future shipmates with glances critical but friendly. The two forecastle lamps were turned up high, and shed an intense hard glare; shore-going round hats were pushed far on the backs of heads, or rolled about on the deck amongst the chain cables; white collars, undone, stuck out on each side of red faces; big arms in white sleeves gesticulated; the growling voices hummed steady amongst bursts of laughter and hoarse calls. "Here, sonny, take that bunk! . . . Don't you do it! . . . What's your last ship? . . . I know her. . . . Three years ago, in Puget Sound. . . . This here berth leaks, I tell you! . . . Come on; give us a chance to swing that chest! . . . Did you bring a bottle, any of you shore toffs? . . . Give us a bit of 'baccy. . . . I know her; her skipper drank himself to death. . . . He was a dandy boy! . . . Liked his lotion inside, he did! . . . No! . . . Hold your row, you chaps! . . . I tell you, you came on board a hooker, where they get their money's worth out of poor Jack by——! . . ."

A little fellow, called Craik and nicknamed Belfast, abused the ship violently, romancing on principle, just to give the new hands something to think over. Archie, sitting aslant on his sea-chest, kept his knees out of the way, and pushed the needle steadily through a white patch in a pair of blue trousers. Men in black jackets and stand-up collars, mixed with men bare-footed, bare-armed, with colored shirts open on hairy chests, pushed against one another in the middle of the forecastle. The group swayed, reeled, turning upon itself with the motion of a scrimmage, in a haze of tobacco smoke. All were speaking together, swearing at every second word. A Russian Finn, wearing a yellow shirt with pink stripes, stared upwards, dreamy-eyed, from under a mop of tumbled hair. Two young giants with smooth, baby faces—two Scandinavians—helped each other to spread their bedding, silent, and smiling placidly at the tempest of good-humored and meaningless curses. Old Singleton, the oldest able seaman in the ship, sat apart on the deck right under the lamps, stripped to the waist, tattooed like a cannibal chief all over his powerful chest and enormous biceps. Between the blue and red patterns his white skin gleamed like satin; his bare back was propped against the heel of the bowsprit, and he held a book at arm's length before his big, sunburnt face. With his spectacles and a venerable white beard, he resembled a learned and savage patriarch, the incarnation of barbarian wisdom serene in the blasphemous turmoil of the world. He was intensely absorbed, and as he turned the pages an expression of grave surprise would pass over his rugged features. He was reading

"Pelham." The popularity of Bulwer-Lytton in the forecastles of Southern-going ships is a wonderful and bizarre phenomenon. What ideas do his polished and so curiously insincere sentences awaken in the simple minds of the big children who people those dark and wandering places of the earth? What meaning can their rough, inexperienced souls find in the elegant verbiage of his pages? What excitement?—what forgetfulness? —what appeasement? Mystery! Is it the fascination of the incomprehensible?—is it the charm of the impossible? Or are those beings who exist beyond the pale of life stirred by his tales as by an enigmatical disclosure of a resplendent world that exists within the frontier of infamy and filth, within that border of dirt and hunger, of misery and dissipation, that comes down on all sides to the water's edge of the incorruptible ocean, and is the only thing they know of life, the only thing they see of surrounding land—those life-long prisoners of the sea? Mystery!

Singleton, who had sailed to the southward since the age of twelve, who in the last forty-five years had lived (as we had calculated from his papers) no more than forty months ashore—old Singleton, who boasted, with the mild composure of long years well spent, that generally from the day he was paid off from one ship till the day he shipped in another he seldom was in a condition to distinguish daylight—old Singleton sat unmoved in the clash of voices and cries, spelling through "Pelham" with slow labor, and lost in an absorption profound enough to resemble a trance. He breathed regularly. Every time he turned the book in his enormous and blackened hands the muscles of his big white arms rolled slightly under the smooth skin. Hidden by the white moustache, his lips, stained with tobacco-juice that trickled down the long beard, moved in inward whisper. His bleared eyes gazed fixedly from behind the glitter of black-rimmed glasses. Opposite to him, and on a level with his face, the ship's cat sat on the barrel of the windlass in the pose of a crouching chimera, blinking its green eyes at its old friend. It seemed to meditate a leap on to the old man's lap over the bent back of the ordinary seaman who sat at Singleton's feet. Young Charley was lean and long-necked. The ridge of his backbone made a chain of small hills under the old shirt. His face of a street-boy—a face precocious, sagacious, and ironic, with deep downward folds on each side of the thin, wide mouth—hung low over his bony knees. He was learning to make a lanyard knot with a bit of an old rope. Small drops of perspiration stood out on his bulging forehead; he sniffed strongly from time to time, glancing out of the corners of his restless eyes at the old seaman, who took no notice of the puzzled youngster muttering at his work.

The noise increased. Little Belfast seemed, in the heavy heat of the forecastle, to boil with facetious fury. His eyes danced; in the crimson of his face, comical as a mask, the mouth yawned black, with strange grimaces. Facing him, a half-undressed man held his sides, and, throwing his head back, laughed with wet eyelashes. Others stared with amazed eyes. Men sitting doubled up in the upper bunks smoked short pipes, swinging bare brown feet above the heads of those who, sprawling below on sea-chests, listened, smiling stupidly or scornfully. Over the white rims of berths stuck out heads with blinking eyes; but the bodies were lost in the gloom of those places, that resembled narrow niches for coffins in a whitewashed and lighted mortuary. Voices buzzed louder. Archie, with compressed lips, drew himself in, seemed to shrink into a smaller space, and sewed steadily, industrious and dumb. Belfast shrieked like an inspired Dervish:—". . . So I seez to him, boys, seez I, 'Beggin' yer pardon, sorr,' seez I to that second mate of that steamer—'beggin' your-r-r pardon, sorr, the Board of Trade must 'ave been drunk when they granted you your certificate!' 'What do you say, you—!' seez he, comin' at me like a mad bull . . . all in his white clothes; and I up with my tar-pot and capsizes it all over his blamed lovely face and his lovely jacket. . . . 'Take that!' seez I. 'I am a sailor, anyhow, you nosing, skipper-licking, useless, sooperfloos bridge-stanchion, you! That's the kind of man I am!' shouts I. . . . You should have seed him skip, boys! Drowned, blind with tar, he was! So . . ."

"Don't 'ee believe him! He never upset no tar; I was there!" shouted somebody. The two Norwegians sat on a chest side by side, alike and placid, resembling a pair of love-birds on a perch, and with round eyes stared innocently; but the Russian Finn, in the racket of explosive shouts and rolling laughter, remained motionless, limp and dull, like a deaf man without a backbone. Near him Archie smiled at his needle. A broad-chested, slow-eyed newcomer spoke deliberately to Belfast during an exhausted lull in the noise:—"I wonder any of the mates here are alive yet with such a chap as you on board! I concloode they ain't that bad now, if you had the taming of them, sonny."

"Not bad! Not bad!" screamed Belfast. "If it wasn't for us sticking together. . . . Not bad! They ain't never bad when they ain't got a chawnce, blast their black 'arts. . . ." He foamed, whirling his arms, then suddenly grinned and, taking a tablet of black tobacco out of his pocket, bit a piece off with a funny show of ferocity. Another new hand—a man with shifty eyes and a yellow hatchet face, who had been listening open-mouthed in the shadow of the midship locker—observed in a squeaky voice:—"Well, it's a 'omeward trip, anyhow. Bad or good, I can do it on my 'ed—s'long as I get 'ome. And I can look after my rights! I will show 'em!" All the heads turned towards him. Only the ordinary seaman and the cat took no notice. He stood with arms akimbo, a little fellow with white eyelashes. He looked as if he had known all the degradations and all the furies. He looked as if he had been cuffed, kicked, rolled in the mud; he looked as if he had been scratched, spat upon, pelted with unmentionable filth . . . and he smiled with a sense of security at the faces around. His ears were bending down under the weight of his battered felt hat. The torn tails of his black coat flapped in fringes about the calves of his legs. He unbuttoned the only two buttons that remained and every one saw that he had no shirt under it. It was his deserved misfortune that those rags which nobody could possibly be supposed to own looked on him as if they had been stolen. His neck was long and thin; his eyelids were red; rare hairs hung about his jaws; his shoulders were peaked and drooped like the broken wings of a bird; all his left side was caked with mud which showed that he had lately slept in a wet ditch. He had saved his inefficient carcass from violent destruction by running away from an American ship where, in a moment of forgetful folly, he had dared to engage himself; and he had knocked about for a fortnight ashore in the native quarter, cadging for drinks, starving, sleeping on rubbish-heaps, wandering in sun-shine: a startling visitor from a world of nightmares. He stood repulsive and smiling in the sudden silence. This clean white forecastle was his refuge; the place where he could be lazy; where he could wallow, and lie and eat—and curse the food he ate; where he could display his talents for shirking work, for cheating, for cadging; where he could find surely some one to wheedle and some one to bully—and where he would be paid for doing all this. They all knew him. Is there a spot on earth where such a man is unknown, an ominous survival testifying to the eternal fitness of lies and impudence? A taciturn long-armed shellback, with hooked fingers, who had been lying on his back smoking, turned in his bed to examine him dispassionately, then, over his head, sent a long jet of clear saliva towards the door. They all knew him! He was the man that cannot steer, that cannot splice, that dodges the work on dark nights; that, aloft, holds on frantically with both arms and legs, and swears at the wind, the sleet, the darkness; the man who curses the sea while others work. The man who is the last out and the first in when all hands are called. The man who can't do most things and won't do the rest. The pet of philanthropists and self-seeking landlubbers. The sympathetic and deserving creature that knows all about his rights, but knows nothing of courage, of endurance, and of the unexpressed faith, of the unspoken loyalty that knits together a ship's company. The independent offspring of the ignoble freedom of the slums full of disdain and hate for the austere servitude of the sea.

Some one cried at him: "What's your name?"—"Donkin," he said, looking round with cheerful effrontery.—"What are you?" asked another voice.—"Why, a sailor like you, old man," he replied, in a tone that meant to be hearty but was impudent.— "Blamme if you don't look a blamed sight worse than a broken-down fireman," was the comment in a convinced mutter. Charley lifted his head and piped in a cheeky voice: "He is a man and a sailor"—then wiping his nose with the back of his hand bent down industriously over his bit of rope. A few laughed. Others stared doubtfully. The ragged newcomer was indignant—"That's a fine way to welcome a chap into a fo'c'sle," he snarled. "Are you men or a lot of 'artless cannybals?"—"Don't take your shirt off for a word, shipmate," called out Belfast, jumping up in front, fiery, menacing, and friendly at the same time.—"Is that 'ere bloke blind?" asked the indomitable scarecrow, looking right and left with affected surprise. "Can't 'ee see I 'aven't got no shirt?"

He held both his arms out crosswise and shook the rags that hung over his bones with dramatic effect.

" 'Cos why?" he continued very loud. "The bloody Yankees been tryin' to jump my guts out 'cos I stood up for my rights like a good 'un. I am an Englishman, I am. They set upon me an' I 'ad to run. That's why. A'n't yer never seed a man 'ard up? Yah! What kind of blamed ship is this? I'm dead broke. I 'aven't got nothink. No bag, no bed, no blanket, no shirt—not a bloomin' rag but what I stand in. But I 'ad the 'art to stand up agin' them Yankees. 'As any of you 'art enough to spare a pair of old pants for a chum?"

He knew how to conquer the naïve instincts of that crowd. In a moment they gave him their compassion, jocularly, contemptuously, or surlily; and at first it took the shape of a blanket thrown at him as he stood there with the white skin of his limbs showing his human kinship through the black fantasy of his rags. Then a pair of old shoes fell at his muddy feet. With a cry:—"From under," a rolled-up pair of canvas trousers, heavy with tar stains, struck him on the shoulder. The gust of their benevolence sent a wave of sentimental pity through their doubting hearts. They were touched by their own readiness to alleviate a shipmate's misery. Voices cried:—"We will fit you out, old man." Murmurs: "Never seed seech a hard case. . . . Poor beggar. . . . I've got an old singlet. . . . Will that be of any use to you? . . . Take it, matey. . . ." Those friendly murmurs filled the forecastle. He pawed around with his naked foot, gathering the things in a heap and looked about for more. Unemotional Archie perfunctorily contributed to the pile an old cloth cap with the peak torn off. Old Singleton, lost in the serene regions of fiction, read on unheeding. Charley, pitiless with the wisdom of youth, squeaked:—"If you want brass buttons for your new uniforms I've got two for you." The filthy object of universal charity shook his fist at the youngster.—"I'll make you keep this 'ere fo'c'sle clean, young feller," he snarled viciously. "Never you fear. I will learn you to be civil to an able seaman, you ignerant ass." He glared harmfully, but saw Singleton shut his book, and his little beady eyes began to roam from berth to berth.—"Take that bunk by the door there— it's pretty fair," suggested Belfast. So advised, he gathered the gifts at his feet, pressed them in a bundle against his breast, then looked cautiously at the Russian Finn, who stood on one side with an unconscious gaze, contemplating, perhaps, one of those weird visions that haunt the men of his race.—"Get out of my road, Dutchy," said the victim of Yankee brutality. The Finn did not move—did not hear. "Get out, blast ye," shouted the other, shoving him aside with his elbow. "Get out, you blanked deaf and dumb fool. Get out." The man staggered, recovered himself, and gazed at the speaker in silence.—"Those damned furriners should be kept under," opined the amiable Donkin to the forecastle. "If you don't teach em their place they put on you like anythink." He flung all his worldly possessions into the empty bedplace, gauged with another shrewd look the risks of the proceeding, then leaped up to the Finn, who stood pensive and dull.—"I'll teach you to swell around," he yelled. "I'll plug your eyes for you, you blooming squarehead." Most of the men were now in their bunks and the two had the forecastle clear to themselves. The development of the destitute Donkin aroused interest. He danced all in tatters before the amazed Finn, squaring from a distance at the heavy, unmoved face. One or two men cried encouragingly: "Go it, Whitechapel!" settling themselves luxuriously in their beds to survey the fight. Others shouted: "Shut yer row! . . . Go an' put yer 'ed in a bag! . . ." The hubbub was recommencing. Suddenly many heavy blows struck with a handspike on the deck above boomed like discharges of small cannon through the forecastle. Then the boatswain's voice rose outside the door with an authoritative note in its drawl:—"D'ye hear, below there? Lay aft! Lay aft to muster all hands!"

There was a moment of surprised stillness. Then the forecastle floor disappeared under men whose bare feet flopped on the planks as they sprang clear out of their berths. Caps were rooted for amongst tumbled blankets. Some, yawning, buttoned waistbands. Half-smoked pipes were knocked hurriedly against woodwork and stuffed under pillows. Voices growled:—"What's up? . . . Is there no rest for us?" Donkin yelped:—"If that's the way of this ship, we'll 'ave to change all that. . . . You leave me alone. . . . I will soon. . . ." None of the crowd noticed him. They were lurching in twos and threes through the doors, after the manner of merchant Jacks who cannot go out of a door fairly, like mere landsmen. The votary of change followed them. Singleton, struggling into his jacket, came last, tall and fatherly, bearing high his head of a weather-beaten sage on the body of an old athlete. Only Charley remained alone in the white glare of the empty place, sitting between the two rows of iron links that stretched into the narrow gloom forward. He pulled hard at the strands in a hurried endeavor to finish his knot. Suddenly he started up, flung the rope at the cat, and skipped after the black tom which went off leaping sedately over chain compressors, with its tail carried stiff and upright, like a small flagpole.

Outside the glare of the steaming forecastle the serene purity of the night enveloped the seamen with its soothing breath, with its tepid breath flowing under the stars that hung countless above the mastheads in a thin cloud of luminous dust. On the town side the blackness of the water was streaked with trails of light which undulated gently on slight ripples, similar to filaments that float rooted to the shore. Rows of other lights stood away in straight lines as if drawn up on parade between towering buildings; but on the other side of the harbor sombre hills arched high their black spines, on which, here and there, the point of a star resembled a spark fallen from the sky. Far off, Byculla way, the electric lamps at the dock gates shone on the end of lofty standards with a glow blinding and frigid like captive ghosts of some evil moons. Scattered all over the dark polish of the roadstead, the ships at anchor floated in perfect stillness under the feeble gleam of their riding-lights, looming up, opaque and bulky, like strange and monumental structures abandoned by men to an everlasting repose.

Before the cabin door Mr. Baker was mustering the crew. As they stumbled and lurched along past the mainmast, they could see aft his round, broad face with a white paper before it, and beside his shoulder the sleepy head, with dropped eyelids, of the boy, who held, suspended at the end of his raised arm, the luminous globe of a lamp. Even before the shuffle of naked soles had ceased along the decks, the mate began to call over the names. He called distinctly in a serious tone befitting this roll-call to unquiet loneliness, to inglorious and obscure struggle, or to the more trying endurance of small privations and wearisome duties. As the chief mate read out a name, one of the men would answer: "Yes, sir!" or "Here!" and, detaching himself from the shadowy mob of heads visible above the blackness of starboard bulwarks, would step barefooted into the circle of light, and in two noiseless strides pass into the shadows on the port side of the quarter-deck. They answered in divers tones: in thick mutters, in clear, ringing voices; and some, as if the whole thing had been an outrage on their feelings, used an injured intonation: for discipline is not ceremonious in merchant ships, where the sense of hierarchy is weak, and where all feel themselves equal before the unconcerned immensity of the sea and the exacting appeal of the work.

Mr. Baker read on steadily:—"Hanse—Campbell—Smith—Wamibo. Now, then,

Wamibo. Why don't you answer? Always got to call your name twice." The Finn emitted at last an uncouth grunt, and, stepping out, passed through the patch of light, weird and gaudy, with the face of a man marching through a dream. The mate went on faster:—"Craik—Singleton—Donkin. . . . O Lord!" he involuntarily ejaculated as the incredibly dilapidated figure appeared in the light. It stopped; it uncovered pale gums and long, upper teeth in a malevolent grin.—"Is there anythink wrong with me, Mister Mate?" it asked, with a flavor of insolence in the forced simplicity of its tone. On both sides of the deck subdued titters were heard.—"That'll do. Go over," growled Mr. Baker, fixing the new hand with steady blue eyes. And Donkin vanished suddenly out of the light into the dark group of mustered men, to be slapped on the back and to hear flattering whispers:—"He ain't afeard, he'll give sport to 'em, see if he don't. . . . Reg'lar Punch and Judy show. . . . Did ye see the mate start at him? . . . Well! Damme, if I ever! . . ."

The last man had gone over, and there was a moment of silence while the mate peered at his list.—"Sixteen, seventeen," he muttered. "I am one hand short, bo'sun," he said aloud. The big west-countryman at his elbow, swarthy and bearded like a gigantic Spaniard, said in a rumbling bass:—"There's no one left forward, sir. I had a look round. He ain't aboard, but he may turn up before daylight."—"Ay. He may or he may not," commented the mate, "can't make out that last name. It's all a smudge. . . . That will do, men. Go below."

The distinct and motionless group stirred, broke up, began to move forward.

"Wait!" cried a deep, ringing voice.

All stood still. Mr. Baker, who had turned away yawning, spun round open-mouthed. At last, furious, he blurted out:—"What's this? Who said 'Wait'? What . . ."

But he saw a tall figure standing on the rail. It came down and pushed through the crowd, marching with a heavy tread towards the light on the quarter-deck. Then again the sonorous voice said with insistence:—"Wait!" The lamplight lit up the man's body. He was tall. His head was away up in the shadows of lifeboats that stood on skids above the deck. The whites of his eyes and his teeth gleamed distinctly, but the face was indistinguishable. His hands were big and seemed gloved.

Mr. Baker advanced intrepidly. "Who are you? How dare you . . ." he began.

The boy, amazed like the rest, raised the light to the man's face. It was black. A surprised hum—a faint hum that sounded like the suppressed mutter of the word "Nigger"—ran along the deck and escaped out into the night. The nigger seemed not to hear. He balanced himself where he stood in a swagger that marked time. After a moment he said calmly:—"My name is Wait—James Wait."

"Oh!" said Mr. Baker. Then, after a few seconds of smouldering silence, his temper blazed out. "Ah! Your name is Wait. What of that? What do you want? What do you mean, coming shouting here?"

The nigger was calm, cool, towering, superb. The men had approached and stood behind him in a body. He overtopped the tallest by half a head. He said: "I belong to the ship." He enunciated distinctly, with soft precision. The deep, rolling tones of his

voice filled the deck without effort. He was naturally scornful, unaffectedly condescending, as if from his height of six foot three he had surveyed all the vastness of
human folly and had made up his mind not to be too hard on it. He went on:—"The
captain shipped me this morning. I couldn't get aboard sooner. I saw you all aft as I
came up the ladder, and could see directly you were mustering the crew. Naturally I
called out my name. I thought you had it on your list, and would understand. You
misapprehended." He stopped short. The folly around him was confounded. He was
right as ever, and as ever ready to forgive. The disdainful tones had ceased, and,
breathing heavily, he stood still, surrounded by all these white men. He held his head
up in the glare of the lamp—a head vigorously modeled into deep shadows and
shining lights—a head powerful and misshapen with a tormented and flattened face—
a face pathetic and brutal: the tragic, the mysterious, the repulsive mask of a nigger's
soul.

Mr. Baker, recovering his composure, looked at the paper close. "Oh, yes; that's so.
All right, Wait. Take your gear forward," he said.

Suddenly the nigger's eyes rolled wildly, became all whites. He put his hand to his
side and coughed twice, a cough metallic, hollow, and tremendously loud; it resounded
like two explosions in a vault; the dome of the sky rang to it, and the iron plates of the
ship's bulwarks seemed to vibrate in unison, then he marched off forward with the
others. The officers lingering by the cabin door could hear him say: "Won't some of
you chaps lend a hand with my dunnage? I've got a chest and a bag." The words,
spoken sonorously, with an even intonation, were heard all over the ship, and the
question was put in a manner that made refusal impossible. The short, quick shuffle of
men carrying something heavy went away forward, but the tall figure of the nigger
lingered by the main hatch in a knot of smaller shapes. Again he was heard asking: "Is
your cook a colored gentleman?" Then a disappointed and disapproving "Ah! h'm!"
was his comment upon the information that the cook happened to be a mere white
man. Yet, as they went all together towards the forecastle, he condescended to put his
head through the galley door and boom out inside a magnificent "Good evening,
doctor!" that made all the saucepans ring. In the dim light the cook dozed on the coal
locker in front of the captain's supper. He jumped up as if he had been cut with a
whip, and dashed wildly on deck to see the backs of several men going away laughing.
Afterwards, when talking about that voyage, he used to say:—"The poor fellow had
scared me. I thought I had seen the devil." The cook had been seven years in the ship
with the same captain. He was a serious-minded man with a wife and three children,
whose society he enjoyed on an average one month out of twelve. When on shore he
took his family to church twice every Sunday. At sea he went to sleep every evening
with his lamp turned up full, a pipe in his mouth, and an open Bible in his hand.
Some one had always to go during the night to put out the light, take the book from
his hand, and the pipe from between his teeth. "For"—Belfast used to say, irritated
and complaining—"some night, you stupid cookie, you'll swallow your old clay, and
we will have no cook."—"Ah! sonny, I am ready for my Maker's call . . . wish you
all were," the other would answer with a benign serenity that was altogether imbecile

and touching. Belfast outside the galley door danced with vexation. "You holy fool! I don't want you to die," he howled, looking up with furious, quivering face and tender eyes. "What's the hurry? You blessed wooden-headed ould heretic, the divvle will have you soon enough. Think of Us . . . of Us . . . of Us!" And he would go away, stamping, spitting aside, disgusted and worried; while the other, stepping out, saucepan in hand, hot, begrimed and placid, watched with a superior, cocksure smile the back of this "queer little man" reeling in a rage. They were great friends.

Mr. Baker, lounging over the after-hatch, sniffed the humid night in the company of the second mate.—"Those West India niggers run fine and large—some of them . . . Ough! . . . Don't they? A fine, big man that, Mr. Creighton. Feel him on a rope. Hey? Ough! I will take him into my watch, I think." The second mate, a fair, gentlemanly young fellow, with a resolute face and a splendid physique, observed quietly that it was just about what he expected. There could be felt in his tone some slight bitterness which Mr. Baker very kindly set himself to argue away. "Come, come, young man," he said, grunting between the words. "Come! Don't be too greedy. You had that big Finn in your watch all the voyage. I will do what's fair. You may have those two young Scandinavians and I . . . Ough! . . . I get the nigger, and will take that . . . Ough! that cheeky costermonger chap in a black frockcoat. I'll make him . . . Ough! . . . make him toe the mark, or my . . . Ough! . . . name isn't Baker. Ough! Ough! Ough!"

He grunted thrice—ferociously. He had that trick of grunting so between his words and at the end of sentences. It was a fine, effective grunt that went well with his menacing utterance, with his heavy, bull-necked frame, his jerky, rolling gait; with his big, seamed face, his steady eyes, and sardonic mouth. But its effect had been long ago discounted by the men. They liked him; Belfast—who was a favorite, and knew it—mimicked him, not quite behind his back. Charley—but with greater caution—imitated his rolling gait. Some of his sayings became established, daily quotations in the forecastle. Popularity can go no farther! Besides, all hands were ready to admit that on a fitting occasion the mate could "jump down a fellow's throat in a reg'lar Western Ocean style."

Now he was giving his last orders. "Ough! . . . You, Knowles! Call all hands at four. I want . . . Ough! . . . to heave short before the tug comes. Look out for the captain. I am going to lie down in my clothes. . . . Ough! . . . Call me when you see the boat coming. Ough! Ough! . . . The old man is sure to have something to say when he gets aboard," he remarked to Creighton. "Well, good-night. . . . Ough! A long day before us to-morrow. . . . Ough! . . . Better turn in now. Ough. Ough!"

Upon the dark deck a band of light flashed, then a door slammed, and Mr. Baker was gone into his neat cabin. Young Creighton stood leaning over the rail, and looked dreamily into the night of the East. And he saw in it a long country lane, a lane of waving leaves and dancing sunshine. He saw stirring boughs of old trees outspread, and framing in their arch the tender, the caressing blueness of an English sky. And through the arch a girl in a light dress, smiling under a sunshade, seemed to be stepping out of the tender sky.

At the other end of the ship the forecastle, with only one lamp burning now, was going to sleep in a dim emptiness traversed by loud breathings, by sudden short sighs. The double row of berths yawned black, like graves tenanted by uneasy corpses. Here and there a curtain of gaudy chintz, half drawn, marked the resting-place of a sybarite. A leg hung over the edge very white and lifeless. An arm stuck straight out with a dark palm turned up, and thick fingers half closed. Two light snores, that did not synchronise, quarrelled in funny dialogue. Singleton stripped again—the old man suffered much from prickly heat—stood cooling his back in the doorway, with his arms crossed on his bare and adorned chest. His head touched the beam of the deck above. The nigger, half undressed, was busy casting adrift the lashing of his box, and spreading his bedding in an upper berth. He moved about in his socks, tall and noiseless, with a pair of braces beating about his calves. Amongst the shadows of stanchions and bowsprit, Donkin munched a piece of hard ship's bread, sitting on the deck with upturned feet and restless eyes; he held the biscuit up before his mouth in the whole fist and snapped his jaws at it with a raging face. Crumbs fell between his outspread legs. Then he got up.

"Where's our water-cask?" he asked in a contained voice.

Singleton, without a word, pointed with a big hand that held a short smouldering pipe. Donkin bent over the cask, drank out of the tin, splashing the water, turned round and noticed the nigger looking at him over the shoulder with calm loftiness. He moved up sideways.

"There's a blooming supper for a man," he whispered bitterly. "My dorg at 'ome wouldn't 'ave it. It's fit enouf for you an' me. 'Ere's a big ship's fo'c'sle! . . . Not a blooming scrap of meat in the kids. I've looked in all the lockers. . . ."

The nigger stared like a man addressed unexpectedly in a foreign language. Donkin changed his tone:—"Giv' us a bit of 'baccy, mate," he breathed out confidentially, "I 'aven't 'ad smoke or chew for the last month. I am rampin' mad for it. Come on, old man!"

"Don't be familiar," said the nigger. Donkin started and sat down on a chest near by, out of sheer surprise. "We haven't kept pigs together," continued James Wait in a deep undertone. "Here's your tobacco." Then, after a pause, he inquired:—"What ship?"—"*Golden State*," muttered Donkin indistinctly, biting the tobacco. The nigger whistled low.—"Ran?" he said curtly. Donkin nodded: one of his cheeks bulged out. "In course I ran," he mumbled. "They booted the life hout of one Dago chap on the passage 'ere, then started on me. I cleared hout 'ere."—"Left your dunnage behind?"— "Yes, dunnage and money," answered Donkin, raising his voice a little; "I got nothink. No clothes, no bed. A bandy-legged little Hirish chap 'ere 'as give me a blanket. . . . Think I'll go an' sleep in the fore topmast staysail to-night."

He went on deck trailing behind his back a corner of the blanket. Singleton, without a glance, moved slightly aside to let him pass. The nigger put away his shore togs and sat in clean working clothes on his box, one arm stretched over his knees.

After staring at Singleton for some time he asked without emphasis:—"What kind of ship is this? Pretty fair? Eh?"

Singleton didn't stir. A long while after he said, with unmoved face:—"Ship! . . . Ships are all right. It is the men in them!"

He went on smoking in the profound silence. The wisdom of half a century spent in listening to the thunder of the waves had spoken unconsciously through his old lips. The cat purred on the windlass. Then James Wait had a fit of roaring, rattling cough, that shook him, tossed him like a hurricane, and flung him panting with staring eyes headlong on his sea-chest. Several men woke up. One said sleepily out of his bunk: " 'Struth! what a blamed row!"—"I have a cold on my chest," gasped Wait.—"Cold! you call it," grumbled the man; "Should think 'twas something more. . . ."—"Oh! you think so," said the nigger upright and loftily scornful again. He climbed into his berth and began coughing persistently while he put his head out to glare all round the forecastle. There was no further protest. He fell back on the pillow, and could be heard there wheezing regularly like a man oppressed in his sleep.

Singleton stood at the door with his face to the light and his back to the darkness. And alone in the dim emptiness of the sleeping forecastle he appeared bigger, colossal, very old; old as Father Time himself, who should have come there into this place as quiet as a sepulchre to contemplate with patient eyes the short victory of sleep, the consoler. Yet he was only a child of time, a lonely relic of a devoured and forgotten generation. He stood, still strong, as ever unthinking; a ready man with a vast empty past and with no future, with his childlike impulses and his man's passions already dead within his tattooed breast. The men who could understand his silence were gone —those men who knew how to exist beyond the pale of life and within sight of eternity. They had been strong, as those are strong who know neither doubts nor hopes. They had been impatient and enduring, turbulent and devoted, unruly and faithful. Well-meaning people had tried to represent those men as whining over every mouthful of their food; as going about their work in fear of their lives. But in truth they had been men who knew toil, privation, violence, debauchery—but knew not fear, and had no desire of spite in their hearts. Men hard to manage, but easy to inspire; voiceless men—but men enough to scorn in their hearts the sentimental voices that bewailed the hardness of their fate. It was a fate unique and their own; the capacity to bear it appeared to them the privilege of the chosen! Their generation lived inarticulate and indispensable, without knowing the sweetness of affections or the refuge of a home—and died free from the dark menace of a narrow grave. They were the everlast-ing children of the mysterious sea. Their successors are the grown-up children of a discontented earth. They are less naughty, but less innocent; less profane, but perhaps also less believing; and if they have learned how to speak they have also learned how to whine. But the others were strong and mute; they were effaced, bowed and enduring, like stone caryatides that hold up in the night the lighted halls of a resplendent and glorious edifice. They are gone now—and it does not matter. The sea and the earth are unfaithful to their children: a truth, a faith, a generation of men goes—and is forgotten, and it does not matter! Except, perhaps, to the few of those who believed the truth, confessed the faith—or loved the men.

A breeze was coming. The ship that had been lying tide-rode swung to a heavier puff; and suddenly the slack of the chain cable between the windlass and the hawse-pipe clinked, slipped forward an inch, and rose gently off the deck with a startling suggestion as of unsuspected life that had been lurking stealthily in the iron. In the hawse-pipe the grinding links sent through the ship a sound like a low groan of a man sighing under a burden. The strain came on the windlass, the chain tautened like a string, vibrated—and the handle of the screw-brake moved in slight jerks. Singleton stepped forward.

Till then he had been standing meditative and unthinking, reposeful and hopeless, with a face grim and blank—a sixty-year-old child of the mysterious sea. The thoughts of all his lifetime could have been expressed in six words, but the stir of those things that were as much part of his existence as his beating heart called up a gleam of alert understanding upon the sternness of his aged face. The flame of the lamp swayed, and the old man, with knitted and bushy eyebrows, stood over the brake, watchful and motionless in the wild saraband of dancing shadows. Then the ship, obedient to the call of her anchor, forged ahead slightly and eased the strain. The cable relieved, hung down, and after swaying imperceptibly to and fro dropped with a loud tap on the hard wood planks. Singleton seized the high lever, and, by a violent throw forward of his body, wrung out another half-turn from the brake. He recovered himself, breathed largely, and remained for a while glaring down at the powerful and compact engine that squatted on the deck at his feet like some quiet monster—a creature amazing and tame.

"You . . . hold!" he growled at it masterfully, in the incult tangle of his white beard.

II

Next morning, at daylight, the *Narcissus* went to sea. A slight haze blurred the horizon. Outside the harbor the measureless expanse of smooth water lay sparkling like a floor of jewels, and as empty as the sky. The short black tug gave a pluck to windward, in the usual way, then let go the rope, and hovered for a moment on the quarter with her engines stopped; while the slim, long hull of the ship moved ahead slowly under lower topsails. The loose upper canvas blew out in the breeze with soft round contours, resembling small white clouds snared in the maze of ropes. Then the sheets were hauled home, the yards hoisted, and the ship became a high and lonely pyramid, gliding, all shining and white, through the sunlit mist. The tug turned short round and went away towards the land. Twenty-six pairs of eyes watched her low broad stern crawling languidly over the smooth swell between the two paddle-wheels that turned fast, beating the water with fierce hurry. She resembled an enormous and aquatic black beetle, surprised by the light, overwhelmed by the sunshine, trying to escape with ineffectual effort into the distant gloom of the land. She left a lingering smudge of smoke on the sky, and two vanishing trails of foam on the water. On the place where she had stopped a round black patch of soot remained, undulating on the swell—an unclean mark of the creature's rest.

The *Narcissus* left alone, heading south, seemed to stand resplendent and still upon the restless sea, under the moving sun. Flakes of foam swept past her sides; the water struck her with flashing blows; the land glided away slowly fading; a few birds screamed on motionless wings over the swaying mastheads. But soon the land disappeared, the birds went away; and to the west the pointed sail of an Arab dhow running for Bombay rose triangular and upright above the sharp edge of the horizon, lingered, and vanished like an illusion. Then the ship's wake, long and straight, stretched itself out through a day of immense solitude. The setting sun, burning on the level of the water, flamed crimson below the blackness of heavy rain clouds. The sunset squall, coming up from behind, dissolved itself into the short deluge of a hissing shower. It left the ship glistening from trucks to waterline, and with darkened sails. She ran easily before a fair monsoon, with her decks cleared for the night; and, moving along with her, was heard the sustained and monotonous swishing of the waves, mingled with the low whispers of men mustered aft for the setting of watches; the short plaint of some block aloft; or, now and then, a loud sigh of wind.

Mr. Baker, coming out of his cabin, called out the first name sharply before closing the door behind him. He was going to take charge of the deck. On the homeward trip, according to an old custom of the sea, the chief officer takes the first night-watch—from eight till midnight. So Mr. Baker, after he had heard the last "Yes, sir!" said moodily, "Relieve the wheel and look-out"; and climbed with heavy feet the poop ladder to windward. Soon after Mr. Creighton came down, whistling softly, and went into the cabin. On the doorstep the steward lounged, in slippers, meditative, and with his shirt-sleeves rolled up to the armpits. On the main deck the cook, locking up the galley doors, had an altercation with young Charley about a pair of socks. He could be heard saying impressively, in the darkness amidships: "You don't deserve a kindness. I've been drying them for you, and now you complain about the holes—and you swear, too! Right in front of me! If I hadn't been a Christian—which you ain't, you young ruffian—I would give you a clout on the head. . . . Go away!" Men in couples or threes stood pensive or moved silently along the bulwarks in the waist. The first busy day of a homeward passage was sinking into the dull peace of resumed routine. Aft, on the high poop, Mr. Baker walked shuffling and grunted to himself in the pauses of his thoughts. Forward, the look-out man, erect between the flukes of the two anchors, hummed an endless tune, keeping his eyes fixed dutifully ahead in a vacant stare. A multitude of stars coming out into the clear night peopled the emptiness of the sky. They glittered, as if alive above the sea; they surrounded the running ship on all sides; more intense than the eyes of a staring crowd, and as inscrutable as the souls of men.

The passage had begun, and the ship, a fragment detached from the earth, went on lonely and swift like a small planet. Round her the abysses of sky and sea met in an unattainable frontier. A great circular solitude moved with her, ever changing and ever the same, always monotonous and always imposing. Now and then another wandering white speck, burdened with life, appeared far off—disappeared; intent on its own destiny. The sun looked upon her all day, and every morning rose with a burning, round stare of undying curiosity. She had her own future; she was alive with the lives of those beings who trod her decks; like that earth which had given her up to the sea, she had an intolerable load of regrets and hopes. On her lived timid truth and audacious lies; and, like the earth, she was unconscious, fair to see—and condemned by men to an ignoble fate. The august loneliness of her path lent dignity to the sordid inspiration of her pilgrimage. She drove foaming to the southward, as if guided by the courage of a high endeavor. The smiling greatness of the sea dwarfed the extent of time. The days raced after one another, brilliant and quick like the flashes of a lighthouse, and the nights, eventful and short, resembled fleeting dreams.

The men had shaken into their places, and the half-hourly voice of the bells ruled their life of unceasing care. Night and day the head and shoulders of a seaman could be seen aft by the wheel, outlined high against sunshine or starlight, very steady above the stir of revolving spokes. The faces changed, passing in rotation. Youthful faces, bearded faces, dark faces: faces serene, or faces moody, but all akin with the brotherhood of the sea; all with the same attentive expression of eyes, carefully watching the compass or the sails. Captain Allistoun, serious, and with an old red muffler round his throat, all day long pervaded the poop. At night, many times he rose out of the darkness of the companion, such as a phantom above a grave, and stood watchful and mute under the stars, his night-shirt fluttering like a flag—then, without a sound, sank down again. He was born on the shores of the Pentland Firth. In his youth he attained the rank of harpooner in Peterhead whalers. When he spoke of that time his restless grey eyes became still and cold, like the loom of ice. Afterwards he went into the East Indian trade for the sake of change. He had commanded the *Narcissus* since she was built. He loved his ship, and drove her unmercifully; for his secret ambition was to make her accomplish some day a brilliantly quick passage which would be mentioned in nautical papers. He pronounced his owner's name with a sardonic smile, spoke but seldom to his officers, and reproved errors in a gentle voice, with words that cut to the quick. His hair was iron-grey, his face hard and of the color of pump-leather. He shaved every morning of his life—at six—but once (being caught in a fierce hurricane eighty miles southwest of Mauritius) he had missed three consecutive days. He feared naught but an unforgiving God, and wished to end his days in a little house, with a plot of ground attached—far in the country—out of sight of the sea.

He, the ruler of that minute world, seldom descended from the Olympian heights of his poop. Below him—at his feet, so to speak—common mortals led their busy and insignificant lives. Along the main deck, Mr. Baker grunted in a manner bloodthirsty and innocuous; and kept all our noses to the grindstone, being—as he once remarked —paid for doing that very thing. The men working about the deck were healthy and contented—as most seamen are, when once well out to sea. The true peace of God begins at any spot a thousand miles from the nearest land; and when He sends there the messengers of His might it is not in terrible wrath against crime, presumption, and folly, but paternally, to chasten simple hearts—ignorant hearts that know nothing of life, and beat undisturbed by envy or greed.

In the evening the cleared decks had a reposeful aspect, resembling the autumn of the earth. The sun was sinking to rest, wrapped in a mantle of warm clouds. Forward, on the end of the spare spars, the boatswain and the carpenter sat together with crossed arms; two men friendly, powerful, and deep-chested. Beside them the short, dumpy sailmaker—who had been in the Navy—related, between the whiffs of his pipe, impossible stories about Admirals. Couples tramped backwards and forwards, keeping step and balance without effort, in a confined space. Pigs grunted in the big pigsty. Belfast, leaning thoughtfully on his elbow, above the bars, communed with them through the silence of his meditation. Fellows with shirts open wide on sunburnt breasts sat upon the mooring bits, and all up the steps of the forecastle ladders. By the foremast a few discussed in a circle the characteristics of a gentleman. One said:—"It's money as does it." Another maintained:—"No, it's the way they speak." Lame Knowles stumped up with an unwashed face (he had the distinction of being the dirty man of the forecastle), and showing a few yellow fangs in a shrewd smile, explained craftily that he "had seen some of their pants." The backsides of them—he had observed—were thinner than paper from constant sitting down in offices, yet otherwise they looked first-rate and would last for years. It was all appearance. "It was," he said, "bloomin' easy to be a gentleman when you had a clean job for life." They disputed endlessly, obstinate and childish; they repeated in shouts and with inflamed faces their amazing arguments; while the soft breeze, eddying down the enormous cavity of the foresail, distended above their bare heads, stirred the tumbled hair with a touch passing and light like an indulgent caress.

They were forgetting their toil, they were forgetting themselves. The cook approached to hear, and stood by, beaming with the inward consciousness of his faith, like a conceited saint unable to forget his glorious reward; Donkin, solitary and brooding over his wrongs on the forecastle-head, moved closer to catch the drift of the discussion below him; he turned his sallow face to the sea, and his thin nostrils moved, sniffing the breeze, as he lounged negligently by the rail. In the glow of sunset faces shone with interest, teeth flashed, eyes sparkled. The walking couples stood still suddenly, with broad grins; a man, bending over a washtub, sat up, entranced, with the soapsuds flecking his wet arms. Even the three petty officers listened leaning back, comfortably propped, and with superior smiles. Belfast left off scratching the ear of his favorite pig, and, open mouthed, tried with eager eyes to have his say. He lifted his arms, grimacing and baffled. From a distance Charley screamed at the ring:—"I know about gentlemen more'n any of you. I've been intermit with 'em. . . . I've blacked their boots." The cook, craning his neck to hear better, was scandalized. "Keep your mouth shut when your elders speak, you impudent young heathen—you." "All right, old Hallelujah, I'm done," answered Charley, soothingly. At some opinion of dirty Knowles, delivered with an air of supernatural cunning, a ripple of laughter ran along, rose like a wave, burst with a startling roar. They stamped with both feet; they turned their shouting faces to the sky; many, spluttering, slapped their thighs; while one or two, bent double, gasped, hugging themselves with both arms like men in pain. The carpenter and the boatswain, without changing their attitude, shook with laughter where they sat; the sailmaker, charged with an anecdote about a Commodore, looked sulky; the cook was wiping his eyes with a greasy rag; and lame Knowles, astonished at his own success, stood in their midst showing a slow smile.

Suddenly the face of Donkin leaning high-shouldered over the after-rail became grave. Something like a weak rattle was heard through the forecastle door. It became a murmur; it ended in a sighing groan. The washerman plunged both his arms into the tub abruptly; the cook became more crestfallen than an exposed backslider; the boatswain moved his shoulders uneasily; the carpenter got up with a spring and walked away—while the sailmaker seemed mentally to give his story up, and began to puff at his pipe with somber determination. In the blackness of the doorway a pair of eyes glimmered white, and big, and staring. Then James Wait's head protruding, became visible, as if suspended between the two hands that grasped a doorpost on each side of the face. The tassel of his blue woolen nightcap, cocked forward, danced gaily over his left eyelid. He stepped out in a tottering stride. He looked powerful as ever, but showed a strange and affected unsteadiness in his gait; his face was perhaps a trifle thinner, and his eyes appeared rather startlingly prominent. He seemed to hasten the retreat of departing light by his very presence; the setting sun dipped sharply, as though fleeing before our nigger; a black mist emanated from him; a subtle and dismal influence; a something cold and gloomy that floated out and settled on all the faces like a mourning veil. The circle broke up. The joy of laughter died on stiffened lips. There was not a smile left among all the ship's company. Not a word was spoken. Many turned their backs, trying to look unconcerned; others, with averted heads, sent half-reluctant glances out of the corners of their eyes. They resembled criminals conscious of misdeeds more than honest men distracted by doubt; only two or three stared frankly, but stupidly, with lips slightly open. All expected James Wait to say something, and, at the same time, had the air of knowing beforehand what he would say. He leaned his back against the doorpost, and with heavy eyes swept over them a glance domineering and pained, like a sick tyrant overawing a crowd of abject but untrustworthy slaves.

No one went away. They waited in fascinated dread. He said ironically, with gasps between the words:—

"Thank you . . . chaps. You . . . are nice . . . and . . . quiet . . . you are! Yelling so . . . before . . . the door. . . ."

He made a longer pause, during which he worked his ribs in an exaggerated labor of breathing. It was intolerable. Feet were shuffled. Belfast let out a groan; but Donkin above blinked his red eyelids with invisible eyelashes, and smiled bitterly over the nigger's head.

The nigger went on again with surprising ease. He gasped no more, and his voice rang, hollow and loud, as though he had been talking in an empty cavern. He was contemptuously angry.

"I tried to get a wink of sleep. You know I can't sleep o' nights. And you come jabbering near the door here like a blooming lot of old women. . . . You think yourselves good shipmates. Do you? . . . Much you care for a dying man!"

Belfast spun away from the pigsty. "Jimmy," he cried tremulously, "if you hadn't been sick I would—"

He stopped. The nigger waited awhile, then said, in a gloomy tone:—"You would. . . . What? Go an' fight another such one as yourself. Leave me alone. It won't be for long. I'll soon die. . . . It's coming right enough!"

Men stood around very still and with exasperated eyes. It was just what they had expected, and hated to hear, that idea of a stalking death, thrust at them many times a day like a boast and like a menace by this obnoxious nigger. He seemed to take a pride in that death which, so far, had attended only upon the ease of his life; he was overbearing about it, as if no one else in the world had ever been intimate with such a companion; he paraded it unceasingly before us with an affectionate persistence that made its presence indubitable, and at the same time incredible. No man could be suspected of such monstrous friendship! Was he a reality—or was he a sham—this ever-expected visitor of Jimmy's? We hesitated between pity and mistrust, while, on the slightest provocation, he shook before our eyes the bones of his bothersome and infamous skeleton. He was for ever trotting him out. He would talk of that coming death as though it had been already there, as if it had been walking the deck outside, as if it would presently come in to sleep in the only empty bunk; as if it had sat by his side at every meal. It interfered daily with our occupations, with our leisure, with our amusements. We had no songs and no music in the evening, because Jimmy (we all lovingly called him Jimmy, to conceal our hate of his accomplice) had managed, with that prospective decease of his, to disturb even Archie's mental balance. Archie was the owner of the concertina; but after a couple of stinging lectures from Jimmy he refused to play any more. He said:—"Yon's an uncanny joker. I dinna ken what's wrang wi' him, but there's something verra wrang, verra wrang. It's nae manner of use asking me. I won't play." Our singers became mute because Jimmy was a dying man. For the same reason no chap—as Knowles remarked—could "drive in a nail to hang his few poor rags upon," without being made aware of the enormity he committed in disturbing Jimmy's interminable last moments. At night, instead of the cheerful yell, "One bell! Turn out! Do you hear there? Hey! hey! hey! Show leg!" the watches were called man by man, in whispers, so as not to interfere with Jimmy's, possibly, last slumber on earth. True, he was always awake, and managed, as we sneaked out on deck, to plant in our backs some cutting remark that, for the moment, made us feel as if we had been brutes, and afterwards made us suspect ourselves of being fools. We spoke in low tones within that fo'c'sle as though it had been a church. We ate our meals in silence and dread, for Jimmy was capricious with his food, and railed bitterly at the salt meat, at the biscuits, at the tea, as at articles unfit for human consumption—"let alone for a dying man!" He would say:—"Can't you find a better slice of meat for a sick man who's trying to get home to be cured—or buried? But there! If I had a chance, you fellows would do away with it. You would poison me. Look at what you have given me!" We served him in his bed with rage and humility, as though we had been the base courtiers of a hated prince; and he rewarded us by his unconciliating criticism. He had found the secret of keeping for ever on the run the fundamental imbecility of man-kind; he had the secret of life, that confounded dying man, and he made himself master of every moment of our existence. We grew desperate, and remained submis-sive. Emotional little Belfast was for ever on the verge of assault or on the verge of tears. One evening he confided to Archie:—"For a ha'penny I would knock his ugly black head off—the skulking dodger!" And the straightforward Archie pretended to be shocked! Such was the infernal spell which that casual St. Kitt's nigger had cast upon our guileless manhood! But the same night Belfast stole from the galley the officers' Sunday fruit pie, to tempt the fastidious appetite of Jimmy. He endangered not only his long friendship with the cook but also—as it appeared—his eternal welfare. The cook was overwhelmed with grief; he did not know the culprit but he knew that wickedness flourished; he knew that Satan was aboard amongst those men, whom he looked upon as in some way under his spiritual care. Whenever he saw three or four of us standing together he would leave his stove, to run out and preach. We fled from him; and only Charley (who knew the thief) affronted the cook with a candid gaze which irritated the good man. "It's you, I believe," he groaned, sorrowful and with a patch of soot on his chin. "It's you. You are a brand for the burning! No more of *your* socks in my galley." Soon, unofficially, the information was spread about that, should there be another case of stealing, our marmalade (an extra allowance: half a pound per man) would be stopped. Mr. Baker ceased to heap jocular abuse upon his favorites, and grunted suspiciously at all. The captain's cold eyes, high up on the poop, glittered mistrustful, as he surveyed us trooping in a small mob from halyards to braces for the usual evening pull at all the ropes. Such stealing in a merchant ship is difficult to check, and may be taken as a declaration by men of their dislike for their officers. It is a bad symptom. It may end in God knows what trouble. The *Narcissus* was still a peaceful ship, but mutual confidence was shaken. Donkin did not conceal his delight. We were dismayed.

Then illogical Belfast reproached our nigger with great fury. James Wait, with his elbow on the pillow, choked, gasped out:—"Did I ask you to bone the dratted thing? Blow your blamed pie. It has made me worse—you little Irish lunatic, you!" Belfast, with scarlet face and trembling lips, made a dash at him. Every man in the forecastle rose with a shout. There was a moment of wild tumult. Some one shrieked piercingly: —"Easy, Belfast! Easy! . . ." We expected Belfast to strangle Wait without more ado. Dust flew. We heard through it the nigger's cough, metallic and explosive like a gong. Next moment we saw Belfast hanging over him. He was saying plaintively:—"Don't! Don't, Jimmy! Don't be like that. An angel couldn't put up with ye—sick as ye are." He looked round at us from Jimmy's bedside, his comical mouth twitching, and through tearful eyes; then he tried to put straight the disarranged blankets. The unceasing whisper of the sea filled the forecastle. Was James Wait frightened, or touched, or repentant? He lay on his back with a hand to his side, and as motionless as if his expected visitor had come at last. Belfast fumbled about his feet, repeating with

emotion:—"Yes. We know. Ye are bad, but. . . . Just say what ye want done, and
. . . We all know ye are bad—very bad. . . ." No! Decidedly James Wait was not
touched or repentant. Truth to say, he seemed rather startled. He sat up with incredible suddenness and ease. "Ah! You think I am bad, do you?" he said gloomily, in his
clearest baritone voice (to hear him speak sometimes you would never think there was
anything wrong with that man). "Do you? . . . Well, act according! Some of you
haven't sense enough to put a blanket shipshape over a sick man. There! Leave it alone!
I can die anyhow!" Belfast turned away limply with a gesture of discouragement. In the
silence of the forecastle, full of interested men, Donkin pronounced distinctly:—
"Well, I'm blowed!" and sniggered. Wait looked at him. He looked at him in a quite
friendly manner. Nobody could tell what would please our incomprehensible invalid:
but for us the scorn of that snigger was hard to bear.

Donkin's position in the forecastle was distinguished but unsafe. He stood on the
bad eminence of a general dislike. He was left alone; and in his isolation he could do
nothing but think of the gales of the Cape of Good Hope and envy us the possession
of warm clothing and waterproofs. Our sea-boots, our oilskin coats, our well-filled
sea-chests, were to him so many causes for bitter meditation: he had none of those
things, and he felt instinctively that no man, when the need arose, would offer to share
them with him. He was impudently cringing to us and systematically insolent to the
officers. He anticipated the best results, for himself, from such a line of conduct—and
was mistaken. Such natures forget that under extreme provocation men will be just—
whether they want to be so or not. Donkin's insolence to long-suffering Mr. Baker
became at last intolerable to us, and we rejoiced when the mate, one dark night, tamed
him for good. It was done neatly, with great decency and decorum, and with little
noise. We had been called—just before midnight—to trim the yards, and Donkin—as
usual—made insulting remarks. We stood sleepily in a row with the forebrace in our
hands waiting for the next order, and heard in the darkness a scuffly trampling of feet,
an exclamation of surprise, sounds of cuffs and slaps, suppressed, hissing whispers:—
"Ah!   Will   you!" . . . "Don't . . . Don't" . . . "Then   behave." . . . "Oh!
Oh! . . ." Afterwards there were soft thuds mixed with the rattle of iron things as if a
man's body had been tumbling helplessly amongst the main-pump rods. Before we
could realize the situation, Mr. Baker's voice was heard very near and a little impatient:
—"Haul away, men! Lay back on that rope!" And we did lay back on the rope with
great alacrity. As if nothing had happened, the chief mate went on trimming the yards
with his usual and exasperating fastidiousness. We didn't at the time see anything of
Donkin, and did not care. Had the chief officer thrown him overboard, no man would
have said as much as "Hallo! he's gone!" But, in truth, no great harm was done—even
if Donkin did lose one of his front teeth. We perceived this in the morning, and
preserved a ceremonious silence: the etiquette of the forecastle commanded us to be
blind and dumb in such a case, and we cherished the decencies of our life more than
ordinary landsmen respect theirs. Charley, with unpardonable want of *savoir vivre*, yelled
out:—" 'Ave you been to your dentyst? . . . Hurt ye, didn't it?" He got a box on the
ear from one of his best friends. The boy was surprised, and remained plunged in grief

for at least three hours. We were sorry for him, but youth requires even more discipline than age. Donkin grinned venomously. From that day he became pitiless; told Jimmy that he was a "black fraud"; hinted to us that we were an imbecile lot, daily taken in by a vulgar nigger. And Jimmy seemed to like the fellow!

Singleton lived untouched by human emotions. Taciturn and unsmiling, he breathed amongst us—in that alone resembling the rest of the crowd. We were trying to be decent chaps, and found it jolly difficult; we oscillated between the desire of virtue and the fear of ridicule; we wished to save ourselves from the pain of remorse, but did not want to be made the contemptible dupes of our sentiment. Jimmy's hateful accomplice seemed to have blown with his impure breath undreamt-of subtleties into our hearts. We were disturbed and cowardly. That we knew. Singleton seemed to know nothing, understand nothing. We had thought him till then as wise as he looked, but now we dared, at times, suspect him of being stupid—from old age. One day, however, at dinner, as we sat on our boxes round a tin dish that stood on the deck within the circle of our feet, Jimmy expressed his general disgust with men and things in words that were particularly disgusting. Singleton lifted his head. We became mute. The old man, addressing Jimmy, asked:—"Are you dying?" Thus interrogated, James Wait appeared horribly startled and confused. We all were startled. Mouths remained open; hearts thumped, eyes blinked; a dropped tin fork rattled in the dish; a man rose as if to go out, and stood still. In less than a minute Jimmy pulled himself together:— "Why? Can't you see I am?" he answered shakily. Singleton lifted a piece of soaked biscuit ("his teeth"—he declared—"had no edge on them now") to his lips.—"Well, get on with your dying," he said with venerable mildness; "don't raise a blamed fuss with us over that job. We can't help you." Jimmy fell back in his bunk, and for a long time lay very still wiping the perspiration off his chin. The dinner-tins were put away quickly. On deck we discussed the incident in whispers. Some showed a chuckling exultation. Many looked grave. Wamibo, after long periods of staring dreaminess, attempted abortive smiles; and one of the young Scandinavians, much tormented by doubt, ventured in the second dog-watch to approach Singleton (the old man did not encourage us much to speak to him) and ask sheepishly:—"You think he will die?" Singleton looked up.—"Why, of course he will die," he said deliberately. This seemed decisive. It was promptly imparted to everyone by him who had consulted the oracle. Shy and eager, he would step up and with averted gaze recite his formula:—"Old Singleton says he will die." It was a relief! At last we knew that our compassion would not be misplaced, and we could again smile without misgivings—but we reckoned without Donkin. Donkin "didn't want to 'ave no truck with 'em dirty furriners." When Nilsen came to him with the news: "Singleton says he will die," he answered him by a spiteful "And so will you—you fat-headed Dutchman. Wish you Dutchmen were all dead—'stead comin' takin' our money inter your starvin' country." We were appalled. We perceived that after all Singleton's answer meant nothing. We began to hate him for making fun of us. All our certitudes were going; we were on doubtful terms with our officers; the cook had given us up for lost; we had overheard the boatswain's opinion that "we were a crowd of softies." We suspected Jimmy, one another, and even our very selves. We did not know what to do. At every insignificant turn of our humble life we met Jimmy overbearing and blocking the way, arm-in-arm with his awful and veiled familiar. It was a weird servitude.

It began a week after leaving Bombay and came on us stealthily like any other great misfortune. Every one had remarked that Jimmy from the first was very slack at his work; but we thought it simply the outcome of his philosophy of life. Donkin said:— "You put no more weight on a rope than a bloody sparrer." He disdained him. Belfast, ready for a fight, exclaimed provokingly:—"You don't kill yourself, old man!"— "Would you?" he retorted with extreme scorn—and Belfast retired. One morning, as we were washing decks, Mr. Baker called to him:—"Bring your broom over here, Wait." He strolled languidly. "Move yourself! Ough!" grunted Mr. Baker; "what's the matter with your hind legs?" He stopped dead short. He gazed slowly with eyes that bulged out with an expression audacious and sad.—"It isn't my legs," he said, "it's my lungs." Everybody listened.—"What's . . . Ough! . . . What's wrong with them?" inquired Mr. Baker. All the watch stood around on the wet deck, grinning, and with brooms or buckets in their hands. He said mournfully:—"Going—or gone. Can't you see I'm a dying man? I know it!" Mr. Baker was disgusted.—"Then why the devil did you ship aboard here?"—"I must live till I die—mustn't I?" he replied. The grins became audible.—"Go off the deck—get out of my sight," said Mr. Baker. He was nonplussed. It was a unique experience. James Wait, obedient, dropped his broom, and walked slowly forward. A burst of laughter followed him. It was too funny. All hands laughed. . . . They laughed! . . . Alas!

He became the tormentor of all our moments; he was worse than a nightmare. You couldn't see that there was anything wrong with him: a nigger does not show. He was not very fat—certainly—but then he was no leaner than other niggers we had known. He coughed often, but the most prejudiced person could perceive that, mostly, he coughed when it suited his purpose. He wouldn't, or couldn't, do his work—and he wouldn't lie-up. One day he would skip aloft with the best of them, and next time we would be obliged to risk our lives to get his limp body down. He was reported, he was examined; he was remonstrated with, threatened, cajoled, lectured. He was called into the cabin to interview the captain. There were wild rumors. It was said he had cheeked the old man; it was said he had frightened him. Charley maintained that the "skipper, weepin', 'as giv' 'im 'is blessin' an' a pot of jam." Knowles had it from the steward that the unspeakable Jimmy had been reeling against the cabin furniture; that he had groaned; that he had complained of general brutality and disbelief and had ended by coughing all over the old man's meteorological journals which were then spread on the table. At any rate, Wait returned forward supported by the steward, who, in a pained and shocked voice, entreated us:—"Here! Catch hold of him, one of you. He is to lie-up." Jimmy drank a tin mugful of coffee, and, after bullying first one and then another, went to bed. He remained there most of the time, but when it suited him would come on deck and appear amongst us. He was scornful and brooding; he looked ahead upon the sea, and no one could tell what was the meaning of that black man sitting apart in a meditative attitude and as motionless as a carving.

He refused steadily all medicine; he threw sago and cornflour overboard till the steward got tired of bringing it to him. He asked for paregoric. They sent him a big bottle; enough to poison a wilderness of babies. He kept it between his mattress and the deal lining of the ship's side; and nobody ever saw him take a dose. Donkin abused him to his face, jeered at him while he gasped; and the same day Wait would lend him a warm jersey. Once Donkin reviled him for half an hour; reproached him with the extra work his malingering gave to the watch; and ended by calling him "a black-faced swine." Under the spell of our accursed perversity we were horror-struck. But Jimmy positively seemed to revel in that abuse. It made him look cheerful—and Donkin had a pair of old sea-boots thrown at him. "Here, you East-end trash," boomed Wait, "you may have that."

At last Mr. Baker had to tell the captain that James Wait was disturbing the peace of the ship. "Knock discipline on the head—he will, Ough," grunted Mr. Baker. As a matter of fact, the starboard watch came as near as possible to refusing duty, when ordered one morning by the boatswain to wash out their forecastle. It appears Jimmy objected to a wet floor—and that morning we were in a compassionate mood. We thought the boatswain a brute, and, practically, told him so. Only Mr. Baker's delicate tact prevented an all-fired row: he refused to take us seriously. He came bustling forward, and called us many unpolite names but in such a hearty and seamanlike manner that we began to feel ashamed of ourselves. In truth, we thought him much too good a sailor to annoy him willingly: and after all Jimmy might have been a fraud —probably was! The forecastle got a clean up that morning; but in the afternoon a sick-bay was fitted up in the deck-house. It was a nice little cabin opening on deck, and with two berths. Jimmy's belongings were transported there, and then—notwithstanding his protests—Jimmy himself. He said he couldn't walk. Four men carried him on a blanket. He complained that he would have to die there alone, like a dog. We grieved for him, and were delighted to have him removed from the forecastle. We attended him as before. The galley was next door, and the cook looked in many times a day. Wait became a little more cheerful. Knowles affirmed having heard him laugh to himself in peals one day. Others had seen him walking about on deck at night. His little place, with the door ajar on a long hook, was always full of tobacco smoke. We spoke through the crack cheerfully, sometimes abusively, as we passed by, intent on our work. He fascinated us. He would never let doubt die. He overshadowed the ship. Invulnerable in his promise of speedy corruption he trampled on our self-respect, he demonstrated to us daily our want of moral courage; he tainted our lives. Had we been a miserable gang of wretched immortals, unhallowed alike by hope and fear, he could not have lorded it over us with a more pitiless assertion of his sublime privilege.

III

Meantime the *Narcissus*, with square yards, ran out of the fair monsoon. She drifted slowly, swinging round and round the compass, through a few days of baffling light airs. Under the patter of short warm showers, grumbling men whirled the heavy yards from side to side; they caught hold of the soaked ropes with groans and sighs, while their officers, sulky and dripping with rain water, unceasingly ordered them about in wearied voices. During the short respites they looked with disgust into the smarting palms of their stiff hands, and asked one another bitterly:—"Who would be a sailor if he could be a farmer?" All the tempers were spoilt, and no man cared what he said. One black night, when the watch, panting in the heat and half-drowned with the rain, had been through four mortal hours hunted from brace to brace, Belfast declared that he would "chuck the sea for ever and go in a steamer." This was excessive, no doubt. Captain Allistoun, with great self-control, would mutter sadly to Mr. Baker:—"It is not so bad—not so bad," when he had managed to shove, and dodge, and maneuver his smart ship through sixty miles in twenty-four hours. From the doorstep of the little cabin, Jimmy, chin in hand, watched our distasteful labors with insolent and melancholy eyes. We spoke to him gently—and out of his sight exchanged sour smiles.

Then, again, with a fair wind and under a clear sky, the ship went on piling up the South Latitude. She passed outside Madagascar and Mauritius without a glimpse of the land. Extra lashings were put on the spare spars. Hatches were looked to. The steward in his leisure moments and with a worried air tried to fit washboards to the cabin doors. Stout canvas was bent with care. Anxious eyes looked to the westward, towards the cape of storms. The ship began to dip into a southwest swell, and the softly luminous sky of low latitudes took on a harder sheen from day to day above our heads: it arched high above the ship vibrating and pale, like an immense dome of steel, resonant with the deep voice of freshening gales. The sunshine gleamed cold on the white curls of black waves. Before the strong breath of westerly squalls the ship, with reduced sail, lay slowly over, obstinate and yielding. She drove to and fro in the unceasing endeavor to fight her way through the invisible violence of the winds: she pitched headlong into dark smooth hollows; she struggled upwards over the snowy ridges of great running seas; she rolled, restless, from side to side, like a thing in pain. Enduring and valiant, she answered to the call of men; and her slim spars waving for ever in abrupt semicircles, seemed to beckon in vain for help towards the stormy sky.

It was a bad winter off the Cape that year. The relieved helmsmen came off flapping their arms, or ran stamping hard and blowing into swollen, red fingers. The watch on deck dodged the sting of cold sprays or, crouching in sheltered corners, watched dismally the high and merciless seas boarding the ship time after time in unappeasable fury. Water tumbled in cataracts over the forecastle doors. You had to dash through a waterfall to get into your damp bed. The men turned in wet and turned out stiff to face the redeeming and ruthless exactions of their glorious and obscure fate. Far aft, and peering watchfully to windward, the officers could be seen through the mist of squalls. They stood by the weather-rail, holding on grimly, straight and glistening in their long coats; and in the disordered plunges of the hard-driven ship, they appeared high up, attentive, tossing violently above the grey line of a clouded horizon in motionless attitudes.

They watched the weather and the ship as men on shore watch the momentous chances of fortune. Captain Allistoun never left the deck, as though he had been part of the ship's fittings. Now and then the steward, shivering, but always in shirt-sleeves, would struggle towards him with some hot coffee, half of which the gale blew out of the cup before it reached the master's lips. He drank what was left gravely in one long gulp, while heavy sprays pattered loudly on his oilskin coat, the seas swishing broke about his high boots; and he never took his eyes off the ship. He kept his gaze riveted upon her as a loving man watches the unselfish toil of a delicate woman upon the slender thread of whose existence is hung the whole meaning and joy of the world. We all watched her. She was beautiful and had a weakness. We loved her no less for that. We admired her qualities aloud, we boasted of them to one another, as though they had been our own, and the consciousness of her only fault we kept buried in the silence of our profound affection. She was born in the thundering peal of hammers beating upon iron, in black eddies of smoke, under a grey sky, on the banks of the Clyde. The clamorous and sombre stream gives birth to things of beauty that float away into the sunshine of the world to be loved by men. The *Narcissus* was one of that perfect brood. Less perfect than many perhaps, but she was ours, and, consequently, incomparable. We were proud of her. In Bombay, ignorant landlubbers alluded to her as that "pretty grey ship." Pretty! A scurvy meed of commendation! We knew she was the most magnificent sea-boat ever launched. We tried to forget that, like many good seaboats, she was at time rather crank. She was exacting. She wanted care in loading and handling, and no one knew exactly how much care would be enough. Such are the imperfections of mere men! The ship knew, and sometimes would correct the presumptuous human ignorance by the wholesome discipline of fear. We had heard ominous stories about past voyages. The cook (technically a seaman, but in reality no sailor)—the cook, when unstrung by some misfortune, such as the rolling over of a saucepan, would mutter gloomily while he wiped the floor:—"There! Look at what she has done! Some voy'ge she will drown all hands! You'll see if she won't." To which the steward, snatching in the galley a moment to draw breath in the hurry of his worried life, would remark philosophically:—"Those that see won't tell, anyhow. I don't want to see it." We derided those fears. Our hearts went out to the old man when he pressed her hard so as to make her hold her own, hold to every inch gained to windward; when he made her, under reefed sails, leap obliquely at enormous waves. The men, knitted together aft into a ready group by the first sharp order of an officer coming to take charge of the deck in bad weather:—"Keep handy the watch," stood admiring her valiance. Their eyes blinked in the wind; their dark faces were wet with drops of water more salty and bitter than human tears; beards and mustaches, soaked, hung straight and dripping like fine seaweed. They were fantastically misshapen; in high boots, in hats like helmets, and swaying clumsily, stiff and bulky in glistening oilskins, they resembled men strangely equipped for some fabulous adventure. Whenever she rose easily to a towering green sea, elbows dug ribs, faces brightened, lips murmured:—"Didn't she do it cleverly," and all the heads turning like one watched with sardonic grins the foiled wave go roaring to leeward, white with the foam of a monstrous rage. But when she had not been quick enough and, struck heavily, lay over trembling under the blow, we clutched at ropes, and looking up at the narrow bands of drenched and strained sails waving desperately aloft, we thought in our hearts:—"No wonder. Poor thing!"

The thirty-second day out of Bombay began inauspiciously. In the morning a sea smashed one of the galley doors. We dashed in through lots of steam and found the cook very wet and indignant with the ship:—"She's getting worse every day. She's trying to drown me in front of my own stove!" He was very angry. We pacified him, and the carpenter, though washed away twice from there, managed to repair the door. Through that accident our dinner was not ready till late, but it didn't matter in the end because Knowles, who went to fetch it, got knocked down by a sea and the dinner went over the side. Captain Allistoun, looking more hard and thin-lipped than ever, hung on to full topsails and foresail, and would not notice that the ship, asked to do too much, appeared to lose heart altogether for the first time since we knew her. She refused to rise, and bored her way sullenly through the seas. Twice running, as though she had been blind or weary of life, she put her nose deliberately into a big wave and swept the decks from end to end. As the boatswain observed with marked annoyance, while we were splashing about in a body to try and save a worthless washtub:—"Every blooming thing in the ship is going overboard this afternoon." Venerable Singleton broke his habitual silence and said with a glance aloft:—"The old man's in a temper with the weather, but it's no good bein' angry with the winds of heaven." Jimmy had shut his door, of course. We knew he was dry and comfortable within his little cabin, and in our absurd way were pleased one moment, exasperated the next, by that certitude. Donkin skulked shamelessly, uneasy and miserable. He grumbled:—"I'm perishin' with cold outside in bloomin' wet rags, an' that 'ere black sojer sits dry on a blamed chest full of bloomin' clothes; blank his black soul!" We took no notice of him; we hardly gave a thought to Jimmy and his bosom friend. There was no leisure for idle probing of hearts. Sails blew adrift. Things broke loose. Cold and wet, we were washed about the deck while trying to repair damages. The ship tossed about, shaken furiously, like a toy in the hand of a lunatic. Just at sunset there was a rush to shorten sail before the menace of a sombre hail cloud. The hard gust of wind came brutal like the blow of a fist. The ship relieved of her canvas in time received it pluckily: she yielded reluctantly to the violent onset; then, coming up with a stately and irresistible motion, brought her spars to windward in the teeth of the screeching squall. Out of the abysmal darkness of the black cloud overhead white hail streamed on her, rattled on the rigging, leaped in handfuls off the yards, rebounded on the deck —round and gleaming in the murky turmoil like a shower of peas. It passed away. For a moment a livid sun shot horizontally the last rays of sinister light between the hills of steep, rolling waves. Then a wild night rushed in—stamped out in a great howl that dismal remnant of a stormy day.

There was no sleep on board that night. Most seamen remember in their life one or two such nights of a culminating gale. Nothing seems left of the whole universe but darkness, clamor, fury—and the ship. And like the last vestige of a shattered creation she drifts, bearing an anguished remnant of sinful mankind, through the distress, tumult, and pain of an avenging terror. No one slept in the forecastle. The tin oil-lamp suspended on a long string, smoking, described wide circles; wet clothing made dark heaps on the glistening floor; a thin layer of water rushed to and fro. In the bed-places men lay booted, resting on elbows and with open eyes. Hung-up suits of oilskin swung out and in, lively and disquieting like reckless ghosts of decapitated seamen dancing in a tempest. No one spoke and all listened. Outside the night moaned and sobbed to the accompaniment of a continuous loud tremor as of innumerable drums beating far off. Shrieks passed through the air. Tremendous dull blows made the ship tremble while she rolled under the weight of the seas toppling on her deck. At times she soared up swiftly as if to leave this earth for ever, then during interminable moments fell through a void with all the hearts on board of her standing still, till a frightful shock, expected and sudden, started them off again with a big thump. After every dislocating jerk of the ship, Wamibo, stretched full length, his face on the pillow, groaned slightly with the pain of his tormented universe. Now and then, for the fraction of an intolerable second, the ship, in the fiercer burst of a terrible uproar, remained on her side, vibrating and still, with a stillness more appalling than the wildest motion. Then upon all those prone bodies a stir would pass, a shiver of suspense. A man would protrude his anxious head and a pair of eyes glistened in the sway of light glaring wildly. Some moved their legs a little as if making ready to jump out. But several, motionless on their backs and with one hand gripping hard the edge of the bunk, smoked nervously with quick puffs, staring upwards; immobilized in a great craving for peace.

At midnight, orders were given to furl the fore and mizen topsails. With immense efforts men crawled aloft through a merciless buffeting, saved the canvas and crawled down almost exhausted, to bear in panting silence the cruel battering of the seas. Perhaps for the first time in the history of the merchant service the watch, told to go below, did not leave the deck, as if compelled to remain there by the fascination of a venomous violence. At every heavy gust men, huddled together, whispered to one another:—"It can blow no harder"—and presently the gale would give them the lie with a piercing shriek, and drive their breath back into their throats. A fierce squall seemed to burst asunder the thick mass of sooty vapors; and above the wrack of torn clouds glimpses could be caught of the high moon rushing backwards with frightful speed over the sky, right into the wind's eye. Many hung their heads, muttering that it "turned their inwards out" to look at it. Soon the clouds closed up and the world again became a raging, blind darkness that howled, flinging at the lonely ship salt sprays and sleet.

About half-past seven the pitchy obscurity round us turned a ghastly grey, and we knew that the sun had risen. This unnatural and threatening daylight, in which we could see one another's wild eyes and drawn faces, was only an added tax on our endurance. The horizon seemed to have come on all sides within arm's length of the ship. Into that narrowed circle furious seas leaped in, struck, and leaped out. A rain of salt, heavy drops flew aslant like mist. The main-topsail had to be goose-winged, and with stolid resignation every one prepared to go aloft once more; but the officers yelled, pushed back, and at last we understood that no more men would be allowed to go on the yard than were absolutely necessary for the work. As at any moment the masts were likely to be jumped out or blown overboard, we concluded that the captain didn't want to see all his crowd go over the side at once. That was reasonable. The watch then on duty, led by Mr. Creighton, began to struggle up the rigging. The wind flattened them against the ratlines; then, easing a little, would let them ascend a couple of steps; and again, with a sudden gust, pin all up the shrouds the whole crawling line in attitudes of crucifixion. The other watch plunged down on the main deck to haul up the sail. Men's heads bobbed up as the water flung them irresistibly from side to side. Mr. Baker grunted encouragingly in our midst, spluttering and blowing amongst the tangled ropes like an energetic porpoise. Favored by an ominous and untrustworthy lull, the work was done without any one being lost either off the deck or from the yard. For the moment the gale seemed to take off, and the ship, as if grateful for our efforts, plucked up heart and made better weather of it.

At eight the men off duty, watching their chance, ran forward over the flooded deck to get some rest. The other half of the crew remained aft for their turn of "seeing her through her trouble," as they expressed it. The two mates urged the master to go below. Mr. Baker grunted in his ear:—"Ough! surely now . . . Ough! . . . confidence in us . . . nothing more to do . . . she must lay it out or go. Ough! Ough!" Tall young Mr. Creighton smiled down at him cheerfully:—". . . She's as right as a trivet! Take a spell, sir." He looked at them stonily with bloodshot, sleepless eyes. The rims of his eyelids were scarlet, and he moved his jaws unceasingly with a slow effort, as though he had been masticating a lump of india-rubber. He shook his head. He repeated:—"Never mind me. I must see it out—I must see it out," but he consented to sit down for a moment on the skylight, with his hard face turned unflinchingly to windward. The sea spat at it—and stoical, it streamed with water as though he had been weeping. On the weather side of the poop the watch, hanging on to the mizen rigging and to one another, tried to exchange encouraging words. Singleton, at the wheel, yelled out:—"Look out for yourselves!" His voice reached them in a warning whisper. They were startled.

A big, foaming sea came out of the mist; it made for the ship, roaring wildly, and in its rush it looked as mischievous and discomposing as a madman with an axe. One or two, shouting, scrambled up the rigging; most, with a convulsive catch of the breath, held on where they stood. Singleton dug his knees under the wheel-box, and carefully eased the helm to the headlong pitch of the ship, but without taking his eyes off the coming wave. It towered close-to and high, like a wall of green glass topped with snow. The ship rose to it as though she had soared on wings, and for a moment rested poised upon the foaming crest as if she had been a great sea-bird. Before we could draw breath a heavy gust struck her, another roller took her unfairly under the weather bow, she gave a toppling lurch, and filled her decks. Captain Allistoun leaped up, and fell; Archie rolled over him, screaming:—"She will rise!" She gave another lurch to leeward; the lower deadeyes dipped heavily; the men's feet flew from under them, and they hung kicking above the slanting poop. They could see the ship putting her side in the water, and shouted all together:—"She's going!" Forward the forecastle doors flew open, and the watch below were seen leaping out one after another, throwing their arms up; and, falling on hands and knees, scrambled aft on all fours along the high side of the deck, sloping more than the roof of a house. From leeward the seas rose, pursuing them; they looked wretched in a hopeless struggle, like vermin fleeing before a flood; they fought up the weather ladder of the poop one after another, half naked and staring wildly; and as soon as they got up they shot to leeward in clusters, with closed eyes, till they brought up heavily with their ribs against the iron stanchions of the rail; then, groaning, they rolled in a confused mass. The immense volume of water thrown forward by the last scend of the ship had burst the lee door of the forecastle. They could see their chests, pillows, blankets, clothing, come out floating upon the sea. While they struggled back to windward they looked in dismay. The straw beds swam high, the blankets, spread out, undulated; while the chests, waterlogged and with a heavy list, pitched heavily like dismasted hulks, before they sank; Archie's big coat passed with outspread arms, resembling a drowned seaman floating with his head under water. Men were slipping down while trying to dig their fingers into the planks; others, jammed in corners, rolled enormous eyes. They all yelled unceasingly:—"The masts! Cut! Cut! . . ." A black squall howled low over the ship, that lay on her side with the weather yard-arms pointing to the clouds; while the tall masts, inclined nearly to the horizon, seemed to be of an immeasurable length. The carpenter let go his hold, rolled against the skylight, and began to crawl to the cabin entrance, where a big axe was kept ready for just such an emergency. At that moment the topsail sheet parted, the end of the heavy chain racketed aloft, and sparks of red fire streamed down through the flying sprays. The sail flapped once with a jerk that seemed to tear our hearts out through our teeth, and instantly changed into a bunch of fluttering narrow ribbons that tied themselves into knots and became quiet along the yard. Captain Allistoun struggled, managed to stand up with his face near the deck, upon which men swung on the ends of ropes, like nest robbers upon a cliff. One of his feet was on somebody's chest, his face was purple; his lips moved. He yelled also; he yelled, bending down:—"No! No!" Mr. Baker, one leg over the binnacle-stand, roared out:— "Did you say no? Not cut?" He shook his head madly. "No! No!" Between his legs the crawling carpenter heard, collapsed at once, and lay full length in the angle of the skylight. Voices took up the shout—"No! No!" then all became still. They waited for the ship to turn over altogether, and shake them out into the sea; and upon the terrific noise of wind and sea not a murmur of remonstrance came out from those men, who each would have given ever so many years of life to see "them damned sticks go overboard!" They all believed it their only chance; but a little hard-faced man shook his grey head and shouted "No!" without giving them as much as a glance. They were silent, and gasped. They gripped rails, they had wound ropes'-ends under their arms; they clutched ringbolts, they crawled in heaps where there was foothold; they held on with both arms, hooked themselves to anything to windward with elbows, with chins, almost with their teeth: and some, unable to crawl away from where they had been flung, felt the sea leap up, striking against their backs as they struggled upwards. Singleton had stuck to the wheel. His hair flew out in the wind; the gale seemed to take its life-long adversary by the beard and shake his old head. He wouldn't let go, and, with his knees forced between the spokes, flew up and down like a man on a bough. As Death appeared unready, they began to look about. Donkin, caught by one foot in a loop of some rope, hung, head down, below us, and yelled, with his face to the deck:—"Cut! Cut!" Two men lowered themselves cautiously to him; others hauled on the rope. They caught him up, shoved him into a safer place, held him. He shouted curses at the master, shook his fist at him with horrible blasphemies, called upon us in filthy words to "Cut! Don't mind that murdering fool! Cut, some of you!" One of his rescuers struck him a back-handed blow over the mouth; his head banged on the deck, and he became suddenly very quiet, with a white face, breathing hard, and with a few drops of blood trickling from his cut lip. On the lee side another man could be seen stretched out as if stunned; only the washboard prevented him from going over the side. It was the steward. We had to sling him up like a bale, for he was paralyzed with fright. He had rushed up out of the pantry when he felt the ship go over, and had rolled down helplessly, clutching a china mug. It was not broken. With difficulty we tore it away from him, and when he saw it in our hands he was amazed. "Where did you get that thing?" he kept on asking us in a trembling voice. His shirt was blown to shreds; the ripped sleeves flapped like wings. Two men made him fast, and, doubled over the rope that held him, he resembled a bundle of wet rags. Mr. Baker crawled along the line of men, asking:—"Are you all there?" and looking them over. Some blinked vacantly, others shook convulsively; Wamibo's head hung over his breast; and in painful attitudes, cut by lashings, exhausted with clutching, screwed up in corners, they breathed heavily. Their lips twitched and at every sickening heave of the over-turned ship they opened them wide as if to shout. The cook, embracing a wooden stanchion, unconsciously repeated a prayer. In every short interval of the fiendish noises around he could be heard there, without cap or slippers, imploring in that storm the Master of our lives not to lead him into temptation. Soon he also became silent. In all that crowd of cold and hungry men, waiting wearily for a violent death, not a voice was heard; they were mute, and in somber thoughtfulness listened to the horrible imprecations of the gale.

Hours passed. They were sheltered by the heavy inclination of the ship from the wind that rushed in one long unbroken moan above their heads, but cold rain showers fell at times into the uneasy calm of their refuge. Under the torment of that new infliction a pair of shoulders would writhe a little. Teeth chattered. The sky was clearing, and bright sunshine gleamed over the ship. After every burst of battering seas, vivid and fleeting rainbows arched over the drifting hull in the flick of sprays. The gale was ending in a clear blow, which gleamed and cut like a knife. Between two bearded shellbacks Charley, fastened with somebody's long muffler to a deck ringbolt, wept quietly, with rare tears wrung out by bewilderment, cold, hunger, and general misery. One of his neighbors punched him in the ribs asking roughly:—"What's the matter with your cheek? In fine weather there's no holding you, youngster." Turning about with prudence he worked himself out of his coat and threw it over the boy. The other man closed up, muttering:—" 'Twill make a bloomin' man of you, sonny." They flung their arms over and pressed against him. Charley drew his feet up and his eyelids dropped. Sighs were heard, as men, perceiving that they were not to be "drowned in a hurry," tried easier positions. Mr. Creighton, who had hurt his leg, lay amongst us with compressed lips. Some fellows belonging to his watch set about securing him better. Without a word or a glance he lifted his arms one after another to facilitate the operation, and not a muscle moved in his stern, young face. They asked him with solicitude:—"Easier now, sir?" He answered with a curt:—"That'll do." He was a hard young officer, but many of his watch used to say they liked him well enough because he had "such a gentlemanly way of damning us up and down the deck." Others unable to discern such fine shades of refinement respected him for his smartness. For the first time since the ship had gone on her beam ends Captain Allistoun gave a short glance down at his men. He was almost upright—one foot against the side of the skylight, one knee on the deck; and with the end of the vang round his waist swung back and forth with his gaze fixed ahead, watchful, like a man looking out for a sign. Before his eyes the ship, with half her deck below water, rose and fell on heavy seas that rushed from under her flashing in the cold sunshine. We began to think she was wonderfully buoyant—considering. Confident voices were heard shouting:—"She'll do, boys!" Belfast exclaimed with fervor:—"I would giv' a month's pay for a draw at a pipe!" One or two, passing dry tongues on their salt lips, muttered something about a "drink of water." The cook, as if inspired, scrambled up with his breast against the poop water-cask and looked in. There was a little at the bottom. He yelled, waving his arms, and two men began to crawl backwards and forwards with the mug. We had a good mouthful all round. The master shook his head impatiently, refusing. When it came to Charley one of his neighbors shouted:—"That bloomin' boy's asleep." He slept as though he had been dosed with narcotics. They let him be. Singleton held to the wheel with one hand while he drank, bending down to shelter his lips from the wind. Wamibo had to be poked and yelled at before he saw the mug held before his eyes. Knowles said sagaciously:—"It's better'n a tot o' rum." Mr. Baker grunted:—"Thank ye." Mr. Creighton drank and nodded. Donkin gulped greedily, glaring over the rim. Belfast made us laugh when with grimacing mouth he shouted:—"Pass it this way. We're all tay-tottlers here." The master, presented with the mug again by a crouching man, who screamed up at him:—"We all had a drink, captain," groped for it without ceasing to look ahead, and handed it back stiffly as though he could not spare half a glance away from the ship. Faces brightened. We shouted to the cook:—"Well done, doctor!" He sat to leeward, propped by the water-cask and yelled back abundantly, but the seas were breaking in thunder just then, and we only caught snatches that sounded like: "Providence" and "born again." He was at the old game of preaching. We made friendly but derisive gestures at him, and from below he lifted one arm, holding on with the other, moved his lips; he beamed up to us, straining his voice—earnest, and ducking his head before the sprays.

Suddenly some one cried:—"Where's Jimmy?" and we were appalled once more. On the end of the row the boatswain shouted hoarsely:—"Has anyone seed him come out?" Voices exclaimed dismally:—"Drowned—is he? . . . No! In his cabin! . . .

Good Lord! . . . Caught like a bloomin' rat in a trap. . . . Couldn't open his door
. . . Aye! She went over too quick and the water jammed it . . . Poor beggar! . . .
No help for 'im. . . . Let's go and see . . ." "Damn him, who could go?" screamed
Donkin.—"Nobody expects you to," growled the man next to him: "you're only a
thing."—"Is there half a chance to get at 'im?" inquired two or three men together.
Belfast untied himself with blind impetuosity, and all at once shot down to leeward
quicker than a flash of lightning. We shouted all together with dismay; but with his
legs overboard he held and yelled for a rope. In our extremity nothing could be
terrible; so we judged him funny kicking there, and with his scared face. Some one
began to laugh, and, as if hysterically infected with screaming merriment, all those
haggard men went off laughing, wild-eyed, like a lot of maniacs tied up on a wall. Mr.
Baker swung off the binnacle-stand and tendered him one leg. He scrambled up rather
scared, and consigning us with abominable words to the "divvle." "You are. . . .
Ough! You're a foul-mouthed beggar, Craik," grunted Mr. Baker. He answered, stut-
tering with indignation:—"Look at 'em, sorr. The bloomin' dirty images! laughing at
a chum going overboard. Call themselves men, too." But from the break of the poop
the boatswain called out:—"Come along," and Belfast crawled away in a hurry to join
him. The five men, poised and gazing over the edge of the poop, looked for the best
way to get forward. They seemed to hesitate. The others, twisting in their lashings,
turning painfully, stared with open lips. Captain Allistoun saw nothing; he seemed
with his eyes to hold the ship up in a superhuman concentration of effort. The wind
screamed loud in sunshine; columns of spray rose straight up; and in the glitter of
rainbows bursting over the trembling hull the men went over cautiously, disappearing
from sight with deliberate movements.

They went swinging from belaying pin to cleat above the seas that beat the half-
submerged deck. Their toes scraped the planks. Lumps of green cold water toppled
over the bulwark and on their heads. They hung for a moment on strained arms, with
the breath knocked out of them, and with closed eyes—then, letting go with one hand,
balanced with lolling heads, trying to grab some rope or stanchion further forward.
The long-armed and athletic boatswain swung quickly, gripping things with a fist hard
as iron, and remembering suddenly snatches of the last letter from his "old woman."
Little Belfast scrambled in a rage spluttering "cursed nigger." Wamibo's tongue hung
out with excitement; and Archie, intrepid and calm, watched his chance to move with
intelligent coolness.

When above the side of the house, they let go one after another, and falling heavily,
sprawled, pressing their palms to the smooth teak wood. Round them the backwash of
waves seethed white and hissing. All the doors had become trap-doors, of course. The
first was the galley door. The galley extended from side to side, and they could hear
the sea splashing with hollow noises in there. The next door was that of the carpenter's shop. They lifted it, and looked down. The room seemed to have been devastated
by an earthquake. Everything in it had tumbled on the bulkhead facing the door, and
on the other side of that bulkhead there was Jimmy dead or alive. The bench, a half-
finished meat-safe, saws, chisels, wire rods, axes, crowbars, lay in a heap besprinkled

with loose nails. A sharp adze stuck up with a shining edge that gleamed dangerously down there like a wicked smile. The men clung to one another, peering. A sickening, sly lurch of the ship nearly sent them overboard in a body. Belfast howled "Here goes!" and leaped down. Archie followed cannily, catching at shelves that gave way with him, and eased himself in a great crash of ripped wood. There was hardly room for three men to move. And in the sunshiny blue square of the door, the boatswain's face, bearded and dark, Wamibo's face, wild and pale, hung over—watching.

Together they shouted: "Jimmy! Jim!" From above the boatswain contributed a deep growl: "You . . . Wait!" In a pause, Belfast entreated: "Jimmy, darlin', are ye aloive?" The boatswain said: "Again! All together, boys!" All yelled excitedly. Wamibo made noises resembling loud barks. Belfast drummed on the side of the bulkhead with a piece of iron. All ceased suddenly. The sound of screaming and hammering went on thin and distinct—like a solo after a chorus. He was alive. He was screaming and knocking below us with the hurry of a man prematurely shut up in a coffin. We went to work. We attacked with desperation the abominable heap of things heavy, of things sharp, of things clumsy to handle. The boatswain crawled away to find somewhere a flying end of a rope; and Wamibo, held back by shouts:—"Don't jump! . . . Don't come in here, muddlehead!"—remained glaring above us—all shining eyes, gleaming fangs, tumbled hair; resembling an amazed and half-witted fiend gloating over the extraordinary agitation of the damned. The boatswain adjured us to "bear a hand," and a rope descended. We made things fast to it and they went up spinning, never to be seen by man again. A rage to fling things overboard possessed us. We worked fiercely, cutting our hands and speaking brutally to one another. Jimmy kept up a distracting row; he screamed piercingly, without drawing breath, like a tortured woman; he banged with hands and feet. The agony of his fear wrung our hearts so terribly that we longed to abandon him, to get out of that place deep as a well and swaying like a tree, to get out of his hearing, back on the poop where we could wait passively for death in incomparable repose. We shouted to him to "shut up, for God's sake." He redoubled his cries. He must have fancied we could not hear him. Probably he heard his own clamor but faintly. We could picture him crouching on the edge of the upper berth, letting out with both fists at the wood, in the dark, and with his mouth wide open for that unceasing cry. Those were loathsome moments. A cloud driving across the sun would darken the doorway menacingly. Every movement of the ship was pain. We scrambled about with no room to breathe, and felt frightfully sick. The boatswain yelled down at us:—"Bear a hand! Bear a hand! We two will be washed away from here directly if you ain't quick!" Three times a sea leaped over the high side and flung bucketfuls of water on our heads. Then Jimmy, startled by the shock, would stop his noise for a moment—waiting for the ship to sink, perhaps—and began again, distressingly loud, as if invigorated by the gust of fear. At the bottom the nails lay in a layer several inches thick. It was ghastly. Every nail in the world, not driven in firmly somewhere, seemed to have found its way into that carpenter's shop. There they were, of all kinds, the remnants of stores from seven voyages. Tin-tacks, copper tacks (sharp as needles); pump nails with big heads, like tiny iron mushrooms; nails without any heads (horrible); French nails polished and slim. They lay in a solid mass more inabordable than a hedgehog. We hesitated, yearning for a shovel, while Jimmy below us yelled as though he had been flayed. Groaning, we dug our fingers in, and very much hurt, shook our hands, scattering nails and drops of blood. We passed up our hats full of assorted nails to the boatswain, who, as if performing a mysterious and appeasing rite, cast them wide upon a raging sea.

We got to the bulkhead at last. Those were stout planks. She was a ship, well finished in every detail—the *Narcissus* was. They were the stoutest planks ever put into a ship's bulkhead—we thought—and then we perceived that, in our hurry, we had sent all the tools overboard. Absurd little Belfast wanted to break it down with his own weight, and with both feet leaped straight up like a springbok, cursing the Clyde shipwrights for not scamping their work. Incidentally he reviled all North Britain, the rest of the earth, the sea—and all his companions. He swore, as he alighted heavily on his heels, that he would never, never any more associate with any fool that "hadn't savee enough to know his knee from his elbow." He managed by his thumping to scare the last remnant of wits out of Jimmy. We could hear the object of our exasperated solicitude darting to and fro under the planks. He had cracked his voice at last, and could only squeak miserably. His back or else his head rubbed the planks, now here, now there, in a puzzling manner. He squeaked as he dodged the invisible blows. It was more heartrending even than his yells. Suddenly Archie produced a crowbar. He had kept it back; also a small hatchet. We howled with satisfaction. He struck a mighty blow and small chips flew at our eyes. The boatswain above shouted:—"Look out! Look out there. Don't kill the man. Easy does it!" Wamibo, maddened with excitement, hung head down and insanely urged us:—"Hoo! Strook 'im! Hoo! Hoo!" We were afraid he would fall in and kill one of us and, hurriedly, we entreated the boatswain to "shove the blamed Finn overboard." Then, all together, we yelled down at the planks:—"Stand from under! Get forward," and listened. We only heard the deep hum and moan of the wind above us, the mingled roar and hiss of the seas. The ship, as if overcome with despair, wallowed lifelessly, and our heads swam with that unnatural motion. Belfast clamored:—"For the love of God, Jimmy, where are ye? . . . Knock! Jimmy darlint! . . . Knock! You bloody black beast! Knock!" He was as quiet as a dead man inside a grave; and, like men standing above a grave, we were on the verge of tears—but with vexation, the strain, the fatigue; with the great longing to be done with it, to get away, and lie down to rest somewhere where we could see our danger and breathe. Archie shouted:—"Gi'e me room!" We crouched behind him, guarding our heads, and he struck time after time in the joint of planks. They cracked. Suddenly the crowbar went halfway in through a splintered oblong hole. It must have missed Jimmy's head by less than an inch. Archie withdrew it quickly, and that infamous nigger rushed at the hole, put his lips to it, and whispered "Help," in an almost extinct voice; he pressed his head to it, trying madly to get out through that opening one inch wide and three inches long. In our disturbed state we were absolutely paralyzed by his incredible action. It seemed impossible to drive him away. Even Archie at last lost his composure. "If ye don't clear oot I'll drive the crowbar thro' your head," he shouted in a determined voice. He meant what he said, and his earnestness seemed to make an impression on Jimmy. He disappeared suddenly, and we set to prising and tearing at the planks with the eagerness of men trying to get at a mortal enemy, and spurred by the desire to tear him limb from limb. The wood split, cracked, gave way. Belfast plunged in head and shoulders and groped viciously. "I've got 'im! Got 'im," he shouted. "Oh! There! . . . He's gone; I've got 'im! . . . Pull at my legs! . . . Pull!" Wamibo hooted unceasingly. The boatswain shouted directions:— "Catch hold of his hair, Belfast; pull straight up, you two! . . . Pull fair!" We pulled fair. We pulled Belfast out with a jerk, and dropped him with disgust. In a sitting posture, purple-faced, he sobbed despairingly:—"How can I hold on to 'is blooming short wool?" Suddenly Jimmy's head and shoulders appeared. He stuck half-way, and with rolling eyes foamed at our feet. We flew at him with brutal impatience, we tore the shirt off his back, we tugged at his ears, we panted over him; and all at once he came away in our hands as though somebody had let go his legs. With the same movement, without a pause, we swung him up. His breath whistled, he kicked our upturned faces, he grasped two pairs of arms above his head, and he squirmed up with such precipitation that he seemed positively to escape from our hands like a bladder full of gas. Streaming with perspiration, we swarmed up the rope, and, coming into the blast of cold wind, gasped like men plunged into icy water. With burning faces we shivered to the very marrow of our bones. Never before had the gale seemed to us more furious, the sea more mad, the sunshine more merciless and mocking, and the position of the ship more hopeless and appalling. Every movement of her was ominous of the end of her agony and of the beginning of ours. We staggered away from the door, and, alarmed by a sudden roll, fell down in a bunch. It appeared to us that the side of the house was more smooth than glass and more slippery than ice. There was nothing to hang on to but a long brass hook used sometimes to keep back an open door. Wamibo held on to it and we held on to Wamibo, clutching our Jimmy. He had completely collapsed now. He did not seem to have the strength to close his hand. We stuck to him blindly in our fear. We were not afraid of Wamibo letting go (we remembered that the brute was stronger than any three men in the ship), but we were afraid of the hook giving way, and we also believed that the ship had made up her mind to turn over at last. But she didn't. A sea swept over us. The boatswain spluttered:—"Up and away. There's a lull. Away aft with you, or we will all go to the devil here." We stood up surrounding Jimmy. We begged him to hold up, to hold on, at least. He glared with his bulging eyes, mute as a fish, and with all the stiffening knocked out of him. He wouldn't stand; he wouldn't even as much as clutch at our necks; he was only a cold black skin loosely stuffed with soft cotton wool; his arms and legs swung jointless and pliable; his head rolled about; the lower lip hung down, enormous and heavy. We pressed round him, bothered and dismayed; sheltering him we swung here and there in a body; and on the very brink of eternity we tottered all together with concealing and absurd gestures, like a lot of drunken men embarrassed with a stolen corpse.

Something had to be done. We had to get him aft. A rope was tied slack under his armpits, and, reaching up at the risk of our lives, we hung him on the foresheet cleat. He emitted no sound; he looked as ridiculously lamentable as a doll that had lost half its sawdust, and we started on our perilous journey over the main deck, dragging along with care that pitiful, that limp, that hateful burden. He was not very heavy, but had he weighed a ton he could not have been more awkward to handle. We literally passed him from hand to hand. Now and then we had to hang him up on a handy belaying-pin, to draw a breath and re-form the line. Had the pin broken he would have irretrievably gone into the Southern Ocean, but he had to take his chance of that; and after a little while, becoming apparently aware of it, he groaned slightly, and with a great effort whispered a few words. We listened eagerly. He was reproaching us with our carelessness in letting him run such risks: "Now, after I got myself out from there," he breathed out weakly. "There" was his cabin. And he got himself out. We had nothing to do with it apparently! . . . No matter. . . . We went on and let him take his chances, simply because we could not help it; for though at that time we hated him more than ever—more than anything under heaven—we did not want to lose him. We had so far saved him; and it had become a personal matter between us and the sea. We meant to stick to him. Had we (by an incredible hypothesis) undergone similar toil and trouble for an empty cask, that cask would have become as precious to us as Jimmy was. More precious, in fact, because we would have had no reason to hate the cask. And we hated James Wait. We could not get rid of the monstrous suspicion that this astounding black-man was shamming sick, had been malingering heartlessly in the face of our toil, of our scorn, of our patience—and now was malingering in the face of our devotion—in the face of death. Our vague and imperfect morality rose with disgust at his unmanly lie. But he stuck to it manfully— amazingly. No! It couldn't be. He was at all extremity. His cantankerous temper was only the result of the provoking invincibleness of that death he felt by his side. Any man may be angry with such a masterful chum. But, then, what kind of men were we —with our thoughts! Indignation and doubt grappled within us in a scuffle that trampled upon the finest of our feelings. And we hated him because of the suspicion; we detested him because of the doubt. We could not scorn him safely—neither could we pity him without risk to our dignity. So we hated him, and passed him carefully from hand to hand. We cried, "Got him?"—"Yes. All right. Let go." And he swung from one enemy to another, showing about as much life as an old bolster would do. His eyes made two narrow white slits in the black face. The air escaped through his lips with a noise like the sound of bellows. We reached the poop ladder at last, and it being a comparatively safe place, we lay for a moment in an exhausted heap to rest a little. He began to mutter. We were always incurably anxious to hear what he had to say. This time he mumbled peevishly, "It took you some time to come. I began to think the whole smart lot of you had been washed overboard. What kept you back? Hey? Funk?" We said nothing. With sighs we started again to drag him up. The secret and ardent desire of our hearts was the desire to beat him viciously with our fists about the head; and we handled him as tenderly as though he had been made of glass. . . .

The return on the poop was like the return of wanderers after many years amongst people marked by the desolation of time. Eyes were turned slowly in their sockets, glancing at us. Faint murmurs were heard, "Have you got 'im after all?" The well-known faces looked strange and familiar; they seemed faded and grimy; they had a mingled expression of fatigue and eagerness. They seemed to have become much thinner during our absence, as if all these men had been starving for a long time in their abandoned attitudes. The captain, with a round turn of a rope on his wrist, and kneeling on one knee, swung with a face cold and stiff; but with living eyes he was still holding the ship up, heeding no one, as if lost in the unearthly effort of that endeavor. We fastened up James Wait in a safe place. Mr. Baker scrambled along to lend a hand. Mr. Creighton, on his back, and very pale, muttered, "Well done," and gave us, Jimmy and the sky, a scornful glance, then closed his eyes slowly. Here and there a man stirred a little, but most of them remained apathetic, in cramped positions, muttering between shivers. The sun was setting. A sun enormous, unclouded and red, declining low as if bending down to look into their faces. The wind whistled across long sunbeams that, resplendent and cold, struck full on the dilated pupils of staring eyes without making them wink. The wisps of hair and the tangled beards were grey with the salt of the sea. The faces were earthy, and the dark patches under the eyes extended to the ears, smudged into the hollows of sunken cheeks. The lips were livid and thin, and when they moved it was with difficulty, as though they had been glued to the teeth. Some grinned sadly in the sunlight, shaking with cold. Others were sad and still. Charley, subdued by the sudden disclosure of the insignificance of his youth, darted fearful glances. The two smooth-faced Norwegians resembled decrepit children, star-ing stupidly. To leeward, on the edge of the horizon, black seas leaped up towards the glowing sun. It sank slowly, round and blazing, and the crests of waves splashed on the edge of the luminous circle. One of the Norwegians appeared to catch sight of it, and after giving a violent start, began to speak. His voice, startling the others, made them stir. They moved their heads stiffly, or turning with difficulty, looked at him with surprise, with fear, or in grave silence. He chattered at the setting sun, nodding his head, while the big seas began to roll across the crimson disc; and over miles of turbulent waters the shadows of high waves swept with a running darkness the faces of men. A crested roller broke with a loud hissing roar, and the sun, as if put out, disappeared. The chattering voice faltered, went out together with the light. There were sighs. In the sudden lull that follows the crash of a broken sea a man said wearily, "Here's that blooming Dutchman gone off his chump." A seaman, lashed by the middle, tapped the deck with his open hand with unceasing quick flaps. In the gathering greyness of twilight a bulky form was seen rising aft, and began marching on all fours with the movements of some big cautious beast. It was Mr. Baker passing along the line of men. He grunted encouragingly over every one, felt their fastenings. Some, with half-open eyes, puffed like men oppressed by heat; others mechanically and in dreamy voices answered him, "Aye! aye! sir!" He went from one to another grunting, "Ough! . . . See her through it yet"; and unexpectedly, with loud angry outbursts, blew up Knowles for cutting off a long piece from the fall of the relieving tackle.

"Ough!——Ashamed of yourself——Relieving tackle——Don't you know better!——Ough!——Able seaman! Ough!" The lame man was crushed. He muttered,
"Get som'think for a lashing for myself, sir."—"Ough! Lashing——yourself. Are you
a tinker or a sailor——What? Ough!——May want that tackle directly——
Ough!——More use to the ship than your lame carcass. Ough!——Keep it!——
Keep it, now you've done it." He crawled away slowly, muttering to himself about
some men being "worse than children." It had been a comforting row. Low exclamations were heard "Hallo . . . Hallo." . . . Those who had been painfully dozing
asked with convulsive starts, "What's up? . . . What is it?" The answers came with
unexpected cheerfulness: "The mate is going bald-headed for lame Jack about something or other." "No!" . . . "What 'as he done?" Some one even chuckled. It was like
a whiff of hope, like a reminder of safe days. Donkin, who had been stupefied with
fear, revived suddenly and began to shout:—" 'Ear 'im; that's the way they tawlk to us.
Vy donch 'ee 'it 'im—one ov yer! 'It 'im. 'It 'im! Comin' the mate over us. We are as
good men as 'ee! We're all goin' to 'ell now. We 'ave been starved in this rotten ship,
an' now we're goin' to be drowned for them black 'earted bullies! 'It 'im!" He shrieked
in the deepening gloom, he blubbered and sobbed, screaming:—" 'It 'im! 'It 'im!" The
rage and fear of his disregarded right to live tried the steadfastness of hearts more than
the menacing shadows of the night that advanced through the unceasing clamor of the
gale. From aft Mr. Baker was heard:—"Is one of you men going to stop him—must I
come along?" "Shut up!" . . . "Keep quiet!" cried various voices, exasperated, trembling with cold.—"You'll get one across the mug from me directly," said an invisible
seaman, in a weary tone, "I won't let the mate have the trouble." He ceased and lay still
with the silence of despair. On the black sky the stars, coming out, gleamed over an
inky sea that, speckled with foam, flashed back at them the evanescent and pale light
of a dazzling whiteness born from the black turmoil of the waves. Remote in the
eternal calm they glittered hard and cold above the uproar of the earth; they surrounded the vanquished and tormented ship on all sides: more pitiless than the eyes of
a triumphant mob, and as unapproachable as the hearts of men.

The icy south wind howled exultingly under the somber splendor of the sky. The
cold shook the men with a resistless violence as though it had tried to shake them to
pieces. Short moans were swept unheard off the stiff lips. Some complained in mutters
of "not feeling themselves below the waist"; while those who had closed their eyes,
imagined they had a block of ice on their chests. Others, alarmed at not feeling any
pain in their fingers, beat the deck feebly with their hands—obstinate and exhausted.
Wamibo stared vacant and dreamy. The Scandinavians kept on a meaningless mutter
through chattering teeth. The spare Scotchmen, with determined efforts, kept their
lower jaws still. The West-country men lay big and stolid in an invulnerable surliness.
A man yawned and swore in turns. Another breathed with a rattle in his throat. Two
elderly hard-weather shellbacks, fast side by side, whispered dismally to one another
about the landlady of a boarding-house in Sunderland, whom they both knew. They
extolled her motherliness and her liberality; they tried to talk about the joint of beef
and the big fire in the downstairs kitchen. The words dying faintly on their lips ended

in light sighs. A sudden voice cried into the cold night, "O Lord!" No one changed his position or took any notice of the cry. One or two passed, with a repeated and vague gesture, their hands over their faces, but most of them kept very still. In the benumbed immobility of their bodies they were excessively wearied by their thoughts, which rushed with the rapidity and vividness of dreams. Now and then, by an abrupt and startling exclamation, they answered the weird hail of some illusion; then, again, in silence contemplated the vision of known faces and familiar things. They recalled the aspect of forgotten shipmates and heard the voice of dead and gone skippers. They remembered the noise of gaslit streets, the steamy heat of tap-rooms or the scorching sunshine of calm days at sea.

Mr. Baker left his insecure place, and crawled, with stoppages, along the poop. In the dark and on all fours he resembled some carnivorous animal prowling amongst corpses. At the break, propped to windward of a stanchion, he looked down on the main deck. It seemed to him that the ship had a tendency to stand up a little more. The wind had eased a little, he thought, but the sea ran as high as ever. The waves foamed viciously, and the lee side of the deck disappeared under a hissing whiteness as of boiling milk, while the rigging sang steadily with a deep vibrating note, and, at every upward swing of the ship, the wind rushed with a long-drawn clamor amongst the spars. Mr. Baker watched very still. A man near him began to make a blabbing noise with his lips, all at once and very loud, as though the cold had broken brutally through him. He went on:—"Ba—ba—ba—brr—brr—ba—ba."—"Stop that!" cried Mr. Baker, groping in the dark. "Stop it!" He went on shaking the leg he found under his hand.—"What is it, sir?" called out Belfast, in the tone of a man awakened suddenly; "We are looking after that 'ere Jimmy."—"Are you? Ough! Don't make that row then. Who's that near you?"—"It's me—the boatswain, sir," growled the West-country man; "we are trying to keep life in that poor devil."—"Aye, aye!" said Mr. Baker. "Do it quietly, can't you?"—"He wants us to hold him up above the rail," went on the boatswain, with irritation, "says he can't breathe here under our jackets."—"If we lift 'im, we drop 'im overboard," said another voice, "we can't feel our hands with cold."—"I don't care. I am choking!" exclaimed James Wait in a clear tone.—"Oh, no, my son," said the boatswain, desperately, "you don't go till we all go on this fine night."—"You will see yet many a worse," said Mr. Baker, cheerfully.—"It's no child's play, sir!" answered the boatswain. "Some of us further aft, here, are in a pretty bad way."—"If the blamed sticks had been cut out of her she would be running along on her bottom now like any decent ship, an' giv' us all a chance," said some one, with a sigh.—"The old man wouldn't have it . . . much he cares for us," whispered an-other.—"Care for you!" exclaimed Mr. Baker, angrily. "Why should he care for you? Are you a lot of women passengers to be taken care of? We are here to take care of the ship—and some of you ain't up to that. Ough! . . . What have you done so very smart to be taken care of? Ough! . . . Some of you can't stand a bit of a breeze without crying over it."—"Come, sorr. We ain't so bad," protested Belfast, in a voice shaken by shivers; "we ain't . . . brr . . ."—"Again," shouted the mate, grabbing at the shadowy form; "again! . . . Why, you're in your shirt! What have you done?"—

"I've put my oilskin and jacket over that half-dead nayggur—and he says he chokes," said Belfast, complainingly—"You wouldn't call me nigger if I wasn't half dead, you Irish beggar!" boomed James Wait, vigorously.—"You . . . brr . . . You wouldn't be white if you were ever so well . . . I will fight you . . . brrr . . . in fine weather . . . brrr . . . with one hand tied behind my back . . . brrrrr . . ."—"I don't want your rags—I want air," gasped out the other faintly, as if suddenly exhausted.

The sprays swept over whistling and pattering. Men disturbed in their peaceful torpor by the pain of quarrelsome shouts, moaned, muttering curses. Mr. Baker crawled off a little way to leeward where a watercask boomed up big, with something white against it. "Is it you, Podmore?" asked Mr. Baker. He had to repeat the question twice before the cook turned, coughing feebly.—"Yes, sir. I've been praying in my mind for a quick deliverance; for I am prepared for any call. . . . I——"—"Look here, cook," interrupted Mr. Baker, "the men are perishing with cold."—"Cold!" said the cook, mournfully; "they will be warm enough before long."—"What?" asked Mr. Baker, looking along the deck into the faint sheen of frothing water.—"They are a wicked lot," continued the cook solemnly, but in an unsteady voice, "about as wicked as any ship's company in this sinful world! Now, I"—he trembled so that he could hardly speak; his was an exposed place, and in a cotton shirt, a thin pair of trousers, and with his knees under his nose, he received, quaking, the flicks of stinging, salt drops; his voice sounded exhausted—"now, I—any time . . . My eldest youngster, Mr. Baker . . . a clever boy . . . last Sunday on shore before this voyage he wouldn't go to church, sir. Says I, 'You go and clean yourself, or I'll know the reason why!' What does he do? . . . Pond, Mr. Baker—fell into the pond in his best rig, sir! . . . Accident? . . . 'Nothing will save you, fine scholar though you are!' says I. . . . Accident! . . . I whopped him, sir, till I couldn't lift my arm. . . ." His voice faltered. "I whopped 'im!" he repeated, rattling his teeth; then, after a while, let out a mournful sound that was half a groan, half a snore. Mr. Baker shook him by the shoulders. "Hey! Cook! Hold up, Podmore! Tell me—is there any fresh water in the galley tank? The ship is lying along less, I think; I would try to get forward. A little water would do them good. Hallo! Look out! Look out!" The cook struggled.—"Not you, sir—not you!" He began to scramble to windward. "Galley! . . . my business!" he shouted.—"Cook's going crazy now," said several voices. He yelled:—"Crazy, am I? I am more ready to die than any of you, officers incloosive—there! As long as she swims I will cook! I will get you coffee."—"Cook, ye are a gentleman!" cried Belfast. But the cook was already going over the weather-ladder. He stopped for a moment to shout back on the poop:—"As long as she swims I will cook!" and disappeared as though he had gone overboard. The men who had heard sent after him a cheer that sounded like a wail of sick children. An hour or more afterwards some one said distinctly: "He's gone for good."—"Very likely," assented the boatswain; "even in fine weather he was as smart about the deck as a milch-cow on her first voyage. We ought to go and see." Nobody moved. As the hours dragged slowly through the darkness Mr. Baker crawled back and forth along the poop several times. Some men fancied they had heard him exchange murmurs with the master, but at that time the memories were incomparably more vivid than anything actual, and they were not certain whether the murmurs were heard now or many years ago. They did not try to find out. A mutter more or less did not matter. It was too cold for curiosity, and almost for hope. They could not spare a moment or a thought from the great mental occupation of wishing to live. And the desire of life kept them alive, apathetic and enduring, under the cruel persistence of wind and cold; while the bestarred black dome of the sky revolved slowly above the ship, that drifted, bearing their patience and their suffering, through the stormy solitude of the sea.

Huddled close to one another, they fancied themselves utterly alone. They heard sustained loud noises, and again bore the pain of existence through long hours of profound silence. In the night they saw sunshine, felt warmth, and suddenly, with a start, thought that the sun would never rise upon a freezing world. Some heard laughter, listened to songs; others, near the end of the poop, could hear loud human shrieks, and opening their eyes, were surprised to hear them still, though very faint, and far away. The boatswain said:—"Why, it's the cook, hailing from forward. I think." He hardly believed his own words or recognized his own voice. It was a long time before the man next to him gave a sign of life. He punched hard his other neighbor and said:—"The cook's shouting!" Many did not understand, others did not care; the majority further aft did not believe. But the boatswain and another man had the pluck to crawl away forward to see. They seemed to have been gone for hours, and were very soon forgotten. Then suddenly men who had been plunged in a hopeless resignation became as if possessed with a desire to hurt. They belabored one another with fists. In the darkness they struck persistently anything soft they could feel near, and with a greater effort than for a shout, whispered excitedly:—"They've got some hot coffee. . . . Boss'en got it. . . ." "No! . . . Where?" . . . "It's coming! Cook made it." James Wait moaned. Donkin scrambled viciously, caring not where he kicked, and anxious that the officers should have none of it. It came in a pot, and they drank in turns. It was hot, and while it blistered the greedy palates, it seemed incredible. The men sighed out parting with the mug:—"How 'as he done it?" Some cried weakly:—"Bully for you, doctor!"

He had done it somehow. Afterwards Archie declared that the thing was "meeraculous." For many days we wondered, and it was the one ever-interesting subject of conversation to the end of the voyage. We asked the cook, in fine weather, how he felt when he saw his stove "reared up on end." We inquired, in the north-east trade and on serene evenings, whether he had to stand on his head to put things right somewhat. We suggested he had used his bread-board for a raft, and from there comfortably had stoked his grate; and we did our best to conceal our admiration under the wit of fine irony. He affirmed not to know anything about it, rebuked our levity, declared himself, with solemn animation, to have been the object of a special mercy for the saving of our unholy lives. Fundamentally he was right, no doubt; but he need not have been so offensively positive about it—he need not have hinted so often that it would have gone hard with us had he not been there, meritorious and pure, to receive the inspiration and the strength for the work of grace. Had we been saved by his recklessness or his agility, we could have at length become reconciled to the fact; but to admit our obligation to anybody's virtue and holiness alone was as difficult for us as for any other handful of mankind. Like many benefactors of humanity, the cook took himself too seriously, and reaped the reward of irreverence. We were not ungrateful, however. He remained heroic. His saying—*the* saying of his life—became proverbial in the mouth of men as are the sayings of conquerors or sages. Later, whenever one of us was puzzled by a task and advised to relinquish it, he would express his determination to persevere and to succeed by the words:—"As long as she swims I will cook!"

The hot drink helped us through the bleak hours that precede the dawn. The sky low by the horizon took on the delicate tints of pink and yellow like the inside of a rare shell. And higher, where it glowed with a pearly sheen, a small black cloud appeared, like a forgotten fragment of the night set in a border of dazzling gold. The beams of light skipped on the crests of waves. The eyes of men turned to the eastward. The sunlight flooded their weary faces. They were giving themselves up to fatigue as though they had done for ever with their work. On Singleton's black oilskin coat the dried salt glistened like hoar frost. He hung on by the wheel, with open and lifeless eyes. Captain Allistoun, unblinking, faced the rising sun. His lips stirred, opened for the first time in twenty-four hours, and with a fresh firm voice he cried, "Wear ship!"

The commanding sharp tones made all these torpid men start like a sudden flick of a whip. Then again, motionless where they lay, the force of habit made some of them repeat the order in hardly audible murmurs. Captain Allistoun glanced down at his crew, and several, with fumbling fingers and hopeless movements, tried to cast themselves adrift. He repeated impatiently, "Wear ship. Now then, Mr. Baker, get the men along. What's the matter with them?"—"Wear ship. Do you hear there?—Wear ship!" thundered out the boatswain suddenly. His voice seemed to break through a deadly spell. Men began to stir and crawl.—"I want the fore-topmast staysail run up smartly," said the master, very loudly; "if you can't manage it standing up you must do it lying down—that's all. Bear a hand!"—"Come along! Let's give the old girl a chance," urged the boatswain.—"Aye! aye! Wear ship!" exclaimed quavering voices. The forecastle men, with reluctant faces, prepared to go forward. Mr. Baker pushed ahead, grunting, on all fours to show the way, and they followed him over the break. The others lay still with a vile hope in their hearts of not being required to move till they got saved or drowned in peace.

After some time they could be seen forward appearing on the forecastle head, one by one in unsafe attitudes; hanging on to the rails, clambering over the anchors; embracing the cross-head of the windlass or hugging the fore-capstan. They were restless with strange exertions, waved their arms, knelt, lay flat down, staggered up, seemed to strive their hardest to go overboard. Suddenly a small white piece of canvas fluttered amongst them, grew larger, beating. Its narrow head rose in jerks—and at last it stood distended and triangular in the sunshine.—"They have done it!" cried the voices aft. Captain Allistoun let go the rope he had round his wrist and rolled to leeward headlong. He could be seen casting the lee main braces off the pins while the

backwash of waves splashed over him.—"Square the main yard!" he shouted up to us
—who stared at him in wonder. We hesitated to stir. "The main brace, men. Haul!
haul anyhow! Lay on your backs and haul!" he screeched, half drowned down there.
We did not believe we could move the main yard, but the strongest and the less
discouraged tried to execute the order. Others assisted half-heartedly. Singleton's eyes
blazed suddenly as he took a fresh grip of the spokes. Captain Allistoun fought his
way up to windward.—"Haul, men! Try to move it! Haul, and help the ship." His
hard face worked, suffused and furious. "Is she going off, Singleton?" he cried.—"Not
a move yet, sir," croaked the old seaman in a horribly hoarse voice.—"Watch the helm,
Singleton," spluttered the master. "Haul, men! Have you no more strength than rats?
Haul, and earn your salt." Mr. Creighton, on his back, with a swollen leg and a face as
white as a piece of paper, blinked his eyes; his bluish lips twitched. In the wild
scramble men grabbed at him, crawled over his hurt leg, knelt on his chest. He kept
perfectly still, setting his teeth without a moan, without a sigh. The master's ardor, the
cries of that silent man inspired us. We hauled and hung in bunches on the rope. We
heard him say with violence to Donkin, who sprawled abjectly on his stomach—"I
will brain you with this belaying pin if you don't catch hold of the brace," and that
victim of men's injustice, cowardly and cheeky, whimpered:—"Are you goin' to murder
us now?" while with sudden desperation he gripped the rope. Men sighed, shouted,
hissed meaningless words, groaned. The yards moved, came slowly square against the
wind, that hummed loudly on the yard-arms.—"Going off, sir," shouted Singleton,
"she's just started."—"Catch a turn with that brace. Catch a turn!" clamored the
master. Mr. Creighton, nearly suffocated and unable to move, made a mighty effort,
and with his left hand managed to nip the rope—"All fast!" cried some one. He
closed his eyes as if going off into a swoon, while huddled together about the brace we
watched with scared looks what the ship would do now.

She went off slowly as though she had been weary and disheartened like the men
she carried. She paid off very gradually, making us hold our breath till we choked, and
as soon as she had brought the wind abaft the beam she started to move, and fluttered
our hearts. It was awful to see her, nearly overturned, begin to gather way and drag her
submerged side through the water. The dead-eyes of the rigging churned the breaking
seas. The lower half of the deck was full of mad whirlpools and eddies; and the long
line of the lee rail could be seen showing black now and then in the swirls of a field of
foam as dazzling and white as a field of snow. The wind sang shrilly amongst the
spars; and at every slight lurch we expected her to slip to the bottom sideways from
under our backs. When dead before it she made the first distinct attempt to stand up,
and we encouraged her with a feeble and discordant howl. A great sea came running up
aft and hung for a moment over us with a curling top; then crashed down under the
counter and spread out on both sides into a great sheet of bursting froth. Above its
fierce hiss we heard Singleton's croak:—"She is steering!" He had both his feet now
planted firmly on the grating, and the wheel spun fast as he eased the helm.—"Bring
the wind on the port quarter and steady her!" called out the master, staggering to his
feet, the first man up from amongst our prostrate heap. One or two screamed with

excitement:—"She rises!" Far away forward, Mr. Baker and three others were seen erect and black on the clear sky, lifting their arms, and with open mouths as though they had been shouting all together. The ship trembled, trying to lift her side, lurched back, seemed to give up with a nerveless dip, and suddenly with an unexpected jerk swung violently to windward, as though she had torn herself out from a deadly grasp. The whole immense volume of water, lifted by her deck, was thrown bodily across to starboard. Loud cracks were heard. Iron ports breaking open thundered with ringing blows. The water topped over the starboard rail with the rush of a river falling over a dam. The sea on deck, and the seas on every side of her, mingled together in a deafening roar. She rolled violently. We got up and were helplessly run or flung about from side to side. Men, rolling over and over, yelled,—"The house will go!"—"She clears herself!" Lifted by a towering sea she ran along with it for a moment, spouting thick streams of water through every opening of her wounded sides. The lee braces having been carried away or washed off the pins, all the ponderous yards on the fore swung from side to side and with appalling rapidity at every roll. The men forward were seen crouching here and there with fearful glances upwards at the enormous spars that whirled about over their heads. The torn canvas and the ends of broken gear streamed in the wind like wisps of hair. Through the clear sunshine, over the flashing turmoil and uproar of the seas, the ship ran blindly, dishevelled and headlong, as if fleeing for her life; and on the poop we spun, we tottered about, distracted and noisy. We all spoke at once in a thin babble; we had the aspect of invalids and the gestures of maniacs. Eyes shone, large and haggard, in smiling, meager faces that seemed to have been dusted over with powdered chalk. We stamped, clapped our hands, feeling ready to jump and do anything; but in reality hardly able to keep on our feet. Captain Allistoun, hard and slim, gesticulated madly from the poop at Mr. Baker: "Steady these foreyards! Steady them the best you can!" On the main deck, men excited by his cries, splashed, dashing aimlessly here and there with the foam swirling up to their waists. Apart, far aft, and alone by the helm, old Singleton had deliberately tucked his white beard under the top button of his glistening coat. Swaying upon the din and tumult of the seas, with the whole battered length of the ship launched forward in a rolling rush before his steady old eyes, he stood rigidly still, forgotten by all, and with an attentive face. In front of his erect figure only the two arms moved crosswise with a swift and suddenly readiness, to check or urge again the rapid stir of circling spokes. He steered with care.

I V

On men reprieved by its disdainful mercy, the immortal sea confers in its justice the full privilege of desired unrest. Through the perfect wisdom of its grace they are not permitted to meditate at ease upon the complicated and acrid savor of existence. They must without pause justify their life to the eternal pity that commands toil to be hard and unceasing, from sunrise to sunset, from sunset to sunrise; till the weary succession of nights and days tainted by the obstinate clamor of sages, demanding bliss and empty heaven, is redeemed at last by the vast silence of pain and labor, by the dumb fear and the dumb courage of men obscure, forgetful, and enduring.

The master and Mr. Baker coming face to face stared for a moment, with the intense and amazed looks of men meeting unexpectedly after years of trouble. Their voices were gone, and they whispered desperately at one another.—"Any one missing?" asked Captain Allistoun.—"No. All there."—"Anybody hurt?"—"Only the second mate."—"I will look after him directly. We're lucky."—"Very," articulated Mr. Baker, faintly. He gripped the rail and rolled bloodshot eyes. The little grey man made an effort to raise his voice above a dull mutter, and fixed his chief mate with a cold gaze, piercing like a dart.—"Get sail on the ship," he said, speaking authoritatively and with an inflexible snap of his thin lips. "Get sail on her as soon as you can. This is a fair wind. At once, sir—Don't give the men time to feel themselves. They will get done up and stiff, and we will never . . . We must get her along now" . . . He reeled to a long heavy roll; the rail dipped into the glancing, hissing water. He caught a shroud, swung helplessly against the mate . . . "now we have a fair wind at last—Make—sail." His head rolled from shoulder to shoulder. His eyelids began to beat rapidly. "And the pumps—pumps, Mr. Baker." He peered as though the face within a foot of his eyes had been half a mile off. "Keep the men on the move to—to get her along," he mumbled in a drowsy tone, like a man going off into a doze. He pulled himself together suddenly. "Mustn't stand. Won't do," he said with a painful attempt at a smile. He let go his hold, and, propelled by the dip of the ship, ran aft unwillingly, with small steps, till he brought up against the binnacle stand. Hanging on there he looked up in an aimless manner at Singleton, who, unheeding him, watched anxiously the end of the jib-boom—"Steering gear works all right?" he asked. There was a noise in the old seaman's throat, as though the words had been rattling together before they could come out.—"Steers . . . like a little boat," he said, at last, with hoarse tenderness, without giving the master as much as half a glance—then, watchfully, spun the wheel down, steadied, flung it back again. Captain Allistoun tore himself away from the delight of leaning against the binnacle, and began to walk the poop, swaying and reeling to preserve his balance. . . .

The pump-rods, clanking, stamped in short jumps while the fly-wheels turned smoothly, with great speed, at the foot of the mainmast, flinging back and forth with a regular impetuosity two limp clusters of men clinging to the handles. They abandoned themselves, swaying from the hip with twitching faces and stony eyes. The carpenter, sounding from time to time, exclaimed mechanically: "Shake her up! Keep her going!" Mr. Baker could not speak, but found his voice to shout; and under the goad of his objurgations, men looked to the lashings, dragged out new sails; and thinking themselves unable to move, carried heavy blocks aloft—overhauled the gear. They went up the rigging with faltering and desperate efforts. Their heads swam as they shifted their hold, stepped blindly on the yards like men in the dark; or trusted themselves to the first rope at hand with the negligence of exhausted strength. The narrow escapes from falls did not disturb the languid beat of their hearts; the roar of the seas seething far below them sounded continuous and faint like an indistinct noise from another world:

278   NOVELS

the wind filled their eyes with tears, and with heavy gusts tried to push them off from where they swayed in insecure positions. With streaming faces and blowing hair they flew up and down between sky and water, bestriding the ends of yard-arms, crouching on foot-ropes, embracing lifts to have their hands free, or standing up against chain ties. Their thoughts floated vaguely between the desire of rest and the desire of life, while their stiffened fingers cast off head-earrings, fumbled for knives, or held with tenacious grip against the violent shocks of beating canvas. They glared savagely at one another, made frantic signs with one hand while they held their life in the other, looked down on the narrow strip of flooded deck, shouted along to leeward: "Light-to!" . . . "Haul out!" . . . "Make fast!" Their lips moved, their eyes started, furious and eager with the desire to be understood, but the wind tossed their words unheard upon the disturbed sea. In an unendurable and unending strain they worked like men driven by a merciless dream to toil in an atmosphere of ice or flame. They burnt and shivered in turns. Their eyeballs smarted as if in the smoke of a conflagration; their heads were ready to burst with every shout. Hard fingers seemed to grip their throats. At every roll they thought: Now I must let go. It will shake us all off—and thrown about aloft they cried wildly: "Look out there—catch the end." . . . "Reeve clear" . . . "Turn this block. . . ." They nodded desperately; shook infuriated faces, "No! No! From down up." They seemed to hate one another with a deadly hate. The longing to be done with it all gnawed their breasts, and the wish to do things well was a burning pain. They cursed their fate, contemned their life, and wasted their breath in deadly imprecations upon one another. The sailmaker, with his bald head bared, worked feverishly, forgetting his intimacy with so many admirals. The boatswain, climbing up with marlin-spikes and bunches of spunyarn rovings, or kneeling on the yard and ready to take a turn with the midship-stop, had acute and fleeting visions of his old woman and the youngsters in a moorland village. Mr. Baker, feeling very weak, tottered here and there, grunting and inflexible, like a man of iron. He waylaid those who, coming from aloft, stood gasping for breath. He ordered, encouraged, scolded. "Now then—to the main topsail now! Tally on to that gantline. Don't stand about there!"—"Is there no rest for us?" muttered voices. He spun round fiercely, with a sinking heart.—"No! No rest till the work is done. Work till you drop. That's what you're here for." A bowed seaman at his elbow gave a short laugh.—"Do or die," he croaked bitterly, then spat into his broad palms, swung up his long arms, and grasping the rope high above his head sent out a mournful, wailing cry for a pull all together. A sea boarded the quarter-deck and sent the whole lot sprawling to leeward. Caps, handspikes floated. Clenched hands, kicking legs, with here and there a spluttering face, stuck out of the white hiss of foaming water. Mr. Baker, knocked down with the rest, screamed—"Don't let go that rope! Hold on to it! Hold!" And sorely bruised by the brutal fling, they held on to it, as though it had been the fortune of their life. The ship ran, rolling heavily, and the topping crests glanced past port and starboard flashing their white heads. Pumps were freed. Braces were rove. The three topsails and foresail were set. She spurted faster over the water, outpacing the swift rush of waves. The menacing thunder of distanced seas rose behind her—filled the air with the tremendous vibrations of its voice. And devastated, battered, and wounded she drove foaming to the northward, as though inspired by the courage of a high endeavor. . . .

The forecastle was a place of damp desolation. They looked at their dwelling with dismay. It was slimy, dripping; it hummed hollow with the wind, and was strewn with shapeless wreckage, like a half-tide cavern in a rocky and exposed coast. Many had lost all they had in the world, but most of the starboard watch had preserved their chests; thin streams of water trickled out of them, however. The beds were soaked; the blankets spread out and saved by some nails squashed under foot. They dragged wet rags from evil-smelling corners, and wringing the water out, recognized their property. Some smiled stiffly. Others looked round blank and mute. There were cries of joy over old waistcoats, and groans of sorrow over shapeless things found among the splinters of smashed bed boards. One lamp was discovered jammed under the bowsprit. Charley whimpered a little. Knowles stumped here and there, sniffing, examining dark places for salvage. He poured dirty water out of a boot, and was concerned to find the owner. Those who, overwhelmed by their losses, sat on the forepeak hatch, remained elbows on knees, and, with a fist against each cheek, disdained to look up. He pushed it under their noses. "Here's a good boot. Yours?" They snarled, "No—get out." One snapped at him, "Take it to hell out of this." He seemed surprised. "Why? It's a good boot," but remembering suddenly that he had lost every stitch of his clothing, he dropped his find and began to swear. In the dim light cursing voices clashed. A man came in and, dropping his arms, stood still, repeating from the doorstep, "Here's a bloomin' old go! Here's a bloomin' old go!" A few rooted anxiously in flooded chests for tobacco. They breathed hard, clamored with heads down. "Look at that Jack!" . . . "Here! Sam! Here's my shore-going rig spoilt for ever." One blasphemed tearfully, holding up a pair of dripping trousers. No one looked at him. The cat came out from somewhere. He had an ovation. They snatched him from hand to hand, caressed him in a murmur of pet names. They wondered where he had "weathered it out"; disputed about it. A squabbling argument began. Two men brought in a bucket of fresh water, and all crowded round it; but Tom, lean and mewing, came up with every hair astir and had the first drink. A couple of hands went aft for oil and biscuits.

Then in the yellow light and in the intervals of mopping the deck they crunched hard bread, arranging to "worry through somehow." Men chummed as to beds. Turns were settled for wearing boots and having the use of oilskin coats. They called one another "old man" and "sonny" in cheery voices. Friendly slaps resounded. Jokes were shouted. One or two stretched on the wet deck, slept with heads pillowed on their bent arms, and several, sitting on the hatch, smoked. Their weary faces appeared through a thin blue haze, pacified and with sparkling eyes. The boatswain put his head through the door. "Relieve the wheel, one of you"—he shouted inside—"it's six. Blamme if that old Singleton hasn't been there more'n thirty hours. You are a fine lot." He slammed the door again. "Mate's watch on deck," said some one. "Hey, Donkin, it's your relief!" shouted three or four together. He had crawled into an empty bunk and on wet planks lay still. "Donkin, your wheel." He made no sound. "Donkin's dead," guffawed some one. "Sell 'is bloomin' clothes," shouted another. "Donkin, if ye don't go to the bloomin' wheel they will sell your clothes—d'ye hear?" jeered a third. He groaned from his dark hole. He complained about pains in all his bones, he whimpered pitifully. "He won't go," exclaimed a contemptuous voice, "your turn, Davis." The young seaman rose painfully, squaring his shoulders. Donkin stuck his head out, and it appeared in the yellow light, fragile and ghastly. "I will giv' yer a pound of tobaccer," he whined in a conciliating voice, "so soon as I draw it from aft. I will—s'elp me . . ." Davis swung his arm backhanded and the head vanished. "I'll go," he said, "but you will pay for it." He walked unsteady but resolute to the door. "So I will," yelped Donkin, popping out behind him. "So I will—s'elp me . . . a pound . . . three bob they chawrge." Davis flung the door open. "You will pay my price . . . in fine weather," he shouted over his shoulder. One of the men unbuttoned his wet coat rapidly, threw it at his head. "Here, Taffy—take that, you thief!" "Thank you!" he cried from the darkness above the swish of rolling water. He could be heard splashing; a sea came on board with a thump. "He's got his bath already," remarked a grim shellback. "Aye, aye!" grunted others. Then, after a long silence, Wamibo made strange noises. "Hallo, what's up with you?" said some one grumpily. "He says he would have gone for Davy," explained Archie, who was the Finn's interpreter generally. "I believe him!" cried voices. . . . Never mind, Dutchy . . . You'll do, muddle-head. . . . Your turn will come soon enough . . . You don't know when ye're well off." They ceased, and all together turned their faces to the door. Singleton stepped in, advanced two paces, and stood swaying slightly. The sea hissed, flowed roaring past the bows, and the forecastle trembled, full of deep murmurs; the lamp flared, swinging like a pendulum. He looked with a dreamy and puzzled stare, as though he could not distinguish the still men from their restless shadows. There were awestruck exclamations:—"Hallo, hallo" . . . "How does it look outside now, Singleton?" Those who sat on the hatch lifted their eyes in silence, and the next oldest seaman in the ship (those two understood one another, though they hardly exchanged three words in a day) gazed up at his friend attentively for a moment, then taking a short clay pipe out of his mouth, offered it without a word. Singleton put out his arm towards it, missed, staggered, and suddenly fell forward, crashing down, stiff and headlong like an uprooted tree. There was a swift rush. Men pushed, crying:—"He's done!" . . . "Turn him over!" . . . "Stand clear there!" Under a crowd of startled faces bending over him he lay on his back, staring upwards in a continuous and intolerable manner. In the breathless silence of a general consternation, he said in a grating murmur:—"I am all right," and clutched with his hands. They helped him up. He mumbled despondently:—"I am getting old . . . old."—"Not you," cried Belfast, with ready tact. Supported on all sides, he hung his head.—"Are you better?" they asked. He glared at them from under his eyebrows with large black eyes, spreading over his chest the bushy whiteness of a beard long and thick.—"Old! old!" he repeated sternly. Helped along, he reached his bunk. There was in it a slimy soft heap of something that smelt, as does at dead low water a muddy foreshore. It was his soaked straw bed. With a convulsive effort he pitched himself on it, and in the darkness of the narrow place could be heard growling angrily, like an irritated and savage animal

uneasy in its den:—"Bit of breeze . . . small thing . . . can't stand up . . . old!"
He slept at last, high-booted, sou'wester on head, and his oilskin clothes rustled, when
with a deep sighing groan he turned over. Men conversed about him in quiet concerned whispers. "This will break 'im up" . . . "Strong as a horse" . . . "Aye. But
he ain't what he used to be." . . . In sad murmurs they gave him up. Yet at midnight
he turned out to duty as if nothing had been the matter, and answered to his name
with a mournful "Here!" He brooded alone more than ever, in an impenetrable silence
and with a saddened face. For many years he had heard himself called "Old Singleton,"
and had serenely accepted the qualification, taking it as a tribute of respect due to a
man who through half a century had measured his strength against the favors and the
rages of the sea. He had never given a thought to his mortal self. He lived unscathed,
as though he had been indestructible, surrendering to all the temptations, weathering
many gales. He had panted in sunshine; shivered in the cold; suffered hunger, thirst,
debauch; passed through many trials—known all the furies. Old! It seemed to him he
was broken at last. And like a man bound treacherously while he sleeps, he woke up
fettered by the long chain of disregarded years. He had to take up at once the burden
of all his existence, and found it almost too heavy for his strength. Old! He moved his
arms, shook his head, felt his limbs. Getting old . . . and then? He looked upon the
immortal sea with the awakened and groping perception of its heartless might; he saw
it unchanged, black and foaming under the eternal scrutiny of the stars; he heard its
impatient voice calling for him out of a pitiless vastness full of unrest, of turmoil, and
of terror. He looked afar upon it, and he saw an immensity tormented and blind,
moaning and furious, that claimed all the days of his tenacious life, and, when life was
over, would claim the worn-out body of its slave. . . .

     This was the last of the breeze. It veered quickly, changed to a black south-easter,
and blew itself out, giving the ship a famous shove to the northward into the joyous
sunshine of the trade. Rapid and white she ran homewards in a straight path, under a
blue sky and upon the plain of a blue sea. She carried Singleton's completed wisdom,
Donkin's delicate susceptibilities, and the conceited folly of us all. The hours of
ineffective turmoil were forgotten; the fear and anguish of these dark moments were
never mentioned in the glowing peace of fine days. Yet from that time our life seemed
to start afresh as though we had died and had been resuscitated. All the first part of
the voyage, the Indian Ocean on the other side of the Cape, all that was lost in a haze,
like an ineradicable suspicion of some previous existence. It had ended—then there
were blank hours: a livid blur—and again we lived! Singleton was possessed of sinister
truth; Mr. Creighton of a damaged leg; the cook of fame—and shamefully abused the
opportunities of his distinction. Donkin had an added grievance. He went about
repeating with insistence: " 'E said 'e would brain me—did yer 'ear? They are goin' to
murder us now for the least little thing." We began at last to think it was rather awful.
And we were conceited! We boasted of our pluck, of our capacity for work, of our
energy. We remembered honorable episodes: our devotion, our indomitable perseverance—and were proud of them as though they had been the outcome of our unaided

impulses. We remembered our danger, our toil—and conveniently forgot our horrible scare. We decried our officers—who had done nothing—and listened to the fascinating Donkin. His care for our rights, his disinterested concern for our dignity, were not discouraged by the invariable contumely of our words, by the disdain of our looks. Our contempt for him was unbounded—and we could not but listen with interest to that consummate artist. He told us we were good men—a "bloomin' condemned lot of good men." Who thanked us? Who took any notice of our wrongs? Didn't we lead a "dorg's loife for two poun' ten a month?" Did we think that miserable pay enough to compensate us for the risk to our lives and for the loss of our clothes? "We've lost every rag!" he cried. He made us forget that he, at any rate, had lost nothing of his own. The younger men listened, thinking this 'ere Donkin's a long-headed chap, though no kind of man, anyhow. The Scandinavians were frightened at his audacities; Wamibo did not understand; and the older seamen thoughtfully nodded their heads making the thin gold earrings glitter in the fleshy lobes of hairy ears. Severe, sunburnt faces were propped meditatively on tattooed forearms. Veined, brown fists held in their knotted grip the dirty white clay of smoldering pipes. They listened, impenetrable, broad-backed, with bent shoulders, and in grim silence. He talked with ardor, despised and irrefutable. His picturesque and filthy loquacity flowed like a troubled stream from a poisoned source. His beady little eyes danced, glancing right and left, ever on the watch for the approach of an officer. Sometimes Mr. Baker going forward to take a look at the head sheets would roll with his uncouth gait through the sudden stillness of the men; or Mr. Creighton limped along, smooth-faced, youthful, and more stern than ever, piercing our short silence with a keen glance of his clear eyes. Behind his back Donkin would begin again darting stealthy, sidelong looks.—" 'Ere's one of 'em. Some of yer 'as made 'im fast that day. Much thanks yer got for it. Ain't 'ee a-drivin' yer wusse'n ever? . . . Let 'im slip overboard. . . . Vy not? It would 'ave been less trouble. Vy not?" He advanced confidentially, backed away with great effect; he whispered, he screamed, waved his miserable arms no thicker than pipestems—stretched his lean neck—spluttered—squinted. In the pauses of his impassioned orations the wind sighed quietly aloft, the calm sea unheeded murmured in a warning whisper along the ship's side. We abominated the creature and could not deny the luminous truth of his contentions. It was all so obvious. We were indubitably good men; our deserts were great and our pay small. Through our exertions we had saved the ship and the skipper would get the credit of it. What had he done? we wanted to know. Donkin asked:— "What 'ee could do without hus?" and we could not answer. We were oppressed by the injustice of the world, surprised to perceive how long we had lived under its burden without realizing our unfortunate state, annoyed by the uneasy suspicion of our undiscerning stupidity. Donkin assured us it was all our "good 'eartedness," but we would not be consoled by such shallow sophistry. We were men enough to courageously admit to ourselves our intellectual shortcomings; though from that time we refrained from kicking him, tweaking his nose, or from accidentally knocking him about, which last, after we had weathered the Cape, had been rather a popular amusement. Davis ceased to talk at him provokingly about black eyes and flattened noses.

Charley, much subdued since the gale, did not jeer at him. Knowles deferentially and with a crafty air propounded questions such as:—"Could we all have the same grub as the mates? Could we all stop ashore till we got it? What would be the next thing to try for if we got that?" He answered readily with contemptuous certitude; he strutted with assurance in clothes that were much too big for him as though he had tried to disguise himself. These were Jimmy's clothes mostly—though he would accept anything from anybody; but nobody, except Jimmy, had anything to spare. His devotion to Jimmy was unbounded. He was for ever dodging in the little cabin, ministering to Jimmy's wants, humoring his whims, submitting to his exacting peevishness, often laughing with him. Nothing could keep him away from the pious work of visiting the sick, especially when there was some heavy hauling to be done on deck. Mr. Baker had on two occasions jerked him out from there by the scruff of the neck to our inexpressible scandal. Was a sick chap to be left without attendance? Were we to be ill-used for attending a shipmate?—"What?" growled Mr. Baker, turning menacingly at the mutter, and the whole half-circle like one man stepped back a pace. "Set the topmast stunsail. Away aloft, Donkin, overhaul the gear," ordered the mate inflexibly. "Fetch the sail along; bend the down-haul clear. Bear a hand." Then, the sail set, he would go slowly aft and stand looking at the compass for a long time, careworn, pensive, and breathing hard as if stifled by the taint of unaccountable ill-will that pervaded the ship. "What's up amongst them?" he thought. "Can't make out this hanging back and growling. A good crowd, too, as they go nowadays." On deck the men exchanged bitter words, suggested by a silly exasperation against something unjust and irremediable that would not be denied, and would whisper into their ears long after Donkin had ceased speaking. Our little world went on its curved and unswerving path carrying a discontented and aspiring population. They found comfort of a gloomy kind in an interminable and conscientious analysis of their unappreciated worth; and inspired by Donkin's hopeful doctrines they dreamed enthusiastically of the time when every lonely ship would travel over a serene sea, manned by a wealthy and well-fed crew of satisfied skippers.

It looked as if it would be a long passage. The southeast trades, light and unsteady, were left behind; and then, on the equator and under a low grey sky, the ship, in close heat, floated upon a smooth sea that resembled a sheet of ground glass. Thunder squalls hung on the horizon, circled round the ship, far off and growling angrily, like a troop of wild beasts afraid to charge home. The invisible sun, sweeping above the upright masts, made on the clouds a blurred stain of rayless light, and a similar patch of faded radiance kept pace with it from east to west over the unglittering level of the waters. At night, through the impenetrable darkness of earth and heaven, broad sheets of flame waved noiselessly; and for half a second the becalmed craft stood out with its masts and rigging, with every sail and every rope distinct and black in the center of a fiery outburst, like a charred ship enclosed in a globe of fire. And, again, for long hours she remained lost in a vast universe of night and silence where gentle sighs, wandering here and there like forlorn souls, made the still sails flutter as in sudden fear, and the ripple of a beshrouded ocean whisper its compassion afar—in a voice mournful, immense, and faint. . . .

When the lamp was put out, and through the door thrown wide open, Jimmy, turning on his pillow, could see vanishing beyond the straight line of top-gallant rail, the quick, repeated visions of a fabulous world made up of leaping fire and sleeping water. The lightning gleamed in his big sad eyes that seemed in a red flicker to burn themselves out in his black face, and then he would lie blinded and invisible in the midst of an intense darkness. He could hear on the quiet deck soft footfalls, the breathing of some man lounging on the doorstep; the low creak of swaying masts; or the calm voice of the watch-officer reverberating aloft, hard and loud, amongst the unstirring sails. He listened with avidity, taking a rest in the attentive perception of the slightest sound from the fatiguing wanderings of his sleeplessness. He was cheered by the rattling of blocks, reassured by the stir and murmur of the watch, soothed by the slow yawn of some sleepy and weary seaman settling himself deliberately for a snooze on the planks. Life seemed an indestructible thing. It went on in darkness, in sunshine, in sleep; tireless, it hovered affectionately round the imposture of his ready death. It was bright, like the twisted flare of lightning, and more full of surprises than the dark night. It made him safe, and the calm of its overpowering darkness was as precious as its restless and dangerous light.

But in the evening, in the dog-watches, and even far into the first night-watch, a knot of men could always be seen congregated before Jimmy's cabin. They leaned on each side of the door peacefully interested and with crossed legs; they stood astride the doorstep discoursing, or sat in silent couples on his sea-chest; while against the bulwark along the spare topmast, three or four in a row stared meditatively; with their simple faces lit up by the projected glare of Jimmy's lamp. The little place, repainted white, had, in the night, the brilliance of a silver shrine where a black idol, reclining stiffly under a blanket, blinked its weary eyes and received our homage. Donkin officiated. He had the air of a demonstrator showing a phenomenon, a manifestation bizarre, simple, and meritorious that, to the beholders, should be a profound and an everlasting lesson. "Just look at 'im, 'ee knows what's what—never fear!" he exclaimed now and then, flourishing a hand hard and fleshless like the claw of a snipe. Jimmy, on his back, smiled with reserve and without moving a limb. He affected the langor of extreme weakness, so as to make it manifest to us that our delay in hauling him out from his horrible confinement, and then that night spent on the poop among our selfish neglect of his needs, had "done for him." He rather liked to talk about it, and of course we were always interested. He spoke spasmodically, in fast rushes with long pauses between, as a tipsy man walks. . . . "Cook had just given me a pannikin of hot coffee. . . . Slapped it down there, on my chest—banged the door to. . . . I felt a heavy roll coming; tried to save my coffee, burnt my fingers . . . and fell out of my bunk . . . She went over so quick. . . . Water came in through the ventilator. . . . I couldn't move the door . . . dark as a grave . . . tried to scramble up into the upper berth. . . . Rats . . . a rat bit my finger as I got up. . . . I could hear him swimming below me. . . . I thought you would never come . . . I thought you

were all gone overboard . . . of course . . . Could hear nothing but the wind. . . .
Then you came . . . to look for the corpse, I suppose. A little more and . . ."

"Man! But ye made a rare lot of noise in here," observed Archie, thoughtfully.

"You chaps kicked up such a confounded row above. . . . Enough to scare any
one. . . . I didn't know what you were up to. . . . Bash in the blamed planks . . .
my head. . . . Just what a silly, scary gang of fools would do. . . . Not much good
to me anyhow. . . . Just as well . . . drown. . . . Pah."

He groaned, snapped his big white teeth, and gazed with scorn. Belfast lifted a pair
of dolorous eyes, with a broken-hearted smile, clenched his fists stealthily; blue-eyed
Archie caressed his red whiskers with a hesitating hand; the boatswain at the door
stared a moment, and brusquely went away with a loud guffaw. Wamibo dreamed.
. . . Donkin felt all over his sterile chin for the few rare hairs, and said, triumphantly,
with a sidelong glance at Jimmy:—"Look at 'im! Wish I was 'arf has 'ealthy as 'ee is—
I do." He jerked a short thumb over his shoulder towards the after end of the ship.
"That's the blooming way to do 'em!" he yelped, with forced heartiness. Jimmy said:
—"Don't be a dam' fool," in a pleasant voice. Knowles, rubbing his shoulder against
the doorpost, remarked shrewdly:—"We can't all go an' be took sick—it would be
mutiny."—"Mutiny—gawn!" jeered Donkin, "there's no bloomin' law against bein'
sick."—"There's six weeks' hard work for refoosing dooty," argued Knowles, "I mind I
once seed in Cardiff the crew of an overloaded ship—leastways she weren't overloaded,
only a fatherly old gentleman with a white beard and an umbreller came along the quay
and talked to the hands. Said as how it was crool hard to be drowned in winter just for
the sake of a few pounds more for the owner—he said. Nearly cried over them—he
did; and he had a square mainsail coat, and a gaff-topsail hat too—all proper. So they
chaps they said they wouldn't go to be drownded in winter—depending upon that 'ere
Plimsoll man to see 'em through the court. They thought to have a bloomin' lark and
two or three days' spree. And the beak giv' 'em six weeks—coss the ship warn't
overloaded. Anyways they made it out in court that she wasn't. There wasn't one
overloaded ship in Penarth Dock at all. 'Pears that old coon he was only on pay and
allowance from some kind people, under orders to look for overloaded ships, and he
couldn't see no further than the length of his umbreller. Some of us in the boarding-
house, where I live when I'm looking for a ship in Cardiff, stood by to duck that old
weeping spunger in the dock. We kept a good look-out, too—but he topped his boom
directly he was outside the court. . . . Yes. They got six weeks' hard. . . ."

They listened, full of curiosity, nodding in the pauses their rough pensive faces.
Donkin opened his mouth once or twice, but restrained himself. Jimmy lay still with
open eyes and not at all interested. A seaman emitted the opinion that after a verdict
of atrocious partiality "the bloomin' beaks go an' drink at the skipper's expense."
Others assented. It was clear, of course. Donkin said:—"Well, six weeks ain't much
trouble. You sleep all night in, reg'lar, in chokey. Do it on my 'ead." "You are used to
it ainch'ee, Donkin?" asked somebody. Jimmy condescended to laugh. It cheered up
every one wonderfully. Knowles, with surprising mental agility, shifted his ground. "If
we all went sick what would become of the ship? eh?" He posed the problem and

grinned all round.—"Let 'er go to 'ell," sneered Donkin. "Damn 'er. She ain't yourn."
—"What? Just let her drift?" insisted Knowles in a tone of unbelief.—"Aye! Drift, an'
be blowed," affirmed Donkin with fine recklessness. The other did not see it—
meditated.—"The stores would run out," he muttered, "and . . . never get anywhere
. . . And what about pay-day?" he added with greater assurance.—"Jack likes a good
pay-day," exclaimed a listener on the doorstep. "Aye, because then the girls put one
arm round his neck an' t'other in his pocket, and call him ducky. Don't they, Jack?"—
"Jack, you're a terror with the gals."—"He takes three of 'em in tow to once, like one
of 'em Watkinses two-funnel tugs waddling away with three schooners behind."—
"Jack, you're a lame scamp."—"Jack, tell us about that one with a blue eye and a black
eye. Do."—"There's plenty of girls with one black eye along the Highway by . . ."—
"No, that's a speshul one—come, Jack." Donkin looked severe and disgusted; Jimmy
very bored; a grey-haired sea-dog shook his head slightly, smiling at the bowl of his
pipe, discreetly amused. Knowles turned about bewildered; stammered first at one,
then at another.—"No! . . . I never! . . . can't talk sensible sense midst you. . . .
Always on the kid." He retired bashfully—muttering and pleased. They laughed,
hooting in the crude light, around Jimmy's bed, when on a white pillow his hollowed
black face moved to and fro restlessly. A puff of wind came, made the flame of the
lamp leap, and outside, high up, the sails fluttered, while near by the block of the
foresheet struck a ringing blow on the iron bulwark. A voice far off cried, "Helm up!"
another, more faint, answered, "Hard-up, sir!" They became silent—waited expectantly. The grey-haired seaman knocked his pipe on the doorstep and stood up. The
ship leaned over gently and the sea seemed to wake up, murmuring drowsily. "Here's a
little wind comin'," said some one very low. Jimmy turned over slowly to face the
breeze. The voice in the night cried loud and commanding:—"Haul the spanker out."
The group before the door vanished out of the light. They could be heard tramping
aft while they repeated with varied intonations:—"Spanker out!" . . . "Out spanker,
sir!" Donkin remained alone with Jimmy. There was a silence. Jimmy opened and shut
his lips several times as if swallowing draughts of fresher air; Donkin moved the toes
of his bare feet and looked at them thoughtfully.

"Ain't you going to give them a hand with the sail?" asked Jimmy.

"No. If six ov 'em ain't 'nough beef to set that blamed, rotten spanker, they ain't fit
to live," answered Donkin in a bored, far-away voice, as though he had been talking
from the bottom of a hole. Jimmy considered the conical, fowl-like profile with a
queer kind of interest; he was leaning out of his bunk with the calculating, uncertain
expression of a man who reflects how best to lay hold of some strange creature that
looks as though it could sting or bite. But he said only:—"The mate will miss you—
and there will be ructions."

Donkin got up to go. "I will do for 'im some dark night; see if I don't," he said
over his shoulder.

Jimmy went on quickly:—"You're like a poll-parrot, like a screechin' poll-parrot."
Donkin stopped and cocked his head attentively on one side. His big ears stood out,
transparent and veined, resembling the thin wings of a bat.

"Yuss?" he said, with his back towards Jimmy.

"Yes! Chatter out all you know—like . . . like a dirty white cockatoo."

Donkin waited. He could hear the other's breathing, long and slow; the breathing of a man with a hundred-weight or so on the breastbone. Then he asked calmly:— "What do I know?"

"What? . . . What I tell you . . . not much. What do you want . . . to talk about my health so . . ."

"It's a blooming imposyshun. A bloomin', stinkin', first-class imposyshun—but it don't tyke me in. Not it."

Jimmy kept still. Donkin put his hands in his pockets, and in one slouching stride came up to the bunk.

"I talk—what's the odds. They ain't men 'ere—sheep they are. A driven lot of sheep. I 'old you up . . . Vy not? You're well orf."

"I am . . . I don't say anything about that. . . ."

"Well. Let 'em see it. Let 'em larn what a man can do. I am a man, I know all about yer. . . ." Jimmy threw himself further away on the pillow; the other stretched out his skinny neck, jerked his bird face down at him as though pecking at the eyes. "I am a man. I've seen the inside of every chokey in the Colonies rather'n give up my rights. . . ."

"You are a jail-prop," said Jimmy, weakly.

"I am . . . an' proud of it, too. You! You 'aven't the bloomin' nerve—so you inventyd this 'ere dodge. . . ." He paused; then with marked afterthought accentuated slowly:—"Yer ain't sick—are yer?"

"No," said Jimmy, firmly. "Been out of sorts now and again this year," he mumbled with a sudden drop in his voice.

Donkin closed one eye, amicable and confidential. He whispered:—"Ye 'ave done this afore 'aven'tchee?" Jimmy smiled—then as if unable to hold back he let himself go:—"Last ship—yes. I was out of sorts on the passage. See? It was easy. They paid me off in Calcutta, and the skipper made no bones about it either. . . . I got my money all right. Laid up fifty-eight days! The fools! O Lord! The fools! Paid right off." He laughed spasmodically. Donkin chimed in giggling. Then Jimmy coughed violently. "I am as well as ever," he said, as soon as he could draw breath.

Donkin made a derisive gesture. "In course," he said, profoundly, "any one can see that."—"They don't," said Jimmy, gasping like a fish.—"They would swallow any yarn," affirmed Donkin.—"Don't you let on too much," admonished Jimmy in an exhausted voice.—"Your little gyme? Eh?" commented Donkin, jovially. Then with sudden disgust: "Yer all for yerself, s'long as ye're right. . . ."

So charged with egoism James Wait pulled the blanket up to his chin and lay still for a while. His heavy lips protruded in an everlasting black pout. "Why are you so hot on making trouble?" he asked without much interest.

" 'Cos it's a bloomin' shayme. We are put upon . . . bad food, bad pay . . . I want us to kick up a bloomin' row; a blamed 'owling row that would make 'em remember! Knocking people about . . . brain us . . . indeed! Ain't we men?" His

altruistic indignation blazed. Then he said calmly:—"I've been airing yer clothes."—
"All right," said Jimmy, languidly, "bring them in."—"Giv' us the key of your chest,
I'll put 'em away for yer," said Donkin with friendly eagerness.—"Bring 'em in, I will
put them away myself," answered James Wait with severity. Donkin looked down,
muttering. . . . "What d'you say? What d'you say?" inquired Wait anxiously.—
"Nothink. The night's dry, let 'em 'ang out till the morning," said Donkin, in a
strangely trembling voice, as though restraining laughter or rage. Jimmy seemed satisfied.—"Give me a little water for the night in my mug—there," he said. Donkin took
a stride over the doorstep.—"Git it yourself," he replied in a surly tone. "You can do it,
unless you *are* sick."—"Of course I can do it," said Wait, "only . . ."—"Well, then,
do it," said Donkin, viciously, "if yer can look after yer clothes, yer can look after
yerself." He went on deck without a look back.

Jimmy reached out for the mug. Not a drop. He put it back gently with a faint sigh
—and closed his eyes. He thought:—That lunatic Belfast will bring me some water if
I ask. Fool. I am very thirsty. . . . It was very hot in the cabin, and it seemed to turn
slowly round, detach itself from the ship, and swing out smoothly into a luminous,
arid space where a black sun shone, spinning very fast. A place without any water! No
water! A policeman with the face of Donkin drank a glass of beer by the side of an
empty well, and flew away flapping vigorously. A ship whose mastheads protruded
through the sky and could not be seen was discharging grain, and the wind whirled the
dry husks in spirals along the quay of a dock with no water in it. He whirled along
with the husks—very tired and light. All his inside was gone. He felt lighter than the
husks—and more dry. He expanded his hollow chest. The air streamed in, carrying
away in its rush a lot of strange things that resembled houses, trees, people, lampposts.
. . . No more! There was no more air—and he had not finished drawing his long
breath. But he was in jail! They were locking him up. A door slammed. They turned
the key twice, flung a bucket of water over him—Phoo! What for?

He opened his eyes, thinking the fall had been very heavy for an empty man—
empty—empty. He was in his cabin. Ah! All right! His face was streaming with
perspiration, his arms heavier than lead. He saw the cook standing in the doorway, a
brass key in one hand and a bright tin hook-pot in the other.

"I have locked up the galley for the night," said the cook, beaming benevolently.
"Eight bells just gone. I brought you a pot of cold tea for your night's drinking,
Jimmy. I sweetened it with some white cabin sugar, too. Well—it won't break the
ship."

He came in, hung the pot on the edge of the bunk, asked perfunctorily, "How goes
it?" and sat down on the box.—"H'm," grunted Wait, inhospitably. The cook wiped
his face with a dirty cotton rag, which, afterwards, he tied round his neck.—"That's
how them firemen do in steamboats," he said, serenely, and much pleased with himself.
"My work is as heavy as theirs—I'm thinking—and longer hours. Did you ever see
them down the stokehold? Like fiends they look—firing—firing—firing—down
there."

He pointed his forefinger at the deck. Some gloomy thought darkened his shining face, fleeting, like the shadow of a traveling cloud over the light of a peaceful sea. The relieved watch tramped noisily forward, passing in a body across the sheen of the doorway. Some one cried, "Good-night!" Belfast stopped for a moment and looked at Jimmy, quivering and speechless with repressed emotion. He gave the cook a glance charged with dismal foreboding, and vanished. The cook cleared his throat. Jimmy stared upwards and kept as still as a man in hiding.

The night was clear, with a gentle breeze. Above the mastheads the resplendent curve of the Milky Way spanned the sky like a triumphal arch of eternal light, thrown over the dark pathway of the earth. On the forecastle head a man whistled with loud precision a lively jig, while another could be heard faintly, shuffling and stamping in time. There came from forward a confused murmur of voices, laughter—snatches of song. The cook shook his head, glanced obliquely at Jimmy, and began to mutter. "Aye. Dance and sing. That's all they think of. I am surprised that Providence don't get tired. . . . They forget the day that's sure to come . . . but you. . . ."

Jimmy drank a gulp of tea, hurriedly, as though he had stolen it, and shrank under his blanket, edging away towards the bulkhead. The cook got up, closed the door, then sat down again and said distinctly:—

"Whenever I poke my galley fire I think of you chaps—swearing, stealing, lying, and worse—as if there was no such thing as another world. . . . Not bad fellows, either, in a way," he conceded, slowly; then, after a pause of regretful musing, he went on in a resigned tone:—"Well, well. They will have a hot time of it. Hot! Did I say? The furnaces of one of them White Star boats ain't nothing to it."

He kept very quiet for a while. There was a great stir in his brain; an addled vision of bright outlines; an exciting row of rousing songs and groans of pain. He suffered, enjoyed, admired, approved. He was delighted, frightened, exalted—as on that evening (the only time in his life—twenty-seven years ago; he loved to recall the number of years) when as a young man he had—through keeping bad company—become intoxicated in an East-end music-hall. A tide of sudden feeling swept him clean out of his body. He soared. He contemplated the secret of the hereafter. It commended itself to him. It was excellent; he loved it, himself, all hands, and Jimmy. His heart overflowed with tenderness, with comprehension, with the desire to meddle, with anxiety for the soul of that black man, with the pride of possessed eternity, with the feeling of might. Snatch him up in his arms and pitch him right into the middle of salvation. . . . The black soul—blacker—body—rot—Devil. No! Talk—strength—Samson. . . . There was a great din as of cymbals in his ears; he flashed through an ecstatic jumble of shining faces, lilies, prayer-books, unearthly joy, white skirts, gold harps, black coats, wings. He saw flowing garments, clean shaved faces, a sea of light—a lake of pitch. There were sweet scents, a smell of sulphur—red tongues of flame licking a white mist. An awesome voice thundered! . . . It lasted three seconds.

"Jimmy!" he cried in an inspired tone. Then he hesitated. A spark of human pity glimmered yet through the infernal fog of his supreme conceit.

"What?" said James Wait, unwillingly. There was a silence. He turned his head just the least bit, and stole a cautious glance. The cook's lips moved without a sound; his face was rapt, his eyes turned up. He seemed to be mentally imploring deck beams, the brass hook of the lamp, two cockroaches.

"Look here," said Wait, "I want to go to sleep. I think I could."

"This is no time for sleep!" exclaimed the cook, very loud. He had prayerfully divested himself of the last vestige of his humanity. He was a voice—a fleshless and sublime thing, as on that memorable night—the night when he went walking over the sea to make coffee for perishing sinners. "This is no time for sleeping," he repeated with exaltation. "I can't sleep."

"Don't care a damn," said Wait, with factitious energy. "I can. Go an' turn in."

"Swear . . . in the very jaws! . . . In the very jaws! Don't you see the everlasting fire . . . don't you feel it? Blind, chockful of sin! Repent, repent! I can't bear to think of you. I hear the call to save you. Night and day. Jimmy, let me save you!" The words of entreaty and menace broke out of him in a roaring torrent. The cockroaches ran away. Jimmy perspired, wriggling stealthily under his blanket. The cook yelled. . . . "Your days are numbered! . . ."—"Get out of this," boomed Wait, courageously.— "Pray with me! . . ."—"I won't! . . ." The little cabin was as hot as an oven. It contained an immensity of fear and pain; an atmosphere of shrieks and moans; prayers vociferated like blasphemies and whispered curses. Outside, the men called by Charley, who informed them in tones of delight that there was a holy row going on in Jimmy's place, crowded before the closed door, too startled to open it. All hands were there. The watch below had jumped out on deck in their shirts, as after a collision. Men running up asked:—"What is it?" Others said:—"Listen!" The muffled screaming went on:—"On your knees! On your knees!"—"Shut up!"—"Never! You are delivered into my hands. . . . Your life has been saved. . . . Purpose. . . . Mercy. . . . Repent."—"You are a crazy fool! . . ."—"Account of you . . . you . . . Never sleep in this world, if I . . ."—"Leave off."—"No! . . . stokehold . . . only think! . . ." Then an impassioned screeching babble where words pattered like hail.— "No!" shouted Wait.—"Yes. You are! . . . No help. . . . Everybody says so."— "You lie!"—"I see you dying this minnyt . . . before my eyes . . . as good as dead already."—"Help!" shouted Jimmy, piercingly.—"Not in this valley. . . . look up-wards," howled the other.—"Go away! Murder! Help!" clamored Jimmy. His voice broke. There were moanings, low mutters, a few sobs.

"What's the matter now?" said a seldom-heard voice.—"Fall back, men! Fall back, there!" repeated Mr. Creighton, sternly, pushing through.—"Here's the old man," whispered some.—"The cook's in there, sir," exclaimed several, backing away. The door clattered open; a broad stream of light darted out on wondering faces: a warm whiff of vitiated air passed. The two mates towered head and shoulders above the spare, grey-haired man who stood revealed between them, in shabby clothes, stiff and angular, like a small carved figure, and with a thin, composed face. The cook got up from his knees. Jimmy sat high in the bunk, clasping his drawn-up legs. The tassel of the blue night-cap almost imperceptibly trembled over his knees. They gazed aston-ished at his long, curved back, while the white corner of one eye gleamed blindly at them. He was afraid to turn his head, he shrank within himself; and there was an aspect astounding and animal-like in the perfection of his expectant immobility. A thing of instinct—the unthinking stillness of a scared brute.

"What are you doing here?" asked Mr. Baker, sharply.—"My duty," said the cook, with ardor.—"Your . . . what?" began the mate. Captain Allistoun touched his arm lightly.—"I know his caper," he said, in a low voice. "Come out of that, Podmore," he ordered, aloud.

The cook wrung his hands, shook his fists above his head, and his arms dropped as if too heavy. For a moment he stood distracted and speechless.—"Never," he stammered, "I . . . he . . . I."—"What—do—you—say?" pronounced Captain Allistoun. "Come out at once—or . . ."—"I am going," said the cook, with a hasty and somber resignation. He strode over the doorstep firmly—hesitated—made a few steps. They looked at him in silence.—"I make you responsible!" he cried, desperately, turning half round. "That man is dying. I make you . . ."—"You there yet?" called the master in a threatening tone.—"No, sir," he exclaimed, hurriedly, in a startled voice. The boatswain led him away by the arm; some one laughed; Jimmy lifted his head for a stealthy glance, and in one unexpected leap sprang out of his bunk; Mr. Baker made a clever catch and felt him very limp in his arms; the group at the door grunted with surprise.—"He lies," gasped Wait, "he talked about black devils—he is a devil—a white devil—I am all right." He stiffened himself, and Mr. Baker, experimentally, let him go. He staggered a pace or two; Captain Allistoun watched him with a quiet and penetrating gaze; Belfast ran to his support. He did not appear to be aware of any one near him; he stood silent for a moment, battling singlehanded with a legion of nameless terrors, amidst the eager looks of excited men who watched him far off, utterly alone in the impenetrable solitude of his fear. The sea gurgled through the scuppers as the ship heeled over to a short puff of wind.

"Keep him away from me," said James Wait at last in his fine baritone voice, and leaning with all his weight on Belfast's neck. "I've been better this last week . . . I am well . . . I was going back to duty . . . tomorrow—now if you like—Captain." Belfast hitched his shoulders to keep him upright.

"No," said the master, looking at him, fixedly.

Under Jimmy's armpit Belfast's red face moved uneasily. A row of eyes gleaming stared on the edge of light. They pushed one another with elbows, turned their heads, whispered. Wait let his chin fall on his breast and, with lowered eyelids, looked round in a suspicious manner.

"Why not?" cried a voice from the shadows, "the man's all right, sir."

"I am all right," said Wait, with eagerness. "Been sick . . . better . . . turn-to now." He sighed.—"Howly Mother!" exclaimed Belfast with a heave of the shoulders, "stand up, Jimmy."—"Keep away from me then," said Wait, giving Belfast a petulant push, and reeling fetched against the doorpost. His cheekbones glistened as though they had been varnished. He snatched off his night-cap, wiped his perspiring face with it, flung it on the deck. "I am coming out," he declared without stirring.

"No. You don't," said the master, curtly. Bare feet shuffled, disapproving voices murmured all round; he went on as if he had not heard:—"You have been skulking nearly all the passage and now you want to come out. You think you are near enough to the paytable now. Smell the shore, hey?"

"I've been sick . . . now—better," mumbled Wait, glaring in the light.—"You have been shamming sick," retorted Captain Allistoun with severity; "Why . . ." he hesitated for less than half a second. "Why, anybody can see that. There's nothing the matter with you, but you choose to lie-up to please yourself—and now you shall lie-up to please me. Mr. Baker, my orders are that this man is not to be allowed on deck to the end of the passage."

There were exclamations of surprise, triumph, indignation. The dark group of men swung across the light. "What for?" "Told you so . . ." "Bloomin' shame . . ."—"We've got to say somethink about that," screeched Donkin from the rear.—"Never mind, Jim—we will see you righted," cried several together. An elderly seaman stepped to the front. "D'ye mean to say, sir," he asked, ominously, "that a sick chap ain't allowed to get well in this 'ere hooker?" Behind him Donkin whispered excitedly amongst a staring crowd where no one spared him a glance, but Captain Allistoun shook a forefinger at the angry bronzed face of the speaker.—"You—you hold your tongue," he said, warningly.—"This isn't the way," clamored two or three younger men.—"Are we bloomin' masheens?" inquired Donkin in a piercing tone, and dived under the elbows of the front rank.—"Soon show 'im we ain't boys . . ."—"The man's a man if he is black."—"We ain't goin' to work this bloomin' ship shorthanded if Snowball's all right . . ."—"He says he is."—"Well then, strike, boys, strike!"—"That's the bloomin' ticket." Captain Allistoun said sharply to the second mate: "Keep quiet, Mr. Creighton," and stood composed in the tumult, listening with profound attention to mixed growls and screeches, to every exclamation and every curse of the sudden outbreak. Somebody slammed the cabin door to with a kick; the darkness full of menacing mutters leaped with a short clatter over the streak of light, and the men became gesticulating shadows that growled, hissed, laughed excitedly. Mr. Baker whispered:—"Get away from them, sir." The big shape of Mr. Creighton hovered silently about the slight figure of the master.—"We have been hymposed upon all this voyage," said a gruff voice, "but this 'ere fancy takes the cake."—"That man is a shipmate."—"Are we bloomin' kids?"—"The port watch will refuse duty." Charley carried away by his feeling whistled shrilly, then yelped:—"Giv' us our Jimmy!" This seemed to cause a variation in the disturbance. There was a fresh burst of squabbling uproar. A lot of quarrels were set going at once.—"Yes."—"No."—"Never been sick."—"Go for them to once."—"Shut yer mouth, youngster—this is men's work."—"Is it?" muttered Captain Allistoun, bitterly. Mr. Baker grunted: "Ough! They're gone silly. They've been simmering for the last month."—"I did notice," said the master.—"They have started a row amongst themselves now," said Mr. Creighton with disdain, "better get aft, sir. We will soothe them." "Keep your temper, Creighton," said the master. And the three men began to move slowly towards the cabin door.

In the shadows of the fore rigging a dark mass stamped, eddied, advanced, retreated. There were words of reproach, encouragement, unbelief, execration. The elder seamen, bewildered and angry, growled their determination to go through with something or other; but the younger school of advanced thought exposed their and Jimmy's wrongs with confused shouts arguing amongst themselves. They clustered round that moribund carcass, the fit emblem of their aspirations, and encouraging one another they swayed, they tramped on one spot, shouting that they would not be "put upon." Inside the cabin, Belfast, helping Jimmy into his bunk, twitched all over in his desire not to miss all the row, and with difficulty restrained the tears of his facile emotion. James Wait, flat on his back under the blanket, gasped complaints.—"We will back you up, never fear," assured Belfast, busy about his feet.—"I'll come out tomorrow morning—take my chance—you fellows must—" mumbled Wait, "I come out tomorrow—skipper or no skipper." He lifted one arm with great difficulty, passed the hand over his face; "Don't you let that cook . . ." he breathed out.—"No, no," said Belfast, turning his back on the bunk, "I will put a head on him if he comes near you." —"I will smash his mug!" faintly Wait exclaimed, enraged and weak; "I don't want to kill a man, but . . ." He panted fast like a dog after a run in sunshine. Some one just outside the door shouted, "He's as fit as any ov us!" Belfast put his hand on the door-handle.—"Here!" called James Wait, hurriedly, and in such a clear voice that the other spun round with a start. James Wait, stretched out black and deathlike in the dazzling light, turned his head on the pillow. His eyes stared at Belfast, appealing and impudent. "I am rather weak from lying-up so long," he said, distinctly. Belfast nodded. "Getting quite well now," insisted Wait.—"Yes. I noticed you getting better this . . . last month," said Belfast, looking down. "Hallo! What's this?" he shouted and ran out.

He was flattened directly against the side of the house by two men who lurched against him. A lot of disputes seemed to be going on all round. He got clear and saw three indistinct figures standing along in the fainter darkness under the arched foot of the mainsail, that rose above their heads like a convex wall of a high edifice. Donkin hissed:—"Go for them . . . it's dark!" The crowd took a short run aft in a body—then there was check. Donkin, agile and thin, flitted past with his right arm going like a windmill—and then stood still suddenly with his arm pointing rigidly above his head. The hurtling flight of some heavy object was heard; it passed between the heads of the two mates, bounded heavily along the deck, struck the after-hatch with a ponderous and deadened blow. The bulky shape of Mr. Baker grew distinct. "Come to your senses, men!" he cried, advancing at the arrested crowd. "Come back, Mr. Baker!" called the master's quiet voice. He obeyed unwillingly. There was a minute of silence, then a deafening hubbub arose. Above it Archie was heard energetically:—"If ye go oot ageen I wull tell!" There were shouts. "Don't" "Drop it!"—"We ain't that kind!" The black cluster of human forms reeled against the bulwark, back again towards the house. Ringbolts rang under stumbling feet.—"Drop it!" "Let me!"—"No!"—"Curse you . . . hah!" Then sounds as of some one's face being slapped; a piece of iron fell on the deck; a short scuffle, and some one's shadowy body scuttled rapidly across the main hatch before the shadow of a kick. A raging voice sobbed out a torrent of filthy language . . .—"Throwing things—good God!" grunted Mr. Baker in dismay.— "That was meant for me," said the master, quietly; "I felt the wind of that thing; what was it—an iron belaying-pin?"—"By Jove!" muttered Mr. Creighton. The confused voices of men talking amidships mingled with the wash of the sea, ascended between the silent and distended sails—seemed to flow away into the night, further than the horizon, higher than the sky. The stars burned steadily over the inclined mastheads. Trails of light lay on the water, broke before the advancing hull, and, after she had passed, trembled for a long time as if in awe of the murmuring sea.

Meantime the helmsman, anxious to know what the row was about, had let go the wheel, and, bent double, ran with long, stealthy footsteps to the break of the poop. The *Narcissus*, left to herself, came up gently to the wind without any one being aware of it. She gave a slight roll, and the sleeping sails woke suddenly, coming all together with a mighty flap against the masts, then filled again one after another in a quick succession of loud reports that ran down the lofty spars, till the collapsed mainsail flew out last with a violent jerk. The ship trembled from trucks to keel; the sails kept on rattling like a discharge of musketry; the gin blocks groaned. It was as if an invisible hand had given the ship an angry shake to recall the men that peopled her decks to the sense of reality, vigilance, and duty.—"Helm up!" cried the master, sharply. "Run aft, Mr. Creighton, and see what that fool there is up to."—"Flatten in the head sheets. Stand by the weather forebraces," growled Mr. Baker. Startled men ran swiftly repeating the orders. The watch below, abandoned all at once by the watch on deck, drifted towards the forecastle in twos and three, arguing noisily as they went—"We shall see tomorrow!" cried a loud voice, as if to cover with a menacing hint an inglorious retreat. And then only orders were heard, the falling of heavy coils of rope, the rattling of blocks. Singleton's white head flitted here and there in the night, high above the deck, like the ghost of a bird.—"Going off, sir!" shouted Mr. Creighton from aft.— "Full again."—"All right . . ."—"Ease off the head sheets. That will do the braces. Coil the ropes up," grunted Mr. Baker, bustling about.

Gradually the tramping noises, the confused sound of voices, died out, and the officers, coming together on the poop, discussed the events. Mr. Baker was bewildered and grunted; Mr. Creighton was calmly furious; but Captain Allistoun was composed and thoughtful. He listened to Mr. Baker's growling argumentation, to Creighton's interjected and severe remarks, while looking down on the deck he weighed in his hand the iron belaying-pin—that a moment ago had just missed his head—as if it had been the only tangible fact of the whole transaction. He was one of those commanders who speak little, seem to hear nothing, look at no one—and know everything, hear every whisper, see every fleeting shadow of their ship's life. His two big officers towered above his lean, short figure; they talked over his head; they were dismayed, surprised, and angry, while between them the little quiet man seemed to have found his taciturn serenity in the profound depths of a larger experience. Lights were burning in the forecastle; now and then a loud gust of babbling chatter came from forward, swept over the decks, and became faint, as if the unconscious ship, gliding gently through the great peace of the sea, had left behind and for ever the foolish noise of turbulent mankind. But it was renewed again and again. Gesticulating arms, profiles of heads with open mouths appeared for a moment in the illuminated squares of doorways; black fists darted—withdrew . . . "Yes. It was most damnable to have such an unprovoked row sprung on one," assented the master. . . . A tumult of yells rose in the light, abruptly ceased. . . . He didn't think there would be any further trouble just then. . . . A bell was struck aft, another, forward, answered in a deeper tone, and the clamor of ringing metal spread round the ship in a circle of wide vibrations that ebbed away into the immeasurable night of an empty sea. . . . Didn't he know them! Didn't he! In past years. Better men, too. Real men to stand by one in a tight place. Worse than devils too sometimes—downright, horned devils. Pah! This—nothing. A miss as good as a mile. . . . The wheel was being relieved in the usual way.—"Full and by," said, very loud, the man going off.—"Full and by," repeated the other, catching hold of the spokes.—"This head wind *is* my trouble," exclaimed the master, stamping his foot in sudden anger; "head wind! all the rest is nothing." He was calm again in a moment. "Keep them on the move tonight, gentlemen; just to let them feel we've got hold all the time—quietly, you know. Mind you keep your hands off them, Creighton. Tomorrow I will talk to them like a Dutch Uncle. A crazy crowd of tinkers! Yes, tinkers! I could count the real sailors amongst them on the fingers of one hand. Nothing will do but a row—if—you—please." He paused. "Did you think I had gone wrong there, Mr. Baker?" He tapped his forehead, laughed short. "When I saw him standing there, three parts dead and so scared—black amongst that gaping lot —no grit to face what's coming to us all—the notion came to me all at once, before I could think. Sorry for him—like you would be for a sick brute. If ever creature was in a mortal funk to die! . . . I thought I would let him go out in his own way. Kind of impulse. It never came into my head, those fools. . . . H'm! Stand to it now—of course." He stuck the belaying-pin in his pocket, seemed ashamed of himself, then sharply:—"If you see Podmore at his tricks again tell him I will have him put under the pump. Had to do it once before. The fellow breaks out like that now and then. Good cook tho'." He walked away quickly, came back to the companion. The two mates followed him through the starlight with amazed eyes. He went down three steps, and changing his tone, spoke with his head near the deck:—"I shan't turn in tonight, in case of anything; just call out if . . . Did you see the eyes of that sick nigger, Mr. Baker? I fancied he begged me for something. What? Past all help. One lone black beggar amongst the lot of us, and he seemed to look through me into the very hell. Fancy, this wretched Podmore! Well, let him die in peace. I am master here after all. Let him be. He might have been half a man once . . . Keep a good look-out." He disappeared down below, leaving his mates facing one another, and more impressed than if they had seen a stone image shed a miraculous tear of compassion over the incertitudes of life and death. . . .

In the blue mist spreading from twisted threads that stood upright in the bowls of pipes, the forecastle appeared as vast as a hall. Between the beams a heavy cloud stagnated; and the lamps surrounded by halos burned each at the core of a purple glow in two lifeless flames without rays. Wreaths drifted in denser wisps. Men sprawled about on the deck, sat in negligent poses, or, bending a knee, drooped with one shoulder against a bulkhead. Lips moved, eyes flashed, waving arms made sudden eddies in the smoke. The murmur of voices seemed to pile itself higher and higher as if unable to run out quick enough through the narrow doors. The watch below in their shirts, and striding on long white legs, resembled raving somnambulists; while now and then one of the watch on deck would rush in, looking strangely overdressed, listen a moment, fling a rapid sentence into the noise and run out again; but a few remained near the door, fascinated, and with one ear turned to the deck. "Stick together, boys," roared Davis. Belfast tried to make himself heard. Knowles grinned in a slow, dazed way. A short fellow with a thick clipped beard kept on yelling periodically:—"Who's afeard? Who's afeard?" Another one jumped up, excited, with glazing eyes, sent out a string of unattached curses and sat down quietly. Two men discussed familiarly, striking one another's breast in turn, to clinch arguments. Three others, with their heads in a bunch, spoke all together with a confidential air, and at the top of their voices. It was a stormy chaos of speech where intelligible fragments, tossing, struck the ear. One could hear:—"In the last ship"—"Who cares? Try it on any one of us if—." "Knock under"—"Not a hand's turn"—"He says he is all right"—"I always thought" —"Never mind. . . ." Donkin, crouching all in a heap against the bowsprit, hunched his shoulderblades as high as his ears, and hanging a peaked nose, resembled a sick vulture with ruffled plumes. Belfast, straddling his legs, had a face red with yelling, and with arms thrown up, figured a Maltese cross. The two Scandinavians, in a corner, had a dumbfounded and distracted aspect of men gazing at a cataclysm. And, beyond the light, Singleton stood in the smoke, monumental, indistinct, with his head touching the beam; like a statue of heroic size in the gloom of a crypt.

He stepped forward, impassive and big. The noise subsided like a broken wave: but Belfast cried once more with uplifted arms:—"The man is dying, I tell ye!" then sat down suddenly on the hatch and took his head between his hands. All looked at Singleton, gazing upwards from the deck, staring out of dark corners, or turning their heads with curious glances. They were expectant and appeased as if that old man, who looked at no one, had possessed the secret of their uneasy indignations and desires, a sharper vision, a clearer knowledge. And indeed standing there amongst them, he had the uninterested appearance of one who had seen multitudes of ships, had listened many times to voices such as theirs, had already seen all that could happen on the wide seas. They heard his voice rumble in his broad chest as though the words had been rolling towards them out of a rugged past. "What do you want to do?" he asked. No one answered. Only Knowles muttered—"Aye, aye," and somebody said low:—"It's a bloomin' shame." He waited, made a contemptuous gesture.—"I have seen rows aboard ship before some of you were born," he said, slowly, "for something or nothing; but never for such a thing."—"The man is dying, I tell ye," repeated Belfast, woefully, sitting at Singleton's feet.—"And a black fellow, too," went on the old seaman, "I have seen them die like flies." He stopped, thoughtful, as if trying to recollect gruesome things, details of horrors, hecatombs of niggers. They looked at him fascinated. He was old enough to remember slavers, bloody mutinies, pirates perhaps; who could tell through what violences and terrors he had lived! What would he say? He said:—"You can't help him; die he must." He made another pause. His moustache and beard stirred. He chewed words, mumbled behind tangled white hairs;

incomprehensible and exciting, like an oracle behind a veil. . . . —"Stop ashore—
sick.—Instead—bringing all this head wind. Afraid. The sea will have her own.—Die
in sight of land. Always so. They know it—long passage—more days, more dollars.—
You keep quiet.—What do you want? Can't help him." He seemed to wake up from a
dream. "You can't help yourselves," he said, austerely, "Skipper's no fool. He has
something in his mind. Look out—I say! I know 'em!" With eyes fixed in front he
turned his head from right to left, from left to right, as if inspecting a long row of
astute skippers.—" 'Ee said 'ee would brain me!" cried Donkin in a heartrending tone.
Singleton peered downwards with puzzled attention, as though he couldn't find him.
—"Damn you!" he said, vaguely, giving it up. He radiated unspeakable wisdom, hard
unconcern, the chilling air of resignation. Round him all the listeners felt themselves
somehow completely enlightened by their disappointment, and mute, they lolled about
with the careless ease of men who can discern perfectly the irremediable aspect of their
existence. He, profound and unconscious, waved his arm once, and strode out on deck
without another word.

Belfast was lost in a round-eyed meditation. One or two vaulted heavily into upper
berths, and, once there, sighed; others dived head first inside lower bunks—swift, and
turning round instantly upon themselves, like animals going into lairs. The grating of
a knife scraping burnt clay was heard. Knowles grinned no more. Davis said, in a tone
of ardent conviction: "Then our skipper's looney." Archie muttered: "My faith! we
haven't heard the last of it yet!" Four bells were struck.—"Half our watch below
gone!" cried Knowles in alarm, then reflected. "Well, two hours' sleep is something
towards a rest," he observed, consolingly. Some already pretended to slumber; and
Charley, sound asleep, suddenly said a few slurred words in an arbitrary, blank voice.
—"This blamed boy has worrums!" commented Knowles from under a blanket, in a
learned manner. Belfast got up and approached Archie's berth.—"We pulled him out,"
he whispered, sadly.—"What?" said the other, with sleepy discontent.—"And now we
will have to chuck him overboard," went on Belfast, whose lower lip trembled.—
"Chuck what?" asked Archie.—"Poor Jimmy," breathed out Belfast.—"He be
blowed!" said Archie with untruthful brutality, and sat up in his bunk; "It's all through
him. If it hadn't been for me, there would have been murder on board this ship!"—
" 'Tain't his fault, is it?" argued Belfast, in a murmur; "I've put him to bed . . . an'
he ain't no heavier than an empty beef-cask," he added, with tears in his eyes. Archie
looked at him steadily, then turned his nose to the ship's side with determination.
Belfast wandered about as though he had lost his way in the dim forecastle, and nearly
fell over Donkin. He contemplated him from on high for a while. "Ain't ye going to
turn in?" he asked. Donkin looked up hopelessly.—"That black'earted Scotch son of a
thief kicked me!" he whispered from the floor, in a tone of utter desolation.—"And a
good job, too!" said Belfast, still very depressed; "You were as near hanging as damn-it
tonight, sonny. Don't you play any of your murthering games around my Jimmy! You
haven't pulled him out. You just mind! 'Cos if I start to kick you"—he brightened up
a bit—"if I start to kick you, it will be Yankee fashion—to break something!" He
tapped lightly with his knuckles the top of the bowed head. "You moind that, my

bhoy!" he concluded, cheerily. Donkin let it pass.—"Will they split on me?" he asked with pained anxiety.—"Who—split?" hissed Belfast, coming back a step. "I would split your nose this minyt if I hadn't Jimmy to look after! Who d'ye think we are?" Donkin rose and watched Belfast's back lurch through the doorway. On all sides invisible men slept, breathing calmly. He seemed to draw courage and fury from the peace around him. Venomous and thin-faced, he glared from the ample misfit of borrowed clothes as if looking for something he could smash. His heart leaped wildly in his narrow chest. They slept! He wanted to wring necks, gouge eyes, spit on faces. He shook a dirty pair of meager fists at the smoking lights. "Ye're no men!" he cried, in a deadened tone. No one moved. "Yer 'aven't the pluck of a mouse!" His voice rose to a husky screech. Wamibo darted out a disheveled head, and looked at him wildly. "Ye're sweepings ov ships! I 'ope you will all rot before you die!" Wamibo blinked, uncomprehending but interested. Donkin sat down heavily; he blew with force through quivering nostrils, he ground and snapped his teeth, and, with the chin pressed hard against the breast, he seemed busy gnawing his way through it, as if to get at the heart within. . . .

In the morning the ship, beginning another day of her wandering life, had an aspect of sumptuous freshness, like the spring-time of the earth. The washed decks glistened in a long clear stretch; the oblique sunlight struck the yellow brasses in dazzling splashes, darted over the polished rods in lines of gold, and the single drops of salt water forgotten here and there along the rail were as limpid as drops of dew, and sparkled more than scattered diamonds. The sails slept, hushed by a gentle breeze. The sun, rising lonely and splendid in the blue sky, saw a solitary ship gliding close-hauled on the blue sea.

The men pressed three deep abreast of the mainmast and opposite the cabin-door. They shuffled, pushed, had an irresolute mien and stolid faces. At every slight movement Knowles lurched heavily on his short leg. Donkin glided behind backs, restless and anxious, like a man looking for an ambush. Captain Allistoun came out on the quarter-deck suddenly. He walked to and fro before the front. He was grey, slight, alert, shabby in the sunshine, and as hard as adamant. He had his right hand in the side-pocket of his jacket, and also something heavy in there that made folds all down that side. One of the seamen cleared his throat ominously.—"I haven't till now found fault with you men," said the master, stopping short. He faced them with his worn, steely gaze, that by a universal illusion looked straight into every individual pair of the twenty pairs of eyes before his face. At his back Mr. Baker, gloomy and bull-necked, grunted low; Mr. Creighton, fresh as paint, had rosy cheeks and a ready, resolute bearing. "And I don't now," continued the master; "but I am here to drive this ship and keep every man-jack aboard of her up to the mark. If you knew your work as well as I do mine, there would be no trouble. You've been braying in the dark about 'See tomorrow morning!' Well, you see me now. What do you want?" He waited, stepping quickly to and fro, giving them searching glances. What did they want? They shifted from foot to foot, they balanced their bodies; some, pushing back their caps, scratched their heads. What did they want? Jimmy was forgotten; no one thought of him, alone forward in his cabin, fighting great shadows, clinging to brazen lies, chuckling painfully over his transparent deceptions. No, not Jimmy; he was more forgotten than if he had been dead. They wanted great things. And suddenly all the simple words they knew seemed to be lost for ever in the immensity of their vague and burning desire. They knew what they wanted, but they could not find anything worth saying. They stirred on one spot, swinging, at the end of muscular arms, big tarry hands with crooked fingers. A murmur died out.—"What is it—food?" asked the master. "You know the stores have been spoiled off the Cape."—"We know that sir," said a bearded shell-back in the front rank.—"Work too hard—eh? Too much for your strength?" he asked again. There was an offended silence.—"We don't want to go shorthanded, sir," began at last Davis in a wavering voice, "and this 'ere black— . . ."—"Enough!" cried the master. He stood scanning them for a moment, then walking a few steps this way and that began to storm at them coldly, in gusts violent and cutting like the gales of those icy seas that had known his youth.—"Tell you what's the matter? Too big for your boots. Think yourselves damn good men. Know half your work. Do half your duty. Think it too much. If you did ten times as much it wouldn't be enough."—"We did our best by her, sir," cried some one with shaky exasperation.—"Your best," stormed on the master; "You hear a lot on shore, don't you? They don't tell you there your best isn't much to boast of. I tell you—your best is no better than bad. You can do no more? No, I know, and say nothing. But you stop your caper or I will stop it for you. I am ready for you! Stop it!" He shook a finger at the crowd. "As to that man," he raised his voice very much; "as to that man, if he puts his nose out on deck without my leave I will clap him in irons. There!" The cook heard him forward, ran out of the galley lifting his arms, horrified, unbelieving, amazed, and ran in again. There was a moment of profound silence during which a bow-legged seaman, stepping aside, expectorated decorously into the scupper. "There is another thing," said the master, calmly. He made a quick stride and with a swing took an iron belaying-pin out of his pocket. "This!" His movement was so unexpected and sudden that the crowd stepped back. He gazed fixedly at their faces, and some at once put on a surprised air as though they had never seen a belaying-pin before. He held it up. "This is my affair. I don't ask you any questions, but you all know it; it has got to go where it came from." His eyes became angry. The crowd stirred uneasily. They looked away from the piece of iron, they appeared shy, they were embarrassed and shocked as though it had been something horrid, scandalous, or indelicate, that in common decency should not have been flourished like this in broad daylight. The master watched them attentively. "Donkin," he called out in a short, sharp tone.

Donkin dodged behind one, then behind another, but they looked over their shoulders and moved aside. The ranks kept on opening before him, closing behind, till at last he appeared alone before the master as though he had come up through the deck. Captain Allistoun moved close to him. They were much of a size; and at short range the master exchanged a deadly glance with the beady eyes. They wavered.—"You know this?" asked the master.—"No, I don't," answered the other, with cheeky trepidation.—"You are a cur. Take it," ordered the master. Donkin's arms seemed glued to his thighs; he stood, eyes front, as if drawn on parade. "Take it," repeated the master, and stepped closer; they breathed on one another. "Take it," said Captain Allistoun again, making a menacing gesture. Donkin tore away one arm from his side.—"Vy are yer down on me?" he mumbled with effort and as if his mouth had been full of dough. —"If you don't . . ." began the master. Donkin snatched at the pin as though his intention had been to run away with it, and remained stock still holding it like a candle. "Put it back where you took it from," said Captain Allistoun, looking at him fiercely. Donkin stepped back opening wide eyes. "Go, you blackguard, or I will make you," cried the master, driving him slowly backwards by a menacing advance. He dodged, and with the dangerous iron tried to guard his head from a threatening fist. Mr. Baker ceased grunting for a moment.—"Good! By Jove," murmured appreciatively Mr. Creighton in the tone of a connoisseur.—"Don't tech me," snarled Donkin, backing away.—"Then go. Go faster."—"Don't yer 'it me. . . . I will pull yer up afore the magistryt. . . . I'll show yer up." Captain Allistoun made a long stride, and Donkin, turning his back fairly, ran off a little, then stopped and over his shoulder showed yellow teeth.—"Further on, fore-rigging," urged the master, pointing with his arm.—"Are yer goin' to stand by and see me bullied?" screamed Donkin at the silent crowd that watched him. Captain Allistoun walked at him smartly. He started off again with a leap, dashed at the fore-rigging, rammed the pin into its hole violently. "I'll be even with yer yet," he screamed at the ship at large and vanished beyond the foremast. Captain Allistoun spun round and walked back aft with a composed face, as though he had already forgotten the scene. Men moved out of his way. He looked at no one.—"That will do, Mr. Baker. Send the watch below," he said, quietly. "And you men try to walk straight for the future," he added in a calm voice. He looked pensively for a while at the backs of the impressed and retreating crowd. "Breakfast, steward," he called in a tone of relief through the cabin door.—"I didn't like to see you—Ough!— give that pin to that chap, sir," observed Mr. Baker; "he could have bust—Ough!— bust your head like an eggshell with it."—"O! he!" muttered the master, absently. "Queer lot," he went on in a low voice. "I suppose it's all right now. Can never tell tho', nowadays, with such a . . . Years ago; I was a young master then—one China voyage I had a mutiny; real mutiny, Baker. Different men tho'. I knew what they wanted: they wanted to broach the cargo and get at the liquor. Very simple. . . . We knocked them about for two days, and when they had enough—gentle as lambs. Good crew. And a smart trip I made." He glanced aloft at the yards braced sharp up. "Head wind day after day," he exclaimed, bitterly. "Shall we never get a decent slant this passage?"—"Ready, sir," said the steward, appearing before them as if by magic and with a stained napkin in his hand.—"Ah! All right. Come along, Mr. Baker—it's late —with all this nonsense."

V

A heavy atmosphere of oppressive quietude pervaded the ship. In the afternoon men
went about washing clothes and hanging them out to dry in the unprosperous breeze
with the meditative langor of disenchanted philosophers. Very little was said. The
problem of life seemed too voluminous for the narrow limits of human speech, and by
common consent it was abandoned to the great sea that had from the beginning
enfolded it in its immense grip; to the sea that knew all, and would in time infallibly
unveil to each the wisdom hidden in all the errors, the certitude that lurks in doubts,
the realm of safety and peace beyond the frontiers of sorrow and fear. And in the
confused current of impotent thoughts that set unceasingly this way and that through
bodies of men, Jimmy bobbed up upon the surface, compelling attention, like a black
buoy chained to the bottom of a muddy stream. Falsehood triumphed. It triumphed
through doubt, through stupidity, through pity, through sentimentalism. We set ourselves to bolster it up, from compassion, from recklessness, from a sense of fun.
Jimmy's steadfastness to his untruthful attitude in the face of the inevitable truth had
the proportions of a colossal enigma—of a manifestation grand and incomprehensible
that at times inspired a wondering awe; and there was also, to many, something
exquisitely droll in fooling him thus to the top of his bent. The latent egoism of
tenderness to suffering appeared in the developing anxiety not to see him die. His
obstinate nonrecognition of the only certitude whose approach we could watch from
day to day was as disquieting as the failure of some law of nature. He was so utterly
wrong about himself that one could not but suspect him of having access to some
source of supernatural knowledge. He was absurd to the point of inspiration. He was
unique, and as fascinating as only something inhuman could be; he seemed to shout
his denials already from beyond the awful border. He was becoming immaterial like an
apparition; his cheekbones rose, the forehead slanted more; the face was all hollows,
patches of shade; and the fleshless head resembled a disinterred black skull, fitted with
two restless globes of silver in the sockets of eyes. He was demoralizing. Through him
we were becoming highly humanized, tender, complex, excessively decadent: we understood the subtlety of his fear, sympathized with all his repulsions, shrinkings, evasions,
delusions—as though we had been overcivilized, and rotten, and without any knowledge of the meaning of life. We had the air of being initiated in some infamous
mysteries; we had the profound grimaces of conspirators, exchanged meaning glances,
significant short words. We were inexpressibly vile and very much pleased with ourselves. We lied to him with gravity, with emotion, with unction, as if performing some
moral trick with a view to an eternal reward. We made a chorus of affirmation to his
wildest assertions, as though he had been a millionaire, a politician, or a reformer—
and we a crowd of ambitious lubbers. When we ventured to question his statements
we did it after the manner of obsequious sycophants, to the end that his glory should
be augmented by the flattery of our dissent. He influenced the moral tone of our
world as though he had it in his power to distribute honors, treasures, or pain; and he
could give us nothing but his contempt. It was immense; it seemed to grow gradually
larger, as his body day by day shrank a little more, while we looked. It was the only

thing about him—of him—that gave the impression of durability and vigor. It lived within him with an unquenchable life. It spoke through the eternal pout of his black lips; it looked at us through the impertinent mournfulness of his languid and enormous stare. We watched him intently. He seemed unwilling to move, as if distrustful of his own solidity. The slightest gesture must have disclosed to him (it could not surely be otherwise) his bodily weakness, and caused a pang of mental suffering. He was chary of movements. He lay stretched out, chin on blanket, in a kind of sly, cautious immobility. Only his eyes roamed over faces: his eyes disdainful, penetrating and sad.

It was at that time that Belfast's devotion—and also his pugnacity—secured universal respect. He spent every moment of his spare time in Jimmy's cabin. He tended him, talked to him; was as gentle as a woman, as tenderly gay as an old philanthropist, as sentimentally careful of his nigger as a model slave-owner. But outside he was irritable, explosive as gunpowder, somber, suspicious, and never more brutal than when most sorrowful. With him it was a tear and a blow: a tear for Jimmy, a blow for any one who did not seem to take a scrupulously orthodox view of Jimmy's case. We talked about nothing else. The two Scandinavians, even, discussed the situation—but it was impossible to know in what spirit, because they quarreled in their own language. Belfast suspected one of them of irreverence, and in this incertitude thought that there was no option but to fight them both. They became very much terrified by his truculence, and henceforth lived amongst us, dejected, like a pair of mutes. Wamibo never spoke intelligibly, but he was as smileless as an animal—seemed to know much less about it all than the cat—and consequently was safe. Moreover, he had belonged to the chosen band of Jimmy's rescuers, and was above suspicion. Archie was silent generally, but often spent an hour or so talking to Jimmy quietly with an air of proprietorship. At any time of the day and often through the night some man could be seen sitting on Jimmy's box. In the evening, between six and eight, the cabin was crowded, and there was an interested group at the door. Every one stared at the nigger.

He basked in the warmth of our interest. His eyes gleamed ironically, and in a weak voice he reproached us with our cowardice. He would say, "If you fellows had stuck out for me I would be now on deck." We hung our heads. "Yes, but if you think I am going to let them put me in irons just to show you sport. . . . Well, no. . . . It ruins my health, this lying-up, it does. You don't care." We were as abashed as if it had been true. His superb impudence carried all before it. We would not have dared to revolt. We didn't want to, really. We wanted to keep him alive till home—to the end of the voyage.

Singleton as usual held aloof, appearing to scorn the insignificant events of an ended life. Once only he came along, and unexpectedly stopped in the doorway. He peered at Jimmy in profound silence, as if desirous to add that black image to the crowd of Shades that peopled his old memory. We kept very quiet, and for a long time Singleton stood there as though he had come by appointment to call for some one, or to see some important event. James Wait lay perfectly still, and apparently not aware of the gaze scrutinizing him with a steadiness full of expectation. There was a sense of a

contest in the air. We felt the inward strain of men watching a wrestling bout. At last
Jimmy with perceptible apprehension turned his head on the pillow.—"Good evening," he said in a conciliating tone.—"H'm," answered the old seaman, grumpily. For
a moment longer he looked at Jimmy with severe fixity, then suddenly went away. It
was a long time before any one spoke in the little cabin, though we all breathed more
freely as men do after an escape from some dangerous situation. We all knew the old
man's ideas about Jimmy, and nobody dared to combat them. They were unsettling,
they caused pain; and, what was worse, they might have been true for all we knew.
Only once did he condescend to explain them fully, but the impression was lasting. He
said that Jimmy was the cause of head winds. Mortally sick men—he maintained—
linger till the first sight of land, and then die; and Jimmy knew that the very first land
would draw his life from him. It is so in every ship. Didn't we know it? He asked us
with austere contempt: what did we know? What would we doubt next? Jimmy's desire
encouraged by us and aided by Wamibo's (he was a Finn—wasn't he? Very well!) by
Wamibo's spells delayed the ship in the open sea. Only lubberly fools couldn't see it.
Whoever heard of such a run of calms and head winds? It wasn't natural. . . . We
could not deny that it was strange. We felt uneasy. The common saying, "More days,
more dollars," did not give the usual comfort because the stores were running short.
Much had been spoiled off the Cape, and we were on half allowance of biscuit. Peas,
sugar and tea had been finished long ago. Salt meat was giving out. We had plenty of
coffee but very little water to make it with. We took up another hole in our belts and
went on scraping, polishing, painting the ship from morning to night. And soon she
looked as though she had come out of a band-box; but hunger lived on board of her.
Not dead starvation, but steady, living hunger that stalked about the decks, slept in the
forecastle; the tormentor of waking moments, the disturber of dreams. We looked to
windward for signs of change. Every few hours of night and day we put her round with
the hope that she would come up on that tack at last! She didn't. She seemed to have
forgotten the way home; she rushed to and fro, heading northwest, heading east; she
ran backwards and forwards, distracted, like a timid creature at the foot of a wall.
Sometimes, as if tired to death, she would wallow languidly for a day in the smooth
swell of an unruffled sea. All up the swinging masts the sails thrashed furiously
through the hot stillness of the calm. We were weary, hungry, thirsty; we commenced
to believe Singleton, but with unshaken fidelity dissembled to Jimmy. We spoke to
him with jocose allusiveness, like cheerful accomplices in a clever plot; but we looked
to the westward over the rail with longing eyes for a sign of hope, for a sign of fair
wind; even if its first breath should bring death to our reluctant Jimmy. In vain! The
universe conspired with James Wait. Light airs from the northward sprang up again;
the sky remained clear; and round our weariness the glittering sea, touched by the
breeze, basked voluptuously in the great sunshine, as though it had forgotten our life
and trouble.

Donkin looked out for a fair wind along with the rest. No one knew the venom of
his thoughts now. He was silent, and appeared thinner, as if consumed slowly by an
inward rage at the injustice of men and of fate. He was ignored by all and spoke to no

one, but his hate for every man dwelt in his furtive eyes. He talked with the cook only, having somehow persuaded the good man that he—Donkin—was a much calumniated and persecuted person. Together they bewailed the immorality of the ship's company. There could be no greater criminals than we, who by our lies conspired to send the unprepared soul of a poor ignorant black man to everlasting perdition. Podmore cooked what there was to cook, remorsefully, and felt all the time that by preparing the food of such sinners he imperilled his own salvation. As to the Captain —he had sailed with him for seven years, now, he said, and would not have believed it possible that such a man . . . "Well. Well . . . There it was . . . Can't get out of it. Judgment capsized all in a minute . . . Struck in all his pride . . . More like a sudden visitation than anything else." Donkin, perched sullenly on the coal-locker, swung his legs and concurred. He paid in the coin of spurious assent for the privilege to sit in the galley; he was disheartened and scandalized; he agreed with the cook; could find no words severe enough to criticize our conduct; and when in the heat of reprobation he swore at us, Podmore, who would have liked to swear also if it hadn't been for his principles, pretended not to hear. So Donkin, unrebuked, cursed enough for two, cadged for matches, borrowed tobacco, and loafed for hours, very much at home, before the stove. From there he could hear us on the other side of the bulkhead, talking to Jimmy. The cook knocked the saucepans about, slammed the oven door, muttered prophesies of damnation for all the ship's company; and Donkin, who did not admit of any hereafter (except for purpose of blasphemy) listened, concentrated and angry, gloating fiercely over a called-up image of infinite torment—as men gloat over the accursed images of cruelty and revenge, of greed, and of power. . . .

On clear evenings the silent ship, under the cold sheen of the dead moon, took on a false aspect of passionless repose resembling the winter of the earth. Under her a long band of gold barred the black disc of the sea. Footsteps echoed on her quiet decks. The moonlight clung to her like a frosted mist, and the white sails stood out in dazzling cones as of stainless snow. In the magnificence of the phantom rays the ship appeared pure like a vision of ideal beauty, illusive like a tender dream of serene peace. And nothing in her was real, nothing was distinct and solid but the heavy shadows that filled her decks with their unceasing and noiseless stir: the shadows darker than the night and more restless than the thoughts of men.

Donkin prowled spiteful and alone amongst the shadows, thinking that Jimmy too long delayed to die. That evening land had been reported from aloft, and the master, while adjusting the tubes of the long glass, had observed with quiet bitterness to Mr. Baker that, after fighting our way inch by inch to the Western Islands, there was nothing to expect now but a spell of calm. The sky was clear and the barometer high. The light breeze dropped with the sun, and an enormous stillness, forerunner of a night without wind, descended upon the heated waters of the ocean. As long as daylight lasted, the hands collected on the forecastle-head watched on the eastern sky the island of Flores, that rose above the level expanse of the sea with irregular and broken outlines like a somber ruin upon a vast and deserted plain. It was the first land seen for nearly four months. Charley was excited, and in the midst of general indulgence took liberties with his betters. Men strangely elated without knowing why talked in groups, and pointed with bared arms. For the first time that voyage Jimmy's sham existence seemed for a moment forgotten in the face of a solid reality. We had got so far anyhow. Belfast discoursed, quoting imaginary examples of short homeward runs from the Islands. "Them smart fruit schooners do it in five days," he affirmed. "What do you want?—only a good little breeze." Archie maintained that seven days was the record passage, and they disputed amicably with insulting words. Knowles declared he could already smell home from there, and with a heavy list on his short leg laughed fit to split his sides. A group of grizzled seadogs looked out for a time in silence and with grim absorbed faces. One said suddenly—" 'Tain't far to London now."—"My first night ashore, blamme if I haven't steak and onions for supper . . . and a pint of bitter," said another.—"A barrel ye mean," shouted someone.—"Ham an' eggs three times a day. That's the way I live!" cried an excited voice. There was a stir, appreciative murmurs; eyes began to shine; jaws champed; short, nervous laughs were heard. Archie smiled with reserve all to himself. Singleton came up, gave a careless glance, and went down again without saying a word, indifferent, like a man who had seen Flores an incalculable number of times. The night traveling from the East blotted out of the limpid sky the purple stain of the high land. "Dead calm," said somebody quietly. The murmur of lively talk suddenly wavered, died out; the clusters broke up; men began to drift away one by one, descending the ladders slowly and with serious faces as if sobered by that reminder of their dependence upon the invisible. And when the big yellow moon ascended gently above the sharp rim of the clear horizon it found the ship wrapped up in a breathless silence; a fearless ship that seemed to sleep profoundly, dreamlessly on the bosom of the sleeping and terrible sea.

Donkin chafed at the peace—at the ship—at the sea that stretching away on all sides merged into the illimitable silence of all creation. He felt himself pulled up sharp by unrecognized grievances. He had been physically cowed, but his injured dignity remained indomitable, and nothing could heal his lacerated feelings. Here was land already—home very soon—a bad payday—no clothes—more hard work. How offensive all this was. Land. The land that draws away life from sick sailors. That nigger there had money—clothes—easy times; and would not die. Land draws life away. . . . He felt tempted to go and see whether it did. Perhaps already . . . It would be a bit of luck. There was money in the beggar's chest. He stepped briskly out of the shadows into the moonlight, and instantly, his craving, hungry face from sallow became livid. He opened the door of the cabin and had a shock. Sure enough, Jimmy was dead! He moved no more than a recumbent figure with clasped hands, carved on the lid of a stone coffin. Donkin glared with avidity. Then Jimmy, without stirring, blinked his eyelids, and Donkin had another shock. Those eyes were rather startling. He shut the door behind his back with gentle care, looking intently the while at James Wait as though he had come in there at a great risk to tell some secret of startling importance. Jimmy did not move but glanced languidly out of the corners of his eyes. —"Calm?" he asked.—"Yuss," said Donkin, very disappointed, and sat down on the box.

Jimmy was used to such visits at all times of night or day. Men succeeded one another. They spoke in clear voices, pronounced cheerful words, repeated old jokes, listened to him; and each, going out, seemed to leave behind a little of his own vitality, surrender some of his own strength, renew the assurance of life—the indestructible thing! He did not like to be alone in his cabin, because, when he was alone, it seemed to him as if he hadn't been there at all. There was nothing. No pain. Not now. Perfectly right—but he couldn't enjoy his healthful repose unless some one was by to see it. This man would do as well as anybody. Donkin watched him stealthily:—"Soon home now," observed Wait.—"Vy d'yer whisper?" asked Donkin with interest, "can't yer speak up?" Jimmy looked annoyed and said nothing for a while; then in a lifeless, unringing voice:—"Why should I shout? You ain't deaf that I know."—"Oh! I can 'ear right enough," answered Donkin in a low tone, and looked down. He was thinking sadly of going out when Jimmy spoke again.—"Time we did get home . . . to get something decent to eat . . . I am always hungry." Donkin felt angry all of a sudden. —"What about me," he hissed, "I am 'ungry too an' got ter work. You, 'ungry!"— "Your work won't kill you," commented Wait, feebly; "there's a couple of biscuits in the lower bunk there—you may have one. I can't eat them." Donkin dived in, groped in the corner and when he came up again his mouth was full. He munched with ardor. Jimmy seemed to doze with open eyes. Donkin finished his hard bread and got up.— "You're not going?" asked Jimmy, staring at the ceiling.—"No," said Donkin, impulsively, and instead of going out leaned his back against the closed door. He looked at James Wait, and saw him long, lean, dried up, as though all his flesh had shriveled on his bones in the heat of a white furnace; the meager fingers of one hand moved lightly upon the edge of the bunk playing an endless tune. To look at him was irritating and fatiguing; he could last like this for days; he was outrageous—belonging wholly neither to death nor life, and perfectly invulnerable in his apparent ignorance of both. Donkin felt tempted to enlighten him.—"What are yer thinkin' of?" he asked, surlily. James Wait had a grimacing smile that passed over the deathlike impassiveness of his bony face, incredible and frightful as would, in a dream, have been the sudden smile of a corpse.

"There is a girl," whispered Wait. . . . "Canton Street girl.—She chucked a third engineer of a Rennie boat—for me. Cooks oysters just as I like . . . She says—she would chuck—any toff—for a colored gentleman. . . . That's me. I am kind to wimmen," he added, a shade louder.

Donkin could hardly believe his ears. He was scandalized—"Would she? Yer wouldn't be any good to 'er," he said with unrestrained disgust. Wait was not there to hear him. He was swaggering up the East India Dock Road; saying kindly, "Come along for a treat," pushing glass swing-doors, posing with superb assurance in the gaslight above a mahogany counter.—"D'yer think yer will ever get ashore?" asked Donkin, angrily. Wait came back with a start.—"Ten days," he said, promptly, and returned at once to the regions of memory that know nothing of time. He felt untired, calm, and safely withdrawn within himself beyond the reach of every grave incertitude. There was something of the immutable quality of eternity in the slow moments of his complete restfulness. He was very quiet and easy amongst his vivid reminiscences which he mistook joyfully for images of an undoubted future. He cared for no one. Donkin felt this vaguely like a blind man feeling in his darkness the fatal antagonism of all the surrounding existences, that to him shall for ever remain irrealizable, unseen and enviable. He had a desire to assert his importance, to break, to crush; to be even with everybody for everything; to tear the veil, unmask, expose, leave no refuge—a perfidious desire of truthfulness! He laughed in a mocking splutter and said:

"Ten days. Strike me blind if I ever! . . . You will be dead by this time tomorrow p'r'aps. Ten days!" He waited for a while. "D'ye 'ear me? Blamme if yer don't look dead already."

Wait must have been collecting his strength, for he said almost aloud—"You're a stinking, cadging liar. Every one knows you." And sitting up, against all probability, startled his visitor horribly. But very soon Donkin recovered himself. He blustered, "What? What? Who's a liar? You are—the crowd are—the skipper—everybody. I ain't! Putting on airs! Who's yer?" He nearly choked himself with indignation. "Who's yer to put on airs," he repeated, trembling. " 'Ave one—'ave one, says 'ee—an' cawn't eat 'em 'isself. Now I'll 'ave both. By Gawd—I will! Yer nobody!"

He plunged into the lower bunk, rooted in there and brought to light another dusty biscuit. He held it up before Jimmy—then took a bite defiantly.

"What now?" he asked with feverish impudence. "Yer may take one—says yer. Why not giv' me both? No. I'm a mangy dorg. One fur a mangy dorg. I'll tyke both. Can yer stop me? Try. Come on. Try."

Jimmy was clasping his legs and hiding his face on the knees. His shirt clung to him. Every rib was visible. His emaciated back was shaken in repeated jerks by the panting catches of his breath.

"Yer won't? Yer can't! What did I say?" went on Donkin, fiercely. He swallowed another dry mouthful with a hasty effort. The other's silent helplessness, his weakness, his shrinking attitude exasperated him. "Ye're done!" he cried. "Who's yer to be lied to; to be waited on 'and an' foot like a bloomin' ymperor. Yer nobody. Yer no one at all!" he spluttered with such a strength of unerring conviction that it shook him from head to foot in coming out, and left him vibrating like a released string.

James Wait rallied again. He lifted his head and turned bravely at Donkin, who saw a strange face, an unknown face, a fantastic and grimacing mask of despair and fury. Its lips moved rapidly; and hollow, moaning, whistling sounds filled the cabin with a vague mutter full of menace, complaint and desolation, like the far-off murmur of a rising wind. Wait shook his head; rolled his eyes; he denied, cursed, threatened—and not a word had the strength to pass beyond the sorrowful pout of those black lips. It was incomprehensible and disturbing; a gibberish of emotions, a frantic dumb show of speech pleading for impossible things, promising a shadowy vengeance. It sobered Donkin into a scrutinizing watchfulness.

"Yer can't 'oller. See? What did I tell yer?" he said, slowly, after a moment of attentive examination. The other kept on headlong and unheard, nodding passionately, grinning with grotesque and appalling flashes of big white teeth. Donkin, as if fascinated by the dumb eloquence and anger of that black phantom, approached, stretching his neck out with distrustful curiosity; and it seemed to him suddenly that he was looking only at the shadow of a man crouching high in the bunk on the level with his eyes.—"What? What?" he said. He seemed to catch the shape of some words in the continuous panting hiss. "Yer will tell Belfast! Will yer? Are ye a bloomin' kid?" He trembled with alarm and rage, "Tell yer gran'mother! Yer afeard! Who's yer ter be afeard more'n any one." His passionate sense of his own importance ran away with a last remnant of caution. "Tell an' be damned! Tell, if yer can!" he cried. "I've been treated worser'n a dorg by your blooming back-lickers. They 'as set me on, only to turn aginst me. I am the only man 'ere. They clouted me, kicked me—an' yer laffed— yer black, rotten incumbrance, you! You will pay fur it. They giv' yer their grub, their water—yer will pay fur it to me, by Gawd! Who axed me ter 'ave a drink of water? They put their bloomin' rags on yer that night, an' what did they giv' ter me—a clout on the bloomin' mouth—blast their . . . S'elp me! . . . Yer will pay fur it with yer money. I'm goin' ter 'ave it in a minyte; as soon has ye're dead, yer bloomin' useless fraud. That's the man I am. An' ye're a thing—a bloody thing. Yah—you corpse!"

He flung at Jimmy's head the biscuit he had been all the time clutching hard, but it only grazed, and striking with a loud crack the bulkhead beyond burst like a hand-grenade into flying pieces. James Wait, as if wounded mortally, fell back on the pillow. His lips ceased to move and the rolling eyes became quiet and stared upwards with an intense and steady persistence. Donkin was surprised; he sat suddenly on the chest, and looked down, exhausted and gloomy. After a moment, he began to mutter to himself, "Die, you beggar—die. Somebody'll come in . . . I wish I was drunk . . . Ten days . . . oysters . . ." He looked up and spoke louder. "No . . . No more for yer . . . no more bloomin' gals that cook oysters . . . Who's yer? It's my turn now . . . I wish I was drunk; I would soon giv' you a leg up. That's where yer bound to go. Feet fust, through a port . . . Splash! Never see yer any more. Overboard! Good 'nuff fur yer."

Jimmy's head moved slightly and he turned his eyes to Donkin's face; a gaze unbelieving, desolated and appealing, of a child frightened by the menace of being shut up alone in the dark. Donkin observed him from the chest with hopeful eyes; then, without rising, tried the lid. Locked. "I wish I was drunk," he muttered and getting up listened anxiously to the distant sound of footsteps on the deck. They approached—ceased. Some one yawned interminably just outside the door, and the footsteps went away shuffling lazily. Donkin's fluttering heart eased its pace, and when he looked towards the bunk again Jimmy was staring as before at the white beam.— " 'Ow d'yer feel now?" he asked.—"Bad," breathed out Jimmy.

Donkin sat down patient and purposeful. Every half-hour the bells spoke to one another ringing along the whole length of the ship. Jimmy's respiration was so rapid that it couldn't be counted, so faint that it couldn't be heard. His eyes were terrified as though he had been looking at unspeakable horrors; and by his face one could see that he was thinking of abominable things. Suddenly with an incredibly strong and heart-breaking voice he sobbed out:

"Overboard! . . . I! . . . My God!"

Donkin writhed a little on the box. He looked unwillingly. James Wait was mute. His two long bony hands smoothed the blanket upwards, as though he had wished to gather it all up under his chin. A tear, a big solitary tear, escaped from the corner of his eye and, without touching the hollow cheek, fell on the pillow. His throat rattled faintly.

And Donkin, watching the end of that hateful nigger, felt the anguishing grasp of a great sorrow on his heart at the thought that he himself, some day, would have to go through it all—just like this—perhaps! His eyes became moist. "Poor beggar," he murmured. The night seemed to go by in a flash; it seemed to him he could hear the irremediable rush of precious minutes. How long would this blooming affair last? Too long surely. No luck. He could not restrain himself. He got up and approached the bunk. Wait did not stir. Only his eyes appeared alive and his hands continued their smoothing movement with a horrible and tireless industry. Donkin bent over.

"Jimmy," he called low. There was no answer, but the rattle stopped. "D'yer see me?" he asked, trembling. Jimmy's chest heaved. Donkin, looking away, bent his ear to Jimmy's lips, and heard a sound like the rustle of a single dry leaf driven along the smooth sand of a beach. It shaped itself.

"Light . . . the lamp . . . and . . . go," breathed out Wait.

Donkin, instinctively, glanced over his shoulder at the brilliant flame; then, still looking away, felt under the pillow for a key. He got it at once and for the next few minutes remained on his knees shakily but swiftly busy inside the box. When he got up, his face—for the first time in his life—had a pink flush—perhaps of triumph.

He slipped the key under the pillow again, avoiding to glance at Jimmy, who had not moved. He turned his back squarely from the bunk, and started to the door as though he were going to walk a mile. At his second stride he had his nose against it. He clutched the handle cautiously, but at that moment he received the irresistible impression of something happening behind his back. He spun round as though he had been tapped on the shoulder. He was just in time to see Wait's eyes blaze up and go out at once, like two lamps overturned together by a sweeping blow. Something resembling a scarlet thread hung down his chin out of the corner of his lips—and he had ceased to breathe.

Donkin closed the door behind him gently but firmly. Sleeping men, huddled under jackets, made on the lighted deck shapeless dark mounds that had the appearance of neglected graves. Nothing had been done all through the night and he hadn't been missed. He stood motionless and perfectly astounded to find the world outside as he had left it; there was the sea, the ship—sleeping men; and he wondered absurdly at it, as though he had expected to find the men dead, familiar things gone for ever: as though, like a wanderer returning after many years, he had expected to see bewildering changes. He shuddered a little in the penetrating freshness of the air, and hugged himself forlornly. The declining moon drooped sadly in the western board as if withered by the cold touch of a pale dawn. The ship slept. And the immortal sea stretched away, immense and hazy, like the image of life, with a glittering surface and lightless depths. Donkin gave it a defiant glance and slunk off noiselessly as if judged and cast out by the august silence of its might.

Jimmy's death, after all, came as a tremendous surprise. We did not know till then how much faith we had put in his delusions. We had taken his chances of life so much at his own valuation that his death, like the death of an old belief, shook the foundations of our society. A common bond was gone; the strong, effective and respectable bond of a sentimental lie. All that day we mooned at our work, with suspicious looks and a disabused air. In our hearts we thought that in the matter of his departure Jimmy had acted in a perverse and unfriendly manner. He didn't back us up, as a shipmate should. In going he took away with himself the gloomy and solemn shadow in which our folly had posed, with humane satisfaction, as a tender arbiter of fate. And now we saw it was no such thing. It was just common foolishness; a silly and ineffectual meddling with issues of majestic import—that is, if Podmore was right. Perhaps he was? Doubt survived Jimmy; and, like a community of banded criminals disintegrated by a touch of grace, we were profoundly scandalized with each other. Men spoke unkindly to their best chums. Others refused to speak at all. Singleton only was not surprised. "Dead—is he? Of course," he said, pointing at the island right abeam: for the calm still held the ship spell-bound within sight of Flores. Dead—of course. *He* wasn't surprised. Here was the land, and there, on the forehatch and waiting for the sailmaker—there was that corpse. Cause and effect. And for the first time that voyage, the old seaman became quite cheery and garrulous, explaining and illustrating from the stores of experience how, in sickness, the sight of an island (even a very small one) is generally more fatal than the view of a continent. But he couldn't explain why.

Jimmy was to be buried at five, and it was a long day till then—a day of mental disquiet and even of physical disturbance. We took no interest in our work and, very properly, were rebuked for it. This, in our constant state of hungry irritation, was exasperating. Donkin worked with his brow bound in a dirty rag, and looked so ghastly that Mr. Baker was touched with compassion at the sight of this plucky suffering.—"Ough! You, Donkin! Put down your work and go lay-up this watch. You look ill."—"I am bad, sir—in my 'ead," he said in a subdued voice, and vanished speedily. This annoyed many, and they thought the mate "bloomin' soft today." Captain Allistoun could be seen on the poop watching the sky to the southwest, and it soon got to be known about the decks that the barometer had begun to fall in the night, and that a breeze might be expected before long. This, by a subtle association of ideas, led to violent quarreling as to the exact moment of Jimmy's death. Was it before or after "that 'ere glass started down?" It was impossible to know, and it caused much contemptuous growling at one another. All of a sudden there was a great tumult forward. Pacific Knowles and good-tempered Davis had come to blows over it. The watch below interfered with spirit, and for ten minutes there was a noisy scrimmage round the hatch, where, in the balancing shade of the sails, Jimmy's body, wrapped up in a white blanket, was watched over by the sorrowful Belfast, who, in his desolation, disdained the fray. When the noise had ceased, and the passions had calmed into surly silence, he stood up at the head of the swathed body, lifting both arms on high, cried with pained indignation:—"You ought to be ashamed of yourselves! . . ." We were.

Belfast took his bereavement very hard. He gave proofs of unextinguishable devotion. It was he, and no other man, who would help the sailmaker to prepare what was left of Jimmy for a solemn surrender to the insatiable sea. He arranged the weights carefully at the feet: two holystones, an old anchor-shackle without its pin, some broken links of a worn-out stream cable. He arranged them this way, then that. "Bless my soul! you aren't afraid he will chafe his heel?" said the sailmaker, who hated the job. He pushed the needle, puffing furiously, with his head in a cloud of tobacco smoke; he turned the flaps over, pulled at the stitches, stretched at the canvas. "Lift his shoulders. . . . Pull to you a bit. . . . So—o—o. Steady." Belfast obeyed, pulled, lifted, overcome with sorrow, dropping tears on the tarred twine.—"Don't you drag the canvas too taut over his poor face, Sails," he entreated, tearfully.—"What are you fashing yourself for? He will be comfortable enough," assured the sailmaker, cutting the threat after the last stitch, which came about the middle of Jimmy's forehead. He rolled up the remaining canvas, put away the needles. "What makes you take on so?" he asked. Belfast looked down at the long package of grey sailcloth.—"I pulled him out," he whispered, "and he did not want to go. If I had sat up with him last night he would have kept alive for me . . . but something made me tired." The sailmaker took vigorous draws at his pipe and mumbled:—"When I . . . West India Station . . . In the *Blanche* frigate . . . Yellow Jack . . . sewed in twenty men a week . . . Portsmouth-Devonport men—townies—knew their fathers, mothers, sisters—the whole boiling of 'em. Thought nothing of it. And these niggers like this one—you don't know where it comes from. Got nobody. No use to nobody. Who will miss him?"—"I do—I pulled him out," mourned Belfast dismally.

On two planks nailed together and apparently resigned and still under the folds of the Union Jack with a white border, James Wait, carried aft by four men, was deposited slowly, with his feet pointing at an open port. A swell had set in from the westward, and following on the roll of the ship, the red ensign, at half-mast, darted out and collapsed again on the grey sky, like a tongue of flickering fire; Charley tolled the bell; and at every swing to starboard the whole vast semicircle of steely waters visible on that side seemed to come up with a rush to the edge of the port, as if impatient to get at our Jimmy. Every one was there but Donkin, who was too ill to come; the Captain and Mr. Creighton stood bareheaded on the break of the poop; Mr. Baker, directed by the master, who had said to him gravely:—"You know more about the prayer book than I do," came out of the cabin door quickly and a little embarrassed. All the caps went off. He began to read in a low tone, and with his usual harmlessly menacing utterance, as though he had been for the last time reproving confidentially that dead seaman at his feet. The men listened in scattered groups; they leaned on the fife rail, gazing on the deck; they held their chins in their hands thoughtfully, or, with crossed arms and one knee slightly bent, hung their heads in an attitude of upright meditation. Wamibo dreamed. Mr. Baker read on, grunting reverently at the turn of every page. The words, missing the unsteady hearts of men, rolled out to wander without a home upon the heartless sea; and James Wait, silenced for ever, lay uncritical and passive under the hoarse murmur of despair and hopes.

Two men made ready and waited for those words that send so many of our brothers to their last plunge. Mr. Baker began the passage. "Stand by," muttered the boatswain. Mr. Baker read out: "To the deep," and paused. The men lifted the inboard end of the planks, the boatswain snatched off the Union Jack, and James Wait did not move.—"Higher," muttered the boatswain angrily. All the heads were raised; every man stirred uneasily, but James Wait gave no sign of going. In death and swathed up for all eternity, he yet seemed to cling to the ship with the grip of an undying fear. "Higher! Lift!" whispered the boatswain, fiercely.—"He won't go," stammered one of the men, shakily, and both appeared ready to drop everything. Mr. Baker waited, burying his face in the book, and shuffling his feet nervously. All the men looked profoundly disturbed; from their midst a faint humming noise spread out—growling louder. . . ."Jimmy!" cried Belfast in a wailing tone, and there was a second of shuddering dismay.

"Jimmy, be a man!" he shrieked, passionately. Every mouth was wide open, not an eyelid winked. He stared wildly, twitching all over; he bent his body forward like a man peering at a horror. "Go!" he shouted, and sprang out of the crowd with his arm extended. "Go, Jimmy!—Jimmy, go! Go!" His fingers touched the head of the body, and the grey package started reluctantly to whizz off the lifted planks all at once, with the suddenness of a flash of lightning. The crowd stepped forward like one man; a deep Ah—h—h! came out vibrating from the broad chests. The ship rolled as if relieved of an unfair burden; the sails flapped. Belfast, supported by Archie, gasped hysterically; and Charley, who, anxious to see Jimmy's last dive, leaped headlong on the rail, was too late to see anything but the faint circle of a vanishing ripple.

Mr. Baker, perspiring abundantly, read out the last prayer in a deep rumor of excited men and fluttering sails. "Amen!" he said in an unsteady growl, and closed the book.

"Square the yards!" thundered a voice above his head. All hands gave a jump; one or two dropped their caps; Mr. Baker looked up surprised. The master, standing on the break of the poop, pointed to the westward. "Breeze coming," he said, "Man the weather braces." Mr. Baker crammed the book hurriedly into his pocket. "Forward, there—let go the foretack!" he hailed joyfully, bareheaded and brisk; "Square the foreyard, you port-watch!"—"Fair wind—fair wind," muttered the men going to the braces.—"What did I tell you?" mumbled old Singleton, flinging down coil after coil with hasty energy; "I knowed it—he's gone, and here it comes."

It came with the sound of a lofty and powerful sigh. The sails filled, the ship gathered way, and the waking sea began to murmur sleepily of home to the ears of men.

That night, while the ship rushed foaming to the Northward before a freshening gale, the boatswain unbosomed himself to the petty officers' berth:—"The chap was nothing but trouble," he said, "from the moment he came aboard—d'ye remember—that night in Bombay? Been bullying all that softy crowd—cheeked the old man—we had to go fooling all over a half-drowned ship to save him. Dam' nigh a mutiny all for him—and now the mate abused me like a pickpocket for forgetting to dab a lump of grease on them planks. So I did, but you ought to have known better, too, than to leave a nail sticking up—hey, Chips?"

"And you ought to have known better than to chuck all my tools overboard for 'im, like a skeary greenhorn," retorted the morose carpenter. "Well—he's gone after 'em now," he added in an unforgiving tone.—"On the China Station, I remember once, the Admiral he says to me . . ." began the sailmaker.

A week afterwards the *Narcissus* entered the chops of the Channel.

Under white wings she skimmed low over the blue sea like a great tired bird speeding to its nest. The clouds raced with her mastheads; they rose astern enormous and white, soared to the zenith, flew past, and falling down the wide curve of the sky seemed to dash headlong into the sea—the clouds swifter than the ship, more free, but without a home. The coast to welcome her stepped out of space into the sunshine. The lofty headlands trod masterfully into the sea; the wide bays smiled in the light; the shadows of homeless clouds ran along the sunny plains, leaped over valleys, without a check darted up the hills, rolled down the slopes; and the sunshine pursued them with patches of running brightness. On the brows of dark cliffs white light-houses shone in pillars of light. The Channel glittered like a blue mantle shot with gold and starred by the silver of the capping seas. The *Narcissus* rushed past the headlands and the bays. Outward-bound vessels crossed her track, lying over, and with their masts stripped for a slogging fight with the hard sou'wester. And, inshore, a string of smoking steamboats waddled, hugging the coast, like migrating and amphibious monsters, distrustful of the restless waves.

At night the headlands retreated, the bays advanced into one unbroken line of gloom. The lights of the earth mingled with the lights of heaven; and above the tossing lanterns of a trawling fleet a great lighthouse shone steadily, like an enormous riding light burning above a vessel of fabulous dimensions. Below its steady glow, the coast, stretching away straight and black, resembled the high side of an indestructible craft riding motionless upon the immortal and unresting sea. The dark land lay alone in the midst of waters, like a mighty ship bestarred with vigilant lights—a ship carrying the burden of millions of lives—a ship freighted with dross and with jewels, with gold and with steel. She towered up immense and strong, guarding priceless traditions and untold suffering, sheltering glorious memories and base forgetfulness, ignoble virtues and splendid transgressions. A great ship! For ages had the ocean battered in vain her enduring sides; she was there when the world was vaster and darker, when the sea was great and mysterious, and ready to surrender the prize of fame to audacious men. A ship mother of fleets and nations! The great flagship of the race; stronger than the storms! and anchored in the open sea.

The *Narcissus*, heeling over to off-shore gusts, rounded the South Foreland, passed through the Downs, and, in tow, entered the river. Shorn of the glory of her white wings, she wound obediently after the tug through the maze of invisible channels. As she passed them the red-painted light-vessels swung at their moorings, seemed for an instant to sail with great speed in the rush of tide, and the next moment were left hopelessly behind. The big buoys on the tails of banks slipped past her sides very low, and, dropping in her wake, tugged at their chains like fierce watchdogs. The reach narrowed; from both sides the land approached the ship. She went steadily up the river. On the riverside slopes the houses appeared in groups—seemed to stream down the declivities at a run to see her pass, and, checked by the mud of the foreshore, crowded on the banks. Further on, the tall factory chimneys appeared in insolent bands and watched her go by, like a straggling crowd of slim giants, swaggering and upright under the black plummets of smoke, cavalierly aslant. She swept round the bends; an impure breeze shrieked a welcome between her stripped spars; and the land, closing in, stepped between the ship and the sea.

A low cloud hung before her—a great opalescent and tremulous cloud, that seemed to rise from the steaming brows of millions of men. Long drifts of smoky vapors soiled it with livid trails; it throbbed to the beat of millions of hearts, and from it came an immense and lamentable murmur—the murmur of millions of lips praying, cursing, sighing, jeering—the undying murmur of folly, regret, and hope exhaled by the crowds of the anxious earth. The *Narcissus* entered the cloud; the shadows deepened; on all sides there was the clang of iron, the sound of mighty blows, shrieks, yells. Black barges drifted stealthily on the murky stream. A mad jumble of begrimed walls loomed up vaguely in the smoke, bewildering and mournful, like a vision of disaster. The tugs backed and filled in the stream, to hold the ship steady at the dock-gates; from her bows two lines went through the air whistling, and struck at the land viciously, like a pair of snakes. A bridge broke in two before her, as if by enchantment; big hydraulic capstans began to turn all by themselves, as though animated by a mysterious and unholy spell. She moved through a narrow lane of water between two low walls of granite, and men with check-ropes in their hands kept pace with her, walking on the broad flagstones. A group waited impatiently on each side of the vanished bridge: rough heavy men in caps; sallow-faced men in high hats; two bareheaded women; ragged children, fascinated, and with wide eyes. A cart coming at a jerky trot pulled up sharply. One of the women screamed at the silent ship—"Hallo, Jack!" without looking at any one in particular, and all hands looked at her from the forecastle-head.—"Stand clear! Stand clear of that rope!" cried the dockmen, bending over stone posts. The crowd murmured, stamped where they stood.—"Let go your quarter-checks! Let go!" sang out a ruddy-faced old man on the quay. The ropes splashed heavily falling in the water, and the *Narcissus* entered the dock.

The stony shores ran away right and left in straight lines, enclosing a somber and rectangular pool. Brick walls rose high above the water—soulless walls, staring through hundreds of windows as troubled and dull as the eyes of over-fed brutes. At their base monstrous iron cranes crouched, with chains hanging from their long necks, balancing cruel-looking hooks over the decks of lifeless ships. A noise of wheels rolling over stones, the thump of heavy things falling, the racket of feverish winches, the grinding of strained chains, floated on the air. Between high buildings the dust of all the continents soared in short flights; and a penetrating smell of perfumes and dirt, of spices and hides, of things costly and of things filthy, pervaded the space, made for it an atmosphere precious and disgusting. The *Narcissus* came gently into her berth; the shadows of soulless walls fell upon her, the dust of all the continents leaped upon her deck, and a swarm of strange men, clambering up her sides, took possession of her in the name of the sordid earth. She had ceased to live.

A toff in a black coat and high hat scrambled with agility, came up to the second mate, shook hands, and said:—"Hallo, Herbert." It was his brother. A lady appeared suddenly. A real lady, in a black dress and with a parasol. She looked extremely elegant in the midst of us, and as strange as if she had fallen there from the sky. Mr. Baker touched his cap to her. It was the master's wife. And very soon the Captain, dressed very smartly and in a white shirt, went with her over the side. We didn't recognize him at all till, turning on the quay, he called to Mr. Baker:—"Don't forget to wind up the chronometers tomorrow morning." An underhand lot of seedy-looking chaps with shifty eyes wandered in and out of the forecastle looking for a job—they said.— "More likely for something to steal," commented Knowles, cheerfully. Poor beggars. Who cared? Weren't we home! But Mr. Baker went for one of them who had given him some cheek, and we were delighted. Everything was delightful.—"I've finished aft, sir," called out Mr. Creighton.—"No water in the well, sir," reported for the last time the carpenter, sounding-rod in hand. Mr. Baker glanced along the decks at the expectant group of sailors, glanced aloft at the yards.—"Ough! That will do, men," he grunted. The group broke up. The voyage was ended.

Rolled-up beds went flying over the rail; lashed chests went sliding down the gangway—mighty few of both at that. "The rest is having a cruise off the Cape," explained Knowles enigmatically to a dockloafer with whom he had struck a sudden friendship. Men ran, calling to one another, hailing utter strangers to "lend a hand with the dunnage," then with sudden decorum approached the mate to shake hands before going ashore.—"Good-bye, sir," they repeated in various tones. Mr. Baker grasped hard palms, grunted in a friendly manner at every one, his eyes twinkled.— "Take care of your money, Knowles. Ough! Soon get a nice wife if you do." The lame man was delighted.—"Good-bye, sir," said Belfast, with emotion, wringing the mate's hand, and looked up with swimming eyes. "I thought I would take 'im ashore with me," he went on, plaintively. Mr. Baker did not understand, but said kindly:—"Take care of yourself, Craik," and the bereaved Belfast went over the rail mourning and alone.

Mr. Baker, in the sudden peace of the ship, moved about solitary and grunting, trying door-handles, peering into dark places, never done—a model chief mate! No one waited for him ashore. Mother dead; father and two brothers, Yarmouth fishermen, drowned together on the Dogger Bank; sister married and unfriendly. Quite a lady. Married to the leading tailor of a little town, and its leading politician, who did not think his sailor brother-in-law quite respectable enough for him. Quite a lady, quite a lady, he thought, sitting down for a moment's rest on the quarter-hatch. Time enough to go ashore and get a bite and sup, and a bed somewhere. He didn't like to part with a ship. No one to think about then. The darkness of a misty evening fell, cold and damp, upon the deserted deck; and Mr. Baker sat smoking, thinking of all the successive ships to whom through many long years he had given the best of a seaman's care. And never a command in sight. Not once!—"I haven't somehow the cut of a skipper about me," he meditated, placidly, while the shipkeeper (who had taken possession of the galley), a wizened old man with bleared eyes, cursed him in whispers for "hanging about so."—"Now, Creighton," he pursued the unenvious train of thought, "quite a gentleman . . . swell friends . . . will get on. Fine young fellow . . . a little more experience." He got up and shook himself. "I'll be back first thing tomorrow morning for the hatches. Don't you let them touch anything before I come, shipkeeper," he called out. Then, at last, he also went ashore—a model chief mate!

The men scattered by the dissolving contact of the land came together once more in the shipping office.—"The *Narcissus* pays off," shouted outside a glazed door a brass-bound old fellow with a crown and the capitals B. T. on his cap. A lot trooped in at once but many were late. The room was large, white-washed, and bare; a counter surmounted by a brass-wire grating fenced off a third of the dusty space, and behind the grating a pasty-faced clerk, with his hair parted in the middle, had the quick, glittering eyes and the vivacious, jerky movements of a caged bird. Poor Captain Allistoun also in there, and sitting before a little table with piles of gold and notes on it, appeared subdued by his captivity. Another Board of Trade bird was perching on a high stool near the door: an old bird that did not mind the chaff of elated sailors. The crew of the *Narcissus*, broken up into knots, pushed in the corners. They had new shore togs, smart jackets that looked as if they had been shaped with an axe, glossy trousers that seemed made of crumpled sheet-iron, collarless flannel shirts, shiny new boots. They tapped on shoulders, button-holed one another, asked:—"Where did you sleep last night?" whispered gaily, slapped their thighs with bursts of subdued laughter. Most had clean, radiant faces; only one or two turned up disheveled and sad; the two young Norwegians looked tidy, meek, and altogether of a promising material for the kind ladies who patronize the Scandinavian Home. Wamibo, still in his working clothes, dreamed, upright and burly in the middle of the room, and, when Archie came in, woke up for a smile. But the wide-awake clerk called out a name, and the paying-off business began.

One by one they came up to the pay-table to get the wages of their glorious and obscure toil. They swept the money with care into broad palms, rammed it trustfully into trousers' pockets, or, turning their backs on the table, reckoned with difficulty in the hollow of their stiff hands.—"Money right? Sign the release. There—there," repeated the clerk, impatiently. "How stupid those sailors are!" he thought. Singleton came up, venerable—and uncertain as to daylight; brown drops of tobacco juice hung in his white beard; his hands, that never hesitated in the great light of the open sea, could hardly find the small pile of gold in the profound darkness of the shore. "Can't write?" said the clerk, shocked. "Make a mark, then." Singleton painfully sketched in a heavy cross, blotted the page. "What a disgusting old brute," muttered the clerk.

Somebody opened the door for him, and the patriarchal seaman passed through unsteadily, without as much as a glance at any of us.

Archie displayed a pocket-book. He was chaffed. Belfast, who looked wild, as though he had already luffed up through a public-house or two, gave signs of emotion and wanted to speak to the Captain privately. The master was surprised. They spoke through the wires, and we could hear the Captain saying:—"I've given it up to the Board of Trade." "I should've liked to get something of his," mumbled Belfast. "But you can't, my man. It's given up, locked and sealed, to the Marine Office," expostulated the master; and Belfast stood back, with drooping mouth and troubled eyes. In a pause of the business we heard the master and the clerk talking. We caught: "James Wait—deceased—found no papers of any kind—no relations—no trace—the Office must hold his wages then." Donkin entered. He seemed out of breath, was grave, full of business. He went straight to the desk, talked with animation to the clerk, who thought him an intelligent man. They discussed the account, dropping h's against one another as if for a wager—very friendly. Captain Allistoun paid. "I give you a bad discharge," he said, quietly. Donkin raised his voice:—"I don't want your bloomin' discharge—keep it. I'm goin' ter 'ave a job ashore." He turned to us. "No more bloomin' sea fur me," he said, aloud. All looked at him. He had better clothes, had an easy air, appeared more at home than any of us; he stared with assurance, enjoying the effect of his declaration. "Yuss. I 'ave friends well off. That's more'n you got. But I am a man. Yer shipmates for all that. Who's comin' fur a drink?"

No one moved. There was a silence; a silence of blank faces and stony looks. He waited a moment, smiled bitterly, and went to the door. There he faced round once more. "You won't? You bloomin' lot of yrpocrits. No? What 'ave I done to yer? Did I bully yer? Did I 'urt yer? Did I? . . . You won't drink? . . . No! . . . Then may ye die of thirst, every mother's son of yer! Not one of yer 'as the sperrit of a bug. Ye're the scum of the world. Work and starve!"

He went out, and slammed the door with such violence that the old Board of Trade bird nearly fell off his perch.

"He's mad," declared Archie. "No! No! He's drunk," insisted Belfast, lurching about, and in a maudlin tone. Captain Allistoun sat smiling thoughtfully at the cleared pay-table.

Outside, on Tower Hill, they blinked, hesitated clumsily, as if blinded by the strange quality of the hazy light, as if discomposed by the view of so many men; and they who could hear one another in the howl of gales seemed deafened and distracted by the dull roar of the busy earth.—"To the Black Horse! To the Black Horse!" cried some. "Let us have a drink together before we part." They crossed the road, clinging to one another. Only Charley and Belfast wandered off alone. As I came up I saw a red-faced, blowsy woman, in a grey shawl, and with dusty, fluffy hair, fall on Charley's neck. It was his mother. She slobbered over him:—"O, my boy! My boy!"—"Leggo of me," said Charley, "Leggo, mother!" I was passing him at the time, and over the untidy head of the blubbering woman he gave me a humorous smile and a glance ironic, courageous, and profound, that seemed to put all my knowledge of life to shame. I nodded and passed on, but heard him say again, good-naturedly:—"If you leggo of me this minyt—ye shall'ave a bob for a drink out of my pay." In the next few steps I came upon Belfast. He caught my arm with tremulous enthusiasm.—"I couldn't go wi' 'em," he stammered, indicating by a nod our noisy crowd, that drifted slowly along the other sidewalk. "When I think of Jimmy . . . Poor Jim! When I think of him I have no heart for drink. You were his chum, too . . . but I pulled him out . . . didn't I? Short wool he had. . . . Yes. And I stole the blooming pie. . . . He wouldn't go. . . . He wouldn't go for nobody." He burst into tears. "I never touched him— never—never!" he sobbed. "He went for me like . . . like . . . a lamb."

I disengaged myself gently. Belfast's crying fits generally ended in a fight with some one, and I wasn't anxious to stand the brunt of his inconsolable sorrow. Moreover, two bulky policemen stood near by, looking at us with a disapproving and incorrupt- ible gaze.—"So long!" I said, and went on my way.

But at the corner I stopped to take my last look at the crew of the *Narcissus.* They were swaying irresolute and noisy on the broad flagstones before the Mint. They were bound for the Black Horse, where men, in fur caps with brutal faces and in shirt sleeves, dispense out of varnished barrels the illusions of strength, mirth, happiness; the illusion of splendour and poetry of life, to the paid-off crews of southern-going ships. From afar I saw them discoursing, with jovial eyes and clumsy gestures, while the sea of life thundered into their ears ceaseless and unheeded. And swaying about there on the white stones, surrounded by the hurry and clamour of men, they appeared to be creatures of another kind—lost, alone, foregetful, and doomed; they were like cast- aways, like reckless and joyous castaways, like mad castaways making merry in the storm and upon an insecure ledge of a treacherous rock. The roar of the town resembled the roar of topping breakers, merciless and strong, with a loud voice and cruel purpose; but overhead the clouds broke; a flood of sunshine streamed down the walls of grimy houses. The dark knot of seamen drifted in sunshine. To the left of them the trees in Tower Gradens sighed, the stones of the Tower, gleaming, seemed to stir in the play of light, as if remembering suddenly all the great joys and sorrows of the past, the fighting prototypes of these men; press-gangs; mutinous cries; the wailing of women by the riverside, and the shouts of men welcoming victories. The sunshine of heaven fell like a gift of grace on the mud of the earth, on the remembering and mute stones, on greed, selfishness; on the anxious faces of forgetful men. And to the right of the dark group the stained front of the Mint, cleansed by the flood of light, stood out for a moment dazzling and white like a marble palace in a fairy tale. The crew of the *Narcissus* drifted out of sight.

I never saw them again. The sea took some, the steamers took others, the grave- yards of the earth will account for the rest. Singleton has no doubt taken with him the long record of his faithful work into the peaceful depths of an hospitable sea. And Donkin, who never did a decent day's work in his life, no doubt earns his living by discoursing with filthy eloquence upon the right of labor to live. So be it! Let the earth and the sea each have its own.

A gone shipmate, like any other man, is gone for ever: and I never met one of them again. But at times the spring-flood of memory sets with force up the dark River of the Nine Bends. Then on the waters of the forlorn stream drifts a ship—a shadowy ship manned by a crew of Shades. They pass and make a sign, in a shadowy hail. Haven't we, together and upon the immortal sea, wrung out a meaning from our sinful lives? Good-bye, brothers! You were a good crowd. As good a crowd as ever fisted with wild cries the beating canvas of a heavy foresail; or tossing aloft, invisible in the night, gave back yell for yell to a westerly gale.

LORD JIM

A Tale

Author's Note

hen this novel first appeared in book form a notion got about that I had been bolted away with. Some reviewers maintained that the work starting as a short story had got beyond the writer's control. One or two discovered internal evidence of the fact, which seemed to amuse them. They pointed out the limitations of the narrative form. They argued that no man could have been expected to talk all that time, and other men to listen so long. It was not, they said, very credible.

After thinking it over for something like sixteen years I am not so sure about that. Men have been known, both in the tropics and in the temperate zone, to sit up half the night "swapping yarns." This, however, is but one yarn, yet with interruptions affording some measure of relief; and in regard to the listeners' endurance, the postulate must be accepted that the story *was* interesting. It is the necessary preliminary assumption. If I hadn't believed that it *was* interesting I could never have begun to write it. As to the mere physical possibility we all know that some speeches in Parliament have taken nearer six than three hours in delivery; whereas all that part of the book which is Marlow's narrative can be read through aloud, I should say, in less than three hours. Besides—though I have kept strictly all such insignificant details out of the tale—we may presume that there must have been refreshments on that night, a glass of mineral water of some sort to help the narrator on.

But, seriously, the truth of the matter is, that my first thought was of a short story, concerned only with the pilgrim ship episode; nothing more. And that was a legitimate conception. After writing a few pages, however, I became for some reason discontented and I laid them aside for a time. I didn't take them out of the drawer till the late Mr. Williams Blackwood suggested I should give something again to his magazine.

It was only then that I perceived that the pilgrim ship episode was a good starting-point for a free and wandering tale; that it was an event, too, which could conceivably color the whole "sentiment of existence" in a simple and sensitive character. But all these preliminary moods and stirrings of spirit were rather obscure at the time, and they do not appear clearer to me now after the lapse of so many years.

The few pages I had laid aside were not without their weight in the choice of subject. But the whole was rewritten deliberately. When I sat down to it I knew it would be a long book, though I didn't foresee that it would spread itself over thirteen numbers of "Maga."

I have been asked at times whether this was not the book of mine I liked best. I am a great foe to favoritism in public life, in private life, and even in the delicate relationship of an author to his works. As a matter of principle I will have no favorites; but I don't go so far as to feel grieved and annoyed by the preference some people give to my Lord Jim. I won't even say that I "fail to understand. . . ." No! But once I had occasion to be puzzled and surprised.

A friend of mine returning from Italy had talked with a lady there who did not like the book. I regretted that, of course, but what surprised me was the ground of her dislike. "You know," she said, "it is all so morbid."

The pronouncement gave me food for an hour's anxious thought. Finally I arrived at the conclusion that, making due allowances for the subject itself being rather foreign to women's normal sensibilities, the lady could not have been an Italian. I wonder whether she was European at all? In any case, no Latin temperament would have perceived anything morbid in the acute consciousness of lost honor. Such a consciousness may be wrong, or it may be right, or it may be condemned as artificial; and, perhaps, my Jim is not a type of wide commonness. But I can safely assure my readers that he is not the product of coldly perverted thinking. He's not a figure of Northern Mists either. One sunny morning in the commonplace surroundings of an Eastern roadstead, I saw his form pass by—appealing—significant—under a cloud—perfectly silent. Which is as it should be. It was for me, with all the sympathy of which I was capable, to seek fit words for his meaning. He was "one of us."

J. C.
June, 1917

It is certain my Conviction gains infinitely,

the moment another soul will believe in it.

Novalis

e was an inch, perhaps two, under six feet, powerfully built, and he advanced straight at you with a slight stoop of the shoulders, head forward, and a fixed from-under stare which made you think of a charging bull. His voice was deep, loud, and his manner displayed a kind of dogged self-assertion which had nothing aggressive in it. It seemed a necessity, and it was directed apparently as much at himself as at anybody else. He was spotlessly neat, appareled in immaculate white from shoes to hat, and in the various Eastern ports where he got his living as ship-chandler's water-clerk he was very popular.

A water-clerk need not pass an examination in anything under the sun, but he must have Ability in the abstract and demonstrate it practically. His work consists in racing under sail, steam, or oars against other water-clerks for any ship about to anchor, greeting her captain cheerily, forcing upon him a card—the business card of the ship-chandler—and on his first visit on shore piloting him firmly but without ostentation to a vast, cavern-like shop which is full of things that are eaten and drunk on board ship; where you can get everything to make her seaworthy and beautiful, from a set of chain-hooks for her cable to a book of gold-leaf for the carvings of her stern; and where her commander is received like a brother by a ship-chandler he has never seen before. There is a cool parlor, easy-chairs, bottles, cigars, writing implements, a copy of harbor regulations, and a warmth of welcome that melts the salt of a three months' passage out of a seaman's heart. The connection thus begun is kept up, as long as the ship remains in harbor, by the daily visits of the water-clerk. To the captain he is faithful like a friend and attentive like a son, with the patience of Job, the unselfish devotion of a woman, and the jollity of a boon companion. Later on the bill is sent in. It is a beautiful and humane occupation. Therefore good water-clerks are scarce. When a water-clerk who possesses Ability in the abstract has also the advantage of having been brought up to the sea, he is worth to his employer a lot of money and some humoring. Jim had always good wages and as much humoring as would have bought the fidelity of a fiend. Nevertheless, with black ingratitude he would throw up the job suddenly and depart. To his employers the reasons he gave were obviously inadequate. They said "Confounded fool!" as soon as his back was turned. This was their criticism on his exquisite sensibility.

To the white men in the waterside business and to the captains of ships he was just Jim—nothing more. He had, of course, another name, but he was anxious that it should not be pronounced. His incognito, which had as many holes as a sieve, was not meant to hide a personality but a fact. When the fact broke through the incognito he would leave suddenly the seaport where he happened to be at the time and go to another—generally farther east. He kept to seaports because he was a seaman in exile from the sea, and had Ability in the abstract, which is good for no other work but that of a water-clerk. He retreated in good order towards the rising sun, and the fact followed him casually but inevitably. Thus in the course of years he was known successively in Bombay, in Calcutta, in Rangoon, in Penang, in Batavia—and in each of these halting-places was just Jim the water-clerk. Afterwards, when his keen perception of the Intolerable drove him away for good from seaports and white men, even into the virgin forest, the Malays of the jungle village, where he had elected to conceal his deplorable faculty, added a word to the monosyllable of his incognito. They called him Tuan Jim: as one might say—Lord Jim.

Originally he came from a parsonage. Many commanders of fine merchant-ships come from these abodes of piety and peace. Jim's father possessed such certain knowledge of the Unknowable as made for the righteousness of people in cottages without disturbing the ease of mind of those whom an unerring Providence enables to live in mansions. The little church on a hill had the mossy greyness of a rock seen through a ragged screen of leaves. It had stood there for centuries, but the trees around probably remembered the laying of the first stone. Below, the red front of the rectory gleamed with a warm tint in the midst of grass-plots, flowerbeds, and fir-trees, with an orchard at the back, a paved stable-yard to the left, and the sloping glass of greenhouses tacked along a wall of bricks. The living had belonged to the family for generations; but Jim was one of five sons, and when after a course of light holiday literature his vocation for the sea had declared itself, he was sent at once to a "training-ship for officers of the mercantile marine."

He learned there a little trigonometry and how to cross top-gallant yards. He was generally liked. He had the third place in navigation and pulled stroke in the first cutter. Having a steady head with an excellent physique, he was very smart aloft. His station was in the fore-top, and often from there he looked down, with the contempt of a man destined to shine in the midst of dangers, at the peaceful multitude of roofs cut in two by the brown tide of the stream, while scattered on the outskirts of the surrounding plain the factory chimneys rose perpendicular against a grimy sky, each slender like a pencil, and belching out smoke like a volcano. He could see the big ships departing, the broad-beamed ferries constantly on the move, the little boats floating far below his feet, with the hazy splendor of the sea in the distance, and the hope of a stirring life in the world of adventure.

On the lower deck in the babel of two hundred voices he would forget himself, and beforehand live in his mind the sea-life of light literature. He saw himself saving people from sinking ships, cutting away masts in a hurricane, swimming through a surf with a line; or as a lonely castaway, barefooted and half naked, walking on uncovered reefs in search of shellfish to stave off starvation. He confronted savages on tropical shores, quelled mutinies on the high seas, and in a small boat upon the ocean kept up the hearts of despairing men—always an example of devotion to duty, and as unflinching as a hero in a book.

"Something's up. Come along."

He leaped to his feet. The boys were streaming up the ladders. Above could be heard a great scurrying about and shouting, and when he got through the hatchway he stood still—as if confounded.

It was the dusk of a winter's day. The gale had freshened since noon, stopping the traffic on the river and now blew with the strength of a hurricane in fitful bursts that boomed like salvoes of great guns firing over the ocean. The rain slanted in sheets that flicked and subsided, and between whiles Jim had threatening glimpses of the tumbling tide, the small craft jumbled and tossing along the shore, the motionless buildings in the driving mist, the broad ferryboats pitching ponderously at anchor, the vast landing-stages heaving up and down and smothered in sprays. The next gust seemed to blow all this away. The air was full of flying water. There was a fierce purpose in the gale, a furious earnestness in the screech of the wind, in the brutal tumult of earth and sky, that seemed directed at him, and made him hold his breath in awe. He stood still. It seemed to him he was whirled around.

He was jostled. "Man the cutter!" Boys rushed past him. A coaster running in for shelter had crashed through a schooner at anchor, and one of the ship's instructors had seen the accident. A mob of boys clambered on the rails, clustered round the davits. "Collision. Just ahead of us. Mr. Symons saw it." A push made him stagger against the mizzen-mast, and he caught hold of a rope. The old training-ship chained to her moorings quivered all over, bowing gently head to wind, and with her scanty rigging humming in a deep bass the breathless song of her youth at sea. "Lower away!" He saw the boat, manned, drop swiftly below the rail, and rushed after her. He heard a splash. "Let go; clear the falls!" He leaned over. The river alongside seethed in frothy streaks. The cutter could be seen in the falling darkness under the spell of tide and wind, that for a moment held her bound, and tossing abreast of the ship. A yelling voice in her reached him faintly: "Keep stroke, you young whelps, if you want to save anybody! Keep stroke!" And suddenly she lifted high her bow, and, leaping with raised oars over a wave, broke the spell cast upon her by the wind and tide.

Jim felt his shoulder gripped firmly. "Too late, youngster." The captain of the ship laid a restraining hand on that boy, who seemed on the point of leaping overboard, and Jim looked up with the pain of conscious defeat in his eyes. The captain smiled sympathetically. "Better luck next time. This will teach you to be smart."

A shrill cheer greeted the cutter. She came dancing back half full of water, and with two exhausted men washing about on her bottom boards. The tumult and the menace of wind and sea now appeared very contemptible to Jim, increasing the regret of his awe at their inefficient menace. Now he knew what to think of it. It seemed to him he cared nothing for the gale. He could affront greater perils. He would do so—better than anybody. Not a particle of fear was left. Nevertheless he brooded apart that evening while the bowman of the cutter—a boy with a face like a girl's and big grey eyes—was the hero of the lower deck. Eager questioners crowded round him. He narrated: "I just saw his head bobbing, and I dashed my boat-hook in the water. It caught in his breeches and I nearly went overboard, as I thought I would, only old Symons let go the tiller and grabbed my legs—the boat nearly swamped. Old Symons is a fine old chap. I don't mind a bit him being grumpy with us. He swore at me all the time he held my leg, but that was only his way of telling me to stick to the boat-hook. Old Symons is awfully excitable—isn't he? No—not the little fair chap—the other, the big one with a beard. When we pulled him in he groaned, 'Oh, my leg! oh, my leg!' and turned up his eyes. Fancy such a big chap fainting like a girl. Would any of you fellows faint for a jab with a boat-hook?—I wouldn't. It went into his leg so far." He showed the boat-hook, which he had carried below for the purpose and produced a sensation. "No, silly! It was not his flesh that held him—his breeches did. Lots of blood, of course."

Jim thought it a pitiful display of vanity. The gale had ministered to a heroism as spurious as its own pretence of terror. He felt angry with the brutal tumult of earth and sky for taking him unawares and checking unfairly a generous readiness for narrow escapes. Otherwise he was rather glad he had not gone into the cutter, since a lower achievement had served the turn. He had enlarged his knowledge more than those who had done the work. When all men flinched, then—he felt sure—he alone would know how to deal with the spurious menace of wind and seas. He knew what to think of it. Seen dispassionately, it seemed contemptible. He could detect no trace of emotion in himself, and the final effect of a staggering event was that, unnoticed and apart from the noisy crowd of boys, he exulted with fresh certitude in his avidity for adventure, and in a sense of many-sided courage.

II

After two years of training he went to sea, and entering the regions so well known to his imagination, found them strangely barren of adventure. He made many voyages. He knew the magic monotony of existence between sky and water: he had to bear the criticism of men, the exactions of the sea, and the prosaic severity of the daily task that gives bread—but whose only reward is in the perfect love of the work. This reward eluded him. Yet he could not go back, because there is nothing more enticing, disenchanting, and enslaving than the life at sea. Besides, his prospects were good. He was gentlemanly, steady, tractable, with a thorough knowledge of his duties; and in time, when yet very young, he became chief mate of a fine ship, without ever having been tested by those events of the sea that show in the light of day the inner worth of a man, the edge of his temper, and the fiber of his stuff; that reveal the quality of his resistance and the secret truth of his pretences, not only to others but also to himself.

Only once in all that time he had again the glimpse of the earnestness in the anger of the sea. That truth is not so often made apparent as people might think. There are many shades in the danger of adventures and gales, and it is only now and then that there appears on the face of facts a sinister violence of intention—that indefinable something which forces it upon the mind and the heart of a man, that this complication of accidents or these elemental furies are coming at him with a purpose of malice, with a strength beyond control, with an unbridled cruelty that means to tear out of him his hope and his fear, the pain of his fatigue and his longing for rest: which means to smash, to destroy, to annihilate all he has seen, known, loved, enjoyed, or hated; all that is priceless and necessary—the sunshine, the memories, the future,—which means to sweep the whole precious world utterly away from his sight by the simple and appalling act of taking his life.

Jim, disabled by a falling spar at the beginning of a week of which his Scottish captain used to say afterwards, "Man! it's a pairfect meeracle to me how she lived through it!" spent many days stretched on his back, dazed, battered, hopeless, and tormented as if at the bottom of an abyss of unrest. He did not care what the end would be, and in his lucid moments overvalued his indifference. The danger, when not seen, has the imperfect vagueness of human thought. The fear grows shadowy; and Imagination, the enemy of men, the father of all terrors, unstimulated, sinks to rest in the dulness of exhausted emotion. Jim saw nothing but the disorder of his tossed cabin. He lay there battened down in the midst of a small devastation, and felt secretly glad he had not to go on deck. But now and again an uncontrollable rush of anguish would grip him bodily, make him gasp and writhe under the blankets, and then the unintelligent brutality of an existence liable to the agony of such sensations filled him with a despairing desire to escape at any cost. Then fine weather returned, and he thought no more about it.

His lameness, however, persisted, and when the ship arrived at an Eastern port he had to go to the hospital. His recovery was slow, and he was left behind.

There were only two other patients in the white men's ward: the purser of a gunboat, who had broken his leg falling down a hatchway; and a kind of railway contractor from a neighboring province, afflicted by some mysterious tropical disease, who held the doctor for an ass, and indulged in secret debaucheries of patent medicine which his Tamil servant used to smuggle in with unwearied devotion. They told each other the story of their lives, played cards a little, or, yawning and in pajamas, lounged through the day in easy-chairs without saying a word. The hospital stood on a hill, and a gentle breeze entering through the windows, always flung wide open, brought into the bare room the softness of the sky, the languor of the earth, the bewitching breath of the Eastern waters. There were perfumes in it, suggestions of infinite repose, the gift of endless dreams. Jim looked every day over the thickets of gardens, beyond the roofs of the town, over the fronds of palms growing on the shore, at that roadstead which is a thoroughfare to the East,—at the roadstead dotted by garlanded islets, lighted by festal sunshine, its ships like toys, its brilliant activity resembling a holiday pageant, with the eternal serenity of the Eastern sky overhead and the smiling peace of the Eastern seas possessing the space as far as the horizon.

Directly he could walk without a stick, he descended into the town to look for some opportunity to get home. Nothing offered just then, and, while waiting, he associated naturally with the men of his calling in the port. These were of two kinds. Some, very few and seen there but seldom, led mysterious lives, had preserved an undefaced energy with the temper of buccaneers and the eyes of dreamers. They appeared to live in a crazy maze of plans, hopes, dangers, enterprises, ahead of civilization, in the dark places of the sea, and their death was the only event of their fantastic existence that seemed to have a reasonable certitude of achievement. The majority were men who, like himself, thrown there by some accident, had remained as officers of country ships. They had now a horror of the home service, with its harder conditions, severer view of duty, and the hazard of stormy oceans. They were attuned to the eternal peace of Eastern sky and sea. They loved short passages, good deck-chairs, large native crews, and the distinction of being white. They shuddered at the thought of hard work, and led precariously easy lives, always on the verge of dismissal, always on the verge of engagement, serving Chinamen, Arabs, half-castes—would have served the devil himself had he made it easy enough. They talked everlastingly of turns of luck: how So-and-so got charge of a boat on the coast of China—a soft thing; how this one had an easy billet in Japan somewhere, and that one was doing well in the Siamese navy; and in all they said—in their actions, in their looks, in their persons—could be detected the soft spot, the place of decay, the determination to lounge safely through existence.

To Jim that gossiping crowd, viewed as seamen, seemed at first more unsubstantial than so many shadows. But at length he found a fascination in the sight of those men, in their appearance of doing so well on such a small allowance of danger and toil. In time, beside the original disdain there grew up slowly another sentiment; and suddenly, giving up the idea of going home, he took a berth as chief mate of the *Patna*.

The *Patna* was a local steamer as old as the hills, lean like a greyhound, and eaten up with rust worse than a condemned water-tank. She was owned by a Chinaman, chartered by an Arab, and commanded by a sort of renegade New South Wales German, very anxious to curse publicly his native country, but who, apparently on the strength of Bismarck's victorious policy, brutalized all those he was not afraid of, and wore a "blood-and-iron" air, combined with a purple nose and a red moustache. After she had been painted outside and whitewashed inside, eight hundred pilgrims (more or less) were driven on board of her as she lay with steam up alongside a wooden jetty.

They streamed aboard over three gangways, they streamed in urged by faith and the hope of paradise, they streamed in with a continuous tramp and shuffle of bare feet, without a word, a murmur, or a look back; and when clear of confining rails spread on all sides over the deck, flowed forward and aft, overflowed down the yawning hatchways, filled the inner recesses of the ship—like water filling a cistern, like water flowing into crevices and crannies, like water rising silently even with the rim. Eight hundred men and women with faith and hopes, with affections and memories, they had collected there, coming from north and south and from the outskirts of the East, after treading the jungle paths, descending the rivers, coasting in praus along the shallows, crossing in small canoes from island to island, passing through suffering, meeting strange sights, beset by strange fears, upheld by one desire. They came from solitary huts in the wilderness, from populous campongs, from villages by the sea. At the call of an idea they had left their forests, their clearings, the protection of their rulers, their prosperity, their poverty, the surroundings of their youth and the graves of their fathers. They came covered with dust, with sweat, with grime, with rags—the strong men at the head of family parties, the lean old men pressing forward without hope of return; young boys with fearless eyes glancing curiously, shy little girls with tumbled long hair; the timid women muffled up and clasping to their breasts, wrapped in loose ends of soiled head-cloths, their sleeping babies, the unconscious pilgrims of an exacting belief.

"Look at dese cattle," said the German skipper to his new chief mate.

An Arab, the leader of that pious voyage, came last. He walked slowly aboard, handsome and grave in his white gown and large turban. A string of servants followed, loaded with his luggage; the *Patna* cast off and backed away from the wharf.

She was headed between two small islets, crossed obliquely the anchoring-ground of sailing-ships, swung through half a circle in the shadow of a hill, then ranged close to a ledge of foaming reefs. The Arab standing up aft, recited aloud the prayer of travelers by sea. He invoked the favor of the Most High upon that journey, implored His blessing on men's toil and on the secret purposes of their hearts; the steamer pounded in the dusk the calm water of the Strait; and far astern of the pilgrim ship a screw-pile lighthouse, planted by unbelievers on a treacherous shoal, seemed to wink at her its eye of flame, as if in derision of her errand of faith.

She cleared the Strait, crossed the bay, continued on her way through the "One-degree" passage. She held on straight for the Red Sea under a serene sky, under a sky scorching and unclouded, enveloped in a fulgor of sunshine that killed all thought, oppressed the heart, withered all impulses of strength and energy. And under the sinister splendor of that sky the sea, blue and profound, remained still, without a stir, without a ripple, without a wrinkle—viscous, stagnant, dead. The *Patna*, with a slight hiss, passed over that plain luminous and smooth, unrolled a black ribbon of smoke across the sky, left behind her on the water a white ribbon of foam that vanished at once, like the phantom of a track drawn upon a lifeless sea by the phantom of a steamer.

Every morning the sun, as if keeping pace in his revolutions with the progress of the pilgrimage, emerged with a silent burst of light exactly at the same distance astern of the ship, caught up with her at noon, pouring the concentrated fire of his rays on the pious purposes of the men, glided past on his descent, and sank mysteriously into the sea evening after evening, preserving the same distance ahead of her advancing bows. The five whites on board lived amid-ships, isolated from the human cargo. The awnings covered the deck with a white roof from stem to stern, and a faint hum, a low murmur of sad voices, alone revealed the presence of a crowd of people upon the great blaze of the ocean. Such were the days, still, hot, heavy, disappearing one by one into the past, as if falling into an abyss for ever open in the wake of the ship; and the ship, lonely under a wisp of smoke, held on her steadfast way black and smoldering in a luminous immensity, as if scorched by a flame flicked at her from a heaven without pity.

The nights descended on her like a benediction.

III

A marvelous stillness pervaded the world, and the stars, together with the serenity of their rays, seemed to shed upon the earth the assurance of everlasting security. The young moon recurved, and shining low in the west, was like a slender shaving thrown up from a bar of gold, and the Arabian Sea smooth and cool to the eye like a sheet of ice, extended its perfect level to the perfect circle of a dark horizon. The propeller turned without a check, as though its beat had been part of the scheme of a safe universe; and on each side of the *Patna* two deep folds of water, permanent and somber on the unwrinkled shimmer, enclosed within their straight and diverging ridges a few white swirls of foam bursting in a low hiss, a few wavelets, a few ripples, a few undulations that, left behind, agitated the surface of the sea for an instant after the passage of the ship, subsided splashing gently, calmed down at last into the circular stillness of water and sky with the black speck of the moving hull remaining everlastingly in its center.

Jim on the bridge was penetrated by the great certitude of unbounded safety and peace that could be read on the silent aspect of nature like the certitude of fostering love upon the placid tenderness of a mother's face. Below the roof of awnings, surrendered to the wisdom of white men and to their courage, trusting the power of their unbelief and the iron shell of their fire-ship, the pilgrims of an exacting faith slept on mats, on blankets, on bare planks, on every deck, in all the dark corners, wrapped in dyed cloths, muffled in soiled rags, with their heads resting on small bundles, with their faces pressed to bent forearms: the men, the women, the children; the old with the young, the decrepit with the lusty—all equal before sleep, death's brother.

A draught of air, fanned from forward by the speed of the ship, passed steadily through the long gloom between the high bulwarks, swept over the rows of prone bodies; a few dim flames in globe-lamps were hung short here and there under the ridge-poles, and in the blurred circles of light thrown down and trembling slightly to the unceasing vibration of the ship appeared a chin upturned, two closed eyelids, a dark hand with silver rings, a meager limb draped in a torn covering, a head bent back, a naked foot, a throat bared and stretched as if offering itself to the knife. The well-to-do had made for their families shelters with heavy boxes and dusty mats; the poor reposed side by side with all they had on earth tied up in a rag under their heads; the lone old men slept, with drawn-up legs, upon their prayer-carpets, with their hands over their ears and one elbow on each side of the face; a father, his shoulders up and his knees under his forehead, dozed dejectedly by a boy who slept on his back with tousled hair and one arm commandingly extended; a woman covered from head to foot, like a corpse, with a piece of white sheeting, had a naked child in the hollow of each arm; the Arab's belongings, piled right aft, made a heavy mound of broken outlines, with a cargo-lamp swung above, and a great confusion of vague forms behind: gleams of paunchy brass pots, the foot-rest of a deck-chair, blades of spears, the straight scabbard of an old sword leaning against a heap of pillows, the spout of a tin coffee-pot. The patent log on the taffrail periodically rang a single tinkling stroke for every mile traversed on an errand of faith. Above the mass of sleepers a faint and patient sigh at times floated, the exhalation of a troubled dream; and short metallic clangs bursting out suddenly in the depths of the ship, the harsh scrape of a shovel, the violent slam of a furnace-door, exploded brutally, as if the men handling the mysterious things below had their breasts full of fierce anger: while the slim high hull of the steamer went on evenly ahead, without a sway of her bare masts, cleaving continuously the great calm of the waters under the inaccessible serenity of the sky.

Jim paced athwart, and his footsteps in the vast silence were loud to his own ears, as if echoed by the watchful stars: his eyes roaming about the line of the horizon, seemed to gaze hungrily into the unattainable, and did not see the shadow of the coming event. The only shadow on the sea was the shadow of the black smoke pouring heavily from the funnel its immense streamer, whose end was constantly dissolving in the air. Two Malays, silent and almost motionless, steered, one on each side of the wheel, whose brass rim shone fragmentarily in the oval of light thrown out by the binnacle. Now and then a hand, with black fingers alternately letting go and catching hold of revolving spokes, appeared in the illumined part; the links of wheel-chains ground heavily in the grooves of the barrel. Jim would glance at the compass, would glance around the unattainable horizon, would stretch himself till his joints cracked with a leisurely twist of the body, in the very excess of well-being; and, as if made audacious by the invincible aspect of the peace, he felt he cared for nothing that could happen to him to the end of his days. From time to time he glanced idly at a chart pegged out with four drawing-pins on a low three-legged table abaft the steering-gear case. The sheet of paper portraying the depths of the sea presented a shiny surface under the light of a bull's-eye lamp lashed to a stanchion, a surface as level and smooth as the glimmering surface of the waters. Parallel rulers with a pair of dividers reposed on it; the ship's position at last noon was marked with a small black cross, and the straight pencil-line drawn firmly as far as Perim figured the course of the ship—the path of souls towards the holy place, the promise of salvation, the reward of eternal life —while the pencil with its sharp end touching the Somali coast lay round and still like a naked ship's spar floating in the pool of a sheltered dock. "How steady she goes," thought Jim with wonder, with something like gratitude for this high peace of sea and sky. At such times his thoughts would be full of valorous deeds: he loved these dreams and the success of his imaginary achievements. They were the best parts of life, its secret truth, its hidden reality. They had a gorgeous virility, the charm of vagueness, they passed before him with a heroic tread; they carried his soul away with them and made it drunk with the divine philter of an unbounded confidence in itself. There was nothing he could not face. He was so pleased with the idea that he smiled, keeping perfunctorily his eyes ahead; and when he happened to glance back he saw the white streak of the wake drawn as straight by the ship's keel upon the sea as the black line drawn by the pencil upon the chart.

The ash-buckets racketed, clanking up and down the stokehold ventilators, and this tin-pot clatter warned him the end of his watch was near. He sighed with content, with regret as well at having to part from that serenity which fostered the adventurous freedom of his thoughts. He was a little sleepy, too, and felt a pleasurable languor running through every limb as though all the blood in his body had turned to warm milk. His skipper had come up noiselessly, in pajamas and with his sleeping-jacket flung wide open. Red of face, only half awake, the left eye partly closed, the right staring stupid and glassy, he hung his big head over the chart and scratched his ribs sleepily. There was something obscene in the sight of his naked flesh. His bared breast glistened soft and greasy as though he had sweated out his fat in his sleep. He pronounced a professional remark in a voice harsh and dead, resembling the rasping sound of a wood-file on the edge of a plank; the fold of his double chin hung like a bag triced up close under the hinge of his jaw. Jim started, and his answer was full of deference; but the odious and fleshy figure, as though seen for the first time in a revealing moment, fixed itself in his memory for ever as the incarnation of everything vile and base that lurks in the world we love: in our own hearts we trust for our salvation in the men that surround us, in the sights that fill our eyes, in the sounds that fill our ears, and in the air that fills our lungs.

The thin gold shaving of the moon floating slowly downwards had lost itself on the darkened surface of the waters, and the eternity beyond the sky seemed to come down nearer to the earth, with the augmented glitter of the stars, with the more profound somberness in the luster of the half-transparent dome covering the flat disc of an opaque sea. The ship moved so smoothly that her onward motion was imperceptible to the senses of men, as though she had been a crowded planet speeding through the dark spaces of ether behind the swarm of suns, in the appalling and calm solitudes awaiting the breath of future creations. "Hot is no name for it down below," said a voice.

Jim smiled without looking round. The skipper presented an unmoved breadth of back: it was the renegade's trick to appear pointedly unaware of your existence unless it suited his purpose to turn at you with a devouring glare before he let loose a torrent of foamy, abusive jargon that came like a gush from a sewer. Now he emitted only a sulky grunt; the second engineer at the head of the bridge-ladder, kneading with damp palms a dirty sweat-rag, unabashed, continued the tale of his complaints. The sailors had a good time of it up here, and what was the use of them in the world he would be blowed if he could see. The poor devils of engineers had to get the ship along anyhow, and they could very well do the rest too; by gosh they——"Shut up" growled the German stolidly. "Oh yes! Shut up—and when anything goes wrong you fly to us, don't you?" went on the other. He was more than half cooked, he expected; but anyway, now, he did not mind how much he sinned, because these last three days he had passed through a fine course of training for the place where the bad boys go when they die—b'gosh, he had—besides being made jolly well deaf by the blasted racket below. The durned, compound, surface-condensing, rotten scrap-heap rattled and banged down there like an old deck-winch, only more so; and what made him risk his life every night and day that God made amongst the refuse of a breaking-up yard flying round at fifty-seven revolutions, was more than *he* could tell. He must have been born reckless, b'gosh. He . . ."Where did you get drink?" inquired the German, very savage, but motionless in the light of the binnacle, like a clumsy effigy of a man cut out of a block of fat. Jim went on smiling at the retreating horizon; his heart was full of generous impulses, and his thought was contemplating his own superiority. "Drink!" repeated the engineer with amiable scorn: he was hanging on with both hands to the rail, a shadowy figure with flexible legs. "Not from you, captain. You're far too mean, b'gosh. You would let a good man die sooner than give him a drop of schnaps. That's what you Germans call economy. Penny wise, pound foolish." He became sentimental. The chief had given him a four-finger nip about ten o'clock— "only one, s'elp me!"—good old chief; but as to getting the old fraud out of his bunk —a five-ton crane couldn't do it. Not it. Not tonight anyhow. He was sleeping sweetly like a little child, with a bottle of prime brandy under his pillow. From the thick throat of the commander of the *Patna* came a low rumble, on which the sound of the word *schwein* fluttered high and low like a capricious feather in a faint stir of air. He and the chief engineer had been cronies for a good few years—serving the same jovial, crafty, old Chinaman, with horn-rimmed goggles and strings of red silk plaited into the venerable gray hairs of his pigtail. The quay-side opinion in the *Patna's* home-port was that these two in the way of brazen peculation "had done together pretty well every-thing you can think of." Outwardly they were badly matched: one dull-eyed, malevo-lent, and of soft fleshy curves; the other lean, all hollows, with a head long and bony like the head of an old horse, with sunken cheeks, with sunken temples, with an indifferent glazed glance of sunken eyes. He had been stranded out East somewhere— in Canton, in Shanghai, or perhaps in Yokohama; he probably did not care to remem-ber himself the exact locality, nor yet the cause of his shipwreck. He had been, in mercy to his youth, kicked quietly out of his ship twenty years ago or more, and it might have been so much worse for him that the memory of the episode had in it hardly a trace of misfortune. Then, steam navigation expanding in these seas and men of his craft being scarce at first, he had "got on" after a sort. He was eager to let strangers know in a dismal mumble that he was "an old stager out here." When he moved a skeleton seemed to sway loose in his clothes; his walk was mere wandering, and he was given to wander thus around the engineroom skylight, smoking, without relish, doctored tobacco in a brass bowl at the end of a cherrywood stem four feet long, with the imbecile gravity of a thinker evolving a system of philosophy from the hazy glimpse of a truth. He was usually anything but free with his private store of liquor; but on that night he had departed from his principles, so that his second, a weak-headed child of Wapping, what with the unexpectedness of the treat and the strength of the stuff, had become very happy, cheeky, and talkative. The fury of the New South Wales German was extreme; he puffed like an exhaust-pipe, and Jim, faintly amused by the scene, was impatient for the time when he could get below: the last ten minutes of the watch were irritating like a gun that hangs fire; those men did not belong to the world of heroic adventure; they weren't bad chaps though. Even the skipper himself . . . His gorge rose at the mass of panting flesh from which issued gurgling mutters, a cloudy trickle of filthy expressions; but he was too pleasurably languid to dislike actively this or any other thing. The quality of these men did not matter; he rubbed shoulders with them, but they could not touch him; he shared the air they breathed, but he was different. . . . Would the skipper go for the engineer? . . . The life was easy and he was too sure of himself—too sure of himself to . . . The line dividing his meditation from a surreptitious doze on his feet was thinner than a thread in a spider's web.

The second engineer was coming by easy transition to the consideration of his finances and of his courage.

"Who's drunk? I? No, no, captain! That won't do. You ought to know by this time the chief ain't free-hearted enough to make a sparrow drunk, b'gosh. I've never been the worse for liquor in my life; the stuff ain't made yet that would make *me* drunk. I could drink liquid fire against your whisky peg for peg, b'gosh, and keep as cool as a cucumber. If I thought I was drunk I would jump overboard—do away with myself, b'gosh. I would! Straight! And I won't go off the bridge. Where do you expect me to take the air on a night like this, eh? On deck amongst that vermin down there? Likely —ain't it! And I am not afraid of anything you can do."

The German lifted two heavy fists to heaven and shook them a little without a word.

"I don't know what fear is," pursued the engineer, with the enthusiasm of sincere conviction. "I am not afraid of doing all the bloomin' work in this rotten hooker, b'gosh! And a jolly good thing for you that there are some of us about the world that aren't afraid of their lives, or where would you be—you and this old thing here with her plates like brown paper—brown paper, s'elp me? It's all very fine for you—you get a power of pieces out of her one way and another; but what about me—what do I get? A measly hundred and fifty dollars a month and find yourself. I wish to ask you respectfully—respectfully, mind—who wouldn't chuck a dratted job like this? 'Tain't safe, s'elp me, it ain't! Only I am one of them fearless fellows. . . ."

He let go the rail and made ample gestures as if demonstrating in the air the shape and extent of his valor; his thin voice darted in prolonged squeaks upon the sea, he tiptoed back and forth for the better emphasis of utterance, and suddenly pitched down head-first as though he had been clubbed from behind. He said "Damn!" as he tumbled; an instant of silence followed upon his screeching: Jim and the skipper staggered forward by common accord, and catching themselves up, stood very stiff and still gazing, amazed, at the undisturbed level of the sea. Then they looked upwards at the stars.

What had happened? The wheezy thump of the engines went on. Had the earth been checked in her course? They could not understand; and suddenly the calm sea, the sky without a cloud, appeared formidably insecure in their immobility, as if poised on the brow of yawning destruction. The engineer rebounded vertically full length and collapsed again into a vague heap. This heap said "What's that?" in the muffled accents of profound grief. A faint noise as of thunder, of thunder infinitely remote, less than a sound, hardly more than a vibration, passed slowly, and the ship quivered in response, as if the thunder had growled deep down in the water. The eyes of the two Malays at the wheel glittered towards the white men, but their dark hands remained closed on the spokes. The sharp hull driving on its way seemed to rise a few inches in succession through its whole length, as though it had become pliable, and settled down again rigidly to its work of cleaving the smooth surface of the sea. Its quivering stopped, and the faint noise of thunder ceased all at once, as though the ship had steamed across a narrow belt of vibrating water and of humming air.

IV

A month or so afterwards, when Jim, in answer to pointed questions, tried to tell honestly the truth of this experience, he said, speaking of the ship: "She went over whatever it was as easy as a snake crawling over a stick." The illustration was good: the questions were aiming at facts, and the official Inquiry was being held in the police court of an Eastern port. He stood elevated in the witness-box, with burning cheeks in a cool lofty room: the big framework of punkahs moved gently to and fro high above his head, and from below many eyes were looking at him out of dark faces, out of white faces, out of red faces, out of faces attentive, spellbound, as if all these people sitting in orderly rows upon narrow benches had been enslaved by the fascination of his voice. It was very loud, it rang startling in his own ears, it was the only sound audible in the world, for the terribly distinct questions that extorted his answers seemed to shape themselves in anguish and pain within his breast,—came to him poignant and silent like the terrible questioning of one's conscience. Outside the court the sun blazed—within was the wind of great punkahs that made you shiver, the shame that made you burn, the attentive eyes whose glance stabbed. The face of the presiding magistrate, clean shaved and impassible, looked at him deadly pale between the red faces of the two nautical assessors. The light of a broad window under the ceiling fell from above on the heads and shoulders of the three men, and they were fiercely distinct in the half-light of the big courtroom where the audience seemed composed of staring shadows. They wanted facts. Facts! They demanded facts from him, as if facts could explain anything!

"After you had concluded you had collided with something floating awash, say a water-logged wreck, you were ordered by your captain to go forward and ascertain if there was any damage done. Did you think it likely from the force of the blow?" asked the assessor sitting to the left. He had a thin horseshoe beard, salient cheekbones and with both elbows on the desk clasped his rugged hands before his face, looking at Jim with thoughtful blue eyes; the other, a heavy, scornful man, throw back in his seat, his left arm extended full length, drummed delicately with his fingertips on a blotting-pad: in the middle the magistrate upright in the roomy armchair, his head inclined slightly on the shoulder, had his arms crossed on his breast and a few flowers in a glass vase by the side of his inkstand.

"I did not," said Jim. "I was told to call no one and to make no noise for fear of creating a panic. I thought the precaution reasonable. I took one of the lamps that were hung under the awnings and went forward. After opening the forepeak hatch I heard splashing in there. I lowered then the lamp the whole drift of its lanyard, and saw that the forepeak was more than half full of water already. I knew then there must be a big hole below the waterline." He paused.

"Yes," said the big assessor, with a dreamy smile at the blotting-pad; his fingers played incessantly, touching the paper without noise.

"I did not think of danger just then. I might have been a little startled: all this happened in such a quiet way and so very suddenly. I knew there was no other bulkhead in the ship but the collision bulkhead separating the forepeak from the forehold. I went back to tell the captain. I came upon the second engineer getting up at the foot of the bridge-ladder: he seemed dazed, and told me he thought his left arm was broken; he had slipped on the top step when getting down while I was forward. He exclaimed, 'My God! That rotten bulkhead'll give way in a minute, and the damned thing will go down under us like a lump of lead.' He pushed me away with his right arm and ran before me up the ladder, shouting as he climbed. His left arm hung by his side. I followed up in time to see the captain rush at him and knock him down flat on his back. He did not strike him again: he stood bending over him and speaking angrily but quite low. I fancy he was asking him why the devil he didn't go and stop the engines, instead of making a row about it on deck. I heard him say, 'Get up! Run! fly!' He swore also. The engineer slid down the starboard ladder and bolted around the skylight to the engine-room companion which was on the port-side. He moaned as he ran. . . ."

He spoke slowly; he remembered swiftly and with extreme vividness; he could have reproduced like an echo the moaning of the engineer for the better information of these men who wanted facts. After his first feeling of revolt he had come around to the view that only a meticulous precision of statement would bring out the true horror behind the appalling face of things. The facts those men were so eager to know had been visible, tangible, open to the senses, occupying their place in space and time, requiring for their existence a fourteen-hundred-ton steamer and twenty-seven minutes by the watch; they made a whole that had features, shades of expression, a complicated aspect that could be remembered by the eye, and something else besides, something invisible, a directing spirit of perdition that dwelled within, like a malevolent soul in a detestable body. He was anxious to make this clear. This had not been a common affair, everything in it had been of the utmost importance, and fortunately he remembered everything. He wanted to go on talking for truth's sake, perhaps for his own sake also; and while his utterance was deliberate, his mind positively flew round and round the serried circle of facts that had surged up all about him to cut him off from the rest of his kind: it was like a creature that, finding itself imprisoned within an enclosure of high stakes, dashes round and round, distracted in the night, trying to find a weak spot, a crevice, a place to scale, some opening through which it may squeeze itself and escape. This awful activity of mind made him hesitate at times in his speech. . . .

"The captain kept on moving here and there on the bridge; he seemed calm enough, only he stumbled several times; and once as I stood speaking to him he walked right into me as though he had been stone-blind. He made no definite answer to what I had to tell. He mumbled to himself; all I heard of it were a few words that sounded like 'confounded steam!' and 'infernal steam!'—something about steam. I thought . . ."

He was becoming irrelevant; a question to the point cut short his speech, like a pang of pain, and he felt extremely discouraged and weary. He was coming to that, he was coming to that—and now, checked brutally, he had to answer by yes or no. He answered truthfully by a curt "Yes, I did"; and fair of face, big of frame, with young, gloomy eyes, he held his shoulders upright above the box while his soul writhed within him. He was made to answer another question so much to the point and so useless, then waited again. His mouth was tastelessly dry, as though he had been eating dust, then salt and bitter as after a drink of sea-water. He wiped his damp forehead, passed his tongue over parched lips, felt a shiver run down his back. The big assessor had dropped his eyelids, and drummed on without a sound, careless and mournful; the eyes of the other above the sunburned, clasped fingers seemed to glow with kindliness; the magistrate had swayed forward; his pale face hovered near the flowers, and then dropping sideways over the arm of his chair, he rested his temple in the palm of his hand. The wind of the punkahs eddied down on the heads, on the dark-faced natives wound about in voluminous draperies, on the Europeans sitting together very hot and in drill suits that seemed to fit them as close as their skins, and holding their round pith hats on their knees; while gliding along the walls the court peons, buttoned tight in long white coats, flitted rapidly to and fro, running on bare toes, red-sashed, red turban on head, as noiseless as ghosts, and on the alert like so many retrievers.

Jim's eyes, wandering in the intervals of his answers, rested upon a white man who sat apart from the others, with his face worn and clouded, but with quiet eyes that glanced straight, interested and clear. Jim answered another question and was tempted to cry out, "What's the good of this! what's the good!" He tapped with his foot slightly, bit his lip, and looked away over the heads. He met the eyes of the white man. The glance directed at him was not the fascinated stare of the others. It was an act of intelligent volition. Jim between two questions forgot himself so far as to find leisure for a thought. This fellow—ran the thought—looks at me as though he could see somebody or something past my shoulder. He had come across that man before—in the street perhaps. He was positive he had never spoken to him. For days, for many days, he had spoken to no one, but had held silent, incoherent, and endless converse with himself, like a prisoner alone in his cell or like a wayfarer lost in a wilderness. At present he was answering questions that did not matter though they had a purpose, but he doubted whether he would ever again speak out as long as he lived. The sound of his own truthful statements confirmed his deliberate opinion that speech was of no use to him any longer. That man there seemed to be aware of his hopeless difficulty. Jim looked at him, then turned away resolutely, as after a final parting.

And later on, many times, in distant parts of the world, Marlow showed himself willing to remember Jim, to remember him at length, in detail and audibly.

Perhaps it would be after dinner, on a verandah draped in motionless foliage and crowned with flowers, in the deep dusk speckled by fiery cigar-ends. The elongated bulk of each cane-chair harbored a silent listener. Now and then a small red glow would move abruptly, and expanding light up the fingers of a languid hand, part of a face in profound repose, or flash a crimson gleam into a pair of pensive eyes overshadowed by a fragment of an unruffled forehead; and with the very first word uttered Marlow's body, extended at rest in the seat, would become very still, as though his spirit had winged its way back into the lapse of time and were speaking through his lips from the past.

<h1 style="text-align:center">V</h1>

"Oh yes. I attended the inquiry," he would say, "and to this day I haven't left off wondering why I went. I am willing to believe each of us has a guardian angel, if you fellows will concede to me that each of us has a familiar devil as well. I want you to own up, because I don't like to feel exceptional in any way, and I know I have him— the devil, I mean. I haven't seen him, of course, but I go upon circumstantial evidence. He is there right enough, and, being malicious, he lets me in for that kind of thing. What kind of thing, you ask? Why, the inquiry thing, the yellow-dog thing—you wouldn't think a mangy, native tyke would be allowed to trip up people in the verandah of a magistrate's court, would you?—the kind of thing that by devious, unexpected, truly diabolical ways causes me to run up against men with soft spots, with hard spots, with hidden plague spots, by Jove! and loosens their tongues at the sight of me for their infernal confidences; as though, forsooth, I had no confidences to make to myself, as though—God help me!—I didn't have enough confidential information about myself to harrow my own soul till the end of my appointed time. And what I have done to be thus favored I want to know. I declare I am as full of my own concerns as the next man, and I have as much memory as the average pilgrim in this valley, so you see I am not particularly fit to be a receptacle of confessions. Then why? Can't tell—unless it be to make time pass away after dinner. Charley, my dear chap, your dinner was extremely good, and in consequence these men here look upon a quiet rubber as a tumultuous occupation. They wallow in your good chairs and think to themselves, 'Hang exertion. Let that Marlow talk.'

"Talk! So be it. And it's easy enough to talk of Master Jim, after a good spread, two hundred feet above the sea-level, with a box of decent cigars handy, on a blessed evening of freshness and starlight that would make the best of us forget we are only on sufferance here and got to pick our way in cross lights, watching every precious minute and every irremediable step, trusting we shall manage yet to go out decently in the end —but not so sure of it after all—and with dashed little help to expect from those we touch elbows with right and left. Of course there are men here and there to whom the whole of life is like an after-dinner hour with a cigar; easy, pleasant, empty, perhaps enlivened by some fable of strife to be forgotten before the end is told—before the end is told—even if there happens to be any end to it.

"My eyes met his for the first time at that inquiry. You must know that everybody connected in any way with the sea was there, because the affair had been notorious for days, ever since that mysterious cable message came from Aden to start us all cackling. I say mysterious, because it was so in a sense though it contained a naked fact, about as naked and ugly as a fact can well be. The whole waterside talked of nothing else. First thing in the morning as I was dressing in my state-room, I would hear through the bulkhead my Parsee Dubash jabbering about the *Patna* with the steward, while he drank a cup of tea, by favor, in the pantry. No sooner on shore I would meet some acquaintance, and the first remark would be, 'Did you ever hear of anything to beat this?' and according to his kind the man would smile cynically, or look sad, or let out a swear or two. Complete strangers would accost each other familiarly, just for the sake of easing their minds on the subject: every confounded loafer in the town came in for a harvest of drinks over this affair: you heard of it in the harbor office, at every ship-broker's, at your agent's, from whites, from natives, from half-castes, from the very boatmen squatting half-naked on the stone steps as you went up—by Jove! There was some indignation, not a few jokes, and no end of discussions as to what had become of them, you know. This went on for a couple of weeks or more, and the opinion that whatever was mysterious in this affair would turn out to be tragic as well, began to prevail, when one fine morning, as I was standing in the shade by the steps of the harbor office, I perceived four men walking towards me along the quay. I wondered for a while where that queer lot had sprung from, and suddenly, I may say, I shouted to myself, 'Here they are!'

"There they were, sure enough, three of them as large as life, and one much larger of girth than any living man has a right to be, just landed with a good breakfast inside of them from an outward-bound Dale Line steamer that had come in about an hour after sunrise. There could be no mistake; I spotted the jolly skipper of the *Patna* at the first glance: the fattest man in the whole blessed tropical belt clear around that good old earth of ours. Moreover, nine months or so before, I had come across him in Samarang. His steamer was loading in the Roads, and he was abusing the tyrannical institutions of the German empire, and soaking himself in beer all day long and day after day in De Jongh's back-shop, till De Jongh, who charged a guilder for every bottle without as much as the quiver of an eyelid, would beckon me aside, and, with his little leathery face all puckered up, declare confidentially, 'Business is business, but this man, captain, he make me very sick. Tfui!'

"I was looking at him from the shade. He was hurrying on a little in advance, and the sunlight beating on him brought out his bulk in a startling way. He made me think of a trained baby elephant walking on hind-legs. He was extravagantly gorgeous too—got up in a soiled sleeping-suit, bright green and deep orange vertical stripes, with a pair of ragged straw slippers on his bare feet, and somebody's castoff pith hat, very dirty and two sizes too small for him, tied up with a manila rope-yarn on the top of his big head. You understand a man like that hasn't the ghost of a chance when it comes to borrowing clothes. Very well. On he came in hot haste, without a look right or left, passed within three feet of me, and in the innocence of his heart went on pelting upstairs in the harbor office to make his deposition, or report, or whatever you like to call it.

"It appears he addressed himself in the first instance to the principal shipping-master. Archie Ruthvel had just come in, and, as his story goes, was about to begin his arduous day by giving a dressing-down to his chief clerk. Some of you might have known him—an obliging little Portuguese half-caste with a miserably skinny neck, and always on the hop to get something from the shipmasters in the way of eatables—a piece of salt pork, a bag of biscuits, a few potatoes, or what not. One voyage, I recollect, I tipped him a live sheep out of the remnant of my sea-stock: not that I wanted him to do anything for me—he couldn't, you know—but because his childlike belief in the sacred right to perquisites quite touched my heart. It was so strong as to be almost beautiful. The race—the two races rather—and the climate . . . However, never mind. I know where I have a friend for life.

"Well, Ruthvel says he was giving him a severe lecture—on official morality, I suppose—when he heard a kind of subdued commotion at his back, and turning his head he saw, in his own words, something round and enormous, resembling a sixteen-hundred-weight sugar-hogshead wrapped in striped flannelette, up-ended in the middle of the large floor space in the office. He declares he was so taken aback that for quite an appreciable time he did not realize the thing was alive, and sat still wondering for what purpose and by what means that object had been transported in front of his desk. The archway from the anteroom was crowded with punkah-pullers, sweepers, police peons, the coxswain and crew of the harbor steam-launch, all craning their necks and almost climbing on each other's backs. Quite a riot. By that time the fellow had managed to tug and jerk his hat clear of his head, and advanced with slight bows at Ruthvel, who told me the sight was so discomposing that for some time he listened quite unable to make out what that apparition wanted. It spoke in a voice harsh and lugubrious but intrepid, and little by little it dawned upon Archie that this was a development of the *Patna* case. He says that as soon as he understood who it was before him he felt quite unwell—Archie is so sympathetic and easily upset—but pulled himself together and shouted 'Stop! I can't listen to you. You must go to the Master Attendant. I can't possibly listen to you. Captain Elliot is the man you want to see. This way, this way.' He jumped up, ran around that long counter, pulled, shoved: the other let him, surprised but obedient at first, and only at the door of the private office some sort of animal instinct made him hang back and snort like a frightened bullock. 'Look here! what's up? Let go! Look here!' Archie flung open the door without knocking. 'The master of the *Patna*, sir,' he shouts. 'Go in, captain.' He saw the old man lift his head from some writing so sharp that his nose-nippers fell off, banged the door to, and fled to his desk, where he had some papers waiting for his signature: but he says the row that burst out in there was so awful that he couldn't collect his senses sufficiently to remember the spelling of his own name. Archie's the most sensitive shipping-master in the two hemispheres. He declares he felt as though he had thrown a man to a hungry lion. No doubt the noise was great. I heard it down below, and I have every reason to believe it was heard clear across the Esplanade as far as the bandstand. Old father Elliot had a great stock of works and could shout—and didn't mind who he shouted at either. He would have shouted at the Viceroy himself. As he used to tell me: 'I am as high as I can get; my pension is safe. I've a few pounds laid by, and if they don't like my notions of duty I would just as soon go home as not. I am an old man, and I have always spoken my mind. All I care for now is to see my girls married before I die.' He was a little crazy on that point. His three daughters were awfully nice, though they resemble him amazingly, and on the mornings he woke up with a gloomy view of their matrimonial prospects the office would read it in his eye and tremble, because, they said, he was sure to have somebody for breakfast. However, that morning he did not eat the renegade, but, if I may be allowed to carry on the metaphor, chewed him up very small, so to speak, and—ah! ejected him again.

"Thus in a very few moments I saw his monstrous bulk descend in haste and stand still on the outer steps. He had stopped close to me for the purpose of profound meditation: his large purple cheeks quivered. He was biting his thumb, and after a while noticed me with a sidelong vexed look. The other three chaps that had landed with him made a little group waiting at some distance. There was a sallow-faced, mean little chap with his arm in a sling, and a long individual in a blue flannel coat, as dry as a chip and no stouter than a broomstick, with drooping gray mustaches, who looked about him with an air of jaunty imbecility. The third was an upstanding, broad-shouldered youth, with his hands in his pockets, turning his back on the other two who appeared to be talking together earnestly. He stared across the empty Esplanade. A ramshackle gharry, all dust and venetian blinds, pulled up short opposite the group, and the driver, throwing up his right foot over his knee, gave himself up to the critical examination of his toes. The young chap, making no movement, not even stirring his head, just stared into the sunshine. This was my first view of Jim. He looked as unconcerned and unapproachable as only the young can look. There he stood, clean-limbed, clean-faced, firm on his feet, as promising a boy as the sun ever shone on; and, looking at him, knowing all he knew and a little more too, I was as angry as though I had detected him trying to get something out of me by false pretenses. He had no business to look so sound. I thought to myself—well, if this sort can go wrong like that . . . and I felt as though I could fling down my hat and dance on it from sheer mortification, as I once saw the skipper of an Italian barque do because his duffer of a mate got into a mess with his anchors when making a flying moor in a roadstead full of ships. I asked myself, seeing him there apparently so much at ease—is he silly? is he callous? He seemed ready to start whistling a tune. And note, I did not care a rap about the behavior of the other two. Their persons somehow fitted the tale that was public property, and was going to be the subject of an official inquiry. 'That old mad rogue upstairs called me a hound,' said the captain of the *Patna*. I can't tell whether he recognized me—I rather think he did; but at any rate our glances met. He glared—I smiled; hound was the very mildest epithet that had reached me through the open window. 'Did he?' I said from some strange inability to hold my tongue. He nodded, bit his thumb again, swore under his breath: then lifting his head and looking at me with sullen and passionate impudence—'Bah! the Pacific is big, my friendt. You damned Englishmen can do your worst; I know where there's plenty of room for a man like me: I am well aguaindt in Apia, in Honolulu, in . . .' He paused reflectively, while without effort I could depict to myself the sort of people he was 'aguaindt' with in those places. I won't make a secret of it that I had been 'aguaindt' with not a few of that sort myself. There are times when a man must act as though life were equally sweet in any company. I've known such a time, and, what's more I shan't now pretend to pull a long face over my necessity, because a good many of that bad company from want of moral—moral—what shall I say?—posture, or from some other equally profound cause, were twice as instructive and twenty times more amusing than the usual respectable thief of commerce you fellows ask to sit at your table without any real necessity—from habit, from cowardice, from good-nature, from a hundred sneaking and inadequate reasons.

" 'You Englishmen are all rogues,' went on my patriotic Flensborg or Stettin Australian. I really don't recollect now what decent little port on the shores of the Baltic was defiled by being the nest of that precious bird. 'What are you to shout? Eh? You tell me? You no better than other people, and that old rogue he make Gottam fuss with me.' His thick carcass trembled on its legs that were like a pair of pillars; it trembled from head to foot. 'That's what you English always make—make a tam' fuss —for any little thing, because I was not born in your tam' country. Take away my certificate. Take it. I don't want the certificate. A man like me don't want your verfluchte certificate. I shpit on it.' He spat. 'I vill an Amerigan citizen begome,' he cried, fretting and fuming and shuffling his feet as if to free his ankles from some invisible and mysterious grasp that would not let him get away from that spot. He made himself so warm that the top of his bullet head positively smoked. Nothing mysterious prevented me from going away: curiosity is the most obvious of sentiments, and it held me there to see the effect of a full information upon that young fellow who, hands in pockets, and turning his back upon the sidewalk, gazed across the grass-plots of the Esplanade at the yellow portico of the Malabar Hotel with the air of a man about to go for a walk as soon as his friend is ready. That's how he looked, and it was odious. I waited to see him overwhelmed, confounded, pierced through and through, squirming like an impaled beetle—and I was half afraid to see it too—if you understand what I mean. Nothing more awful than to watch a man who has been found out, not in a crime but in a more than criminal weakness. The commonest sort of fortitude prevents us from becoming criminals in a legal sense; it is from weakness unknown, but perhaps suspected, as in some parts of the world you suspect a deadly snake in every bush—from weakness that may lie hidden, watched or unwatched, prayed against or manfully scorned, repressed or maybe ignored more than half a lifetime, not one of us is safe. We are snared into doing things for which we get called names, and things for which we get hanged, and yet the spirit may well survive— survive the condemnations, survive the halter, by Jove! And there are things—they look small enough sometimes too—by which some of us are totally and completely un-done. I watched the youngster there. I liked his appearance; I knew his appearance; he came from the right place; he was one of us. He stood there for all the parentage of his kind, for men and women by no means clever or amusing, but whose very existence is based upon honest faith, and upon the instinct of courage. I don't mean military courage, or civil courage, or any special kind of courage. I mean just that inborn ability to look temptations straight in the face—a readiness unintellectual enough, goodness knows, but without pose—a power of resistance, don't you see, ungracious if you like, but priceless—an unthinking and blessed stiffness before the outward and inward terrors, before the might of nature, and the seductive corruption of men—backed by a faith invulnerable to the strength of facts, to the contagion of example, to the solicita-tion of ideas. Hang ideas! They are tramps, vagabonds, knocking at the back door of your mind, each taking a little of your substance, each carrying away some crumb of that belief in a few simple notions you must cling to if you want to live decently and would like to die easy!

"This has nothing to do with Jim, directly; only he was outwardly so typical of that good, stupid kind we like to feel marching right and left of us in life, of the kind that is not disturbed by the vagaries of intelligence and the perversions of—of nerves, let us say. He was the kind of fellow you would, on the strength of his looks, leave in charge of the deck—figuratively and professionally speaking. I say I would, and I ought to know. Haven't I turned out youngsters enough in my time, for the service of the Red Rag, to the craft of the sea, to the craft whose whole secret could be expressed in one short sentence, and yet must be driven afresh every day into young heads till it becomes the component part of every waking thought—till it is present in every dream of their young sleep! The sea has been good to me, but when I remember all these boys that passed through my hands, some grown up now and some drowned by this time, but all good stuff for the sea, I don't think I have done badly by it either. Were I to go home tomorrow, I bet that before two days passed over my head some sunburned young chief mate would overtake me at some dock gateway or other, and a fresh deep voice speaking above my hat would ask: 'Don't you remember me, sir? Why! little So-and-so. Such and such a ship. It was my first voyage.' And I would remember a bewildered little shaver, no higher than the back of this chair, with a mother and perhaps a big sister on the quay, very quiet but too upset to wave their handkerchiefs at the ship that glides out gently between the pier-heads: or perhaps some decent middle-aged father who has come early with his boy to see him off, and stays all the morning because he is interested in the windlass apparently, and stays too long, and has got to scramble ashore at last with no time at all to say good-bye. The mud pilot on the poop sings out to me in a drawl, 'Hold her with the check line for a moment, Mister Mate. There's a gentleman wants to get ashore. . . . Up with you, sir. Nearly got carried off to Talcahuano, didn't you? Now's your time; easy does it. . . . All right. Slack away again forward there.' The tugs, smoking like the pit of perdition, get hold and churn the old river into fury; the gentleman ashore is dusting his knees—the benevolent steward has shied his umbrella after him. All very proper. He has offered his bit of sacrifice to the sea, and now he may go home pretending he thinks nothing of it; and the little willing victim shall be very seasick before next morning. By-and-by, when he has learned all the little mysteries and the one great secret of the craft, he shall be fit to live or die as the sea may decree; and the man who had taken a hand in this fool game, in which the sea wins every toss, will be pleased to have his back slapped by a heavy young hand, and to hear a cheery sea-puppy voice: 'Do you remember me, sir? The little So-and-so.'

"I tell you this is good; it tells you that once in your life at least you had gone the right way to work. I have been thus slapped, and I have winced, for the slap was heavy, and I have glowed all day long and gone to bed feeling less lonely in the world by virtue of that hearty thump. Don't I remember the little So-and-so's! I tell you I ought to know the right kind of looks. I would have trusted the deck to that youngster on the strength of a single glance, and gone to sleep with both eyes—and, by Jove! it wouldn't have been safe. There are depths of horror in that thought. He looked as genuine as a new sovereign, but there was some infernal alloy in his metal. How much? The least thing—the least drop of something rare and accursed; the least drop!—but he made you—standing there with his don't-care-hang air—he made you wonder whether perchance he were nothing more rare than brass.

"I couldn't believe it. I tell you I wanted to see him squirm for the honor of the craft. The other two no-account chaps spotted their captain, and began to move slowly towards us. They chatted together as they strolled, and I did not care any more than if they had not been visible to the naked eye. They grinned at each other—might have been exchanging jokes, for all I know. I saw that with one of them it was the case of a broken arm; and as to the long individual with gray mustaches he was the chief engineer, and in various ways a pretty notorious personality. They were nobodies. They approached. The skipper gazed in an inanimate way between his feet: he seemed to be swollen to an unnatural size by some awful disease, by the mysterious action of an unknown poison. He lifted his head, saw the two before him waiting, opened his mouth with an extraordinary, sneering contortion of his puffed face—to speak to them, I suppose—and then a thought seemed to strike him. His thick, purplish lips came together without a sound, he went off in a resolute waddle to the gharry and began to jerk at the door handle with such a blind brutality of impatience that I expected to see the whole concern overturned on its side, pony and all. The driver, shaken out of his meditation over the sole of his foot, displayed at once all the signs of intense terror, and held with both hands, looking around from his box at this vast carcass forcing its way into his conveyance. The little machine shook and rocked tumultuously, and the crimson nape of that lowered neck, the size of those straining thighs, the immense heaving of that dingy, striped green-and-orange back, the whole burrowing effort of that gaudy and sordid mass troubled one's sense of probability with a droll and fearsome effect, like one of those grotesque and distinct visions that scare and fascinate one in a fever. He disappeared. I half expected the roof to split in two, the little box on wheels to burst open in the manner of a ripe cotton-pod—but it only sank with a click of flattened springs, and suddenly one venetian blind rattled down. His shoulders reappeared, jammed in the small opening; his head hung out, distended and tossing like a captive balloon, perspiring, furious, spluttering. He reached for the gharry-wallah with vicious flourishes of a fist as dumpy and red as a lump of raw meat. He roared at him to be off, to go on. Where? Into the Pacific, perhaps. The driver lashed; the pony snorted, reared once, and darted off at a gallop. Where? To Apia? to Honolulu? He had 6,000 miles of tropical belt to disport himself in, and I did not hear the precise address. A snorting pony snatched him into 'ewig-keit' in the twinkling of an eye, and I never saw him again; and, what's more, I don't know of anybody that ever had a glimpse of him after he departed from my knowledge sitting inside a ramshackle little gharry that fled around the corner in a white smother of dust. He departed, disappeared, vanished, absconded; and absurdly enough it looked as though he had taken that gharry with him, for never again did I come across a sorrel pony with a slit ear and a lackadaisical Tamil driver afflicted by a sore foot. The Pacific is indeed big; but whether he found a place for a display of his talents in it or not, the fact remains he had flown into space like a witch on a broomstick. The little chap with his arm in a sling started to run after the carriage, bleating, 'Captain! I say, Captain! I sa-a-ay!'—but after a few steps stopped short, hung his head, and walked back slowly. At the sharp rattle of the wheels the young fellow spun around where he stood. He made no other movement, no gesture, no sign, and remained facing in the new direction after the gharry had swung out of sight.

"All this happened in much less time than it takes to tell, since I am trying to interpret for you into slow speech the instantaneous effect of visual impressions. Next moment the half-caste clerk, sent by Archie to look a little after the poor castaways of the *Patna*, came upon the scene. He ran out eager and bareheaded, looking right and left, and very full of his mission. It was doomed to be a failure as far as the principal person was concerned, but he approached the others with fussy importance, and, almost immediately, found himself involved in a violent altercation with the chap that carried his arm in a sling and who turned out to be extremely anxious for a row. He wasn't going to be ordered about—'not he, b'gosh." He wouldn't be terrified with a pack of lies by a cocky half-breed little quill-driver. He was not going to be bullied by 'no object of that sort,' if the story were true 'ever so!' He bawled his wish, his desire, his determination to go to bed. 'If you weren't a God-forsaken Portuguese,' I heard him yell, 'you would know that the hospital is the right place for me.' He pushed the fist of his sound arm under the other's nose; a crowd began to collect; the half-caste, flustered, but doing his best to appear dignified, tried to explain his intentions. I went away without waiting to see the end.

"But it so happened that I had a man in the hospital at the time, and going there to see about him the day before the opening of the Inquiry, I saw in the white men's ward that little chap tossing on his back, with his arm in splints, and quite lightheaded. To my great surprise the other one, the long individual with drooping white mustache, had also found his way there. I remembered I had seen him slinking away during the quarrel, in a half prance, half shuffle, and trying very hard not to look scared. He was no stranger to the port, it seems, and in his distress was able to make tracks straight

for Mariani's billiard-room and grog-shop near the bazaar. That unspeakable vagabond, Mariani, who had known the man and had ministered to his vices in one or two
other places, kissed the ground, in a manner of speaking, before him, and shut him up
with a supply of bottles in an upstairs room of his infamous hovel. It appears he was
under some hazy apprehension as to his personal safety, and wished to be concealed.
However, Mariani told me a long time after (when he came on board one day to dun
my steward for the price of some cigars) that he would have done more for him
without asking any questions, from gratitude for some unholy favor received very many
years ago—as far as I could make out. He thumped twice his brawny chest, rolled
enormous black and white eyes glistening with tears: 'Antonio never forget—Antonio
never forget!' What was the precise nature of the immoral obligation I never learned,
but be it what it may, he had every facility given him to remain under lock and key,
with a chair, a table, a mattress in a corner, and a litter of fallen plaster on the floor, in
an irrational state of funk, and keeping up his pecker with such tonics as Mariani
dispensed. This lasted till the evening of the third day, when, after letting out a few
horrible screams, he found himself compelled to seek safety in flight from a legion of
centipedes. He burst the door open, made one leap for dear life down the crazy little
stairway, landed bodily on Mariani's stomach, picked himself up, and bolted like a
rabbit into the streets. The police plucked him off a garbage-heap in the early morning. At first he had a notion they were carrying him off to be hanged, and fought for
liberty like a hero, but when I sat down by his bed he had been very quiet for two
days. His lean bronzed head, with white mustaches, looked fine and calm on the
pillow, like the head of a war-worn soldier with a childlike soul, had it not been for a
hint of spectral alarm that lurked in the blank glitter of his glance, resembling a
nondescript form of a terror crouching silently behind a pane of glass. He was so
extremely calm, that I began to indulge in the eccentric hope of hearing something
explanatory of the famous affair from his point of view. Why I longed to go grubbing
into the deplorable details of an occurrence which, after all, concerned me no more
than as a member of an obscure body of men held together by a community of
inglorious toil and by fidelity to a certain standard of conduct, I can't explain. You
may call it an unhealthy curiosity if you like; but I have a distinct notion I wished to
find something. Perhaps, unconsciously, I hoped I would find that something, some
profound and redeeming cause, some merciful explanation, some convincing shadow of
an excuse. I see well enough now that I hoped for the impossible—for the laying of
what is the most obstinate ghost of man's creation, of the uneasy doubt uprising like a
mist, secret and gnawing like a worm, and more chilling than the certitude of death—
the doubt of the sovereign power enthroned in a fixed standard of conduct. It is the
hardest thing to stumble against; it is the thing that breeds yelling panics and good
little quiet villainies; it's the true shadow of calamity. Did I believe in a miracle? and
why did I desire it so ardently? Was it for my own sake that I wished to find some
shadow of an excuse for that young fellow whom I had never seen before, but whose
appearance alone added a touch of personal concern to the thoughts suggested by the
knowledge of his weakness—made it a thing of mystery and terror—like a hint of a

destructive fate ready for us all whose youth—in its day—had resembled his youth? I fear that such was the secret motive of my prying. I was, and no mistake, looking for a miracle. The only thing that at this distance of time strikes me as miraculous is the extent of my imbecility. I positively hoped to obtain from that battered and shady invalid some exorcism against the ghost of doubt. I must have been pretty desperate too, for, without a loss of time, after a few indifferent and friendly sentences which he answered with languid readiness, just as any decent sick man would do, I produced the word *Patna* wrapped up in a delicate question as in a wisp of floss silk. I was delicate selfishly; I did not want to startle him; I had no solicitude for him; I was not furious with him and sorry for him: his experience was of no importance, his redemption would have had no point for me. He had grown old in minor iniquities, and could no longer inspire aversion or pity. He repeated *Patna?* interrogatively, seemed to make a short effort of memory and said: 'Quite right. I am an old stager out here. I saw her go down.' I made ready to vent my indignation at such a stupid lie, when he added smoothly, 'She was full of reptiles.'

"This made me pause. What did he mean? The unsteady phantom of terror behind his glassy eyes seemed to stand still and look into mine wistfully. 'They turned me out of my bunk in the middle watch to look at her sinking,' he pursued in a reflective tone. His voice sounded alarmingly strong all at once. I was sorry for my folly. There was no snowy-winged coif of a nursing sister to be seen flitting in the perspective of the ward; but away in the middle of a long row of empty iron bedsteads an accident case from some ship in the Roads sat up brown and gaunt with a white bandage set rakishly on the forehead. Suddenly my interesting invalid shot out an arm thin like a tentacle and clawed my shoulder. 'Only my eyes were good enough to see. I am famous for my eyesight. That's why they called me, I expect. None of them was quick enough to see her go, but they saw that she was gone right enough, and sang out together—like this.' . . . A wolfish howl searched the very recesses of my soul. 'Oh! make 'im dry up,' whined the accident case irritably. 'You don't believe me, I suppose,' went on the other, with an air of ineffable conceit. 'I tell you there are no such eyes as mine this side of the Persian Gulf. Look under the bed.'

"Of course I stooped instantly. I defy anybody not to have done so. 'What can you see?' he asked. 'Nothing,' I said, feeling awfully ashamed of myself. He scrutinized my face with wild and withering contempt. 'Just so,' he said, 'but if I were to look I could see—there's no eyes like mine, I tell you.' Again he clawed, pulling at me downwards in his eagerness to relieve himself by a confidential communication. 'Millions of pink toads. There's no eyes like mine. Millions of pink toads. It's worse than seeing a ship sink. I could look at sinking ships and smoke my pipe all day long. Why don't they give me back my pipe? I would get a smoke while I watched these toads. The ship was full of them. They've got to be watched, you know.' He winked facetiously. The perspiration dripped on him off my head, my drill coat clung to my wet back: the afternoon breeze swept impetuously over the row of bedsteads, the stiff folds of curtains stirred perpendicularly, rattling on brass rods, the covers of empty beds blew about noiselessly near the bare floor all along the line, and I shivered to the very marrow. The soft wind of the tropics played in that naked ward as bleak as a winter's gale in an old barn at home. 'Don't you let him start his hollering, mister,' hailed from afar the accident case in a distressed angry shout that came ringing between the walls like a quavering call down a tunnel. The clawing hand hauled at my shoulder; he leered at me knowingly. 'The ship was full of them, you know, and we had to clear out on the strict Q. T.,' he whispered with extreme rapidity. 'All pink. All pink—as big as mastiffs, with an eye on the top of the head and claws all around their ugly mouths. Ough! Ough!' Quick jerks as of galvanic shocks disclosed under the flat coverlet the outlines of meager and agitated legs; he let go my shoulder and reached after something in the air; his body trembled tensely like a released harp-string; and while I looked down, the spectral horror in him broke through his glassy gaze. Instantly his face of an old soldier, with its noble and calm outlines, became decomposed before my eyes by the corruption of stealthy cunning, of an abominable caution and of desperate fear. He restrained a cry—'Ssh! what are they doing now down there?' he asked, pointing to the floor with fantastic precautions of voice and gesture, whose meaning, borne upon my mind in a lurid flash, made me very sick of my cleverness. 'They are all asleep,' I answered, watching him narrowly. That was it. That's what he wanted to hear; these were the exact words that could calm him. He drew a long breath. 'Ssh! Quiet, steady. I am an old stager out here. I know them brutes. Bash in the head of the first that stirs. There's too many of them, and she won't swim more than ten minutes.' He panted again. 'Hurry up,' he yelled suddenly, and went on in a steady scream: 'They are all awake—millions of them. They are trampling on me! Wait! Oh, wait! I'll smash them in heaps like flies. Wait for me! Help! H-e-elp!' An interminable and sustained howl completed my discomfiture. I saw in the distance the accident case raise deplorably both his hands to his bandaged head; a dresser, aproned to the chin, showed himself in the vista of the ward, as if seen in the small end of a telescope. I confessed myself fairly routed, and without more ado, stepping out through one of the long windows, escaped into the outside gallery. The howl pursued me like a vengeance. I turned into a deserted landing, and suddenly all became very still and quiet around me, and I descended the bare and shiny staircase in a silence that enabled me to compose my distracted thoughts. Down below I met one of the resident surgeons who was crossing the courtyard and stopped me. 'Been to see your man, Captain? I think we may let him go tomorrow. These fools have no notion of taking care of themselves, though. I say, we've got the chief engineer of that pilgrim ship here. A curious case. D. T.'s of the worst kind. He has been drinking hard in that Greek's or Italian's grog-shop for three days. What can you expect? Four bottles of that kind of brandy a day, I am told. Wonderful, if true. Sheeted with boiler-iron inside, I should think. The head, ah! the head, of course, gone, but the curious part is there's some sort of method in his raving. I am trying to find out. Most unusual—that thread of logic in such a delirium. Traditionally he ought to see snakes, but he doesn't. Good old tradition's at a discount nowadays. Eh! His—er—visions are batrachian. Ha! ha! No, seriously, I never remem-bered being so interested in a case of jim-jams before. He ought to be dead, don't you know, after such a festive experiment. Oh! he is a tough object. Four-and-twenty years of the tropics too. You ought really to take a peep at him. Noble-looking old boozer. Most extraordinary man I ever met—medically, of course. Won't you?'

"I had been all along exhibiting the usual polite signs of interest, but now assuming an air of regret I murmured of want of time, and shook hands in a hurry. 'I say,' he cried after me, 'he can't attend that inquiry. Is his evidence material, you think?'

" 'Not in the least,' I called back from the gateway."

VI

"The authorities were evidently of the same opinion. The inquiry was not adjourned. It was held on the appointed day to satisfy the law, and it was well attended because of its human interest, no doubt. There was no incertitude as to facts—as to the one material fact, I mean. How the *Patna* came by her hurt it was impossible to find out; the court did not expect to find out; and in the whole audience there was not a man who cared. Yet, as I've told you, all the sailors in the port attended, and the waterside business was fully represented. Whether they knew it or not, the interest that drew them there was purely psychological—the expectation of some essential disclosure as to the strength, the power, the horror, of human emotions. Naturally nothing of the kind could be disclosed. The examination of the only man able and willing to face it was beating futilely around the well-known fact, and the play of questions upon it was as instructive as the tapping with a hammer on an iron box, were the object to find out what's inside. However, an official inquiry could not be any other thing. Its object was not the fundamental why, but the superficial how, of this affair.

"The young chap could have told them, and, though that very thing was the thing that interested the audience, the questions put to him necessarily led him away from what to me, for instance, would have been the only truth worth knowing. You can't expect the constituted authorities to inquire into the state of a man's soul—or is it only of his liver? Their business was to come down upon the consequences, and frankly, a casual police magistrate and two nautical assessors are not much good for anything else. I don't mean to imply these fellows were stupid. The magistrate was very patient. One of the assessors was a sailing-ship skipper with a reddish beard, and of a pious disposition. Brierly was the other. Big Brierly. Some of you must have heard of Big Brierly—the captain of the crack ship of the Blue Star line. That's the man.

"He seemed consumedly bored by the honor thrust upon him. He had never in his life made a mistake, never had an accident, never a mishap, never a check in his steady rise, and he seemed to be one of those lucky fellows who know nothing of indecision, much less of self-mistrust. At thirty-two he had one of the best commands going in the Eastern trade—and, what's more, he thought a lot of what he had. There was nothing like it in the world, and I suppose if you had asked him point-blank he would have confessed that in his opinion there was not such another commander. The choice had fallen upon the right man. The rest of mankind that did not command the sixteen-knot steel steamer *Ossa* were rather poor creatures. He had saved lives at sea, had rescued ships in distress, had a gold chronometer presented to him by the under-writers, and a pair of binoculars with a suitable inscription from some foreign Government, in commemoration of these services. He was acutely aware of his merits and of his rewards. I liked him well enough, though some I know—meek, friendly men at first —couldn't stand him at any price. I haven't the slightest doubt he considered himself vastly my superior—indeed, had you been Emperor of East and West, you could not have ignored your inferiority in his presence—but I couldn't get up any real sentiment of offense. He did not despise me for anything I could help, for anything I was— don't you know? I was negligible quantity simply because I was not *the* fortunate man of the earth, not Montague Brierly in command of the *Ossa*, not the owner of an inscribed gold chronometer and of silver-mounted binoculars testifying to the excellence of my seamanship and to my indomitable pluck; not possessed of an acute sense of my merits and of my rewards, besides the love and worship of a black retriever, the most wonderful of its kind—for never was such a man loved thus by such a dog. No doubt, to have all this forced upon you was exasperating enough; but when I reflected that I was associated in these fatal disadvantages with twelve hundred millions of other more or less human beings, I found I could bear my share of his good-natured and contemptuous pity for the sake of something indefinite and attractive in the man. I have never defined to myself this attraction, but there were moments when I envied him. The sting of life could do no more to his complacent soul than the scratch of a pin to the smooth face of a rock. This was enviable. As I looked at him flanking on one side the unassuming pale-faced magistrate who presided at the inquiry, his self-satisfaction presented to me and to the world a surface as hard as granite. He committed suicide very soon after.

"No wonder Jim's case bored him, and while I thought with something akin to fear of the immensity of his contempt for the young man under examination, he was probably holding silent inquiry into his own case. The verdict must have been of unmitigated guilt, and he took the secret of the evidence with him in that leap into the sea. If I understand anything of men, the matter was no doubt of the gravest import, one of those trifles that awaken ideas—start into life some thought with which a man unused to such a companionship finds it impossible to live. I am in a position to know that it wasn't money, and it wasn't drink, and it wasn't woman. He jumped overboard at sea barely a week after the end of the inquiry, and less than three days after leaving port on his outward passage; as though on that exact spot in the midst of waters he had suddenly perceived the gates of the other world flung open wide for his reception.

"Yet it was not a sudden impulse. His gray-headed mate, a first-rate sailor and a nice old chap with strangers, but in his relations with his commander the surliest chief officer I've ever seen, would tell the story with tears in his eyes. It appears that when he came on deck in the morning Brierly had been writing in the chart-room. 'It was ten minutes to four,' he said, 'and the middle watch was not relieved yet of course. He heard my voice on the bridge speaking to the second mate, and called me in. I was loath to go, and that's the truth, Captain Marlow—I couldn't stand poor Captain Brierly, I tell you with shame; we never know what a man is made of. He had been promoted over too many heads, not counting my own, and he had a damnable trick of making you feel small, nothing but by the way he said "Good morning." I never addressed him, sir, but on matters of duty, and then it was as much as I could do to keep a civil tongue in my head.' (He flattered himself there. I often wondered how Brierly could put up with his manners for more than half a voyage.) 'I've a wife and children,' he went on, 'and I had been ten years in the Company, always expecting the next command—more fool I. Says he, just like this: "Come in here, Mr. Jones," in that swagger voice of his—"Come in here, Mr. Jones." In I went. "We'll lay down her position," says he, stooping over the chart, a pair of dividers in hand. By the standing orders, the officer going off duty would have done that at the end of his watch. However, I said nothing, and looked on while he marked off the ship's position with a tiny cross and wrote the date and the time. I can see him this moment writing his neat figures: seventeen, eight, four A.M. The year would be written in red ink at the top of the chart. He never used his charts more than a year, Captain Brierly didn't. I've the chart now. When he had done he stands looking down at the mark he had made and smiling to himself, then looks up at me. "Thirty-two miles more as she goes," says he, "and then we shall be clear, and you may alter the course twenty degrees to the southward."

" 'We were passing to the north of the Hector Bank that voyage. I said, "All right, sir," wondering what he was fussing about, since I had to call him before altering the course anyhow. Just then eight bells were struck: we came out on the bridge, and the second mate before going off mentions in the usual way—"Seventy-one on the log." Captain Brierly looks at the compass and then all around. It was dark and clear, and all the stars were out as plain as on a frosty night in high latitudes. Suddenly he says with a sort of a little sigh: "I am going aft, and shall set the log at zero for you myself, so that there can be no mistake. Thirty-two miles more on this course and then you are safe. Let's see—the correction on the log is six per cent. additive; say, then, thirty by the dial to run, and you may come twenty degrees to starboard at once. No use losing any distance—is there?" I had never heard him talk so much at a stretch, and to no purpose as it seemed to me. I said nothing. He went down the ladder, and the dog, that was always at his heels whenever he moved, night or day, followed, sliding nose first, after him. I heard his boot-heels tap, tap on the after-deck, then he stopped and spoke to the dog—"Go back, Rover. On the bridge, boy! Go on—get." The he calls out to me from the dark, "Shut that dog up in the chart-room, Mr. Jones—will you?"

" 'This was the last time I heard his voice, Captain Marlow. These are the last words he spoke in the hearing of any living human being, sir.' At this point the old chap's voice got quite unsteady. 'He was afraid the poor brute would jump after him, don't you see?' he pursued with a quaver. 'Yes, Captain Marlow. He set the log for me; he—would you believe it?—he put a drop of oil in it too. There was the oil-feeder where he left it near by. The boatswain's mate got the hose along aft to wash down at half-past five; by-and-by he knocks off and runs up on the bridge—"Will you please come aft, Mr. Jones," he says. "There's a funny thing. I don't like to touch it." It was Captain Brierly's gold chronometer watch carefully hung under the rail by its chain.

" 'As soon as my eyes fell on it something struck me, and I knew, sir. My legs got soft under me. It was as if I had seen him go over; and I could tell how far behind he was left too. The taffrail-log marked eighteen miles and three-quarters, and four iron belaying-pins were missing around the mainmast. Put them in his pockets to help him down, I suppose; but, Lord! what's four iron pins to a powerful man like Captain Brierly. Maybe his confidence in himself was just shook a bit at the last. That's the only sign of fluster he gave in his whole life, I should think; but I am ready to answer for him, that once over he did not try to swim a stroke, the same as he would have had pluck enough to keep up all day long on the bare chance had he fallen overboard accidentally. Yes, sir. He was second to none—if he said so himself, as I heard him once. He had written two letters in the middle watch, one to the Company and the other to me. He gave me a lot of instructions as to the passage—I had been in the trade before he was out of his time—and no end of hints as to my conduct with our people in Shanghai, so that I should keep the command of the *Ossa*. He wrote like a father would to a favorite son, Captain Marlow, and I was five-and-twenty years his senior and had tasted salt water before he was fairly breeched. In his letter to the owners—it was left open for me to see—he said that he had always done his duty by them—up to that moment—and even now he was not betraying their confidence, since he was leaving the ship to as competent a seaman as could be found—meaning me, sir, meaning me! He told them that if the last act of his life didn't take away all his credit with them, they would give weight to my faithful service and to his warm recommendation, when about to fill the vacancy made by his death. And much more like this, sir. I couldn't believe my eyes. It made me feel queer all over,' went on the old chap in great perturbation, and squashing something in the corner of his eye with the end of a thumb as broad as a spatula. 'You would think, sir, he had jumped overboard only to give an unlucky man a last show to get on. What with the shock of him going in this awful rash way, and thinking myself a made man by that chance, I was nearly off my chump for a week. But no fear. The captain of the *Pelion* was shifted into the *Ossa*—came aboard in Shanghai—a little popinjay, sir, in a gray check suit, with his hair parted in the middle. "Aw—I am—aw—your new captain, Mister—Mister—aw —Jones." He was drowned in scent—fairly stunk with it, Captain Marlow. I daresay it was the look I gave him that made him stammer. He mumbled something about my natural disappointment—I had better know at once that his chief officer got the promotion to the *Pelion*—he had nothing to do with it, of course—supposed the office knew best—sorry. . . . Says I, "Don't you mind old Jones, sir; damn his soul, he's used to it." I could see directly I had shocked his delicate ear, and while we sat at our first tiffin together he began to find fault in a nasty manner with this and that in the ship. I never heard such a voice out of a Punch and Judy show. I set my teeth hard, and glued my eyes to my plate, and held my peace as long as I could; but at last I had to say something: up he jumps tiptoeing, ruffling all his pretty plumes, like a little fighting cock. "You'll find you have a different person to deal with than the late Captain Brierly." "I've found it," says I, very glum, but pretending to be mighty busy with my steak. "You are an old ruffian, Mr.—aw—Jones; and what's more, you are known for an old ruffian in the employ," he squeaks at me. The damned bottle-washers stood about listening with their mouths stretched from ear to ear. "I may be a hard case," answers I, "but I ain't so far gone as to put up with the sight of you sitting in Captain Brierly's chair." With that I lay down my knife and fork. "You would like to sit in it yourself—that's where the shoe pinches," he sneers. I left the saloon, got my rags together, and was on the quay with all my dunnage about my feet before the stevedores had turned to again. Yes. Adrift—on shore—after ten years' service—and with a poor woman and four children six thousand miles off depending on my half-pay for every mouthful they ate. Yes, sir! I chucked it rather than hear Captain Brierly abused. He left me his night-glasses—here they are; and he wished me to take care of the dog—here he is. Hallo, Rover, poor boy. Where's the captain, Rover?' The dog looked up at us with mournful eyes, gave one desolate bark, and crept under the table.

"All this was taking place, more than two years afterwards, on board that nautical ruin the *Fire-Queen* this Jones had got charge of—quite by a funny accident, too—from Matherson—mad Matherson they generally called him—the same who used to hang out in Haï-phong, you know, before the occupation days. The old chap snuffled on—

" 'Ay, sir, Captain Brierly will be remembered here, if there's no other place on earth. I wrote fully to his father and did not get a word in reply—neither Thank you, nor Go to the devil!—nothing! Perhaps they did not want to know.'

"The sight of that watery-eyed old Jones mopping his bald head with a red cotton handkerchief, the sorrowing yelp of the dog, the squalor of that flyblown cuddy which was the only shrine of his memory, threw a veil of inexpressibly mean pathos over Brierly's remembered figure, the posthumous revenge of fate for that belief in his own splendor which had almost cheated his life of its legitimate terrors. Almost! Perhaps wholly. Who can tell what flattering view he had induced himself to take of his own suicide?

" 'Why did he commit the rash act, Captain Marlow—can you think?' asked Jones, pressing his palms together. 'Why? It beats me! Why?' He slapped his low and wrinkled forehead. 'If he had been poor and old and in debt—and never a show—or else mad. But he wasn't of the kind that goes mad, not he. You trust me. What a mate don't know about his skipper isn't worth knowing. Young, healthy, well off, no cares. . . . I sit here sometimes thinking, thinking, till my head fairly begins to buzz. There was some reason.'

" 'You may depend on it, Captain Jones,' said I, 'it wasn't anything that would have disturbed much either of us two,' I said; and then, as if a light had been flashed into the muddle of his brain, poor old Jones found a last word of amazing profundity. He blew his nose, nodding at me dolefully:

'Ay, ay! neither you nor I, sir, had ever thought so much of ourselves.'

"Of course the recollection of my last conversation with Brierly is tinged with the knowledge of his end that followed so close upon it. I spoke with him for the last time during the progress of the inquiry. It was after the first adjournment, and he came up with me in the street. He was in a state of irritation, which I noticed with surprise, his usual behavior when he condescended to converse being perfectly cool, with a trace of amused tolerance, as if the existence of his interlocutor had been a rather good joke.

'They caught me for that inquiry, you see,' he began, and for a while enlarged com-plainingly upon the inconveniences of daily attendance in court. 'And goodness knows how long it will last. Three days, I suppose.' I heard him out in silence; in my then opinion it was a way as good as another of putting on side. 'What's the use of it? It is the stupidest set out you can imagine,' he pursued, hotly. I remarked that there was no option. He interrupted me with a sort of pent-up violence. 'I feel like a fool all the time.' I looked up at him. This was going very far—for Brierly—when talking of Brierly. He stopped short, and seized the lapel of my coat, gave it a slight tug. 'Why are we tormenting that young chap?' he asked. This question chimed in so well to the tolling of a certain thought of mine that, with the image of the absconding renegade in my eye, I answered at once, 'Hanged if I know, unless it be that he lets you.' I was astonished to see him fall into line, so to speak, with that utterance, which ought to have been tolerably cryptic. He said angrily, 'Why, yes. Can't he see that wretched skipper of his has cleared out? What does he expect to happen? Nothing can save him. He's done for.' We walked on in silence a few steps. 'Why eat all that dirt?' he exclaimed, with an oriental energy of expression—about the only sort of energy you can find a trace of east of the fiftieth meridian. I wondered greatly at the direction of his thoughts, but now I strongly suspect it was strictly in character: at bottom poor Brierly must have been thinking of himself. I pointed out to him that the skipper of the *Patna* was known to have feathered his nest pretty well, and could procure almost anywhere the means of getting away. With Jim it was otherwise: the Government was keeping him in the Sailors' Home for the time being, and probably he hadn't a penny in his pocket to bless himself with. It costs some money to run away. 'Does it? Not always,' he said, with a bitter laugh, and to some further remark of mine—'Well, then, let him creep twenty feet underground and stay there! By heavens! *I* would.' I don't know why his tone provoked me, and I said, 'There is a kind of courage in facing it out as he does, knowing very well that if he went away nobody would trouble to run after him.' 'Courage be hanged!' growled Brierly. 'That sort of courage is of no use to keep a man straight, and I don't care a snap for such courage. If you were to say it was a kind of cowardice now—of softness, I tell you what, I will put up two hundred rupees if you put up another hundred and undertake to make the beggar clear out early tomorrow morning. The fellow's a gentleman if he ain't fit to be touched—he will understand. He must! This infernal publicity is too shocking: there he sits while all these confounded natives, serangs, lascars, quartermasters, are giving evidence that's enough to burn a man to ashes with shame. This is abominable. Why, Marlow, don't you think, don't you feel, that this is abominable; don't you now—come—as a seaman? If he went away all this would stop at once.' Brierly said these words with a most unusual animation, and made as if to reach after his pocketbook. I restrained him, and declared coldly that the cowardice of these four men did not seem to me a matter of such great importance. 'And you call yourself a seaman, I suppose,' he pronounced, angrily. I said that's what I called myself, and I hoped I was too. He heard me out, and made a gesture with his big arm that seemed to deprive me of my individuality, to push me away into the crowd. 'The worst of it,' he said, 'is that all you fellows have no sense of dignity; you don't think enough of what you are supposed to be.'

"We had been walking slowly meantime, and now stopped opposite the harbor office, in sight of the very spot from which the immense captain of the *Patna* had vanished as utterly as a tiny feather blown away in a hurricane. I smiled. Brierly went on: 'This is a disgrace. We've got all kinds amongst us—some anointed scoundrels in the lot; but, hang it, we must preserve professional decency or we become no better than so many tinkers going about loose. We are trusted. Do you understand?— trusted! Frankly, I don't care a snap for all the pilgrims that ever came out of Asia, but a decent man would not have behaved like this to a full cargo of old rags in bales. We aren't an organized body of men, and the only thing that holds us together is just the name for that kind of decency. Such an affair destroys one's confidence. A man may go pretty near through his whole sea-life without any call to show a stiff upper lip. But when the call comes . . . Aha! . . . If I . . .'

"He broke off, and in a changed tone, 'I'll give you two hundred rupees now, Marlow, and you just talk to that chap. Confound him! I wish he had never come out here. Fact is, I rather think some of my people know his. The old man's a parson, and I remember now I met him once when staying with my cousin in Essex last year. If I am not mistaken, the old chap seemed rather to fancy his sailor son. Horrible. I can't do it myself—but you . . .'

"Thus, apropos of Jim, I had a glimpse of the real Brierly a few days before he committed his reality and his sham together to the keeping of the sea. Of course I declined to meddle. The tone of this last 'but you' (poor Brierly couldn't help it), that seemed to imply I was no more noticeable than an insect, caused me to look at the proposal with indignation, and on account of that provocation, or for some other reason, I became positive in my mind that the inquiry was a severe punishment to that Jim, and that his facing it—practically of his own free will—was a redeeming feature in his abominable case. I hadn't been so sure of it before. Brierly went off in a huff. At the time his state of mind was more of a mystery to me than it is now.

"Next day, coming into court late, I sat by myself. Of course I could not forget the conversation I had with Brierly, and now I had them both under my eyes. The demeanor of one suggested gloomy impudence and of the other a contemptuous boredom; yet one attitude might not have been truer than the other, and I was aware that one was not true. Brierly was not bored—he was exasperated; and if so, then Jim might not have been impudent. According to my theory he was not. I imagined he was hopeless. Then it was that our glances met. They met, and the look he gave me was discouraging of any intention I might have had to speak to him. Upon either hypothe- sis—insolence or despair—I felt I could be of no use to him. This was the second day of the proceedings. Very soon after that exchange of glances the inquiry was adjourned again to the next day. The white men began to troop out at once. Jim had been told to stand down some time before, and was able to leave amongst the first. I saw his broad shoulders and his head outlined in the light of the door, and while I made my way slowly out talking with some one—some stranger who had addressed me casually—I could see him from within the courtroom resting both elbows on the balustrade of the verandah and turning his back on the small stream of people trickling down the few steps. There was a murmur of voices and a shuffle of boots.

"The next case was that of assault and battery committed upon a money-lender, I believe; and the defendant—a venerable villager with a straight white beard—sat on a mat just outside the door with his sons, daughters, sons-in-law, their wives, and, I should think, half the population of his village besides, squatting or standing around him. A slim dark woman, with part of her back and one black shoulder bared, and with a thin gold ring in her nose, suddenly began to talk in a high-pitched, shrewish tone. The man with me instinctively looked up at her. We were then just through the door, passing behind Jim's burly back.

"Whether those villagers had brought the yellow dog with them, I don't know. Anyhow, a dog was there, weaving himself in and out amongst people's legs in that mute stealthy way native dogs have and my companion stumbled over him. The dog leaped away without a sound; the man, raising his voice a little, said with a slow laugh, 'Look at that wretched cur,' and directly afterwards we became separated by a lot of people pushing in. I stood back for a moment against the wall while the stranger managed to get down the steps and disappeared. I saw Jim spin around. He made a step forward and barred my way. We were alone; he glared at me with an air of stubborn resolution. I became aware I was being held up, so to speak, as if in a wood. The verandah was empty by then, the noise and movement in court had ceased: a great silence fell upon the building, in which, somewhere far within, an oriental voice began to whine abjectly. The dog in the very act of trying to sneak in at the door, sat down hurriedly to hunt for fleas.

" 'Did you speak to me?' asked Jim very low, and bending forward, not so much towards me but at me, if you know what I mean. I said 'No' at once. Something in the sound of that quiet tone of his warned me to be on my defense. I watched him. It was very much like a meeting in a wood, only more uncertain in its issue, since he could possibly want neither my money nor my life—nothing that I could simply give up or defend with a clear conscience. 'You say you didn't,' he said, very somber. 'But I heard.' 'Some mistake,' I protested, utterly at a loss, and never taking my eyes off him. To watch his face was like watching a darkening sky before a clap of thunder, shade upon shade imperceptibly coming on, the gloom growing mysteriously intense in the calm of maturing violence.

" 'As far as I know, I haven't opened my lips in your hearing,' I affirmed with perfect truth. I was getting a little angry, too, at the absurdity of this encounter. It strikes me now I have never in my life been so near a beating—I mean it literally; a beating with fists. I suppose I had some hazy prescience of that eventuality being in the air. Not that he was actively threatening me. On the contrary, he was strangely passive—don't you know? but he was lowering, and, though not exceptionally big, he looked generally fit to demolish a wall. The most reassuring symptom I noticed was a kind of slow and ponderous hesitation, which I took as a tribute to the evident sincerity of my manner and of my tone. We faced each other. In the court the assault case was proceeding. I caught the words: 'Well—buffalo—stick—in the greatness of my fear. . . .'

" 'What did you mean by staring at me all the morning?' said Jim at last. He looked up and looked down again. 'Did you expect us all to sit with downcast eyes out of regard for your susceptibilities?' I retorted sharply. I was not going to submit meekly to any of his nonsense. He raised his eyes again, and this time continued to look me straight in the face. 'No. That's all right,' he pronounced with an air of deliberating with himself upon the truth of this statement—'that's all right. I am going through with that. Only'—and there he spoke a little faster—'I won't let any man call me names outside this court. There was a fellow with you. You spoke to him —oh, yes—I know; 'tis all very fine. You spoke to him, but you meant me to hear. . . .'

"I assured him he was under some extraordinary delusion. I had no conception how it came about. 'You thought I would be afraid to resent this,' he said, with just a faint tinge of bitterness. I was interested enough to discern the slightest shades of expression, but I was not in the least enlightened; yet I don't know what in these words, or perhaps just the intonation of that phrase, induced me suddenly to make all possible allowances for him. I ceased to be annoyed at my unexpected predicament. It was some mistake on his part; he was blundering and I had an intuition that the blunder was of an odious, of an unfortunate nature. I was anxious to end this scene on grounds of decency, just as one is anxious to cut short some unprovoked and abominable confidence. The funniest part was, that in the midst of all these considerations of the higher order I was conscious of a certain trepidation as to the possibility—nay, likelihood—of this encounter ending in some disreputable brawl which could not possibly be explained, and would make me ridiculous. I did not hanker after a three days' celebrity as the man who got a black eye or something of the sort from the mate of the *Patna*. He, in all probability, did not care what he did, or at any rate would be fully justified in his own eyes. It took no magician to see he was amazingly angry about something, for all his quiet and even torpid demeanor. I don't deny I was extremely desirous to pacify him at all costs, had I only known what to do. But I didn't know, as you may well imagine. It was blackness without a single gleam. We confronted each other in silence. He hung fire for about fifteen seconds, then made a step nearer, and I made ready to ward off a blow, though I don't think I moved a muscle. 'If you were as big as two men and as strong as six,' he said very softly, 'I would tell you what I think of you. You . . .' 'Stop!' I exclaimed. This checked him for a second. 'Before you tell me what you think of me,' I went on, quickly, 'will you kindly tell me what it is I've said or done?' During the pause that ensued he surveyed me with indignation, while I made supernatural efforts of memory, in which I was hindered by the oriental voice within the courtroom expostulating with impassioned volubility against a charge of falsehood. Then we spoke almost together. 'I will soon show you I am not,' he said, in a tone suggestive of a crisis. 'I declare I don't know,' I protested earnestly at the same time. He tried to crush me by the scorn of his glance. 'Now that you see I am not afraid you try to crawl out of it,' he said. 'Who's a cur now—hey?' Then, at last, I understood.

"He had been scanning my features as though looking for a place where he would plant his fist. 'I will allow no man,' . . . he mumbled, threateningly. It was, indeed, a hideous mistake; he had given himself away utterly. I can't give you an idea how shocked I was. I suppose he saw some reflection of my feelings in my face, because his expression changed just a little. 'Good God!' I stammered, 'you don't think I . . .' 'But I am sure I've heard,' he persisted, raising his voice for the first time since the beginning of this deplorable scene. Then with a shade of disdain he added, 'It wasn't you, then? Very well; I'll find the other.' 'Don't be a fool,' I cried in exasperation; 'it wasn't that at all.' 'I've heard,' he said again with an unshaken and somber perseverance.

"There may be those who could have laughed at his pertinacity. I didn't. Oh, I didn't! There had never been a man so mercilessly shown up by his own natural impulse. A single word had stripped him of his discretion—and that discretion which is more necessary to the decencies of our inner being than clothing is to the decorum of our body. 'Don't be a fool,' I repeated. 'But the other man said it, you don't deny that?' he pronounced, distinctly, and looking in my face without flinching. 'No, I don't deny,' said I, returning his gaze. At last his eyes followed downwards the direction of my pointing finger. He appeared at first uncomprehending, then confounded, and at last amazed and scared as though a dog had been a monster and he had never seen a dog before. 'Nobody dreamt of insulting you,' I said.

"He contemplated the wretched animal, that moved no more than an effigy: it sat with ears pricked and its sharp muzzle pointed into the doorway, and suddenly snapped at a fly like a piece of mechanism.

"I looked at him. The red of his fair sunburned complexion deepened suddenly under the down of his cheeks, invaded his forehead, spread to the roots of his curly hair. His ears became intensely crimson, and even the clear blue of his eyes was darkened many shades by the rush of blood to his head. His lips pouted a little, trembling as though he had been on the point of bursting into tears. I perceived he was incapable of pronouncing a word from the excess of his humiliation. From disappointment too—who knows? Perhaps he looked forward to that hammering he was going to give me for rehabilitation, for appeasement? Who can tell what relief he expected from this chance of a row? He was naïve enough to expect anything; but he had given himself away for nothing in this case. He had been frank with himself—let alone with me—in the wild hope of arriving in that way at some effective refutation, and the stars had been ironically unpropitious. He made an inarticulate noise in his throat like a man imperfectly stunned by a blow on the head. It was pitiful.

"I didn't catch up again with him till well outside the gate. I had even to trot a bit at the last, but when, out of breath at his elbow, I taxed him with running away, he said, 'Never!' and at once turned at bay. I explained I never meant to say he was running away from *me*. 'From no man—from not a single man on earth,' he affirmed with a stubborn mien. I forebore to point out the one obvious exception which would hold good for the bravest of us; I thought he would find out by himself very soon. He looked at me patiently while I was thinking of something to say, but I could find nothing on the spur of the moment, and he began to walk on. I kept up, and anxious not to lose him, I said hurriedly that I couldn't think of leaving him under a false impression of my—of my—I stammered. The stupidity of the phrase appalled me while I was trying to finish it, but the power of sentences has nothing to do with their sense or the logic of their construction. My idiotic mumble seemed to please him. He cut it short by saying, with courteous placidity that argued an immense power of self-control or else a wonderful elasticity of spirits—'Altogether my mistake.' I marveled greatly at this expression: he might have been alluding to some trifling occurrence. Hadn't he understood its deplorable meaning? 'You may well forgive me,' he continued, and went on a little moodily, 'All these staring people in court seemed such fools that—that it might have been as I supposed.'

"This opened suddenly a new view of him to my wonder. I looked at him curiously and met his unabashed and impenetrable eyes. 'I can't put up with this kind of thing,' he said, very simply, 'and I don't mean to. In court it's different; I've got to stand that —and I can do it too.'

"I don't pretend I understood him. The views he let me have of himself were like those glimpses through the shifting rents in a thick fog—bits of vivid and vanishing detail, giving no connected idea of the general aspect of a country. They fed one's curiosity without satisfying it; they were no good for purposes of orientation. Upon the whole he was misleading. That's how I summed him up to myself after he left me late in the evening. I had been staying at the Malabar House for a few days, and on my pressing invitation he dined with me there."

VII

"An outward-bound mail-boat had come in that afternoon, and the big dining-room of the hotel was more than half full of people with a hundred pounds round-the-world tickets in their pockets. There were married couples looking domesticated and bored with each other in the midst of their travels; there were small parties and large parties, and lone individuals dining solemnly or feasting boisterously, but all thinking, conversing, joking, or scowling as was their wont at home; and just as intelligently receptive of new impressions as their trunks upstairs. Henceforth they would be labeled as having passed through this and that place and so would be their luggage. They would cherish this distinction of their persons, and preserve the gummed tickets on their portmanteaus as documentary evidence, as the only permanent trace of their improving enterprise. The dark-faced servants tripped without noise over the vast and polished floor; now and then a girl's laugh would be heard, as innocent and empty as her mind, or, in a sudden hush of crockery, a few words in an affected drawl from some wit embroidering for the benefit of a grinning tableful the last funny story of shipboard scandal. Two nomadic old maids, dressed up to kill, worked acrimoniously through the bill of fare, whispering to each other with faded lips, wooden-faced and bizarre, like two sumptuous scarecrows. A little wine opened Jim's heart and loosened

his tongue. His appetite was good, too, I noticed. He seemed to have buried somewhere the opening episode of our acquaintance. It was like a thing of which there
would be no more question in this world. And all the time I had before me these blue,
boyish eyes looking straight into mine, this young face, these capable shoulders, the
open bronzed forehead with a white line under the roots of clustering fair hair, this
appearance appealing at sight to all my sympathies: this frank aspect, the artless smile,
the youthful seriousness. He was of the right sort; he was one of us. He talked soberly,
with a sort of composed unreserve, and with a quiet bearing that might have been the
outcome of manly self-control, of impudence, of callousness, of a colossal uncon-
sciousness, of a gigantic deception. Who can tell! From our tone we might have been
discussing a third person, a football match, last year's weather. My mind floated in a
sea of conjectures till the turn of the conversation enabled me, without being offensive,
to remark that, upon the whole, this inquiry must have been pretty trying to him. He
darted his arm across the tablecloth, and clutching my hand by the side of my plate,
glared fixedly. I was startled. 'It must be awfully hard,' I stammered, confused by this
display of speechless feeling. 'It is—hell,' he burst out in a muffled voice.

"This movement and these words caused two well-groomed male globetrotters at a
neighboring table to look up in alarm from their iced pudding. I rose, and we passed
into the front gallery for coffee and cigars.

"On little octagon tables candles burned in glass globes; clumps of stiff-leaved
plants separated sets of cozy wicker chairs; and between the pairs of columns, whose
reddish shafts caught in a long row the sheen from the tall windows, the night,
glittering and somber, seemed to hang like a splendid drapery. The riding lights of
ships winked afar like setting stars, and the hills across the roadstead resembled
rounded black masses of arrested thunder-clouds.

" 'I couldn't clear out,' Jim began. 'The skipper did—that's all very well for him. I
couldn't, and I wouldn't. They all got out of it in one way or another, but it wouldn't
do for me.'

"I listened with concentrated attention, not daring to stir in my chair; I wanted to
know—and to this day I don't know, I can only guess. He would be confident and
depressed all in the same breath, as if some conviction of innate blamelessness had
checked the truth writhing within him at every turn. He began by saying, in the tone
in which a man would admit his inability to jump a twenty-foot wall, that he could
never go home now; and this declaration recalled to my mind what Brierly had said,
'that the old parson in Essex seemed to fancy his sailor son not a little.'

"I can't tell you whether Jim knew he was especially 'fancied,' but the tone of his
references to 'my Dad' was calculated to give me a notion that the good old rural dean
was about the finest man that ever had been worried by the cares of a large family since
the beginning of the world. This, though never stated, was implied with an anxiety
that there should be no mistake about it, which was really very true and charming, but
added a poignant sense of lives far off to the other elements of the story. 'He has seen
it all in the home papers by this time,' said Jim. 'I can never face the poor old chap.' I
did not dare to lift my eyes at this till I heard him add, 'I could never explain. He

wouldn't understand.' Then I looked up. He was smoking reflectively, and after a moment, rousing himself, began to talk again. He discovered at once a desire that I should not confound him with his partners in—in crime, let us call it. He was not one of them; he was altogether of another sort. I gave no sign of dissent. I had no intention, for the sake of barren truth, to rob him of the smallest particle of any saving grace that would come in his way. I didn't know how much of it he believed himself. I didn't know what he was playing up to—if he was playing up to anything at all—and I suspect he did not know either; for it is my belief no man ever understands quite his own artful dodges to escape from the grim shadow of self-knowledge. I made no sound all the time he was wondering what he had better do after 'that stupid inquiry was over.'

"Apparently he shared Brierly's contemptuous opinion of these proceedings ordained by law. He would not know where to turn, he confessed, clearly thinking aloud rather than talking to me. Certificate gone, career broken, no money to get away, no work that he could obtain as far as he could see. At home he could perhaps get something; but it meant going to his people for help, and that he would not do. He saw nothing for it but ship before the mast—could get perhaps a quartermaster's billet in some steamer. Would do for a quartermaster. . . . 'Do you think you would?' I asked, pitilessly. He jumped up, and going to the stone balustrade looked out into the night. In a moment he was back, towering above my chair with his youthful face clouded yet by the pain of a conquered emotion. He had understood very well I did not doubt his ability to steer a ship. In a voice that quavered a bit he asked me, 'Why did I say that? I had been "no end kind" to him. I had not even laughed at him when' —here he began to mumble—'that mistake, you know—made a confounded ass of myself.' I broke in by saying rather warmly that for me such a mistake was not a matter to laugh at. He sat down and drank deliberately some coffee, emptying the small cup to the last drop. 'That does not mean I admit for a moment the cap fitted,' he declared, distinctly. 'No?' I said. 'No,' he affirmed with quiet decision. 'Do you know what *you* would have done? Do you? And you don't think yourself' . . . he gulped something . . . 'you don't think yourself a—a—cur?'

"And with this—upon my honor!—he looked up at me inquisitively. It was a question it appears—a *bonâ-fide* question! However, he didn't wait for an answer. Before I could recover he went on, with his eyes straight before him, as if reading off something written on the body of the night. 'It is all in being ready. I wasn't; not—not then. I don't want to excuse myself; but I would like to explain—I would like somebody to understand—somebody—one person at least! You! Why not you?'

"It was solemn, and a little ridiculous, too, as they always are, those struggles of an individual trying to save from the fire his idea of what his moral identity should be, this precious notion of a convention, only one of the rules of the game, nothing more, but all the same so terribly effective by its assumption of unlimited power over natural instincts, by the awful penalties of its failure. He began his story quietly enough. On board that Dale Line steamer that had picked up these four floating in a boat upon the discreet sunset glow of the sea, they had been after the first day looked askance upon.

The fat skipper told some story, the others had been silent, and at first it had been accepted. You don't cross-examine poor castaways you had the good luck to save, if not from cruel death, then at least from cruel suffering. Afterwards, with time to think it over, it might have struck the officers of the *Avondale* that there was 'something fishy' in the affair; but of course they would keep their doubts to themselves. They had picked up the captain, the mate, and two engineers of the steamer *Patna* sunk at sea, and that, very properly, was enough for them. I did not ask Jim about the nature of his feelings during the ten days he spent on board. From the way he narrated that part I was at liberty to infer he was partly stunned by the discovery he had made—the discovery about himself—and no doubt was at work trying to explain it away to the only man who was capable of appreciating all its tremendous magnitude. You must understand he did not try to minimize its importance. Of that I am sure; and therein lies his distinction. As to what sensations he experienced when he got ashore and heard the unforeseen conclusion of the tale in which he had taken such a pitiful part, he told me nothing of them, and it is difficult to imagine. I wonder whether he felt the ground cut from under his feet? I wonder? But no doubt he managed to get a fresh foothold very soon. He was ashore a whole fortnight waiting in the Sailors' Home, and as there were six or seven men staying there at the time, I had heard of him a little. Their languid opinion seemed to be that in addition to his other shortcomings, he was a sulky brute. He had passed these days on the verandah, buried in a long chair, and coming out of his place of sepulture only at meal-times or late at night, when he wandered on the quays all by himself, detached from his surroundings, irresolute and silent, like a ghost without a home to haunt. 'I don't think I've spoken three words to a living soul in all that time,' he said, making me very sorry for him; and directly he added, 'One of these fellows would have been sure to blurt out something I had made up my mind not to put up with, and I didn't want a row. No! Not then. I was too— too . . . I had no heart for it.' 'So that bulkhead held out after all,' I remarked, cheerfully. 'Yes,' he murmured, 'it held. And yet I swear to you I felt it bulge under my hand.' 'It's extraordinary what strains old iron will stand sometimes,' I said. Thrown back in his seat, his legs stiffly out and arms hanging down, he nodded slightly several times. You could not conceive a sadder spectacle. Suddenly he lifted his head; he sat up; he slapped his thigh. 'Ah! what a chance missed! My God! what a chance missed!' he blazed out, but the ring of the last 'missed' resembled a cry wrung out by pain.

"He was silent again with a still, far-away look of fierce yearning after that missed distinction, with his nostrils for an instant dilated, sniffing the intoxicating breath of that wasted opportunity. If you think I was either surprised or shocked you do me an injustice in more ways than one! Ah, he was an imaginative beggar! He would give himself away; he would give himself up. I could see in his glance darted into the night all his inner being carried on, projected headlong into the fanciful realm of recklessly heroic aspirations. He had no leisure to regret what he had lost, he was so wholly and naturally concerned for what he had failed to obtain. He was very far away from me who watched him across three feet of space. With every instant he was penetrating deeper into the impossible world of romantic achievements. He got to the heart of it at last! A strange look of beatitude overspread his features, his eyes sparkled in the light of the candle burning between us; he positively smiled! He had penetrated to the very heart—to the very heart. It was an ecstatic smile that your faces—or mine either —will never wear, my dear boys. I whisked him back by saying, 'If you had stuck to the ship, you mean!'

"He turned upon me, his eyes suddenly amazed and full of pain, with a bewildered, startled, suffering face, as though he had tumbled down from a star. Neither you nor I will ever look like this on any man. He shuddered profoundly, as if a cold fingertip had touched his heart. Last of all he sighed.

"I was not in a merciful mood. He provoked one by his contradictory indiscretions. 'It is unfortunate you didn't know beforehand!' I said with every unkind intention; but the perfidious shaft fell harmless—dropped at his feet like a spent arrow, as it were, and he did not think of picking it up. Perhaps he had not even seen it. Presently, lolling at ease, he said, 'Dash it all! I tell you it bulged. I was holding up my lamp along the angle-iron in the lower deck when a flake of rust as big as the palm of my hand fell off the plate, all of itself.' He passed his hand over his forehead. 'The thing stirred and jumped off like something alive while I was looking at it.' 'That made you feel pretty bad,' I observed, casually. 'Do you suppose,' he said, 'that I was thinking of myself, with a hundred and sixty people at my back, all fast asleep in that fore-'tween-deck alone—and more of them aft; more on the deck—sleeping—knowing nothing about it—three times as many as there were boats for, even if there had been time? I expected to see the iron open out as I stood there and the rush of water going over them as they lay. . . . What could I do—what?'

"I can easily picture him to myself in the peopled gloom of the cavernous place, with the light of the bulk-lamp falling on a small portion of the bulkhead that had the weight of the ocean on the other side, and the breathing of unconscious sleepers in his ears. I can see him glaring at the iron, startled by the falling rust, overburdened by the knowledge of an imminent death. This, I gathered, was the second time he had been sent forward by that skipper of his, who, I rather think, wanted to keep him away from the bridge. He told me that his first impulse was to shout and straight away make all those people leap out of sleep into terror; but such an overwhelming sense of his helplessness came over him that he was not able to produce a sound. This is, I suppose, what people mean by the tongue cleaving to the roof of the mouth. 'Too dry,' was the concise expression he used in reference to this state. Without a sound, then, he scrambled out on deck through the number one hatch. A wind-sail rigged down there swung against him accidentally, and he remembered that the light touch of the canvas on his face nearly knocked him off the hatchway ladder.

"He confessed that his knees wobbled a good deal as he stood on the foredeck looking at another sleeping crowd. The engines having been stopped by that time, the steam was blowing off. Its deep rumble made the whole night vibrate like a bass string. The ship trembled to it.

"He saw here and there a head lifted off a mat, a vague form uprise in sitting posture, listen sleepily for a moment, sink down again into the billowy confusion of boxes, steam-winches, ventilators. He was aware all these people did not known enough to take intelligent notice of that strange noise. The ship of iron, the men with white faces, all the sights, all the sounds, everything on board to that ignorant and pious multitude was strange alike, and as trustworthy as it would for ever remain incomprehensible. It occurred to him that the fact was fortunate. The idea of it was simply terrible.

"You must remember he believed, as any other man would have done in his place, that the ship would go down at any moment; the bulging, rust-eaten plates that kept back the ocean, fatally must give way, all at once like an undermined dam, and let in a sudden and overwhelming flood. He stood still looking at these recumbent bodies, a doomed man aware of his fate, surveying the silent company of the dead. They were dead! Nothing could save them! There were boats enough for half of them perhaps, but there was no time. No time! No time! It did not seem worthwhile to open his lips, to stir hand or foot. Before he could shout three words, or make three steps, he would be floundering in a sea whitened awfully by the desperate struggles of human beings, clamorous with the distress of cries for help. There was no help. He imagined what would happen perfectly; he went through it all motionless by the hatchway with the lamp in his hand—he went through it to the very last harrowing detail. I think he went through it again while he was telling me these things he could not tell the court.

" 'I saw as clearly as I see you now that there was nothing I could do. It seemed to take all life out of my limbs. I thought I might just as well stand where I was and wait. I did not think I had many seconds . . .' Suddenly the steam ceased blowing off. The noise, he remarked, had been distracting, but the silence at once became intolerably oppressive.

" 'I thought I would choke before I got drowned,' he said.

"He protested he did not think of saving himself. The only distinct thought formed, vanishing, and reforming in his brain, was: eight hundred people and seven boats; eight hundred people and seven boats.

" 'Somebody was speaking aloud inside my head,' he said a little wildly. 'Eight hundred people and seven boats—and no time! Just think of it.' He leaned towards me across the little table, and I tried to avoid his stare. 'Do you think I was afraid of death?' he asked in a voice very fierce and low. He brought down his open hand with a bang that made the coffee cups dance. 'I am ready to swear I was not—I was not. . . . By God—no!' He hitched himself upright and crossed his arms; his chin fell on his breast.

"The soft clashes of crockery reached us faintly through the high windows. There was a burst of voices, and several men came out in high good-humor into the gallery. They were exchanging jocular reminiscences of the donkeys in Cairo. A pale anxious youth stepping softly on long legs was being chaffed by a strutting and rubicund globetrotter about his purchases in the bazaar. 'No, really—do you think I've been done to that extent?' he inquired very earnest and deliberate. The band moved away dropping into chairs as they went; matches flared, illuminating for a second faces without the ghost of an expression and the flat glaze of white shirt-fronts; the hum of many conversations animated with the ardor of feasting sounded to me absurd and infinitely remote.

" 'Some of the crew were sleeping on the number one hatch within reach of my arm,' began Jim again.

"You must know they kept Kalashee watch in that ship, all hands sleeping through the night, and only the reliefs of quartermasters and look-out men being called. He was tempted to grip and shake the shoulder of the nearest lascar, but he didn't. Something held his arms down along his sides. He was not afraid—oh no! only he just couldn't—that's all. He was not afraid of death perhaps, but I'll tell you what, he was afraid of the emergency. His confounded imagination had evoked for him all the horrors of panic, the trampling rush, the pitiful screams, boats swamped—all the appalling incidents of a disaster at sea he had ever heard of. He might have been resigned to die but I suspect he wanted to die without added terrors, quietly, in a sort of peaceful trance. A certain readiness to perish is not so very rare, but it is seldom that you meet men whose souls, steeled in the impenetrable armor of resolution, are ready to fight a losing battle to the last, the desire of peace waxes stronger as hope declines, till at last it conquers the very desire of life. Which of us here has not observed this, or maybe experienced something of that feeling in his own person—this extreme weariness of emotions, the vanity of effort, the yearning for rest? Those striving with unreasonable forces know it well,—the shipwrecked castaways in boats, wanderers lost in a desert, men battling against the unthinking might of nature, or the stupid brutality of crowds."

VIII

"How long he stood stock-still by the hatch expecting every moment to feel the ship dip under his feet and the rush of water to take him at the back and toss him like a chip, I cannot say. Not very long—two minutes perhaps. A couple of men he could not make out began to converse drowsily, and also, he could not tell where, he detected a curious noise of shuffling feet. Above these faint sounds there was that awful stillness preceding a catastrophe, that trying silence of the moment before the crash; then it came into his head that perhaps he would have time to rush along and cut all the lanyards of the grips, so that the boats would float off as the ship went down.

"The *Patna* had a long bridge, and all the boats were up there, four on one side and three on the other—the smallest of them on the port-side and nearly abreast of the steering gear. He assured me, with evident anxiety to be believed, that he had been most careful to keep them ready for instant service. He knew his duty. I dare say he was a good enough mate as far as that went. 'I always believed in being prepared for the worst,' he commented, staring anxiously in my face. I nodded my approval of the sound principle, averting my eyes before the subtle unsoundness of the man.

"He started unsteadily to run. He had to step over legs, avoid stumbling against the heads. Suddenly someone caught hold of his coat from below, and a distressed voice spoke under his elbow. The light of the lamp he carried in his right hand fell upon an upturned dark face whose eyes entreated him together with the voice. He had picked up enough of the language to understand the word water, repeated several times in a tone of insistence, of prayer, almost of despair. He gave a jerk to get away, and felt an arm embrace his leg.

" 'The beggar clung to me like a drowning man,' he said, impressively. 'Water, water! What water did he mean? What did he know? As calmly as I could I ordered him to let go. He was stopping me, time was pressing, other men began to stir; I wanted time—time to cut the boats adrift. He got hold of my hand now, and I felt that he would begin to shout. It flashed upon me it was enough to start a panic, and I hauled off with my free arm and slung the lamp in his face. The glass jingled, the light went out, but the blow made him let go, and I ran off—I wanted to get at the boats; I wanted to get at the boats. He leaped after me from behind. I turned on him. He would not keep quiet; he tried to shout; I had half throttled him before I made out what he wanted. He wanted some water—water to drink; they were on strict allowance, you know, and he had with him a young boy I had noticed several times. His child was sick—and thirsty. He had caught sight of me as I passed by, and was begging for a little water. That's all. We were under the bridge, in the dark. He kept on snatching at my wrists; there was no getting rid of him. I dashed into my berth, grabbed my water-bottle, and thrust it into his hands. He vanished. I didn't find out till then how much I was in want of a drink myself.' He leaned on one elbow with a hand over his eyes.

"I felt a creepy sensation all down my backbone; there was something peculiar in all this. The fingers of the hand that shaded his brow trembled slightly. He broke the short silence.

" 'These things happen only once to a man and . . . Ah! well! When I got on the bridge at last the beggars were getting one of the boats off the chocks. A boat! I was running up the ladder when a heavy blow fell on my shoulder, just missing my head. It didn't stop me, and the chief engineer—they had got him out of his bunk by then—raised the boat-stretcher again. Somehow I had no mind to be surprised at anything. All this seemed natural—and awful—and awful. I dodged that miserable maniac, lifted him off the deck as though he had been a little child, and he started whispering in my arms: "Don't! don't! I thought you were one of them niggers." I flung him away, he skidded along the bridge and knocked the legs from under the little chap—the second. The skipper, busy about the boat, looked around and came at me head down, growling like a wild beast. I flinched no more than a stone. I was as solid standing there as this,' he tapped lightly with his knuckles the wall beside his chair. 'It was as though I had heard it all, seen it all, gone through it all twenty times already. I wasn't afraid of them. I drew back my fist and he stopped short, muttering—

" ' "Ah! it's you. Lend a hand quick."

" 'That's what he said. Quick! As if anybody could be quick enough. "Aren't you going to do something?" I asked. "Yes. Clear out," he snarled over his shoulder.

" 'I don't think I understood then what he meant. The other two had picked themselves up by that time, and they rushed together to the boat. They tramped, they wheezed, they shoved, they cursed the boat, the ship, each other—cursed me. All in mutters. I didn't move, I didn't speak. I watched the slant of the ship. She was as still as if landed on the blocks in a dry dock—only she was like this.' He held up his hand, palm under, the tips of the fingers inclined downwards. 'Like this,' he repeated. 'I could see the line of the horizon before me, as clear as a bell, above her stem-head; I could see the water far off there black and sparkling, and still—still as a pond, deadly still, more still than ever sea was before—more still than I could bear to look at. Have you watched a ship floating head down, checked in sinking by a sheet of old iron too rotten to stand being shored up. Have you? Oh yes, shored up? I thought of that—I thought of every mortal thing; but can you shore up a bulkhead in five minutes—or in fifty for that matter? Where was I going to get men that would go down below? And the timber—the timber! Would you have had the courage to swing the maul for the first blow if you had seen that bulkhead? Don't say you would: you had not seen it; nobody would. Hang it—to do a thing like that you must believe there is a chance, one in a thousand, at least, some ghost of a chance; and you would not have believed. Nobody would have believed. You think me a cur for standing there, but what would you have done? What! You can't tell—nobody can tell. One must have time to turn around. What would you have me do? Where was the kindness in making crazy with fright all those people I could not save single-handed—that nothing could save? Look here! As true as I sit on this chair before you . . .'

"He drew quick breaths at every few words and shot quick glances at my face, as though in his anguish he were watchful of the effect. He was not speaking to me, he was only speaking before me, in a dispute with an invisible personality, an antagonistic and inseparable partner of his existence—another possessor of his soul. These were issues beyond the competency of a court of inquiry: it was a subtle and momentous quarrel as to the true essence of life, and did not want a judge. He wanted an ally, a helper, an accomplice. I felt the risk I ran of being circumvented, blinded, decoyed, bullied, perhaps, into taking a definite part in a dispute impossible of decision if one had to be fair to all the phantoms in possession—to the reputable that had its claims and to the disreputable that had its exigencies. I can't explain to you who haven't seen him and who hear his words only at second hand the mixed nature of my feelings. It seemed to me I was being made to comprehend the Inconceivable—and I know of nothing to compare with the discomfort of such a sensation. I was made to look at the convention that lurks in all truth and on the essential sincerity of falsehood. He appealed to all sides at once—to the side turned perpetually to the light of day, and to that side of us which, like the other hemisphere of the moon, exists stealthily in perpetual darkness, with only a fearful ashy light falling at times on the edge. He swayed me. I own to it, I own up. The occasion was obscure, insignificant—what you will: a lost youngster, one in a million—but then he was one of us; an incident as completely devoid of importance as the flooding of an ant-heap, and yet the mystery of his attitude got hold of me as though he had been an individual in the forefront of his kind, as if the obscure truth involved were momentous enough to affect mankind's conception of itself. . . ."

Marlow paused to put new life into his expiring cheroot, seemed to forget all about the story, and abruptly began again.

"My fault of course. One has no business really to get interested. It's a weakness of mine. His was of another kind. My weakness consists in not having a discriminating eye for the incidental—for the externals—no eye for the hod of the rag-picker or the fine linen of the next man. Next man—that's it. I have me so many men," he pursued, with momentary sadness—"met them, too, with a certain—certain—impact, let us say; like this fellow, for instance—and in each case all I could see was merely the human being. A confounded democratic quality of vision which may be better than total blindness, but has been of no advantage to me, I can assure you. Men expect one to take into account their fine linen. But I never could get up any enthusiasm about these things. Oh! it's a failing; it's a failing; and then comes a soft evening; a lot of men too indolent for whist—and a story. . . ."

He paused again to wait for an encouraging remark perhaps, but nobody spoke; only the host, as if reluctantly performing a duty, murmured—

"You are so subtle, Marlow."

"Who? I?" said Marlow in a low voice. "Oh, no! But *he* was; and try as I may for the success of this yarn I am missing innumerable shades—they were so fine, so difficult to render in colorless words. Because he complicated matters by being so simple, too—the simplest poor devil! . . . By Jove! he was amazing. There he sat telling me that just as I saw him before my eyes he wouldn't be afraid to face anything —and believing in it, too. I tell you it was fabulously innocent and it was enormous, enormous! I watched him covertly, just as though I had suspected him of an intention to take a jolly good rise out of me. He was confident that, on the square, 'on the square, mind!' there was nothing he couldn't meet. Ever since he had been 'so high'— 'quite a little chap,' he had been preparing himself for all the difficulties that can beset one on land and water. He confessed proudly to this kind of foresight. He had been elaborating dangers and defenses, expecting the worst, rehearsing his best. He must have led a most exalted existence. Can you fancy it? A succession of adventures, so much glory, such a victorious progress! and the deep sense of his sagacity crowning every day of his inner life. He forgot himself; his eyes shone; and with every word my heart, searched by the light of his absurdity, was growing heavier in my breast. I had no mind to laugh, and lest I should smile I made for myself a stolid face. He gave signs of irritation.

" 'It is always the unexpected that happens,' I said in a propitiatory tone. My obtuseness provoked him into a contemptuous 'Pshaw!' I suppose he meant that the unexpected couldn't touch him; nothing less than the unconceivable itself could get over his perfect state of preparation. He had been taken unawares—and he whispered to himself a malediction upon the waters and the firmament, upon the ship, upon the men. Everything had betrayed him! He had been tricked into that sort of high-minded resignation which prevented him lifting as much as his little finger, while these others who had a very clear perception of the actual necessity were tumbling against each other and sweating desperately over that boat business. Something had gone wrong there at the last moment. It appears that in their flurry they had contrived in some mysterious way to get the sliding bolt of the foremost boat-chock jammed tight, and forthwith had gone out of the remnants of their minds over the deadly nature of that incident. It must have been a pretty sight, the fierce industry of these beggars toiling on a motionless ship that floated quietly in the silence of a world asleep, fighting against time for the freeing of that boat, groveling on all fours, standing up in despair, tugging, pushing, snarling at each other venomously, ready to kill, ready to weep, and only kept from flying at each other's throats by the fear of death that stood silent behind them like an inflexible and cold-eyed taskmaster. Oh, yes! It must have been a pretty sight. He saw it all, he could talk about it with scorn and bitterness; he had a minute knowledge of it by means of some sixth sense, I conclude, because he swore to me he had remained apart without a glance at them and at the boat—without one single glance. An I believe him. I should think he was too busy watching the threatening slant of the ship, the suspended menace discovered in the midst of the most perfect security—fascinated by the sword hanging by a hair over his imaginative head.

"Nothing in the world moved before his eyes, and he could depict to himself without hindrance the sudden swing upwards of the dark skyline, the sudden tilt up of the vast plain of the sea, the swift still rise, the brutal fling, the grasp of the abyss, the struggle without hope, the starlight closing over his head forever like the vault of a tomb—the revolt of his young life—the black end. He could! By Jove! who couldn't? And you must remember he was a finished artist in that peculiar way, he was a gifted poor devil with the faculty of swift and forestalling vision. The sights it showed him had turned him into cold stone from the soles of his feet to the nape of his neck; but there was a hot dance of thoughts in his head, a dance of lame, blind, mute thoughts —a whirl of awful cripples. Didn't I tell you he confessed himself before me as though I had the power to bind and to loose? He burrowed deep, deep, in the hope of my absolution, which would have been of no good to him. This was one of those cases which no solemn deception can palliate, which no man can help; where his very Maker seems to abandon a sinner to his own devices.

"He stood on the starboard side of the bridge, as far as he could get from the struggle for the boat, which went on with the agitation of madness and the stealthiness of a conspiracy. The two Malays had meantime remained holding to the wheel. Just picture to yourselves the actors in that, thank God! unique, episode of the sea, four beside themselves with fierce and secret exertions, and three looking on in complete immobility, above the awnings covering the profound ignorance of hundreds of human beings, with their weariness, with their dreams, with their hopes, arrested, held by an invisible hand on the brink of annihilation. For that they were so, makes no doubt to me: given the state of the ship, this was the deadliest possible description of accident that could happen. These beggars by the boat had every reason to go distracted with funk. Frankly, had I been there I would not have given as much as a counterfeit farthing for the ship's chance to keep above water to the end of each successive second. And still she floated! These sleeping pilgrims were destined to accomplish their whole pilgrimage to the bitterness of some other end. It was as if the Omnipotence whose mercy they confessed had needed their humble testimony on earth for a while longer, and had looked down to make a sign, 'Thou shalt not!' to the ocean. Their escape would trouble me as a prodigiously inexplicable event, did I not know how tough old iron can be—as tough sometimes as the spirit of some men we meet now and then, worn to a shadow and breasting the weight of life. Not the least wonder of these twenty minutes, to my mind, is the behavior of the two helmsmen. They were among the native batch of all sorts brought over from Aden to give evidence at the inquiry. One of them, laboring under intense bashfulness, was very young, and with his smooth, yellow, cheery countenance looked even younger than he was. I remember perfectly Brierly asking him, through the interpreter, what he thought of it at the time, and the interpreter, after a short colloquy, turning to the court with an important air—

" 'He says he thought nothing.'

"The other with patient blinking eyes, a blue cotton handkerchief, faded with much washing, bound with a smart twist over a lot of gray wisps, his face shrunk into grim hollows, his brown skin made darker by a mesh of wrinkles, explained that he had a knowledge of some evil thing befalling the ship, but there had been no order; he could not remember an order; why should he leave the helm? To some further questions he jerked back his spare shoulders, and declared it never came into his mind then that the white men were about to leave the ship through fear of death. He did not believe it now. There might have been secret reasons. He wagged his old chin knowingly. Aha! secret reasons. He was a man of great experience, and he wanted *that* white Tuan to know—he turned towards Brierly, who didn't raise his head—that he had acquired a knowledge of many things by serving white men on the sea for a great number of years —and, suddenly, with shaky excitement he poured upon our spellbound attention a lot of queer-sounding names, names of dead-and-gone skippers, names of forgotten country ships, names of familiar and distorted sound, as if the hand of dumb time had been at work on them for ages. They stopped him at last. A silence fell upon the court,—a silence that remained unbroken for at least a minute, and passed gently into a deep murmur. This episode was *the* sensation of the second day's proceedings— affecting all the audience, affecting everybody except Jim, who was sitting moodily at the end of the first bench, and never looked up at this extraordinary and damning witness that seemed possessed of some mysterious theory of defense.

"So these two lascars stuck to the helm of that ship without steerage-way, where death would have found them if such had been their destiny. The whites did not give them half a glance, had probably forgotten their existence. Assuredly Jim did not remember it. He remembered he could do nothing; he could do nothing, now he was alone. There was nothing to do but to sink with the ship. No use making a disturbance about it. Was there? He waited upstanding, without a sound, stiffened in the idea of some sort of heroic discretion. The first engineer ran cautiously across the bridge to tug at his sleeve.

" 'Come and help! For God's sake, come and help!'

"He ran back to the boat on the points of his toes, and returned directly to worry at his sleeve, begging and cursing at the same time.

" 'I believe he would have kissed my hands,' said Jim, savagely, 'and, next moment, he starts foaming and whispering in my face. "If I had the time I would like to crack your skull for you." I pushed him away. Suddenly he caught hold of me around the neck. Damn him! I hit him. I hit out without looking. "Won't you save your own life —you infernal coward?" he sobs. Coward! He called me an infernal coward! Ha! ha! ha! ha! He called me—ha! ha! ha! . . .'

"He had thrown himself back and was shaking with laughter. I had never in my life heard anything so bitter as that noise. It felt like a blight on all the merriment about donkeys, pyramids, bazaars, or what not. Along the whole dim length of the gallery the voices dropped, the pale blotches of faces turned our way with one accord, and the silence became so profound that the clear tinkle of a teaspoon falling on the tesselated floor of the verandah rang out like a tiny and silvery scream.

" 'You mustn't laugh like this, with all these people about," I remonstrated. 'It isn't nice for them, you know.'

"He gave no sign of having heard at first, but after a while, with a stare that, missing me altogether, seemed to probe the heart of some awful vision, he muttered carelessly—'Oh! they'll think I am drunk.'

"And after that you would have thought from his appearance he would never make a sound again. But—no fear! He could no more stop telling now than he could have stopped living by the mere exertion of his will."

IX

" 'I was saying to myself, "Sink—curse you! Sink!" ' These were the words with which he began again. He wanted it over. He was severely left alone, and he formulated in his head this address to the ship in a tone of imprecation, while at the same time he enjoyed the privilege of witnessing scenes—as far as I can judge—of low comedy. They were still at that bolt. The skipper was ordering. 'Get under and try to lift;' and the others naturally shirked. You understand that to be squeezed flat under the keel of a boat wasn't a desirable position to be caught in if the ship went down suddenly. 'Why don't you—you the strongest?' whined the little engineer. 'Gott-for-dam! I am too thick,' spluttered the skipper in despair. It was funny enough to make angels weep. They stood idle for a moment, and suddenly the chief engineer rushed again at Jim.

" 'Come and help, man! Are you mad to throw your only chance away? Come and help, man! Man! Look there—look!'

"And at last Jim looked astern where the other pointed with maniacal insistence. He saw a silent black squall which had eaten up already one-third of the sky. You know how these squalls come up there about that time of the year. First you see a darkening of the horizon—no more; then a cloud rises opaque like a wall. A straight edge of vapor lined with sickly whitish gleams flies up from the southwest, swallowing the stars in whole constellations; its shadow flies over the waters, and confounds sea and sky into one abyss of obscurity. And all is still. No thunder, no wind, no sound;

not a flicker of lightning. Then in the tenebrous immensity a livid arch appears; a swell or two like undulations of the very darkness run past, and suddenly, wind and rain strike together with a peculiar impetuosity as if they had burst through something solid. Such a cloud had come up while they weren't looking. They had just noticed it, and were perfectly justified in surmising that if in absolute stillness there was some chance for the ship to keep afloat a few minutes longer, the least disturbance of the sea would make an end of her instantly. Her first nod to the swell that precedes the burst of such a squall would be also her last, would become a plunge, would, so to speak, be prolonged into a long dive, down, down to the bottom. Hence these new capers of their fright, these new antics in which they displayed their extreme aversion to die.

" 'It was black, black,' pursued Jim with moody steadiness. 'It had sneaked upon us from behind. The infernal thing! I suppose there had been at the back of my head some hope yet. I don't know. But that was all over anyhow. It maddened me to see myself caught like this. I was angry, as though I had been trapped. I *was* trapped! The night was hot, too, I remember. Not a breath of air.'

"He remembered so well that, gasping in the chair, he seemed to sweat and choke before my eyes. No doubt it maddened him; it knocked him over afresh—in a manner of speaking—but it made him also remember that important purpose which had sent him rushing on that bridge only to slip clean out of his mind. He had intended to cut the lifeboats clear of the ship. He whipped out his knife and went to work slashing as though he had seen nothing, had heard nothing, had known of no one on board. They thought him hopelessly wrong-headed and crazy, but dared not protest noisily against this useless loss of time. When he had done he returned to the very same spot from which he had started. The chief was there, ready with a clutch at him to whisper close to his head, scathingly, as though he wanted to bite his ear—

" 'You silly fool! do you think you'll get the ghost of a show when all that lot of brutes is in the water? Why, they will batter your head for you from these boats.'

"He wrung his hands, ignored, at Jim's elbow. The skipper kept up a nervous shuffle in one place and mumbled, 'Hammer! hammer! Mein Gott! Get a hammer.'

"The little engineer whimpered like a child, but broken arm and all, he turned out the least craven of the lot as it seems, and, actually, mustered enough pluck to run an errand to the engine-room. No trifle, it must be owned in fairness to him. Jim told me he darted desperate looks like a cornered man, gave one low wail, and dashed off. He was back instantly clambering, hammer in hand, and without a pause flung himself at the bolt. The others gave up Jim at once and ran off to assist. He heard the tap, tap of the hammer, the sound of the released chock falling over. The boat was clear. Only then he turned to look—only then. But he kept his distance—he kept his distance. He wanted me to know he had kept his distance; that there was nothing in common between him and these men—who had the hammer. Nothing whatever. It is more than probable he thought himself cut off from them by a space that could not be traversed, by an obstacle that could not be overcome, by a chasm without bottom. He was as far as he could get from them—the whole breadth of the ship.

"His feet were glued to that remote spot and his eyes to their indistinct group bowed together and swaying strangely in the common torment of fear. A hand-lamp lashed to a stanchion above a little table rigged up on the bridge—the *Patna* had no chart-room amidships—threw a light on their laboring shoulders, on their arched and bobbing backs. They pushed at the bow of the boat; they pushed out into the night; the pushed, and would no more look back at him. They had given him up as if indeed he had been too far, too hopelessly separated from themselves, to be worth an appealing word, a glance, or a sign. They had no leisure to look back upon his passive heroism, to feel the sting of his abstention. The boat was heavy; they pushed at the bow with no breath to spare for an encouraging word: but the turmoil of terror that had scattered their self-control like chaff before the wind, converted their desperate exertions into a bit of fooling, upon my word fit for knockabout clowns in a farce. They pushed with their hands, with their heads, they pushed for dear life with all the weight of their bodies, they pushed with all the might of their souls—only no sooner had they succeeded in canting the stem clear of the davit than they would leave off like one man and start a wild scramble into her. As a natural consequence that boat would swing in abruptly, driving them back, helpless and jostling against each other. They would stand nonplussed for a while, exchanging in fierce whispers all the infamous names they could call to mind, and go at it again. Three times this occurred. He described it to me with morose thoughtfulness. He hadn't lost a single movement of that comic business. 'I loathed them. I hated them. I had to look at all that,' he said without emphasis, turning upon me a somberly watchful glance. 'Was ever there any one so shamefully tried!'

"He took his head in his hands for a moment, like a man driven to distraction by some unspeakable outrage. These were things he could not explain to the court—and not even to me; but I would have been little fitted for the reception of his confidences had I not been able at times to understand the pauses between the words. In this assault upon his fortitude there was the jeering intention of a spiteful and vile vengeance; there was an element of burlesque in his ordeal—a degradation of funny grimaces in the approach of death or dishonor.

"He related facts which I have not forgotten, but at this distance of time I couldn't recall his very words: I only remember that he managed wonderfully to convey the brooding rancor of his mind into the bare recital of events. Twice, he told me, he shut his eyes in the certitude that the end was upon him already, and twice he had to open them again. Each time he noted the darkening of the great stillness. The shadow of the silent cloud had fallen upon the ship from the zenith, and seemed to have extinguished every sound of her teeming life. He could no longer hear the voices under the awnings. He told me that each time he closed his eyes a flash of thought showed him that crowd of bodies, laid out for death, as plain as daylight. When he opened them, it was to see the dim struggle of four men fighting like mad with a stubborn boat. 'They would fall back before it time after time, stand swearing at each other, and suddenly make another rush in a bunch. . . . Enough to make you die laughing,' he commented with downcast eyes; then raising them for a moment to my face with a dismal smile, 'I ought to have a merry life of it, by God! for I shall see that funny sight a good many times yet before I die.' His eyes fell again. 'See and hear. . . . See and hear,' he repeated twice, at long intervals, filled by vacant staring.

"He roused himself.

" 'I made up my mind to keep my eyes shut,' he said, 'and I couldn't. I couldn't, and I don't care who knows it. Let them go through that kind of thing before they talk. Just let them—and do better—that's all. The second time my eyelids flew open and my mouth too. I had felt the ship move. She just dipped her bows—and lifted them gently—and slow! everlastingly slow; and ever so little. She hadn't done that much for days. The cloud had raced ahead, and this first swell seemed to travel upon a sea of lead. There was no life in that stir. It managed, though, to knock over something in my head. What would you have done? You are sure of yourself—aren't you? What would you do if you felt now—this minute—the house here move, just move a little under your chair. Leap! By heavens! you would take one spring from where you sit and land in that clump of bushes yonder.'

"He flung his arm out at the night beyond the stone balustrade. I held my peace. He looked at me very steadily, very severe. There could be no mistake: I was being bullied now, and it behooved me to make no sight lest by a gesture or a word I should be drawn into a fatal admission about myself which would have had some bearing on the case. I was not disposed to take any risk of that sort. Don't forget I had him before me, and really he was too much like one of us not to be dangerous. But if you want to know I don't mind telling you that I did, with a rapid glance, estimate the distance to the mass of denser blackness in the middle of the grass plot before the verandah. He exaggerated. I would have landed short by several feet—and that's the only thing of which I am fairly certain.

"The last moment had come, as he thought, and he did not move. His feet remained glued to the planks if his thoughts were knocking about loose in his head. It was at this moment, too, that he saw one of the men around the boat step backwards suddenly, clutch at the air with raised arms, totter and collapse. He didn't exactly fall, he only slid gently into a sitting posture, all hunched up and with his shoulders propped against the side of the engine-room skylight. 'That was the donkey-man. A haggard, white-faced chap with a ragged mustache. Acted third engineer,' he explained.

" 'Dead,' I said. We had heard something of that in court.

" 'So they say,' he pronounced with somber indifference. 'Of course I never knew. Weak heart. The man had been complaining of being out of sorts for some time before. Excitement. Overexertion. Devil only knows. Ha! ha! ha! It was easy to see he did not want to die either. Droll, isn't it? May I be shot if he hadn't been fooled into killing himself! Fooled—neither more nor less. Fooled into it, by heavens! just as I . . . Ah! If he had only kept still; if he had only told them to go to the devil when they came to rush him out of his bunk because the ship was sinking! If he had only stood by with his hands in his pockets and called them names!'

"He got up, shook his fist, glared at me, and sat down.

" 'A chance missed, eh?' I murmured.

" 'Why don't you laugh?" he said, 'A joke hatched in hell. Weak heart! . . . I wish sometimes mine had been.'

"This irritated me. 'Do you?' I exclaimed with deep-rooted irony. 'Yes! Can't *you* understand?' he cried. 'I don't know what more you could wish for,' I said, angrily. He gave me an utterly uncomprehending glance. This shaft had also gone wide of the mark, and he was not the man to bother about stray arrows. Upon my word, he was too unsuspecting; he was not fair game. I was glad that my missile had been thrown away,—that he had not even heard the twang of the bow.

"Of course he could not know at the time the man was dead. The next minute— his last on board—was crowded with a tumult of events and sensations which beat about him like the sea upon a rock. I use the simile advisedly, because from his relation I am forced to believe he had preserved through it all a strange illusion of passiveness, as though he had not acted but had suffered himself to be handled by the infernal powers who had selected him for the victim of their practical joke. The first thing that came to him was the grinding surge of the heavy davits swinging out at last—a jar which seemed to enter his body from the deck through the soles of his feet, and travel up his spine to the crown of his head. Then, the squall being very near now, another and a heavier swell lifted the passive hull in a threatening heave that checked his breath, while his brain and his heart together were pierced as with daggers by panic-stricken screams. 'Let go! For God's sake, let go! Let go! She's going.' Following upon that the boat-falls ripped through the blocks, and a lot of men began to talk in startled tones under the awnings. 'When these beggars did break out, their yelps were enough to wake the dead,' he said. Next after the splashing shock of the boat literally dropped in the water, came the hollow noises of stamping and tumbling in her, mingled with confused shouts: 'Unhook! Unhook! Shove! Unhook! Shove for your life! Here's the squall down on us. . . .' He heard, high above his head, the faint muttering of the wind; he heard below his feet a cry of pain. A lost voice alongside started cursing a swivel hook. The ship began to buzz fore and aft like a disturbed hive, and, as quietly as he was telling me all of this—because just then he was very quiet in attitude, in face, in voice—he went on to say without the slightest warning as it were, 'I stumbled over his legs.'

"This was the first I heard of his having moved at all. I could not restrain a grunt of surprise. Something had started him off at last, but of the exact moment, of the cause that tore him out of his immobility, he knew no more than the uprooted tree knows of the wind that laid it low. All this had come to him: the sounds, the sights, the legs of the dead man—by Jove! The internal joke was being crammed devilishly down his throat, but—look you—he was not going to admit of any sort of swallowing motion in his gullet. It's extraordinary how he could cast upon you the spirit of his illusion. I listened as if to a tale of black magic at work upon a corpse.

" 'He went over sideways, very gently, and this is the last thing I remember seeing on board,' he continued. 'I did not care what he did. It looked as though he were picking himself up: I thought he was picking himself up, of course: I expected him to bolt past me over the rail and drop into the boat after the others. I could hear them knocking about, down there, and a voice as if crying up a shaft called out "George." Then three voices together raised a yell. They came to me separately: one bleated, another screamed, one howled. Ough!'

"He shivered a little, and I beheld him rise slowly as if a steady hand from above had been pulling him out of the chair by his hair. Up, slowly—to his full height, and when his knees had locked stiff the hand let him go, and he swayed a little on his feet. There was a suggestion of awful stillness in his face, in his movements, in his very voice when he said 'They shouted'—and involuntarily I pricked up my ears for the ghost of that shout that would be heard directly through the false effect of silence. 'There were eight hundred people in that ship,' he said, impaling me to the back of my seat with an awful blank stare. 'Eight hundred living people, and they were yelling after the one dead man to come down and be saved. "Jump, George! Jump! Oh, jump!" I stood by with my hand on the davit. I was very quiet. It had come over pitch dark. You could see neither sky nor sea. I heard the boat alongside go bump, bump, and not another sound down there for a while, but the ship under me was full of talking noises. Suddenly the skipper howled, "Mein Gott! The squall! The squall! Shove off!" With the first hiss of rain, and the first gust of wind, they screamed, "Jump, George! We'll catch you! Jump!" The ship began a slow plunge; the rain swept over her like a broken sea; my cap flew off my head; my breath was driven back into my throat. I heard as if I had been on the top of a tower another wild screech, "Geo-o-o-orge! Oh, jump!" She was going down, down, head first under me. . . .

"He raised his hand deliberately to his face, and made picking motions with his fingers as though he had been bothered with cobwebs, and afterwards he looked into the open palm for quite half a second before he blurted out—

" 'I had jumped . . .' He checked himself, averted his gaze. . . . 'It seems,' he added.

"His clear blue eyes turned to me with a piteous stare, and looking at him standing before me, dumbfounded and hurt, I was oppressed by a sad sense of resigned wisdom, mingled with the amused and profound pity of an old man helpless before a childish disaster.

" 'Looks like it,' I muttered.

" 'I knew nothing about it till I looked up,' he explained, hastily. And that's possible, too. You had to listen to him as you would to a small boy in trouble. He didn't know. It had happened somehow. It would never happen again. He had landed partly on somebody and fallen across a thwart. He felt as though all his ribs on his left side must be broken; then he rolled over, and saw vaguely the ship he had deserted uprising above him, with the red side-light glowing large in the rain like a fire on the brow of a hill seen through a mist. 'She seemed higher than a wall; she loomed like a cliff over the boat. . . . I wished I could die,' he cried. 'There was no going back. It was as if I had jumped into a well—into an everlasting deep hole. . . .' "

X

"He locked his fingers together and tore them apart. Nothing could be more true: he had indeed jumped into an everlasting deep hole. He had tumbled from a height he could never scale again. By that time the boat had gone driving forward past the bows. It was too dark just then for them to see each other, and, moreover, they were blinded and half drowned with rain. He told me it was like being swept by a flood through a cavern. They turned their backs to the squall; the skipper, it seems, got an oar over the stern to keep the boat before it, and for two or three minutes the end of the world had come through a deluge in a pitchy blackness. The sea hissed 'like twenty thousand kettles.' That's his simile, not mine. I fancy there was not much wind after the first gust; and he himself had admitted at the inquiry that the sea never got up that night to any extent. He crouched down in the bows and stole a furtive glance back. He saw just one yellow gleam of the masthead light high up and blurred like a last star ready to dissolve. 'It terrified me to see it was still there,' he said. That's what he said. What terrified him was the thought that the drowning was not over yet. No doubt he wanted to be done with that abomination as quickly as possible. Nobody in the boat made a sound. In the dark she seemed to fly, but of course she could not have had much way. Then the shower swept ahead, and the great, distracting, hissing noise followed the rain into distance and died out. There was nothing to be heard then but the slight wash about the boat's sides. Somebody's teeth were chattering violently. A hand touched his back. A faint voice said, 'You there?' Another cried out, shakily, 'She's gone!' and they all stood up together to look astern. They saw no lights. All was black. A thin cold drizzle was driving into their faces. The boat lurched slightly. The teeth chattered faster, stopped, and began again twice before the man could master his shiver sufficiently to say, 'Ju-ju-st in ti-ti-me. . . . Brrrr.' He recognized the voice of the chief engineer saying surlily, 'I saw her go down. I happened to turn my head.' The wind had dropped almost completely.

"They watched in the dark with their heads half turned to windward as if expecting to hear cries. At first he was thankful the night had covered up the scene before his eyes, and then to know of it and yet to have seen and heard nothing appeared somehow the culminating-point of an awful misfortune. 'Strange, isn't it?' he murmured, interrupting himself in his disjointed narrative.

"It did not seem so strange to me. He must have had an unconscious conviction that the reality could not be half as bad, not half as anguishing, appalling, and vengeful as the created terror of his imagination. I believe that, in this first moment, his heart was wrung with all the suffering, that his soul knew the accumulated savor of all the fear, all the horror, all the despair of eight hundred human beings pounced upon in the night by a sudden and violent death, else why should he have said, 'It seemed to me that I must jump out of that accursed boat and swim back to see—half a mile— more—any distance—to the very spot . . .'? Why this impulse? Do you see the significance? Why back to the very spot? Why not drown alongside—if he meant drowning? why back to the very spot, to see—as if his imagination had to be soothed by the assurance that all was over before death could bring relief? I defy any one of you to offer another explanation. It was one of those bizarre and exciting glimpses through the fog. It was an extraordinary disclosure. He let it out as the most natural thing one could say. He fought down that impulse and then he became conscious of the silence. He mentioned this to me. A silence of the sea, of the sky, merged into one indefinite immensity still as death around these saved, palpitating lives. 'You might have heard a pin drop in the boat,' he said with a queer contraction of his lips, like a man trying to master his sensibilities while relating some extremely moving fact. A silence! God alone, who had willed him as he was, knows what he made of it in his heart. 'I don't think any spot on earth could be so still,' he said. 'You couldn't distinguish the sea from the sky; there was nothing to see and nothing to hear. Not a glimmer, not a shape, not a sound. You could have believed that every bit of dry land had gone to the bottom; that every man on earth but I and these beggars in the boat had got drowned.' He leaned over the table with his knuckles propped amongst coffee-cups, liqueur-glasses, cigar-ends. 'I seemed to believe it. Everything was gone and—all was over . . .' he fetched a deep sigh . . . 'with me.' "

Marlow sat up abruptly and flung away his cheroot with force. It made a darting red trail like a toy rocket fired through the drapery of creepers. Nobody stirred.

"Hey, what do you think of it?" he cried with sudden animation. "Wasn't he true to himself, wasn't he? His saved life was over for want of ground under his feet, for want of sights for his eyes, for want of voices in his ears. Annihilation—hey! And all the time it was only a clouded sky, a sea that did not break, the air that did not stir. Only a night; only a silence.

"It lasted for a while, and then they were suddenly and unanimously moved to make a noise over their escape. 'I knew from the first she would go.' 'Not a minute too soon.' 'A narrow squeak, b'gosh!' He said nothing, but the breeze that had dropped came back, a gentle draft freshened steadily, and the sea joined its murmuring voice to this talkative reaction succeeding the dumb moments of awe. She was gone! She was gone! Not a doubt of it. Nobody could have helped. They repeated the same words over and over again as though they couldn't stop themselves. Never doubted she would go. The lights were gone. No mistake. The lights were gone. Couldn't expect anything else. She had to go. . . . He noticed that they talked as though they had left behind them nothing but an empty ship. They concluded she would not have been long when she once started. It seemed to cause them some sort of satisfaction. They assured each other that she couldn't have been long about it—'Just shot down like a flat-iron.' The chief engineer declared that the masthead light at the moment of sinking seemed to drop 'like a lighted match you throw down.' At this the second laughed hysterically. 'I am g-g-glad, I am gla-a-ad.' His teeth went on 'like an electric rattle,' said Jim, 'and all at once he began to cry. He wept and blubbered like a child, catching his breath and sobbing. "Oh, dear! oh, dear! oh, dear!" He would be quiet for a while and start suddenly, "Oh, my poor arm! oh, my poor a-a-a-arm!" I felt I could knock him down. Some of them sat in the stern-sheets. I could just make out their shapes. Voices came to me, mumble, mumble, grunt, grunt. All this seemed very heard to bear. I was cold, too. And I could do nothing. I thought that if I moved I would have to go over the side and . . .'

"His hand groped stealthily, came in contact with a liqueur-glass, and was withdrawn suddenly as if it had touched a red-hot coal. I pushed the bottle slightly. 'Won't you have some more?' I asked. He looked at me angrily. 'Don't you think I can tell you what there is to tell without screwing myself up?' he asked. The squad of globetrotters had gone to bed. We were alone but for a vague white form erect in the shadow, that, being looked at, cringed forward, hesitated, backed away silently. It was getting late, but I did not hurry my guest.

"In the midst of his forlorn state he heard his companions begin to abuse some one. 'What kept you from jumping, you lunatic?' said a scolding voice. The chief engineer left the stern-sheets, and could be heard clambering forward as if with hostile intentions against 'the greatest idiot that ever was.' The skipper shouted with rasping effort offensive epithets from where he sat at the oars. He lifted his head at that uproar, and heard the name 'George,' while a hand in the dark struck him on the breast. 'What have you got to say for yourself, you fool?' queried somebody, with a sort of virtuous fury. 'They were after me,' he said. 'They were abusing me—abusing me . . . by the name of George.'

"He paused to stare, tried to smile, turned his eyes away and went on. 'That little second puts his head right under my nose, "Why, it's that blasted mate!" "What!" howls the skipper from the other end of the boat. "No!" shrieks the chief. And he, too, stopped to look at my face.'

"The wind had left the boat suddenly. The rain began to fall again, and the soft, uninterrupted, a little mysterious sound with which the sea receives a shower arose on all sides in the night. 'They were too taken aback to say anything more at first,' he narrated steadily, 'and what could I have to say to them?' He faltered for a moment, and made an effort to go on. 'They called me horrible names.' His voice, sinking to a whisper, now and then would leap up suddenly, hardened by the passion of scorn, as though he had been talking of secret abominations. 'Never mind what they called me,' he said, grimly. 'I could hear hate in their voices. A good thing, too. They could not forgive me for being in that boat. They hated it. It made them mad. . . .' He laughed short. . . . 'But it kept me from—Look! I was sitting with my arms crossed, on the gunwale! . . .' He perched himself smartly on the edge of the table and crossed his arms. . . . 'Like this—see? One little tilt backwards and I would have been gone—after the others. One little tilt—the least bit—the least bit.' He frowned, and tapping his forehead with the tip of his middle finger, 'It was there all the time,' he said, impressively. 'All the time—that notion. And the rain—cold, thick, cool as melted snow—colder—on my thin cotton clothes—I'll never be so cold again in my life, I know. And the sky was black, too—all black. Not a star, not a light anywhere. Nothing outside that confounded boat and those two yapping before me like a couple of mean mongrels at a treed thief. Yap! yap! "What you doing here? You're a fine sort! Too much of a bloomin' gentleman to put his hand to it. Come out of your trance, did you? To sneak in? Did you?" Yap! yap! "You ain't fit to live!" Yap! yap! Two of them together trying to out-bark each other. The other would bay from the stern through the rain—couldn't see him—couldn't make out—some of his filthy jargon. Yap! yap! Bow-ow-ow-ow-ow! Yap! yap! It was sweet to hear them; it kept me alive, I tell you. It saved my life. At it they went, as if trying to drive me overboard with the noise! . . . "I wonder you had pluck enough to jump. You ain't wanted here. If I had known who it was, I would have tipped you over—you skunk. What have you done with the other? Where did you get the pluck to jump—you coward? What's to prevent us three from firing you overboard?" . . . They were out of breath; the shower passed away upon the sea. Then nothing. There was nothing around the boat, not even a sound. Wanted to see me overboard, did they? Upon my soul! I think they would have had their wish if they had only kept quiet. Fire me overboard! Would they! "Try," I said. "I would for twopence." "Too good for you," they screeched together. It was so dark that it was only when one or the other of them moved that I was quite sure of seeing him. By heavens! I only wish they had tried.'

"I couldn't help exclaiming, 'What an extraordinary affair.'

" 'Not bad—eh?' he said, as if in some sort astounded. 'They pretended to think I had done away with that donkey-man for some reason or other. Why should I? And how the devil was I to know? Didn't I get somehow into that boat? into that boat—I . . .' The muscles around his lips contracted into an unconscious grimace that tore through the mask of his usual expression—something violent, short-lived, and illuminating like a twist of lightning that admits the eye for an instant into the secret convolutions of a cloud. 'I did. I was plainly there with them—wasn't I? Isn't it awful a man should be driven to do a thing like that—and be responsible? What did I know about their George they were howling after? I remembered I had seen him curled up on the deck. "Murdering coward!" the chief kept on calling me. He didn't seem able to remember any other two words. I didn't care, only his noise began to worry me. "Shut up," I said. At that he collected himself for a confounded screech. "You killed him. You killed him." "No," I shouted, "but I will kill you directly." I jumped up, and he fell backwards over a thwart with an awful loud thump. I don't know why. Too dark. Tried to step back, I suppose. I stood still facing aft, and the wretched little second began to whine, "You ain't going to hit a chap with a broken arm—and you call yourself a gentleman, too." I heard a heavy tramp—one—two—and wheezy grunting. The other beast was coming at me, clattering his oar over the stern. I saw him moving, big, big—as you see a man in a mist, in a dream. "Come on," I cried. I would have tumbled him over like a bale of shakings. He stopped, muttered to himself, and went back. Perhaps he had heard the wind. I didn't. It was the last heavy gust we had. He went back to his oar. I was sorry. I would have tried to—to . . .'

"He opened and closed his curved fingers, and his hands had an eager and cruel flutter. 'Steady, steady,' I murmured.

" 'Eh? What? I am not excited,' he remonstrated, awfully hurt, and with a convulsive jerk of his elbow knocked over the cognac-bottle. I started forward, scraping my chair. He bounced off the table as if a mine had been exploded behind his back, and half turned before he alighted, crouching on his feet to show me a startled pair of eyes and a face white about the nostrils. A look of intense annoyance succeeded. 'Awfully sorry. How clumsy of me!' he mumbled very vexed, while the pungent odor of spilled alcohol enveloped us suddenly with an atmosphere of a low drinking-bout in the cool, pure darkness of the night. The lights had been put out in the dining-hall; our candle glimmered solitary in the long gallery, and the columns had turned black from pediment to capital. On the vivid stars the high corner of the Harbor Office stood out distinct across the Esplanade, as though the somber pile had glided nearer to see and hear.

"He assumed an air of indifference.

" 'I dare say I am less calm now than I was then. I was ready for anything. These were trifles. . . .'

" 'You had a lively time of it in that boat,' I remarked.

" 'I was ready,' he repeated. 'After the ship's lights had gone, anything might have happened in that boat—anything in the world—and the world no wiser. I felt this, and I was pleased. It was just dark enough, too. We were like men walled up quick in a roomy grave. No concern with anything on earth. Nobody to pass an opinion. Nothing mattered.' For the third time during this conversation he laughed harshly, but there was no one about to suspect him of being only drunk. 'No fear, no law, no sounds, no eyes—not even our own, till—till sunrise at least.'

"I was struck by the suggestive truth of his words. There is something peculiar in a small boat upon the wide seas. Over the lives borne from under the shadow of death there seems to fall the shadow of madness. When your ship fails you, your whole world seems to fail you; the world that made you, restrained you, has taken care of you. It is as if the souls of men floating on an abyss and in touch with immensity had been set free for any excess of heroism, absurdity, or abomination. Of course, as with belief, thought, love, hate, conviction, or even the visual aspect of material things, there are as many shipwrecks as there are men, and in this one there was something abject which made the isolation more complete—there was a villainy of circumstances that cut these men off more completely from the rest of mankind, whose ideal of conduct had never undergone the trial of a fiendish and appalling joke. They were exasperated with him for being a half-hearted shirker: he focused on them his hatred of the whole thing; he would have liked to take a signal revenge for the abhorrent opportunity they had put in his way. Trust a boat on the high seas to bring out the Irrational that lurks at the bottom of every thought, sentiment, sensation, emotion. It was part of the burlesque meanness pervading that particular disaster at sea that they did not come to blows. It was all threats, all a terribly effective feint, a sham from beginning to end, planned by the tremendous disdain of the Dark Powers whose real terrors, always on the verge of triumph, are perpetually foiled by the steadfastness of men. I asked, after waiting for a while, 'Well, what happened?' A futile question. I knew too much already to hope for the grace of a single uplifting touch, for the favor of hinted madness, of shadowed horror. 'Nothing,' he said. 'I meant business, but they meant noise only. Nothing happened.'

"And the rising sun found him just as he had jumped up first in the bows of the boat. What a persistence of readiness! He had been holding the tiller in his hand, too, all the night. They had dropped the rudder overboard while attempting to ship it, and I suppose the tiller got kicked forward somehow while they were rushing up and down that boat trying to do all sorts of things at once so as to get clear of the side. It was a long heavy piece of hard wood, and apparently he had been clutching it for six hours or so. If you don't call that being ready! Can you imagine him, silent and on his feet half the night, his face to the gusts of rain, staring at somber forms, watchful of vague movements, straining his ears to catch rare low murmurs in the stern-sheets! Firmness of courage or effort of fear? What do you think? And the endurance is undeniable, too. Six hours more or less on the defensive; six hours of alert immobility while the boat drove slowly or floated arrested according to the caprice of the wind; while the sea, calmed, slept at last; while the clouds passed above his head; while the sky from an immensity lusterless and black, diminished to a somber and lustrous vault, scintillated with a greater brilliance, faded to the east, paled at the zenith; while the dark shapes blotting the low stars astern got outlines, relief; became shoulders, heads, faces, features,—confronted him with dreary stares, had disheveled hair, torn clothes, blinked red eyelids at the white dawn. 'They looked as though they had been knocking about drunk in gutters for a week,' he described graphically; and then he muttered something about the sunrise being of a kind that foretells a calm day. You know that sailor habit of referring to the weather in every connection. And on my side his few mumbled words were enough to make me see the lower limb of the sun clearing the line of the horizon, the tremble of a vast ripple running over all the visible expanse of the sea, as if the waters had shuddered, giving birth to the globe of light, while the last puff of the breeze would stir the air in a sigh of relief.

" 'They sat in the stern shoulder to shoulder, with the skipper in the middle, like three dirty owls, and stared at me,' I heard him say with an intention of hate that distilled a corrosive virtue into the commonplace words like a drop of powerful poison falling into a glass of water; but my thoughts dwelled upon that sunrise. I could imagine under the pellucid emptiness of the sky these four men imprisoned in the solitude of the sea, the lonely sun, regardless of the speck of life, ascending the clear curve of the heaven as if to gaze ardently from a greater height at his own splendor reflected in the still ocean. 'They called out to me from aft,' said Jim, 'as though we had been chums together. I heard them. They were begging me to be sensible and drop that "blooming piece of wood." Why *would* I carry on so? They hadn't done me any harm—had they? There had been no harm. . . . No harm!'

"His face crimsoned as though he could not get rid of the air in his lungs.

" 'No harm!' he burst out. 'I leave it to you. You can understand. Can't you? You see it—don't you? No harm! Good God! What more could they have done? Oh, yes, I know very well—I jumped. Certainly. I jumped! I told you I jumped; but I tell you they were too much for any man. It was their doing as plainly as if they had reached up with a boathook and pulled me over. Can't you see it? You must see it. Come. Speak—straight out.'

"His uneasy eyes fastened upon mine, questioned, begged, challenged, entreated.

For the life of me I couldn't help murmuring, 'You've been tried.' 'More than is fair,' he caught up, swiftly. 'I wasn't given half a chance—with a gang like that. And now they were friendly—oh, so damnably friendly! Chums, shipmates. All in the same boat. Make the best of it. They hadn't meant anything. They didn't care a hang for George. George had gone back to his berth for something at the last moment and got caught. The man was a manifest fool. Very sad, of course. . . . Their eyes looked at me; their lips moved; they wagged their heads at the other end of the boat—three of them; they beckoned—to me. Why not? Hadn't I jumped? I said nothing. There were no words for the sort of things I wanted to say. If I had opened my lips just then I would have simply howled like an animal. I was asking myself when I would wake up. They urged me aloud to come aft and hear quietly what the skipper had to say. We were sure to be picked up before the evening—right in the track of all the Canal traffic; there was smoke to the northwest now.

" 'It gave me an awful shock to see this faint, faint blur, this low trail of brown mist through which you could see the boundary of sea and sky. I called out to them that I could hear very well where I was. The skipper started swearing, as hoarse as a crow. He wasn't going to talk at the top of his voice for *my* accommodation. "Are you afraid they will hear you on shore?" I asked. He glared as if he would have liked to claw me to pieces. The chief engineer advised him to humor me. He said I wasn't right in my head yet. The other rose astern, like a thick pillar of flesh—and talked—talked. . . .'

"Jim remained thoughtful. 'Well?' I asked. 'What did I care what story they agreed to make up?' he cried, recklessly. 'They could tell what they jolly well liked. It was their business. I knew the story. Nothing they could make people believe could alter it for me. I let him talk, argue—talk, argue. He went on and on and on. Suddenly I felt my legs give way under me. I was sick, tired—tired to death. I let fall the tiller, turned my back on them, and sat down on the foremost thwart. I had enough. They called to me to know if I understood—wasn't it true, every word of it? It was true, by God! after their fashion. I did not turn my head. I heard them palavering together. "The silly ass won't say anything." "Oh, he understands well enough." "Let him be; he will be all right." "What can he do?" What could I do? Weren't we all in the same boat? I tried to be deaf. The smoke had disappeared to the northward. It was a dead calm. They had a drink from the water-breaker, and I drank, too. Afterwards they made a great business of spreading the boat-sail over the gunwales. Would I keep a look-out? They crept under, out of my sight, thank God! I felt weary, weary, done up, as if I hadn't had one hour's sleep since the day I was born. I couldn't see the water for the glitter of the sunshine. From time to time one of them would creep out, stand up to take a look all around, and get under again. I could hear spells of snoring below the sail. Some of them could sleep. One of them at least. I couldn't! All was light, light, and the boat seemed to be falling through it. Now and then I would feel quite surprised to find myself sitting on a thwart. . . .'

"He began to walk with measured steps to and fro before my chair, one hand in his trousers-pocket, his head bent thoughtfully, and his right arm at long intervals raised for a gesture that seemed to put out of his way an invisible intruder.

" 'I suppose you think I was going mad,' he began in a changed tone. 'And well you may, if you remember I had lost my cap. The sun crept all the way from east to west over my bare head, but that day I could not come to any harm, I suppose. The sun could not make me mad. . . .' His right arm put aside the idea of madness. . . . 'Neither could it kill me. . . .' Again his arm repulsed a shadow. . . . '*That* rested with me.'

" 'Did it?' I said, inexpressibly amazed at this new turn, and I looked at him with the same sort of feeling I might be fairly conceived to experienced had he, after spinning around on his heel, presented an altogether new face.

" 'I didn't get brain fever, I did not drop dead either,' he went on. 'I didn't bother myself at all about the sun over my head. I was thinking as coolly as any man that ever sat thinking in the shade. That greasy beast of a skipper poked his big cropped head from under the canvas and screwed his fish eyes up at me. "Donnerwetter! you will die," he growled, and drew in like a turtle. I had seen him. I had heard him. He didn't interrupt me. I was thinking just then that I wouldn't.'

"He tried to sound my thought with an attentive glance dropped on me in passing. 'Do you mean to say you had been deliberating with yourself whether you would die?' I asked in as impenetrable a tone as I could command. He nodded without stopping. 'Yes, it had come to that as I sat there alone,' he said. He passed on a few steps to the imaginary end of his beat, and when he flung around to come back both his hands were thrust deep into his pockets. He stopped short in front of my chair and looked down. 'Don't you believe it?' he inquired with tense curiosity. I was moved to make a solemn declaration of my readiness to believe implicitly anything he thought fit to tell me."

XI

"He heard me out with his head on one side, and I had another glimpse through a rent in the mist in which he moved and had his being. The dim candle spluttered within the ball of glass, and that was all I had to see him by; at his back was the dark night with the clear stars, whose distant glitter disposed in retreating planes lured the eye into the depths of a greater darkness; and yet a mysterious light seemed to show me his boyish head, as if in that moment the youth within him had, for a moment, gleamed and expired. 'You are an awful good sort to listen like this,' he said. 'It does me good. You don't know what it is to me. You don't' . . . words seemed to fail him. It was a distinct glimpse. He was a youngster of the sort you like to see about you; of the sort you like to imagine yourself to have been; of the sort whose appearance claims the fellowship of these illusions you had thought gone out, extinct, cold, and which, as if rekindled at the approach of another flame, give a flutter deep, deep down somewhere, give a flutter of light . . . of heat! . . . Yes; I had a glimpse of him then . . . and it was not the last of that kind. . . . 'You don't know what it is for a fellow in my position to be believed—make a clean breast of it to an elder man. It is so difficult—so awfully unfair—so hard to understand.'

"The mists were closing again. I don't know how old I appeared to him—and how much wise. Not half as old as I felt just then; not half as uselessly wise as I knew myself to be. Surely in no other craft as in that of the sea do the hearts of those already launched to sink or swim go out so much to the youth on the brink, looking with shining eyes upon that glitter of the vast surface which is only a reflection of his own glances full of fire. There is such magnificent vagueness in the expectations that had driven each of us to sea, such a glorious indefiniteness, such a beautiful greed of adventures that are their own and only reward! What we get—well, we won't talk of that; but can one of us restrain a smile? In no other kind of life is the illusion more wide of reality—in no other is the beginning *all* illusion—the disenchantment more swift—the subjugation more complete. Hadn't we all commenced with the same desire, ended with the same knowledge, carried the memory of the same cherished glamour through the sordid days of imprecation? What wonder that when some heavy prod gets home the bond is found to be close; that besides the fellowship of the craft there is felt the strength of a wider feeling—the feeling that binds a man to a child. He was there before me, believing that age and wisdom can find a remedy against the pain of truth, giving me a glimpse of himself as a young fellow in a scrape that is the very devil of a scrape, the sort of scrape graybeards wag at solemnly while they hide a smile. And he had been deliberating upon death—confound him! He had found *that* to meditate about because he thought he had saved his life, while all its glamour had gone with the ship in the night. What more natural! It was tragic enough and funny enough in all conscience to call aloud for compassion, and in what was I better than the rest of us to refuse him my pity? And even as I looked at him the mists rolled into the rent, and his voice spoke—

" 'I was so lost, you know. It was the sort of thing one does not expect to happen to one. It was not like a fight, for instance.'

" 'It was not,' I admitted. He appeared changed as if he had suddenly matured.

" 'One couldn't be sure,' he muttered.

" 'Ah! You were not sure,' I said, and was placated by the sound of a faint sigh that passed between us like the flight of a bird in the night.

" 'Well, I wasn't," he said, courageously. 'It was something like that wretched story they made up. It was not a lie—but it wasn't truth all the same. It was something. . . . One knows a downright lie. There was not the thickness of a sheet of paper between the right and wrong of this affair.'

" 'How much more did you want?' I asked; but I think I spoke so low that he did not catch what I said. He had advanced his argument as though life had been a network of paths separated by chasms. His voice sounded reasonable.

" 'Suppose I had not—I mean to say, suppose I had stuck to the ship? Well. How much longer? Say a minute—half a minute. Come. In thirty seconds, as it seemed certain then, I would have been overboard; and do you think I would not have laid hold of the first thing that came in my way—oar, life-buoy, grating—anything? Wouldn't you?'

" 'And be saved,' I interjected.

" 'I would have meant to be,' he retorted. 'And that's more than I meant when I'

. . . he shivered as if about to swallow some nauseous drug . . . 'jumped,' he pronounced with a convulsive effort, whose stress, as if propagated by the waves of the air, made my body stir a little in the chair. He fixed me with lowering eyes. 'Don't you believe me?' he cried. 'I swear! . . . Confound it! You got me here to talk, and . . . You must! . . . You said you would believe.' 'Of course I do,' I protested in a matter-of-fact tone which produced a calming effect. 'Forgive me,' he said. 'Of course I wouldn't have talked to you about all this if you had not been a gentleman. I ought to have known . . . I am—I am—a gentleman, too . . .' 'Yes, yes,' I said, hastily. He was looking me squarely in the face and withdrew his gaze slowly. 'Now you understand why I didn't after all . . . didn't go out in that way. I wasn't going to be frightened at what I had done. And, anyhow, if I had stuck to the ship I would have done my best to be saved. Men have been known to float for hours—in the open sea —and be picked up not much the worse for it. I might have lasted it out better than many others. There's nothing the matter with *my* heart.' He withdrew his right fist from his pocket, and the blow he struck on his chest resounded like a muffled detonation in the night.

" 'No,' I said. He meditated, with his legs slightly apart and his chin sunk. 'A hair's breadth,' he muttered. 'Not the breadth of a hair between this and that. And at the time . . .'

" 'It is difficult to see a hair at midnight,' I put in, a little viciously I fear. Don't you see what I mean by the solidarity of the craft? I was aggrieved against him, as though he had cheated me—me!—of a splendid opportunity to keep up the illusion of my beginnings, as though he had robbed our common life of the last spark of its glamour. 'And so you cleared out—at once.'

" 'Jumped,' he corrected me incisively. 'Jumped—mind!' he repeated, and I wondered at the evident but obscure intention. 'Well, yes! Perhaps I could not see then. But I had plenty of time and any amount of light in that boat. And I could think, too. Nobody would know, of course, but this did not make it any easier for me. You've got to believe that, too. I did not want all this talk. . . . No . . . Yes . . . I won't lie . . . I wanted it: it is the very thing I wanted—there. Do you think you or anybody could have made me if I . . . I am—I am not afraid to tell. And I wasn't afraid to think either. I looked it in the face. I wasn't going to run away. At first—at night, if it hadn't been for these fellows I might have . . . No! by heavens! I was not going to give them that satisfaction. They had done enough. They made up a story, and believed it for all I know. But I knew the truth, and I would live it down—alone, with myself. I wasn't going to give in to such a beastly unfair thing. What did it prove after all? I was confoundedly cut up. Sick of life—to tell you the truth; but what would have been the good to shirk it—in—in—that way? That was not the way. I believe—I believe it would have—it would have ended—nothing.'

"He had been walking up and down but with the last word he turned short at me.

" 'What do *you* believe?' he asked with violence. A pause ensued, and suddenly I felt myself overcome by a profound and hopeless fatigue, as though his voice had startled me out of a dream of wandering through empty spaces whose immensity had harassed my soul and exhausted my body.

" '. . . Would have ended nothing,' he muttered over me obstinately, after a little while. 'No! the proper thing was to face it out—alone for myself—wait for another chance—find out . . .' "

XII

"All around everything was still as far as the eye could reach. The mist of his feelings shifted between us, as if disturbed by his struggles, and in the rifts of the immaterial veil he would appear to my staring eyes distinct of form and pregnant with vague appeal like a symbolic figure in a picture. The chill air of the night seemed to lie on my limbs as heavy as a slab of marble.

" 'I see,' I murmured, more to prove to myself that I could break my state of numbness than for any other reason.

" 'The *Avondale* picked us up just before sunset,' he remarked, moodily. 'Steamed right straight for us. We had only to sit and wait.'

"After a long interval, he said, 'They told their story.' And again there was that oppressive silence. 'Then only I knew what it was I had made up my mind to,' he added.

" 'You said nothing,' I whispered.

" 'What could I say?' he asked, in the same low tone. . . . 'Shock slight. Stopped the ship. Ascertained the damage. Took measures to get the boats out without creating a panic. As the first boat was lowered ship went down in a squall. Sank like lead. . . . What could be more clear' . . . he hung his head . . . 'and more awful?' His lips quivered while he looked straight into my eyes. 'I had jumped—hadn't I?' he asked, dismayed. 'That's what I had to live down. The story didn't matter.' . . . He clasped his hands for an instant, glanced right and left into the gloom: 'It was like cheating the dead,' he stammered.

" 'And there were no dead,' I said.

"He went away from me at this. That is the only way I can describe it. In a moment I saw his back close to the balustrade. He stood there for some time, as if admiring the purity and the peace of the night. Some flowering-shrub in the garden below spread its powerful scent through the damp air. He returned to me with hasty steps.

" 'And that did not matter,' he said, as stubbornly as you please.

" 'Perhaps not,' I admitted. I began to have a notion he was too much for me. After all, what did *I* know?

" 'Dead or not dead, I could not get clear,' he said. 'I had to live; hadn't I?'

" 'Well, yes—if you take it in that way,' I mumbled.

" 'I was glad, of course,' he threw out carelessly with his mind fixed on something else. 'The exposure,' he pronounced, slowly, and lifted his head. 'Do you know what was my first thought when I heard? I was relieved. I was relieved to learn that those shouts—did I tell you I heard shouts? No? Well, I did. Shouts for help . . . blown

along with the drizzle. Imagination I suppose. And yet I can hardly . . . How stupid.
. . . The others did not. I asked them afterwards. They all said No. No? And I was
hearing them even then! I might have known—but I didn't think—I only listened.
Very faint screams—day after day. Then that little half-caste chap here came up and
spoke to me. "The *Patna* . . . French gunboat . . . towed successfully to Aden . . .
Investigation . . . Marine Office . . . Sailors' Home . . . arrangements made for
your board and lodging!" I walked along with him, and I enjoyed the silence. So there
had been no shouting. Imagination. I had to believe him. I could hear nothing any
more. I wonder how long I could have stood it. It was getting worse, too . . . I mean
—louder.'

"He fell into thought.

" 'And I had heard nothing! Well—so be it. But the lights! The lights did go! We
did not see them. They were not there. If they had been, I would have swam back—I
would have gone back and shouted along side—I would have begged them to take me
on board. . . . I would have had my chance. . . . You doubt me? . . . How do
you know how I felt? . . . What right have you to doubt? . . . I very nearly did it
as it was—do you understand?' His voice fell. 'There was not a glimmer—not a
glimmer,' he protested, mournfully. 'Don't you understand that if there had been, you
would not have seen me here? You see me—and you doubt.'

"I shook my head negatively. This question of the lights being lost sight of when
the boat could not have been more than a quarter of a mile from the ship was a matter
for much discussion. Jim stuck to it that there was nothing to be seen after the first
shower had cleared away; and the others had affirmed the same thing to the officers of
the *Avondale.* Of course people shook their heads and smiled. One old skipper who sat
near me in court tickled my ear with his white beard to murmur, 'Of course they
would lie.' As a matter of fact nobody lied; not even the chief engineer with his story
of the masthead light dropping like a match you throw down. Not consciously, at
least. A man with his liver in such a state might very well have seen a floating spark in
the corner of his eye when stealing a hurried glance over his shoulder. They had seen
no light of any sort though they were well within range, and they could only explain
this in one way: the ship had gone down. It was obvious and comforting. The foreseen
fact coming so swiftly had justified their haste. No wonder they did not cast about for
any other explanation. Yet the true one was very simple, and as soon as Brierly
suggested it the court ceased to bother about the question. If you remember, the ship
had been stopped and was lying with her head on the course steered through the night,
with her stern canted high and her bows brought low down in the water through the
filling of the fore-compartment. Being thus out of trim, when the squall struck her a
little on the quarter, she swung head to wind as sharply as though she had been at
anchor. By this change in her position all her lights were in a very few moments shut
off from the boat to leeward. It may very well be that, had they been seen, they would
have had the effect of a mute appeal—that their glimmer lost in the darkness of the
cloud would have had the mysterious power of the human glance that can awaken the
feelings of remorse and pity. It would have said, 'I am here—still here' . . . and what

more can the eye of the most forsaken of human beings say? But she turned her back on them as if in disdain of their fate: she had swung around, burdened, to glare stubbornly at the new danger of the open sea which she so strangely survived to end her days in a breaking-up yard, as if it had been her recorded fate to die obscurely under the blows of many hammers. What were the various ends their destiny provided for the pilgrims I am unable to say; but the immediate future brought, at about nine o'clock next morning, a French gunboat homeward bound from Réunion. The report of her commander was public property. He had swept a little out of his course to ascertain what was the matter with that steamer floating dangerously by the head upon a still and hazy sea. There was an ensign, union down, flying at her main gaff (the serang had the sense to make a signal of distress at daylight); but the cooks were preparing the food in the cooking-boxes forward as usual. The decks were packed as close as a sheep-pen: there were people perched all along the rails, jammed on the bridge in a solid mass; hundreds of eyes stared, and not a sound was heard when the gunboat ranged abreast, as if all that multitude of lips had been sealed by a spell.

"The Frenchman hailed, could get no intelligible reply, and after ascertaining through his binoculars that the crowd on deck did not look plague-stricken, decided to send a boat. Two officers came on board, listened to the serang, tried to talk with the Arab, couldn't make head or tail of it: but of course the nature of the emergency was obvious enough. They were also very much struck by discovering a white man, dead and curled up peacefully on the bridge. '*Fort intrigués par ce cadavre,*' as I was informed a long time after by an elderly French lieutenant whom I came across one afternoon in Sydney, by the merest chance, in a sort of café, and who remembered the affair perfectly. Indeed this affair, I may notice in passing, has an extraordinary power of defying the shortness of memories and the length of time: it seemed to live, with a sort of uncanny vitality, in the minds of men, on the tips of their tongues. I've had the questionable pleasure of meeting it often, years afterwards, thousands of miles away, emerging from the remotest possible talk, coming to the surface of the most distant allusions. Has it not turned up tonight between us? And I am the only seaman here. I am the only one to whom it is a memory. And yet it has made its way out! But if two men who, unknown to each other, knew of this affair met accidentally on any spot of this earth, the thing would pop up between them as sure as fate, before they parted. I had never seen that Frenchman before, and at the end of an hour we had done with each other for life: he did not seem particularly talkative either; he was a quiet, massive chap in a creased uniform sitting drowsily over a tumbler half full of some dark liquid. His shoulder-straps were a bit tarnished, his clean-shaved cheeks were large and sallow; he looked like a man who would be given to taking snuff—don't you know? I won't say he did; but the habit would have fitted that kind of man. It all began by his handing me a number of *Home News*, which I didn't want, across the marble table. I said, 'Merci.' We exchanged a few apparently innocent remarks, and suddenly, before I knew how it had come about, we were in the midst of it, and he was telling me how much they had been 'intrigued by that corpse.' It turned out he had been one of the boarding officers.

"In the establishment where we sat one could get a variety of foreign drinks which were kept for the visiting naval officers, and he took a sip of the dark medical-looking stuff, which probably was nothing more nasty than *cassis à l'eau*, and glancing with one eye into the tumbler, shook his head slightly. '*Impossible de comprendre—vous concevez*,' he said, with a curious mixture of unconcern and thoughtfulness. I could very easily conceive how impossible it had been for them to understand. Nobody in the gunboat knew enough English to get hold of the story as told by the serang. There was a good deal of noise, too, around the two officers. 'They crowded upon us. There was a circle around that dead man (*autour de ce mort*),' he described. 'One had to attend to the most pressing. These people were beginning to agitate themselves—*Parbleu!* A mob like that —don't you see?' he interjected with philosophic indulgence. As to the bulkhead, he had advised his commander that the safest thing was to leave it alone, it was so villainous to look at. They got two hawsers on board promptly (*en toute hâte*) and took the *Patna* in tow—stern foremost at that—which, under the circumstances, was not so foolish, since the rudder was too much out of the water to be of any great use for steering, and this maneuver eased the strain on the bulkhead, whose state, he expounded with stolid glibness, demanded the greatest care (*éxigeait les plus grands ménagements*). I could not help thinking that my new acquaintance must have had a voice in most of these arrangements: he looked a reliable officer, no longer very active, and he was seamanlike, too, in a way, though, as he sat there, with his thick fingers clasped lightly on his stomach, he reminded you of one of those snuffy, quiet village priests, into whose ears are poured the sins, the sufferings, the remorse of peasant generations, on whose faces the placid and simple expression is like a veil thrown over the mystery of pain and distress. He ought to have had a threadbare black *soutane* buttoned smoothly up to his ample chin, instead of a frockcoat with shoulder-straps and brass buttons. His broad bosom heaved regularly while he went on telling me that it had been the very devil of a job, as doubtless (*sans doute*) I could figure to myself in my quality of the seaman (*en votre qualité de marin*). At the end of the period he inclined his body slightly towards me, and, pursing his shaved lips, allowed the air to escape with a gentle hiss. 'Luckily,' he continued, 'the sea was level like this table, and there was no more wind than there is here.' . . . The place struck me as indeed intolerably stuffy, and very hot; my face burned as though I had been young enough to be embarrassed and blushing. They had directed their course, he pursued, to the nearest English port '*naturellement*,' where their responsibility ceased '*Dieu merci.*' . . . He blew out his flat cheeks a little. . . . 'Because, mind you (*notez bien*), all the time of towing we had two quartermasters stationed with axes by the hawsers, to cut us clear of our tow in case she . . .' He fluttered downwards his heavy eyelids, making his meaning as plain as possible. . . . 'What would you! One does what one can (*on fait ce qu'on peut*),' and for a moment he managed to invest his ponderous immobility with an air of resignation. 'Two quartermasters—thirty hours—always there. Two!' he repeated, lifting up his right hand a little, and exhibiting two fingers. This was absolutely the first gesture I saw him make. It gave me the opportunity to 'note' a starred scar on the back of his hand—effect of a gunshot clearly; and, as if my sight had been made more acute by this discovery, I perceived also the seam of an old wound, beginning a little below the temple and going out of sight under the short gray hair at the side of his head—the graze of a spear or the cut of a saber. He clasped his hands on his stomach again. 'I remained on board that—that—my memory is going (*s'en va*). *Ah! Patt-nà. C'est bien ça. Patt-nà. Merci.* It is droll how one forgets. I stayed on that ship thirty hours. . . .'

" 'You did!' I exclaimed. Still gazing at his hands, he pursed his lips a little, but this time made no hissing sound. 'It was judged proper,' he said, lifting his eyebrows dispassionately, 'that one of the officers should remain to keep an eye open (*pour ouvrir l'oeil*)' . . . he sighed idly . . . 'and for communicating by signals with the towing ship—do you see?—and so on. For the rest, it was my opinion, too. We made our boats ready to drop over—and I also on that ship took measures. . . . *Enfin!* One has done one's possible. It was a delicate position. Thirty hours. They prepared me some food. As for the wine—go and whistle for it—not a drop.' In some extraordinary way, without any marked change in his inert attitude and in the placid expression of his face, he managed to convey the idea of profound disgust. 'I—you know—when it comes to eating without my glass of wine—I am nowhere.'

"I was afraid he would enlarge upon the grievance, for he didn't stir a limb or twitch a feature, he made one aware how much he was irritated by the recollection. But he seemed to forget all about it. They delivered their charge to the 'port authorities,' as he expressed it. He was struck by the calmness with which it had been received. 'One might have thought they had such a droll find (*drôle de trouvaille*) brought them every day. You are extraordinary—you others,' he commented, with his back propped against the wall, and looking himself as incapable of an emotional display as a sack of meal. There happened to be a man-of-war and an Indian Marine steamer in the harbor at the time, and he did not conceal his admiration of the efficient manner in which the boats of these two ships cleared the *Patna* of her passengers. Indeed his torpid demeanor concealed nothing: it had that mysterious, almost miraculous, power of producing striking effects by means impossible of detection which is the last word of the highest art. 'Twenty-five minutes—watch in hand—twenty-five, no more.' . . . He unclasped and clasped again his fingers without removing his hands from his stomach, and made it infinitely more effective than if he had thrown up his arms to heaven in amazement. . . . 'All that lot (*tout ce monde*) on shore—with their little affairs— nobody left but a guard of seamen (*marins de l'État*) and that interesting corpse (*cet intéressant cadavre*). Twenty-five minutes.' . . . With downcast eyes and his head tilted slightly on one side he seemed to roll knowingly on his tongue the savor of a smart bit of work. He persuaded one without any further demonstration that his approval was eminently worth having, and resuming his hardly interrupted immobility, he went on to inform me that, being under orders to make the best of their way to Toulon, they left in two hours' time, 'so that (*de sorte que*) there are many things in this incident of my life (*dans cet épisode de ma vie*) which have remained obscure.' "

XIII

"After these words, and without a change of attitude, he, so to speak, submitted himself passively to a state of silence. I kept him company; and suddenly, but not abruptly, as if the appointed time had arrived for his moderate and husky voice to come out of his immobility, he pronounced, *'Mon Dieu!* how the time passes!' Nothing could have been more commonplace than this remark; but its utterance coincided for me with a moment of vision. It's extraordinary how we go through life with eyes half shut, with dull ears, with dormant thoughts. Perhaps it's just as well; and it may be that it is this very dullness that makes life to the incalculable majority so supportable and so welcome. Nevertheless, there can be but few of us who had never known one of these rare moments of awakening when we see, hear, understand ever so much— everything—in a flash—before we fall back again into our agreeable somnolence. I raised my eyes when he spoke, and I saw him as though I had never seen him before. I saw his chin sunk on his breast, the clumsy folds of his coat, his clasped hands, his motionless pose, so curiously suggestive of his having been simply left there. Time had passed indeed: it had overtaken him and gone ahead. It had left him hopelessly behind with a few poor gifts: the iron-gray hair, the heavy fatigue of the tanned face, two scars, a pair of tarnished shoulder-straps; one of those steady, reliable men who are the raw material of great reputations, one of those uncounted lives that are buried without drums and trumpets under the foundations of monumental successes. 'I am now third lieutenant of the *Victorieuse'* (she was the flagship of the French Pacific squadron at the time), he said, detaching his shoulders from the wall a couple of inches to introduce himself. I bowed slightly on my side of the table, and told him I commanded a merchant vessel at present anchored in Ruschcutters' Bay. He had 'remarked' her,—a pretty little craft. He was very civil about it in his impassive way. I even fancy he went the length of tilting his head in compliment as he repeated, breathing visibly the while, 'Ah, yes. A little craft painted black—very pretty—very pretty *(très coquet).'* After a time he twisted his body slowly to face the glass door on our right. 'A dull town *(triste ville),'* he observed, staring into the street. It was a brilliant day; a southerly buster was raging, and we could see the passersby, men and women, buffeted by the wind on the sidewalks, the sunlit fronts of the houses across the road blurred by the tall whirls of dust. 'I descended on shore,' he said, 'to stretch my legs a little, but . . .' He didn't finish, and sank into the depths of his repose. 'Pray—tell me,' he began, coming up ponderously, 'what was there at the bottom of this affair—precisely *(au juste)?* It is curious. That dead man, for instance—and so on.'

" 'There were living men, too,' I said; 'much more curious.'

" 'No doubt, no doubt,' he agreed half audibly, then, as if after mature consideration, murmured, 'Evidently.' I made no difficulty in communicating to him what had interested me most in this affair. It seemed as though he had a right to know: hadn't he spent thirty hours on board the *Patna*—had he not taken the succession, so to speak, had he not done 'his possible'? He listened to me, looking more priest-like than ever, and with what—probably on account of his downcast eyes—had the appearance of devout concentration. Once or twice he elevated his eyebrows (but without raising his eyelids), as one would say 'The devil!' Once he calmly exclaimed, 'Ah, bah!' under his breath, and when I had finished he pursed his lips in a deliberate way and emitted a sort of sorrowful whistle.

"In any one else it might have been an evidence of boredom, a sign of indifference; but he, in his occult way, managed to make his immobility appear profoundly responsive, and as full of valuable thoughts as an egg is of meat. What he said at last was nothing more than a 'very interesting,' pronounced politely, and not much above a whisper. Before I got over my disappointment he added, but as if speaking to himself, 'That's it. That *is* it.' His chin seemed to sink lower on his breast, his body to weigh heavier on his seat. I was about to ask him what he meant when a sort of preparatory tremor passed over his whole person, as a faint ripple may be seen upon stagnant water even before the wind is felt. 'And so that poor young man ran away along with the others,' he said, with grave tranquillity.

"I don't know what made me smile: it is the only genuine smile of mine I can remember in connection with Jim's affair. But somehow this simple statement of the matter sounded funny in French. . . . *'S'est enfui avec les autres,'* had said the lieutenant. And suddenly I began to admire the discrimination of the man. He had made out the point at once: he did get hold of the only thing I cared about. I felt as though I were taking professional opinion on the case. His imperturbable and mature calmness was that of an expert in possession of the facts, and to whom one's perplexities are mere child's-play. 'Ah! The young, the young,' he said, indulgently. 'And after all, one does not die of it.' 'Die of what?' I asked, swiftly. 'Of being afraid.' He elucidated his meaning and sipped his drink.

"I perceived that the three last fingers of his wounded hand were stiff and could not move independently of each other, so that he took up his tumbler with an ungainly clutch. 'One is always afraid. One may talk, but . . .' He put down the glass awkwardly. . . . 'The fear, the fear—look you—it is always there.' . . . He touched his breast near a brass button on the very spot where Jim had given a thump to his own when protesting that there was nothing the matter with his heart. I suppose I made some sign of dissent, because he insisted, 'Yes! yes! One talks, one talks; this is all very fine; but at the end of the reckoning one is no cleverer than the next man—and no more brave. Brave! This is always to be seen. I have rolled my hump *(roulé ma bosse),'* he said, using the slang expression with imperturbable seriousness, 'in all parts of the world; I have known brave men—famous ones! *Allez!'* . . . He drank carelessly. . . . 'Brave—you conceive—in the Service—one has got to be—the trade demands it *(le métier veux ça).* Is it not so?' he appealed to me reasonably. *'Eh bien!* Each of them—I say each of them, if he were an honest man—*bien entendu*—would confess that there is a point—there is a point—for the best of us—there is somewhere a point when you let go of everything *(vous lachez tout).* And you have got to live with that truth—do you see? Given a certain combination of circumstances, fear is sure to come. Abominable funk *(un trac épouvantable).* And even for those who do not believe this truth there is fear all the same—the fear of themselves. Absolutely so. Trust me. Yes. Yes. . . . At my age one knows what one is talking about—*que diable?'* . . . He had delivered himself of all this as immovably as though he had been the mouthpiece of abstract wisdom, but at this point he heightened the effect of detachment by beginning to twirl his thumbs slowly. 'It's evident—*parbleu!*' he continued; 'for, make up your mind as much as you like, even a simple headache or a fit of indigestion (*un dérangement d'estomac*) is enough to . . . Take me, for instance—I have made my proofs. *Eh bien!* I, who am speaking to you, once . . .'

"He drained his glass and returned to his twirling. 'No, no; one does not die of it,' he pronounced, finally, and when I found he did not mean to proceed with the personal anecdote, I was extremely disappointed; the more so as it was not the sort of story, you know, one could very well press him for. I sat silent, and he too, as if nothing could please him better. Even his thumbs were still now. Suddenly his lips began to move. 'That is so,' he resumed, placidly. 'Man is born a coward (*l'homme est né poltron*). It is a difficulty—*parbleu!* It would be too easy otherwise. But habit—habit—necessity do you see?—the eye of others—*voilà.* One puts up with it. And then the example of others who are no better than yourself, and yet make good countenance. . . .'

"His voice ceased.

" 'That young man—you will observe—had none of these inducements—at least at the moment,' I remarked.

"He raised his eyebrows forgivingly: 'I don't say; I don't say. The young man in question might have had the best dispositions—the best dispositions,' he repeated, wheezing a little.

" 'I am glad to see you taking a lenient view,' I said. 'His own feeling in the matter was—ah!—hopeful, and . . .'

"The shuffle of his feet under the table interrupted me. He drew up his heavy eyelids. Drew up, I say—no other expression can describe the steady deliberation of the act—and at last was disclosed completely to me. I was confronted by two narrow gray circlets, like two tiny steel rings around the profound blackness of the pupils. The sharp glance, coming from that massive body, gave a notion of extreme efficiency, like a razor-edge on a battle-ax. 'Pardon,' he said, punctiliously. His right hand went up, and he swayed forward. 'Allow me . . . I contended that one may get on knowing very well that one's courage does not come of itself (*ne vient pas tout seul*). There's nothing much in that to get upset about. One truth the more ought not to make life impossible. . . . But the honor—the honor, monsieur! . . . The honor . . . that is real—that is! And what life may be worth when' . . . he got on his feet with a ponderous impetuosity, as a startled ox might scramble up from the grass . . . 'when the honor is gone—*ah ça! par exemple*—I can offer no opinion. I can offer no opinion—because—monsieur—I know nothing of it.'

"I had risen, too, and, trying to throw infinite politeness into our attitudes, we faced each other mutely, like two china dogs on a mantlepiece. Hang the fellow! he had pricked the bubble. The blight of futility that lies in wait for men's speeches had fallen upon our conversation, and made it a thing of empty sounds. 'Very well,' I said, with a disconcerted smile, 'but couldn't it reduce itself to not being found out?' He made as if to retort readily, but when he spoke he had changed his mind. 'This, monsieur, is too fine for me—much above me—I don't think about it.' He bowed heavily over his cap, which he held before him by the peak, between the thumb and the forefinger of his wounded hand. I bowed, too. We bowed together: we scraped out feet at each other with much ceremony, while a dirty specimen of a waiter looked on critically, as though he had paid for the performance. 'Serviteur,' said the Frenchman. Another scrape. 'Monsieur' . . . 'Monsieur' . . . The glass door swung behind his burly back. I saw the southerly buster get hold of him and drive him down wind with his hand to his head, his shoulders braced, and the tails of his coat blown hard against his legs.

"I sat down again alone and discouraged—discouraged about Jim's case. If you wonder that after more than three years it had preserved its actuality, you must know that I had seen him only very lately. I had come straight from Samarang, where I had loaded a cargo for Sydney: an utterly uninteresting bit of business,—what Charley here would call one of my rational transactions—and in Samarang I had seen something of Jim. He was then working for De Jongh, on my recommendation. Water-clerk. 'My representative afloat,' as De Jongh called him. You can't imagine a mode of life more barren of consolation, less capable of being invested with a spark of glamour—unless it be the business of an insurance canvasser. Little Bob Stanton—Charley here knew him well—had gone through that experience. The same who got drowned afterwards trying to save a lady's-maid in the *Sephora* disaster. A case of collision on a hazy morning off the Spanish coast you may remember. All the passengers had been packed tidily into the boats and shoved clear of the ship when Bob sheered alongside again and scrambled back on deck to fetch that girl. How she had been left behind I can't make out; anyhow, she had gone completely crazy—wouldn't leave the ship—held to the rail like grim death. The wrestling-match could be seen plainly from the boats; but poor Bob was the shortest chief mate in the merchant service, and the woman stood five feet ten in her shoes and was as strong as a horse, I've been told. So it went on, pull devil, pull baker, the wretched girl screaming all the time, and Bob letting out a yell now and then to warn his boat to keep clear of the ship. One of the hands told me, hiding a smile at the recollection, 'It was for all the world, sir, like a naughty youngster fighting with his mother.' The same old chap said that 'At the last we could see that Mr. Stanton had given up hauling at the gal, and just stood by looking at her, watchful like. We thought afterwards he must 've been reckoning that, maybe, the rush of water would tear her away from the rail by and by and give him a show to save her. We daren't come alongside for our life; and after a bit the old ship went down all on a sudden with a lurch to starboard—plop. The suck in was something awful. We never saw anything alive or dead come up.' Poor Bob's spell of shore-life had been one of the complications of a love affair, I believe. He fondly hoped he had done with the sea forever, and made sure he had got hold of all the bliss on earth, but it came to canvassing in the end. Some cousin of his in Liverpool put him up to it. He used to tell us his experiences in that line. He made us laugh till we cried, and, not altogether displeased at the effect, undersized and bearded to the waist like a gnome, he would tiptoe among us and say, 'It's all very well for you beggars to laugh, but my immortal soul was shriveled down to the size of a parched pea after a week of that work.' I don't know how Jim's soul accommodated itself to the new conditions of his life—I was kept too busy in getting him something to do that would keep body and soul together —but I am pretty certain his adventurous fancy was suffering all the pangs of starvation. It had certainly nothing to feed upon in this new calling. It was distressing to see him at it, though he tackled it with a stubborn serenity for which I must give him full credit. I kept my eye on his shabby plodding with a sort of notion that it was a punishment for the heroics of his fancy—an expiation for his craving after more glamour than he could carry. He had loved too well to imagine himself a glorious racehorse, and now he was condemned to toil without honor like a costermonger's donkey. He did it very well. He shut himself in, put his head down, said never a word. Very well; very well indeed—except for certain fantastic and violent outbreaks, on the deplorable occasions when the irrepressible *Patna* case cropped up. Unfortunately that scandal of the Eastern seas would not die out. And this is the reason why I could never feel I had done with Jim for good.

"I sat thinking of him after the French lieutenant had left, not, however, in connection with De Jongh's cool and gloomy backshop, where we had hurriedly shaken hands not very long ago, but as I had seen him years before in the last flickers of the candle, alone with me in the long gallery of the Malabar House, with the chill and the darkness of the night at his back. The respectable sword of his country's law was suspended over his head. Tomorrow—or was it today? (midnight had slipped by long before we parted)—the marble-faced police magistrate, after distributing fines and terms of imprisonment in the assault-and-battery case, would take up the awful weapon and smite his bowed neck. Our communion in the night was uncommonly like a last vigil with a condemned man. He was guilty, too. He was guilty—as I had told myself repeatedly, guilty and done for; nevertheless, I wished to spare him the mere detail of a formal execution. I don't pretend to explain the reasons of my desire—I don't think I could; but if you haven't got a sort of notion by this time, then I must have been very obscure in my narrative, or you too sleepy to seize upon the sense of my words. I don't defend my morality. There was no morality in the impulse which induced me to lay before him Brierly's plan of evasion—I may call it—in all its primitive simplicity. There were the rupees—absolutely ready in my pocket and very much at his service. Oh! a loan; a loan of course—and if an introduction to a man (in Rangoon) who could put some work in his way . . . Why! with the greatest pleasure. I had pen, ink, and paper in my room on the first floor. And even while I was speaking I was impatient to begin the letter: day, month, year, 2:30 A.M. . . . for the sake of our old friendship I ask you to put some work in the way of Mr. James So-and-so, in whom, etc., etc. . . . I was even ready to write in that strain about him. If he had not enlisted my sympathies he had done better for himself—he had gone to the very front and origin of that sentiment, he had reached the secret sensibility of my egoism. I am concealing nothing from you, because were I to do so my action would appear more unintelligible than any man's action has the right to be, and—in the second place—tomorrow you shall forget my sincerity along with the other lessons of the past. In this transaction, to speak grossly and precisely, I was the irreproachable man: but the subtle intentions of my immorality were defeated by the moral simplicity of the criminal. No doubt he was selfish, too, but his selfishness had a higher origin, a more lofty aim. I discovered that, say what I would, he was eager to go through the ceremony of execution; and I didn't say much, for I felt that in argument his youth would tell against me heavily: he believed where I had already ceased to doubt. There was something fine in the wildness of his unexpressed, hardly formulated hope. 'Clear out! Couldn't think of it,' he said, with a shake of the head. 'I make you an offer for which I neither demand or expect any sort of gratitude,' I said; 'you shall repay the money when convenient, and . . .' 'Awfully good of you,' he muttered without looking up. I watched him narrowly: the future must have appeared horribly uncertain to him; but he did not falter, as though indeed there had been nothing wrong with his heart. I felt angry—not for the first time that night. 'The whole wretched business,' I said, 'is bitter enough, I should think, for a man of your kind . . .' 'It is, it is,' he whispered twice, with his eyes fixed on the floor. It was heartrending. He towered above the light, and I could see the down on his cheek, the color mantling warm under the smooth skin of his face. Believe me or not, I say it was outrageously heartrending. It provoked me to brutality. 'Yes,' I said; 'and allow me to confess that I am totally unable to imagine what advantage you can expect from this licking of the dregs.' 'Advantage!' he murmured out of his stillness. 'I am dashed if I do,' I said, enraged. 'I've been trying to tell you all there is in it,' he went on, slowly, as if meditating something unanswerable. 'But after all, it is *my* trouble.' I opened my mouth to retort, and discovered suddenly that I'd lost all confidence in myself; and it was as if he, too, had given me up, for he mumbled like a man thinking half aloud. 'Went away . . . went into hospitals. . . . Not one of them would face it. . . . They! . . .' He moved his hand slightly to imply disdain. 'But I've got to get over this thing, and I mustn't shirk any of it or . . . I won't shirk any of it.' He was silent. He gazed as though he had been haunted. His unconscious face reflected the passing expressions of scorn, of despair, of resolution,—reflected them in turn, as a magic mirror would reflect the gliding passage of unearthly shapes. He lived surrounded by deceitful ghosts, by austere shades. 'Oh! nonsense, my dear fellow,' I began. He had a movement of impatience. 'You don't seem to understand,' he said, incisively; then looking at me without a wink, 'I may have jumped, but I don't run away.' 'I meant no offense' I said; and added stupidly, 'Better men than you have found it expedient to run, at times.' He colored all over, while in my confusion I half-choked myself with my own tongue. 'Perhaps so,' he said at last; 'I am not good enough; I can't afford it. I am bound to fight this thing down—I am fighting it *now*.' I got out of my chair and felt stiff all over. The silence was embarrassing, and to put an end to it I imagined nothing better but to remark, 'I had no idea it was so late,' in an airy tone. . . . 'I daresay you have had enough of this,' he said, brusquely: 'and to tell you the truth'—he began to look around for his hat—'so have I.'

"Well! he had refused this unique offer. He had struck aside my helping hand; he was ready to go now, and beyond the balustrade the night seemed to wait for him very still, as though he had been marked down for its prey. I heard his voice. 'Ah! here it is.' He had found his hat. For a few seconds we hung in the wind. 'What will you do after —after . . .' I asked very low. 'Go to the dogs as likely as not,' he answered in a gruff manner. I had recovered my wits in a measure, and judged best to take it lightly. 'Pray remember,' I said, 'that I should like very much to see you again before you go.' 'I don't know what's to prevent you. The damned thing won't make me invisible,' he said with intense bitterness—'no such luck.' And then at the moment of taking leave he treated me to a ghastly muddle of dubious stammers and movements, to an awful display of hesitations. God forgive him—me! He had taken it into his fanciful head that I was likely to make some difficulty as to shaking hands. It was too awful for words. I believe I shouted suddenly at him as you would bellow to a man you saw about to walk over a cliff; I remember our voices being raised, the appearance of a miserable grin on his face, a crushing clutch on my hand, a nervous laugh. The candle spluttered out, and the thing was over at last, with a groan that floated up to me in the dark. He got himself away somehow. The night swallowed his form. He was a horrible bungler. Horrible. I heard the quick crunch-crunch of the gravel under his boots. He was running. Absolutely running, with nowhere to go to. And he was not yet four-and-twenty."

XIV

"I slept little, hurried over my breakfast, and after a slight hesitation gave up my early morning visit to my ship. It was really very wrong of me, because, though my chief mate was an excellent man all around, he was the victim of such black imaginings that if he did not get a letter from his wife at the expected time he would go quite distracted with rage and jealousy, lose all grip on the work, quarrel with all hands, and either weep in his cabin or develop such a ferocity of temper as all but drove the crew to the verge of mutiny. The thing had always seemed inexplicable to me: they had been married thirteen years; I had a glimpse of her once, and, honestly, I couldn't conceive a man abandoned enough to plunge into sin for the sake of such an unattractive person. I don't know whether I have not done wrong by refraining from putting that view before poor Selvin: the man made a little hell on earth for himself, and I also suffered indirectly, but some sort of, no doubt, false delicacy prevented me. The marital relations of seamen would make an interesting subject, and I could tell you instances. . . . However, this is not the place, nor the time, and we are concerned with Jim— who was unmarried. If his imaginative conscience or his pride; if all the extravagant ghosts and austere shades that were the disastrous familiars of his youth would not let him run away from the block, I, who of course can't be suspected of such familiars, was irresistibly impelled to go and see his head roll off. I wended my way towards the court. I didn't hope to be very much impressed or edified, or interested or even frightened—though, as long as there is any life before one, a jolly good fright now and then is a salutary discipline. But neither did I expect to be so awfully depressed. The bitterness of his punishment was in its chill and mean atmosphere. The real significance of crime is in its being a breach of faith with the community of mankind, and from that point of view he was no mean traitor, but his execution was a hole-and-corner affair. There was no high scaffolding, no scarlet cloth (did they have scarlet cloth on Tower Hill? They should have had), no awestricken multitude to be horrified at his guilt and be moved to tears at his fate—no air of somber retribution. There was, as I walked along, the clear sunshine, a brilliance too passionate to be consoling, the streets full of jumbled bits of color like a damaged kaleidoscope: yellow, green, blue, dazzling white, the brown nudity of an undraped shoulder, a bullock-cart with a red canopy, a company of native infantry in a drab body with dark heads marching in dusty laced boots, a native policeman in a somber uniform of scanty cut and belted in patent leather, who looked up at me with orientally pitiful eyes as though his migrating spirit were suffering exceedingly from that unforeseen—what d'ye call 'em?—avatar—incarnation. Under the shade of a lonely tree in the courtyard, the villagers connected with the assault case sat in a picturesque group, looking like a chromo-lithograph of a camp in a book of Eastern travel. One missed the obligatory thread of smoke in the foreground and the pack-animals grazing. A blank yellow wall rose behind overtopping the tree, reflecting the glare. The courtroom was somber, seemed more vast. High up in the dim space the punkahs were swaying short to and fro, to and fro. Here and there a draped figure, dwarfed by the bare walls, remained without stirring among the rows of empty benches, as if absorbed in pious meditation. The plaintiff, who had been beaten, an obese chocolate-colored man with shaved head, one fat breast bare and a bright yellow caste-mark above the bridge of his nose, sat in pompous immobility; only his eyes glittered, rolling in the gloom, and the nostrils dilated and collapsed violently as he breathed. Brierly dropped into his seat looking done up, as though he had spent the night in sprinting on a cinder-track. The pious sailing-ship skipper appeared excited and made uneasy movements, as if restraining with difficulty an impulse to stand up and exhort us earnestly to prayer and repentance. The head of the magistrate, delicately pale under the neatly arranged hair, resembled the head of a hopeless invalid after he had been washed and brushed and propped up in bed. He moved aside the vase of flowers—a bunch of purple with a few pink blossoms on long stalks—and seizing in both hands a long sheet of bluish paper, ran his eye over it, propped his forearms on the edge of the desk, and began to read aloud in an even, distinct, and careless voice.

"By Jove! for all my foolishness about scaffolds and heads rolling off—I assure you it was infinitely worse than a beheading. A heavy sense of finality brooded over all this, unrelieved by the hope of rest and safety following the fall of the ax. These proceedings had all the cold vengefulness of a death-sentence, had all the cruelty of a sentence of exile. This is how I looked at it that morning—and even now I seem to see an undeniable vestige of truth in that exaggerated view of a common occurrence. You may imagine how strongly I felt this at the time. Perhaps it is for that reason that I could not bring myself to admit the finality. The thing was always with me, I was always eager to take opinion on it, as though it had not been practically settled: individual opinion—international opinion—by Jove! That Frenchman's, for instance. His own country's pronouncement was uttered in the passionless and definite phraseology a machine would use, if machines could speak. The head of the magistrate was half hidden by the paper, his brow was like alabaster.

"There were several questions before the Court. The first as to whether the ship was in every respect fit and seaworthy for the voyage. The court found she was not. The next point, I remember, was, whether up to the time of the accident the ship had been navigated with proper and seamanlike care. They said Yes to that, goodness knows why, and then they declared that there was no evidence to show the exact cause of the accident. A floating derelict probably. I myself remember that a Norwegian barque bound out with a cargo of pitch-pine had been given up as missing about that time, and it was just the sort of craft that would capsize in a squall and float bottom up for months—a kind of maritime ghoul on the prowl to kill ships in the dark. Such wandering corpses are common enough in the North Atlantic, which is haunted by all the terrors of the sea,—fogs, icebergs, dead ships bent upon mischief, and long sinister gales that fasten upon one like a vampire till all the strength and the spirit and even hope are gone, and one feels like the empty shell of a man. But there—in those seas— the incident was rare enough to resemble a special arrangement of a malevolent providence, which, unless it had for its object the killing of a donkeyman and the bringing of worse than death upon Jim, appeared an utterly aimless piece of devilry. This view occurring to me took off my attention. For a time I was aware of the magistrate's voice as a sound merely; but in a moment it shaped itself into distinct words . . . 'in utter disregard of their plain duty,' it said. The next sentence escaped me somehow, and then . . . 'abandoning in the moment of danger the lives and property confided to their charge' . . . went on the voice evenly, and stopped. A pair of eyes under the white forehead shot darkly a glance above the edge of the paper. I looked for Jim hurriedly, as though I had expected him to disappear. He was very still —but he was there. He sat pink and fair and extremely attentive. 'Therefore, . . .' began the voice emphatically. He stared with parted lips, hanging upon the words of the man behind the desk. These came out into the stillness wafted on the wind made by the punkahs, and I, watching for their effect upon him, caught only the fragments of official language. . . . 'The Court . . . Gustav So-and-so master . . . native of Germany . . . James So-and-so . . . mate . . . certificates canceled.' A silence fell. The magistrate had dropped the paper, and leaning sideways on the arm of his chair, began to talk with Brierly easily. People started to move out; others were pushing in, and I also made for the door. Outside I stood still, and when Jim passed me on his way to the gate, I caught at his arm and detained him. The look he gave discomposed me, as though I had been responsible for his state: he looked at me as if I had been the embodied evil of life. 'It's all over,' I stammered. 'Yes,' he said, thickly. 'And now let no man . . .' He jerked his arm out of my grasp. I watched his back as he went away. It was a long street, and he remained in sight for some time. He walked rather slow, and straddling his legs a little, as if he had found it difficult to keep a straight line. Just before I lost him I fancied he staggered a bit.

" 'Man overboard,' said a deep voice behind me. Turning around, I saw a fellow I

knew slightly, a West Australian; Chester was his name. He, too, had been looking
after Jim. He was a man with an immense girth of chest, a rugged, clean-shaved face of
mahogany color, and two blunt tufts of iron-gray, thick wiry hairs on his upper lip.
He had been pearler, wrecker, trader, whaler, too, I believe; in his own words—
anything and everything a man may be at sea, but a pirate. The Pacific, north and
south, was his proper hunting-ground; but he had wandered so far afield looking for a
cheap steamer to buy. Lately he had discovered—so he said—a guano island somewhere, but its approaches were dangerous, and the anchorage, such as it was, could not
be considered safe, to say the least of it. 'As good as a gold-mine,' he would exclaim.
'Right bang in the middle of the Walpole Reefs, and if it's true enough that you can
get no holding-ground anywhere in less than forty fathom, then what of that? There
are the hurricanes, too. But it's a first-rate thing. As good as a gold-mine—better! Yet
there's not a fool of them that will see it. I can't get a skipper or a shipowner to go
near the place. So I made up my mind to cart the blessed stuff myself.' . . . This was
what he required a steamer for, and I knew he was just then negotiating enthusiastically with a Parsee firm for an old, brig-rigged, sea-anachronism of ninety horsepower.
We had met and spoken together several times. He looked knowingly after Jim. 'Takes
it to heart?' he asked scornfully. 'Very much,' I said. 'Then he's no good,' he opined.
'What's all the to-do about? A bit of ass's skin. That never yet made a man. You must
see things exactly as they are—if you don't, you may just as well give in at once. You
will never do anything in this world. Look at me. I made it a practice never to take
anything to heart.' 'Yes,' I said, 'you see things as they are.' 'I wish I could see my
partner coming along, that's what I wish to see,' he said. 'Know my partner? Old
Robinson. Yes; *the* Robinson. Don't *you* know? The notorious Robinson. The man
who smuggled more opium and bagged more seals in his time than any loose Johnny
now alive. They say he used to board the sealing-schooners up Alaska way when the
fog was so thick that the Lord God, He alone, could tell one man from another. Holy-
Terror Robinson. That's the man. He is with me in that guano thing. The best chance
he ever came across in his life.' He put his lips to my ear. 'Cannibal?—well, they used
to give him the name years and years ago. You remember the story? A shipwreck on the
west side of Stewart Island; that's right; seven of them got ashore, and it seems they
did not get on very well together. Some men are too cantankerous for anything—don't
know how to make the best of a bad job—don't see things as they are—as they *are*, my
boy! And then what's the consequence? Obvious! Trouble, trouble; as likely as not a
knock on the head; and serve 'em right, too. That sort is the most useful when it's
dead. The story goes that a boat of Her Majesty's ship *Wolverine* found him kneeling
on the kelp, naked as the day he was born, and chanting some psalm-tune or other;
light snow was falling at the time. He waited till the boat was an oar's length from the
shore, and then up and away. They chased him for an hour up and down the boulders,
till a marine flung a stone that took him behind the ear providentially and knocked
him senseless. Alone? Of course. But that's like that tale of sealing-schooners; the Lord
God knows the right and the wrong of that story. The cutter did not investigate much.
They wrapped him in a boat-cloak and took him off as quick as they could, with a

dark night coming on, the weather threatening, and the ship firing recall guns every five minutes. Three weeks afterwards he was as well as ever. He didn't allow any fuss that was made on shore to upset him; he just shut his lips tight, and let people screech. It was bad enough to have lost his ship, and all he was worth besides, without paying attention to the hard names they called him. That's the man for me.' He lifted his arm for a signal to some one down the street. 'He's got a little money, so I had to let him into my thing. Had to! It would have been sinful to throw away such a find, and I was cleaned out myself. It cut me to the quick, but I could see the matter just as it was, and if I *must* share—thinks I—with any man, then give me Robinson. I left him at breakfast in the hotel to come to court, because I've an idea. . . . Ah! Good morning, Captain Robinson. . . . Friend of mine, Captain Robinson.'

"An emaciated patriarch in a suit of white drill, a solah topi with a green-lined rim on a head trembling with age, joined us after crossing the street in a trotting shuffle, and stood propped with both hands on the handle of an umbrella. A white beard with amber streaks hung lumpily down to his waist. He blinked his creased eyelids at me in a bewildered way. 'How do you do? how do you do?' he piped, amiably, and tottered. 'A little deaf,' said Chester aside. 'Did you drag him over six thousand miles to get a cheap steamer?' I asked. 'I would have taken him twice around the world as soon as look at him,' said Chester with immense energy. 'The steamer will be the making of us, my lad. Is it my fault that every skipper and shipowner in the whole of blessed Australasia turns out a blamed fool? Once I talked for three hours to a man in Auckland. "Send a ship," I said, "send a ship. I'll give you half of the first cargo for yourself, free gratis for nothing—just to make a good start." Says he, "I wouldn't do it if there was no other place on earth to send a ship to." Perfect ass, of course. Rocks, currents, no anchorage, sheer cliff to lay to, no insurance company would take the risk, didn't see how he could get loaded under three years. Ass! I nearly went on my knees to him. "But look at the thing as it is," says I. "Damn rocks and hurricanes. Look at it as it is. There's guano there Queensland sugar-planters would fight for—fight for on the quay, I tell you." . . . What can you do with a fool? . . . "That's one of your little jokes, Chester," he says. . . . Joke! I could have wept. Ask Captain Robinson here. . . . And there was another shipowning fellow—a fat chap in a white waistcoat in Wellington, who seemed to think I was up to some swindle or other. "I don't know what sort of fool you're looking for," he says, "but I am busy just now. Good morning." I longed to take him in my two hands and smash him through the window of his own office. But I didn't. I was as mild as a curate. "Think of it," says I. "*Do* think it over. I'll call tomorrow." He grunted something about being "out all day." On the stairs I felt ready to beat my head against the wall from vexation. Captain Robinson here can tell you. It was awful to think of all that lovely stuff lying waste under the sun—stuff that would send the sugar-cane shooting sky-high. The making of Queensland! The making of Queensland! And in Brisbane, where I went to have a last try, they gave me the name of a lunatic. Idiots! The only sensible man I came across was the cabman who drove me about. A broken-down swell he was, I fancy. Hey! Captain

Robinson? You remember I told you about my cabby in Brisbane—don't you? The chap had a wonderful eye for things. He saw it all in a jiffy. It was a real pleasure to talk with him. One evening after a devil of a day among shipowners I felt so bad that, says I, "I must get drunk. Come along; I must get drunk, or I'll go mad." "I am your man," he says; "go ahead." I don't know what I would have done without him. Hey! Captain Robinson.'

"He poked the ribs of his partner. 'He! he! he!' laughed the Ancient, looked aimlessly down the street, then peered at me doubtfully with sad, dim pupils. . . . 'He! he! he!' . . . He leaned heavier on the umbrella, and dropped his gaze on the ground. I needn't tell you I had tried to get away several times, but Chester had foiled every attempt by simply catching hold of my coat. 'One minute. I've a notion.' 'What's your infernal notion?' I exploded at last. 'If you think I am going with you . . .' 'No, no, my boy. Too late, if you wanted ever so much. We've got a steamer.' 'You've got the ghost of a steamer,' I said. 'Good enough for a start—there's no superior nonsense about us. Is there, Captain Robinson?' 'No! no! no!' croaked the old man without lifting his eyes, and the senile tremble of his head became almost fierce with determination. 'I understand you know that young chap,' said Chester, with a nod at the street from which Jim had disappeared long ago. 'He's been having grub with you in the Malabar last night—so I was told.'

"I said that was true, and after remarking that he, too, liked to live well and in style, only that, for the present, he had to be saving of every penny—'none too many for the business! Isn't that so, Captain Robinson?'—he squared his shoulders and stroked his dumpy mustache, while the notorious Robinson, coughing at his side, clung more than ever to the handle of the umbrella, and seemed ready to subside passively into a heap of old bones. 'You see, the old chap has all the money,' whispered Chester, confidentially. 'I've been cleaned out trying to engineer the dratted thing. But wait a bit, wait a bit. The good time is coming.' . . . He seemed suddenly astonished at the signs of impatience I gave. 'Oh, crakee!' he cried; 'I am telling you of the biggest thing that ever was, and you . . .' 'I have an appointment,' I pleaded mildly. 'What of that?' he asked with genuine surprise; 'let it wait.' 'That's exactly what I am doing now,' I remarked; 'hadn't you better tell me what it is you want?' 'Buy twenty hotels like that,' he growled to himself; 'and every joker boarding in them, too—twenty times over.' He lifted his head smartly. 'I want that young chap.' 'I don't understand,' I said. 'He's no good, is he?' said Chester, crisply. 'I know nothing about it,' I protested. 'Why, you told me yourself he was taking it to heart,' argued Chester. 'Well, in my opinion a chap who . . . Anyhow, he can't be much good; but then you see I am on the look-out for somebody, and I've just got a thing that will suit him. I'll give him a job on my island.' He nodded significantly. 'I'm going to dump forty coolies there—if I've got to steal 'em. Somebody must work the stuff. Oh! I mean to act square: wooden shed, corrugated-iron roof—I know a man in Hobart who will take my bill at six months for the materials. I do. Honor bright. Then there's the water-supply. I'll have to fly around and get somebody to trust me for half-a-dozen second-hand iron tanks. Catch rainwater, hey? Let him take charge. Make him supreme boss over the coolies. Good idea, isn't it? What do you say?' 'There are whole years when not a drop of rain falls on Walpole,' I said, too amazed to laugh. He bit his lip and seemed bothered. 'Oh, well, I will fix up something for them—or land a supply. Hang it all! That's not the question.'

"I said nothing. I had a rapid vision of Jim perched on a shadowless rock, up to his knees in guano, with the screams of sea-birds in his ears, the incandescent ball of the sun above his head; the empty sky and the empty ocean all a-quiver, shimmering together in the heat as far as the eye could reach. 'I wouldn't advise my worst enemy . . .' I began. 'What's the matter with you?' cried Chester; 'I mean to give him a good screw—that is, as soon as the thing is set going, of course. It's as easy as falling off a log. Simply nothing to do; two six-shooters in his belt. . . . Surely he wouldn't be afraid of anything forty coolies could do—with two six-shooters and he the only armed man, too! It's much better than it looks. I want you to help me to talk him over.' 'No!' I shouted. Old Robinson lifted his bleared eyes dismally for a moment, Chester looked at me with infinite contempt. 'So you wouldn't advise him?' he uttered, slowly. 'Certainly not,' I answered, as indignant as though he had requested me to help murder somebody; 'moreover, I am sure he wouldn't. He is badly cut up, but he isn't mad as far as I know.' 'He is no earthly good for anything,' Chester mused aloud. 'He would just have done for me. If you only could see a thing as it is, you would see it's the very thing for him. And besides . . . Why! it's the most splendid, sure chance' . . . He got angry suddenly. 'I must have a man. There! . . .' He stamped his foot and smiled unpleasantly. 'Anyhow, I could guarantee the island wouldn't sink under him—and I believe he is a bit particular on that point.' 'Good morning,' I said, curtly. He looked at me as though I had been an incomprehensible fool. . . . 'Must be moving, Captain Robinson,' he yelled suddenly into the old man's ear. 'These Parsee Johnnies are waiting for us to clinch the bargain.' He took his partner under the arm with a firm grip, swung him around, and, unexpectedly, leered at me over his shoulder. 'I was trying to do him a kindness,' he asserted with an air and tone that made my blood boil. 'Thank you for nothing—in his name,' I rejoined. 'Oh! you are devilish smart,' he sneered; 'but you are like the rest of them. Too much in the clouds. See what *you* will do with him.' 'I don't know that I want to do anything with him.' 'Don't you?' he sputtered; his gray mustache bristled with anger, and by his side the notorious Robinson, propped on the umbrella, stood with his back to me, as patient and still as a worn-out cab-horse. 'I haven't found a guano island,' I said. 'It's my belief you wouldn't know one if you were led right up to it by the hand,' he riposted quickly; 'and in this world you've got to see a thing first, before you can make use of it. Got to see it through and through at that, neither more nor less.' 'And get others to see it, too,' I insinuated, with a glance at the bowed back by his side. Chester snorted at me. 'His eyes are right enough—don't you worry. He ain't a puppy.' 'Oh, dear, no!' I said. 'Come along, Captain Robinson,' he shouted, with a sort of bullying deference under the rim of the old man's hat; the Holy Terror gave a submissive little jump. The ghost of a steamer was waiting for them. Fortune on that fair isle! They made a curious pair of Argonauts. Chester strode on leisurely, well set up, portly, and of conquering mien; the other, long, wasted, drooping, and hooked to his arm, shuffled his withered shanks with desperate haste.'"

XV

"I did not start in search of Jim at once, only because I had really an appointment which I could not neglect. Then, as ill-luck would have it, in my agent's office I was fastened upon by a fellow fresh from Madagascar with a little scheme for a wonderful piece of business. It had something to do with cattle and cartridges and a Prince Ravonalo something; but the pivot of the whole affair was the stupidity of some admiral—Admiral Pierre, I think. Everything turned on that, and the chap couldn't find words strong enough to express his confidence. He had globular eyes starting out of his head with a fishy glitter, bumps on his forehead, and wore his long hair brushed back without a parting. He had a favorite phrase which he kept on repeating triumphantly, 'The minimum of risk with the maximum of profit is my motto. What?' He made my head ache, spoiled my tiffin, but got his own out of me all right; and as soon as I had shaken him off, I made straight for the water-side. I caught sight of Jim leaning over the parapet of the quay. Three native boatmen quarreling over five annas were making an awful row at his elbow. He didn't hear me come up, but spun around as if the slight contact of my finger had released a catch. 'I was looking,' he stammered. I don't remember what I said, not much anyhow, but he made no difficulty in following me to the hotel.

"He followed me as manageable as a little child, with an obedient air, with no sort of manifestation, rather as though he had been waiting for me there to come along and carry him off. I need not have been so surprised as I was at his tractability. On all the round earth, which to some seems to big and that others affect to consider as rather smaller than a mustard-seed, he had no place where he could—what shall I say?— where he could withdraw. That's it! Withdraw—be alone with his loneliness. He walked by my side very calm, glancing here and there, and once turned his head to look after a Sidiboy fireman in a cutaway coat and yellowish trousers, whose black face had silky gleams like a lump of anthracite coal. I doubt, however, whether he saw anything, or even remained all the time aware of my companionship, because if I had not edged him to the left here, or pulled him to the right there, I believe he would have gone straight before him in any direction till stopped by a wall or some other obstacle. I steered him into my bedroom, and sat down at once to write letters. This was the only place in the world (unless, perhaps, the Walpole Reef—but that was not so handy) where he could have it out with himself without being bothered by the rest of the universe. The damned thing—as he had expressed it—had not made him invisible, but I behaved exactly as though he were. No sooner in my chair I bent over my writing-desk like a medieval scribe, and, but for the movement of the hand holding the pen, remained anxiously quiet. I can't say I was frightened; but I certainly kept as still as if there had been something dangerous in the room, that at the first hint of a movement on my part would be provoked to pounce upon me. There was not much in the room—you know how these bedrooms are—a sort of four-poster bedstead under a mosquito-net, two or three chairs, the table I was writing at, a bare floor. A glass door opened on an upstairs verandah, and he stood with his face to it, having a hard time with all possible privacy. Dusk fell; I lit a candle with the greatest economy of movement and as much prudence as though it were an illegal proceeding. There is no doubt that he had a very hard time of it, and so had I, even to the point, I must own, of wishing him to the devil, or on Walpole Reef at least. It occurred to me once or twice that, after all, Chester was, perhaps, the man to deal effectively with such a disaster. That strange idealist had found a practical use for it at once—unerring, as it were. It was enough to make one suspect that, maybe, he really could see the true aspect of things that appeared mysterious or utterly hopeless to less imaginative persons. I wrote and wrote; I liquidated all the arrears of my correspondence, and then went on writing to people who had no reason whatever to expect from me a gossipy letter about nothing at all. At times I stole a sidelong glance. He was rooted to the spot, but convulsive shudders ran down his back; his shoulders would heave suddenly. He was fighting, he was fighting—mostly for his breath, as it seemed. The massive shadows, cast all one way from the straight flame of the candle, seemed possessed of gloomy consciousness; the immobility of the furniture had to my furtive eye an air of attention. I was becoming fanciful in the midst of my industrious scribbling; and though, when the scratching of my pen stopped for a moment, there was complete silence and stillness in the room, I suffered from that profound disturbance and confusion of thought which is caused by a violent and menacing uproar—of a heavy gale at sea, for instance. Some of you may know what I mean,—that mingled anxiety, distress, and irritation with a sort of craven feeling creeping in—not pleasant to acknowledge, but which gives a quite special merit to one's endurance. I don't claim any merit for standing the stress of Jim's emotions; I could take refuge in the letters; I could have written to strangers if necessary. Suddenly, as I was taking up a fresh sheet of notepaper, I heard a low sound, the first sound that, since we had ben shut up together, had come to my ears in the dim stillness of the room. I remained with my head down, with my hand arrested. Those who have kept vigil by a sickbed have heard such faint sounds in the stillness of the night watches, sounds wrung from a racked body, from a weary soul. He pushed the glass door with such force that all the panes rang: he stepped out, and I held my breath, straining my ears without knowing what else I expected to hear. He was really taking too much to heart an empty formality which to Chester's rigorous criticism seemed unworthy the notice of a man who could see things as they were. An empty formality; a piece of parchment. Well, well. As to the inaccessible guano deposit, that was another story altogether. One could intelligibly break one's heart over that. A feeble burst of many voices mingled with the tinkle of silver and glass floated up from the dining-room below; through the open door the outer edge of the light from my candle fell on his back faintly; beyond all was black; he stood on the brink of a vast obscurity, like a lonely figure by the shore of a somber and hopeless ocean. There was the Walpole Reef in it—to be sure—a speck in the dark void, a straw for the drowning man. My compassion for him took the shape of the thought that I wouldn't have liked his people to see him at that moment. I found it trying myself. His back was no longer shaken by his gasps; he stood straight as an arrow, faintly visible and still; and the meaning of this stillness sank to the bottom of my soul like lead into the water, and made it so heavy that for a second I wished heartily that the only course left open for me were to pay for his funeral. Even the law had done with him. To bury him would have been such an easy kindness! It would have been so much in accordance with the wisdom of life, which consists in putting out of sight all the reminders of our folly, of our weakness, of our mortality; all that makes against our efficiency—the memory of our failures, the hints of our undying fears, the bodies of our dead friends. Perhaps he did not take it too much to heart. And if so then—Chester's offer. . . . At this point I took up a fresh sheet and began to write resolutely. There was nothing but myself between him and the dark ocean. I had a sense of responsibility. If I spoke, would that motionless and suffering youth leap into the obscurity—clutch at the straw? I found out how difficult it may be sometimes to make a sound. There is a weird power in a spoken word. And why the devil not? I was asking myself persistently while I drove on with my writing. All at once, on the blank page, under the very point of the pen, the two figures of Chester and his antique partner, very distinct and complete, would lodge into view with stride and gestures, as if reproduced in the field of some optical toy. I would watch them for a while. No! They were too phantasmal and extravagant to enter into any one's fate. And a word carries far—very far—deals destruction through time as the bullets go flying through space. I said nothing; and he, out there with his back to the light, as if bound and gagged by all the invisible foes of man, made no stir and made no sound."

XVI

"The time was coming when I should see him loved, trusted, admired, with a legend of strength and prowess forming around his name as though he had been the stuff of a hero. It's true—I assure you; as true as I'm sitting here talking about him in vain. He, on his side, had that faculty of beholding at a hint the face of his desire and the shape of his dream, without which the earth would know no lover and no adventurer. He captured much honor and an Arcadian happiness (I won't say anything about inno-cence) in the bush, and it was as good to him as the honor and the Arcadian happiness of the streets to another man. Felicity, felicity—how shall I say it?—is quaffed out of a golden cup in every latitude: the flavor is with you—with you alone, and you can make it as intoxicating as you please. He was of the sort that would drink deep, as you may guess from what went before. I found him, if not exactly intoxicated, then at least flushed with the elixir at his lips. He had not obtained it at once. There had been, as you know, a period of probation among infernal ship-chandlers, during which he had suffered and I had worried about—about—my trust—you may call it. I don't know that I am completely reassured now, after beholding him in all his brilliance. That was my last view of him—in a strong light, dominating, and yet in complete accord with his surroundings—with the life of the forests and with the life of men. I own that I was impressed, but I must admit to myself that after all this is not the lasting impression. He was protected by his isolation, alone of his own superior kind, in close touch with Nature, that keeps faith on such easy terms with her lovers. But I cannot fix before my eye the image of his safety. I shall always remember him as seen through the open door of my room, taking, perhaps, too much to heart the mere consequences of his failure. I am pleased, of course, that some good—and even some splendor—came out of my endeavors; but at times it seems to me it would have been better for my peace of mind if I had not stood between him and Chester's confoundedly generous offer. I wonder what his exuberant imagination would have made of Walpole islet— that most hopelessly forsaken crumb of dry land on the face of the waters. It is not likely I would ever have heard, for I must tell you that Chester, after calling at some Australian port to patch up his brig-rigged sea-anachronism, steamed out into the Pacific with a crew of twenty-two hands all told, and the only news having a possible bearing upon the mystery of his fate was the news of a hurricane which is supposed to have swept in its course over the Walpole shoals, a month or so afterwards. Not a vestige of the Argonauts ever turned up; not a sound came out of the waste. Finis! The Pacific is the most discreet of live, hot-tempered oceans: the chilly Antarctic can keep a secret, too, but more in the manner of a grave.

"And there is a sense of blessed finality in such discretion, which is what we all more or less sincerely are ready to admit—for what else is it that makes the idea of death supportable? End! Finis! the potent word that exorcises from the house of life the haunting shadow of fate. This is what—notwithstanding the testimony of my eyes and his own earnest assurances—I miss when I look back upon Jim's success. While there's life there is hope, truly; but there is fear, too. I don't mean to say that I regret my action, nor will I pretend that I can't sleep o' nights in consequence; still the idea obtrudes itself that he made so much of his disgrace while it is the guilt alone that matters. He was not—if I may say so—clear to me. He was not clear. And there is a suspicion he was not clear to himself either. There were his fine sensibilities, his fine feelings, his fine longings—a sort of sublimated, idealized selfishness. He was—if you allow me to say so—very fine; very fine—and very unfortunate. A little coarser nature would not have borne the strain; it would have had to come to terms with itself—with a sigh, with a grunt, or even with a guffaw; a still coarser one would have remained invulnerably ignorant and completely uninteresting.

"But he was too interesting or too unfortunate to be thrown to the dogs, or even to Chester. I felt this while I sat with my face over the paper and he fought and gasped, struggling for his breath in that terrible stealthy way, in my room; I felt it when he rushed out on the verandah as if to fling himself over—and didn't; I felt it more and more all the time he remained outside, faintly lighted on the background of night, as if standing on the shore of a somber and hopeless sea.

"An abrupt heavy rumble made me lift my head. The noise seemed to roll away, and suddenly a searching and violent glare fell on the blind face of the night. The sustained and dazzling flickers seemed to last for an unconscionable time. The growl of the thunder increased steadily while I looked at him, distinct and black, planted solidly upon the shores of a sea of light. At the moment of greatest brilliance the darkness leaped back with a culminating crash, and he vanished before my dazzled eyes as utterly as though he had been blown to atoms. A blustering sigh passed; furious hands seemed to tear at the shrubs, shake the tops of the trees below, slam doors, break window-panes, all along the front of the building. He stepped in, closing the door behind him, and found me bending over the table; my sudden anxiety as to what he would say was very great, and akin to a fright. 'May I have a cigarette?' he asked. I gave a push to the box without raising my head. 'I want—want—tobacco,' he muttered. I became extremely buoyant. 'Just a moment,' I grunted, pleasantly. He took a few steps here and there. 'That's over,' I heard him say. A single distant clap of thunder came from the sea like a gun of distress. 'The monsoon breaks up early this year,' he remarked, conversationally, somewhere behind me. This encouraged me to turn around, which I did as soon as I had finished addressing the last envelope. He was smoking greedily in the middle of the room, and though he heard the stir I made, he remained with his back to me for a time.

" 'Come—I carried it off pretty well,' he said, wheeling suddenly. 'Something's paid off—not much. I wonder what's to come.' His face did not show any emotion, only it appeared a little darkened and swollen, as though he had been holding his breath. He smiled reluctantly as it were, and went on while I gazed up at him mutely. . . . 'Thank you, though—your room—jolly convenient—for a chap—badly hipped.' . . . The rain pattered and swished in the garden; a water-pipe (it must have had a hole in it) performed just outside the window a parody of blubbering woe with funny sobs and gurgling lamentations, interrupted by jerky spasms of silence. . . . 'A bit of shelter,' he mumbled and ceased.

"A flash of faded lightning darted in through the black framework of the windows and ebbed out without any noise. I was thinking how I had best approach him (I did not want to be flung off again) when he gave a little laugh. 'No better than a vagabond now' . . . the end of the cigarette smoldered between his fingers . . . 'without a single—single,' he pronounced slowly; 'and yet . . .' He paused; the rain fell with redoubled violence. 'Some say one's bound to come upon some sort of chance to get it all back again. Must!' he whispered, distinctly, glaring at my boots.

"I did not even know what it was he wished so much to regain, what it was he had so terribly missed. It might have been so much that it was impossible to say. A piece of ass's skin, according to Chester. . . . He looked up at me inquisitively. 'Perhaps. If life's long enough,' I muttered through my teeth with unreasonable animosity. 'Don't reckon too much of it.'

" 'Jove! I feel as if nothing could ever touch me,' he said in a tone of somber conviction. 'If this business couldn't knock me over, then there's no fear of there being not enough time to—climb out, and . . .' He looked upwards.

"It struck me that it is from such as he that the great army of waifs and strays is recruited, the army that marches down, down into all the gutters of the earth. As soon as he left my room, that 'bit of shelter,' he would take his place in the ranks, and begin the journey towards the bottomless pit. I at least had no illusions; but it was I, too, who a moment ago had been so sure of the power of words, and now was afraid to speak, in the same way one dares not move for fear of losing a slippery hold. It is when we try to grapple with another man's intimate need that we perceive how incomprehensible, wavering, and misty are the beings that share with us the sight of the stars and the warmth of the sun. It is as if loneliness were a hard and absolute condition of existence; the envelope of flesh and blood on which our eyes are fixed melts before the outstretched hand, and there remains only the capricious, unconsolable, and elusive spirit that no eye can follow, no hand can grasp. It was the fear of losing him that kept me silent, for it was borne upon me suddenly and with unaccountable force that should I let him slip away into the darkness I would never forgive myself.

" 'Well. Thanks—once more. You've been—er—uncommonly—really there's no word to . . . Uncommonly! I don't know why, I am sure. I am afraid I don't feel as grateful as I would if the whole thing hadn't been so brutally sprung on me. Because at bottom . . . you, yourself . . .' He stuttered.

" 'Possibly,' I struck in. He frowned.

" 'All the same, one is responsible.' He watched me like a hawk.

" 'And that's true, too,' I said.

" 'Well. I've gone with it to the end, and I don't intend to let any may cast it in my teeth without—without—resenting it.' He clenched his fist.

" 'There's yourself,' I said with a smile—mirthless enough, God knows—but he looked at me menacingly. 'That's my business,' he said. An air of indomitable resolution came and went upon his face like a vain and passing shadow. Next moment he looked a dear good boy in trouble, as before. He flung away the cigarette. 'Good-bye,' he said, with the sudden haste of a man who had lingered too long in view of a pressing bit of work waiting for him; and then for a second or so he made not the slightest movement. The downpour fell with the heavy uninterrupted rush of a sweeping flood, with a sound of unchecked overwhelming fury that called to one's mind the images of collapsing bridges, of uprooted trees, of undermined mountains. No man could breast the colossal and headlong stream that seemed to break and swirl against the dim stillness in which we were precariously sheltered as if on an island. The perforated pipe gurgled, choked, spat, and splashed in odious ridicule of a swimmer fighting for his life. 'It is raining,' I remonstrated, 'and I . . .' 'Rain or shine,' he began, brusquely, checked himself, and walked to the window. 'Perfect deluge,' he muttered after a while: he leaned his forehead on the glass. 'It's dark, too.'

" 'Yes, it is very dark,' I said.

"He pivoted on his heels, crossed the room, and had actually opened the door leading into the corridor before I leaped up from my chair. 'Wait,' I cried, 'I want you to . . .' 'I can't dine with you again tonight,' he flung at me, with one leg out of the room already. 'I haven't the slightest intention to ask you,' I shouted. At this he drew back his foot, but remained mistrustfully in the very doorway. I lost no time in entreating him earnestly not to be absurd; to come in and shut the door."

XVII

"He came in at last; but I believe it was mostly the rain that did it; it was falling just then with a devastating violence which quieted down gradually while we talked. His manner was very sober and set; his bearing was that of a naturally taciturn man possessed by an idea. My talk was of the material aspect of his position; it had the sole aim of saving him from the degradation, ruin, and despair that out there close so swiftly upon a friendless, homeless man; I pleaded with him to accept my help; I argued reasonably: and every time I looked up at that absorbed smooth face, so grave and youthful, I had a disturbing sense of being no help but rather an obstacle to some mysterious, inexplicable, impalpable striving of his wounded spirit.

" 'I suppose you intend to eat and drink and to sleep under shelter in the usual way,' I remember saying with irritation. 'You say you won't touch the money that is due to you.' . . . He came as near as his sort can to making a gesture of horror. (There were three weeks and five days' pay owing him as mate of the *Patna.*) 'Well, that's too little to matter anyhow; but what will you do tomorrow? Where will you turn? You must live . . .' 'That isn't the thing,' was the comment that escaped him under his breath. I ignored it, and went on combating what I assumed to be the scruples of an exaggerated delicacy. 'On every conceivable ground,' I concluded, 'you must let me help you.' 'You can't,' he said very simply and gently, and holding fast to some deep idea which I could detect shimmering like a pool of water in the dark, but which I despaired of ever approaching near enough to fathom. I surveyed his well-proportioned bulk. 'At any rate,' I said, 'I am able to help what I can see of you. I don't pretend to do more.' He shook his head skeptically without looking at me. I got very warm. 'But I can,' I insisted. 'I can do even more. I *am* doing more. I am trusting you . . .' 'The money . . .' he began. 'Upon my word you deserve being told to go to the devil,' I cried, forcing the note of indignation. He was startled, smiled, and I pressed my attack home. 'It isn't a question of money at all. You are too superficial,' I said (and at the same time I was thinking to myself: Well, here goes! And perhaps he is after all). 'Look at the letter I want you to take. I am writing to a man of whom I've never asked a favor, and I am writing about you in terms that one only ventures to use when speaking of an intimate friend. I make myself unreservedly responsible for you. That's what I am doing. And really if you will only reflect a little what that means . . .'

"He lifted his head. The rain had passed away; only the water-pipe went on shedding tears with an absurd drip, drip outside the window. It was very quiet in the room, whose shadows huddled together in corners, away from the still flame of the candle flaring upright in the shape of a dagger; his face after a while seemed suffused by a reflection of a soft light as if the dawn had broken already.

" 'Jove!' he gasped out. 'It is noble of you!'

"Had he suddenly put out his tongue at me in derision, I could not have felt more humiliated. I thought to myself—Serve me right for a sneaking humbug. . . . His eyes shone straight into my face, but I perceived it was not a mocking brightness. All at once he sprang into jerky agitation, like one of those flat wooden figures that are worked by a string. His arms went up, then came down with a slap. He became another man altogether. 'And I had never seen,' he shouted; then suddenly bit his lip and frowned. 'What a bally ass I've been,' he cried very slow in an awed tone. . . . 'You are a brick,' he cried next in a muffled voice. He snatched my hand as though he had just then seen it for the first time, and dropped it at once. 'Why! this is what I— you—I . . .' he stammered, and then with a return of his old stolid, I may say mulish, manner he began heavily, 'I would be a brute now if I . . .' and then his voice seemed to break. 'That's all right,' I said. I was almost alarmed by this display of feeling, through which pierced a strange elation. I had pulled the string accidentally, as it were; I did not fully understand the working of the toy. 'I must go now,' he said. 'Jove! You *have* helped me. Can't sit still. The very thing . . .' He looked at me with puzzled admiration. 'The very thing . . .'

"Of course it was the thing. It was ten to one that I had saved him from starvation —of that peculiar sort that is almost invariably associated with drink. That was all. I had not a single illusion on that score, but looking at him, I allowed myself to wonder at the nature of the one he had, within the last three minutes, so evidently taken into his bosom. I had forced into his hand the means to carry on decently the serious business of life, to get food, drink, and shelter of the customary kind while his wounded spirit, like a bird with a broken wing, might hop and flutter into some hole to die quietly of inanition there. This is what I had thrust upon him: a definitely small thing; and—behold!—by the manner of its reception it loomed in the dim light of the candle like a big, indistinct, perhaps a dangerous shadow. 'You don't mind me not saying anything appropriate,' he burst out. 'There isn't anything one could say. Last night already you had done me no end of good. Listening to me—you know. I give you my word I've thought more than once the top of my head would fly off . . .' He darted—positively darted—here and there, rammed his hands into his pockets, jerked them out again, flung his cap on his head. I had no idea it was in him to be so airily brisk. I thought of a dry leaf imprisoned in an eddy of wind, while a mysterious apprehension, a load of indefinite doubt, weighed me down in my chair. He stood stock-still, as if struck motionless by a discovery. 'You have given me confidence,' he declared, soberly. 'Oh! for God's sake, my dear fellow—don't!' I entreated, as though he had hurt me. 'All right. I'll shut up now and henceforth. Can't prevent me thinking though. . . . Never mind! . . . I'll show yet . . .' He went to the door in a hurry, paused with his head down, and came back, stepping deliberately. 'I always thought that if a fellow could begin with a clean slate . . . And now you . . . in a measure . . . yes . . . clean slate.' I waved my hand, and he marched out without looking back; the sound of his footfalls died out gradually behind the closed door—the unhesitating tread of a man walking in broad daylight.

"But as to me, left alone with the solitary candle, I remained strangely unenlightened. I was no longer young enough to behold at every turn the magnificence that besets our insignificant footsteps in good and in evil. I smiled to think that, after all, it was yet he, of us two, who had the light. And I felt sad. A clean slate, did he say? As if the initial word of each our destiny were not graven in imperishable characters upon the face of a rock."

XVIII

"Six months afterwards my friend (he was a cynical, more than middle-aged bachelor, with a reputation for eccentricity, and owned a rice-mill) wrote to me, and judging, from the warmth of my recommendation, that I would like to hear, enlarged a little upon Jim's perfections. These were apparently of a quiet and effective sort. 'Not having been able so far to find more in my heart than a resigned toleration for any individual of my kind, I have lived till now alone in a house that even in this steaming climate could be considered as too big for one man. I have had him to live with me for some time past. It seems I haven't made a mistake.' It seemed to me on reading this letter that my friend had found in his heart more than tolerance for Jim,—that there were the beginnings of active liking. Of course he stated his grounds in a characteristic way. For one thing, Jim kept his freshness in the climate. Had he been a girl—my friend wrote—one could have said he was blooming—blooming modestly—like a violet, not like some of these blatant tropical flowers. He had been in the house for six weeks, and had not as yet attempted to slap him on the back, or address him as 'old boy,' or try to make him feel a superannuated fossil. He had nothing of the exasperating young man's chatter. He was good-tempered, had not much to say for himself, was not clever by any means, thank goodness—wrote my friend. It appeared, however, that Jim was clever enough to be quietly appreciative of his wit, while, on the other hand, he amused him by his naïveness. 'The dew is yet on him, and since I had the bright idea of giving him a room in the house and having him at meals I feel less withered myself. The other day he took it into his head to cross the room with no other purpose but to open a door for me; and I felt more in touch with mankind than I had been for years. Ridiculous, isn't it? Of course I guess there is something—some awful little scrape—which you know all about—but if I am sure that it is terribly heinous, I fancy one could manage to forgive it. For my part, I declare I am unable to imagine him guilty of anything much more than robbing an orchard. Is *it* much worse? Perhaps you ought to have told me; but it is such a long time since we both turned saints that you may have forgotten we, too, had sinned in our time? It may be that some day I shall have to ask you, and then I shall expect to be told. I don't care to question him myself till I have some idea what it is. Moreover, it's too soon as yet. Let him open the door a few times more for me. . . .' Thus my friend. I was trebly pleased—at Jim's shaping so well, at the tone of the letter, at my own cleverness. Evidently I had known what I was doing. I had read characters aright, and so on. And what if something unexpected and wonderful were to come of it? That evening, reposing in a deck-chair under the shade of my own poop awning (it was in Hong Kong harbor), I laid on Jim's behalf the first stone of a castle in Spain.

"I made a trip to the northward, and when I returned I found another letter from my friend awaiting for me. It was the first envelope I tore open. 'There are no spoons missing, as far as I know,' ran the first line; 'I haven't been interested enough to inquire. He is gone, leaving on the breakfast-table a formal little note of apology, which is either silly or heartless. Probably both—and it's all one to me. Allow me to say, lest you should have some more mysterious young men in reserve, that I have shut up shop, definitely and forever. This is the last eccentricity I shall be guilty of. Do not imagine for a moment that I care a hang; but he is very much regretted at tennis-parties, and for my own sake I've told a plausible lie at the club. . . .' I flung the letter aside and started looking through the batch on my table, till I came upon Jim's handwriting. Would you believe it? One chance in a hundred! But it is always that hundredth chance! That little second engineer of the *Patna* had turned up in a more or less destitute state, and got a temporary job of looking after the machinery of the mill. 'I couldn't stand the familiarity of the little beast,' Jim wrote from a seaport seven hundred miles south of the place where he should have been in clover. 'I am now for the time with Egström & Blake, ship-chandlers, as their—well—runner, to call the thing by its right name. For reference I gave them your name, which they know of course, and if you could write a word in my favor it would be a permanent employment.' I was utterly crushed under the ruins of my castle, but of course I wrote as desired. Before the end of the year my new charter took me that way, and I had an opportunity of seeing him.

"He was still with Egström & Blake, and we met in what they called 'our parlor' opening out of the store. He had that moment come in from boarding a ship, and confronted me head down, ready for a tussle. 'What have you got to say for yourself?' I began as soon as we had shaken hands. 'What I wrote you—nothing more,' he said stubbornly. 'Did the fellow blab—or what?' I asked. He looked up at me with a troubled smile. 'Oh, no! He didn't. He made it a kind of confidential business between us. He was most damnably mysterious whenever I came over to the mill; he would wink at me in a respectful manner—as much as to say, "We know what we know." Infernally fawning and familiar—and that sort of thing.' He threw himself into a chair and stared down his legs. 'One day we happened to be alone and the fellow had the cheek to say, "Well, Mr. James"—I was called Mr. James there as if I had been the son —"here we are together once more. This is better than the old ship—ain't it?" . . . Wasn't it appalling, eh? I looked at him, and he put on a knowing air. "Don't you be uneasy, sir," he says. "I know a gentleman when I see one, and I know how a gentleman feels. I hope, though, you will be keeping me on this job. I had a hard time of it, too, along of that rotten old *Patna* racket." Jove! It was awful. I don't know what I should have said or done if I had not just then heard Mr. Denver calling me in the passage. It was tiffin-time, and we walked together across the yard and through the garden to the bungalow. He began to chaff me in this kindly way . . . I believe he liked me . . .'

"Jim was silent for a while.

" 'I know he liked me. That's what made it so hard. Such a splendid man! That morning he slipped his hand under my arm. . . . He, too, was familiar with me.' He burst into a short laugh, and dropped his chin on his breast. 'Pah! When I remembered how that mean little beast had been talking to me,' he began suddenly in a vibrating voice, 'I couldn't bear to think of myself . . . I suppose you know . . .' I nodded. . . . 'More like a father,' he cried; his voice sank. 'I would have had to tell him. I couldn't let it go on—could I?' 'Well?' I murmured, after waiting a while. 'I preferred to go,' he said, slowly; 'this thing must be buried.'

"We could hear in the shop Blake upbraiding Egström in an abusive, strained voice. They had been associated for many years, and every day from the moment the doors were opened to the last minute before closing, Blake, a little man with sleek, jetty hair and unhappy, beady eyes, could be heard rowing his partner incessantly with a sort of scathing and plaintive fury. The sound of that everlasting scolding was part of the place like the other fixtures; even strangers would very soon come to disregard it completely unless it be perhaps to mutter 'Nuisance,' or to get up suddenly and shut the door of the 'parlor.' Egström himself, a raw-boned, heavy Scandinavian, with a busy manner and immense blond whiskers, went on directing his people, checking parcels, making out bills or writing letters at a stand-up desk in the shop, and comported himself in that clatter exactly as though he had been stone-deaf. Now and again he would emit a bothered perfunctory 'Sssh,' which neither produced nor was expected to produce the slightest effect. 'They are very decent to me here,' said Jim. 'Blake's a little cad, but Egström's all right.' He stood up quickly, and walking with measured steps to a tripod telescope standing in the window and pointed at the roadstead, he applied his eye to it. 'There's that ship which had been becalmed outside all the morning has got a breeze now and is coming in,' he remarked, patiently; 'I must go and board.' We shook hands in silence, and he turned to go. 'Jim!' I cried. He looked round with his hand on the lock. 'You—you have thrown away something like a fortune.' He came back to me all the way from the door. 'Such a splendid old chap,' he said. 'How could I? How could I?' His lips twitched. 'Here it does not matter.' 'Oh! you—you———' I began, and had to cast about for a suitable word, but before I became aware that there was no name that would just do, he was gone. I heard outside Egström's deep gentle voice saying cheerily, 'That's the *Sarah W. Granger*, Jimmy. You must manage to be first aboard'; and directly Blake struck in, screaming after the manner of an outraged cockatoo, 'Tell the captain we've got some of his mail here. That'll fetch him. D'ye hear, Mister What's-your-name?' And there was Jim answering Egström with something boyish in his tone. 'All right. I'll make a race of it.' He seemed to take refuge in the boat-sailing part of that sorry business.

"I did not see him again that trip, but on my next (I had a six months' charter) I went up to the store. Ten yards away from the door Blake's scolding met my ears, and when I came in he gave me a glance of utter wretchedness; Egström, all smiles, advanced, extending a large bony hand. 'Glad to see you, captain. . . . Sssh. . . . Been thinking you were about due back here. What did you say, sir? . . . Sssh. . . . Oh! him! He has left us. Come into the parlor.'. . . . After the slam of the door Blake's strained voice became faint, as the voice of one scolding desperately in a wilderness. . . . 'Put us to a great inconvenience, too. Used us badly—I must say . . .' 'Where's he gone to? Do you know?' I asked. 'No. It's no use asking either,' said Egström, standing bewhiskered and obliging before me with his arms hanging down his sides clumsily and a thin silver watch-chain looped very low on a rucked-up blue serge waistcoat. 'A man like that don't go anywhere in particular.' I was too concerned at the news to ask for the explanation of that pronouncement, and he went on. 'He left—let's see—the very day a steamer with returning pilgrims from the Red Sea put in here with two blades of her propeller gone. Three weeks ago now.' 'Wasn't there something said about the *Patna* case?' I asked, fearing the worst. He gave a start, and looked at me as if I had been a sorcerer. 'Why, yes! How do you know? Some of them were talking about it here. There was a captain or two, the manager of Vanlo's engineering shop at the harbor, two or three others, and myself. Jim was in here, too, having a sandwich and a glass of beer; when we are busy—you see, captain—there's no time for a proper tiffin. He was standing by this table eating sandwiches, and the rest of us were round the telescope watching that steamer come in; and by and by Vanlo's manager began to talk about the chief of the *Patna;* he had done some repairs for him once, and from that he went on to tell us what an old ruin she was, and the money that had been made out of her. He came to mention her last voyage, and then we all struck in. Some said one thing and some another—not much—what you or any other man might say; and there was some laughing. Captain O'Brien of the *Sarah W. Granger,* a large, noisy old man with a stick—he was sitting listening to us in this armchair here —he let drive suddenly with his stick at the floor, and roars out, "Skunks!" . . . Made us all jump. Vanlo's manager winks at us and asks, "What's the matter, Captain O'Brien?" "Matter! matter!" the old man began to shout; "what are you Injuns laugh-ing at? It's no laughing matter. It's a disgrace to human natur'—that's what it is. I would despise being seen in the same room with one of those men. Yes, sir!" He seemed to catch my eye like, and I had to speak out of civility. "Skunks!" says I, "of course, Captain O'Brien, and I wouldn't care to have them here myself, so you're quite safe in this room, Captain O'Brien. Have a little something cool to drink." "Dam' your drink, Egström," says he, with a twinkle in his eye; "when I want a drink I will shout for it. I am going to quit. It stinks here now." At this all the others burst out laughing, and out they go after the old man. And then, sir, that blasted Jim he puts down the sandwich he had in his hand and walks around the table to me; there was his glass of beer poured out quite full. "I am off," he says—just like this. "It isn't half-past one yet," says I; "you might snatch a smoke first." I thought he meant it was time for him to go down to his work. When I understood what he was up to, my arms fell —so! Can't get a man like that every day, you know, sir; a regular devil for sailing a boat; ready to go out miles to sea to meet ships in any sort of weather. More than once a captain would come in here full of it and the first thing he would say would be, "That's a reckless sort of a lunatic you've got for water-clerk, Egström. I was feeling my way in at daylight under short canvas when there comes flying out of the mist right under my forefoot a boat half under water, sprays going over the masthead, two frightened niggers on the bottom boards, a yelling fiend at the tiller. Hey! hey! Ship ahoy! ahoy! Captain! Hey! hey! Egström & Blake's man first to speak to you! Hey! hey! Egström & Blake! Hallo! hey! whoop! Kick the niggers—out reefs—a squall on at the time—shoots ahead whooping and yelling to me to make sail and he would give me a lead in—more like a demon than a man. Never saw a boat handled like that in all my life. Couldn't have been drunk—was he? Such a quiet, soft-spoken chap, too—blush like a girl when he came on board. . . .' I tell you, Captain Marlow, nobody had a chance against us with a strange ship when Jim was out. The other ship-chandlers just kept their old customers, and . . .'

"Egström appeared overcome with emotion.

" 'Why, sir—it seemed as though he wouldn't mind going a hundred miles out to sea in an old shoe to nab a ship for the firm. If the business had been his own and all to make yet, he couldn't have done more in that way. And now . . . all at once . . . like this! Thinks I to myself: "Oho! a rise in the screw—that's the trouble—is it? All right," says I, "no need of all that fuss with me, Jimmy. Just mention your figure. Anything in reason." He looks at me as if he wanted to swallow something that stuck in his throat. "I can't stop with you." "What's that blooming joke?" I asks. He shakes his head, and I could see in his eye he was as good as gone already, sir. So I turned to him and slanged him till all was blue. "What is it you're running away from?" I asks. "Who has been getting at you? What scared you? You haven't as much sense as a rat; they don't clear out from a good ship. Where do you expect to get a better berth?— you this and you that." I made him look sick, I can tell you. "This business ain't going to sink," says I. He gave a big jump. "Good-bye," he says, nodding at me like a lord; "you ain't half a bad chap, Egström. I give you my word that if you knew my reasons you wouldn't care to keep me." "That's the biggest lie you ever told in your life," says I; "I know my own mind." He made me so mad that I had to laugh. "Can't you really stop long enough to drink this glass of beer here, you funny beggar, you?" I don't know what came over him; he didn't seem able to find the door; something comical, I can tell you, captain. I drank the beer myself. "Well, if you're in such a hurry, here's luck to you in your own drink," says I; "only, you mark my words, if you keep up this game you'll very soon find that the earth ain't big enough to hold you—that's all." He gave me one black look, and out he rushed with a face fit to scare little children.'

"Egström snorted bitterly, and combed one auburn whisker with knotty fingers. 'Haven't been able to get a man that was any good since. It's nothing but worry, worry, worry in business. And where might you have come across him, captain, if it's fair to ask?'

" 'He was the mate of the *Patna* that voyage,' I said, feeling that I owed some explanation. For a time Egström remained very still, with his fingers plunged in the hair at the side of his face, and then exploded. 'And who the devil cares about that?' 'I daresay no one,' I began . . . 'And what the devil is he—anyhow—for to go on like this?' He stuffed suddenly his left whisker into his mouth and stood amazed. 'Jee!' he exclaimed, 'I told him the earth wouldn't be big enough to hold his caper.' "

XIX

"I have told you these two episodes at length to show his manner of dealing with himself under the new conditions of his life. There were many others of the sort, more than I could count on the fingers of my two hands.

"They were all equally tinged by a high-minded absurdity of intention which made their futility profound and touching. To fling away your daily bread so as to get your hands free for a grapple with a ghost may be an act of prosaic heroism. Men had done it before (though we who have lived know full well that it is not the haunted soul but the hungry body that makes an outcast), and men who had eaten and meant to eat every day had applauded the creditable folly. He was indeed unfortunate, for all his recklessness could not carry him out from under the shadow. There was always a doubt of his courage. The truth seems to be that it for myself; but only think, captain, if everybody started such games! Why, the man might have been drowned! And here I can't run out into the next street and buy a new cue. I've got to write to Europe for them. No, no! A temper like that won't do!' . . . He was extremely sore on the subject.

"This was the worst incident of all in his—his retreat. Nobody could deplore it more than myself; for if, as somebody said hearing him mentioned, 'Oh, yes! I know. He has knocked about a good deal out here,' yet he had somehow avoided being battered and chipped in the process. This last affair, however, made me seriously uneasy, because if his exquisite sensibilities were to go the length of involving him in pot-house shindies, he would lose his name of an inoffensive, if aggravating, fool, and acquire that of a common loafer. For all my confidence in him I could not help reflecting that in such cases from the name to the thing itself is but a step. I suppose you will understand that by that time I could not think of washing my hands of him. I took him away from Bangkok in my ship, and we had a longish passage. It was pitiful to see how he shrank within himself. A seaman, even if a mere passenger, takes an interest in a ship, and looks at the sealife around him with the critical enjoyment of a painter, for instance, looking at another man's work. In every sense of the expression he is 'on deck'; but my Jim, for the most part, skulked down below as though he had been a stowaway. He infected me so that I avoided speaking on professional matters, such as would suggest themselves naturally to two sailors during a passage. For whole days we did not exchange a word; I felt extremely unwilling to give orders to my officers in his presence. Often, when alone with him on deck or in the cabin, we didn't know what to do with our eyes.

"I placed him with De Jongh, as you know, glad enough to dispose of him in any way, yet persuaded that his position was now growing intolerable. He had lost some of that elasticity which had enabled him to rebound back into his uncompromising position after every overthrow. One day, coming ashore, I saw him standing on the quay; the water of the roadstead and the sea in the offing made one smooth ascending plane, and the outermost ships at anchor seemed to ride motionless in the sky. He was waiting for his boat, which was being loaded at our feet with packages of small stores for some vessel ready to leave. After exchanging greetings, we remained silent—side by side. 'Jove!' he said, suddenly, 'this is killing work.'

"He smiled at me; I must say he generally could manage a smile. I made no reply. I knew very well he was not alluding to his duties; he had an easy time of it with De Jongh. Nevertheless, as soon as he had spoken I became completely convinced that the work was killing. I did not even look at him. 'Would you like,' said I, 'to leave this part of the world altogether; try California or the West Coast? I'll see what I can do . . .' He interrupted me a little scornfully. 'What difference would it make?' . . . I felt at once convinced that he was right. It would make no difference; it was not relief he wanted; I seemed to perceive dimly that what he wanted, what he was, as it were, waiting for, was something not easy to define—something in the nature of an opportunity. I had given him many opportunities, but they had been merely opportunities to earn his bread. Yet what more could any man do? The position struck me as hopeless, and poor Brierly's saying recurred to me, 'Let him creep twenty feet underground and stay there.' Better that, I thought, than this waiting above ground for the impossible. Yet one could not be sure even of that. There and then, before his boat was three oars' lengths away from the quay, I had made up my mind to go and consult Stein in the evening.

"This Stein was a wealthy and respected merchant. His 'house' (because it was a house, Stein & Co., and there was some sort of partner who, as Stein said, 'looked after the Moluccas') had a large interisland business, with a lot of trading posts established in the most out-of-the-way places for collecting the produce. His wealth and his respectability were not exactly the reasons why I was anxious to seek his advice. I desired to confide my difficulty to him because he was one of the most trustworthy men I had ever known. The gentle light of a simple unwearied, as it were, and intelligent good-nature illumined his long hairless face. It had deep downward folds, and was pale as of a man who had always led a sedentary life—which was indeed very far from being the case. His hair was thin, and brushed back from a massive and lofty forehead. One fancied that at twenty he must have looked very much like what he was now at threescore. It was a student's face; only the eyebrows nearly all white, thick and bushy, together with the resolute searching glance that came from under them, were not in accord with his, I may say, learned appearance. He was tall and loose-jointed; his slight stoop, together with an innocent smile, made him appear benevolently ready to lend you his ear; his long arms with pale big hands had rare deliberate gestures of a pointing out, demonstrating kind. I speak of him at length, because under this exterior, and in conjunction with an upright and indulgent nature, this man possessed an intrepidity of spirit and a physical courage that could have been called reckless had it not been like a natural function of the body—say good digestion, for instance—completely unconscious of itself. It is sometimes said of a man that he carries his life in his hand. Such a saying would have been inadequate if applied to him; during the early part of his existence in the East he had been playing ball with it. All this was in the past, but I knew the story of his life and the origin of his fortune. He was also a naturalist of some distinction, or perhaps I should say a learned collector. Entomology was his special study. His collection of *Buprestidœ* and *Longicorns*—beetles all— horrible miniature monsters, looking malevolent in death and immobility, and his cabinet of butterflies, beautiful and hovering under the glass of cases on lifeless wings, had spread his fame far over the earth. The name of this merchant, adventurer, sometime adviser of a Malay sultan (to whom he never alluded otherwise than as 'my poor Mohammed Bonso'), had, on account of a few bushels of dead insects, become known to learned persons in Europe, who could have had no conception, and certainly would not have cared to know anything, of his life or character. I, who knew, considered him an eminently suitable person to receive my confidences about Jim's difficulties as well as my own."

XX

"Late in the evening I entered his study, after traversing an imposing but empty dining-room very dimly lit. The house was silent. I was preceded by an elderly grim Javanese servant in a sort of livery of white jacket and yellow sarong, who, after throwing the door open, exclaimed low, 'O master!' and stepping aside, vanished in a mysterious way as though he had been a ghost only momentarily embodied for that particular service. Stein turned round with the chair, and in the same movement his spectacles seemed to get pushed up on his forehead. He welcomed me in his quiet and humorous voice. Only one corner of the vast room, the corner in which stood his writing-desk, was strongly lighted by a shaded reading-lamp, and the rest of the spacious apartment melted into shapeless gloom like a cavern. Narrow shelves filled with dark boxes of uniform shape and color ran around the walls, not from floor to ceiling, but in a somber belt about four feet broad. Catacombs of beetles. Wooden tablets were hung above at irregular intervals. The light reached one of them, and the word *Coleoptera* written in gold letters glittered mysteriously upon a vast dimness. The glass cases containing the collection of butterflies were ranged in three long rows upon slender-legged little tables. One of these cases had been removed from its place and stood on the desk, which was bestrewn with oblong slips of paper blackened with minute handwriting.

" 'So you see me—so,' he said. His hand hovered over the case where a butterfly in solitary grandeur spread out dark bronze wings, seven inches or more across, with exquisite white veinings and a gorgeous border of yellow spots. 'Only one specimen like this they have in *your* London, and then—no more. To my small native town this my collection I shall bequeath. Something of me. The best.'

"He bent forward in the chair and gazed intently, his chin over the front of the case. I stood at his back. 'Marvelous,' he whispered, and seemed to forget my presence. His history was curious. He had been born in Bavaria, and when a youth of twenty-two had taken an active part in the revolutionary movement of 1848. Heavily compromised, he managed to make his escape, and at first found a refuge with a poor republican watchmaker in Trieste. From there he made his way to Tripoli with a stock of cheap watches to hawk about,—not a very great opening truly, but it turned out lucky enough, because it was there he came upon a Dutch traveler—a rather famous man, I believe, but I don't remember his name. It was that naturalist who, engaging him as a sort of assistant, took him to the East. They traveled in the Archipelago together and separately, collecting insects and birds, for four years or more. Then the naturalist went home, and Stein, having no more home to go to, remained with an old trader he had come across in his journeys in the interior of Celebes—if Celebes may be said to have an interior. This old Scotsman, the only white man allowed to reside in the country at the time, was a privileged friend of the chief ruler of Wajo States, who was a woman. I often heard Stein relate how that chap, who was slightly paralyzed on one side, had introduced him to the native court a short time before another stroke carried him off. He was a heavy man with a patriarchal white beard, and of imposing stature. He came into the council-hall where all the rajahs, pangerans, and headmen were assembled, with the queen, a fat wrinkled woman (very free in her speech, Stein said), reclining on a high couch under a canopy. He dragged his leg, thumping with his stick, and grasped Stein's arm, leading him right up to the couch. 'Look, queen, and you rajahs, this is my son,' he proclaimed in a stentorian voice. 'I have traded with your fathers, and when I die he shall trade with you and your sons.'

"By means of this simple formality Stein inherited the Scotsman's privileged position and all his stock-in-trade, together with a fortified house on the banks of the only navigable river in the country. Shortly afterwards the old queen, who was so free in her speech, died, and the country became disturbed by various pretenders to the throne. Stein joined the party of a younger son, the one of whom thirty years later he never spoke otherwise but as 'my poor Mohammed Bonso.' They both became the heroes of innumerable exploits; they had wonderful adventures, and once stood a siege in the Scotsman's house for a month, with only a score of followers against a whole army. I believe the natives talk of that war to this day. Meantime, it seems, Stein never failed to annex on his own account every butterfly or beetle he could lay hands on. After some eight years of war, negotiations, false truces, sudden outbreaks, reconciliation, treachery, and so on, and just as peace seemed at last permanently established, his 'poor Mohammed Bonso' was assassinated at the gate of his own royal residence while dismounting in the highest spirits on his return from a successful deerhunt. This event rendered Stein's position extremely insecure, but he would have stayed perhaps had it not been that a short time afterwards he lost Mohammed's sister ('my dear wife the princess,' he used to say solemnly), by whom he had had a daughter—mother and child both dying within three days of each other from some infectious fever. He left the country, which this cruel loss had made unbearable to him. Thus ended the first and adventurous part of his existence. What followed was so different that, but for the reality of sorrow which remained with him, this strange part must have resembled a dream. He had a little money; he started life afresh, and in the course of years acquired a considerable fortune. At first he had traveled a good deal amongst the islands, but age had stolen upon him, and of late he seldom left his spacious house three miles out of town, with an extensive garden, and surrounded by stables, offices, and bamboo cottages for his servants and dependants, of whom he had many. He drove in his buggy every morning to town, where he had an office with white and Chinese clerks.

He owned a small fleet of schooners and native craft, and dealt in island produce on a large scale. For the rest he lived solitary, but not misanthropic, with his books and his collection, classing and arranging specimens, corresponding with entomologists in Europe, writing up a descriptive catalog of his treasures. Such was the history of the man whom I had come to consult upon Jim's case without any definite hope. Simply to hear what he would have to say would have been a relief. I was very anxious, but I respected the intense, almost passionate, absorption with which he looked at a butterfly, as though on the bronze sheen of these frail wings, in the white tracings, in the gorgeous markings, he could see other things, an image of something as perishable and defying destruction as these delicate and lifeless tissues displaying a splendor unmarred by death.

" 'Marvelous!' he repeated, looking up at me. 'Look! The beauty—but that is nothing—look at the accuracy, the harmony. And so fragile! And so strong! And so exact! This is Nature—the balance of colossal forces. Every star is so—and every blade of grass stands so—and the mighty Kosmos in perfect equilibrium produces—this. This wonder; this masterpiece of Nature—the great artist.'

" 'Never heard an entomologist go on like this,' I observed, cheerfully. 'Masterpiece! And what of man?'

" 'Man is amazing, but he is not a masterpiece,' he said, keeping his eyes fixed on the glass case. 'Perhaps the artist was a little mad. Eh? What do you think? Sometimes it seems to me that man is come where he is not wanted, where there is no place for him; for if not, why should he want all the place? Why should he run about here and there making a great noise about himself, talking about the stars, disturbing the blades of grass? . . .'

" 'Catching butterflies,' I chimed in.

"He smiled, threw himself back in his chair, and stretched his legs. 'Sit down,' he said. 'I captured this rare specimen myself one very fine morning. And I had a very big emotion. You don't know what it is for a collector to capture such a rare specimen. You can't know.'

"I smiled at my ease in a rocking-chair. His eyes seemed to look far beyond the wall at which they stared; and he narrated how, one night, a messenger arrived from his 'poor Mohammed,' requiring his presence at the 'residenz'—as he called it—which was distant some nine or ten miles by a bridlepath over a cultivated plain, with patches of forest here and there. Early in the morning he started from his fortified house, after embracing his little Emma, and leaving the 'princess,' his wife, in command. He described how she came with him as far as the gate, walking with one hand on the neck of his horse; she had on a white jacket, gold pins in her hair, and a brown leather belt over her left shoulder with a revolver in it. 'She talked as women will talk,' he said, 'telling me to be careful, and to try to get back before dark, and what a great wickedness it was for me to go alone. We were at war, and the country was not safe; my men were putting up bullet-proof shutters to the house and loading their rifles, and she begged me to have no fear for her. She could defend the house against anybody till I returned. And I laughed with pleasure a little. I liked to see her so brave and young and strong. I, too, was young then. At the gate she caught hold of my hand and gave it one squeeze and fell back. I made my horse stand still outside till I heard the bars of the gate put up behind me. There was a great enemy of mine, a great noble —and a great rascal, too—roaming with a band in the neighborhood. I cantered for four or five miles; there had been rain in the night, but the mists had gone up, up— and the face of the earth was clean; it lay smiling to me, so fresh and innocent—like a little child. Suddenly somebody fires a volley—twenty shots at least it seemed to me. I hear bullets sing in my ear, and my hat jumps to the back of my head. It was a little intrigue, you understand. They got my poor Mohammed to send for me and then laid that ambush. I see it all in a minute, and I think—— This wants a little management. My pony snort, jump, and stand, and I fall slowly, forward with my head on his mane. He begins to walk, and with one eye I could see over his neck a faint cloud of smoke hanging in front of a clump of bamboos to my left. I think—— Aha! my friends, why you not wait long enough before you shoot? This is not yet *gelungen*. Oh, no! I get hold of my revolver with my right hand—quiet—quiet. After all, there were only seven of these rascals. They get up from the grass and start running with their sarongs tucked up, waving spears above their heads, and yelling to each other to look out and catch the horse, because I was dead. I let them come as close as the door here, and then bang, bang, bang—take aim each time, too. One more shot I fire at a man's back, but I miss. Too far already. And then I sit alone on my horse with the clean earth smiling at me, and there are the bodies of three men lying on the ground. One was curled up like a dog, another on his back had an arm over his eyes as if to keep off the sun, and the third man he draws up his leg very slowly and makes it with one kick straight again. I watch him very carefully from my horse, but there is no more—*bleibt ganz ruhig*—keep still, so. And as I looked at his face for some sign of life I observed something like a faint shadow pass over his forehead. It was the shadow of this butterfly. Look at the form of the wing. This species fly high with a strong flight. I raised my eyes and I saw him fluttering away. I think—— Can it be possible? And then I lost him. I dismounted and went on very slow, leading my horse and holding my revolver with one hand and my eyes darting up and down and right and left, everywhere! At last I saw him sitting on a small heap of dirt ten feet away. At once my heart began to beat quick. I let go my horse, keep my revolver in one hand, and with the other snatch my soft felt hat off my head. One step. Steady. Another step. Flop! I got him! When I got up I shook like a leaf with excitement, and when I opened these beautiful wings and made sure what a rare and so extraordinary perfect specimen I had, my head went around and my legs became so weak with emotion that I had to sit on the ground. I had greatly desired to possess myself of a specimen of that species when collecting for the professor. I took long journeys and underwent great privations; I had dreamed of him in my sleep, and here suddenly I had him in my fingers—for myself! In the words of the poet' (he pronounced it 'boet')—

> So halt' ich's endlich denn in meinen Händen,
> Und nenn' es in gewissem Sinne mein.

He gave to the last word the emphasis of a suddenly lowered voice, and withdrew his eyes slowly from my face. He began to charge a long-stemmed pipe busily and in silence, then, pausing with his thumb on the orifice of the bowl, looked again at me significantly.

" 'Yes, my good friend. On that day I had nothing to desire; I had greatly annoyed my principal enemy; I was young, strong; I had friendship; I had the love' (he said 'lof') 'of woman, a child I had, to make my heart very full—and even what I had once dreamed in my sleep had come into my hand, too!'

"He struck a match, which flared violently. His thoughtful placid face twitched once.

" 'Friend, wife, child,' he said, slowly, gazing at the small flame—'phoo!' The match was blown out. He sighed and turned again to the glass case. The frail and beautiful wings quivered faintly, as if his breath had for an instant called back to life that gorgeous object of his dreams.

" 'The work,' he began, suddenly, pointing to the scattered slips, and in his usual gentle and cheery tone, 'is making great progress. I have been this rare specimen describing. . . . Na! And what is your good news?'

" 'To tell you the truth, Stein,' I said with an effort that surprised me, 'I came here to describe a specimen. . . .'

" 'Butterfly?' he asked, with an unbelieving and humorous eagerness.

" 'Nothing so perfect,' I answered, feeling suddenly dispirited with all sorts of doubts. 'A man!'

" '*Ach* so?' he murmured, and his smiling countenance, turned to me, became grave. Then after looking at me for a while he said slowly, 'Well—I am a man, too.'

"Here you have him as he was; he knew how to be so generously encouraging as to make a scrupulous man hesitate on the brink of confidence; but if I did hesitate it was not for long.

"He heard me out, sitting with crossed legs. Sometimes his head would disappear completely in a great eruption of smoke, and a sympathetic growl would come out from the cloud. When I finished he uncrossed his legs, laid down his pipe, leaned forward towards me earnestly with his elbows on the arms of his chair, the tips of his fingers together.

" 'I understand very well. He is romantic.'

"He had diagnosed the case for me, and at first I was quite startled to find how simple it was; and indeed our conference resembled so much a medical consultation—Stein, of learned aspect, sitting in an armchair before his desk; I, anxious, in another, facing him, but a little to one side—that it seemed natural to ask—

" 'What's good for it?'

"He lifted up a long forefinger.

" 'There is only one remedy! One thing alone can us from being ourselves cure!' The finger came down on the desk with a smart rap. The case which he had made to look so simple before became if possible still simpler—and altogether hopeless. There was a pause. 'Yes,' said I, 'strictly speaking, the question is not how to get cured, but how to live.'

"He approved with his head, a little sadly as it seemed. *Ja! ja!* In general, adapting the words of your great poet: That is the question. . . .' He went on nodding sympathetically. . . . 'How to be! *Ach!* How to be.'

"He stood up with the tips of his fingers resting on the desk.

" 'We want in so many different ways to be,' he began again. 'This magnificent butterfly finds a little heap of dirt and sits still on it; but man he will never on his heap of mud keep still. He want to be so, and again he want to be so. . . .' He moved his hand up, then down. . . . 'He wants to be a saint, and he wants to be a devil—and every time he shuts his eyes he sees himself as a very fine fellow—so fine as he can never be. . . . In a dream. . . .'

"He lowered the glass lid, the automatic lock clicked sharply, and taking up the case in both hands he bore it religiously away to its place, passing out of the bright circle of the lamp into the ring of fainter light—into shapeless dusk at last. It had an odd effect—as if these few steps had carried him out of this concrete and perplexed world. His tall form, as though robbed of its substance, hovered noiselessly over invisible things with stooping and indefinite movements; his voice, heard in that remoteness where he could be glimpsed mysteriously busy with immaterial cares, was no longer incisive, seemed to roll voluminous and grave—mellowed by distance.

" 'And because you not always can keep your eyes shut there comes the real trouble —the heart pain—the world pain. I tell you, my friend, it is not good for you to find you cannot make your dream come true, for the reason that you not strong enough are, or not clever enough. *Ja!* . . . And all the time you are such a fine fellow, too! *Wie? Was? Gott in Himmel!* How can that be? Ha! ha! ha!'

"The shadow prowling amongst the graves of butterflies laughed boisterously.

" 'Yes! Very funny this terrible thing is. A man that is born falls into a dream like a man who falls into the sea. If he tries to climb out into the air as inexperienced people endeavor to do, he drowns—*nicht wahr?* . . . No! I tell you! The way is to the destructive element submit yourself, and with the exertions of your hands and feet in the water make the deep, deep sea keep you up. So if you ask me—how to be?'

"His voice leaped up extraordinarily strong, as though away there in the dusk he had been inspired by some whisper of knowledge. 'I will tell you! For that, too, there is only one way.'

"With a hasty swish swish of his slippers he loomed up in the ring of faint light, and suddenly appeared in the bright circle of the lamp. His extended hand aimed at my breast like a pistol; his deep-set eyes seemed to pierce through me, but his twitching lips uttered no word, and the austere exaltation of a certitude seen in the dusk vanished from his face. The hand that had been pointing at my breast fell, and by-and-by, coming a step nearer, he laid it gently on my shoulder. There were things, he said mournfully, that perhaps could never be told, only he had lived so much alone that sometimes he forgot—he forgot. The light had destroyed the assurance which had inspired him in the distant shadows. He sat down and, with both elbows on the desk, rubbed his forehead. 'And yet it is true—it is true. In the destructive element immerse.' . . . He spoke in a subdued tone, without looking at me, one hand on each side of his face. 'That was the way. To follow the dream, and again to follow the dream—and so—*ewig*—*usque ad finem.* . . .' The whisper of his conviction seemed to open before me a vast and uncertain expanse, as of a crepuscular horizon on a plain at dawn—or was it, perchance, at the coming of the night? One had not the courage to decide; but it was a charming and deceptive light, throwing the impalpable poesy of its dimness over pitfalls—over graves. His life had begun in sacrifice, in enthusiasm for generous ideas; he had traveled very far, on various ways, on strange paths, and whatever he followed it had been without faltering, and therefore without shame and without regret. In so far he was right. That was the way, no doubt. Yet for all that the great plain on which men wander amongst graves and pitfalls remained very desolate under the impalpable poesy of its crepuscular light, overshadowed in the center, circled with a bright edge as if surrounded by an abyss full of flames. When at last I broke the silence it was to express the opinion that no one could be more romantic than himself.

"He shook his head slowly, and afterwards looked at me with a patient and inquiring glance. It was a shame, he said. There we were sitting and talking like two boys, instead of putting our heads together to find something practical—a practical remedy—for the evil—for the great evil—he repeated, with a humorous and indulgent smile. For all that, our talk did not grow more practical. We avoided pronouncing Jim's name as though we had tried to keep flesh and blood out of our discussion, or he were nothing but an erring spirit, a suffering and nameless shade. 'Na!' said Stein, rising. 'Tonight you sleep here, and in the morning we shall do something practical—practical. . . .' He lit a two-branched candlestick and led the way. We passed through empty dark rooms, escorted by gleams from the lights Stein carried. They glided along the waxed floors, sweeping here and there over the polished surface of the table, leaped upon a fragmentary curve of a piece of furniture, or flashed perpendicularly in and out of distant mirrors, while the forms of two men and the flicker of two flames could be seen for a moment stealing silently across the depths of a crystaline void. He walked slowly a pace in advance with stooping courtesy; there was a profound, as it were a listening, quietude on his face; the long flaxen locks mixed with white threads were scattered thinly upon his slightly bowed neck.

" 'He is romantic—romantic,' he repeated. 'And that is very bad—very bad. . . . Very good, too,' he added. 'But *is he?*' I queried.

" '*Gewiss*,' he said, and stood still holding up the candelabrum, but without looking at me. 'Evident! What is it that by inward pain makes him know himself? What is it that for you and me makes him—exist?'

"At that moment it was difficult to believe in Jim's existence—starting from a country parsonage, blurred by crowds of men as by clouds of dust, silenced by the clashing claims of life and death in a material world—but his imperishable reality came to me with a convincing, with an irresistible force! I saw it vividly, as though in our progress through the lofty silent rooms amongst fleeting gleams of light and the sudden revelations of human figures stealing with flickering flames within unfathomable and pellucid depths, we had approached nearer to absolute Truth, which, like Beauty itself, floats elusive, obscure, half submerged, in the silent still waters of mystery. 'Perhaps he is,' I admitted with a slight laugh, whose unexpectedly loud reverberation made me lower my voice directly; 'but I am sure you are.' With his head dropping on his breast and the light held high he began to walk again. 'Well—I exist, too,' he said.

"He preceded me. My eyes followed his movements, but what I did see was not the head of the firm, the welcome guest at afternoon receptions, the correspondent of learned societies, the entertainer of stray naturalists; I saw only the reality of his destiny, which he had known how to follow with unfaltering footsteps, that life begun in humble surroundings, rich in generous enthusiasms, in friendship, love, war—in all the exalted elements of romance. At the door of my room he faced me. 'Yes,' I said, as though carrying on a discussion, 'and amongst other things you dreamed foolishly of a certain butterfly; but when one fine morning your dream came in your way you did not let the splendid opportunity escape. Did you? Whereas he . . .' Stein lifted his hand. 'And do you know how many opportunities I let escape; how many dreams I had lost that had come in my way?' He shook his head regretfully. 'It seems to me that some would have been very fine—if I had made them come true. Do you know how many? Perhaps I myself don't know.' 'Whether his were fine or not,' I said, 'he knows of one which he certainly did not catch.' 'Everybody knows of one or two like that,' said Stein; 'and that is the trouble—the great trouble. . . .'

"He shook hands on the threshold, peered into my room under his raised arm. 'Sleep well. And tomorrow we must do something practical—practical. . . .'

"Though his own room was beyond mine I saw him return the way he came. He was going back to his butterflies."

XXI

"I don't suppose any of you had ever heard of Patusan?" Marlow resumed, after a silence occupied in the careful lighting of a cigar. "It does not matter; there's many a heavenly body in the lot crowding upon us of a night that mankind had never heard of, it being outside the sphere of its activities and of no earthly importance to anybody but to the astronomers who are paid to talk learnedly about its composition, weight, path—the irregularities of its conduct, the aberrations of its light—a sort of scientific scandalmongering. Thus with Patusan. It was referred to knowingly in the inner government circles in Batavia, especially as to its irregularities and aberrations, and it was known by name to some few, very few, in the mercantile world. Nobody, however, had been there, and I suspect no one desired to go there in person, just as an astronomer, I should fancy, would strongly object to being transported into a distant heavenly body, where, parted from his earthly emoluments, he would be bewildered by the view of an unfamiliar heavens. However, neither heavenly bodies nor astronomers have anything to do with Patusan. It was Jim who went there. I only meant you to understand that had Stein arranged to send him into a star of the fifth magnitude the change could not have been greater. He left his earthly failings behind him and that sort of reputation he had, and there was a totally new set of conditions for his imaginative faculty to work upon. Entirely new, entirely remarkable. And he got hold of them in a remarkable way.

"Stein was the man who knew more about Patusan than anybody else. More than was known in the government circles I suspect. I have no doubt he had been there, either in his butterfly-hunting days or later on, when he tried in his incorrigible way to season with a pinch of romance the fattening dishes of his commercial kitchen. There were very few places in the Archipelago he had not seen in the original dusk of their being, before light (and even electric light) had been carried into them for the sake of better morality and—and—well—the greater profit, too. It was at breakfast of the morning following our talk about Jim that he mentioned the place, after I had quoted poor Brierly's remark: 'Let him creep twenty feet underground and stay there.' He looked up at me with interested attention, as though I had been a rare insect. 'This could be done, too,' he remarked, sipping his coffee. 'Bury him in some sort,' I explained. 'One doesn't like to do it of course, but it would be the best thing, seeing what he is.' 'Yes; he is young,' Stein mused. 'The youngest human being now in existence,' I affirmed. '*Schön.* There's Patusan,' he went on in the same tone. . . . 'And the woman is dead now,' he added incomprehensibly.

"Of course I don't know that story; I can only guess that once before Patusan had been used as a grave for some sin, transgression, or misfortune. It is impossible to suspect Stein. The only woman that had ever existed for him was the Malay girl he called 'My wife the princess,' or, more rarely in moments of expansion, 'the mother of my Emma.' Who was the woman he had mentioned in connection with Patusan I can't say; but from his allusions I understand she had been an educated and very good-looking Dutch-Malay girl, with a tragic or perhaps only a pitiful history, whose most painful part no doubt was her marriage with a Malacca Portuguese who had been clerk in some commercial house in the Dutch colonies. I gathered from Stein that this man was an unsatisfactory person in more ways than one, all being more or less indefinite and offensive. It was solely for his wife's sake that Stein had appointed him manager of Stein & Co.'s trading post in Patusan; but commercially the arrangement was not a success, at any rate for the firm, and now the woman had died, Stein was disposed to try another agent there. The Portuguese, whose name was Cornelius, considered himself a very deserving but ill-used person, entitled by his abilities to a better position. This man Jim would have to relieve. 'But I don't think he will go away from the place,' remarked Stein. 'That has nothing to do with me. It was only for the sake of the woman that I . . . But as I think there is a daughter left, I shall let him, if he likes to stay, keep the old house.'

"Patusan is a remote district of a native-ruled State, and the chief settlement bears the same name. At a point on the river about forty miles from the sea, where the first houses come into view, there can be seen rising above the level of the forests the summits of two steep hills very close together, and separated by what looks like a deep fissure, the cleavage of some mighty stroke. As a matter of fact, the valley between is nothing but a narrow ravine; the appearance from the settlement is of one irregularly conical hill split in two, and with the two halves leaning slightly apart. On the third day after the full, the moon, as seen from the open space in front of Jim's house (he had a very fine house in the native style when I visited him), rose exactly behind these hills, its diffused light at first throwing the two masses into intensely black relief, and then the nearly perfect disc, glowing ruddily, appeared, gliding upwards between the sides of the chasm, till it floated away above the summits, as if escaping from a yawning grave in gentle triumph. 'Wonderful effect,' said Jim by my side. 'Worth seeing. Is it not?'

"And this question was put with a note of personal pride that made me smile, as though he had had a hand in regulating that unique spectacle. He had regulated so many things in Patusan! Things that would have appeared as much beyond his control as the motions of the moon and the stars.

"It was inconceivable. That was the distinctive quality of the part into which Stein and I had tumbled him unwittingly, with no other notion than to get him out of the way; out of his own way, be it understood. That was our main purpose, though, I own, I might have had another motive which had influenced me a little. I was about to go home for a time; and it may be I desired, more than I was aware of myself, to dispose of him—to dispose of him, you understand—before I left. I was going home, and he had come to me from there, with his miserable trouble and his shadowy claim, like a man panting under a burden in a mist. I cannot say I had ever seen him distinctly— not even to this day, after I had my last view of him; but it seemed to me that the less I understood the more I was bound to him in the name of that doubt which is the inseparable part of our knowledge. I did not know so much more about myself. And then, I repeat, I was going home—to that home distant enough for all its hearthstones to be like one hearthstone, by which the humblest of us has the right to sit. We wander in our thousands over the face of the earth, the illustrious and the obscure, earning beyond the seas our fame, our money, or only a crust of bread; but it seems to me that for each of us going home must be like going to render an account. We return to face our superiors, our kindred, our friends—those whom we obey, and those whom we love, but even they who have neither, the most free, lonely, irresponsible and bereft of ties,—even those for whom home holds no dear face, no familiar voice,— even they have to meet the spirit that dwells within the land, under its sky, in its air, in its valleys, and on its rises, in its fields, in its waters and its trees—a mute friend, judge, and inspirer. Say what you like, to get its joy, to breathe its peace, to face its truth, one must return with a clear consciousness. All this may seem to you sheer sentimentalism; and indeed very few of us have the will or the capacity to look consciously under the surface of familiar emotions. There are the girls we love, the men we look up to, the tenderness, the friendships, the opportunities, the pleasures! But the fact remains that you must touch your reward with clean hands, lest it turn to dead leaves, to thorns, in your grasp. I think it is the lonely, without a fireside or an affection they may call their own, those who return not to a dwelling but to the land itself, to meet its disembodied, eternal, and unchangeable spirit—it is those who understand best its severity, its saving power, the grace of its secular right to our fidelity, to our obedience. Yes! few of us understand, but we all feel it though, and I say *all* without exception, because those who do not feel do not count. Each blade of grass has its spot on earth whence it draws its life, its strength; and so is man rooted to the land from which he draws his faith together with his life. I don't know how much Jim understood; but I know he felt, he felt confusedly but powerfully, the demand of some such truth or some such illusion—I don't care how you call it, there is so little difference, and the difference means so little. The thing is that in virtue of his feeling he mattered. He would never go home now. Not he. Never. Had he been capable of picturesque manifestations he would have shuddered at the thought and made you shudder, too. But he was not of that sort, though he was expressive enough in his way. Before the idea of going home he would grow desperately stiff and immovable, with lowered chin and pouted lips, and with those candid blue eyes of his glowering darkly under a frown, as if before something unbearable, as if before something revolting. There was imagination in that hard skull of his, over which the thick clustering hair fitted like a cap. As to me, I have no imagination (I would be more certain about him today, if I had), and I do not mean to imply that I figured to myself the spirit of the land uprising above the white cliffs of Dover, to ask me what I— returning with no bones broken, so to speak—had done with my very young brother. I could not make such a mistake. I knew very well he was of those about whom there is no inquiry; I had seen better men go out, disappear, vanish utterly, without provoking a sound of curiosity or sorrow. The spirit of the land, as becomes the ruler of great enterprises, is careless of innumerable lives. Woe to the stragglers! We exist only in so far as we hang together. He had straggled in a way; he had not hung on; but he was aware of it with an intensity that made him touching, just as a man's more intense life makes his death more touching than the death of a tree. I happened to be handy, and I happened to be touched. That's all there is to it. I was concerned as to the way he would go out. It would have hurt me if, for instance, he had taken to drink. The earth is so small that I was afraid of, some day, being waylaid by a bleary-eyed, swollen-faced, besmirched loafer, with no soles to his canvas shoes, and with a flutter of rags about the elbows, who, on the strength of old acquaintance, would ask for a loan of five dollars. You know the awful jaunty bearing of these scarecrows coming to you from a decent past, the rasping careless voice, the half-averted impudent glances— those meetings more trying to a man who believes in the solidarity of our lives than the sight of an impenitent deathbed to a priest. That, to tell you the truth, was the only danger I could see for him and for me; but I also mistrusted my want of imagination. It might even come to something worse, in some way it was beyond my powers of fancy to foresee. He wouldn't let me forget how imaginative he was, and your imaginative people swing farther in any direction, as if given a longer scope of cable in the uneasy anchorage of life. They do. They take to drink, too. It may be I was belittling him by such a fear. How could I tell? Even Stein could say no more than that he was romantic. I only knew he was one of us. And what business had he to be romantic? I am telling you so much about my own instinctive feelings and bemused reflections because there remains so little to be told of him. He existed for me, and after all it is only through me that he exists for you. I've led him out by the hand; I have paraded him before you. Were my commonplace fears unjust? I won't say—not even now. You may be able to tell better, since the proverb has it that the onlookers see most of the game. At any rate, they were superfluous. He did not go out, not at all; on the contrary, he came on wonderfully, came on straight as a die and in excellent form, which showed that he could stay as well as spurt. I ought to be delighted, for it is a victory in which I had taken my part; but I am not so pleased as I would have expected to be. I ask myself whether his rush had really carried him out of that mist in which he loomed interesting if not very big, with floating outlines—a straggler yearning inconsolably for his humble place in the ranks. And besides, the last word is not said,—probably shall never be said. Are not our lives too short for that full utterance which through all our stammerings is of course our only and abiding intention? I have given up expecting those last words, whose ring, if they could only be pronounced, would shake both heaven and earth. There is never time to say our last word—the last word of our love, of our desire, faith, remorse, submission, revolt. The heaven and the earth must not be shaken. I suppose—at least, not by us who know so many truths about either. My last words about Jim shall be few. I affirm he had achieved greatness; but the thing would be dwarfed in the telling, or rather in the hearing. Frankly, it is not my words that I mistrust but your minds. I could be eloquent were I not afraid you fellows had starved your imaginations to feed your bodies. I do not mean to be offensive; it is respectable to have no illusions—and safe—and profitable—and dull. Yet you, too, in your time must have known the intensity of life, that light of glamor created in the shock of trifles, as amazing as the glow of sparks struck from a cold stone—and as short-lived, alas!"

XXII

The conquest of love, honor, men's confidence—the pride of it, the power of it, are fit materials for a heroic tale; only our minds are struck by the externals of such a success, and to Jim's successes there were no externals. Thirty miles of forest shut it off from the sight of an indifferent world, and the noise of the white surf along the coast overpowered the voice of fame. The stream of civilization, as if divided on a headland a hundred miles north of Patusan, branches east and southeast, leaving its plains and valleys, its old trees and its old mankind, neglected and isolated, such as an insignificant and crumbling islet between the two branches of a mighty, devouring stream. You find the name of the country pretty often in collections of old voyages. The seventeenth-century traders went there for pepper, because the passion for pepper seemed to burn like a flame of love in the breast of Dutch and English adventurers about the time of James the First. Where wouldn't they go for pepper? For a bag of pepper they would cut each other's throats without hesitation, and would foreswear their souls, of which they were so careful otherwise: the bizarre obstinacy of that desire made them defy death in a thousand shapes; the unknown seas, the loathesome and strange diseases; wounds, captivity, hunger, pestilence, and despair. It made them great! By heavens! It made them heroic; and it made them pathetic, too, in their craving for trade with the inflexible death levying its toll on young and old. It seems impossible to believe that mere greed could hold men to such a steadfastness of purpose, to such a blind persistence in endeavor and sacrifice. And indeed those who adventured their persons and lives risked all they had for a slender reward. They left their bones to lie bleaching on distant shores, so that wealth might flow to the living at home. To us, their less tried successors, they appear magnified, not as agents of trade but as instruments of a recorded destiny, pushing out into the unknown in obedience to an inward voice, to an impulse beating in the blood, to a dream of the future. They were wonderful; and it must be owned they were ready for the wonderful. They recorded it complacently in their sufferings, in the aspect of the seas, in the customs of strange nations, in the glory of splendid rulers.

"In Patusan they had found lots of pepper, and had been impressed by the magnificence and the wisdom of the Sultan; but somehow, after a century of checkered intercourse, the country seems to drop gradually out of the trade. Perhaps the pepper had given out. Be it as it may, nobody cares for it now; the glory has departed, the Sultan is an imbecile youth with two thumbs on his left hand and an uncertain and beggarly revenue extorted from a miserable population and stolen from him by his many uncles.

"This of course I have from Stein. He gave me their names and a short sketch of the life and character of each. He was as full of information about native States as an official report, but infinitely more amusing. He *had* to know. He traded in so many, and in some districts—as in Patusan, for instance—his firm was the only one to have an agency by special permit from the Dutch authorities. The Government trusted his discretion, and it was understood that he took all the risks. The men he employed understood that, too, but he made it worth their while apparently. He was perfectly frank with me over the breakfast-table in the morning. As far as he was aware (the last news was thirteen months old, he stated precisely), utter insecurity for life and property was the normal condition. There were in Patusan antagonistic forces, and one of them was Rajah Allang, the worst of the Sultan's uncles, the governor of the river, who did the extorting and the stealing, and ground down to the point of extinction the country-born Malays, who, utterly defenseless, had not even the resource of emigrating,—'for indeed,' as Stein remarked, 'where could they go, and how could they get away?' No doubt they did not even desire to get away. The world (which is circumscribed by lofty impassable mountains) has been given into the hand of the high-born, and *this* Rajah they knew: he was of their own royal house. I had the pleasure of meeting the gentleman later on. He was a dirty, little, used-up old man with evil eyes and a weak mouth, who swallowed an opium pill every two hours, and in defiance of common decency wore his hair uncovered and falling in wild stringy locks about his wizened grimy face. When giving audience he would clamber upon a sort of narrow stage erected in a hall like a ruinous barn with a rotten bamboo floor, through the cracks of which you could see twelve or fifteen feet below the heaps of refuse and garbage of all kinds lying under the house. That is where and how he received us when, accompanied by Jim, I paid him a visit of ceremony. There were about forty people in the room, and perhaps three times as many in the great courtyard below. There was constant movement, coming and going, pushing and murmuring, at our backs. A few youths in gay silks glared from the distance; the majority, slaves and humble dependants, were half naked, in ragged sarongs, dirty with ashes and mud-stains. I had never seen Jim look so grave, so self-possessed, in an impenetrable, impressive way. In the midst of these dark-faced men, his stalwart figure in white apparel, the gleaming clusters of his fair hair, seemed to catch all the sunshine that trickled through the cracks in the closed shutters of that dim hall, with its walls of mats and a roof of thatch. He appeared like a creature not only of another kind but of another essence. Had they not seen him come up in a canoe they might have thought he had descended upon them from the clouds. He did, however, come in a crazy dug-out, sitting (very still and with his knees together, for fear of overturning the thing)—sitting on a tin box—which I had lent him—nursing on his lap a revolver of the Navy pattern— presented by me on parting—which, through an interposition of Providence, or through some wrong-headed notion, that was just like him, or else from sheer instinctive sagacity, he had decided to carry unloaded. That's how he ascended the Patusan river. Nothing could have been more prosaic and more unsafe, more extravagantly casual, more lonely. Strange, this fatality that would cast the complexion of a flight upon all his acts, of impulsive unreflecting desertion—of a jump into the unknown.

"It is precisely the casualness of it that strikes me most. Neither Stein nor I had a clear conception of what might be on the other side when we, metaphorically speaking, took him up and hove him over the wall with scant ceremony. At the moment I merely wished to achieve his disappearance. Stein characteristically enough had a sentimental motive. He had a notion of paying off (in kind, I suppose) the old debt he had never forgotten. Indeed he had been all his life especially friendly to anybody from the British Isles. His late benefactor, it is true, was a Scot—even to the length of being called Alexander M'Neil—and Jim came from a long way south of the Tweed; but at the distance of six or seven thousand miles Great Britain, though never diminished, looks foreshortened enough even to its own children to rob such details of their importance. Stein was excusable, and his hinted intentions were so generous that I begged him most earnestly to keep them secret for a time. I felt that no consideration of personal advantage should be allowed to influence Jim; that not even the risk of such influence should be run. We had to deal with another sort of reality. He wanted a refuge, and a refuge at the cost of danger should be offered him—nothing more.

"Upon every other point I was perfectly frank with him, and I even (as I believed at the time) exaggerated the danger of the undertaking. As a matter of fact I did not do it justice; his first day in Patusan was nearly his last—would have been his last if he had not been so reckless or so hard on himself and had condescended to load that revolver. I remember, as I unfolded our precious scheme for his retreat, how his stubborn but weary resignation was gradually replaced by surprise, interest, wonder, and by boyish eagerness. This was a chance he had been dreaming of. He couldn't think how he merited that I . . . He would be shot if he could see to what he owed . . . And it was Stein, Stein the merchant, who . . . but of course it was me he had to . . . I cut him short. He was not articulate, and his gratitude caused me inexplicable pain. I told him that if he owed this chance to any one especially, it was to an old Scot of whom he had never heard, who had died many years ago, of whom little was remembered besides a roaring voice and a rough sort of honesty. There was really no one to receive his thanks. Stein was passing on to a young man the help he had received in his own young days, and I had done no more than to mention his name. Upon this he colored, and, twisting a bit of paper in his fingers, he remarked bashfully that I had always trusted him.

"I admitted that such was the case, and added after a pause that I wished he had been able to follow my example. 'You think I don't?' he asked uneasily, and remarked in a mutter that one had to get some sort of show first; then brightening up, and in a loud voice he protested he would give me no occasion to regret my confidence, which —which . . .

" 'Do not misapprehend,' I interrupted. 'It is not in your power to make me regret anything.' There would be no regrets; but if there were, it would be altogether my own affair: on the other hand, I wished him to understand clearly that this arrangement, this—this—experiment, was his own doing; he was responsible for it and no one else. 'Why? Why,' he stammered, 'this is the very thing that I . . .' I begged him not to be dense, and he looked more puzzled than ever. He was in a fair way to make life intolerable to himself. . . . 'Do you think so?' he asked, disturbed; but in a moment added confidently, 'I was going on though. Was I not?' It was impossible to be angry with him: I could not help a smile, and told him that in the old days people who went on like this were on the way of becoming hermits in a wilderness. 'Hermits be hanged!' he commented with engaging impulsiveness. Of course he didn't mind a wilderness. . . . 'I was glad of it,' I said. That was where he would be going to. He would find it lively enough, I ventured to promise. 'Yes, yes,' he said, keenly. He had shown a desire, I continued inflexibly, to go out and shut the door after him. . . . 'Did I?' he interrupted in a strange access of gloom that seemed to envelop him from head to foot like the shadow of a passing cloud. He was wonderfully expressive after all. Wonderfully! 'Did I?' he repeated, bitterly. 'You can't say I made much noise about it. And I can keep it up, too—only, confound it! you show me a door.' . . . 'Very well. Pass on,' I struck in. I could make him a solemn promise that it would be shut behind him with a vengeance. His fate, whatever it was, would be ignored, because the country, for all its rotten state, was not judged ripe for interference. Once he got in, it would be for the outside world as though he had never existed. He would have nothing but the soles of his two feet to stand upon, and he would have first to find his ground at that. 'Never existed—that's it, by Jove!' he murmured to himself. His eyes, fastened upon my lips, sparkled. If he had thoroughly understood the conditions, I concluded, he had better jump into the first gharry he could see and drive on to Stein's house for his final instructions. He flung out of the room before I had fairly finished speaking."

XXIII

He did not return till next morning. He had been kept to dinner and for the night. There never had been such a wonderful man as Mr. Stein. He had in his pocket a letter for Cornelius ('the Johnnie who's going to get the sack,' he explained with a momentary drop in his elation), and he exhibited with glee a silver ring, such as natives use, worn down very thin and showing faint traces of chasing.

"This was his introduction to an old chap called Doramin—one of the principal men out there—a big pot—who had been Mr. Stein's friend in that country where he had all these adventures. Mr. Stein called him 'war-comrade.' War-comrade was good. Wasn't it? And didn't Mr. Stein speak English wonderfully well? Said he had learned it in Celebes—of all places! That was awfully funny. Was it not? He did not speak with an accent—a twang—did I notice? That chap Doramin had given him the ring. They had exchanged presents when they parted for the last time. Sort of promising eternal friendship. He called it fine—did I not? They had to make a dash for dear life out of the country when that Mohammed—Mohammed—What's-his-name had been killed. I knew the story, of course. Seemed a beastly shame, didn't it? . . .

"He ran on like this, forgetting his plate, with a knife and fork in hand (he had found me at tiffin), slightly flushed, and with his eyes darkened many shades, which was with him a sign of excitement. The ring was a sort of credential—('It's like something you read of in books,' he threw in appreciatively) and Doramin would do his best for him. Mr. Stein had been the means of saving that chap's life on some occasion; purely by accident, Mr. Stein had said, but he—Jim—had his own opinion about that. Mr. Stein was just the man to look out for such accidents. No matter. Accident or purpose, this would serve his turn immensely. Hoped to goodness the jolly old beggar had not gone off the hooks meantime. Mr. Stein could not tell. There had been no news for more than a year; they were kicking up no end of an all-fired row amongst themselves, and the river was closed. Jolly awkward, this; but, no fear; he would manage to find a crack to get in.

"He impressed, almost frightened, me with his elated rattle. He was voluble like a youngster on the eve of a long holiday with a prospect of delightful scrapes, and such an attitude of mind in a grown man and in this connection had in it something phenomenal, a little mad, dangerous, unsafe. I was on the point of entreating him to take things seriously when he dropped his knife and fork (he had begun eating, or rather swallowing food, as it were, unconsciously), and began a search all around his plate. The ring! The ring! Where the devil . . . Ah! Here it was. . . . He closed his big hand on it, and tried all his pockets one after another. Jove! wouldn't do to lose the thing. He meditated gravely over his fist. Had it? Would hang the bally affair round his neck! And he proceeded to do this immediately, producing a string (which looked like a bit of a cotton shoelace) for the purpose. There! That would do the trick! It would be the deuce if . . . He seemed to catch sight of my face for the first time, and it steadied him a little. I probably didn't realize, he said with a naïve gravity, how much importance he attached to that token. It meant a friend; and it is a good thing to have a friend. He knew something about that. He nodded at me expressively, but before my disclaiming gesture he leaned his head on his hand and for a while sat silent, playing thoughtfully with the breadcrumbs on the cloth. . . . 'Slam the door—that was jolly well put,' he cried, and jumping up, began to pace the room, reminding me by the set of the shoulders, the turn of his head, the headlong and uneven stride, of that night when he had paced thus, confessing, explaining—what you will—but, in the last instance, living—living before me, under his own little cloud, with all his unconscious subtlety which could draw consolation from the very source of sorrow. It was the same mood, the same and different, like a fickle companion that today guiding you on the true path, with the same eyes, the same step, the same impulse, tomorrow will lead you hopelessly astray. His tread was assured, his straying, darkened eyes seemed to search the room for something. One of his footfalls somehow sounded louder than the other—the fault of his boots probably—and gave a curious impression of an invisible halt in his gait. One of his hands was rammed deep into his trousers-pocket, the other waved suddenly above his head. 'Slam the door!' he shouted. 'I've been waiting for that. I'll show yet . . . I'll . . . I'm ready for any confounded thing. . . . I've been dreaming of it . . . Jove! Get out of this. Jove! This is luck at last. . . . You wait. I'll . . .'

"He tossed his head fearlessly, and I confess that for the first and last time in our acquaintance I perceived myself unexpectedly to be thoroughly sick of him. Why these vaporings? He was stumping about the room flourishing his arm absurdly, and now and then feeling on his breast for the ring under his clothes. Where was the sense of such exaltation in a man appointed to be a trading-clerk, and in a place where there was no trade—at that? Why hurl defiance at the universe? This was not a proper frame of mind to approach any undertaking; an improper frame of mind not only for him, I said, but for any man. He stood still over me. Did I think so? he asked, by no means subdued, and with a smile in which I seemed to detect suddenly something insolent. But then I am twenty years his senior. Youth *is* insolent; it is its right—its necessity; it has got to assert itself, and all assertion in this world of doubts is a defiance, is an insolence. He went off into a far corner, and coming back, he, figuratively speaking, turned to rend me. I spoke like that because I—even I, who had been no end kind to him—even I remembered—remembered—against him—what—what had happened. And what about others—the—the—world? Where's the wonder he wanted to get out, meant to get out, meant to stay out—by heavens! And I talked about proper frames of mind!

" 'It is not I or the world who remember,' I shouted. 'It is you—you, who remember.'

"He did not flinch, and went on with heat, 'Forget everything, everybody, everybody.' . . . His voice fell. . . . 'But you,' he added.

" 'Yes—me, too—if it would help,' I said, also in a low tone. After this we remained silent and languid for a time as if exhausted. Then he began again, composedly, and told me that Mr. Stein had instructed him to wait for a month or so, to see whether it was possible for him to remain, before he began building a new house for himself, so as to avoid 'vain expense.' He did make use of funny expressions—Stein did. 'Vain expense' was good. . . . Remain? Why! of course. He would hang on. Let him only get in—that's all; he would answer for it he would remain. Never get out. It was easy enough to remain.

" 'Don't be foolhardy,' I said, rendered uneasy by his threatening tone. 'If you only live long enough you will want to come back.'

" 'Come back to what?' he asked, absently, with his eyes fixed upon the face of a clock on the wall.

"I was silent for a while. 'Is it to be never, then?' I said. 'Never,' he repeated, dreamily, without looking at me, and then flew into sudden activity. 'Jove! Two o'clock, and I sail at four!'

"It was true. A brigantine of Stein's was leaving for the westward that afternoon, and he had been instructed to take his passage in her, only no orders to delay the sailing had been given. I suppose Stein forgot. He made a rush to get his things while I went aboard my ship, where he promised to call on his way to the outer roadster. He turned up accordingly in a great hurry and with a small leather valise in his hand. This wouldn't do, and I offered him an old tin trunk of mine supposed to be water-tight, or at least damp-tight. He effected the transfer by the simple process of shooting out the contents of his valise as you would empty a sack of wheat. I saw three books in the tumble; two small, in dark covers, and a thick green-and-gold volume—a half-crown complete Shakespeare. 'You read this?' I asked. 'Yes. Best thing to cheer up a fellow,' he said, hastily. I was struck by this appreciation, but there was no time for Shakespearian talk. A heavy revolver and two small boxes of cartridges were lying on the cuddy-table. 'Pray take this,' I said. 'It may help you to remain.' No sooner were these words out of my mouth that I perceived what grim meaning they could bear. 'May help you to get in,' I corrected myself, remorsefully. He, however, was not troubled by obscure meanings; he thanked me effusively and bolted out, calling Good-bye over his shoulder. I heard his voice through the ship's side urging his boatmen to give way, and looking out of the sternport I saw the boat rounding under the counter. He sat in her leaning forward, exciting his men with voice and gestures; and as he had kept the revolver in his hand and seemed to be presenting it at their heads, I shall never forget the scared faces of the four Javanese, and the frantic swing of their stroke which snatched that vision from under my eyes. Then turning away, the first thing I saw were the two boxes of cartridges on the cuddy-table. He had forgotten to take them.

"I ordered my gig manned at once; but Jim's rowers, under the impression that their lives hung on a thread while they had that madman in the boat, made such excellent time that before I had traversed half the distance between the two vessels I caught sight of him clambering over the rail, and of his box being passed up. All the brigantine's canvas was loose, her mainsail was set, and the windlass was just beginning to clink as I stepped upon her deck: her master, a dapper little half-caste of forty or so, in a blue flannel suit, with lively eyes, his round face the color of lemon-peel, and with a thin little black moustache drooping on each side of his thick, dark lips, came forward smirking. He turned out, notwithstanding his self-satisfied and cheery exterior, to be of a careworn temperament. In answer to a remark of mine (while Jim had gone below

for a moment) he said, 'Oh, yes. Patusan.' He was going to carry the gentleman to the
mouth of the river, but would 'never ascend.' His flowing English seemed to be derived
from a dictionary compiled by a lunatic. Had Mr. Stein desired him to 'ascend,' he
would have 'reverentially'—(I think he wanted to say respectfully—but devil only
knows)—'reverentially made objects for the safety of properties.' If disregarded, he
would have presented 'resignation to quit.' Twelve months ago he had made his last
voyage there, and though Mr. Cornelius 'propitiated many offertories' to Mr. Rajah
Allang and the 'principal populations,' on conditions which made the trade 'a snare
and ashes in the mouth,' yet his ship had been fired upon from the woods by
'irresponsive parties' all the way down the river; which causing his crew 'from exposure
to limb to remain silent in hidings,' the brigantine was nearly stranded on a sandbank
at the bar, where she 'would have been perishable beyond the act of man.' The angry
disgust at the recollection, the pride of his fluency, to which he turned an attentive ear,
struggled for the possession of his broad simple face. He scowled and beamed at me,
and watched with satisfaction the undeniable effect of his phraseology. Dark frowns
ran swiftly over the placid sea, and the brigantine, with her foretopsail to the mast and
her mainboom amidships, seemed bewildered amongst the cat's-paws. He told me
further, gnashing his teeth, that the Rajah was a 'laughable hyena' (can't imagine how
he got hold of hyenas); while somebody else was many times falser than the 'weapons
of a crocodile.' Keeping one eye on the movements of his crew forward, he let loose his
volubility—comparing the place to a 'cage of beasts made ravenous by long impeni-
tence.' I fancy he meant impunity. He had no intention, he cried, to 'exhibit himself to
be made attached purposefully to robbery.' The long-drawn wails, giving the time for
the pull of the men catting the anchor, came to an end, and he lowered his voice.
'Plenty too much enough of Patusan,' he concluded, with energy.

"I heard afterwards he had been so indiscreet as to get himself tied up by the neck
with a rattan halter to a post planted in the middle of a mud-hole before the Rajah's
house. He spent the best part of a day and a whole night in that unwholesome
situation, but there is every reason to believe the thing had been meant as a sort of
joke. He brooded for a while over that horrid memory, I suppose, and then addressed
in a quarrelsome tone the man coming aft to the helm. When he turned to me again it
was to speak judicially, without passion. He would take the gentleman to the mouth of
the river at Batu Kring (Patusan town 'being situated internally,' he remarked, 'thirty
miles'). But in his eyes, he continued—a tone of bored, weary conviction replacing his
previous voluble delivery—the gentleman was already 'in the similitude of a corpse.'
'What? What do you say?' I asked. He assumed a startlingly ferocious demeanor, and
imitated to perfection the act of stabbing from behind. 'Already like the body of one
deported,' he explained, with the insufferably conceited air of his kind after what they
imagine a display of cleverness. Behind him I perceived Jim smiling silently at me, and
with a raised hand checking the exclamation on my lips.

"Then, while the half-caste, bursting with importance, shouted his orders, while the
yards swung creaking and the heavy boom came surging over, Jim and I, alone as it
were, to leeward of the mainsail, clasped each other's hands and exchanged the last

hurried words. My heart was freed from that dull resentment which had existed side by side with interest in his fate. The absurd chatter of the half-caste had given more reality to the miserable dangers of his path than Stein's careful statements. On that occasion the sort of formality that had been always present in our intercourse vanished from our speech; I believe I called him 'dear boy,' and he tacked on the words 'old man' to some half-uttered expression of gratitude, as though his risk set off against my years had made us more equal in age and in feeling. There was a moment of real and profound intimacy, unexpected and short-lived like a glimpse of some everlasting, of some saving truth. He exerted himself to soothe me as though he had been the more mature of the two. 'All right, all right,' he said, rapidly, and with feeling. 'I promise to take care of myself. Yes; I won't take any risks. Not a single blessed risk. Of course not. I mean to hang out. Don't you worry. Jove! I feel as if nothing could touch me. Why! this is luck from the word Go. I wouldn't spoil such a magnificent chance!' . . . A magnificent chance! Well, it *was* magnificent, but chances are what men make them, and how was I to know? As he had said, even I—even I remembered—his—his misfortunes against him. It was true. And the best thing for him was to go.

"My gig had dropped in the wake of the brigantine, and I saw him aft detached upon the light of the westering sun, raising his cap high above his head. I heard an indistinct shout, 'You—shall—hear—of—me.' Of me, or from me, I don't know which. I think it must have been *of* me. My eyes were too dazzled by the glitter of the sea below his feet to see him clearly; I am fated never to see him clearly; but I can assure you no man could have appeared less 'in the similitude of a corpse,' as that half-caste croaker had put it. I could see the little wretch's face, the shape and color of a ripe pumpkin, poked out somewhere under Jim's elbow. He, too, raised his arm as if for a downward thrust. *Absit omen!*"

XXIV

"The coast of Patusan (I saw it nearly two years afterwards) is straight and somber, and faces a misty ocean. Red trails are seen like cataracts of rust streaming under the dark-green foliage of bushes and creepers clothing the low cliffs. Swampy plains open out at the mouth of rivers, with a view of jagged blue peaks beyond the vast forests. In the offing a chain of islands, dark, crumbling shapes, stand out in the everlasting sunlit haze like the remnants of a wall breached by the sea.

"There is a village of fisherfolk at the mouth of the Batu Kring branch of the estuary. The river, which had been closed so long, was open then, and Stein's little schooner, in which I had my passage, worked her way up in three tides without being exposed to a fusillade from 'irresponsive parties.' Such a state of affairs belonged already to ancient history, if I could believe the elderly headman of the fishing village, who came on board to act as a sort of pilot. He talked to me (the second white man he had ever seen) with confidence, and most of his talk was about the first white man he had ever seen. He called him Tuan Jim, and the tone of his references was made remarkable by a strange mixture of familiarity and awe. They, in the village, were under that lord's special protection, which showed that Jim bore no grudge. If he had warned me that I would hear of him it was perfectly true. I was hearing of him. There was already a story that the tide had turned two hours before its time to help him on his journey up the river. The talkative old man himself had steered the canoe and had marveled at the phenomenon. Moreover, all the glory was in his family. His son and his son-in-law had paddled; but they were only youths without experience, who did not notice the speed of the canoe till he pointed out to them the amazing fact.

"Jim's coming to that fishing village was a blessing; but to them, as to many of us, the blessing came heralded by terrors. So many generations had been released since the last white man had visited the river that the very tradition had been lost. The appearance of the being that descended upon them and demanded inflexibly to be taken up to Patusan was discomposing; his insistence was alarming; his generosity more than suspicious. It was an unheard-of request. There was no precedent. What would the Rajah say to this? What would he do to them? The best part of the night was spent in consultation; but the immediate risk from the anger of that strange man seemed so great that at last a cranky dugout was got ready. The women shrieked with grief as it put off. A fearless old hag cursed the stranger.

"He sat in it, as I've told you, on his tin box, nursing the unloaded revolver on his lap. He sat with precaution—than which there is nothing more fatiguing—and thus entered the land he was destined to fill with the fame of his virtues, from the blue peaks inland to the white ribbon of surf on the coast. At the first bend he lost sight of the sea with its laboring waves for ever rising, sinking, and vanishing to rise again—the very image of struggling mankind—and faced the immovable forests rooted deep in the soil, soaring towards the sunshine, everlasting in the shadowy might of their tradition, like life itself. And his opportunity sat veiled by his side like an Eastern bride waiting to be uncovered by the hand of the master. He, too, was the heir of a shadowy and mighty tradition! He told me, however, that he had never in his life felt so depressed and tired as in that canoe. All the movement he dared to allow himself was to reach, as it were by stealth, after the shell of half a coconut floating between his shoes, and bale some of the water out with a carefully restrained action. He discovered how hard the lid of a block-tin case was to sit upon. He had heroic health; but several times during that journey he experienced fits of giddiness, and between whiles he speculated hazily as to the size of the blister the sun was raising on his back. For amusement he tried by looking ahead to decide whether the muddy object he saw lying on the water's edge was a log of wood or an alligator. Only very soon he had to give that up. No fun in it. Always alligator. One of them flopped into the river and all but capsized the canoe. But this excitement was over directly. Then in a long empty reach he was very grateful to a troop of monkeys who came right down on the bank and made an insulting hullabaloo on his passage. Such was the way in which he was approaching greatness as genuine as any man ever achieved. Principally, he longed for sunset; and meantime his three paddlers were preparing to put into execution their plan of delivering him up to the Rajah.

" 'I suppose I might have been stupid with fatigue, or perhaps I did doze off for a time,' he said. The first thing he knew was his canoe coming to the bank. He became instantaneously aware of the forest having been left behind, of the first houses being visible higher up, of a stockade on his left, and of his boatmen leaping out together upon a low point of land and taking to their heels. Instinctively he leaped out after them. At first he thought himself deserted for some inconceivable reason, but he heard excited shouts, a gate swung open, and a lot of people poured out, making towards him. At the same time a boat full of armed men appeared on the river and came alongside his empty canoe, thus shutting off his retreat.

" 'I was too startled to be quite cool—don't you know? and if that revolver had been loaded I would have shot somebody—perhaps two, three bodies, and that would have been the end of me. But it wasn't. . . .' 'Why not?' I asked. 'Well, I couldn't fight the whole population, and I wasn't coming to them as if I were afraid of my life,' he said, with just a faint hint of his stubborn sulkiness in the glance he gave me. I refrained from pointing out to him that they could not have known the chambers were actually empty. He had to satisfy himself in his own way. . . . 'Anyhow it wasn't,' he repeated, good-humoredly, 'and so I just stood still and asked them what was the matter. That seemed to strike them dumb. I saw some of these thieves going off with my box. That long-legged old scoundrel Kassim (I'll show him to you tomorrow) ran out fussing at me about the Rajah wanting to see me. I said, "All right;" I, too, wanted to see the Rajah, and I simply walked in through the gate and—and—here I am.' He laughed, and then with unexpected emphasis, 'and do you know what's the best in it?' he asked. 'I'll tell you. It's the knowledge that had I been wiped out it is this place that would have been the loser.'

"He spoke thus to me before his house on that evening I've mentioned—after we had watched the moon float away above the chasm between the hills like an ascending spirit out of a grave; its sheen descended, cold and pale, like the ghost of dead sunlight. There is something haunting in the light of the moon; it has all the dispassionateness of a disembodied soul, and something of its inconceivable mystery. It is to our sunshine, which—say what you like—is all we have to live by, what the echo is to the sound: misleading and confusing whether the note be mocking or sad. It robs all forms of matter—which, after all, is our domain—of their substance, and gives a sinister reality to shadows alone. And the shadows were very real around us, but Jim by my side looked very stalwart, as though nothing—not even the occult power of moonlight—could rob him of his reality in my eyes. Perhaps, indeed, nothing could touch him since he had survived the assault of the dark powers. All was silent, all was still; even on the river the moonbeams slept as on a pool. It was the moment of high water, a moment of immobility that accentuated the utter isolation of this lost corner of the earth. The houses crowding along the wide shining sweep without ripple or glitter, stepping into the water in a line of jostling, vague, grey, silvery forms mingled with black masses of shadow, were like a spectral herd of shapeless creatures pressing forward to drink in a spectral and lifeless stream. Here and there a red gleam twinkled within the bamboo walls, warm, like a living spark, significant of human affections, of shelter, of repose.

"He confessed to me that he often watched these tiny warm gleams go out one by one, that he loved to see people go to sleep under his eyes, confident in the security of tomorrow. 'Peaceful here, eh?' he asked. He was not eloquent, but there was a deep meaning in the words that followed. 'Look at these houses; there's not one where I am not trusted. Jove! I told you I would hang on. Ask any man, woman, or child . . .' He paused. 'Well, I am all right anyhow.'

"I observed quickly that he had found that out in the end. I had been sure of it, I added. He shook his head. 'Were you?' He pressed my arm lightly above the elbow. 'Well, then—you were right.'

"There was elation and pride, there was awe almost, in that low exclamation. 'Jove!' he cried, 'only think what it is to me.' Again he pressed my arm. 'And you asked me whether I thought of leaving. Good God! I! want to leave! Especially now after what you told me of Mr. Stein's . . . Leave! Why! That's what I was afraid of. It would have been—it would have been harder than dying. No—on my word. Don't laugh. I must feel—every day, every time I open my eyes—that I am trusted—that nobody has a right—don't you know? Leave! For where? What for? To get what?'

"I had told him (indeed it was the main object of my visit) that it was Stein's intention to present him at once with the house and the stock of trading goods, on certain easy conditions which would make the transaction perfectly regular and valid. He began to snort and plunge at first. 'Confound your delicacy!' I shouted. 'It isn't Stein at all. It's giving you what you had made for yourself. And in any case keep your remarks for M'Neil—when you meet him in the other world. I hope it won't happen soon. . . .' He had to give in to my arguments, because all his conquests, the trust, the fame, the friendships, the love—all these things that made him master had made him a captive, too. He looked with an owner's eye at the peace of the evening, at the river, at the houses, at the everlasting life of the forests, at the life of the old mankind, at the secrets of the land, at the pride of his own heart: but it was they that possessed him and made him their own to the innermost thought, to the slightest stir of blood, to his last breath.

"It was something to be proud of. I, too, was proud—for him, if not so certain of the fabulous value of the bargain. It was wonderful. It was not so much of his fearlessness that I thought. It is strange how little account I took of it: as if it had been something too conventional to be at the root of the matter. No. I was more struck by the other gifts he had displayed. He had proved his grasp of the unfamiliar situation, his intellectual alertness in that field of thought. There was his readiness, too! Amazing. And all this had come to him in a manner like keen scent to a well-bred hound. He was not eloquent, but there was a dignity in this constitutional reticence, there was a high seriousness in his stammerings. He had still his old trick of stubborn blushing. Now and then, though, a word, a sentence, would escape him that showed how deeply, how solemnly, he felt about that work which had given him the certitude of rehabilitation. That is why he seemed to love the land and the people with a sort of fierce egoism, with a contemptuous tenderness."

XXV

" 'This is where I was prisoner for three days,' he murmured to me (it was on the occasion of our visit to the Rajah), while we were making our way slowly through a kind of awestruck riot of dependants across Tunku Allang's courtyard. 'Filthy place, isn't it? And I couldn't get anything to eat either, unless I made a row about it, and then it was only a small plate of rice and a fried fish not much bigger than a stickleback—confound them! Jove! *I've* been hungry prowling inside this stinking enclosure with some of these vagabonds shoving their mugs right under my nose. I had given up that famous revolver of yours at the first demand. Glad to get rid of the bally thing. Look like a fool walking about with an empty shooting-iron in my hand.' At that moment we came into the presence, and he became unflinchingly grave and complimentary with his late captor. Oh! magnificent! I want to laugh when I think of it. But I was impressed, too. The old disreputable Tunku Allang could not help showing his fear (he was no hero, for all the tales of his hot youth he was fond of telling); and at the same time there was a wistful confidence in his manner towards his late prisoner. Note! Even where he would be most hated he was still trusted. Jim—as far as I could follow the conversation—was improving the occasion by the delivery of a lecture. Some poor villagers had been waylaid and robbed while on their way to Doramin's house with a few pieces of gum or beeswax which they wished to exchange for rice. 'It was Doramin who was a thief,' burst out the Rajah. A shaking fury seemed to enter that old frail body. He writhed weirdly on his mat, gesticulating with his hands and feet, tossing the tangled strings of his mop—an impotent incarnation of rage. There were staring eyes and dropping jaws all around us. Jim began to speak. Resolutely, coolly, and for some time he enlarged upon the text that no man should be prevented from getting his food and his children's food honestly. The other sat like a tailor at his board, one palm on each knee, his head low, and fixing Jim through the grey hair that fell over his very eyes. When Jim had done there was a great stillness. Nobody seemed to breathe even; no one made a sound till the old Rajah sighed faintly, and looking up, with a toss of his head, said quickly, 'You hear, my people! No more of these little games.' This decree was received in profound silence. A rather heavy man, evidently in a position of confidence, with intelligent eyes, a bony, broad, very dark face, and a cheerily officious manner (I learned later on he was the executioner), presented to us two cups of coffee on a brass tray, which he took from the hands of an inferior attendant. 'You needn't drink,' muttered Jim very rapidly. I didn't perceive the meaning at first, and only looked at him. He took a good sip and sat composedly, holding the saucer in his left hand. In a moment I felt excessively annoyed. 'Why the devil,' I whispered, smiling at him amiably, 'do you expose me to such a stupid risk?' I drank, of course, there was nothing for it, while he gave no sign, and almost immediately afterwards we took our leave. While we were going down the courtyard to our boat, escorted by the intelligent and cheery executioner, Jim said he was very sorry. It was the barest chance, of course. Personally he thought nothing of poison. The remotest chance. He was—he assured me—considered to be infinitely more useful than dangerous, and so . . . 'But the Rajah is afraid of you abominably.

Anybody can see that,' I argued, with, I own, a certain peevishness, and all the time watching anxiously for the first twist of some sort of ghastly colic. I was awfully disgusted. 'If I am to do any good here and preserve my position,' he said, taking his seat by my side in the boat, 'I must stand the risk: I take it once every month, at least. Many people trust me to do that—for them. Afraid of me! That's just it. Most likely he is afraid of me because I am not afraid of his coffee.' Then showing me a place on the north front of the stockade where the pointed tops of several stakes were broken, 'This is where I leaped over on my third day in Patusan. They haven't put new stakes there yet. Good leap, eh?' A moment later we passed the mouth of a muddy creek. 'This is my second leap. I had a bit of a run and took this one flying, but fell short. Thought I would leave my skin there. Lost my shoes struggling. And all the time I was thinking to myself how beastly it would be to get a jab with a bally long spear while sticking in the mud like this. I remember how sick I felt wriggling in that slime. I mean really sick—as if I had bitten something rotten."

"That's how it was—and the opportunity ran by his side, leaped over the gap, floundered in the mud . . . still veiled. The unexpectedness of his coming was the only thing, you understand, that saved him from being at once dispatched with krises and flung into the river. They had him, but it was like getting hold of an apparition, a wraith, a portent. What did it mean? What to do with it? Was it too late to conciliate him? Hadn't he better be killed without more delay? But what would happen then? Wretched old Allang went nearly mad with apprehension and through the difficulty of making up his mind. Several times the council was broken up, and the advisers made a break helter-skelter for the door and out on to the veranda. One—it is said—even jumped down to the ground—fifteen feet, I should judge—and broke his leg. The royal governor of Patusan had bizarre mannerisms, and one of them was to introduce boastful rhapsodies into every arduous discussion, when, getting gradually excited, he would end by flying off his perch with a kris in his hand. But, barring such interruptions, the deliberations upon Jim's fate went on night and day.

"Meanwhile he wandered about the courtyard, shunned by some, glared at by others, but watched by all, and practically at the mercy of the first casual ragamuffin with a chopper, in there. He took possession of a small tumbledown shed to sleep in; the effluvia of filth and rotten matter incommoded him greatly: it seems he had not lost his appetite though, because—he told me—he had been hungry all the blessed time. Now and again 'some fussy ass' deputed from the council-room would come out running to him, and in honeyed tones would administer amazing interrogatories: 'Were the Dutch coming to take the country? Would the white man like to go back down the river? What was the object of coming to such a miserable country? The Rajah wanted to know whether the white man could repair a watch? They did actually bring out to him a nickel clock of New England make, and out of sheer unbearable boredom he busied himself in trying to get the alarm to work. It was apparently when thus occupied in his shed that the true perception of his extreme peril dawned upon him. He dropped the thing—he says—'like a hot potato,' and walked out hastily, without the slightest idea of what he would, indeed could, do. He only knew that the position was intolerable. He strolled aimlessly beyond a sort of ramshackle little granary on posts, and his eyes fell on the broken stakes of the palisade; and then—he says—at once, without any mental process as it were, without any stir of emotion, he set about his escape as if executing a plan matured for a month. He walked off carelessly to give himself a good run and when he faced about there was some dignitary, with two spearmen in attendance, close at his elbow ready with a question. He started off 'from under his very nose,' went over 'like a bird,' and landed on the other side with a fall that jarred all his bones and seemed to split his head. He picked himself up instantly. He never thought of anything at the time; all he could remember —he said—was a great yell; the first houses of Patusan were before him four hundred yards away; he saw the creek, and as it were mechanically put on more pace. The earth seemed fairly to fly backwards under his feet. He took off from the last dry spot, felt himself flying through the air, felt himself, without any shock, planted upright in an extremely soft and sticky mudbank. It was only when he tried to move his legs and found he couldn't that, in his own words, 'he came to himself.' He began to think of the 'bally long spears.' As a matter of fact, considering that the people inside the stockade had to run to the gate, then get down to the landing-place, get into boats, and pull round a point of land, he had more advance than he imagined. Besides, it being low water, the creek was without water—you couldn't call it dry—and practically he was safe for a time from everything but a very long shot perhaps. The higher firm ground was about six feet in front of him. 'I thought I would have to die there all the same,' he said. He reached and grabbed desperately with his hands, and only succeeded in gathering a horrible cold shiny heap of slime against his breast—up to his very chin. It seemed to him he was burying himself alive, and then he struck out madly, scattering the mud with his fists. It fell on his head, on his face, over his eyes, into his mouth. He told me that he remembered suddenly the courtyard, as you remember a place where you have been very happy years ago. He longed—so he said— to be back there again, mending the clock. Mending the clock—that was the idea. He made efforts, tremendous sobbing, gasping efforts, efforts that seemed to burst his eyeballs in their sockets and make him blind, and culminating into one mighty supreme effort in the darkness to crack the earth asunder, to throw it off his limbs—and he felt himself creeping feebly up the bank. He lay full length on the firm ground and saw the light, the sky. Then as a sort of happy thought the notion came to him that he would go to sleep. He will have it that he *did* actually go to sleep; that he slept— perhaps for a minute, perhaps for twenty seconds, or only for one second, but he recollects distinctly the violent convulsive start of awakening. He remained lying still for a while, and then he arose muddy from head to foot and stood there, thinking he was alone of his kind for hundreds of miles, alone, with no help, no sympathy, no pity to expect from any one, like a hunted animal. The first houses were not more than twenty yards from him; and it was the desperate screaming of a frightened woman trying to carry off a child that started him again. He pelted straight on in his socks, be plastered with filth out of all semblance to a human being. He traversed more than half the length of the settlement. The nimbler women fled right and left, the slower

men just dropped whatever they had in their hands, and remained petrified with
dropping jaws. He was a flying terror. He says he noticed the little children trying to
run for life, falling on their little stomachs and kicking. He swerved between two
houses up a slope, clambered in desperation over a barricade of felled trees (there
wasn't a week without some fight in Patusan at that time), burst through a fence into a
maize-patch, where a scared boy flung a stick at him, blundered upon a path, and ran
all at once into the arms of several startled men. He just had breath enough to gasp
out, 'Doramin! Doramin!' He remembers being half-carried, half-rushed to the top of
the slope, and in a vast enclosure with palms and fruit-trees being run up to a large
man sitting massively in a chair in the midst of the greatest possible commotion and
excitement. He fumbled in mud and clothes to produce the ring, and, finding himself
suddenly on his back, wondered who had knocked him down. They had simply let
him go—don't you know?—but he couldn't stand. At the foot of the slope random
shots were fired, and above the roofs of the settlement there rose a dull roar of
amazement. But he was safe. Doramin's people were barricading the gate and pouring
water down his throat; Doramin's old wife, full of business and commiseration, was
issuing shrill orders to her girls. 'The old woman,' he said, softly, 'made a to-do over
me as if I had been her own son. They put me into an immense bed—her state bed—
and she ran in and out wiping her eyes to give me pats on the back. I must have been a
pitiful object. I just lay there like a log for I don't know how long.'

"He seemed to have a great liking for Doramin's old wife. She on her side had
taken a motherly fancy to him. She had a round, nut-brown, soft face, all fine wrinkles,
large, bright red lips (she chewed betel assiduously), and screwed-up, winking, benevolent eyes. She was constantly in movement, scolding busily and ordering unceasingly a
troop of young women with clear brown faces and big grave eyes, her daughters, her
servants, her slave-girls. You know how it is in these households: it's generally impossible to tell the difference. She was very spare, and even her ample outer garment,
fastened in front with jeweled clasps, had somehow a skimpy effect. Her dark bare feet
were thrust into yellow straw slippers of Chinese make. I have seen her myself flitting
about with her extremely thick, long, grey hair falling about her shoulders. She uttered
homely shrewd sayings, was of noble birth, and was eccentric and arbitrary. In the
afternoon she would sit in a very roomy arm-chair, opposite her husband, gazing
steadily through a wide opening in the wall which gave an extensive view of the
settlement and the river.

"She invariably tucked up her feet under her, but old Doramin sat squarely, sat
imposingly as a mountain sits on a plain. He was only of the *nakhoda* or merchant class,
but the respect shown to him and the dignity of his bearing were very striking. He was
the chief of the second power in Patusan. The immigrants from Celebes (about sixty
families that, with dependents and so on, could muster some one hundred men
'wearing the kris') had elected him years ago for their head. The men of that race are
intelligent, enterprising, revengeful, but with a more frank courage than the other
Malays, and restless under oppression. They formed the party opposed to the Rajah.
Of course the quarrels were for trade. This was the primary cause of faction fights, of

the sudden outbreaks that would fill this or that part of the settlement with smoke, flame, the noise of shots and shrieks. Villages were burnt, men were dragged into the Rajah's stockade to be killed or tortured for the crime of trading with anybody else but himself. Only a day or two before Jim's arrival several heads of households in the very fishing village that was afterwards taken under his especial protection had been driven over the cliffs by a party of the Rajah's spearmen, on suspicion of having been collecting edible birds' nests for a Celebes trader. Rajah Allang pretended to be the only trader in his country, and the penalty for the breach of the monopoly was death; but his idea of trading was indistinguishable from the commonest forms of robbery. His cruelty and rapacity had no other bounds than his cowardice, and he was afraid of the organized power of the Celebes men, only—till Jim came—he was not afraid enough to keep quiet. He struck at them through his subjects, and thought himself pathetically in the right. The situation was complicated by a wandering stranger, an Arab half-breed, who, I believe, on purely religious grounds, had incited the tribes in the interior (the bush-folk, as Jim himself called them) to rise, and had established himself in a fortified camp on the summit of one of the twin hills. He hung over the town of Patusan like a hawk over a poultry-yard, but he devastated the open country. Whole villages, deserted, rotted on their blackened posts over the banks of clear streams, dropping piecemeal into the water the grass of their walls, the leaves of their roofs, with a curious effect of natural decay as if they had been a form of vegetation stricken by a blight at its very root. The two parties in Patusan were not sure which one this partisan most desired to plunder. The Rajah intrigued with him feebly. Some of the Bugis settlers, weary with endless insecurity, were half inclined to call him in. The younger spirits amongst them, chaffing, advised to 'get Sherif Ali with his wild men and drive the Rajah Allang out of the country.' Doramin restrained them with difficulty. He was growing old, and, though his influence had not diminished, the situation was getting beyond him. This was the state of affairs when Jim, bolting from the Rajah's stockade, appeared before the chief of the Bugis, produced the ring, and was received, in a manner of speaking, into the heart of the community."

XXVI

"Doramin was one of the most remarkable men of his race I had ever seen. His bulk for a Malay was immense, but he did not look merely fat; he looked imposing, monumental. This motionless body, clad in rich stuffs, colored silks, gold embroideries; this huge head, enfolded in a red-and-gold head-kerchief; the flat, big, round face, wrinkled, furrowed, with two semicircular heavy folds starting on each side of wide, fierce nostrils, and enclosing a thick-lipped mouth; the throat like a bull; the vast corrugated brow overhanging the staring proud eyes—made a whole that, once seen, can never be forgotten. His impassive repose (he seldom stirred a limb when once he sat down) was like a display of dignity. He was never known to raise his voice. It was a hoarse and powerful murmur, slightly veiled as if heard from a distance. When he walked, two short, sturdy young fellows, naked to the waist, in white sarongs and with black skull-caps on the backs of their heads, sustained his elbows; they would ease him down and stand behind his chair till he wanted to rise, when he would turn his head slowly, as if with difficulty, to the right and to the left, and then they would catch him under his armpits and help him up. For all that, there was nothing of a cripple about him: on the contrary, all his ponderous movements were like manifestations of a mighty deliberate force. It was generally believed he consulted his wife as to public affairs; but nobody, as far as I know, had ever heard them exchange a single word. When they sat in state by the wide opening it was in silence. They could see below them in the declining light the vast expanse of the forest country, a dark sleeping sea of somber green undulating as far as the violet and purple range of mountains; the shining sinuosity of the river like an immense letter S of beaten silver; the brown ribbon of houses following the sweep of both banks, overtopped by the twin hills uprising above the nearer tree-tops. They were wonderfully contrasted: she, light, delicate, spare, quick, a little witch-like, with a touch of motherly fussiness in her repose; he, facing her, immense and heavy, like a figure of a man roughly fashioned of stone, with something magnanimous and ruthless in his immobility. The son of these old people was a most distinguished youth.

"They had him late in life. Perhaps he was not really so young as he looked. Four- or five-and-twenty is not so young when a man is already father of a family at eighteen. When he entered the large room, lined and carpeted with fine mats, and with a high ceiling of white sheeting, where the couple sat in state surrounded by a most deferential retinue, he would make his way straight to Doramin, to kiss his hand—which the other abandoned to him majestically—and then would step across to stand by his mother's chair. I suppose I may say they idolized him, but I never caught them giving him an overt glance. Those, it is true, were public functions. The room was generally thronged. The solemn formality of greetings and leave-takings, the profound respect expressed in gestures, on the faces, in the low whispers, is simply indescribable. 'It's well worth seeing,' Jim had assured me while we were crossing the river, on our way back. 'They are like people in a book, aren't they?' he said triumphantly. 'And Dain Waris—their son—is the best friend (barring you) I ever had. What Mr. Stein would call a good "war-comrade." I was in luck. Jove! I was in luck when I tumbled amongst them at my last gasp.' He meditated with bowed head, then rousing himself he added:

" 'Of course I didn't go to sleep over it, but . . .' He paused again. 'It seemed to come to me,' he murmured. 'All at once I saw what I had to do . . .'

"There was no doubt that it had come to him; and it had come through the war, too, as is natural, since this power that came to him was the power to make peace. It is in this sense alone that might so often *is* right. You must not think he had seen his way at once. When he arrived the Bugis community was in a most critical position. 'They were all afraid,' he said to me—'each man afraid of himself; while I could see as plain as possible that they must do something at once, if they did not want to go under one after another, what between the Rajah and that vagabond Sherif.' But to see that was nothing. When he got his idea he had to drive it into reluctant minds, through the bulwarks of fear, of selfishness. He drove it in at last. And that was nothing. He had to devise the means. He devised them—an audacious plan; and his task was only half done. He had to inspire with his own confidence a lot of people who had hidden and absurd reasons to hang back; he had to conciliate imbecile jealousies, and argue away all sorts of senseless mistrusts. Without the weight of Doramin's authority and his son's fiery enthusiasm, he would have failed. Dain Waris, the distinguished youth, was the first to believe in him; theirs was one of those strange, profound, rare friendships between brown and white, in which the very difference of race seems to draw two human beings closer by some mystic element of sympathy. Of Dain Waris, his own people said with pride that he knew how to fight like a white man. This was true; he had that sort of courage—the courage in the open, I may say—but he had also a European mind. You meet them sometimes like that, and are surprised to discover unexpectedly a familiar turn of thought, an unobscured vision, a tenacity of purpose, a touch of altruism. Of small stature, but admirably well proportioned, Dain Waris had a proud carriage, a polished, easy bearing, a temperament like a clear flame. His dusky face, with big black eyes, was in action expressive, and in repose thoughtful. He was of a silent disposition; a firm glance, an ironic smile, a courteous deliberation of manner seemed to hint at great reserves of intelligence and power. Such beings open to the Western eye, so often concerned with mere surfaces, the hidden possibilities of races and lands over which hangs the mystery of unrecorded ages. He not only trusted Jim, he understood him, I firmly believe. I speak of him because he had captivated me. His —if I may say so—his caustic placidity, and, at the same time, his intelligent sympathy with Jim's aspirations, appealed to me. I seemed to behold the very origin of friendship. If Jim took the lead, the other had captivated his leader. In fact, Jim the leader was a captive in every sense. The land, the people, the friendship, the love, were like the jealous guardians of his body. Every day added a link to the fetters of that strange freedom. I felt convinced of it, as from day to day I learned more of the story.

"The story! Haven't I heard the story? I've heard it on the march, in camp (he made me scour the country after invisible game); I've listened to a good part of it on one of the twin summits, after climbing the last hundred feet or so on my hands and knees. Our escort (we had volunteer followers from village to village) had camped meantime on a bit of level ground half-way up the slope, and in the still breathless evening the smell of wood-smoke reached our nostrils from below with the penetrating delicacy of some choice scent. Voices also ascended, wonderful in their distinct and immaterial clearness. Jim sat on the trunk of a felled tree, and pulling out his pipe began to smoke. A new growth of grass and bushes was springing up; there were traces of an earthwork under a mass of thorny twigs. 'It all started from here,' he said, after a long and meditative silence. On the other hill, two hundred yards across a somber precipice, I saw a line of high blackened stakes, showing here and there ruinously—the remnants of Sherif Ali's impregnable camp.

"But it had been taken though. That had been his idea. He had mounted Doramin's old ordnance on the top of that hill; two rusty iron 7-pounders, a lot of small brass cannon—currency cannon. But if the brass guns represent wealth, they can also, when crammed recklessly to the muzzle, send a solid shot to some little distance. The thing was to get them up there. He showed me where he had fastened the cables, explained how he had improvised a rude capstan out of a hollowed log turning upon a pointed stake, indicated with the bowl of his pipe the outline of the earth-work. The last hundred feet of the ascent had been the most difficult. He had made himself responsible for success on his own head. He had induced the war party to work hard all night. Big fires lighted at intervals blazed all down the slope, 'but up here,' he explained, 'the hoisting gang had to fly around in the dark.' From the top he saw men moving on the hillside like ants at work. He himself on that night had kept on rushing down and climbing up like a squirrel, directing, encouraging, watching all along the line. Old Doramin had himself carried up the hill in his arm-chair. They put him down on the level place upon the slope, and he sat there in the light of one of the big fires—'amazing old chap—real old chieftain,' said Jim, 'with his little fierce eyes—a pair of immense flintlock pistols on his knees. Magnificent things, ebony, silver-mounted, with beautiful locks and a caliber like an old blunderbuss. A present from Stein, it seems—in exchange for that ring, you know. Used to belong to good old M'Neil. God only knows how *he* came by them. There he sat, moving neither hand nor foot, a flame of dry bushwood behind him, and lots of people rushing about, shouting and pulling around him—the most solemn, imposing old chap you can imagine. *He* wouldn't have had much chance if Sherif Ali had let his infernal crew loose at us and stampeded my lot. Eh? Anyhow, he had come up there to die if anything went wrong. No mistake! Jove! It thrilled me to see him there—like a rock. But the Sherif must have thought us mad, and never troubled to come and see how we got on. Nobody believed it could be done. Why! I think the very chaps who pulled and shoved and sweated over it did not believe it could be done! Upon my word I don't think they did. . . .'

"He stood erect, the smoldering brier-wood in his clutch, with a smile on his lips and a sparkle in his boyish eyes. I sat on the stump of a tree at his feet, and below us stretched the land, the great expanse of the forests, somber under the sunshine, rolling like a sea, with glints of winding rivers, the grey spots of villages, and here and there a clearing, like an islet of light amongst the dark waves of continuous tree-tops. A brooding gloom lay over this vast and monotonous landscape; the light fell on it as if into an abyss. The land devoured the sunshine; only far off, along the coast, the empty ocean, smooth and polished within the faint haze, seemed to rise up to the sky in a wall of steel.

"And there I was with him, high in the sunshine on the top of that historic hill of his. He dominated the forest, the secular gloom, the old mankind. He was like a figure set up on a pedestal, to represent in his persistent youth the power, and perhaps the virtues, of races that never grow old, that have emerged from the gloom. I don't know why he should always have appeared to me symbolic. Perhaps this is the real cause of my interest in his fate. I don't know whether it was exactly fair to him to remember the incident which had given a new direction to his life, but at that very moment I remembered very distinctly. It was like a shadow in the light."

XXVII

"Already the legend had gifted him with supernatural powers. Yes, it was said, there had been many ropes cunningly disposed, and a strange contrivance that turned by the efforts of many men, and each gun went up tearing slowly through the bushes, like a wild pig rooting its way in the undergrowth, but . . . and the wisest shook their heads. There was something occult in all this, no doubt; for what is the strength of ropes and of men's arms? There is a rebellious soul in things which must be overcome by powerful charms and incantations. Thus old Sura—a very respectable householder of Patusan—with whom I had a quiet chat one evening. However, Sura was a professional sorcerer also, who attended all the rice sowings and reapings for miles around for the purpose of subduing the stubborn soul of things. This occupation he seemed to think a most arduous one, and perhaps the souls of things are more stubborn than the souls of men. As to the simple folk of outlying villages, they believed and said (as the most natural thing in the world) that Jim had carried the guns up the hill on his back—two at a time.

"This would make Jim stamp his foot in vexation and exclaim with an exasperated little laugh, 'What can you do with such silly beggars? They will sit up half the night talking bally rot, and the greater the lie the more they seem to like it.' You could trace the subtle influence of his surroundings in this irritation. It was part of his captivity. The earnestness of his denials was amusing, and at last I said, 'My dear fellow, you don't suppose *I* believe this.' He looked at me quite startled. 'Well, no! I suppose not,' he said, and burst into a Homeric peal of laughter. 'Well, anyhow the guns were there, and went off together at sunrise. Jove! You should have seen the splinters fly,' he cried. By his side Dain Waris, listening with a quiet smile, dropped his eyelids and shuffled his feet a little. It appears that the success in mounting the guns had given Jim's people such a feeling of confidence that he ventured to leave the battery under charge of two elderly Bugis who had seen some fighting in their day, and went to join Dain Waris and the storming party who were concealed in the ravine. In the small hours they began creeping up, and when two-thirds of the way up, lay in the wet grass waiting for the appearance of the sun, which was the agreed signal. He told me with what impatient anguishing emotion he watched the swift coming of the dawn; how, heated with the work and the climbing, he felt the cold dew chilling his very bones; how afraid he was he would begin to shiver and shake like a leaf before the time came for the advance. 'It was the slowest half-hour in my life,' he declared. Gradually the silent stockade came out on the sky above him. Men scattered all down the slope were crouching amongst the dark stones and dripping bushes. Dain Waris was lying flattened by his side. 'We looked at each other,' Jim said, resting a gentle hand on his friend's shoulder. 'He smiled at me as cheery as you please, and I dared not stir my lips for fear I would break out into a shivering fit. 'Pon my word, it's true! I had been streaming with perspiration when we took cover—so you may imagine . . .' He declared, and I believe him, that he had no fears as to the result. He was only anxious as to his ability to repress these shivers. He didn't bother about the result. He was bound to get to the top of that hill and stay there, whatever might happen. There could be no going back for him. Those people had trusted him implicitly. Him alone! His bare word. . . .

"I remember how, at this point, he paused with his eyes fixed upon me. 'As far as he knew, they never had an occasion to regret it yet,' he said. 'Never. He hoped to God they never would. Meantime—worse luck!—they had got into the habit of taking his word for anything and everything. I could have no idea! Why? Only the other day an old fool he had never seen in his life came from some village miles away to find out if he should divorce his wife. Fact. Solemn word. That's the sort of thing. . . . He wouldn't have believed it. Would I? Squatted on the veranda chewing betel-nut, sighing and spitting all over the place for more than an hour, and as glum as an undertaker before he came out with that dashed conundrum. That's the kind of thing that isn't so funny as it looks. What was a fellow to say?—Good wife?—Yes. Good wife—old though; started a confounded long story about some brass pots. Been living together for fifteen years—twenty years—could not tell. A long, long time. Good wife. Beat her a little—not much—just a little, when she was young. Had to—for the sake of his honor. Suddenly in her old age she goes and lends three brass pots to her sister's son's wife, and begins to abuse him every day in a loud voice. His enemies jeered at him; his face was utterly blackened. Pots totally lost. Awfully cut up about it. Impossible to fathom a story like that; told him to go home, and promised to come along myself and settle it all. It's all very well to grin, but it was the dashedest nuisance! A day's journey through the forest, another day lost in coaxing a lot of silly villagers to get at the rights of the affair. There was the making of a sanguinary shindy in the thing. Every bally idiot took sides with one family or the other, and one half of the village was ready to go for the other half with anything that came handy. Honor bright! No joke! . . . Instead of attending to their bally crops. Got him the infernal pots back of course—and pacified all hands. No trouble to settle it. Of course not. Could settle the deadliest quarrel in the country by crooking his little finger. The trouble was to get at the truth of anything. Was not sure to this day whether he had been fair to all parties. It worried him. And the talk! Jove! There didn't seem to be any head or tail to it. Rather storm a twenty-foot-high old stockade any day. Much! Child's play to that other job. Wouldn't take so long either. Well, yes; a funny set out, upon the whole—the fool looked old enough to be his grandfather. But from another point of view it was no joke. His word decided everything—ever since the smashing of Sherif Ali. An awful responsibility,' he repeated. 'No, really—joking apart, had it been three lives instead of three rotten brass pots it would have been the same. . . .'

"Thus he illustrated the moral effect of his victory in war. It was in truth immense. It had led him from strife to peace, and through death into the innermost life of the people; but the gloom of the land spread out under the sunshine preserved its appearance of inscrutable, of secular repose. The sound of his fresh young voice—it's extraordinary how very few signs of wear he showed—floated lightly, and passed away over the unchanged face of the forests like the sound of the big guns on that cold dewy morning when he had no other concern on earth but the proper control of the chills in his body. With the first slant of sun-rays along these immovable tree-tops the summit of one hill wreathed itself, with heavy reports, in white clouds of smoke, and the other burst into an amazing noise of yells, war-cries, shouts of anger, of surprise, of dismay. Jim and Dain Waris were the first to lay their hands on the stakes. The popular story has it that Jim with a touch of one finger had thrown down the gate. He was, of course, anxious to disclaim this achievement. The whole stockade—he would insist on explaining to you—was a poor affair (Sherif Ali trusted mainly to the inaccessible position); and, anyway, the thing had been already knocked to pieces and only hung together by a miracle. He put his shoulder to it like a little fool and went in head over heels. Jove! If it hadn't been for Dain Waris, a pock-marked tattooed vagabond would have pinned him with his spear to a baulk of timber like one of Stein's beetles. The third man in, it seems, had been Tamb' Itam, Jim's own servant. This was a Malay from the north, a stranger who had wandered into Patusan, and had been forcibly detained by Rajah Allang as paddler of one of the state boats. He had made a bolt of it at the first opportunity, and finding a precarious refuge (but very little to eat) amongst the Bugis settlers, had attached himself to Jim's person. His complexion was very dark, his face flat, his eyes prominent and injected with bile. There was something excessive, almost fanatical, in his devotion to his 'white lord.' He was inseparable from Jim like a morose shadow. On state occasions he would tread on his master's heels, one hand on the haft of his kris, keeping the common people at a distance by his truculent brooding glances. Jim had made him the headman of his establishment, and all Patusan respected and courted him as a person of much influence. At the taking of the stockade he had distinguished himself greatly by the methodical ferocity of his fighting. The storming-party had come on so quick—Jim said—that notwithstanding the panic of the garrison, there was a 'Hot five minutes hand-to-hand inside that stockade, till some bally ass set fire to the shelters of boughs and dry grass, and we all had to clear out for dear life.'

"The rout, it seems, had been complete. Doramin waiting immovably in his chair on the hillside, with the smoke of the guns spreading slowly above his big head, received the news with a deep grunt. When informed that his son was safe and leading the pursuit, he, without another sound, made a mighty effort to rise; his attendants hurried to his help, and, held up reverently, he shuffled with great dignity into a bit of shade where he laid himself down to sleep covered entirely with a piece of white sheeting. In Patusan the excitement was intense. Jim told me that from the hill, turning his back on the stockade with its embers, black ashes, and half-consumed corpses, he could see time after time the open spaces between the houses on both sides of the stream fill suddenly with a seething rush of people and get empty in a moment. His ears caught feebly from below the tremendous din of gongs and drums; the wild shouts of the crowd reached him in bursts of faint roaring. A lot of streamers made a flutter as of little white, red, yellow birds amongst the brown ridges of roofs. 'You must have enjoyed it,' I murmured, feeling the stir of sympathetic emotion.

" 'It was . . . it was immense! Immense!' he cried aloud, flinging his arms open. The sudden movement startled me as though I had seen him bare the secrets of his breast to the sunshine, to the brooding forests, to the steely sea. Below us the town reposed in easy curves upon the banks of a stream whose current seemed to sleep. 'Immense!' he repeated for a third time, speaking in a whisper, for himself alone.

"Immense! No doubt it was immense; the seal of success upon his words, the conquered ground for the soles of his feet, the blind trust of men, the belief in himself snatched from the fire, the solitude of his achievement. All this, as I've warned you, gets dwarfed in the telling. I can't with mere words convey to you the impression of his total and utter isolation. I know, of course, he was in every sense alone of his kind there, but the unsuspected qualities of his nature had brought him in such close touch with his surroundings that this isolation seemed only the effect of his power. His loneliness added to his stature. There was nothing within sight to compare him with, as though he had been one of those exceptional men who can be only measured by the greatness of their fame; and his fame, remember, was the greatest thing around for many a day's journey. You would have to paddle, pole, or track a long weary way through the jungle before you passed beyond the reach of its voice. Its voice was not the trumpeting of the disreputable goddess we all know—not blatant—not brazen. It took its tone from the stillness and gloom of the land without a past, where his word was the one truth of every passing day. It shared something of the nature of that silence through which it accompanied you into unexplored depths, heard continuously by your side, penetrating, far-reaching—tinged with wonder and mystery on the lips of whispering men."

XXVIII

"The defeated Sherif Ali fled the country without making another stand, and when the miserable hunted villagers began to crawl out of the jungle back to their rotting houses, it was Jim who, in consultation with Dain Waris, appointed the headmen. Thus he became the virtual ruler of the land. As to old Tunku Allang, his fears at first had known no bounds. It is said that at the intelligence of the successful storming of the hill he flung himself, face down, on the bamboo floor of his audience-hall, and lay motionless for a whole night and a whole day, uttering stifled sounds of such an appalling nature that no man dared approach his prostrate form nearer than a spear's length. Already he could see himself driven ignominiously out of Patusan, wandering abandoned, stripped, without opium, without his women, without followers, a fair game for the first comer to kill. After Sherif Ali his turn would come, and who could resist an attack led by such a devil? And indeed he owed his life and such authority as he still possessed at the time of my visit to Jim's idea of what was fair alone. The Bugis had been extremely anxious to pay off old scores, and the impassive old Doramin cherished the hope of yet seeing his son ruler of Patusan. During one of our interviews he deliberately allowed me to get a glimpse of his secret ambition. Nothing could be finer in its way than the dignified wariness of his approaches. He himself—he began by declaring—had used his strength in his young days, but now he had grown old and tired. . . . With his imposing bulk and haughty little eyes darting sagacious, inquisitive glances, he reminded one irresistibly of a cunning old elephant; the slow rise and fall of his vast breast went on powerful and regular, like the heave of a calm sea.

He, too, as he protested, had an unbounded confidence in Tuan Jim's wisdom. If he could only obtain a promise! One word would be enough! . . . His breathing silences, the low rumblings of his voice, recalled the last efforts of a spent thunderstorm.

"I tried to put the subject aside. It was difficult, for there could be no question that Jim had the power; in his new sphere there did not seem to be anything that was not his to hold or to give. But that, I repeat, was nothing in comparison with the notion, which occurred to me, while I listened with a show of attention, that he seemed to have come very near at last to mastering his fate. Doramin was anxious about the future of the country, and I was struck by the turn he gave to the argument. The land remains where God had put it; but white men—he said—they come to us and in a little while they go. They go away. Those they leave behind do not know when to look for their return. They go to their own land, to their people, and so this white man, too, would. . . . I don't know what induced me to commit myself at this point by a vigorous 'No, no.' The whole extent of this indiscretion became apparent when Doramin, turning full upon me his face, whose expression, fixed in rugged deep folds, remained unalterable, like a huge brown mask, said that this was good news indeed, reflectively; and then wanted to know why.

"His little, motherly witch of a wife sat on my other hand, with her head covered and her feet tucked up, gazing through the great shutter-hole. I could only see a straying lock of grey hair, a high cheek-bone, the slight masticating motion of the sharp chin. Without removing her eyes from the vast prospect of forests stretching as far as the hills, she asked me in a pitying voice why was it that he so young had wandered from his home, coming so far, through so many dangers? Had he no household there, no kinsmen in his own country? Had he no old mother, who would always remember his face? . . .

"I was completely unprepared for this. I could only mutter and shake my head vaguely. Afterwards I am perfectly aware I cut a very poor figure trying to extricate myself out of this difficulty. From that moment, however, the old *nakhoda* became taciturn. He was not very pleased, I fear, and evidently I had given him food for thought. Strangely enough, on the evening of that very day (which was my last in Patusan) I was once more confronted with the same question, with the unanswerable why of Jim's fate. And this brings me to the story of his love.

"I suppose you think it is a story that you can imagine for yourselves. We have heard so many such stories, and the majority of us don't believe them to be stories of love at all. For the most part we look upon them as stories of opportunities: episodes of passion at best, or perhaps only of youth and temptation, doomed to forgetfulness in the end, even if they pass through the reality of tenderness and regret. This view mostly is right, and perhaps in this case, too. . . . Yet I don't know. To tell this story is by no means so easy as it should be—were the ordinary standpoint adequate. Apparently it is a story very much like the others: for me, however, there is visible in its background the melancholy figure of a woman, the shadow of a cruel wisdom buried in a lonely grave, looking on wistfully, helplessly, with sealed lips. The grave itself, as I came upon it during an early morning stroll, was a rather shapeless brown mound, with an inlaid neat border of white lumps of coral at the base, and enclosed within a circular fence made of split saplings, with the bark left on. A garland of leaves and flowers was woven about the heads of the slender posts—and the flowers were fresh.

"Thus, whether the shadow is of my imagination or not, I can at all events point out the significant fact of an unforgotten grave. When I tell you besides that Jim with his own hands had worked at the rustic fence, you will perceive directly the difference, the individual side of the story. There is in his espousal of memory and affection belonging to another human being something characteristic of his seriousness. He had a conscience, and it was a romantic conscience. Through her whole life the wife of the unspeakable Cornelius had no other companion, confidante, and friend but her daughter. How the poor woman had come to marry the awful Malacca Portuguese—after the separation from the father of her girl—and how that separation had been brought about, whether by death, which can be sometimes merciful, or by the merciless pressure of conventions, is a mystery to me. From the little which Stein (who knew so many stories) had let drop in my hearing, I am convinced that she was no ordinary woman. Her own father had been a white; a high official; one of the brilliantly endowed men who are not dull enough to nurse a success, and whose careers so often end under a cloud. I suppose she, too, must have lacked the saving dullness—and her career ended in Patusan. Our common fate . . . for where is the man—I mean a real sentient man—who does not remember vaguely having been deserted in the fullness of possession by some one or something more precious than life? . . . our common fate fastens upon the women with a peculiar cruelty. It does not punish like a master, but inflicts lingering torment, as if to gratify a secret, unappeasable spite. One would think that, appointed to rule on earth, it seeks to revenge itself upon the beings that come nearest to rising above the trammels of earthly caution; for it is only women who manage to put at times into their love an element just palpable enough to give one a fright—an extra-terrestrial touch. I ask myself with wonder—how the world can look to them—whether it has the shape and substance we know, the air we breathe! Sometimes I fancy it must be a region of unreasonable sublimities seething with the excitement of their adventurous souls, lighted by the glory of all possible risks and renunciations. However, I suspect there are very few women in the world, though of course I am aware of the multitudes of mankind and of the equality of sexes in point of numbers—that is. But I am sure that the mother was as much of a woman as the daughter seemed to be. I cannot help picturing to myself these two, at first the young woman and the child, then the old woman and the young girl, the awful sameness and the swift passage of time, the barrier of forest, the solitude and the turmoil round these two lonely lives, and every word spoken between them penetrated with sad meaning. There must have been confidences, not so much of fact, I suppose, as of innermost feelings—regrets—fears—warnings, no doubt: warnings that the younger did not fully understand till the elder was dead—and Jim came along. Then I am sure she understood much—not everything—the fear mostly, it seems. Jim called her by a word that means precious, in the sense of a precious gem—jewel. Pretty, isn't it? But he was capable of anything. He was equal to his fortune, as he—after all—must have been equal to his misfortune. Jewel he called her; and he would say this as he might have said 'Jane,' don't you know—with a marital, homelike, peaceful effect. I heard the name for the first time ten minutes after I had landed in his courtyard, when, after nearly shaking my arm off, he darted up the steps and began to make a joyous, boyish disturbance at the door under the heavy eaves. 'Jewel! O Jewel! Quick! Here's a friend come,' . . . and suddenly peering at me in the dim veranda, he mumbled earnestly, 'You know—this—no confounded nonsense about it—can't tell you how much I owe to her—and so—you understand—I—exactly as if . . .' His hurried, anxious whispers were cut short by the flitting of a white form within the house, a faint exclamation, and a childlike but energetic little face with delicate features and a profound, attentive glance peeped out of the inner gloom, like a bird out of the recess of a nest. I was struck by the name, of course; but it was not till later on that I connected it with an astonishing rumor that had met me on my journey, at a little place on the coast about 230 miles south of Patusan river. Stein's schooner, in which I had my passage, put in there, to collect some produce, and going ashore, I found to my great surprise that the wretched locality could boast of a third-class deputy-assistant resident, a big, fat, greasy, blinking fellow of mixed descent, with turned-out, shiny lips. I found him lying extended on his back in a cane chair, odiously unbuttoned, with a large green leaf of some sort on the top of his steaming head, and another in his hand which he used lazily as a fan. . . . Going to Patusan? Oh, yes. Stein's Trading Company. He knew. Had a permission? No business of his. It was not so bad there now, he remarked negligently, and, he went on drawling, 'There's some sort of white vagabond has got in there, I hear. . . . Eh? What you say? Friend of yours? So! . . . Then it was true there was one of these *verdamte*—What was he up to? Found his way in, the rascal. Eh? I had not been sure. Patusan—they cut throats there—no business of ours.' He interrupted himself to groan. 'Phoo! Almighty! The heat! The heat! Well, then, there might be something in the story, too, after all, and . . .' He shut one of his beastly glassy eyes (the eyelid went on quivering), while he leered at me atrociously with the other. 'Look here,' says he, mysteriously, 'if—do you understand?—if he has really got hold of something fairly good—none of your bits of green glass—understand?—I am a government official—you tell the rascal . . . Eh? What? Friend of yours?' . . . He continued wallowing calmly in the chair. . . . 'You said so; that's just it; and I am pleased to give you the hint. I suppose you, too, would like to get something out of it? Don't interrupt. You just tell him I've heard the tale, but to my government I have made no report. Not yet. See? Why make a report? Eh? Tell him to come to me if they let him get alive out of the country. He had better look out for himself. Eh? I promise to ask no questions. On the quiet—you understand? You, too—you shall get something from me. Small commission for the trouble. Don't interrupt. I am a government official, and make no report. That's business. Understand? I know some good people that will buy anything worth having, and can give him more money than the scoundrel ever saw in his life. I know his sort.' He fixed me steadfastly with both his eyes open, while I stood over him utterly amazed and asking myself whether he was mad or drunk. He perspired, puffed, moaning feebly, and scratching himself with such horrible composure that I could not bear the sight long enough to find out. Next day, talking casually with the people of the little native court of the place, I discovered that a story was traveling slowly down the coast about a mysterious white man in Patusan who had got hold of an extraordinary gem—namely, an emerald of an enormous size, and altogether priceless. The emerald seems to appeal more to the Eastern imagination than any other precious stone. The white man had obtained it, I was told, partly by the exercise of his wonderful strength and partly by cunning, from the ruler of a distant country, whence he had fled instantly, arriving in Patusan in utmost distress, but frightening the people by his extreme ferocity, which nothing seemed able to subdue. Most of my informants were of the opinion that the stone was probably unlucky,—like the famous stone of the Sultan of Succadana, which in the old times had brought wars and untold calamities upon that country. Perhaps it was the same stone—one couldn't say. Indeed the story of a fabulously large emerald is as old as the arrival of the first white men in the Archipelago; and the belief in it is so persistent that less than forty years ago there had been an official Dutch inquiry into the truth of it. Such a jewel—it was explained to me by the old fellow from whom I heard most of this amazing Jim-myth—a sort of scribe to the wretched little Rajah of the place;—such a jewel, he said, cocking his poor purblind eyes up at me (he was sitting on the cabin floor out of respect), is best preserved by being concealed about the person of a woman. Yet it is not every woman that would do. She must be young—he sighed deeply—and insensible to the seductions of love. He shook his head skeptically. But such a woman seemed to be actually in existence. He had been told of a tall girl, whom the white man treated with great respect and care, and who never went forth from the house unattended. People said the white man could be seen with her almost any day; they walked side by side, openly, he holding her arm under his—pressed to his side— thus—in a most extraordinary way. This might be a lie, he conceded, for it was indeed a strange thing for any one to do: on the other hand, there could be no doubt she wore the white man's jewel concealed upon her bosom."

XXIX

"This was the theory of Jim's marital evening walks. I made a third on more than one occasion, unpleasantly aware every time of Cornelius, who nursed the aggrieved sense of his legal paternity, slinking in the neighborhood with that peculiar twist of his mouth as if he were perpetually on the point of gnashing his teeth. But do you notice how, three hundred miles beyond the end of telegraph cables and mail-boat lines, the haggard utilitarian lies of our civilization wither and die, to be replaced by pure exercises of imagination, that have the futility, often the charm, and sometimes the deep hidden truthfulness, of works of art? Romance had singled Jim for its own—and that was the true part of the story, which otherwise was all wrong. He did not hide his jewel. In fact, he was extremely proud of it.

"It comes to me now that I had, on the whole, seen very little of her. What I remember best is the even, olive pallor of her complexion, and the intense blue-black gleams of her hair, flowing abundantly from under a small crimson cap she wore far back on her shapely head. Her movements were free, assured, and she blushed a dusky red. While Jim and I were talking, she would come and go with rapid glances at us, leaving on her passage an impression of grace and charm and a distinct suggestion of watchfulness. Her manner presented a curious combination of shyness and audacity. Every pretty smile was succeeded swiftly by a look of silent, repressed anxiety, as if put to flight by the recollection of some abiding danger. At times she would sit down with us and, with her soft cheek dimpled by the knuckles of her little hand, she would listen to our talk; her big clear eyes would remain fastened on our lips, as though each pronounced word had a visible shape. Her mother had taught her to read and write; she had learned a good bit of English from Jim, and she spoke it most amusingly, with his own clipping, boyish intonation. Her tenderness hovered over him like a flutter of wings. She lived so completely in his contemplation that she had acquired something of his outward aspect, something that recalled him in her movements, in the way she stretched her arm, turned her head, directed her glances. Her vigilant affection had an intensity that made it almost perceptible to the senses; it seemed actually to exist in the ambient matter of space, to envelop him like a peculiar fragrance, to dwell in the sunshine like a tremulous, subdued, and impassioned note. I suppose you think that I, too, am romantic, but it is a mistake. I am relating to you the sober impressions of a bit of youth, of a strange uneasy romance that had come in my way. I observed with interest the work of his—well—good fortune. He was jealously loved, but why she should be jealous, and of what, I could not tell. The land, the people, the forests were her accomplices, guarding him with vigilant accord, with an air of seclusion, of mystery, of invincible possession. There was no appeal, as it were; he was imprisoned within the very freedom of his power, and she, though ready to make a footstool of her head for his feet, guarded her conquest inflexibly—as though he were hard to keep. The very Tamb' Itam, marching on our journeys upon the heels of his white lord, with his head thrown back, truculent and be-weaponed like a janissary, with kris, chopper, and lance (besides carrying Jim's gun); even Tamb' Itam allowed himself to put on the airs of uncompromising guardianship, like a surly devoted jailer ready to lay down his life for his captive. On the evenings when we sat up late his silent, indistinct form would pass and repass under the veranda, with noiseless footsteps, or lifting my head I would unexpectedly make him out standing rigidly erect in the shadow. As a general rule he would vanish after a time, without a sound; but when we rose he would spring up close to us as if from the ground, ready for any orders Jim might wish to give. The girl, too, I believe, never went to sleep till we had separated for the night. More than once I saw her and Jim through the window of my room come out together quietly and lean on the rough balustrade—two white forms very close, his arm about her waist, her head on his shoulder. Their soft murmurs reached me, penetrating, tender, with a calm sad note in the stillness of the night, like a self-communion of one being carried on in two tones. Later on, tossing on my bed under the mosquito-net, I was sure to hear slight creakings, faint breathing, a throat cleared cautiously—and I would know that Tamb' Itam was still on the prowl. Though he had (by the favor of the white lord) a house in the compound, had 'taken wife,' and had lately been blessed with a child, I believe that, during my stay at all events, he slept on the veranda every night. It was very difficult to make this faithful and grim retainer talk. Even Jim himself was answered in jerky short sentences, under protest as it were. Talking, he seemed to imply, was no business of his. The longest speech I heard him volunteer was one morning when, suddenly extending his hand towards the courtyard, he pointed at Cornelius and said, 'Here comes the Nazarene.' I don't think he was addressing me, though I stood at his side; his object seemed rather to awaken the indignant attention of the universe. Some muttered allusions, which followed, to dogs and the smell of roast-meat, struck me as singularly felicitous. The courtyard, a large square space, was one torrid glaze of sunshine, and, bathed in intense light, Cornelius was creeping across in full view with an inexpressible effect of stealthiness, of dark and secret slinking. He reminded one of everything that is unsavory. His slow laborious walk resembled the creeping of a repulsive beetle, the legs alone moving with horrid indus-try while the body glided evenly. I suppose he made straight enough for the place where he wanted to get to, but his progress with one shoulder carried forward seemed oblique. He was often seen circling slowly amongst the sheds, as if following a scent; passing before the veranda with upward stealthy glances; disappearing without haste round the corner of some hut. That he seemed free of the place demonstrated Jim's absurd carelessness or else his infinite disdain, for Cornelius had played a very dubious part (to say the least of it) in a certain episode which might have ended fatally for Jim. As a matter of fact, it had redounded to his glory. But everything redounded to his glory; and it was the irony of his good fortune that he, who had been too careful of it once, seemed to bear a charmed life.

"You must know he had left Doramin's place very soon after his arrival—much too soon, in fact, for his safety, and of course a long time before the war. In this he was actuated by a sense of duty; he had to look after Stein's business, he said. Hadn't he? To that end, with an utter disregard of his personal safety, he crossed the river and took up his quarters with Cornelius. How the latter had managed to exist through the troubled times I can't say. As Stein's agent, after all, he must have had Doramin's protection in a measure; and in one way or another he had managed to wriggle through all the deadly complications, while I have no doubt that his conduct, whatever line he was forced to take, was marked by that abjectness which was like the stamp of the man. That was his characteristic; he was fundamentally and outwardly abject, as other men are markedly of a generous, distinguished, or venerable appearance. It was the element of his nature which permeated all his acts and passions and emotions; he raged abjectly, smiled abjectly, was abjectly sad; his civilities and his indignations were alike abject. I am sure his love would have been the most abject of sentiments—but can one imagine a loathsome insect in love? And his loathsomeness, too, was abject, so that a simply disgusting person would have appeared noble by his side. He has his place neither in the background nor in the foreground of the story; he is simply seen skulking on its outskirts, enigmatical and unclean, tainting the fragrance of its youth and of its naïveness.

"His position in any case could not have been other than extremely miserable, yet it may very well be that he found some advantages in it. Jim told me he had been received at first with an abject display of the most amicable sentiments. 'The fellow apparently couldn't contain himself for joy,' said Jim with disgust. 'He flew at me every morning to shake both my hands—confound him! but I could never tell whether there would be any breakfast. If I got three meals in two days I considered myself jolly lucky, and he made me sign a chit for ten dollars every week. Said he was sure Mr. Stein did not mean him to keep me for nothing. Well—he kept me on nothing as near as possible. Put it down to the unsettled state of the country, and made as if to tear his hair out, begging my pardon twenty times a day, so that I had at last to entreat him not to worry. It made me sick. Half the roof of his house had fallen in, and the whole place had a mangy look, with wisps of dry grass sticking out and the corners of broken mats flapping on every wall. He did his best to make out that Mr. Stein owed him money on the last three years' trading, but his books were all torn, and some were missing. He tried to hint it was his late wife's fault. Disgusting scoundrel! At last I had to forbid him to mention his late wife at all. It made Jewel cry. I couldn't discover what became of all the trade-goods; there was nothing in the store but rats, having a high old time amongst a litter of brown paper and old sacking. I was assured on every hand that he had a lot of money buried somewhere, but of course could get nothing out of him. It was the most miserable existence I led there in that wretched house. I tried to do my duty by Stein, but I had also other matters to think of. When I escaped to Doramin old Tunku Allang got frightened and returned all my things. It was done in a roundabout way, and with no end of mystery, through a Chinaman who keeps a small shop here; but as soon as I left the Bugis quarter and went to live with Cornelius it began to be said openly that the Rajah had made up his mind to have me killed before long. Pleasant, wasn't it? And I couldn't see what there was to prevent him if he really *had* made up his mind. The worst of it was, I couldn't help feeling I wasn't doing any good either for Stein or for myself. Oh! it was beastly—the whole six weeks of it.' "

XXX

"He told me further that he didn't know what made him hang on—but of course we may guess. He sympathized deeply with the defenseless girl, at the mercy of that 'mean, cowardly scoundrel.' It appears Cornelius led her an awful life, stopping only short of actual ill-usage, for which he had not the pluck, I suppose. He insisted upon her calling him father—'and with respect, too—with respect,' he would scream, shaking a little yellow fist in her face. 'I am a respectable man, and what are you? Tell me— what are you? You think I am going to bring up somebody else's child and not to be treated with respect? You ought to be glad I let you. Come—say Yes, father. . . . No? . . . You wait a bit.' Thereupon he would begin to abuse the dead woman, till the girl would run off with her hands to her head. He pursued her, dashing in and out and round the house and amongst the sheds, would drive her into some corner, where she would fall on her knees stopping her ears, and then he would stand at a distance and declaim filthy denunciations at her back for half an hour at a stretch. 'Your mother was a devil, a deceitful devil—and you, too, are a devil,' he would shriek in a final outburst, pick up a bit of dry earth or a handful of mud (there was plenty of mud around the house), and fling it into her hair. Sometimes, though, she would hold out full of scorn, confronting him in silence, her face somber and contracted, and only now and then uttering a word or two that would make the other jump and writhe with the sting. Jim told me these scenes were terrible. It was indeed a strange thing to come upon in the wilderness. The endlessness of such a subtly cruel situation was appalling —if you think of it. The respectable Cornelius (Inchi 'Nelyus the Malays called him, with a grimace that meant many things) was a much-disappointed man. I don't know what he had expected would be done for him in consideration of his marriage; but evidently the liberty to steal, and embezzle, and appropriate to himself for many years and in any way that suited him best, the goods of Stein's Trading Company (Stein kept the supply up unfalteringly as long as he could get his skippers to take it there) did not seem to him a fair equivalent for the sacrifice of his honorable name. Jim would have enjoyed exceedingly thrashing Cornelius within an inch of his life; on the other hand, the scenes were of so painful a character, so abominable, that his impulse would be to get out of earshot, in order to spare the girl's feelings. They left her agitated, speechless, clutching her bosom now and then with a stony, desperate face, and then Jim would lounge up and say unhappily, 'Now—come—really—what's the use—you must try to eat a bit,' or give some such mark of sympathy. Cornelius would keep on slinking through the doorways, across the veranda and back again, as mute as a fish, and with malevolent, mistrustful, underhand glances. 'I can stop his game,' Jim said to her once. 'Just say the word.' And do you know what she answered? She said— Jim told me impressively—that if she had not been sure he was intensely wretched himself, she would have found the courage to kill him with her own hands. 'Just fancy that! The poor devil of a girl, almost a child, being driven to talk like that,' he exclaimed in horror. It seemed impossible to save her not only from that mean rascal but even from herself! It wasn't that he pitied her so much, he affirmed; it was more than pity; it was as if he had something on his conscience, while that life went on. To leave the house would have appeared a base desertion. He had understood at last that there was nothing to expect from a longer stay, neither accounts nor money, nor truth of any sort, but he stayed on, exasperating Cornelius to the verge, I won't say of insanity, but almost of courage. Meantime he felt all sorts of dangers gathering obscurely about him. Doramin had sent over twice a trusty servant to tell him seriously that he could do nothing for his safety unless he would recross the river again and live amongst the Bugis as at first. People of every condition used to call, often in the dead of night, in order to disclose to him plots for his assassination. He was to be poisoned. He was to be stabbed in the bath-house. Arrangements were being made to have him shot from a boat on the river. Each of these informants professed himself to be his very good friend. It was enough—he told me—to spoil a fellow's rest for ever. Something of the kind was extremely possible—nay, probable—but the lying warnings gave him only the sense of deadly scheming going on all around him, on all sides, in the dark. Nothing more calculated to shake the best of nerve. Finally, one night, Cornelius himself, with a great apparatus of alarm and secrecy, unfolded in solemn wheedling tones a little plan wherein for one hundred dollars—or even for eighty; let's say eighty—he, Cornelius, would procure a trustworthy man to smuggle Jim out of the river, all safe. There was nothing else for it now—if Jim cared a pin for his life. What's eighty dollars? A trifle. An insignificant sum. While he, Cornelius, who had to remain behind, was absolutely courting death by his proof of devotion to Mr. Stein's young friend. The sight of his abject grimacing was—Jim told me—very hard to bear: he clutched at his hair, beat his breast, rocked himself to and fro with his hands pressed to his stomach, and actually pretended to shed tears. 'Your blood be on your own head,' he squeaked at last, and rushed out. It is a curious question how far Cornelius was sincere in that performance. Jim confessed to me that he did not sleep a wink after the fellow had gone. He lay on his back on a thin mat spread over the bamboo flooring, trying idly to make out the bare rafters, and listening to the rustlings in the torn thatch. A star suddenly twinkled through a hole in the roof. His brain was in a whirl; but, nevertheless, it was on that very night that he matured his plan for overcoming Sherif Ali. It had been the thought of all the moments he could spare from the hopeless investigation into Stein's affairs, but the notion—he says—came to him then all at once. He could see, as it were, the guns mounted on the top of the hill. He got very hot and excited lying there; sleep was out of the question more than ever. He jumped up, and went out barefooted on the veranda. Walking silently, he came upon the girl, motionless against the wall, as if on the watch. In his then state of mind it did not surprise him to see her up, nor yet to hear her ask in an anxious whisper where Cornelius could be. He simply said he did not know. She moaned a little, and peered into the *campong*. Everything was very quiet. He was possessed by his new idea, and so full of it that he could not help telling the girl all about it at once. She listened, clapped her hands lightly, whispered softly her admiration, but was evidently on the alert all the time. It seems he had been used to make a confidante of her all along— and that she on her part could and did give him a lot of useful hints as to Patusan affairs there is no doubt. He assured me more than once that he had never found himself the worse for her advice. At any rate, he was proceeding to explain his plan fully to her there and then, when she pressed his arm once, and vanished from his side. Then Cornelius appeared from somewhere, and, perceiving Jim, ducked sideways, as though he had been shot at, and afterwards stood very still in the dusk. At last he came forward prudently, like a suspicious cat. 'There were some fishermen there—with fish,' he said in a shaky voice. 'To sell fish—you understand.' . . . It must have been then two o'clock in the morning—a likely time for anybody to hawk fish about!

"Jim, however, let the statement pass, and did not give it a single thought. Other matters occupied his mind, and besides he had neither seen or heard anything. He contented himself by saying, 'Oh!' absently, got a drink of water out of a pitcher standing there, and leaving Cornelius a prey to some inexplicable emotion—that made him embrace with both arms the worm-eaten rail of the veranda as if his legs had failed—went in again and lay down on his mat to think. By-and-by he heard stealthy footsteps. They stopped. A voice whispered tremulously through the wall, 'Are you asleep?' 'No! What is it?' he answered, briskly, and there was an abrupt movement outside, and then all was still, as if the whisperer had been startled. Extremely annoyed at this, Jim came out impetuously, and Cornelius with a faint shriek fled along the veranda as far as the steps, where he hung on to the broken banister. Very puzzled, Jim called out to him from the distance to know what the devil he meant. 'Have you given your consideration to what I spoke to you about?' asked Cornelius, pronouncing the words with difficulty, like a man in the cold fit of a fever. 'No!' shouted Jim in a passion. 'I did not, and I don't intend to. I am going to live here, in Patusan.' 'You shall d-d-die h-h-here.' answered Cornelius, still shaking violently, and in a sort of expiring voice. The whole performance was so absurd and provoking that Jim didn't know whether he ought to be amused or angry. 'Not till I have seen you tucked away, you bet,' he called out, exasperated yet ready to laugh. Half seriously (being excited with his own thoughts, you know) he went on shouting, 'Nothing can touch me! You can do your damnedest.' Somehow the shadowy Cornelius far off there seemed to be the hateful embodiment of all the annoyances and difficulties he had found in his path. He let himself go—his nerves had been over-wrought for days—and called him many pretty names,—swindler, liar, sorry rascal: in fact, carried on in an extraordinary way. He admits he passed all bounds, that he was quite beside himself—defied all Patusan to scare him away—declared he would make them all dance to his own tune yet, and so on, in a menacing, boasting strain. Perfectly bombastic and ridiculous, he said. His ears burned at the bare recollection. Must have been off his chump in some way. . . . The girl, who was sitting with us, nodded her little head at me quickly, frowned faintly, and said, 'I heard him,' with childlike solemnity. He laughed and blushed. What stopped him at last, he said, was the silence, the complete deathlike silence, of the indistinct figure far over there, that seemed to hang collapsed, doubled over the rail in a weird immobility. He came to his senses, and ceasing suddenly, wondered greatly at himself. He watched for a while. Not a stir, not a sound. 'Exactly as if the chap had died while I had been making all that noise,' he said. He was so ashamed of himself that he went indoors in a hurry without another word, and flung himself down again. The row seemed to have done him good though, because he went to sleep for the rest of the night like a baby. Hadn't slept like that for weeks. 'But *I* didn't sleep,' struck in the girl, one elbow on the table and nursing her cheek. 'I watched.' Her big eyes flashed, rolling a little, and then she fixed them on my face intently."

XXXI

"You may imagine with what interest I listened. All these details were perceived to have some significance twenty-four hours later. In the morning Cornelius made no allusion to the events of the night. 'I suppose you will come back to my poor house,' he muttered, surlily, slinking up just as Jim was entering the canoe to go over to Doramin's *campong*. Jim only nodded, without looking at him. 'You find it good fun, no doubt,' muttered the other in a sour tone. Jim spent the day with the old *nakhoda*,

preaching the necessity of vigorous action to the principal men of the Bugis community, who had been summoned for a big talk. He remembered with pleasure how very
eloquent and persuasive he had been. 'I managed to put some backbone into them that
time, and no mistake,' he said. Sherif Ali's last raid had swept the outskirts of the
settlement, and some women belonging to the town had been carried off to the
stockade. Sherif Ali's emissaries had been seen in the marketplace the day before,
strutting about haughtily in white cloaks, and boasting of the Rajah's friendship for
their master. One of them stood forward in the shade of a tree, and, leaning on the
long barrel of a rifle, exhorted the people to prayer and repentance, advising them to
kill all the strangers in their midst, some of whom, he said, were infidels and others
even worse—children of Satan in the guise of Moslems. It was reported that several of
the Rajah's people amongst the listeners had loudly expressed their approbation. The
terror amongst the common people was intense. Jim, immensely pleased with his day's
work, crossed the river again before sunset.

"As he had got the Bugis irretrievably committed to action and had made himself
responsible for success on his own head, he was so elated that in the lightness of his
heart he absolutely tried to be civil with Cornelius. But Cornelius became wildly jovial
in response, and it was almost more than he could stand, he says, to hear his little
squeaks of false laughter, to see him wriggle and blink, and suddenly catch hold of his
chin and crouch low over the table with a distracted stare. The girl did not show
herself, and Jim retired early. When he rose to say good-night, Cornelius jumped up,
knocking his chair over, and ducked out of sight as if to pick up something he had
dropped. His good-night came huskily from under the table. Jim was amazed to see
him emerge out with a dropping jaw, and staring, stupidly frightened eyes. He clutched
the edge of the table. 'What's the matter? Are you unwell?' asked Jim. 'Yes, yes, yes. A
great colic in my stomach,' says the other; and it is Jim's opinion that it was perfectly
true. If so, it was, in view of his contemplated action, an abject sign of a still imperfect
callousness for which he must be given all due credit.

"Be it as it may, Jim's slumbers were disturbed by a dream of heavens like brass
resounding with a great voice, which called upon him to Awake! Awake! so loud that,
notwithstanding his desperate determination to sleep on, he did wake up in reality.
The glare of a red spluttering conflagration going on in mid-air fell on his eyes. Coils
of black thick smoke curved round the head of some apparition, some unearthly being,
all in white, with a severe, drawn, anxious face. After a second or so he recognized the
girl. She was holding a dammar torch at arm's-length aloft, and in a persistent, urgent
monotone she was repeating, 'Get up! Get up! Get up!'

"Suddenly he leaped to his feet; at once she put into his hand a revolver, his own
revolver, which had been hanging on a nail, but loaded this time. He gripped it in
silence, bewildered, blinking in the light. He wondered what he could do for her.

"She asked rapidly and very low, 'Can you face four men with this?' He laughed
while narrating this part at the recollection of his polite alacrity. It seems he made a
great display of it. 'Certainly—of course—certainly—command me.' He was not
properly awake, and had a notion of being very civil in these extraordinary circum-

stances, of showing his unquestioning, devoted readiness. She left the room, and he followed her; in the passage they disturbed an old hag who did the casual cooking of the household, though she was so decrepit as to be hardly able to understand human speech. She got up and hobbled behind them, mumbling toothlessly. On the veranda a hammock of sailcloth, belonging to Cornelius, swayed lightly to the touch of Jim's elbow. It was empty.

"The Patusan establishment, like all the posts of Stein's Trading Company, had originally consisted of four buildings. Two of them were represented by two heaps of sticks, broken bamboos, rotten thatch, over which the four cornerposts of hardwood leaned sadly at different angles: the principal storeroom, however, stood yet, facing the agent's house. It was an oblong hut, built of mud and clay: it had at one end a wide door of stout planking, which so far had not come off the hinges, and in one of the side walls there was a square aperture, a sort of window, with three wooden bars. Before descending the few steps the girl turned her face over her shoulder and said quickly, 'You were to be set upon while you slept.' Jim tells me he experienced a sense of deception. It was the old story. He was weary of these attempts upon his life. He had had his fill of these alarms. He was sick of them. He assured me he was angry with the girl for deceiving him. He had followed her under the impression that it was she who wanted his help, and now he had half a mind to turn on his heel and go back in disgust. 'Do you know,' he commented, profoundly, 'I rather think I was not quite myself for whole weeks on end about that time.' 'Oh, yes. You were though,' I couldn't help contradicting.

"But she moved on swiftly, and he followed her into the courtyard. All its fences had fallen in a long time ago; the neighbors' buffaloes would pace in the morning across the open space, snorting profoundly, without haste; the very jungle was invading it already. Jim and the girl stopped in the rank grass. The light in which they stood made a dense blackness all round, and only above their heads there was an opulent glitter of stars. He told me it was a beautiful night—quite cool, with a little stir of breeze from the river. It seems he noticed its friendly beauty. Remember this is a love story I am telling you now. A lovely night that seemed to breathe on them a soft caress. The flame of the torch streamed now and then with a fluttering noise like a flag, and for a time this was the only sound. 'They are in the storeroom waiting,' whispered the girl; 'they are waiting for the signal.' 'Who's to give it?' he asked. She shook the torch, which blazed up after a shower of sparks. 'Only you have been sleeping so restlessly,' she continued in a murmur. 'I watched your sleep, too.' 'You!' he exclaimed, craning his neck to look about him. 'You think I watched on this night only!' she said, with a sort of despairing indignation.

"He says it was as if he had received a blow on the chest. He gasped. He thought he had been an awful brute somehow, and he felt remorseful, touched, happy, elated. This, let me remind you again, is a love story; you can see it by the imbecility, not a repulsive imbecility, the exalted imbecility of these proceedings, this station in torch-light, as if they had come there on purpose to have it out for the edification of concealed murderers. If Sherif Ali's emissaries had been possessed—as Jim remarked

—of a pennyworth of spunk, this was the time to make a rush. His heart was thumping—not with fear—but he seemed to hear the grass rustle, and he stepped smartly out of the light. Something dark, imperfectly seen, flitted rapidly out of sight. He called out in a strong voice, 'Cornelius! O Cornelius!' A profound silence succeeded: his voice did not seem to have carried twenty feet. Again the girl was by his side. 'Fly!' she said. The old woman was coming up; her broken figure hovered in crippled little jumps on the edge of the light; they heard her mumbling, and a light, moaning sigh. 'Fly!' repeated the girl, excitedly. 'They are frightened now—this light —the voices. They know you are awake now—they know you are big, strong, fearless . . .' 'If I am all that,' he began, but she interrupted him. 'Yes—tonight! But what of tomorrow night? Of the next night? Of the night after—of all the many, many nights? Can I be always watching?' A sobbing catch of her breath affected him beyond the power of words.

"He told me that he had never felt so small, so powerless—and as to courage, what was the good of it? he thought. He was so helpless that even flight seemed of no use; and though she kept on whispering, 'Go to Doramin, go to Doramin,' with feverish insistence, he realized that for him there was no refuge from that loneliness which centupled all his dangers except—in her. 'I thought,' he said to me, 'that if I went away from her it would be the end of everything somehow.' Only as they couldn't stop there for ever in the middle of that courtyard, he made up his mind to go and look into the storehouse. He let her follow him without thinking of any protest, as if they had been indissolubly united. 'I am fearless—am I?' he muttered through his teeth. She restrained his arm. 'Wait till you hear my voice,' she said, and, torch in hand, ran lightly round the corner. He remained alone in the darkness, his face to the door: not a sound, not a breath came from the other side. The old hag let out a dreary groan somewhere behind his back. He heard a high-pitched almost screaming call from the girl. 'Now! Push!' he pushed violently; the door swung with a creak and a clatter, disclosing to his intense astonishment the low dungeon-like interior illuminated by a lurid, wavering glare. A turmoil of smoke eddied down upon an empty wooden crate in the middle of the floor, a litter of rags and straw tried to soar, but only stirred feebly in the draught. She had thrust the light through the bars of the window. He saw her bare round arm extended and rigid, holding up the torch with the steadiness of an iron bracket. A conical ragged heap of old mats cumbered a distant corner almost to the ceiling, and that was all.

"He explained to me that he was bitterly disappointed at this. His fortitude had been tried by so many warnings, he had been for weeks surrounded by so many hints of danger, that he wanted the relief of some reality, of something tangible that he could meet. 'It would have cleared the air for a couple of hours at least, if you know what I mean,' he said to me. 'Jove! I had been living for days with a stone on my chest.' Now at last he had thought he would get hold of something, and—nothing! Not a trace, not a sign of anybody. He had raised his weapon as the door flew open, but now his arm fell. 'Fire! Defend yourself,' the girl outside cried in an agonizing voice. She being in the dark and with her arm thrust in to the shoulder through the small hole, couldn't see what was going on, and she dared not withdraw the torch now to run round. 'There's nobody here!' yelled Jim, contemptuously, but his impulse to burst into a resentful exasperated laugh died without a sound: he had perceived in the very act of turning away that he was exchanging glances with a pair of eyes in the heap of mats. He saw a shifting gleam of whites. 'Come out!' he cried in a fury, a little doubtful, and a dark-faced head, a head without a body, shaped itself in the rubbish, a strangely detached head, that looked at him with a steady scowl. Next moment the whole mound stirred, and with a low grunt a man emerged swiftly, and bounded towards Jim. Behind him the mats as it were jumped and flew, his right arm was raised with a crooked elbow, and the dull blade of a kris protruded from his fist held off, a little above his head. A cloth wound tight round his loins seemed dazzlingly white on his bronze skin; his naked body glistened as if wet.

"Jim noted all this. He told me he was experiencing a feeling of unutterable relief, of vengeful elation. He held his shot, he says, deliberately. He held it for the tenth part of a second, for three strides of the man—an unconscionable time. He held it for the pleasure of saying to himself, That's a dead man! He was absolutely positive and certain. He let him come on because it did not matter. A dead man, anyhow. He noticed the dilated nostrils, the wide eyes, the intent, eager stillness of the face, and then he fired.

"The explosion in that confined space was stunning. He stepped back a pace. He saw the man jerk his head up, fling his arms forward, and drop the kris. He ascertained afterwards that he had shot him through the mouth, a little upwards, the bullet coming out high at the back of the skull. With the impetus of his rush the man drove straight on, his face suddenly gaping disfigured, with his hands open before him gropingly, as though blinded, and landed with terrific violence on his forehead, just short of Jim's bare toes. Jim says he didn't lose the smallest detail of all this. He found himself calm, appeased, without rancor, without uneasiness, as if the death of that man had atoned for everything. The place was getting very full of sooty smoke from the torch, in which the unswaying flame burned blood-red without a flicker. He walked in resolutely, striding over the dead body, and covered with his revolver another naked figure out-lined vaguely at the other end. As he was about to pull the trigger, the man threw away with force a short heavy spear, and squatted submissively on his hams, his back to the wall and his clasped hands between his legs. 'You want your life?' Jim said. The other made no sound. 'How many more of you?' asked Jim again. 'Two more, Tuan,' said the man very softly, looking with big fascinated eyes into the muzzle of the revolver. Accordingly two more crawled from under the mats, holding out ostentatiously their empty hands."

XXXII

"Jim took up an advantageous position and shepherded them out in a bunch through the doorway: all that time the torch had remained vertical in the grip of a little hand, without so much as a tremble. The three men obeyed him, perfectly mute, moving automatically. He ranged them in a row. 'Link arms!' he ordered. They did so. 'The first who withdraws his arm or turns his head is a dead man,' he said. 'March!' They stepped out together, rigidly; he followed, and at the side the girl, in a trailing white gown, her black hair falling as low as her waist, bore the light. Erect and swaying, she seemed to glide without touching the earth; the only sound was the silky swish and rustle of the long grass. 'Stop!' cried Jim.

"The river-bank was steep; a great freshness ascended, the light fell on the edge of smooth dark water frothing without a ripple; right and left the shapes of the houses ran together below the sharp outlines of the roofs. 'Take my greetings to Sherif Ali— till I come myself,' said Jim. Not one head of the three budged. 'Jump!' he thundered. The three splashes made one splash, a shower flew up, black heads bobbed convulsively, and disappeared; but a great blowing and spluttering went on, growing faint, for they were diving industriously in great fear of a parting shot. Jim turned to the girl, who had been a silent and attentive observer. His heart seemed suddenly to grow too big for his breast and choke him in the hollow of his throat. This probably made him speechless for so long, and after returning his gaze she flung the burning torch with a wide sweep of the arm into the river. The ruddy fiery glare, taking a long flight through the night, sank with a vicious hiss, and the calm soft starlight descended upon them, unchecked.

"He did not tell me what it was he said when at last he recovered his voice. I don't suppose he could be very eloquent. The world was still, the night breathed on them, one of those nights that seem created for the sheltering of tenderness, and there are moments when our souls, as if freed from their dark envelope, glow with an exquisite sensibility that makes certain silences more lucid than speeches. As to the girl, he told me, 'She broke down a bit. Excitement—don't you know. Reaction. Deucedly tired she must have been—and all that kind of thing. And—and—hang it all—she was fond of me, don't you see. . . . I, too . . . didn't know, of course . . . never entered my head. . . .'

"There he got up and began to walk about in some agitation. 'I—I love her dearly. More than I could tell. Of course one cannot tell. You take a different view of your actions when you come to understand, when you are *made* to understand every day that your existence is necessary—you see, absolutely necessary—to another person. I am made to feel that. Wonderful. But only try to think what her life had been. It is too extravagantly awful! Isn't it? And me finding her here like this—as you may go out for a stroll and come suddenly upon somebody drowning in a lonely dark place. Jove! No time to lose. Well, it is a trust, too . . . I believe I am equal to it. . . .'

"I must tell you the girl had left us to ourselves some time before. He slapped his chest. 'Yes! I feel that, but I believe I am equal to all my luck!' He had the gift of finding a special meaning in everything that happened to him. This was the view he took of his love-affair; it was idyllic, a little solemn, and also true, since his belief had all the unshakable seriousness of youth. Some time after, on another occasion, he said to me, 'I've been only two years here, and now, upon my word, I can't conceive being able to live anywhere else. The very thought of the world outside is enough to give me a fright; because, don't you see,' he continued, with downcast eyes watching the action of his boot busied in squashing thoroughly a tiny bit of dried mud (we were strolling on the river-bank)—'because I have not forgotten why I came here. Not yet!'

"I refrained from looking at him, but I think I heard a short sigh; we took a turn or two in silence. 'Upon my soul and conscience,' he began again, 'if such a thing can be forgotten, then I think I have a right to dismiss it from my mind. Ask any man here' . . . his voice changed. 'Is it not strange,' he went on in a gentle, almost yearning tone, 'that all these people, all these people who would do anything for me, can never be made to understand? Never! If you disbelieve me I could not call them up. It seems hard, somehow. I am stupid, am I not? What more can I want? If you ask them who is brave—who is true—who is just—who is it they would trust with their lives?—they would say, Tuan Jim. And yet they can never know the real, real truth. . . .'

"That's what he said to me on my last day with him. I did not let a murmur escape me: I felt he was going to say more, and come no nearer to the root of the matter. The sun, whose concentrated glare dwarfs the earth into a restless mote of dust, had sunk behind the forest, and the diffused light from an opal sky seemed to cast upon a world without shadows and without brilliance the illusion of a calm and pensive greatness. I don't know why, listening to him, I should have noted so distinctly the gradual darkening of the river, of the air; the irresistible slow work of the night settling silently on all the visible forms, effacing the outlines, burying the shapes deeper and deeper, like a steady fall of impalpable black dust.

" 'Jove!' he began, abruptly, 'there are days when a fellow is too absurd for anything; only I know I can tell you what I like. I talk about being done with it—with the bally thing at the back of my head. . . . Forgetting. . . . Hang me if I know! I can think of it quietly. After all, what has it proved? Nothing. I suppose you don't think so. . . .'

"I made a protesting murmur.

" 'No matter,' he said. 'I am satisfied . . . nearly. I've got to look only at the face of the first man that comes along, to regain my confidence. They can't be made to understand what is going on in me. What of that? Come! I haven't done so badly.'

" 'Not so badly,' I said.

" 'But all the same, you wouldn't like to have me aboard your own ship—hey?'

" 'Confound you!' I cried. 'Stop this.'

" 'Aha! You see,' he cried, crowing, as it were, over me placidly. 'Only,' he went on, 'you just try to tell this to any of them here. They would think you a fool, a liar, or worse. And so I can stand it. I've done a thing or two for them, but this is what they have done for me.'

" 'My dear chap,' I cried, 'you shall always remain for them an insoluble mystery.' Thereupon we were silent.

" 'Mystery,' he repeated, before looking up. 'Well, then let me always remain here.'

"After the sun had set, the darkness seemed to drive upon us, borne in every faint puff of the breeze. In the middle of a hedged path I saw the arrested, gaunt, watchful, and apparently one-legged silhouette of Tamb' Itam; and across the dusky space my eye detected something white moving to and fro behind the supports of the roof. As soon as Jim, with Tamb' Itam at his heels, had started upon his evening rounds, I went up to the house alone, and, unexpectedly, found myself waylaid by the girl, who had been clearly waiting for this opportunity.

"It is hard to tell you what it was precisely she wanted to wrest from me. Obviously it would be something very simple—the simplest impossibility in the world; as, for instance, the exact description of the form of a cloud. She wanted an assurance, a statement, a promise, an explanation—I don't know how to call it: the thing has no name. It was dark under the projecting roof, and all I could see were the flowing lines of her gown, the pale small oval of her face, with the white flash of her teeth, and, turned towards me, the big somber orbits of her eyes, where there seemed to be a faint stir, such as you may fancy you can detect when you plunge your gaze to the bottom of an immensely deep well. What is it that moves there? you ask yourself. Is it a blind monster or only a lost gleam from the universe? It occurred to me—don't laugh—that all things being dissimilar, she was more inscrutable in her childish ignorance than the Sphinx propounding childish riddles to wayfarers. She had been carried off to Patusan before her eyes were open. She had grown up there; she had seen nothing, she had known nothing, she had no conception of anything. I ask myself whether she were sure that anything else existed. What notions she may have formed of the outside world is to me inconceivable: all that she knew of its inhabitants were a betrayed woman and a sinister pantaloon. Her lover also came to her from there, gifted with irresistible seductions; but what would become of her if he should return to these inconceivable regions that seemed always to claim back their own? Her mother had warned her of this with tears, before she died. . . .

"She had caught hold of my arm firmly, and as soon as I had stopped she had withdrawn her hand in haste. She was audacious and shrinking. She feared nothing, but she was checked by the profound incertitude and the extreme strangeness—a brave person groping in the dark. I belonged to this Unknown that might claim Jim for its own at any moment. I was, as it were, in the secret of its nature and of its intentions; —the confidant of a threatening mystery;—armed with its power perhaps! I believe she supposed I could with a word whisk Jim away out of her very arms; it is my sober conviction she went through agonies of apprehension during my long talks with Jim; through a real and intolerable anguish that might have conceivably driven her into plotting my murder, had the fierceness of her soul been equal to the tremendous situation it had created. This is my impression, and it is all I can give you: the whole thing dawned gradually upon me, and as it got clearer and clearer I was overwhelmed by a slow incredulous amazement. She made me believe her, but there is no word that on my lips could render the effect of the headlong and vehement whisper, of the soft, passionate tones, of the sudden breathless pause and the appealing movement of the white arms extended swiftly. They fell; the ghostly figure swayed like a slender tree in the wind, the pale oval of the face drooped; it was impossible to distinguish her features, the darkness of the eyes was unfathomable; two wide sleeves uprose in the dark like unfolding wings, and she stood silent, holding her head in her hands."

XXXIII

"I was immensely touched: her youth, her ignorance, her ignorance, her pretty beauty, which had the simple charm and the delicate vigor of a wild-flower, her pathetic pleading, her helplessness, appealed to me with almost the strength of her own unreasonable and natural fear. She feared the unknown as we all do, and her ignorance made the unknown infinitely vast. I stood for it, for myself, for you fellows, for all the world that neither cared for Jim nor needed him in the least. I would have been ready enough to answer for the indifference of the teeming earth but for the reflection that he, too, belonged to this mysterious unknown of her fears, and that, however much I stood for, I did not stand for him. This made me hesitate. A murmur of hopeless pain unsealed my lips. I began by protesting that I at least had come with no intention to take Jim away.

"Why did I come, then? After a slight movement she was as still as a marble statue in the night. I tried to explain briefly: friendship, business; if I had any wish in the matter it was rather to see him stay. . . . 'They always leave us,' she murmured. The breath of sad wisdom from the grave which her piety wreathed with flowers seemed to pass in a faint sigh. . . . Nothing, I said, could separate Jim from her.

"It is my firm conviction now; it was my conviction at the time; it was the only possible conclusion from the facts of the case. It was not made more certain by her whispering in a tone in which one speaks to oneself, 'He swore this to me.' 'Did you ask him?' I said.

"She made a step nearer. 'No. Never!' She had asked him only to go away. It was that night on the river-bank, after he had killed the man—after she had flung the torch in the water because he was looking at her so. There was too much light, and the danger was over then—for a little time—for a little time. He said then he would not abandon her to Cornelius. She had insisted. She wanted him to leave her. He said that he could not—that it was impossible. He trembled while he said this. She had felt him tremble. . . . One does not require much imagination to see the scene, almost to hear their whispers. She was afraid for him, too. I believe that then she saw in him only a predestined victim of dangers which she understood better than himself. Though by nothing but his mere presence he had mastered her heart, had filled all her thoughts, and had possessed himself of all her affections, she under-estimated his chances of success. It is obvious that at about that time everybody was inclined to under-estimate his chances. Strictly speaking he didn't seem to have any. I know this was Cornelius's view. He confessed that much to me in extenuation of the shady part he had played in Sherif Ali's plot to do away with the infidel. Even Sheriff Ali himself, as it seems certain now, had nothing but contempt for the white man. Jim was to be murdered mainly on religious grounds, I believe. A simple act of piety (and so far infinitely meritorious), but otherwise without much importance. In the last part of this opinion Cornelius concurred. 'Honorable sir,' he argued abjectly on the only occasion he managed to have me to himself—'Honorable sir, how was I to know? Who was he? What could he do to make people believe him? What did Mr. Stein mean sending a boy like that to talk big to an old servant? I was ready to save him for eighty dollars.

Only eighty dollars. Why didn't the fool go? Was I to get stabbed myself for the sake of a stranger?' He groveled in spirit before me, with his body doubled up insinuatingly and his hands hovering about my knees, as though he were ready to embrace my legs. 'What's eighty dollars? An insignificant sum to give to a defenseless old man ruined for life by a deceased she-devil.' Here he wept. But I anticipate. I didn't that night chance upon Cornelius till I had had it out with the girl.

"She was unselfish when she urged Jim to leave her, and even to leave the country. It was his danger that was foremost in her thoughts—even if she wanted to save herself, too—perhaps unconsciously: but then look at the warning she had, look at the lesson that could be drawn from every moment of the recently ended life in which all her memories were centered. She fell at his feet—she told me so—there by the river, in the discreet light of stars which showed nothing except great masses of silent shadows, indefinite open spaces, and trembling faintly upon the broad stream made it appear as wide as the sea. He had lifted her up. He lifted her up, and then she would struggle no more. Of course not. Strong arms, a tender voice, a stalwart shoulder to rest her poor lonely little head upon. The need—the infinite need—of all this for the aching heart, for the bewildered mind;—the promptings of youth—the necessity of the moment. What would you have? One understands—unless one is incapable of understanding anything under the sun. And so she was content to be lifted up—and held. 'You know —Jove! this is serious—no nonsense in it!' as Jim had whispered hurriedly with a troubled concerned face on the threshold of his house. I don't know so much about nonsense, but there was nothing lighthearted in their romance: they came together under the shadow of a life's disaster, like knight and maiden meeting to exchange vows amongst haunted ruins. The starlight was good enough for that story, a light so faint and remote that it cannot resolve shadows into shapes, and show the other shore of a stream. I did look upon the stream that night and from the very place; it rolled silent and as black as Styx: the next day I went away, but I am not likely to forget what it was she wanted to be saved from when she entreated him to leave her while there was time. She told me what it was, calmed—she was now too passionately interested for mere excitement—in a voice as quiet in the obscurity as her white half-lost figure. She told me, 'I didn't want to die weeping.' I thought I had not heard aright.

" 'You did not want to die weeping?' I repeated after her. 'Like my mother,' she added readily. The outlines of her white shape did not stir in the least. 'My mother had wept bitterly before she died,' she explained. An inconceivable calmness seemed to have risen from the ground around us, imperceptibly, like the still rise of a flood in the night, obliterating the familiar landmarks of emotions. There came upon me, as though I had felt myself losing my footing in the midst of waters, a sudden dread, the dread of the unknown depths. She went on explaining that, during the last moments, being alone with her mother, she had to leave the side of the couch to go and set her back against the door, in order to keep Cornelius out. He desired to get in, and kept on drumming with both fists, only desisting now and again to shout huskily, 'Let me in! Let me in! Let me in!' In a far corner upon a few mats the moribund woman, already speechless and unable to lift her arm, rolled her head over, and with a feeble movement of her hand seemed to command—'No! No!' and the obedient daughter, setting her shoulders with all her strength against the door, was looking on. 'The tears fell from her eyes—and then she died,' concluded the girl in an imperturbable monotone, which more than anything else, more than the white statuesque immobility of her person, more than mere words could do, troubled my mind profoundly with the passive, irremediable horror of the scene. It had the power to drive me out of my conception of existence, out of that shelter each of us makes for himself to creep under in moments of danger, as a tortoise withdraws within its shell. For a moment I had a view of a world that seemed to wear a vast and dismal aspect of disorder, while, in truth, thanks to our unwearied efforts, it is as sunny an arrangement of small conveniences as the mind of man can conceive. But still—it was only a moment: I went back into my shell directly. One *must*—don't you know?—though I seemed to have lost all my words in the chaos of dark thoughts I had contemplated for a second or two beyond the pale. These came back, too, very soon, for words also belong to the sheltering conception of light and order which is our refuge. I had them ready at my disposal before she whispered softly, 'He swore he would never leave me, when we stood there alone! He swore to me!' . . . 'And is it possible that you—you! do not believe him?' I asked, sincerely reproachful, genuinely shocked. Why couldn't she believe? Wherefore this craving for incertitude, this clinging to fear, as if incertitude and fear had been the safeguards of her love. It was monstrous. She should have made for herself a shelter of inexpugnable peace out of that honest affection. She had not the knowledge—not the skill perhaps. The night had come on apace; it had grown pitch-dark where we were, so that without stirring she had faded like the intangible form of a wistful and perverse spirit. And suddenly I heard her quiet whisper again, 'Other men had sworn the same thing.' It was like a meditative comment on some thoughts full of sadness, of awe. And she added, still lower if possible, 'My father did.' She paused the time to draw an inaudible breath. 'Her father, too.' . . . These were the things she knew! At once I said, 'Ah! but he is not like that.' This, it seemed, she did not intend to dispute; but after a time the strange still whisper wandering dreamily in the air stole into my ears. 'Why is he different? Is he better? Is here . . .' 'Upon my word of honor,' I broke in, 'I believe he is.' We subdued our tones to a mysterious pitch. Amongst the huts of Jim's workmen (they were mostly liberated slaves from the Sherif's stockade) somebody started a shrill, drawling song. Across the river a big fire (at Doramin's, I think) made a glowing ball, completely isolated in the night. 'Is he more true?' she murmured. 'Yes,' I said. 'More true than any other man,' she repeated in lingering accents. 'Nobody here,' I said, 'would dream of doubting his word— nobody would dare—except you.'

"I think she made a movement at this. 'More brave,' she went on in a changed tone. 'Fear shall never drive him away from you,' I said a little nervously. The song stopped short on a shrill note, and was succeeded by several voices talking in the distance. Jim's voice, too. I was struck by her silence. 'What has he been telling you? He has been telling you something?' I asked. There was no answer. 'What is it he told you?' I insisted.

" 'Do you think I can tell you? How am I to know? How am I to understand?' she cried at last. There was a stir. I believe she was wringing her hands. 'There is something he can never forget.'

" 'So much the better for you,' I said, gloomily.

" 'What is it? What is it?' she put an extraordinary force of appeal into her supplicating tone. 'He says he had been afraid. How can I believe this? Am I a mad woman to believe this? You all remember something! You all go back to it. What is it? You tell me! What is this thing? Is it alive?—is it dead? I hate it. It is cruel. Has it got a face and a voice—this calamity? Will he see it—will he hear it? In his sleep perhaps when he cannot see me—and then arise and go. Ah! I shall never forgive him. My mother had forgiven—but I, never! Will it be a sign—a call?'

"It was a wonderful experience. She mistrusted his very slumbers—and she seemed to think I could tell her why! Thus a poor mortal seduced by the charm of an apparition might have tried to wring from another ghost the tremendous secret of the claim the other world holds over a disembodied soul astray amongst the passions of this earth. The very ground on which I stood seemed to melt under my feet. And it was so simple, too; but if the spirits evoked by our fears and our unrest have ever to vouch for each other's constancy before the forlorn magicians that we are, then I—I alone of us dwellers in the flesh—have shuddered in the hopeless chill of such a task. A sign, a call! How telling in its expression was her ignorance. A few words! How she came to know them, how she came to pronounce them, I can't imagine. Women find their inspiration in the stress of moments that for us are merely awful, absurd, or futile. To discover that she had a voice at all was enough to strike awe into the heart. Had a spurned stone cried out in pain it could not have appeared a greater and more pitiful miracle. These few sounds wandering in the dark had made their two benighted lives tragic to my mind. It was impossible to make her understand. I chafed silently at my impotence. And Jim, too—poor devil! Who would need him? Who would remember him? He had what he wanted. His very existence probably had been forgotten by this time. They had mastered their fates. They were tragic.

"Her immobility before me was clearly expectant, and my part was to speak for my brother from the realm of forgetful shades. I was deeply moved at my responsibility and at her distress. I would have given anything for the power to soothe her frail soul, tormenting itself in its invincible ignorance like a small bird beating about the cruel wires of a cage. Nothing easier than to say, Have no fear! Nothing more difficult. How does one kill fear, I wonder? How do you shoot a specter through the heart, slash off its spectral head, take it by its spectral throat? It is an enterprise you rush into while you dream, and are glad to make your escape with wet hair and every limb shaking. The bullet is not run, the blade not forged, the man not born; even the winged words of truth drop at your feet like lumps of lead. You require for such a desperate encounter an enchanted and poisoned shaft dipped in a lie too subtle to be found on earth. An enterprise for a dream, my masters!

"I began my exorcism with a heavy heart, with a sort of sullen anger in it, too. Jim's voice, suddenly raised with a stern intonation, carried across the courtyard, reproving the carelessness of some dumb sinner by the river-side. Nothing—I said, speaking in a distinct murmur—there could be nothing, in that unknown world she fancied so eager to rob her of her happiness, there was nothing neither living nor dead, there was no face, no voice, no power, that could tear Jim from her side. I drew breath and she whispered softly, 'He told me so.' 'He told you the truth,' I said. 'Nothing,' she sighed out, and abruptly turned upon me with a barely audible intensity of tone: 'Why did you come to us from out there? He speaks of you too often. You make me afraid. Do you—do you want him?' A sort of stealthy fierceness had crept into our hurried mutters. 'I shall never come again,' I said, bitterly. 'And I don't want him. No one wants him.' 'No one,' she repeated in a tone of doubt. 'No one,' I affirmed, feeling myself swayed by some strange excitement. 'You think him strong, wise, courageous, great—why not believe him to be true, too? I shall go tomorrow—and that is the end. You shall never be troubled by a voice from there again. This world you don't know is too big to miss him. You understand? Too big. You've got his heart in your hand. You must feel that. You must know that.' 'Yes, I know that,' she breathed out, hard and still, as a statue might whisper.

"I felt I had done nothing. And what is it that I had wished to do? I am not sure now. At the time I was animated by an inexplicable ardor, as if before some great and necessary task—the influence of the moment upon my mental and emotional state. There are in all our lives such moments, such influences, coming from the outside, as it were, irresistible, incomprehensible—as if brought about by the mysterious conjunctions of the planets. She owned, as I had put it to her, his heart. She had that and everything else—if she could only believe it. What I had to tell her was that in the whole world there was no one who ever would need his heart, his mind, his hand. It was a common fate, and yet it seemed an awful thing to say of any man. She listened without a word, and her stillness now was like the protest of an invincible unbelief. What need she care for the world beyond the forests? I asked. From all the multitudes that peopled the vastness of that unknown there would come, I assured her, as long as he lived, neither a call nor a sign for him. Never. I was carried away. Never! Never! I remember with wonder the sort of dogged fierceness I displayed. I had the illusion of having got the specter by the throat at last. Indeed the whole real thing has left behind the detailed and amazing impression of a dream. Why should she fear? She knew him to be strong, true, wise, brave. He was all that. Certainly. He was more. He was great —invincible—and the world did not want him, it had forgotten him, it would not even know him.

"I stopped; the silence over Patusan was profound, and the feeble dry sound of a paddle striking the side of a canoe somewhere in the middle of the river seemed to make it infinite. 'Why?' she murmured. I felt that sort of rage one feels during a hard tussle. The specter was trying to slip out of my grasp. 'Why?' she repeated louder; 'tell me!' And as I remained confounded, she stamped with her foot like a spoilt child. 'Why? Speak.' 'You want to know?' I asked in a fury. 'Yes!' she cried. 'Because he is not good enough,' I said, brutally. During the moment's pause I noticed the fire on the other shore blaze up, dilating the circle of its glow like an amazed stare, and contract

suddenly to a red pin-point. I only knew how close to me she had been when I felt the
clutch of her fingers on my forearm. Without raising her voice, she threw into it an
infinity of scathing contempt, bitterness, and despair.

" 'This is the very thing he said. . . . You lie!'

"The last two words she cried at me in the native dialect. 'Hear me out!' I
entreated; she caught her breath tremulously, flung my arm away. 'Nobody, nobody is
good enough,' I began with the greatest earnestness. I could hear the sobbing labor of
her breath frightfully quickened. I hung my head. What was the use? Footsteps were
approaching; I slipped away without another word. . . ."

<h1 style="text-align:center">XXXIV</h1>

Marlow swung his legs out, got up quickly, and staggered a little, as though he had
been set down after a rush through space. He leaned his back against the balustrade
and faced a disordered array of long cane-chairs. The bodies prone in them seemed
startled out of their torpor by his movement. One or two sat up as if alarmed; here
and there a cigar glowed yet; Marlow looked at them all with the eyes of a man
returning from the excessive remoteness of a dream. A throat was cleared; a calm voice
encouraged negligently, "Well."

"Nothing," said Marlow with a slight start. "He had told her—that's all. She did
not believe him—nothing more. As to myself, I do not know whether it be just,
proper, decent for me to rejoice or to be sorry. For my part, I cannot say what I
believed—indeed I don't know to this day, and never shall probably. But what did the
poor devil believe himself? Truth shall prevail—don't you know *Magna est veritas et* . . .
Yes, when it gets a chance. There is a law, no doubt—and likewise a law regulates your
luck in the throwing of dice. It is not Justice the servant of men, but accident, hazard,
Fortune—the ally of patient Time—that holds an even and scrupulous balance. Both
of us had said the very same thing. Did we both speak the truth—or one of us did—
or neither? . . ."

Marlow paused, crossed his arms on his breast, and in a changed tone—

"She said we lied. Poor soul. Well—let's leave it to Chance, whose ally is Time that
cannot be hurried, and whose enemy is Death, that will not wait. I had retreated—a
little cowed, I must own. I had tried a fall with fear itself and got thrown—of course. I
had only succeeded in adding to her anguish the hint of some mysterious collusion, of
an inexplicable and incomprehensible conspiracy to keep her for ever in the dark. And
it had come easily, naturally, unavoidably, by his act, by her own act! It was as though I
had been shown the working of the implacable destiny of which we are the victims—
and the tools. It was appalling to think of the girl whom I had left standing there
motionless; Jim's footsteps had a fateful sound as he tramped by, without seeing me,
in his heavy laced boots. 'What? No lights!' he said in a loud, surprised voice. 'What
are you doing in the dark—you two?' Next moment he caught sight of her, I suppose.
'Hallo, girl!' he cried, cheerily. 'Hallo, boy!' she answered at once, with amazing pluck.

"This was their usual greeting to each other, and the bit of swagger she would put
into her rather high but sweet voice was very droll, pretty, and childlike. It delighted

Jim greatly. This was the last occasion on which I heard them exchange this familiar hail, and it struck a chill into my heart. There was the high sweet voice, the pretty effort, the swagger; but it all seemed to die out prematurely, and the playful call sounded like a moan. It was too confoundedly awful. 'What have you done with Marlow?' Jim was asking; and then, 'Gone down—has he? Funny I didn't meet him. . . . You there, Marlow?'

"I didn't answer. I wasn't going in—not yet at any rate. I really couldn't. While he was calling me I was engaged in making my escape through a little gate leading out upon a stretch of newly cleared ground. No; I couldn't face them yet. I walked hastily with lowered head along a trodden path. The ground rose gently, the few big trees had been felled, the undergrowth had been cut down and the grass fired. He had a mind to try a coffee-plantation there. The big hill, rearing its double summit coal-black in the clear yellow glow of the rising moon, seemed to cast its shadow upon the ground prepared for that experiment. He was going to try ever so many experiments; I had admired his energy, his enterprise, and his shrewdness. Nothing on earth seemed less real now than his plans, his energy, and his enthusiasm; and raising my eyes, I saw part of the moon glittering through the bushes at the bottom of the chasm. For a moment it looked as though the smooth disc, falling from its place in the sky upon the earth, had rolled to the bottom of that precipice: its ascending movement was like a leisurely rebound; it disengaged itself from the tangle of twigs; the bare contorted limb of some tree, growing on the slope, made a black crack right across its face. It threw its level rays afar as if from a cavern, and in this mournful eclipse-like light the stumps of felled trees uprose very dark, the heavy shadows fell at my feet on all sides, my own moving shadow, and across my path the shadow of the solitary grave perpetually garlanded with flowers. In the darkened moonlight the interlaced blossoms took on shapes foreign to one's memory and colors indefinable to the eye, as though they had been special flowers gathered by no man, grown not in this world, and destined for the use of the dead alone. Their powerful scent hung in the warm air, making it thick and heavy like the fumes of incense. The lumps of white coral shone round the dark mound like a chaplet of bleached skulls, and everything around was so quiet that when I stood still all sound and all movements in the world seemed to come to an end.

"It was a great peace, as if the earth had been one grave, and for a time I stood there thinking mostly of the living who, buried in remote places out of the knowledge of mankind, still are fated to share in its tragic or grotesque miseries. In its noble struggles, too—who knows? The human heart is vast enough to contain all the world. It is valiant enough to bear the burden, but where is the courage that would cast it off?

"I suppose I must have fallen into a sentimental mood; I only know that I stood there long enough for the sense of utter solitude to get hold of me so completely that all I had lately seen, all I had heard, and the very human speech itself, seemed to have passed away out of existence, living only for a while longer in my memory, as though I had been the last of mankind. It was a strange and melancholy illusion, evolved half-consciously like all our illusions, which I suspect only to be visions of remote unattainable truth, seen dimly. This was, indeed, one of the lost, forgotten, unknown places of the earth; I had looked under its obscure surface; and I felt that when tomorrow I had left it forever, it would slip out of existence, to live only in my memory till I myself passed into oblivion. I have that feeling about me now; perhaps it is that feeling which has incited me to tell you the story, to try to hand over to you, as it were, its very existence, its reality—the truth disclosed in a moment of illusion.

"Cornelius broke upon it. He bolted out, vermin-like, from the long grass growing in a depression of the ground. I believe his house was rotting somewhere near by, though I've never seen it, not having been far enough in that direction. He ran towards me upon the path; his feet, shod in dirty white shoes, twinkled on the dark earth: he pulled himself up, and began to whine and cringe under a tall stovepipe hat. His dried-up little carcass was swallowed up, totally lost, in a suit of black broadcloth. That was his costume for holidays and ceremonies, and it reminded me that this was the fourth Sunday I had spent in Patusan. All the time of my stay I had been vaguely aware of his desire to confide in me, if he only could get me all to himself. He hung about with an eager craving look on his sour yellow little face; but his timidity had kept him back as much as my natural reluctance to have anything to do with such an unsavory creature. He would have succeeded, nevertheless, had he not been so ready to slink off as soon as you looked at him. He would slink off before Jim's severe gaze, before my own, which I tried to make indifferent, even before Tamb' Itam's surly, superior glance. He was perpetually slinking away; whenever seen he was seen moving off deviously, his face over his shoulder, with either a mistrustful snarl or a woe-begone, piteous, mute aspect; but no assumed expression could conceal this innate irremediable abjectness of his nature, any more than an arrangement of clothing can conceal some monstrous deformity of the body.

"I don't know whether it was the demoralization of my utter defeat in my encounter with a specter of fear less than an hour ago, but I let him capture me without even a show of resistance. I was doomed to be the recipient of confidences, and to be confronted with unanswerable questions. It was trying; but the contempt, the unreasoned contempt, the man's appearance provoked, made it easier to bear. He couldn't possibly matter. Nothing mattered, since I had made up my mind that Jim, for whom alone I cared, had at last mastered his fate. He had told me he was satisfied . . . nearly. This is going further than most of us dare. I—who have the right to think myself good enough—dare not. Neither does any of you here, I suppose? . . ."

Marlow paused, as if expecting an answer. Nobody spoke.

"Quite right," he began again. "Let no soul know, since the truth can be wrung out of us only by some cruel, little, awful catastrophe. But he is one of us, and he could say he was satisfied . . . nearly. Just fancy this! Nearly satisfied. One could almost envy him his catastrophe. Nearly satisfied. After this nothing could matter. It did not matter who suspected him, who trusted him, who loved him, who hated him—especially as it was Cornelius who hated him.

"Yet after all this was a kind of recognition. You shall judge of a man by his foes as well as by his friends, and this enemy of Jim was such as no decent man would be ashamed to own, without, however, making too much of him. This was the view Jim took, and in which I shared; but Jim disregarded him on general grounds. 'My dear Marlow,' he said, 'I feel that if I go straight nothing can touch me. Indeed I do. Now you have been long enough here to have a good look around—and, frankly, don't you think I am pretty safe? It all depends upon me, and, by Jove! I have lots of confidence in myself. The worst thing he could do would be to kill me, I suppose. I don't think for a moment he would. He couldn't, you know—not if I were myself to hand him a loaded rifle for the purpose, and then turn my back on him. That's the sort of thing he is. And suppose he would—suppose he could? Well—what of that? I didn't come here flying for my life—did I? I came here to set my back against the wall, and I am going to stay here . . .'

" 'Till you are *quite* satisfied,' I struck in.

"We were sitting at the time under the roof in the stern of his boat; twenty paddles flashed like one, ten on a side, striking the water with a single splash, while behind our backs Tamb' Itam dipped silently right and left, and stared right down the river, attentive to keep the long canoe in the greatest strength of the current. Jim bowed his head, and our last talk seemed to flicker out for good. He was seeing me off as far as the mouth of the river. The schooner had left the day before, working down and drifting on the ebb, while I had prolonged my stay overnight. And now he was seeing me off.

"Jim had been a little angry with me for mentioning Cornelius at all. I had not, in truth, said much. The man was too insignificant to be dangerous, though he was as full of hate as he could hold. He had called me 'honorable sir' at every second sentence, and had whined at my elbow as he followed me from the grave of his 'late wife' to the gate of Jim's compound. He declared himself the most unhappy of men, a victim, crushed like a worm; he entreated me to look at him. I wouldn't turn my head to do so; but I could see out of the corner of my eye his obsequious shadow gliding after mine, while the moon, suspended on our right hand, seemed to gloat serenely upon the spectacle. He tried to explain—as I've told you—his share in the events of the memorable night. It was a matter of expediency. How could he know who was going to get the upper hand? 'I would have saved him, honorable sir! I would have saved him for eighty dollars,' he protested in dulcet tones, keeping a pace behind me. 'He has saved himself,' I said, 'and he has forgiven you.' I heard a sort of tittering, and turned upon him; at once he appeared ready to take to his heels. 'What are you laughing at?' I asked, standing still. 'Don't be deceived, honorable sir!' he shrieked, seemingly losing all control over his feelings. '*He* save himself! He knows nothing, honorable sir—nothing whatever. Who is he? What does he want here—the big thief? What does he want here? He throws dust into everybody's eyes; he throws dust into your eyes, honorable sir; but he can't throw dust into my eyes. He is a big fool, honorable sir.' I laughed contemptuously, and, turning on my heel, began to walk on again. He ran up to my elbow and whispered forcibly, 'He's no more than a little child here—like a little child—a little child.' Of course I didn't take the slightest notice, and seeing the time pressed, because we were approaching the bamboo fence that glittered over the blackened ground of the clearing, he came to the point. He commenced by being abjectly lachrymose. His great misfortunes had affected his head. He hoped I would kindly forget what nothing but his troubles made him say. He didn't mean anything by it; only the honorable sir did not know what it was to be ruined, broken down, trampled upon. After this introduction he approached the matter near his heart, but in such a rambling, ejaculatory, craven fashion, that for a long time I couldn't make out what he was driving at. He wanted me to intercede with Jim in his favor. It seemed, too, to be some sort of money affair. I heard time and again the words, 'Moderate provision—suitable present.' He seemed to be claiming value for something, and he even went the length of saying with some warmth that life was not worth having if a man were to be robbed of everything. I did not breathe a word, of course, but neither did I stop my ears. The gist of the affair, which became clear to me gradually, was in this, that he regarded himself as entitled to some money in exchange for the girl. He had brought her up. Somebody else's child. Great trouble and pains—old man now—suitable present. If the honorable sir would say a word. . . . I stood still to look at him with curiosity, and fearful lest I should think him extortionate, I suppose, he hastily brought himself to make a concession. In consideration of a 'suitable present' given at once, he would, he declared, be willing to undertake the charge of the girl, 'without any other provision—when the time came for the gentleman to go home.' His little yellow face, all crumpled as though it had been squeezed together, expressed the most anxious, eager avarice. His voice whined coaxingly, 'No more trouble—natural guardian—a sum of money. . . .'

"I stood there and marveled. That kind of thing, with him, was evidently a vocation. I discovered suddenly in his cringing attitude a sort of assurance, as though he had been all his life dealing in certitudes. He must have thought I was dispassionately considering his proposal, because he became as sweet as honey. 'Every gentleman made a provision when the time came to go home,' he began, insinuatingly. I slammed the little gate. 'In this case, Mr. Cornelius,' I said, 'the time shall never come.' He took a few seconds to gather this in. 'What!' he fairly squealed. 'Why,' I continued from my side of the gate, 'haven't you heard him say so himself? He will never go home.' 'Oh! this is too much,' he shouted. He would not address me as 'honored sir' any more. He was very still for a time, and then without a trace of humility began very low. 'Never go—ah! He—he—he comes here devil knows from where—comes here—devil knows why—to trample on me till I die—ah—trample' (he stamped softly with both feet), 'trample like this—nobody knows why—till I die. . . .' His voice became quite extinct; he was bothered by a little cough; he came up close to the fence and told me, dropping into a confidential and piteous tone, that he would not be trampled upon. 'Patience—patience,' he muttered, striking his breast. I had done laughing at him, but unexpectedly he treated me to a wild cracked burst of it. 'Ha! ha! ha! We shall see! We shall see! What! Steal from me? Steal from me everything! Everything! Everything!' His head drooped on one shoulder, his hands were hanging before him lightly clasped. One would have thought he had cherished the girl with surpassing love, that his spirit had been crushed and his heart broken by the most cruel of spoliations. Suddenly he lifted his head and shot out an infamous word. 'Like her mother—she is like her deceitful mother. Exactly. In her face, too. In her face. The devil!' He leaned his forehead against the fence, and in that position uttered threats and horrible blasphemies in Portuguese in very weak ejaculations, mingled with miserable plaints and groans, coming out with a heave of the shoulders as though he had been overtaken by a deadly fit of sickness. It was an inexpressibly grotesque and vile performance, and I hastened away. He tried to shout something after me. Some disparagement of Jim, I believe—not too loud though, we were too near the house. All I heard distinctly was, 'No more than a little child—a little child.' "

XXXV

"But next morning, at the first bend of the river shutting off the houses of Patusan, all this dropped out of my sight bodily, with its color, its design, and its meaning, like a picture created by fancy on a canvas, upon which, after long contemplation, you turn your back for the last time. It remains in the memory motionless, unfaded, with its life arrested, in an unchanging light. There are the ambitions, the fears, the hate, the hopes, and they remain in my mind just as I had seen them—intense and as if for ever suspended in their expression. I had turned away from the picture and was going back to the world where events move, men change, light flickers, life flows in a clear stream, no matter whether over mud or over stones. I wasn't going to dive into it; I would have enough to do to keep my head above the surface. But as to what I was leaving behind, I cannot imagine any alteration. The immense and magnanimous Doramin and his little motherly witch of a wife, gazing together upon the land and nursing secretly their dreams of parental ambition; Tunku Allang, wizened and greatly perplexed; Dain Waris, intelligent and brave, with his faith in Jim, with his firm glance and his ironic friendliness; the girl, absorbed in her frightened, suspicious adoration; Tamb' Itam, surly and faithful; Cornelius, leaning his forehead against the fence under the moonlight—I am certain of them. They exist as if under an enchanter's wand. But the figure round which all these are grouped—that one lives, and I am not certain of him. No magician's wand can immobilize him under my eyes. He is one of us.

"Jim, as I've told you, accompanied me on the first stage of my journey back to the world he had renounced, and the way at times seemed to lead through the very heart of untouched wilderness. The empty reaches sparkled under the high sun; between the high walls of vegetation the heat drowsed upon the water, and the boat, impelled vigorously, cut her way through the air that seemed to have settled dense and warm under the shelter of lofty trees.

"The shadow of the impending separation had already put an immense space between us, and when we spoke it was with an effort, as if to force our low voices across a vast and increasing distance. The boat fairly flew; we sweltered side by side in the stagnant superheated air; the smell of mud, of marsh, the primeval smell of fecund earth, seemed to sting our faces; till suddenly at a bend it was as if a great hand far away had lifted a heavy curtain, had flung open an immense portal. The light itself seemed to stir, the sky above our heads widened, a far-off murmur reached our ears, a freshness enveloped us, filled our lungs, quickened our thoughts, our blood, our regrets —and, straight ahead, the forests sank down against the dark-blue ridge of the sea.

"I breathed deeply, I reveled in the vastness of the opened horizon, in the different atmosphere that seemed to vibrate with a toil of life, with the energy of an impeccable world. This sky and this sea were open to me. The girl was right—there was a sign, a call in them—something to which I responded with every fiber of my being. I let my eyes roam through space, like a man released from bonds who stretches his cramped limbs, runs, leaps, responds to the inspiring elation of freedom. 'This is glorious!' I cried, and then I looked at the sinner by my side. He sat with his head sunk on his breast and said 'Yes,' without raising his eyes, as if afraid to see writ large on the clear sky of the offing the reproach of his romantic conscience.

"I remember the smallest details of that afternoon. We landed on a bit of white beach. It was backed by a low cliff wooded on the brow, draped in creepers to the very foot. Below us the plain of the sea, of a serene and intense blue, stretched with a slight upward tilt to the thread-like horizon drawn at the height of our eyes. Great waves of glitter blew lightly along the pitted dark surface, as swift as feathers chased by the breeze. A chain of islands sat broken and massive facing the wide estuary, displayed in a sheet of pale glassy water reflecting faithfully the contour of the shore. High in the colorless sunshine a solitary bird, all black, hovered, dropping and soaring above the same spot with a slight rocking motion of the wings. A ragged, sooty bunch of flimsy mat hovels was perched over its own inverted image upon a crooked multitude of high piles the color of ebony. A tiny black canoe put off from amongst them with two tiny men, all black, who toiled exceedingly, striking down at the pale water: and the canoe seemed to slide painfully on a mirror. This bunch of miserable hovels was the fishing village that boasted of the white lord's especial protection, and the two men crossing over were the old headman and his son-in-law. They landed and walked up to us on the white sand, lean, dark-brown as if dried in smoke, with ashy patches on the skin of their naked shoulders and breasts. Their heads were bound in dirty but carefully folded handkerchiefs, and the old man began at once to state a complaint, voluble, stretching a lank arm, screwing up at Jim his old bleared eyes confidently. The Rajah's people would not leave them alone; there had been some trouble about a lot of turtles' eggs his people had collected on the islets there—and leaning at arm's-length upon his paddle, he pointed with a brown skinny hand over the sea. Jim listened for a time without looking up, and at last told him gently to wait. He would hear him by-and-by. They withdrew obediently to some little distance, and sat on their heels, with their paddles lying before them on the sand; the silvery gleams in their eyes followed our movements patiently; and the immensity of the outspread sea, the stillness of the coast, passing north and south beyond the limits of my vision, made up one colossal Presence watching us four dwarfs isolated on a strip of glistening sand.

" 'The trouble is,' remarked Jim, moodily, 'that for generations these beggars of fishermen in that village there had been considered as the Rajah's personal slaves—and the old rip can't get it into his head that . . .'

"He paused. 'That you have changed all that,' I said.

" 'Yes. I've changed all that,' he muttered in a gloomy voice.

" 'You have had your opportunity,' I pursued.

" 'Had I?' he said. 'Well, yes. I suppose so. Yes. I have got back my confidence in myself—a good name—yet sometimes I wish . . . No! I shall hold what I've got. Can't expect anything more.' He flung his arm out towards the sea. 'Not out there anyhow.' He stamped his foot upon the sand. 'This is my limit, because nothing less will do.'

"We continued pacing the beach. 'Yes, I've changed all that,' he went on, with a sidelong glance at the two patient squatting fishermen; 'but only try to think what it would be if I went away. Jove! can't you see it? Hell loose. No! Tomorrow I shall go and take my chance of drinking that silly old Tunku Allang's coffee, and I shall make no end of fuss over these rotten turtles' eggs. No. I can't say—enough. Never. I must go on, go on for ever holding up my end, to feel sure that nothing can touch me. I must stick to their belief in me to feel safe and to—to' . . . He cast about for a word, seemed to look for it on the sea . . . 'to keep in touch with' . . . His voice sank suddenly to a murmur . . . 'with those whom, perhaps, I shall never see any more. With—with—you, for instance.'

"I was profoundly humbled by his words. 'For God's sake,' I said, 'don't set me up, my dear fellow; just look to yourself.' I felt a gratitude, an affection, for that straggler whose eyes had singled me out, keeping my place in the ranks of an insignificant multitude. How little that was to boast of, after all! I turned my burning face away; under the low sun, glowing, darkened and crimson, like an ember snatched from the fire, the sea lay outspread, offering all its immense stillness to the approach of the fiery orb. Twice he was going to speak, but checked himself: at last, as if he had found a formula—

" 'I shall be faithful,' he said, quietly. 'I shall be faithful,' he repeated, without looking at me, but for the first time letting his eyes wander upon the waters, whose blueness had changed to a gloomy purple under the fires of sunset. Ah! he was romantic, romantic. I recalled some words of Stein's. . . . 'In the destructive element immerse! . . . To follow the dream, and again to follow the dream—and so—always —usque ad finem . . .' He was romantic, but none the less true. Who could tell what forms, what faces, what visions, what forgiveness he could see in the glow of the west! . . . A small boat, leaving the schooner, moved slowly, with a regular beat of two oars, towards the sandbank to take me off. 'And then there's Jewel,' he said, out of the great silence of earth, sky, and sea, which had mastered my very thoughts so that his voice made me start. 'There's Jewel.' 'Yes,' I murmured. 'I need not tell you what she is to me,' he pursued. 'You've seen. In time she will come to understand . . .' 'I hope so,' I interrupted. 'She trusts me, too,' he mused, and then changed his tone. 'When shall we meet next, I wonder?' he said.

" 'Never—unless you come out,' I answered, avoiding his glance. He didn't seem to be surprised; he kept very quiet for a while.

" 'Good-bye, then,' he said, after a pause. 'Perhaps it's just as well.'

"We shook hands, and I walked to the boat, which waited with her nose on the beach. The schooner, her mainsail set and jib-sheet to windward, curveted on the purple sea; there was a rosy tinge on her sails. 'Will you be going home again soon?' asked Jim, just as I swung my leg over the gunwale. 'In a year or so if I live,' I said. The forefoot grated on the sand, the boat floated, the wet oars flashed and dipped once, twice. Jim, at the water's edge, raised his voice. 'Tell them . . .' he began. I signed to the men to cease rowing, and waited in wonder. Tell who? The half-submerged sun faced him; I could see its red gleam in his eyes that looked dumbly at me. . . . 'No —nothing,' he said, and with a slight wave of his hand motioned the boat away. I did not look again at the shore till I had clambered on board the schooner.

"By that time the sun had set. The twilight lay over the east, and the coast, turned black, extended infinitely its somber wall that seemed the very stronghold of the night; the western horizon was one great blaze of gold and crimson in which a big detached cloud floated dark and still, casting a slaty shadow on the water beneath, and I saw Jim on the beach watching the schooner fall off and gather headway.

"The two half-naked fishermen had arisen as soon as I had gone; they were no doubt pouring the plaint of their trifling, miserable, oppressed lives into the ears of the white lord, and no doubt he was listening to it, making it his own, for was it not a part of his luck—the luck 'from the word Go'—the luck to which he had assured me he was so completely equal? They, too, I should think, were in luck, and I was sure their pertinacity would be equal to it. Their dark-skinned bodies vanished on the dark background long before I had lost sight of their protector. He was white from head to foot, and remained persistently visible with the stronghold of the night at his back, the sea at his feet, the opportunity by his side—still veiled. What do you say? Was it still veiled? I don't know. For me that white figure in the stillness of coast and sea seemed to stand at the heart of a vast enigma. The twilight was ebbing fast from the sky above his head, the strip of sand had sunk already under his feet, he himself appeared no bigger than a child—then only a speck, a tiny white speck, that seemed to catch all the light left in a darkened world. . . . And, suddenly, I lost him. . . ."

XXXVI

With these words Marlow had ended his narrative, and his audience had broken up forthwith, under his abstract, pensive gaze. Men drifted off the veranda in pairs or alone without loss of time, without offering a remark, as if the last image of that incomplete story, its incompleteness itself, and the very tone of the speaker, had made discussion vain and comment impossible. Each of them seemed to carry away his own impression, to carry it away with him like a secret; but there was only one man of all these listeners who was ever to hear the last word of the story. It came to him at home, more than two years later, and it came contained in a thick packet addressed in Marlow's upright and angular handwriting.

The privileged man opened the packet, looked in, then, laying it down, went to the window. His rooms were in the highest flat of a lofty building, and his glance could travel afar beyond the clear panes of glass, as though he were looking out of the lantern of a lighthouse. The slopes of the roofs glistened, the dark broken ridges succeeded each other without end like somber, uncrested waves, and from the depths of the town under his feet ascended a confused and unceasing mutter. The spires of churches, numerous, scattered haphazard, uprose like beacons on a maze of shoals without a channel; the driving rain mingled with the falling dusk of a winter's evening; and the booming of a big clock on a tower striking the hour, rolled past in voluminous, austere bursts of sound, with a shrill vibrating cry at the core. He drew the heavy curtains.

The light of his shaded reading-lamp slept like a sheltered pool, his footfalls made no sound on the carpet, his wandering days were over. No more horizons as boundless as hope, no more twilights within the forests as solemn as temples, in the hot quest of the Ever-undiscovered Country over the hill, across the stream, beyond the wave. The hour was striking! No more! No more!—but the opened packet under the lamp brought back the sounds, the visions, the very savor of the past—a multitude of fading faces, a tumult of low voices, dying away upon the shores of distant seas under a passionate and unconsoling sunshine. He sighed and sat down to read.

At first he saw three distinct enclosures. A good many pages closely blackened and pinned together; a loose square sheet of grayish paper with a few words traced in a handwriting he had never seen before, and an explanatory letter from Marlow. From this last fell another letter, yellowed by time and frayed on the folds. He picked it up and, laying it aside, turned to Marlow's message, ran swiftly over the opening lines, and, checking himself, thereafter read on deliberately, like one approaching with slow feet and alert eyes the glimpse of an undiscovered country.

". . . I don't suppose you've forgotten," went on the letter. "You alone have showed an interest in him that survived the telling of his story, though I remember well you would not admit he had mastered his fate. You prophesied for him the disaster of weariness and of disgust with acquired honor, with the self-appointed task, with the love sprung from pity and youth. You had said you knew so well 'that kind of thing,' its illusory satisfaction, its unavoidable deception. You said also—I call to mind—that 'giving your life up to them' (*them* meaning all of mankind with skins brown, yellow, or black in color) 'was like selling your soul to a brute.' You contended that 'that kind of thing' was only endurable and enduring when based on a firm conviction in the truth of ideas racially our own, in whose name are established the order, the mortality of an ethical progress. 'We want its strength at our backs,' you had said. 'We want a belief in its necessity and its justice, to make a worthy and conscious sacrifice of our lives. Without it the sacrifice is only forgetfulness, the way of offering is no better than the way to perdition.' In other words, you maintained that we must fight in the ranks or our lives don't count. Possibly! You ought to know—be it said without malice—you who have rushed into one or two places single-handed and came out cleverly, without singeing your wings. The point, however, is that of all mankind Jim had no dealings but with himself, and the question is whether at the last he had not confessed to a faith mightier than the laws of order and progress.

"I affirm nothing. Perhaps you may pronounce—after you've read. There is much truth—after all—in the common expression 'under a cloud.' It is impossible to see him clearly—especially as it is through the eyes of others that we take our last look at him. I have no hesitation in imparting to you all I know of the last episode that, as he used to say, had 'come to him.' One wonders whether this was perhaps that supreme opportunity, that last and satisfying test for which I had always suspected him to be waiting, before he could frame a message to the impeccable world. You remember that when I was leaving him for the last time he had asked whether I would be going home soon, and suddenly cried after me, 'Tell them!' . . . I had waited—curious I'll own, and hopeful, too—only to hear him shout, 'No. Nothing.' That was all then—and there shall be nothing more; there shall be no message, unless such as each of us can interpret for himself from the language of facts, that are so often more enigmatic than the craftiest arrangement of words. He made, it is true, one more attempt to deliver himself; but that, too, failed, as you may perceive if you look at the sheet of grayish foolscap enclosed here. He had tried to write; do you notice the commonplace hand? It is headed 'The Fort, Patusan.' I suppose he had carried out his intention of making out of his house a place of defense. It was an excellent plan: a deep ditch, an earth wall topped by a palisade, and at the angles guns mounted on platforms to sweep each side of the square. Doramin had agreed to furnish him the guns; and so each man of his party would know there was a place of safety, upon which every faithful partisan could rally in case of some sudden danger. All this showed his judicious foresight, his faith in the future. What he called 'my own people'—the liberated captives of the Sherif— were to make a distinct quarter of Patusan, with their huts and little plots of ground under the walls of the stronghold. Within he would be an invincible host in himself. 'The Fort, Patusan.' No date, as you observe. What is a number and a name to a day of days? It is also impossible to say whom he had in his mind when he seized the pen: Stein—myself—the world at large—or was this only the aimless startled cry of a solitary man confronted by his fate? 'An awful thing has happened,' he wrote before he flung the pen down for the first time; look at the ink blot resembling the head of an arrow under these words. After a while he had tried again, scrawling heavily, as if with a hand of lead, another line. 'I must now at once . . .' The pen had spluttered, and that time he gave it up. There's nothing more; he had seen a broad gulf that neither eye nor voice could span. I can understand this. He was overwhelmed by the inexplicable; he was overwhelmed by his own personality—the gift of that destiny which he had done his best to master.

"I send you also an old letter—a very old letter. It was found carefully preserved in his writing-case. It is from his father, and by the date you can see he must have received it a few days before he joined the *Patna*. Thus it must be the last letter he ever had from home. He had treasured it all these years. The good old parson fancied his sailor-son. I've looked in at a sentence here and there. There is nothing in it except just affection. He tells his 'dear James' that the last long letter from him was very 'honest and entertaining.' He would not have him 'judge men harshly or hastily.' There are four pages of it, easy morality and family news. Tom had 'taken orders.' Carrie's husband had 'money losses.' The old chap goes on equably trusting Providence and the established order of the universe, but alive to its small dangers and its small mercies. One can almost see him, grey-haired and serene in the inviolable shelter of his book-lined, faded, and comfortable study, where for forty years he had conscientiously gone over and over again the round of his little thoughts about faith and virtue, about the conduct of life and the only proper manner of dying; where he had written so many sermons, where he sits talking to his boy, over there, on the other side of the earth. But what of the distance? Virtue is one all over the world, and there is only one faith, one conceivable conduct of life, one manner of dying. He hopes his 'dear James' will never forget that 'who once gives way to temptation, in the very instant hazards his total depravity and everlasting ruin. Therefore resolve fixedly never, through any possible motives, to do anything which you believe to be wrong.' There is also some news of a favorite dog; and a pony, 'which all you boys used to ride had gone blind from old age and had to be shot. The old chap invokes Heaven's blessing; the mother and all the girls then at home send their love. . . . No, there is nothing much in that yellow frayed letter fluttering out of his cherishing grasp after so many years. It was never answered, but who can say what converse he may have held with all these placid colorless forms of men and women peopling that quiet corner of the world as free of danger or strife as a tomb, and breathing equably the air of undisturbed rectitude. It seems amazing that he should belong to it, he to whom so many things 'had come.' Nothing ever came to them; they would never be taken unawares, and never be called upon to grapple with fate. Here they all are, evoked by the mild gossip of the father, all these brothers and sisters, bone of his bone and flesh of his flesh, gazing with clear unconscious eyes while I seem to see him, returned at last, no longer a mere white speck at the heart of an immense mystery, but of full stature, standing disregarded amongst their untroubled shapes, with a stern and romantic aspect, but always muted dark—under a cloud.

"The story of the last events you shall find in the few pages enclosed here. You must admit that it is romantic beyond the wildest dreams of his boyhood, and yet there is to my mind a sort of profound and terrifying logic in it as if it were our imagination alone that could set loose upon us the might of an overwhelming destiny. The imprudence of our thoughts recoils upon our heads; who toys with the sword shall perish by the sword. This astounding adventure of which the most astounding part is that it is true, come on as an unavoidable consequence. Something of the sort had to happen. You repeat this to yourself while you marvel that such a thing could happen in the year of grace before last. But it has happened—and there is no disputing its logic.

"I put it down here for you as though I had been an eyewitness. My information was fragmentary, but I've fitted the pieces together, and there is enough of them to make an intelligible picture. I wonder how he would have related it himself. He has confided so much in me that at times it seems as though he must come in presently and tell the story in his own words, in his careless yet feeling voice, with his offhand manner, a little puzzled, a little bothered, a little hurt, but now and then by a word or a phrase giving one of these glimpses of his very own self that were never any good for purposes of orientation. It's difficult to believe he will never come. I shall never hear his voice again, nor shall I see his smooth tan-and-pink face with a white line on the forehead, and the youthful eyes darkened by excitement to a profound, unfathomable blue."

XXXVII

"It all begins with a remarkable exploit of a man called Brown, who stole with complete success a Spanish schooner out of a small bay near Zamboanga. Till I discovered the fellow my information was incomplete, but most unexpectedly I did come upon him a few hours before he gave up his arrogant ghost. Fortunately he was willing and able to talk between the choking fits of asthma, and his racked body writhed with malicious exultation at the bare thought of Jim. He exulted thus at the idea that he had 'paid out the stuck-up beggar after all.' He gloated over his action. I had to bear the sunken glare of his fierce crow-footed eyes if I wanted to know; and so I bore it, reflecting how much certain forms of evil are akin to madness, derived from intense egoism, inflamed by resistance, tearing the soul to pieces, and giving factitious vigor to the body. The story also reveals unsuspected depths of cunning in the wretched Cornelius, whose abject and intense hate acts like a subtle inspiration, pointing out an unerring way towards revenge.

" 'I could see directly I set my eyes on him what sort of a fool he was,' gasped the dying Brown. 'He a man! Hell! He was a hollow sham. As if he couldn't have said straight out, "Hands off my plunder!" blast him! That would have been like a man! Rot his superior soul! He had me there—but he hadn't devil enough in him to make an end of me. Not he! A thing like that letting me off as if I wasn't worth a kick! . . .' Brown struggled desperately for breath. . . . 'Fraud. . . . Letting me off. . . . And so I did make an end of him after all. . . .' He choked again. . . . 'I expect this thing'll kill me, but I shall die easy now. You . . . you hear . . . I don't know your name—I would give you a five-pound note if—if I had it—for the news— or my name's not Brown. . . .' He grinned horribly. . . . 'Gentleman Brown.'

"He said all these things in profound gasps, staring at me with his yellow eyes out of a long, ravaged brown face; he jerked his left arm; a pepper-and-salt matted beard hung almost into his lap; a dirty ragged blanket covered his legs. I had found him out in Bangkok through that busybody Schomberg, the hotelkeeper, who had, confidentially, directed me where to look. It appears that a sort of loafing, fuddled vagabond— a white man living amongst the natives with a Siamese woman—had considered it a great privilege to give a shelter to the last days of the famous Gentleman Brown. While he was talking to me in the wretched hovel, and, as it were, fighting for every minute of his life, the Siamese woman, with big bare legs and a stupid coarse face, sat in a dark corner chewing betel stolidly. Now and then she would get up for the purpose of shooing a chicken away from the door. The whole hut shook when she walked. An ugly yellow child, naked and pot-bellied like a little heathen god, stood at the foot of the couch, finger in mouth, lost in a profound and calm contemplation of the dying man.

"He talked feverishly; but in the middle of a word, perhaps, an invisible hand would take him by the throat, and he would look at me dumbly with an expression of doubt and anguish. He seemed to fear that I would get tired of waiting and go away, leaving him with his tale untold, with his exultation unexpressed. He died during the night, I believe, but by that time I had nothing more to learn.

"So much as to Brown, for the present.

"Eight months before this, coming into Samarang, I went as usual to see Stein. On the garden side of the house a Malay on the veranda greeted me shyly, and I remembered that I had seen him in Patusan, in Jim's house, amongst other Bugis men who used to come in the evening to talk interminably over their war reminiscences and to discuss State affairs. Jim had pointed him out to me once as a respectable petty trader owning a small seagoing native craft, who had showed himself 'one of the best at the taking of the stockade.' I was not very surprised to see him, since any Patusan trader venturing as far as Samarang would naturally find his way to Stein's house. I returned his greeting and passed on. At the door of Stein's room I came upon another Malay in whom I recognized Tamb' Itam.

"I asked him at once what he was doing there; it occurred to me that Jim might have come on a visit. I own I was pleased and excited at the thought. Tamb' Itam looked as if he did not know what to say. 'Is Tuan Jim inside?' I asked, impatiently. 'No,' he mumbled, hanging his head for a moment, and then with sudden earnestness, 'He would not fight. He would not fight,' he repeated twice. As he seemed unable to say anything else, I pushed him aside and went in.

"Stein, tall and stooping, stood alone in the middle of the room between the rows of butterfly cases. '*Ach!* is it you, my friend?' he said, sadly, peering through his glasses. A drab sack-coat of alpaca hung, unbuttoned, down to his knees. He had a Panama hat on his head, and there were deep furrows on his pale cheeks. 'What's the matter now?' I asked, nervously. 'There's Tamb' Itam there. . . .' 'Come and see the girl. Come and see the girl. She is here,' he said, with a half-hearted show of activity. I tried to detain him, but with gentle obstinacy he would take no notice of my eager questions. 'She is here, she is here,' he repeated, in great perturbation. 'They came here two days ago. An old man like me, a stranger—*sehen Sie*—cannot do much. . . . Come this way. . . . Young hearts are unforgiving. . . .' I could see he was in utmost distress. . . . 'The strength of life in them, the cruel strength of life. . . .' He mumbled, leading me round the house; I followed him, lost in dismal and angry conjectures. At the door of the drawing-room he barred my way. 'He loved her very much?' he said interrogatively, and I only nodded, feeling so bitterly disappointed that I would not trust myself to speak. 'Very frightful,' he murmured. 'She can't understand me. I am only a strange old man. Perhaps you . . . she knows you. Talk to her. We can't leave it like this. Tell her to forgive him. It was very frightful.' 'No doubt,' I said, exasperated at being in the dark; 'but have *you* forgiven him?' He looked at me queerly. 'You shall hear,' he said, and opening the door, absolutely pushed me in.

"You know Stein's big house and the two immense reception-rooms, uninhabited and uninhabitable, clean, full of solitude and of shining things that look as if never beheld by the eye of man? They are cool on the hottest days, and you enter them as you would a scrubbed cave underground. I passed through one, and in the other I saw the girl sitting at the end of a big mahogany table, on which she rested her head, the face hidden in her arms. The waxed floor reflected her dimly as though it had been a sheet of frozen water. The rattan screens were down, and through the strange greenish gloom made by the foliage of the trees outside, a strong wind blew in gusts, swaying the long draperies of windows and doorways. Her white figure seemed shaped in snow; the pendent crystals of a great chandelier clicked above her head like glittering icicles. She looked up and watched my approach. I was chilled as if these vast apartments had been the cold abode of despair.

"She recognized me at once, and as soon as I had stopped, looking down at her: 'He has left me,' she said, quietly; 'you always leave us—for your own ends.' Her face was set. All the heat of life seemed withdrawn within some inaccessible spot in her breast. 'It would have been easy to die with him,' she went on, and made a slight weary gesture as if giving up the incomprehensible. 'He would not! It was like a blindness— and yet it was I who was speaking to him; it was I who stood before his eyes; it was at me that he looked all the time! Ah! you are hard, treacherous, without truth, without compassion. What makes you so wicked? Or is it that you are all mad?'

"I took her hand; it did not respond, and when I dropped it, it hung down to the floor. That indifference, more awful than tears, cries, and reproaches, seemed to defy time and consolation. You felt that nothing you could say would reach the seat of the still and benumbing pain.

"Stein had said, 'You shall hear.' I did hear. I heard it all, listening with amazement, with awe, to the tones of her inflexible weariness. She could not grasp the real sense of what she was telling me, and her resentment filled me with pity for her—for him, too. I stood rooted to the spot after she had finished. Leaning on her arm, she stared with hard eyes, and the wind passed in gusts, the crystals kept on clicking in the greenish gloom. She went on whispering to herself; 'And yet he was looking at me! He could see my face, hear my voice, hear my grief! When I used to sit at his feet, with my cheek against his knee and his hand on my head, the curse of cruelty and madness was already within him, waiting for the day. The day came! . . . and before the sun had set he could not see me any more—he was made blind and deaf and without pity, as you all are. He shall have no tears from me. Never, never. Not one tear. I will not! He went away from me as if I had been worse than death. He fled as if driven by some accursed thing he had heard or seen in his sleep. . . .'

"Her steady eyes seemed to strain after the shape of a man torn out of her arms by the strength of a dream. She made no sign to my silent bow. I was glad to escape.

"I saw her once again, the same afternoon. On leaving her I had gone in search of Stein, whom I could not find indoors; and I wandered out, pursued by distressful thoughts, into the gardens, those famous gardens of Stein, in which you can find every plant and tree of tropical lowlands. I followed the course of the canalized stream, and sat for a long time on a shaded bench near the ornamental pond, where some water- fowl with clipped wings were diving and splashing noisily. The branches of casuarinatrees behind me swayed lightly, incessantly, reminding me of the soughing of fir-trees at home.

"This mournful and restless sound was a fit accompaniment to my meditations. She had said he had been driven away from her by a dream,—and there was no answer one could make her—there seemed to be no forgiveness for such a transgression. And yet is not mankind itself, pushing on its blind way, driven by a dream of its greatness and its power upon the dark paths of excessive cruelty and of excessive devotion. And what is the pursuit of truth, after all?

"When I rose to get back to the house I caught sight of Stein's drab coat through a gap in the foliage, and very soon at a turn of the path I came upon him walking with the girl. Her little hand rested on his forearm, and under the broad, flat rim of his Panama hat he bent over her, grey-haired, paternal, with compassionate and chivalrous deference. I stood aside, but they stopped, facing me. His gaze was bent on the ground at his feet; the girl, erect and slight on his arm, stared somberly beyond my shoulder with black, clear, motionless eyes. 'Schrecklich,' he murmured. 'Terrible! Terrible! What can one do?' He seemed to be appealing to me, but her youth, the length of the days suspended over her head, appealed to me more; and suddenly, even as I realized that nothing could be said, I found myself pleading his cause for her sake. 'You must forgive him,' I concluded, and my own voice seemed to me muffled, lost in an irresponsive deaf immensity. 'We all want to be forgiven,' I added after a while.

" 'What have I done?' she asked with her lips only.

" 'You always mistrusted him,' I said.

" 'He was like the others,' she pronounced slowly.

" 'Not like the others,' I protested, but she continued evenly, without any feeling—

" 'He was false.' And suddenly Stein broke in. "No! no! no! My poor child! . . .' He patted her hand lying passively on his sleeve. 'No! no! Not false! True! true! true!' He tried to look into her stony face. 'You don't understand. Ach! Why you do not understand? . . . Terrible,' he said to me. 'Some day she *shall* understand.'

" 'Will *you* explain?' I asked, looking hard at him. They moved on.

"I watched them. Her gown trailed on the path, her black hair fell loose. She walked upright and light by the side of the tall man, whose long shapeless coat hung in perpendicular folds from the stooping shoulders, whose feet moved slowly. They disappeared beyond that spinney (you may remember) where sixteen different kinds of bamboo grow together, all distinguishable to the learned eye. For my part, I was fascinated by the exquisite grace and beauty of that fluted grove, crowned with pointed leaves and feathery heads, the lightness, the vigor, the charm as distinct as a voice of that unperplexed luxuriating life. I remember staying to look at it for a long time, as one would linger within reach of a consoling whisper. The sky was pearly grey. It was one of those overcast days so rare in the tropics, in which memories crowd upon one, memories of other shores, of other faces.

"I drove back to town the same afternoon, taking with me Tamb' Itam and the other Malay, in whose seagoing craft they had escaped in the bewilderment, fear, and gloom of the disaster. The shock of it seemed to have changed their natures. It had turned her passion into stone, and it made the surly taciturn Tamb' Itam almost loquacious. His surliness, too, was subdued into puzzled humility, as though he had seen the failure of a potent charm in a supreme moment. The Bugis trader, a shy hesitating man, was very clear in the little he had to say. Both were evidently overawed by a sense of deep inexpressible wonder, by the touch of an inscrutable mystery."

There with Marlow's signature the letter proper ended. The privileged reader screwed up his lamp, and solitary above the billowy roofs of the town, like a light-house-keeper above the sea, he turned to the pages of the story.

XXXVIII

"It all begins, as I've told you, with the man called Brown," ran the opening sentence of Marlow's narrative. "You who have knocked about the Western Pacific must have heard of him. He was the show ruffian on the Australian coast—not that he was often to be seen there, but because he was always trotted out in the stories of lawless life a visitor from home is treated to; and the mildest of these stories which were told about him from Cape York to Eden Bay was more than enough to hang a man if told in the right place. They never failed to let you know, too, that he was supposed to be the son of a baronet. Be it as it may, it is certain he had deserted from a home ship in the early gold-digging days, and in a few years became talked about as the terror of this or that group of islands in Polynesia. He would kidnap natives, he would strip some lonely white trader to the very pajamas he stood in, and after he had robbed the poor devil, he would as likely as not invite him to fight a duel with shot-guns on the beach—which would have been fair enough as these things go, if the other man hadn't been by that time already half-dead with fright. Brown was a latter-day buccaneer, sorry enough, like his more celebrated prototypes; but what distinguished him from his contemporary brother ruffians, like Bully Hayes or the mellifluous Pease, or that perfumed, Dundreary-whiskered, dandified scoundrel known as Dirty Dick, was the arrogant temper of his misdeeds and a vehement scorn for mankind at large and for his victims in particular. The others were merely vulgar and greedy brutes, but he seemed moved by some complex intention. He would rob a man as if only to demon-strate his poor opinion of the creature, and he would bring to the shooting or maiming of some quiet, unoffending stranger a savage and vengeful earnestness fit to terrify the most reckless of desperados. In the days of his greatest glory he owned an armed barque, manned by a mixed crew of Kanakas and runaway whalers, and boasted, I don't know with what truth, of being financed on the quiet by a most respectable firm of copra merchants. Later on he ran off—it was reported—with the wife of a missionary, a very young girl from Clapham way, who had married the mild, flat-footed fellow in a moment of enthusiasm, and suddenly transplanted to Melanesia, lost her bearings somehow. It was a dark story. She was ill at the time he carried her off, and died on board his ship. It is said—as the most wonderful part of the tale—that over her body he gave way to an outburst of somber and violent grief. His luck left him, too, very soon after. He lost his ship on some rocks off Malaita, and disappeared for a time as though he had gone down with her. He is heard of next at

Nuka-Hiva, where he bought an old French schooner out of Government service. What creditable enterprise he might have had in view when he made that purchase I can't say, but it is evident that what with High Commissioners, consuls, men-of-war, and international control, the South Seas were getting too hot to hold gentlemen of his kidney. Clearly he must have shifted the scene of his operations farther west, because a year later he plays an incredibly audacious, but not a very profitable part, in a serio-comic business in Manila Bay, in which a peculating governor and an absconding treasurer are the principal figures; thereafter he seems to have hung around the Philippines in his rotten schooner, battling with an adverse fortune, till at last, running his appointed course, he sails into Jim's history, a blind accomplice of the Dark Powers.

"His tale goes that when a Spanish patrol cutter captured him he was simply trying to run a few guns for the insurgents. If so, then I can't understand what he was doing off the south coast of Mindanao. My belief, however, is that he was blackmailing the native villages along the coast. The principal thing is that the cutter, throwing a guard on board, made him sail in company towards Zamboanga. On the way, for some reason or other, both vessels had to call at one of these new Spanish settlements— which never came to anything in the end—where there was not only a civil official in charge on shore, but a good stout coasting schooner lying at anchor in the little bay; and this craft, in every way much better than his own, Brown made up his mind to steal.

"He was down on his luck—as he told me himself. The world he had bullied for twenty years with fierce, aggressive disdain, had yielded him nothing in the way of material advantage except a small bag of silver dollars, which was concealed in his cabin so that 'the devil himself couldn't smell it out.' And that was all—absolutely all. He was tired of his life, and not afraid of death. But this man, who would stake his existence on a whim with a bitter and jeering recklessness, stood in mortal fear of imprisonment. He had an unreasoning cold-sweat, nerve-shaking, blood-to-water-turning sort of horror at the bare possibility of being locked up—the sort of terror a superstitious man would feel at the thought of being embraced by a specter. Therefore the civil official who came on board to make a preliminary investigation into the capture, investigated arduously all day long, and only went ashore after dark, muffled up in a cloak, and taking great care not to let Brown's little all clink in its bag. Afterwards, being a man of his word, he contrived (the very next evening, I believe) to send off the Government cutter on some urgent bit of special service. As her commander could not spare a prize crew, he contented himself by taking away before he left all the sails of Brown's schooner to the very last rag, and took good care to tow his two boats on to the beach a couple of miles off.

"But in Brown's crew there was a Solomon Islander, kidnapped in his youth and devoted to Brown, who was the best man of the whole gang. That fellow swam off to the coaster—five hundred yards or so—with the end of a warp made up of all the running gear unrove for the purpose. The water was smooth, and the bay dark, 'like the inside of a cow,' as Brown described it. The Solomon Islander clambered over the bulwarks with the end of the rope in his teeth. The crew of the coaster—all Tagals—

were ashore having a jollification in the native village. The two shipkeepers left on
board woke up suddenly and saw the devil. It had glittering eyes and leaped quick as
lightning about the deck. They fell on their knees, paralyzed with fear, crossing
themselves and mumbling prayers. With a long knife he found in the caboose the
Solomon Islander, without interrupting their orisons, stabbed first one, then the other;
with the same knife he set to sawing patiently at the coir cable till suddenly it parted
under the blade with a splash. Then in the silence of the bay he let out a cautious
shout, and Brown's gang, who meantime had been peering and straining their hopeful
ears in the darkness, began to pull gently at their end of the warp. In less than five
minutes the two schooners came together with a slight shock and a creak of spars.

"Brown's crowd transferred themselves without losing an instant, taking with them
their firearms and a large supply of ammunition. They were sixteen in all: two runaway
blue-jackets, a lanky deserter from a Yankee man-of-war, a couple of simple, blond
Scandinavians, a mulatto of sorts, one bland Chinaman who cooked—and the rest of
the nondescript spawn of the South Seas. None of them cared; Brown bent them to
his will, and Brown, indifferent to gallows, was running away from the specter of a
Spanish prison. He didn't give them the time to trans-ship enough provisions; the
weather was calm, the air was charged with dew, and when they cast off the ropes and
set sail to a faint offshore draught there was no flutter in the damp canvas; their old
schooner seemed to detach itself gently from the stolen craft and slip away silently,
together with the black mass of the coast, into the night.

"They got clear away. Brown related to me in detail their passage down the Straits
of Macassar. It is a harrowing and desperate story. They were short of food and water;
they boarded several native craft and got a little from each. With a stolen ship Brown
did not dare to put into any port, of course. He had no money to buy anything, no
papers to show, and no lie plausible enough to get him out again. An Arab barque,
under the Dutch flag, surprised one night at anchor off Poulo Laut, yielded a little
dirty rice, a bunch of bananas, and a cask of water; three days of squally misty weather
from the north-east shot the schooner across the Java Sea. The yellow muddy waves
drenched that collection of hungry ruffians. They sighted mail-boats moving on their
appointed routes; passed well-found home ships with rusty iron sides anchored in the
shallow sea waiting for a change of weather or the turn of the tide; an English gunboat,
white and trim, with two slim masts, crossed their bows one day in the distance; and
on another occasion a Dutch corvette, black and heavily sparred, loomed upon their
quarter, steaming dead slow in the mist. They slipped through unseen or disregarded,
a wan, sallow-faced band of utter outcasts, enraged with hunger and hunted by fear.
Brown's idea was to make for Madagascar, where he expected, on grounds not altogether illusory, to sell the schooner in Tamatave, and no questions asked, or perhaps
obtain some more or less forged papers for her. Yet before he could face the long
passage across the Indian Ocean food was wanted—water, too.

"Perhaps he had heard of Patusan—or perhaps he just only happened to see the
name written in small letters on the chart—probably that of a largish village up a river
in a native state, perfectly defenseless, far from the beaten tracks of the sea and from

the ends of submarine cables. He had done that kind of thing before—in the way of business; and this now was an absolute necessity, a question of life and death—or rather of liberty. Of liberty! He was sure to get provisions—bullocks—rice—sweet-potatoes. The sorry gang licked their chops. A cargo of produce for the schooner perhaps could be extorted—and, who knows?—some real ringing coined money! Some of these chiefs and village headmen can be made to part freely. He told me he would have roasted their toes rather than be baulked. I believe him. His men believed him too. They didn't cheer aloud, being a dumb pack, but made ready wolfishly.

"Luck served him as to weather. A few days of calm would have brought unmentionable horrors on board that schooner, but with the help of land and sea breezes, in less than a week after clearing the Sunda Straits, he anchored off the Batu Kring mouth within a pistol-shot of the fishing village.

"Fourteen of them packed into the schooner's longboat (which was big, having been used for cargo-work) and started up the river, while two remained in charge of the schooner with food enough to keep starvation off for ten days. The tide and wind helped, and early one afternoon the big white boat under a ragged sail shouldered its way before the sea breeze into Patusan Reach, manned by fourteen assorted scarecrows glaring hungrily ahead, and fingering the breech-blocks of cheap rifles. Brown calculated upon the terrifying surprise of his appearance. They sailed in with the last of the flood; the Rajah's stockade gave no sign; the first houses on both sides of the stream seemed deserted. A few canoes were seen up the reach in full flight. Brown was astonished at the size of the place. A profound silence reigned. The wind dropped between the houses; two oars were got out and the boat held on upstream, the idea being to effect a lodgment in the center of the town before the inhabitants could think of resistance.

"It seems, however, that the headman of the fishing village at Batu Kring had managed to send off a timely warning. When the long-boat came abreast of the mosque (which Doramin had built: a structure with gables and roof finials of carved coral) the open space before it was full of people. A shout went up, and was followed by a clash of gongs all up the river. From a point above two little brass six-pounders were discharged, and the round-shot came skipping down the empty reach, spiriting glittering jets of water in the sunshine. In front of the mosque a shouting lot of men began firing in volleys that whipped athwart the current of the river; an irregular, rolling fusillade was opened on the boat from both banks, and Brown's men replied with a wild, rapid fire. The oars had been got in.

"The turn of the tide at high water comes on very quick in that river, and the boat in midstream, nearly hidden in smoke, began to drift back stern foremost. Along both shores the smoke thickened also, lying below the roofs in a level streak as you may see a long cloud cutting the slope of a mountain. A tumult of war-cries, the vibrating clang of gongs, the deep snoring of drums, yells of rage, crashes of volley-firing, made an awful din, in which Brown sat confounded but steady at the tiller, working himself into a fury of hate and rage against those people who dared to defend themselves. Two of his men had been wounded, and he saw his retreat cut off below the town by some boats that had put off from Tunku Allang's stockade. There were six of them full of men. While he was thus beset he perceived the entrance of the narrow creek (the same which Jim had jumped at low water). It was then brim full. Steering the long-boat in, they landed, and, to make a long story short, they established themselves on a little knoll about 900 yards from the stockade, which, in fact, they commanded from that position. The slopes of the knoll were bare, but there were a few trees on the summit. They went to work cutting these down for a breastwork, and were fairly intrenched before dark; meantime the Rajah's boats remained in the river with curious neutrality. When the sun set the glare of many brushwood blazes lighted on the river-front, and between the double line of houses on the land side threw into black relief the roofs, the groups of slender palms, the heavy clumps of fruit-trees. Brown ordered the grass round his position to be fired; a low ring of thin flames under the slow, ascending smoke wriggled rapidly down the slopes of the knoll; here and there a dry bush caught with a tall, vicious roar. The conflagration made a clear zone of fire for the rifles of the small party, and expired smoldering on the edge of the forests and along the muddy bank of the creek. A strip of jungle luxuriating in a damp hollow between the knoll and the Rajah's stockade stopped it on that side with a great crackling and detonations of bursting bamboo stems. The sky was somber, velvety, and swarming with stars. The blackened ground smoked quietly with low creeping wisps, till a little breeze came on and blew everything away. Brown expected an attack to be delivered as soon as the tide had flowed enough again to enable the war-boats which had cut off his retreat to enter the creek. At any rate he was sure there would be an attempt to carry off his long-boat, which lay below the hill, a dark high lump on the feeble sheen of a wet mud-flat. But no move of any sort was made by the boats in the river. Over the stockade and the Rajah's buildings Brown saw their lights on the water. They seemed to be anchored across the stream. Other lights afloat were moving in the reach, crossing and recrossing from side to side. There were also lights twinkling motionless upon the long walls of houses up the reach, as far as the bend, and more still beyond, others isolated inland. The loom of the big fires disclosed buildings, roofs, black piles as far as he could see. It was an immense place. The fourteen desperate invaders lying flat behind the felled trees raised their chins to look over at the stir of that town that seemed to extend up-river for miles and swarm with thousands of angry men. They did not speak to each other. Now and then they would hear a loud yell, or a single shot rang out, fired very far somewhere. But round their position everything was still, dark, silent. They seemed to be forgotten, as if the excitement keeping awake all the population had nothing to do with them, as if they had been dead already."

XXXIX

"All the events of that night have a great importance, since they brought about a situation which remained unchanged till Jim's return. Jim had been away in the interior for more than a week, and it was Dain Waris who had directed the first repulse. That brave and intelligent youth ('who knew how to fight after the manner of white men') wished to settle the business off-hand, but his people were too much for him. He had not Jim's racial prestige and the reputation of invincible, supernatural power. He was not the visible, tangible incarnation of unfailing truth and of unfailing victory. Beloved, trusted, and admired as he was, he was still one of *them*, while Jim was one of *us*. Moreover, the white man, a tower of strength in himself, was invulnerable, while Dain Waris could be killed. Those unexpressed thoughts guided the opinions of the chief men of the town, who elected to assemble in Jim's fort for deliberation upon the emergency, as if expecting to find wisdom and courage in the dwelling of the absent white man. The shooting of Brown's ruffians was so far good, or lucky, that there had been half-a-dozen casualties amongst the defenders. The wounded were lying on the veranda tended by their womenfolk. The women and children from the lower part of the town had been sent into the fort at the first alarm. There Jewel was in command, very efficient and high-spirited, obeyed by Jim's 'own people,' who, quitting in a body their little settlement under the stockade, had gone in to form the garrison. The refugees crowded round her; and through the whole affair, to the very disastrous last, she showed an extraordinary martial ardor. It was to her that Dain Waris had gone at once at the first intelligence of danger, for you must know that Jim was the only one in Patusan who possessed a store of gunpowder. Stein, with whom he had kept up intimate relations by letters, had obtained from the Dutch Government a special authorization to export five hundred kegs of it to Patusan. The powder-magazine was a small hut of rough logs covered entirely with earth, and in Jim's absence the girl had the key. In the council, held at eleven o'clock in the evening in Jim's dining-room, she backed up Waris's advice for immediate and vigorous action. I am told that she stood up by the side of Jim's empty chair at the head of the long table and made a warlike impassioned speech, which for the moment extorted murmurs of approbation from the assembled headmen. Old Doramin, who had not showed himself outside his own gate for more than a year, had been brought across with great difficulty. He was, of course, the chief man there. The temper of the council was very unforgiving, and the old man's word would have been decisive; but it is my opinion that, well aware of his son's fiery courage, he dared not pronounce the word. More dilatory counsels prevailed. A certain Haji Saman pointed out at great length that 'these tyrannical and ferocious men had delivered themselves to a certain death in any case. They would stand fast on their hill and starve, or they would try to regain their boat and be shot from ambushes across the creek, or they would break and fly into the forest and perish singly there.' He argued that by the use of proper stratagems these evil-minded strangers could be destroyed without the risk of a battle, and his words had a great weight, especially with the Patusan men proper. What unsettled the minds of the townsfolk was the failure of the Rajah's boats to act at the decisive moment. It was the diplomatic Kassim who represented the Rajah at the council. He spoke very little, listened smilingly, very friendly and impenetrable. During the sitting messengers kept arriving every few minutes almost, with reports of the invaders' proceedings. Wild and exaggerated rumors were flying: there was a large ship at the mouth of the river with big guns and many more men—some white, others with black skins and of blood-thirsty appearance. They were coming with many more boats to exterminate every living thing. A sense of near, incomprehensible danger affected the common people. At one moment there was a panic in the courtyard amongst the women; shrieking; a rush; children crying—Haji Saman went out to quiet them. Then a fort sentry fired at something moving on the river, and nearly killed a villager bringing in his women-folk in a canoe together with the best of his domestic utensils and a dozen fowls. This caused more confusion. Meantime the palaver inside Jim's house went on in the presence of the girl. Doramin sat fierce-faced, heavy, looking at the speakers in turn, and breathing slow like a bull. He didn't speak till the last, after Kassim had declared that the Rajah's boats would be called in because the men were required to defend his master's stockade. Dain Waris in his father's presence would offer no opinion, though the girl entreated him in Jim's name to speak out. She offered him Jim's own men in her anxiety to have these intruders driven out at once. He only shook his head, after a glance or two at Doramin. Finally, when the council broke up it had been decided that the houses nearest the creek should be strongly occupied to obtain the command of the enemy's boat. The boat itself was not to be interfered with openly, so that the robbers on the hill should be tempted to embark, when a well directed fire would kill most of them, no doubt. To cut the escape of those who might survive, and to prevent more of them coming up, Dain Waris was ordered by Doramin to take an armed party of Bugis down the river to a certain spot ten miles below Patusan, and there form a camp on the shore and blockade the stream with the canoes. I don't believe for a moment that Doramin feared the arrival of fresh forces. My opinion is, that his conduct was guided solely by his wish to keep his son out of harm's way. To prevent a rush being made into the town the construction of a stockade was to be commenced at daylight at the end of the street on the left bank. The old *nakhoda* declared his intention to command there himself. A distribution of powder, bullets, and percussion caps was made immediately under the girl's supervision. Several messengers were to be dispatched in different directions after Jim, whose exact whereabouts were unknown. These men started at dawn, but before that time Kassim had managed to open communications with the besieged Brown.

"That accomplished diplomatist and confidant of the Rajah, on leaving the fort to go back to his master, took into his boat Cornelius, whom he found slinking mutely amongst the people in the courtyard. Kassim had a little plan of his own and wanted him for an interpreter. Thus it came about that towards morning Brown, reflecting upon the desperate nature of his position, heard from the marshy overgrown hollow an amicable, quavering, strained voice crying—in English—for permission to come up, under a promise of personal safety and on a very important errand. He was overjoyed. If he was spoken to he was no longer a hunted wild beast. These friendly sounds took off at once the awful stress of vigilant watchfulness as of so many blind men not knowing whence the deathblow might come. He pretended a great reluctance. The voice declared itself 'a white man. A poor, ruined, old man who had been living here for years.' A mist, wet and chilly, lay on the slopes of the hill, and after some more shouting from one to the other, Brown called out, 'Come on, then, but alone, mind!' As a matter of fact—he told me, writhing with rage at the recollection of his helplessness—it made no difference. They couldn't see more than a few yards before them, and no treachery could make their position worse. By-and-by Cornelius, in his week-day attire of a ragged dirty shirt and pants, barefooted, with a broken-rimmed pith hat on his head, was made out vaguely, sidling up to the defenses, hesitating, stopping to listen in a peering posture. 'Come along! You are safe,' yelled Brown, while his men stared. All their hopes of life became suddenly centered in that dilapidated, mean newcomer, who in profound silence clambered clumsily over a felled tree-trunk, and shivering, with his sour mistrustful face, looked about at the knot of bearded, anxious, sleepless desperados.

"Half an hour's confidential talk with Cornelius opened Brown's eyes as to the home affairs of Patusan. He was on the alert at once. There were possibilities, im-mense possibilities; but before he would talk over Cornelius's proposals he demanded that some food should be sent up as a guarantee of good faith. Cornelius went off, creeping sluggishly down the hill on the side of the Rajah's palace, and after some delay a few of Tunku Allang's men came up, bringing a scanty supply of rice, chillies, and dried fish. This was immeasurably better than nothing. Later on Cornelius re-turned accompanying Kassim, who stepped out with an air of perfect good-humored trustfulness, in sandals, and muffled up from neck to ankles in dark-blue sheeting. He shook hands with Brown discreetly, and the three drew aside for a conference. Brown's men, recovering their confidence, were slapping each other on the back, and cast knowing glances at their captain while they busied themselves with preparations for cooking.

"Kassim disliked Doramin and his Bugis very much, but he hated the new order of things still more. It had occurred to him that these whites, together with the Rajah's followers, could attack and defeat the Bugis before Jim's return. Then, he reasoned, general defection of the townsfolk was sure to follow, and the reign of the white man who protected poor people would be over. Afterwards the new allies could be dealt with. They would have no friends. The fellow was perfectly able to perceive the difference of character, and had seen enough of white men to know that these new-comers were outcasts, men without country. Brown preserved a stern and inscrutable demeanor. When he first heard Cornelius's voice demanding admittance, it brought merely the hope of a loophole for escape. In less than an hour other thoughts were seething in his head. Urged by an extreme necessity, he had come there to steal food, a few tons of rubber or gum maybe, perhaps a handful of dollars, and had found himself enmeshed by deadly dangers. Now in consequence of these overtures from Kassim he began to think of stealing the whole country. Some confounded fellow had apparently accomplished something of the kind—single-handed at that. Couldn't have done it very well though. Perhaps they could work together—squeeze everything dry and then go out quietly. In the course of his negotiations with Kassim he became aware that he was supposed to have a big ship with plenty of men outside. Kassim begged him earnestly to have this big ship with his many guns and men brought up the river without delay for the Rajah's service. Brown professed himself willing, and on this basis the negotiation was carried on with mutual distrust. Three times in the course of the morning the courteous and active Kassim went down to consult the Rajah and came up busily with his long stride. Brown, while bargaining, had a sort of grim enjoyment in thinking of his wretched schooner, with nothing but a heap of dirt in her hold, that stood for an armed ship, and a Chinaman and a lame ex-beachcomber of Levuka on board, who represented all his many men. In the afternoon he obtained further doles of food, a promise of some money, and a supply of mats for his men to make shelters for themselves. They lay down and snored, protected from the burning sunshine; but Brown, sitting fully exposed on one of the felled trees, feasted his eyes upon the view of the town and the river. There was much loot here. Cornelius, who had made himself at home in the camp, talked at his elbow, pointing out the localities, imparting advice, giving his own version of Jim's character, and commenting in his own fashion upon the events of the last three years. Brown, who, apparently indifferent and gazing away, listened with attention to every word, could not make out clearly what sort of man this Jim could be. 'What's his name? Jim! Jim! That's not enough for a man's name.' 'They call him,' said Cornelius, scornfully, 'Tuan Jim here. As you may say Lord Jim.' 'What is he? Where does he come from?' inquired Brown. 'What sort of man is he? Is he an Englishman?' 'Yes, yes, he's an Englishman. I am an Englishman, too. From Malacca. He is a fool. All you have to do is to kill him and then you are king here. Everything belongs to him,' explained Cornelius. 'It strikes me he may be made to share with somebody before very long,' commented Brown half aloud. 'No, no. The proper way is to kill him the first chance you get, and then you can do what you like,' Cornelius would insist earnestly. 'I have lived for many years here, and I am giving you a friend's advice.'

"In such converse and in gloating over the view of Patusan, which he had deter-mined in his mind should become his prey, Brown whiled away most of the afternoon, his men, meantime, resting. On that day Dain Waris's fleet of canoes stole one by one under the shore farthest from the creek, and went down to close the river against his retreat. Of this Brown was not aware, and Kassim, who came up the knoll an hour before sunset, took good care not to enlighten him. He wanted the white man's ship to come up the river, and this news, he feared, would be discouraging. He was very pressing with Brown to send the 'order,' offering at the same time a trusty messenger, who for greater secrecy (as he explained) would make his way by land to the mouth of the river and deliver the 'order' on board. After some reflection Brown judged it expedient to tear a page out of his pocketbook, on which he simply wrote, 'We are getting on. Big job. Detain the man.' The stolid youth selected by Kassim for that service performed it faithfully, and was rewarded by being suddenly tipped, head first, into the schooner's empty hold by the ex-beachcomber and the Chinaman, who thereupon hastened to put on the hatches. What became of him afterwards Brown did not say."

X L

"Brown's object was to gain time by fooling with Kassim's diplomacy. For doing a real stroke of business he could not help thinking the white man was the person to work with. He could not imagine such a chap (who must be confoundedly clever after all to get hold of the natives like that) refusing a help that would do away with the necessity for slow, cautious, risky cheating, that imposed itself as the only possible line of conduct for a single-handed man. He, Brown, would offer him the power. No man could hesitate. Everything was in coming to a clear understanding. Of course they would share. The idea of there being a fort—all ready to his hand—a real fort, with artillery (he knew this from Cornelius), excited him. Let him only once get in and . . . He would impose modest conditions. Not too low, though. The man was no fool, it seemed. They would work like brothers till . . . till the time came for a quarrel and a shot that would settle all accounts. With grim impatience of plunder he wished himself to be talking with the man now. The land already seemed to be his to tear to pieces, squeeze, and throw away. Meantime Kassim had to be fooled for the sake of food first—and for a second string. But the principal thing was to get something to eat from day to day. Besides, he was not averse to begin fighting on that Rajah's account, and teach a lesson to those people who had received him with shots. The lust of battle was upon him.

"I am sorry that I can't give you this part of the story, which of course I have mainly from Brown, in Brown's own words. There was in the broken, violent speech of that man, unveiling before me his thoughts with the very hand of Death upon his throat, an undisguised ruthlessness of purpose, a strange vengeful attitude towards his own past, and a blind belief in the righteousness of his will against all mankind, something of that feeling which could induce the leader of a horde of wandering cut-throats to call himself proudly the Scourge of God. No doubt the natural senseless ferocity which is the basis of such a character was exasperated by failure, ill-luck, and the recent privations, as well as by the desperate position in which he found himself; but what was most remarkable of all was this, that while he planned treacherous alliances, had already settled in his own mind the fate of the white man, and intrigued in an overbearing, offhand manner with Kassim, one could perceive that what he had really desired, almost in spite of himself, was to play havoc with that jungle town which had defied him, to see it strewn over with corpses and enveloped in flames. Listening to his pitiless, panting voice, I could imagine how he must have looked at it from the hillock, peopling it with images of murder and rapine. The part nearest to the creek wore an abandoned aspect, though as a matter of fact every house concealed a few armed men on the alert. Suddenly beyond the stretch of waste ground, interspersed with small patches of low dense bush, excavations, heaps of rubbish, with trodden paths between, a man, solitary and looking very small, strolled out into the deserted opening of the street between the shut-up, dark, lifeless buildings at the end. Perhaps one of the inhabitants, who had fled to the other bank of the river, coming back for some object of domestic use. Evidently he supposed himself quite safe at that distance from the hill on the other side of the creek. A light stockade, set up hastily, was just round the turn of the street, full of his friends. He moved leisurely. Brown saw him, and instantly called to his side the Yankee deserter, who acted as a sort of second in command. This lanky, loose-jointed fellow came forward, wooden-faced, trailing his rifle lazily. When he understood what was wanted from him a homicidal and conceited smile uncovered his teeth, making two deep folds down his sallow, leathery cheeks. He prided himself on being a dead shot. He dropped on one knee, and taking aim from a steady rest through the unlopped branches of a felled tree, fired, and at once stood up to look. The man, far away, turned his head to the report, made another step forward, seemed to hesitate, and abruptly got down on his hands and knees. In the silence that fell upon the sharp crack of the rifle, the dead shot, keeping his eyes fixed upon the quarry, guessed that 'this there coon's health would never be a source of anxiety to his friends any more.' The man's limbs were seen to move rapidly under his body in an endeavor to run on all-fours. In that empty space arose a multitudinous shout of dismay and surprise. The man sank flat, face down, and moved no more. 'That showed them what we could do,' said Brown to me. 'Struck the fear of sudden death into them. That was what we wanted. They were two hundred to one, and this gave them something to think over for the night. Not one of them had an idea of such a long shot before. That beggar belonging to the Rajah scouted downhill with his eyes hanging out of his head.'

"As he was telling me this he tried with a shaking hand to wipe the thin foam on his blue lips. 'Two hundred to one. Two hundred to one . . . strike terror . . . terror, terror, I tell you. . . .' His own eyes were starting out of their sockets. He fell back, clawing the air with skinny fingers, sat up again, bowed and hairy, glared at me sideways like some man-beast of folklore, with open mouth in his miserable and awful agony before he got his speech back after that fit. There are sights one never forgets.

"Furthermore, to draw the enemy's fire and locate such parties as might have been hiding in the bushes along the creek. Brown ordered the Solomon Islander to go down to the boat and bring an oar, as you send a spaniel after a stick into the water. This failed, and the fellow came back without a single shot having been fired at him from anywhere. 'There's nobody,' opined some of the men. It is 'onnattural,' remarked the Yankee. Kassim had gone, by that time, very much impressed, pleased, too, and also uneasy. Pursuing his tortuous policy, he had dispatched a message to Dain Waris warning him to look out for the white men's ship, which, he had had information, was about to come up the river. He minimized its strength and exhorted him to oppose its passage. This double-dealing answered his purpose, which was to keep the Bugis forces divided and to weaken them by fighting. On the other hand, he had in the course of that day sent word to the assembled Bugis chiefs in town, assuring them that he was trying to induce the invaders to retire; his messages to the fort asked earnestly for powder for the Rajah's men. It was a long time since Tunku Allang had had ammunition for the score or so of old muskets rusting in their arm-racks in the audience-hall. The open intercourse between the hill and the palace unsettled all the minds. It was already time for men to take sides, it began to be said. There would soon be much bloodshed, and thereafter great trouble for many people. The social fabric of orderly, peaceful life, when every man was sure of tomorrow, the edifice raised by Jim's hands, seemed on that evening ready to collapse into a ruin reeking with blood. The poorer folk were already taking to the bush or flying up the river. A good many of the upper class judged it necessary to go and pay their court to the Rajah. The Rajah's youths jostled them rudely. Old Tunku Allang, almost out of his mind with fear and indecision, either kept a sullen silence or abused them violently for daring to come with empty hands: they departed very much frightened; only old Doramin kept his countrymen together and pursued his tactics inflexibly. Enthroned in a big chair behind the improvised stockade, he issued his orders in a deep veiled rumble, unmoved, like a deaf man, in the flying rumors.

"Dusk fell, hiding first the body of the dead man, which had been left lying with arms outstretched as if nailed to the ground, and then the revolving sphere of the night rolled smoothly over Patusan and came to a rest, showering the glitter of countless worlds upon the earth. Again, in the exposed part of the town big fires blazed along the only street, revealing from distance to distance upon their glares the falling straight lines of roofs, the fragments of wattled walls jumbled in confusion, here and there a whole hut elevated in the glow upon the vertical black stripes of a group of high piles: and all this line of dwellings, revealed in patches by the swaying flames, seemed to flicker tortuously away upriver into the gloom at the heart of the land. A great silence, in which the looms of successive fires played without noise, extended into the darkness at the foot of the hill; but the other bank of the river, all dark save for a solitary bonfire at the river-front before the fort, sent out into the air an increasing tremor that might have been the stamping of a multitude of feet, the hum of many voices, or the fall of an immensely distant waterfall. It was then, Brown confessed to me, while, turning his back on his men, he sat looking at it all, that notwithstanding his disdain, his ruthless faith in himself, a feeling came over him that at last he had run his head against a stone wall. Had his boat been afloat at the time, he believed he would have tried to steal away, taking his chances of a long chase down the river and of starvation at sea. It was very doubtful whether he would have succeeded in getting away. However, he didn't try this. For another moment he had a passing thought of trying to rush the town, but he perceived very well that in the end he would find himself in the lighted street, where they would be shot down like dogs from the houses. They were two hundred to one—he thought, while his men, huddling round two heaps of smoldering embers, munched the last of the bananas and roasted the few yams they owed to Kassim's diplomacy. Cornelius sat amongst them dozing sulkily.

"Then one of the whites remembered that some tobacco had been left in the boat, and, encouraged by the impunity of the Solomon Islander, said he would go to fetch it. At this all the others shook off their despondency. Brown applied to, said, 'Go, and be d—d to you,' scornfully. He didn't think there was any danger in going to the creek in the dark. The man threw a leg over the tree-trunk and disappeared. A moment later he was heard clambering into the boat and then clambering out. 'I've got it,' he cried. A flash and a report at the very foot of the hill followed. 'I am hit,' yelled the man.

'Look out, look out—I am hit,' and instantly all the rifles went off. The hill squirted fire and noise into the night like a little volcano, and when Brown and the Yankee with curses and cuffs stopped the panic-stricken firing, a profound, weary groan floated up from the creek, succeeded by a plaint whose heart-rending sadness was like some poison turning the blood cold in the veins. Then a strong voice pronounced several distinct incomprehensible words somewhere beyond the creek. 'Let no one fire,' shouted Brown. 'What does it mean?' . . . 'Do you hear on the hill? Do you hear? Do you hear?' repeated the voice three times. Cornelius translated, and then prompted the answer. 'Speak,' cried Brown, 'we hear.' Then the voice, declaiming in the sonorous inflated tone of a herald, and shifting continually on the edge of the vague wasteland, proclaimed that between the men of the Bugis nation living in Patusan and the white men on the hill and those with them, there would be no faith, no compassion, no speech, no peace. A bush rustled; a haphazard volley rang out. 'Dam' foolishness,' muttered the Yankee, vexedly grounding the butt. Cornelius translated. The wounded man below the hill, after crying out twice, 'Take me up! take me up!' went on complaining in moans. While he had kept on the blackened earth of the slope and afterwards crouching in the boat, he had been safe enough. It seems that in his joy at finding tobacco he forgot himself and jumped out on her off-side, as it were. The white boat, lying high and dry, showed him up; the creek was no more than seven yards wide in that place, and there happened to be a man crouching in the bush on the other bank.

"He was a Bugis of Tondano only lately come to Patusan, and a relation of the man shot in the afternoon. That famous long shot had indeed appalled the beholders. The man in utter security had been struck down, in full view of his friends, dropping with a joke on his lips, and they seemed to see in the act an atrocity which had stirred a bitter rage. That relation of his, Si-Lapa by name, was then with Doramin in the stockade only a few feet away. You who know these chaps must admit that the fellow showed an unusual pluck by volunteering to carry the message, alone, in the dark. Creeping across the open ground, he had deviated to the left and found himself opposite the boat. He was startled when Brown's man shouted. He came to a sitting position with his gun to his shoulder, and when the other jumped out, exposing himself, he pulled the trigger and lodged three jagged slugs point-blank into the poor wretch's stomach. Then, lying flat on his face, he gave himself up for dead, while a thin hail of lead chopped and swished the bushes close on his right hand; afterwards he delivered his speech shouting, bent double, dodging all the time in cover. With the last word he leaped sideways, lay close for a while, and afterwards got back to the houses unharmed, having achieved on that night such a renown as his children will not willingly allow to die.

"And on the hill the forlorn band let the two little heaps of embers go out under their bowed heads. They sat dejected on the ground with compressed lips and down-cast eyes, listening to their comrade below. He was a strong man and died hard, with moans now loud, now sinking to a strange confidential note of pain. Sometimes he shrieked, and again, after a period of silence, he could be heard muttering deliriously a long and unintelligible complaint. Never for a moment did he cease.

" 'What's the good?' Brown had said unmoved once, seeing the Yankee, who had been swearing under his breath, prepare to go down. 'That's so,' assented the deserter, reluctantly desisting. 'There's no encouragement for wounded men here. Only his noise is calculated to make all the others think too much of the hereafter, cap'n.' 'Water!' cried the wounded man in an extraordinarily clear vigorous voice, and then went off moaning feebly. 'Ay, water. Water will do it,' muttered the other to himself, resignedly. 'Plenty by-and-by. The tide is flowing.'

"At last the tide flowed, silencing the plaint and the cries of pain, and the dawn was near when Brown, sitting with his chin in the palm of his hand before Patusan, as one might stare at the unscalable side of a mountain, heard the brief ringing bark of a brass six-pounder far away in town somewhere. 'What's this?' he asked of Cornelius, who hung about him. Cornelius listened. A muffled roaring shout rolled down-river over the town; a big drum began to throb, and others responded, pulsating and droning. Tiny scattered lights began to twinkle in the dark half of the town, while the part lighted by the loom of fires hummed with a deep and prolonged murmur. 'He has come,' said Cornelius. 'What? Already? Are you sure?' Brown asked. 'Yes! yes! Sure. Listen to the noise.' 'What are they making that row about?' pursued Brown. 'For joy,' snorted Cornelius; 'he is a very great man but all the same, he knows no more than a child, and so they make a great noise to please him, because they known no better.' 'Look here,' said Brown, 'how is one to get at him?' 'He shall come to talk to you,' Cornelius declared 'What do you mean? Come down here strolling as it were?' Cornelius nodded vigorously in the dark. 'Yes. He will come straight here and talk to you. He is just like a fool. You shall see what a fool he is.' Brown was incredulous. 'You shall see; you shall see,' repeated Cornelius. 'He is not afraid—not afraid of anything. He will come and order you to leave his people alone. Everybody must leave his people alone. He is like a little child. He will come to you straight.' Alas he knew Jim well—that 'mean little skunk,' as Brown called him to me. 'Yes, certainly,' he pursued with ardor, 'and then, captain, you tell that tall man with a gun to shoot him. Just you kill him, and you shall frighten everybody so much that you can do anything you like with them afterwards—get what you like—go away when you like. Ha! ha! ha! Fine. . . .' He almost danced with impatience and eagerness; and Brown, looking over his shoulder at him, could see, shown up by the pitiless dawn, his men drenched with dew, sitting amongst the cold ashes and the litter of the camp, haggard, cowed, and in rags."

XLI

"To the very last moment, till the full day came upon them with a spring, the fires on the west bank blazed bright and clear; and then Brown saw in a knot of colored figures motionless between the advanced houses a man in European clothes, in a helmet, all white. 'That's him; look! look!' Cornelius said excitedly. All Brown's men had sprung up and crowded at his back with lusterless eyes. The group of vivid colors and dark faces with the white figure in the midst were observing the knoll. Brown could see naked arms being raised to shade the eyes and other brown arms pointing. What should he do? He looked around, and the forests that faced him on all sides walled the cock-pit of an unequal contest. He looked once more at his men. A contempt, a weariness, the desire of life, the wish to try for one more chance—for some other grave—struggled in his breast. From the outline the figure presented it seemed to him that the white man there, backed up by all the power of the land, was examining his position through binoculars. Brown jumped up on the log, throwing his arms up, the palms outwards. The colored group closed round the white man, and fell back twice before he got clear of them, walking slowly alone. Brown remained standing on the log till Jim, appearing and disappearing between the patches of thorny scrub, had nearly reached the creek; then Brown jumped off and went down to meet him on his side.

"They met, I should think, not very far from the place, perhaps on the very spot, where Jim took the second desperate leap of his life—the leap that landed him into the life of Patusan, into the trust, the love, the confidence of the people. They faced each other across the creek, and with steady eyes tried to understand each other before they opened their lips. Their antagonism must have been expressed in their glances; I know that Brown hated Jim at first sight. Whatever hopes he might have had vanished at once. This was not the man he had expected to see. He hated him for this—and in a checked flannel shirt with sleeves cut off at the elbows, grey bearded, with a sunken, sun-blackened face—he cursed in his heart the other's youth and assurance, his clear eyes and his untroubled bearing. That fellow had got in a long way before him! He did not look like a man who would be willing to give anything for assistance. He had all the advantages on his side—possession, security, power; he was on the side of an overwhelming force! He was not hungry and desperate, and he did not seem in the least afraid. And there was something in the very neatness of Jim's clothes, from the white helmet to the canvas leggings and the pipe-clayed shoes, which in Brown's somber irritated eyes seemed to belong to things he had in the very shaping of his life condemned and flouted.

" 'Who are you?' asked Jim at last, speaking in his usual voice. 'My name's Brown,' answered the other, loudly; 'Captain Brown. What's yours?' and Jim after a little pause went on quietly, as if he had not heard: 'What made you come here?' 'You want to know,' said Brown bitterly. 'It's easy to tell. Hunger. And what made you?'

" 'The fellow started at this,' said Brown, relating to me the opening of this strange conversation between those two men, separated only by the muddy bed of a creek, but standing on the opposite poles of that conception of life which includes all mankind —'The fellow started at this and got very red in the face. Too big to be questioned, I suppose. I told him that if he looked upon me as a dead man with whom you may take liberties, he himself was not a whit better off really. I had a fellow up there who had a bead drawn on him all the time, and only waited for a sign from me. There was nothing to be shocked at in this. He had come down of his own freewill. "Let us agree," said I, "that we are both dead men, and let us talk on that basis, as equals. We are all equal before death," I said. I admitted I was there like a rat in a trap, but we had been driven to it, and even a trapped rat can give a bite. He caught me up in a moment. "Not if you don't go near the trap till the rat is dead." I told him that sort of game was good enough for these native friends of his, but I would have thought him too white to serve even a rat so. Yes, I had wanted to talk with him. Not to beg for my life, though. My fellows were—well—what they were—men like himself, anyhow. All we wanted from him was to come on in the devil's name and have it out. "God d—n it," said I, while he stood there as still as a wooden post, "you don't want to come out here every day with your glasses to count how many of us are left on our feet. Come. Either bring your infernal crowd along or let us go out and starve in the open sea, by God! You have been white once, for all your tall talk of this being your own people and you being one with them. Are you? And what the devil do you get for it; what is it you've found here that is so d—d precious? Hey? You don't want us to come down here perhaps—do you? You are two hundred to one. You don't want us to come down into the open. Ah! I promise you we shall give you some sport before you've done. You talk about me making a cowardly set upon unoffending people. What's that to me that they are unoffending when I am starving for next to no offense? But I am not a coward. Don't you be one. Bring them along or, by all the fiends, we shall yet manage to send half your unoffending town to heaven with us in smoke!' "

"He was terrible—relating this to me—this tortured skeleton of a man drawn up together with his face over his knees, upon a miserable bed in that wretched hovel, and lifting his head to look at me with malignant triumph.

" 'That's what I told him—I knew what to say,' he began again, feebly at first, but working himself up with incredible speed into a fiery utterance of his scorn. 'We aren't going into the forest to wander like a string of living skeletons dropping one after another for ants to go to work upon us before we are fairly dead. Oh, no! . . .' "You don't deserve a better fate," he said. "And what do you deserve," I shouted at him, "you that I find skulking here with your mouth full of your responsibility, of innocent lives, of your infernal duty? What do you know more of me than I know of you? I came here for food. D'ye hear?—food to fill our bellies. And what did *you* come for? What did you ask for when you came here? We don't ask you for anything but to give us a fight or a clear road to go back whence we came. . . ." "I would fight with you now," says he, pulling at his little mustache. "And I would let you shoot me, and welcome," I said. "This is as good a jumping-off place for me as another. I am sick of my infernal luck. But it would be too easy. There are my men in the same boat—and, by God, I am not the sort to jump out of trouble and leave them in a d—d lurch," I said. He stood thinking for a while and then wanted to know what I had done ("out there," he says, tossing his head down-stream) to be hazed about so. "Have we met to tell each other the story of our lives?" I asked him. "Suppose you begin. No? Well, I am sure I don't want to hear. Keep it to yourself. I know it is no better than mine. I've lived—and so did you though you talk as if you were one of those people that should have wings so as to go about without touching the dirty earth. Well—it is dirty. I haven't got any wings. I am here because I was afraid once in my life. Want to know what of? Of a prison. That scares me, and you may know it—if it's any good to you. I won't ask you what scared you into this infernal hole, where you seem to have found pretty pickings. That's your luck and this is mine—the privilege to beg for the favor of being shot quickly, or else kicked out to go free and starve in my own way." ' . . .

"His debilitated body shook with an exultation so vehement, so assured, and so malicious that it seemed to have driven off the death waiting for him in that hut. The corpse of his mad self-love uprose from rags and destitution as from the dark horrors of a tomb. It is impossible to say how much he lied to Jim then, how much he lied to me now—and to himself always. Vanity plays lurid tricks with our memory, and the truth of every passion wants some pretense to make it live. Standing at the gate of the other world in the guise of a beggar, he had slapped this world's face, he had spat on it, he had thrown upon it an immensity of scorn and revolt at the bottom of his misdeeds. He had overcome them all—men, women, savages, traders, ruffians, missionaries—and Jim—that beefy-faced beggar. I did not begrudge him this triumph *in articulo mortis*, this almost posthumous illusion of having trampled all the earth under his feet. While he was boasting to me, in his sordid and repulsive agony, I couldn't help thinking of the chuckling talk relating to the time of his greatest splendor when, during a year or more, Gentleman Brown's ship was to be seen, for many days on end, hovering off an islet befringed with green upon azure, with the dark dot of the mission-house on a white beach; while Gentleman Brown, ashore, was casting his spells over a romantic girl for whom Melanesia had been too much, and giving hopes of a remarkable conversion to her husband. The poor man, some time or other, had been heard to express the intention of winning 'Captain Brown to a better way of life.' . . . 'Bag Gentleman Brown for Glory'—as a leery-eyed loafer expressed it once—'just to let them see up above what a Western Pacific trading skipper looks like.' And this was the man, too, who had run off with a dying woman, and had shed tears over her body. 'Carried on like a big baby,' his then mate was never tired of telling, 'and where the fun came in may I be kicked to death by diseased Kanakas if *I* know. Why, gents! she was too far gone when he brought her aboard to know him; she just lay there on her back in his bunk staring at the beam with awful shining eyes—and then she died. Dam' bad sort of fever, I guess. . . .' I remembered all these stories while, wiping his matted lump of a beard with a livid hand, he was telling me from his noisome couch how he got round, got in, got home, on the confounded, immaculate, don't-you-touch-me sort of fellow. He admitted that he couldn't be scared, but there was a way, 'as broad as a turnpike, to get in and shake his twopenny soul around and inside out and upside down—by God!' "

XLII

"I don't think he could do more than perhaps look upon that straight path. He seemed to have been puzzled by what he saw, for he interrupted himself in his narrative more than once to exclaim, 'He nearly slipped from me there. I could not make him out. Who was he?' And after glaring at me wildly he would go on, jubilating and sneering. To me the conversation of these two across the creek appears now as the deadliest kind of duel on which Fate looked on with her cold-eyed knowledge of the end. No, he didn't turn Jim's soul inside out, but I am much mistaken if the spirit so utterly out of his reach had not been made to taste to the full the bitterness of that contest. These were the emissaries with whom the world he had renounced was pursuing him in his retreat. White men from 'out there' where he did not think himself good enough to live. This was all that came to him—a menace, a shock, a danger to his work. I suppose it is this sad, half-resentful, half-resigned feeling, piercing through the few words Jim said now and then, that puzzled Brown so much in the reading of his character. Some great men owe most of their greatness to the ability of detecting in those they destine for their tools the exact quality of strength that matters for their work, and Brown, as though he had been really great, had a satanic gift of finding out the best and the weakest spot in his victims. He admitted to me that Jim wasn't of the sort that can be got over by truckling, and accordingly he took care to show himself as a man confronting without dismay ill-luck, censure, and disaster. The smuggling of a few guns was no great crime, he pointed out. As to coming to Patusan, who had the right to say he hadn't come to beg? The infernal people here let loose at him from both banks without staying to ask questions. He made the point brazenly, for, in truth, Dain Waris's energetic action had prevented the greatest calamities; because Brown told me distinctly that, perceiving the size of the place, he had resolved instantly in his mind that as soon as he had gained a footing he would set fire right and left, and begin by shooting down everything living in sight, in order to cow and terrify the population. The disproportion of forces was so great that this was the only way giving him the slightest chance of attaining his ends—he argued in a fit of coughing. But he didn't tell Jim this. As to the hardships and starvation they had gone through, these had been very real; it was enough to look at his band. He made, at the sound of a shrill whistle, all his men appear standing in a row on the logs in full view, so that Jim could see them. For the killing of the man, it had been done —well, it had—but was not this war, bloody war—in a corner? and the fellow had been killed cleanly, shot through the chest, not like that poor devil of his lying now in the creek. They had to listen to him dying for six hours, with his entrails torn with slugs. At any rate this was a life for a life. . . . And all this was said with the weariness, with the recklessness of a man spurred on and on by ill-luck till he cares not where he runs. When he asked Jim, with a sort of brusque despairing frankness, whether he himself—straight now—didn't understand that when 'it came to saving one's life in the dark, one didn't care who else went—three, thirty, three hundred people'—it was as if a demon had been whispering advice in his ear. 'I made him wince,' boasted Brown to me. 'He very soon left off coming the righteous over me. He just stood there with nothing to say, and looking as black as thunder—not at me—on the ground.' He asked Jim whether he had nothing fishy in his life to remember that he was so damnedly hard upon a man trying to get out of a deadly hole by the first means that came to hand—and so on, and so on. And there ran through the rough talk a vein of subtle reference to their common blood, an assumption of common experience; a sickening suggestion of common guilt, of secret knowledge that was like a bond of their minds and of their hearts.

"At last Brown threw himself down full length and watched Jim out of the corners

of his eyes. Jim on his side of the creek stood thinking and switching his leg. The
houses in view were silent, as if a pestilence had swept them clean of every breath of
life; but many invisible eyes were turned, from within, upon the two men with the
creek between them, a stranded white boat, and the body of the third man half sunk in
the mud. On the river canoes were moving again, for Patusan was recovering its belief
in the stability of earthly institutions since the return of the white lord. The right
bank, the platforms of the houses, the rafts moored along the shores, even the roofs of
bathing-huts, were covered with people that, far away out of earshot and almost out of
sight, were straining their eyes towards the knoll beyond the Rajah's stockade. Within
the wide irregular ring of forests broken in two places by the sheen of the river there
was a silence. 'Will you promise to leave the coast?' Jim asked. Brown lifted and let fall
his hand, giving everything up as it were—accepting the inevitable. 'And surrender
your arms?' Jim went on. Brown sat up and glared across. 'Surrender our arms! Not till
you come to take them out of our stiff hands. You think I am gone crazy with funk?
Oh, no! That and the rags I stand in is all I have got in the world, besides a few more
breechloaders on board; and I expect to sell the lot in Madagascar, if I ever get so far
—begging my way from ship to ship.'

"Jim said nothing to this. At last, throwing away the switch he held in his hand, he
said, as if speaking to himself, 'I don't know whether I have the power.' . . . 'You
don't know! And you wanted me just now to give up my arms! That's good, too,' cried
Brown. 'Suppose they say one thing to you, and do the other thing to me.' He calmed
down markedly. 'I daresay you have the power, or what's the meaning of all this talk?'
he continued. 'What did you come down here for? To pass the time of day?'

" 'Very well,' said Jim, lifting his head suddenly after a long silence. 'You shall have
a clear road or else a clear fight.' He turned on his heel and walked away.

"Brown got up at once, but he did not go up the hill till he had seen Jim disappear
between the first houses. He never set his eyes on him again. On his way back he met
Cornelius slouching down with his head between his shoulders. He stopped before
Brown. 'Why didn't you kill him?' he demanded in a sour, discontented voice. 'Because
I could do better than that,' Brown said with an amused smile. 'Never! never!' protested Cornelius with energy. 'Couldn't. I have lived here for many years.' Brown
looked up at him curiously. There were many sides to the life of that place in arms
against him; things he would never find out. Cornelius slunk past dejectedly in the
direction of the river. He was now leaving his new friends; he accepted the disappointing course of events with a sulky obstinacy which seemed to draw more together
his little yellow old face; and as he went down he glanced askant here and there, never
giving up his fixed idea.

"Henceforth events move fast without a check, flowing from the very hearts of men
like a stream from a dark source, and we see Jim amongst them, mostly through Tamb'
Itam's eyes. The girl's eyes had watched him, too, but her life is too much entwined
with his: there is her passion, her wonder, her anger, and, above all, her fear and her
unforgiving love. Of the faithful servant, uncomprehending as the rest of them, it is the
fidelity alone that comes into play; a fidelity and a belief in his lord so strong that even

amazement is subdued to a sort of saddened acceptance of a mysterious failure. He has eyes only for one figure, and through all the mazes of bewilderment he preserves his air of guardianship, of obedience, of care.

"His master came back from his talk with the white men, walking slowly towards the stockade in the street. Everybody was rejoiced to see him return, for while he was away every man had been afraid not only of him being killed, but also of what would come after. Jim went into one of the houses, where old Doramin had retired, and remained alone for a long time with the head of the Bugis settlers. No doubt he discussed the course to follow with him then, but no man was present at the conversation. Only Tamb' Itam, keeping as close to the door as he could, heard his master say, 'Yes. I shall let all the people know that such is my wish; but I spoke to you, O Doramin, before all the others, and alone; for you know my heart as well as I know yours and its greatest desire. And you know well also that I have no thought but for the people's good.' Then his master, lifting the sheeting in the doorway, went out, and he, Tamb' Itam, had a glimpse of old Doramin within, sitting in the chair with his hands on his knees, and looking between his feet. Afterwards he followed his master to the fort, where all the principal Bugis and Patusan inhabitants had been summoned for a talk. Tamb' Itam himself hoped there would be some fighting. 'What was it but the taking of another hill?' he exclaimed regretfully. However, in the town many hoped that the rapacious strangers would be induced, by the sight of so many brave men making ready to fight, to go away. It would be a good thing if they went away. Since Jim's arrival had been made known before daylight by the gun fired from the fort and the beating of the big drum there, the fear that had hung over Patusan had broken and subsided like a wave on a rock, leaving the seething foam of excitement, curiosity, and endless speculation. Half of the population had been ousted out of their homes for purposes of defense, and were living in the street on the left side of the river, crowding around the fort, and in momentary expectation of seeing their abandoned dwellings on the threatened bank burst into flames. The general anxiety was to see the matter settled quickly. Food, through Jewel's care, had been served out to the refugees. Nobody knew what their white man would do. Some remarked that it was worse than in Sherif Ali's war. Then many people did not care; now everybody had something to lose. The movements of canoes passing to and fro between the two parts of the town were watched with interest. A couple of Bugis warboats lay anchored in the middle of the stream to protect the river, and a thread of smoke stood at the bow of each; the men in them were cooking their midday rice when Jim, after his interviews with Brown and Doramin, crossed the river and entered by the water-gate of his fort. The people inside crowded round him so that he could hardly make his way to the house. They had not seen him before, because on his arrival during the night he had only exchanged a few words with the girl, who had come down to the landing-stage for the purpose, and had then gone on at once to join the chiefs and the fighting men on the other bank. People shouted greetings after him. One old woman raised a laugh by pushing her way to the front madly and enjoining him in a scolding voice to see to it that her two sons, who were with Doramin, did not come to harm at the hands of the robbers.

Several of the bystanders tried to pull her away, but she struggled and cried, 'Let me go. What is this, O Muslims? This laughter is unseemly. Are they not cruel, blood-thirsty robbers bent on killing?' 'Let her be,' said Jim, and as a silence fell suddenly, he said slowly, 'Everybody shall be safe.' He entered the house before the great sigh, and the loud murmurs of satisfaction, had died out.

"There's no doubt his mind was made up that Brown should have his way clear back to the sea. His fate, revolted, was forcing his hand. He had for the first time to affirm his will in the face of out-spoken opposition. 'There was much talk, and at first my master was silent,' Tamb' Itam said. 'Darkness came, and then I lit the candles on the long table. The chiefs sat on each side, and the lady remained by my master's right hand.'

"When he began to speak the unaccustomed difficulty seemed only to fix his resolve more immovably. The white men were now waiting for his answer on the hill. Their chief had spoken to him in the language of his own people, making clear many things difficult to explain in any other speech. They were erring men whom suffering had made blind to right and wrong. It is true that lives had been lost already, but why lose more? He declared to his hearers, the assembled heads of the people, that their welfare was his welfare, their losses his losses, their mourning his mourning. He looked round at the grave listening faces and told them to remember that they had fought and worked side by side. They knew his courage . . . Here a murmur interrupted him . . . And that he had never deceived them. For many years they had dwelt together. He loved the land and the people living in it with a very great love. He was ready to answer with his life for any harm that should come to them if the white men with beards were allowed to retire. They were evil-doers, but their destiny had been evil, too. Had he ever advised them ill? Had his words ever brought suffering to the people? he asked. He believed that it would be best to let these whites and their followers go with their lives. It would be a small gift. 'I whom you have tried and found always true ask you to let them go.' He turned to Doramin. The old *nakhoda* made no movement. 'Then,' said Jim, 'call in Dain Waris, your son, my friend, for in this business I shall not lead.' "

XLIII

"Tamb' Itam behind his chair was thunderstruck. The declaration produced an im-mense sensation. 'Let them go because this is best in my knowledge which has never deceived you,' Jim insisted. There was a silence. In the darkness of the courtyard could be heard the subdued whispering, shuffling noise of many people. Doramin raised his heavy head and said that there was no more reading of hearts than touching the sky with the hand, but—he consented. The others gave their opinion in turn. 'It is best,' 'Let them go,' and so on. But most of them simply said that they 'believed Tuan Jim.'

"In this simple form of assent to his will lies the whole gist of the situation; their creed, his truth; and the testimony to that faithfulness which made him in his own eyes the equal of the impeccable men who never fall out of the ranks. Stein's words, 'Romantic!—Romantic!' seem to ring over those distances that will never give him up now to a world indifferent to his failing and his virtues, and to that ardent and clinging affection that refuses him the dole of tears in the bewilderment of a great grief and of eternal separation. From the moment the sheer truthfulness of his last three years of life carries the day against the ignorance, the fear, and the anger of men, he appears no longer to me as I saw him last—a white speck catching all the dim light left upon a somber coast and the darkened sea—but greater and more pitiful in the loneliness of his soul, that remains even for her who loved him best a cruel and insoluble mystery.

"It is evident that he did not mistrust Brown; there was no reason to doubt the story, whose truth seemed warranted by the rough frankness, by a sort of virile sincerity in accepting the morality and the consequences of his acts. But Jim did not know the almost inconceivable egotism of the man which made him, when resisted and foiled in his will, mad with the indignant and revengeful rage of a thwarted autocrat. But if Jim did not mistrust Brown, he was evidently anxious that some misunderstanding should not occur, ending perhaps in collision and bloodshed. It was for this reason that directly the Malay chiefs had gone he asked Jewel to get him something to eat, as he was going out of the fort to take command in the town. On her remonstrating against this on the score of his fatigue, he said that something might happen for which he would never forgive himself. 'I am responsible for every life in the land,' he said. He was moody at first; she served him with her own hands, taking the plates and dishes (of the dinner-service presented him by Stein) from Tamb' Itam. He brightened up after a while; told her she would be again in command of the fort for another night. 'There's no sleep for us, old girl,' he said, 'while our people are in danger.' Later on he said jokingly that she was the best man of them all. 'If you and Dain Waris had done what you wanted, not one of these poor devils would be alive today.' 'Are they very bad?' she asked, leaning over his chair. 'Men act badly sometimes without being much worse than others,' he said after some hesitation.

"Tamb' Itam followed his master to the landing-stage outside the fort. The night was clear, but without a moon, and the middle of the river was dark, while the water under each bank reflected the light of many fires 'as on a night of Ramadan,' Tamb' Itam said. Warboats drifted silently in the dark lane or, anchored, floated motionless with a loud ripple. That night there was much paddling in a canoe and walking at his master's heels for Tamb' Itam: up and down the street they tramped, where the fires were burning, inland on the outskirts of the town where small parties of men kept guard in the fields. Tuan Jim gave his orders and was obeyed. Last of all they went to the Rajah's stockade, which a detachment of Jim's people manned on that night. The old Rajah had fled early in the morning with most of his women to a small house he had near a jungle village on a tributary stream. Kassim, left behind, had attended the council with his air of diligent activity to explain away the diplomacy of the day before. He was considerably cold-shouldered, but managed to preserve his smiling, quiet alertness, and professed himself highly delighted when Jim told him sternly that he proposed to occupy the stockade on that night with his own men. After the council broke up he was heard outside accosting this and that departing chief, and speaking in a loud, gratified tone of the Rajah's property being protected in the Rajah's absence.

"About ten or so Jim's men marched in. The stockade commanded the mouth of the creek, and Jim meant to remain there till Brown had passed below. A small fire was lit on the flat, grassy point outside the wall of stakes, and Tamb' Itam placed a little folding-stool for his master. Jim told him to try and sleep. Tamb' Itam got a mat and lay down a little way off; but he could not sleep, though he knew he had to go on an important journey before the night was out. His master walked to and fro before the fire with bowed head and with his hands behind his back. His face was sad. Whenever his master approached him Tamb' Itam pretended to sleep, not wishing his master to know he had been watched. At last his master stood still, looking down on him as he lay, and said softly, 'It is time.'

"Tamb' Itam arose directly and made his preparations. His mission was to go down the river, preceding Brown's boat by an hour or more, to tell Dain Waris finally and formally that the whites were to be allowed to pass out unmolested. Jim would not trust anybody else with that service. Before starting Tamb' Itam, more as a matter of form (since his position about Jim made him perfectly known), asked for a token. 'Because, Tuan,' he said, 'the message is important, and these are thy very words I carry.' His master first put his hand into one pocket, then into another, and finally took off his forefinger Stein's silver ring, which he habitually wore, and gave it to Tamb' Itam. When Tamb' Itam left on his mission, Brown's camp on the knoll was dark but for a single small glow shining through the branches of one of the trees the white men had cut down.

"Early in the evening Brown had received from Jim a folded piece of paper on which was written, 'You get the clear road. Start as soon as your boat floats on the morning tide. Let your men be careful. The bushes on both sides of the creek and the stockade at the mouth are full of well-armed men. You would have no chance, but I don't believe you want bloodshed.' Brown read it, tore the paper into small pieces, and, turning to Cornelius, who had brought it, said jeeringly, 'Good-bye, my excellent friend.' Cornelius had been in the fort, and had been sneaking around Jim's house during the afternoon. Jim chose him to carry the note because he could speak English, was known to Brown, and was not likely to be shot by some nervous mistake of one of the men as a Malay, approaching in the dusk, perhaps might have been.

"Cornelius didn't go away after delivering the paper. Brown was sitting up over a tiny fire; all the others were lying down. 'I could tell you something you would like to know,' Cornelius mumbled crossly. Brown paid no attention. 'You did not kill him,' went on the other, 'and what do you get for it? You might have had money from the Rajah, besides the loot of all the Bugis houses, and now you get nothing.' 'You had better clear out from here,' growled Brown, without even looking at him. But Cornelius let himself drop by his side and began to whisper very fast, touching his elbow from time to time. What he had to say made Brown sit up at first, with a curse. He had simply imformed him of Dain Waris's armed party down the river. At first Brown saw himself completely sold and betrayed, but a moment's reflection convinced him that there could be no treachery intended. He said nothing, and after a while Cornelius remarked, in a tone of complete indifference, that there was another way out of the river which he knew very well. 'A good thing to know, too,' said Brown, pricking up his ears; and Cornelius began to talk of what went on in town and repeated all that had been said in council, gossiping in an even undertone at Brown's ear as you talk amongst sleeping men you do not wish to wake. 'He thinks he has made me harmless, does he?' mumbled Brown very low. . . . 'Yes. He is a fool. A little child. He came here and robbed me,' droned on Cornelius, 'and he made all the people believe him. But if something happened that they did not believe him any more, where would he be? And the Bugis Dain who is waiting for you down the river there, captain, is the very man who chased you up here when you first came.' Brown observed nonchalantly that it would be just as well to avoid him, and with the same detached, musing air Cornelius declared himself acquainted with a backwater broad enough to take Brown's boat past Waris's camp. 'You will have to be quiet,' he said as an afterthought, 'for in one place we pass close behind his camp. Very close. They are camped ashore with their boat hauled up.' 'Oh, we know how to be as quiet as mice; never fear,' said Brown. Cornelius stipulated that in case he were to pilot Brown out, his canoe should be towed. 'I'll have to get back quick,' he explained.

"It was two hours before the dawn when word was passed to the stockade from outlying watchers that the white robbers were coming down to their boat. In a very short time every armed man from one end of Patusan to the other was on the alert, yet the banks of the river remained so silent that but for the fires burning with sudden blurred flares the town might have been asleep as if in peacetime. A heavy mist lay very low on the water, making a sort of illusive grey light that showed nothing. When Brown's longboat glided out of the creek into the river, Jim was standing on the low point of land before the Rajah's stockade—on the very spot where for the first time he put his foot on Patusan shore. A shadow loomed up, moving in the greyness, solitary, very bulky, and yet constantly eluding the eye. A murmur of low talking came out of it. Brown at the tiller heard Jim speak calmly: 'A clear road. You had better trust to the current while the fog lasts; but this will lift presently.' 'Yes, presently we shall see clear,' replied Brown.

"The thirty or forty men standing with muskets at ready outside the stockade held their breath. The Bugis owner of the prau, whom I saw on Stein's verandah, and who was amongst them, told me that the boat, shaving the low point close, seemed for a moment to grow big and hang over it like a mountain. 'If you think it worth your while to wait a day outside,' called out Jim, 'I'll try to send you down something— bullock, some yams—what I can.' The shadow went on moving. 'Yes. Do,' said a voice, blank and muffled out of the fog. Not one of the many attentive listeners understood what the words meant; and then Brown and his men in their boat floated away, fading spectrally without the slightest sound.

"Thus Brown, invisible in the mist, goes out of Patusan elbow to elbow with Cornelius in the stern-sheets of the longboat. 'Perhaps you shall get a small bullock,' said Cornelius. 'Oh, yes. Bullock. Yam. You'll get it if *he* said so. He always speaks the truth. He stole everything I had. I suppose you like a small bullock better than the loot of many houses.' 'I would advise you to hold your tongue, or somebody here may fling you overboard into this damned fog,' said Brown. The boat seemed to be standing still; nothing could be seen, not even the river alongside, only the water-dust flew and trickled, condensed, down their beards and faces. It was weird, Brown told me. Every individual man of them felt as though he were adrift alone in a boat, haunted by an almost imperceptible suspicion of sighing, muttering ghosts. 'Throw me out, would you? But I would know where I was,' mumbled Cornelius, surlily. 'I've lived many years here.' 'Not long enough to see through a fog like this,' Brown said, lolling back with his arm swinging to and fro on the useless tiller. 'Yes. Long enough for that,' snarled Cornelius. 'That's very useful,' commented Brown. 'Am I to believe you could find that backway you spoke of blindfold, like this?' Cornelius grunted. 'Are you too tired to row?' he asked after a silence. 'No, by God!' shouted Brown suddenly. 'Out with your oars there.' There was a great knocking in the fog, which after a while settled into a regular grind of invisible sweeps against invisible thole-pins. Otherwise nothing was changed, and but for the slight splash of a dipped blade it was like rowing a balloon car in a cloud, said Brown. Thereafter Cornelius did not open his lips except to ask querulously for somebody to bale out his canoe, which was towing behind the long-boat. Gradually the fog whitened and became luminous ahead. To the left Brown saw a darkness as though he had been looking at the back of the departing night. All at once a big bough covered with leaves appeared above his head, and ends of twigs, dripping and still, curved slenderly close alongside. Cornelius, without a word, took the tiller from his hand."

XLIV

"I don't think they spoke together again. The boat entered a narrow by-channel, where it was pushed by the oar-blades set into crumbling banks, and there was a gloom as if enormous black wings had been outspread above the mist that filled its depth to the summits of the trees. The branches overhead showered big drops through the gloomy fog. At a mutter from Cornelius, Brown ordered his men to load. 'I'll give you a chance to get even with them before we're done, you dismal cripples, you,' he said to his gang. 'Mind you don't throw it away—you hounds.' Low growls answered that speech. Cornelius showed much fussy concern for the safety of his canoe.

"Meantime Tamb' Itam had reached the end of his journey. The fog had delayed him a little, but he had paddled steadily, keeping in touch with the south bank. By-and-by daylight came like a glow in a ground glass globe. The shores made on each side of the river a dark smudge, in which one could detect hints of columnar forms and shadows of twisted branches high up. The mist was still thick on the water, but a good watch was being kept, for as Tamb' Itam approached the camp the figures of two men emerged out of the white vapor, and voices spoke to him boisterously. He answered, and presently a canoe lay alongside, and he exchanged news with the paddlers. All was well. The trouble was over. Then the men in the canoe let go their grip on the side of his dug-out and incontinently fell out of sight. He pursued his way till he heard voices coming to him quietly over the water, and saw, under the now lifting, swirling mist, the glow of many little fires burning on a sandy stretch, backed by lofty thin timber and bushes. There again a look-out was kept, for he was challenged. He shouted his name as the two last sweeps of his paddle ran his canoe up on the strand. It was a big camp. Men crouched in many knots under a subdued murmur of early morning talk. Many thin threads of smoke curled slowly on the white mist. Little shelters, elevated above the ground, had been built for the chiefs. Muskets were stacked in small pyramids, and long spears were stuck singly into the sand near the fires.

"Tamb' Itam, assuming an air of importance, demanded to be led to Dain Waris. He found the friend of his white lord lying on a raised couch made of bamboo, and sheltered by a sort of shed of sticks covered with mats. Dain Waris was awake, and a bright fire was burning before his sleeping-place, which resembled a rude shrine. The only son of Nakhoda Doramin answered his greeting kindly. Tamb' Itam began by handing him the ring which vouched for the truth of the messenger's words. Dain Waris, reclining on his elbow, bade him speak and tell all the news. Beginning with the consecrated formula, 'The news is good,' Tamb' Itam delivered Jim's own words. The white men, departing with the consent of all the chiefs, were to be allowed to pass down the river. In answer to a question or two Tamb' Itam then reported the proceedings of the last council. Dain Waris listened attentively to the end, toying with the ring which ultimately he slipped on the forefinger of his right hand. After hearing all he had to say he dismissed Tamb' Itam to have food and rest. Orders for the return in the afternoon were given immediately. Afterwards Dain Waris lay down again, open-eyed, while his personal attendants were preparing his food at the fire, by which Tamb' Itam also sat talking to the men who lounged up to hear the latest intelligence from the town. The sun was eating up the mist. A good watch was kept upon the reach of the main stream where the boat of the whites was expected to appear every moment.

"It was then that Brown took his revenge upon the world which, after twenty years of contemptuous and reckless bullying, refused him the tribute of a common robber's success. It was an act of cold-blooded ferocity, and it consoled him on his deathbed like a memory of an indomitable defiance. Stealthily he landed his men on the other side of the island opposite to the Bugis camp, and led them across. After a short but quite silent scuffle, Cornelius, who had tried to slink away at the moment of landing, resigned himself to show the way where the undergrowth was most sparse. Brown held both his skinny hands together behind his back in the grip of one vast fist, and now and then impelled him forward with a fierce push. Cornelius remained as mute as a fish, abject but faithful to his purpose, whose accomplishment loomed before him dimly. At the edge of the patch of forest Brown's men spread themselves out in cover and waited. The camp was plain from end to end before their eyes, and no one looked their way. Nobody even dreamed that the white men could have any knowledge of the narrow channel at the back of the island. When he judged the moment come, Brown yelled, 'Let them have it,' and fourteen shots rang out like one.

"Tamb' Itam told me the surprise was so great that, except for those who fell dead or wounded, not a soul of them moved for quite an appreciable time after the first discharge. Then a man screamed, and after that scream a great yell of amazement and fear went up from all the throats. A blind panic drove these men in a surging swaying mob to and fro along the shore like a herd of cattle afraid of the water. Some few jumped into the river then, but most of them did so only after the last discharge. Three times Brown's men fired into the ruck, Brown, the only one in view, cursing and yelling, 'Aim low! aim low!'

"Tamb' Itam says that, as for him, he understood at the first volley what had happened. Though untouched he fell down and lay as if dead, but with his eyes open. At the sound of the first shots Dain Waris, reclining on the couch, jumped up and ran out upon the open shore, just in time to receive a bullet in his forehead at the second discharge. Tamb' Itam saw him fling his arms wide open before he fell. Then, he says, a great fear came upon him—not before. The white men retired as they had come— unseen.

"Thus Brown balanced his account with the evil fortune. Notice that even in this awful outbreak there is a superiority as of a man who carries right—the abstract thing —within the envelope of his common desires. It was not a vulgar and treacherous massacre; it was a lesson, a retribution—a demonstration of some obscure and awful attribute of our nature which, I am afraid, is not so very far under the surface as we like to think.

"Afterwards the whites depart unseen by Tamb' Itam, and seem to vanish from before men's eyes altogether; and the schooner, too, vanishes after the manner of stolen goods. But a story is told of a white long-boat picked up a month later in the Indian Ocean by a cargo-steamer. Two parched, yellow, glassy-eyed, whispering skeletons in her recognized the authority of a third, who declared that his name was Brown. His schooner, he reported, bound south with a cargo of Java sugar, had sprung a bad leak and sank under his feet. He and his companions were the survivors of a crew of six. The two died on board the steamer which rescued them. Brown lived to be seen by me, and I can testify that he had played his part to the last.

"It seems, however, that in going away they had neglected to cast off Cornelius's canoe. Cornelius himself Brown had let go at the beginning of the shooting, with a kick for a parting benediction. Tamb' Itam, after arising from amongst the dead, saw the Nazarene running up and down the shore amongst the corpses and the expiring fires. He uttered little cries. Suddenly he rushed to the water, and made frantic efforts to get one of the Bugis boats into the water. 'Afterwards, till he had seen me,' related Tamb' Itam, 'he stood looking at the heavy canoe and scratching his head.' 'What became of him?' I asked. Tamb' Itam, staring at me, made an expressive gesture with his right arm. 'Twice I struck, Tuan,' he said. 'When he beheld me approaching he cast himself violently on the ground and made a great outcry, kicking. He screeched like a frightened hen till he felt the point; then he was still, and lay staring at me while his life went out of his eyes.'

"This done, Tamb' Itam did not tarry. He understood the importance of being the first with the awful news at the fort. There were, of course, many survivors of Dain Waris's party; but in the extremity of panic some had swum across the river, others had bolted into the bush. The fact is that they did not know really who struck that blow—whether more white robbers were not coming, whether they had not already got hold of the whole land. They imagined themselves to be the victims of a vast treachery, and utterly doomed to destruction. It is said that some small parties did not come in till three days afterwards. However, a few tried to make their way back to Patusan at once, and one of the canoes that were patrolling the river that morning was in sight of the camp at the very moment of the attack. It is true that at first the men in her leaped overboard and swam to the opposite bank, but afterwards they returned to their boat and started fearfully upstream. Of these Tamb' Itam had an hour's advance."

XLV

"When Tamb' Itam, paddling madly, came into the town-reach, the women, thronging the platforms before the houses, were looking out for the return of Dain Waris's little fleet of boats. The town had a festive air; here and there men, still with spears or guns in their hands, could be seen moving or standing on the shore in groups. Chinamen's shops had been opened early; but the market-place was empty, and a sentry, still posted at the corner of the fort, made out Tamb' Itam, and shouted to those within. The gate was wide open. Tamb' Itam jumped ashore and ran in headlong. The first person he met was the girl coming down from the house.

"Tamb' Itam, disordered, panting, with trembling lips and wild eyes, stood for a time before her as if a sudden spell had been laid on him. Then he broke out very quickly: 'They have killed Dain Waris and many more.' She clapped her hands, and her first words were, 'Shut the gates.' Most of the fortmen had gone back to their houses, but Tamb' Itam hurried on the few who remained for their turn of duty within. The girl stood in the middle of the courtyard, while the others ran about. 'Doramin,' she cried despairingly, as Tamb' Itam passed her. Next time he went by he answered her thought rapidly, 'Yes. But we have all the powder in Patusan.' She caught him by the arm, and, pointing at the house, 'Call him out,' she whispered, trembling.

"Tamb' Itam ran up the steps. His master was sleeping. 'It is I, Tamb' Itam,' he cried at the door, 'with tidings that cannot wait.' He saw Jim turn over on the pillow and open his eyes, and he burst out at once. 'This, Tuan, is a day of evil, an accursed day.' His master raised himself on his elbow to listen—just as Dain Waris had done. And then Tamb' Itam began his tale, trying to relate the story in order, calling Dain Waris Panglima, and saying: 'The Panglima then called out to the chief of his own boatmen, "Give Tamb' Itam something to eat" '—when his master put his feet to the ground and looked at him with such a discomposed face that the words remained in his throat.

" 'Speak out,' said Jim. 'Is he dead?' 'May you live long,' cried Tamb' Itam. 'It was a most cruel treachery. He ran out at the first shots and fell. . . .' His master walked to the window and with his fist struck at the shutter. The room was made light; and then in a steady voice, but speaking fast, he began to give him orders to assemble a fleet of boats for immediate pursuit, go to this man, to the other—send messengers; and as he talked he sat down on the bed, stooping to lace his boots hurriedly, and suddenly looked up. 'Why do you stand here?' he asked very red-faced. 'Waste no time.' Tamb' Itam did not move. 'Forgive me, Tuan, but . . . but,' he began to stammer. 'What?' cried his master aloud, looking terrible, leaning forward with his hands gripping the edge of the bed. 'It is not safe for thy servant to go out amongst the people,' said Tamb' Itam, after hesitating a moment.

"Then Jim understood. He had retreated from one world, for a small matter of an impulsive jump, and now the other, the work of his own hands, had fallen in ruins upon his head. It was not safe for his servant to go out amongst his own people! I believe that in that very moment he had decided to defy the disaster in the only way it occurred to him such a disaster could be defied; but all I know is that, without a word, he came out of his room and sat before the long table, at the head of which he was accustomed to regulate the affairs of his world, proclaiming daily the truth that surely lived in his heart. The dark powers should not rob him twice of his peace. He sat like a stone figure. Tamb' Itam, deferential, hinted at preparations for defense. The girl he loved came in and spoke to him, but he made a sign with his hand, and she was awed by the dumb appeal for silence in it. She went out on the verandah and sat on the threshold, as if to guard him with her body from dangers outside.

"What thoughts passed through his head—what memories? Who can tell? Everything was gone, and he who had been once unfaithful to his trust had lost again all men's confidence. It was then, I believe, he tried to write—to somebody—and gave it up. Loneliness was closing on him. People had trusted him with their lives—only for that; and yet they could never, as he had said, never be made to understand him. Those without did not hear him make a sound. Later, towards the evening, he came to the door and called for Tamb' Itam. 'Well?' he asked. 'There is much weeping. Much anger, too,' said Tamb' Itam. Jim looked up at him. 'You know,' he murmured. 'Yes, Tuan,' said Tamb' Itam. 'Thy servant does know, and the gates are closed. We shall have to fight.' 'Fight! What for?' he asked. 'For our lives.' 'I have no life,' he said. Tamb' Itam heard a cry from the girl at the door. 'Who knows?' said Tamb' Itam. 'By audacity and cunning we may even escape. There is much fear in men's hearts, too.' He went out, thinking vaguely of boats and of open sea, leaving Jim and the girl together.

"I haven't the heart to set down here such glimpses as she had given me of the hour or more she has passed in there wrestling with him for the possession of her happiness. Whether he had any hope—what he expected, what he imagined—it is impossible to say. He was inflexible, and with the growing loneliness of his obstinacy his spirit seemed to rise above the ruins of his existence. She cried 'Fight!' into his ear. She could not understand. There was nothing to fight for. He was going to prove his power in another way and conquer the fatal destiny itself. He came out into the courtyard, and behind him, with streaming hair, wild of face, breathless, she staggered out and leaned on the side of the doorway. 'Open the gates,' he ordered. Afterwards, turning to those of his men who were inside, he gave them leave to depart to their homes. 'For how long, Tuan?' asked one of them timidly. 'For all life,' he said, in a somber tone.

"A hush had fallen upon the town after the outburst of wailing and lamentation that had swept over the river, like a gust of wind from the opened abode of sorrow. But rumors flew in whispers, filling the hearts with consternation and horrible doubts. The robbers were coming back, bringing many others with them, in a great ship, and there would be no refuge in the land for any one. A sense of utter insecurity as during an earthquake pervaded the minds of men, who whispered their suspicions, looking at each other as if in the presence of some awful portent.

"The sun was sinking towards the forests when Dain Waris's body was brought into Doramin's *campong*. Four men carried it in, covered decently with a white sheet which the old mother had sent out down to the gate to meet her son on his return. They laid him at Doramin's feet, and the old man sat still for a long time, one hand on each knee, looking down. The fronds of palms swayed gently, and the foliage of fruit-trees stirred above his head. Every single man of his people was there, fully armed, when the old *nakhoda* at last raised his eyes. He moved them slowly over the crowd, as if seeking for a missing face. Again his chin sank on his breast. The whispers of many men mingled with the slight rustling of the leaves.

"The Malay who had brought Tamb' Itam and the girl to Samarang was there, too. 'Not so angry as many,' he said to me, but struck with a great awe and wonder at the 'suddenness of men's fate, which hangs over their heads like a cloud charged with thunder.' He told me that when Dain Waris's body was uncovered at a sign of Doramin's, he whom they often called the white lord's friend was disclosed lying unchanged with his eyelids a little open as if about to wake. Doramin leaned forward a little more, like one looking for something fallen on the ground. His eyes searched the body from its feet to its head, for the wound maybe. It was in the forehead and small; and there was no word spoken while one of the bystanders, stooping, took off the silver ring from the cold stiff hand. In silence he held it up before Doramin. A murmur of dismay and horror ran through the crowd at the sight of that familiar token. The old *nakhoda* stared at it, and suddenly let out one great fierce cry, deep from the chest, a roar of pain and fury, as mighty as the bellow of a wounded bull, bringing great fear into men's hearts, by the magnitude of his anger and his sorrow that could be plainly discerned without words. There was a great stillness afterwards for a space, while the body was being borne aside by four men. They laid it down under a tree, and on the instant, with one long shriek, all the women of the household began to wail together; they mourned with shrill cries; the sun was setting, and in the intervals of screamed lamentations the high singsong voices of two old men intoning the Koran chanted alone.

"About this time Jim, leaning on a gun-carriage, looked at the river, and turned his back on the house; and the girl, in the doorway, panting as if she had run herself to a standstill, was looking at him across the yard. Tamb' Itam stood not far from his master, waiting patiently for what might happen. All at once Jim, who seemed to be lost in quiet thought, turned to him and said, 'Time to finish this.'

" 'Tuan?' said Tamb' Itam, advancing with alacrity. He did not know what his master meant, but as soon as Jim made a movement the girl started, too, and walked down into the open space. It seems that no one else of the people of the house was in sight. She tottered slightly, and about half-way down called out to Jim, who had apparently resumed his peaceful contemplation of the river. He turned round, setting his back against the gun. 'Will you fight?' she cried. 'There is nothing to fight for,' he said; 'nothing is lost.' Saying this he made a step towards her. 'Will you fly?' she cried again. 'There is no escape,' he said, stopping short, and she stood still also, silent, devouring him with her eyes. 'And you shall go?' she said, slowly. He bent his head. 'Ah!' she exclaimed, peering at him as it were, 'you are mad or false. Do you remember the night I prayed you to leave me, and you said that you could not? That it was impossible! Impossible! Do you remember you said you would never leave me? Why? I asked you for no promise. You promised unasked—remember.' 'Enough, poor girl,' he said. 'I should not be worth having.'

"Tamb' Itam said that while they were talking she would laugh loud and senselessly like one under the visitation of God. His master put his hands to his head. He was fully dressed as for every day, but without a hat. She stopped laughing suddenly, 'For the last time,' she cried, menacingly, 'will you defend yourself?' 'Nothing can touch me,' he said in a last flicker of superb egoism. Tamb' Itam saw her lean forward where she stood, open her arms, and run at him swiftly. She flung herself upon his breast and clasped him round the neck.

" 'Ah! but I shall hold thee thus,' she cried. . . . 'Thou art mine!'

"She sobbed on his shoulder. The sky over Patusan was blood-red, immense, streaming like an open vein. An enormous sun nestled crimson amongst the tree-tops, and the forest below had a black and forbidding face.

"Tamb' Itam tells me that on that evening the aspect of the heavens was angry and frightful. I may well believe it, for I know that on that very day a cyclone passed within sixty miles of the coast, though there was hardly more than a languid stir of air in the place.

"Suddenly Tamb' Itam saw Jim catch her arms, trying to unclasp her hands. She hung on them with her head fallen back; her hair touched the ground. 'Come here!' his master called, and Tamb' Itam helped to ease her down. It was difficult to separate her fingers. Jim, bending over her, looked earnestly upon her face, and all at once ran to the landing-stage. Tamb' Itam followed him, but turning his head, he saw that she had struggled up to her feet. She ran after them a few steps, then fell down heavily on her knees. 'Tuan! Tuan!' called Tamb' Itam, 'look back;' but Jim was already in a canoe, standing up paddle in hand. He did not look back. Tamb' Itam had just time to scramble in after him when the canoe floated clear. The girl was then on her knees, with clasped hands, at the water-gate. She remained thus for a time in a supplicating attitude before she sprang up. 'You are false!' she screamed out after Jim. 'Forgive me,' he cried. 'Never! Never!' she called back.

"Tamb' Itam took the paddle from Jim's hands, it being unseemly that he should sit while his lord paddled. When they reached the other shore his master forbade him to come any farther; but Tamb' Itam did follow him at a distance, walking up the slope to Doramin's *campong*.

"It was beginning to grow dark. Torches twinkled here and there. Those they met seemed awestruck, and stood aside hastily to let Jim pass. The wailing of women came from above. The courtyard was full of armed Bugis with their followers, and of Patusan people.

"I do not know what this gathering really meant. Were these preparations for war, or for vengeance, or to repulse a threatened invasion? Many days elapsed before the people had ceased to look out, quaking, for the return of the white men with long beards and in rags, whose exact relation to their own white man they could never understand. Even for those simple minds poor Jim remains under a cloud.

"Doramin, alone, immense and desolate, sat in his armchair with the pair of flintlock pistols on his knees, faced by an armed throng. When Jim appeared, at somebody's exclamation, all the heads turned round together, and then the mass opened right and left, and he walked up a lane of averted glances. Whispers followed him; murmurs: 'He has worked all the evil.' 'He hath a charm.' . . . He heard them —perhaps!

"When he came up into the light of torches the wailing of the women ceased suddenly. Doramin did not lift his head, and Jim stood silent before him for a time. Then he looked to the left, and moved in that direction with measured steps. Dain Waris's mother crouched at the head of the body, and the grey disheveled hair concealed her face. Jim came up slowly, looked at his dead friend, lifting the sheet, then dropped it without a word. Slowly he walked back.

" 'He came! He came!' was running from lip to lip, making a murmur to which he moved. 'He hath taken it upon his own head,' a voice said aloud. He heard this and turned to the crowd. 'Yes. Upon my head.' A few people recoiled. Jim waited awhile before Doramin, and then said gently, 'I am come in sorrow.' He waited again. 'I am come ready and unarmed,' he repeated.

"The unwieldy old man, lowering his big forehead like an ox under a yoke, made an effort to rise, clutching at the flintlock pistols on his knees. From his throat came gurgling, choking, inhuman sounds, and his two attendants helped him from behind. People remarked that the ring which he had dropped on his lap fell and rolled against the foot of the white man, and that poor Jim glanced down at the talisman that had opened for him the door of fame, love, and success within the wall of forests fringed with white foam, within the coast that under the western sun looks like the very stronghold of the night. Doramin, struggling to keep his feet, made with his two supporters a swaying, tottering group; his little eyes stared with an expression of mad pain, of rage, with a ferocious glitter, which the bystanders noticed; and then, while Jim stood stiffened and with bared head in the light of torches, looking him straight in the face, he clung heavily with his left arm round the neck of a bowed youth, and lifting deliberately his right, shot his son's friend through the chest.

"The crowd, which had fallen apart behind Jim as soon as Doramin had raised his hand, rushed tumultuously forward after the shot. They say that the white man sent right and left at all those faces a proud and unflinching glance. Then with his hand over his lips he fell forward dead.

"And that's the end. He passes away under a cloud, inscrutable at heart, forgotten, unforgiven, and excessively romantic. Not in the wildest days of his boyish visions could he have seen the alluring shape of such an extraordinary success! For it may very well be that in the short moment of his last proud and unflinching glance, he had beheld the face of that opportunity which, like an Eastern bride, had come veiled to his side.

"But we can see him, an obscure conqueror of fame, tearing himself out of the arms of a jealous love at the sign, at the call of his exalted egoism. He goes away from a living woman to celebrate his pitiless wedding with a shadowy ideal of conduct. Is he satisfied—quite, now, I wonder? We ought to know. He is one of us—and have I not stood up once, like an evoked ghost, to answer for his eternal constancy? Was I so very wrong after all? Now he is no more, there are days when the reality of his existence comes to me with an immense, with an overwhelming force; and yet upon my honor there are moments, too, when he passes from my eyes like a disembodied spirit astray amongst the passions of this earth, ready to surrender himself faithfully to the claim of his own world of shades.

"Who knows? He is gone, inscrutable at heart, and the poor girl is leading a sort of soundless, inert life in Stein's house. Stein has aged greatly of late. He feels it himself, and says often that he is 'preparing to leave all this; preparing to leave . . .' while he waves his hand sadly at his butterflies."

NOSTROMO

A Tale of the Seaboard

Author's Note

ostromo is the most anxiously meditated of the longer novels which belong to the period following upon the publication of the *Typhoon* volume of short stories.

I don't mean to say that I became then conscious of any impending change in my mentality and in my attitude towards the tasks of my writing life. And perhaps there was never any change, except in that mysterious, extraneous thing which has nothing to do with the theories of art; a subtle change in the nature of the inspiration; a phenomenon for which I can not in any way be held responsible. What, however, did cause me some concern was that after finishing the last story of the *Typhoon* volume it seemed somehow that there was nothing more in the world to write about.

This so strangely negative but disturbing mood lasted some little time; and then, as with many of my longer stories, the first hint for *Nostromo* came to me in the shape of a vagrant anecdote completely destitute of valuable details.

As a matter of fact in 1875 or '76, when very young, in the West Indies or rather in the Gulf of Mexico, for my contacts with land were short, few, and fleeting, I heard the story of some man who was supposed to have stolen single-handed a whole lighterful of silver, somewhere on the Tierra Firme seaboard during the troubles of a revolution.

On the face of it this was something of a feat. But I heard no details, and having no particular interest in crime *qua* crime I was not likely to keep that one in mind. And I forgot it till twenty-six or -seven years afterwards I came upon the very thing in a shabby volume picked up outside a second-hand bookshop. It was the life story of an American seaman written by himself with the assistance of a journalist. In the course of his wanderings that American sailor worked for some months on board a schooner, the master and owner of which was the thief of whom I had heard in my very young

533

days. I have no doubt of that because there could hardly have been two exploits of that peculiar kind in the same part of the world and both connected with a South American revolution.

The fellow had actually managed to steal a lighter with silver, and this, it seems, only because he was implicitly trusted by his employers, who must have been singularly poor judges of character. In the sailor's story he is represented as an unmitigated rascal, a small cheat, stupidly ferocious, morose, of mean appearance, and altogether unworthy of the greatness this opportunity had thrust upon him. What was interesting was that he would boast of it openly.

He used to say: "People think I make a lot of money in this schooner of mine. But that is nothing. I don't care for that. Now and then I go away quietly and lift a bar of silver. I must get rich slowly—you understand."

There was also another curious point about the man. Once in the course of some quarrel the sailor threatened him: "What's to prevent me reporting ashore what you have told me about that silver?"

The cynical ruffian was not alarmed in the least. He actually laughed. "You fool, if you dare talk like that on shore about me you will get a knife stuck in your back. Every man, woman, and child in that port is my friend. And who's to prove the lighter wasn't sunk? I didn't show you where the silver is hidden. Did I? So you know nothing. And suppose I lied? Eh?"

Ultimately the sailor, disgusted with the sordid meanness of that impenitent thief, deserted from the schooner. The whole episode takes about three pages of his autobiography. Nothing to speak of; but as I looked them over, the curious confirmation of the few casual words heard in my early youth evoked the memories of that distant time when everything was so fresh, so surprising, so venturesome, so interesting; bits of strange coasts under the stars, shadows of hills in the sunshine, men's passions in the dusk, gossip half-forgotten, faces grown dim. . . . Perhaps, perhaps, there still was in the world something to write about. Yet I did not see anything at first in the mere story. A rascal steals a large parcel of a valuable commodity—so people say. It's either true or untrue; and in any case it has no value in itself. To invent a circumstantial account of the robbery did not appeal to me, because my talents not running that way I did not think that the game was worth the candle. It was only when it dawned upon me that the purloiner of the treasure need not necessarily be a confirmed rogue, that he could be even a man of character, an actor, and possibly a victim in the changing scenes of a revolution, it was only then that I had the first vision of a twilight country which was to become the province of Sulaco, with its high shadowy Sierra and its misty Campo for mute witnesses of events flowing from the passions of men shortsighted in good and evil.

Such are in very truth the obscure origins of *Nostromo*—the book. From that moment, I suppose, it had to be. Yet even then I hesitated, as if warned by the instinct of self-preservation from venturing on a distant and toilsome journey into a land full of intrigues and revolutions. But it had to be done.

It took the best part of the years 1903–4 to do; with many intervals of renewed hesitation, lest I should lose myself in the ever-enlarging vistas opening before me as I progressed deeper in my knowledge of the country. Often, also, when I had thought myself to a standstill over the tangled-up affairs of the Republic, I would, figuratively speaking, pack my bag, rush away from Sulaco for a change of air, and write a few pages of *The Mirror of the Sea.* But generally, as I've said before, my sojourn on the continent of Latin America, famed for its hospitality, lasted for about two years. On my return I found (speaking somewhat in the style of Captain Gulliver) my family all well, my wife heartily glad to learn that the fuss was all over, and our small boy considerably grown during my absence.

My principal authority for the history of Costaguana is, of course, my venerated friend, the late Don José Avellanos, Minister to the Courts of England and Spain, etc., etc., in his impartial and eloquent *History of Fifty Years of Misrule.* That work was never published—the reader will discover why—and I am in fact the only person in the world possessed of its contents. I have mastered them in not a few hours of earnest meditation, and I hope that my accuracy will be trusted. In justice to myself, and to allay the fears of prospective readers, I beg to point out that the few historical allusions are never dragged in for the sake of parading my unique erudition, but that each of them is closely related to actuality; either throwing a light on the nature of current events or affecting directly the fortunes of the people of whom I speak.

As to their own histories I have tried to set them down. Aristocracy and People, men and women, Latin and Anglo-Saxon, bandit and politician, with as cool a hand as was possible in the heat and clash of my own conflicting emotions. And after all this is also the story of their conflicts. It is for the reader to say how far they are deserving of interest in their actions and in the secret purposes of their hearts revealed in the bitter necessities of the time. I confess that, for me, that time is the time of firm friendships and unforgotten hospitalities. And in my gratitude I must mention here Mrs. Gould, 'the first lady of Sulaco,' whom we may safely leave to the secret devotion of Dr. Monygham, and Charles Gould, the Idealist-creator of Material Interests whom we must leave to his Mine—from which there is no escape in this world.

About Nostromo, the second of the two racially and socially contrasted men, both captured by the silver of the San Tomé Mine, I feel bound to say something more.

I did not hesitate to make that central figure an Italian. First of all the thing is perfectly credible: Italians were swarming into the Occidental Province at the time, as anybody who will read further can see; and secondly, there was no one who could stand so well by the side of Giorgio Viola, the Garibaldino, the Idealist of the old, humanitarian revolutions. For myself I needed there a man of the People as free as possible from his class-conventions and all settled modes of thinking. This is not a side-snarl at conventions. My reasons were not moral but artistic. Had he been an Anglo-Saxon he would have tried to get into local politics. But Nostromo does not aspire to be a leader in a personal game. He does not want to raise himself above the mass. He is content to feel himself a power—within the People.

But mainly Nostromo is what he is because I received the inspiration for him in my early days from a Mediterranean sailor. Those who have read certain pages of mine will see at once what I mean when I say that Dominic, the *padrone* of the *Tremolino*, might under given circumstances have been a Nostromo. At any rate Dominic would have understood the younger man perfectly—if scornfully. He and I were engaged together in a rather absurd adventure, but the absurdity does not matter. It is a real satisfaction to think that in my very young days there must, after all, have been something in me worthy to command that man's half-bitter fidelity, his half-ironic devotion. Many of Nostromo's speeches I have heard first in Dominic's voice. His hand on the tiller and his fearless eyes roaming the horizon from within the monkish hood shadowing his face, he would utter the usual exordium of his remorseless wisdom: *"Vous autres gentilhommes!"* in a caustic tone that hangs on my ear yet. Like Nostromo! *"You hombres finos!"* Very much like Nostromo. But Dominic the Corsican nursed a certain pride of ancestry from which my Nostromo is free; for Nostromo's lineage had to be more ancient still. He is a man with the weight of countless generations behind him and no parentage to boast of . . . like the People.

In his firm grip on the earth he inherits, in his improvidence and generosity, in his lavishness with his gifts, in his manly vanity, in the obscure sense of his greatness, and in his faithful devotion with something despairing as well as desperate in its impulses, he is a Man of the People, their very own unenvious force, disdaining to lead but ruling from within. Years afterwards, grown older as the famous Captain Fidanza, with a stake in the country, going about his many affairs followed by respectful glances in the modernized streets of Sulaco, calling on the widow of the *cargador*, attending the Lodge, listening in unmoved silence to anarchist speeches at the meeting, the enigmatical patron of the new revolutionary agitation, the trusted, the wealthy comrade Fidanza with the knowledge of his moral ruin locked up in his breast, he remains essentially a Man of the People. In his mingled love and scorn of life and in the bewildered conviction of having been betrayed, of dying betrayed he hardly knows by what or by whom, he is still of the People, their undoubted Great Man—with a private history of his own.

One more figure of those stirring times I would like to mention: and that is Antonia Avellanos—the 'beautiful Antonia.' Whether she is a possible variation of Latin-American girlhood I wouldn't dare to affirm. But, for me, she *is*. Always a little in the background by the side of her father (my venerated friend) I hope she has yet relief enough to make intelligible what I am going to say. Of all the people who had seen with me the birth of the Occidental Republic, she is the only one who has kept in my memory the aspect of continued life. Antonia the Aristocrat and Nostromo the Man of the People are the artisans of the New Era, the true creators of the New State; he by his legendary and daring feat, she, like a woman, simply by the force of what she is: the only being capable of inspiring a sincere passion in the heart of a trifler.

If anything could induce me to revisit Sulaco (I should hate to see all these changes) it would be Antonia. And the true reason for that—why not be frank about it?—the true reason is that I have modeled her on my first love. How we, a band of tallish schoolboys, the chums of her two brothers, how we used to look up to that girl just out of the schoolroom herself, as the standard-bearer of a faith to which we all were born but which she alone knew how to hold aloft with an unflinching hope! She had perhaps more glow and less serenity in her soul than Antonia, but she was an uncompromising Puritan of patriotism with no taint of the slightest worldliness in her thoughts. I was not the only one in love with her; but it was I who had to hear oftenest her scathing criticism of my levities—very much like poor Decoud—or stand the brunt of her austere, unanswerable invective. She did not quite understand—but never mind. That afternoon when I came in, a shrinking yet defiant sinner, to say the final good-bye I received a hand-squeeze that made my heart leap and saw a tear that took my breath away. She was softened at the last as though she had suddenly perceived (we were such children still!) that I was really going away for good, going very far away— even as far as Sulaco, lying unknown, hidden from our eyes in the darkness of the Placid Gulf.

That's why I long sometimes for another glimpse of the "beautiful Antonia" (or can it be the Other?) moving in the dimness of the great cathedral, saying a short prayer at the tomb of the first and last Cardinal-Archbishop of Sulaco, standing absorbed in filial devotion before the monument of Don José Avellanos, and, with a lingering, tender, faithful glance at the medallion-memorial to Martin Decoud, going out serenely into the sunshine of the Plaza with her upright carriage and her white head; a relic of the past disregarded by men awaiting impatiently the Dawns of other New Eras, the coming of more Revolutions.

But this is the idlest of dreams; for I did understand perfectly well at the time that the moment the breath left the body of the Magnificent Capataz, the Man of the People, freed at last from the toils of love and wealth, there was nothing more for me to do in Sulaco.

J .C.
October 1917

To John Galsworthy

"so foul a sky

clears not

without a storm"

Shakespeare

CONTENTS

Nostromo

Part I

THE SILVER OF THE MINE

I

In the time of Spanish rule, and for many years afterwards, the town of Sulaco—the luxuriant beauty of the orange gardens bears witness to its antiquity—had never been commercially anything more important than a coasting port with a fairly large local trade in ox-hides and indigo. The clumsy deep-sea galleons of the conquerors that, needing a brisk gale to move at all, would lie becalmed, where your modern ship built on clipper lines forges ahead by the mere flapping of her sails, had been barred out of Sulaco by the prevailing calms of its vast gulf. Some harbors of the earth are made difficult of access by the treachery of sunken rocks and the tempests of their shores. Sulaco had found an inviolable sanctuary from the temptations of a trading world in the solemn hush of the deep Golfo Placido as if within an enormous semi-circular and unroofed temple open to the ocean, with its walls of lofty mountains hung with the mourning draperies of cloud.

On one side of this broad curve in the straight seaboard of the Republic of Costaguana, the last spur of the coast range forms an insignificant cape whose name is Punta Mala. From the middle of the gulf the point of the land itself is not visible at all; but the shoulder of a steep hill at the back can be made out faintly like a shadow on the sky.

On the other side, what seems to be an isolated patch of blue mist floats lightly on the glare of the horizon. This is the peninsula of Azuera, a wild chaos of sharp rocks and stony levels cut about by vertical ravines. It lies far out to sea like a rough head of stone stretched from a green-clad coast at the end of a slender neck of sand covered with thickets of thorny scrub. Utterly waterless, for the rainfall runs off at once on all sides into the sea, it has not soil enough—it is said—to grow a single blade of grass, as if it were blighted by a curse. The poor, associating by an obscure instinct of consolation the ideas of evil and wealth, will tell you that it is deadly because of its forbidden treasures. The common folk of the neighborhood, peons of the *estancias*, *vaqueros* of the seaboard plains, tame Indians coming miles to market with a bundle of sugar-cane or a basket of maize worth about threepence, are well aware that heaps of shining gold lie in the gloom of the deep precipices cleaving the stony levels of Azuera. Tradition has it that many adventurers of olden time had perished in the search. The story goes also that within men's memory two wandering sailors—*Americanos*, perhaps, but *gringos* of some sort for certain—talked over a gambling, good-for-nothing *mozo*, and the three stole a donkey to carry for them a bundle of dry sticks, a water-skin, and provisions enough to last a few days. Thus accompanied, and with revolvers at their belts, they had started to chop their way with machetes through the thorny scrub on the neck of the peninsula.

On the second evening an upright spiral of smoke (it could only have been from their camp-fire) was seen for the first time within memory of man standing up faintly upon the sky above a razor-backed ridge on the stony head. The crew of a coasting schooner, lying becalmed three miles off the shore, stared at it with amazement till dark. A Negro fisherman, living in a lonely hut in a little bay near by, had seen the start and was on the lookout for some sign. He called to his wife just as the sun was about to set. They had watched the strange portent with envy, incredulity, and awe.

The impious adventurers gave no other sign. The sailors, the Indian, and the stolen *burro* were never seen again. As to the *mozo*, a Sulaco man—his wife paid for some Masses, and the poor four-footed beast, being without sin, had been probably permitted to die; but the two *gringos*, spectral and alive, are believed to be dwelling to this day amongst the rocks, under the fatal spell of their success. Their souls cannot tear themselves away from their bodies mounting guard over the discovered treasure. They are now rich and hungry and thirsty—a strange theory of tenacious *gringo* ghosts suffering in their starved and parched flesh of defiant heretics, where a Christian would have renounced and been released.

These, then, are the legendary inhabitants of Azuera guarding its forbidden wealth; and the shadow on the sky on one side, with the round patch of blue haze blurring the bright skirt of the horizon on the other, mark the two outermost points of the bend which bears the name of Golfo Placido, because never a strong wind had been known to blow upon its waters.

On crossing the imaginary line drawn from Punta Mala to Azuera the ships from Europe bound to Sulaco lose at once the strong breezes of the ocean. They become the prey of capricious airs that play with them for thirty hours at a stretch sometimes. Before them the head of the calm gulf is filled on most days of the year by a great body of motionless and opaque clouds. On the rare clear mornings another shadow is cast upon the sweep of the gulf. The dawn breaks high behind the towering and serrated wall of the Cordillera, a clear-cut vision of dark peaks rearing their steep slopes on a lofty pedestal of forest rising from the very edge of the shore. Amongst them the white head of Higuerota rises majestically upon the blue. Bare clusters of enormous rocks sprinkle with tiny black dots the smooth dome of snow.

Then, as the midday sun withdraws from the gulf the shadow of the mountains, the clouds begin to roll out of the lower valleys. They swathe in somber tatters the naked crags of precipices above the wooded slopes, hide the peaks, smoke in stormy trails across the snows of Higuerota. The Cordillera is gone from you as if it had dissolved itself into great piles of gray and black vapors that travel out slowly to seaward and vanish into thin air all along the front before the blazing heat of the day. The wasting edge of the cloud-bank always strives for, but seldom wins, the middle of the gulf. The sun—as the sailors say—is eating it up. Unless perchance a somber thunder-head breaks away from the main body to career all over the gulf till it escapes into the offing beyond Azuera, where it bursts suddenly into flame and crashes like a sinister pirate-ship of the air, hove-to above the horizon, engaging the sea.

At night the body of clouds advancing higher up the sky smothers the whole quiet gulf below with an impenetrable darkness, in which the sound of the falling showers can be heard beginning and ceasing abruptly—now here, now there. Indeed, these cloudy nights are proverbial with the seamen along the whole west coast of a great continent. Sky, land, and sea disappear together out of the world when the Placido— as the saying is—goes to sleep under its black poncho. The few stars left below the seaward frown of the vault shine feebly as into the mouth of a black cavern. In its vastness your ship floats unseen under your feet, her sails flutter invisible above your head. The eye of God Himself—they add with grim profanity—could not find out what work a man's hand is doing in there; and you would be free to call the devil to your aid with impunity if even his malice were not defeated by such a blind darkness.

The shores on the gulf are steep-to all around; three uninhabited islets basking in the sunshine just outside the cloud veil, and opposite the entrance to the harbor of Sulaco, bear the name of "The Isabels."

There is the Great Isabel; the Little Isabel, which is round; and Hermosa, which is the smallest.

That last is no more than a foot high, and about seven paces across, a mere flat top of a gray rock which smokes like a hot cinder after a shower, and where no man would care to venture a naked sole before sunset. On the Little Isabel an old ragged palm with a thick bulging trunk rough with spines, a very witch amongst palm trees, rustles a dismal bunch of dead leaves above the coarse sand. The Great Isabel has a spring of fresh water issuing from the overgrown side of a ravine. Resembling an emerald green wedge of land a mile long, and laid flat upon the sea, it bears two forest trees standing close together, with a wide spread of shade at the foot of their smooth trunks. A ravine extending the whole length of the island is full of bushes; and presenting a deep tangled cleft on the high side spreads itself out on the other into a shallow depression abutting on a small strip of sandy shore.

From that low end of the Great Isabel the eye plunges through an opening two miles away, as abrupt as if chopped with an axe out of the regular sweep of the coast, right into the harbor of Sulaco. It is an oblong, lake-like piece of water. On one side the short wooded spurs and valleys of the Cordillera come down at right angles to the very strand; on the other the open view of the great Sulaco plain passes into the opal mystery of great distances overhung by dry haze. The town of Sulaco itself—tops of walls, a great cupola, gleams of white miradors in a vast grove of orange trees—lies between the mountains and the plain, at some little distance from its harbor and out of the direct line of sight from the sea.

II

The only sign of commercial activity within the harbor, visible from the beach of the Great Isabel, is the square blunt end of the wooden jetty which the Oceanic Steam Navigation Company (the O.S.N. of familiar speech) had thrown over the shallow part of the bay soon after they had resolved to make of Sulaco one of their ports of call for the Republic of Costaguana. The State possesses several harbors on its long seaboard, but except Cayta, an important place, all are either small and inconvenient inlets in an iron-bound coast—like Esmeralda, for instance, sixty miles to the south—or else mere open roadsteads exposed to the winds and fretted by the surf.

Perhaps the very atmospheric conditions which had kept away the merchant fleets of bygone ages induced the O.S.N. Company to violate the sanctuary of peace sheltering the calm existence of Sulaco. The variable airs sporting lightly with the vast semicircle of waters within the head of Azuera could not baffle the steam power of their excellent fleet. Year after year the black hulls of their ships had gone up and down the coast, in and out, past Azuera, past the Isabels, past Punta Mala—disregarding everything but the tyranny of time. Their names, the names of all mythology, became the household words of a coast that had never been ruled by the gods of Olympus. The *Juno* was known only for her comfortable cabins amidships, the *Saturn* for the geniality of her captain and the painted and gilt luxuriousness of her saloon, whereas the *Ganymede* was fitted out mainly for cattle transport, and to be avoided by coastwise passengers. The humblest Indian in the obscurest village on the coast was familiar with the *Cerberus*, a little black puffer without charm or living accommodation to speak of, whose mission was to creep inshore along the wooded beaches close to mighty ugly rocks, stopping obligingly before every cluster of huts to collect produce, down to three-pound parcels of india rubber bound in a wrapper of dry grass.

And as they seldom failed to account for the smallest package, rarely lost a bullock, and had never drowned a single passenger, the name of the O.S.N. stood very high for trustworthiness. People declared that under the Company's care their lives and property were safer on the water than in their own houses on shore.

The O.S.N.'s superintendent in Sulaco for the whole Costaguana section of the service was very proud of his Company's standing. He resumed it in a saying which was very often on his lips, "We never make mistakes." To the Company's officers it took the form of a severe injunction. "We must make no mistakes. I'll have no mistakes here, no matter what Smith may do at his end."

Smith, on whom he had never set eyes in his life, was the other superintendent of the service, quartered some fifteen hundred miles away from Sulaco. "Don't talk to me of your Smith."

Then, calming down suddenly, he would dismiss the subject with studied negligence.

"Smith knows no more of this continent than a baby."

"Our excellent Señor Mitchell" for the business and official world of Sulaco; "Fussy Joe" for the commanders of the Company's ships, Captain Joseph Mitchell prided himself on his profound knowledge of men and things in the country—*cosas de Costaguana*. Amongst these last he accounted as most unfavorable to the orderly working of his Company the frequent changes of government brought about by revolutions of the military type.

The political atmosphere of the Republic was generally stormy in these days. The fugitive patriots of the defeated party had the knack of turning up again on the coast with half a steamer's load of small arms and ammunition. Such resourcefulness Captain Mitchell considered as perfectly wonderful in view of their utter destitution at the time of the flight. He had observed that "they never seemed to have enough change about them to pay for their passage ticket out of the country." And he could speak with knowledge; for on a memorable occasion he had been called upon to save the life of a dictator, together with the lives of a few Sulaco officials—the political chief, the director of the customs, and the head of police—belonging to an overturned government. Poor Señor Ribiera (such was the dictator's name) had come pelting eighty miles over mountain tracks after the lost battle of Socorro, in the hope of outdistancing the fatal news—which, of course, he could not manage to do on a lame mule. The animal, moreover, expired under him at the end of the Alameda, where the military band plays sometimes in the evenings between the revolutions. "Sir," Captain Mitchell would pursue with portentous gravity, "the ill-timed end of that mule attracted attention to the unfortunate rider. His features were recognized by several deserters from the Dictatorial army amongst the rascally mob already engaged in smashing the windows of the Intendencia."

Early on the morning of that day the local authorities of Sulaco had fled for refuge to the O.S.N. Company's offices, a strong building near the shore end of the jetty, leaving the town to the mercies of a revolutionary rabble; and as the Dictator was execrated by the populace on account of the severe recruitment law his necessities had compelled him to enforce during the struggle, he stood a good chance of being torn to pieces. Providentially, Nostromo—invaluable fellow—with some Italian workmen, imported to work upon the National Central Railway, was at hand, and managed to snatch him away—for the time at least. Ultimately, Captain Mitchell succeeded in taking everybody off in his own gig to one of the Company's steamers—it was the *Minerva*—just then, as luck would have it, entering the harbor.

He had to lower these gentlemen at the end of a rope out of a hole in the wall at the back, while the mob which, pouring out of the town, had spread itself all along the shore, howled and foamed at the foot of the building in front. He had to hurry them then the whole length of the jetty; it had been a desperate dash, neck or nothing—and again it was Nostromo, a fellow in a thousand, who, at the head, this time, of the Company's body of lightermen, held the jetty against the rushes of the rabble, thus giving the fugitives time to reach the gig lying ready for them at the other end with the Company's flag at the stern. Sticks, stones, shots flew; knives, too, were thrown.

Captain Mitchell exhibited willingly the long cicatrice of a cut over his left ear and temple, made by a razor-blade fastened to a stick—a weapon, he explained, very much in favor with the "worst kind of nigger out here."

Captain Mitchell was a thick, elderly man, wearing high, pointed collars and short side-whiskers, partial to white waistcoats, and really very communicative under his air of pompous reserve.

"These gentlemen," he would say, staring with great solemnity, "had to run like rabbits, sir. I ran like a rabbit myself. Certain forms of death are—er—distasteful to a —a—er respectable man. They would have pounded me to death, too. A crazy mob, sir, does not discriminate. Under providence we owed our preservation to my Capataz de Cargadores, as they called him in the town, a man who, when I discovered his value, sir, was just the bos'n of an Italian ship, a big Genoese ship, one of the few European ships that ever came to Sulaco with a general cargo before the building of the National Central. He left her on account of some very respectable friends he made here, his own countrymen, but also, I suppose, to better himself. Sir, I am a pretty good judge of character. I engaged him to be the foreman of our lightermen, and caretaker of our jetty. That's all that he was. But without him Señor Ribiera would have been a dead man. This Nostromo, sir, a man absolutely above reproach, became the terror of all the thieves in the town. We were infested, infested, overrun, sir, here at that time by *ladrones* and *matreros,* thieves and murderers from the whole province. On this occasion they had been flocking into Sulaco for a week past. They had scented the end, sir. Fifty per cent of that murdering mob were professional bandits from the Campo, sir, but there wasn't one that hadn't heard of Nostromo. As to the town *leperos,* sir, the sight of his black whiskers and white teeth was enough for them. They quailed before him, sir. That's what the force of character will do for you."

It could very well be said that it was Nostromo alone who saved the lives of these gentlemen. Captain Mitchell, on his part, never left them till he had seen them collapse, panting, terrified, and exasperated, but safe, on the luxurious velvet sofas in the first-class saloon of the *Minerva*. To the very last he had been careful to address the ex-Dictator as "Your Excellency."

"Sir, I could do no other. The man was down—ghastly, livid, one mass of scratches."

The *Minerva* never let go her anchor that call. The superintendent ordered her out of the harbor at once. No cargo could be landed, of course, and the passengers for Sulaco naturally refused to go ashore. They could hear the firing and see plainly the fight going on at the edge of the water. The repulsed mob devoted its energies to an attack upon the Custom House, a dreary, unfinished-looking structure with many windows two hundred yards away from the O.S.N. Offices, and the only other build-ing near the harbor. Captain Mitchell, after directing the commander of the *Minerva* to land "these gentlemen" in the first port of call outside Costaguana, went back in his gig to see what could be done for the protection of the Company's property. That and the property of the railway were preserved by the European residents; that is, by Captain Mitchell himself and the staff of engineers building the road, aided by the

Italian and Basque workmen who rallied faithfully round their English chiefs. The Company's lightermen, too, natives of the Republic, behaved very well under their Capataz. An outcast lot of very mixed blood, mainly Negroes, everlastingly at feud with the other customers of low grog shops in the town, they embraced with delight this opportunity to settle their personal scores under such favorable auspices. There was not one of them that had not, at some time or other, looked with terror at Nostromo's revolver poked very close at his face, or been otherwise daunted by Nostromo's resolution. He was "much of a man," their Capataz was, they said, too scornful in his temper ever to utter abuse, a tireless taskmaster, and the more to be feared because of his aloofness. And behold! there he was that day, at their head, condescending to make jocular remarks to this man or the other.

Such leadership was inspiriting, and in truth all the harm the mob managed to achieve was to set fire to one—only one—stack of railway-sleepers, which, being creosoted, burned well. The main attack on the railway yards, on the O.S.N. Offices, and especially on the Custom House, whose strong-room, it was well known, contained a large treasure in silver ingots, failed completely. Even the little hotel kept by old Giorgio, standing alone half-way between the harbor and the town, escaped looting and destruction, not by a miracle, but because with the safes in view they had neglected it at first, and afterwards found no leisure to stop. Nostromo, with his *cargadores*, was pressing them too hard then.

III

It might have been said that there he was only protecting his own. From the first he had been admitted to live in the intimacy of the family of the hotel-keeper who was a countryman of his. Old Giorgio Viola, a Genoese with a shaggy white leonine head— often called simply "the Garibaldino" (as Mohammedans are called after their prophet)—was, to use Captain Mitchell's own words, the "respectable married friend" by whose advice Nostromo had left his ship to try for a run of shore luck in Costaguana.

The old man, full of scorn for the populace, as your austere republican so often is, had disregarded the preliminary sounds of trouble. He went on that day as usual pottering about the *casa* in his slippers, muttering angrily to himself his contempt of the non-political nature of the riot, and shrugging his shoulders. In the end he was taken unawares by the out-rush of the rabble. It was too late then to remove his family, and, indeed, where could he have run to with the portly Signora Teresa and two little girls on that great plain? So, barricading every opening, the old man sat down sternly in the middle of the darkened café with an old shot-gun on his knees. His wife sat on another chair by his side, muttering pious invocations to all the saints of the calendar.

The old republican did not believe in saints, or in prayers, or in what he called "priests' religion." Liberty and Garibaldi were his divinities; but he tolerated "superstition" in women, preserving in these matters a lofty and silent attitude.

His two girls, the eldest fourteen, and the other two years younger, crouched on the sanded floor, on each side of the Signora Teresa, with their heads on their mother's lap, both scared, but each in her own way, the dark-haired Linda indignant and angry, the fair Giselle, the younger, bewildered and resigned. The Padrona removed her arms, which embraced her daughters, for a moment to cross herself and wring her hands hurriedly. She moaned a little louder.

"Oh! Gian' Battista, why art thou not here? Oh! why art thou not here?"

She was not then invoking the saint himself, but calling upon Nostromo, whose patron he was. And Giorgio, motionless on the chair by her side, would be provoked by these reproachful and distracted appeals.

"Peace, woman! Where's the sense of it? There's his duty," he murmured in the dark; and she would retort, panting:

"Eh! I have no patience. Duty! What of the woman who has been like a mother to him? I bent my knee to him this morning; don't you go out, Gian' Battista—stop in the house. Battistino—look at those two little innocent children!"

Mrs. Viola was an Italian, too, a native of Spezzia, and though considerably younger than her husband, already middle-aged. She had a handsome face, whose complexion had turned yellow because the climate of Sulaco did not suit her at all. Her voice was a rich contralto. When, with her arms folded tight under her ample bosom, she scolded the squat, thick-legged China girls handling linen, plucking fowls, pounding corn in wooden mortars amongst the mud outbuildings at the back of the house, she could bring out such an impassioned, vibrating, sepulchral note that the chained watch-dog bolted into his kennel with a great rattle. Luis, a cinnamon-colored mulatto with a sprouting mustache and thick, dark lips, would stop sweeping the café with a broom of palm-leaves to let a gentle shudder run down his spine. His languishing almond eyes would remain closed for a long time.

This was the staff of the Casa Viola, but all these people had fled early that morning at the first sounds of the riot, preferring to hide on the plain rather than trust themselves in the house; a preference for which they were in no way to blame, since, whether true or not, it was generally believed in the town that the Garibaldino had some money buried under the clay floor of the kitchen. The dog, an irritable, shaggy brute, barked violently and whined plaintively in turns at the back, running in and out of his kennels as rage or fear prompted him.

Bursts of great shouting rose and died away, like wild gusts of wind on the plain round the barricaded house; the fitful popping of shots grew louder above the yelling. Sometimes there were intervals of unaccountable stillness outside, and nothing could have been more gaily peaceful than the narrow bright lines of sunlight from the cracks in the shutters, ruled straight across the café over the disarranged chairs and tables to the wall opposite. Old Giorgio had chosen that bare, whitewashed room for a retreat. It had only one window, and its only door swung out upon the track of thick dust fenced by aloe hedges between the harbor and the town, where clumsy carts used to creak along behind slow yokes of oxen guided by boys on horseback.

In a pause of stillness Giorgio cocked his gun. The ominous sound wrung a low moan from the rigid figure of the woman sitting by his side. A sudden outbreak of defiant yelling quite near the house sank all at once to a confused murmur of growls.

Somebody ran along; the loud catching of his breath was heard for an instant passing the door; there were hoarse mutters and footsteps near the wall; a shoulder rubbed against the shutter, effacing the bright lines of sunshine pencilled across the whole breadth of the room. Signora Teresa's arms thrown about the kneeling forms of her daughters embraced them closer with a convulsive pressure.

The mob, driven away from the Custom House, had broken up into several bands, retreating across the plain in the direction of the town. The subdued crash of irregular volleys fired in the distance was answered by faint yells far away. In the intervals the single shots rang feebly, and the low, long, white building blinded in every window seemed to be the center of a turmoil widening in a great circle about its closed-up silence. But the cautious movements and whispers of a routed party seeking a momentary shelter behind the wall made the darkness of the room, striped by threads of quiet sunlight, alight with evil, stealthy sounds. The Violas had them in their ears as though invisible ghosts hovering about their chairs had consulted in mutters as to the advisability of setting fire to this foreigner's *casa*.

It was trying to the nerves. Old Viola had risen slowly, gun in hand, irresolute, for he did not see how he could prevent them. Already voices could be heard talking at the back. Signora Teresa was beside herself with terror.

"Ah! the traitor! the traitor!" she mumbled, almost inaudibly. "Now we are going to be burned; and I bent my knee to him. No! he must run at the heels of his English."

She seemed to think that Nostromo's mere presence in the house would have made it perfectly safe. So far, she, too, was under the spell of that reputation the Capataz de Cargadores had made for himself by the waterside, along the railway line, with the English, and with the populace of Sulaco. To his face, and even against her husband, she invariably affected to laugh it to scorn, sometimes good-naturedly, more often with a curious bitterness. But then women are unreasonable in their opinions, as Giorgio used to remark calmly on fitting occasions. On this occasion, with his gun held at ready before him, he stooped down to his wife's head, and, keeping his eyes steadfastly on the barricaded door, he breathed out into her ear that Nostromo would have been powerless to help. What could two men shut up in a house do against twenty or more bent upon setting fire to the roof? Gian' Battista was thinking of the *casa* all the time, he was sure.

"He think of the *casa*! He!" gasped Signora Viola, crazily. She struck her breast with her open hands. "I know him. He thinks of nobody but himself."

A discharge of firearms nearby made her throw her head back and close her eyes. Old Giorgio set his teeth hard under his white mustache, and his eyes began to roll fiercely. Several bullets struck the end of the wall together; pieces of plaster could be heard falling outside; a voice screamed "Here they come!" and after a moment of uneasy silence there was a rush of running feet along the front.

Then the tension of old Giorgio's attitude relaxed, and a smile of contemptuous relief came upon his lips of an old fighter with a leonine face. These were not a people striving for justice, but thieves. Even to defend his life against them was a sort of degradation for a man who had been one of Garibaldi's immortal thousand in the conquest of Sicily. He had an immense scorn for this outbreak of scoundrels and *leperos,* who did not know the meaning of the word "liberty."

He grounded his old gun, and, turning his head, glanced at the colored lithograph of Garibaldi in a black frame on the white wall; a thread of strong sunshine cut it perpendicularly. His eyes, accustomed to the luminous twilight, made out the high coloring of the face, the red of the shirt, the outlines of the square shoulders, the black patch of the Bersagliere hat with cock's feathers curling over the crown. An immortal hero! This was your liberty; it gave you not only life, but immortality as well!

For that one man his fanaticism had suffered no diminution. In the moment of relief from the apprehension of the greatest danger, perhaps, his family had been exposed to in all their wanderings, he had turned to the picture of his old chief, first and only, then laid his hand on his wife's shoulder.

The children kneeling on the floor had not moved. Signora Teresa opened her eyes a little, as though he had awakened her from a very deep and dreamless slumber. Before he had time in his deliberate way to say a reassuring word she jumped up, with the children clinging to her, one on each side, gasped for breath, and let out a hoarse shriek.

It was simultaneous with the bang of a violent blow struck on the outside of the shutter. They could hear suddenly the snorting of a horse, the restive tramping of hoofs on the narrow, hard path in front of the house; the toe of a boot struck at the shutter again; a spur jingled at every blow, and an excited voice shouted, "Hola! hola, in there!"

I V

All the morning Nostromo had kept his eye from afar on the Casa Viola, even in the thick of the hottest scrimmage near the Custom House. "If I see smoke rising over there," he thought to himself, "they are lost." Directly the mob had broken he pressed with a small band of Italian workmen in that direction, which, indeed, was the shortest line towards the town. That part of the rabble he was pursuing seemed to think of making a stand under the house; a volley fired by his followers from behind an aloe hedge made the rascals fly. In a gap chopped out for the rails of the harbor branch-line Nostromo appeared, mounted on his silver-gray mare. He shouted, sent after them one shot from his revolver, and galloped up to the café window. He had an idea that old Giorgio would choose that part of the house for a refuge.

His voice had penetrated to them, sounding breathlessly hurried: *"Hola! vecchio! O, vecchio!* Is it all well with you in there?"

"You see—" murmured old Viola to his wife.

Signora Teresa was silent now. Outside Nostromo laughed.

"I can hear the *padrona* is not dead."

"You have done your best to kill me with fear," cried Signora Teresa. She wanted to say something more, but her voice failed her.

Linda raised her eyes to her face for a moment, but old Giorgio shouted apologetically:

"She is a little upset."

Outside Nostromo shouted back with another laugh:

"She cannot upset me."

Signora Teresa found her voice.

"It is what I say. You have no heart—and you have no conscience, Gian' Battista—"

They heard him wheel his horse away from the shutters. The party he led were babbling excitedly in Italian and Spanish, inciting each other to the pursuit. He put himself at their head, crying, *"Avanti!"*

"He has not stopped very long with us. There is no praise from strangers to be got here," Signora Teresa said, tragically. *"Avanti!* Yes! That is all he cares for. To be first somewhere—somehow—to be first with these English. They will be showing him to everybody. 'This is our Nostromo!' " She laughed ominously. "What a name! What is that? Nostromo? He would take a name that is properly no word from them."

Meantime Giorgio, with tranquil movements, had been unfastening the door; the flood of light fell on Signora Teresa, with her two girls gathered to her side, a picturesque woman in a pose of maternal exaltation. Behind her the wall was dazzlingly white, and the crude colors of the Garibaldi lithograph paled in the sunshine.

Old Viola, at the door, moved his arm upwards as if referring all his quick, fleeting thoughts to the picture of his old chief on the wall. Even when he was cooking for the *"signori inglesi"*—the engineers (he was a famous cook, though the kitchen was a dark place)—he was, as it were, under the eye of the great man who had led him in a glorious struggle where, under the walls of Gaeta, tyranny would have expired for ever had it not been for that accursed Piedmontese race of kings and ministers. When sometimes a frying-pan caught fire during a delicate operation with some shredded onions, and the old man was seen backing out of the doorway, swearing and coughing violently in an acrid cloud of smoke, the name of Cavour—the arch intriguer sold to kings and tyrants—could be heard involved in imprecations against the China girls, cooking in general, and the brute of a country where he was reduced to live for the love of liberty that traitor had strangled.

Then Signora Teresa, all in black, issuing from another door, advanced, portly and anxious, inclining her fine, black-browed head, opening her arms, and crying in a profound tone—

"Giorgio! thou passionate man! *Misericordia divina!* In the sun like this! He will make himself ill."

At her feet the hens made off in all directions, with immense strides; if there were any engineers from up the line staying in Sulaco, a young English face or two would appear at the billiard-room occupying one end of the house; but at the other end, in the café, Luis, the mulatoo, took good care not to show himself. The Indian girls, with hair like flowing black manes, and dressed only in a shift and short petticoat, stared dully from under the square-cut fringes on their foreheads; the noisy frizzling of fat had stopped, the fumes floated upwards in sunshine, a strong smell of burnt onions hung in the drowsy heat, enveloping the house; and the eye lost itself in a vast flat expanse of grass to the west, as if the plain between the Sierra overtopping Sulaco and the coast range away there towards Esmeralda had been as big as half the world.

Signora Teresa, after an impressive pause, remonstrated:

"Eh, Giorgio! Leave Cavour alone and take care of yourself now we are lost in this country all alone with the two children, because you cannot live under a king."

And while she looked at him she would sometimes put her hand hastily to her side with a short twitch of her fine lips and a knitting of her black, straight eyebrows like a flicker of angry pain or an angry thought on her handsome, regular features.

It was pain; she suppressed the twinge. It had come to her first a few years after they had left Italy to emigrate to America and settle at last in Sulaco after wandering from town to town, trying shopkeeping in a small way here and there; and once an organized enterprise of fishing—in Maldonado—for Giorgio, like the great Garibaldi, had been a sailor in his time.

Sometimes she had no patience with pain. For years its gnawing had been part of the landscape embracing the glitter of the harbor under the wooded spurs of the range; and the sunshine itself was heavy and dull—heavy with pain—not like the sunshine of her girlhood, in which middle-aged Giorgio had wooed her gravely and passionately on the shores of the gulf of Spezzia.

"You go in at once, Giorgio," she directed. "One would think you do not wish to have any pity on me—with four Signori Inglesi staying in the house."

"*Va bene, va bene,*" Giorgio would mutter.

He obeyed. The Signori Inglesi would require their midday meal presently. He had been one of the immortal and invincible band of liberators who had made the mercenaries of tyranny fly like chaff before a hurricane, "*un uragano terribile.*" But that was before he was married and had children; and before tyranny had reared its head again amongst the traitors who had imprisoned Garibaldi, his hero.

There were three doors in the front of the house, and each afternoon the Garibaldino could be seen at one or another of them with his big bush of white hair, his arms folded, his legs crossed, leaning back his leonine head against the lintel, and looking up the wooded slopes of the foothills at the snowy dome of Higuerota. The front of his house threw off a black long rectangle of shade, broadening slowly over the soft ox-cart track. Through the gaps, chopped out in the oleander hedges, the harbor branch railway, laid out temporarily on the level of the plain, curved away its shining parallel ribbons on a belt of scorched and withered grass within sixty yards of the end of the house. In the evening the empty material trains of flat cars circled round the dark green grove of Sulaco, and ran, undulating slightly with white jets of steam, over the plain towards the Casa Viola, on their way to the railway yards by the harbor. The Italian drivers saluted him from the footplate with raised hand, while the Negro brakesmen sat carelessly on the brakes, looking straight forward, with the rims of their big hats flapping in the wind. In return Giorgio would give a slight sideways jerk of the head, without unfolding his arms.

On this memorable day of the riot his arms were not folded on his chest. His hand grasped the barrel of the gun grounded on the threshold; he did not look up once at the white dome of Higuerota, whose cool purity seemed to hold itself aloof from a hot earth. His eyes examined the plain curiously. Tall trails of dust subsided here and there. In a speckless sky the sun hung clear and blinding. Knots of men ran headlong; others made a stand; and the irregular rattle of firearms came rippling to his ears in the fiery, still air. Single figures on foot raced desperately. Horsemen galloped towards each other, wheeled round together, separated at speed. Giorgio saw one fall, rider and horse disappearing as if they had galloped into a chasm, and the movements of the animated scene were like the passages of a violent game played upon the plain by dwarfs mounted and on foot, yelling with tiny throats, under the mountain that seemed a colossal embodiment of silence. Never before had Giorgio seen this bit of plain so full of active life; his gaze could not take in all its details at once; he shaded his eyes with his hand, till suddenly the thundering of many hoofs near by startled him.

A troop of horses had broken out of the fenced paddock of the Railway Company. They came on like a whirlwind, and dashed over the line snorting, kicking, squealing in a compact, piebald, tossing mob of bay, brown, gray backs, eyes staring, necks extended, nostrils red, long tails streaming. As soon as they had leaped upon the road the thick dust flew upwards from under their hoofs, and within six yards of Giorgio only a brown cloud with vague forms of necks and cruppers rolled by, making the soil tremble on its passage.

Viola coughed, turning his face away from the dust, and shaking his head slightly.

"There will be some horse-catching to be done before tonight," he muttered.

In the square of sunlight falling through the door Signora Teresa, kneeling before the chair, had bowed her head, heavy with a twisted mass of ebony hair streaked with silver, into the palm of her hands. The black lace shawl she used to drape about her face dropped to the ground by her side. The two girls had got up, hand-in-hand, in short skirts, their loose hair falling in disorder. The younger had thrown her arm across her eyes, as if afraid to face the light. Linda, with her hand on the other's shoulder, stared fearlessly. Viola looked at his children.

The sun brought out the deep lines on his face, and, energetic in expression, it had the immobility of a carving. It was impossible to discover what he thought. Bushy gray eyebrows shaded his dark glance.

"Well! And do you not pray like your mother?"

Linda pouted, advancing her red lips, which were almost too red; but she had admirable eyes, brown, with a sparkle of gold in the irises, full of intelligence and meaning, and so clear that they seemed to throw a glow upon her thin, colorless face. There were bronze glints in the somber clusters of her hair, and the eyelashes, long and coal black, made her complexion appear still more pale.

"Mother is going to offer up a lot of candles in the church. She always does when Nostromo has been away fighting. I shall have some to carry up to the Chapel of the Madonna in the Cathedral."

She said all this quickly, with great assurance, in an animated, penetrating voice. Then, giving her sister's shoulder a slight shake, she added:

"And she will be made to carry one, too!"

"Why made?" inquired Giorgio, gravely. "Does she not want to?"

"She is timid," said Linda, with a little burst of laughter. "People notice her fair hair as she goes along with us. They call out after her, 'Look at the *rubia!* Look at the *rubiacita!*' They call out in the streets. She is timid."

"And you? You are not timid—eh?" the father pronounced, slowly.

She tossed back all her dark hair.

"Nobody calls out after me."

Old Giorgio contemplated his children thoughtfully. There was two years difference between them. They had been born to him late, years after the boy had died. Had he lived he would have been nearly as old as Gian' Battista—he whom the English called Nostromo; but as to his daughters, the severity of his temper, his advancing age, his absorption in his memories, had prevented his taking much notice of them. He loved his children, but girls belong more to the mother, and much of his affection had been expended in the worship and service of liberty.

When quite a youth he had deserted from a ship trading to La Plata, to enlist in the navy of Montevideo, then under the command of Garibaldi. Afterwards, in the Italian legion of the Republic struggling against the encroaching tyranny of Rosas, he had taken part, on great plains, on the banks of immense rivers, in the fiercest fighting perhaps the world had ever known. He had lived amongst men who had declaimed about liberty, suffered for liberty, died for liberty, with a desperate exaltation, and with their eyes turned towards an oppressed Italy. His own enthusiasm had been fed on scenes of carnage, on the examples of lofty devotion, on the din of armed struggle, on the inflamed language of proclamations. He had never parted from the chief of his choice—the fiery apostle of independence—keeping by his side in America and in Italy till after the fatal day of Aspromonte, when the treachery of kings, emperors, and ministers had been revealed to the world in the wounding and imprisonment of his hero—a catastrophe that had instilled into him a gloomy doubt of ever being able to understand the ways of divine justice.

He did not deny it, however. It required patience, he would say. Though he disliked priests, and would not put his foot inside a church for anything, he believed in God. Were not the proclamations against tyrants addressed to the peoples in the name of God and liberty? "God for men—religions for women," he muttered sometimes. In Sicily, an Englishman who had turned up in Palermo after its evacuation by the army of the king, had given him a Bible in Italian—the publication of the British and Foreign Bible Society, bound in a dark leather cover. In periods of political adversity, in the pauses of silence when the revolutionists issued no proclamations, Giorgio earned his living with the first work that came to hand—as sailor, as dock laborer on the quays of Genoa, once as a hand on a farm in the hills above Spezzia—and in his spare time he studied the thick volume. He carried it with him into battles. Now it was his only reading, and in order not to be deprived of it (the print was small) he had consented to accept the present of a pair of silver-mounted spectacles from Señora

Emilia Gould, the wife of the Englishman who managed the silver mine in the mountains three leagues from the town. She was the only Englishwoman in Sulaco.

Giorgio Viola had a great consideration for the English. This feeling, born on the battlefields of Uruguay, was forty years old at the very least. Several of them had poured their blood for the cause of freedom in America, and the first he had ever known he remembered by the name of Samuel; he commanded a Negro company under Garibaldi, during the famous siege of Montevideo, and died heroically with his Negroes at the fording of the Boyana. He, Giorgio, had reached the rank of ensign— *alferez*—and cooked for the general. Later, in Italy, he, with the rank of lieutenant, rode with the staff and still cooked for the general. He had cooked for him in Lombardy through the whole campaign; on the march to Rome he had lassoed his beef in the Campagna after the American manner; he had been wounded in the defense of the Roman Republic; he was one of the four fugitives who, with the general, carried out of the woods the inanimate body of the general's wife into the farmhouse where she died, exhausted by the hardships of that terrible retreat. He had survived that disastrous time to attend his general in Palermo when the Neapolitan shells from the castle crashed upon the town. He had cooked for him on the field of Volturno after fighting all day. And everywhere he had seen Englishmen in the front rank of the army of freedom. He respected their nation because they loved Garibaldi. Their very countesses and princesses had kissed the general's hands in London, it was said. He could well believe it; for the nation was noble, and the man was a saint. It was enough to look once at his face to see the divine force of faith in him and his great pity for all that was poor, suffering, and oppressed in this world.

The spirit of self-forgetfulness, the simple devotion to a vast humanitarian idea which inspired the thought and stress of that revolutionary time, had left its mark upon Giorgio in a sort of austere contempt for all personal advantage. This man, whom the lowest class in Sulaco suspected of having a buried hoard in his kitchen, had all his life despised money. The leaders of his youth had lived poor, had died poor. It had been a habit of his mind to disregard tomorrow. It was engendered partly by an existence of excitement, adventure, and wild warfare. But mostly it was a matter of principle. It did not resemble the carelessness of a *condottiere*, it was a puritanism of religion.

This stern devotion to a cause had cast a gloom upon Giorgio's old age. It cast a gloom because the cause seemed lost. Too many kings and emperors flourished yet in the world which God had meant for the people. He was sad because of his simplicity. Though always ready to help his countrymen, and greatly respected by the Italian emigrants wherever he lived (in his exile he called it), he could not conceal from himself that they cared nothing for the wrongs of down-trodden nations. They listened to his tales of war readily, but seemed to ask themselves what he had got out of it after all. There was nothing that they could see. "We wanted nothing, we suffered for the love of all humanity!" he cried out furiously sometimes, and the powerful voice, the blazing eyes, the shaking of the white mane, the brown, sinewy hand pointing upwards as if to call heaven to witness, impressed his hearers. After the old man had broken off abruptly with a jerk of the head and a movement of the arm, meaning clearly, "But what's the good of talking to you?" they nudged each other. There was in old Giorgio an energy of feeling, a personal quality of conviction, something they called *"terribilita"*—"an old lion," they used to say of him. Some slight incident, a chance word, would set him off talking on the beach to the Italian fishermen of Maldonado; in the little shop he kept afterwards (in Valparaiso) to his countrymen customers; of an evening, suddenly, in the café at one end of the Casa Viola (the other was reserved for the English engineers) to the select clientele of engine-drivers and foremen of the railway shops.

With their handsome, bronzed, lean faces, shiny black ringlets, glistening eyes, broad-chested, bearded, sometimes a tiny gold ring in the lobe of the ear, the aristocracy of the railway works listened to him, turning away from their cards or dominoes. Here and there a fair-haired Basque studied his hand meantime, waiting without protest. No native of Costaguana intruded there. This was the Italian stronghold. Even the Sulaco policemen on a night patrol let their horses pace softly by, bending low in the saddle to glance through the window at the heads in a fog of smoke; and the drone of old Giorgio's declamatory narrative seemed to sink behind them into the plain. Only now and then the assistant of the chief of police, some broad-faced, brown little gentleman, with a great deal of Indian in him, would put in an appearance. Leaving his man outside with the horses he advanced with a confident, sly smile, and without a word up to the long trestle table. He pointed to one of the bottles on the shelf; Giorgio, thrusting his pipe into his mouth abruptly, served him in person. Nothing would be heard but the slight jingle of the spurs. His glass emptied, he would take a leisurely, scrutinizing look all round the room, go out, and ride away slowly, circling towards the town.

V

In this way only was the power of the local authorities vindicated amongst the great body of strong-limbed foreigners who dug the earth, blasted the rocks, drove the engines for the "progressive and patriotic undertaking." In these very words eighteen months before the Excellentissimo Señor don Vincente Ribiera, the Dictator of Costaguana, had described the National Central Railway in his great speech at the turning of the first sod.

He had come on purpose to Sulaco, and there was a one-o'clock dinner-party, a *convité* offered by the O.S.N. Company on board the *Juno* after the function on shore. Captain Mitchell had himself steered the cargo lighter, all draped with flags, which, in tow of the *Juno*'s steam launch, took the Excellentissimo from the jetty to the ship. Everybody of note in Sulaco had been invited—the one or two foreign merchants, all the representatives of the old Spanish families then in town, the great owners of estates on the plain, grave, courteous, simple men, *caballeros* of pure descent, with small hands and feet, conservative, hospitable, and kind. The Occidental Province was their stronghold; their Blanco party had triumphed now; it was their President-Dictator, a Blanco of the Blancos, who sat smiling urbanely between the representatives of two friendly foreign powers. They had come with him from Sta Marta to countenance by their presence the enterprise in which the capital of their countries was engaged.

The only lady of that company was Mrs. Gould, the wife of Don Carlos, the administrator of the San Tomé silver mine. The ladies of Sulaco were not advanced enough to take part in the public life to that extent. They had come out strongly at the great ball at the Intendencia the evening before, but Mrs. Gould alone had appeared, a bright spot in the group of black coats behind the President-Dictator, on the crimson cloth-covered stage erected under a shady tree on the shore of the harbor, where the ceremony of turning the first sod had taken place. She had come off in the cargo lighter, full of notabilities, sitting under the flutter of gay flags, in the place of honor by the side of Captain Mitchell, who steered, and her clear dress gave the only truly festive note to the somber gathering in the long, gorgeous saloon of the *Juno*.

The head of the chairman of the railway board (from London), handsome and pale in a silvery mist of white hair and clipped beard, hovered near her shoulder attentive, smiling, and fatigued. The journey from London to Sta Marta in mail boats and the special carriages of the Sta Marta coast-line (the only railway so far) had been tolerable—even pleasant—quite tolerable. But the trip over the mountains to Sulaco was another sort of experience, in an old *diligencia* over impassable roads skirting awful precipices.

"We have been upset twice in one day on the brink of very deep ravines," he was telling Mrs. Gould in an undertone. "And when we arrived here at last I don't know what we should have done without your hospitality. What an out-of-the-way place Sulaco is!—and for a harbor, too! Astonishing!"

"Ah, but we are very proud of it. It used to be historically important. The highest ecclesiastical court, for two viceroyalties, sat here in the olden time," she instructed him with animation.

"I am impressed. I didn't mean to be disparaging. You seem very patriotic."

"The place is lovable, if only by its situation. Perhaps you don't know what an old resident I am."

"How old, I wonder," he murmured, looking at her with a slight smile. Mrs. Gould's appearance was made youthful by the mobile intelligence of her face. "We can't give you your ecclesiastical court back again; but you shall have more steamers, a railway, a telegraph-cable—a future in the great world which is worth infinitely more than any amount of ecclesiastical past. You shall be brought in touch with something greater than two viceroyalties. But I had no notion that a place on a sea-coast could remain so isolated from the world. If it had been a thousand miles inland now—most remarkable! Has anything ever happened here for a hundred years before today?"

While he talked in a slow, humorous tone, she kept her little smile. Agreeing ironically, she assured him that certainly not—nothing ever happened in Sulaco. Even the revolutions, of which there had been two in her time, had respected the repose of the place. Their course ran in the more populous southern parts of the Republic, and in the great valley of Sta Marta, which was like one great battlefield of the parties, with the possession of the capital for a prize and an outlet to another ocean. They were more advanced over there. Here in Sulaco they heard only the echoes of these great questions, and, of course, their official world changed each time, coming to them over their rampart of mountains which he himself had traversed in an old *diligencia*, with such a risk to life and limb.

The chairman of the railway had been enjoying her hospitality for several days, and he was really grateful for it. It was only since he had left Sta Marta that he had utterly lost touch with the feeling of European life on the background of his exotic surroundings. In the capital he had been the guest of the Legation, and had been kept busy negotiating with the members of Don Vincente's Government—cultured men, men to whom the conditions of civilized business were not unknown.

What concerned him most at the time was the acquisition of land for the railway. In the Sta Marta Valley, where there was already one line in existence, the people were tractable, and it was only a matter of price. A commission had been nominated to fix the values, and the difficulty resolved itself into the judicious influencing of the Commissioners. But in Sulaco—the Occidental Province for whose very development the railway was intended—there had been trouble. It had been lying for ages ensconced behind its natural barriers, repelling modern enterprise by the precipices of its mountain range, by its shallow harbor opening into the everlasting calms of a gulf full of clouds, by the benighted state of mind of the owners of its fertile territory—all these aristocratic old Spanish families, all these Don Ambrosios this and Don Fernandos that, who seemed actually to dislike and distrust the coming of the railway over their lands. It had happened that some of the surveying parties scattered all over the province had been warned off with threats of violence. In other cases outrageous pretensions as to price had been raised. But the man of railways prided himself on being equal to every emergency. Since he was met by the inimical sentiment of blind conservatism in Sulaco he would meet it by sentiment, too, before taking his stand on his right alone. The Government was bound to carry out its part of the contract with the board of the new railway company, even if it had to use force for the purpose. But he desired nothing less than an armed disturbance in the smooth working of his plans. They were much too vast and far reaching, and too promising to leave a stone unturned; and so he imagined to get the President-Dictator over there on a tour of ceremonies and speeches, culminating in a great function at the turning of the first sod by the harbor shore. After all he was their own creature—that Don Vincente. He was the embodied triumph of the best elements in the State. These were facts, and, unless facts meant nothing, Sir John argued to himself, such a man's influence must be real, and his personal action would produce the conciliatory effect he required. He had succeeded in arranging the trip with the help of a very clever advocate, who was known in Sta Marta as the agent of the Gould silver mine, the biggest thing in Sulaco, and even in the whole Republic. It was indeed a fabulously rich mine. Its so-called agent, evidently a man of culture and ability, seemed, without official position, to possess an extraordinary influence in the highest Government spheres. He was able to assure Sir John that the President-Dictator would make the journey. He regretted, however, in the course of the same conversation, that General Montero insisted upon going, too.

General Montero, whom the beginning of the struggle had found an obscure army captain employed on the wild eastern frontier of the State, had thrown in his lot with the Ribiera party at a moment when special circumstances had given that small adhesion a fortuitous importance. The fortunes of war served him marvelously, and the victory of Rio Seco (after a day of desperate fighting) put a seal to his success. At the end he emerged General, Minister of War, and the military head of the Blanco party, although there was nothing aristocratic in his descent. Indeed, it was said that he and his brother, orphans, had been brought up by the munificence of a famous European traveler, in whose service their father had lost his life. Another story was that their father had been nothing but a charcoal burner in the woods, and their mother a baptized Indian woman from the far interior.

However that might be, the Costaguana Press was in the habit of styling Montero's forest march from his commandancia to join the Blanco forces at the beginning of the troubles, the "most heroic military exploit of modern times." About the same time, too, his brother had turned up from Europe, where he had gone apparently as secretary to a consul. Having, however, collected a small band of outlaws, he showed some talent as guerrilla chief and had been rewarded at the pacification by the post of Military Commandant of the capital.

The Minister of War, then, accompanied the Dictator. The board of the O.S.N. Company, working hand-in-hand with the railway people for the good of the Republic, had on this important occasion instructed Captain Mitchell to put the mailboat *Juno* at the disposal of the distinguished party. Don Vincente, journeying south from Sta Marta, had embarked at Cayta, the principal port of Costaguana, and came to Sulaco by sea. But the chairman of the railway company had courageously crossed the mountains in a ramshackle *diligencia*, mainly for the purpose of meeting his engineer-in-chief engaged in the final survey of the road.

For all the indifference of a man of affairs to nature, whose hostility can always be overcome by the resources of finance, he could not help being impressed by his surroundings during his halt at the surveying camp established at the highest point his railway was to reach. He spent the night there, arriving just too late to see the last dying glow of sunlight upon the snowy flank of Higuerota. Pillared masses of black basalt framed like an open portal a portion of the white field lying aslant against the west. In the transparent air of the high altitudes everything seemed very near, steeped in a clear stillness as in an imponderable liquid; and with his ear ready to catch the first sound of the expected *diligencia* the engineer-in-chief, at the door of a hut of rough stones, had contemplated the changing hues on the enormous side of the mountain, thinking that in this sight, as in a piece of inspired music, there could be found together the utmost delicacy of shaded expression and a stupendous magnificence of effect.

Sir John arrived too late to hear the magnificent and inaudible strain sung by the sunset amongst the high peaks of the Sierra. It had sung itself out into the breathless pause of deep dusk before, climbing down the fore wheel of the *diligencia* with stiff limbs, he shook hands with the engineer.

They gave him his dinner in a stone hut like a cubical boulder, with no door or windows in its two openings; a bright fire of sticks (brought on muleback from the first valley below) burning outside sent in a wavering glare; and two candles in tin candlesticks lighted, it was explained to him, in his honor—stood on a sort of rough camp table, at which he sat on the right hand of the chief. He knew how to be amiable; and the young men of the engineering staff, for whom the surveying of the railway track had the glamour of the first steps on the path of life, sat there, too, listening modestly, with their smooth faces tanned by the weather, and very pleased to witness so much affability in so great a man.

Afterwards, late at night, pacing to and fro outside, he had a long talk with his chief engineer. He knew him well of old. This was not the first undertaking in which their gifts, as elementally different as fire and water, had worked in conjunction. From the contact of these two personalities, who had not the same vision of the world, there was generated a power for the world's service—a subtle force that could set in motion mighty machines, men's muscles, and awaken also in human breasts an unbounded devotion to the task. Of the young fellows at the table, to whom the survey of the track was like the tracing of the path of life, more than one would be called to meet death before the work was done. But the work would be done: the force would be almost as strong as a faith. Not quite, however. In the silence of the sleeping camp upon the moonlit plateau forming the top of the pass like the floor of a vast arena surrounded by the basalt walls of precipices, two strolling figures in thick ulsters stood still, and the voice of the engineer pronounced distinctly the words:

"We can't move mountains!"

Sir John, raising his head to follow the pointing gesture, felt the full force of the words. The white Higuerota soared out of the shadows of rock and earth like a frozen bubble under the moon. All was still, till near by, behind the wall of a corral for the camp animals, built roughly of loose stones in the form of a circle, a pack mule stamped his forefoot and blew heavily twice.

The engineer-in-chief had used the phrase in answer to the chairman's tentative suggestion that the tracing of the line could, perhaps, be altered in deference to the prejudices of the Sulaco landowners. The chief engineer believed that the obstinacy of men was the lesser obstacle. Moreover, to combat that they had the great influence of Charles Gould, whereas tunneling under Higuerota would have been a colossal under-taking.

"Ah, yes! Gould. What sort of a man is he?"

Sir John had heard much of Charles Gould in Sta Marta, and wanted to know more. The engineer-in-chief assured him that the administrator of the San Tomé silver mine had an immense influence over all these Spanish Dons. He had also one of the best houses in Sulaco, and the Gould hospitality was beyond all praise.

"They received me as if they had known me for years," he said. "The little lady is kindness personified. I stayed with them for a month. He helped me to organize the surveying parties. His practical ownership of the San Tomé silver mine gives him a special position. He seems to have the ear of every provincial authority apparently, and, as I said, he can wind all the *hidalgos* of the province round his little finger. If you follow his advice the difficulties will fall away, because he wants the railway. Of course, you must be careful in what you say. He's English, and besides he must be immensely wealthy. The Holroyd house is in with him in that mine, so you may imagine—"

He interrupted himself as, from before one of the little fires burning outside the low wall of the corral, arose the figure of a man wrapped in a poncho up to the neck. The saddle which he had been using for a pillow made a dark patch on the ground against the red glow of embers.

"I shall see Holroyd himself on my way back through the States," said Sir John. "I've ascertained that he, too, wants the railway."

The man who, perhaps disturbed by the proximity of the voices, had arisen from the ground, struck a match to light a cigarette. The flame showed a bronzed, black-whiskered face, a pair of eyes gazing straight; then, rearranging his wrappings, he sank full length and laid his head again on the saddle.

"That's our camp-master, whom I must send back to Sulaco now we are going to carry our survey into the Sta Marta Valley," said the engineer. "A most useful fellow, lent me by Captain Mitchell of the O.S.N. Company. It was very good of Mitchell. Charles Gould told me I couldn't do better than take advantage of the offer. He seems to know how to rule all these muleteers and peons. We had not the slightest trouble with our people. He shall escort your *diligencia* right into Sulaco with some of our railway peons. The road is bad. To have him at hand may save you an upset or two. He promised me to take care of your person all the way down as if you were his father."

This camp-master was the Italian sailor whom all the Europeans in Sulaco, following Captain Mitchell's mispronunciation, were in the habit of calling Nostromo. And indeed, taciturn and ready, he did take excellent care of his charge at the bad parts of the road, as Sir John himself acknowledged to Mrs. Gould afterwards.

V I

At that time Nostromo had been already long enough in the country to raise to the highest pitch Captain Mitchell's opinion of the extraordinary value of his discovery. Clearly he was one of those invaluable subordinates whom to possess is a legitimate cause of boasting. Captain Mitchell plumed himself upon his eye for men—but he was not selfish—and in the innocence of his pride was already developing that mania for "lending you my Capataz de Cargadores" which was to bring Nostromo into personal contact, sooner or later, with every European in Sulaco, as a sort of universal factotum —a prodigy of efficiency in his own sphere of life.

"The fellow is devoted to me, body and soul!" Captain Mitchell was given to affirm; and though nobody, perhaps, could have explained why it should be so, it was impossible on a survey of their relation to throw doubt on that statement, unless, indeed, one were a bitter, eccentric character like Dr. Monygham—for instance— whose short, hopeless laugh expressed somehow an immense mistrust of mankind. Not that Dr. Monygham was a prodigal either of laughter or of words. He was bitterly taciturn when at his best. At his worst people feared the open scornfulness of his tongue. Only Mrs. Gould could keep his unbelief in men's motives within due bounds; but even to her (on an occasion not connected with Nostromo, and in a tone which for him was gentle), even to her, he had said once, "Really, it is most unreasonable to demand that a man should think of other people so much better than he is able to think of himself."

And Mrs. Gould had hastened to drop the subject. There were strange rumors of the English doctor. Years ago, in the time of Guzman Bento, he had been mixed up, it was whispered, in a conspiracy which was betrayed and as people expressed it, drowned in blood. His hair had turned gray, his hairless, seamed face was of a brick-dust color; the large check pattern of his flannel shirt and his old stained Panama hat were an established defiance to the conventionalities of Sulaco. Had it not been for the immaculate cleanliness of his apparel he might have been taken for one of those shiftless Europeans that are a moral eyesore to the respectability of a foreign colony in almost every exotic part of the world. The young ladies of Sulaco, adorning with clusters of pretty faces the balconies along the Street of the Constitution, when they saw him pass, with his limping gait and bowed head, a short linen jacket drawn on carelessly over the flannel check shirt, would remark to each other, "Here is the Señor Doctor going to call on Doña Emilia. He has got his little coat on." The inference was true. Its deeper meaning was hidden from their simple intelligence. Moreover, they expended no store of thought on the doctor. He was old, ugly, learned—and a little *loco* —mad, if not a bit of a sorcerer, as the common people suspected him of being. The little white jacket was in reality a concession to Mrs. Gould's humanizing influence. The doctor, with his habit of skeptical, bitter speech, had no other means of showing his profound respect for the character of the woman who was known in the country as the English Señora. He presented this tribute very seriously indeed; it was no trifle for a man of his habits. Mrs. Gould felt that, too, perfectly. She would never have thought of imposing upon him this marked show of deference.

She kept her old Spanish house (one of the finest specimens in Sulaco) open for the dispensation of the small graces of existence. She dispensed them with simplicity and charm because she was guided by an alert perception of values. She was highly gifted in the art of human intercourse which consists in delicate shades of self-forgetfulness and in the suggestion of universal comprehension. Charles Gould (the Gould family, established in Costaguana for three generations, always went to England for their education and for their wives) imagined that he had fallen in love with a girl's sound common sense like any other man, but these were not exactly the reasons why, for instance, the whole surveying camp, from the youngest of the young men to their mature chief, should have found occasion to allude to Mrs. Gould's house so frequently amongst the high peaks of the Sierra. She would have protested that she had done nothing for them, with a low laugh and a surprised widening of her gray eyes, had anybody told her how convincingly she was remembered on the edge of the snow-line above Sulaco. But directly, with a little capable air of setting her wits to work, she would have found an explanation. "Of course, it was such a surprise for these boys to find any sort of welcome here. And I suppose they are homesick. I suppose everybody must be always just a little homesick."

She was always sorry for homesick people.

Born in the country, as his father before him, spare and tall, with a flaming mustache, a neat chin, clear blue eyes, auburn hair, and a thin, fresh, red face, Charles Gould looked like a new arrival from over the sea. His grandfather had fought in the cause of independence under Bolívar, in that famous English legion which on the battlefield of Carabobo had been saluted by the great Liberator as Saviors of his country. One of Charles Gould's uncles had been the elected President of that very province of Sulaco (then called a State) in the days of Federation, and afterwards had been put up against the wall of a church and shot by the order of the barbarous Unionist general, Guzman Bento. It was the same Guzman Bento who, becoming later Perpetual President, famed for his ruthless and cruel tyranny, reached his apotheosis in the popular legend of a sanguinary land-haunting specter whose body had been carried off by the devil in person from the brick mausoleum in the nave of the Church of Assumption in Sta Marta. Thus, at least, the priests explained its disappearance to the barefooted multitude that streamed in, awestruck, to gaze at the hole in the side of the ugly box of bricks before the great altar.

Guzman Bento of cruel memory had put to death great numbers of people besides Charles Gould's uncle; but with a relative martyred in the cause of aristocracy, the Sulaco Oligarchs (this was the phraseology of Guzman Bento's time; now they were called Blancos, and had given up the federal idea), which meant the families of pure Spanish descent, considered Charles as one of themselves. With such a family record, no one could be more of a Costaguanero than Don Carlos Gould; but his aspect was so characteristic that in the talk of common people he was just the *Inglés*—the Englishman of Sulaco. He looked more English than a casual tourist, a sort of heretic pilgrim, however, quite unknown in Sulaco. He looked more English than the last arrived batch of young railway engineers, than anybody out of the hunting-field pictures in the numbers of *Punch* reaching his wife's drawing-room two months or so after date. It astonished you to hear him talk Spanish (Castillan, as the natives say) or the Indian dialect of the country-people so naturally. His accent had never been English; but there was something so indelible in all these ancestral Goulds—liberators, explorers, coffee planters, merchants, revolutionists—of Costaguana, that he, the only representative of the third generation in a continent possessing its own style of horsemanship, went on looking thoroughly English even on horseback. This is not said of him in the mocking spirit of the *llaneros*—men of the great plains—who think that no one in the world knows how to sit a horse but themselves. Charles Gould, to use the suitably lofty phrase, rode like a centaur. Riding for him was not a special form of exercise; it was a natural faculty, as walking straight is to all men sound of mind and limb; but, all the same, when cantering beside the rutty ox-cart track to the mine he looked in his English clothes and with his imported saddlery as though he had come this moment to Costaguana at his easy swift *pasotrote*, straight out of some green meadow at the other side of the world.

His way would lie along the old Spanish road—the Camino Real of popular speech—the only remaining vestige of a fact and name left by that royalty old Giorgio Viola hated, and whose very shadow had departed from the land; for the big equestrian statue of Charles IV at the entrance of the alameda, towering white against the trees, was only known to the folk from the country and to the beggars of the town that slept on the steps around the pedestal, as the Horse of Stone. The other Carlos, turning off to the left with a rapid clatter of hoofs on the disjointed pavement—Don Carlos Gould, in his English clothes, looked as incongruous, but much more at home than the kingly cavalier reining in his steed on the pedestal above the sleeping *leperos*, with his marble arm raised towards the marble rim of a plumed hat.

The weather-stained effigy of the mounted king, with its vague suggestion of a saluting gesture, seemed to present an inscrutable breast to the political changes which had robbed it of its very name; but neither did the other horseman, well known to the people, keen and alive on his well-shaped, slate-colored beast with a white eye, wear his heart on the sleeve of his English coat. His mind preserved its steady poise as if sheltered in the passionless stability of private and public decencies at home in Europe. He accepted with a like calm the shocking manner in which the Sulaco ladies smothered their faces with pearl powder till they looked like white plaster casts with beautiful living eyes, the peculiar gossip of the town, and the continuous political changes, the constant "saving of the country," which to his wife seemed a puerile and bloodthirsty game of murder and rapine played with terrible earnestness by depraved children. In the early days of her Costaguana life, the little lady used to clench her hands with exasperation at not being able to take the public affairs of the country as seriously as the incidental atrocity of methods deserved. She saw in them a comedy of naïve pretenses, but hardly anything genuine except her own appalled indignation. Charles, very quiet and twisting his long mustaches, would decline to discuss them at all. Once, however, he observed to her gently:

"My dear, you seem to forget that I was born here."

These few words made her pause as if they had been a sudden revelation. Perhaps the mere fact of being born in the country did make a difference. She had a great confidence in her husband; it had always been very great. He had struck her imagination from the first by his unsentimentalism, by that very quietude of mind which she had erected in her thought for a sign of perfect competency in the business of living. Don José Avellanos, their neighbor across the street, a statesman, a poet, a man of culture, who had represented his country at several European Courts (and had suffered untold indignities as a state prisoner in the time of the tyrant Guzman Bento), used to declare in Doña Emilia's drawing-room that Carlos had all the English qualities of character with a truly patriotic heart.

Mrs. Gould, raising her eyes to her husband's thin, red and tan face, could not detect the slightest quiver of a feature at what he must have heard said of his patriotism. Perhaps he had just dismounted on his return from the mine; he was English enough to disregard the hottest hours of the day. Basilio, in a livery of white linen and a red sash, had squatted for a moment behind his heels to unstrap the heavy, blunt spurs in the patio; and then the Señor Administrator would go up the staircase into the gallery. Rows of plants in pots, ranged on the balustrade between the pilasters of the arches, screened the *corredor* with their leaves and flowers from the quadrangle below, whose paved space is the true hearthstone of a South American house, where the quiet hours of domestic life are marked by the shifting of light and shadow on the flagstones.

Señor Avellanos was in the habit of crossing the patio at five o'clock almost every day. Don José chose to come over at teatime because the English rite at Doña Emilia's house reminded him of the time when he lived in London as Minister Plenipotentiary to the Court of St. James. He did not like tea; and, usually, rocking his American chair, his neat little shiny boots crossed on the foot-rest, he would talk on and on with a sort of complacent virtuosity wonderful in a man of his age, while he held the cup in his hands for a long time. His close-cropped head was perfectly white; his eyes coal-black.

On seeing Charles Gould step into the *sala* he would nod provisionally and go on to the end of the oratorical period. Only then he would say:

"Carlos, my friend, you have ridden from San Tomé in the heat of the day. Always the true English activity. No? What?"

He drank up all the tea at once in one draught. This performance was invariably followed by a slight shudder and a low, involuntary "br-r-r-r," which was not covered by the hasty exclamation, "Excellent!"

Then giving up the empty cup into his young friend's hand, extended with a smile, he continued to expatiate upon the patriotic nature of the San Tomé mine for the simple pleasure of talking fluently, it seemed, while his reclining body jerked backwards and forwards in a rocking-chair of the sort exported from the United States. The ceiling of the largest drawing-room of the Casa Gould extended its white level far above his head. The loftiness dwarfed the mixture of heavy, straight-backed Spanish chairs of brown wood with leathern seats, and European furniture, low, and cushioned all over, like squat little monsters gorged to bursting with steel springs and horsehair. There were knick-knacks on little tables, mirrors let into the wall above marble consoles, square spaces of carpet under the two groups of armchairs, each presided over by a deep sofa; smaller rugs scattered all over the floor of red tiles; three windows from ceiling down to the ground, opening on a balcony, and flanked by the perpendicular folds of the dark hangings. The stateliness of ancient days lingered between the four high, smooth walls, tinted a delicate primrose-color; and Mrs. Gould, with her little head and shining coils of hair, sitting in a cloud of muslin and lace before a slender mahogany table, resembled a fairy posed lightly before dainty philters dispensed out of vessels of silver and porcelain.

Mrs. Gould knew the history of the San Tomé mine. Worked in the early days mostly by means of lashes on the backs of slaves, its yield had been paid for in its own weight of human bones. Whole tribes of Indians had perished in the exploitation; and then the mine was abandoned, since with this primitive method it had ceased to make a profitable return, no matter how many corpses were thrown into its maw. Then it became forgotten. It was rediscovered after the War of Independence. An English company obtained the right to work it, and found so rich a vein that neither the exactions of successive governments, nor the periodical raids of recruiting officers upon the population of paid miners they had created, could discourage their perseverance. But in the end, during the long turmoil of *pronunciamientos* that followed the death of the famous Guzman Bento, the native miners, incited to revolt by the emissaries sent out from the capital, had risen upon their English chiefs and murdered them to a man. The decree of confiscation which appeared immediately afterwards in the *Diario Oficial*, published in Sta Marta, began with the words:

> Justly incensed at the grinding oppression of foreigners, actuated by sordid motives of gain rather than by love for a country where they come impoverished to seek their fortunes, the mining population of San Tomé, etc. . . .

and ended with the declaration:

> The chief of the State has resolved to exercise to the full his power of clemency. The mine, which by every law, international, human, and divine, reverts now to the Government as national property, shall remain closed till the sword drawn for the sacred defense of liberal principles has accomplished its mission of securing the happiness of our beloved country.

And for many years this was the last of the San Tomé mine. What advantage that Government had expected from the spoliation, it is impossible to tell now. Costaguana was made with difficulty to pay a beggarly money compensation to the families of the victims, and then the matter dropped out of diplomatic dispatches. But afterwards another Government bethought itself of that valuable asset. It was an ordinary Costaguana Government—the fourth in six years—but it judged of its opportunities sanely. It remembered the San Tomé mine with a secret conviction of its worthlessness in their own hands, but with an ingenious insight into the various uses a silver mine can be put to, apart from the sordid process of extracting the metal from under the ground. The father of Charles Gould, for a long time one of the most wealthy merchants of Costaguana, had already lost a considerable part of his fortune in forced loans to the successive Governments. He was a man of calm judgment, who never dreamed of pressing his claims; and when, suddenly, the perpetual concession of the San Tomé mine was offered to him in full settlement, his alarm became extreme. He was versed in the ways of Governments. Indeed, the intention of this affair, though no doubt deeply meditated in the closet, lay open on the surface of the document presented urgently for his signature. The third and most important clause stipulated that the concession-holder should pay at once to the Government five years' royalties on the estimated output of the mine.

Mr. Gould, senior, defended himself from this fatal favor with many arguments and entreaties, but without success. He knew nothing of mining; he had no means to put his concession on the European market; the mine as a working concern did not exist. The buildings had been burst down, the mining plant had been destroyed, the mining population had disappeared from the neighborhood years and years ago; the very road had vanished under a flood of tropical vegetation as effectually as if swallowed by the sea; and the main gallery had fallen in within a hundred yards from the entrance. It was no longer an abandoned mine; it was a wild, inaccessible, and rocky gorge of the Sierra, where vestiges of charred timber, some heaps of smashed bricks, and a few shapeless pieces of rusty iron could have been found under the matted mass of thorny creepers covering the ground. Mr. Gould, senior, did not desire the perpetual possession of that desolate locality; in fact, the mere vision of it arising before his mind in the still watches of the night had the power to exasperate him into hours of hot and agitated insomnia.

It so happened, however, that the Finance Minister of the time was a man to whom, in years gone by, Mr. Gould had, unfortunately, declined to grant some small pecuniary assistance, basing his refusal on the ground that the applicant was a notorious gambler and cheat, besides being more than half suspected of a robbery with violence on a wealthy *ranchero* in a remote country district, where he was actually exercising the function of a judge. Now, after reaching his exalted position, that politician had proclaimed his intention to repay evil with good to Señor Gould—the poor man. He affirmed and reaffirmed this resolution in the drawing-rooms of Sta Marta, in a soft and implacable voice, and with such malicious glances that Mr. Gould's best friends advised him earnestly to attempt no bribery to get the matter dropped. It would have been useless. Indeed, it would not have been a very safe proceeding. Such was also the opinion of a stout, loud-voiced lady of French extraction, the daughter, she said, of an officer of high rank (*officier supérieur de l'armée*), who was accommodated with lodgings within the walls of a secularized convent next door to the Ministry of Finance. That florid person, when approached on behalf of Mr. Gould in a proper manner, and with a suitable present, shook her head despondently. She was good-natured, and her despondency was genuine. She imagined she could not take money in consideration of something she could not accomplish. The friend of Mr. Gould, charged with the delicate mission, used to say afterwards that she was the only honest person closely or remotely connected with the Government he had ever met. "No go," she had said with a cavalier, husky intonation which was natural to her, and using turns of expression more suitable to a child of parents unknown than to the orphaned daughter of a general officer. "No; it's no go. *Pas moyen, mon garçon. C'est dommage, tout de même. Ah! zut! Je ne vole pas mon monde. Je ne suis pas ministre—moi! Vous pouvez emporter votre petit sac.*"

For a moment, biting her carmine lip, she deplored inwardly the tyranny of the rigid principles governing the sale of her influence in high places. Then, significantly, and with a touch of impatience, *"Allez,"* she added, *"et dites bien à votre bonhomme— entendez-vous?—qu'il faut avaler la pilule."*

After such a warning there was nothing for it but to sign and pay. Mr. Gould had swallowed the pill, and it was as though it had been compounded of some subtle poison that acted directly on his brain. He became at once mine-ridden, and as he was well read in light literature it took to his mind the form of the Old Man of the Sea fastened upon his shoulders. He also began to dream of vampires. Mr. Gould exaggerated to himself the disadvantages of his new position, because he viewed it emotionally. His position in Costaguana was no worse than before. But man is a desperately conservative creature, and the extravagant novelty of this outrage upon his purse distressed his sensibilities. Everybody around him was being robbed by the grotesque and murderous bands that played their game of governments and revolutions after the death of Guzman Bento. His experience had taught him that, however short the plunder might fall of their legitimate expectations, no gang in possession of the Presidential Palace would be so incompetent as to suffer itself to be baffled by the want of a pretext. The first casual colonel of the barefooted army of scarecrows that came along was able to expose with force and precision to any mere civilian his titles to a sum of ten thousand dollars; the while his hope would be immutably fixed upon a gratuity, at any rate, of no less than a thousand. Mr. Gould knew that very well, and, armed with resignation, had waited for better times. But to be robbed under the forms of legality and business was intolerable to his imagination. Mr. Gould, the father, had one fault in his sagacious and honorable character: he attached too much importance to form. It is a failing common to mankind, whose views are tinged by prejudices. There was for him in that affair a malignancy of perverted justice which, by means of a moral shock, attacked his vigorous physique. "It will end by killing me," he used to affirm many times a day. And, in fact, since that time he began to suffer from fever, from liver pains, and mostly from a worrying inability to think of anything else. The Finance Minister could have formed no conception of the profound subtlety of his revenge. Even Mr. Gould's letters to his fourteen-year-old boy Charles, then away in England for his education, came at last to talk of practically nothing but the mine. He groaned over the injustice, the persecution, the outrage of that mine; he occupied whole pages in the exposition of the fatal consequences attaching to the possession of that mine from every point of view, with every dismal inference, with words of horror at the apparently eternal character of that curse. For the Concession had been granted to him and his descendants for ever. He implored his son never to return to Costaguana, never to claim any part of his inheritance there, because it was tainted by the infamous Concession; never to touch it, never to approach it, to forget that America existed, and pursue a mercantile career in Europe. And each letter ended with bitter self-reproaches for having stayed too long in that cavern of thieves, intriguers, and brigands.

To be told repeatedly that one's future is blighted because of the possession of a silver mine is not, at the age of fourteen, a matter of prime importance as to its main statement; but in its form it is calculated to excite a certain amount of wonder and attention. In course of time the boy, at first only puzzled by the angry jeremiads, but rather sorry for his dad, began to turn the matter over in his mind in such moments as he could spare from play and study. In about a year he had evolved from the lecture of the letters a definite conviction that there was a silver mine in the Sulaco province of the Republic of Costaguana, where poor Uncle Harry had been shot by soldiers a great many years before. There was also connected closely with that mine a thing called the "iniquitous Gould Concession," apparently written on a paper which his father desired ardently to "tear and fling into the faces" of presidents, members of judicature, and ministers of State. And this desire persisted, though the names of these people, he noticed, seldom remained the same for a whole year together. This desire (since the thing was iniquitous) seemed quite natural to the boy, though why the affair was iniquitous he did not know. Afterwards, with advancing wisdom, he managed to clear the plain truth of the business from the fantastic intrusions of the Old Man of the Sea, vampires, and ghouls, which had lent to his father's correspondence the flavor of a gruesome Arabian Nights tale. In the end, the growing youth attained to as close an intimacy with the San Tomé mine as the old man who wrote these plaintive and enraged letters on the other side of the sea. He had been made several times already to pay heavy fines for neglecting to work the mine, he reported, besides other sums extracted from him on account of future royalties, on the ground that a man with such a valuable concession in his pocket could not refuse his financial assistance to the Government of the Republic. The last of his fortune was passing away from him against worthless receipts, he wrote, in a rage, whilst he was being pointed out as an individual who had known how to secure enormous advantages from the necessities of his country. And the young man in Europe grew more and more interested in that thing which could provoke such a tumult of words and passion.

He thought of it every day; but he thought of it without bitterness. It might have been an unfortunate affair for his poor dad, and the whole story threw a queer light upon the social and political life of Costaguana. The view he took of it was sympathetic to his father, yet calm and reflective. His personal feelings had not been outraged, and it is difficult to resent with proper and durable indignation the physical or mental anguish of another organism, even if that other organism is one's own father. By the time he was twenty Charles Gould had, in his turn, fallen under the spell of the San Tomé mine. But it was another form of enchantment, more suitable to his youth, into whose magic formula there entered hope, vigor, and self-confidence, instead of weary indignation and despair. Left after he was twenty to his own guidance (except for the severe injunction not to return to Costaguana), he had pursued his studies in Belgium and France with the idea of qualifying for a mining engineer. But this scientific aspect of his labors remained vague and imperfect in his mind. Mines had acquired for him a dramatic interest. He studied their peculiarities from a personal point of view, too, as one would study the varied characters of men. He visited them as one goes with curiosity to call upon remarkable persons. He visited mines in Germany, in Spain, in Cornwall. Abandoned workings had for him strong fascination. Their desolation appealed to him like the sight of human misery, whose causes are varied and profound. They might have been worthless, but also they might have been misunderstood. His future wife was the first, and perhaps the only person to detect this secret mood which governed the profoundly sensible, almost voiceless attitude of this man towards the world of material things. And at once her delight in him, lingering with half-open wings like those birds that cannot rise easily from a flat level, found a pinnacle from which to soar up into the skies.

They had become acquainted in Italy, where the future Mrs. Gould was staying with an old and pale aunt who, years before, had married a middle-aged, impoverished Italian marquis. She now mourned that man, who had known how to give up his life to the independence and unity of his country, who had known how to be as enthusiastic in his generosity as the youngest of those who fell for that very cause of which old Giorgio Viola was a drifting relic, as a broken spar is suffered to float away disregarded after a naval victory. The Marchesa led a still, whispering existence, nun-like in her black robes and a white band over the forehead, in a corner of the first floor of an ancient and ruinous palace, whose big, empty halls downstairs sheltered under their painted ceilings the harvests, the fowls, and even the cattle, together with the whole family of the tenant farmer.

The two young people had met in Lucca. After that meeting Charles Gould visited no mines, though they went together in a carriage, once, to see some marble quarries, where the work resembled mining in so far that it also was the tearing of the raw material of treasure from the earth. Charles Gould did not open his heart to her in any set speeches. He simply went on acting and thinking in her sight. This is the true method of sincerity. One of his frequent remarks was, "I think sometimes that poor father takes a wrong view of that San Tomé business." And they discussed that opinion long and earnestly, as if they could influence a mind across half the globe; but in reality they discussed it because the sentiment of love can enter into any subject and live ardently in remote phrases. For this natural reason these discussions were precious to Mrs. Gould in her engaged state. Charles feared that Mr. Gould, senior, was wasting his strength and making himself ill by his efforts to get rid of the Concession. "I fancy that this is not the kind of handling it requires," he mused aloud, as if to himself. And when she wondered frankly that a man of character should devote his energies to plotting and intrigues, Charles would remark, with a gentle concern that understood her wonder, "You must not forget that he was born there."

She would set her quick mind to work upon that, and then make the inconsequent retort, which he accepted as perfectly sagacious, because, in fact, it was so—

"Well, and you? You were born there, too."

He knew his answer.

"That's different. I've been away ten years. Dad never had such a long spell; and it was more than thirty years ago."

She was the first person to whom he opened his lips after receiving the news of his father's death.

"It has killed him!" he said.

He had walked straight out of town with the news, straight out before him in the noonday sun on the white road, and his feet had brought him face to face with her in the hall of the ruined *palazzo*, a room magnificent and naked, with here and there a long strip of damask, black with damp and age, hanging down on a bare panel of the wall. It was furnished with exactly one gilt armchair, with a broken back, and an octagon columnar stand bearing a heavy marble vase ornamented with sculptured masks and garlands of flowers, and cracked from top to bottom. Charles Gould was dusty with the white dust of the road lying on his boots, on his shoulders, on his cap with two peaks. Water dripped from under it all over his face, and he grasped a thick oaken cudgel in his bare right hand.

She went very pale under the roses of her big straw hat, gloved, swinging a clear sunshade, caught just as she was going out to meet him at the bottom of the hill, where three poplars stand near the wall of a vineyard.

"It has killed him!" he repeated. "He ought to have had many years yet. We are a long-lived family."

She was too startled to say anything; he was contemplating with a penetrating and motionless stare the cracked marble urn as though he had resolved to fix its shape for ever in his memory. It was only when, turning suddenly to her, he blurted out twice, "I've come to you—I've come straight to you—," without being able to finish his phrase, that the great pitifulness of that lonely and tormented death in Costaguana came to her with the full force of its misery. He caught hold of her hand, raised it to his lips, and at that she dropped her parasol to pat him on the cheek, murmured "Poor boy," and began to dry her eyes under the downward curve of her hat-brim, very small in her simple, white frock, almost like a lost child crying in the degraded grandeur of the noble hall, while he stood by her, again perfectly motionless in the contemplation of the marble urn.

Afterwards they went out for a long walk, which was silent till he exclaimed suddenly:

"Yes. But if he had only grappled with it in a proper way!"

And then they stopped. Everywhere there were long shadows lying on the hills, on the roads, on the enclosed fields of olive trees; the shadows of poplars, of wide chestnuts, of farm buildings, of stone walls; and in mid-air the sound of a bell, thin and alert, was like the throbbing pulse of the sunset glow. Her lips were slightly parted as though in surprise that he should not be looking at her with his usual expression. His usual expression was unconditionally approving and attentive. He was in his talks with her the most anxious and deferential of dictators, an attitude that pleased her immensely. It affirmed her power without detracting from his dignity. That slight girl, with her little feet, little hands, little face attractively overweighted by great coils of hair; with a rather large mouth, whose mere parting seemed to breathe upon you the fragrance of frankness and generosity, had the fastidious soul of an experienced woman. She was, before all things and all flatteries, careful of her pride in the object of her choice. But now he was actually not looking at her at all; and his expression was tense and irrational, as is natural in a man who elects to stare at nothing past a young girl's head.

"Well, yes. It was iniquitous. They corrupted him thoroughly, the poor old boy. Oh! why wouldn't he let me go back to him? But now I shall know how to grapple with this."

After pronouncing these words with immense assurance, he glanced down at her, and at once fell a prey to distress, incertitude, and fear.

The only thing he wanted to know now, he said, was whether she did love him enough—whether she would have the courage to go with him so far away? He put these questions to her in a voice that trembled with anxiety—for he was a determined man.

She did. She would. And immediately the future hostess of all the Europeans in Sulaco had the physical experience of the earth falling away from under her. It vanished completely, even to the very sound of the bell. When her feet touched the ground again, the bell was still ringing in the valley; she put her hands up to her hair, breathing quickly, and glanced up and down the stony lane. It was reassuringly empty. Meantime, Charles, stepping with one foot into a dry and dusty ditch, picked up the open parasol, which had bounded away from them with a martial sound of drum taps. He handed it to her soberly, a little crestfallen.

They turned back, and after she had slipped her hand on his arm, the first words he pronounced were:

"It's lucky that we shall be able to settle in a coast town. You've heard its name. It is Sulaco. I am so glad poor Father did get that house. He bought a big house there years ago, in order that there should always be a Casa Gould in the principal town of what used to be called the Occidental Province. I lived there once, as a small boy, with my dear mother, for a whole year, while poor Father was away in the United States on business. You shall be the new mistress of the Casa Gould."

And later, in the inhabited corner of the *palazzo* above the vineyards, the marble hills, the pines and olives of Lucca, he also said:

"The name of Gould has been always highly respected in Sulaco. My uncle Harry was chief of the State for some time, and has left a great name amongst the first families. By this I mean the pure Creole families, who take no part in the miserable farce of governments. Uncle Harry was no adventurer. In Costaguana we Goulds are no adventurers. He was of the country, and he loved it, but he remained essentially an Englishman in his ideas. He made use of the political cry of his time. It was Federation. But he was no politician. He simply stood up for social order out of pure love for rational liberty and from his hate of oppression. There was no nonsense about him. He went to work in his own way because it seemed right, just as I feel I must lay hold of that mine."

In such words he talked to her because his memory was very full of the country of his childhood, his heart of his life with that girl, and his mind of the San Tomé Concession. He added that he would have to leave her for a few days to find an American, a man from San Francisco, who was still somewhere in Europe. A few months before he had made his acquaintance in an old historic German town, situated in a mining district. The American had his womankind with him, but seemed lonely while they were sketching all day long the old doorways and the turreted corners of the medieval houses. Charles Gould had with him the inseparable companionship of the mine. The other man was interested in mining enterprises, knew something of

Costaguana, and was no stranger to the name of Gould. They had talked together with some intimacy which was made possible by the difference of their ages. Charles wanted now to find that capitalist of shrewd mind and accessible character. His father's fortune in Costaguana, which he had supposed to be still considerable, seemed to have melted in the rascally crucible of revolutions. Apart from some ten thousand pounds deposited in England, there appeared to be nothing left except the house in Sulaco, a vague right of forest exploitation in a remote and savage district, and the San Tomé Concession, which had attended his poor father to the very brink of the grave.

He explained those things. It was late when they parted. She had never before given him such a fascinating vision of herself. All the eagerness of youth for a strange life, for great distances, for a future in which there was an air of adventure, of combat—a subtle thought of redress and conquest—had filled her with an intense excitement, which she returned to the giver with a more open and exquisite display of tenderness.

He left her to walk down the hill, and directly he found himself alone he became sober. That irreparable change a death makes in the course of our daily thoughts can be felt in a vague and poignant discomfort of mind. It hurt Charles Gould to feel that never more, by no effort of will, would he be able to think of his father in the same way he used to think of him when the poor man was alive. His breathing image was no longer in his power. This consideration, closely affecting his own identity, filled his breast with a mournful and angry desire for action. In this his instinct was unerring. Action is consolatory. It is the enemy of thought and the friend of flattering illusions. Only in the conduct of our action can we find the sense of mastery over the Fates. For his action, the mine was obviously the only field. It was imperative sometimes to know how to disobey the solemn wishes of the dead. He resolved firmly to make his disobedience as thorough (by way of atonement) as it well could be. The mine had been the cause of an absurd moral disaster; its working must be made a serious and moral success. He owed it to the dead man's memory. Such were the—properly speaking—emotions of Charles Gould. His thoughts ran upon the means of raising a large amount of capital in San Francisco or elsewhere; and incidentally there occurred to him also the general reflection that the counsel of the departed must be an unsound guide. Not one of them could be aware beforehand what enormous changes the death of any given individual may produce in the very aspect of the world.

The latest phase in the history of the mine Mrs. Gould knew from personal experience. It was in essence the history of her married life. The mantle of the Goulds' hereditary position in Sulaco had descended amply upon her little person; but she would not allow the peculiarities of the strange garment to weigh down the vivacity of her character, which was the sign of no mere mechanical sprightliness, but of an eager intelligence. It must not be supposed that Mrs. Gould's mind was masculine. A woman with a masculine mind is not a being of superior efficiency; she is simply a phenomenon of imperfect differentiation—interestingly barren and without impor-tance. Doña Emilia's intelligence being feminine led her to achieve the conquest of Sulaco, simply by lighting the way for her unselfishness and sympathy. She could converse charmingly, but she was not talkative. The wisdom of the heart having no

concern with the erection or demolition of theories any more than with the defense of
prejudices, has no random words at its command. The words it pronounces have the
value of acts of integrity, tolerance, and compassion. A woman's true tenderness, like
the true virility of man, is expressed in action of a conquering kind. The ladies of
Sulaco adored Mrs. Gould. "They still look upon me as something of a monster,"
Mrs. Gould had said pleasantly to one of the three gentlemen from San Francisco she
had to entertain in her new Sulaco house just about a year after her marriage.

They were her first visitors from abroad, and they had come to look at the San
Tomé mine. She jested most agreeably, they thought; and Charles Gould, besides
knowing thoroughly what he was about, had shown himself a real hustler. These facts
caused them to be well disposed towards his wife. An unmistakable enthusiasm,
pointed by a slight flavor of irony, made her talk of the mine absolutely fascinating to
her visitors, and provoked them to grave and indulgent smiles in which there was a
good deal of deference. Perhaps had they known how much she was inspired by an
idealistic view of success they would have been amazed at the state of her mind as the
Spanish-American ladies had been amazed at the tireless activity of her body. She
would—in her own words—have been for them "something of a monster." However,
the Goulds were in essentials a reticent couple, and their guests departed without the
suspicion of any other purpose but simple profit in the working of a silver mine. Mrs.
Gould had out her own carriage, with two white mules, to drive them down to the
harbor, whence the *Ceres* was to carry them off into the Olympus of plutocrats.
Captain Mitchell had snatched at the occasion of leave-taking to remark to Mrs.
Gould, in a low, confidential mutter, "This marks an epoch."

Mrs. Gould loved the patio of her Spanish house. A broad flight of stone steps was
overlooked silently from a niche in the wall by a Madonna in blue robes with the
crowned child sitting on her arm. Subdued voices ascended in the early mornings from
the paved well of the quadrangle, with the stamping of horses and mules led out in
pairs to drink at the cistern. A tangle of slender bamboo stems drooped its narrow,
blade-like leaves over the square pool of water, and the fat coachman sat muffled up on
the edge, holding lazily the ends of halters in his hand. Barefooted servants passed to
and fro, issuing from dark, low doorways below; two laundry girls with baskets of
washed linen; the baker with the tray of bread made for the day; Leonarda—her own
camerista—bearing high up, swung from her hand raised above her raven black head, a
bunch of starched underskirts dazzlingly white in the slant of sunshine. Then the old
porter would hobble in, sweeping the flagstones, and the house was ready for the day.
All the lofty rooms on three sides of the quadrangle opened into each other and into
the *corredor*, with its wrought-iron railings and a border of flowers, whence, like the lady
of the medieval castle, she could witness from above all the departures and arrivals of
the Casa, to which the sonorous arched gateway lent an air of stately importance.

She had watched her carriage roll away with the three guests from the north. She
smiled. Their three arms went up simultaneously to their three hats. Captain Mitchell,
the fourth, in attendance, had already begun a pompous discourse. Then she lingered.
She lingered, approaching her face to the clusters of flowers here and there as if to give

time to her thoughts to catch up with her slow footsteps along the straight vista of the corridor.

A fringed Indian hammock from Aroa, gay with colored featherwork, had been swung judiciously in a corner that caught the early sun; for the mornings are cool in Sulaco. The cluster of *flor de noche buena* blazed in great masses before the open glass doors of the reception-rooms. A big green parrot, brilliant like an emerald in a cage that flashed like gold, screamed out ferociously, *"Viva Costaguana!"* then called twice mellifluously, *"Leonarda! Leonarda!"* in imitation of Mrs. Gould's voice, and suddenly took refuge in immobility and silence. Mrs. Gould reached the end of the gallery and put her head through the door of her husband's room.

Charles Gould, with one foot on a low wooden stool, was already strapping his spurs. He wanted to hurry back to the mine. Mrs. Gould, without coming in, glanced about the room. One tall, broad bookcase, with glass doors, was full of books; but in the other, without shelves, and lined with red baize, were arranged firearms: Winchester carbines, revolvers, a couple of shot-guns, and even two pairs of double-barrelled holster pistols. Between them, by itself, upon a strip of scarlet velvet, hung an old cavalry saber, once the property of Don Enrique Gould, the hero of the Occidental Province, presented by Don José Avellanos, the hereditary friend of the family.

Otherwise, the plastered white walls were completely bare, except for a water-color sketch of the San Tomé mountain—the work of Doña Emilia herself. In the middle of the red-tiled floor stood two long tables littered with plans and papers, a few chairs, and a glass show-case containing specimens of ore from the mine. Mrs. Gould, looking at all these things in turn, wondered aloud why the talk of these wealthy and enterprising men discussing the prospects, the working, and the safety of the mine rendered her so impatient and uneasy, whereas she could talk of the mine by the hour with her husband with unwearied interest and satisfaction.

And dropping her eyelids expressively, she added:

"What do *you* feel about it, Charley?"

Then, surprised at her husband's silence, she raised her eyes, opened wide, as pretty as pale flowers. He had done with the spurs, and, twisting his mustache with both hands, horizontally, he contemplated her from the height of his long legs with a visible appreciation of her appearance. The consciousness of being thus contemplated pleased Mrs. Gould.

"They are considerable men," he said.

"I know. But have you listened to their conversation? They don't seem to have understood anything they have seen here."

"They have seen the mine. They have understood that to some purpose," Charles Gould interjected, in defense of the visitors; and then his wife mentioned the name of the most considerable of the three. He was considerable in finance and in industry. His name was familiar to many millions of people. He was so considerable that he would never have traveled so far away from the center of his activity if the doctors had not insisted, with veiled menaces, on his taking a long holiday.

"Mr. Holroyd's sense of religion," Mrs. Gould pursued, "was shocked and disgusted at the tawdriness of the dressed-up saints in the cathedral—the worship, he called it, of wood and tinsel. But it seemed to me that he looked upon his own God as a sort of influential partner, who gets his share of profits in the endowment of churches. That's a sort of idolatry. He told me he endowed churches every year, Charley."

"No end of them," said Mr. Gould, marveling inwardly at the mobility of her physiognomy. "All over the country. He's famous for that sort of munificence."

"Oh, he didn't boast," Mrs. Gould declared, scrupulously. "I believe he's really a good man, but so stupid! A poor Cholo who offers a little silver arm or leg to thank his god for a cure is as rational and more touching."

"He's at the head of immense silver and iron interests," Charles Gould observed.

"Ah, yes! The religion of silver and iron. He's a very civil man, though he looked awfully solemn when he first saw the Madonna on the staircase, who's only wood and paint; but he said nothing to me. My dear Charley, I heard those men talk among themselves. Can it be that they really wish to become, for an immense consideration, drawers of water and hewers of wood to all the countries and nations of the earth."

"A man must work to some end," Charles Gould said, vaguely.

Mrs. Gould, frowning, surveyed him from head to foot. With his riding-breeches, leather leggings (an article of apparel never before seen in Costaguana), a Norfolk coat of gray flannel, and those great flaming mustaches, he suggested an officer of cavalry turned gentleman farmer. This combination was gratifying to Mrs. Gould's tastes. "How thin the poor boy is!" she thought. "He overworks himself." But there was no denying that his fine-drawn, keen red face, and his whole, long-limbed, lank person had an air of breeding and distinction. And Mrs. Gould relented.

"I only wondered what you felt," she murmured, gently.

During the last few days, as it happened, Charles Gould had been kept too busy thinking twice before he spoke to have paid much attention to the state of his feelings. But theirs was a successful match, and he had no difficulty in finding his answer.

"The best of my feelings are in your keeping, my dear," he said lightly; and there was so much truth in that obscure phrase that he experienced towards her at the moment a great increase of gratitude and tenderness.

Mrs. Gould, however, did not seem to find this answer in the least obscure. She brightened up delicately; already he had changed his tone.

"But there are facts. The worth of the mine—as a mine—is beyond doubt. It shall make us very wealthy. The mere working of it is a matter of technical knowledge, which I have—which ten thousand other men in the world have. But its safety, its continued existence as an enterprise, giving a return to men—to strangers, comparative strangers—who invest money in it, is left altogether in my hands. I have inspired confidence in a man of wealth and position. You seem to think this perfectly natural —do you? Well, I don't know. I don't know why I have; but it is a fact. This fact makes everything possible, because without it I would never have thought of disregarding my father's wishes. I would never have disposed of the Concession as a speculator disposes of a valuable right to a company—for cash and shares, to grow rich eventually if possible, but at any rate to put some money at once in his pocket. No. Even if it had been feasible—which I doubt—I would not have done so. Poor Father did not understand. He was afraid I would hang on to the ruinous thing, waiting for just some such chance, and waste my life miserably. That was the true sense of his prohibition, which we have deliberately set aside."

They were walking up and down the corridor. Her head just reached to his shoulder. His arm, extended downwards, was about her waist. His spurs jingled slightly.

"He had not seen me for ten years. He did not know me. He parted from me for my sake, and he would never let me come back. He was always talking in his letters of leaving Costaguana, of abandoning everything and making his escape. But he was too valuable a prey. They would have thrown him into one of their prisons at the first suspicion."

His spurred feet clinked slowly. He was bending over his wife as they walked. The big parrot, turning its head askew, followed their pacing figures with a round, unblinking eye.

"He was a lonely man. Ever since I was ten years old he used to talk to me as if I had been grown up. When I was in Europe he wrote to me every month. Ten, twelve pages every month of my life for ten years. And, after all, he did not know me! Just think of it—ten whole years away; the years I was growing up into a man. He could not know me. Do you think he could?"

Mrs. Gould shook her head negatively; which was just what her husband had expected from the strength of the argument. But she shook her head negatively only because she thought that no one could know her Charles—really know him for what he was but herself. The thing was obvious. It could be felt. It required no argument. And poor Mr. Gould, senior, who had died too soon to ever hear of their engagement, remained too shadowy a figure for her to be credited with knowledge of any sort whatever.

"No, he did not understand. In my view this mine could never have been a thing to sell. Never! After all his misery I simply could not have touched it for money alone," Charles Gould pursued: and she pressed her head to his shoulder approvingly.

These two young people remembered the life which had ended wretchedly just when their own lives had come together in that splendor of hopeful love, which to the most sensible minds appears like a triumph of good over all the evils of the earth. A vague idea of rehabilitation had entered the plan of their life. That it was so vague as to elude the support of argument made it only the stronger. It had presented itself to them at the instant when the woman's instinct of devotion and the man's instinct of activity receive from the strongest of illusions their most powerful impulse. The very prohibition imposed the necessity of success. It was as if they had been morally bound to make good their vigorous view of life against the unnatural error of weariness and despair. If the idea of wealth was present to them it was only so far as it was bound with that other success. Mrs. Gould, an orphan from early childhood and without fortune, brought up in an atmosphere of intellectual interests, had never considered the aspects of great wealth. They were too remote, and she had not learned that they were desirable. On the other hand, she had not known anything of absolute want. Even the very poverty of her aunt, the Marchesa, had nothing intolerable to a refined mind; it seemed in accord with a great grief; it had the austerity of a sacrifice offered to a noble ideal. Thus even the most legitimate touch of materialism was wanting in Mrs. Gould's character. The dead man of whom she thought with tenderness (because he was Charley's father), and with some impatience (because he had been weak), must be put completely in the wrong. Nothing else would do to keep their prosperity without a stain on its only real, on its immaterial side!

Charles Gould, on his part, had been obliged to keep the idea of wealth well to the fore; but he brought it forward as a means, not as an end. Unless the mine was good business it could not be touched. He had to insist on that aspect of the enterprise. It was his lever to move men who had capital. And Charles Gould believed in the mine. He knew everything that could be known of it. His faith in the mine was contagious, though it was not served by a great eloquence; but businessmen are frequently as sanguine and imaginative as lovers. They are affected by a personality much oftener than people would suppose; and Charles Gould, in his unshaken assurance, was absolutely convincing. Besides, it was a matter of common knowledge to the men to whom he addressed himself that mining in Costaguana was a game that could be made considerably more than worth the candle. The men of affairs knew that very well. The real difficulty in touching it was elsewhere. Against that there was an implication of calm and implacable resolution in Charles Gould's very voice. Men of affairs venture sometimes on acts that the common judgment of the world would pronounce absurd; they make their decisions on apparently impulsive and human grounds. "Very well," had said the considerable personage to whom Charles Gould on his way out through San Francisco had lucidly exposed his point of view. "Let us suppose that the mining affairs of Sulaco are taken in hand. There would then be in it: first, the house of Holroyd, which is all right; then, Mr. Charles Gould, a citizen of Costaguana, who is also all right; and, lastly, the Government of the Republic. So far this resembles the first start of the Atacama nitrate fields, where there was a financing house, a gentleman of the name of Edwards, and—a Government; or, rather, two Governments—two South American Governments. And you know what came of it. War came of it; devastating and prolonged war came of it, Mr. Gould. However, here we possess the advantage of having only one South American Government hanging around for plunder out of the deal. It is an advantage; but then there are degrees of badness, and that Government is the Costaguana Government."

Thus spoke the considerable personage, the millionaire endower of churches on a scale befitting the greatness of his native land—the same to whom the doctors used the language of horrid and veiled menaces. He was a big-limbed, deliberate man, whose quiet burliness lent to an ample silk-faced frockcoat a superfine dignity. His hair was iron gray, his eyebrows were still black, and his massive profile was the profile of a Caesar's head on an old Roman coin. But his parentage was German and Scotch and English, with remote strains of Danish and French blood, giving him the temperament of a Puritan and an insatiable imagination of conquest. He was completely unbending to his visitor, because of the warm introduction the visitor had brought from Europe, and because of an irrational liking for earnestness and determination wherever met, to whatever end directed.

"The Costaguana Government shall play its hand for all it's worth—and don't you forget it, Mr. Gould. Now, what is Costaguana? It is the bottomless pit of ten-percent loans and other fool investments. European capital has been flung into it with both hands for years. Not ours, though. We in this country know just about enough to keep indoors when it rains. We can sit and watch. Of course, some day we shall step in. We are bound to. But there's no hurry. Time itself has got to wait on the greatest country in the whole of God's Universe. We shall be giving the word for everything: industry, trade, law, journalism, art, politics, and religion, from Cape Horn clear over to Smith's Sound, and beyond, too, if anything worth taking hold of turns up at the North Pole. And then we shall have the leisure to take in hand the outlying islands and continents of the earth. We shall run the world's business whether the world likes it or not. The world can't help it—and neither can we, I guess."

By this he meant to express his faith in destiny in words suitable to his intelligence, which was unskilled in the presentation of general ideas. His intelligence was nourished on facts; and Charles Gould, whose imagination had been permanently affected by the one great fact of a silver mine, had no objection to this theory of the world's future. If it had seemed distasteful for a moment it was because the sudden statement of such vast eventualities dwarfed almost to nothingness the actual matter in hand. He and his plans and all the mineral wealth of the Occidental Province appeared suddenly robbed of every vestige of magnitude. The sensation was disagreeable; but Charles Gould was not dull. Already he felt that he was producing a favorable impression; the consciousness of that flattering fact helped him to a vague smile, which his big interlocutor took for a smile of discreet and admiring assent. He smiled quietly, too; and immediately Charles Gould, with that mental agility mankind will display in defense of a cherished hope, reflected that the very apparent insignificance of his aim would help him to success. His personality and his mine would be taken up because it was a matter of no great consequence, one way or another, to a man who referred his action to such a prodigious destiny. And Charles Gould was not humiliated by this consideration, because the thing remained as big as ever for him. Nobody else's vast conceptions of destiny could diminish the aspect of his desire for the redemption of the San Tomé mine. In comparison to the correctness of his aim, definite in space and absolutely attainable within a limited time, the other man appeared for an instant as a dreamy idealist of no importance.

The great man, massive and benignant, had been looking at him thoughtfully; when he broke the short silence it was to remark that concessions flew about thick in the air of Costaguana. Any simple soul that just yearned to be taken in could bring down a concession at the first shot.

"Our consuls get their mouths stopped with them," he continued, with a twinkle of genial scorn in his eyes. But in a moment he became grave. "A conscientious, upright man, that cares nothing for boodle, and keeps clear of their intrigues, conspiracies, and factions, soon gets his passports. See that, Mr. Gould? *Persona non grata.* That's the reason our Government is never properly informed. On the other hand, Europe must be kept out of this continent, and for proper interference on our part the time is not yet ripe, I dare say. But we here—we are not this country's Government, neither are we simple souls. Your affair is all right. The main question for us is whether the second partner, and that's you, is the sort to hold his own against the third and unwelcome partner, which is one or another of the high and mighty robber gangs that run the Costaguana Government. What do you think, Mr. Gould, eh?"

He bent forward to look steadily into the unflinching eyes of Charles Gould, who, remembering the large box full of his father's letters, put the accumulated scorn and bitterness of many years into the tone of his answer:

"As far as the knowledge of these men and their methods and their politics is concerned, I can answer for myself. I have been fed on that sort of knowledge since I was a boy. I am not likely to fall into mistakes from excess of optimism."

"Not likely, eh? That's all right. Tact and a stiff upper lip is what you'll want; and you could bluff a little on the strength of your backing. Not too much, though. We will go with you as long as the thing runs straight. But we won't be drawn into any large trouble. This is the experiment which I am willing to make. There is some risk, and we will take it; but if you can't keep up your end, we will stand our loss, of course, and then—we'll let the thing go. This mine can wait; it has been shut up before, you know. You must understand that under no circumstances will we consent to throw good money after bad."

Thus the great personage had spoken then, in his own private office, in a great city where other men (very considerable in the eyes of a vain populace) waited with alacrity upon a wave of his hand. And rather more than a year later, during his unexpected appearance in Sulaco, he had emphasized his uncompromising attitude with a freedom of sincerity permitted to his wealth and influence. He did this with the less reserve, perhaps, because the inspection of what had been done, and more still the way in which successive steps had been taken, had impressed him with the conviction that Charles Gould was perfectly capable of keeping up his end.

"This young fellow," he thought to himself, "may yet become a power in the land."

This thought flattered him, for hitherto the only account of this young man he could give to his intimates was:

"My brother-in-law met him in one of these one-horse old German towns, near some mines, and sent him on to me with a letter. He's one of the Costaguana Goulds, pure-bred Englishmen, but all born in the country. His uncle went into politics, was the last Provincial President of Sulaco, and got shot after a battle. His father was a prominent businessman in Sta Marta, tried to keep clear of their politics, and died ruined after a lot of revolutions. And that's your Costaguana in a nutshell."

Of course, he was too great a man to be questioned as to his motives, even by his intimates. The outside world was at liberty to wonder respectfully at the hidden meaning of his actions. He was so great a man that his lavish patronage of the "purer forms of Christianity" (which in its naïve form of church-building amused Mrs. Gould) was looked upon by his fellow-citizens as the manifestation of a pious and humble spirit. But in his own circles of the financial world the taking up of such a thing as the San Tomé mine was regarded with respect, indeed, but rather as a subject for discreet jocularity. It was a great man's caprice. In the great Holroyd building (an enormous pile of iron, glass, and blocks of stone at the corner of two streets, cob-webbed aloft by the radiation of telegraph wires) the heads of principal departments exchanged humorous glances, which meant that they were not let into the secrets of the San Tomé business. The Costaguana mail (it was never large—one fairly heavy enve-lope) was taken unopened straight into the great man's room, and no instructions dealing with it had ever been issued thence. The office whispered that he answered personally—and not by dictation either, but actually writing in his own hand, with pen and ink, and, it was to be supposed, taking a copy in his own private press copybook, inaccessible to profane eyes. Some scornful young men, insignificant pieces of minor machinery in that eleven-story-high workshop of great affairs, expressed frankly their private opinion that the great chief had done at last something silly, and was ashamed of his folly; others, elderly and insignificant, but full of romantic rever-ence for the business that had devoured their best years, used to mutter darkly and knowingly that this was a portentous sign; that the Holroyd connection meant by-and-by to get hold of the whole Republic of Costaguana, lock, stock, and barrel. But, in fact, the hobby theory was the right one. It interested the great man to attend personally to the San Tomé mine; it interested him so much that he allowed this hobby to give a direction to the first complete holiday he had taken for quite a startling number of years. He was not running a great enterprise there; no mere railway board or individual corporation. He was running a man! A success would have pleased him very much on refreshingly novel grounds; but, on the other side of the same feeling, it was incumbent upon him to cast it off utterly at the first sign of failure. A man may be thrown off. The papers had unfortunately trumpeted all over the land his journey to Costaguana. If he was pleased at the way Charles Gould was going on, he infused an added grimness into his assurances of support. Even at the very last interview, half an hour or so before he rolled out of the patio, hat in hand, behind Mrs. Gould's white mules, he had said in Charles's room:

"You go ahead in your own way, and I shall know how to help you as long as you hold your own. But you may rest assured that in a given case we shall know how to drop you in time."

To this Charles Gould's only answer had been: "You may begin sending out the machinery as soon as you like."

And the great man had liked this imperturbable assurance. The secret of it was that to Charles Gould's mind these uncompromising terms were agreeable. Like this the mine preserved its identity, with which he had endowed it as a boy; and it remained dependent on himself alone. It was a serious affair, and he, too, took it grimly.

"Of course," he said to his wife, alluding to this last conversation with the departed guest, while they walked slowly up and down the corridor, followed by the irritated eye of the parrot—"of course, a man of that sort can take up a thing or drop it when he likes. He will suffer from no sense of defeat. He may have to give in, or he may have to die tomorrow, but the great silver and iron interests shall survive, and some day shall get hold of Costaguana along with the rest of the world."

They had stopped near the cage. The parrot, catching the sound of a word belonging to his vocabulary, was moved to interfere. Parrots are very human.

"*Viva Costaguana!*" he shrieked, with intense self-assertion, and, instantly ruffling up his feathers, assumed an air of puffed-up somnolence behind the glittering wires.

"And do you believe that, Charley?" Mrs. Gould asked. "This seems to me most awful materialism, and—"

"My dear, it's nothing to me," interrupted her husband, in a reasonable tone. "I make use of what I see. What's it to me whether his talk is the voice of destiny or simply a bit of clap-trap eloquence? There's a good deal of eloquence of one sort or another produced in both Americas. The air of the New World seems favorable to the art of declamation. Have you forgotten how dear Avellanos can hold forth for hours here—?"

"Oh, but that's different," protested Mrs. Gould, almost shocked. The allusion was not to the point. Don José was a dear good man, who talked very well, and was enthusiastic about the greatness of the San Tomé mine. "How can you compare them, Charles?" she exclaimed, reproachfully. "He has suffered—and yet he hopes."

The working competence of men—which she never questioned—was very surprising to Mrs. Gould, because upon so many obvious issues they showed themselves strangely muddle-headed.

Charles Gould, with a careworn calmness which secured for him at once his wife's anxious sympathy, assured her that he was not comparing. He was an American himself, after all, and perhaps he could understand both kinds of eloquence—"if it were worth while to try," he added, grimly. But he had breathed the air of England longer than any of his people had done for three generations, and really he begged to be excused. His poor father could be eloquent, too. And he asked his wife whether she remembered a passage in one of his father's last letters where Mr. Gould had expressed the conviction that "God looked wrathfully at these countries, or else He would let some ray of hope fall through a rift in the appalling darkness of intrigue, bloodshed, and crime that hung over the Queen of Continents."

Mrs. Gould had not forgotten. "You read it to me, Charley," she murmured. "It was a striking pronouncement. How deeply your father must have felt its terrible sadness!"

"He did not like to be robbed. It exasperated him," said Charles Gould. "But the image will serve well enough. What is wanted here is law, good faith, order, security. Anyone can declaim about these things, but I pin my faith to material interests. Only let the material interests once get a firm footing, and they are bound to impose the conditions on which alone they can continue to exist. That's how your money-making is justified here in the face of lawlessness and disorder. It is justified because the security which it demands must be shared with an oppressed people. A better justice will come afterwards. That's your ray of hope." His arm pressed her slight form closer to his side for a moment. "And who knows whether in that sense even the San Tomé mine may not become that little rift in the darkness which poor Father despaired of ever seeing?"

She glanced up at him with admiration. He was competent; he had given a vast shape to the vagueness of her unselfish ambitions.

"Charley," she said, "you are splendidly disobedient."

He left her suddenly in the *corredor* to go and get his hat, a soft, gray sombrero, an article of national costume which combined unexpectedly well with his English get-up. He came back, a riding-whip under his arm, buttoning up a dogskin glove; his face reflected the resolute nature of his thoughts. His wife had waited for him at the head of the stairs, and before he gave her the parting kiss he finished the conversation:

"What should be perfectly clear to us," he said, "is the fact that there is no going back. Where could we begin life afresh? We are in now for all that there is in us."

He bent over her upturned face very tenderly and a little remorsefully. Charles Gould was competent because he had no illusions. The Gould Concession had to fight for life with such weapons as could be found at once in the mire of corruption that was so universal as to almost lose its significance. He was prepared to stoop for his weapons. For a moment he felt as if the silver mine, which had killed his father, had decoyed him further than he meant to go; and with the roundabout logic of emotions, he felt that the worthiness of his life was bound up with success. There was no going back.

VII

Mrs. Gould was too intelligently sympathetic not to share that feeling. It made life exciting, and she was too much of a woman not to like excitement. But it frightened her, too, a little; and when Don José Avellanos, rocking in the American chair, would go so far as to say, "Even, my dear Carlos, if you had failed; even if some untoward event were yet to destroy your work—which God forbid!—you would have deserved well of your country," Mrs. Gould would look up from the tea-table profoundly at her unmoved husband stirring the spoon in the cup as though he had not heard a word.

Not that Don José anticipated anything of the sort. He could not praise enough dear Carlos's tact and courage. His English, rocklike quality of character was his best safeguard, Don José affirmed; and, turning to Mrs. Gould, "As to you, Emilia, my soul"—he would address her with the familiarity of his age and old friendship—"you are as true a patriot as though you had been born in our midst."

This might have been less or more than the truth. Mrs. Gould, accompanying her husband all over the province in the search for labor, had seen the land with a deeper glance than a trueborn Costaguana could have done. In her travel-worn riding habit, her face powdered white like a plaster cast, with a further protection of a small silk mask during the heat of the day, she rode on a well-shaped, light-footed pony in the center of a little cavalcade. Two *mozos de campo*, picturesque in great hats, with spurred bare heels, in white embroidered *calzoneras*, leather jackets, and striped ponchos, rode

ahead with carbines across their shoulders, swaying in unison to the pace of the horses.
A *tropilla* of pack mules brought up the rear in charge of a thin brown muleteer, sitting
his long-eared beast very near the tail, legs thrust far forward, the wide brim of his hat
set far back, making a sort of halo for his head. An old Costaguana officer, a retired
senior major of humble origins, but patronized by the first families on account of his
Blanco opinions, had been recommended by Don José for commissary and organizer
of that expedition. The points of his gray mustache hung far below his chin, and,
riding on Mrs. Gould's left hand, he looked about with kindly eyes, pointing out the
features of the country, telling the names of the little *pueblos* and of the estates, of
the smooth-walled *haciendas* like long fortresses crowning the knolls above the level of
the Sulaco Valley. It unrolled itself, with green young crops, plains, woodland, and
gleams of water, park-like, from the blue vapor of the distant sierra to an immense
quivering horizon of grass and sky, where big white clouds seemed to fall slowly into
the darkness of their own shadows.

Men ploughed with wooden ploughs and yoked oxen, small on a boundless expanse, as if attacking immensity itself. The mounted figures of *vaqueros* galloped in the
distance, and the great herds fed with all their horned heads one way, in one single
wavering line as far as eye could reach across the broad *potreros*. A spreading cotton-
wool tree shaded a thatched *rancho* by the road; the trudging files of burdened Indians,
taking off their hats, would lift sad, mute eyes to the cavalcade raising the dust of the
crumbling *camino real* made by the hands of their enslaved forefathers. And Mrs. Gould,
with each day's journey, seemed to come nearer to the soul of the land in the
tremendous disclosure of this interior unaffected by the slight European veneer of the
coast towns, a great land of plain and mountain and people, suffering and mute,
waiting for the future in a pathetic immobility of patience.

She knew its sights and its hospitality, dispensed with a sort of slumbrous dignity
in those great houses presenting long, blind walls and heavy portals to the windswept
pastures. She was given the head of the tables, where masters and dependants sat in a
simple and patriarchal state. The ladies of the house would talk softly in the moonlight under the orange trees of the courtyards, impressing upon her the sweetness of
their voices and the something mysterious in the quietude of their lives. In the morning the gentlemen, well mounted in braided *sombreros* and embroidered riding-suits,
with much silver on the trappings of their horses, would ride forth to escort the
departing guests before committing them, with grave good-byes, to the care of God at
the boundary pillars of their estates. In all these households she could hear stories of
political outrage; friends, relatives, ruined, imprisoned, killed in the battles of senseless
civil wars, barbarously executed in ferocious proscriptions, as though the government
of the country had been a struggle of lust between bands of absurd devils let loose
upon the land with sabers and uniforms and grandiloquent phrases. And on all the
lips she found a weary desire for peace, the dread of officialdom with its nightmarish
parody of administration without law, without security, and without justice.

She bore a whole two months of wandering very well; she had that power of
resistance to fatigue which one discovers here and there in some quite frail-looking

women with surprise—like a state of possession by a remarkably stubborn spirit. Don Pepe—the old Costaguana major—after much display of solicitude for the delicate lady, had ended by conferring upon her the name of the "Never-tired Señora." Mrs. Gould was indeed becoming a Costaguanera. Having acquired in southern Europe a knowledge of true peasantry, she was able to appreciate the great worth of the people. She saw the man under the silent, sad-eyed beast of burden. She saw them on the road carrying loads, lonely figures upon the plain, toiling under great straw hats, with their white clothing flapping about their limbs in the wind; she remembered the villages by some group of Indian women at the fountain impressed upon her memory, by the face of some young Indian girl with a melancholy and sensual profile, raising an earthen-ware vessel of cool water at the door of a dark hut with a wooden porch cumbered with great brown jars. The solid wooden wheels of an ox-cart, halted with its shafts in the dust, showed the strokes of the axe; and a party of charcoal carriers, with each man's load resting above his head on the top of the low mud wall, slept stretched in a row within the strip of shade.

The heavy stonework of bridges and churches left by the conquerors proclaimed the disregard of human labor, the tribute-labor of vanished nations. The power of king and church was gone, but at the sight of some heavy ruinous pile overtopping from a knoll the low mud walls of a village, Don Pepe would interrupt the tale of his campaigns to exclaim:

"Poor Costaguana! Before, it was everything for the padres, nothing for the people; and now it is everything for these great *políticos* in Sta Marta, for Negroes and thieves."

Charles talked with the *alcades*, with the *fiscales*, with the principal people in towns, and with the *caballeros* on the estates. The *comandantes* of the districts offered him escorts —for he could show an authorization from the Sulaco political chief of the day. How much the document had cost him in gold twenty-dollar pieces was a secret between himself, a great man in the United States (who condescended to answer the Sulaco mail with his own hand), and a great man of another sort, with a dark olive complex-ion and shifty eyes, inhabiting then the Palace of the Intendencia in Sulaco, and who piqued himself on his culture and Europeanism generally in a rather French style because he had lived in Europe for some years—in exile, he said. However, it was pretty well known that just before this exile he had incautiously gambled away all the cash in the Custom House of a small port where a friend in power had procured for him the post of subcollector. That youthful indiscretion had, amongst other inconve-niences, obliged him to earn his living for a time as a café waiter in Madrid; but his talents must have been great, after all, since they had enabled him to retrieve his political fortunes so splendidly. Charles Gould, exposing his business with an imper-turbable steadiness, called him Excellency.

The provincial Excellency assumed a weary superiority, tilting his chair far back near an open window in the true Costaguana manner. The military band happened to be braying operatic selections on the *plaza* just then, and twice he raised his hand imperatively for silence in order to listen to a favorite passage.

"Exquisite, delicious!" he murmured; while Charles Gould waited, standing by with inscrutable patience. "Lucia, Lucia di Lammermoor! I am passionate for music. It transports me. Ha! the divine—ha!—Mozart. *Si!* divine. . . . What is it you were saying?"

Of course, rumors had reached him already of the newcomer's intentions. Besides, he had received an official warning from Sta Marta. His manner was intended simply to conceal his curiosity and impress his visitor. But after he had locked up something valuable in the drawer of a large writing-desk in a distant part of the room, he became very affable, and walked back to his chair smartly.

"If you intend to build villages and assemble a population near the mine, you shall require a decree of the Minister of the Interior for that," he suggested in a businesslike manner.

"I have already sent a memorial," said Charles Gould, steadily, "and I reckon now confidently upon your Excellency's favorable conclusions."

The Excellency was a man of many moods. With the receipt of the money a great mellowness had descended upon his simple soul. Unexpectedly he fetched a deep sigh.

"Ah, Don Carlos! What we want is advanced men like you in the province. The lethargy—the lethargy of these aristocrats! The want of public spirit! The absence of all enterprise! I, with my profound studies in Europe, you understand—"

With one hand thrust into his swelling bosom, he rose and fell on his toes, and for ten minutes, almost without drawing breath, went on hurling himself intellectually to the assault of Charles Gould's polite silence; and when, stopping abruptly, he fell back into his chair, it was as though he had been beaten off from a fortress. To save his dignity he hastened to dismiss this silent man with a solemn inclination of the head and the words, pronounced with moody, fatigued condescension:

"You may depend upon my enlightened goodwill as long as your conduct as a good citizen deserves it."

He took up a paper fan and began to cool himself with a consequential air, while Charles Gould bowed and withdrew. Then he dropped the fan at once, and stared with an appearance of wonder and perplexity at the closed door for quite a long time. At last he shrugged his shoulders as if to assure himself of his disdain. Cold, dull. No intellectuality. Red hair. A true Englishman. He despised him.

His face darkened. What meant this unimpressed and frigid behavior? He was the first of the successive politicians sent out from the capital to rule the Occidental Province whom the manner of Charles Gould in official intercourse was to strike as offensively independent.

Charles Gould assumed that if the appearance of listening to deplorable balderdash must form part of the price he had to pay for being left unmolested, the obligation of uttering balderdash personally was by no means included in the bargain. He drew the line there. To these provincial autocrats, before whom the peaceable population of all classes had been accustomed to tremble, the reserve of that English-looking engineer caused an uneasiness which swung to and fro between cringing and truculence. Gradually all of them discovered that, no matter what party was in power, that man remained in most effective touch with the higher authorities in Sta Marta.

This was a fact, and it accounted perfectly for the Goulds being by no means so wealthy as the engineer-in-chief on the new railway could legitimately suppose. Following the advice of Don José Avellanos, who was a man of good counsel (though rendered timid by his horrible experiences of Guzman Bento's time), Charles Gould had kept clear of the capital; but in the current gossip of the foreign residents there he was known (with a good deal of seriousness underlying the irony) by the nickname of "King of Sulaco." An advocate of the Costaguana Bar, a man of reputed ability and good character, member of the distinguished Moraga family possessing extensive estates in the Sulaco Valley, was pointed out to strangers, with a shade of mystery and respect, as the agent of the San Tomé mine—"political, you know." He was tall, black-whiskered, and discreet. It was known that he had easy access to ministers, and that the numerous Costaguana generals were always anxious to dine at his house. Presidents granted him audience with facility. He corresponded actively with his maternal uncle, Don José Avellanos; but his letters—unless those expressing formally his dutiful affection—were seldom entrusted to the Costaguana post office. There the envelopes are opened, indiscriminately, with the frankness of a brazen and childish impudence characteristic of some Spanish-American Governments. But it must be noted that at about the time of the reopening of the San Tomé mine the muleteer who had been employed by Charles Gould in his preliminary travels on the Campo added his small train of animals to the thin stream of traffic carried over the mountain passes between the Sta Marta upland and the Valley of Sulaco. There are no travelers by that arduous and unsafe route unless under very exceptional circumstances, and the state of inland trade did not visibly require additional transport facilities; but the man seemed to find his account in it. A few packages were always found for him whenever he took the road. Very brown and wooden, in goatskin breeches with the hair outside, he sat near the tail of his own smart mule, his great hat turned against the sun, an expression of blissful vacancy on his long face, humming day after day a love-song in a plaintive key, or, without a change of expression, letting out a yell at his small *tropilla* in front. A round little guitar hung high up on his back; and there was a place scooped out artistically in the wood of one of his pack-saddles where a tightly rolled piece of paper could be slipped in, the wooden plug replaced, and the coarse canvas nailed on again. When in Sulaco it was his practice to smoke and doze all day long (as though he had no care in the world) on a stone bench outside the doorway of the Casa Gould and facing the windows of the Avellanos house. Years and years ago his mother had been chief laundry-woman in that family—very accomplished in the matter of clear-starching. He himself had been born on one of their *haciendas*. His name was Bonifacio, and Don José, crossing the street about five o'clock to call on Doña Emilia, always acknowledged his humble salute by some movement of hand or head. The porters of both houses conversed lazily with him in tones of grave intimacy. His evenings he devoted to gambling and to calls in a spirit of generous festivity upon the *peyne d'oro* girls in the more remote side-streets of the town. But he, too, was a discreet man.

VIII

Those of us whom business or curiosity took to Sulaco in these years before the first advent of the railway can remember the steadying effect of the San Tomé mine upon the life of that remote province. The outward appearances had not changed then as they have changed since, as I am told, with cable cars running along the streets of the Constitution, and carriage roads far into the country, to Rincón and other villages, where the foreign merchants and the *ricos* generally have their modern villas, and a vast railway goods-yard by the harbor, which has a quayside, a long range of warehouses, and quite serious, organized labor troubles of its own.

Nobody had ever heard of labor troubles then. The Cargadores of the port formed, indeed, an unruly brotherhood of all sorts of scum, with a patron saint of their own. They went on strike regularly (every bullfight day), a form of trouble that even Nostromo at the height of his prestige could never cope with efficiently; but the morning after each fiesta, before the Indian market-women had opened their mat parasols on the *plaza*, when the snows of Higuerota gleamed pale over the town on a yet black sky, the appearance of a phantom-like horseman mounted on a silver-gray mare solved the problem of labor without fail. His steed paced the lanes of the slums and the weed-grown enclosures within the old ramparts, between the black, lightless cluster of huts, like cow-byres, like dog-kennels. The horseman hammered with the butt of a heavy revolver at the doors of low *pulperías*, of obscene lean-to sheds sloping against the tumble-down piece of a noble wall, at the wooden sides of dwellings so flimsy that the sound of snores and sleepy mutters within could be heard in the pauses of the thundering clatter of his blows. He called out men's names menacingly from the saddle, once, twice. The drowsy answers—grumpy, conciliating, savage, jocular, or deprecating—came out into the silent darkness in which the horseman sat still, and presently a dark figure would flit out coughing in the still air. Sometimes a low-toned woman cried through the window-hole softly, "He's coming directly, *señor*," and the horseman waited silent on a motionless horse. But if perchance he had to dismount, then, after a while, from the door of that hovel or of that *pulpería*, with a ferocious scuffle and stifled imprecations, a *cargador* would fly out head first and hands abroad, to sprawl under the forelegs of the silver-gray mare, who only pricked forward her sharp little ears. She was used to that work; and the man, picking himself up, would walk away hastily from Nostromo's revolver, reeling a little along the street and snarling low curses. At sunrise Captain Mitchell, coming out anxiously in his night attire on to the wooden balcony running the whole length of the O.S.N. Company's lonely building by the shore, would see the lighters already under way, figures moving busily about the cargo cranes, perhaps hear the invaluable Nostromo, now dismounted and in the checked shirt and red sash of a Mediterranean sailor, bawling orders from the end of the jetty in a stentorian voice. A fellow in a thousand!

The material apparatus of perfected civilization which obliterates the individuality of old towns under the stereotyped conveniences of modern life had not intruded as yet; but over the worn-out antiquity of Sulaco, so characteristic with its stuccoed houses and barred windows, with the great yellow-white walls of abandoned convents behind the rows of somber green cypresses, that fact—very modern in its spirit—the San Tomé mine had already thrown its subtle influence. It had altered, too, the outward character of the crowds on feast days on the *plaza* before the open portal of the cathedral, by the number of white ponchos with a green stripe affected as holiday wear by the San Tomé miners. They had also adopted white hats with green cord and braid—articles of good quality, which could be obtained in the storehouse of the administration for very little money. A peaceable *cholo* wearing these colors (unusual in Costaguana) was somehow very seldom beaten to within an inch of his life on a charge of disrespect to the town police; neither ran he much risk of being suddenly lassoed on the road by a recruiting party of *lanceros*—a method of voluntary enlistment looked upon as almost legal in the Republic. Whole villages were known to have volunteered for the army in that way; but, as Don Pepe would say with a hopeless shrug to Mrs. Gould, "What would you! Poor people! *Pobrecitos! Pobrecitos!* But the State must have its soldiers."

Thus professionally spoke Don Pepe, the fighter, with pendent mustaches, a nut-brown, lean face, and a clean run of a cast-iron jaw, suggesting the type of a cattle-herd horseman from the great Llanos of the South. "If you will listen to an old officer of Paez, *señores,*" was the exordium of all his speeches in the Aristocratic Club of Sulaco, where he was admitted on account of his past services to the extinct cause of Federation. The club, dating from the days of the proclamation of Costaguana's independence, boasted many names of liberators amongst its first founders. Suppressed arbitrarily innumerable times by various Governments, with memories of proscriptions and of at least one wholesale massacre of its members, sadly assembled for a banquet by the order of a zealous military *comandante* (their bodies were afterwards stripped naked and flung into the *plaza* out of the windows by the lowest scum of the populace), it was again flourishing, at that period, peacefully. It extended to strangers the large hospitality of the cool, big rooms of its historic quarters in the front part of a house, once the residence of a high official of the Holy Office. The two wings, shut up, crumbled behind the nailed doors, and what may be described as a grove of young orange trees grown in the unpaved *patio* concealed the utter ruin of the back part facing the gate. You turned in from the street, as if entering a secluded orchard, where you came upon the foot of a disjointed staircase, guarded by a moss-stained effigy of some saintly bishop, mitred and staffed, and bearing the indignity of a broken nose meekly, with his fine stone hands crossed on his breast. The chocolate-colored faces of servants with mops of black hair peeped at you from above; the click of billiard balls came to your ears, and ascending the steps, you would perhaps see in the first *sala*, very stiff upon a straight-backed chair, in a good light, Don Pepe moving his long mustaches as he spelled his way, at arm's length, through an old Sta Marta newspaper. His horse—a stony-hearted but persevering black brute with a hammer head—you would have seen in the street dozing motionless under an immense saddle, with its nose almost touching the curbstone of the sidewalk.

Don Pepe, when "down from the mountain," as the phrase, often heard in Sulaco, went, could also be seen in the drawing-room of the Casa Gould. He sat with modest assurance at some distance from the tea-table. With his knees close together, and a kindly twinkle of drollery in his deep-set eyes, he would throw his small and ironic pleasantries into the current of conversation. There was in that man a sort of sane, humorous shrewdness, and a vein of genuine humanity so often found in simple old soldiers of proved courage who have seen much desperate service. Of course he knew nothing whatever of mining, but his employment was of a special kind. He was in charge of the whole population in the territory of the mine, which extended from the head of the gorge to where the cart-track from the foot of the mountain enters the plain, crossing a stream over a little wooden bridge painted green—green, the color of hope, being also the color of the mine.

It was reported in Sulaco that up there "at the mountain" Don Pepe walked about precipitous paths, girt with a great sword and in a shabby uniform with tarnished bullion epaulettes of a senior major. Most miners being Indians, with big wild eyes, addressed him as "Taita" (father), as these barefooted people of Costaguana will address anybody who wears shoes; but it was Basilio, Mr. Gould's own *mozo* and the head servant of the Casa, who, in all good faith and from a sense of propriety, announced him once in the solemn words, "El Señor Gobernador has arrived."

Don José Avellanos, then in the drawing-room, was delighted beyond measure at the aptness of the title, with which he greeted the old major banteringly as soon as the latter's soldierly figure appeared in the doorway. Don Pepe only smiled in his long mustaches, as much as to say, "You might have found a worse name for an old soldier."

And "El Señor Gobernador" he had remained, with his small jokes upon his function and upon his domain, where he affirmed with humorous exaggeration to Mrs. Gould:

"No two stones could come together anywhere without the Gobernador hearing the click, *señora.*"

And he would tap his ear with the tip of his forefinger knowingly. Even when the number of the miners alone rose to over six hundred he seemed to know each of them individually, all the innumerable Josés, Manuels, Ignacios, from the villages *primero— segundo—*or *tercero* (there were three mining villages) under his government. He could distinguish them not only by their flat, joyless faces, which to Mrs. Gould looked all alike, as if run into the same ancestral mold of suffering and patience, but apparently also by the infinitely graduated shades of reddish-brown, of blackish-brown, of coppery-brown backs, as the two shifts, stripped to linen drawers and leather skull-caps, mingled together with a confusion of naked limbs, of shouldered picks, swinging lamps, in a great shuffle of sandalled feet on the open plateau before the entrance of the main tunnel. It was a time of pause. The Indian boys leaned idly against the long line of little cradle wagons standing empty; the screeners and ore-breakers squatted on their heels smoking long cigars; the great wooden shoots slanting over the edge of the tunnel plateau were silent; and only the ceaseless, violent rush of water in the open flumes could be heard, murmuring fiercely, with the splash and rumble of revolving turbine-wheels, and the thudding march of the stamps pounding to powder the treasure rock on the plateau below. The heads of gangs, distinguished by brass medals hanging on their bare breasts, marshaled their squads; and at last the mountain would swallow one half of the silent crowd, while the other half would move off in long files down the zigzag paths leading to the bottom of the gorge. It was deep; and, far below, a thread of vegetation winding between the blazing rock faces resembled a slender green cord, in which three lumpy knots of banana patches, palm-leaf roots, and shady trees marked the Village One, Village Two, Village Three, housing the miners of the Gould Concession.

Whole families had been moving from the first towards the spot in the Higuerota range, whence the rumor of work and safety had spread over the pastoral Campo, forcing its way also, even as the waters of a high flood, into the nooks and crannies of the distant blue walls of the Sierras. Father first, in a pointed straw hat, then the mother with the bigger children, generally also a diminutive donkey, all under burdens, except the leader himself, or perhaps some grown girl, the pride of the family, stepping barefooted and straight as an arrow, with braids of raven hair, a thick, haughty profile, and no load to carry but the small guitar of the country and a pair of soft leather sandals tied together on her back. At the sight of such parties strung out on the cross trails between the pastures, or camped by the side of the royal road, travelers on horseback would remark to each other:

"More people going to the San Tomé mine. We shall see others tomorrow."

And spurring on in the dusk they would discuss the great news of the province, the news of San Tomé mine. A rich Englishman was going to work it—and perhaps not an Englishman, *Quién sabe!* A foreigner with much money. Oh, yes, it had begun. A party of men who had been to Sulaco with a herd of black bulls for the next *corrida* had reported that from the porch of the *posada* in Rincón, only a short league from the town, the lights on the mountain were visible, twinkling above the trees. And there was a woman seen riding a horse sideways, not in the chair seat, but upon a sort of saddle, and a man's hat on her head. She walked about, too, on foot up the mountain paths. A woman engineer, it seemed she was.

"What an absurdity! Impossible, *señor!*"

"*Sí! Sí! Una americana del Norte.*"

"Ah, well! if your worship is informed. *Una Americana;* it need be something of that sort."

And they would laugh a little with astonishment and scorn, keeping a wary eye on the shadows of the road, for one is liable to meet bad men when traveling late on the Campo.

And it was not only the men that Don Pepe knew so well, but he seemed able, with one attentive, thoughtful glance, to classify each woman, girl, or growing youth of his domain. It was only the small fry that puzzled him sometimes. He and the padre could be seen frequently side by side, meditative and gazing across the street of a village at a lot of sedate brown children, trying to sort them out, as it were, in low, consulting tones, or else they would together put searching questions as to the parentage of some small, staid urchin met wandering, naked and grave, along the road with a cigar in his baby mouth, and perhaps his mother's rosary, purloined for purposes of ornamentation, hanging in a loop of beads low down on his rotund little stomach. The spiritual and temporal pastors of the mine flock were very good friends. With Dr. Monygham, the medical pastor, who had accepted the charge from Mrs. Gould, and lived in the hospital building, they were on not so intimate terms. But no one could be on intimate terms with El Señor Doctor, who, with his twisted shoulders, drooping head, sardonic mouth, and side-long bitter glance, was mysterious and uncanny. The other two authorities worked in harmony. Father Román, dried-up, small, alert, wrinkled, with big round eyes, a sharp chin, and a great snuff-taker, was an old campaigner, too; he had shriven many simple souls on the battlefields of the Republic, kneeling by the dying on hillsides, in the long grass, in the gloom of the forests, to hear the last confession with the smell of gunpowder smoke in his nostrils, the rattle of muskets, the hum and spatter of bullets in his ears. And where was the harm if, at the presbytery, they had a game with a pack of greasy cards in the early evening, before Don Pepe went his last rounds to see that all the watchmen of the mine—a body organized by himself—were at their posts? For that last duty before he slept Don Pepe did actually gird his old sword on the veranda of an unmistakable American white frame-house, which Father Román called the presbytery. Near by, a long, low, dark building, steeple-roofed, like a vast barn with a wooden cross over the gable, was the miners' chapel. There Father Román said Mass every day before a somber altarpiece representing the Resurrection, the gray slab of the tombstone balanced on one corner, a figure soaring upwards, long-limbed and vivid, in an oval of pallid light, and a helmeted brown legionary smitten down, right across the bituminous foreground. "This picture, my children, *muy linda e maravillosa*," Father Román would say to some of his flock, "which you behold here through the munificence of the wife of our Señor Administrator, has been painted in Europe, a country of saints and miracles, and much greater than our Costaguana." And he would take a pinch of snuff with unction. But when once an inquisitive spirit desired to know in what direction this Europe was situated, whether up or down the coast, Father Román, to conceal his perplexity, became very reserved and severe. "No doubt it is extremely far away. But ignorant sinners like you of the San Tomé mine should think earnestly of everlasting punishment instead of inquiring into the magnitude of the earth, with its countries and populations altogether beyond your understanding."

With a "Good night Padre," "Good night, Don Pepe," the Gobernador would go off, holding up his saber against his side, his body bent forward, with a long, plodding stride in the dark. The jocularity proper to an innocent card game for a few cigars or a bundle of yerba was replaced at once by the stern duty mood of an officer setting out to visit the outposts of an encamped army. One loud blast of the whistle that hung from his neck provoked instantly a great shrilling of responding whistles, mingled with the barking of dogs, that would calm down slowly at last, away up at the head of the gorge; and in the stillness two *serenos*, on guard by the bridge, would appear walking noiselessly towards him. On one side of the road a long frame-building—the store—would be closed and barricaded from end to end; facing it another white frame-house, still longer, and with a veranda—the hospital—would have lights in the two windows of Dr. Monygham's quarters. Even the delicate foliage of a clump of pepper trees did not stir, so breathless would be the darkness warmed by the radiation of the over-heated rocks. Don Pepe would stand still for a moment with the two motionless *serenos* before him, and, abruptly, high up on the sheer face of the mountain, dotted with single torches, like drops of fire fallen from the two great blazing clusters of lights above, the ore shoots would begin to rattle. The great clattering, shuffling noise, gathering speed and weight, would be caught up by the walls of the gorge, and sent upon the plain in a growl of thunder. The *posadero* in Rincón swore that on calm nights, by listening intently, he could catch the sound in his doorway as of a storm in the mountains.

To Charles Gould's fancy it seemed that the sound must reach the uttermost limits of the province. Riding at night towards the mine, it would meet him at the edge of a little wood just beyond Rincón. There was no mistaking the growling mutter of the mountain pouring its stream of treasure under the stamps; and it came to his heart with the peculiar force of a proclamation thundered forth over the land and the marvelousness of an accomplished fact fulfilling an audacious desire. He had heard this desire. He had heard this very sound in his imagination on that far-off evening when his wife and himself, after a tortuous ride through a strip of forest, had reined in their horses near the stream, and had gazed for the first time upon the jungle-grown solitude of the gorge. The head of a palm rose here and there. In a high ravine round the corner of the San Tomé mountain (which is square like a blockhouse) the thread of a slender waterfall flashed bright and glassy through the dark green of the heavy fronds of tree-ferns. Don Pepe, in attendance, rode up, and, stretching his arm up the gorge, had declared with mock solemnity, "Behold the very paradise of snakes, *señora.*"

And then they had wheeled their horses and ridden back to sleep that night at Rincón. The *alcalde*—an old, skinny Moreno, a sergeant of Guzman Bento's time—had cleared respectfully out of his house with his three pretty daughters, to make room for the foreign *señora* and their worships the *caballeros.* All he asked Charles Gould (whom he took for a mysterious and official person) to do for him was to remind the supreme Government—*el Gobierno supremo*—of a pension (amounting to about a dollar a month) to which he believed himself entitled. It had been promised to him, he affirmed, straightening his bent back martially, "many years ago, for my valor in the wars with the wild *indios* when a young man, *señor.*"

The waterfall existed no longer. The tree-ferns that had luxuriated in its spray had dried around the dried-up pool, and the high ravine was only a big trench half filled up with the refuse of excavations and tailings. The torrent, dammed up above, sent its water rushing along the open flumes of scooped tree trunks striding on trestle-legs to the turbines working the stamps on the lower plateau—the *mesa grande* of the San Tomé mountain. Only the memory of the waterfall, with its amazing fernery, like a hanging garden above the rocks of the gorge, was preserved in Mrs. Gould's water-color sketch; she had made it hastily one day from a cleared patch in the bushes, sitting in the shade of a roof of straw erected for her on three rough poles under Don Pepe's direction.

Mrs. Gould had seen it all from the beginning: the clearing of the wilderness, the making of the road, the cutting of new paths up the cliff face of San Tomé. For weeks together she had lived on the spot with her husband; and she was so little in Sulaco during that year that the appearance of the Gould carriage on the Alameda would cause social excitement. From the heavy family coaches full of stately *señoras* and black-eyed *señoritas* rolling solemnly in the shaded alley white hands were waved towards her with animation in a flutter of greetings. Doña Emilia was "down from the mountain."

But not for long. Doña Emilia would be gone "up to the mountain" in a day or two, and her sleek carriage mules would have an easy time of it for another spell. She had watched the erection of the first frame-house put up on the lower *mesa* for an office and Don Pepe's quarters; she heard with a thrill of thankful emotion the first wagon-load of ore rattle down the then only shoot; she had stood by her husband's side perfectly silent, and gone cold all over with excitement at the instant when the first battery of only fifteen stamps was put in motion for the first time. On the occasion when the fires under the first set of retorts in their shed had glowed far into the night she did not retire to rest on the rough cadre set up for her in the as yet bare frame-house till she had seen the first spongy lump of silver yielded to the hazards of the world by the dark depths of the Gould Concession; she had laid her unmercenary hands, with an eagerness that made them tremble, upon the first silver ingot turned out still warm from the mold; and by her imaginative estimate of its power she endowed that lump of metal with a justificative conception, as though it were not a mere fact, but something farreaching and impalpable, like the true expression of an emotion or the emergence of a principle.

Don Pepe, extremely interested, too, looked over her shoulder with a smile that, making longitudinal folds on his face, caused it to resemble a leathern mask with a benignantly diabolic expression.

"Would not the *muchachos* of Hernandez like to get hold of this insignificant object, that looks, *por Dios*, very much like a piece of tin?" he remarked, jocularly.

Hernandez, the robber, had been an inoffensive, small *ranchero*, kidnapped in circumstances of peculiar atrocity from his home during one of the civil wars, and forced to serve in the army. There his conduct as soldier was exemplary, till, watching his chance, he killed his colonel, and managed to get clear away. With a band of deserters, who chose him for their chief, he had taken refuge beyond the wild and waterless Bolson de Tonoro. The *haciendas* paid him blackmail in cattle and horses; extraordinary stories were told of his powers and of his wonderful escapes from capture. He used to ride, single-handed, into the villages and the little towns on the Campo, driving a pack mule before him, with two revolvers in his belt, go straight to the shop or store, select what he wanted, and ride away unopposed because of the terror his exploits and his audacity inspired. Poor country people he usually left alone; the upper class were often stopped on the roads and robbed; but any unlucky official that fell into his hands was sure to get a severe flogging. The army officers did not like his name to be mentioned in their presence. His followers, mounted on stolen horses, laughed at the pursuit of the regular cavalry sent to hunt them down, and whom they took pleasure to ambush most scientifically in the broken ground of their own fastness. Expeditions had been fitted out; a price had been put upon his head; even attempts had been made, treacherously of course, to open negotiations with him, without in the slightest way affecting the even tenor of his career. At last, in true Costaguana fashion, the Fiscal of Tonoro, who was ambitious of the glory of having reduced the famous Hernandez, offered him a sum of money and a safe conduct out of the country for the betrayal of his band. But Hernandez evidently was not of the stuff of which the distinguished military politicians and conspirators of Costaguana are made. This clever but common device (which frequently works like a charm in putting down revolutions) failed with the chief of vulgar Salteadores. It promised well for the Fiscal at first, but ended very badly for the squadron of *lanceros* posted (by the Fiscal's directions) in a fold of the ground into which Hernandez had promised to lead his unsuspecting followers. They came, indeed, at the appointed time, but creeping on their hands and knees through the bush, and only let their presence be known by a general discharge of firearms, which emptied many saddles. The troopers who escaped came riding very hard into Tonoro. It is said that their commanding officer (who, being better mounted, rode far ahead of the rest) afterwards got into a state of despairing intoxication and beat the ambitious Fiscal severely with the flat of his saber in the presence of his wife and daughters, for bringing this disgrace upon the National Army. The highest civil official of Tonoro, falling to the ground in a swoon, was further kicked all over the body and roweled with sharp spurs about the neck and face because of the great sensitiveness of his military colleague. This gossip of the inland Campo, so characteristic of the rulers of the country and its story of oppression, inefficiency, fatuous methods, treachery, and savage brutality, was perfectly known to Mrs. Gould. That it should be accepted with no indignant comment by people of intelligence, refinement, and character as something inherent in the nature of things was one of the symptoms of degradation that had the power to exasperate her almost to the verge of despair. Still looking at the ingot of silver, she shook her head at Don Pepe's remark:

"If it had not been for the lawless tyranny of your Government, Don Pepe, many an outlaw now with Hernandez would be living peaceably and happy by the honest work of his hands."

"*Señora*," cried Don Pepe, with enthusiasm, "it is true! It is as if God had given you the power to look into the very breasts of people. You have seen them working round you, Doña Emilia—meek as lambs, patient like their own *burros,* brave like lions. I have led them to the very muzzles of guns—I, who stand here before you, *señora*—in the time of Paez, who was full of generosity, and in courage only approached by the uncle of Don Carlos here, as far as I know. No wonder there are bandits in the Campo when there are none but thieves, swindlers, and sanguinary *macaques* to rule us in Sta Marta. However, all the same, a bandit is a bandit, and we shall have a dozen good straight Winchesters to ride with the silver down to Sulaco."

Mrs. Gould's ride with the first silver escort to Sulaco was the closing episode of what she called "my camp life" before she had settled in her town-house permanently, as was proper and even necessary for the wife of the administrator of such an important institution as the San Tomé mine. For the San Tomé mine was to become an institution, a rallying-point for everything in the province that needed order and stability to live. Security seemed to flow upon this land from the mountain-gorge. The authorities of Sulaco had learned that the San Tomé mine could make it worth their while to leave things and people alone. This was the nearest approach to the rule of common sense and justice Charles Gould felt it possible to secure at first. In fact, the mine, with its organization, its population growing fiercely attached to their position of privileged safety, with its armory, with its Don Pepe, with its armed body of *serenos* (where, it was said, many an outlaw and deserter—and even some members of Hernandez's band—had found a place), the mine was a power in the land. As a certain prominent man in Sta Marta had exclaimed with a hollow laugh, once, when discussing the line of action taken by the Sulaco authorities at a time of political crisis:

"You call these men Government officials? They? Never! They are officials of the mine—officials of the Concession—I tell you."

The prominent man (who was then a person in power, with a lemon-colored face and a very short and curly, not to say woolly, head of hair) went so far in his temporary discontent as to shake his yellow fist under the nose of his interlocutor, and shriek:

"Yes! All! Silence! All! I tell you! The political *jefe*, the chief of the police, the chief of the customs, the general, all, all are the officials of that Gould."

Thereupon an intrepid but low and argumentative murmur would flow on for a space of the ministerial cabinet, and the prominent man's passion would end in a cynical shrug of the shoulders. After all, he seemed to say, what did it matter as long as the minister himself was not forgotten during his brief day of authority? But all the same, the unofficial agent of the San Tomé mine, working for a good cause, had his moments of anxiety, which were reflected in his letters to Don José Avellanos, his maternal uncle.

"No sanguinary *macaque* from Sta Marta shall set foot on that part of Costaguana which lies beyond the San Tomé bridge," Don Pepe used to assure Mrs. Gould. "Except, of course, as an honored guest—for our Señor Administrador is a deep *político*." But to Charles Gould, in his own room, the old Major would remark with a grim and soldierly cheeriness, "We are all playing our heads at this game."

Don José Avellanos would mutter *"Imperium in imperio*, Emilia, my soul," with an air of profound self-satisfaction which, somehow, in a curious way, seemed to contain a queer admixture of bodily discomfort. But that, perhaps, could only be visible to the initiated.

And for the initiated it was a wonderful place, this drawing-room of the Casa Gould, with its momentary glimpses of the master—El Señor Administrador—older, harder, mysteriously silent, with the lines deepened on his English, ruddy, out-of-doors complexion; flitting on his thin cavalryman's legs across the doorways, either just "back from the mountain" or with jingling spurs and riding-whip under his arm, on the point of starting "for the mountain." Then Don Pepe, modestly martial in his chair, the *llanero* who seemed somehow to have found his martial jocularity, his knowledge of the world, and his manner perfect for his station, in the midst of savage armed contests with his kind; Avellanos, polished and familiar, the diplomatist with his loquacity covering much caution and wisdom in delicate advice, with his manuscript of a historical work on Costaguana, entitled *Fifty Years of Misrule,* which, at present, he thought it was not prudent (even if it were possible) "to give to the world;" these three, and also Doña Emilia amongst them, gracious, small, and fairy-like, before the glittering tea-set, with one common master-thought in their heads, with one common feeling of a tense situation, with one ever-present aim to preserve the inviolable character of the mine at every cost. And there was also to be seen Captain Mitchell, a little apart, near one of the long windows, with an air of old-fashioned neat old bachelorhood about him, slightly pompous, in a white waistcoat, a little disregarded and unconscious of it; utterly in the dark, and imagining himself to be in the thick of things. The good man, having spent a clear thirty years of his life on the high seas before getting what he called a "shore billet," was astonished at the importance of transactions (other than relating to shipping) which take place on dry land. Almost every event out of the usual daily course "marked an epoch" for him or else was "history;" unless with his pomposity struggling with a discomfited droop of his rubicund, rather handsome face, set off by snow-white close hair and short whiskers, he would mutter:

"Ah, that! That, sir, was a mistake."

The reception of the first consignment of San Tomé silver for shipment to San Francisco in one of O.S.N. Company's mailboats had, of course, "marked an epoch" for Captain Mitchell. The ingots packed in boxes of stiff ox-hide with plaited handles, small enough to be carried easily by two men, were brought down by the *serenos* of the mine walking in careful couples down the half mile or so of steep, zigzag paths to the foot of the mountain. There they would be loaded into a string of two-wheeled carts, resembling roomy coffers with a door at the back, and harnessed tandem with two mules each, waiting under the guard of armed and mounted *serenos.* Don Pepe padlocked each door in succession, and at the signal of his whistle the string of carts would move off, closely surrounded by the clank of spur and carbine, with jolts and cracking of whips, with a sudden deep rumble over the boundary bridge ("into the land of thieves and sanguinary *macaques,*" Don Pepe defined that crossing); hats bobbing in the first light of the dawn, on the heads of cloaked figures; Winchesters on hip; bridle hands protruding lean and brown from under the falling folds of the ponchos. The convoy, skirting a little wood, along the mine trail, between the mud huts and low walls of Rincón, increased its pace on the *camino real,* mules urged to speed, escort galloping, Don Carlos riding alone ahead of a dust storm affording a vague vision of long ears of mules, of fluttering little green and white flags stuck upon each cart; of raised arms in a mob of *sombreros* with the white gleam of ranging eyes; and Don Pepe, hardly visible in the rear of that rattling dust trail, with a stiff seat and impassive face, rising and falling rhythmically on a ewe-necked silver-bitted black brute with a hammer head.

The sleepy people in the little clusters of huts, in the small *ranchos* near the road, recognized by the headlong sound the charge of the San Tomé silver escort towards the crumbling wall of the city on the Campo side. They came to the doors to see it dash by over ruts and stones, with a clatter and clank and cracking of whips, with the reckless rush and precise driving of a field battery hurrying into action, and the solitary English figure of the Señor Administrador riding far ahead in the lead.

In the fenced roadside paddocks loose horses galloped wildly for a while; the heavy cattle stood up breast deep in the grass, lowing mutteringly at the flying noise; a meek Indian villager would glance back once and hasten to shove his loaded little donkey bodily against a wall, out of the way of the San Tomé silver escort going to the sea; a small knot of chilly *leperos* under the Stone Horse of the Alameda would mutter: *"Caramba!"* on seeing it take a wide curve at a gallop and dart into the empty street of the Constitution; for it was considered the correct thing, the only proper style by the mule-drivers of the San Tomé mine to go through the waking town from end to end without a check in the speed as if chased by a devil.

The early sunshine glowed on the delicate primrose, pale pink, pale blue fronts of the big houses with all their gates shut yet, and no face behind the iron bars of the windows. In the whole sunlit range of empty balconies along the street only one white figure would be visible high up above the clear pavement—the wife of the Señor Administrador—leaning over to see the escort go by to the harbor, a mass of heavy, fair hair twisted up negligently on her little head, and a lot of lace about the neck of her muslin wrapper. With a smile to her husband's single, quick, upward glance, she would watch the whole thing stream past below her feet with an orderly uproar, till she answered by a friendly sign the salute of the galloping Don Pepe, the stiff, deferential inclination with a sweep of the hat below the knee.

The string of padlocked carts lengthened, the size of the escort grew bigger as the years went on. Every three months an increasing stream of treasure swept through the streets of Sulaco on its way to the strong room in the O.S.N. Company's building by the harbor, there to await shipment for the north. Increasing in volume, and of immense value also; for, as Charles Gould told his wife once with some exultation, there had never been seen anything in the world to approach the vein of the Gould Concession. For them both, each passing of the escort under the balconies of the Casa Gould was like another victory gained in the conquest of peace for Sulaco.

No doubt the initial action of Charles Gould had been helped at the beginning by a period of comparative peace which occurred just about that time; and also by the general softening of manners as compared with the epoch of civil wars whence had emerged the iron tyranny of Guzman Bento of fearful memory. In the contests that broke out at the end of his rule (which had kept peace in the country for a whole fifteen years) there was more fatuous imbecility, plenty of cruelty and suffering still, but much less of the old-time fierce and blindly ferocious political fanaticism. It was all more vile, more base, more contemptible, and infinitely more manageable in the very outspoken cynicism of motives. It was more clearly a brazen-faced scramble for a constantly diminishing quantity of booty; since all enterprise had been stupidly killed in the land. Thus it came to pass that the province of Sulaco, once the field of cruel party vengeances, had become in a way one of the considerable prizes of political career. The great of the earth (in Sta Marta) reserved the posts in the old Occidental State to those nearest and dearest to them; nephews, brothers, husbands of favorite sisters, bosom friends, trusty supporters—or prominent supporters of whom perhaps they were afraid. It was the blessed province of great opportunities and of largest salaries; for the San Tomé mine had its own unofficial pay list, whose items and amounts, fixed in consultation by Charles Gould and Señor Avellanos, were known to a prominent businessman in the United States, who for twenty minutes or so in every month gave his undivided attention to Sulaco affairs. At the same time the material interests of all sorts, backed up by the influence of the San Tomé mine, were quietly gathering substance in that part of the Republic. If, for instance, the Sulaco Collector-ship was generally understood, in the political world of the capital, to open the way to the Ministry of Finance, and so on for every official post, then, on the other hand, the despondent business circles of the Republic had come to consider the Occidental Province as the promised land of safety, especially if a man managed to get on good terms with the administration of the mine. "Charles Gould; excellent fellow! Abso-lutely necessary to make sure of him before taking a single step. Get an introduction to him from Moraga if you can—the agent of the King of Sulaco, don't you know."

No wonder, then, that Sir John, coming from Europe to smooth the path for his railway, had been meeting the name (and even the nickname) of Charles Gould at every turn in Costaguana. The agent of San Tomé Administration in Sta Marta (a polished, well-informed gentleman, Sir John thought him) had certainly helped so greatly in bringing about the presidential tour that he began to think that there was something in the faint whispers hinting at the immense occult influence of the Gould Concession. What was currently whispered was this—that the San Tomé Administra-tion had, in part, at least, financed the last revolution, which had brought into a five-year dictatorship Don Vincente Ribiera, a man of culture and of unblemished charac-ter, invested with a mandate of reform by the best elements of the State. Serious, well-informed men seemed to believe the fact, to hope for better things, for the establish-ment of legality, of good faith and order in public life. So much the better, then, thought Sir John. He worked always on a great scale; there was a loan to the State, and a project for systematic colonization of the Occidental Province, involved in one vast scheme with the construction of the National Central Railway. Good faith, order, honesty, peace, were badly wanted for this great development of material interests. Anybody on the side of these things, and especially if able to help, had an importance in Sir John's eyes. He had not been disappointed in the "King of Sulaco." The local difficulties had fallen away, as the engineer-in-chief had foretold they would, before Charles Gould's mediation. Sir John had been extremely fêted in Sulaco, next to the President-Dictator, a fact which might have accounted for the evident ill-humor Gen-eral Montero displayed at lunch given on board the *Juno* just before she was to sail, taking away from Sulaco the President-Dictator and the distinguished foreign guests in his train.

The Excellentissimo ("the hope of honest men," as Don José had addressed him in a public speech delivered in the name of the Provincial Assembly of Sulaco) sat at the head of the long table; Captain Mitchell, positively stony-eyed and purple in the face with the solemnity of this "historical event," occupied the foot as the representative of the O.S.N. Company in Sulaco, the hosts of that informal function, with the captain of the ship and some minor officials from the shore around him. Those cheery, swarthy little gentlemen cast jovial side-glances at the bottles of champagne beginning to pop behind the guests' backs in the hands of the ship's stewards. The amber wine creamed up to the rims of the glasses.

Charles Gould had his place next to a foreign envoy, who, in a listless undertone, had been talking to him fitfully of hunting and shooting. The well-nourished, pale face, with an eye-glass and drooping yellow moustache, made the Señor Administrador appear by contrast twice as sunbaked, more flaming red, a hundred times more intensely and silently alive. Don José Avellanos touched elbows with the other foreign diplomat, a dark man with a quiet, watchful, self-confident demeanor, and a touch of reserve. All etiquette being laid aside on the occasion, General Montero was the only one there in full uniform, so stiff with embroideries in front that his broad chest seemed protected by a cuirass of gold. Sir John at the beginning had got away from high places for the sake of sitting near Mrs. Gould.

The great financier was trying to express to her his grateful sense of her hospitality and of his obligation to her husband's "enormous influence in this part of the country," when she interrupted him by a low "Hush!" The President was going to make an informal pronouncement.

The Excellentissimo was on his legs. He said only a few words, evidently deeply felt, and meant perhaps mostly for Avellanos—his old friend—as to the necessity of unremitting effort to secure the lasting welfare of the country emerging after this last struggle, he hoped, into a period of peace and material prosperity.

Mrs. Gould, listening to the mellow, slightly mournful voice, looking at this rotund, dark, spectacled face, at the short body, obese to the point of infirmity, thought that this man of delicate and melancholy mind, physically almost a cripple, coming out of his retirement into a dangerous strife at the call of his fellows, had the right to speak with the authority of his self-sacrifice. And yet she was made uneasy. He was more pathetic than promising, this first civilian Chief of the State Costaguana had ever known, pronouncing, glass in hand, his simple watchwords of honesty, peace, respect for law, political good faith abroad and at home—the safeguards of national honor.

He sat down. During the respectful, appreciative buzz of voices that followed the speech, General Montero raised a pair of heavy, drooping eyelids and rolled his eyes with a sort of uneasy dullness from face to face. The military backwoods hero of the party, though secretly impressed by the sudden novelties and splendors of his position (he had never been on board a ship before, and had hardly ever seen the sea except from a distance), understood by a sort of instinct the advantage his surly, unpolished attitude of a savage fighter gave him amongst all these refined Blanco aristocrats. But why was it that nobody was looking at him? he wondered to himself angrily. He was able to spell out the print of newspapers, and knew that he had performed the "greatest military exploit of modern times."

"My husband wanted the railway," Mrs. Gould said to Sir John in the general murmur of resumed conversations. "All this brings nearer the sort of future we desire for the country, which has waited for it in sorrow long enough, God knows. But I will confess that the other day, during my afternoon drive when I suddenly saw an Indian boy ride out of a wood with the red flag of a surveying party in his hand, I felt something of a shock. The future means change—an utter change. And yet even here there are simple and picturesque things that one would like to preserve."

Sir John listened, smiling. But it was his turn now to hush Mrs. Gould.

"General Montero is going to speak," he whispered, and almost immediately added, in comic alarm, "Heavens! he's going to propose my own health, I believe."

General Montero had risen with a jingle of steel scabbard and a ripple of glitter on his gold-embroidered breast; a heavy swordhilt appeared at his side above the edge of the table. In this gorgeous uniform, with his bull neck, his hooked nose flattened on the tip upon a blue-black, dyed moustache, he looked like a disguised and sinister *vaquero*. The drone of his voice had a strangely rasping, soulless ring. He floundered, lowering, through a few vague sentences; then suddenly raising his big head and his voice together, burst out harshly:

"The honor of the country is in the hands of the army. I assure you I shall be faithful to it." He hesitated till his roaming eyes met Sir John's face, upon which he fixed a lurid, sleepy glance; and the figure of the lately negotiated loan came into his mind. He lifted his glass. "I drink to the health of the man who brings us a million and a half of pounds."

He tossed off his champagne, and sat down heavily with a half-surprised, half-bullying look all round the faces in the profound, as if appalled, silence which succeeded the felicitous toast. Sir John did not move.

"I don't think I am called upon to rise," he murmured to Mrs. Gould. "That sort of thing speaks for itself." But Don José Avellanos came to the rescue with a short oration, in which he alluded pointedly to England's goodwill towards Costaguana—"a goodwill," he continued significantly, "of which I, having been in my time accredited to the Court of St. James, am able to speak with some knowledge."

Only then Sir John thought fit to respond, which he did gracefully in bad French, punctuated by bursts of applause and the "Hear! Hears!" of Captain Mitchell, who was able to understand a word now and then. Directly he had done, the financier of railways turned to Mrs. Gould:

"You were good enough to say that you intended to ask me for something," he reminded her, gallantly. "What is it? Be assured that any request from you would be considered in the light of a favor to myself."

She thanked him by a gracious smile. Everybody was rising from the table.

"Let us go on deck," she proposed, "where I'll be able to point out to you the very object of my request."

An enormous national flag of Costaguana, diagonal red and yellow, with two green palm trees in the middle, floated lazily at the mainmast head of the *Juno*. A multitude of fireworks being let off in their thousands at the water's edge in honor of the President kept up a mysterious crepitating noise half round the harbor. Now and then a lot of rockets, swishing upwards invisibly, detonated overhead with only a puff of smoke in the bright sky. Crowds of people could be seen between the town gate and the harbor, under the bunches of multicolored flags fluttering on tall poles. Faint bursts of military music would be heard suddenly, and the remote sound of shouting. A knot of ragged Negroes at the end of the wharf kept on loading and firing a small iron cannon time after time. A grayish haze of dust hung thin and motionless against the sun.

Don Vincente Ribiera made a few steps under the deck-awning, leaning on the arm of Señor Avellanos; a wide circle was formed round him, where the mirthless smile of his dark lips and the sightless glitter of his spectacles could be seen turning amiably from side to side. The informal function arranged on purpose on board the *Juno* to give the President-Dictator an opportunity to meet intimately some of his most notable adherents in Sulaco was drawing to an end. On one side, General Montero, his bald head covered now by a plumed cocked hat, remained motionless on a skylight seat, a pair of big gauntleted hands folded on the hilt of the saber standing upright between his legs. The white plume, the coppery tint of his broad face, the blue-black of the moustaches under the curved beak, the mass of gold on sleeves and breast, the high shining boots with enormous spurs, the working nostrils, the imbecile and domineering stare of the glorious victor of Rio Seco had in them something ominous and incredible; the exaggeration of a cruel caricature, the fatuity of solemn masquerading, the atrocious grotesqueness of some military idol of Aztec conception and European bedecking, awaiting the homage of worshippers. Don José approached diplomatically this weird and inscrutable portent, and Mrs. Gould turned her fascinated eyes away at last.

Charles, coming up to take leave of Sir John, heard him say, as he bent over his wife's hand, "Certainly. Of course, my dear Mrs. Gould, for a protégé of yours! Not the slightest difficulty. Consider it done."

Going ashore in the same boat with the Goulds, Don José Avellanos was very silent. Even in the Gould carriage he did not open his lips for a long time. The mules trotted slowly away from the wharf between the extended hands of the beggars, who for that day seemed to have abandoned in a body the portals of churches. Charles Gould sat on the back seat and looked away upon the plain. A multitude of booths made of green boughs, of rushes, of odd pieces of plank eked out with bits of canvas had been erected all over it for the sale of cana, of dulces, of fruit, of cigars. Over little heaps of glowing charcoal Indian women, squatting on mats, cooked food in black earthen pots, and boiled the water for the maté gourds, which they offered in soft, caressing voices to the country people. A racecourse had been staked out for the *vaqueros;* and away to the left, from where the crowd was massed thickly about a huge temporary erection, like a circus tent of wood with a conical grass roof, came the resonant twanging of harp strings, the sharp ping of guitars, with the grave drumming throb of an Indian gombo pulsating steadily through the shrill choruses of the dancers.

Charles Gould said presently:

"All this piece of land belongs now to the Railway Company. There will be no more popular feasts held here."

Mrs. Gould was rather sorry to think so. She took this opportunity to mention how she had just obtained from Sir John the promise that the house occupied by Giorgio Viola should not be interfered with. She declared she could never understand why the survey engineers ever talked of demolishing that old building. It was not in the way of the projected harbor branch of the line in the least.

She stopped the carriage before the door to reassure at once the old Genoese, who came out bare-headed and stood by the carriage step. She talked to him in Italian, of course, and he thanked her with calm dignity. An old Garibaldino was grateful to her from the bottom of his heart for keeping the roof over the heads of his wife and children. He was too old to wander any more.

"And is it for ever, *signora?*" he asked.

"For as long as you like."

"*Bene.* Then the place must be named. It was not worth while before."

He smiled ruggedly, with a running together of wrinkles at the corners of his eyes. "I shall set about the painting of the name tomorrow."

"And what is it going to be, Giorgio?"

"Albergo d'Italia Una," said the old Garibaldino, looking away for a moment. "More in memory of those who have died," he added, "than for the country stolen from us soldiers of liberty by the craft of that accursed Piedmontese race of kings and ministers."

Mrs. Gould smiled slightly, and, bending over a little, began to inquire about his wife and children. He had sent them into town on that day. The *padrona* was better in health; many thanks to the *signora* for inquiring.

People were passing in twos and threes, in whole parties of men and women attended by trotting children. A horseman mounted on a silver-gray mare drew rein quietly in the shade of the house after taking off his hat to the party in the carriage, who returned smiles and familiar nods. Old Viola, evidently very pleased with the news he had just heard, interrupted himself for a moment to tell him rapidly that the house was secured, by the kindness of the English *signora*, for as long as he liked to keep it. The other listened attentively, but made no response.

When the carriage moved on he took off his hat again, a gray *sombrero* with a silver cord and tassels. The bright colors of a Mexican *serape* twisted on the cantle, the enormous silver buttons on the embroidered leather jacket, the row of tiny silver buttons down the seam of the trousers, the snowy linen, a silk sash with embroidered ends, the silver plates on headstall and saddle, proclaimed the unapproachable style of the famous Capataz de Cargadores—a Mediterranean sailor—got up with more finished splendor than any well-to-do young *ranchero* of the Campo had ever displayed on a high holiday.

"It is a great thing for me," murmured old Giorgio, still thinking of the house, for now he had grown weary of change. "The *signora* just said a word to the Englishman."

"The old Englishman who has enough money to pay for a railway? He is going off in an hour," remarked Nostromo, carelessly. "*Buon viaggio,* then. I've guarded his bones all the way from the Entrada pass down to the plain and into Sulaco, as though he had been my own father."

Old Giorgio only moved his head sideways absently. Nostromo pointed after the Goulds' carriage, nearing the grass-grown gate in the old town wall that was like a wall of matted jungle.

"And I have sat alone at night with my revolver in the Company's warehouse time and again by the side of that other Englishman's heap of silver, guarding it as though it had been my own."

Viola seemed lost in thought. "It is a great thing for me," he repeated again, as if to himself.

"It is," agreed the magnificent Capataz de Cargadores, calmly. "Listen, *vecchio*—go in and bring me out a cigar, but don't look for it in my room. There's nothing there."

Viola stepped into the café and came out directly, still absorbed in this idea, and tendered him a cigar, mumbling thoughtfully in his moustache. "Children growing up —and girls, too! Girls!" He sighed and fell silent.

"What, only one?" remarked Nostromo, looking down with a sort of comic inquisitiveness at the unconscious old man. "No matter," he added, with lofty negligence; "one is enough till another is wanted."

He lit and let the match drop from his passive fingers. Giorgio Viola looked up, and said abruptly:

"My son would have been just such a fine young man as you, Gian' Battista, if he had lived."

"What? Your son? But you are right, *padrone.* If he had been like me he would have been a man."

He turned his horse slowly, and paced on between the booths, checking the mare almost to a standstill now and then for children, for the groups of people from the distant Campo, who stared after him with admiration. The Company's lightermen saluted him from afar; and the greatly envied Capataz de Cargadores advanced, amongst murmurs of recognition and obsequious greetings, towards the huge circus-like erection. The throng thickened; the guitars tinkled louder; other horsemen sat motionless, smoking calmly above the heads of the crowd; it eddied and pushed before the doors of the high-roofed building, whence issued a shuffle and thumping of feet in time to the dance music vibrating and shrieking with a racking rhythm, overhung by the tremendous, sustained, hollow roar of the gombo. The barbarous and imposing noise of the big drum, that can madden a crowd, and that even Europeans cannot hear without a strange emotion, seemed to draw Nostromo on to its source, while a man, wrapped up in a faded, torn poncho, walked by his stirrup, and, buffeted right and left, begged "his worship" insistently for employment on the wharf. He whined, offering the Señor Capataz half his daily pay for the privilege of being admitted to the swaggering fraternity of *cargadores*; the other half would be enough for him, he protested. But Captain Mitchell's right-hand man—"invaluable for our work—a perfectly incorruptible fellow"—after looking down critically at the ragged *mozo*, shook his head without a word in the uproar going on around.

The man fell back; and a little farther on Nostromo had to pull up. From the doors of the dance-hall men and women emerged tottering, streaming with sweat, trembling in every limb, to lean, panting, with staring eyes and parted lips, against the wall of the structure, where the harps and guitars played on with mad speed in an incessant roll of thunder. Hundreds of hands clapped in there; voices shrieked, and then all at once would sink low, chanting in unison the refrain of a love song, with a dying fall. A red flower, flung with a good aim from somewhere in the crowd, struck the resplendent Capataz on the cheek.

He caught it as it fell, neatly, but for some time did not turn his head. When at last he condescended to look round, the throng near him had parted to make way for a pretty Morenita, her hair held up by a small golden comb, who was walking towards him in the open space.

Her arms and neck emerged plump and bare from a snowy chemisette; the blue woollen skirt, with all the fullness gathered in front, scanty on the hips and tight across the back, disclosed the provoking action of her walk. She came straight on and laid her hand on the mare's neck with a timid, coquettish look upwards out of the corner of her eyes.

"*Querido*," she murmured, caressingly, "why do you pretend not to see me when I pass?"

"Because I don't love thee any more," said Nostromo, deliberately, after a moment of reflective silence.

The hand on the mare's neck trembled suddenly. She dropped her head before all the eyes in the wide circle formed round the generous, the terrible, the inconstant Capataz de Cargadores, and his Morenita.

Nostromo, looking down, saw tears beginning to fall down her face.

"Has it come true, then, ever beloved of my heart?" she whispered. "Is it true?"

"No," said Nostromo, looking away carelessly. "It was a lie. I love thee as much as ever."

"Is that true?" she cooed, joyously, her cheeks still wet with tears.

"It is true."

"True on the life?"

"As true as that; but thou must not ask me to swear it on the Madonna that stands in thy room." And the Capataz laughed a little in response to the grins of the crowd.

She pouted—very pretty—a little uneasy.

"No, I will not ask for that. I can see love in your eyes." She laid her hand on his knee. "Why are you trembling like this? From love?" she continued, while the cavernous thundering of the gombo went on without a pause. "But if you love her as much as that, you must give your Paquita a gold-mounted rosary of beads for the neck of her Madonna."

"No," said Nostromo, looking into her uplifted, begging eyes, which suddenly turned stony with surprise.

"No? Then what else will your worship give me on the day of the fiesta?" she asked, angrily; "so as not to shame me before all these people."

"There is no shame for thee in getting nothing from thy lover for once."

"True! The shame is your worship's—my poor lover's," she flared up, sarcastically.

Laughs were heard at her anger, at her retort. What an audacious spitfire she was! The people aware of this scene were calling out urgently to others in the crowd. The circle round the silver-gray mare narrowed slowly.

The girl went off a pace or two, confronting the mocking curiosity of the eyes, then flung back to the stirrup, tiptoeing, her enraged face turned up to Nostromo with a pair of blazing eyes. He bent low to her in the saddle.

"Juan," she hissed, "I could stab thee to the heart!"

The dreaded Capataz de Cargadores, magnificent and carelessly public in his amours, flung his arm round her neck and kissed her spluttering lips. A murmur went round.

"A knife!" he demanded at large, holding her firmly by the shoulder.

Twenty blades flashed out together in the circle. A young man in holiday attire, bounding in, thrust one in Nostromo's hand and bounded back into the ranks, very proud of himself. Nostromo had not even looked at him.

"Stand on my foot," he commanded the girl, who, suddenly subdued, rose lightly, and when he had her up, encircling her waist, her face near to his, he pressed the knife into her little hand.

"No, Morenita! You shall not put me to shame," he said. "You shall have your present; and so that everyone should know who is your lover today, you may cut all the silver buttons off my coat."

There were shouts of laughter and applause at this witty freak, while the girl passed the keen blade, and the impassive rider jingled in his palm the increasing hoard of silver buttons. He eased her to the ground with both her hands full. After whispering for a while with a very strenuous face, she walked away, staring haughtily, and vanished into the crowd.

The circle had broken up, and the lordly Capataz de Cargadores, the indispensable man, the tried and trusty Nostromo, the Mediterranean sailor come ashore casually to try his luck in Costaguana, rode slowly towards the harbor. The *Juno* was just then swinging round; and even as Nostromo reined up again to look on, a flag ran up on the improvised flagstaff erected in an ancient and dismantled little fort at the harbor entrance. Half a battery of field guns had been hurried over there from the Sulaco barracks for the purpose of firing the regulation salutes for the President-Dictator and the War Minister. As the mail-boat headed through the pass, the badly timed reports announced the end of Don Vincente Ribiera's first official visit to Sulaco, and for Captain Mitchell the end of another "historic occasion." Next time when the "Hope of honest men" was to come that way, a year and a half later, it was unofficially, over the mountain tracks, fleeing after a defeat on a lame mule, to be only just saved by Nostromo from an ignominious death at the hands of a mob. It was a very different event, of which Captain Mitchell used to say:

"It was history—history, sir! And that fellow of mine, Nostromo, you know, was right in it. Absolutely making history, sir."

But this event, creditable to Nostromo, was to lead immediately to another, which could not be classed either as "history" or as "a mistake" in Captain Mitchell's phraseology. He had another word for it.

"Sir," he used to say afterwards, "that was no mistake. It was a fatality. A misfortune, pure and simple, sir. And that poor fellow of mine was right in it—right in the middle of it! A fatality, if ever there was one—and to my mind he has never been the same man since."

Part II
THE ISABELS

I

hrough good and evil report in the varying fortune of that struggle which Don José had characterized in the phrase, "the fate of national honesty trembles in the balance," the Gould Concession, "*Imperium in Imperio*," had gone on working; the square mountain had gone on pouring its treasure down the wooden shoots to the unresting batteries of stamps; the lights of San Tomé had twinkled night after night upon the great, limitless shadow of the Campo; every three months the silver escort had gone down to the sea as if neither the war nor its consequences could ever affect the ancient Occidental State secluded beyond its high barrier of the Cordillera. All the fighting took place on the other side of that mighty wall of serrated peaks lorded over by the white dome of Higuerota and as yet breached by the railway, of which only the first part, the easy Campo part from Sulaco to the Ivie Valley at the foot of the pass, had been laid. Neither did the telegraph line cross the mountains yet; its poles, like slender beacons on the plain, penetrated into the forest fringe of the foothills cut by the deep avenue of the track; and its wire ended abruptly in the construction camp at a white deal table supporting a Morse apparatus, in a long hut of planks with a corrugated-iron roof overshadowed by gigantic cedar trees—the quarters of the engineer in charge of the advance section.

The harbor was busy, too, with the traffic in railway material, and with the movements of troops along the coast. The O.S.N. Company had found much occupation for its fleet. Costaguana had no navy, and, apart from a few coastguard cutters, there were no national ships except a couple of old merchant steamers used as transports.

Captain Mitchell, feeling more and more in the thick of history, found time for an hour or so during an afternoon in the drawing-room of the Casa Gould, where, with a strange ignorance of the real forces at work around him, he professed himself delighted to get away from the strain of affairs. He did not know what he would have done

613

without his invaluable Nostromo, he declared. Those confounded Costaguana politics gave him more work—he confided to Mrs. Gould—than he had bargained for.

Don José Avellanos had displayed in the service of the endangered Ribiera Government an organizing activity and an eloquence of which the echoes reached even Europe. For, after the new loan to the Ribiera Government, Europe had become interested in Costaguana. The Sala of the Provincial Assembly (in the Municipal Buildings of Sulaco), with its portraits of the Liberators on the walls and an old flag of Cortés preserved in a glass case above the President's chair, had heard all these speeches—the early one containing the impassioned declaration "Militarism is the enemy," the famous one of the "trembling balance" delivered on the occasion of the vote for the raising of a second Sulaco regiment in the defense of the reforming Government; and when the provinces again displayed their old flags (proscribed in Guzman Bento's time) there was another of those great orations, when Don José greeted these old emblems of the war of Independence, brought out again in the name of new Ideals. The old idea of Federalism had disappeared. For his part he did not wish to revive old political doctrines. They were perishable. They died. But the doctrine of political rectitude was immortal. The second Sulaco regiment, to whom he was presenting this flag, was going to show its valor in a contest for order, peace, progress; for the establishment of national self-respect without which—he declared with energy—"we are a reproach and a byword amongst the powers of the world."

Don José Avellanos loved his country. He had served it lavishly with his fortune during his diplomatic career, and the later story of his captivity and barbarous ill-usage under Guzman Bento was well known to his listeners. It was a wonder that he had not been a victim of the ferocious and summary executions which marked the course of that tyranny; for Guzman had ruled the country with the somber imbecility of political fanaticism. The power of Supreme Government had become in his dull mind an object of strange worship, as if it were some sort of cruel deity. It was incarnated in himself, and his adversaries, the Federalists, were the supreme sinners, objects of hate, abhorrence, and fear, as heretics would be to a convinced Inquisitor. For years he had carried about at the tail of the Army of Pacification, all over the country, a captive band of such atrocious criminals, who considered themselves most unfortunate at not having been summarily executed. It was a diminishing company of nearly naked skeletons, loaded with irons, covered with dirt, with vermin, with raw wounds, all men of positions, of education, of wealth, who had learned to fight amongst themselves for scraps of rotten beef thrown to them by soldiers, or to beg a Negro cook for a drink of muddy water in pitiful accents. Don José Avellanos, clanking his chains amongst the others, seemed only to exist in order to prove how much hunger, pain, degradation, and cruel torture a human body can stand without parting with the last spark of life. Sometimes interrogatories, backed by some primitive method of torture, were administered to them by a commission of officers hastily assembled in a hut of sticks and branches, and made pitiless by the fear for their own lives. A lucky one or two of that spectral company of prisoners would perhaps be led tottering behind a bush to be shot by a file of soldiers. Always an army chaplain—some unshaven, dirty man, girt with a sword and with a tiny cross embroidered in white cotton on the left breast of a lieutenant's uniform—would follow, cigarette in the corner of the mouth, wooden stool in hand, to hear the confession and give absolution; for the Citizen Savior of the Country (Guzman Bento was called thus officially in petitions) was not averse from the exercise of rational clemency. The irregular report of the firing squad would be heard, followed sometimes by a single finishing shot; a little bluish cloud of smoke would float up above the green bushes, and the Army of Pacification would move on over the savannas, through the forests, crossing rivers, invading rural *pueblos*, devastating the *haciendas* of the horrid aristocrats, occupying the inlaid towns in the fulfilment of its patriotic mission, and leaving behind a united land wherein the evil taint of Federalism could no longer be detected in the smoke of burning houses and the smell of spilt blood.

Don José Avellanos had survived that time.

Perhaps, when contemptuously signifying to him his release, the Citizen Savior of the Country might have thought this benighted aristocrat too broken in health and spirit and fortune to be any longer dangerous. Or, perhaps, it may have been a simple caprice. Guzman Bento, usually full of fanciful fears and brooding suspicions, had sudden accesses of unreasonable self-confidence when he perceived himself elevated on a pinnacle of power and safety beyond the reach of mere mortal plotters. At such times he would impulsively command the celebration of a solemn Mass of thanksgiving which would be sung in great pomp in the cathedral of Sta Marta by the trembling, subservient Archbishop of his creation. He heard it sitting in a gilt armchair placed before the high altar, surrounded by the civil and military heads of his Government. The unofficial world of Sta Marta would crowd into the cathedral, for it was not quite safe for anybody of mark to stay away from these manifestations of presidential piety. Having thus acknowledged the only power he was at all disposed to recognize as above himself, he would scatter acts of political grace in a sardonic wantonness of clemency. There was no other way left now to enjoy his power but by seeing his crushed adversaries crawl impotently into the light of day out of the dark, noisome cells of the Collegio. Their harmlessness fed his insatiable vanity, and they could always be got hold of again. It was the rule for all the women of their families to present thanks afterwards in a special audience. The incarnation of that strange god, El Gobierno Supremo, received them standing, cocked hat on head, and exhorted them in a menacing mutter to show their gratitude by bringing up their children in fidelity to the democratic form of government, "which I have established for the happiness of our country." His front teeth having been knocked out in some accident of his former herdsman's life, his utterance was spluttering and indistinct. He had been working for Costaguana alone in the midst of treachery and opposition. Let it cease now lest he should become weary of forgiving!

Don José Avellanos had known this forgiveness.

He was broken in health and fortune deplorably enough to present a truly gratifying spectacle to the supreme chief of democratic institutions. He retired to Sulaco. His wife had an estate in that province, and she nursed him back to life out of the house of death and captivity. When she died, their daughter, an only child, was old enough to devote herself to "poor papa."

Miss Avellanos, born in Europe and educated partly in England, was a tall, grave girl, with a self-possessed manner, a wide, white forehead, a wealth of rich brown hair, and blue eyes.

The other young ladies of Sulaco stood in awe of her character and accomplishments. She was reputed to be terribly learned and serious. As to pride, it was well known that all the Corbeláns were proud, and her mother was a Corbelán. Don José Avellanos depended very much upon the devotion of his beloved Antonia. He accepted it in the benighted way of men, who, though made in God's image, are like stone idols without sense before the smoke of certain burnt offerings. He was ruined in every way, but a man possessed of passion is not a bankrupt in life. Don José Avellanos desired passionately for his country: peace, prosperity, and (as the end of the preface to *Fifty Years of Misrule* has it) "an honorable place in the comity of civilized nations." In this last phrase the Minister Plenipotentiary, cruelly humiliated by the bad faith of his Government towards the foreign bondholders, stands disclosed in the patriot.

The fatuous turmoil of greedy factions succeeding the tyranny of Guzman Bento seemed to bring his desire to the very door of opportunity. He was too old to descend personally into the center of the arena at Sta Marta. But the men who acted there sought his advice at every step. He himself thought that he could be most useful at a distance, in Sulaco. His name, his connections, his former position, his experience commanded the respect of his class. The discovery that this man, living in dignified poverty in the Corbelán town residence (opposite the Casa Gould), could dispose of material means towards the support of the cause increased his influence. It was his open letter of appeal that decided the candidature of Don Vincente Ribiera for the Presidency. Another of these informal State papers drawn up by Don José (this time in the shape of an address from the Province) induced that scrupulous constitutionalist to accept the extraordinary powers conferred upon him for five years by an overwhelming vote of congress in Sta Marta. It was a specific mandate to establish the prosperity of the people on the basis of firm peace at home, and to redeem the national credit by the satisfaction of all just claims abroad.

In the afternoon the news of that vote had reached Sulaco by the usual roundabout postal way through Cayta, and up the coast by steamer. Don José, who had been waiting for the mail in the Gould's drawing-room, got out of the rocking-chair, letting his hat fall off his knees. He rubbed his silvery, short hair with both hands, speechless with the excess of joy.

"Emilia, my soul," he had burst out, "let me embrace you! Let me—"

Captain Mitchell, had he been there, would no doubt have made an apt remark about the dawn of a new era; but if Don José thought something of the kind, his eloquence failed him on this occasion. The inspirer of that revival of the Blanco party tottered where he stood. Mrs. Gould moved forward quickly and, as she offered her cheek with a smile to her old friend, managed very cleverly to give him the support of her arm he really needed.

Don José had recovered himself at once, but for a time he could do no more than murmur, "Oh, you two patriots! Oh, you two patriots!"—looking from one to the other. Vague plans of another historical work, wherein all the devotions to the regeneration of the country he loved would be enshrined for the reverent worship of posterity, flitted through his mind. The historian who had enough elevation of soul to write of Guzman Bento: "Yet this monster, imbrued in the blood of his countrymen, must not be held unreservedly to the execration of future years. It appears to be true that he, too, loved his country. He had given it twelve years of peace; and, absolute master of lives and fortunes as he was, he died poor. His worst fault, perhaps, was not his ferocity, but his ignorance"; the man who could write thus of a cruel persecutor (the passage occurs in his *History of Misrule*) felt at the foreshadowing of success an almost boundless affection for his two helpers, for these two young people from over the sea.

Just as years ago, calmly, from the conviction of practical necessity, stronger than any abstract political doctrine, Henry Gould had drawn the sword, so now, the times being changed, Charles Gould had flung the silver of the San Tomé into the fray. The Inglés of Sulaco, the "Costaguana Englishman" of the third generation, was as far from being a political intriguer as his uncle from a revolutionary swashbuckler. Springing from the instinctive uprightness of their natures their action was reasoned. They saw an opportunity and used the weapon to hand.

Charles Gould's position—a commanding position in the background of that attempt to retrieve the peace and the credit of the Republic—was very clear. At the beginning he had had to accommodate himself to existing circumstances of corruption so naïvely brazen as to disarm the hatred of a man courageous enough not to be afraid of its irresponsible potency to ruin everything it touched. It seemed to him too contemptible for hot anger even. He made use of it with a cold, fearless scorn, manifested rather than concealed by the forms of stony courtesy which did away with much of the ignominy of the situation. At bottom, perhaps, he suffered from it, for he was not a man of cowardly illusions, but he refused to discuss the ethical view with his wife. He trusted that, though a little disenchanted, she would be intelligent enough to understand that his character safeguarded the enterprise of their lives as much as or more than his policy. The extraordinary development of the mine had put a great power into his hands. To feel that prosperity always at the mercy of unintelligent greed had grown irksome to him. To Mrs. Gould it was humiliating. At any rate, it was dangerous. In the confidential communications passing between Charles Gould, the King of Sulaco, and the head of the silver and steel interests far away in California, the conviction was growing that any attempt made by men of education and integrity ought to be discreetly supported. "You may tell your friend Avellanos that I think so," Mr. Holroyd had written at the proper moment from his inviolable sanctuary within the eleven-story-high factory of great affairs. And shortly afterwards, with a credit opened by the Third Southern Bank (located next door but one to the Holroyd Building), the Ribierist party in Costaguana took a practical shape under the eye of the administrator of the San Tomé mine. And Don José, the hereditary friend of the Gould family, could say: "Perhaps, my dear Carlos, I shall not have believed in vain."

II

After another armed struggle, decided by Montero's victory of Río Seco, had been added to the tale of civil wars, the "honest men," as Don José called them, could breathe freely for the first time in half a century. The Five-Year-Mandate law became the basis of that regeneration, the passionate desire and hope for which had been like the elixir of everlasting youth for Don José Avellanos.

And when it was suddenly—and not quite unexpectedly—endangered by that "brute Montero," it was a passionate indignation that gave him a new lease of life, as it were. Already, at the time of the President-Dictator's visit to Sulaco, Moraga had sounded a note of warning from Sta Marta about the War Minister. Montero and his brother made the subject of an earnest talk between the Dictator-President and the Nestor-inspirer of the party. But Don Vincente, a doctor of philosophy from the Cordova University, seemed to have an exaggerated respect for military ability, whose mysteriousness—since it appeared to be altogether independent of intellect—imposed upon his imagination. The Victor of Río Seco was a popular hero. His services were so recent that the President-Dictator quailed before the obvious charge of political ingratitude. Great regenerating transactions were being initiated—the fresh loan, a new railway line, a vast colonization scheme. Anything that could unsettle the public opinion in the capital was to be avoided. Don José bowed to these arguments and tried to dismiss from his mind the gold-laced portent in boots, and with a saber, made meaningless now at last, he hoped, in the new order of things.

Less than six months after the President-Dictator's visit, Sulaco learned with stupefaction of the military revolt in the name of national honor. The Minister of War, in a barrack-square allocution to the officers of the artillery regiment he had been inspecting, had declared the national honor sold to foreigners. The Dictator, by his weak compliance with the demands of the European powers—for the settlement of long outstanding money claims—had showed himself unfit to rule. A letter from Moraga explained afterwards that the initiative, and even the very text, of the incendiary allocution came, in reality, from the other Montero, the *ex-guerrillero*, the Commandante de Plaza. The energetic treatment of Dr. Monygham, sent for in haste "to the mountain," who came galloping three leagues in the dark, saved Don José from a dangerous attack of jaundice.

After getting over the shock, Don José refused to let himself be prostrated. Indeed, better news succeeded at first. The revolt in the capital had been suppressed after a night of fighting in the streets. Unfortunately, both the Monteros had been able to make their escape south, to their native province of Entre-Montes. The hero of the forest march, the victor of Rio Seco, had been received with frenzied acclamations in Nicoya, the provincial capital. The troops in garrison there had gone to him in a body. The brothers were organizing an army, gathering malcontents, sending emissaries primed with patriotic lies to the people, and with promises of plunder to the wild *llaneros*. Even a Monterist press had come into existence, speaking oracularly of the secret promises of support given by "our great sister Republic of the North" against the sinister land-grabbing designs of European powers, cursing in every issue the "miserable Ribiera," who had plotted to deliver his country, bound hand and foot, for a prey to foreign speculators.

Sulaco, pastoral and sleepy, with its opulent Campo and the rich silver mine, heard the din of arms fitfully in its fortunate isolation. It was nevertheless in the very forefront of the defense with men and money; but the very rumors reached it circuitously—from abroad even, so much was it cut off from the rest of the Republic, not only by natural obstacles, but also by the vicissitudes of the war. The Monteristos were besieging Cayta, an important postal link. The overland couriers ceased to come across the mountains, and no muleteer would consent to risk the journey at last; even Bonifacio on one occasion failed to return from Sta Marta, either not daring to start, or perhaps captured by the parties of the enemy raiding the country between the Cordillera and the capital. Monterist publications, however, found their way into the province, mysteriously enough; and also Monterist emissaries preaching death to aristocrats in the villages and towns of the Campo. Very early, at the beginning of the trouble, Hernandez, the bandit, had proposed (through the agency of an old priest of a village in the wilds) to deliver two of them to the Ribierist authorities in Tonoro. They had come to offer him a free pardon and the rank of colonel from General Montero in consideration of joining the rebel army with his mounted band. No notice was taken at the time of the proposal. It was joined, as an evidence of good faith, to a petition praying the Sulaco Assembly for permission to enlist, with all his followers, in the forces being then raised in Sulaco for the defense of the Five-Year-Mandate of its regeneration. The petition, like everything else, had found its way into Don José's hands. He had showed to Mrs. Gould these pages of dirty-grayish rough paper (perhaps looted in some village store), covered with the crabbed, illiterate handwriting of the old padre, carried off from his hut by the side of a mud-walled church to be the secretary of the dreaded *Salteador*. They had both bent in the lamplight of the Gould drawing-room over the document containing the fierce and yet humble appeal of the man against the blind and stupid barbarity turning an honest *ranchero* into a bandit. A postscript of the priest stated that, but for being deprived of his liberty for ten days, he had been treated with humanity and the respect due to his sacred calling. He had been, it appears, confessing and absolving the chief and most of the band, and he guaranteed the sincerity of their good disposition. He had distributed heavy penances, no doubt in the way of litanies and fasts; but he argued shrewdly that it would be difficult for them to make their peace with God durably till they made peace with men.

Never before, perhaps, had Hernandez's head been in less jeopardy than when he petitioned humbly for permission to buy a pardon for himself and his gang of deserters by armed service. He could range afar from the waste lands protecting his fastness, unchecked, because there were no troops left in the whole province. The usual garrison of Sulaco had gone south to the war, with its brass band playing the "Bolívar March" on the bridge of one of the O.S.N. Company's steamers. The great family coaches drawn up along the shore of the harbor were made to rock on the high leathern springs by the enthusiasm of the *señoras* and the *señoritas* standing up to wave their lace handkerchiefs, as lighter after lighter packed full of troops left the end of the jetty.

Nostromo directed the embarkation, under the superintendence of Captain Mitchell, red-faced in the sun, conspicuous in a white waistcoat, representing the allied and anxious goodwill of all the material interests of civilization. General Barrios, who commanded the troops, assured Don José on parting that in three weeks he would have Montero in a wooden cage drawn by three pair of oxen ready for a tour through all the towns of the Republic.

"And then, *señora*," he continued, baring his curly iron-gray head to Mrs. Gould in her landau—"and then, *señora*, we shall convert our swords into ploughshares and grow rich. Even I, myself, as soon as this little business is settled, shall open a *fundación* on some land I have on the *llanos* and try to make a little money in peace and quietness. *Señora*, you know, all Costaguana knows—what do I say?—this whole South American continent knows, that Pablo Barrios has had his fill of military glory."

Charles Gould was not present at the anxious and patriotic send-off. It was not his part to see the soldiers embark. It was neither his part, nor his inclination, nor his policy. His part, his inclination, and his policy were united in one endeavor to keep unchecked the flow of treasure he had started single-handed from the re-opened scar in the flank of the mountain. As the mine developed he had trained for himself some native help. There were foremen, artificers, and clerks, with Don Pepe for the *gobernador* of the mining population. For the rest his shoulders alone sustained the whole weight of the *"Imperium in Imperio,"* the great Gould Concession whose mere shadow had been enough to crush the life out of his father.

Mrs. Gould had no silver mine to look after. In the general life of the Gould Concession she was represented by her two lieutenants, the doctor and the priest, but she fed her woman's love for excitement on events whose significance was purified to her by the fire of her imaginative purpose. On that day she had brought the Avellanos, father and daughter, down to the harbor with her.

Amongst his other activities of that stirring time, Don José had become the chairman of a Patriotic Committee which had armed a great proportion of troops in the Sulaco command with an improved model of a military rifle. It had been just discarded for something still more deadly by one of the great European powers. How much of the market-price for second-hand weapons was covered by the voluntary contributions of the principal families, and how much came from those funds Don José was understood to command abroad, remained a secret which he alone could have disclosed; but the *ricos*, as the populace called them, had contributed under the pressure of their Nestor's eloquence. Some of the more enthusiastic ladies had been moved to bring offerings of jewels into the hands of the man who was the life and soul of the party.

There were moments when both his life and his soul seemed overtaxed by so many years of undiscouraged belief in regeneration. He appeared almost inanimate, sitting rigidly by the side of Mrs. Gould in the landau, with his fine, old, clean-shaven face of a uniform tint as if modeled in yellow wax, shaded by a soft felt hat, the dark eyes looking out fixedly. Antonia, the beautiful Antonia, as Miss Avellanos was called in

Sulaco, leaned back, facing them; and her full figure, the grave oval of her face with full red lips, made her look more mature than Mrs. Gould, with her mobile expression and small, erect person under a slightly swaying sunshade.

Whenever possible Antonia attended her father; her recognized devotion weakened the shocking effect of her scorn for the rigid conventions, regulating the life of Spanish-American girlhood. And, in truth, she was no longer girlish. It was said that she often wrote State papers from her father's dictation, and was allowed to read all the books in his library. At the receptions—where the situation was saved by the presence of a very decrepit old lady (a relation of the Corbeláns), quite deaf and motionless in an armchair—Antonia could hold her own in a discussion with two or three men at a time. Obviously she was not the girl to be content with peeping through a barred window at a cloaked figure of a lover ensconced in a doorway opposite—which is the correct form of Costaguana courtship. It was generally believed that with her foreign upbringing and foreign ideas the learned and proud Antonia would never marry—unless, indeed, she married a foreigner from Europe or North America, now that Sulaco seemed on the point of being invaded by all the world.

III

When General Barrios stopped to address Mrs. Gould, Antonia raised negligently her hand holding an open fan, as if to shade from the sun her head, wrapped in a light lace shawl. The clear gleam of her blue eyes gliding behind the black fringe of eyelashes paused for a moment upon her father, then traveled farther to the figure of a young man of thirty at most, of medium height, rather thick-set, wearing a light overcoat. Bearing down with the open palm of his hand upon the knob of a flexible cane, he had been looking on from a distance; but directly he saw himself noticed, he approached quietly and put his elbow over the door of the landau.

The shirt collar, cut low in the neck, the big bow of his cravat, the style of his clothing, from the round hat to the varnished shoes, suggested an idea of French elegance; but otherwise he was the very type of a fair Spanish creole. The fluffy moustache and the short, curly, golden beard did not conceal his lips, rosy, fresh, almost pouting in expression. His full, round face was of that warm, healthy creole white which is never tanned by its native sunshine. Martin Decoud was seldom exposed to the Costaguana sun under which he was born. His people had been long settled in Paris, where he had studied law, had dabbled in literature, had hoped now and then in moments of exaltation to become a poet like that other foreigner of Spanish blood, José Maria Heredia. In other moments he had, to pass the time, condescended to write articles on European affairs for the *Semenario*, the principal newspaper in Sta Marta, which printed them under the heading "From our special correspondent." though the authorship was an open secret. Everybody in Costaguana, where the tale of compatriots in Europe is jealously kept, knew that it was "the son Decoud," a talented young man, supposed to be moving in the higher spheres of Society. As a matter of fact, he was an idle boulevardier, in touch with some smart journalists, made free of a few newspaper offices, and welcomed in the pleasure-haunts of pressmen. This life, whose dreary superficiality is covered by the glitter of universal *blague*, like the stupid clowning of a harlequin by the spangles of a motley costume, induced in him a Frenchified—but most un-French—cosmopolitanism, in reality a mere barren indifferentism posing as intellectual superiority. Of his own country he used to say to his French associates: "Imagine an atmosphere of *opéra bouffe* in which all the comic business of stage statesmen, brigands, etc., etc., all their farcical stealing, intriguing, and stabbing is done in dead earnest. It is screamingly funny, the blood flows all the time, and the actors believe themselves to be influencing the fate of the universe. Of course, government in general, any government anywhere, is a thing of exquisite comicality to a discerning mind; but really we Spanish-Americans do over-step the bounds. No man of ordinary intelligence can take part in the intrigues of *une farce macabre*. However, these Ribierists, of whom we hear so much just now, are really trying in their own comical way to make the country habitable, and even to pay some of its debts. My friends, you had better write up Señor Ribiera all you can in kindness to your own bondholders. Really, if what I am told in my letters is true, there is some chance for them at last."

And he would explain with railing verve what Don Vincente Ribiera stood for—a mournful little man oppressed by his own good intentions, the significance of battles won, who Montero was (*un grotesque vaniteux et féroce*), and the manner of the new loan connected with railway development, and the colonization of vast tracts of land in one great financial scheme.

And his French friends would remark that evidently this little fellow Decoud *connaissait la question à fond*. An important Parisian review asked him for an article on the situation. It was composed in a serious tone and in a spirit of levity. Afterwards he asked one of his intimates:

"Have you read my thing about the regeneration of Costaguana—*une bonne blague, hein?*"

He imagined himself Parisian to the tips of his fingers. But far from being that he was in danger of remaining a sort of nondescript dilettante all his life. He had pushed the habit of universal raillery to a point where it blinded him to the genuine impulses of his own nature. To be suddenly selected for the executive member of the patriotic small-arms committee of Sulaco seemed to him the height of the unexpected, one of those fantastic moves of which only his "dear countrymen" were capable.

"It's like a tile falling on my head. I—I—executive member! It's the first I hear of it! What do I know of military rifles? *C'est funambulesque!*" he had exclaimed to his favorite sister; for the Decoud family—except the old father and mother—used the French language amongst themselves. "And you should see the explanatory and confidential letter! Eight pages of it—no less!"

This letter, in Antonia's handwriting, was signed by Don José, who appealed to the "young and gifted Costaguanero" on public grounds, and privately opened his heart to his talented godson, a man of wealth and leisure, with wide relations, and by his parentage and bringing-up worthy of all confidence.

"Which means," Martin commented, cynically, to his sister, "that I am not likely to misappropriate the funds, or go blabbing to our Chargé d'Affaires here."

The whole thing was being carried out behind the back of the War Minister, Montero, a mistrusted member of the Ribiera Government, but difficult to get rid of at once. He was not to know anything of it till the troops under Barrio's command had the new rifle in their hands. The President-Dictator, whose position was very difficult, was alone in the secret.

"How funny!" commented Martin's sister and confidant; to which the brother, with an air of best Parisian *blague*, had retorted:

"It's immense! The idea of that Chief of the State engaged, with the help of private citizens, in digging a mine under his own indispensable War Minister. No! We are unapproachable!" And he laughed immoderately.

Afterwards his sister was surprised at the earnestness and ability he displayed in carrying out his mission, which circumstances made delicate, and his want of special knowledge rendered difficult. She had never seen Martin take so much trouble about anything in his whole life.

"It amuses me," he had explained, briefly. "I am beset by a lot of swindlers trying to sell all sorts of gaspipe weapons. They are charming; they invite me to expensive luncheons; I keep up their hopes; it's extremely entertaining. Meanwhile, the real affair is being carried through in quite another quarter."

When the business was concluded he declared suddenly his intention of seeing the precious consignment delivered safely in Sulaco. The whole burlesque business, he thought, was worth following up to the end. He mumbled his excuses, tugging at his golden beard, before the acute young lady who (after the first wide stare of astonishment) looked at him with narrowed eyes, and pronounced slowly:

"I believe you want to see Antonia."

"What Antonia?" asked the Costaguana boulevardier, in a vexed and disdainful tone. He shrugged his shoulders, and spun round on his heel. His sister called out after him joyously:

"The Antonia you used to know when she wore her hair in two plaits down her back."

He had known her some eight years since, shortly before the Avellanos had left Europe for good, as a tall girl of sixteen, youthfully austere, and of a character already so formed that she ventured to treat slightingly his pose of disabused wisdom. On one occasion, as though she had lost all patience, she flew out at him about the aimlessness of his life and the levity of his opinions. He was twenty then, an only son, spoiled by his adoring family. This attack disconcerted him so greatly that he had faltered in his affection of amused superiority before that insignificant chit of a school-girl. But the impression left was so strong that ever since all the girl friends of his sisters recalled to him Antonia Avellanos by some faint resemblance, or by the great force of contrast. It was, he told himself, like a ridiculous fatality. And, of course, in the news the Decouds received regularly from Costaguana, the name of their friends, the Avellanos, cropped up frequently—the arrest and the abominable treatment of the ex-Minister, the dangers and hardships endured by the family, its withdrawal in poverty to Sulaco, the death of the mother.

The Monterist *pronunciamiento* had taken place before Martin Decoud reached Costaguana. He came out in a roundabout way, through Magellan's Straits by the main line and the West Coast Service of the O.S.N. Company. His precious consignment arrived just in time to convert the first feelings of consternation into a mood of hope and resolution. Publicly he was made much of by the *familias principales*. Privately Don José, still shaken and weak, embraced him with tears in his eyes.

"You have come out yourself! No less could be expected from a Decoud. Alas! our worst fears have been realized," he moaned, affectionately. And again he hugged his godson. This was indeed the time for men of intellect and conscience to rally round the endangered cause.

It was then that Martin Decoud, the adopted child of Western Europe, felt the absolute change of atmosphere. He submitted to being embraced and talked to without a word. He was moved in spite of himself by that note of passion and sorrow unknown on the more refined stage of European politics. But when the tall Antonia, advancing with her light step in the dimness of the big bare *sala* of the Avellanos house, offered him her hand (in her emancipated way), and murmured, "If am glad to see you here, Don Martin," he felt how impossible it would be to tell these two people that he had intended to go away by the next month's packet. Don José, meantime, continued his praises. Every accession added to public confidence, and, besides, what an example to the young men at home from the brilliant defender of the country's regeneration, the worthy expounder of the party's political faith before the world! Everybody had read the magnificent article in the famous *Parisian Review*. The world was now informed: and the author's appearance at this moment was like a public act of faith. Young Decoud felt overcome by a feeling of impatient confusion. His plan had been to return by way of the United States through California, visit Yellowstone Park, see Chicago, Niagara, have a look at Canada, perhaps make a short stay in New York, a longer one in Newport, use his letters of introduction. The pressure of Antonia's hand was so frank, the tone of her voice was so unexpectedly unchanged in its approving warmth, that all he found to say after his low bow was:

"I am inexpressibly grateful for your welcome; but why need a man be thanked for returning to his native country? I am sure Doña Antonia does not think so."

"Certainly not, *señor*," she said, with that perfectly calm openness of manner which characterized all her utterances. "But when he returns, as you return, one may be glad —for the sake of both."

Martin Decoud said nothing of his plans. He not only never breathed a word of them to anyone, but only a fortnight later asked the mistress of the Casa Gould (where he had of course obtained admission at once), leaning forward in his chair with an air of well-bred familiarity, whether she could not detect in him that day a marked change —an air, he explained, of more excellent gravity. At this Mrs. Gould turned her face full towards him with the silent inquiry of slightly widened eyes and the merest ghost of a smile, a habitual movement with her, which was very fascinating to men by something subtly devoted, finely self-forgetful in its lively readiness of attention. Because, Decoud continued imperturbably, he felt no longer an idle cumberer of the earth. She was, he assured her, actually beholding at that moment the Journalist of Sulaco. At once Mrs. Gould glanced towards Antonia, posed upright in the corner of a high, straight-backed Spanish sofa, a large black fan waving slowly against the curves of her fine figure, the tips of crossed feet peeping from under the hem of the black skirt. Decoud's eyes also remained fixed there, while in an undertone he added that Miss Avellanos was quite aware of his new and unexpected vocation, which in Costaguana was generally the speciality of half-educated Negroes and wholly penniless lawyers. Then, confronting with a sort of urbane effrontery Mrs. Gould's gaze, now turned sympathetically upon himself, he breathed out the words, *"Pro patria!"*

What had happened was that he had all at once yielded to Don José's pressing entreaties to take the direction of a newspaper that would "voice the aspirations of the province." It had been Don José's old and cherished idea. The necessary plant (on a modest scale) and a large consignment of paper had been received from America some time before; the right man alone was wanted. Even Señor Moraga in Sta Marta had not been able to find one, and the matter was now becoming pressing; some organ was absolutely needed to counteract the effect of the lies disseminated by the Monterist Press: the atrocious calumnies, the appeals of the people calling upon them to rise with their knives in their hands and put an end once for all to the Blancos, to these Gothic remnants, to these sinister mummies, these impotent *paralíticos,* who plotted with foreigners for the surrender of the lands and the slavery of the people.

The clamor of this "Negro Liberalism" frightened Señor Avellanos. A newspaper was the only remedy. And now that the right man had been found in Decoud, great black letters appeared painted between the windows above the arcaded ground floor of a house on the Plaza. It was next to Anzani's great emporium of boots, silks, ironware, muslins, wooden toys, tiny silver arms, legs, heads, hearts (for ex-voto offerings), rosaries, champagne, women's hats, patent medicines, even a few dusty books in paper covers and mostly in the French language. The big black letters formed the words, "Offices of the *Porvenir.*" From these offices a single folded sheet of Martin's journalism issued three times a week; and the sleek yellow Anzani prowling in a suit of ample black and carpet slippers, before the many doors of his establishment, greeted by a deep, side-long inclination of his body the Journalist of Sulaco going to and fro on the business of his august calling.

IV

Perhaps it was in the exercise of his calling that he had come to see the troops depart. The *Porvenir* of the day after next would no doubt relate the event, but its editor, leaning his side against the landau, seemed to look at nothing. The front rank of the company of infantry drawn up three deep across the shore-end of the jetty when pressed too close would bring their bayonets to the charge ferociously, with an awful rattle; and then the crowd of spectators swayed back bodily, even under the noses of the big white mules. Notwithstanding the great multitude there was only a low, muttering noise; the dust hung in a brown haze, in which the horsemen, wedged in the throng here and there, towered from the hips upwards, gazing all one way over the heads. Almost every one of them had mounted a friend, who steadied himself with both hands grasping his shoulders from behind; and the rims of their hats touching, made like one disc sustaining the cones of two pointed crowns with a double face underneath. A hoarse *mozo* would bawl out something to an acquaintance in the ranks, or a woman would shriek suddenly the word *Adiós!* followed by the Christian name of a man.

General Barrios, in a shabby blue tunic and white peg-top trousers falling upon strange red boots, kept his head uncovered and stooped slightly, propping himself up with a thick stick. No! He had earned enough military glory to satiate any man, he insisted to Mrs. Gould, trying at the same time to put an air of gallantry into his attitude. A few jetty hairs hung sparsely from his upper lip, he had a salient nose, a thin, long jaw, and a black silk patch over one eye. His other eye, small and deep-set, twinkled erratically in all directions, aimlessly affable. The few European spectators, all men, who had naturally drifted into the neighborhood of the Gould carriage, betrayed by the solemnity of their faces their impression that the general must have had too much punch (Swedish punch, imported in bottles by Anzani) at the Amarilla Club before he had started with his Staff on a furious ride to the harbor. But Mrs. Gould bent forward, self-possessed, and declared her conviction that still more glory awaited the general in the near future.

"*Señora!*" he remonstrated, with great feeling, "in the name of God, reflect! How can there be any glory for a man like me in overcoming that bald-headed *embustero* with the dyed moustaches?"

Pablo Ignacio Barrios, son of a village *alcalde*, general of division, commanding in chief the Occidental Military district, did not frequent the higher society of the town. He preferred the unceremonious gatherings of men where he could tell jaguar-hunt stories, boast of his powers with the lasso, with which he could perform extremely difficult feats of the sort "no married man should attempt," as the saying goes amongst the *llaneros;* relate tales of extraordinary night rides, encounters with wild bulls, struggles with crocodiles, adventures in the great forests, crossings of swollen rivers. And it was not mere boastfulness that prompted the general's reminiscences, but a genuine love of that wild life which he had led in his young days before he turned his back for ever on the thatched roof of the parental *toldería* in the woods. Wandering away as far as Mexico he had fought against the French by the side (as he said) of Juarez, and was the only military man of Costaguana who had ever encountered European troops in the field. That fact shed a great luster upon his name till it became eclipsed by the rising star of Montero. All his life he had been an inveterate gambler. He alluded himself quite openly to the current story how once, during some campaign (when in command of a brigade), he had gambled away his horses, pistols, and accoutrements, to the very epaulettes, playing *monte* with his colonels the night before the battle. Finally, he had sent under escort his sword (a presentation sword, with a gold hilt) to the town in the rear of his position to be immediately pledged for five hundred pesetas with a sleepy and frightened shopkeeper. By daybreak he had lost the last of that money, too, when his only remark, as he rose calmly, was, "Now let us go and fight to the death." From that time he had become aware that a general could lead his troops into battle very well with a simple stick in his hand. "It has been my custom ever since," he would say.

He was always overwhelmed with debts; even during the periods of splendor in his varied fortunes of a Costaguana general, when he held high military commands, his gold-laced uniforms were almost always in pawn with some tradesman. And at last, to avoid the incessant difficulties of costume caused by the anxious lenders, he had assumed a disdain of military trappings, an eccentric fashion of shabby old tunics, which had become like a second nature. But the faction Barrios joined needed to fear no political betrayal. He was too much of a real soldier for the ignoble traffic of buying and selling victories. A member of the foreign diplomatic body in Sta Marta had once passed a judgment upon him: "Barrios is a man of perfect honesty and even of some talent for war, *mais il manque de tenue.*" After the triumph of the Ribierists he had obtained the reputedly lucrative Occidental command, mainly through the exertions of his creditors (the Sta Marta shopkeepers, all great politicians), who moved heaven and earth in his interest publicly, and privately besieged Señor Moraga, the influential agent of the San Tomé mine, with the exaggerated lamentations that if the general were passed over, "we shall all be ruined." An incidental but favorable mention of his name in Mr. Gould senior's long correspondence with his son had something to do with his appointment, too; but most of all undoubtedly his established political honesty. No one questioned the personal bravery of the Tiger-killer, as the populace called him. He was, however, said to be unlucky in the field—but this was to be the beginning of an era of peace. The soldiers liked him for his humane temper, which was like a strange and precious flower unexpectedly blooming on the hotbed of corrupt revolutions; and when he rode slowly through the streets during some military display, the contemptuous good humor of his solitary eye roaming over the crowds extorted the acclamations of the populace. The women of that class especially seemed positively fascinated by the long drooping nose, the peaked chin, the heavy lower lip, the black silk eye-patch and band slanting rakishly over the forehead. His high rank always procured an audience of *caballeros* for his sporting stories, which he detailed very well with a simple, grave enjoyment. As to the society of ladies, it was irksome by the restraints it imposed without any equivalent, as far as he could see. He had not, perhaps, spoken three times on the whole to Mrs. Gould since he had taken up his high command; but he had observed her frequently riding with the Señor Administrador, and had pronounced that there was more sense in her little bridle-hand than in all the female heads in Sulaco. His impulse had been to be very civil on parting to a woman who did not wobble in the saddle, and happened to be the wife of a personality very important to a man always short of money. He even pushed his attentions so far as to desire the aide-de-camp at his side (a thick-set, short captain with a Tartar physiognomy) to bring along a corporal with a file of men in front of the carriage, lest the crowd in its backward surges would "incommode the mules of the *señora.*" Then, turning to the small knot of silent Europeans looking on within earshot, he raised his voice protectingly:

"*Señores*, have no apprehension. Go on quietly making your Ferro Carril—your railways, your telegraphs. Your—There's enough wealth in Costaguana to pay for everything—or else you would not be here. Ha! ha! Don't mind this little *picardía* of my friend Montero. In a little while you shall behold his dyed mustaches through the bars of a strong wooden cage. *Sí, señores!* Fear nothing, develop the country, work, work!"

The little group of engineers received this exhortation without a word, and after waving his hand at them loftily, he addressed himself again to Mrs. Gould:

"That is what Don José says we must do. Be enterprising! Work! Grow rich! To put Montero in a cage is my work; and when that insignificant piece of business is done, then, as Don José wishes us, we shall grow rich, one and all, like so many Englishmen, because it is money that saves a country, and—"

But a young officer in a very new uniform, hurrying up from the direction of the jetty, interrupted his interpretation of Señor Avellanos's ideals. The general made a movement of impatience; the other went on talking to him insistently, with an air of respect. The horses of the Staff had been embarked, the steamer's gig was awaiting the general at the boat steps; and Barrios, after a fierce stare of his one eye, began to take leave. Don José roused himself for an appropriate phrase pronounced mechanically. The terrible strain of hope and fear was telling on him, and he seemed to husband the last sparks of his fire for those oratorical efforts of which even the distant Europe was to hear. Antonia, her red lips firmly closed, averted her head behind the raised fan; and young Decoud, though he felt the girl's eyes upon him, gazed away persistently, hooked on his elbow, with a scornful and complete detachment. Mrs. Gould heroically concealed her dismay at the appearance of men and events so remote from her racial conventions, dismay too deep to be uttered in words even to her husband. She understood his voiceless reserve better now. Their confidential intercourse fell, not in moments of privacy, but precisely in public, when the quick meeting of their glances would comment upon some fresh turn of events. She had gone to his school of uncompromising silence, the only one possible, since so much that seemed shocking, weird, and grotesque in the working out of their purposes had to be accepted as normal in this country. Decidedly, the stately Antonia looked more mature and infinitely calm; but she would never have known how to reconcile the sudden sinkings of her heart with an amiable mobility of expression.

Mrs. Gould smiled a good-bye at Barrios, nodded round to the Europeans (who raised their hats simultaneously) with an engaging invitation. "I hope to see you all presently, at home," then said nervously to Decoud, "Get in, Don Martin," and heard him mutter to himself in French, as he opened the carriage door, *"Le sort en est jeté."* She heard him with a sort of exasperation. Nobody ought to have known better than himself that the first cast of dice had been already thrown long ago in a most desperate game. Distant acclamations, words of command yelled out, and a roll of drums on the jetty greeted the departing general. Something like a slight faintness came over her, and she looked blankly at Antonia's face, wondering what would happen to Charley if that absurd man failed. *"A la casa, Ignacio,"* she cried at the motionless broad back of the coachman, who gathered the reins without haste, mumbling to himself under his breath, *"Sí, la casa. Sí, sí, niña."*

The carriage rolled noiselessly on the soft track, the shadows fell long on the dusty little plain interspersed with dark bushes, mounds of turned-up earth, low wooden buildings with iron roofs of the Railway Company; the sparse row of telegraph poles strode obliquely clear of the town, bearing a single, almost invisible wire far into the great *campo*—like a slender, vibrating feeler of that progress waiting outside for a moment of peace to enter and twine itself about the weary heart of the land.

The café window of the Albergo d'Italia Una was full of sunburnt, whiskered faces of railway men. But at the other end of the house, the end of the Signori Inglesi, old Giorgio, at the door with one of his girls on each side, bared his bushy head, as white as the snows of Higuerota. Mrs. Gould stopped the carriage. She seldom failed to speak to the protégé; moreover, the excitement, the heat, and the dust had made her thirsty. She asked for a glass of water. Giorgio sent the children indoors for it, and approached with pleasure expressed in his whole rugged countenance. It was not often that he had occasion to see his benefactress, who was also an Englishwoman—another title to his regard. He offered some excuses for his wife. It was a bad day with her; her oppressions—he tapped his own broad chest. She could not move from her chair that day.

Decoud, ensconced in the corner of his seat, observed gloomily Mrs. Gould's old revolutionist, then, offhand:

"Well, and what do you think of it all, Garibaldino?"

Old Giorgio, looking at him with some curiosity, said civilly that the troops had marched very well. One-eyed Barrios and his officers had done wonders with the recruits in a short time. Those *Indios*, only caught the other day, had gone swinging past in double-quick time, like *bersaglieri*; they looked well fed, too, and had whole uniforms. "Uniforms!" he repeated with a half-smile of pity. A look of grim retrospect stole over his piercing, steady eyes. It had been otherwise in his time when men fought against tyranny, in the forests of Brazil, or on the plains of Uruguay, starving on half-raw beef without salt, half naked, with often only a knife tied to a stick for a weapon. "And yet we used to prevail against the oppressor," he concluded, proudly.

His animation fell; the slight gesture of his hand expressed discouragement; but he added that he had asked one of the sergeants to show him the new rifle. There was no such weapon in his fighting days; and if Barrios could not—

"Yes, yes," broke in Don José, almost trembling with eagerness. "We are safe. The good Señor Viola is a man of experience. Extremely deadly—is it not so? You have accomplished your mission admirably, my dear Martin."

Decoud, lolling back moodily, contemplated old Viola.

"Ah! Yes. A man of experience. But who are you for, really, in your heart?"

Mrs. Gould leaned over to the children. Linda had brought out a glass of water on a tray, with extreme care; Giselle presented her with a bunch of flowers gathered hastily.

"For the people," declared old Viola, sternly.

"We are all for the people—in the end."

"Yes," muttered old Viola, savagely. "And meantime they fight for you. Blind. *Esclavos!*"

At that moment young Scarfe of the railway staff emerged from the door of the part reserved for the Signori Inglesi. He had come down to headquarters from somewhere up the line on a light engine, and had had just time to get a bath and change his clothes. He was a nice boy, and Mrs. Gould welcomed him.

"It's a delightful surprise to see you, Mrs. Gould. I've just come down. Usual luck. Missed everything, of course. This show is just over, and I hear there has been a great dance at Don Juste Lopez's last night. Is it true?"

"The young patricians," Decoud began suddenly in his precise English, "have indeed been dancing before they started off to the war with the Great Pompey."

Young Scarfe stared, astounded. "You haven't met before," Mrs. Gould intervened. "Mr. Decoud—Mr. Scarfe."

"Ah! But we are not going to Pharsalia," protested Don José, with nervous haste, also in English. "You should not jest like this, Martin."

Antonia's breast rose and fell with a deeper breath. The young engineer was utterly in the dark. "Great what?" he muttered, vaguely.

"Luckily, Montero is not a Caesar," Decoud continued. "Not the two Monteros put together would make a decent parody of a Caesar." He crossed his arms on his breast, looking at Señor Avellanos, who had returned to his immobility. "It is only you, Don José, who are a genuine old Roman—*vir Romanus*—eloquent and inflexible."

Since he had heard the name of Montero pronounced, young Scarfe had been eager to express his simple feelings. In a loud and youthful tone he hoped that this Montero was going to be licked once for all and done with. There was no saying what would happen to the railway if the revolution got the upper hand. Perhaps it would have to be abandoned. It would not be the first railway gone to pot in Costaguana. "You know, it's one of their so-called national things," he ran on, wrinkling up his nose as if the world had a suspicious flavor to his profound experience of South American affairs. And, of course, he chatted with animation, it had been such an immense piece of luck for him at his age to get appointed on the staff "of a big thing like that—don't you know." It would give him the pull over a lot of chaps all through life, he asserted. "Therefore—down with Montero! Mrs. Gould." His artless grin disappeared slowly before the unanimous gravity of the faces turned upon him from the carriage; only that "old chap," Don José, presenting a motionless, waxy profile, stared straight on as if deaf. Scarfe did not know the Avellanos very well. They did not give balls, and Antonia never appeared at a ground-floor window, as some other young ladies used to do attended by elder women, to chat with the *caballeros* on horseback in the *calle*. The stares of these creoles did not matter much; but what on earth had come to Mrs. Gould? She said, "Go on, Ignacio," and gave him a slow inclination of the head. He heard a short laugh from that round-faced, Frenchified fellow. He colored up to the eyes, and stared at Giorgio Viola, who had fallen back with the children, hat in hand.

"I shall want a horse presently," he said with some asperity to the old man.

"*Sí, señor.* There are plenty of horses," muttered the Garibaldino, smoothing absently, with his brown hands, the two heads, one dark with bronze glints, the other fair with a coppery ripple, of the two girls by his side. The returning stream of sightseers raised a great dust on the road. Horsemen noticed the group. "Go to your mother," he said. "They are growing up as I am growing older, and there is nobody—"

He looked at the young engineer and stopped, as if awakened from a dream; then, folding his arms on his breast, took up his usual position, leaning back in the doorway with an upward glance fastened on the white shoulder of Higuerota far away.

In the carriage Martin Decoud, shifting his position as though he could not make himself comfortable, muttered as he swayed towards Antonia, "I suppose you hate me." Then in a loud voice he began to congratulate Don José upon all the engineers being convinced Ribierists. The interest of all those foreigners was gratifying. "You have heard this one. He is an enlightened well-wisher. It is pleasant to think that the prosperity of Costaguana is of some use to the world."

"He is very young," Mrs. Gould remarked, quietly.

"And so very wise for his age," retorted Decoud. "But here we have the naked truth from the mouth of that child. You are right, Don José. The natural treasures of Costaguana are of importance to the progressive Europe represented by this youth, just as three hundred years ago the wealth of our Spanish fathers was a serious object to the rest of Europe—as represented by the bold buccaneers. There is a curse of futility upon our character: Don Quixote and Sancho Panza, chivalry and materialism, high-sounding sentiments and a supine morality, violent efforts for an idea and a sullen acquiescence in every form of corruption. We convulsed a continent for our independence only to become the passive prey of a democratic parody, the helpless victims of scoundrels and cut-throats, our institutions a mockery, our laws a farce—a Guzman Bento our master! And we have sunk so low that when a man like you has awakened our conscience, a stupid barbarian of a Montero—Great Heavens! a Montero!— becomes a deadly danger, and an ignorant, boastful *indio*, like Barrios, is our defender."

But Don José, disregarding the general indictment as though he had not heard a word of it, took up the defense of Barrios. The man was competent enough for his special task in the plan of campaign. It consisted in an offensive movement, with Cayta as base, upon the flank of the revolutionist forces advancing from the south against Sta Marta, which was covered by another army with the President-Dictator in its midst. Don José became quite animated with a great flow of speech, bending forward anxiously under the steady eyes of his daughter. Decoud, as if silenced by so much ardor, did not make a sound. The bells of the city were striking the hour of *Oración* when the carriage rolled under the old gateway facing the harbor like a shapeless monument of leaves and stones. The rumble of wheels under the sonorous arch was traversed by a strange, piercing shriek, and Decoud, from his back seat, had a view of the people behind the carriage trudging along the road outside, all turning their heads, in *sombreros* and *rebozos*, to look at a locomotive which rolled quickly out of sight behind Giorgio Viola's house, under a white trail of steam that seemed to vanish in the breathless, hysterically prolonged scream of warlike triumph. And it was all like a fleeting vision, the shrieking ghost of a railway engine fleeing across the frame of the archway, behind the startled movement of the people streaming back from a military spectacle with silent footsteps on the dust of the road. It was a material train returning from the Campo to the palisaded yards. The empty cars rolled lightly on the single track; there was no rumble of wheels, no tremor on the ground. The engine-driver, running past the Casa Viola with the salute of an uplifted arm, checked his speed smartly before entering the yard; and when the ear-splitting screech of the steam-whistle for the brakes had stopped, a series of hard, battering shocks, mingled with the clanking of chain-couplings, made a tumult of blows and shaken fetters under the vault of the gate.

V

The Gould carriage was the first to return from the harbor to the empty town. On the ancient pavement, laid out in patterns, sunk into ruts and holes, the portly Ignacio, mindful of the springs of the Parisian-built landau, had pulled up to a walk, and Decoud in his corner contemplated moodily the inner aspect of the gate. The squat turreted sides held up between them a mass of masonry with bunches of grass growing at the top, and a gray, heavily scrolled armorial shield of stone above the apex of the arch with the arms of Spain nearly smoothed out as if in readiness for some new device typical of the impending progress.

The explosive noise of the railway trucks seemed to augment Decoud's irritation. He muttered something to himself, then began to talk aloud in curt, angry phrases thrown at the silence of the two women. They did not look at him at all; while Don José, with his semi-translucent, waxy complexion, overshadowed by the soft gray hat, swayed a little to the jolts of the carriage by the side of Mrs. Gould.

"This sound puts a new edge on a very old truth."

Decoud spoke in French, perhaps because of Ignacio on the box above him; the old coachman, with his broad back filling a short, silver-braided jacket, had a big pair of ears, whose thick rims stood well away from his cropped head.

"Yes, the noise outside the city wall is new, but the principle is old."

He ruminated his discontent for a while, then began afresh with a sidelong glance at Antonia:

"No, but just imagine our forefathers in morions and corselets drawn up outside this gate, and a band of adventurers just landed from their ships in the harbor there. Thieves, of course. Speculators, too. Their expeditions, each one, were the speculations of grave and reverend persons in England. That is history, as that absurd sailor Mitchell is always saying."

"Mitchell's arrangements for the embarkation of the troops were excellent!" exclaimed Don José.

"That!—that! oh, that's really the work of that Genoese seaman! But to return to my noises; there used to be in the old days the sound of trumpets outside that gate.

War trumpets! I'm sure they were trumpets. I have read somewhere that Drake, who was the greatest of these men, used to dine alone in his cabin on board ship to the sound of trumpets. In those days this town was full of wealth. Those men came to take it. Now the whole land is like a treasure-house, and all these people are breaking into it, whilst we are cutting each other's throats. The only thing that keeps them out is mutual jealousy. But they'll come to an agreement some day—and by the time we've settled our quarrels and become decent and honorable, there'll be nothing left for us. It has always been the same. We are a wonderful people, but it has always been our fate to be"—he did not say "robbed," but added, after a pause—"exploited!"

Mrs. Gould said, "Oh, this is unjust!" And Antonia interjected, "Don't answer him, Emilia. He is attacking me."

"You surely do not think I was attacking Don Carlos!" Decoud answered.

And then the carriage stopped before the door of the Casa Gould. The young man offered his hand to the ladies. They went in first together; Don José walked by the side of Decoud, and the gouty old porter tottered after them with some light wraps on his arm.

Don José slipped his hand under the arm of the journalist of Sulaco.

"The *Porvenir* must have a long and confident article upon Barrios and the irresistibleness of his army of Cayta! The moral effect should be kept up in the country. We must cable encouraging extracts to Europe and the United States to maintain a favorable impression abroad."

Decoud muttered, "Oh, yes, we must comfort our friends, the speculators."

The long open gallery was in shadow, with its screen of plants in vases along the balustrade, holding out motionless blossoms, and all the glass doors of the reception-rooms thrown open. A jingle of spurs died out at the farther end.

Basilio, standing aside against the wall, said in a soft tone to the passing ladies, "The Señor Administrador is just back from the mountain."

In the great *sala*, with its group of ancient Spanish and modern European furniture making as if different centers under the high white spread of the ceiling, the silver and porcelain of the tea-service gleamed among a cluster of dwarf chairs, like a bit of a lady's boudoir, putting in a note of feminine and intimate delicacy.

Don José in his rocking-chair placed his hat on his lap, and Decoud walked up and down the whole length of the room, passing between tables loaded with knick-knacks and almost disappearing behind the high backs of leathern sofas. He was thinking of the angry face of Antonia; he was confident that he would make his peace with her. He had not stayed in Sulaco to quarrel with Antonia.

Martin Decoud was angry with himself. All he saw and heard going on around him exasperated the preconceived views of his European civilization. To contemplate revolutions from the distance of the Parisian Boulevards was quite another matter. Here on the spot it was not possible to dismiss their tragic comedy with the expression, *"Quelle farce!"*

The reality of the political action, such as it was, seemed closer, and acquired poignancy by Antonia's belief in the cause. Its crudeness hurt his feelings. He was surprised at his own sensitiveness.

"I suppose I am more of a Costaguanero than I would have believed possible," he thought to himself.

His disdain grew like a reaction of his skepticism against the action into which he was forced by his infatuation for Antonia. He soothed himself by saying he was not a patriot, but a lover.

The ladies came in bareheaded, and Mrs. Gould sank low before the little tea-table. Antonia took up her usual place at the reception hour—the corner of a leathern couch, with a rigid grace in her pose and a fan in her hand. Decoud, swerving from the straight line of his march, came to lean over the high back of her seat.

For a long time he talked into her ear from behind, softly, with a half smile and an air of apologetic familiarity. Her fan lay half grasped on her knees. She never looked at him. His rapid utterance grew more and more insistent and caressing. At last he ventured a slight laugh.

"No, really. You must forgive me. One must be serious sometimes." He paused. She turned her head a little; her blue eyes glided slowly towards him, slightly upwards, mollified and questioning.

"You can't think I am serious when I call Montero a *gran' bestia* every second day in the *Porvenir?* That is not a serious occupation. No occupaion is serious, not even when a bullet through the heart is the penalty of failure!"

Her hand closed firmly on her fan.

"Some reason, you understand, I mean some sense, may creep into thinking; some glimpse of truth. I mean some effective truth, for which there is no room in politics or journalism. I happen to have said what I thought. And you are angry! If you do me the kindness to think a little you will see that I spoke like a patriot."

She opened her red lips for the first time, not unkindly.

"Yes, but you never see the aim. Men must be used as they are. I suppose nobody is really disinterested, unless, perhaps, you, Don Martin."

"God forbid! It's the last thing I should like you to believe of me." He spoke lightly, and paused.

She began to fan herself with a slow movement without raising her hand. After a time he whispered passionately:

"Antonia!"

She smiled, and extended her hand after the English manner towards Charles Gould, who was bowing before her, while Decoud, with his elbows spread on the back of the sofa, dropped his eyes and murmured, *"Bonjour."*

The Señor Administrador of the San Tomé mine bent over his wife for a moment. They exchanged a few words, of which only the phrase, "The greatest enthusiasm," pronounced by Mrs. Gould, could be heard.

"Yes," Decoud began in a murmur. "Even he!"

"This is sheer calumny," said Antonia, not very severely.

"You just ask him to throw his mine into the melting-pot for the great cause," Decoud whispered.

Don José had raised his voice. He rubbed his hands cheerily. The excellent aspect of the troops and the great quantity of new deadly rifles on the shoulders of those brave men seemed to fill him with an ecstatic confidence.

Charles Gould, very tall and thin before his chair, listened, but nothing could be discovered in his face except a kind of deferential attention.

Meantime, Antonia had risen, and, crossing the room, stood looking out of one of the three long windows giving on the street. Decoud followed her. The window was thrown open, and he leaned against the thickness of the wall. The long folds of the damask curtain, falling straight from the broad brass cornice, hid him partly from the room. He folded his arms on his breast, and looked steadily at Antonia's profile.

The people returning from the harbor filled the pavements; the shuffle of sandals and a low murmur of voices ascended to the window. Now and then a coach rolled slowly along the disjointed roadway of the Calle de la Constición. There were not many private carriages in Sulaco; at the most crowded hour on the Alameda they could be counted with one glance of the eye. The great family arks swayed on high leathern springs, full of pretty powdered faces in which the eyes looked intensely alive and black. And first Don Juste Lopez, the President of the Provincial Assembly, passed with his three lovely daughters, solemn in a black frock-coat and stiff white tie, as when directing a debate from a high tribune. Though they all raised their eyes, Antonia did not make the usual greeting gesture of a fluttered hand, and they affected not to see the two young people, Costaguaneros with European manners, whose eccentricities were discussed behind the barred windows of the first families in Sulaco. And then the widowed Señora Gavilaso de Valdes rolled by, handsome and dignified, in a great machine in which she used to travel to and from her country house, surrounded by an armed retinue in leather suits and big sombreros, with carbines at the bows of their saddles. She was a woman of most distinguished family, proud, rich, and kind-hearted. Her second son, Jaime, had just gone off on the Staff of Barrios. The eldest, a worthless fellow of a moody disposition, filled Sulaco with the noise of his dissipations, and gambled heavily at the club. The two youngest boys, with yellow Ribierist cockades in their caps, sat on the front seat. She, too, affected not to see the Señor Decoud talking publicly with Antonia in defiance of every convention. And he not even her *novio* as far as the world knew! Though, even in that case, it would have been scandal enough. But the dignified old lady, respected and admired by the first families, would have been still more shocked if she could have heard the words they were exchanging.

"Did you say I lost sight of the aim? I have only one aim in the world."

She made an almost imperceptible negative movement of her head, still staring across the street at the Avellanos's house, gray, marked with decay, and with iron bars like a prison.

"And it would be so easy of attainment," he continued, "this aim which, whether knowingly or not, I have always had in my heart—ever since the day when you snubbed me so horribly once in Paris, you remember."

A slight smile seemed to move the corner of the lip that was on his side.

"You know you were a very terrible person, a sort of Charlotte Corday in a schoolgirl's dress; a ferocious patriot. I suppose you would have stuck a knife into Guzman Bento?"

She interrupted him. "You do me too much honor."

"At any rate," he said, changing suddenly to a tone of bitter levity, "you would have sent me to stab him without compunction."

"Ah, *par exemple!*" she murmured in a shocked tone.

"Well," he argued, mockingly, "you do keep me here writing deadly nonsense. Deadly to me! It has already killed my self-respect. And you may imagine," he continued, his tone passing into light banter, "that Montero, should he be successful, would get even with me in the only way such a brute can get even with a man of intelligence who condescends to call him a *gran' bestia* three times a week. It's a sort of intellectual death; but there is the other one in the background for a journalist of my ability."

"If he is successful," said Antonia, thoughtfully.

"You seem satisfied to see my life hang on a thread," Decoud replied, with a broad smile. "And the other Montero, the 'my trusted brother' of the proclamations, the *guerrillero*—haven't I written that he was taking the guests' overcoats and changing plates in Paris at our Legation in the intervals of spying on our refugees there, in the time of Rojas? He will wash out that sacred truth in blood. In my blood! Why do you look annoyed? This is simply a bit of the biography of one of our great men. What do you think he will do to me? There is a certain convent wall round the corner of the Plaza, opposite the door of the Bull Ring. You know? Opposite the door with the inscription, 'Intrada de la Sombra.' Appropriate, perhaps! That's where the uncle of our host gave up his Anglo-South-American soul. And, note, he might have run away. A man who has fought with weapons may run away. You might have let me go with Barrios if you had cared for me. I would have carried one of those rifles, in which Don José believes, with the greatest satisfaction, in the ranks of poor peons and *indios*, that know nothing either of reason or politics. The most forlorn hope in the most forlorn army on earth would have been safer than that for which you made me stay here. When you make war you may retreat, but not when you spend your time in inciting poor ignorant fools to kill and to die."

His tone remained light, and as if unaware of his presence she stood motionless, her hands clasped lightly, the fan hanging down from her interlaced fingers. He waited for a while, and then:

"I shall go to the wall," he said, with a sort of jocular desperation.

Even that declaration did not make her look at him. Her head remained still, her eyes fixed upon the house of the Avellanos, whose chipped pilasters, broken cornices, the whole degradation of dignity was hidden now by the gathering dusk of the street. In her whole figure her lips alone moved, forming the words:

"Martin, you will make me cry."

He remained silent for a minute, startled, as if overwhelmed by a sort of awed happiness, with the lines of the mocking smile still stiffened about his mouth, and incredulous surprise in his eyes. The value of a sentence is in the personality which utters it, for nothing new can be said by man or woman; and those were the last words, it seemed to him, that could ever have been spoken by Antonia. He had never made it up with her so completely in all their intercourse of small encounters; but even before she had time to turn towards him, which she did slowly with a rigid grace, he had begun to plead:

"My sister is only waiting to embrace you. My father is transported with joy. I won't say anything of my mother! Our mothers were like sisters. There is the mail-boat for the south next week—let us go. That Morago is a fool! A man like Montero is bribed. It's the practice of the country. It's tradition—it's politics. Read *Fifty Years of Misrule*."

"Leave poor papa alone, Don Martin. He believes—"

"I have the greatest tenderness for your father," he began, hurriedly. "But I love you, Antonia! And Moraga has miserably mismanaged this business. Perhaps your father did, too; I don't know. Montero was bribable. Why, I suppose he only wanted his share of this famous loan for national development. Why didn't the stupid Sta Marta people give him a mission to Europe, or something? He would have taken five years' salary in advance, and gone on loafing in Paris, this stupid, ferocious *indio!*"

"The man," she said, thoughtfully, and very calm before this outburst, "was intoxicated with vanity. We had all the information, not from Moragao only; from others, too. There was his brother intriguing, too."

"Oh, yes!" he said. "Of course you know. You know everything. You read all the correspondence, you write all the papers—all those State papers that are inspired here, in this room, in blind deference to a theory of political purity. Hadn't you Charles Gould before you eyes? 'Rey de Sulaco!' He and his mine are the practical demonstration of what could have been done. Do you think he succeeded by his fidelity to a theory of virtue? And all those railway people, with their honest work! Of course, their work is honest! But what if you cannot work honestly till the thieves are satisfied? Could he not, a gentleman, have told this Sir John what's-his-name that Montero had to be bought off—he and all his Negro liberals hanging on to his gold-laced sleeve? He ought to have been bought off with his own stupid weight of gold—his weight of gold, I tell you, boots, saber, spurs, cocked hat, and all."

She shook her head slightly. "It was impossible," she murmured.

"He wanted the whole lot? What?"

She was facing him now in the deep recess of the window, very close and motionless. Her lips moved rapidly. Decoud, leaning his back against the wall, listened with crossed arms and lowered eyelids. He drank the tones of her even voice, and watched the agitated life of her throat, as if waves of emotion had run from her heart to pass out into the air in her reasonable words. He also had his aspirations, he aspired to carry her away out of these deadly futilities of *pronunciamientos* and reforms. All this was wrong—utterly wrong; but she fascinated him, and sometimes the sheer sagacity of a phrase would break the charm, replace the fascination by a sudden unwilling thrill of interest. Some women hovered, as it were, on the threshold of genius, he reflected. They did not want to know, or think, or understand. Passion stood for all that, and he was ready to believe that some startlingly profound remark, some appreciation of character, or a judgment upon an event, bordered on the miraculous. In the mature Antonia he could see with an extraordinary vividness the austere schoolgirl of the earlier days. She seduced his attention; sometimes he could not restrain a murmur of assent; now and then he advanced an objection quite seriously. Gradually they began to argue; the curtain half hid them from the people in the *sala.*

Outside it had grown dark. From the deep trench of shadow between the houses, lit up vaguely by the glimmer of street lamps, ascended the evening silence of Sulaco; the silence of a town with a few carriages, of unshod horses, and a softly sandalled population. The windows of the Casa Gould flung their shining parallelograms upon the house of Avellanos. Now and then a shuffle of feet passed below with the pulsating red glow of a cigarette at the foot of the walls; and the night air, as if cooled by the snows of Higuerota, refreshed their faces.

"We Occidentals," said Martin Decoud, using the usual term the provincials of Sulaco applied to themselves, "have been always distinct and separated. As long as we hold Cayta nothing can reach us. In all our troubles no army has marched over those mountains. A revolution in the central provinces isolated us at once. Look how complete it is now! The news of Barrios's movement will be cabled to the United States, and only in that way will it reach Sta Marta by the cable from the other seaboard. We have the greatest riches, the greatest fertility, the purest blood in our great families, the most laborious population. The Occidental Province should stand alone. The early Federalism was not bad for us. Then came this union which Don Henrique Gould resisted. It opened the road to tyranny; and, ever since, the rest of Costaguana hangs like a millstone round our necks. The Occidental territory is large enough to make any man's country. Look at the mountains! Nature itself seems to cry to us 'Separate!' "

She made an energetic gesture of negation. A silence fell.

"Oh, yes, I know it's contrary to the doctrine laid down in the *History of Fifty Years' Misrule.* I am only trying to be sensible. But my sense seems always to give you cause for offense. Have I startled you very much with this perfectly reasonable aspiration?"

She shook her head. No, she was not startled, but the idea shocked her early convictions. Her patriotism was larger. She had never considered that possibility.

"It may yet be the means of saving some of your convictions," he said, prophetically.

She did not answer. She seemed tired. They leaned side by side on the rail of the little balcony, very friendly, having exhausted politics, giving themselves up to the silent feeling of their nearness, in one of those profound pauses that fall upon the rhythm of passion. towards the *plaza* end of the street the glowing coals in the *brazeros* of the market women cooking their evening meal gleamed red along the edge of the pavement. A man appeared without a sound in the light of a street lamp, showing the colored inverted triangle of his bordered poncho, square on his shoulders, hanging to a point below his knees. From the harbor end of the *calle* a horseman walked his soft-stepping mount, gleaming silver-gray abreast each lamp under the dark shape of the rider.

"Behold the illustrious Capataz de Cargadores," said Decoud, gently, "coming in all his splendor after his work is done. The next great man of Sulaco after Don Carlos Gould. But he is good-natured, and let me make friends with him."

"Ah, indeed!" said Antonia. "How did you make friends?"

"A journalist ought to have his finger on the popular pulse, and this man is one of the leaders of the populace. A journalist ought to know remarkable men—and this man is remarkable in his way."

"Ah, yes!" said Antonia, thoughtfully. "It is known that this Italian has a great influence."

The horseman had passed below them, with a gleam of dim light on the shining broad quarters of the gray mare, on a bright heavy stirrup, on a long silver spur; but the short flick of yellowish flame in the dusk was powerless against the muffled-up mysteriousness of the dark figure with an invisible face concealed by a great *sombrero*.

Decoud and Antonia remained leaning over the balcony, side by side, touching elbows, with their heads overhanging the darkness of the street, and the brilliantly lighted *sala* at their backs. This was a *tête-à-tête* of extreme impropriety; something of which in the whole extent of the Republic only the extraordinary Antonia could be capable—the poor, motherless girl, never accompanied, with a careless father, who had thought only of making her learned. Even Decoud himself seemed to feel that this was as much as he could expect of having her to himself till—till the revolution was over and he could carry her off to Europe, away from the endlessness of civil strife, whose folly seemed even harder to bear than its ignominy. After one Montero there would be another, the lawlessness of a populace of all colors and races, barbarism, irremediable tyranny. As the great Liberator Bolívar had said in the bitterness of his spirit, "America is ungovernable. Those who worked for her independence have ploughed the sea." He did not care, he declared boldly; he seized every opportunity to tell her that though she had managed to make a Blanco journalist of him, he was no patriot. First of all, the word had no sense for cultured minds, to whom the narrowness of every belief is odious; and secondly, in connection with the everlasting troubles of this unhappy country it was hopelessly besmirched; it had been the cry of dark barbarism, the cloak of lawlessness, of crimes, of rapacity, of simple thieving.

He was surprised at the warmth of his own utterance. He had no need to drop his voice; it had been low all the time, a mere murmur in the silence of dark houses with their shutters closed early against the night air, as is the custom of Sulaco. Only the *sala* of the Casa Gould flung out defiantly the blaze of its four windows, the bright appeal of light in the whole dumb obscurity of the street. And the murmur on the little balcony went on after a short pause.

"But we are laboring to change all that," Antonia protested. "It is exactly what we desire. It is our object. It is the great cause. And the word you despise has stood also for sacrifice, for courage, for constancy, for suffering. Papa, who—"

"Ploughing the sea," interrupted Decoud, looking down.

There was below the sound of hasty and ponderous footsteps.

"Your uncle, the Grand Vicar of the cathedral, has just turned under the gate," observed Decoud. "He said Mass for the troops in the Plaza this morning. They had built for him an altar of drums, you know. And they brought outside all the painted blocks to take the air. All the wooden saints stood militarily in a row at the top of the great flight of steps. They looked like a gorgeous escort attending the Vicar-General. I saw the great function from the windows of the *Porvenir*. He is amazing, your uncle, the last of the Corbeláns. He glittered exceedingly in his vestments with a great crimson velvet cross down his back. And all the time our savior Barrios sat in the Amarilla Club drinking punch at an open window. *Espirit fort*—our Barrios. I expected every moment your uncle to launch an ex-communication there and then at the black eye-patch in the window across the Plaza. But not at all. Ultimately the troops marched off. Later Barrios came down with some of the officers, and stood with his uniform all unbuttoned, discoursing at the edge of the pavement. Suddenly your uncle appeared, no longer glittering, but all black, at the cathedral door with that threatening aspect he has—you know, like a sort of avenging spirit. He gives one look, strides over straight at the group of uniforms, and leads away the general by the elbow. He walked him for a quarter of an hour in the shade of a wall. Never let go his elbow for a moment, talking all the time with exaltation, and gesticulating with a long black arm. It was a curious scene. The officers seemed struck with astonishment. Remarkable man, your missionary uncle. He hates an infidel much less than a heretic, and prefers a heathen many times to an infidel. He condescends graciously to call me a heathen, sometimes, you know."

Antonia listened with her hands over the balustrade, opening and shutting the fan gently; and Decoud talked a little nervously, as if afraid that she would leave him at the first pause. Their comparative isolation, the precious sense of intimacy, the slight contact of their arms, affected him softly; for now and then a tender inflection crept into the flow of his ironic murmurs.

"Any slight sign of favor from a relative of yours is welcome, Antonia. And perhaps he understands me, after all! But I know him, too, our Padre Corbelán. The idea of political honor, justice, and honesty for him consists in the restitution of the confiscated Church property. Nothing else could have drawn that fierce converter of savage Indians out of the wilds to work for the Ribierist cause! Nothing else but that wild hope! He would make a *pronunciamiento* himself for such an object against any Government if he could only get followers! What does Don Carlos Gould think of that? But, of course, with his English impenetrability, nobody can tell what he thinks. Probably he thinks of nothing apart from his mine; of his 'Imperium in Imperio'. As to Mrs. Gould, she thinks of her schools, of her hospitals, of the mothers with the young babies, of every sick old man in the three villages. If you were to turn your head now you would see her extracting a report from that sinister doctor in a check shirt—

what's his name? Monygham—or else catechizing Don Pepe or perhaps listening to Padre Román. They are all down here today—all her ministers of state. Well, she is a sensible woman, and perhaps Don Carlos is a sensible man. It's a part of solid English sense not to think too much; to see only what may be of practical use at the moment. These people are not like ourselves. We have no political reason; we have political passions—sometimes. What is a conviction? A particular view of our personal advantage either practical or emotional. No one is a patriot for nothing. The word serves us well. But I am clear-sighted, and I shall not use that word to you, Antonia! I have no patriotic illusions. I have only the supreme illusion of a lover."

He paused, then muttered almost inaudibly, "That can lead one very far, though."

Behind their backs the political tide that once in every twenty-four hours set with a strong flood through the Gould drawing-room could be heard, rising higher in a hum of voices. Men had been dropping in singly, or in twos and threes: the higher officials of the province, engineers of the railway, sunburnt and in tweeds, with the frosted head of their chief smiling with slow, humorous indulgence amongst the young eager faces. Scarfe, the lover of fandangos, had already slipped out in search of some dance, no matter where, on the outskirts of the town. Don Juste Lopez, after taking his daughters home, had entered solemnly, in a black creased coat buttoned up under his spreading brown beard. The few members of the Provincial Assembly present clustered at once around their President to discuss the news of the war and the last proclamation of the rebel Montero, the miserable Montero, calling in the name of "a justly incensed democracy" upon all the Provincial Assemblies of the Republic to suspend their sittings till his sword had made peace and the will of the people could be consulted. It was practically an invitation to dissolve: an unheard-of audacity of that evil madman.

The indignation ran high in the knot of deputies behind José Avellanos. Don José, lifting up his voice, cried out to them over the high back of his chair, "Sulaco has answered by sending today an army upon his flank. If all the other provinces show only half as much patriotism as we, Occidentals—"

A great outburst of acclamations covered the vibrating treble of the life and soul of the party. Yes! Yes! This was true! A great truth! Sulaco was in the forefront as ever! It was a boastful tumult, the hopefulness inspired by the event of the day breaking out amongst those *caballeros* of the Campo thinking of their herds, of their lands, of the safety of their families. Everything was at stake. . . . No! It was impossible that Montero should succeed! This criminal, this shameless *indio!* The clamor continued for some time, everybody else in the room looking towards the group where Don Juste had put on his air of impartial solemnity as if presiding at a sitting of the Provincial Assembly. Decoud had turned round at the noise, and, leaning his back on the balustrade, shouted into the room with all the strength of his lungs, *"Gran' bestia!"*

This unexpected cry had the effect of stilling the noise. All the eyes were directed to the window with an approving expectation; but Decoud had already turned his back upon the room, and was again leaning out over the quiet street.

"This is the quintessence of my journalism; this is the supreme argument," he said to Antonia. "I have invented this definition, this last word on a great question. But I am no patriot. I am no more of a patriot than the Capataz of the Sulaco Cargadores, this Genoese who has done such great things for this harbor—this active usher-in of the material implements for our progress. You have heard Captain Mitchell confess over and over again that till he got this man he could never tell how long it would take to unload a ship. That is bad for progress. You have seen him pass by after his labors on his famous horse to dazzle the girls in some ballroom with an earthen floor. He is a fortunate fellow! His work is an exercise of personal powers; his leisure is spent in receiving the marks of extraordinary adulation. And he likes it, too. Can anybody be more fortunate? To be feared and admired is—"

"And are these your highest aspirations, Don Martin?" interrupted Antonia.

"I was speaking of a man of that sort," said Decoud, curtly. "The heroes of the world have been feared and admired. What more could he want?"

Decoud had often felt his familiar habit of ironic thought fall shattered against Antonia's gravity. She irritated him as if she, too, had suffered from that inexplicable feminine obtuseness which stands so often between a man and a woman of the more ordinary sort. But he overcame his vexation at once. He was very far from thinking Antonia ordinary, whatever verdict his skepticism might have pronounced upon himself. With a touch of penetrating tenderness in his voice he assured her that his only aspiration was to a felicity so high that it seemed almost unrealizable on this earth.

She colored invisibly, with a warmth against which the breeze from the sierra seemed to have lost its cooling power in the sudden melting of the snows. His whisper could not have carried so far, though there was enough ardor in his tone to melt a heart of ice. Antonia turned away abruptly, as if to carry his whispered assurance into the room behind, full of light, noisy with voices.

The tide of political speculation was beating high within the four walls of the great *sala*, as if driven beyond the marks by a great gust of hope. Don Juste's fan-shaped beard was still the center of loud and animated discussions. There was a self-confident ring in all the voices. Even the few Europeans around Charles Gould—a Dane, a couple of Frenchmen, a discreet fat German, smiling, with down-cast eyes, the representatives of those material interests that had got a footing in Sulaco under the protecting might of the San Tomé mine—had infused a lot of good humor into their deference. Charles Gould, to whom they were paying their court, was the visible sign of the stability that could be achieved on the shifting ground of revolutions. They felt hopeful about their various undertakings. One of the two Frenchmen, small, black, with glittering eyes lost in an immense growth of bushy beard, waved his tiny brown hands and delicate wrists. He had been traveling in the interior of the province for a syndicate of European capitalists. His forcible *"Monsieur l'Administrateur"* returning every minute shrilled above the steady hum of conversations. He was relating his discoveries. He was ecstatic. Charles Gould glanced down at him courteously.

At a given moment of these necessary receptions it was Mrs. Gould's habit to withdraw quietly into a little drawing-room, especially her own, next to the great *sala*. She had risen, and, waiting for Antonia, listened with a slightly worried graciousness to the engineer-in-chief of the railway, who stooped over her, relating slowly, without the slightest gesture, something apparently amusing, for his eyes had a humorous twinkle. Antonia, before she advanced into the room to join Mrs. Gould, turned her head over her shoulder towards Decoud, only for a moment.

"Why should any one of us think his aspirations unrealizable?" she said, rapidly.

"I am going to cling to mine to the end, Antonia," he answered, through clenched teeth, then bowed very low, a little distantly.

The engineer-in-chief had not finished telling his amusing story. The humors of railway building in South America appealed to his keen appreciation of the absurd, and he told his instances of ignorant prejudice and as ignorant cunning very well. Now, Mrs. Gould gave him all her attention as he walked by her side escorting the ladies out of the room. Finally all three passed unnoticed through the glass doors in the gallery. Only a tall priest stalking silently in the noise of the *sala* checked himself to look after them. Father Corbelán, whom Decoud had seen from the balcony turning into the gateway of the Casa Gould, had addressed no one since coming in. The long, skimpy soutane accentuated the tallness of his stature; he carried his powerful torso thrown forward; and the straight, black bar of his joined eyebrows, the pugnacious outline of the bony face, the white spot of a scar on the bluish shaven cheeks (a testimonial to his apostolic zeal from a party of unconverted Indians), suggested something unlawful behind his priesthood, the idea of a chaplain of bandits.

He separated his bony knotted hands clasped behind his back, to shake his finger at Martin.

Decoud had stepped into the room after Antonia. But he did not go far. He had remained just within, against the curtain, with an expression of not quite genuine gravity, like a grown-up person taking part in a game of children. He gazed quietly at the threatening finger.

"I have watched your reverence converting General Barrios by a special sermon on the Plaza," he said, without making the slightest movement.

"What miserable nonsense!" Father Corbelán's deep voice resounded all over the room, making all the heads turn on the shoulders. "The man is a drunkard. *Señores*, the God of your General is a bottle!"

His contemptuous, arbitrary voice caused an uneasy suspension of every sound, as if the self-confidence of the gathering had been staggered by a blow. But nobody took up Father Corbelán's declaration.

It was known that Father Corbelán had come out of the wilds to advocate the sacred rights of the Church with the same fanatical fearlessness with which he had gone preaching to bloodthirsty savages, devoid of human compassion or worship of any kind. Rumors of legendary proportions told of his successes as a missionary beyond the eye of Christian men. He had baptized whole nations of Indians, living with them like a savage himself. It was related that the padre used to ride with his Indians for days, half naked, carrying a bullock-hide shield, and, no doubt, a long lance, too—who knows? That he had wandered clothed in skins, seeking for proselytes somewhere near the snow line of the Cordillera. Of these exploits Padre Corbelán himself was never known to talk. But he made no secret of his opinion that the politicians of Sta Marta had harder hearts and more corrupt minds than the heathen to whom he had carried the word of God. His injudicious zeal for the temporal welfare of the Church was damaging the Ribierist cause. It was common knowledge that he had refused to be made titular bishop of the Occidental diocese till justice was done to a despoiled Church. The political *jefe* of Sulaco (the same dignitary whom Captain Mitchell saved from the mob afterwards) hinted with naïve cynicism that doubtless their Excellencies the Ministers sent the padre over the mountains to Sulaco in the worst season of the year in the hope that he would be frozen to death by the icy blasts of the high *páramos.* Every year a few hardy muleteers—men inured to exposure —were known to perish in that way. But what would you have? Their Excellencies possibly had not realized what a tough priest he was. Meantime, the ignorant were beginning to murmur that the Ribierist reforms meant simply the taking away of the land from the people. Some of it was to be given to foreigners who made the railway; the greater part was to go to the padres.

These were the results of the Grand Vicar's zeal. Even from the short allocution to the troops on the Plaza (which only the first ranks could have heard) he had not been able to keep out his fixed idea of an outraged Church waiting for reparation from a penitent country. The political *jefe* had been exasperated. But he could not very well throw the brother-in-law of Don José into the prison of the Cabildo. The chief magistrate, an easy-going and popular official, visited the Casa Gould, walking over after sunset from the Intendencia, unattended, acknowledging with dignified courtesy the salutations of high and low alike. That evening he had walked up straight to Charles Gould and had hissed out to him that he would have liked to deport the Grand Vicar out of Sulaco, anywhere, to some desert island, to the Isabels, for instance. "The one without water preferably—eh, Don Carlos?" he had added in a tone between jest and earnest. This uncontrollable priest, who had rejected his offer of the episcopal palace for a residence and preferred to hang his shabby hammock amongst the rubble and spiders of the sequestrated Dominican Convent, had taken into his head to advocate an unconditional pardon for Hernandez the Robber! And this was not enough; he seemed to have entered into communication with the most audacious criminal the country had known for years. The Sulaco police knew, of course, what was going on. Padre Corbelán had got hold of that reckless Italian, the Capataz de Cargadores, the only man fit for such an errand, and had sent a message through him. Father Corbelán had studied in Rome, and could speak Italian. The Capataz was known to visit the old Dominican Convent at night. An old woman who served the Grand Vicar had heard the name of Hernandez pronounced; and only last Saturday afternoon the Capataz had been observed galloping out of town. He did not return for two days. The police would have laid the Italian by the heels if it had not been for fear of the *cargadores,* a turbulent body of men, quite apt to raise a tumult. Nowadays it was not so easy to govern Sulaco. Bad characters flocked into it, attracted by the money in the pockets of the railway workmen. The populace was made restless by Father Corbelán's discourses. And the first magistrate explained to Charles Gould that now the province was stripped of troops any outbreak of lawlessness would find the authorities with their boots off, as it were.

Then he went away moodily to sit in an armchair, smoking a long, thin cigar, not very far from Don José, with whom, bending over sideways, he exchanged a few words from time to time. He ignored the entrance of the priest, and whenver Father Corbelán's voice was raised behind him, he shrugged his shoulders impatiently.

Father Corbelán had remained quite motionless for a time with that something vengeful in his immobility which seemed to characterize all his attitudes. A lurid glow of strong convictions gave its peculiar aspect to the black figure. But its fierceness became softened as the padre, fixing his eyes upon Decoud, raised his long, black arm slowly, impressively:

"And you—you are a perfect heathen," he said, in a subdued, deep voice.

He made a step nearer, pointing a forefinger at the young man's breast. Decoud, very calm, felt the wall behind the curtain with the back of his head. Then, with his chin tilted well up, he smiled.

"Very well," he agreed with the slightly weary nonchalance of a man well used to these passages. "But is it perhaps that you have not discovered yet what is the God of my worship? It was an easier task with our Barrios."

The priest suppressed a gesture of discouragement. "You believe neither in stick nor stone," he said.

"Nor bottle," added Decoud without stirring. "Neither does the other of your reverence's confidants. I mean the Capataz of the Cargadores. He does not drink. Your reading of my character does honor to your perspicacity. But why call me a heathen?"

"True," retorted the priest. "You are ten times worse. A miracle could not convert you."

"I certainly do not believe in miracles," said Decoud, quietly. Father Corbelán shrugged his high, broad shoulders doubtfully.

"A sort of Frenchman—godless—a materialist," he pronounced slowly, as if weighing the terms of a careful analysis. "Neither the son of his own country nor of any other," he continued thoughtfully.

"Scarcely human, in fact," Decoud commented under his breath, his head at rest against the wall, his eyes gazing up at the ceiling.

"The victim of his faithless age," Father Corbelán resumed in a deep but subdued voice.

"But of some use as a journalist," Decoud changed his pose and spoke in a more animated tone. "Has your worship neglected to read the last number of the *Porvenir?* I assure you it is just like the others. On the general policy it continues to call Montero a *gran' bestia,* and stigmatize his brother, the *guerrillero,* for a combination of lackey and spy. What could be more effective? In local affairs it urges the Provincial Government to enlist bodily into the national army the band of Hernandez the Robber—who is apparently the protégé of the Church—or at least of the Great Vicar. Nothing could be more sound."

The priest nodded and turned on the heels of his square-toed shoes with big steel buckles. Again, with his hands clasped behind his back, he paced to and fro, planting his feet firmly. When he swung about, the skirt of his soutane was inflated slightly by the brusqueness of his movements.

The great *sala* had been emptying itself slowly. When the Jefe Politico rose to go, most of those still remaining stood up suddenly in sign of respect, and Don José Avellanos stopped the rocking of the chair. But the good-natured First Official made a deprecatory gesture, waved his hand to Charles Gould, and went out discreetly.

In the comparative peace of the room the screaming *"Monsieur l'Administrateur"* of the frail, hairy Frenchman seemed to acquire a preternatural shrillness. The explorer of the Capitalist syndicate was still enthusiastic. "Ten million dollars' worth of copper practically in sight, *Monsieur l'Administrateur.* Ten millions in sight! And a railway coming—a railway! They will never believe my report. *C'est trop beau."* He fell a prey to a screaming ecstasy, in the midst of sagely nodding heads, before Charles Gould's imperturbable calm.

And only the priest continued his pacing, flinging round the skirt of his soutane at each end of his beat. Decoud murmured to him ironically: "Those gentlemen talk about their gods."

Father Corbelán stopped short, looked at the journalist of Sulaco fixedly for a moment, shrugged his shoulders slightly, and resumed his plodding walk of an obstinate traveler.

And now the Europeans were dropping off from the group around Charles Gould till the Administrator of the Great Silver Mine could be seen in his whole lank length, from head to foot, left stranded by the ebbing tide of his guests on the great square of carpet, as it were a multi-colored shoal of flowers and arabesques under his brown boots. Father Corbelán approached the rocking-chair of Don José Avellanos.

"Come, brother," he said, with kindly brusqueness and a touch of relieved impatience a man may feel at the end of a perfectly useless ceremony. *"A la casa! A la Casa!* This has been all talk. Let us now go and think and pray for guidance from Heaven."

He rolled his black eyes upwards. By the side of the frail diplomatist—the life and soul of the party—he seemed gigantic, with a gleam of fanaticism in the glance. But the voice of the party, or, rather, its mouthpiece, the "son Decoud" from Paris, turned journalist for the sake of Antonia's eyes, knew very well that it was not so, that he was only a strenuous priest with one idea, feared by the women and execrated by the men of the people. Martin Decoud, the dilettante in life, imagined himself to derive an artistic pleasure from watching the picturesque extreme of wrong-headedness into which an honest, almost sacred, conviction may drive a man. "It is like madness. It must be—because it's self-destructive," Decoud had said to himself often. It seemed to him that every conviction, as soon as it became effective, turned into that form of dementia the gods send upon those they wish to destroy. But he enjoyed the bitter flavor of that example with the zest of a connoisseur in the art of his choice. Those two men got on well together, as if each had felt respectively that a masterful conviction, as well as utter skepticism, may lead a man very far on the by-paths of political action.

Don José obeyed the touch of the big hairy hand. Decoud followed out the brothers-in-law. And there remained only one visitor in the vast empty *sala*, bluishly hazy with tobacco smoke, a heavy-eyed, round-cheeked man, with a drooping mustache, a hide merchant from Esmeralda, who had come overland to Sulaco, riding with a few peons across the coast range. He was very full of his journey, undertaken mostly for the purpose of seeing the Señor Administrador of San Tomé in relation to some assistance he required in his hide-exporting business. He hoped to enlarge it greatly now that the country was going to be settled. It was going to be settled, he repeated several times, degrading by a strange, anxious whine the sonority of the Spanish language, which he pattered rapidly, like some sort of cringing jargon. A plain man could carry on his little business now in the country, and even think of enlarging it—with safety. Was it not so? He seemed to beg Charles Gould for a confirmatory word, a grunt of assent, a simple nod even.

He could get nothing. His alarm increased, and in the pauses he would dart his eyes here and there; then, loth to give up, he would branch off into feeling allusion to the dangers of his journey. The audacious Hernandez, leaving his usual haunts, had crossed the Campo of Sulaco, and was known to be lurking in the ravines of the coast range. Yesterday, when distant only a few hours from Sulaco, the hide merchant and his servants had seen three men on the road arrested suspiciously, with their horses' heads together. Two of these rode off at once and disappeared in a shallow *quebrada* to the left. "We stopped," continued the man from Esmeralda, "and I tried to hide behind a small bush. But none of my *mozos* would go forward to find out what it meant, and the third horseman seemed to be waiting for us to come up. It was no use. We had been seen. So we rode slowly on, trembling. He let us pass—a man on a gray horse with his hat down on his eyes—without a word of greeting; but by-and-by we heard him galloping after us. We faced about, but that did not seem to intimidate him. He rode up at speed, and touching my foot with the toe of his boot, asked me for a cigar, with a blood-curdling laugh. He did not seem armed, but when he put his hand back to reach for the matches I saw an enormous revolver strapped to his waist. I shuddered. He had very fierce whiskers, Don Carlos, and as he did not offer to go on we dared not move. At last, blowing the smoke of my cigar into the air through his nostrils, he said, 'Señor, it would be perhaps better for you if I rode behind your party. You are not very far from Sulaco now. Go you with God.' What would you? We went on. There was no resisting him. He might have been Hernandez himself; though my servant, who has been many times to Sulaco by sea, assured me that he had recognized him very well for the Capataz of the Steamship Company's *cargadores*. Later, that same evening, I saw that very man at the corner of the Plaza talking to a girl, a Morenita, who stood by the stirrup with her hand on the gray horse's mane."

"I assure you, Señor Hirsch," murmured Charles Gould, "that you ran no risk on this occasion."

"That may be, *señor*, though I tremble yet. A most fierce man—to look at. And what does it mean? A person employed by the Steamship Company talking with *salteadores*—no less, *señor*; the other horsemen were *salteadores*—in a lonely place, and behaving like a robber himself! A cigar is nothing, but what was there to prevent him asking me for my purse?"

"No, no, Señor Hirsch," Charles Gould murmured, letting his glance stray away a little vacantly from the round face, with its hooked beak upturned towards him in an almost childlike appeal. "If it was the Capataz de Cargadores you met—and there is no doubt, is there?—you were perfectly safe."

"Thank you. You are very good. A very fierce-looking man, Don Carlos. He asked me for a cigar in a most familiar manner. What would have happened if I had not had a cigar? I shudder yet. What business had he to be talking with robbers in a lonely place?"

But Charles Gould, openly preoccupied now, gave not a sign, made no sound. The impenetrability of the embodied Gould Concession had its surface shades. To be dumb is merely a fatal affliction; but the King of Sulaco had words enough to give him all the mysterious weight of a taciturn force. His silences, backed by the power of speech, had as many shades of significance as uttered words in the way of assent, of doubt, of negation—even of simple comment. Some seemed to say plainly, "Think it over"; others meant clearly "Go ahead," a simple, low "I see," with an affirmative nod, at the end of a patient listening half-hour was the equivalent of a verbal contract, which men had learned to trust implicitly, since behind it all there was the great San Tomé mine, the head and front of the material interests, so strong that it depended on no man's goodwill in the whole length and breadth of the Occidental Province—that is, on no goodwill which it could not buy ten times over. But to the little hook-nosed man from Esmeralda, anxious about the export of hides, the silence of Charles Gould portended a failure. Evidently this was no time for extending a modest man's business. He enveloped in a swift mental malediction the whole country, with all its inhabitants, partisans of Ribiera and Montero alike; and there were incipient tears in his mute anger at the thought of the innumerable ox-hides going to waste upon the dreamy expanse of the Campo, with its single palms rising like ships at sea within the perfect circle of the horizon, its clumps of heavy timber motionless like solid islands of leaves above the running waves of grass. There were hides there, rotting, with no profit to anybody—rotting where they had been dropped by men called away to attend the urgent necessities of political revolutions. The practical, mercantile soul of Señor Hirsch rebelled against all that foolishness, while he was taking a respectful but disconcerted leave of the might and majesty of the San Tomé mine in the person of Charles Gould. He could not restrain a heart-broken murmur, wrung out of his very aching heart, as it were.

"It is a great, great foolishness, Don Carlos, all this. The price of hides in Hamburg is gone way up—up. Of course the Ribierist Government will do away with all that— when it gets established firmly, Meantime—"

He sighed.

"Yes, meantime," repeated Charles Gould, inscrutably.

The other shrugged his shoulders. But he was not ready to go yet. There was a little matter he would like to mention very much if permitted. It appeared he had some good friends in Hamburg (he murmured the name of the firm) who were very anxious to do business, in dynamite, he explained. A contract for dynamite with the San Tomé mine, and then, perhaps, later on, other mines, which were sure to—the little man from Esmeralda was ready to enlarge, but Charles interrupted him. It seemed as though the patience of the Señor Administrador was giving way at last.

"Señor Hirsch," he said, "I have enough dynamite stored up at the mountain to send it down crashing into the valley"—his voice rose a little—"to send half Sulaco into the air if I liked."

Charles Gould smiled at the round, startled eyes of the dealer in hides, who was murmuring hastily, "Just so. Just so." And now he was going. It was impossible to do business in explosives with an Administrador so well provided and so discouraging. He had suffered agonies in the saddle and had exposed himself to the atrocities of the bandit Hernandez for nothing at all. Neither hides nor dynamite—and the very shoulders of the enterprising Israelite expressed dejection. At the door he bowed low to the engineer-in-chief. But at the bottom of the stairs in the patio he stopped short, with his pudgy hand over his lips in attitude of meditative astonishment.

"What does he want to keep so much dynamite for?" he muttered. "And why does he talk like this to me?"

The engineer-in-chief, looking in at the door of the empty *sala*, whence the political tide had ebbed out to the last insignificant drop, nodded familiarly to the master of the house, standing motionless like a tall beacon amongst the deserted shoals of furniture.

"Good night, I am going. Got my bike downstairs. The railway will know where to go for dynamite should we get short at any time. We have done cutting and chopping for a while now. We shall begin soon to blast our way through."

"Don't come to me," said Charles Gould, with perfect serenity. "I shan't have an ounce to spare for anybody. Not an ounce. Not for my own brother, if I had a brother, and he were the engineer-in-chief of the most promising railway in the world."

"What's that?" asked the engineer-in-chief, with equanimity. "Unkindness?"

"No," said Charles Gould, stolidly. "Policy."

"Radical, I should think," the engineer-in-chief observed from the doorway.

"Is that the right name?" Charles Gould said, from the middle of the room.

"I mean, going to the roots, you know," the engineer explained, with an air of enjoyment.

"Why, yes," Charles pronounced, slowly. "The Gould Concession has struck such deep roots in this country, in this province, in that gorge of the mounains, that nothing but dynamite shall be allowed to dislodge it from there. It's my choice. It's my last card to play."

The engineer-in-chief whistled low. "A pretty game," he said, with a shade of discretion. "And have you told Holroyd of that extraordinary trump card you hold in your hand?"

"Card only when it's played; when it falls at the end of the game. Till then you may call it a—a—"

"Weapon," suggested the railway man.

"No. You may call it rather an argument," corrected Charles Gould, gently. "And that's how I've presented it to Mr. Holroyd."

"And what did he say to it?" asked the engineer, with undisguised interest.

"He"—Charles Gould spoke after a slight pause—"he said something about holding on like grim death and putting our trust in God. I should imagine he must have been rather startled. But then"—pursued the Administrador of the San Tomé mine—"but then, he is very far away, you know, and, as they say in this country, God is very high above."

The engineer's appreciative laugh died away down the stairs, where the Madonna with the Child on her arm seemed to look after his shaking broad back from her shallow niche.

VI

A profound stillness reigned in the Casa Gould. The master of the house, walking along the corridor, opened the door of his room, and saw his wife sitting in a big armchair—his own smoking armchair—thoughtful, contemplating her little shoes. And she did not raise her eyes when he walked in.

"Tired?" asked Charles Gould.

"A little," said Mrs. Gould. Still without looking up, she added with feeling, "There is an awful sense of unreality about all this."

Charles Gould, before the long table strewn with papers, on which lay a hunting crop and a pair of spurs, stood looking at his wife: "The heat and dust must have been awful this afternoon by the waterside," he murmured, sympathetically. "The glare on the water must have been simply terrible."

"One could close one's eyes to the glare," said Mrs. Gould. "But, my dear Charley, it is impossible for me to close my eyes to our position; to this awful . . ."

She raised her eyes and looked at her husband's face, from which all sign of sympathy or any other feeling had disappeared. "Why don't you tell me something?" she almost wailed.

"I thought you had understood me perfectly from the first," Charles Gould said, slowly. "I thought we had said all there was to say a long time ago. There is nothing to say now. There were things to be done. We have done them; we have gone on doing them. There is no going back now. I don't suppose that, even from the first, there was really any possible way back. And, what's more, we can't even afford to stand still."

"Ah, if one only knew how far you mean to go," said his wife, inwardly trembling, but in an almost playful tone.

"Any distance, any length, of course," was the answer, in a matter-of-fact tone, which caused Mrs. Gould to make another effort to repress a shudder.

She stood up, smiling graciously, and her little figure seemed to be diminished still more by the heavy mass of her hair and the long train of her gown.

""But always to success," she said, persuasively.

Charles Gould, enveloping her in the steely blue glance of his attentive eyes, answered without hesitation:

"Oh, there is no alternative."

He put an immense assurance into his tone. As to the words, this was all that his conscience would allow him to say.

Mrs. Gould's smile remained a shade too long upon her lips. She murmured:

"I will leave you; I've a slight headache. The heat, the dust, were indeed—I suppose you are going back to the mine before the morning?"

"At midnight," said Charles Gould. "We are bringing down the silver tomorrow. Then I shall take three whole days off in town with you."

"Ah, you are going to meet the escort. I shall be on the balcony at five o'clock to see you pass. Till then, good-bye."

Charles Gould walked rapidly round the table, and, seizing her hands, bent down, pressing them both to his lips. Before he straightened himself up again to his full height she had disengaged one to smooth his cheek with a light touch, as if he were a little boy.

"Try to get some rest for a couple of hours," she murmured, with a glance at a hammock stretched in a distant part of the room. Her long train swished softly after her on the red tiles. At the door she looked back.

Two big lamps with unpolished glass globes bathed in a soft and abundant light the four white walls of the room, with a glass case of arms, the brass hilt of Henry Gould's cavalry saber on its square of velvet, and the water-color sketch of the San Tomé gorge. And Mrs. Gould, gazing at the last in its black wooden frame, sighed out:

"Ah, if we had left it alone, Charley!"

"No," Charles Gould said, moodily; "it was impossible to leave it alone."

"Perhaps it was impossible," Mrs. Gould admitted, slowly. Her lips quivered a little, but she smiled with an air of dainty bravado. "We have disturbed a good many snakes in that Paradise, Charley, haven't we?"

"Yes, I remember," said Charles Gould, "it was Don Pepe who called the gorge the Paradise of snakes. No doubt we have disturbed a great many. But remember, my dear, that it is not now as it was when you made that sketch." He waved his hand towards the small water-color hanging alone upon the great bare wall. "It is no longer a Paradise of snakes. We have brought mankind into it, and we cannot turn our backs upon them to go and begin a new life elsewhere."

He confronted his wife with a firm, concentrated gaze, which Mrs. Gould returned with a brave assumption of fearlessness before she went out, closing the door gently after her.

In contrast with the white glaring room the dimly lit corridor had the restful mysteriousness of a forest glade, suggested by the stems and the leaves of the plants ranged along the balustrade of the open side. In the streaks of light falling through the open doors of the reception-rooms, the blossoms, white and red and pale lilac, came out vivid with the brilliance of flowers in a stream of sunshine; and Mrs. Gould, passing on, had the vividness of a figure seen in the clear patches of sun that checker the gloom of open glades in the woods. The stones in the rings upon her hand pressed to her forehead glittered in the lamplight abreast of the door of the *sala*.

"Who's there?" she asked, in a startled voice. "Is that you, Basilio?" She looked in, and saw Martin Decoud walking about, with an air of having lost something, amongst the chairs and tables.

"Antonia has forgotten her fan in here," said Decoud, with a strange air of distraction; "so I entered to see."

But, even as he said this, he had obviously given up his search, and walked straight towards Mrs. Gould, who looked at him with doubtful surprise.

"*Señora*," he began, in a low voice.

"What is it, Don Martin?" asked Mrs. Gould. And then she added, with a slight laugh, "I am so nervous today," as if to explain the eagerness of the question.

"Nothing immediately dangerous," said Decoud, who now could not conceal his agitation. "Pray don't distress yourself. No, really, you must not distress yourself."

Mrs. Gould, with her candid eyes very wide open, her lips composed into a smile, was steadying herself in the doorway with a little bejewelled hand.

"Perhaps you don't know how alarming you are, appearing like this unexpectedly—"

"I! Alarming!" he protested, sincerely vexed and surprised. "I assure you that I am not in the least alarmed myself. A fan is lost; well, it will be found again. But I don't think it is here. It is a fan I am looking for. I cannot understand how Antonia could— Well! Have you found it, *amigo?*"

"No, *señor*," said behind Mrs. Gould the soft voice of Basilio, the head servant of the Casa. "I don't think the *señorita* could have left it in this house at all."

"Go and look for it in the patio again. Go now, my friend; look for it on the steps, under the gate; examine every flagstone; search for it till I come down again . . . That fellow"—he addressed himself in English to Mrs. Gould—"is always stealing up behind one's back on his bare feet. I set him to look for that fan directly I came in to justify my reappearance, my sudden return."

He paused and Mrs. Gould said, amiably, "You are always welcome." She paused for a second, too. "But I am waiting to learn the cause of your return."

Decoud affected suddenly the utmost nonchalance.

"I can't bear to be spied upon. Oh, the cause? Yes, there is a cause; there is something else that is lost besides Antonia's favorite fan. As I was walking home after seeing Don José and Antonia to their house, the Capataz de Cargadores, riding down the street, spoke to me."

"Has anything happened to the Violas?" inquired Mrs. Gould.

"The Violas? You mean the old Garibaldino who keeps the hotel where the engineers live? Nothing happened there. The Capataz said nothing of them; he only told me that the telegraphist of the Cable Company was walking on the Plaza, bareheaded, looking out for me. This is news from the interior, Mrs. Gould. I should rather say rumors of news."

"Good news?" said Mrs. Gould in a low voice.

"Worthless, I should think. But if I must define them, I would say bad. They are to the effect that a two days' battle has been fought near Sta Marta, and that the Ribierists are defeated. It must have happened a few days ago—perhaps a week. The rumor has just reached Cayta, and the man in charge of the cable station there has telegraphed the news to his colleague here. We might just as well have kept Barrios in Sulaco."

"What's to be done now?" murmured Mrs. Gould.

"Nothing. He's at sea with the troops. He will get to Cayta in a couple of days' time and learn the news there. What he will do then, who can say? Hold Cayta? Offer his submission to Montero? Disband his army—this last most likely, and go himself in one of the O.S.N. Company's steamers, north or south—to Valparaiso or to San Francisco, no matter where. Our Barrios has a great practice in exiles and repatriations, which mark the points in the political game."

Decoud, exchanging a steady stare with Mrs. Gould, added, tentatively, as it were, "And yet, if we had Barrios with his 2,000 improved rifles here, something could have been done."

"Montero victorious, completely victorious!" Mrs. Gould breathed out in a tone of unbelief.

"A canard, probably. That sort of a bird is hatched in great numbers is such times as these. And even if it were true? Well, let us put things at their worst, let us say it is true."

"Then everything is lost," said Mrs. Gould, with the calmness of despair.

Suddenly she seemed to divine, she seemed to see Decoud's tremendous excitement under its cloak of studied carelessness. It was, indeed, becoming visible in his audacious and watchful stare, in the curve, half-reckless, half-contemptuous, of his lips. And a French phrase came upon them as if, for this Costaguanero of the Boulevard, that had been the only forcible language:

"Non, Madame. Rien n'est perdu."

It electrified Mrs. Gould out of her benumbed attitude, and she said, vivaciously: "What would you think of doing?"

But already there was something of mockery in Decoud's suppressed excitement.

"What would you expect a true Costaguanero to do? Another revolution, of course. On my word of honor, Mrs. Gould, I believe I am a true hijo del pais, a true son of the country, whatever Father Corbelán may say. And I'm not so much of an unbeliever as not to have faith in my own ideas, in my own remedies, in my own desires."

"Yes," said Mrs. Gould, doubtfully.

"You don't seem convinced," Decoud went on again in French. "Say, then, in my passions."

Mrs. Gould received this addition unflinchingly. To understand it thoroughly she did not require to hear his muttered assurance:

"There is nothing I would not do for the sake of Antonia. There is nothing I am not prepared to undertake. There is no risk I am not ready to run."

Decoud seemed to find a fresh audacity in this voicing of his thoughts. "You would not believe me if I were to say that it is the love of the country which—"

She made a sort of discouraged protest with her arm, as if to express that she had given up expecting that motive from anyone.

"A Sulaco revolution," Decoud pursued in a forcible undertone. "The Great Cause may be served here, on the very spot of its inception, in the place of its birth, Mrs. Gould."

Frowning, and biting her lower lip thoughtfully, she made a step away from the door.

"You are not going to speak to your husband?" Decoud arrested her anxiously.

"But you will need his help?"

"No doubt," Decoud admitted without hesitation. "Everything turns upon the San Tomé mine, but I would rather he didn't know anything as yet of my—my hopes."

A puzzled look came upon Mrs. Gould's face, and Decoud, approaching, explained confidentially:

"Don't you see, he's such an idealist."

Mrs. Gould flushed pink, and her eyes grew darker at the same time.

"Charley an idealist!" she said, as if to herself, wonderingly. "What on earth do you mean?"

"Yes," conceded Decoud, "it's a wonderful thing to say with the sight of the San Tomé mine, the greatest fact in the whole of South America, perhaps, before our very eyes. But look even at that, he has idealized this fact to a point—" He paused. "Mrs. Gould, are you aware to what point he has idealized the existence, the worth, the meaning of the San Tomé mine? Are you aware of it?"

He must have known what he was talking about.

The effect he expected was produced. Mrs. Gould, ready to take fire, gave it up suddenly with a low little sound that resembled a moan.

"What do you know?" she asked in a feeble voice.

"Nothing," answered Decoud, firmly. "But, then, don't you see, he's an Englishman?"

"Well, what of that?" asked Mrs. Gould.

"Simply that he cannot act or exist without idealizing every simple feeling, desire, or achievement. He could not believe his own motives if he did not make them first a part of some fairy tale. The earth is not quite good enough for him, I fear. Do you excuse my frankness? Besides, whether you excuse it or not, it is part of the truth of things which hurts me—what do you call them?—the Anglo-Saxon's susceptibilities, and at the present moment I don't feel as if I could treat seriously either his conception of things or—if you allow me to say so—or yet yours."

Mrs. Gould gave no sign of being offended. "I suppose Antonia understands you thoroughly?"

"Understands? Well, yes. But I am not sure that she approves. That, however, makes no difference. I am honest enough to tell you that, Mrs. Gould."

"Your idea, of course, is separation," she said.

"Separation, of course," declared Martin. "Yes; separation of the whole Occidental Province from the rest of the unquiet body. But my true idea, the only one I care for, is not to be separated from Antonia."

"And that is all?" asked Mrs. Gould, without severity.

"Absolutely. I am not deceiving myself about my motives. She won't leave Sulaco for my sake, therefore Sulaco must leave the rest of the Republic to its fate. Nothing could be clearer than that. I like a clearly defined situation. I cannot part with Antonia, therefore the one and indivisible Republic of Costaguana must be made to part with its western province. Fortunately it happens to be also a sound policy. The richest, the most fertile part of this land may be saved from anarchy. Personally, I care little, very little; but it's a fact that the establishment of Montero in power would mean death to me. In all the proclamations of general pardon which I have seen, my name, with a few others, is specially excepted. The brothers hate me, as you know very well, Mrs. Gould; and behold, here is the rumor of them having won a battle. You say that supposing it is true, I have plenty of time to run away."

The slight, protesting murmur on the part of Mrs. Gould made him pause for a moment, while he looked at her with a sombre and resolute glance.

"Oh, but I would, Mrs. Gould. I would run away if it served that which at present is my only desire. I am courageous enough to say that, and to do it, too. But women, even our women, are idealists. It is Antonia that won't run away. A novel sort of vanity."

"You call it vanity," said Mrs. Gould, in a shocked voice.

"Say pride, then, which, Father Corbelán would tell you, is a mortal sin. But I am not proud. I am simply too much in love to run away. At the same time I want to live. There is no love for a dead man. Therefore it is necessary that Sulaco should not recognize the victorious Montero."

"And you think my husband will give you his support?"

"I think he can be drawn into it, like all idealists, when he once sees a sentimental basis for his action. But I wouldn't talk to him. Mere clear facts won't appeal to his sentiment. It is much better for him to convince himself in his own way. And, frankly, I could not, perhaps, just now pay sufficient respect to either his motives or even, perhaps, to yours, Mrs. Gould."

It was evident that Mrs. Gould was very determined not to be offended. She smiled vaguely, while she seemed to think the matter over. As far as she could judge from the girl's half-confidences, Antonia understood that young man. Obviously there was promise of safety in his plan, or rather in his idea. Moreover, right or wrong, the idea could do no harm. And it was quite possible, also, that the rumor was false.

"You have some sort of a plan," she said.

"Simplicity itself. Barrios has started, let him go on then; he will hold Cayta, which is the door of the sea route to Sulaco. They cannot send a sufficient force over the mountains. No; not even to cope with the band of Hernandez. Meantime we shall organize our resistance here. And for that, this very Hernandez will be useful. He has defeated troops as a bandit; he will no doubt accomplish the same thing if he is made a colonel or even a general. You know the country well enough not to be shocked by what I say, Mrs. Gould. I have heard you assert that this poor bandit was the living, breathing example of cruelty, injustice, stupidity, and oppression, that ruin men's souls as well as their fortunes in this country. Well, there would be some poetical retribution in that man arising to crush the evils which had driven an honest *ranchero* into a life of crime. A fine idea of retribution in that, isn't there?"

Decoud had dropped easily into English, which he spoke with precision, very correctly, but with too many *z* sounds.

"Think also of your hospitals, of your schools, of your ailing mothers and feeble old men, of all that population which you and your husband have brought into the rocky gorge of San Tomé. Are you not responsible to your conscience for all these people? Is it not worth while to make another effort, which is not at all so desperate as it looks, rather than—"

Decoud finished his thought with an upward toss of the arm, suggesting annihilation; and Mrs. Gould turned away her head with a look of horror.

"Why don't you say all this to my husband?" she asked, without looking at Decoud, who stood watching the effect of his words.

"Ah! But Don Carlos is so English," he began. Mrs. Gould interrupted:

"Leave that alone, Don Martin. He's as much a Costaguanero—No! He's more of a Costaguanero than yourself."

"Sentimentalist, sentimentalist," Decoud almost cooed, in a tone of gentle and soothing deference. "Sentimentalist, after the amazing manner of your people. I have been watching El Rey de Sulaco since I came here on a fool's errand, and perhaps impelled by some treason of fate lurking behind the unaccountable turns of a man's life. But I don't matter, I am not a sentimentalist, I cannot endow my personal desires with a shining robe of silk and jewels. Life is not for me a moral romance derived from the tradition of a pretty fairy tale. No, Mrs. Gould; I am practical. I am not afraid of my motives. But, pardon me, I have been rather carried away. What I wish to say is that I have been observing. I won't tell you what I have discovered—"

"No. That is unnecessary," whispered Mrs. Gould, once more averting her head.

"It is. Except one little fact, that your husband does not like me. It's a small matter, which, in the circumstances, seems to acquire a perfectly ridiculous importance. Ridiculous and immense; for, clearly, money is required for my plan," he reflected; then added, meaningly, "and we have two sentimentalists to deal with."

"I don't know that I understand you, Don Martin," said Mrs. Gould, coldly, preserving the low key of their conversation. "But, speaking as if I did, who is the other?"

"The great Holroyd in San Francisco, of course," Decoud whispered, lightly. "I think you understand me very well. Women are idealists; but then they are so perspicacious."

But whatever was the reason of that remark, disparaging and complimentary at the same time, Mrs. Gould seemed not to pay attention to it. The name of Holroyd had given a new tone to her anxiety.

"The silver escort is coming down to the harbor tomorrow; a whole six months' working, Don Martin!" she cried in dismay.

"Let it come down, then," breathed out Decoud, earnestly, almost into her ear.

"But if the rumor should get about, and especially if it turned out true, troubles might break out in the town," objected Mrs. Gould.

Decoud admitted that it was possible. He knew well the town children of the Sulaco Campo: sullen, thievish, vindictive, and bloodthirsty, whatever great qualities their brothers of the plain might have had. But then there was that other sentimentalist, who attached a strangely idealistic meaning to concrete facts. This stream of silver must be kept flowing north to return in the form of financial backing from the great house of Holroyd. Up at the mountain in the strong-room of the mine the silver bars were worth less for his purpose than so much lead, from which at least bullets may be run. Let it come down to the harbor, ready for shipment.

The next north-going steamer would carry it off for the very salvation of the San Tomé mine, which has produced so much treasure. And, moreover, the rumor was probably false, he remarked, with much conviction in his hurried tone.

"Besides, *señora,*" concluded Decoud, "we may suppress it for many days. I have been talking with the telegraphist in the middle of the Plaza Mayor; thus I am certain that we could not have been overheard. There was not even a bird in the air near us. And also let me tell you something more. I have been making friends with this man called Nostromo, the Capataz. We had a conversation this very evening, I walking by the side of his horse as he rode slowly out of the town just now. He promised me that if a riot took place for any reason—even for the most political of reasons, you understand—his *cargadores,* an important part of the populace, you will admit, should be found on the side of the Europeans."

"He has promised you that?" Mrs. Gould inquired, with interest. "What made him make that promise to you?"

"Upon my word, I don't know," declared Decoud, in a slightly surprised tone. "He certainly promised me that, but now you ask me why I certainly could not tell you his reasons. He talked with his usual carelessness, which, if he had been anything else but a common sailor, I would call a pose or an affectation."

Decoud, interrupting himself, looked at Mrs. Gould curiously.

"Upon the whole," he continued, "I suppose he expects something to his advantage from it. You mustn't forget that he does not exercise his extraordinary power over the lower classes without a certain amount of personal risk and without a great profusion in spending his money. One must pay in some way or other for such a solid thing as individual prestige. He told me after we made friends at a dance, in a *posada* kept by a Mexican just outside the walls, that he had come here to make his fortune. I suppose he looks upon his prestige as a sort of investment."

"Perhaps he prizes it for its own sake," Mrs. Gould said in a tone as if she were repelling an undeserved aspersion. "Viola, the Garibaldino, with whom he has lived for some years, calls him the Incorruptible."

"Ah! he belongs to the group of your protégés out there towards the harbor, Mrs.

Gould. *Muy bien.* And Captain Mitchell calls him wonderful. I have heard no end of tales of his strength, his audacity, his fidelity. No end of fine things. H'm! incorruptible! It is indeed a name of honor for the Capataz of the Cargadores of Sulaco. Incorruptible! Fine, but vague. However, I suppose he's sensible, too. And I talked to him upon that sane and practical assumption."

"I prefer to think him disinterested, and therefore trustworthy," Mrs. Gould said, with the nearest approach to curtness it was in her nature to assume.

"Well, if so, then the silver will be still more safe. Let it come down, *señora.* Let it come down, so that it may go north and return to us in the shape of credit."

Mrs. Gould glanced along the corridor towards the door of her husband's room. Decoud, watching her as if she had his fate in her hands, detected an almost imperceptible nod of assent. He bowed with a smile, and, putting his hand into the breast pocket of his coat, pulled out a fan of light feathers set upon painted leaves of sandal-wood. "I had it in my pocket," he murmured, triumphantly, "for a plausible pretext." He bowed again. "Good night, *señora.*"

Mrs. Gould continued along the corridor away from her husband's room. The fate of the San Tomé mine was lying heavy upon her heart. It was a long time now since she had begun to fear it. It had been an idea. She had watched it with misgivings turning into a fetish, and now the fetish had grown into a monstrous and crushing weight. It was as if the inspiration of their early years had left her heart to turn into a wall of silver-bricks, erected by the silent work of evil spirits, between her and her husband. He seemed to dwell alone within a circumvallation of precious metal, leaving her outside with her school, her hospital, the sick mothers, and the feeble old men, mere insignificant vestiges of the initial inspiration. "Those poor people!" she murmured to herself.

Below she heard the voice of Martin Decoud in the patio speaking loudly:

"I have found Doña Antonia's fan, Basilio. Look, here it is!"

VII

It was part of what Decoud would have called his sane materialism that he did not believe in the possibility of friendship between man and woman.

The one exception he allowed confirmed, he maintained, that absolute rule. Friendship was possible between brother and sister, meaning by friendship the frank unreserve, as before another human being, of thoughts and sensations; all the objectless and necessary sincerity of one's innermost life trying to react upon the profound sympathies of another existence.

His favorite sister, the handsome, slightly arbitrary, and resolute angel, ruling the father and mother Decoud in the first-floor apartments of a very fine Parisian house, was the recipient of Martin Decoud's confidences as to his thoughts, actions, purposes, doubts, and even failures . . .

> Prepare our little circle in Paris for the birth of another South American Republic. One more or less, what does it matter? They may come into the

world like evil flowers on a hotbed of rotten institutions; but the seed of this one has germinated in your brother's brain, and that will be enough for your devoted assent. I am writing this to you by the light of a single candle, in a sort of inn, near the harbor, kept by an Italian called Viola, a protégé of Mrs. Gould. The whole building, which, for all I know, may have been contrived by a Conquistador farmer of the pearl fishery three hundred years ago, is perfectly silent. So is the plain between the town and the harbor; silent, but not so dark as the house, because the pickets of Italian workmen guarding the railway have lighted little fires all along the line. It was not so quiet around here yesterday. We had an awful riot—a sudden outbreak of the populace, which was not suppressed till late today. Its object, no doubt, was loot, and that was defeated, as you must have learned already from the cablegram sent via San Francisco and New York last night, when the cables were still open. You have read already there that the energetic action of the Europeans of the railway has saved the town from destruction, and you may believe that. I wrote out the cable myself. We have no Reuter's agency man here. I have also fired at the mob from the windows of the club, in company with some other young men of position. Our object was to keep the Calle de la Constitución clear for the exodus of the ladies and children, who have taken refuge on board a couple of cargo ships now in the harbor here. That was yesterday. You should also have learned from the cable that the missing President, Ribiera, who had disappeared after the battle of Sta Marta, has turned up here in Sulaco by one of those strange coincidences that are almost incredible, riding on a lame mule into the very midst of the street fighting. It appears that he had fled, in company with a muleteer called Bonifacio, across the mountains from the threats of Montero into the arms of an enraged mob.

The Capataz of Cargadores, that Italian sailor of whom I have written to you before, has saved him from an ignoble death. That man seems to have a particular talent for being on the spot whenever there is something pictur-esque to be done.

He was with me at four o'clock in the morning at the offices of the *Porvenir*, where he had turned up so early in order to warn me of the coming trouble, and also to assure me that he would keep his *cargadores* on the side of order. When the full daylight came we were looking together at the crowd on foot and on horseback, demonstrating on the Plaza and shying stones at the windows of the Intendencia. Nostromo (that is the name they call him by here) was pointing out to me his *cargadores* interspersed in the mob.

The sun shines late upon Sulaco, for it has first to climb above the mountains. In that clear morning light, brighter than twilight, Nostromo saw right across the vast Plaza, at the end of the street beyond the cathedral, a mounted man apparently in difficulties with a yelling knot of *leperos*. At once he said to me, "That's a stranger. What is it they are doing to him?" Then he took out the silver whistle he is in the habit of using on the wharf (this man seems to disdain the use of any metal less precious than silver) and blew into it twice, evidently a preconcerted signal for his *cargadores*. He ran out immediately, and they rallied round him. I ran out, too, but was too late to follow them and help in the rescue of the stranger, whose animal had fallen. I was set upon at once as a hated aristocrat, and was only too glad to get to the club, where Don Jaime Berges (you may remember him visiting at our house in Paris some three years ago) thrust a sporting gun into my hands. They were already firing from the windows. There were little heaps of cartridges lying about on the open card-tables. I remember a couple of overturned chairs, some bottles rolling on the floor amongst the packs of cards scattered suddenly as the *caballeros* rose from their game to open fire upon the mob. Most of the young men had spent the night at the club in the expectation of some such disturbance. In two of the candelabra, on the consoles, the candles were burning down in their sockets. A large iron nut, probably stolen from the railway workshops, flew in from the street as I entered, and broke one of the large mirrors set in the wall. I noticed also one of the club servants tied up hand and foot with the cords of the curtain and flung in a corner. I have a vague recollection of Don Jaime assuring me hastily that the fellow had been detected putting poison into the dishes at supper. But I remember distinctly he was shrieking for mercy, without stopping at all, continuously, and so absolutely disregarded that nobody even took the trouble to gag him. The noise he made was so disagreeable that I had half a mind to do it myself. But there was no time to waste on such trifles. I took my place at one of the windows and began firing.

I didn't learn till later in the afternoon whom it was that Nostromo, with his *cargadores* and some Italian workmen as well, had managed to save from those drunken rascals. That man has a peculiar talent when anything striking to the imagination has to be done. I made that remark to him afterwards when we met after some sort of order had been restored in the town, and the answer he made rather surprised me. He said quite moodily, "And how much do I get for that, *señor?*" Then it dawned upon me that perhaps this man's vanity has been satiated by the adulation of the common people and the confidences of his superiors!

Decoud paused to light a cigarette, then, with his head still over his writing, he blew a cloud of smoke, which seemed to rebound from the paper. He took up the pencil again.

That was yesterday evening on the Plaza, while he sat on the steps of the cathedral, his hands between his knees, holding the bridle of his famous silver-gray mare. He had led his body of *cargadores* splendidly all day long. He looked fatigued. I don't know how I looked. Very dirty, I suppose. But I suppose I also looked pleased. From the time the fugitive President had been got off to the S.S. *Minerva*, the tide of success had turned against the mob. They had been driven off the harbor, and out of the better streets of the town, into their own maze of ruins and *tolderías*. You must understand that this riot, whose primary object was undoubtedly the getting hold of the San Tomé silver stored in the lower rooms of the Custom House (besides the general looting of the *ricos*), had acquired a political coloring from the fact of two Deputies to the Provincial Assembly, Señores Gamacho and Fuentes, both from Bolson, putting themselves at the head of it—late in the afternoon, it is true, when the mob, disappointed in their hopes of loot, made a stand in the narrow streets to the cries of *"Viva la libertad!* Down with Feudalism!"* (I wonder what they imagine feudalism to be?) "Down with the Goths and Paralytics." I suppose the Señores Gamacho and Fuentes knew what they were doing. They are prudent gentlemen. In the Assembly they called themselves Moderates, and opposed every energetic measure with philanthropic pensiveness. At the first rumors of Monter's victory, they began to show a subtle change of the pensive temper, and began to defy poor Don Juste Lopez in his Presidential tribune with an effrontery to which the poor man could only respond by a dazed smoothing of his beard and ringing of the Presidential bell. Then, when the downfall of the Ribierist cause became confirmed beyond the shadow of a doubt, they have blossomed into convinced Liberals, acting together as if they were Siamese twins, and ultimately taking charge, as it were, of the riot in the name of Monterist principles.

Their last move of eight o'clock last night was to organize themselves into a Monterist Committee which sits, as far as I know, in a *posada* kept by a retired Mexican bull-fighter, a great politician, too, whose name I have forgotten. Thence they have issued a communication to us, the Goths and Paralytics of the Amarilla Club (who have our own committee), inviting us to come to some provisional understanding for a truce, in order, they have the impudence to say, that the noble cause of Liberty "should not be stained by the criminal excesses of Conservative selfishness!" As I came out to sit with Nostromo on the cathedral steps the club was busy considering a proper reply in the principal room, littered with exploded cartridges, with a lot of broken glass, blood smears, candlesticks, and all sorts of wreckage on the floor. But all this is nonsense. Nobody in the town has any real power except the railway engineers, whose men occupy the dismantled houses acquired by the Company for their town station on one side of the Plaza, and Nostromo, whose *cargadores* were sleeping under the arcades along the front of Anzani's shops. A fire of broken furniture out of the Intendencia saloons, mostly gilt, was burning on the Plaza, in a high flame swaying right upon the statue of Charles IV. The dead body of a man was lying on the steps of the pedestal, his arms thrown wide open, and his *sombrero* covering his face—the attention of some friend, perhaps. The light of the flame touched the foliage of the first trees on the Alameda, and played on the end of a side-street near by, blocked up by a jumble of ox-carts and dead bullocks. Sitting on one of the carcases, a *lepero*, muffled up, smoked a cigarette. It was a truce, you understand. The only other living being on the Plaza besides ourselves was a *cargador* walking to and fro, with a long, bare knife in his hand, like a sentry before the Arcades, where his friends were sleeping. And the only other spot of light in the dark town were the lighted windows of the club, at the corner of the Calle.

After having written so far, Don Martin Decoud, the exotic dandy of the Parisian boulevard, got up and walked across the sanded floor of the café at one end of the Albergo of United Italy, kept by Giorgio Viola, the old companion of Garibaldi. The highly colored lithograph of the Faithful Hero seemed to look dimly, in the light of one candle, at the man with no faith in anything except the truth of his own sensations. Looking out of the window, Decoud was met by a darkness so impenetrable that he could see neither the mountains nor the town, nor yet the buildings near the harbor; and there was not a sound, as if the tremendous obscurity of the Placid Gulf, spreading from the waters over the land, had made it dumb as well as blind. Presently Decoud felt a light tremor of the floor and a distant clank of iron. A bright white light appeared, deep in the darkness, growing bigger with a thundering noise. The rolling stock usually kept on the sidings in Rincón was being run back to the yards for safe keeping. Like a mysterious stirring of the darkness behind the headlight of the engine, the train passed in a gust of hollow uproar, by the end of the house, which seemed to vibrate all over in response. And nothing was clearly visible but, on the end of the last car, a Negro, in white trousers and naked to the waist, swinging a blazing torch basket incessantly with a circular movement of his bare arm. Decoud did not stir.

Behind him, on the back of the chair from which he had risen, hung his elegant Parisian overcoat, with a pearl-gray silk lining. But when he turned back to come to the table the candlelight fell upon a face that was grimy and scratched. His rosy lips were blackened with heat, the smoke of gun-powder. Dirt and rust tarnished the luster of his short beard. His shirt collar and cuffs were crumpled; the blue silken tie hung down his breast like a rag; a greasy smudge crossed his white brow. He had not taken off his clothing nor used water, except to snatch a hasty drink greedily, for some forty hours. An awful restlessness had made him its own, had marked him with all the signs of desperate strife, and put a dry, sleepless stare into his eyes. He murmured to himself in a hoarse voice, "I wonder if there's any bread here," looked vaguely about him, then dropped into the chair and took the pencil up again. He became aware he had not eaten anything for many hours.

It occurred to him that no one could understand him so well as his sister. In the most skeptical heart there lurks at such moments, when the chances of existence are involved, a desire to leave a correct impression of the feelings, like a light by which the action may be seen when personality is gone, gone where no light of investigation can ever reach the truth which every death takes out of the world. Therefore, instead of looking for something to eat, or trying to snatch an hour or so of sleep, Decoud was filling the pages of a large pocket-book with a letter to his sister.

In the intimacy of that intercourse he could not keep out his weariness, his great fatigue, the close touch of his bodily sensations. He began again as if he were talking to her. With almost an illusion of her presence, he wrote the phrase, "I am very hungry."

> I have the feeling of a great solitude around me [he continued]. Is it, perhaps, because I am the only man with a definite idea in his head, in the complete collapse of every resolve, intention, and hope about me? But the solitude is also very real. All the engineers are out, and have been for two days, looking after the property of the National Central Railway, of that great Costaguana undertaking which is to put money into the pockets of Englishmen, Frenchmen, Americans, Germans, and God knows who else. The silence about me is ominous. There is above the middle part of this house a sort of first floor, with narrow openings like loopholes for windows, probably used in old times for the better defense against the savages, when the persistent barbarism of our native continent did not wear the black coats of politicians, but went about yelling, half-naked, with bows and arrows in its hands. The woman of the house is dying up there, I believe, all alone with her old husband. There is a narrow staircase, the sort of staircase one man could easily defend against a mob, leading up there, and I have just heard, through the thickness of the wall, the old fellow going down into their kitchen for something or other. It was a sort of noise a mouse might make behind the plaster of a wall. All the servants they had ran away yesterday and have not returned yet, if ever they do. For the rest, there are only two children here, two girls. The father has sent them downstairs, and they have crept into this café, perhaps because I am here. They huddle together in a corner, in each other's arms; I just noticed them a few minutes ago, and I feel more lonely than ever.

Decoud turned half round in his chair, and asked, "Is there any bread here?"

Linda's dark head was shaken negatively in response, above the fair head of her sister nestling on her breast.

"You couldn't get me some bread?" insisted Decoud. The child did not move; he saw her large eyes stare at him very dark from the corner. "You're not afraid of me?" he said.

"No," said Linda, "we are not afraid of you. You came here with Gian' Battista."

"You mean Nostromo?" said Decoud.

"The English call him so, but that is no name either for man or beast," said the girl, passing her hand gently over her sister's hair.

"But he lets people call him so," remarked Decoud.

"Not in this house," retorted the child.

"Ah! well, I shall call him the Capataz then."

Decoud gave up the point, and after writing steadily for a while turned round again.

"When do you expect him back?" he asked.

"After he brought you here he rode off to fetch the Señor Doctor from the town for mother. He will be back soon."

"He stands a good chance of getting shot somewhere on the road," Decoud murmured to himself audibly; and Linda declared in her high-pitched voice:

"Nobody would dare to fire a shot at Gian' Battista."

"You believe that," asked Decoud, "do you?"

"I know it," said the child, with conviction. "There is no one in this place brave enough to attack Gian' Battista."

"It doesn't require much bravery to pull a trigger behind a bush," muttered Decoud to himself. "Fortunately, the night is dark, or there would be but little chance of saving the silver of the mine."

He turned again to his pocket-book, glanced back through the pages, and again started his pencil.

> That was the position yesterday, after the *Minerva* with the fugitive President had gone out of harbor, and the rioters had been driven back into the side-lanes of the town. I sat on the steps of the cathedral with Nostromo, after sending out the cable message for the information of a more or less attentive world. Strangely enough, though the offices of the Cable Company are in the same building as the *Porvenir,* the mob, which has thrown my presses out of the window and scattered the type all over the Plaza, has been kept from interfering with the instruments on the other side of the courtyard. As I sat talking with Nostromo, Bernhardt, the telegraphist, came out from under the Arcades with a piece of paper in his hand. The little man had tied himself up to an enormous sword and was hung all over with revolvers. He is ridiculous, but the bravest German of his size that ever tapped the key of a Morse transmitter. He had received the message from Cayta reporting the transports with Barrios's army just entering the port, and ending with the words, "The greatest enthusiasm prevails." I walked off to drink some water at the fountain, and I was shot at from the Alameda by somebody hiding behind a tree. But I drank, and didn't care; with Barrios in Cayta and the great Cordillera between us and Montero's victorious army I seemed, notwithstanding Messrs. Gamacho and Fuentes, to hold my new State in the hollow of my hand. I was ready to sleep, but when I got as far as the Casa Gould I found the patio full of wounded laid out on straw. Lights were burning, and in that enclosed courtyard on that hot night a faint odor of chloroform and blood hung about. At one end Dr. Monygham, the doctor of the mine, was dressing the wounds; at the other, near the stairs, Father Corbelán, kneeling, listened to the confession of a dying *cargador.* Mrs. Gould was walking about through these shambles with a large bottle in one hand and a lot of cotton wool in the

other. She just looked at me and never even winked. Her *camerista* was following her, also holding a bottle, and sobbing gently to herself.

I busied myself for some time in fetching water from the cistern for the
wounded. Afterwards I wandered upstairs, meeting some of the first ladies of
Sulaco, paler than I had ever seen them before, with bandages over their arms.
Not all of them had fled to the ships. A good man had taken refuge for the
day in the Casa Gould. On the landing a girl, with her hair half down, was
kneeling against the wall under the niche where stands a Madonna in blue
robes and a gilt crown on her head. I think it was the eldest Miss Lopez; I
couldn't see her face, but I remember looking at the high French heel of her
little shoe. She did not make a sound, she did not stir, she was not sobbing;
she remained there, perfectly still, all black against the white wall, a silent
figure of passionate piety. I am sure she was no more frightened than the
other white-faced ladies I met carrying bandages. One was sitting on the top
step tearing a piece of linen hastily into strips—the young wife of an elderly
man of fortune here. She interrupted herself to wave her hand to my bow, as
though she were in her carriage on the Alameda. The women of our country
are worth looking at during a revolution. The rouge and pearl powder fall off,
together with that passive attitude towards the outer world which education,
tradition, custom impose upon them from the earliest infancy. I thought of
your face, which from your infancy had the stamp of intelligence instead of
that patient and resigned cast which appears when some political commotion
tears down the veil of cosmetics and usage.

In the great *sala* upstairs a sort of Junta of Notables was sitting, the
remnant of the vanished Provincial Assembly. Don Juste Lopez had had half
his beard singed off at the muzzle of a *trabuco* loaded with slugs, of which
every one missed him, providentially. And as he turned his head from side to
side it was exactly as if there had been two men inside his frock-coat, one
nobly whiskered and solemn, the other untidy and scared.

They raised a cry of "Decoud! Don Martin!" at my entrance. I asked
them, "What are you deliberating upon, gentlemen?" There did not seem to
be any president, though Don José Avellanos sat at the head of the table.
They all answered together, "On the preservation of life and property." "Till
the new officials arrive," Don Juste explained to me, with the solemn side of
his face offered to my view. It was as if a stream of water had been poured
upon my glowing idea of a new State. There was a hissing sound in my ears,
and the room grew dim, as if suddenly filled with vapor.

I walked up to the table blindly, as though I had been drunk. "You are
deliberating upon surrender," I said. They all sat still, with their noses over
the sheet of paper each had before him, God only knows why. Only Don José
hid his face in his hands, muttering, "Never, never!" But as I looked at him, it
seemed to me that I could have blown him away with my breath, he looked so
frail, so weak, so worn out. Whatever happens, he will not survive. The

deception is too great for a man of his age; and hasn't he seen the sheets of *Fifty Years of Misrule*, which we have begun printing on the presses of the *Porvenir*, littering the Plaza, floating in the gutters, fired out as wads for trabucos loaded with handfuls of type, blown in the wind, trampled in the mud? I have seen pages floating upon the very waters of the harbor. It would be unreasonable to expect him to survive. It would be cruel.

"Do you know," I cried, "what surrender means to you, to your women, to your children, to your property?"

I declaimed for five minutes without drawing breath, it seems to me, harping on our best chances, on the ferocity of Montero, whom I made out to be as great a beast as I have no doubt he would like to be if he had intelligence enough to conceive a systematic reign of terror. And then for another five minutes or more I poured out an impassioned appeal to their courage and manliness, with all the passion of my love for Antonia. For if ever man spoke well, it would be from a personal feeling, denouncing an enemy, defending himself, or pleading for what really may be dearer than life. My dear girl, I absolutely thundered at them. It seemed as if my voice would burst the walls asunder, and when I stopped I saw all their scared eyes looking at me dubiously. And that was all the effect I had produced! Only Don José's head had sunk lower and lower on his breast. I bent my ear to his withered lips, and made out his whisper, something like, "In God's name, then, Martin, my son!" I don't know exactly. There was the name of God in it, I am certain. It seems to me I have caught his last breath—the breath of his departing soul on his lips.

He lives yet, it is true. I have seen him since; but it was only a senile body, lying on its back, covered to the chin, with open eyes, and so still that you might have said it was breathing no longer. I left him thus, with Antonia kneeling by the side of the bed, just before I came to this Italian's *posada*, where the ubiquitous death is also waiting. But I know that Don José has really died there, in the Casa Gould, with that whisper urging me to attempt what no doubt his soul, wrapped up in the sanctity of diplomatic treaties and solem declarations, must have abhorred. I had exclaimed very loud, "There is never any God in a country where men will not help themselves."

Meanwhile, Don Juste had begun a pondered oration whose solemn effect was spoiled by the ridiculous disaster to his beard. I did not wait to make it out. He seemed to argue that Montero's (he called him The General) intentions were probably not evil, though, he went on, "that distinguished man" (only a week ago we used to call him a *gran' bestia*) "was perhaps mistaken as to the true means." As you may imagine, I didn't stay to hear the rest. I know the intentions of Montero's brother, Pedrito, the *guerrillero*, whom I exposed in Paris, some years ago, in a café frequented by South American students, where he tried to pass himself off for a Secretary of Legation. He used to come in and talk for hours, twisting his felt hat in his hairy paws, and his ambition seemed to be to become a sort of Duc de Morny to a sort of Napoleon. Already, then, he used to talk of his brother in inflated terms. He seemed fairly safe from being found out, because the students, all of the Blanco families, did not, as you may imagine, frequent the Legation. It was only Decoud, a man without faith and principles, as they used to say, that went in there sometimes for the sake of the fun, as it were to an assembly of trained monkeys. I know his intentions. I have seen him change the plates at table. Whoever is allowed to live on in terror, I must die the death.

No, I didn't stay to the end to hear Don Juste Lopez trying to persuade himself in a grave oration of the clemency and justice, and honesty, and purity of the brothers Montero. I went out abruptly to seek Antonia. I saw her in the gallery. As I opened the door, she extended to me her clasped hands.

"What are they doing in there?" she asked.

"Talking," I said, with my eyes looking into hers.

"Yes, yes, but—"

"Empty speeches," I interrupted her. "Hiding their fears behind imbecile hopes. They are all great Parliamentarians there—on the English model, as you know." I was so furious that I could hardly speak. She made a gesture of despair.

Through the door I held a little ajar behind me, we heard Don Juste's measured mouthing monotone go on from phrase to phrase, like a sort of awful and solemn madness.

"After all, the Democratic aspirations have, perhaps, their legitimacy. The ways of human progress are inscrutable, and if the fate of the country is in the hand of Montero, we ought—"

I crashed the door to on that; it was enough; it was too much. There was never a beautiful face expressing more horror and despair than the face of Antonia. I couldn't bear it; I seized her wrists.

"Have they killed my father in there?" she asked.

Her eyes blazed with indignation, but as I looked on, fascinated, the light in them went out.

"It is a surrender," I said. And I remember I was shaking her wrists I held apart in my hands. "But it's more than talk. Your father told me to go on in God's name."

My dear girl, there is that in Antonia which would make me believe in the feasibility of anything. One look at her face is enough to set my brain on fire. And yet I love her as any other man would—with the heart, and with that alone. She is more to me than his Church to Father Corbelán (the Grand Vicar disappeared last night from the town; perhaps gone to join the band of Hernandez). She is more to me than his precious mine to that sentimental Englishman. I won't speak of his wife. She may have been sentimental once. The San Tomé mine stands now between those two people. "Your father himself, Antonia," I repeated; "your father, do you understand? has told me to go on."

She averted her face, and in a pained voice—

"He has?" she cried. "Then, indeed, I fear he will never speak again."

She freed her wrists from my clutch and began to cry in her handkerchief. I disregarded her sorrow; I would rather see her miserable than not see her at all, never any more; for whether I escaped or stayed to die, there was for us no coming together, no future. And that being so, I had no pity to waste upon the passing moments of her sorrow. I sent her off in tears to fetch Doña Emilia and Don Carlos, too. Their sentiment was necessary to the very life of my plan; the sentimentalism of the people that will never do anything for the sake of their passionate desire, unless it comes to them clothed in the fair robes of an idea.

Late at night we formed a small junta of four—the two women, Don Carlos, and myself—in Mrs. Gould's blue-and-white boudoir.

El Rey de Sulaco thinks himself, no doubt, a very honest man. And so he is, if one could look behind his taciturnity. Perhaps he thinks that this alone makes his honesty unstained. Those Englishmen live on illusions which somehow or other help them to get a firm hold of the substance. When he speaks it is by a rare "yes" or "no" that seems as impersonal as the words of an oracle. But he could not impose on me by his dumb reserve. I knew what he had in his head; he has his mine in his head; and his wife had nothing in her head but his precious person, which he has bound up with the Gould Concession and tied to that little woman's neck. No matter. The thing was to make him present the affair to Holroyd (the Steel and Silver King) in such a manner as to secure his financial support. At that time last night, just twenty-four hours ago, we thought the silver of the mine safe in the Custom House vaults till the northbound steamer came to take it away. And as long as the treasure flowed north, without a break, that utter sentimentalist, Holroyd, would not drop his idea of introducing, not only justice, industry, peace, to the benighted continents, but also that pet dream of his of a purer form of Christianity. Later on, the principal European really in Sulaco, the engineer-in-chief of the railway, came riding up the *calle*, from the harbor, and was admitted to our conclave. Meantime, the Junta of the Notables in the great *sala* was still deliberating; only, one of them had run out in the corridor to ask the servant whether something to eat couldn't be sent in. The first words the engineer-in-chief said as he came into the boudoir were, "What is your house, dear Mrs. Gould? A war hospital below, and apparently a restaurant above. I saw them carrying trays full of good things into the *sala.*"

"And here, in this boudoir," I said, "you behold the inner cabinet of the Occidental Republic that is to be."

He was so preoccupied that he didn't smile at that, he didn't even look surprised.

He told us that he was attending to the general dispositions for the defense of the railway property at the railway yards when he was sent for to go into the railway telegraph office. The engineer of the railhead, at the foot of the mountains, wanted to talk to him from his end of the wire. There was nobody in the office but himself and the operator of the railway telegraph, who read off the clicks aloud as the tape coiled its length upon the floor. And the purport of that talk, clicked nervously from a wooden shed in the depths of the forests, had informed the chief that President Ribiera had been, or was being, pursued. This was news, indeed, to all of us in Sulaco, Ribiera himself, when rescued, revived, and soothed by us, had been inclined to think that he had not been pursued.

Ribiera had yielded to the urgent solicitations of his friends, and had left the headquarters of his discomfited army alone, under the guidance of Bonifacio, the muleteer, who had been willing to take the responsibility with the risk. He had departed at daybreak of the third day. His remaining forces had melted away during the night. Bonifacio and he rode hard on horses towardss the Cordillera; then they obtained mules, entered the passes, and crossed the Paramo of Ivie just before a freezing blast swept over that stony plateau, burying in a drift of snow the little shelter-hut of stones in which they had spent the night. Afterwards poor Ribiera had many adventures, got separated from his guide, lost his mount, struggled down to the Campo on foot, and if he had not thrown himself on the mercy of a *ranchero* would have perished a long way from Sulaco. That man, who, as a matter of fact, recognized him at once, let him have a fresh mule, which the fugitive, heavy and unskillful, had ridden to death. And it was true he had been pursued by a party commanded by no less than a person than Pedro Montero, the brother of the general. The cold wind of the Paramo luckily caught the pursuers on the top of the pass. Some few men, and all the animals, perished in the icy blast. The stragglers died, but the main body kept on. They found poor Bonifacio lying half-dead at the foot of a snow slope, and bayoneted him promptly in the true Civil War style. They would have had Ribiera, too, if they had not, for some reason or other, turned off the track of the old *camino real*, only to lose their way in the forests at the foot of the lower slopes. And there they were at last, having stumbled in unexpectedly upon the construction camp. The engineer at the railhead told his chief by wire that he had Pedro Montero absolutely there, in the very office, listening to the clicks. He was going to take possession of Sulaco in the name of the Democracy. He was very overbearing. His men slaughtered some of the Railway Company's cattle without asking leave, and went to work broiling the meat on the embers. Pedrito made many pointed inquiries as to the silver mine, and what had become of the product of the last six months' working. He had said peremptorily, "Ask your chief up there by wire, he ought to know; tell him that Don Pedro Montero, Chief of the Campo and Minister of the Interior of the new Government, desires to be correctly informed."

He had his feet wrapped up in blood-stained rags, a lean, haggard face, ragged beard and hair, and had walked in limping, with a crooked branch of a tree for a staff. His followers were, perhaps, in a worse plight, but apparently they had not thrown away their arms, and, at any rate, not all their ammunition. Their lean faces filled the door and the windows of the telegraph hut. As it was at the same time the bedroom of the engineer-in-charge there, Montero had thrown himself on his clean blankets and lay there shivering and dictating requisitions to be transmitted by wire to Sulaco. He demanded a train of cars to be sent down at once to transport his men up.

"To this I answered from my end," the engineer-in-chief related to us, "that I dared not risk the rolling-stock in the interior, as there had been attempts to wreck trains all along the line several times. I did that for your sake, Gould," said the chief engineer. "The answer to this was, in the words of my subordinate, 'The filthy brute on my bed said, "Suppose I were to have you shot?"' To which my subordinate, who, it appears, was himself operating, remarked that it would not bring the cars up. Upon that, the other, yawning, said, 'Never mind, there is no lack of horses on the Campo.' And, turning over, went to sleep on Harris's bed."

That is why, my dear girl, I am a fugitive tonight. The last wire from the railhead says that Pedro Montero and his men left at daybreak, after feeding on *asado* beef all night. They took all the horses; they will find more on the road; they'll be here in less than thirty hours, and thus Sulaco is no place either for me or the great store of silver belonging to the Gould Concession.

But that is not the worst. The garrison of Esmeralda has gone over to the victorious party. We have heard this by means of the telegraphist of the Cable Company, who came to the Casa Gould in the early morning with the news. In fact, it was so early that the day had not yet quite broken over Sulaco. His colleague in Esmeralda had called him up to say that the Garrison, after shooting some of their officers, had taken possession of a Government steamer laid up in the harbor. It is really a heavy blow for me. I thought I could depend on every man in this province. It was a mistake. It was a Monterist Revolution in Esmeralda, just such as was attempted in Sulaco, only that *that* one came off. The telegraphist was signaling to Bernhardt all the time, and his last transmitted words were, "They are bursting in the door, and taking possession of the cable office. You are cut off. Can do no more."

But, as a matter of fact, he managed somehow to escape the vigilance of his captors, who had tried to stop the communication with the outer world. He did manage it. How it was done I don't know, but a few hours afterwards he called up Sulaco again, and what he said was, "The insurgent army has taken possession of the Government transport in the bay and are filling her with troops, with the intention of going round the coast to Sulaco. Therefore look out for yourselves. They will be ready to start in a few hours, and may be upon you before daybreak."

This is all he could say. They drove him away from his instrument this time for good, because Bernhardt has been calling up Esmeralda ever since without getting an answer.

After setting these words down in the pocket-book which he was filling up for the benefit of his sister, Decoud lifted his head to listen. But there were no sounds, neither in the room nor in the house, except the drip of the water from the filter into the vast earthenware jar under the wooden stand. And outside the house there was a great silence. Decoud lowered his head again over the pocket-book.

I am not running away, you understand [he wrote on]. I am simply going away with that great treasure of silver which must be saved at all costs. Pedro Montero from the Campo and the revolted garrison of Esmeralda from the sea are converging upon it. That it is there lying ready for them is only an accident. The real objective is the San Tomé mine itself, as you may well imagine; otherwise the Occidental Province would have been, no doubt, left alone for many weeks, to be gathered at leisure into the arms of the victorious party. Don Carlos Gould will have enough to do to save his mine, with its organization and its people; this *"Imperium in Imperio,"* this wealth-producing thing, to which his sentimentalism attaches a strange idea of justice. He holds to it as some men hold to the idea of love or revenge. Unless I am much mistaken in the man, it must remain inviolate or perish by an act of his will alone. A passion has crept into his cold and idealistic life. A passion which I can only comprehend intellectually. A passion that is not like the passions we know, we men of another blood. But it is as dangerous as any of ours.

His wife has understood it, too. That is why she is such a good ally of mine. She seizes upon all my suggestions with a sure instinct that in the end they make for the safety of the Gould Concession. And he defers to her because he trusts her perhaps, but I fancy more rather as if he wished to make up for some subtle wrong, for that sentimental unfaithfulness which surrenders her happiness, her life, to the seduction of an idea. The little woman has discovered that he lives for the mine rather than for her. But let them be. To each his fate, shaped by passion or sentiment. The principal thing is that she has backed up my advice to get the silver out of the town, out of the country, at once, at any cost, at any risk. Don Carlos's mission is to preserve unstained the fair name of his mine; Mrs. Gould's mission is to save him from the effects of that cold and overmastering passion, which she dreads more than if it were an infatuation for another woman. Nostromo's mission is to save the silver. The plan is to load it into the largest of the Company's lighters, and send it across the gulf to a small port out of Costaguana territory just on the other side of the Azuera, where the first northbound steamer will get orders to pick it up. The waters here are calm. We shall slip away into the darkness of the gulf before the Esmeralda rebels arrive; and by the time the day breaks over the ocean we shall be out of sight, invisible, hidden by Azuera, which itself looks from the Sulaco shore like a faint blue cloud on the horizon.

The incorruptible Capataz de Cargadores is the man for that work; and I, the man with a passion, but without a mission, I go with him to return—to play my part in the farce to the end, and if successful, to receive my reward, which no one but Antonia can give me.

I shall not see her again now before I depart. I left her, as I have said, by Don José's bedside. The street was dark, the houses shut up, and I walked out of the town in the night. Not a single street-lamp had been lit for two days, and the archway of the gate was only a mass of darkness in the vague form of a tower, in which I heard low, dismal groans that seemed to answer the murmurs of a man's voice.

I recognized something impassive and careless in the tone, characteristic of that Genoese sailor who, like me, has come casually here to be drawn into the events for which his skepticism as well as mine seems to entertain a sort of passive contempt. The only thing he seems to care for, as far as I have been able to discover, is to be well spoken of. An ambition fit for noble souls, but also a profitable one for an exceptionally intelligent scoundrel. Yes. His very words, "To be well spoken of. *Sí, señor.*" He does not seem to make any difference between speaking and thinking. Is it sheer naïveness or the practical point of view, I wonder? Exceptional individualities always interest me, because they are true to the general formula expressing the moral state of humanity.

He joined me on the harbor road after I had passed them under the dark archway without stopping. It was a woman in trouble he had been talking to. Through discretion I kept silent while he walked by my side. After a time he began to talk himself. It was not what I expected. It was only an old woman, an old lace-maker, in search of her son, one of the street-sweepers employed by the municipality. Friends had come the day before at daybreak to the door of their hovel calling him out. He had gone with them, and she had not seen him since; so she had left the food she had been preparing half-cooked on the extinct embers and had crawled out as far as the harbor, where she had heard that some town *mozos* had been killed on the morning of the riot. One of the *cargadores* guarding the Custom House had brought out a lantern, and had helped her to look at the few dead left lying about there. Now she was creeping back, having failed in her search. So she sat down on the stone seat under the arch, moaning, because she was very tired. The Capataz had questioned her, and after hearing her broken and groaning tale had advised her to go and look amongst the wounded in the patio of the Casa Gould. He had also given her a quarter dollar, he mentioned carelessly.

"Why did you do that?" I asked. "Do you know her?"

"No, *señor*. I don't suppose I have ever seen her before. How should I? She has not probably been out in the streets for years. She is one of those old women that you find in this country at the back of huts, crouching over fireplaces, with a stick on the ground by their side, and almost too feeble to drive away the stray dogs from their cooking-pots. *Caramaba!* I could tell by her voice that death had forgotten her. But, old or young, they like money, and will speak well of the man who gives it to them." He laughed a little. "*Señor*, you should have felt the clutch of her paw as I put the piece in her palm." He paused. "My last, too," he added.

I made no comment. He's known for his liberality, and his bad luck at the game of *monte*, which keeps him as poor as when he first came here.

"I suppose, Don Martin," he began, in a thoughtful, speculative tone, "that the Señor Administrador of San Tomé will reward me some day if I save his silver?"

I said that it could not be otherwise, surely. He walked on, muttering to himself. "*Sí, sí*, without doubt, without doubt; and, look you, *Señor* Martin, what it is to be well spoken of! There is not another man that could have been even thought of for such a thing. I shall get something great for it some day. And let it come soon," he mumbled. "Time passes in this country as quick as anywhere else."

This, *soeur chérie*, is my companion in the great escape for the sake of the great cause. He is more naïve than shrewd, more masterful than crafty, more generous with his personality than the people who make use of him are with their money. At least, that is what he thinks himself with more pride than sentiment. I am glad I have made friends with him. As a companion he acquires more importance than he ever had as a sort of minor genius in his way—as an original Italian sailor whom I allowed to come in in the small hours and talk familiarly to the editor of the *Porvenir* while the paper was going through the press. And it is curious to have met a man for whom the value of life seems to consist in personal prestige.

I am waiting for him here now. On arriving at the *posada* kept by Viola we found the children alone down below, and the old Genoese shouted to his countryman to go and fetch the doctor. Otherwise we would have gone on to the wharf, where it appears Captain Mitchell with some volunteer Europeans and a few picked *cargadores* are loading the lighter with the silver that must be saved from Montero's clutches in order to be used for Montero's defeat. Nostromo galloped furiously back towards the town. He has been long gone already. This delay gives me time to talk to you. By the time this pocket-book reaches your hands much will have happened. But now it is a pause under the hovering wing of death in that silent house buried in the black night, with this dying woman, the two children crouching without a sound, and that old man whom I can hear through the thickness of the wall passing up and down with a light rubbing noise no louder than a mouse. And I, the only other with them, don't really know whether to count myself with the living or with the dead. *"Quién sabe?"* as the people here are prone to say in answer to every question. But no! feeling for you is certainly not dead, and the whole thing, the house, the dark night, the silent children in this dim room, my very presence here—all this is life, must be life, since it is so much like a dream.

With the writing of the last line there came upon Decoud a moment of sudden and complete oblivion. He swayed over the table as if struck by a bullet. The next moment he sat up, confused, with the idea that he had heard his pencil roll on the floor. The low door of the café, wide open, was filled with the glare of a torch in which was visible half of a horse, switching its tail against the leg of a rider with a long iron spur strapped to the naked heel. The two girls were gone, and Nostromo, standing in the middle of the room, looked at him from under the round brim of the *sombrero* low down over his brow.

"I have brought that sour-faced English doctor in Señora Gould's carriage," said Nostromo. "I doubt if, with all his wisdom, he can save the Padrona this time. They have sent for the children. A bad sign that."

He sat down on the end of a bench. "She wants to give them her blessing, I suppose."

Dazedly Decoud observed that he must have fallen sound asleep, and Nostromo said, with a vague smile, that he had looked in at the window and had seen him lying still across the table with his head on his arms. The English *señora* had also come in the carriage, and went upstairs at once with the doctor. She had told him not to wake up Don Martin yet; but when they sent for the children he had come into the café.

The half of the horse with its half of the rider swung round outside the door; the torch of tow and resin in her iron basket which was carried on a stick at the saddle-bow flared right into the room for a moment, and Mrs. Gould entered hastily with a very white, tired face. The hood of her dark, blue cloak had fallen back. Both men rose.

"Teresa wants to see you, Nostromo," she said.

The Capataz did not move. Decoud, with his back to the table, began to button up his coat.

"The silver, Mrs. Gould, the silver," he murmured in English. "Don't forget that the Esmeralda garrison have got a steamer. They may appear at any moment at the harbor entrance."

"The doctor says there is no hope," Mrs. Gould spoke rapidly, also in English. "I shall take you down to the wharf in my carriage and then come back to fetch away the girls." She changed swiftly into Spanish to address Nostromo. "Why are you wasting time? Old Giorgio's wife wishes to see you."

"I am going to her, *señora*," muttered the Capataz.

Dr. Monygham now showed himself, bringing back the children. To Mrs. Gould's inquiring glance he only shook his head and went outside at once, followed by Nostromo.

The horse of the torch-bearer, motionless, hung his head low, and the rider had dropped the reins to light a cigarette. The glare of the torch played on the front of the house crossed by the big black letters of its inscription in which only the word ITALIA was lighted fully. The patch of wavering glare reached as far as Mrs. Gould's carriage waiting on the road, with the yellow-faced, portly Ignacio apparently dozing on the box. By his side Basilio, dark and skinny, held a Winchester carbine in front of him, with both hands, and peered fearfully into the darkness. Nostromo touched lightly the doctor's shoulder.

"Is she really dying, Señor Doctor?"

"Yes,' said the doctor, with a strange twitch of his scarred cheek. "And why she wants to see you I cannot imagine."

"She has been like that before," suggested Nostromo, looking away.

"Well, Capataz, I can assure you she will never be like that again," snarled Dr. Monygham. "You may go to her or stay away. There is very little to be got from talking to the dying. But she told Doña Emilia in my hearing that she has been like a mother to you ever since you first set foot ashore here."

"Sí! And she never had a good word to say for me to anybody. It is more as if she could not forgive me for being alive, and such a man, too, as she would have liked her son to be."

"Maybe!" exclaimed a mournful deep voice near them. "Women have their own ways of tormenting themselves." Giorgio Viola had come out of the house. He threw a heavy black shadow in the torchlight, and the glare fell on his big face, on the great bushy head of white hair. He motioned the Capataz indoors with his extended arm.

Dr. Monygham, after busying himself with a little medicament box of polished wood on the seat of the landau, turned to old Giorgio and thrust into his big, trembling hand one of the glass-stoppered bottles out of the case.

"Give her a spoonful of this now and then, in water," he said. "It will make her easier."

"And there is nothing more for her?" asked the old man patiently.

"No. Not on earth," said the doctor, with his back to him, clicking the lock of the medicine case.

Nostromo slowly crossed the large kitchen, all dark but for the glow of a heap of charcoal under the heavy mantel of the cooking-range, where water was boiling in an iron pot with a loud bubbling sound. Between the two walls of a narrow staircase a bright light streamed from the sick-room above; and the magnificent Capataz de Cargadores stepping noiselessly in soft leather sandals, bushy whiskered, his muscular neck and bronzed chest bare in the open check shirt, resembled a Mediterranean sailor just come ashore from some wine- or fruit-laden felucca. At the top he paused, broad shouldered, narrow hipped, and supple, looking at the large bed, like a white couch of state, with a profusion of snowy linen, amongst which the Padrona sat unpropped and bowed, her handsome, black-browed face bent over her chest. A mass of raven hair with only a few white threads in it covered her shoulders; one thick strand fallen forward half veiled her cheek. Perfectly motionless in that pose, expressing physical anxiety and unrest, she turned her eyes alone towards Nostromo.

The Capataz had a red sash wound many times round his waist, and a heavy silver ring on the forefinger of the hand he raised to give a twist to his mustache.

"Their revolutions, their revolutions," gasped Señora Teresa. "Look, Gian' Battista, it has killed me at last!"

Nostromo said nothing, and the sick woman with an upward glance insisted. "Look, this one has killed me, while you were away fighting for what did not concern you, foolish man."

"Why talk like this?" mumbled the Capataz between his teeth. "Will you never believe in my good sense? It concerns me to keep on being what I am: every day alike."

"You never change, indeed," she said, bitterly. "Always thinking of yourself and taking your pay out in fine words from those who care nothing for you."

There was between them an intimacy of antagonism as close in its way as the intimacy of accord and affection. He had not walked along the way of Teresa's expectations. It was she who had encouraged him to leave his ship, in the hope of securing a friend and defender for the girls. The wife of old Giorgio was aware of her precarious health, and was haunted by the fear of her aged husband's loneliness and the unprotected state of the children. She had wanted to annex that apparently quiet and steady young man, affectionate and pliable, an orphan from his tenderest age, as he had told her, with no ties in Italy except an uncle, owner and master of a felucca, from whose ill-usage he had run away before he was fourteen. He had seemed to her courageous, a hard worker, determined to make his way in the world. From gratitude and the ties of habit he would become like a son to herself and Giorgio; and then, who knows, when Linda had grown up. . . . Ten years' difference between husband and wife was not so much. Her own great man was nearly twenty years older than herself. Gian' Battista was an attractive young fellow, besides; attractive to men, women, and children, just by that profound quietness of personality which, like a serene twilight, rendered more seductive the promise of his vigorous form and the resolution of his conduct.

Old Giorgio, in profound ignorance of his wife's views and hopes, had a great regard for his young countryman. "A man ought not to be tame," he used to tell her, quoting the Spanish proverb in defense of the splendid Capataz. She was growing jealous of his success. He was escaping from her, she feared. She was practical, and he seemed to her to be an absurd spendthrift of these qualities which made him so valuable. He got too little for them. He scattered them with both hands amongst too many people, she thought. He laid no money by. She railed at his poverty, his exploits, his adventures, his loves, and his reputation; but in her heart she had never given him up, as though, indeed, he had been her son.

Even now, ill as she was, ill enough to feel the chill, black breath of the approaching end, she had wished to see him. It was like putting out her benumbed hand to regain her hold. But she had presumed too much on her strength. She could not command her thoughts; they had become dim, like her vision. The words faltered on her lips, and only the paramount anxiety and desire of her life seemed to be too strong for death.

The Capataz said, "I have heard these things many times. You are unjust, but it does not hurt me. Only now you do not seem to have much strength to talk, and I have but little time to listen. I am engaged in a work of very great moment."

She made an effort to ask him whether it was true that he had found time to go and fetch a doctor for her. Nostromo nodded affirmatively.

She was pleased: it relieved her sufferings to know that the man had condescended to do so much for those who really wanted his help. It was a proof of his friendship. Her voice became stronger.

"I want a priest more than a doctor," she said, pathetically. She did not move her head; only her eyes ran into the corners to watch the Capataz standing by the side of her bed. "Would you go to fetch a priest for me now? Think! A dying woman asks you!"

Nostromo shook his head resolutely. He did not believe in priests in their sacerdotal character. A doctor was an efficacious person; but a priest, as priest, was nothing, incapable of doing either good or harm. Nostromo did not even dislike the sight of them as old Giorgio did. The utter uselessness of the errand was what struck him most.

"Padrona," he said, "you have been like this before, and got better after a few days. I have given you already the very last moments I can spare. Ask Señora Gould to send you one."

He was feeling uneasy at the impiety of this refusal. The Padrona believed in priests, and confessed herself to them. But all women did that. It could not be of much consequence. And yet his heart felt oppressed for a moment—at the thought of what absolution would mean to her if she believed in it only ever so little. No matter. It was quite true that he had given her already the very last moment he could spare.

"You refuse to go?" she gasped. "Ah! you are always yourself, indeed."

"Listen to reason, Padrona," he said. "I am needed to save the silver of the mine. Do you hear? A greater treasure than the one which they say is guarded by ghosts and devils in Azuera. It is true. I am resolve to make this the most desperate affair I was ever engaged on in my whole life."

She felt a despairing indignation. The supreme test had failed. Standing above her, Nostromo did not see the distorted features of her face, distorted by a paroxysm of pain and anger. Only she began to tremble all over. Her bowed head shook. The broad shoulders quivered.

"Then God, perhaps, will have some mercy upon me! But do you look to it, man, that you get something for yourself out of it, besides the remorse that shall overtake you some day."

She laughed feebly. "Get riches at least for once, you indispensable, admired Gian' Battista, to whom the peace of a dying woman is less than the praise of people who have given you a silly name—and nothing besides—in exchange for your soul and body."

The Captain de Cargadores swore to himself under his breath.

"Leave my soul alone, Padrona, and I shall know how to take care of my body. Where is the harm of people having need of me? What are you envying me that I have robbed you and the children of? Those very people you are throwing in my teeth have done more for old Giorgio than they ever thought of doing for me."

He struck his breast with his open palm; his voice had remained low though he had spoken in a forcible tone. He twisted his mustaches one after another, and his eyes wandered a little about the room.

"Is it my fault that I am the only man for their purposes? What angry nonsense are you talking, mother? Would you rather have me timid and foolish, selling watermelons on the market-place or rowing a boat for passengers along the harbor, like a soft Neapolitan without courage or reputation? Would you have a young man live like a monk? I do not believe it. Would you want a monk for your eldest girl? Let her grow. What are you afraid of? You have been angry with me for everything I did for years; ever since you first spoke to me, in secret from old Giorgio, about your Linda. Husband to one and brother to the other, did you say? Well, why not! I like the little ones, and a man must marry some time. But ever since that time you have been making little of me to everyone. Why? Did you think you could put a collar and chain on me as if I were one of the watchdogs they keep over there in the railway yards? Look here, Padrona, I am the same man who came ashore one evening and sat down in the thatched *rancho* you lived in at that time on the other side of the town and told you all about himself. You were not unjust to me then. What has happened since? I am no longer an insignificant youth. A good name, Giorgio says, is a treasure, Padrona."

"They have turned your head with their praises," gasped the sick woman. "They have been paying you with words. Your folly shall betray you into poverty, misery, starvation. The very *leperos* shall laugh at you—the great Capataz."

Nostromo stood for a time as if struck dumb. She never looked at him. A self-confident, mirthless smile passed quickly from his lips, and then he backed away. His disregarded figure sank down beyond the doorway. He descended the stairs backwards, with the usual sense of having been somehow baffled by this woman's disparagement of this reputation he had obtained and desired to keep.

Downstairs in the big kitchen a candle was burning, surrounded by the shadows of the walls, of the ceiling, but no ruddy glare filled the open square of the outer door. The carriage with Mrs. Gould and Don Martin, preceded by the horseman bearing the torch, had gone on to the jetty. Dr. Monygham, who had remained, sat on the corner of a hard wood table near the candlestick, his seamed, shaved face inclined sideways, his arms crossed on his breast, his lips pursed up, and his prominent eyes glaring stonily upon the floor of black earth. Near the overhanging mantel of the fireplace, where the pot of water was still boiling violently, old Giorgio held his chin in his hand, one foot advanced, as if arrested by a sudden thought.

"*Adios, viejo,*" said Nostromo, feeling the handle of his revolver in the belt and loosening his knife in its sheath. He picked up a blue poncho lined with red from the table, and put it over his head. "*Adios,* look after my things in my sleeping-room, and if you hear from me no more, give up the box to Paquita. There is not much of value there, except my new serape from Mexico, and a few silver buttons on my best jacket. No matter! The things will look well enough on the next lover she gets, and the man need not be afraid I shall linger on earth after I am dead, like those *gringos* that haunt the Azuera."

Dr. Monygham twisted his lips into a bitter smile. After old Giorgio, with an almost imperceptible nod and without a word, had gone up the narrow stairs, he said:

"Why, Capataz! I thought you could never fail in anything."

Nostromo, glancing contemptuously at the doctor, lingered in the doorway rolling a cigarette, then struck a match, and, after lighting it, held the burning piece of wood above his head till the flame nearly touched his fingers.

"No wind!" he muttered to himself. "Look here, *señor*—do you know the nature of my undertaking?"

Dr. Monygham nodded sourly.

"It is as if I were taking up a curse upon me, Señor Doctor. A man with a treasure on this coast will have every knife raised against him in every place upon the shore. You see that, Señor Doctor? I shall float along with a spell upon my life till I meet somewhere the north-bound steamer of the Company, and then indeed they will talk about the Capataz of the Sulaco Cargadores from one end of America to another."

Dr. Monygham laughed his short, throaty laugh. Nostromo turned round in the doorway.

"But if your worship can find any other man ready and fit for such business I will stand back. I am not exactly tired of my life, though I am so poor that I can carry all I have with myself on my horse's back."

"You gamble too much, and never say 'no' to a pretty face, Capataz," said Dr. Monygham, with sly simplicity. "That's not the way to make a fortune. But nobody that I know ever suspected you of being poor. I hope you have made a good bargain in case you come back safe from this adventure."

"What bargain would your worship have made?" asked Nostromo, blowing the smoke out of his lips through the doorway.

Dr. Monygham listened up the staircase for a moment before he answered, with another of his short, abrupt laughs:

"Illustrious Capataz, for taking the curse of death upon my back, as you call it, nothing else but the whole treasure would do."

Nostromo vanished out of the doorway with a grunt of discontent at his jeering answer. Dr. Monygham heard him gallop away. Nostromo rode furiously in the dark. There were lights in the buildings of the O.S.N. Company near the wharf, but before he got there he met the Gould carriage. The horseman preceded it with the torch, whose light showed the white mules trotting, the portly Ignacio driving, and Basilio with the carbine on the box. From the dark body of the landau Mrs. Gould's voice cried, "They are waiting for you, Capataz!" She was returning, chilly and excited, with Decoud's pocket-book still held in her hand. He had confided it to her to send to his sister. "Perhaps my last words to her," he had said, pressing Mrs. Gould's hand.

The Capataz never checked his speed. At the head of the wharf vague figures with rifles leapt to the head of his horse; others closed upon him—*cargadores* of the company posted by Captain Mitchell on the watch. At a word from him they fell back with subservient murmurs, recognizing his voice. At the other end of the jetty, near a cargo crane, in a dark group with glowing cigars, his name was pronounced in a tone of relief. Most of the Europeans in Sulaco were there, rallied round Charles Gould, as if the silver of the mine had been the emblem of a common cause, the symbol of the supreme importance of material interests. They had loaded it into the lighter with their own hands. Nostromo recognized Don Carlos Gould, a thin, tall shape, standing a little apart and silent, to whom another tall shape, the engineer-in-chief, said aloud, "If it must be lost, it is a million times better that it should go to the bottom of the sea."

Martin Decoud called out from the lighter, *"Au revoir, messieurs,* till we clasp hands again over the new-born Occidental Republic." Only a subdued murmur responded to his clear ringing tones; and then it seemed to him that the wharf was floating away into the night; but it was Nostromo, who was already pushing against a pile with one of the heavy sweeps. Decoud did not move; the effect was that of being launched into space. After a splash or two there was not a sound but the thud of Nostromo's feet leaping about the boat. He hoisted the big sail; a breath of wind fanned Decoud's cheek. Everything had vanished but the light of the lantern Captain Mitchell had hoisted upon the post at the end of the jetty to guide Nostromo out of the harbor.

The two men, unable to see each other, kept silent till the lighter, slipping before the fitful breeze, passed out between almost invisible headlands into the still deeper darkness of the gulf. For a time the lantern on the jetty shone after them. The wind failed, then fanned up again, but so faintly that the big, half-decked boat slipped along with no more noise than if she had been suspended in the air.

"We are out in the gulf now," said the calm voice of Nostromo. A moment after he added, "Señor Mitchell has lowered the light."

"Yes," said Decoud; "nobody can find us now."

A great recrudescence of obscurity embraced the boat. The sea in the gulf was as black as the clouds above. Nostromo, after striking a couple of matches to get a glimpse of the boat-compass he had with him in the lighter, steered by the feel of the wind on his cheek.

It was a new experience for Decoud, this mysteriousness of the great waters spread out strangely smooth, as if their restlessness had been crushed by the weight of that dense night. The Placido was sleeping profoundly under its black poncho.

The main thing now for success was to get away from the coast and gain the middle of the gulf before day broke. The Isabels were somewhere at hand. "On your left as you look forward, *señor,"* said Nostromo, suddenly. When his voice ceased, the enormous stillness, without light or sound, seemed to affect Decoud's senses like a powerful drug. He didn't even know at times whether he were asleep or awake. Like a man lost in slumber, he heard nothing, he saw nothing. Even his hand held before his face did not exist for his eyes. The change from the agitation, the passions and the dangers, from the sights and sounds of the shore, was so complete that it would have resembled death had it not been for the survival of his thoughts. In this foretaste of eternal peace they floated vivid and light, like unearthly clear dreams of earthly things that may haunt the souls freed by death from the misty atmosphere of regrets and hopes. Decoud shook himself, shuddered a bit, though the air that drifted past him was warm. He had the strangest sensation of his soul having just returned into his body from the circumambient darkness in which land, sea, sky, the mountains, and the rocks were as if they had not been.

Nostromo's voice was speaking, though he, at the tiller, was also as if he were not. "Have you been asleep, Don Martin? *Caramba!* If it were possible I would think that I, too, have dozed off. I have a strange notion somehow of having dreamt that there was a sound of blubbering, a sound a sorrowing man could make, somewhere near this boat. Something between a sigh and a sob."

"Strange!" muttered Decoud, stretched upon the pile of treasure boxes covered by many tarpaulins. "Could it be that there is another boat near us in the gulf? We could not see it, you know."

Nostromo laughed a little at the absurdity of the idea. They dismissed it from their minds. The solitude could almost be felt. And when the breeze ceased, the blackness seemed to weigh upon Decoud like a stone.

"This is overpowering," he muttered. "Do we move at all, Capataz?"

"Not so fast as a crawling beetle tangled in the grass," answered Nostromo, and his voice seemed deadened by the thick veil of obscurity that felt warm and hopeless all about them. There were long periods when he made no sound, invisible and inaudible as if he had mysteriously stepped out of the lighter.

In the featureless night Nostromo was not even certain which way the lighter headed after the wind had completely died out. He peered for the islands. There was not a hint of them to be seen, as if they had sunk to the bottom of the gulf. He threw himself down by the side of Decoud at last, and whispered into his ear that if daylight caught them near the Sulaco shore through want of wind, it would be possible to sweep the lighter behind the cliff at the high end of the Great Isabel, where she would lie concealed. Decoud was surprised at the grimness of his anxiety. To him the removal of the treasure was a political move. It was necessary for several reasons that it should not fall into the hands of Montero, but here was a man who took another view of this enterprise. The *caballeros* over there did not seem to have the slightest idea of what they had given him to do. Nostromo, as if affected by the gloom around, seemed nervously resentful. Decoud was surprised. The Capataz, indifferent to those dangers that seemed obvious to his companion, allowed himself to become scornfully exasperated by the deadly nature of the trust put, as a matter of course, into his hands. It was more dangerous, Nostromo said, with a laugh and a curse, than sending a man to get the treasure that people said was guarded by devils and ghosts in the deep ravines of Azuera. *"Señor,"* he said, "we must catch the steamer at sea. We must keep out in the open looking for her till we have eaten and drunk all that has been put on board here. And if we miss her by some mischance, we must keep away from the land till we grow weak, and perhaps mad, and die, and drift dead, until one or another of the steamers of the Compania comes upon the boat with the two dead men who have saved the treasure. That, *señor*, is the only way to save it; for, don't you see? for us to come to the land anywhere in a hundred miles along this coast with this silver in our possession is to run the naked breast against the point of a knife. This thing has been given to me like a deadly disease. If men discover it I am dead, and you, too, *señor*, since you would come with me. There is enough silver to make a whole province rich, let alone a seaboard *pueblo* inhabited by thieves and vagabonds. *Señor*, they would think that heaven itself sent these riches into their hands, and would cut our throats without hesitation. I would trust no fair words from the best man around the shores of this gulf. Reflect that, even by giving up the treasure at the first demand, we would not be able to save our lives. Do you understand this, or must I explain?"

"No, you needn't explain," said Decoud, a little listlessly. "I can see it well enough myself, that the possession of this treasure is very much like a deadly disease for men situated as we are. But it had to be removed from Sulaco, and you were the man for the task."

"I was; but I cannot believe," said Nostromo, "that its loss would have impoverished Don Carlos Gould very much. There is more wealth in the mountain. I have heard it rolling down the shoots on quiet nights when I used to ride to Rincón to see a certain girl, after my work at the harbor was done. For years the rich rocks have been pouring down with a noise like thunder, and the miners say that there is enough at the heart of the mountain to thunder on for years and years to come. And yet, since the day before yesterday, we have been fighting to save it from the mob, and tonight I am sent out with it into this darkness, where there is no wind to get away with; as if it were the last lot of silver on earth to get bread for the hungry with. Ha! ha! Well, I am going to make it the most famous and desperate affair of my life—wind or no wind. It shall be talked about when the little children are grown up and the grown men are old. Aha! the Monterists must not get hold of it, I am told, whatever happens to Nostromo the Capataz; and they shall not have it, I tell you, since it has been tied for safety round Nostromo's neck."

"I see it," murmured Decoud. He saw, indeed, that his companion had his own peculiar view of this enterprise.

Nostromo interrupted his reflections upon the way men's qualities are made use of, without any fundamental knowledge of their nature, by the proposal that they should slip the long oars out and sweep the lighter in the direction of the Isabels. It wouldn't do for daylight to reveal the treasure floating within a mile or so of the harbor entrance. The denser the darkness generally, the smarter were the puffs of wind on which he had reckoned to make his way; but tonight the gulf, under its poncho of clouds, remained breathless, as if dead rather than asleep.

Don Martin's soft hands suffered cruelly, tugging at the thick handle of the enormous oar. He stuck to it manfully, setting his teeth. He, too, was in the toils of an imaginative existence, and that strange work of pulling a lighter seemed to belong naturally to the inception of a new state, and acquired an ideal meaning from his love for Antonia. For all their efforts, the heavily laden lighter hardly moved. Nostromo could be heard swearing to himself between the regular splashes of the sweeps. "We are making a crooked path," he muttered to himself. "I wish I could see the islands."

In his unskilfulness Don Martin over-exerted himself. Now and then a sort of muscular faintness would run from the tips of his aching fingers through every fiber of his body, and pass off in a flush of heat. He had fought, talked, suffered mentally and physically, exerting his mind and body for the last forty-eight hours without intermission. He had had no rest, very little food, no pause in the stress of his thoughts and his feelings. Even his love for Antonia, whence he drew his strength and his inspiration, had reached the point of tragic tension during their hurried interview by Don José's bedside. And now, suddenly, he was thrown out of all this into a dark gulf, whose very gloom, silence, and breathless peace added a torment to the necessity for physical exertion. He imagined the lighter sinking to the bottom with an extraordinary shudder of delight. "I am on the verge of delirium," he thought. He mastered the trembling of all his limbs, of his breast, the inward trembling of all his body exhausted of its nervous force.

"Shall we rest, Capataz?" he proposed in a careless tone. "There are many hours of night yet before us."

"True. It is but a mile or so, I suppose. Rest your arms, señor, if that is what you mean. You will find no other sort of rest, I can promise you, since you let yourself be bound to this treasure whose loss would make no poor man poorer. No, señor; there is no rest till we find a northbound steamer, or else some ship finds us drifting about stretched out dead upon the Englishman's silver. Or rather—no; por Dios! I shall cut down the gunwale with the axe right to the water's edge before thirst and hunger rob me of my strength. By all the saints and devils I shall let the sea have the treasure rather than give it up to any stranger. Since it was the good pleasure of the caballeros to send me off on such an errand, they shall learn I am just the man they take me for."

Decoud lay on the silver boxes panting. All his active sensations and feelings from as far back as he could remember seemed to him the maddest of dreams. Even his passionate devotion to Antonia into which he had worked himself up out of the depths of his skepticism had lost all appearance of reality. For a moment he was the prey of an extremely languid but not unpleasant indifference.

"I am sure they didn't mean you to take such a desperate view of this affair," he said.

"What was it, then? A joke?" snarled the man, who on the paysheets of the O.S.N. Company's establishment in Sulaco was described as "Foreman of the wharf" against hte figure of his wages. "Was it for a joke they woke me up from my sleep after two days of street fighting to make me stake my life upon a bad card? Everybody knows, too, that I am not a lucky gambler."

"Yes, everybody knows of your good luck with women, Capataz," Decoud propitiated his companion in a weary drawl.

"Look here, señor," Nostromo went on. "I never even remonstrated about this affair. Directly I heard what was wanted I saw what a desperate affair it must be, and I made up my mind to see it out. Every minute was of importance. I had to wait for you first. Then, when we arrived at the Italia Una, old Giorgio shouted to me to go for the English doctor. Later on, that poor dying woman wanted to see me, as you know. Señor, I was reluctant to go. I felt already this cursed silver growing heavy upon my back, and I was afraid that, knowing herself to be dying, she would ask me to ride off again for a priest. Father Corbelán, who is fearless, would have come at a word; but Father Corbelán is far away, safe with the band of Hernandez, and the populace, that would have liked to tear him to pieces, are much incensed against the priests. Not a single fat padre would have consented to put his head out of his hiding-place tonight to save a Christian soul, except, perhaps, under my protection. That was in her mind. I pretended I did not believe she was going to die. Señor, I refused to fetch a priest for a dying woman. . . ."

Decoud was heard to stir.

"You did, Capataz!" he exclaimed. His tone changed. "Well, you know—it was rather fine."

"You do not believe in priests, Don Martin? Neither do I. What was the use of wasting time? But she—she believes in them. The thing sticks in my throat. She may be dead already, and here we are floating helpless with no wind at all. Curse on all superstition. She died thinking I deprived her of Paradise, I suppose. It shall be the most desperate affair of my life."

Decoud remained lost in reflection. He tried to analyze the sensations awakened by what he had been told. The voice of the Capataz was heard again:

"Now, Don Martin, let us take up the sweeps and try to find the Isabels. It is either that or sinking the lighter if the day overtakes us. We must not forget that the steamer from Esmeralda with the soldiers may be coming along. We will pull straight on now. I have discovered a bit of a candle here, and we must take the risk of a small light to make a course by the boat compass. There is not enough wind to blow it out—may the curse of Heaven fall upon this blind gulf!"

A small flame appeared burning quite straight. It showed fragmentarily the stout ribs and planking in the hollow, empty part of the lighter. Decoud could see Nostromo standing up to pull. He saw him as high as the red sash on his waist, with a gleam of white-handled revolver and the wooden haft of a long knife protruding on his left side. Decoud nerved himself for the effort of rowing. Certainly there was not enough wind to blow the candle out, but its flame swayed a little to the slow movement of the heavy boat. It was so big that with their utmost efforts they could not move it quicker than about a mile an hour. This was sufficient, however, to sweep them amongst the Isabels long before daylight came. There was a good six hours of darkness before them, and the distance from the harbor to the Great Isabel did not exceed two miles. Decoud put this heavy toil to the account of the Capataz's impatience. Sometimes they paused, and then strained their ears to hear the boat from Esmeralda. In this perfect quietness a steamer moving would have been heard from far off. As to seeing anything it was out of the question. They could not see each other. Even the lighter's sail, which remained set, was invisible. Very often they rested.

"*Caramba!*" said Nostromo, suddenly, during one of those intervals when they lolled idly against the heavy handles of the sweeps. "What is it? Are you distressed, Don Martin?"

Decoud assured him that he was not distressed in the least. Nostromo for a time kept perfectly still, and then in a whisper invited Martin to come aft.

With lips touching Decoud's ear he declared his belief that there was somebody else besides themselves upon the lighter. Twice now he had heard the sound of stifled sobbing.

"*Señor,*" he whispered with awed wonder, "I am certain that there is somebody weeping in this lighter."

Decoud had heard nothing. He expressed his incredulity. However, it was easy to ascertain the truth of the matter.

"It is most amazing," muttered Nostromo. "Could anybody have concealed himself on board while the lighter was lying alongside the wharf?"

"And you say it was like sobbing?" asked Decoud, lowering his voice, too. "If he is weeping, whoever he is he cannot be very dangerous."

Clambering over the precious pile in the middle, they crouched low on the foreside of the mast and groped under the half-deck. Right forward, in the narrowest part, their hands came upon the limbs of a man, who remained as silent as death. Too startled themselves to make a sound, they dragged him aft by one arm and the collar of his coat. He was limp—lifeless.

The light of the bit of candle fell upon a round, hook-nosed face with black mustaches and little side-whiskers. He was extremely dirty. A greasy growth of beard was sprouting on the shaven parts of the cheeks. The thick lips were slightly parted, but the eyes remained closed. Decoud, to his immense astonishment, recognized Señor Hirsch, the hide merchant from Esmeralda. Nostromo, too, had recognized him. And they gazed at each other across the body, lying with its naked feet higher than its head, in an absurd pretence of sleep, faintness, or death.

VIII

For a moment, before this extraordinary find, they forgot their own concerns and sensations. Señor Hirsch's sensations as he lay there must have been those of extreme terror. For a long time he refused to give a sign of life, till at last Decoud's objurgations, and, perhaps more, Nostromo's impatient suggestion that he should be thrown overboard, as he seemed to be dead, induced him to raise one eyelid first, and then the other.

It appeared that he had never found a safe opportunity to leave Sulaco. He lodged with Anzani, the universal storekeeper, on the Plaza Mayor. But when the riot broke out he had made his escape from his host's house before daylight, and in such a hurry that he had forgotten to put on his shoes. He had run out impulsively in his socks, and with his hat in his hand, into the garden of Anzani's house. Fear gave him the necessary agility to climb over several low walls, and afterwards he blundered into the overgrown cloisters of the ruined Franciscan convent in one of the by-streets. He forced himself into the midst of matted bushes with the recklessness of desperation, and this accounted for his scratched body and his torn clothing. He lay hidden there all day, his togue cleaving to the roof of his mouth with all the intensity of thirst engendered by heat and fear. Three times different bands of men invaded the place with shouts and imprecations, looking for Father Corbelán; but towards the evening, still lying on his face in the bushes, he thought he would die from the fear of silence. He was not very clear as to what had induced him to leave the place, but evidently he had got out and slunk successfully out of town along the deserted back lanes. He wandered in the darkness near the railway, so maddened by apprehension that he dared not even approach the fires of the pickets of Italian workmen guarding the line. He had a vague idea evidently of finding refuge in the railway yards, but the dogs rushed upon him, barking; men began to shout; a shot was fired at random. He fled away from the gates. By the merest accident, as it happened, he took the direction of the O.S.N. Company's offices. Twice he stumbled upon the bodies of men killed during the day. But everything living frightened him much more. He crouched, crept, crawled, made dashes, guided by a sort of animal instinct, keeping away from every light and from every sound of voices. His idea was to throw himself at the feet of Captain Mitchell and beg for shelter in the Company's offices. It was all dark there as he approached on his hands and knees, but suddenly someone on guard challenged loudly, "*Quién vive?*" There were more dead men lying about, and he flattened himself down at once by the side of a cold corpse. He heard a voice saying, "Here is one of those wounded rascals crawling about. Shall I go and finish him?" And another voice objected that it was not safe to go out without a lantern upon such an errand; perhaps it was only some Negro liberal looking for a chance to stick a knife into the stomach of an honest man. Hirsch didn't stay to hear any more, but crawling away to the end of the wharf, hid himself amongst a lot of empty casks. After a while some people came along, talking, and with glowing cigarettes. He did not stop to ask himself whether they would be likely to do him any harm, but bolted incontinently along the jetty, saw a lighter lying moored at the end, and threw himself into it. In his desire to find cover he crept right forward under the half-deck, and he had remained there more dead than alive, suffering agonies of hunger and thirst, and almost fainting with terror, when he heard numerous footsteps and the voices of the Europeans who came in a body escorting the wagon-load of treasure, pushed along the rails by a squad of *cargadores.* He understood perfectly what was being done from the talk, but did not disclose his presence from the fear that he would not be allowed to remain. His only idea at the time, overpowering and masterful, was to get away from this terrible Sulaco. And now he regretted it very much. He had heard Nostromo talk to Decoud, and wished himself back on shore. He did not desire to be involved in any desperate affair —in a situation where one could not run away. The involuntary groans of his anguished spirit had betrayed him to the sharp ears of the Capataz.

They had propped him up in a sitting posture against the side of the lighter, and he went on with the moaning account of his adventures till his voice broke, and his head fell forward. "Water," he whispered, with difficulty. Decoud held one of the cans to his lips. He revived after an extraordinarily short time, and scrambled up to his feet wildly. Nostromo, in an angry and threatening voice, ordered him forward. Hirsch was one of those men whom fear lashed like a whip, and he must have had an appalling idea of the Capataz's ferocity. He displayed an extraordinary agility in disappearing forward into the darkness. They heard him getting over the tarpaulin; then there was the sound of a heavy fall, followed by a weary sigh. Afterwards all was still in the forepart of the lighter, as though he had killed himself in his headlong tumble. Nostromo shouted in a menacing voice:

"Lie still there! Do not move a limb. If I hear as much as a loud breath from you I shall come over there and put a bullet through your head."

The mere presence of a coward, however passive, brings an element of treachery into a dangerous situation. Nostromo's nervous impatience passed into gloomy thoughtfulness. Decoud, in an undertone, as if speaking to himself, remarked that, after all, this bizarre event made no great difference. He could not conceive what harm the man could do. At most he would be in the way, like an inanimate and useless object—like a block of wood, for instance.

"I would think twice before getting rid of a piece of wood," said Nostromo, calmly. "Something may happen unexpectedly where you could make use of it. But in an affair like ours a man like this ought to be thrown overboard. Even if he were as brave as a lion we would not want him here. We are not running away for our lives. Señor, there is no harm in a brave man trying to save himself with ingenuity and courage; but you have heard his tale, Don Martin. His being here is a miracle of fear—" Nostromo paused. "There is no room for fear in this lighter," he added through his teeth.

Decoud had no answer to make. It was not a position for argument, for a display of scruples or feelings. There were a thousand ways in which a panic-stricken man could make himself dangerous. It was evident that Hirsch could not be spoken to, reasoned with, or persuaded into a rational line of conduct. The story of his own escape demonstrated that clearly enough. Decoud thought that it was a thousand pities the wretch had not died of fright. Nature, who had made him what he was, seemed to have calculated cruelly how much he could bear in the way of atrocious anguish without actually expiring. Some compassion was due to so much terror. Decoud, though imaginative enough for sympathy, resolved not to interfere with any action that Nostromo would take. But Nostromo did nothing. And the fate of Señor Hirsch remained suspended in the darkness of the gulf at the mercy of events which could not be foreseen.

The Capataz, extending his hand, put out the candle suddenly. It was to Decoud as if his companion had destroyed, by a single touch, the world of affairs, of loves, of revolution, where his complacent superiority analyzed fearlessly all motives and all passions, including his own.

He gasped a little. Decoud was affected by the novelty of his position. Intellectually self-confident, he suffered from being deprived of the only weapon he could use with effect. No intelligence could penetrate the darkness of the Placid Gulf. There remained only one thing he was certain of, and that was the overweening vanity of his companion. It was direct, uncomplicated, naïve, and effectual. Decoud, who had been making use of him, had tried to understand his man thoroughly. He had discovered a complete singleness of motive behind the varied manifestations of a consistent character. This was why the man remained so astonishingly simple in the jealous greatness of his conceit. And now there was a complication. It was evident that he resented having been given a task in which there were so many chances of failure. "I wonder," thought Decoud, "how he would behave if I were not here."

He heard Nostromo mutter again, "No! there is no room for fear on this lighter. Courage itself does not seem good enough. I have a good eye and a steady hand; no man can say he ever saw me tired or uncertain what to do; but *por Dios*, Don Martin, I have been sent out into this black calm on a business where neither a good eye, nor a steady hand, nor judgment are any use. . . ." He swore a string of oaths in Spanish and Italian under his breath. "Nothing but sheer desperation will do for this affair."

These words were in strange contrast to the prevailing peace—to this almost stolid stillness of the gulf. A shower fell with an abrupt whispering sound all round the boat, and Decoud took off his hat, and, letting his head get wet, felt greatly refreshed. Presently a steady little draught of air caressed his cheek. The lighter began to move, but the shower distanced it. The drops ceased to fall upon his head and hands, the whispering died out in the distance. Nostromo emitted a grunt of satisfaction, and grasping the tiller, chirruped softly, as sailors do, to encourage the wind. Never for the last three days had Decoud felt less the need for what the Capataz would call desperation.

"I fancy I hear another shower on the water," he observed in a tone of quiet content. "I hope it will catch us up."

Nostromo ceased chirruping at once. "You hear another shower?" he said, doubtfully. A sort of thinning of the darkness seemed to have taken place, and Decoud could see now the outline of his companion's figure, and even the sail came out of the night like a square block of dense snow.

The sound which Decoud had detected came along the water harshly. Nostromo recognized that noise partaking of a hiss and a rustle which spreads out on all sides of a steamer making her way through a smooth water on a quiet night. It could be nothing else but the captured transport with troops from Esmeralda. She carried no lights. The noise of her steaming, growing louder every minute, would stop at times altogether, and then begin again abruptly, and sound startlingly nearer, as if that invisible vessel, whose position could not be precisely guessed, were making straight for the lighter. Meantime, that last kept on sailing slowly and noiselessly before a breeze so faint that it was only by leaning over the side and feeling the water slip through his fingers that Decoud convinced himself they were moving at all. His drowsy feeling had departed. He was glad to know that the lighter was moving. After so much stillness the noise of the steamer seemed uproarious and distracting. There was a weirdness in not being able to see her. Suddenly all was still. She had stopped, but so close to them that the steam, blowing off, sent its rumbling vibration right over their heads.

"They are trying to make out where they are," said Decoud in a whisper. Again he leaned over and put his fingers into the water. "We are moving quite smartly," he informed Nostromo.

"We seem to be crossing her bows," said the Capataz in a cautious tone. "But this is a blind game with death. Moving on is of no use. We mustn't be seen or heard."

His whisper was hoarse with excitement. Of all his face there was nothing visible but a gleam of white eyeballs. His fingers gripped Decoud's shoulder. "That is the only way to save this treasure from this steamer full of soldiers. Any other would have carried lights. But you observe there is not a gleam to show us where she is."

Decoud stood as if paralyzed; only his thoughts were wildly active. In the space of a second he remembered the desolate glance of Antonia as he left her at the bedside of her father in the gloomy house of Avellanos, with shuttered windows, but all the doors standing open, and deserted by all the servants except an old Negro at the gate. He remembered the Casa Gould on his last visit, the arguments, the tones of his voice, the impenetrable attitude of Charles, Mrs. Gould's face so blanched with anxiety and fatigue that her eyes seemed to have changed color, appearing nearly black by contrast. Even whole sentences of the proclamation which he meant to make Barrios issue from his headquarters at Cayta as soon as he got there passed through his mind; the very germ of the new State, the Separationist proclamation which he had tried before he left to read hurriedly to Don José, stretched out on his bed under the fixed gaze of his daughter. God knows whether the old statesman had understood it; he was unable to speak, but he had certainly lifted his arm off the coverlet; his hand had moved as if to make the sign of the cross in the air, a gesture of blessing, of consent. Decoud had that very draft in his pocket, written in pencil on several loose sheets of paper, with the heavily printed heading, "Administration of the San Tomé Silver Mine. Sulaco, Republic of Costaguana." He had written it furiously, snatching page after page on Charles Gould's table. Mrs. Gould had looked several times over his shoulder as he wrote; but the Señor Administrator, standing straddle-legged, would not even glance at it when it was finished. He had waved it away firmly. It must have been scorn, and not caution, since he never made a remark about the use of the Administration's paper for such a compromising document. And that showed his disdain, the true English disdain of common prudence, as if everything outside the range of their own thoughts and feelings were unworthy of serious recognition. Decoud had the time in a second or two to become furiously angry with Charles Gould, and even resentful against Mrs. Gould, in whose care, tacitly it is true, he had left the safety of Antonia. Better perish a thousand times than owe your preservation to such people, he exclaimed mentally. The grip of Nostromo's fingers never removed from his shoulder, tightening fiercely, recalled him to himself.

"The darkness is our friend," the Capataz murmured into his ear. "I am going to lower the sail, and trust our escape to this black gulf. No eyes could make us out lying silent with a naked mast. I will do it now, before this steamer closes still more upon us. The faint creak of a block would betray us and the San Tomé treasure into the hands of those thieves."

He moved about as warily as a cat. Decoud heard no sound; and it was only by the disappearance of the square blotch of darkness that he knew the yard had come down, lowered as carefully as if it had been made of glass. Next moment he heard Nostromo's quiet breathing by his side.

"You had better not move at all from where you are, Don Martin," advised the Capataz, earnestly. "You might stumble or displace something which would make a noise. The sweeps and the punting poles are lying about. Move not for your life. *Por Dios,* Don Martin," he went on in a keen but friendly whisper, "I am so desperate that if I didn't know your worship to be a man of courage, capable of standing stock still whatever happens, I would drive my knife into your heart."

A deathlike stillness surrounded the lighter. It was difficult to believe that there was near a steamer full of men with many pairs of eyes peering from her bridge for some hint of land in the night. Her steam had ceased blowing off, and she remained stopped too far off apparently for any other sound to reach the lighter.

"Perhaps you would, Capataz," Decoud began in a whisper. "However, you need not trouble. There are other things than the fear of your knife to keep my heart steady. It shall not betray you. Only, have you forgotten—"

"I spoke to you openly as to a man as desperate as myself," explained the Capataz. "The silver must be saved from the Monterists. I told Captain Mitchell three times that I preferred to go alone. I told Don Carlos Gould, too. It was in the Casa Gould. They had sent for me. The ladies were there; and when I tried to explain why I did not wish to have you with me, they promised me, both of them, great rewards for your safety. A strange way to talk to a man you are sending out to an almost certain death. Those gentlefolk do not seem to have sense enough to understand what they are giving one to do. I told them I could do nothing for you. You would have been safer with the bandit Hernandez. It would have been possible to ride out of the town with no greater risk than a chance shot sent after you in the dark. But it was as if they had been deaf. I had to promise I would wait for you under the harbor gate. I did wait. And now because you are a brave man you are as safe as the silver. Neither more nor less."

At that moment, as if by way of comment upon Nostromo's words, the invisible steamer went ahead at half speed only, as could be judged by the leisurely beat of her propeller. The sound shifted its place markedly, but without coming nearer. It even grew a little more distant right abeam of the lighter, and then ceased again.

"They are trying for a sight of the Isabels," muttered Nostromo, "in order to make for the harbor in a straight line and seize the Custom House with the treasure in it. Have you ever seen the Commandant of Esmeralda, Sotillo? A handsome fellow, with a soft voice. When I first came here I used to see him in the Calle talking to the *señoritas* at the windows of the houses, and showing his white teeth all the time. But one of my *cargadores,* who had been a soldier, told me that he had once ordered a man to be flayed alive in the remote Campo, where he was sent recruiting amongst the people of the *estancias.* It has never entered his head that the *compañia* had a man capable of baffling his game."

The murmuring loquacity of the Capataz disturbed Decoud like a hint of weakness. And yet, talkative resolution may be as genuine as grim silence.

"Sotillo is not baffled so far," he said. "Have you forgotten that crazy man forward?"

Nostromo had not forgotten Señor Hirsch. He reproached himself bitterly for not having visited the lighter carefully before leaving the wharf. He reproached himself for not having stabbed and flung Hirsch overboard at the very moment of discovery without even looking at his face. That would have been consistent with the desperate character of the affair. Whatever happened, Sotillo *was* already baffled. Even if that wretch, now as silent as death, did anything to betray the nearness of the lighter, Sotillo—if Sotillo it was in command of the troops on board—would be still baffled of his plunder.

"I have an axe in my hand," Nostromo whispered, wrathfully, "that in three strokes would cut through the side down to the water's edge. Moreover, each lighter has a plug in the stern, and I know exactly where it is. I feel it under the sole of my foot."

Decoud recognized the ring of genuine determination in the nervous murmurs, the vindictive excitement of the famous Capataz. Before the steamer, guided by a shriek or two (for there could be no more than that, Nostromo said, gnashing his teeth audibly), could find the lighter there would be plenty of time to sink this treasure tied up round his neck.

The last words he hissed into Decoud's ear. Decoud said nothing. He was perfectly convinced. The usual characteristic quietness of the man was gone. It was not equal to the situation as he conceived it. Something deeper, something unsuspected by everyone, had come to the surface. Decoud, with careful movements, slipped off his overcoat and divested himself of his boots; he did not consider himself bound in honor to sink with the treasure. His object was to get down to Barrios, in Cayta, as the Capataz knew very well; and he, too, meant, in his own way, to put into that attempt all the desperation of which he was capable. Nostromo muttered, "True, true! You are a politician, *señor*. Rejoin the army, and start another revolution." He pointed out, however, that there was a little boat belonging to every lighter fit to carry two men, if not more. Theirs was towing behind.

Of that Decoud had not been aware. Of course, it was too dark to see, and it was only when Nostromo put his hand upon its painter fastened to a cleat in the stern that he experienced a full measure of relief. The prospect of finding himself in the water and swimming, overwhelmed by ignorance and darkness, probably in a circle, till he sank from exhaustion, was revolting. The barren and cruel futility of such an end intimidated his affectation of careless pessimism. In comparison to it, the chance of being left floating in a boat, exposed to thirst, hunger, discovery, imprisonment, execution, presented itself with an aspect of amenity worth securing even at the cost of some set self-contempt. He did not accept Nostromo's proposal that he should get into the boat at once. "Something sudden may overwhelm us, *señor*," the Capataz remarked promising faithfully, at the same time, to let go the painter at the moment when the necessity became manifest.

But Decoud assured him lightly that he did not mean to take to the boat till the very last moment, and that then he meant the Capataz to come along, too. The darkness of the gulf was no longer for him the end of all things. It was part of a living world since, pervading it, failure and death could be felt at your elbow. And at the same time it was a shelter. He exulted in its impenetrable obscurity. "Like a wall, like a wall," he muttered to himself.

The only thing which checked his confidence was the thought of Señor Hirsch. Not to have bound and gagged him seemed to Decoud now the height of improvident folly. As long as the miserable creature had the power to raise a yell he was a constant danger. His abject terror was mute now, but there was no saying from what cause it might suddenly find vent in shrieks.

This very madness of fear which both Decoud and Nostromo had seen in the wild and irrational glances, and in the continuous twitchings of his mouth, protected Señor Hirsch from the cruel necessities of this desperate affair. The moment of silencing him for ever had passed. As Nostromo remarked, in answer to Decoud's regrets, it was too late! It could not be done without noise, especially in the ignorance of the man's exact position. Wherever he had elected to crouch and tremble, it was too hazardous to go near him. He would begin probably to yell for mercy. It was much better to leave him quite alone since he was keeping so still. But to trust to his silence became every moment a greater strain upon Decoud's composure.

"I wish, Capataz, you had not let the right moment pass," he murmured.

"What! to silence him for ever! I thought it good to hear first how he came to be here. It was too strange. Who could imagine that it was all an accident? Afterwards, señor, when I saw you giving him water to drink, I could not do it. Not after I had seen you holding up the can to his lips as though he were your brother. Señor, that sort of necessity must not be thought of too long. And yet it would have been no cruelty to take away from him his wretched life. It is nothing but fear. Your compassion saved him then, Don Martin, and now it is too late. It couldn't be done without noise."

In the steamer they were keeping a perfect silence, and the stillness was so profound that Decoud felt as if the slightest sound conceivable must travel unchecked and audible to the end of the world. What if Hirsch coughed or sneezed? To feel himself at the mercy of such an idiotic contingency was too exasperating to be looked upon with irony. Nostromo, too, seemed to be getting restless. Was it possible, he asked himself, that the steamer, finding the night too dark altogether, intended to remain stopped where she was till daylight? He began to think that this, after all, was the real danger. He was afraid that the darkness, which was his protection, would, in the end, cause his undoing.

Sotillo, as Nostromo had surmised, was in command on board the transport. The events of the last forty-eight hours in Sulaco were not known to him; neither was he aware that the telegraphist in Esmeralda had managed to warn his colleague in Sulaco. Like a good many officers of the troops garrisoning the province, Sotillo had been influenced in his adoption of the Ribierist cause by the belief that it had the enormous wealth of the Gould Concession on its side. He had been one of the frequenters of the

Casa Gould, where he had aired his Blanco convictions and his ardor for reform before Don José Avellanos, casting frank, honest glances towards Mrs. Gould and Antonia the while. He was known to belong to a good family persecuted and impoverished during the tyranny of Guzman Bento. The opinions he expressed appeared eminently natural and proper in a man of his parentage and antecedents. And he was not a deceiver; it was perfectly natural for him to express elevated sentiments while his whole faculties were taken up with what seemed then a solid and practical notion—the notion that the husband of Antonia Avellanos would be, naturally, the intimate friend of the Gould Concession. He even pointed this out to Anzani once, when negotiating the sixth or seventh small loan in the gloomy, damp apartment with enormous iron bars, behind the principal shop in the whole row under the Arcades. He hinted to the universal shopkeeper at the excellent terms he was on with the emancipated *señorita*, who was like a sister to the Englishwoman. He would advance one leg and put his arms akimbo, posing for Anzani's inspection, and fixing him with a haughty stare.

"Look, miserable shopkeeper! How can a man like me fail with any woman, let alone an emancipated girl living in scandalous freedom?" he seemed to say.

His manner in the Casa Gould was, of course, very different—devoid of all truculence, and even slightly mournful. Like most of his countrymen, he was carried away by the sound of fine words, especially if uttered by himself. He had no convictions of any sort upon anything except as to the irresistible power of his personal advantages. But that was so firm that even Decoud's appearance in Sulaco, and his intimacy with the Goulds and the Avellanos, did not disquiet him. On the contrary, he tried to make friends with that rich Costaguanero from Europe in the hope of borrowing a large sum by-and-by. The only guiding motive of his life was to get money for the satisfaction of his expensive tastes, which he indulged recklessly, having no self-control. He imagined himself a master of intrigue, but his corruption was as simple as an animal instinct. At times, in solitude, he had his moments of ferocity, and also on such occasions as, for instance, when alone in a room with Anzani trying to get a loan.

He had talked himself into the command of the Esmeralda garrison. That small seaport had its importance as the station of the main submarine cable connecting the Occidental Provinces with the outer world, and the junction with it of the Sulaco branch. Don José Avellanos proposed him, and Barrios, with a rude and jeering guffaw, he said, "Oh, let Sotillo go. He is a very good man to keep guard over the cable, and the ladies of Esmeralda ought to have their turn." Barrios, an indubitably brave man, had no great opinion of Sotillo.

It was through the Esmeralda cable alone that the San Tomé mine could be kept in constant touch with the great financier, whose tacit approval made the strength of the Ribierist movement. This movement had its adversaries even there. Sotillo governed Esmeralda with repressive severity till the adverse course of events upon the distant theater of civil war forced upon him the reflection that, after all, the great silver mine was fated to become the spoil of the victors. But caution was necessary. He began by assuming a dark and mysterious attitude towards the faithful Ribierist municipality of Esmeralda. Later on, the information that the commandant was holding assemblies of officers in the dead of night (which had leaked out somehow) caused those gentlemen to neglect their civil duties altogether, and remain shut up in their houses. Suddenly one day all the letters from Sulaco by the overland courier were carried off by a file of soldiers from the post office to the Comandancia, without disguise, concealment, or apology. Sotillo had heard through Cayta of the final defeat of Ribiera.

This was the first open sign of the change in his convictions. Presently notorious democrats, who had been living till then in constant fear of arrest, leg irons, and even floggings, could be observed going in and out at the great door of the Comandancia, where the horses of the orderlies doze under their heavy saddles, while the men, in ragged uniforms and pointed straw hats, lounge on a bench, with their naked feet stuck out beyond the strip of shade; and a sentry, in a red baize coat with holes at the elbows, stands at the top of the steps glaring haughtily at the common people, who uncover their heads to him as they pass.

Sotillo's ideas did not soar above the care for his personal safety and the chance of plundering the town in his charge, but he feared that such a late adhesion would earn but scant gratitude from the victors. He had believed just a little too long in the power of the San Tomé mine. The seized correspondence had confirmed his previous information of a large amount of silver ingots lying in the Sulaco Custom House. To gain possession of it would be a clear Monterist move; a sort of service that would have to be rewarded. With the silver in his hands he could make terms for himself and his soldiers. He was aware neither of the riots, nor of the President's escape to Sulaco and the close pursuit led by Montero's brother, the *guerrillero*. The game seemed in his own hands. The initial moves were the seizure of the cable telegraph office and the securing of the Government steamer lying in the narrow creek which is the harbor of Esmeralda. The last was effected without difficulty by a company of soldiers swarming with a rush over the gangways as she lay alongside the quay; but the lieutenant charged with the duty of arresting the telegraphist halted on the way before the only café in Esmeralda, where he distributed some brandy to his men, and refreshed himself at the expense of the owner, a known Ribierist. The whole party became intoxicated, and proceeded on their mission up the street yelling and firing random shots at the windows. This little festivity, which might have turned out dangerous to the telegraphist's life, enabled him in the end to send his warning to Sulaco. The lieutenant, staggering upstairs with a drawn saber, was before long kissing him on both cheeks in one of those swift changes of mood peculiar to a state of drunkenness. He clasped the telegraphist close round the neck, assuring him that all the officers of the Esmeralda garrison were going to be made colonels, while tears of happiness streamed down his sodden face. Thus it came about that the town major, coming along later, found the whole party sleeping on the stairs and in passages, and the telegraphist (who scorned this chance of escape) very busy clicking the key of the transmitter. The major led him away bareheaded, with his hands tied behind his back, but concealed the truth from Sotillo, who remained in ignorance of the warning dispatched to Sulaco.

The colonel was not the man to let any sort of darkness stand in the way of the planned surprise. It appeared to him a dead certainty; his heart was set upon his object with an ungovernable, childlike impatience. Ever since the steamer had rounded Punta Mala, to enter the deeper shadow of the gulf, he had remained on the bridge in a group of officers as excited as himself. Distracted between the coaxings and menaces of Sotillo and his Staff, the miserable commander of the steamer kept her moving with as much prudence as they would let him exercise. Some of them had been drinking heavily, no doubt; but the prospect of laying hands on so much wealth made them absurdly foolhardy, and, at the same time, extremely anxious. The old major of the battalion, a stupid, suspicious man, who had never been afloat in his life, distinguished himself by putting out suddenly the binnacle light, the only one allowed on board for the necessities of navigation. He could not understand of what use it could be for finding the way. To the vehement protestations of the ship's captain, he stamped his foot and tapped the handle of his sword. "Aha! I have unmasked you," he cried, triumphantly. "You are tearing your hair from despair at my acuteness. Am I a child to believe that a light in that brass box can show you where the harbor is? I am an old soldier, I am. I can smell a traitor a league off. You wanted the gleam to betray our approach to your friend the Englishman. A thing like that show you the way! What a miserable lie! *Que picardía!* You Sulaco people are all in the pay of those foreigners. You deserve to be run through the body with my sword." Other officers, crowding round, tried to calm his indignation, repeating persuasively, "No, no! This is an appliance of the mariners, major. This is no treachery." The captain of the transport flung himself face downwards on the bridge, and refused to rise. "Put an end to me at once," he repeated in a stifled voice. Sotillo had to interfere.

The uproar and confusion on the bridge became so great that the helmsman fled from the wheel. He took refuge in the engine room, and alarmed the engineers, who, disregarding the threats of the soldiers set on guard over them, stopped the engines, protesting that they would rather be shot than run the risk of being drowned down below.

This was the first time Nostromo and Decoud heard the steamer stop. After order had been restored, and the binnacle lamp relighted, she went ahead again, passing wide of the lighter in her search for the Isabels. The group could not be made out, and, at the pitiful entreaties of the captain, Sotillo allowed the engines to be stopped again to wait for one of those periodical lightenings of darkness caused by the shifting of the cloud canopy spread above the waters of the gulf.

Sotillo, on the bridge, muttered from time to time angrily to the captain. The other, in an apologetic and cringing tone, begged *su merced* the colonel to take into consideration the limitations put upon human faculties by the darkness of the night. Sotillo swelled with rage and impatience. It was the chance of a lifetime.

"If your eyes are of no more use to you than this, I shall have them put out," he burst out.

The captain of the steamer made no answer, for just then the mass of the Great Isabel loomed up darkly after a passing shower, then vanished, as if swept away by a wave of greater obscurity preceding another downpour. This was enough for him. In the voice of a man come back to life again, he informed Sotillo that in an hour he would be alongside the Sulaco wharf. The ship was put then full speed on the course, and a great bustle of preparation for landing arose among the soldiers on her deck.

It was heard distinctly by Decoud and Nostromo. The Capataz understood its meaning. They had made out the Isabels, and were going on now in a straight line for Sulaco. He judged that they would pass close; but believed that lying still like this, with the sail lowered, the lighter could not be seen. "No, not even if they rubbed sides with us," he muttered.

The rain began to fall again; first like a wet mist, then with a heavier touch, thickening into a smart, perpendicular downpour; and the hiss and thump of the approaching steamer was coming extremely near. Decoud, with his eyes full of water, and lowered head, asked himself how long it would be before she drew past, when unexpectedly he felt a lurch. An inrush of foam broke swishing over the stern, simultaneously with a crack of timbers and a staggering shock. He had the impression of an angry hand laying hold of the lighter and dragging it along to destruction. The shock, of course, had knocked him down, and he found himself rolling in a lot of water at the bottom of the lighter. A violent churning went on alongside; a strange and amazed voice cried out something above him in the night. He heard a piercing shriek for help from Señor Hirsch. He kept his teeth hard set all the time. It was a collision!

The steamer had struck the lighter obliquely, heeling her over till she was half swamped, starting some of her timbers, and swinging her head parallel to her own course with the force of the blow. The shock of it on board of her was hardly perceptible. All the violence of that collision was, as usual, felt only on board the smaller craft. Even Nostromo himself thought that this was perhaps the end of his desperate adventure. He, too, had been flung away from the long tiller, which took charge of the lurch. Next moment the steamer would have passed on, leaving the lighter to sink or swim after having shouldered her thus out of her way, and without ever getting a glimpse of her form, had it not been that, being deeply laden with stores and the great number of people on board, her anchor was low enough to hook itself into one of the wire shrouds of the lighter's mast. For the space of two or three gasping breaths that new rope held against the sudden strain. It was this that gave Decoud the sensation of the snatching pull, dragging the lighter away to destruction. The cause of it, of course, was inexplicable to him. The whole thing was so sudden that he had no time to think. But all his sensations were perfectly clear; he had kept complete possession of himself; in fact, he was even pleasantly aware of that calmness at the very moment of being pitched head first over the transom, to struggle on his back in a lot of water. Señor Hirsch's shriek he had heard and recognized while he was regaining his feet, always with that mysterious sensation of being dragged headlong through the darkness. Not a word, not a cry escaped him; he had no time to see anything; and following upon the despairing screams for help, the dragging motion ceased so suddenly that he staggered forward with open arms and fell against the pile of the treasure boxes. He clung to them instinctively, in the vague apprehension of being flung about again; and immediately he heard another lot of shrieks for help, prolonged and despairing, not near him at all, but unaccountably in the distance, away from the lighter altogether, as if some spirit in the night were mocking at Señor Hirsch's terror and despair.

Then all was still—as still as when you wake up in your bed in a dark room from a bizarre and agitated dream. The lighter rocked slightly; the rain was still falling. Two groping hands took hold of his bruised sides from behind, and the Capataz's voice whispered, in his ear, "Silence, for your life! Silence! The steamer has stopped."

Decoud listened. The gulf was dumb. He felt the water nearly up to his knees. "Are we sinking?" he asked in a faint breath.

"I don't know," Nostromo breathed back to him. *"Señor,* make not the slightest sound."

Hirsch, when ordered forward by Nostromo, had not returned into his first hiding-place. He had fallen near the mast, and had no strength to rise; moreover, he feared to move. He had given himself up for dead, but not on any rational grounds. It was simply a cruel and terrifying feeling. Whenever he tried to think what would become of him his teeth would start chattering violently. He was too absorbed in the utter misery of his fear to take notice of anything.

Though he was stifling under the lighter's sail which Nostromo had unwittingly lowered on top of him, he did not even dare to put out his head till the very moment of the steamer striking. Then, indeed, he leaped right out, spurred on to new miracles of bodily vigor by this new shape of danger. The inrush of water when the lighter heeled over unsealed his lips. His shriek, "Save me!" was the first distinct warning of the collision for the people on board the steamer. Next moment the wire shroud parted, and the released anchor swept over the lighter's forecastle. It came against the breast of Señor Hirsch, who simply seized hold of it, without in the least knowing what it was, but curling his arms and legs upon the part above the fluke with an invincible, unreasonable tenacity. The lighter yawed off wide, and the steamer, moving on, carried him away, clinging hard, and shouting for help. It was some time, however, after the steamer had stopped that his position was discovered. His sustained yelping for help seemed to come from somebody swimming in the water. At last a couple of men went over the bows and hauled him on board. He was carried straight off to Sotillo on the bridge. His examination confirmed the impression that some craft had been run over and sunk, but it was impracticable on such a dark night to look for the positive proof of floating wreckage. Sotillo was more anxious than ever now to enter the harbor without loss of time; the idea that he had destroyed the principal object of his expedition was too intolerable to be accepted. This feeling made the story he had heard appear the more incredible. Señor Hirsch, after being beaten a little for telling lies, was thrust into the chartroom. But he was beaten only a little. His tale had taken the heart out of Sotillo's Staff, though they all repeated round their chief, "Impossible! impossible!" with the exception of the old major, who triumphed gloomily.

"I told you; I told you," he mumbled. "I could smell some treachery, some *diablería* a league off."

Meantime, the steamer had kept on her way towards Sulaco, where only the truth of that matter could be ascertained. Decoud and Nostromo heard the loud churning of her propeller diminish and die out; and then, with no useless words, busied themselves in making for the Isabels. The last shower had brought with it a gentle but steady breeze. The danger was not over yet, and there was no time for talk. The lighter was leaking like a sieve. They splashed in the water at every step. The Capataz put into Decoud's hands the handle of the pump which was fitted at the side aft, and at once, without question or remark, Decoud began to pump in utter forgetfulness of every desire but that of keeping the treasure afloat. Nostromo hoisted the sail, flew back to the tiller, pulled at the sheet like mad. The short flare of a match (they had been kept dry in a tight tin box, though the man himself was completely wet), the vivid flare of a match, disclosed to the toiling Decoud the eagerness of his face, bent low over the box of the compass, and the attentive stare of his eyes. He knew now where he was, and he hoped to run the sinking lighter ashore in the shallow cove where the high, cliff-like end of the Great Isabel is divided in two equal parts by a deep and overgrown ravine.

Decoud pumped without intermission. Nostromo steered without relaxing for a second the intense, peering effort of his stare. Each of them was as if utterly alone with his task. It did not occur to them to speak. There was nothing in common between them but the knowledge that the damaged lighter must be slowly but surely sinking. In that knowledge, which was like the crucial test of their desires, they seemed to have become completely estranged, as if they had discovered in the very shock of the collision that the loss of the lighter would not mean the same thing to them both. This common danger brought their differences in aim, in view, in character, and in position, into absolute prominence in the private vision of each. There was no bond of conviction, of common idea; they were merely two adventurers pursuing each his own adventure, involved in the same imminence of deadly peril. Therefore they had nothing to say to each other. But this peril, this only incontrovertible truth in which they shared, seemed to act as an inspiration to their mental and bodily powers.

There was certainly something almost miraculous in the way the Capataz made the cove with nothing but the shadowy hint of the island's shape and the vague gleam of a small sandy strip for a guide. Where the ravine opens between the cliffs, and a slender, shallow rivulet meanders out of the bushes to lose itself in the sea, the lighter was run ashore; and the two men, with a taciturn, undaunted energy, began to discharge her precious freight, carrying each ox-hide box up the bed of the rivulet beyond the bushes to a hollow place which the caving in of the soil had made below the roots of a large tree. Its big smooth trunk leaned like a falling column far over the trickle of water running amongst the loose stones.

A couple of years before Nostromo had spent a whole Sunday, all alone, exploring the island. He explained this to Decoud after their task was done, and they sat, weary in every limb, with their legs hanging down the low bank, and their backs against the tree, like a pair of blind men aware of each other and their surroundings by some indefinable sixth sense.

"Yes," Nostromo repeated, "I never forget a place I have carefully looked at once." He spoke slowly, almost lazily, as if there had been a whole leisurely life before him, instead of the scanty two hours before daylight. The existence of the treasure, barely concealed in this improbable spot, laid a burden of secrecy upon every contemplated step, upon every intention and plan of future conduct. He felt the partial failure of this desperate affair entrusted to the great reputation he had known how to make for himself. However, it was also a partial success. His vanity was half appeased. His nervous irritation had subsided.

"You never know what may be of use," he pursued with his usual quietness of tone and manner. "I spent a whole miserable Sunday in exploring this crumb of land."

"A misanthropic sort of occupation," muttered Decoud, viciously. "You had no money, I suppose, to gamble with, and to fling about amongst the girls in your usual haunts, Capataz."

"*È vero!*" exclaimed the Capataz, surprised into the use of his native tongue by so much perspicacity. "I had not! Therefore I did not want to go amongst those beggarly people accustomed to my generosity. It is looked for from the Capataz of the Cargadores, who are the rich men, and, as it were, the *caballeros* amongst the common people. I don't care for cards but as a pastime; and as to those girls that boast of having opened their doors to my knock, you know I wouldn't look at any one of them twice except for what the people would say. They are queer, the good people of Sulaco, and I have got much useful information simply by listening patiently to the talk of the women that everybody believed I was in love with. Poor Teresa could never understand that. On that particular Sunday, *señor*, she scolded so that I went out of the house swearing that I would never darken their door again unless to fetch away my hammock and my chest of clothes. *Señor*, there is nothing more exasperating than to hear a woman you respect rail against your good reputation when you have not a single brass coin in your pocket. I untied one of the small boats and pulled myself out of the harbor with nothing but three cigars in my pocket to help me spend the day on this island. But the water of this rivulet you hear under your feet is cool and sweet and good, *señor*, both before and after a smoke." He was silent for a while, then added reflectively, "That was the first Sunday after I brought the white-whiskered English *rico* all the way down the mountains from the Paramo on the top of the Entrada Pass— and in the coach, too! No coach had gone up or down that mountain road within the memory of man, *señor*, till I brought this one down in charge of fifty peons working like one man with ropes, pick-axes, and poles under my direction. That was the rich Englishman who, as people say, pays for the making of this railway. He was very pleased with me. But my wages were not due till the end of the month."

He slid down the bank suddenly. Decoud heard the splash of his feet in the brook and followed his footsteps down the ravine. His form was lost among the bushes till he had reached the strip of sand under the cliff. As often happens in the gulf when the showers during the first part of the night had been frequent and heavy, the darkness had thinned considerably towards the morning though there were no signs of daylight as yet.

The cargo-lighter, relieved of its precious burden, rocked feebly, half-afloat, with her fore-foot on the sand. A long rope stretched away like a black cotton thread across the strip of white beach to the grapnel Nostromo had carried ashore and hooked to the stem of a tree-like shrub in the very opening of the ravine.

There was nothing for Decoud but to remain on the island. He received from Nostromo's hands whatever food the foresight of Captain Mitchell had put on board the lighter and deposited it temporarily in the little dinghy which on their arrival they had hauled up out of sight amongst the bushes. It was to be left with him. The island was to be a hiding-place, not a prison; he could pull out to a passing ship. The O.S.N. Company's mail boats passed close to the islands when going into Sulaco from the north. But the *Minerva*, carrying off the ex-president, had taken the news up north of the disturbances in Sulaco. It was possible that the next steamer down would get instructions to miss the port altogether since the town, as far as the *Minerva*'s officers knew, was for the time being in the hands of the rabble. This would mean that there would be no steamer for a month, as far as the mail service went; but Decoud had to take his chance of that. The island was his only shelter from the proscription hanging over his head. The Capataz was, of course, going back. The unloaded lighter leaked much less, and he thought that she would keep afloat as far as the harbor.

He passed to Decoud, standing knee-deep alongside, one of the two spades which belonged to the equipment of each lighter for use when ballasting ships. By working with it carefully as soon as there was daylight enough to see, Decoud could loosen a mass of earth and stones overhanging the cavity in which they had deposited the treasure, so that it would look as if it had fallen naturally. It would cover up not only the cavity, but even all traces of their work, the footsteps, the displaced stones, and even the broken bushes.

"Besides, who would think of looking either for you or the treasure here?" Nostromo continued, as if he could not tear himself away from the spot. "Nobody is ever likely to come here. What could any man want with this piece of earth as long as there is room for his feet on the mainland! The people in this country are not curious. There are even no fishermen here to intrude upon your worship. All the fishing that is done in the gulf goes on near Zapiga, over there. *Señor*, if you are forced to leave this island before anything can be arranged for you, do not try to make for Zapiga. It is a settlement of thieves and *matreros*, where they would cut your throat promptly for the sake of your gold watch and chain. And, *señor*, think twice before confiding in anyone whatever; even in the officers of the Company's steamers, if you ever get on board one. Honesty alone is not enough for security. You must look to discretion and prudence in a man. And always remember, *señor*, before you open your lips for a confidence, that this treasure may be left safely here for hundreds of years. Time is on its side, *señor*. And silver is an incorruptible metal that can be trusted to keep its value for ever. . . . An incorruptible metal," he repeated, as if the idea had given him a profound pleasure.

"As some men are said to be," Decoud pronounced, inscrutably, while the Capataz, who busied himself in baling out the lighter with a wooden bucket, went on throwing the water over the side with a regular splash. Decoud, incorrigible in his skepticism, reflected, not cynically, but with general satisfaction, that this man was made incorruptible by his enormous vanity, that finest form of egoism which can take on the aspect of every virtue.

Nostromo ceased baling, and, as if struck with a sudden thought, dropped the bucket with a clatter into the lighter.

"Have you any message?" he asked in a lowered voice. "Remember, I shall be asked questions."

"You must find the hopeful words that ought to be spoken to the people in town. I trust for that your intelligence and your experience, Capataz. You understand?"

"*Si, señor* . . . For the ladies."

"Yes, yes," said Decoud, hastily. "Your wonderful reputation will make them attach great value to your words; therefore be careful what you say. I am looking forward," he continued, feeling the fatal touch of contempt for himself to which his complex nature was subject, "I am looking forward to a glorious and successful ending to my mission. Do you hear, Capataz? Use the words glorious and successful when you speak to the *señorita*. Your own mission is accomplished gloriously and successfully. You have indubitably saved the silver of the mine. Not only this silver, but probably all the silver that shall ever come out of it."

Nostromo detected the ironic tone. "I dare say, Señor Don Martin," he said, moodily. "There are very few things that I am not equal to. Ask the foreign *signori*. I, a man of the people, who cannot always understand what you mean. But as to this lot which I must leave here, let me tell you that I would believe it in greater safety if you had not been with me at all."

An exclamation escaped Decoud, and a short pause followed. "Shall I go back with you to Sulaco?" he asked in an angry tone.

"Shall I strike you dead with my knife where you stand?" retorted Nostromo, contemptuously. "It would be the same thing as taking you to Sulaco. Come, *señor*. Your reputation is in your politics, and mine is bound up with the fate of this silver. Do you wonder I wish there had been no other man to share my knowledge? I wanted no one with me, *señor*."

"You could not have kept the lighter afloat without me," Decoud almost shouted. "You would have gone to the bottom with her."

"Yes," uttered Nostromo, slowly; "alone."

Here was a man, Decoud reflected, that seemed as though he would have preferred to die rather than deface the perfect form of his egoism. Such a man was safe. In silence he helped the Capataz to get the grapnel on board. Nostromo cleared the shelving shore with one push of the heavy oar, and Decoud found himself solitary on the beach like a man in a dream. A sudden desire to hear a human voice once more seized upon his heart. The lighter was hardly distinguishable from the black water upon which she floated.

"What do you think has become of Hirsch?" he shouted.

"Knocked overboard and drowned," cried Nostromo's voice confidently out of the black wastes of sky and sea around the islet. "Keep close in the ravine, *señor*. I shall try to come out to you in a night or two."

A slight swishing rustle showed that Nostromo was setting the sail. It filled all at once with a sound as of a single loud drum-tap. Decoud went back to the ravine. Nostromo, at the tiller, looked back from time to time at the vanishing mass of the Great Isabel, which, little by little, merged into the uniform texture of the night. At last, when he turned his head again, he saw nothing but a smooth darkness, like a solid wall.

Then he, too, experienced that feeling of solitude which had weighed heavily on Decoud after the lighter had slipped off the shore. But while the man on the island was oppressed by a bizarre sense of unreality affecting the very ground upon which he walked, the mind of the Capataz of the Cargadores turned alertly to the problem of future conduct. Nostromo's faculties, working on parallel lines, enabled him to steer straight, to keep a lookout for Hermosa, near which he had to pass, and to try to imagine what would happen tomorrow in Sulaco. Tomorrow, or, as a matter of fact, today, since the dawn was not very far, Sotillo would find out in what way the treasure had gone. A gang of *cargadores* had been employed in loading it into a railway truck from the Custom House storerooms, and running the truck on to the wharf. There would be arrests made, and certainly before noon Sotillo would know in what manner the silver had left Sulaco, and who it was that took it out.

Nostromo's intention had been to sail right into the harbor; but at this thought by a sudden touch of the tiller he threw the lighter into the wind and checked her rapid way. His reappearance with the very boat would raise suspicions, would cause surmises, would absolutely put Sotillo on the track. He himself would be arrested; and once in the *calabozo* there was no saying what they would do to him to make him speak. He trusted himself, but he stood up to look round. Near by, Hermosa showed low its white surface as flat as a table, with the slight run of the sea raised by the breeze washing over its edges noisily. The lighter must be sunk at once.

He allowed her to drift with her sail aback. There was already a good deal of water in her. He allowed her to drift towards the harbor entrance, and, letting the tiller swing about, squatted down and busied himself in loosening the plug. With that out she would fill very quickly, and every lighter carried a little iron ballast—enough to make her go down when full of water. When he stood up again the noisy wash about the Hermosa sounded far away, almost inaudible; and already he could make out the shape of land about the harbor entrance. This was a desperate affair, and he was a good swimmer. A mile was nothing to him, and he knew of an easy place for landing just below the earthworks of the old abandoned fort. It occurred to him with a peculiar fascination that this fort was a good place in which to sleep the day through after so many sleepless nights.

With one blow of the tiller he unshipped for the purpose, he knocked the plug out, but did not take the trouble to lower the sail. He felt the water welling up heavily about his legs before he leaped on to the taffrail. There, upright and motionless, in his shirt and trousers only, he stood waiting. When he had felt her settle he sprang far away with a mighty splash.

At once he turned his head. The gloomy, clouded dawn from behind the mountains showed him on the smooth waters the upper corner of the sail, a dark wet triangle of canvas waving slightly to and fro. He saw it vanish, as if jerked under, and then struck out for the shore.

Part III

THE LIGHTHOUSE

irectly the cargo boat had slipped away from the wharf and got lost in the darkness of the harbor the Europeans of Sulaco separated, to prepare for the coming of the Monterist régime, which was approaching Sulaco from the mountains, as well as from the sea.

This bit of manual work in loading the silver was their last concerted action. It ended the three days of danger, during which, according to the newspaper press of Europe, their energy had preserved the town from the calamities of popular disorder. At the shore end of the jetty, Captain Mitchell said good night and turned back. His intention was to walk the planks of the wharf till the steamer from Esmeralda turned up. The engineers of the railway staff, collecting their Basque and Italian workmen, marched them away to the railway yards, leaving the Custom House, so well defended on the first day of the riot, standing open to the four winds of heaven. Their men had conducted themselves bravely and faithfully during the famous "three days" of Sulaco. In a great part this faithfulness and that courage had been exercised in self-defense rather than in the cause of those material interests to which Charles Gould had pinned his faith. Amongst the cries of the mob not the least loud had been the cry of death to foreigners. It was, indeed, a lucky circumstance for Sulaco that the relations of those imported workmen with the people of the country had been uniformly bad from the first.

Dr. Monygham, going to the door of Viola's kitchen, observed this retreat marking the end of the foreign interference, this withdrawal of the army of material progress from the field of Costaguana revolutions.

Algarroba torches carried on the outskirts of the moving body sent their penetrating aroma into his nostrils. Their light, sweeping along the front of the house, made the letters of the inscription, "Albergo d'Italia Una," leap out black from end to end of the long wall. His eyes blinked in the clear blaze. Several young men, mostly fair and tall, shepherding this mob of dark bronzed heads, surmounted by the glint of slanting rifle barrels, nodded to him familiarly as they went by. The doctor was a well-known character. Some of them wondered what he was doing there. Then, on the flank of their workmen they tramped on, following the line of rails.

"Withdrawing your people from the harbor?" said the doctor, addressing himself to the chief engineer of the railway, who had accompanied Charles Gould so far on his way to the town, walking by the side of the horse, with his hand on the saddlebow. They had stopped just outside the open door to let the workmen cross the road.

"As quick as I can. We are not a political faction," answered the engineer, meaningly. "And we are not going to give our new rulers a handle against the railway. You approve me, Gould?"

"Absolutely," said Charles Gould's impassive voice, high up and outside the dim parallelogram of light falling on the road through the open door.

With Sotillo expected from one side, and Pedro Montero from the other, the engineer-in-chief's only anxiety now was to avoid a collision with either. Sulaco, for him, was a railway station, a terminus, workshops, a great accumulation of stores. As against the mob the railway defended its property, but politically the railway was neutral. He was a brave man; and in that spirit of neutrality he had carried proposals of truce to the self-appointed chiefs of the popular party, the deputies Fuentes and Gamacho. Bullets were still flying about when he had crossed the Plaza on that mission, waving above his head a white napkin belonging to the table linen of the Amarilla Club.

He was rather proud of this exploit; and reflecting that the doctor, busy all day with the wounded in the *patio* of the Casa Gould, had not had time to hear the news, he began a succinct narrative. He had communicated to them the intelligence from the Construction Camp as to Pedro Montero. The brother of the victorious general, he had assured them, could be expected at Sulaco at any time now. This news (as he anticipated), when shouted out of the window by Señor Gamacho, induced a rush of the mob along the Campo Road towards Rincón. The two deputies also, after shaking hands with him effusively, mounted and galloped off to meet the great man. "I have misled them a little as to the time," the chief engineer confessed. "However hard he rides, he can scarcely get here before the morning. But my object is attained. I've secured several hours' peace for the losing party. But I did not tell them anything about Sotillo, for fear they would take it into their heads to try to get hold of the harbor again, either to oppose him or welcome him—there's no saying which. There was Gould's silver, on which rests the remnant of our hopes. Decoud's retreat had to be thought of, too. I think the railway had done pretty well by its friends without compromising itself hopelessly. Now the parties must be left to themselves."

"Costaguana for the Costaguaneros," interjected the doctor, sardonically. "It is a fine country, and they have raised a fine crop of hates, vengeance, murder, and rapine —those sons of the country."

"Well, I am one of them," Charles Gould's voice sounded, calmly, "and I must be going to see to my own crop of trouble. My wife has driven straight on, doctor?"

"Yes. All was quiet on this side. Mrs. Gould has taken the two girls with her."

Charles Gould rode on, and the engineer-in-chief followed the doctor indoors.

"That man is calmness personified," he said, appreciatively, dropping on a bench, and stretching his well-shaped legs in cycling stockings nearly across the doorway. "He must be extremely sure of himself."

"If that's all he is sure of, then he is sure of nothing," said the doctor. He had perched himself again on the end of the table. He nursed his cheek in the palm of one hand, while the other sustained the elbow. "It is the last thing a man ought to be sure of." The candle, half-consumed and burning dimly with a long wick, lighted up from below his inclined face, whose expression, affected by the drawn-in cicatrices in the cheeks, had something vaguely unnatural, an exaggerated remorseful bitterness. As he sat there he had the air of meditating upon sinister things. The engineer-in-chief gazed at him for a time before he protested.

"I really don't see that. For me there seems to be nothing else. However—"

He was a wise man, but he could not quite conceal his contempt for that sort of paradox; in fact, Dr. Monygham was not liked by the Europeans of Sulaco. His outward aspect of an outcast, which he preserved even in Mrs. Gould's drawing-room, provoked unfavorable criticism. There could be no doubt of his intelligence; and as he had lived for over twenty years in the country, the pessimism of his outlook could not be altogether ignored. But instinctively, in self-defense of their activities and hopes, his hearers put it to the account of some hidden imperfection in the man's character. It was known that many years before, when quite young, he had been made by Guzman Bento chief medical officer of the army. Not one of the Europeans then in the service of Costaguana had been so much liked and trusted by the fierce old Dictator.

Afterwards his story was not so clear. It lost itself amongst the innumerable tales of conspiracies and plots against the tyrant as a stream is lost in an arid belt of sandy country before it emerges, diminished and troubled, perhaps, on the other side. The doctor made no secret of it that he had lived for years in the wildest parts of the Republic, wandering with almost unknown Indian tribes in the great forests of the far interior where the great rivers have their sources. But it was mere aimless wandering; he had written nothing, collected nothing, brought nothing for science out of the twilight of the forests, which seemed to cling to his battered personality limping about Sulaco, where it had drifted in casually, only to get stranded on the shores of the sea.

It was also known that he had lived in a state of destitution till the arrival of the Goulds from Europe. Don Carlos and Doña Emilia had taken up the mad English doctor, when it became apparent that for all his savage independence he could be tamed by kindness. Perhaps it was only hunger that had tamed him. In years gone by he had certainly been acquainted with Charles Gould's father in Sta Marta; and now, no matter what were the dark passages of his history, as the medical officer of the San Tomé mine he became a recognized personality. He was recognized, but not unreservedly accepted. So much defiant eccentricity and such an outspoken scorn for mankind seemed to point to mere recklessness of judgment, the bravado of guilt. Besides, since he had become again of some account, vague whispers had been heard that years ago, when fallen into disgrace and thrown into prison by Guzman Bento at the time of the so-called Great Conspiracy, he had betrayed some of his best friends amongst the conspirators. Nobody pretended to believe that whisper; the whole story of the Great Conspiracy was hopelessly involved and obscure; it is admitted in Costaguana that there never had been a conspiracy except in the diseased imagination of the Tyrant; and, therefore, nothing and no one to betray; though the most distinguished Costaguaneros had been imprisoned and executed upon that accusation. The procedure had dragged on for years, decimating the better class like a pestilence. The mere expression of sorrow for the fate of executed kinsmen had been punished with death. Don José Avellanos was perhaps the only one living who knew the whole story of those unspeakable cruelties. He had suffered from them himself, and he, with a shrug of the shoulders and a nervous, jerky gesture of the arm, was wont to put away from him, as it were, every allusion to it. But whatever the reason, Dr. Monygham, a personage in the administration of the Gould Concession, treated with reverent awe by the miners, and indulged in his peculiarities by Mrs. Gould, remained somehow outside the pale.

It was not from any liking for the doctor that the engineer-in-chief had lingered in the inn upon the plain. He liked old Viola much better. He had come to look upon the Albergo d'Italia Una as a dependence of the railway. Many of his subordinates had their quarters there. Mrs. Gould's interest in the family conferred upon it a sort of distinction. The engineer-in-chief, with an army of workers under his orders, appreciated the moral influence of the old Garibaldino upon his countrymen. His austere, old-world Republicanism had a severe, soldier-like standard of faithfulness and duty, as if the world were a battlefield where men had to fight for the sake of universal love and brotherhood, instead of a more or less large share of booty.

"Poor old chap!" he said, after he had heard the doctor's account of Teresa. "He'll never be able to keep the place going by himself. I shall be sorry."

"He's quite alone up there," grunted Dr. Monygham, with a toss of his heavy head towards the narrow staircase. "Every living soul has cleared out, and Mrs. Gould took the girls away just now. It might not be over-safe for them out here before very long. Of course, as a doctor, I can do nothing more here; but she has asked me to stay with old Viola, and as I have no horse to get back to the mine, where I ought to be, I made no difficulty to stay. They can do without me in the town."

"I have a good mind to remain with you, doctor, till we see whether anything happens tonight at the harbor," declared the engineer-in-chief. "He must not be molested by Sotillo's soldiery, who may push on as far as this at once. Sotillo used to be very cordial to me at the Goulds' and at the club. How that man'll ever dare to look any of his friends here in the face I can't imagine."

"He'll no doubt begin by shooting some of them to get over the first awkwardness," said the doctor. "Nothing in this country serves better your military man who has changed sides than a few summary executions." He spoke with a gloomy positive-ness that left no room for protest. The engineer-in-chief did not attempt any. He simply nodded several times regretfully, then said:

"I think we shall be able to mount you in the morning, doctor. Our peons have recovered some of our stampeded horses. By riding hard and taking a wide circuit by Los Hatos and along the edge of the forest, clear of Rincón altogether, you may hope to reach the San Tomé bridge without being interfered with. The mine is just now, to my mind, the safest place for anybody at all compromised. I only wish the railway was as difficult to touch."

"Am I compromised?" Dr. Monygham brought out slowly after a short silence.

"The whole Gould Concession is compromised. I could not have remained for ever outside the political life of the country—if those convulsions may be called life. The thing is—can it be touched? The moment was bound to come when neutrality would become impossible, and Charles Gould understood this well. I believe he is prepared for every extremity. A man of his sort has never contemplated remaining indefinitely at the mercy of ignorance and corruption. It was like being a prisoner in a cavern of *banditti* with the price of your ransom in your pocket, and buying your life from day to day. Your mere safety, not your liberty, mind, doctor. I know what I am talking about. The image at which you shrug your shoulders is perfectly correct, especially if you conceive such a prisoner endowed with the power of replenishing his pocket by means as remote from the faculties of his captors as if they were magic. You must have understood that as well as I do, doctor. He was in the position of the goose with the golden eggs. I broached this matter to him as far back as Sir John's visit here. The prisoner of stupid and greedy *banditti* is always at the mercy of the first imbecile ruffian, who may blow out his brains in a fit of temper or for some prospect of an immediate big haul. The tale of killing the goose with the golden eggs has not been evolved for nothing out of the wisdom of mankind. It is a story that will never grow old. That is why Charles Gould in his deep, dumb way has countenanced the Ribierist Mandate, the first public act that promised him safety on other than venal grounds. Ribierism has failed, as everything merely rational fails in this country. But Gould remains logical in wishing to save this big lot of silver. Decoud's plan of a counter-revolution may be practicable or not, it may have a chance, or it may not have a chance. With all my experience of this revolutionary continent, I can hardly yet look at their methods seriously. Decoud has been reading to us his draft of a proclamation, and talking very well for two hours about his plan of action. He had arguments which should have appeared solid enough if we, members of old, stable political and national organizations, were not startled by the mere idea of a new State evolved like this out of the head of a scoffing young man fleeing for his life, with a proclamation in his pocket, to a rough, jeering, half-bred swashbuckler, who in this part of the world is called a general. It sounds like a comic fairy tale—and behold, it may come off; because it is true to the very spirit of the country."

"Is the silver gone off, then," asked the doctor, moodily.

The chief engineer pulled out his watch. "By Captain Mitchell's reckoning—and he ought to know—it has been gone long enough now to be some three or four miles outside the harbor; and, as Mitchell says, Nostromo is the sort of seaman to make the best of his opportunities." Here the doctor grunted so heavily that the other changed his tone.

"You have a poor opinion of that move, doctor? But why? Charles Gould has got to play his game out, though he is not the man to formulate his conduct even to himself, perhaps, let alone to others. It may be that the game has been partly suggested to him by Holroyd; but it accords with his character, too; and that is why it has been so successful. Haven't they come to calling him 'El Rey de Sulaco' in Sta Marta? A nickname may be the best record of a success. That's what I call putting the face of a joke upon the body of a truth. My dear sir, when I first arrived in Sta Marta I was struck by the way all those journalists, demagogues, members of Congress, and all those generals and judges cringed before a sleepy-eyed advocate without practice simply because he was the plenipotentiary of the Gould Concession. Sir John when he came out was impressed, too."

"A new State, with that plump dandy, Decoud, for the first President," mused Dr. Monygham, nursing his cheek and swinging his legs all the time.

"Upon my word, and why not?" the chief engineer retorted in an unexpectedly earnest and confidential voice. It was as if something subtle in the air of Costaguana had inoculated him with the local faith in *pronunciamientos*. All at once he began to talk, like an expert revolutionist, of the instrument ready to hand in the intact army at Cayta, which could be brought back in a few days to Sulaco if only Decoud managed to make his way at once down the coast. For the military chief there was Barrios, who had nothing but a bullet to expect from Montero, his former professional rival and bitter enemy. Barrios's concurrence was assured. As to his army, it had nothing to expect from Montero either; not even a month's pay. From that point of view the existence of the treasure was of enormous importance. The mere knowledge that it had been saved from the Monterists would be a strong inducement for the Cayta troops to embrace the cause of the new State.

The doctor turned round and contemplated his companion for some time.

"This Decoud, I see, is a persuasive young beggar," he remarked at last. "And pray is it for this, then, that Charles Gould has let the whole lot of ingots go out to sea in charge of that Nostromo?"

"Charles Gould," said the engineer-in-chief, "has said no more about his motive than usual. You know, he doesn't talk. But we all here know his motive, and he has only one—the safety of the San Tomé mine with the preservation of the Gould Concession in the spirit of his compact with Holroyd. Holroyd is another uncommon man. They understand each other's imaginative side. One is thirty, the other nearly sixty, and they have been made for each other. To be a millionaire, and such a millionaire as Holroyd, is like being eternally young. The audacity of youth reckons upon what it fancies an unlimited time at its disposal; but a millionaire has unlimited means in his hand—which is better. One's time on earth is an uncertain quantity, but about the long reach of millions there is no doubt. The introduction of a pure form of Christianity into this continent is a dream for a youthful enthusiast, and I have been trying to explain to you why Holroyd at fifty-eight is like a man on the threshold of life, and better, too. He's not a missionary, but the San Tomé mine holds just that for him. I assure you, in sober truth, that he could not manage to keep this out of a strictly business conference upon the finances of Costaguana he had with Sir John a couple of years ago. Sir John mentioned it with amazement in a letter he wrote to me here, from San Francisco, when on his way home. Upon my word, doctor, things seem to be worth nothing by what they are in themselves. I begin to believe that the only solid thing about them is the spiritual value which everyone discovers in his own form of activity—"

"Bah!" interrupted the doctor, without stopping for an instant the idle swinging movement of his legs. "Self-flattery. Food for that vanity which makes the world go round. Meantime, what do you think is going to happen to the treasure floating about the gulf with the great Capataz and the great politician?"

"Why are you uneasy about it, doctor?"

"I uneasy! And what the devil is it to me? I put no spiritual value into my desires, or my opinions, or my actions. They have not enough vastness to give me room for self-flattery. Look, for instance, I should certainly have liked to ease the last moments of that poor woman. And I can't. It's impossible. Have you met the impossible face to face—or have you, the Napoleon of railways, no such word in your dictionary?"

"Is she bound to have a very bad time of it?" asked the chief engineer, with humane concern.

Slow, heavy footsteps moved across the planks above the heavy hard wood beams of the kitchen. Then down the narrow opening of the staircase made in the thickness of the wall, and narrow enough to be defended by one man against twenty enemies, came the murmur of two voices, one faint and broken, the other deep and gentle answering it, and in its graver tone covering the weaker sound.

The two men remained still and silent till the murmurs ceased, then the doctor shrugged his shoulders and muttered:

"Yes, she's bound to. And I could do nothing if I went up now."

A long period of silence above and below ensued.

"I fancy," began the engineer, in a subdued voice, "that you mistrust Captain Mitchell's Capataz."

"Mistrust him!" muttered the doctor through his teeth. "I believe him capable of anything—even of the most absurd fidelity. I am the last person he spoke to before he left the wharf, you know. The poor woman up there wanted to see him, and I let him go up to her. The dying must not be contradicted, you know. She seemed then fairly calm and resigned, but the scoundrel in those ten minutes or so has done or said something which seems to have driven her into despair. You know," went on the doctor, hesitatingly, "women are so very unaccountable in every position, and at all times of life, that I thought sometimes she was in a way, don't you see? in love with him—the Capataz. The rascal has his own charm indubitably, or he would not have made the conquest of all the populace of the town. No, no, I am not absurd. I may have given a wrong name to some strong sentiment for him on her part, to an unreasonable and simple attitude a woman is apt to take up emotionally towards a man. She used to abuse him to me frequently, which, of course, is not inconsistent with my idea. Not at all. It looked to me as if she were always thinking of him. He was something important in her life. You know, I have seen a lot of those people. Whenever I came down from the mine Mrs. Gould used to ask me to keep my eye on them. She likes Italians; she has lived a long time in Italy, I believe, and she took a special fancy to that old Garibaldino. A remarkable chap enough. A rugged and dreamy character, living in the republicanism of his young days as if in a cloud. He has encouraged much of the Capataz's confounded nonsense—the high-strung, exalted old beggar!"

"What sort of nonsense?" wondered the chief engineer. "I found the Capataz always a very shrewd and sensible fellow, absolutely fearless, and remarkably useful. A perfect handyman. Sir John was greatly impressed by his resourcefulness and attention when he made that overland journey from Sta Marta. Later on, as you might have heard, he rendered us a service by disclosing to the then chief of police the presence in the town of some professional thieves, who came from a distance to wreck and rob our monthly pay train. He has certainly organized the lighterage service of the harbor for the O.S.N. Company with great ability. He knows how to make himself obeyed, foreigner though he is. It is true that the *cargadores* are strangers here, too, for the most part—immigrants, *isleños.*"

"His prestige is his fortune," muttered the doctor, sourly.

"The man has proved his trustworthiness up to the hilt on innumerable occasions and in all sorts of ways," argued the engineer. "When this question of the silver arose, Captain Mitchell naturally was very warmly of the opinion that his Capataz was the only man fit for the trust. As a sailor, of course, I suppose so. But as a man, don't you know, Gould, Decoud, and myself judged that it didn't matter in the least who went. Any boatman would have done just as well. Pray, what could a thief do with such a lot of ingots? If he ran off with them he would have in the end to land somewhere, and how could he conceal his cargo from the knowledge of the people ashore? We dismissed that consideration from our minds. Moreover, Decoud was going. There have been occasions when the Capataz has been more implicitly trusted."

"He took a slightly different view," the doctor said. "I heard him declare in this very room that it would be the most desperate affair of his life. He made a sort of verbal will here in my hearing, appointing old Viola his executor; and, by Jove! do you know, he—he's not grown rich by his fidelity to you good people of the railway and the harbor. I suppose he obtains some—how do you say that?—some spiritual value for his labors, or else I don't know why the devil he should be faithful to you, Gould, Mitchell, or anybody else. He knows this country well. He knows, for instance, that Gamacho, the Deputy from Javira, has been nothing else but a *tramposo* of the commonest sort, a petty peddler of the Campo, till he managed to get enough goods on credit from Anzani to open a little store in the wilds, and got himself elected by the drunken *mozos* that hang about the *estancias* and the poorest sort of *rancheros* who were in his debt. And Gamacho, who tomorrow will be probably one of our high officials, is a stranger, too—an *isleño*. He might have been a *cargador* on the O.S.N. wharf had he not (the *posadero* of Rincón is ready to swear it) murdered a peddler in the woods and stolen his pack to begin life on. And do you think that Gamacho, then, would have ever become a hero with the democracy of this place, like our Capataz? Of course not. He isn't half the man. No; decidedly, I think that Nostromo is a fool."

The doctor's talk was distasteful to the builder of railways. "It is impossible to argue that point," he said, philosophically. "Each man has his gifts. You should have heard Gamacho haranguing his friends in the street. He has a howling voice, and he shouted like mad, lifting his clenched fist right above his head, and throwing his body half out of the window. At every pause the rabble below yelled, 'Down with the Oligarchs! *Viva la libertad!*' Fuentes inside looked extremely miserable. You know, he is the brother of Jorge Fuentes, who has been Minister of the Interior for six months or so, some few years back. Of course, he has no conscience; but he is a man of birth and education—at one time the director of the Customs of Cayta. That idiot-brute Gamacho fastened himself upon him with his following of the lowest rabble. His sickly fear of that ruffian was the most rejoicing sight imaginable."

He got up and went to the door to look out towards the harbor. "All quiet," he said; "I wonder if Sotillo really means to turn up here?"

II

Captain Mitchell, pacing the wharf, was asking himself the same question. There was always the doubt whether the warning of the Esmeralda telegraphist—a fragmentary and interrupted message—had been properly understood. However, the good man had made up his mind not to go to bed till daylight, if even then. He imagined himself to have rendered an enormous service to Charles Gould. When he thought of the saved silver he rubbed his hands together with satisfaction. In his simple way he was proud at being a party to this extremely clever expedient. It was he who had given it a practical shape by suggesting the possibility of intercepting at sea the northbound steamer. And it was advantageous to his Company, too, which would have lost a valuable freight if the treasure had been left ashore to be confiscated. The pleasure of disappointing the Monterists was also very great. Authoritative by temperament and the long habit of command, Captain Mitchell was no democrat. He even went so far as to profess a contempt for parliamentarism itself. "His Excellency Don Vincente Ribiera," he used to say, "whom I and that fellow of mine, Nostromo, had the honor, sir, and the pleasure of saving from a cruel death, deferred too much to his Congress. It was a mistake—a distinct mistake, sir."

The guileless old seaman superintending the O.S.N. service imagined that the last three days had exhausted every startling surprise the political life of Costaguana could offer. He used to confess afterwards that the events which followed surpassed his imagination. To begin with, Sulaco (because of the seizure of the cables and the disorganization of the steam service) remained for a whole fortnight cut off from the rest of the world like a besieged city.

"One would not have believed it possible; but so it was, sir. A full fortnight."

The account of the extraordinary things that happened during that time, and the powerful emotions he experienced, acquired a comic impressiveness from the pompous manner of his personal narrative. He opened it always by assuring his hearer that he was "in the thick of things from first to last." Then he would begin by describing the getting away of the silver, and his natural anxiety lest "his fellow" in charge of the lighter should make some mistake. Apart from the loss of so much precious metal, the life of Señor Martin Decoud, an agreeable, wealthy, and well-informed young gentleman, would have been jeopardized through his falling into the hands of his political enemies. Captain Mitchell also admitted that in his solitary vigil on the wharf he had felt a certain measure of concern for the future of the whole country.

"A feeling, sir," he exclaimed, "perfectly comprehensible in a man properly grateful for the many kindnesses received from the best families of merchants and other native gentlemen of independent means, who, barely saved by us from the excesses of the mob, seemed, to my mind's eye, destined to become the prey in person and fortune of the native soldiery, which, as is well known, behave with regrettable barbarity to the inhabitants during their civil commotions. And then, sir, there were the Goulds, for both of whom, man and wife, I could not but entertain the warmest feelings deserved by their hospitality and kindness. I felt, too, the dangers of the gentlemen of the Amarilla Club, who had made me honorary member, and had treated me with uniform regard and civility, both in my capacity of Consular Agent and as Superintendent of an important Steam Service. Miss Antonia Avellanos, the most beautiful and accomplished young lady whom it had ever been my privilege to speak to, was not a little in my mind, I confess. How the interests of my Company would be affected by the impending change of officials claimed a large share of my attention, too. In short, sir, I was extremely anxious and very tired, as you may suppose, by the exciting and memorable events in which I had taken my little part. The Company's building containing my residence was within five minutes' walk, with the attraction of some supper and of my hammock (I always take my nightly rest in a hammock, as the most suitable to the climate); but somehow, sir, though evidently I could do nothing for anyone by remaining about, I could not tear myself away from that wharf, where the fatigue made me stumble painfully at times. The night was excessively dark—the darkest I remember in my life; so that I began to think that the arrival of the transport from Esmeralda could not possibly take place before daylight, owing to the difficulty of navigating the gulf. The mosquitoes bit like fury. We have been infested here with mosquitoes before the late improvements; a peculiar harbor brand, sir, renowned for its ferocity. They were like a cloud about my head, and I shouldn't wonder that but for their attacks I would have dozed off as I walked up and down, and got a heavy fall. I kept on smoking cigar after cigar, more to protect myself from being eaten up alive than from any real relish for the weed. Then, sir, when perhaps for the twentieth time I was approaching my watch to the lighted end in order to see the time, and observing with surprise that it wanted yet ten minutes to midnight, I heard the splash of a ship's propeller—an unmistakable sound to a sailor's ear on such a calm night. It was faint indeed, because they were advancing with precaution and dead slow, both on account of the darkness and from their desire of not revealing too soon their presence: a very unnecessary care, because, I verily believe, in all the enormous extent of this harbor I was the only living soul about. Even the usual staff of watchmen and others had been absent from their posts for several nights owing to the disturbances. I stood still, after dropping and stamping out my cigar—a circumstance highly agreeable, I should think, to the mosquitoes, if I may judge from the state of my face next morning. But that was a trifling inconvenience in comparison with the brutal proceedings I became victim of on the part of Sotillo. Something utterly inconceivable, sir; more like the proceedings of a maniac than the action of a sane man, however lost to all sense of honor and decency. But Sotillo was furious at the failure of his thievish scheme."

In this Captain Mitchell was right. Sotillo was indeed infuriated. Captain Mitchell, however, had not been arrested at once; a vivid curiosity induced him to remain on the wharf (which is nearly four hundred feet long) to see, or rather hear, the whole process of disembarkation. Concealed by the railway truck used for the silver, which had been run back afterwards to the shore end of the jetty, Captain Mitchell saw the small detachment thrown forward, pass by, taking different directions upon the plain. Meantime, the troops were being landed and formed into a column, whose head crept up gradually so close to him that he made it out, barring nearly the whole width of the wharf, only a very few yards from him. Then the low, shuffling, murmuring, clinking sounds ceased, and the whole mass remained for about an hour motionless and silent, awaiting the return of the scouts. On land nothing was to be heard except the deep baying of the mastiffs at the railway yards, answered by the faint barking of the curs infesting the outer limits of the town. A detached knot of dark shapes stood in front of the head of the column.

Presently the picket at the end of the wharf began to challenge in undertones single figures approaching from the plain. Those messengers sent back from the scouting parties flung to their comrades brief sentences and passed on rapidly, becoming lost in the great motionless mass, to make their report to the Staff. It occurred to Captain Mitchell that his position could become disagreeable and perhaps dangerous, when suddenly, at the head of the jetty, there was a shout of command, a bugle call, followed by a stir and a rattling of arms, and a murmuring noise that ran right up the column. Near by a loud voice directed hurriedly. "Push that railway car out of the way!" At the rush of bare feet to execute the order Captain Mitchell skipped back a pace or two; the car, suddenly impelled by many hands, flew away from him along the rails, and before he knew what had happened he found himself surrounded and seized by his arms and the collar of his coat.

"We have caught a man hiding here, *mi teniente!*" cried one of his captors.

"Hold him on one side till the rearguard comes along," answered the voice. The whole column streamed past Captain Mitchell at a run, the thundering noise of their feet dying away suddenly on the shore. His captors held him tightly, disregarding his declaration that he was an Englishman and his loud demands to be taken at once before their commanding officer. Finally he lapsed into dignified silence. With a hollow rumble of wheels on the planks a couple of field guns, dragged by hand, rolled by. Then, after a small body of men had marched past escorting four or five figures which walked in advance, with a jingle of steel scabbards, he felt a tug at his arms, and was ordered to come along. During the passage from the wharf to the Custom House it is to be feared that Captain Mitchell was subjected to certain indignities at the hands of the soldiers—such as jerks, thumps on the neck, forcible application of the butt of a rifle to the small of his back. Their ideas of speed were not in accord with his notion of his dignity. He became flustered, flushed, and helpless. It was as if the world were coming to an end.

The long building was surrounded by troops, which were already piling arms by companies and preparing to pass the night lying on the ground in their ponchos with their sacks under their heads. Corporals moved with swinging lanterns posting sentries all round the walls wherever there was a door or an opening. Sotillo was taking his measures to protect his conquest as if it had indeed contained the treasure. His desire to make his fortune at one audacious stroke of genius had overmastered his reasoning faculties. He would not believe in the possibility of failure; the mere hint of such a thing made his brain reel with rage. Every circumstance pointing to it appeared incredible. The statement of Hirsch, which was so absolutely fatal to his hopes, could by no means be admitted. It is true, too, that Hirsch's story had been told so incoherently, with such excessive signs of distraction, that it really looked improbable. It was extremely difficult, as the saying is, to make head or tail of it. On the bridge of the steamer, directly after his rescue, Sotillo and his officers, in their impatience and excitement, would not give the wretched man time to collect such few wits as remained to him. He ought to have been quieted, soothed, and reassured, whereas he had been roughly handled, cuffed, shaken, and addressed in menacing tones. His struggles, his wriggles, his attempts to get down on his knees, followed by the most violent efforts to break away, as if he meant incontinently to jump overboard, his shrieks and shrink-ings and cowering wild glances had filled them first with amazement, then with a doubt of his genuineness, as men are wont to suspect the sincerity of every great passion. His Spanish, too, became so mixed up with German that the better half of his statements remained incomprehensible. He tried to propitiate them by calling them *hochwohlgeborene Herren*, which in itself sounded suspicious. When admonished sternly not to trifle he repeated his entreaties and protestations of loyalty and innocence again in German, obstinately, because he was not aware in what language he was speaking. His identity, of course, was perfectly known as an inhabitant of Esmeralda, but this made the matter no clearer. As he kept on forgetting Decoud's name, mixing him up with several other people he had seen in the Casa Gould, it looked as if they all had been in the lighter together; and for a moment Sotillo thought that he had drowned every prominent Ribierist of Sulaco. The improbability of such a thing threw a doubt upon the whole statement. Hirsch was either mad or playing a part—pretending fear and distraction on the spur of the moment to cover the truth. Sotillo's rapacity, excited to the highest pitch by the prospect of an immense booty, could believe in nothing adverse. This Jew might have been very much frightened by the accident, but he knew where the silver was concealed, and had invented this story, with his Jewish cunning, to put him entirely off the track as to what had been done.

Sotillo had taken up his quarters on the upper floor in a vast apartment with heavy black beams. But there was no ceiling, and the eye lost itself in the darkness under the high pitch of the roof. The thick shutters stood open. On a long table could be seen a large inkstand, some stumpy, inky quill pens, and two square wooden boxes, each holding half a hundredweight of sand. Sheets of gray coarse official paper bestrewed the floor. It must have been a room occupied by some higher official of the Customs, because a large leathern armchair stood behind the table, with other high-backed chairs scattered about. A net hammock was swung under one of the beams—for the official's afternoon siesta, no doubt. A couple of candles stuck into tall iron candle-sticks gave a dim reddish light. The colonel's hat, sword, and revolver lay between them, and a couple of his more trusty officers lounged gloomily against the table. The colonel threw himself into the armchair, and a big Negro with a sergeant's stripes on his ragged sleeve, kneeling down, pulled off his boots. Sotillo's ebony moustache contrasted violently with the livid coloring of his cheeks. His eyes were somber and as if sunk very far into his head. He seemed exhausted by his perplexities, languid with disappointment; but when the sentry on the landing thrust his head in to announce the arrival of a prisoner, he revived at once.

"Let him be brought in," he shouted, fiercely.

The door flew open, and Captain Mitchell, bareheaded, his waistcoat open, the bow of his tie under his ear, was hustled into the room.

Sotillo recognized him at once. He could not have hoped for a more precious capture; here was a man who could tell him, if he chose, everything he wished to know —and directly the problem of how to make him talk to the point presented itself to his mind. The resentment of a foreign nation had no terrors for Sotillo. The might of the whole armed Europe would not have protected Captain Mitchell from insults and ill-usage, so well as the quick reflection of Sotillo that this was an Englishman who would most likely turn obstinate under bad treatment, and become quite unmanage-able. At all events, the colonel smoothed the scowl on his brow.

"What! The excellent Señor Mitchell!" he cried, in affected dismay. The pretended anger of his swift advance and of his shout, "Release the *caballero* at once," was so effective that the astounded soldiers positively sprang away from their prisoner. Thus suddenly deprived of forcible support, Captain Mitchell reeled as though about to fall. Sotillo took him familiarly under the arm, led him to a chair, waved his hand at the room. "Go out, all of you," he commanded.

When they had been left alone he stood looking down, irresolute and silent, watching till Captain Mitchell had recovered his power of speech.

Here in his very grasp was one of the men concerned in the removal of the silver. Sotillo's temperament was of that sort that he experienced an ardent desire to beat him; just as formerly when negotiating with difficulty a loan from the cautious Anzani, his fingers always itched to take the shopkeeper by the throat. As to Captain Mitchell, the suddenness, unexpectedness, and general inconceivableness of this experience had confused his thoughts. Moreover, he was physically out of breath.

"I've been knocked down three times between this and the wharf," he gasped out at last. "Somebody shall be made to pay for this." He had certainly stumbled more than once, and had been dragged along for some distance before he could regain his stride. With his recovered breath his indignation seemed to madden him. He jumped up, crimson, all his white hair bristling, his eyes glaring vengefully, and shook violently the flaps of his ruined waistcoat before the disconcerted Sotillo. "Look! Those uniformed thieves of yours downstairs have robbed me of my watch."

The old sailor's aspect was very threatening. Sotillo saw himself cut off from the table on which his saber and revolver were lying.

"I demand restitution and apologies," Mitchell thundered at him, quite beside himself. "From you! Yes, from you!"

For the space of a second or so the colonel stood with a perfectly stony expression of face; then, as Captain Mitchell flung out an arm towards the table as if to snatch up the revolver, Sotillo, with a yell of alarm, bounded to the door and was gone in a flash, slamming it after him. Surprise calmed Captain Mitchell's fury. Behind the closed door Sotillo shouted on the landing, and there was a great tumult of feet on the wooden staircase.

"Disarm him! Bind him!" the colonel could be heard vociferating.

Captain Mitchell had just the time to glance once at the windows, with three perpendicular bars of iron each and some twenty feet from the ground, as he well knew, before the door flew open and the rush upon him took place. In an incredibly short time he found himself bound with many turns of a hide rope to a high-backed chair, so that his head alone remained free. Not till then did Sotillo, who had been leaning in the doorway trembling visibly, venture again within. The soldiers, picking up from the floor the rifles they had dropped to grapple with the prisoner, filed out of the room. The officers remained leaning on their swords and looking on.

"The watch! the watch!" raved the colonel, pacing to and fro like a tiger in a cage. "Give me that man's watch."

It was true, that when searched for arms in the hall downstairs, before being taken into Sotillo's presence, Captain Mitchell had been relieved of his watch and chain; but at the colonel's clamor it was produced quickly enough, a corporal bringing it up, carried carefully in the palms of his joined hands. Sotillo snatched it, and pushed the clenched fist from which it dangled close to Captain Mitchell's face.

"Now then! You arrogant Englishman! You dare to call the soldiers of the army thieves! Behold your watch."

He flourished his fist as if aiming blows at the prisoner's nose. Captain Mitchell, helpless as a swathed infant, looked anxiously at the sixty-guinea gold half-chronometer, presented to him years ago by a Committee of Underwriters for saving a ship from total loss by fire. Sotillo, too, seemed to perceive its valuable appearance. He became silent suddenly, stepped aside to the table, and began a careful examination in the light of the candles. He had never seen anything so fine. His officers closed in and craned their necks behind his back.

He became so interested that for an instant he forgot his precious prisoner. There is always something childish in the rapacity of the passionate, clear-minded, Southern races, wanting in the misty idealism of the Northerners, who at the smallest encouragement dream of nothing less than the conquest of the earth. Sotillo was fond of jewels, gold trinkets, of personal adornment. After a moment he turned about, and with a commanding gesture made all his officers fall back. He laid down the watch on the table, then, negligently, pushed his hat over it.

"Ha!" he began, going up very close to the chair. "You dare call my valiant soldiers of the Esmeralda regiment, thieves. You dare! What impudence! You foreigners come here to rob our country of its wealth. You never have enough! Your audacity knows no bounds."

He looked towards the officers, among whom there was an approving murmur. The older major was moved to declare:

"Sí, mi coronel. They are all traitors."

"I shall say nothing," continued Sotillo, fixing the motionless and powerless Mitchell with an angry but uneasy stare. "I shall say nothing of your treacherous attempt to get possession of my revolver to shoot me while I was trying to treat you with consideration you did not deserve. You have forfeited your life. Your only hope is in my clemency."

He watched for the effect of his words, but there was no obvious sign of fear on Captain Mitchell's face. His white hair was full of dust, which covered also the rest of his helpless person. As if he had heard nothing, he twitched an eyebrow to get rid of a bit of straw which hung amongst the hairs.

Sotillo advanced one leg and put his arms akimbo. "It is you, Mitchell," he said, emphatically, "who are the thief, not my soldiers!" He pointed at his prisoner a forefinger with a long, almond-shaped nail. "Where is the silver of the San Tomé mine? I ask you, Mitchell, where is the silver that was deposited in this Custom House? Answer me that! You stole it. You were a party to stealing it. It was stolen from the Government. Aha! you think I do not know what I say; but I am up to your foreign tricks. It is gone, the silver! No? Gone in one of your *lanchas*, you miserable man! How dared you?"

This time he produced his effect. "How on earth could Sotillo know that?" thought Mitchell. His head, the only part of his body that could move, betrayed his surprise by a sudden jerk.

"Ha! you tremble," Sotillo shouted, suddenly. "It is a conspiracy. It is a crime against the State. Did you not know that the silver belongs to the Republic till the Government claims are satisfied? Where is it? Where have you hidden it, you miserable thief?"

At this question Captain Mitchell's sinking spirits revived. In whatever incomprehensible manner Sotillo had already got his information about the lighter, he had not captured it. That was clear. In his outraged heart, Captain Mitchell had resolved that nothing would induce him to say a word while he remained so disgracefully bound, but his desire to help the escape of the silver made him depart from this resolution. His wits were very much at work. He detected in Sotillo a certain air of doubt, of irresolution.

"That man," he said to himself, "is not certain of what he advances." For all his pomposity in social intercourse, Captain Mitchell could meet the realities of life in a resolute and ready spirit. Now he had got over the first shock of the abominable treatment he was cool and collected enough. The immense contempt he felt for Sotillo steadied him, and he said oracularly, "No doubt it is well concealed by this time."

Sotillo, too, had had time to cool down. *"Muy bien,* Mitchell," he said in a cold and threatening manner. "But can you produce the Government receipt for the royalty and the Custom House permit of embarkation, hey? Can you? No. Then the silver has been removed illegally, and the guilty shall be made to suffer, unless it is produced within five days from this." He gave orders for the prisoner to be unbound and locked up in one of the smaller rooms downstairs. He walked about the room, moody and silent, till Captain Mitchell, with each of his arms held by a couple of men, stood up, shook himself, and stamped his feet.

"How did you like to be tied up, Mitchell?" he asked, derisively.

"It is the most incredible, abominable use of power!" Captain Mitchell declared in a loud voice. "And whatever your purpose, you shall gain nothing from it, I can promise you."

The tall colonel, livid, with his coal-black ringlets and mustache, crouched, as it were, to look into the eyes of the short, thick-set, red-faced prisoner with rumpled white hair.

"That we shall see. You shall know my power a little better when I tie you up to a *potalón* outside in the sun for a whole day." He drew himself up haughtily, and made a sign for Captain Mitchell to be led away.

"What about my watch?" cried Captain Mitchell, hanging back from the efforts of the men pulling him towards the door.

Sotillo turned to his officers. "No! But only listen to this *picaro, caballeros,*" he pronounced with affected scorn, and was answered by a chorus of derisive laughter. "He demands his watch!" . . . He ran up again to Captain Mitchell, for the desire to relieve his feelings by inflicting blows and pain upon this Englishman was very strong within him. "Your watch! You are a prisoner in war time, Mitchell! In war time! You have no rights and no property! *Caramba!* The very breath in your body belongs to me. Remember that."

"Bosh!" said Captain Mitchell, concealing a disagreeable impression.

Down below, in a great hall, with the earthen floor and with a tall mound thrown up by white ants in a corner, the soldiers had kindled a small fire with broken chairs and tables near the arched gateway, through which the faint murmur of the harbor waters on the beach could be heard. While Captain Mitchell was being led down the staircase, an officer passed him, running up to report to Sotillo the capture of more prisoners. A lot of smoke hung about in the vast gloomy place, the fire crackled, and, as if through a haze, Captain Mitchell made out, surrounded by short soldiers with fixed bayonets, the heads of three tall prisoners—the doctor, the engineer-in-chief, and the white leonine mane of old Viola, who stood half-turned away from the others with his chin on his breast and his arms crossed. Mitchell's astonishment knew no bounds. He cried out; the other two exclaimed also. But he hurried, on, diagonally, across the big cavern-like hall. Lots of thoughts, surmises, hints of caution, and so on, crowded his head to distraction.

"Is he actually keeping you?" shouted the chief engineer, whose single eyeglass glittered in the firelight.

An officer from the top of the stairs was shouting urgently, "Bring them all up—all three."

In the clamor of voices and the rattle of arms, Captain Mitchell made himself heard imperfectly: "By heavens! the fellow has stolen my watch."

The engineer-in-chief on the staircase resisted the pressure long enough to shout, "What? What did you say?"

"My chronometer!" Captain Mitchell yelled violently at the very moment of being thrust head foremost through a small door into a sort of cell, perfectly black, and so narrow that he fetched up against the opposite wall. The door had been instantly slammed. He knew where they had put him. This was the strongroom of the Custom House, whence the silver had been removed only a few hours earlier. It was almost as narrow as a corridor, with a small square aperture, barred by a heavy grating, at the distant end. Captain Mitchell staggered for a few steps, then sat down on the earthen floor with his back to the wall. Nothing, not even a gleam of light from anywhere, interfered with Captain Mitchell's meditation. He did some hard but not very extensive thinking. It was not of a gloomy cast. The old sailor, with all his small weaknesses and absurdities, was constitutionally incapable of entertaining for any length of time a fear of his personal safety. It was not so much firmness of soul as the lack of a certain kind of imagination—the kind whose undue development caused intense suffering to Señor Hirsch; that sort of imagination which adds the blind terror of bodily suffering and of death, envisaged as an accident to the body alone, strictly—to all the other apprehensions on which the sense of one's existence is based. Unfortunately, Captain Mitchell had not much penetration of any kind; characteristic, illuminating trifles of expression, action, or movement, escaped him completely. He was too pompously and innocently aware of his own existence to observe that of others. For instance, he could not believe that Sotillo had been really afraid of him, and this simply because it would never have entered into his head to shoot anyone except in the most pressing case of self-defense. Anybody could see he was not a murdering kind of man, he reflected quite gravely. Then why this preposterous and insulting charge? he asked himself. But his thoughts mainly clung around the astounding and unanswerable question: How the devil had the fellow got to know that the silver had gone off in the lighter? It was obvious that he had not captured it. And, obviously, he could not have captured it! In this last conclusion Captain Mitchell was misled by the assumption drawn from his observation of the weather during his long vigil on the wharf. He thought that there had been much more wind than usual that night in the gulf; whereas, as a matter of fact, the reverse was the case.

"How in the name of all that's marvelous did that confounded fellow get wind of the affair?" was the first question he asked directly after the bang, clatter, and flash of the open door (which was closed again almost before he could lift his dropped head) informed him that he had a companion of captivity. Dr. Monygham's voice stopped muttering curses in English and Spanish.

"Is that you, Mitchell?" he made answer, surlily. "I struck my forehead against this confounded wall with enough force to fell an ox. Where are you?"

Captain Mitchell, accustomed to the darkness, could make out the doctor stretching out his hands blindly.

"I am sitting here on the floor. Don't fall over my legs," Captain Mitchell's voice announced with great dignity of tone. The doctor, entreated not to walk about in the dark, sank down to the ground, too. The two prisoners of Sotillo, with their heads nearly touching, began to exchange confidences.

"Yes," the doctor related in a low tone to Captain Mitchell's vehement curiosity, "we have been nabbed in old Viola's place. It seems that one of their pickets, commanded by an officer, pushed as far as the town gate. They had orders not to enter, but to bring along every soul they could find on the plain. We had been talking in there with the door open, and no doubt they saw the glimmer of our light. They must have been making their approaches for some time. The engineer laid himself on a bench in a recess by the fireplace, and I went upstairs to have a look. I hadn't heard any sound from there for a long time. Old Viola, as soon as he saw me come up, lifted his arm for silence. I stole in on tiptoe. By Jove, his wife was lying down and had gone to sleep. The woman had actually dropped off to sleep! 'Señor Doctor,' Viola whispers to me, 'it looks as if her oppression was going to get better.' 'Yes,' I said, very much surprised; 'your wife is a wonderful woman, Giorgio.' Just then a shot was fired in the kitchen, which made us jump and cower as if at a thunder-clap. It seems that the party of soldiers had stolen quite close up, and one of them had crept up to the door. He looked in, thought there was no one there, and, holding his rifle ready, entered quietly. The chief told me that he had just closed his eyes for a moment. When he opened them, he saw the man already in the middle of the room peering into the dark corners. The chief was so startled that, without thinking, he made one leap from the recess right out in front of the fireplace. The soldier, no less startled, ups with his rifle and pulls the trigger, deafening and singeing the engineer, but in his flurry missing him completely. But, look what happens! At the noise of the report the sleeping woman sat up, as if moved by a spring, with a shriek, 'The children, Gian' Battista! Save the children!' I have it in my ears now. It was the truest cry of distress I ever heard. I stood as if paralyzed, but the old husband ran across to the bedside, stretching out his hands. She clung to them! I could see her eyes go glazed; the old fellow lowered her down on the pillows and then looked round at me. She was dead! All this took less than five minutes, and then I ran down to see what was the matter. It was no use thinking of any resistance. Nothing we two could say availed with the officer, so I volunteered to go up with a couple of soldiers and fetch down old Viola. He was sitting at the foot of the bed, looking at his wife's face, and did not seem to hear what I said; but after I had pulled the sheet over her head, he got up and followed us downstairs quietly, in a sort of thoughtful way. They marched us off along the road, leaving the door open and the candle burning. The chief engineer strode on without a word, but I looked back once or twice at the feeble gleam. After we had gone some considerable distance, the Garibaldino, who was walking by my side, suddenly said, 'I have buried many men on battlefields on this continent. The priests talk of consecrated ground! Bah! All the earth made by God is holy; but the sea, which knows nothing of kings and priests and tyrants, is the holiest of all. Doctor! I should like to bury her in the sea. No mummeries, candles, incense, no holy water mumbled over by priests. The spirit of liberty is upon the waters.' . . . Amazing old man. He was saying all this in an undertone as if talking to himself."

"Yes, yes," interrupted Captain Mitchell, impatiently. "Poor old chap! But have you any idea how that ruffian Sotillo obtained his information? He did not get hold of any of our *cargadores* who helped with the truck, did he? But no, it is impossible! These were picked men we've had in our boats for these five years, and I paid them myself specially for the job, with instructions to keep out of the way for twenty-four hours at least. I saw them with my own eyes march on with the Italians to the railway yards. The chief promised to give them rations as long as they wanted to remain there."

"Well," said the doctor, slowly, "I can tell you that you may say good-bye for ever to your best lighter, and to the Capataz of Cargadores."

At this, Captain Mitchell scrambled up to his feet in the excess of his excitement. The doctor, without giving him time to exclaim, stated briefly the part played by Hirsch during the night.

Captain Mitchell was overcome. "Drowned!" he muttered, in a bewildered and appalled whisper. "Drowned!" Afterwards he kept still, apparently listening, but too absorbed in the news of the catastrophe to follow the doctor's narrative with attention.

The doctor had taken up an attitude of perfect ignorance, till at last Sotillo was induced to have Hirsch brought in to repeat the whole story, which was got out of him again with the greatest difficulty, because every moment he would break out into lamentations. At last, Hirsch was led away, looking more dead than alive, and shut up in one of the upstairs rooms to be close at hand. Then the doctor, keeping up his character of a man not admitted to the inner councils of the San Tomé Administration, remarked that the story sounded incredible. Of course, he said, he couldn't tell what had been the action of the Europeans, as he had been exclusively occupied with his own work in looking after the wounded, and also in attending Don José Avellanos. He had succeeded in assuming so well a tone of impartial indifference that Sotillo seemed to be completely deceived. Till then a show of regular inquiry had been kept up; one of the officers sitting at the table wrote down the questions and the answers, the others, lounging about the room, listened attentively, puffing at their long cigars and keeping their eyes on the doctor. But at that point Sotillo ordered everybody out.

III

Directly they were alone, the colonel's severe official manner changed. He rose and approached the doctor. His eyes shone with rapacity and hope; he became confidential. "The silver might have been indeed put on board the lighter, but it was not conceivable that it should have been taken out to sea." The doctor, watching every word, nodded slightly, smoking with apparent relish the cigar which Sotillo had offered him as a sign of his friendly intentions. The doctor's manner of cold detachment from the rest of the Europeans led Sotillo on, till, from conjecture to conjecture, he arrived at hinting that in his opinion this was a put-up job on the part of Charles Gould, in order to get hold of that immense treasure all to himself. The doctor, observant and self-possessed, muttered, "He is very capable of that."

Here Captain Mitchell exclaimed with amazement, amusement, and indignation, "You said that of Charles Gould!" Disgust, and even some suspicion, crept into his tone, for to him, too, as to other Europeans, there appeared to be something dubious about the doctor's personality.

"What on earth made you say that to this watch-stealing scoundrel?" he asked. "What's the object of an infernal lie of that sort? That confounded pickpocket was quite capable of believing you."

He snorted. For a time the doctor remained silent in the dark.

"Yes, that is exactly what I did say," he uttered at last, in a tone which would have made it clear enough to a third party that the pause was not of a reluctant but of a reflective character. Captain Mitchell thought that he had never heard anything so brazenly impudent in his life.

"Well, well!" he muttered to himself, but he had not the heart to voice his thoughts. They were swept away by others full of astonishment and regret. A heavy sense of discomfiture crushed him: the loss of the silver, the death of Nostromo, which was really quite a blow to his sensibilities, because he had become attached to his Capataz as people get attached to their inferiors from love of ease and almost unconscious gratitude. And when he thought of Decoud being drowned, too, his sensibility was almost overcome by this miserable end. What a heavy blow for that poor young woman! Captain Mitchell did not belong to the species of crabbed old bachelors; on the contrary, he liked to see young men paying attentions to young women. It seemed to him a natural and proper thing. Proper especially. As to sailors, it was different; it was not their place to marry, he maintained, but it was on moral grounds as a matter of self-denial, for, he explained, life on board ship is not fit for a woman even at best, and if you leave her on shore, first of all it is not fair, and next she either suffers from it or doesn't care a bit, which, in both cases, is bad. He couldn't have told what upset him most—Charles Gould's immense material loss, the death of Nostromo, which was a heavy loss to himself, or the idea of that beautiful and accomplished young woman being plunged into mourning.

"Yes," the doctor, who had been apparently reflecting some more, began again, "he believed me right enough. I thought he would have hugged me. '*Sí, sí,*' he said, 'he will write to that partner of his, the rich *americano* in San Francisco, that it is all lost. Why not? There is enough to share with many people.' "

"But this is perfectly imbecile!" cried Captain Mitchell.

The doctor remarked that Sotillo *was* imbecile, and that his imbecility was ingenious enough to lead him completely astray. He had helped him only but a little way.

"I mentioned," the doctor said, "in a sort of casual way, that treasure is generally buried in the earth rather than being set afloat upon the sea. At this my Sotillo slapped his forehead. '*Por Dios*, yes,' he said; 'they must have buried it on the shores of this harbor somewhere before they sailed out.' "

"Heavens and earth!" muttered Captain Mitchell, "I should not have believed that anybody could be ass enough—" He paused, then went on mournfully: "But what's the good of all this? It would have been a clever enough lie if the lighter had been still afloat. It would have kept that inconceivable idiot perhaps from sending out the steamer to cruise in the gulf. That was the danger that worried me no end." Captain Mitchell sighed profoundly.

"I had an object," the doctor pronounced, slowly.

"Had you?" muttered Captain Mitchell. "Well, that's lucky, or else I would have thought that you went on fooling him for the fun of the thing. And perhaps that was your object. Well, I must say I personally wouldn't condescend to that sort of thing. It is not to my taste. No, no. Blackening a friend's character is not my idea of fun, if it were to fool the greatest blackguard on earth."

Had it not been for Captain Mitchell's depression, caused by the fatal news, his disgust of Dr. Monygham would have taken a more outspoken shape; but he thought to himself that now it really did not matter what that man, whom he had never liked, would say and do.

"I wonder," he grumbled, "why they have shut us up together, or why Sotillo should have shut you up at all, since it seems to me you have been fairly chummy up there?"

"Yes, I wonder?" said the doctor, grimly.

Captain Mitchell's heart was so heavy that he would have preferred for the time being a complete solitude to the best of company. But any company would have been preferable to the doctor's, at whom he had always looked askance as a sort of beachcomber of superior intelligence partly reclaimed from his abased state. That feeling led him to ask:

"What has that ruffian done with the other two?"

"The chief engineer he wouldn't have let go in any case," said the doctor. "He would like to have a quarrel with the railway upon his hands. Not just yet, at any rate. I don't think, Captain Mitchell, that you understand exactly what Sotillo's position is—"

"I don't see why I should bother my head about it," snarled Captain Mitchell.

"No," assented the doctor, with the same grim composure. "I don't see why you should. It wouldn't help a single human being in the world if you thought ever so hard upon any subject whatever."

"No," said Captain Mitchell, simply, and with evident depression. "A man locked up in a confounded dark hole is not much use to anybody."

"As to old Viola," the doctor continued, as though he had not heard, "Sotillo released him for the same reason he is presently going to release you."

"Eh? What?" exclaimed Captain Mitchell, staring like an owl in the darkness. "What is there in common between me and old Viola? More likely because the old chap has no watch and chain for the pickpocket to steal. And I tell you what, Dr. Monygham," he went on with rising choler, "he will find it more difficult than he thinks to get rid of me. He will burn his fingers over that job yet, I can tell you. To begin with, I won't go without my watch, and as to the rest—we shall see. I dare say it is no great matter for you to be locked up. But Joe Mitchell is a different kind of man, sir. I don't mean to submit tamely to insult and robbery. I am a public character, sir."

And then Captain Mitchell became aware that the bars of the opening had become visible, a black grating upon a square of gray. The coming of the day silenced Captain Mitchell as if by the reflection that now in all the future days he would be deprived of the invaluable services of his Capataz. He leaned against the wall with his arms folded on his breast, and the doctor walked up and down the whole length of the place with his peculiar hobbling gait, as if slinking about on damaged feet. At the end farthest from the grating he would be lost altogether in the darkness. Only the slight limping shuffle could be heard. There was an air of moody detachment in that painful prowl kept up without a pause. When the door of the prison was suddenly flung open and his name shouted out he showed no surprise. He swerved sharply in his walk, and passed out at once, as though much depended upon his speed; but Captain Mitchell remained for some time with his shoulders against the wall, quite undecided in the bitterness of his spirit whether it wouldn't be better to refuse to stir a limb in the way of protest. He had half a mind to get himself carried out, but after the officer at the door had shouted three or four times in tones of remonstrance and surprise he condescended to walk out.

Sotillo's manner had changed. The colonel's offhand civility was slightly irresolute, as though he were in doubt if civility were the proper course in this case. He observed Captain Mitchell attentively before he spoke from the big armchair behind the table in a condescending voice:

"I have concluded not to detain you, Señor Mitchell. I am of a forgiving disposition. I make allowances. Let this be a lesson to you, however."

The peculiar dawn of Sulaco, which seems to break far away to the westward and creep back into the shade of the mountains, mingled with the reddish light of the candles. Captain Mitchell, in sign of contempt and indifference, let his eyes roam all over the room, and he gave a hard stare to the doctor, perched already on the casement of one of the windows, with his eyelids lowered, careless and thoughtful—or perhaps ashamed.

Sotillo, ensconced in the vast armchair, remarked, "I should have thought that the feelings of a *caballero* would have dictated to you an appropriate reply."

He waited for it, but Captain Mitchell remaining mute, more from extreme resentment than from reasoned intention, Sotillo hesitated, glanced towards the doctor, who looked up and nodded, then went on with a slight effort:

"Here, Señor Mitchell, is your watch. Learn how hasty and unjust has been your judgment of my patriotic soldiers."

Lying back in his seat, he extended his arm over the table and pushed the watch away slightly. Captain Mitchell walked up with undisguised eagerness, put it to his ear, then slipped it into his pocket coolly.

Sotillo seemed to overcome an immense reluctance. Again he looked aside at the doctor, who stared at him unwinkingly.

But as Captain Mitchell was turning away, without as much as a nod or a glance, he hastened to say:

"You may go and wait downstairs for the Señor Doctor, whom I am going to liberate, too. You foreigners are insignificant, to my mind."

He forced a slight, discordant laugh out of himself, while Captain Mitchell, for the first time, looked at him with some interest.

"The law shall take note later on of your transgressions," Sotillo hurried on. "But as for me, you can live free, unguarded, unobserved. Do you hear, Señor Mitchell? You may depart to your affairs. You are beneath my notice. My attention is claimed by matters of the very highest importance."

Captain Mitchell was very nearly provoked to an answer. It displeased him to be liberated insultingly; but want of sleep, prolonged anxieties, a profound disappointment with the fatal ending of the silver-saving business weighed upon his spirits. It was as much as he could do to conceal his uneasiness, not about himself perhaps, but about things in general. It occurred to him distinctly that something underhand was going on. As he went out he ignored the doctor pointedly.

"A brute!" said Sotillo, as the door shut.

Dr. Monygham slipped off the window-sill, and, thrusting his hands into the pockets of the long, gray dust coat he was wearing, made a few steps into the room.

Sotillo got up, too, and, putting himself in the way, examined him from head to foot.

"So your countrymen do not confide in you very much, Señor Doctor. They do not love you, eh? Why is that, I wonder?"

The doctor, lifting his head, answered by a long, lifeless stare and the words, "Perhaps because I have lived too long in Costaguana."

Sotillo had a gleam of white teeth under the black mustache.

"Aha! But you love yourself," he said, encouragingly.

"If you leave them alone," the doctor said, looking with the same lifeless stare at Sotillo's handsome face, "they will betray themselves very soon. Meantime, may I try to make Don Carlos speak?"

"Ah, Señor Doctor," said Sotillo, wagging his head, "you are a man of quick intelligence. We were made to understand each other." He turned away. He could bear no longer that expressionless and motionless stare, which seemed to have a sort of impenetrable emptiness like the black depth of an abyss.

Even in a man utterly devoid of moral sense there remains an appreciation of rascality which, being conventional, is perfectly clear. Sotillo thought that Dr. Monygham, so different from all Europeans, was ready to sell his countrymen and Charles Gould, his employer, for some share of the San Tomé silver. Sotillo did not despise him for that. The colonel's want of moral sense was of a profound and innocent character. It bordered upon stupidity, moral stupidity. Nothing that served his ends could appear to him really reprehensible. Nevertheless, he despised Dr. Monygham. He had for him an immense and satisfactory contempt. He despised him with all his heart because he did not mean to let the doctor have any reward at all. He despised him, not as a man without faith and honor, but as a fool. Dr. Monygham's insight into his character had deceived Sotillo completely. Therefore he thought the doctor a fool.

Since his arrival in Sulaco the colonel's ideas had undergone some modification.

He no longer wished for a political career in Montero's administration. He had always doubted the safety of that course. Since he had learned from the chief engineer that at daylight most likely he would be confronted by Pedro Montero his misgivings on that point had considerably increased. The *guerrillero* brother of the general—the Pedrito of popular speech—had a reputation of his own. He wasn't safe to deal with. Sotillo had vaguely planned seizing not only the treasure but the town itself, and then negotiating at leisure. But in the face of facts learned from the chief engineer (who had frankly disclosed to him the whole situation) his audacity, never of a very dashing kind, had been replaced by a most cautious hesitation.

"An army—an army has crossed the mountains under Pedrito already," he had repeated, unable to hide his consternation. "If it had not been that I am given the news by a man of your position I would never have believed it. Astonishing!"

"An armed force," corrected the engineer, suavely.

His aim was attained. It was to keep Sulaco clear of any armed occupation for a few hours longer, to let those whom fear impelled leave the town. In the general dismay there were families hopeful enough to fly upon the road towards Los Hatos, which was left open by the withdrawal of the armed rabble under Señores Fuentes and Gamacho, to Rincón, with their enthusiastic welcome for Pedro Montero. It was a hasty and risky exodus, and it was said that Hernandez, occupying with his band the woods about Los Hatos, was receiving the fugitives. That a good many people he knew were contemplating such a flight had been well known to the chief engineer.

Father Corbelán's efforts in the cause of that most pious robber had not been altogether fruitless. The political chief of Sulaco had yielded at the last moment to the urgent entreaties of the priest, had signed a provisional nomination appointing Hernandez a general, and calling upon him officially in this new capacity to preserve order in the town. The fact is that the political chief, seeing the situation desperate, did not care what he signed. It was the last official document he signed before he left the palace of the Intendencia for the refuge of the O.S.N. Company's office. But even had he meant his act to be effective it was already too late. The riot which he feared and expected broke out in less than an hour after Father Corbelán had left him. Indeed,

Father Corbelán, who had appointed a meeting with Nostromo in the Dominican Convent, where he had his residence in one of the cells, never managed to reach the place. From the Intendencia he had gone straight on to the Avellanos's house to tell his brother-in-law, and though he stayed there no more than half an hour he had found himself cut off from his ascetic abode. Nostromo, after waiting there for some time, watching uneasily the increasing uproar in the street, had made his way to the offices of the *Porvenir*, and stayed there till daylight, as Decoud had mentioned in the letter to his sister. Thus the Capataz, instead of riding towards the Los Hatos woods as bearer of Hernandez's nomination, had remained in town to save the life of the President-Dictator, to assist in repressing the outbreak of the mob, and at last to sail out with the silver of the mine.

But Father Corbelán, escaping to Hernandez, had the document in his pocket, a piece of official writing turning a bandit into a general in a memorable last official act of the Ribierist party, whose watchwords were honesty, peace, and progress. Probably neither the priest nor the bandit saw the irony of it. Father Corbelán must have found messengers to send into the town, for early on the second day of the disturbances there were rumors of Hernandez being on the road to Los Hatos ready to receive those who would put themselves under his protection. A strange-looking horseman, elderly and audacious, had appeared in the town, riding slowly while his eyes examined the fronts of the houses, as though he had never seen such high buildings before. Before the cathedral he had dismounted, and, kneeling in the middle of the Plaza, his bridle over his arm and his hat lying in front of him on the ground, had bowed his head, crossing himself and beating his breast for some little time. Remounting his horse, with a fearless but not unfriendly look round the little gathering formed about his public devotions, he had asked for the Casa Avellanos. A score of hands were extended in answer, with fingers pointing up the Calle de la Constitución.

The horseman had gone on with only a glance of casual curiosity upwards to the windows of the Amarilla Club at the corner. His stentorian voice shouted periodically in the empty street, "Which is the Casa Avellanos?" till an answer came from the scared porter, and he disappeared under the gate. The letter he was bringing, written by Father Corbelán with a pencil by the campfire of Hernandez, was addressed to Don José, of whose critical state the priest was not aware. Antonia read it, and, after consulting Charles Gould, sent it on for the information of the gentlemen garrisoning the Amarilla Club. For herself, her mind was made up; she would rejoin her uncle; she would entrust the last day—the last hours perhaps—of her father's life to the keeping of the bandit, whose existence was a protest against the irresponsible tyranny of all parties alike, against the moral darkness of the land. The gloom of Los Hatos woods was preferable; a life of hardships in the train of a robber band less debasing. Antonia embraced with all her soul her uncle's obstinate defiance of misfortune. It was grounded in the belief in the man whom she loved.

In his message the Vicar-General answered upon his head for Hernandez's fidelity. As to his power, he pointed out that he had remained unsubdued for so many years. In that letter Decoud's idea of the new Occidental State (whose flourishing and stable condition is a matter of common knowledge now) was for the first time made public and used as an argument. Hernandez, ex-bandit and the last general of Ribierist creation, was confident of being able to hold the tract of country between the woods of Los Hatos and the coast range till that devoted patriot, Don Martin Decoud, could bring General Barrios back to Sulaco for the reconquest of the town.

"Heaven itself wills it. Providence is on our side," wrote Father Corbelán; there was no time to reflect upon or to controvert his statement; and if the discussion started upon the reading of that letter in the Amarilla Club was violent, it was also short-lived. In the general bewilderment of the collapse some jumped at the idea with joyful astonishment as upon the amazing discovery of a new hope. Others became fascinated by the prospect of immediate personal safety for their women and children. The majority caught at it as a drowning man catches at a straw. Father Corbelán was unexpectedly offering them a refuge from Pedrito Montero with his *llaneros* allied to Señores Fuentes and Gamacho with their armed rabble.

All the latter part of the afternoon an animated discussion went on in the big rooms of the Amarilla Club. Even those members posted at the windows with rifles and carbines to guard the end of the street in case of an offensive return of the populace shouted their opinions and arguments over their shoulders. As dusk fell Don Juste Lopez, inviting those *caballeros* who were of his way of thinking to follow him, withdrew into the corridor, where at a little table in the light of two candles he busied himself in composing an address, or rather a solemn declaration to be presented to Pedrito Montero by a deputation of such members of Assembly as had elected to remain in town. His idea was to propitiate him in order to save the form at least of parliamentary institutions. Seated before a blank sheet of paper, a goose-quill in his hand, and surged upon from all sides, he turned to the right and to the left, repeating with solemn insistence:

"*Caballeros*, a moment of silence! A moment of silence! We ought to make it clear that we bow in all good faith to the accomplished facts."

The utterance of that phrase seemed to give him a melancholy satisfaction. The hubbub of voices round him was growing strained and hoarse. In the sudden pauses the excited grimacing of the faces would sink all at once into the stillness of profound dejection.

Meantime, the exodus had begun. *Carretas* full of ladies and children rolled swaying across the Plaza, with men walking or riding by their side; mounted parties followed on mules and horses; the poorest were setting out on foot, men and women carrying bundles, clasping babies in their arms, leading old people, dragging along the bigger children. When Charles Gould, after leaving the doctor and the engineer at the Casa Viola, entered the town by the harbor gate, all those that had meant to go were gone, and the others had barricaded themselves in their houses. In the whole dark street there was only one spot of flickering lights and moving figures, where the Señor Administrator recognized his wife's carriage waiting at the door of the Avellanos's house. He rode up, almost unnoticed, and looked on without a word while some of his own servants came out of the gate carrying Don José Avellanos, who, with closed eyes and motionless features, appeared perfectly lifeless. His wife and Antonia walked on each side of the improvised stretcher, which was put at once into the carriage. The two women embraced; while from the other side of the landau Father Corbelán's emissary, with his ragged beard all streaked with gray, and high, bronzed cheek-bones, stared, sitting upright in the saddle. Then Antonia, dry-eyed, got in by the side of the stretcher, and, after making the sign of the cross rapidly, lowered a thick veil upon her face. The servants and the three or four neighbors who had come to assist, stood back, uncovering their heads. On the box, Ignacio, resigned now to driving all night (and to having perhaps his throat cut before daylight) looked back surlily over his shoulder.

"Drive carefully," cried Mrs. Gould in a tremulous voice.

"Sí, carefully, sí niña," he mumbled, chewing his lips, his round leathery cheeks quivering. And the landau rolled slowly out of the light.

"I will see them as far as the ford," said Charles Gould to his wife. She stood on the edge of the sidewalk with her hands clasped lightly, and nodded to him as he followed after the carriage. And now the windows of the Amarilla Club were dark. The last spark of resistance had died out. Turning his head at the corner, Charles Gould saw his wife crossing over to their own gate in the lighted patch of the street. One of their neighbors, a well-known merchant and landowner of the province, followed at her elbow, talking with great gestures. As she passed in all the lights went out in the street, which remained dark and empty from end to end.

The houses of the vast Plaza were lost in the night. High up, like a star, there was a small gleam in one of the towers of the cathedral; and the equestrian statue gleamed pale against the black trees of the Alameda, like a ghost of royalty haunting the scenes of revolution. The rare prowlers they met ranged themselves against the wall. Beyond the last houses the carriage rolled noiselessly on the soft cushion of dust, and with a greater obscurity a feeling of freshness seemed to fall from the foliage of the trees bordering the country road. The emissary from Hernandez's camp pushed his horse close to Charles Gould.

"Caballero," he said in an interested voice, "you are he whom they call the King of Sulaco, the master of the mine? Is it not so?"

"Yes, I am the master of the mine," answered Charles Gould.

The man cantered for a time in silence, then said, "I have a brother, a sereno in your service in the San Tomé valley. You have proved yourself a just man. There had been no wrong done to anyone since you called upon the people to work in the mountains. My brother says that no official of the Government, no oppressor of the Campo, has been seen on your side of the stream. Your own officials do not oppress the people in the gorge. Doubtless they are afraid of your severity. You are a just man and a powerful one," he added.

He spoke in an abrupt, independent tone, but evidently he was communicative with a purpose. He told Charles Gould that he had been a ranchero in one of the lower valleys, far south, a neighbor of Hernandez in the old days, and godfather to his eldest boy; one of those who joined him in his resistance to the recruiting raid which was the beginning of all their misfortunes. It was he that, when his *compadre* had been carried off, had buried his wife and children, murdered by the soldiers.

"*Sí, señor*," he muttered, hoarsely, "I and two or three others, the lucky ones left at liberty, buried them all in one grave near the ashes of their ranch, under the tree that had shaded its roof."

It was to him, too, that Hernandez came after he had deserted, three years afterwards. He had still his uniform on with the sergeant's stripes on the sleeve, and the blood of his colonel upon his hands and breast. Three troopers followed him, of those who had started in pursuit but had ridden on for liberty. And he told Charles Gould how he and a few friends, seeing those soldiers, lay in ambush behind some rocks ready to pull the trigger on them, when he recognized his *compadre* and jumped up from cover, shouting his name, because he knew that Hernandez could not have been coming back on an errand of injustice and oppression. Those three soldiers, together with the party who lay behind the rocks, had formed the nucleus of the famous band and he, the narrator, had been the favorite lieutenant of Hernandez for many, many years. He mentioned proudly that the officials had put a price upon his head, too; but it did not prevent it getting sprinkled with gray upon his shoulders. And now he had lived long enough to see his *compadre* made a general.

He had a burst of muffled laughter. "And now from robbers we have become soldiers. But look, *caballero*, all those who made us soldiers and him a general! Look at these people!"

Ignacio shouted. The light of the carriage lamps, running along the nopal hedges that crowned the bank on each side, flashed upon the scared faces of people standing aside in the road, sunk deep, like an English country lane, into the soft soil of the Campo. They cowered; their eyes glistened very big for a second; and then the light, running on, fell upon the half-denuded roots of a big tree, on another stretch of nopal hedge, caught up another bunch of faces glaring back apprehensively. Three women— of whom one was carrying a child—and a couple of men in civilian dress—one armed with a saber and another with a gun—were grouped about a donkey carrying two bundles tied up in blankets. Farther on Ignacio shouted again to pass a *carreta*, a long wooden box on two high wheels, with the door at the back swinging open. Some ladies in it must have recognized the white mules, because they screamed out, "Is it you, Doña Emilia?"

At the turn of the road the glare of a big fire filled the short stretch vaulted over by the branches meeting overhead. Near the ford of a shallow stream a roadside *rancho* of woven rushes and a roof of grass had been set on fire by accident, and the flames, roaring viciously, lit up an open space blocked with horses, mules, and a distracted, shouting crowd of people. When Ignacio pulled up, several ladies on foot assailed the carriage, begging Antonia for a seat. To their clamor she answered by pointing silently to her father.

"I must leave you here," said Charles Gould, in the uproar. The flames leaped up sky-high, and in the recoil from the scorching heat across the road the stream of fugitives pressed against the carriage. A middle-aged lady dressed in black silk, but with a coarse manta over her head and a rough branch for a stick in her hand, staggered against the front wheel. Two young girls, frightened and silent, were clinging to her arms. Charles Gould knew her very well.

"*Misericordia!* We are getting terribly bruised in this crowd!" she exclaimed, smiling up courageously to him. "We have started on foot. All our servants ran away yesterday to join the democrats. We are going to put ourselves under the protection of Father Corbelán, of your sainted uncle, Antonia. He has wrought a miracle in the heart of a most merciless robber. A miracle!"

She raised her voice gradually up to a scream as she was borne along by the pressure of people getting out of the way of some carts coming up out of the ford at a gallop, with loud yells and cracking of whips. Great masses of sparks mingled with black smoke flew over the road; the bamboos of the walls detonated in the fire with the sound of an irregular fusillade. And then the bright blaze sank suddenly, leaving only a red dusk crowded with aimless dark shadows drifting in contrary directions; the noise of voices seemed to die away with the flame; and the tumult of heads, arms, quarreling, and imprecations passed on fleeing into the darkness.

"I must leave you now," repeated Charles Gould to Antonia. She turned her head slowly and uncovered her face. The emissary and *compadre* of Hernandez spurred his horse close up.

"Has not the master of the mine any message to send to Hernandez, the master of the Campo?"

The truth of the comparison struck Charles Gould heavily. In his determined purpose he held the mine, and the indomitable bandit held the Campo by the same precarious tenure. They were equals before the lawlessness of the land. It was impossible to disentangle one's activity from its debasing contacts. A close-meshed net of crime and corruption lay upon the whole country. An immense and weary discouragement sealed his lips for a time.

"You are a just man," urged the emissary of Hernandez. "Look at those people who made my *compadre* a general and have turned us all into soldiers. Look at those oligarchs fleeing for life, with only the clothes on their backs. My *compadre* does not think of that, but our followers may be wondering greatly, and I would speak for them to you. Listen, *señor!* For many months now the Campo has been our own. We need ask no man for anything; but soldiers must have their pay to live honestly when the wars are over. It is believed that your soul is so just that a prayer from you would cure the sickness of every beast, like the orison of the upright judge. Let me have some words from your lips that would act like a charm upon the doubts of our *partida*, where all are men."

"Do you hear what he says?" Charles Gould said in English to Antonia.

"Forgive us our misery!" she exclaimed, hurriedly. "It is your character that is the inexhaustible treasure which may save us all yet; your character, Carlos, not your wealth. I entreat you to give this man your word that you will accept any arrangement my uncle may make with their chief. One word. He will want no more."

On the site of the roadside hut there remained nothing but an enormous heap of embers, throwing afar a darkening red glow, in which Antonia's face appeared deeply flushed with excitement. Charles Gould, with only a short hesitation, pronounced the required pledge. He was like a man who had ventured on a precipitous path with no room to turn, where the only chance of safety is to press forward. At that moment he understood it thoroughly as he looked down at Don José stretched out, hardly breathing, by the side of the erect Antonia, vanquished in a lifelong struggle with the powers of moral darkness, whose stagnant depths breed monstrous crimes and monstrous illusions. In a few words the emissary from Hernandez expressed his complete satisfaction. Stoically Antonia lowered her veil, resisting the longing to inquire about Decoud's escape. But Ignacio leered morosely over his shoulder.

"Take a good look at the mules, *mi amo*," he grumbled. "You shall never see them again!"

IV

Charles Gould turned towards the town. Before him jagged peaks of the Sierra came out all black in the clear dawn. Here and there a muffled *lepero* whisked round the corner of a grass-grown street before the ringing hoofs of his horse. Dogs barked behind the walls of the gardens; and with the colorless light the chill of the snows seemed to fall from the mountains upon the disjointed pavements and the shuttered houses with broken cornices and the plaster peeling in patches between the flat pilasters of the fronts. The daybreak struggled with the gloom under the arcades on the Plaza, with no signs of country people disposing their goods for the day's market, piles of fruit, bundles of vegetables ornamented with flowers, on low benches under enormous mat umbrellas; with no cheery early-morning bustle of villagers, women, children, and loaded donkeys. Only a few scattered knots of revolutionists stood in the vast space, looking all one way from under their slouched hats for some sign of news from Rincón. The largest of those groups turned about like one man as Charles Gould passed, and shouted, *"Viva la libertad!"* after him in a menacing tone.

Charles Gould rode on, and turned into the archway of his house. In the patio littered with straw, a *practicante*, one of Dr. Monygham's native assistants, sat on the ground with his back against the rim of the fountain, fingering a guitar discreetly, while two girls of the lower class, standing up before him, shuffled their feet a little and waved their arms, humming a popular dance tune. Most of the wounded during the two days of rioting had been taken away already by their friends and relations, but several figures could be seen sitting up balancing their bandaged heads in time to the music. Charles Gould dismounted. A sleepy *mozo* coming out of the bakery door took hold of the horse's bridle; the *practicante* endeavored to conceal his guitar hastily; the girls, unabashed, stepped back smiling; and Charles Gould, on his way to the staircase, glanced into a dark corner of the patio at another group, a mortally wounded *cargador* with a woman kneeling by his side; she mumbled prayers rapidly, trying at the same time to force a piece of orange between the stiffening lips of the dying man.

The cruel futility of things stood unveiled in the levity and sufferings of that incorrigible people; the cruel futility of lives and of deaths thrown away in the vain endeavor to attain an enduring solution of the problem. Unlike Decoud, Charles Gould could not play lightly a part in a tragic farce. It was tragic enough for him in all conscience, but he could see no farcical element. He suffered too much under a conviction of irremediable folly. He was too severely practical and too idealistic to look upon its terrible humors with amusement, as Martin Decoud, the imaginative materialist, was able to do in the dry light of his skepticism. To him, as to all of us, the compromises with his conscience appeared uglier than ever in the light of failure. His taciturnity, assumed with a purpose, had prevented him from tampering openly with his thoughts; but the Gould Concession had insidiously corrupted his judgment. He might have known, he said to himself, leaning over the balustrade of the corridor, that Ribierism could never come to anything. The mine had corrupted his judgment by making him sick of bribing and intriguing merely to have his work left alone from day to day. Like his father, he did not like to be robbed. It exasperated him. He had persuaded himself that, apart from higher considerations, the backing up of Don Jose's hopes of reform was good business. He had gone forth into the senseless fray as his poor uncle, whose sword hung on the wall of his study, had gone forth—in the defense of the commonest decencies of organized society. Only his weapon was the wealth of the mine, more far-reaching and subtle than an honest blade of steel fitted into a simple brass guard.

More dangerous to the wielder, too, this weapon of wealth, double-edged with the cupidity and misery of mankind, steeped in all the vices of self-indulgence as in a concoction of poisonous roots, tainting the very cause for which it is drawn, always ready to turn awkwardly in the hand. There was nothing for it now but to go on using it. But he promised himself to see it shattered into small bits before he let it be wrenched from his grasp.

After all, with his English parentage and English upbringing, he perceived that he was an adventurer in Costaguana, the descendant of adventurers enlisted in a foreign legion, of men who had sought fortune in a revolutionary war, who had planned revolutions, who had believed in revolutions. For all the uprightness of his character, he had something of an adventurer's easy morality which takes count of personal risk in the ethical appraising of his action. He was prepared, if need be, to blow up the whole San Tomé mountain sky high out of the territory of the Republic. This resolution expressed the tenacity of his character, the remorse of that subtle conjugal infidelity through which his wife was no longer the sole mistress of his thoughts, something of his father's imaginative weakness, and something, too, of the spirit of a buccaneer throwing a lighted match into the magazine rather than surrender his ship.

Down below in the patio the wounded *cargador* had breathed his last. The woman cried out once, and her cry, unexpected and shrill, made all the wounded sit up. The *practicante* scrambled up to his feet, and, guitar in hand, gazed steadily in her direction with elevated eyebrows. The two girls—sitting now one on each side of their wounded relative, with their knees drawn up and long cigars between their lips—nodded at each other significantly.

Charles Gould, looking down over the balustrade, saw three men dressed ceremoniously in black frock-coats with white shirts, and wearing European round hats, enter the patio from the street. One of them, head and shoulders taller than the two others, advanced with marked gravity, leading the way. This was Don Juste Lopez, accompanied by two of his friends, members of Assembly, coming to call upon the Administrator of the San Tomé mine at this early hour. They saw him, too, waved their hands to him urgently, walking up the stairs as if in procession.

Don Juste, astonishingly changed by having shaved off altogether his damaged beard, had lost with it nine-tenths of his outward dignity. Even at that time of serious preoccupation Charles Gould could not help noting the revealed ineptitude in the aspect of the man. His companions looked crestfallen and sleepy. One kept on passing the tip of his tongue over his parched lips; the other's eyes strayed dully over the tiled floor of the corridor, while Don Juste, standing a little in advance, harangued the Señor Administrator of the San Tomé mine. It was his firm opinion that forms had to be observed. A new governor is always visited by deputations from the Cabildo, which is the Municipal Council, from the Consulado, the Commercial Board, and it was proper that the Provincial Assembly should send a deputation, too, if only to assert the existence of parliamentary institutions. Don Juste proposed that Don Carlos Gould, as the most prominent citizen of the province, should join the Assembly's deputation. His position was exceptional, his personality known through the length and breadth of the whole Republic. Official courtesies must not be neglected, if they are gone through with a bleeding heart. The acceptance of accomplished facts may save yet the precious vestiges of parliamentary institutions. Don Juste's eyes glowed dully; he believed in parliamentary institutions—and the convinced drone of his voice lost itself in the stillness of the house like the deep buzzing of some ponderous insect.

Charles Gould had turned round to listen patiently, leaning his elbow on the balustrade. He shook his head a little, refusing, almost touched by the anxious gaze of the President of the Provincial Assembly. It was not Charles Gould's policy to make the San Tomé mine a party to any formal proceedings.

"My advice, señores, is that you should wait for your fate in your houses. There is no necessity for you to give yourselves up formally into Montero's hands. Submission to the inevitable, as Don Juste calls it, is all very well, but when the inevitable is called Pedrito Montero there is no need to exhibit pointedly the whole extent of your surrender. The fault of this country is the want of measure in political life. Flat acquiescence in illegality, followed by sanguinary reaction—that, señores, is not the way to a stable and prosperous future."

Charles Gould stopped before the sad bewilderment of the faces, the wondering, anxious glances of the eyes. The feeling of pity for those men, putting all their trust into words of some sort, while murder and rapine stalked over the land, had betrayed him into what seemed empty loquacity. Don Juste murmured:

"You are abandoning us, Don Carlos. . . . And yet, parliamentary institutions—"

He could not finish from grief. For a moment he put his hand over his eyes. Charles Gould, in his fear of empty loquacity, made no answer to the charge. He returned in silence their ceremonious bows. His taciturnity was his refuge. He understood that what they sought was to get the influence of the San Tomé mine on their side. They wanted to go on a conciliating errand to the victor under the wing of the Gould Concession. Other public bodies—the Cabildo, the Consulado—would be coming, too, presently, seeking the support of the most stable, the most effective force they had ever known to exist in their province.

The doctor, arriving with his sharp, jerky walk, found that the master had retired into his own room with orders not to be disturbed on any account. But Dr. Monygham was not anxious to see Charles Gould at once. He spent some time in a rapid examination of his wounded. He gazed down upon each in turn, rubbing his chin between his thumb and forefinger; his steady stare met without expression their silently inquisitive look. All these cases were doing well; but when he came to the dead *cargador* he stopped a little longer, surveying not the man who had ceased to suffer, but the woman kneeling in silent contemplation of the rigid face, with its pinched nostrils and a white gleam in the imperfectly closed eyes. She lifted her head slowly, and said in a dull voice:

"It is not long since he had become a *cargador*—only a few weeks. His worship the Capataz had accepted him after many entreaties."

"I am not responsible for the great Capataz," muttered the doctor, moving off.

Directing his course upstairs towards the door of Charles Gould's room, the doctor at the last moment hesitated; then, turning away from the handle with a shrug of his uneven shoulders, slunk off hastily along the corridor in search of Mrs. Gould's *camerista*.

Leonarda told him that the *señora* had not risen yet. The *señora* had given into her charge the girls belonging to that Italian *posadero*. She, Leonarda, had put them to bed in her own room. The fair girl had cried herself to sleep, but the dark one—the bigger —had not closed her eyes yet. She sat up in bed clutching the sheets right up under her chin and staring before her like a little witch. Leonarda did not approve of the Viola children being admitted to the house. She made this feeling clear by the indifferent tone in which she inquired whether their mother was dead yet. As to the *señora*, she must be asleep. Ever since she had gone into her room after seeing the departure of Doña Antonia with her dying father, there had been no sound behind her door.

The doctor, rousing himself out of profound reflection, told her abruptly to call her mistress at once. He hobbled off to wait for Mrs. Gould in the *sala*. He was very tired, but too excited to sit down. In this great drawing room, now empty, in which his withered soul had been refreshed after many arid years and his outcast spirit had accepted silently the toleration of many side-glances, he wandered haphazardly amongst the chairs and tables till Mrs. Gould, enveloped in a morning wrapper, came in rapidly.

"You know that I never approved of the silver being sent away," the doctor began at once, as a preliminary to the narrative of his night's adventures in association with Captain Mitchell, the engineer-in-chief, and old Viola, at Sotillo's headquarters. To the doctor, with his special conception of this political crisis, the removal of the silver had seemed an irrational and ill-omened measure. It was as if a general were sending the best part of his troops away on the eve of battle upon some recondite pretext. The whole lot of ingots might have been concealed somewhere where they could have been got at for the purpose of staving off the dangers which were menacing the security of the Gould Concession. The Administrator had acted as if the immense and powerful prosperity of the mine had been founded on methods of probity, on the sense of usefulness. And it was nothing of the kind. The method followed had been the only one possible. The Gould Concession had ransomed its way through all those years. It was a nauseous process. He quite understood that Charles Gould had got sick of it and had left the old path to back up that hopeless attempt at reform. The doctor did not believe in the reform of Costaguana. And now the mine was back again in its old path, with the disadvantage that henceforth it had to deal not only with the greed provoked by its wealth, but with the resentment awakened by the attempt to free itself from its bondage to moral corruption. That was the penalty of failure. What made him uneasy was that Charles Gould seemed to him to have weakened at the decisive moment when a frank return to the old methods was the only chance. Listening to Decoud's wild scheme had been a weakness.

The doctor flung up his arms, exclaiming, "Decoud! Decoud!" He hobbled about the room with slight, angry laughs. Many years ago both his ankles had been seriously damaged in the course of a certain investigation conducted in the castle of Sta Marta by a commission composed of military men. Their nomination had been signified to them unexpectedly at the dead of night, with scowling brow, flashing eyes, and in a tempestuous voice, by Guzman Bento. The old tyrant, maddened by one of his sudden accesses of suspicion, mingled spluttering appeals to their fidelity with imprecations and horrible menaces. The cells and casements of the castle on the hill had been already filled with prisoners. The commission was charged now with the task of discovering the iniquitous conspiracy against the Citizen-Saviour of his country.

The dread of the raving tyrant translated itself into a hasty ferocity of procedure. The Citizen-Saviour was not accustomed to wait. A conspiracy had to be discovered. The courtyards of the castle resounded with the clanking of leg-irons, sounds of blows, yells of pain; and the commission of high officers labored feverishly, concealing their distress and apprehensions from each other, and especially from their secretary, Father Berón, an army chaplain, at that time very much in the confidence of the Citizen-Saviour. That priest was a big round-shouldered man, with an unclean-looking, overgrown tonsure on the top of his flat head, of a dingy, yellow complexion, softly fat, with greasy stains all down the front of his lieutenant's uniform, and a small cross embroidered in white cotton on his left breast. He had a heavy nose and a pendant lip. Dr. Monygham remembered him still. He remembered him against all the force of his will striving its utmost to forget. Father Berón had been adjoined to the commission by Guzman Bento expressly for the purpose that his enlightened zeal should assist them in their labors. Dr. Monygham could by no manner of means forget the zeal of Father Berón, or his face, or the pitiless, monotonous voice in which he pronounced the words, "Will you confess now?"

The memory did not make him shudder, but it had made of him what he was in

the eyes of respectable people, a man careless of common decencies, something between a clever vagabond and a disreputable doctor. But not all respectable people
would have had the necessary delicacy of sentiment to understand with what trouble
of mind and accuracy of vision Dr. Monygham, medical officer of the San Tomé mine,
remembered Father Berón, army chaplain, and once a secretary of a military commission. After all these years Dr. Monygham, in his rooms at the end of the hospital
building in the San Tomé gorge, remembered Father Berón as distinctly as ever. He
remembered that priest at night, sometimes, in his sleep. On such nights the doctor
waited for daylight with a candle lighted, and walked the whole length of his rooms to
and fro, staring down at his bare feet, his arms hugging his sides tightly. He would
dream of Father Berón sitting at the end of a long black table, behind which, in a row,
appeared the heads, shoulders, and epaulettes of the military members, nibbling the
feather of a quill pen, and listening with weary and impatient scorn to the protestations of some prisoner calling heaven to witness of his innocence, till he burst out,
"What's the use of wasting time over that miserable nonsense! Let me take him
outside for a while." And Father Berón would go outside after the clanking prisoner,
led away between two soldiers. Such interludes happened on many days, many times,
with many prisoners. When the prisoner returned he was ready to make a full confession, Father Berón would declare, leaning forward with that dull, surfeited look which
can be seen in the eyes of gluttonous persons after a heavy meal.

The priest's inquisitorial instincts suffered but little from the want of classical
apparatus of the Inquisition. At no time of the world's history have men been at a loss
how to inflict mental and bodily anguish upon their fellow-creatures. This aptitude
came to them in the growing complexity of their passions and the early refinement of
their ingenuity. But it may safely be said that primeval man did not go to the trouble
of inventing tortures. He was indolent and pure of heart. He brained his neighbor
ferociously with a stone axe from necessity and without malice. The stupidest mind
may invent a rankling phrase or brand the innocent with a cruel aspersion. A piece of
string and a ramrod; a few muskets in combination with a length of hide rope; or even
a simple mallet of heavy, hard wood applied with a swing to human fingers or to the
joints of a human body is enough for the infliction of the most exquisite torture. The
doctor had been a very stubborn prisoner, and, as a natural consequence of that "bad
disposition" (so Father Berón called it), his subjugation had been very crushing and
very complete. That is why the limp in his walk, the twist of his shoulders, the scars
on his cheeks were so pronounced. His confessions, when they came at last, were very
complete, too. Sometimes on the nights when he walked the floor, he wondered,
grinding his teeth with shame and rage, at the fertility of his imagination when
stimulated by a sort of pain which makes truth, honor, self-respect, and life itself
matters of little moment.

And he could not forget Father Berón with his monotonous phrase, "Will you
confess now?" reaching him in an awful iteration and lucidity of meaning through the
delirious incoherence of unbearable pain. He could not forget. But that was not the
worst. Had he met Father Berón in the street after all these years Dr. Monygham was

sure he would have quailed before him. This contingency was not to be feared now. Father Berón was dead; but the sickening certitude prevented Dr. Monygham from looking anybody in the face.

Dr. Monygham had become, in a manner, the slave of a ghost. It was obviously impossible to take his knowledge of Father Berón home to Europe. When making his extorted confessions to the Military Board, Dr. Monygham was not seeking to avoid death. He longed for it. Sitting half-naked for hours on the wet earth of his prison, and so motionless that the spiders, his companions, attached their webs to his matted hair, he consoled the misery of his soul with acute reasonings that he had confessed to crimes enough for a sentence of death—that they had gone too far with him to let him live to tell the tale.

But, as if by a refinement of cruelty, Dr. Monygham was left for months to decay slowly in the darkness of his grave-like prison. It was no doubt hoped that it would finish him off without the trouble of an execution; but Dr. Monygham had an iron constitution. It was Guzman Bento who died, not by the knife thrust of a conspirator, but from a stroke of apoplexy, and Dr. Monygham was liberated hastily. His fetters were struck off by the light of a candle, which, after months of gloom, hurt his eyes so much that he had to cover his face with his hands. He was raised up. His heart was beating violently with the fear of this liberty. When he tried to walk the extraordinary lightness of his feet made him giddy, and he fell down. Two sticks were thrust into his hands, and he was pushed out of the passage. It was dusk; candles glimmered already in the windows of the officers' quarters round the courtyard; but the twilight sky dazed him by its enormous and overwhelming brilliance. A thin poncho hung over his naked, bony shoulders; the rags of his trousers came down no lower than his knees; an eighteen months' growth of hair fell in dirty gray locks on each side of his sharp cheek-bones. As he dragged himself past the guard-room door, one of the soldiers, lolling outside, moved by some obscure impulse, leaped forward with a strange laugh and rammed a broken old straw hat on his head. And Dr. Monygham, after having tottered, continued on his way. He advanced one stick, then one maimed foot, then the other stick; the other foot followed only a very short distance along the ground, toilfully, as though it were almost too heavy to be moved at all; and yet his legs under the hanging angles of the poncho appeared no thicker than the two sticks in his hands. A ceaseless trembling agitated his bent body, all his wasted limbs, his bony head, the conical ragged crown of the sombrero, whose ample flat rim rested on his shoulders.

In such conditions of manner and attire did Dr. Monygham go forth to take possession of his liberty. And these conditions seemed to bind him indissolubly to the land of Costaguana like an awful procedure of naturalization, involving him deep in the national life, far deeper than any amount of success and honor could have done. They did away with his Europeanism; for Dr. Monygham had made himself an ideal conception of his disgrace. It was a conception eminently fit and proper for an officer and a gentleman. Dr. Monygham, before he went out to Costaguana, had been surgeon in one of Her Majesty's regiments of foot. It was a conception which took no account of physiological facts or reasonable arguments; but it was not stupid for all that. It was simple. A rule of conduct resting mainly on severe rejections is necessarily simple. Dr. Monygham's view of what it behooved him to do was severe; it was an ideal view, in so much that it was the imaginative exaggeration of a correct feeling. It was also, in its force, influence, and persistency, the view of an eminently loyal nature.

There was a great fund of loyalty in Dr. Monygham's nature. He had settled it all on Mrs. Gould's head. He believed her worthy of every devotion. At the bottom of his heart he felt an angry uneasiness before the prosperity of the San Tomé mine, because its growth was robbing her of all peace of mind. Costaguana was no place for a woman of that kind. What could Charles Gould have been thinking of when he brought her out there! It was outrageous! And the doctor had watched the course of events with a grim and distant reserve which, he imagined, his lamentable history imposed upon him.

Loyalty to Mrs. Gould could not, however, leave out of account the safety of her husband. The doctor had contrived to be in town at the critical time because he mistrusted Charles Gould. He considered him hopelessly infected with the madness of revolutions. That is why he hobbled in distress in the drawing-room of the Casa Gould on that morning, exclaiming, "Decoud, Decoud!" in a tone of mournful irritation.

Mrs. Gould, her color heightened, and with glistening eyes, looked straight before her at the sudden enormity of that disaster. The fingertips on one hand rested lightly on a low little table by her side, and the arm trembled right up to the shoulder. The sun, which looks late upon Sulaco, issuing in all the fullness of its power high upon the sky from behind the dazzling snow-edge of Higuerota, had precipitated the delicate, smooth, pearly grayness of light, in which the town lies steeped during the early hours, into sharp-cut masses of black shade and spaces of hot, blinding glare. Three long rectangles of sunshine fell through the windows of the *sala;* while just across the street the front of the Avellanos's house appeared very somber in its own shadow seen through the flood of light.

A voice said at the door, "What of Decoud?"

It was Charles Gould. They had not heard him coming along the corridor. His glance just glided over his wife and struck full at the doctor.

"You have brought some news, doctor?"

Dr. Monygham blurted it all at once, in the rough. For some time after he had done, the Administrator of the San Tomé mine remained looking at him without a word. Mrs. Gould sank into a low chair with her hands lying on her lap. A silence reigned between those three motionless persons. Then Charles Gould spoke:

"You must want some breakfast."

He stood aside to let his wife pass first. She caught up her husband's hand and pressed it as she went out, raising the handkerchief to her eyes. The sight of her husband had brought Antonia's position to her mind, and she could not contain her tears at the thought of the poor girl. When she rejoined the two men in the dining room after having bathed her face, Charles Gould was saying to the doctor across the table:

"No, there does not seem any room for doubt."

And the doctor assented.

"No, I don't see myself how we could question that wretched Hirsch's tale. It's only too true, I fear."

She sat down desolately at the head of the table and looked from one to the other. The two men, without absolutely turning their heads away, tried to avoid her glance. The doctor even made a show of being hungry; he seized his knife and fork, and began to eat with emphasis, as if on the stage. Charles Gould made no pretense of the sort; with his elbows raised squarely, he twisted both ends of his flaming mustaches—they were so long that his hands were quite away from his face.

"I am not surprised," he muttered, abandoning his mustaches and throwing one arm over the back of his chair. His face was calm with that immobility of expression which betrays the intensity of a mental struggle. He felt that this accident had brought to a point all the consequences involved in his line of conduct, with its conscious and subconscious intentions. There must be an end now of this silent reserve, of that air of impenetrability behind which he had been safeguarding his dignity. It was the least ignoble form of dissembling forced upon him by that parody of civilized institutions which offended his intelligence, his uprightness, and his sense of right. He was like his father. He had no ironic eye. He was not amused at the absurdities that prevail in this world. They hurt him in his innate gravity. He felt that the miserable death of that poor Decoud took from him his inaccessible position of a force in the background. It committed him openly unless he wished to throw up the game—and that was impossible. The material interests required from him the sacrifice of his aloofness—perhaps his own safety too. And he reflected that Decoud's separationist plan had not gone to the bottom with the lost silver.

The only thing that was not changed was his position towards Mr. Holroyd. The head of silver and steel interests had entered into Costaguana affairs with a sort of passion. Costaguana had become necessary to his existence; in the San Tomé mine he had found the imaginative satisfaction which other minds would get from drama, from art, or from a risky and fascinating sport. It was a special form of the great man's extravagance, sanctioned by a moral intention, big enough to flatter his vanity. Even in this aberration of his genius he served the progress of the world. Charles Gould felt sure of being understood with precision and judged with the indulgence of their common passion. Nothing now could surprise or startle this great man. And Charles Gould imagined himself writing a letter to San Francisco in some such words: ". . . The men at the head of the movement are dead or have fled; the civil organization of the province is at an end for the present; the Blanco party in Sulaco has collapsed inexcusably, but in the characteristic manner of this country. But Barrios, untouched in Cayta, remains still available. I am forced to take up openly the plan of a provincial revolution as the only way of placing the enormous material interests involved in the prosperity and peace of Sulaco in a position of permanent safety. . . ." That was clear. He saw these words as if written in letters of fire upon the wall at which he was gazing abstractedly.

Mrs. Gould watched his abstraction with dread. It was a domestic and frightful phenomenon that darkened and chilled the house for her like a thunder-cloud passing over the sun. Charles Gould's fits of abstraction depicted the energetic concentration of a will haunted by a fixed idea. A man haunted by a fixed idea is insane. He is dangerous even if that idea is an idea of justice; for may he not bring the heaven down pitilessly upon a loved head? The eyes of Mrs. Gould, watching her husband's profile, filled with tears again. And again she seemed to see the despair of the unfortunate Antonia.

"What would I have done if Charley had been drowned while we were engaged?" she exclaimed, mentally, with horror. Her heart turned to ice, while her cheeks flamed up as if scorched by the blaze of a funeral pyre consuming all her earthly affections. The tears burst out of her eyes.

"Antonia will kill herself!" she cried out.

This cry fell into the silence of the room with strangely little effect. Only the doctor, crumbling up a piece of bread, with his head inclined on one side, raised his face, and the few long hairs sticking out of his shaggy eyebrows stirred in a slight frown. Dr. Monygham thought quite sincerely that Decoud was a singularly unworthy object for any woman's affection. Then he lowered his head again, with a curl of his lip, and his heart full of tender admiration for Mrs. Gould.

"She thinks of that girl," he said to himself; "she thinks of the Viola children; she thinks of me; of the wounded; of the miners; she always thinks of everybody who is poor and miserable! But what will she do if Charles gets the worst of it in this infernal scrimmage those confounded Avellanos have drawn him into? No one seems to be thinking of her."

Charles Gould, staring at the wall, pursued his reflections subtly.

"I shall write to Holroyd that the San Tomé mine is big enough to take in hand the making of a new State. It'll please him. It'll reconcile him to the risk."

But was Barrios really available? Perhaps. But he was inaccessible. To send off a boat to Cayta was no longer possible, since Sotillo was master of the harbor, and had a steamer at his disposal. And now, with all the democrats in the province up, and every Campo township in a state of disturbance, where could he find a man who would make his way successfully overland to Cayta with a message, a ten days' ride at least; a man of courage and resolution, who would avoid arrest or murder, and if arrested would faithfully eat the paper? The Capataz de Cargadores would have been just such a man. But the Capataz of the Cargadores was no more.

And Charles Gould, withdrawing his eyes from the wall, said gently, "That Hirsch! What an extraordinary thing! Saved himself by clinging to the anchor, did he? I had no idea that he was still in Sulaco. I thought he had gone back overland to Esmeralda more than a week ago. He came here once to talk to me about his hide business and some other things. I made it clear to him that nothing could be done."

"He was afraid to start back on account of Hernandez being about," remarked the doctor.

"And but for him we might not have known anything of what has happened," marveled Charles Gould.

Mrs. Gould cried out:

"Antonia must not know! She must not be told. Not now."

"Nobody's likely to carry the news," remarked the doctor. "It's no one's interest. Moreover, the people here are afraid of Hernandez as if he were the devil." He turned to Charles Gould. "It's even awkward, because if you wanted to communicate with the refugees you could find no messenger. When Hernandez was ranging hundreds of miles away from here the Sulaco populace used to shudder at the tales of him roasting his prisoners alive."

"Yes," murmured Charles Gould; "Captain Mitchell's Capataz was the only man in the town who had seen Hernandez eye to eye. Father Corbelán employed him. He opened the communications first. It is a pity that—"

His voice was covered by the booming of the great bell of the cathedral. Three single strokes, one after another, burst out explosively, dying away in deep and mellow vibrations. And then all the bells in the tower of every church, convent, or chapel in town, even those that had remained shut up for years, pealed out together with a crash. In this furious flood of metallic uproar there was a power of suggesting images of strife and violence which blanched Mrs. Gould's cheek. Basilio, who had been waiting at table, shrinking within himself, clung to the sideboard with chattering teeth. It was impossible to hear yourself speak.

"Shut these windows!" Charles Gould yelled at him, angrily. All the other servants, terrified at what they took for the signal of a general massacre, had rushed upstairs, tumbling over each other, men and women, the obscure and generally invisible population of the ground floor on the four sides of the patio. The women, screaming *"Misericordia!"* ran right into the room, and, falling on their knees against the walls, began to cross themselves convulsively. The staring heads of men blocked the doorway in an instant—*mozos* from the stable, gardeners, nondescript helpers living on the crumbs of the munificent house—and Charles Gould beheld all the extent of his domestic establishment, even to the gatekeeper. This was a half-paralyzed old man, whose long white locks fell down to his shoulders: an heirloom taken up by Charles Gould's familial piety. He could remember Henry Gould, an Englishman and a Costaguanero of the second generation, chief of the Sulaco province; he had been his personal *mozo* years and years ago in peace and war; had been allowed to attend his master in prison; had, on the fatal morning, followed the firing-squad; and, peeping from behind one of the cypresses growing along the wall of the Franciscan Convent, had seen, with his eyes starting out of his head, Don Enrique throw up his hands and fall with his face in the dust. Charles Gould noted particularly the big patriarchal head of that witness in the rear of the other servants. But he was surprised to see a shriveled old hag or two, of whose existence within the walls of his house he had not been aware. They must have been the mothers, or even the grandmothers, of some of his people. There were a few children, too, more or less naked, crying and clinging to the legs of their elders. He had never before noticed any sign of a child in his patio. Even

Leonarda, the *camerista*, came in a fright, pushing through, with her spoiled, pouting face of a favorite maid, leading the Viola girls by the hand. The crockery rattled on table and sideboard, and the whole house seemed to sway in the deafening wave of sound.

V

During the night the expectant populace had taken possession of all the belfries in the town in order to welcome Pedrito Montero, who was making his entry after having slept the night in Rincón. And first came straggling in through the land gate the armed mob of all colors, complexions, types, and states of raggedness, calling themselves the Sulaco National Guard, and commanded by Señor Gamacho. Through the middle of the street streamed, like a torrent of rubbish, a mass of straw hats, ponchos, gun-barrels, with an enormous green and yellow flag flapping in their midst, in a cloud of dust, to the furious beating of drums. The spectators recoiled against the walls of the houses shouting their *"Vivas!"* Behind the rabble could be seen the lances of the cavalry, the "army" of Pedro Montero. He advanced between Señores Fuentes and Gamacho at the head of his *llaneros*, who had accomplished the feat of crossing the *páramos* of the Higuerota in a snow-storm. They rode four abreast, mounted on confiscated Campo horses, clad in the heterogeneous stock of roadside stores they had looted hurriedly in their rapid ride through the northern part of the province; for Pedro Montero had been in a great hurry to occupy Sulaco. The handkerchiefs knotted loosely around their bare throats were glaringly new, and all the right sleeves of their cotton shirts had been cut off close to the shoulder for greater freedom in throwing the *lazo*. Emaciated gray-beards rode by the side of lean dark youths, marked by all the hardships of campaigning, with strips of raw beef twined round the crowns of their hats, and huge iron spurs fastened to their naked heels. Those that in the passes of the mountain had lost their lances had provided themselves with the goads used by the Campo cattlemen: slender shafts of palm fully ten feet long, with a lot of loose rings jingling under the ironshod point. They were armed with knives and revolvers. A haggard fearlessness characterized the expression of all these sun-blacked countenances; they glared down haughtily with their scorched eyes at the crowd, or, blinking upwards insolently, pointed out to each other some particular head amongst the women at the windows. When they had ridden into the Plaza and caught sight of the equestrian statue of the King dazzlingly white in the sunshine, towering enormous and motionless above the surges of the crowd, with its eternal gesture of saluting, a murmur of surprise ran through their ranks. "What is that saint in the big hat?" they asked each other.

They were a good sample of the cavalry of the plains with which Pedro Montero had helped so much the victorious career of his brother the general. The influence which that man, brought up in coast towns, acquired in a short time over the plainsmen of the Republic can be ascribed only to a genius for treachery of so effective a kind that it must have appeared to those violent men but little removed from a state of utter savagery, as the perfection of sagacity and virtue. The popular lore of all nations testified that duplicity and cunning, together with bodily strength, were looked upon, even more than courage, as heroic virtues by primitive mankind. To overcome your adversary was the great affair of life. Courage was taken for granted. But the use of intelligence awakened wonder and respect. Stratagems, providing they did not fail, were honorable; the easy massacre of an unsuspecting enemy evoked no feelings but those of gladness, pride, and admiration. Not perhaps that primitive men were more faithless than their descendants of today, but that they went straighter to their aim, and were more artless in their recognition of success as the only standard of morality.

We have changed since. The use of intelligence awakens little wonder and less respect. But the ignorant and barbarous plainsmen engaging in civil strife followed willingly a leader who often managed to deliver their enemies bound, as it were, into their hands. Pedro Montero had a talent for lulling his adversaries into a sense of security. And as men learn wisdom with extreme slowness, and are always ready to believe promises that flatter their secret hopes, Pedro Montero was successful time after time. Whether only a servant or some inferior official in the Costaguana Legation in Paris, he had rushed back to his country directly he heard that his brother had emerged from the obscurity of his frontier *comandancia*. He had managed to deceive by his gift of plausibility the chiefs of the Ribierist movement in his capital, and even the acute agent of the San Tomé mine had failed to understand him thoroughly. At once he had obtained an enormous influence over his brother. They were very much alike in appearance, both bald, with bunches of crisp hair above their ears, arguing the presence of some Negro blood. Only Pedro was smaller than the general, more delicate altogether, with an ape-like faculty for imitating all the outward signs of refinement and distinction, and with a parrot-like talent for languages. Both brothers had received some elementary instruction by the munificence of a great European traveler, to whom their father had been a body-servant during his journeys in the interior of the country. In General Montero's case it enabled him to rise from the ranks. Pedrito, the younger, incorrigibly lazy and slovenly, had drifted aimlessly from one coast town to another, hanging about counting-houses, attaching himself to strangers as a sort of *valet de place*, picking up an easy and disreputable living. His ability to read did nothing for him but fill his head with absurd visions. His actions were usually determined by motives so improbable in themselves as to escape the penetration of a rational person.

Thus at first sight the agent of the Gould Concession in Sta Marta had credited him with the possession of sane views, and even with a restraining power over the general's everlastingly discontented vanity. It could never have entered his head that Pedrito Montero, lackey or inferior scribe, lodged in the garrets of the various Parisian hotels where the Costaguana Legation used to shelter its diplomatic dignity, had been devouring the lighter sort of historical works in the French language, such, for instance, as the books of Imbert de Saint Amand upon the Second Empire. But Pedrito had been struck by the splendor of a brilliant court, and had conceived the idea of an existence for himself where, like the Duc de Morny, he would associate the command of every pleasure with the conduct of political affairs and enjoy power supremely in every way. Nobody could have guessed that. And yet this was one of the immediate causes of the Monterist Revolution. This will appear less incredible by the reflection that the fundamental causes were the same as ever, rooted in the political immaturity of the people, in the indolence of the upper classes and the mental darkness of the lower.

Pedrito Montero saw in the elevation of his brother the road wide open to his wildest imaginings. This was what made the Monterist *pronunciamiento* so unpreventable. The general himself probably could have been bought off, pacified with flatteries, dispatched on a diplomatic mission to Europe. It was his brother who had egged him on from first to last. He wanted to become the most brilliant statesman of South America. He did not desire supreme power. He would have been afraid of its labor and risk, in fact. Before all, Pedrito Montero, taught by his European experience, meant to acquire a serious fortune for himself. With this object in view he obtained from his brother, on the very morrow of the successful battle, the permission to push on over the mountains and take possession of Sulaco. Sulaco was the land of future prosperity, the chosen land of material progress, the only province in the Republic of interest to European capitalists. Pedrito Montero, following the example of the Duc de Morny, meant to have his share of this prosperity. This is what he meant literally. Now his brother was master of the country, whether as president, dictator, or even as Emperor —why not as an Emperor?—he meant to demand a share in every enterprise—in railways, in mines, in sugar estates, in cotton mills, in land companies, in each and every undertaking—as the price of his protection. The desire to be on the spot early was the real cause of the celebrated ride over the mountains with some two hundred *llaneros*, an enterprise of which the dangers had not appeared at first clearly to his impatience. Coming from a series of victories, it seemed to him that a Montero had only to appear to be master of the situation. This illusion had betrayed him into a rashness of which he was becoming aware. As he rode at the head of his *llaneros* he regretted that there were so few of them. The enthusiasm of the populace reassured him. They yelled *"Viva Montero! Viva Pedrito!"* In order to make them still more enthusiastic, and from the natural pleasure he had in dissembling, he dropped the reins on his horse's neck, and with a tremendous effect of familiarity and confidence slipped his hands under the arms of Señores Fuentes and Gamacho. In that posture, with a ragged town *mozo* holding his horse by the bridle, he rode triumphantly across the Plaza to the door of the Intendencia. Its old gloomy walls seemed to shake in the acclamations that rent the air and covered the crashing peals of the cathedral bells.

Pedro Montero, the brother of the general, dismounted into a shouting and perspiring throng of enthusiasts whom the ragged Nationals were pushing back fiercely. Ascending a few steps he surveyed the large crowd gaping at him and the bullet-speckled walls of the houses opposite lightly veiled by a sunny haze of dust. The word "PORVENIR" in immense black capitals, alternating with broken windows, stared at him across the vast space; and he thought with delight of the hour of vengeance, because he was very sure of laying his hands upon Decoud. On his left hand, Gamacho, big and hot, wiping his hairy wet face, uncovered a set of yellow fangs in a grin of stupid hilarity. On his right, Señor Fuentes, small and lean, looked on with compressed lips.

The crowd stared literally open-mouthed, lost in eager stillness, as though they had expected the great *guerrillero*, the famous Pedrito, to begin scattering at once some sort of visible largesse. What he began was a speech. He began it with the shouted word "Citizens!" which reached even those in the middle of the Plaza. Afterwards the greater part of the citizens remained fascinated by the orator's action alone, his tip-toeing, the arms flung above his head with the fists clenched, a hand laid flat upon the heart, the silver gleam of rolling eyes, the sweeping, pointing, embracing gestures, a hand laid familiarly on Gamacho's shoulder; a hand waved formally towards the little black-coated person of Señor Fuentes, advocate and politician and a true friend of the people. The *"Vivas!"* of those nearest to the orator bursting out suddenly propagated themselves irregularly to the confines of the crowd, like flames running over dry grass, and expired in the opening of the streets. In the intervals, over the swarming Plaza brooded a heavy silence, in which the mouth of the orator went on opening and shutting, and detached phrases—"The happiness of the people," "Sons of the country," "The entire world, *el mundo entiero*"—reached even the packed steps of the cathedral with a feeble clear ring, thin as the buzzing of a mosquito. But the orator struck his breast; he seemed to prance between his two supporters. It was the supreme effort of his peroration. Then the two smaller figures disappeared from the public gaze and the enormous Gamacho, left alone, advanced, raising his hat high above his head. Then he covered himself proudly and yelled out, *"Ciudadanos!"* A dull roar greeted Señor Gamacho, ex-pedlar of the Campo, Comandante of the National Guard.

Upstairs Pedrito Montero walked about rapidly from one wrecked room of the Intendencia to another, snarling incessantly:

"What stupidity! What destruction!"

Señor Fuentes, following, would relax his taciturn disposition to murmur:

"It is all the work of Gamacho and his Nationals"; and then, inclining his head on his left shoulder, would press together his lips so firmly that a little hollow would appear at each corner. He had his nomination for Political Chief of the town in his pocket, and was all impatience to enter upon his functions.

In the long audience-room, with its tall mirrors all starred by stones, the hangings torn down, and the canopy over the platform at the upper end pulled to pieces, the vast, deep muttering of the crowd and the howling voice of Gamacho speaking just below reached them through the shutters as they stood idly in dimness and desolation.

"The brute!" observed his Excellency Don Pedro Montero through clenched teeth. "We must contrive as quickly as possible to send him and his Nationals out there to fight Hernandez."

The new Jefe Político only jerked his head sideways, and took a puff at his cigarette in sign of his agreement with this method for ridding the town of Gamacho and his inconvenient rabble.

Pedrito Montero looked with disgust at the absolutely bare floor, and at the belt of heavy gilt picture-frames running round the room, out of which the remnants of torn and slashed canvases fluttered like dingy rags.

"We are not barbarians," he said.

This was what said his Excellency, the popular Pedrito, the *guerrillero* skilled in the art of laying ambushes, charged by his brother at his own demand with the organization of Sulaco on democratic principles. The night before, during the consultation with his partisans, who had come out to meet him in Rincón, he had opened his intentions to Señor Fuentes:

"We shall organize a popular vote, by yes or no, confiding the destinies of our beloved country to the wisdom and valiance of my heroic brother, the invincible general. A plebiscite. Do you understand?"

And Señor Fuentes, puffing out his leathery cheeks, had inclined his head slightly to the left, letting a thin, bluish jet of smoke escape through his pursed lips. He had understood.

His Excellency was exasperated at the devastation. Not a single chair, table, sofa, *étagère*, or console had been left in the state rooms of the Intendencia. His Excellency, though twitching all over with rage, was restrained from bursting into violence by a sense of his remoteness and isolation. His heroic brother was very far away. Meantime, how was he going to take his siesta? He had expected to find comfort and luxury in the Intendencia after a year of hard camp life, ending with the hardships and privations of the daring dash upon Sulaco—upon the province which was worth more in wealth and influence than all the rest of the Republic's territory. He would get even with Gamacho by-and-by. And Señor Gamacho's oration, delectable to popular ears, went on in the heat and glare of the Plaza like the uncouth howlings of an inferior sort of devil cast into a white-hot furnace. Every moment he had to wipe his streaming face with his bare forearm; he had flung off his coat, and had turned up the sleeves of his shirt high above the elbows; but he kept on his head the large cocked hat with white plumes. His ingenuousness cherished this sign of his rank as Comandante of the National Guard. Approving and grave murmurs greeted his periods. His opinion was that war should be declared at once against France, England, Germany, and the United States, who, by introducing railways, mining enterprises, colonization, and under such other shallow pretenses, aimed at robbing poor people of their lands, and with the help of these Goths and paralytics, the aristocrats would convert them into toiling and miserable slaves. And the *leperos,* flinging about the corners of their dirty white mantas, yelled their approbation. General Montero, Gamacho howled with conviction, was the only man equal to the patriotic task. They assented to that, too.

The morning was wearing on; there were already signs of disruption, currents and eddies in the crowd. Some were seeking the shade of the walls and under the trees of the Alameda. Horsemen spurred through, shouting; groups of sombreros set level on heads against the vertical sun were drifting away into the streets, where the open doors of *pulperías* revealed an enticing gloom resounding with the gentle tinkling of guitars. The National Guards were thinking of siesta, and the eloquence of Gamacho, their chief, was exhausted. Later on, when, in the cooler hours of the afternoon, they tried to assemble again for further consideration of public affairs, detachments of Montero's cavalry camped on the Alameda charged them without parley, at speed, with long lances leveled at their flying backs as far as the ends of the streets. The National

Guards of Sulaco were surprised by this proceeding. But they were not indignant. No Costaguanero had ever learned to question the eccentricities of a military force. They were part of the natural order of things. This must be, they concluded, some kind of administrative measure, no doubt. But the motive of it escaped their unaided intelligence, and their chief and orator, Gamacho, Comandante of the National Guard, was lying drunk and asleep in the bosom of his family. His bare feet were upturned in the shadows repulsively, in the manner of a corpse. His eloquent mouth had dropped open. His youngest daughter, scratching her head with one hand, with the other waved a green bough over his scorched and peeling face.

V I

The declining sun had shifted the shadows from west to east amongst the houses of the town. It had shifted them upon the whole extent of the immense Campo, with the white walls of its *haciendas* on the knolls dominating the green distances; with its grass-thatched *ranchos* crouching in the folds of ground by the banks of streams; with the dark islands of clustered trees on a clear sea of grass, and the precipitous range of the Cordillera, immense and motionless, emerging from the billows of the lower forests like the barren coast of a land of giants. The sunset rays striking the snow-slope of Higuerota from afar gave it an air of rosy youth, while the serrated mass of distant peaks remained black, as if calcined in the fiery radiance. The undulating surface of the forests seemed powdered with pale gold dust; and away there, beyond Rincón, hidden from the town by two wooded spurs, the rocks of the San Tomé gorge, with the flat wall of the mountain itself crowned by gigantic ferns, took on warm tones of brown and yellow, with red rusty streaks, and the dark green clumps of bushes rooted in crevices. From the plain the stamp sheds and the houses of the mine appeared dark and small, high up, like the nests of birds clustered on the ledges of a cliff. The zigzag paths resembled faint tracings scratched on the wall of a cyclopean blockhouse. To the two *serenos* of the mine on patrol duty, strolling, carbine in hand, and watchful eyes, in the shade of the trees lining the stream near the bridge, Don Pepe, descending the path from the upper plateau, appeared no bigger than a large beetle.

With his air of aimless, insect-like going to and fro upon the face of the rock, Don Pepe's figure kept on descending steadily, and, when near the bottom, sank at last behind the roofs of storehouses, forges, and workshops. For a time the pair of *serenos* strolled back and forth before the bridge, on which they had stopped a horseman holding a large white envelope in his hand. Then Don Pepe, emerging in the village street from amongst the houses, not a stone's throw from the frontier bridge, approached, striding in wide dark trousers tucked into boots, a white linen jacket, saber at his side, and revolver at his belt. In this disturbed time nothing could find the Señor Gobernador with his boots off, as the saying is.

At a slight nod from one of the *serenos,* the man, a messenger from the town, dismounted, and crossed the bridge, leading his horse by the bridle.

Don Pepe received the letter from his other hand, slapped his left side and his hips in succession, feeling for his spectacle case. After settling the heavy silver-mounted affair astride his nose, and adjusting it carefully behind his ears, he opened the envelope, holding it up at about a foot in front of his eyes. The paper he pulled out contained some three lines of writing. He looked at them for a long time. His gray moustache moved slightly up and down, and the wrinkles, radiating at the corners of his eyes, ran together. He nodded serenely. *"Bueno,"* he said. "There is no answer."

Then, in his quiet, kindly way, he engaged in a cautious conversation with the man, who was willing to talk cheerily, as if something lucky had happened to him recently. He had seen from a distance Sotillo's infantry camped along the shore of the harbor on each side of the Custom House. They had done no damage to the buildings. The foreigners of the railway remained shut up within the yards. They were no longer anxious to shoot poor people. He cursed the foreigners; then he reported Montero's entry and the rumors of the town. The poor were going to be made rich now. That was very good. More he did not know, and, breaking into propitiatory smiles, he intimated that he was hungry and thirsty. The old major directed him to go to the *alcalde* of the first village. The man rode off, and Don Pepe, striding slowly in the direction of a little wooden belfry, looked over a hedge into a little garden, and saw Father Román sitting in a white hammock slung between two orange trees in front of the presbytery.

An enormous tamarind shaded with its dark foliage the whole white frame-house. A young Indian girl with long hair, big eyes, and small hands and feet, carried out a wooden chair, while a thin old woman, crabbed and vigilant, watched her all the time from the veranda.

Don Pepe sat down in the chair and lighted a cigar; the priest drew in an immense quantity of snuff out of the hollow of his palm. On his reddish-brown face, worn, hollowed as if crumbled, the eyes, fresh and candid, sparkled like two black diamonds.

Don Pepe, in a mild and humorous voice informed Father Román that Pedrito Montero, by the hand of Señor Fuentes, had asked him on what terms he would surrender the mine in proper working order to a legally constituted commission of patriotic citizens, escorted by a small military force. The priest cast his eyes up to heaven. However, Don Pepe continued, the *mozo* who brought the letter said that Don Carlos Gould was alive, and so far unmolested.

Father Román expressed in a few words his thankfulness at hearing of the Señor Administrador's safety.

The hour of oration had gone by in silvery ringing of a bell in the little belfry. The belt of forest closing the entrance of the valley stood like a screen between the low sun and the street of the village. At the other end of the rocky gorge, between the walls of basalt and granite, a forest-clad mountain, hiding all the range from the San Tomé dwellers, rose steeply, lighted up and leafy to the very top. Three small rosy clouds hung motionless overhead in the great depth of blue. Knots of people sat in the street between the wattled huts. Before the *casa* of the *alcalde*, the foremen of the night-shift, already assembled to lead their men, squatted on the ground in a circle of leather skull-caps, and, bowing their bronze backs, were passing round the gourd of maté. The *mozo* from the town, having fastened his horse to a wooden post before the door, was telling them the news of Sulaco as the blackened gourd of the decoction passed from hand to hand. The grave *alcalde* himself, in a white waist-cloth and a flowered chintz gown with sleeves, open wide upon his naked stout person with an effect of a gaudy bathing robe, stood by, wearing a rough beaver hat at the back of his head, and grasping a tall staff with a silver knob in his hand. These insignia of his dignity had been conferred upon him by the Administration of the mine, the fountain of honor, of prosperity, and peace. He had been one of the first immigrants into this valley; his sons and sons-in-law worked within the mountain which seemed with its treasures to pour down the thundering ore shoots of the upper *mesa*, the gifts of well-being, security, and justice upon the toilers. He listened to the news from the town with curiosity and indifference, as if concerning another world than his own. And it was true that they appeared to him so. In a very few years the sense of belonging to a powerful organization had been developed in these harassed, half-wild Indians. They were proud of, and attached to, the mine. It had secured their confidence and belief. They invested it with a protecting and invincible virtue as though it were a fetish made by their own hands, for they were ignorant, and in other respects did not differ appreciably from the rest of mankind which puts infinite trust in its own creations. It never entered the *alcalde*'s head that the mine could fail in its protection and force. Politics were good enough for the people of the town and the Campo. His yellow, round face, with wide nostrils, and motionless in expression, resembled a fierce full moon. He listened to the excited vaporings of the *mozo* without misgivings, without surprise, without any active sentiment whatever.

Padre Román sat dejectedly balancing himself, his feet just touching the ground, his hands gripping the edge of the hammock. With less confidence, but as ignorant as his flock, he asked the major what did he think was going to happen now.

Don Pepe, bolt upright in the chair, folded his hands peacefully on the hilt of his sword, standing perpendicular between his thighs, and answered that he did not know. The mine could be defended against any force likely to be sent to take possession. On the other hand, from the arid character of the valley, when the regular supplies from the Campo had been cut off, the population of the three villages could be starved into submission. Don Pepe exposed these contingencies with serenity to Father Román, who, as an old campaigner, was able to understand the reasoning of a military man. They talked with simplicity and directness. Father Román was saddened at the idea of his flock being scattered or else enslaved. He had no illusions as to their fate, not from penetration, but from long experience of political atrocities, which seemed to him fatal and unavoidable in the life of a State. The working of the usual public institutions presented itself to him most distinctly as a series of calamities overtaking private individuals and flowing logically from each other through hate, revenge, folly, and rapacity, as though they had been part of a divine dispensation. Father Román's clearsightedness was served by an uninformed intelligence; but his heart, preserving its tenderness amongst scenes of carnage, spoliation, and violence, abhorred these calamities the more as his association with the victims was closer. He entertained towards the Indians of the valley feelings of paternal scorn. He had been marrying, baptizing, confessing, absolving, and burying the workers of the San Tomé mine with dignity and unction for five years or more; and he believed in the sacredness of these ministrations, which made them his own in a spiritual sense. They were dear to his sacerdotal supremacy. Mrs. Gould's earnest interest in the concerns of these people enhanced their importance in the priest's eyes, because it really augmented his own. When talking over with her the innumerable Marias and Brigidas of the villages, he felt his own humanity expand. Padre Román was incapable of fanaticism to an almost reprehensible degree. The English *señora* was evidently a heretic; but at the same time she seemed to him wonderful and angelic. Whenever that confused state of his feelings occurred to him, while strolling, for instance, his breviary under his arm, in the wide shade of the tamarind, he would stop short to inhale with a strong snuffling noise a large quantity of snuff, and shake his head profoundly. At the thought of what might befall the illustrious *señora* presently, he became gradually overcome with dismay. He voiced it in an agitated murmur. Even Don Pepe lost his serenity for a moment. He leaned forward stiffly.

"Listen, Padre. The very fact that those thieving *macaques* in Sulaco are trying to find out the price of my honor proves that Señor Don Carlos and all in the Casa Gould are safe. As to my honor, that also is safe, as every man, woman, and child knows. But the Negro liberals who have snatched the town by surprise do not know that. *Bueno.* Let them sit and wait. While they wait they can do no harm."

And he regained his composure. He regained it easily, because whatever happened his honor of an old officer of Paez was safe. He had promised Charles Gould that at the approach of an armed force he would defend the gorge just long enough to give himself time to destroy scientifically the whole plant, buildings, and workshops of the mine with heavy charges of dynamite; block with ruins the main tunnel, break down the pathways, blow up the dam of the water-power, shatter the famous Gould Concession into fragments, flying sky-high out of a horrified world. The mine had got hold of Charles Gould with a grip as deadly as ever it had laid upon his father. But this extreme resolution had seemed to Don Pepe the most natural thing in the world. His measures had been taken with judgment. Everything was prepared with a careful completeness. And Don Pepe folded his hands pacifically on his sword hilt, and nodded at the priest. In his excitement, Father Román had flung snuff in handfuls at his face, and, all besmeared with tobacco, round-eyed, and beside himself, had got out of the hammock to walk about, uttering exclamations.

Don Pepe stroked his gray and pendant moustache, whose fine ends hung far below the clean-cut line of his jaw, and spoke with conscious pride in his reputation.

"So, Padre, I don't know what will happen. But I know that as long as I am here Don Carlos can speak to that *macaque*, Pedrito Montero, and threaten the destruction of the mine with perfect assurance that he will be taken seriously. For people know me."

He began to turn the cigar in his lips a little nervously, and went on:

"But that is talk—good for the *políticos.* I am a military man. I do not know what may happen. But I know what ought to be done—the mine should march upon the town with guns, axes, knives tied up to sticks—*por Dios.* That is what should be done. Only—

His folded hands twitched on the hilt. The cigar turned faster in the corner of his lips.

"And who should lead but I? Unfortunately—observe—I have given my word of honor to Don Carlos not to let the mine fall into the hands of these thieves. In war— you know this, Padre—the fate of battles is uncertain, and whom could I leave here to act for me in case of defeat? The explosives are ready. But it would require a man of high honor, of intelligence, of judgment, of courage, to carry out the prepared destruc- tion. Somebody I can trust with my honor as I can trust myself. Another officer of Paez, for instance. Or—or—perhaps one of Paez's old chaplains would do."

He got up, long, lank, upright, hard, with his martial moustache and the bony structure of his face, from which the glance of the sunken eyes seemed to transfix the priest, who stood still, an empty wooden snuff-box held upside down in his hand, and glared back, speechless, at the governor of the mine.

VII

At about that time, in the Intendencia of Sulaco, Charles Gould was assuring Pedrito Montero, who had sent a request for his presence there, that he would never let the mine pass out of his hands for the profit of a Government who had robbed him of it. The Gould Concession could not be resumed. His father had not desired it. The son would never surrender it. He would never surrender it alive. And once dead, where was the power capable of resuscitating such an enterprise in all its vigor and wealth out of the ashes and ruin of destruction? There was no such power in the country. And where was the skill and capital abroad that would condescend to touch such an ill-omened corpse? Charles Gould talked in the impassive tone which had for many years served to conceal his anger and contempt. He suffered. He was disgusted with what he had to say. It was too much like heroics. In him the strictly practical instinct was in profound discord with the almost mystic view he took of his right. The Gould Concession was symbolic of abstract justice. Let the heavens fall. But since the San Tomé mine had developed its world-wide fame his threat had enough force and effectiveness to reach the rudimentary intelligence of Pedro Montero, wrapped up as it was in the futilities of historical anecdotes. The Gould Concession was a serious asset in the country's finance, and, what was more, in the private budgets of many officials as well. It was traditional. It was known. It was said. It was credible. Every Minister of Interior drew a salary from the San Tomé mine. It was natural. And Pedrito intended to be Minister of the Interior and President of the Council in his brother's Government. The Duc de Morny had occupied those high posts during the Second French Empire with conspic- uous advantage to himself.

A table, a chair, a wooden bedstead had been procured for His Excellency, who, after a short siesta, rendered absolutely necessary by the labors and the pomps of his entry into Sulaco, had been getting hold of the administrative machine by making appointments, giving orders, and signing proclamations. Alone with Charles Gould in the audience room, His Excellency managed with his well-known skill to conceal his annoyance and consternation. He had begun at first to talk loftily of confiscation, but the want of all proper feeling and mobility in the Señor Administrador's features ended by affecting adversely his power of masterful expression. Charles Gould had repeated: "The Government can certainly bring about the destruction of the San Tomé mine if it likes; but without me it can do nothing else." It was an alarming pronouncement, and well calculated to hurt the sensibilities of a politician whose mind is bent upon the spoils of victory. And Charles Gould said also that the destruction of the San Tomé mine would cause the ruin of other undertakings, the withdrawal of European capital, the withholding, most probably, of the last install- ment of the foreign loan. That stony fiend of a man said all these things (which were accessible to His Excellency's intelligence) in a cold-blooded manner which made one shudder.

A long course of reading historical works, light and gossipy in tone, carried out in garrets of Parisian hotels, sprawling on an untidy bed, to the neglect of his duties, menial or otherwise, had affected the manners of Pedro Montero. Had he seen around him the splendor of the old Intendencia, the magnificent hangings, the gilt furniture ranged along the walls; had he stood upon a daïs on a noble square of red carpet, he would have probably been very dangerous from a sense of success and elevation. But in this sacked and devastated residence, with the three pieces of common furniture huddled up in the middle of the vast apartment, Pedrito's imagination was subdued by a feeling of insecurity and impermanence. That feeling and the firm attitude of Charles Gould who had not once, so far, pronounced the word "Excellency," dimin- ished him in his own eyes. He assumed the tone of an enlightened man of the world, and begged Charles Gould to dismiss from his mind every cause for alarm. He was now conversing, he reminded him, with the brother of the master of the country, charged with a reorganizing mission. The trusted brother of the master of the country, he repeated. Nothing was farther from the thoughts of that wise and patriotic hero than ideas of destruction. "I entreat you, Don Carlos, not to give way to your anti- democratic prejudices," he cried, in a burst of condescending effusion.

Pedrito Montero surprised one at first sight by the vast development of his bald forehead, a shiny yellow expanse between the crinkly coal-black tufts of hair without any luster, the engaging form of his mouth, and an unexpectedly cultivated voice. But his eyes, very glistening as if freshly painted on each side of his hooked nose, had a round, hopeless, birdlike stare when opened fully. Now, however, he narrowed them agreeably, throwing his square chin up and speaking with closed teeth slightly through the nose, with what he imagined to be the manner of a *grand seigneur*.

In that attitude, he declared suddenly that the highest expression of democracy was Caesarism: the imperial rule based upon the direct popular vote. Caesarism was con- servative. It was strong. It recognized the legitimate needs of democracy which requires orders, titles, and distinctions. They would be showered upon deserving men. Caesar- ism was peace. It was progressive. It secured the prosperity of a country. Pedrito Montero was carried away. Look at what the Second Empire had done in France. It was a régime which delighted to honor men of Don Carlos's stamp. The Second Empire fell, but that was because its chief was devoid of that military genius which had raised General Montero to the pinnacle of fame and glory. Pedrito elevated his hand jerkily to help the idea of pinnacle, of fame. "We shall have many talks yet. We shall understand each other thoroughly, Don Carlos!" he cried in a tone of fellowship. Republicanism had done its work. Imperial democracy was the power of the future. Pedrito, the *guerrillero*, showing his hand, lowered his voice forcibly. A man singled out by his fellow-citizens for the honorable nickname of El Rey de Sulaco could not but receive a full recognition from an imperial democracy as a great captain of industry and a person of weighty counsel, whose popular designation would be soon replaced by a more solid title. "Eh, Don Carlos? No! What do you say? Conde de Sulaco—Eh? —or marquis . . ."

He ceased. The air was cool on the Plaza, where a patrol of cavalry rode round and round without penetrating into the streets, which resounded with shouts and the strumming of guitars issuing from the open doors of *pulperías*. The orders were not to interfere with the enjoyments of the people. And above the roofs, next to the perpendicular lines of the cathedral towers, the snowy curve of Higuerota blocked a large space of darkening blue sky before the windows of the Intendencia. After a time Pedrito Montero, thrusting his hand in the bosom of his coat, bowed his head with slow dignity. The audience was over.

Charles Gould on going out passed his hand over his forehead as if to disperse the mists of an oppressive dream, whose grotesque extravagance leaves behind a subtle sense of bodily danger and intellectual decay. In the passages and on the staircases of the old palace Montero's troopers lounged about insolently, smoking and making way for no one; the clanking of sabers and spurs resounded all over the building. Three silent groups of civilians in severe black waited in the main gallery, formal and helpless, a little huddled up, each keeping apart from the others, as if in the exercise of a public duty they had been overcome by a desire to shun the notice of every eye. These were the deputations waiting for their audience. The one from the Provincial Assembly, more restless and uneasy in its corporate expression, was overtopped by the big face of Don Juste Lopez, soft and white, with prominent eyelids and wreathed in impenetrable solemnity as if in a dense cloud. The President of the Provincial Assembly, coming bravely to save the last shred of parliamentary institutions (on the English model), averted his eyes from the Administrador of the San Tomé mine as a dignified rebuke of his little faith in that only saving principle.

The mournful severity of that reproof did not affect Charles Gould, but he was sensible to the glances of the others directed upon him without reproach, as if only to read their own fate upon his face. All of them had talked, shouted, and declaimed in the great *sala* of the Casa Gould. The feeling of compassion for those men, struck with a strange impotence in the toils of moral degradation, did not induce him to make a sign. He suffered from his fellowship in evil with them too much. He crossed the Plaza unmolested. The Amarilla Club was full of festive ragamuffins. Their frowsy heads protruded from every window, and from within came drunken shouts, the thumping of feet, and the twanging of harps. Broken bottles strewed the pavement below. Charles Gould found the doctor still in his house.

Dr. Monygham came away from the crack in the shutter through which he had been watching the street.

"Ah! You are back at last!" he said in a tone of relief. "I have been telling Mrs. Gould that you were perfectly safe, but I was not by any means certain that the fellow would have let you go."

"Neither was I," confessed Charles Gould, laying his hat on the table.

"You will have to take action."

The silence of Charles Gould seemed to admit that this was the only course. This was as far as Charles Gould was accustomed to go towards expressing his intentions.

"I hope you did not warn Montero of what you mean to do," the doctor said, anxiously.

"I tried to make him see that the existence of the mine was bound up with my personal safety," continued Charles Gould, looking away from the doctor, and fixing his eyes upon the water-color sketch upon the wall.

"He believed you?" the doctor asked, eagerly.

"God knows!" said Charles Gould. "I owed it to my wife to say that much. He is well enough informed. He knows that I have Don Pepe there. Fuentes must have told him. They know that the old major is perfectly capable of blowing up the San Tomé mine without hesitation or compunction. Had it not been for that I don't think I'd have left the Intendencia a free man. He would blow everything up from loyalty and from hate—from hate of these Liberals, as they call themselves. Liberals! The words one knows so well have a nightmarish meaning in this country. Liberty, democracy, patriotism, government—all of them have a flavor of folly and murder. Haven't they, doctor? . . . I alone can restrain Don Pepe. If they were to—to do away with me, nothing could prevent him."

"They will try to tamper with him," the doctor suggested, thoughtfully.

"It is very possible," Charles Gould said very low, as if speaking to himself, and still gazing at the sketch of the San Tomé gorge upon the wall. "Yes, I expect they will try that." Charles Gould looked for the first time at the doctor. "It would give me time," he added.

"Exactly," said Dr. Monygham, suppressing his excitement. "Especially if Don Pepe behaves diplomatically. Why shouldn't he give them some hope of success? Eh? Otherwise you wouldn't gain so much time. Couldn't he be instructed to—"

Charles Gould, looking at the doctor steadily, shook his head, but the doctor continued with a certain amount of fire:

"Yes, to enter into negotiations for the surrender of the mine. It is a good notion. You would mature your plan. Of course, I don't ask what it is. I don't want to know. I would refuse to listen to you if you tried to tell me. I am not fit for confidences."

"What nonsense!" muttered Charles Gould, with displeasure.

He disapproved of the doctor's sensitiveness about that far-off episode of his life. So much memory shocked Charles Gould. It was like morbidness. And again he shook his head. He refused to tamper with the open rectitude of Don Pepe's conduct, both from taste and from policy. Instructions would have to be either verbal or in writing. In either case they ran the risk of being intercepted. It was by no means certain that a messenger could reach the mine; and, besides, there was no one to send. It was on the tip of Charles's tongue to say that only the late Capataz de Cargadores could have been employed with some chance of success and the certitude of discretion. But he did not say that. He pointed out to the doctor that it would have been bad policy. Directly Don Pepe let it be supposed that he could be bought over, the Administrador's personal safety and the safety of his friends would become endangered. For there would be then no reason for moderation. The incorruptibility of Don Pepe was the essential and restraining fact. The doctor hung his head and admitted that in a way it was so.

He couldn't deny to himself that the reasoning was sound enough. Don Pepe's usefulness consisted in his unstained character. As to his own usefulness, he reflected bitterly, it was also his own character. He declared to Charles Gould that he had the means of keeping Sotillo from joining his forces with Montero, at least for the present.

"If you had had all this silver here," the doctor said, "or even if it had been known to be at the mine, you could have bribed Sotillo to throw off his recent Monterism. You could have induced him either to go away in his steamer or even to join you."

"Certainly not that last," Charles Gould declared, firmly. "What could one do with a man like that, afterwards—tell me, doctor? The silver is gone, and I am glad of it. It would have been an immediate and strong temptation. The scramble for that visible plunder would have precipitated a disastrous ending. I would have had to defend it, too. I am glad we've removed it—even if it is lost. It would have been a danger and a curse."

"Perhaps he is right," the doctor, an hour later, said hurriedly to Mrs. Gould, whom he met in the corridor. "The thing is done, and the shadow of the treasure may do just as well as the substance. Let me try to serve you to the whole extent of my evil reputation. I am off now to play my game of betrayal with Sotillo, and keep him off the town."

She put out both her hands impulsively, "Dr. Monygham, you are running a terrible risk," she whispered, averting from his face her eyes, full of tears, for a short glance at the door of her husband's room. She pressed both his hands, and the doctor stood as if rooted to the spot, looking down at her, and trying to twist his lips into a smile.

"Oh, I know you will defend my memory," he uttered at last, and ran tottering down the stairs across the patio, and out of the house. In the street he kept up a great pace with his smart hobbling walk, a case of instruments under his arm. He was known for being *loco*. Nobody interfered with him. From under the seaward gate, across the dusty, arid plain, interspersed with low bushes, he saw, more than a mile away, the ugly enormity of the Custom House, and the two or three other buildings which at that time constituted the seaport of Sulaco. Far away to the south groves of palm trees edged the curve of the harbor shore. The distant peaks of the Cordillera had lost their identity of clearcut shapes in the steadily deepening blue of the eastern sky. The doctor walked briskly. A darkling shadow seemed to fall upon him from the zenith. The sun had set. For a time the snows of Higuerota continued to glow with the reflected glory of the west. The doctor, holding a straight course for the Custom House, appeared lonely, hopping amongst the dark bushes like a tall bird with a broken wing.

Tints of purple, gold, and crimson were mirrored in the clear water of the harbor. A long tongue of land, straight as a wall, with the grass-grown ruins of the fort making a sort of rounded green mound, plainly visible from the inner shore, closed its circuit; while beyond the Placid Gulf repeated those splendors of coloring on a greater scale and with a more somber magnificence. The great mass of cloud filling the head of the gulf had long red smears amongst its convoluted folds of gray and black, as of a floating mantle stained with blood. The three Isabels, overshadowed and clear cut in a great smoothness confounding the sea and sky, appeared suspended, purple-black, in the air. The little wavelets seemed to be tossing tiny red sparks upon the sandy beaches. The glassy bands of water along the horizon gave out a fiery red glow, as if fire and water had been mingled together in the vast bed of the ocean.

At last the conflagration of sea and sky, lying embraced and still in a flaming contact upon the edge of the world, went out. The red sparks in the water vanished together with the stains of blood in the black mantle draping the somber head of the Placid Gulf; a sudden breeze sprang up and died out after rustling heavily the growth of bushes on the ruined earthwork of the fort. Nostromo woke up from a fourteen hours' sleep, and arose full length from his lair in the long grass. He stood knee deep amongst the whispering undulations of the green blades with the lost air of a man just born into the world. Handsome, robust, and supple, he threw back his head, flung his arms open, and stretched himself with a slow twist of the waist and a leisurely growling yawn of white teeth, as natural and free from evil in the moment of waking as a magnificent and unconscious wild beast. Then, in the suddenly steadied glance fixed upon nothing from under a thoughtful frown, appeared the man.

VIII

After landing from his swim Nostromo had scrambled up, all dripping, into the main quadrangle of the old fort; and there, amongst ruined bits of walls and rotting remnants of roofs and sheds, he had slept the day through. He had slept in the shadow of the mountains, in the white blaze of noon, in the stillness and solitude of that overgrown piece of land between the oval of the harbor and the spacious semi-circle of the gulf. He lay as if dead. A *rey zamuro*, appearing like a tiny black speck in the blue, stooped, circling prudently with a stealthiness of flight startling in a bird of that great size. The shadow of his pearly-white body, of his black-tipped wings, fell on the grass no more silently than he alighted himself on a hillock of rubbish within three yards of that man, lying as still as a corpse. The bird stretched his bare neck, craned his bald head, loathsome in the brilliance of varied coloring, with an air of voracious anxiety towards the promising stillness of that prostrate body. Then, sinking his head deeply into his soft plumage, he settled himself to wait. The first thing upon which Nostromo's eyes fell on waking was this patient watcher for the signs of death and corruption. When the man got up the vulture hopped away in great, side-long, fluttering jumps. He lingered for a while, morose and reluctant, before he rose, circling noiselessly with a sinister droop of beak and claws.

Long after he had vanished, Nostromo, lifting his eyes up to the sky, muttered, "I am not dead yet."

The Capataz of the Sulaco Cargadores had lived in splendor and publicity up to the very moment, as it were, when he took charge of the lighter containing the treasure of silver ingots.

The last act he had performed in Sulaco was in complete harmony with his vanity, and as such perfectly genuine. He had given his last dollar to an old woman moaning with the grief and fatigue of a dismal search under the arch of the ancient gate. Performed in obscurity and without witnesses, it had still the characteristics of splendor and publicity, and was in strict keeping with his reputation. But this awakening in solitude, except for the watchful vulture, amongst the ruins of the fort, had no such characteristics. His first confused feeling was exactly this—that it was not in keeping. It was more like the end of things. The necessity of living concealed somehow, for God knows how long, which assailed him on his return to consciousness, made everything that had gone before for years appear vain and foolish, like a flattering dream come suddenly to an end.

He climbed the crumbling slope of the rampart, and, putting aside the bushes, looked upon the harbor. He saw a couple of ships at anchor upon the sheet of water reflecting the last gleams of light, and Sotillo's steamer moored to the jetty. And behind the pale long front of the Custom House, there appeared the extent of the town like a grove of thick timber on the plain with a gateway in front, and the cupolas, towers, and miradors rising above the trees, all dark, as if surrendered already to the night. The thought that it was no longer open to him to ride through the streets, recognized by everyone, great and little, as he used to do every evening on his way to play *monte* in the *posada* of the Mexican Domingo; or to sit in the place of honor, listening to songs and looking at dances, made it appear to him as a town that had no existence.

For a long time he gazed on, then let the parted bushes spring back, and, crossing over to the other side of the fort, surveyed the vaster emptiness of the great gulf. The Isabels stood out heavily upon the narrowing long band of red in the west, which gleamed low between their black shapes, and the Capataz thought of Decoud alone there with the treasure. That man was the only one who cared whether he fell into the hands of the Monterists or not, the Capataz reflected bitterly. And that merely would be an anxiety for his own sake. As to the rest, they neither knew nor cared. What he had heard Giorgio Viola say once was very true. Kings, ministers, aristocrats, the rich in general, kept the people in poverty and subjection; they kept them as they kept dogs, to fight and hunt for their service.

The darkness of the sky had descended to the line of the horizon, enveloping the whole gulf, the islets, and the lover of Antonia alone with the treasure on the Great Isabel. The Capataz, turning his back on these things invisible and existing, sat down and took his face between his fists. He felt the pinch of poverty for the first time in his life. To find himself without money after a run of bad luck at *monte* in the low, smoky room of Domingo's *posada*, where the fraternity of *cargadores* gambled, sang, and danced of an evening; to remain with empty pockets after a burst of public generosity to some *peyne d'oro* girl or other (for whom he did not care), had none of the humiliation of destitution. He remained rich in glory and reputation. But since it was no longer possible for him to parade the streets of the town, and be hailed with respect in the usual haunts of his leisure, this sailor felt himself destitute indeed.

His mouth was dry. It was dry with heavy sleep and extremely anxious thinking, as it had never been dry before. It may be said that Nostromo tasted the dust and ashes of the fruit of life into which he had bitten deeply in his hunger for praise. Without removing his head from between his fists, he tried to spit before him—"Tfui"—and muttered a curse upon the selfishness of all the rich people.

Since everything seemed lost in Sulaco (and that was the feeling of his waking), the idea of leaving the country altogether had presented itself to Nostromo. At that thought he had seen, like the beginning of another dream, a vision of steep and tideless shores, with dark pines on the heights and white houses low down near a very blue sky. He saw the quays of a big port, where the coasting feluccas, with their lateen sails outspread like motionless wings, enter gliding silently between the end of long moles of squared blocks that project angularly towards each other, hugging a cluster of shipping to the superb bosom of a hill covered with palaces. He remembered these sights not without some filial emotion, though he had been habitually and severely beaten as a boy on one of these feluccas by a short-necked, shaven Genoese, with a deliberate and distrustful manner, who (he firmly believed) had cheated him out of his orphan's inheritance. But it is mercifully decreed that the evils of the past should appear but faintly in retrospect. Under the sense of loneliness, abandonment, and failure, the idea of return to these things appeared tolerable. But, what? Return? With bare feet and head, with one check shirt and a pair of cotton *calzoneros* for all worldly possessions?

The renowned Capataz, his elbows on his knees and a fist dug into each cheek, laughed with self-derision, as he had spat with disgust, straight out before him into the night. The confused and intimate impressions of universal dissolution which beset a subjective nature at any strong check to its ruling passion had a bitterness approaching that of death itself. He was simple. He was as ready to become the prey of any belief, superstition, or desire as a child.

The facts of his situation he could appreciate like a man with a distinct experience of the country. He saw them clearly. He was as if sobered after a long bout of intoxication. His fidelity had been taken advantage of. He had persuaded the body of *cargadores* to side with the Blancos against the rest of the people; he had had interviews with Don José; he had been made use of by Father Corbelán for negotiating with Hernandez; it was known that Don Martin Decoud had admitted him to a sort of intimacy, so that he had been free of the offices of the *Porvenir*. All these things had flattered him in the usual way. What did he care about their politics? Nothing at all. And at the end of it all—Nostromo here and Nostromo there—where is Nostromo? Nostromo can do this and that—work all day and ride all night—behold! he found himself a marked Ribierist for any sort of vengeance Gamacho, for instance, would choose to take, now the Montero party had, after all, mastered the town. The Europeans had given up; the *caballeros* had given up. Don Martin had indeed explained it was only temporary—that he was going to bring Barrios to the rescue. Where was that now—with Don Martin (whose ironic manner of talk had always made the Capataz feel vaguely uneasy) stranded on the Great Isabel? Everybody had given up. Even Don Carlos had given up. The hurried removal of the treasure out to sea meant nothing else than that. The Capataz de Cargadores, on a revulsion of subjectiveness, exasperated almost to insanity, beheld all his world without faith and courage. He had been betrayed!

With the boundless shadows of the sea behind him, out of his silence and immobility, facing the lofty shapes of the lower peaks crowded around the white, misty sheen of Higuerota, Nostromo laughed aloud again, sprang abruptly to his feet, and stood still. He must go. But where?

"There is no mistake. They keep us and encourage us as if we were dogs born to fight and hunt for them. The *vecchio* is right," he said, slowly and scathingly. He remembered old Giorgio taking his pipe out of his mouth to throw these words over his shoulder at the café, full of engine-drivers and fitters from the railway workshops. This image fixed his wavering purpose. He would try to find old Giorgio if he could. God knows what might have happened to him! He made a few steps, then stopped again and shook his head. To the left and right, in front and behind him, the scrubby bush rustled mysteriously in the darkness.

"Teresa was right, too," he added in a low tone touched with awe. He wondered whether she was dead in her anger with him or still alive. As if in answer to this thought, half of remorse and half of hope, with a soft flutter and oblique flight, a big owl, whose appalling cry: "Ya-acabo! Ya-acabo!—it is finished; it is finished"—announces calamity and death in the popular belief, drifted vaguely like a large dark ball across his path. In the downfall of all the realities that made his force, he was affected by the superstition, and shuddered slightly. Signora Teresa must have died, then. It could mean nothing else. The cry of the ill-omened bird, the first sound he was to hear on his return, was a fitting welcome for his betrayed individuality. The unseen powers which he had offended by refusing to bring a priest to a dying woman were lifting up their voice against him. She was dead. With admirable and human consistency he referred everything to himself. She had been a woman of good counsel always. And the bereaved old Giorgio remained stunned by his loss just as he was likely to require the advice of his sagacity. The blow would render the dreamy old man quite stupid for a time.

As to Captain Mitchell, Nostromo, after the manner of trusted subordinates, considered him as a person fitted by education perhaps to sign papers in an office and to give orders, but otherwise of no use whatever, and something of a fool. The necessity of winding round his little finger, almost daily, the pompous and testy self-importance of the old seaman had grown irksome with use to Nostromo. At first it had given him an inward satisfaction. But the necessity of overcoming small obstacles becomes wearisome to a self-confident personality as much by the certitude of success as by the monotony of effort. He mistrusted his superior's proneness to fussy action. That old Englishman had no judgment, he said to himself. It was useless to suppose that, acquainted with the true state of the case, he would keep it to himself. He would talk of doing impracticable things. Nostromo feared him as one would fear saddling one's self with some persistent worry. He had no discretion. He would betray the treasure. And Nostromo had made up his mind that the treasure should not be betrayed.

The word had fixed itself tenaciously in his intelligence. His imagination had seized upon the clear and simple notion of betrayal to account for the dazed feeling of enlightenment as to being done for, of having inadvertently gone out of his existence on an issue in which his personality had not been taken into account. A man betrayed is a man destroyed. Signora Teresa (may God have her soul!) had been right. He had never been taken into account. Destroyed! Her white form sitting up bowed in bed, the falling black hair, the wide-browed suffering face raised to him, the anger of her denunciations appeared to him now majestic with the awfulness of inspiration and of death. For it was not for nothing that the evil bird had uttered its lamentable shriek over his head. She was dead—may God have her soul!

Sharing in the anti-priestly freethought of the masses, his mind used the pious formula from the superficial force of habit, but with a deep-seated sincerity. The popular mind is incapable of skepticism; and that incapacity delivers their helpless strength to the wiles of swindlers and to the pitiless enthusiasms of leaders inspired by visions of a high destiny. She was dead. But would God consent to receive her soul? She had died without confession or absolution, because he had not been willing to spare her another moment of his time. His scorn of priests as priests remained; but after all, it was impossible to know whether what they affirmed was not true. Power, punishment, pardon are simple and credible notions. The magnificent Capataz de Cargadores, deprived of certain simple realities, such as the admiration of women, the adulation of men, the admired publicity of his life, was ready to feel the burden of sacrilegious guilt descend upon his shoulders.

Bareheaded, in a thin shirt and drawers, he felt the lingering warmth of the fine sand under the soles of his feet. The narrow strand gleamed far ahead in a long curve, defining the outline of this wild side of the harbor. He flitted along the shore like a pursued shadow between the somber palm-groves and the sheet of water lying as still as death on his right hand. He strode with headlong haste in the silence and solitude as though he had forgotten all prudence and caution. But he knew that on this side of the water he ran no risk of discovery. The only inhabitant was a lonely, silent, apathetic Indian in charge of the *palmarías*, who brought sometimes a load of coconuts to the town for sale. He lived without a woman in an open shed, with a perpetual fire of dry sticks smoldering near an old canoe lying bottom up on the beach. He could be easily avoided.

The barking of the dogs about that man's *ranche* was the first thing that checked his speed. He had forgotten the dogs. He swerved sharply, and plunged into the palm-grove, as into a wilderness of columns in an immense hall, whose dense obscurity seemed to whisper and rustle faintly high above his head. He traversed it, entered a ravine, climbed to the top of a steep ridge free of trees and bushes.

From there, open and vague in the starlight, he saw the plain between the town and the harbor. In the woods above some night-bird made a strange drumming noise. Below beyond the *palmaría* on the beach, the Indian's dogs continued to bark uproari-ously. He wondered what had upset them so much, and, peering down from his elevation, was surprised to detect accountable movements of the ground below, as if several oblong pieces of the plain had been in motion. Those dark, shifting patches, alternately catching and eluding the eye, altered their place always away from the harbor, with a suggestion of consecutive order and purpose. A light dawned upon him. It was a column of infantry on a night march towards the higher broken country at the foot of the hills. But he was too much in the dark about everything for wonder and speculation.

The plain had resumed its shadowy immobility. He descended the ridge and found himself in the open solitude, between the harbor and the town. Its spaciousness, extended indefinitely by an effect of obscurity, rendered more sensible his profound isolation. His pace became slower. No one waited for him; no one thought of him; no one expected or wished his return. "Betrayed! Betrayed!" he muttered to himself. No one cared. He might have been drowned by this time. No one would have cared— unless, perhaps, the children, he thought to himself. But they were with the English *signora*, and not thinking of him at all.

He wavered in his purpose of making straight for the Casa Viola. To what end? What could he expect there? His life seemed to fail him in all its details, even to the scornful reproaches of Teresa. He was aware painfully of his reluctance. Was it that remorse which she had prophesied with, what he saw now, was her last breath?

Meantime, he had deviated from the straight course, inclining by a sort of instinct to the left, towards the jetty and the harbor, the scene of his daily labors. The great length of the Custom House loomed up all at once like the wall of a factory. Not a soul challenged his approach, and his curiosity became excited as he passed cautiously towards the front by the unexpected sight of two lighted windows.

They had the fascination of a lonely vigil kept by some mysterious watcher up there, those two windows shining dimly upon the harbor in the whole vast extent of the abandoned building. The solitude could almost be felt. A strong smell of wood smoke hung about in a thin haze, which was faintly perceptible to his raised eyes against the glitter of the stars. As he advanced in the profound silence, the shrilling of innumerable cicadas in the dry grass seemed positively deafening to his strained ears. Slowly, step by step, he found himself in the great hall, somber and full of acrid smoke.

A fire built against the staircase had burnt down impotently to a low heap of embers. The hard wood had failed to catch; only a few steps at the bottom smoldered, with a creeping glow of sparks defining their charred edges. At the top he saw a streak of light from an open door. It fell upon the vast landing, all foggy with a slow drift of smoke. That was the room. He climbed the stairs, then checked himself, because he had seen within the shadow of a man cast upon one of the walls. It was a shapeless, high-shouldered shadow of somebody standing still, with lowered head, out of his line of sight. The Capataz, remembering that he was totally unarmed, stepped aside, and, effacing himself upright in a dark corner, waited with his eyes fixed on the door.

The whole enormous ruined barrack of a place, unfinished, without ceilings under its lofty roof, was pervaded by the smoke swaying to and fro in the faint cross-draughts playing in the obscurity of many lofty rooms and barnlike passages. Once one of the swinging shutters came against the wall with a single sharp crack, as if pushed by an impatient hand. A piece of paper scurried out from somewhere, rustling along the landing. The man, whoever he was, did not darken the lighted doorway. Twice the Capataz, advancing a couple of steps out of his corner, craned his neck in the hope of catching sight of what he could be at, so quietly, in there. But every time he saw only the distorted shadow of broad shoulders and bowed head. He was doing apparently nothing, and stirred not from the spot, as though he were meditating—or, perhaps, reading a paper. And not a sound issued from the room.

Once more the Capataz stepped back. He wondered who it was—some Monterist? But he dreaded to show himself. To discover his presence on shore, unless after many days, would, he believed, endanger the treasure. With his own knowledge possessing his whole soul, it seemed impossible that anybody in Sulaco should fail to jump at the right surmise. After a couple of weeks or so it would be different. Who could tell he had not returned overland from some port beyond the limits of the Republic? The existence of the treasure confused his thoughts with a peculiar sort of anxiety, as though his life had become bound up with it. It rendered him timorous for a moment before that enigmatic, lighted door. Devil take the fellow! He did not want to see him. There would be nothing to learn from his face, known or unknown. He was a fool to waste his time there in waiting.

Less than five minutes after entering the place the Capataz began his retreat. He got away down the stairs with perfect success, gave one upward look over his shoulder at the light on the landing, and ran stealthily across the hall. But at the very moment he was turning out of the great door, with his mind fixed upon escaping the notice of the man upstairs, somebody he had not heard coming briskly along the front ran full into him. Both muttered a stifled exclamation of surprise, and leaped back and stood still, each indistinct to the other. Nostromo was silent. The other man spoke first, in an amazed and deadened tone.

"Who are you?"

Already Nostromo had seemed to recognize Dr. Monygham. He had no doubt now. He hesitated the space of a second. The idea of bolting without a word presented itself to his mind. No use! An inexplicable repugnance to pronounce the name by which he was known kept him silent a little longer. At last he said in a low voice:

"A *cargador*."

He walked up to the other. Dr. Monygham had received a shock. He flung his arms up and cried out his wonder aloud, forgetting himself before the marvel of this meeting. Nostromo angrily warned him to moderate his voice. The Custom House was not so deserted as it looked. There was somebody in the lighted room above.

There is no more evanescent quality in an accomplished fact than its wonderfulness. Solicited incessantly by the considerations affecting its fears and desires, the human mind turns naturally away from the marvelous side of events. And it was in the most natural way possible that the doctor asked this man whom only two minutes before he believed to have been drowned in the gulf:

"You have seen somebody up there? Have you?"

"No, I have not seen him."

"Then how do you know?"

"I was running away from his shadow when we met."

"His shadow?"

"Yes. His shadow in the lighted room," said Nostromo, in a contemptuous tone. Leaning back with folded arms at the foot of the immense building, he dropped his head, biting his lips slightly, and not looking at the doctor. "Now," he thought to himself, "he will begin asking me about the treasure."

But the doctor's thoughts were concerned with an event not as marvelous as Nostromo's appearance, but in itself much less clear. Why had Sotillo taken himself off with his whole command with this suddenness and secrecy? What did this move portend? However, it dawned upon the doctor that the man upstairs was one of the officers left behind by the disappointed colonel to communicate with him.

"I believe he is waiting for me," he said.

"It is possible."

"I must see. Do not go away yet, Capataz."

"Go away where?" muttered Nostromo.

Already the doctor had left him. He remained leaning against the wall, staring at the dark water of the harbor; the shrilling of cicadas filled his ears. An invincible vagueness coming over his thoughts took from them all power to determine his will.

"Capataz! Capataz!" the doctor's voice called urgently from above.

The sense of betrayal and ruin floated upon his somber indifference as upon a sluggish sea of pitch. But he stepped out from under the wall, and, looking up, saw Dr. Monygham leaning out of a lighted window.

"Come up and see what Sotillo has done. You need not fear the man up here."

He answered by a slight, bitter laugh. Fear a man! The Capataz of the Sulaco Cargadores fear a man! It angered him that anybody should suggest such a thing. It angered him to be disarmed and skulking and in danger because of the accursed treasure, which was of so little account to the people who had tied it round his neck. He could not shake off the worry of it. To Nostromo the doctor represented all these people. . . . And he had never even asked after it. Not a word of inquiry about the most desperate undertaking of his life.

Thinking these thoughts, Nostromo passed again through the cavernous hall, where the smoke was considerably thinned, and went up the stairs, not so warm to his feet now, towards the streak of light at the top. The doctor appeared in it for a moment, agitated and impatient.

"Come up! Come up!"

At the moment of crossing the doorway the Capataz experienced a shock of surprise. The man had not moved. He saw his shadow in the same place. He started, then stepped in with a feeling of being about to solve a mystery.

It was very simple. For an infinitesimal fraction of a second, against the light of two flaring and guttering candles, through a blue, pungent, thin haze which made his eyes smart, he saw the man standing, as he had imagined him, with his back to the door, casting an enormous and distorted shadow upon the wall. Swifter than a flash of lightning followed the impression of his constrained, toppling attitude—the shoulders projecting forward, the head sunk low upon the breast. Then he distinguished the arms behind his back, and wrenched so terribly that the two clenched fists, lashed together, had been forced up higher than the shoulder-blades. From there his eyes traced in one instantaneous glance the hide rope going upwards from the tied wrists over a heavy beam and down to a staple in the wall. He did not want to look at the rigid legs, at the feet hanging down nervelessly, with their bare toes some six inches above the floor, to know that the man had been given the estrapade till he had swooned. His first impulse was to dash forward and sever the rope at one blow. He felt for his knife. He had no knife—not even a knife. He stood quivering, and the doctor, perched on the edge of the table, facing thoughtfully the cruel and lamentable sight, his chin in his hand, uttered, without stirring:

"Tortured—and shot dead through the breast—getting cold."

This information calmed the Capataz. One of the candles flickering in the socket went out. "Who did this?" he asked.

"Sotillo, I tell you. Who else? Tortured—of course. But why shot?" The doctor looked fixedly at Nostromo, who shrugged his shoulders slightly. "And mark, shot suddenly, on impulse. It is evident. I wish I had his secret."

Nostromo had advanced, and stooped slightly to look. "I seem to have seen that face somewhere," he muttered. "Who is he?"

The doctor turned his eyes upon him again. "I may yet come to envying his fate. What do you think of that, Capataz, eh?"

But Nostromo did not even hear these words. Seizing the remaining light, he thrust it under the drooping head. The doctor sat oblivious, with a lost gaze. Then the heavy iron candlestick, as if struck out of Nostromo's hand, clattered on the floor.

"Hullo!" exclaimed the doctor, looking up with a start. He could hear the Capataz stagger against the table and gasp. In the sudden extinction of the light within, the dead blackness sealing the window-frames became alive with stars to his sight.

"Of course, of course," the doctor muttered to himself in English. "Enough to make him jump out of his skin."

Nostromo's heart seemed to force itself into his throat. His head swam. Hirsch! The man was Hirsch! He held on tight to the edge of the table.

"But he was hiding in the lighter," he almost shouted. His voice fell. "In the lighter, and—and—"

"And Sotillo brought him in," said the doctor. "He is no more startling to you than you were to me. What I want to know is how he induced some compassionate soul to shoot him."

"So Sotillo knows—" began Nostromo, in a more equable voice.

"Everything!" interrupted the doctor.

The Capataz was heard striking the table with his fist. "Everything? What are you saying, there? Everything? Know everything? It is impossible! Everything?"

"Of course. What do you mean by impossible? I tell you I have heard this Hirsch questioned last night, here, in this very room. He knew your name, Decoud's name, and all about the loading of the silver. . . . The lighter was cut in two. He was grovelling in abject terror before Sotillo, but he remembered that much. What do you want more? He knew least about himself. They found him clinging to their anchor. He must have caught at it just as the lighter went to the bottom."

"Went to the bottom?" repeated Nostromo, slowly. "Sotillo believes that? *Bueno!*"

The doctor, a little impatiently, was unable to imagine what else anybody could believe. Yes, Sotillo believed that the lighter was sunk, and the Capataz de Cargadores, together with Martin Decoud and perhaps one or two other political fugitives, had been drowned.

"I told you well, Señor Doctor," remarked Nostromo at that point, "that Sotillo did not know everything."

"Eh? What do you mean?"

"He did not know I was not dead."

"Neither did we."

"And you did not care—none of you *caballeros* on the wharf—once you got off a man of flesh and blood like yourselves on a fool's business that could not end well."

"You forget, Capataz, I was not on the wharf. And I did not think well of the business. So you need not taunt me. I tell you what, man, we had but little leisure to think of the dead. Death stands near behind us all. You were gone."

"I went, indeed!" broke in Nostromo. "And for the sake of what—tell me?"

"Ah! that is your own affair," the doctor said, roughly. "Do not ask me."

Their flowing murmurs paused in the dark. Perched on the edge of the table with slightly averted faces, they felt their shoulders touch, and their eyes remained directed towards an upright shape nearly lost in the obscurity of the inner part of the room, that with projecting head and shoulders, in ghastly immobility, seemed intent on catching every word.

"*Muy bien!*" Nostromo muttered at last. "So be it. Teresa was right. It is my own affair."

"Teresa is dead," remarked the doctor, absently, while his mind followed a new line of thought suggested by what might have been called Nostromo's return to life. "She died, the poor woman."

"Without a priest?" the Capataz asked, anxiously.

"What a question! Who could have got a priest for her last night?"

"May God keep her soul!" ejaculated Nostromo, with a gloomy and hopeless fervor which had no time to surprise Dr. Monygham, before, reverting to the previous conversation, he continued in a sinister tone. "*Sí,* Señor Doctor. As you were saying, it is my own affair. A very desperate affair."

"There are no two men in this part of the world that could have saved themselves by swimming as you have done," the doctor said, admiringly.

And again there was silence between those two men. They were both reflecting, and the diversity of their natures made their thoughts born from their meeting swing afar from each other. The doctor, impelled to risky action by his loyalty to the Goulds, wondered with thankfulness at the chain of accident which had brought that man back where he would be of the greatest use in the work of saving the San Tomé mine. The doctor was loyal to the mine. It presented itself to his fifty-year-old eyes in the shape of a little woman in a soft dress with a long train, with a head attractively overweighted by a great mass of fair hair and the delicate preciousness of her inner worth, partaking of a gem and a flower, revealed in every attitude of her person. As the dangers thickened round the San Tomé mine this illusion acquired force, permanency, and authority. It claimed him at last! This claim, exalted by a spiritual detachment from the usual sanctions of hope and reward, made Dr. Monygham's thinking, acting, individuality, extremely dangerous to himself and to others, all his scruples vanishing in the proud feeling that his devotion was the only thing that stood between an admirable woman and a frightful disaster.

It was a sort of intoxication which made him utterly indifferent to Decoud's fate, but left his wits perfectly clear for the appreciation of Decoud's political idea. It was a good idea—and Barrios was the only instrument of its realization. The doctor's soul, withered and shrunk by the shame of moral disgrace, became implacable in the expansion of its tenderness. Nostromo's return was providential. He did not think of him humanely, as of a fellow-creature just escaped from the jaws of death. The Capataz for him was the only possible messenger to Cayta. The very man. The doctor's misanthropic mistrust of mankind (the bitterer because based on personal failure) did not lift him sufficiently above common weaknesses. He was under the spell of an established reputation. Trumpeted by Captain Mitchell, grown in repetition, and fixed in general assent, Nostromo's faithfulness had never been questioned by Dr. Monygham as a fact. It was not likely to be questioned now he stood in desperate need of it himself. Dr. Monygham was human; he accepted the popular conception of the Capataz's incorruptibility simply because no word or fact had ever contradicted a mere affirmation. It seemed to be a part of the man, like his whiskers or his teeth. It was impossible to conceive him otherwise. The question was whether he would consent to go on such a dangerous and desperate errand. The doctor was observant enough to have become aware from the first of something peculiar in the man's temper. He was no doubt sore about the loss of the silver.

"It will be necessary to take him into my fullest confidence," he said to himself, with a certain acuteness of insight into the nature he had to deal with.

On Nostromo's side the silence had been full of black irresolution, anger, and mistrust. He was the first to break it, however.

"The swimming was no great matter," he said. "It is what went before—and what comes after that—"

He did not quite finish what he meant to say, breaking off short, as though his thought had butted against a solid obstacle. The doctor's mind pursued its own schemes with Machiavellian subtlety. He said as sympathetically as he was able:

"It is unfortunate, Capataz. But no one would think of blaming you. Very unfortunate. To begin with, the treasure ought never to have left the mountain. But it was Decoud who—however, he is dead. There is no need to talk of him."

"No," assented Nostromo, as the doctor paused, "there is no need to talk of dead men. But I am not dead yet."

"You are all right. Only a man of your intrepidity could have saved himself."

In this Dr. Monygham was sincere. He esteemed highly the intrepidity of that man, whom he valued but little, being disillusioned as to mankind in general, because of the particular instance in which his own manhood had failed. Having had to encounter single-handed during his period of eclipse many physical dangers, he was well aware of the most dangerous element common to them all: of the crushing, paralyzing sense of human littleness, which is what really defeats a man struggling with natural forces, alone, far from the eyes of his fellows. He was eminently fit to appreciate the mental image he made for himself of the Capataz, after hours of tension and anxiety, precipitated suddenly into an abyss of waters and darkness, without earth or sky, and confronting it not only with an undismayed mind, but with sensible success. Of course, the man was an incomparable swimmer, that was known, but the doctor judged that this instance testified to a still greater intepidity of spirit. It was pleasing to him; he augured well from it for the success of the arduous mission with which he meant to entrust the Capataz so marvelously restored to usefulness. And in a tone vaguely gratified, he observed:

"It must have been terribly dark!"

"It was the worst darkness of the Golfo," the Capataz assented, briefly. He was mollified by what seemed a sign of some faint interest in such things as had befallen him, and dropped a few descriptive phrases with an affected and curt nonchalance. At that moment he felt communicative. He expected the continuance of that interest which, whether accepted or rejected, would have restored to him his personality—the only thing lost in that desperate affair. But the doctor, engrossed by a desperate adventure of his own, was terrible in the pursuit of his idea. He let an exclamation of regret escape him.

"I could almost wish you had shouted and shown a light."

This unexpected utterance astounded the Capataz by its character of cold-blooded atrocity. It was as much as to say, "I wish you had shown yourself a coward; I wish you had had your throat cut for your pains." Naturally he referred it to himself, whereas it related only to the silver, being uttered simply and with many mental reservations. Surprise and rage rendered him speechless, and the doctor pursued, practically unheard by Nostromo, whose stirred blood was beating violently in his ears.

"For I am convinced Sotillo in possession of the silver would have turned short round and made for some small port abroad. Economically it would have been wasteful, but still less wasteful than having it sunk. It was the next best thing to having it at hand in some safe place, and using part of it to buy up Sotillo. But I doubt whether Don Carlos would have ever made up his mind to it. He is not fit for Costaguana, and that is a fact, Capataz."

The Capataz had mastered the fury that was like a tempest in his ears in time to hear the name of Don Carlos. He seemed to have come out of it a changed man—a man who spoke thoughtfully in a soft and even voice.

"And would Don Carlos have been content if I had surrendered this treasure?"

"I should not wonder if they were all of that way of thinking now," the doctor said, grimly. "I was never consulted. Decoud had it his own way. Their eyes are opened by this time, I should think. I for one know that if that silver turned up this moment miraculously ashore I would give it to Sotillo. And, as things stand, I would be approved."

"Turned up miraculously," repeated the Capataz very low; then raised his voice. "That, señor, would be a greater miracle than any saint could perform."

"I believe you, Capataz," said the doctor, drily.

He went on to develop his view of Sotillo's dangerous influence upon the situation. And the Capataz, listening as if in a dream, felt himself of as little account as the indistinct, motionless shape of the dead man whom he saw upright under the beam, with his air of listening also, disregarded, forgotten, like a terrible example of neglect.

"Is it for an unconsidered and foolish whim that they came to me, then?" he interrupted, suddenly. "Had I not done enough for them to be of some account, por Dios? Is it that the hombres finos—the gentlemen—need not think as long as there is a man of the people ready to risk his body and soul? Or, perhaps, we have no souls—like dogs?"

"There was Decoud, too, with his plan," the doctor reminded him again.

"Sí! And the rich man in San Francisco who had something to do with that treasure, too—what do I know? No! I have heard too many things. It seems to me that everything is permitted to the rich."

"I understand, Capataz," the doctor began.

"What Capataz?" broke in Nostromo, in a forcible but even voice. "The Capataz is undone, destroyed. There is no Capataz. Oh, no! You will find the Capataz no more."

"Come, this is childish!" remonstrated the doctor; and the other calmed down suddenly.

"I have been indeed like a little child," he muttered.

And as his eyes met again the shape of the murdered man suspended in his awful immobility, which seemed the uncomplaining immobility of attention, he asked, wondering gently:

"Why did Sotillo give the estrapade to this pitiful wretch? Do you know? No torture could have been worse than his fear. Killing I can understand. His anguish was intolerable to behold. But why should he torment him like this? He could tell no more."

"No; he could tell nothing more. Any sane man would have seen that. He had told him everything. But I tell you what it is, Capataz. Sotillo would not believe what he was told. Not everything."

"What is it he would not believe? I cannot understand."

"I can, because I have seen the man. He refuses to believe that the treasure is lost."

"What?" the Capataz cried out in a discomposed tone.

"That startles you—eh?"

"Am I to understand, señor," Nostromo went on in a deliberate and, as it were, watchful tone, "that Sotillo thinks the treasure has been saved by some means?"

"No! no! That would be impossible," said the doctor, with conviction; and Nostromo emitted a grunt in the dark. "That would be impossible. He thinks that the silver was no longer in the lighter when she was sunk. He has convinced himself that the whole show of getting it away to sea is a mere sham got up to deceive Gamacho and his Nationals, Pedrito Montero, Señor Fuentes, our new Jefe Político, and himself, too. Only, he says, he is no such fool."

"But he is devoid of sense. He is the greatest imbecile that ever called himself a colonel in this country of evil," growled Nostromo.

"He is no more unreasonable than many sensible men," said the doctor. "He has convinced himself that the treasure can be found because he desires passionately to possess himself of it. And he is also afraid of his officers turning upon him and going over to Pedrito, whom he has not the courage either to fight or trust. Do you see that, Capataz? He need fear no desertion as long as some hope remains of that enormous plunder turning up. I have made it my business to keep this very hope up."

"You have!" the Capataz de Cargadores repeated cautiously. "Well, that is wonderful. And how long do you think you are going to keep it up?"

"As long as I can."

"What does that mean?"

"I can tell you exactly. As long as I live," the doctor retorted in a stubborn voice. Then, in a few words, he described the story of his arrest and the circumstances of his release. "I was going back to that silly scoundrel when we met," he concluded.

Nostromo had listened with profound attention. "You have made up your mind, then, to a speedy death," he muttered through his clenched teeth.

"Perhaps, my illustrious Capataz," the doctor said, testily. "You are not the only one here who can look an ugly death in the face."

"No doubt," mumbled Nostromo, loud enough to be overheard. "There may be even more than two fools in this place. Who knows?"

"And that is my affair," said the doctor, curtly.

"As taking out the accursed silver to sea was my affair," retorted Nostromo. "I see. *Bueno.* Each of us has his reasons. But you were the last man I conversed with before I started, and you talked to me as if I were a fool."

Nostromo had a great distaste for the doctor's sardonic treatment of his great reputation. Decoud's faintly ironic recognition used to make him uneasy; but the familiarity of a man like Don Martin was flattering, whereas the doctor was a nobody. He could remember him a penniless outcast, slinking about the streets of Sulaco, without a single friend or acquaintance, till Don Carlos Gould took him into the service of the mine.

"You may be very wise," he went on, thoughtfully, staring into the obscurity of the room, pervaded by the gruesome enigma of the tortured and murdered Hirsch. "But I am not such a fool as when I started. I have learned one thing since, and that is that you are a dangerous man."

Dr. Monygham was too startled to do more than exclaim:

"What is it you say?"

"If he could speak he would say the same thing," pursued Nostromo, with a nod of his shadowy head silhouetted against the starlit window.

"I do not understand you," said Dr. Monygham faintly.

"No? Perhaps, if you had not confirmed Sotillo in his madness, he would have been in no haste to give the estrapade to that miserable Hirsch."

The doctor started at the suggestion. But his devotion, absorbing all his sensibilities, had left his heart steeled against remorse and pity. Still, for complete relief, he felt the necessity of repelling it loudly and contemptuously.

"Bah! You dare to tell me that, with a man like Sotillo. I confess I did not give a thought to Hirsch. If I had it would have been useless. Anybody can see that the luckless wretch was doomed from the moment he caught hold of the anchor. He was doomed, I tell you! Just as I myself am doomed—most probably."

This is what Dr. Monygham said in answer to Nostromo's remark, which was plausible enough to prick his conscience. He was not a callous man. But the necessity, the magnitude, the importance of the task he had taken upon himself dwarfed all merely humane considerations. He had undertaken it in a fanatical spirit. He did not like it. To lie, to deceive, to circumvent even the basest of mankind was odious to him. It was odious to him by training, instinct, and tradition. To do these things in the character of a traitor was abhorrent to his nature and terrible to his feelings. He had made that sacrifice in a spirit of abasement. He had said to himself bitterly, "I am the only one fit for that dirty work." And he believed this. He was not subtle. His simplicity was such that, though he had no sort of heroic idea of seeking death, the risk, deadly enough, to which he exposed himself, had a sustaining and comforting effect. To that spiritual state the fate of Hirsch presented itself as part of the general atrocity of things. He considered that episode practically. What did it mean? Was it a sign of some dangerous change in Sotillo's delusion? That the man should have been killed like this was what the doctor could not understand.

"Yes. But why shot?" he murmured to himself.

Nostromo kept very still.

IX

Distracted between doubts and hopes, dismayed by the sound of bells pealing out the arrival of Pedrito Montero, Sotillo had spent the morning in battling with his thoughts; a contest to which he was unequal, from the vacuity of his mind and the violence of his passions. Disappointment, greed, anger, and fear made a tumult in the colonel's breast louder than the din of bells in the town. Nothing he had planned had come to pass. Neither Sulaco nor the silver of the mine had fallen into his hands. He had performed no military exploit to secure his position, and had obtained no enormous booty to make off with. Pedrito Montero, either as friend or foe, filled him with dread. The sound of bells maddened him.

Imagining at first that he might be attacked at once, he had made his battalion stand to arms on the shore. He walked to and fro all the length of the room, stopping sometimes to gnaw the finger-tips of his right hand with a lurid sideways glare fixed on the floor; then, with a sullen, repelling glance all round, he would resume his tramping in savage aloofness. His hat, horsewhip, sword, and revolver were lying on the table. His officers, crowding the window giving the view of the town gate, disputed amongst themselves the use of his field-glass bought last year on long credit from Anzani. It passed from hand to hand, and the possessor for the time being was besieged by anxious inquiries.

"There is nothing; there is nothing to see!" he would repeat, impatiently.

There was nothing. And when the picket in the bushes near the Casa Viola had been ordered to fall back upon the main body, no stir of life appeared on the stretch of dusty and arid land between the town and the waters of the port. But late in the afternoon a horseman issuing from the gate was made out riding up fearlessly. It was an emissary from Señor Fuentes. Being all alone he was allowed to come on. Dismounting at the great door he greeted the silent bystanders with cheery impudence, and begged to be taken up at once to the "muy valiente" colonel.

Señor Fuentes, on entering upon his functions of Jefe Político, had turned his diplomatic abilities to getting hold of the harbor as well as of the mine. The man he pitched upon to negotiate with Sotillo was a Notary Public, whom the revolution had found languishing in the common jail on a charge of forging documents. Liberated by the mob along with the other "victims of Blanco tyranny," he had hastened to offer his services to the new Government.

He set out determined to display much zeal and eloquence in trying to induce Sotillo to come into town alone for a conference with Pedrito Montero. Nothing was farther from the colonel's intentions. The mere fleeting idea of trusting himself into the famous Pedrito's hands had made him feel unwell several times. It was out of the question—it was madness. And to put himself in open hostility was madness, too. It would render impossible a systematic search for that treasure, for that wealth of silver which he seemed to feel somewhere about, to scent somewhere near.

But where? Where? Heavens! Where? Oh! why had he allowed that doctor to go! Imbecile that he was. But no! It was the only right course, he reflected distractedly, while the messenger waited downstairs chatting agreeably to the officers. It was in that scoundrelly doctor's true interest to return with positive information. But what if anything stopped him? A general prohibition to leave the town, for instance! There would be patrols!

The colonel, seizing his head in his hands, turned in his tracks as if struck with vertigo. A flash of craven inspiration suggested to him an expedient not unknown to European statesmen when they wish to delay a difficult negotiation. Booted and spurred, he scrambled into the hammock with undignified haste. His handsome face had turned yellow with the strain of weighty cares. The ridge of his shapely nose had grown sharp; the audacious nostrils appeared mean and pinched. The velvety, caressing glance of his fine eyes seemed dead and even decomposed; for these almond-shaped, languishing orbs had become inappropriately bloodshot with much sinister sleeplessness. He addressed the surprised envoy of Señor Fuentes in a deadened, exhausted voice. It came pathetically feeble from under a pile of ponchos, which buried his elegant person right up to the black moustaches, uncurled, pendant, in sign of bodily prostration and mental incapacity. Fever, fever—a heavy fever had overtaken the *"muy valiente"* colonel. A wavering wildness of expression, caused by the passing spasms of a slight colic which had declared itself suddenly, and the rattling teeth of repressed panic, had a genuineness which impressed the envoy. It was a cold fit. The colonel explained that he was unable to think, to listen, to speak. With an appearance of superhuman effort the colonel gasped out that he was not in a state to return a suitable reply or to execute any of his Excellency's orders. But tomorrow! Tomorrow! Ah! tomorrow! Let his Excellency Don Pedro be without uneasiness. The brave Esmeralda Regiment held the harbor, held—And closing his eyes, he rolled his aching head like a half-delirious invalid under the inquisitive stare of the envoy, who was obliged to bend down over the hammock in order to catch the painful and broken accents. Meantime, Colonel Sotillo trusted that his Excellency's humanity would permit the doctor, the English doctor, to come out of town with his case of foreign remedies to attend upon him. He begged anxiously his worship the *caballero* now present for the grace of looking in as he passed the Casa Gould, and informing the English doctor, who was probably there, that his services were immediately required by Colonel Sotillo, lying ill of fever in the Custom House. Immediately. Most urgently required. Awaited with extreme impatience. A thousand thanks. He closed his eyes wearily and would not open them again, lying perfectly still, deaf, dumb, insensible, overcome, vanquished, crushed, annihilated by the fell disease.

But as soon as the other had shut after him the door of the landing, the colonel leaped out with a fling of both feet in an avalanche of woollen coverings. His spurs having become entangled in a perfect welter of ponchos he nearly pitched on his head, and did not recover his balance till the middle of the room. Concealed behind the half-closed jalousies he listened to what went on below.

The envoy had already mounted, and turning to the morose officers occupying the great doorway, took off his hat formally.

"*Caballeros,*" he said, in a very loud tone, "allow me to recommend you to take great care of your colonel. It has done me much honor and gratification to have seen you all, a fine body of men exercising the soldierly virtue of patience in this exposed situation, where there is much sun, and no water to speak of, while a town full of wine and feminine charms is ready to embrace you for the brave men you are. *Caballeros,* I have the honor to salute you. There will be much dancing tonight in Sulaco. Good-bye!"

But he reined in his horse and inclined his head sideways on seeing the old major step out, very tall and meager, in a straight narrow coat coming down to his ankles as if it were the casing of the regimental colors rolled round their staff.

The intelligent old warrior, after enunciating in a dogmatic tone the general proposition that the "world was full of traitors," went on pronouncing deliberately a panegyric upon Sotillo. He ascribed to him with leisurely emphasis every virtue under heaven, summing it all up in an absurd colloquialism current amongst the lower class of Occidentals (especially about Esmeralda). "And," he concluded, with a sudden rise in the voice, "a man of many teeth—'*hombre de muchos dientes.*' *Sí, señor.* As to us," he pursued, portentous and impressive, "your worship is beholding the finest body of officers in the Republic, men unequaled for valor and sagacity, '*y hombres de muchos dientes.*' "

"What? All of them?" inquired the disreputable envoy of Señor Fuentes, with a faint, derisive smile.

"*Todos. Sí, señor,*" the major affirmed, gravely, with conviction. "Men of many teeth."

The other wheeled his horse to face the portal resembling the high gate of a dismal barn. He raised himself in his stirrups, extended one arm. He was a facetious scoundrel, entertaining for these stupid Occidentals a feeling of great scorn natural in a native from the central provinces. The folly of Esmeraldians especially aroused his amused contempt. He began an oration upon Pedro Montero, keeping a solemn countenance. He flourished his hand as if introducing him to their notice. And when he saw every face set, all the eyes fixed upon his lips, he began to shout a sort of catalogue of perfections: "Generous, valorous, affable, profound"—he snatched off his hat enthusiastically—"a statesman, an invincible chief of partisans—"He dropped his voice startlingly to a deep, hollow note—"and a dentist."

He was off instantly at a smart walk; the rigid straddle of his legs, the turned-out feet, the stiff back, the rakish slant of the sombrero above the square, motionless set of the shoulders expressing an infinite, awe-inspiring impudence.

Upstairs, behind the jalousies, Sotillo did not move for a long time. The audacity of the fellow appalled him. What were his officers saying below? They were saying nothing. Complete silence. He quaked. It was not thus that he had imagined himself at that stage of the expedition. He had seen himself triumphant, unquestioned, appeased, the idol of the soldiers, weighing in secret complacency the agreeable alternatives of power and wealth open to his choice. Alas! How different! Distracted, restless, supine, burning with fury, or frozen with terror, he felt a dread as fathomless as the sea creep upon him from every side. That rogue of a doctor had to come out with his information. That was clear. It would be of no use to him—alone. He could do nothing with it. Malediction! The doctor would never come out. He was probably under arrest already, shut up together with Don Carlos. He laughed aloud insanely. Ha! ha! ha! ha! It was Pedrito Montero who would get the information. Ha! ha! ha! ha!—and the silver. Ha!

All at once, in the midst of the laugh, he became motionless and silent as if turned into stone. He, too, had a prisoner. A prisoner who must, must know the real truth. He would have to be made to speak. And Sotillo, who all that time had not quite forgotten Hirsch, felt an inexplicable reluctance at the notion of proceeding to extremities.

He felt a reluctance—part of that unfathomable dread that crept on all sides upon him. He remembered reluctantly, too, the dilated eyes of the hide merchant, his contortions, his loud sobs and protestations. It was not compassion or even mere nervous sensibility. The fact was that though Sotillo did never for a moment believe his story—he could not believe it; nobody could believe such nonsense—yet those accents of despairing truth impressed him disagreeably. They made him feel sick. And he suspected also that the man might have gone mad with fear. A lunatic is a hopeless subject. Bah! A pretense. Nothing but a pretense. He would know how to deal with that.

He was working himself up to the right pitch of ferocity. His fine eyes squinted slightly; he clapped his hands; a bare-footed orderly appeared noiselessly; a corporal, with his bayonet hanging on his thigh and a stick in his hand.

The colonel gave his orders, and presently the miserable Hirsch, pushed in by several soldiers, found him frowning awfully in a broad armchair, hat on head, knees wide apart, arms akimbo, masterful, imposing, irresistible, haughty, sublime, terrible.

Hirsch, with his arms tied behind his back, had been bundled violently into one of the smaller rooms. For many hours he remained apparently forgotten, stretched lifelessly on the floor. From that solitude, full of despair and terror, he was torn out brutally, with kicks and blows, passive, sunk in hebetude. He listened to threats and admonitions, and afterwards made his usual answers to questions, with his chin sunk on his breast, his hands tied behind his back, swaying a little in front of Sotillo, and never looking up. When he was forced to hold up his head, by means of a bayonet-point prodding him under the chin, his eyes had a vacant, trance-like stare, and drops of perspiration as big as peas were seen hailing down the dirt, bruises, and scratches of his white face. Then they stopped suddenly.

Sotillo looked at him in silence. "Will you depart from your obstinacy, you rogue?" he asked. Already a rope, whose one end was fastened to Señor Hirsch's wrists, had been thrown over a beam, and three soldiers held the other end, waiting. He made no answer. His heavy lower lip hung stupidly. Sotillo made a sign. Hirsch was jerked up off his feet, and a yell of despair and agony burst out in the room, filled the passages of the great building, rent the air outside, caused every soldier of the camp along the shore to look up at the windows, started some of the officers in the hall babbling excitedly, with shining eyes; others, setting their lips, looked gloomily at the floor.

Sotillo, followed by the soldiers, had left the room. The sentry on the landing presented arms. Hirsch went on screaming all alone behind the half-closed jalousies while the sunshine, reflected from the water of the harbor, made an ever-running ripple of light high up on the wall. He screamed with uplifted eyebrows and a wide-open mouth—incredibly wide, black, enormous, full of teeth—comical.

In the still burning air of the windless afternoon he made the waves of his agony travel as far as the O.S.N. Company's offices. Captain Mitchell on the balcony, trying to make out what went on generally, had heard him faintly but distinctly, and the feeble and appalling sound lingered in his ears after he had retreated indoors with blanched cheeks. He had been driven off the balcony several times during that afternoon.

Sotillo, irritable, moody, walked restlessly about, held consultations with his officers, gave contradictory orders in this shrill clamor pervading the whole empty edifice. Sometimes there would be long and awful silences. Several times he had entered the torture-chamber where his sword, horsewhip, revolver, and field-glass were lying on the table, to ask with forced calmness, "Will you speak the truth now? No? I can wait." But he could not afford to wait much longer. That was just it. Every time he went in and came out with a slam of the door, the sentry on the landing presented arms, and got in return a black, venomous, unsteady glance, which, in reality, saw nothing at all, being merely the reflection of the soul within—a soul of gloomy hatred, irresolution, avarice, and fury.

The sun had set when he went in once more. A soldier carried in two lighted candles and slunk out, shutting the door without noise.

"Speak, thou Jewish child of the devil! The silver! The silver, I say? Where is it? Where have you foreign rogues hidden it? Confess or—"

A slight quiver passed up the taut rope from the racked limbs, but the body of Señor Hirsch, enterprising businessman from Esmeralda, hung under the heavy beam perpendicular and silent, facing the colonel awfully. The inflow of the night air, cooled by the snows of the Sierra, spread gradually a delicious freshness through the close heat of the room.

"Speak—thief—scoundrel—*pícaro*—or—"

Sotillo had seized the riding-whip, and stood with his arm lifted up. For a word, for one little word, he felt he would have knelt, cringed, grovelled on the floor before the drowsy, conscious stare of those fixed eyeballs starting out of the grimy, disheveled head that drooped very still with its mouth closed askew. The colonel ground his teeth with rage and struck. The rope vibrated leisurely to the blow, like the long string of a pendulum starting from a rest. But no swinging motion was imparted to the body of Señor Hirsch, the well-known hide merchant on the coast. With a convulsive effort of the twisted arms it leaped up a few inches, curling upon itself like a fish on the end of a line. Señor Hirsch's head was flung back on his straining throat; his chin trembled.

For a moment the rattle of his chattering teeth pervaded the vast, shadowy room, where the candles made a patch of light round the two flames burning side by side. And as Sotillo, staying his raised hand, waited for him to speak, with the sudden flash of a grin and a straining forward of the wrenched shoulders, he spat violently into his face.

The uplifted whip fell, and the colonel sprang back with a low cry of dismay, as if aspersed by a jet of deadly venom. Quick as thought he snatched up his revolver, and fired twice. The report and the concussion of the shots seemed to throw him at once from ungovernable rage into idiotic stupor. He stood with drooping jaw and stony eyes. What had he done, *sangre de Dios!* What had he done? He was basely appalled at his impulsive act, sealing for ever these lips from which so much was to be extorted. What could he say? How could he explain? Ideas of headlong flight somewhere, anywhere, passed through his mind; even the craven and absurd notion of hiding under the table occurred to his cowardice. It was too late; his officers had rushed in tumultuously, in a great clatter of scabbards, clamoring, with astonishment and wonder. But since they did not immediately proceed to plunge their swords into his breast, the brazen side of his character asserted itself. Passing the sleeve of his uniform over his face he pulled himself together. His truculent glance turned slowly here and there, checked the noise where it fell; and the stiff body of the late Señor Hirsch, merchant, after swaying imperceptibly, made a half turn, and came to a rest in the midst of awed murmurs and uneasy shuffling.

A voice remarked loudly, "Behold a man who will never speak again." And another, from the back row of faces, timid and pressing, cried out:

"Why did you kill him, *mi coronel?*"

"Because he has confessed everything," answered Sotillo, with the hardihood of desperation. He felt himself cornered. He brazened it out on the strength of his reputation with very fair success. His hearers thought him very capable of such an act. They were disposed to believe his flattering tale. There is no credulity so eager and blind as the credulity of covetousness, which, in its universal extent, measures the moral misery and the intellectual destitution of mankind. Ah! he had confessed everything, this fractious Jew, this *bribón.* Good! Then he was no longer wanted. A sudden dense guffaw was heard from the senior captain—a big-headed man, with little round eyes and monstrously fat cheeks which never moved. The old major, tall and fantastically ragged like a scarecrow, walked round the body of the late Señor Hirsch, muttering to himself with ineffable complacency that like this there was no need to guard against any future treacheries of that scoundrel. The others stared, shifting from foot to foot, and whispering short remarks to each other.

Sotillo buckled on his sword and gave curt, peremptory orders to hasten the retirement decided upon in the afternoon. Sinister, impressive, his sombrero pulled right down upon his eyebrows, he marched first through the door in such disorder of mind that he forgot utterly to provide for Dr. Monygham's possible return. As the officers trooped out after him, one or two looked back hastily at the late Señor Hirsch, merchant from Esmeralda, left swinging rigidly at rest, alone with the two burning candles. In the emptiness of the room the burly shadow of head and shoulders on the wall had an air of life.

Below, the troops fell in silently and moved off by companies without drum or trumpet. The old scarecrow major commanded the rearguard; but the party he left behind with orders to fire the Custom House (and "burn the carcass of the treacherous Jew where it hung") failed somehow in their haste to set the staircase properly alight. The body of the late Señor Hirsch dwelt alone for a time in the dismal solitude of the unfinished building, resounding weirdly with sudden slams and clicks of doors and latches, with rustling scurries of torn papers, and the tremulous sighs that at each gust of wind passed under the high roof. The light of the two candles burning before the perpendicular and breathless immobility of the late Señor Hirsch threw a gleam afar over land and water, like a signal in the night. He remained to startle Nostromo by his presence, and to puzzle Dr. Monygham by the mystery of his atrocious end.

"But why shot?" the doctor again asked himself, audibly. This time he was answered by a dry laugh from Nostromo.

"You seem much concerned at a very natural thing, Señor Doctor. I wonder why? It is very likely that before long we shall all get shot one after another, if not by Sotillo, then by Pedrito, or Fuentes, or Gamacho. And we may even get the estrapade, too, or worse—*quién sabe?*—with your pretty tale of the silver you put into Sotillo's head."

"It was in his head already," the doctor protested. "I only—"

"Yes. And you only nailed it there so that the devil himself—"

"That is precisely what I meant to do," caught up the doctor.

"That is what you meant to do. *Bueno.* It is as I say. You are a dangerous man."

Their voices, which without rising had been growing quarrelsome, ceased suddenly. The late Señor Hirsch, erect and shadowy against the stars, seemed to be waiting attentive, in impartial silence.

But Dr. Monygham had no mind to quarrel with Nostromo. At this supremely critical point of Sulaco's fortunes it was borne upon him at last that this man was really indispensable, more indispensable than ever the infatuation of Captain Mitchell, his proud discoverer, could conceive; far beyond what Decoud's best dry raillery about "my illustrious friend, the unique Capataz de Cargadores," had ever intended. The fellow was unique. He was not "one in a thousand." He was absolutely the only one. The doctor surrendered. There was something in the genius of that Genoese seaman which dominated in the destinies of great enterprises and of many people, the fortunes of Charles Gould, the fate of an admirable woman. At this last thought the doctor had to clear his throat before he could speak.

In a completely changed tone he pointed out to the Capataz that, to begin with, he personally ran no great risk. As far as everybody knew he was dead. It was an enormous advantage. He had only to keep out of sight in the Casa Viola, where the old Garibaldino was known to be alone—with his dead wife. The servants had all run away. No one would think of searching for him there, or anywhere else on earth, for that matter.

"That would be very true," Nostromo spoke up, bitterly, "if I had not met you."

For a time the doctor kept silent. "Do you mean to say that you think I may give you away?" he asked in an unsteady voice. "Why? Why should I do that?"

"What do I know? Why not? To gain a day perhaps. It would take Sotillo a day to give me the estrapade, and try some other things perhaps, before he puts a bullet through my heart—as he did to that poor wretch here. Why not?"

The doctor swallowed with difficulty. His throat had gone dry in a moment. It was not from indignation. The doctor, pathetically enough, believed that he had forfeited the right to be indignant with anyone—for anything. It was simple dread. Had the fellow heard his story by some chance? If so, there was an end of his usefulness in that direction. The indispensable man escaped his influence, because of that indelible blot which made him fit for dirty work. A feeling as of sickness came upon the doctor. He would have given anything to know, but he dared not clear up the point. The fanaticism of his devotion, fed on the sense of his abasement, hardened his heart in sadness and scorn.

"Why not, indeed?" he re-echoed, sardonically. "Then the safe thing for you is to kill me on the spot. I would defend myself. But you may just as well know I am going about unarmed."

"Por Dios!" said the Capataz, passionately. "You fine people are all alike. All dangerous. All betrayers of the poor who are your dogs."

"You do not understand," began the doctor, slowly.

"I understand you all!" cried the other with a violent movement, as shadowy to the doctor's eyes as the persistent immobility of the late Señor Hirsch. "A poor man amongst you has got to look after himself. I say that you do not care for those that serve you. Look at me! After all these years, suddenly, here I find myself like one of these curs that bark outside the walls—without a kennel or a dry bone for my teeth. *Caramba!"* But he relented with a contemptuous fairness. "Of course," he went on, quietly, "I do not suppose that you would hasten to give me up to Sotillo, for example. It is not that. It is that I am nothing! Suddenly—" He swung his arm downwards. "Nothing to anyone," he repeated.

The doctor breathed freely. "Listen, Capataz," he said, stretching out his arm almost affectionately towards Nostromo's shoulder. "I am going to tell you a very simple thing. You are safe because you are needed. I would not give you away for any conceivable reason, because I want you."

In the dark Nostromo bit his lip. He had heard enough of that. He knew what that meant. No more of that for him. But he had to look after himself now, he thought. And he thought, too, that it would not be prudent to part in anger from his companion. The doctor, admitted to be a great healer, had, amongst the populace of Sulaco, the reputation of being an evil sort of man. It was based solidly on his personal appearance, which was strange, and on his rough ironic manner—proofs visible, sensible, and incontrovertible of the doctor's malevolent disposition. And Nostromo was of the people. So he only grunted incredulously.

"You, to speak plainly, are the only man," the doctor pursued. "It is in your power to save this town and . . . everybody from the destructive rapacity of men who—"

"No, *señor,*" said Nostromo, sullenly. "It is not in my power to get the treasure back for you to give up to Sotillo, or Pedrito, or Gamacho. What do I know?"

"Nobody expects the impossible," was the answer.

"You have said it yourself—nobody," muttered Nostromo, in a gloomy, threatening tone.

But Dr. Monygham, full of hope, disregarded the enigmatic words and the threatening tone. To their eyes, accustomed to obscurity, the late Señor Hirsch, growing more distinct, seemed to have come nearer. And the doctor lowered his voice in exposing his scheme as though afraid of being overheard.

He was taking the indispensable man into his fullest confidence. Its implied flattery and suggestion of great risks came with a familiar sound to the Capataz. His mind, floating in irresolution and discontent, recognized it with bitterness. He understood well that the doctor was anxious to save the San Tomé mine from annihilation. He would be nothing without it. It was his interest. Just as it had been the interest of Señor Decoud, of the Blancos, and of the Europeans to get his Cargadores on their side. His thoughts became arrested upon Decoud. What would happen to him?

Nostromo's prolonged silence made the doctor uneasy. He pointed out, quite unnecessarily, that though for the present he was safe, he could not live concealed for ever. The choice was between accepting the mission to Barrios, with all its dangers and difficulties, and leaving Sulaco by stealth, ingloriously, in poverty.

"None of your friends could reward you and protect you just now, Capataz. Not even Don Carlos himself."

"I would have none of your protection and none of your rewards. I only wish I could trust your courage and your sense. When I return in triumph, as you say, with Barrios, I may find you all destroyed. You have the knife at your throat now."

It was the doctor's turn to remain silent in the contemplation of horrible contingencies.

"Well, we would trust your courage and your sense. And you, too, have a knife at your throat."

"Ah! And whom am I to thank for that? What are your politics and your mines to me—your silver and your constitutions—your Don Carlos this, and Don José that—"

"I don't know," burst out the exasperated doctor. "There are innocent people in danger whose little finger is worth more than you or I and all the Ribierists together. I don't know. You should have asked yourself before you allowed Decoud to lead you into all this. It was your place to think like a man; but if you did not think, then try to act like a man now. Did you imagine Decoud cared very much for what would happen to you?"

"No more than you care for what will happen to me," muttered the other.

"No; I care for what will happen to you as little as I care for what will happen to myself."

"And all this because you are such a devoted Ribierist?" Nostromo said in an incredulous tone.

"All this because I am such a devoted Ribierist," repeated Dr. Monygham, grimly.

Again Nostromo, gazing abstractedly at the body of the late Señor Hirsch, remained silent, thinking that the doctor was a dangerous person in more than one sense. It was impossible to trust him.

"Do you speak in the name of Don Carlos?" he asked at last.

"Yes. I do," the doctor said, loudly, without hesitation. "He must come forward now. He must," he added in a mutter, which Nostromo did not catch.

"What did you say, *señor?*"

The doctor started. "I say that you must be true to yourself, Capataz. It would be worse than folly to fail now."

"True to myself," repeated Nostromo. "How do you know that I would not be true to myself if I told you to go to the devil with your propositions?"

"I do not know. Maybe you would," the doctor said, with a roughness of tone intended to hide the sinking of his heart and the faltering of his voice. "All I know is that you had better get away from here. Some of Sotillo's men may turn up here looking for me."

He slipped off the table, listened intently. The Capataz, too, stood up.

"Suppose I went to Cayta, what would you do meantime?" he asked.

"I would go to Sotillo directly you had left—in the way I am thinking of."

"A very good way—if only that engineer-in-chief consents. Remind him, *señor*, that I looked after the old rich Englishman who pays for the railway, and that I saved the lives of some of his people that time when a gang of thieves came from the south to wreck one of his pay-trains. It was I who discovered it all at the risk of my life, by pretending to enter into their plans. Just as you are doing with Sotillo."

"Yes. Yes, of course. But I can offer him better arguments," the doctor said, hastily. "Leave it to me."

"Ah, yes! True. I am nothing."

"Not at all. You are everything."

They moved a few paces towards the door. Behind them the late Señor Hirsch preserved the immobility of a disregarded man.

"That will be all right. I know what to say to the engineer," pursued the doctor, in a low tone. "My difficulty will be with Sotillo."

And Dr. Monygham stopped short in the doorway as if intimidated by the difficulty. He had made the sacrifice of his life. He considered this a fitting opportunity. But he did not want to throw his life away too soon. In his quality of betrayer of Don Carlos's confidence, he would have ultimately to indicate the hiding place of the treasure. That would be the end of his deception, and the end of himself as well, at the hands of the infuriated colonel. He wanted to delay him to the very last moment; and he had been racking his brains to invent some place of concealment at once plausible and difficult of access.

He imparted his trouble to Nostromo, and concluded:

"Do you know what, Capataz? I think that when the time comes and some information must be given, I shall indicate the Great Isabel. That is the best place I can think of. What is the matter?"

A low exclamation had escaped Nostromo. The doctor waited, surprised, and after a moment of profound silence, heard a thick voice stammer out "Utter folly," and stop with a gasp.

"Why folly?"

"Ah! You do not see it," began Nostromo, scathingly, gathering scorn as he went on. "Three men in half an hour would see that no ground had been disturbed anywhere on that island. Do you think that such a treasure can be buried without leaving traces of the work—eh! Señor Doctor? Why, you would not gain half a day more before having your throat cut by Sotillo. The Isabel! What stupidity! What miserable invention! Ah! you are all alike, you fine men of intelligence. All you are fit for is to betray men of the people into undertaking deadly risks for objects that you are not even sure about. If it comes off you get the benefit. If not, then it does not matter. He is only a dog. Ah! *Madre de Dios,* I would—" He shook his fists above his head.

The doctor was overwhelmed at first by this fierce, hissing vehemence.

"Well! It seems to me on your own showing that the men of the people are no mean fools, too," he said, sullenly. "No, but come. You are so clever. Have you a better place?"

Nostromo had calmed down as quickly as he had flared up.

"I am clever enough for that," he said, quietly, almost with indifference. "You want to tell him of a hiding-place big enough to take days in ransacking—a place where a treasure of silver ingots can be buried without leaving a sign on the surface."

"And close at hand," the doctor put in.

"Just so, *señor.* Tell him it is sunk."

"This has the merit of being the truth," the doctor said, contemptuously. "He will not believe it."

"You tell him that it is sunk where he may hope to lay his hands on it, and he will believe you quick enough. Tell him it has been sunk in the harbor in order to be recovered afterwards by divers. Tell him you found out that I had orders from Don Carlos Gould to lower the cases quietly overboard somewhere in a line between the end of the jetty and the entrance. The depth is not too great there. He has no divers, but he has a ship, boats, ropes, chains, sailors—of a sort. Let him fish for the silver. Let him set his fools to drag backwards and forwards and crossways while he sits and watches till his eyes drop out of his head."

"Really, this is an admirable idea," muttered the doctor.

"*Sí.* You tell him that, and see whether he will not believe you! He will spend days in rage and torment—and still he will believe. He will have no thought for anything else. He will not give up till he is driven off—why, he may even forget to kill you. He will neither eat nor sleep. He—"

"The very thing! The very thing!" the doctor repeated in an excited whisper. "Capataz, I begin to believe that you are a great genius in your way."

Nostromo had paused; then began again in a changed tone, somber, speaking to himself as though he had forgotten the doctor's existence.

"There is something in a treasure that fastens upon a man's mind. He will pray and blaspheme and still persevere, and will curse the day he ever heard of it, and will let his last hour come upon him unawares, still believing that he missed it only by a foot. He will see it every time he closes his eyes. He will never forget it till he is dead—and even then—Doctor, did you ever hear of the miserable *gringos* on Azuera, that cannot die? Ha! ha! Sailors like myself. There is no getting away from a treasure that once fastens upon your mind."

"You are a devil of a man, Capataz. It is the most plausible thing."

Nostromo pressed his arm.

"It will be worse for him than thirst at sea or hunger in a town full of people. Do you know what that is? He shall suffer greater torments than he inflicted upon that terrified wretch who had no invention. None! none! Not like me. I could have told Sotillo a deadly tale for very little pain."

He laughed wildly and turned in the doorway towards the body of the late Señor Hirsch, an opaque long blotch in the semi-transparent obscurity of the room between the two tall parallelograms of the windows full of stars.

"You man of fear!" he cried. "You shall be avenged by me—Nostromo. Out of my way, doctor! Stand aside—or, by the suffering soul of a woman dead without confession, I will strangle you with my two hands."

He bounded downstairs into the black, smoky hall. With a grunt of astonishment, Dr. Monygham threw himself recklessly into the pursuit. At the bottom of the charred stairs he had a fall, pitching forward on his face with a force that would have stunned a spirit less intent upon a task of love and devotion. He was up in a moment, jarred, shaken, with a queer impression of the terrestrial globe having been flung at his head in the dark. But it wanted more than that to stop Dr. Monygham's body, possessed by the exaltation of self-sacrifice; a reasonable exaltation, determined not to lose whatever advantage chance put into its way. He ran with headlong, tottering swiftness, his arms going like a windmill in his effort to keep his balance on his crippled feet. He lost his hat; the tails of his open gaberdine flew behind him. He had no mind to lose sight of the indispensable man. But it was a long time, and a long way from the Custom House, before he managed to seize his arm from behind, roughly, out of breath.

"Stop! Are you mad?"

Already Nostromo was walking slowly, his head dropping, as if checked in his pace by the weariness of irresolution.

"What is that to you? Ah! I forgot you want me for something. Always. *Siempre Nostromo.*"

"What do you mean by talking of strangling me?" panted the doctor.

"What do I mean? I mean that the king of the devils himself has sent you out of this town of cowards and talkers to meet me tonight of all the nights of my life."

Under the starry sky the Albergo d'Italia Una emerged, black and low, breaking the dark level of the plain. Nostromo stopped altogether.

"The priests say he is a tempter, do they not?" he added, through his clenched teeth.

"My good man, you drivel. The devil has nothing to do with this. Neither has the town, which you may call by what name you please. But Don Carlos Gould is neither a coward nor an empty talker. You will admit that?" He waited. "Well?"

"Could I see Don Carlos?"

"Great heavens! No! Why? What for?" exclaimed the doctor in agitation. "I tell you it is madness. I will not let you go into the town for anything."

"I must."

"You must not!" hissed the doctor, fiercely, almost beside himself with the fear of the man doing away with his usefulness for an imbecile whim of some sort. "I tell you you shall not. I would rather—"

He stopped at a loss for words, feeling fagged out, powerless, holding on to Nostromo's sleeve, absolutely for support after his run.

"I am betrayed!" muttered the Capataz to himself; and the doctor, who overheard the last word, made an effort to speak calmly.

"That is exactly what would happen to you. You would be betrayed."

He thought with a sickening dread that the man was so well known that he could not escape recognition. The house of the Señor Administrador was beset by spies, no doubt. And even the very servants of the *casa* were not to be trusted. "Reflect, Capataz," he said, impressively. . . . "What are you laughing at?"

"I am laughing to think that if somebody that did not approve of my presence in town, for instance—you understand, *señor doctor*—if somebody were to give me up to Pedrito, it would not be beyond my power to make friends even with him. It is true. What do you think of that?"

"You are a man of infinite resource, Capataz," said Dr. Monygham, dismally. "I recognize that. But the town is full of talk about you; and those few *cargadores* that are not in hiding with the railway people have been shouting '*Viva Montero!*' on the Plaza all day."

"My poor *cargadores!*" muttered Nostromo. "Betrayed! Betrayed!"

"I understand that on the wharf you were pretty free in laying about you with a stick amongst your poor *cargadores*," the doctor said in a grim tone, which showed that he was recovering from his exertions. "Make no mistake. Pedrito is furious at Señor Ribiera's rescue, and at having lost the pleasure of shooting Decoud. Already there are rumors in the town of the treasure having been spirited away. To have missed that does not please Pedrito either; but let me tell you that if you had all the silver in your hand for your ransom it would not save you."

Turning swiftly, and catching the doctor by the shoulders, Nostromo thrust his face close to his.

"*Maladetta!* You follow me speaking of the treasure. You have sworn my ruin. You were the last man who looked upon me before I went out with it. And Sidoni the engine-driver says you have an evil eye."

"He ought to know. I saved his broken leg for him last year," the doctor said, stoically. He felt on his shoulders the weight of these hands famed amongst the populace for snapping thick ropes and bending horseshoes. "And to you I offer the best means of saving yourself—let me go—and of retrieving your great reputation. You boasted of making the Capataz de Cargadores famous from one end of America to the other about this wretched silver. But I bring you a better opportunity—let me go, *hombre!*"

Nostromo released him abruptly, and the doctor feared that the indispensable man would run off again. But he did not. He walked on slowly. The doctor hobbled by his side till, within a stone's throw from the Casa Viola, Nostromo stopped again.

Silent in inhospitable darkness, the Casa Viola seemed to have changed its nature; his home appeared to repel him with an air of hopeless and inimical mystery. The doctor said:

"You will be safe there. Go in, Capataz."

"How can I go in?" Nostromo seemed to ask himself in a low, inward tone. "She cannot unsay what she said, and I cannot undo what I have done."

"I tell you it is all right. Viola is all alone in there. I looked in as I came out of the town. You will be perfectly safe in that house till you leave it to make your name famous on the Campo. I am going now to arrange for your departure with the engineer-in-chief, and I shall bring you news here long before daybreak."

Dr. Monygham, disregarding, or perhaps fearing to penetrate the meaning of Nostromo's silence, clapped him lightly on the shoulder, and starting off with his smart, lame walk, vanished utterly at the third or fourth hop in the direction of the railway track. Arrested between the two wooden posts for people to fasten their horses to, Nostromo did not move, as if he, too, had been planted solidly in the ground. At the end of half an hour he lifted his head to the deep baying of the dogs at the railway yards, which had burst out suddenly, tumultuous and deadened as if coming out from under the plain. That lame doctor with the evil eye had got there pretty fast.

Step by step Nostromo approached the Albergo d'Italia Una, which he had never known so lightless, so silent, before. The door, all black in the pale wall, stood open as he had left it twenty-four hours before, when he had nothing to hide from the world. He remained before it, irresolute, like a fugitive, like a man betrayed. Poverty, misery, starvation! Where had he heard these words? The anger of a dying woman had prophesied that fate for his folly. It looked as if it would come true very quickly. And the *leperos* would laugh—she had said. Yes, they would laugh if they knew that the Capataz de Cargadores was at the mercy of the mad doctor whom they could remember, only a few years ago, buying cooked food from a stall on the Plaza for a copper coin—like one of themselves.

At that moment the notion of seeking Captain Mitchell passed through his mind. He glanced in the direction of the jetty and saw a small gleam of light in the O.S.N. Company's building. The thought of lighted windows was not attractive. Two lighted windows had decoyed him into the empty Custom House, only to fall into the clutches of that doctor. No! He would not go near lighted windows again on that night. Captain Mitchell was there. And what could he be told? That doctor would worm it all out of him as if he were a child.

On the threshold he called out "Giorgio!" in an undertone. Nobody answered. He stepped in. *"Olá! viejo!* Are you there? . . ." In the impenetrable darkness his head swam with the illusion that the obscurity of the kitchen was as vast as the Placid Gulf, and that the floor dipped forward like a sinking lighter. *"Olá! viejo!"* he repeated, falteringly, swaying where he stood. His hand, extended to steady himself, fell upon the table. Moving a step forward, he shifted it, and felt a box of matches under his fingers. He fancied he had heard a quiet sigh. He listened for a moment, holding his breath; then, with trembling hands, tried to strike a light.

The tiny piece of wood flamed up quite blindingly at the end of his fingers, raised above his blinking eyes. A concentrated glare fell upon the leonine white head of old Giorgio against the black fireplace—showed him leaning forward in a chair in staring immobility, surrounded, overhung, by great masses of shadow, his legs crossed, his cheek in his hand, and empty pipe in the corner of his mouth. It seemed hours before he attempted to turn his face; at the very moment the match went out, and he disappeared, overwhelmed by the shadows, as if the walls and roof of the desolate house had collapsed upon his white head in ghostly silence.

Nostromo heard him stir and utter dispassionately the words:

"It may have been a vision."

"No," he said, softly. "It is no vision, old man."

A strong chest voice asked in the dark:

"Is that you I hear, Giovann' Battista?"

"Sí, viejo. Steady. Not so loud."

After his release by Sotillo, Giorgio Viola, attended to the very door by the good-natured engineer-in-chief, had re-entered his house, which he had been made to leave almost at the very moment of his wife's death. All was still. The lamp above was burning. He nearly called out to her by name; and the thought that no call from him would ever again evoke the answer of her voice, made him drop heavily into the chair with a loud groan, wrung out by the pain as of a keen blade piercing his breast.

The rest of the night he made no sound. The darkness turned to gray, and on the colorless, clear, glassy dawn the jagged sierra stood out flat and opaque, as if cut out of paper.

The enthusiastic and severe soul of Giorgio Viola, sailor, champion of oppressed humanity, enemy of kings, and, by the grace of Mrs. Gould, hotel-keeper of the Sulaco harbor, had descended into the open abyss of desolation amongst the shattered vestiges of his past. He remembered his wooing between two campaigns a single short week in the season of gathering olives. Nothing approached the grave passion of that time but the deep, passionate sense of his bereavement. He discovered all the extent of his dependence upon the silenced voice of that woman. It was her voice that he missed. Abstracted, busy, lost in inward contemplation, he seldom looked at his wife in those later years. The thought of his girls was a matter of concern, not of consolation. It was her voice that he would miss. And he remembered the other child—the little boy who died at sea. Ah! a man would have been something to lean upon. And, alas! even Gian' Battista—he of whom, and of Linda, his wife had spoken to him so anxiously before she dropped off into her last sleep on earth, he on whom she had called aloud to save the children, just before she died—even he was dead!

And the old man, bent forward, his head in his hand, sat through the day in immobility and solitude. He never heard the brazen roar of the bells in town. When it ceased the earthenware filter in the corner of the kitchen kept on its swift musical drip, drip into the great porous jar below.

Towards sunset he got up, and with slow movements disappeared up the narrow staircase. His bulk filled it; and the rubbing of his shoulders made a small noise as of a mouse running behind the plaster of a wall. While he remained up there the house was as dumb as a grave. Then, with the same faint rubbing noise, he descended. He had to catch at the chairs and tables to regain his seat. He seized his pipe off the high mantel of the fireplace—but made no attempt to reach the tobacco—thrust it empty into the corner of his mouth, and sat down again in the same staring pose. The sun of Pedrito's entry into Sulaco, the last sun of Señor Hirsch's life, the first of Decoud's solitude on the Great Isabel, passed over the Albergo d'Italia Una on its way to the west. The tinkling drip, drip of the filter had ceased, the lamp upstairs had burnt itself out, and the night beset Giorgio Viola and his dead wife with its obscurity and silence that seemed invincible till the Capataz de Cargadores, returning from the dead, put them to flight with the splutter and flare of a match.

"Sí, viejo. It is me. Wait."

Nostromo, after barricading the door and closing the shutters carefully, groped upon a shelf for a candle, and lit it.

Old Viola had risen. He followed with his eyes in the dark the sounds made by Nostromo. The light disclosed him standing without support, as if the mere presence of that man who was loyal, brave, incorruptible, who was all his son would have been, were enough for the support of his decaying strength.

He extended his hand grasping the briar-wood pipe, whose bowl was charred on the edge, and knitted his bushy eyebrows heavily at the light.

"You have returned," he said, with shaky dignity. "Ah! Very well! I—"

He broke off. Nostromo, leaning back against the table, his arms folded on his breast, nodded at him slightly.

"You thought I was drowned! No! The best dog of the rich, of the aristocrats, of these fine men who can only talk and betray the people, is not dead yet."

The Garibaldino, motionless, seemed to drink in the sound of the well-known voice. His head moved slightly once as if in sign of approval; but Nostromo saw clearly that the old man understood nothing of the words. There was no one to understand; no one he could take into the confidence of Decoud's fate, of his own, into the secret of the silver. That doctor was an enemy of the people—a tempter. . . .

Old Giorgio's heavy frame shook from head to foot with the effort to overcome his emotion at the sight of that man, who had shared the intimacies of his domestic life as though he had been a grown-up son.

"She believed you would return," he said, solemnly.

Nostromo raised his head.

"She was a wise woman. How could I fail to come back—?"

He finished the thought mentally: "Since she has prophesied for me an end of poverty, misery, and starvation." These words of Teresa's anger, from the circumstances in which they had been uttered, like the cry of a soul prevented from making its peace with God, stirred the obscure superstition of personal fortune from which even the greatest genius amongst men of adventure and action is seldom free. They reigned over Nostromo's mind with the force of a potent malediction. And what a curse it was that which her words had laid upon him! He had been orphaned so young that he could remember no other woman whom he called mother. Henceforth there would be no enterprise in which he would not fail. The spell was working already. Death itself would elude him now. . . . He said violently:

"Come, *viejo!* Get me something to eat. I am hungry! *Sangre de Dios!* The emptiness of my belly makes me lightheaded."

With his chin dropped again upon his bare breast above his folded arms, barefooted, watching from under a gloomy brow the movements of old Viola foraging amongst the cupboards, he seemed as if indeed fallen under a curse—a ruined and sinister Capataz.

Old Viola walked out of a dark corner, and, without a word, emptied upon the table out of his hollowed palms a few dry crusts of bread and half a raw onion.

While the Capataz began to devour his beggar's fare, taking up with stony-eyed voracity piece after piece lying by his side, the Garibaldino went off, and squatting down in another corner filled an earthenware mug with red wine out of a wicker-covered demijohn. With a familiar gesture, as when serving customers in the café, he had thrust his pipe between his teeth to have his hands free.

The Capataz drank greedily. A slight flush deepened the bronze of his cheek. Before him, Viola, with a turn of his white and massive head towards the staircase, took his empty pipe out of his mouth, and pronounced slowly:

"After the shot was fired down here, which killed her as surely as if the bullet had struck her oppressed heart, she called upon you to save the children. Upon you, Gian' Battista."

The Capataz looked up.

"Did she do that, Padrone? To save the children! They are with the English *señora,* their rich benefactress. Hey! old man of the people. Thy benefactress. . . ."

"I am old," muttered Giorgio Viola. "An Englishwoman was allowed to give a bed to Garibaldi lying wounded in prison. The greatest man that ever lived. A man of the people, too—a sailor. I may let another keep a roof over my head. *Sí* . . . I am old. I may let her. Life lasts too long sometimes."

"And she herself may not have a roof over her head before many days are out, unless I . . . What do you say? Am I to keep a roof over her head? Am I to try—and save all the Blancos together with her?"

"You shall do it," said old Viola in a strong voice. "You shall do it as my son would have. . . ."

"Thy son, *viejo!* . . . There never has been a man like thy son. Ha, I must try.

. . . But what if it were only a part of the curse to lure me on? . . . And so she called upon me to save—and then—?"

"She spoke no more." The heroic follower of Garibaldi, at the thought of the eternal stillness and silence fallen upon the shrouded form stretched out on the bed upstairs, averted his face and raised his hand to his furrowed brow. "She was dead before I could seize her hands," he stammered out, pitifully.

Before the wide eyes of the Capataz, staring at the doorway of the dark staircase, floated the shape of the Great Isabel, like a strange ship in distress, freighted with enormous wealth and the solitary life of a man. It was impossible for him to do anything. He could only hold his tongue, since there was no one to trust. The treasure would be lost, probably—unless Decoud . . . And his thought came abruptly to an end. He perceived that he could not imagine in the least what Decoud was likely to do.

Old Viola had not stirred. And the motionless Capataz dropped his long, soft eyelashes, which gave to the upper part of his fierce, black-whiskered face a touch of feminine ingenuousness. The silence had lasted for a long time.

"God rest her soul!" he murmured, gloomily.

X

The next day was quiet in the morning, except for the faint sound of firing to the northward, in the direction of Los Hatos. Captain Mitchell had listened to it from his balcony anxiously. The phrase "In my delicate position as the only consular agent then in the port, everything, sir, everything was a just cause for anxiety" had its place in the more or less stereotyped relation of the "historical events" which for the next few years was at the service of distinguished strangers visiting Sulaco. The mention of the dignity and neutrality of the flag, so difficult to preserve in his position, "right in the thick of these events between the lawlessness of that piratical villain Sotillo and the more regularly established but scarcely less atrocious tyranny of his Excellency Don Pedro Montero," came next in order. Captain Mitchell was not the man to enlarge upon mere dangers much. But he insisted that it was a memorable day. On that day, towards dusk, he had seen "that poor fellow of mine—Nostromo. The sailor whom I discovered, and, I may say, made, sir. The man of the famous ride to Cayta, sir. An historical event, sir!"

Regarded by the O.S.N. Company as an old and faithful servant, Captain Mitchell was allowed to attain the term of his usefulness in ease and dignity at the head of the enormously extended service. The augmentation of the establishment, with its crowds of clerks, an office in town, the old office in the harbor, the division into departments —passenger, cargo, lighterage, and so on—secured a greater leisure for his last years in the regenerated Sulaco, the capital of the Occidental Republic. Liked by the natives for his good nature and the formality of his manner, self-important and simple, known for years as a "friend of our country," he felt himself a personality of mark in the town. Getting up early for a turn in the marketplace while the gigantic shadow of Higuerota was still lying upon the fruit and flower stalls piled up with masses of gorgeous coloring, attending easily to current affairs, welcomed in houses, greeted by ladies on the Alameda, with his entry into all the clubs and a footing in the Casa Gould, he led his privileged old bachelor, man-about-town existence with great comfort and solemnity. But on mail-boat days he was down at the Harbor Office at an early hour, with his own gig, manned by a smart crew in white and blue, ready to dash off and board the ship directly she showed her bows between the harbor heads.

It would be into the Harbor Office that he would lead some privileged passenger he had brought off in his own boat, and invite him to take a seat for a moment while he signed a few papers. And Captain Mitchell, seating himself at his desk, would keep on talking hospitably:

"There isn't much time if you are to see everything in a day. We shall be off in a moment. We'll have lunch at the Amarilla Club—though I belong also to the Anglo-American—mining engineers and businessmen, don't you know—and to the Mirliflores as well, a new club—English, French, Italians, all sorts—lively young fellows mostly, who wanted to pay a compliment to an old resident, sir. But we'll lunch at the Amarilla. Interest you, I fancy. Real thing of the country. Men of the first families. The President of the Occidental Republic himself belongs to it, sir. Fine old bishop with a broken nose in the patio. Remarkable piece of statuary, I believe. Cavaliere Parrochetti—you know Parrochetti, the famous Italian sculptor—was working here for two years—thought very highly of our old bishop. . . . There! I am very much at your service now."

Proud of his experience, penetrated by the sense of historical importance of men, events, and buildings, he talked pompously in jerky periods, with slight sweeps of his short, thick arm, letting nothing "escape the attention" of his privileged captive.

"Lot of building going on, as you observe. Before the Separation it was a plain of burnt grass smothered in clouds of dust, with an ox-cart track to our Jetty. Nothing more. This is the Harbor Gate. Picturesque, is it not? Formerly the town stopped short there. We enter now the Calle de la Constitución. Observe the old Spanish houses. Great dignity. Eh? I suppose it's just as it was in the time of the Viceroys, except for the pavement. Wood blocks now. Sulaco National Bank there, with the sentry boxes each side of the gate. Casa Avellanos this side, with all the ground-floor windows shuttered. A wonderful woman lives there—Miss Avellanos—the beautiful Antonia. A character, sir! A historical woman! Opposite—Casa Gould. Noble gateway. Yes, *the* Goulds of the original Gould Concession, that all the world knows of now. I hold seventeen of the thousand-dollar shares in the Consolidated San Tomé mines. All the poor savings of my lifetime, sir, and it will be enough to keep me in comfort to the end of my days at home when I retire. I got in on the ground floor, you see. Don Carlos, great friend of mine. Seventeen shares—quite a little fortune to leave behind one, too. I have a niece—married a parson—most worthy man, incumbent of a small parish in Sussex; no end of children. I was never married myself. A sailor should exercise self-denial. Standing under that very gateway, sir, with some young engineer-fellows, ready to defend that house where we had received so much kindness and hospitality, I saw the first and last charge of Pedrito's horsemen upon Barrios's troops, who had just taken the Harbor Gate. They could not stand the new rifles brought out by that poor Decoud. It was a murderous fire. In a moment the street became blocked with a mass of dead men and horses. They never came on again."

And all day Captain Mitchell would talk like this to his more or less willing victim: "The Plaza. I call it magnificent. Twice the area of Trafalgar Square."

From the very center, in the blazing sunshine, he pointed out the buildings:

"The Intendencia, now President's Palace—Cabildo, where the Lower Chamber of Parliament sits. You notice the new houses on that side of the Plaza? Compañia Anzani, a great general store, like those cooperative things at home. Old Anzani was murdered by the National Guards in front of his safe. It was even for that specific crime that the deputy Gamacho, commanding the Nationals, a bloodthirsty and savage brute, was executed publicly by garrotte upon the sentence of a courtmartial ordered by Barrios. Anzani's nephews converted the business into a company. All that side of the Plaza had been burnt; used to be colonnaded before. A terrible fire, by the light of which I saw the last of the fighting, the *llaneros* flying, the Nationals throwing their arms down, and the miners of San Tomé, all Indians from the Sierra, rolling by like a torrent to the sound of pipes and cymbals, green flags flying, a wild mass of men in white ponchos and green hats, on foot, on mules, on donkeys. Such a sight, sir, will never be seen again. The miners, sir, had marched upon the town, Don Pepe leading on his black horse, and their very wives in the rear on *burros*, screaming encouragement, sir, and beating tambourines. I remember one of these women had a green parrot seated on her shoulder, as calm as a bird of stone. They had just saved their Señor Administrador; for Barrios, though he ordered the assault at once, at night, too, would have been too late. Pedrito Montero had Don Carlos led out to be shot—like his uncle many years ago—and then, as Barrios said afterwards, "Sulaco would not have been worth fighting for." Sulaco without the Concession was nothing; and there were tons and tons of dynamite distributed all over the mountain with detonators arranged, and an old priest, Father Román, standing by to annihilate the San Tomé mine at the first news of failure. Don Carlos had made up his mind not to leave it behind, and he had the right men to see to it, too."

Thus Captain Mitchell would talk in the middle of the Plaza, holding over his head a white umbrella with a green lining; but inside the cathedral, in the dim light, with a faint scent of incense floating in the cool atmosphere, and here and there a kneeling female figure, black or all white, with a veiled head, his lowered voice became solemn and impressive.

"Here," he would say, pointing to a niche in the wall of the dusky aisle, "you see the bust of Don José Avellanos, 'Patriot and Statesman,' as the inscription says, 'Minister to Courts of England and Spain, etc., etc., died in the woods of Los Hatos worn out with his life-long struggle for Right and Justice at the dawn of the New Era.' A fair likeness. Parrochetti's work from some old photographs and a pencil sketch by Mrs. Gould. I was well acquainted with that distinguished Spanish-American of the old school, a true *hidalgo*, beloved by everybody who knew him. The marble medallion in the wall, in the antique style, representing a veiled woman seated with her hands clasped loosely over her knees, commemorates that unfortunate young gentleman who sailed out with Nostromo on that fatal night, sir. See, 'To the memory of Martin Decoud, his betrothed Antonia Avellanos.' Frank, simple, noble. There you have that lady, sir, as she is. An exceptional woman. Those who thought she would give way to despair were mistaken, sir. She has been blamed in many quarters for not having taken the veil. It was expected of her. But Doña Antonia is not the stuff they make nuns of. Bishop Corbelán, her uncle, lives with her in the Corbelán town house. He is a fierce sort of priest, everlastingly worrying the Government about the old Church lands and convents. I believe they think a lot of him in Rome. Now let us go to the Amarilla Club, just across the Plaza, to get some lunch."

Directly outside the cathedral on the very top of the noble flight of steps, his voice rose pompously, his arm found again its sweeping gesture.

"*Porvenir*, over there on that first floor, above those French plate-glass shop-fronts; our biggest daily. Conservative, or, rather, I should say, Parliamentary. We have the Parliamentary party here of which the actual Chief of the State, Don Juste Lopez, is the head; a very sagacious man, I think. A first-rate intellect, sir. The Democratic party in opposition rests mostly, I am sorry to say, on these socialist Italians, sir, with their secret societies, *camorras*, and such-like. There are lots of Italians settled here on the railway lands, dismissed navvies, mechanics, and so on, all along the trunk line. There are whole villages of Italians on the Campo. And the natives, too, are being drawn into these ways. . . . American bar? Yes. And over there you can see another. New Yorkers mostly frequent that one—Here we are at the Amarilla. Observe the bishop at the foot of the stairs to the right as we go in."

And the lunch would begin and terminate its lavish and leisurely course at a little table in the gallery. Captain Mitchell nodding, bowing, getting up to speak for a moment to different officials in black clothes, merchants in jackets, officers in uniform, middle-aged *caballeros* from the Campo—sallow, little, nervous men, and fat, placid, swarthy men, and Europeans or North Americans of superior standing, whose faces looked very white amongst the majority of dark complexions and black, glistening eyes.

Captain Mitchell would lie back in the chair, casting around looks of satisfaction, and tender over the table a case full of thick cigars.

"Try a weed with your coffee. Local tobacco. The black coffee you get at the Amarilla, sir, you don't meet anywhere in the world. We get the bean from a famous cafeteria in the foot-hills, whose owner sends three sacks every year as a present to his fellow members in remembrance of the fight against Gamacho's Nationals, carried on from these very windows by the *caballeros*. He was in town at the time, and took part, sir, to the bitter end. It arrives on three mules—not in the common way, by rail; no fear!—right into the patio, escorted by mounted peons, in charge of the Mayoral of his estate, who walks upstairs, booted and spurred, and delivers it to our committee formally with the words, 'For the sake of those fallen the third of May.' We call it 'Tres de Mayo' coffee. Taste it."

Captain Mitchell, with an expression as though making ready to hear a sermon in a church, would lift the tiny cup to his lips. And the nectar would be sipped to the bottom during a restful silence in a cloud of cigar smoke.

"Look at this man in black just going out," he would begin, leaning forward hastily. "This is the famous Hernandez, Minister of War. *The Times's* special correspondent, who wrote that striking series of letters calling the Occidental Republic the 'Treasure House of the World,' gave a whole article to him and the force he has organized—the renowned Carabineers of the Campo."

Captain Mitchell's guest, staring curiously, would see a figure in a long-tailed black coat walking gravely, with downcast eyelids in a long, composed face, a brow furrowed horizontally, a pointed head, whose gray hair, thin at the top, combed down carefully on all sides and rolled at the ends, fell low on the neck and shoulders. This, then, was the famous bandit of whom Europe had heard with interest. He put on a high-crowned sombrero with a wide flat brim; a rosary of wooden beads was twisted about his right wrist. And Captain Mitchell would proceed:

"The protector of the Sulaco refugees from the rage of Pedrito. As general of cavalry with Barrios he distinguished himself at the storming of Tonoro, where Señor Fuentes was killed with the last remnant of the Monterists. He is the friend and humble servant of Bishop Corbelán. Hears three Masses every day. I bet you he will step into the cathedral to say a prayer or two on his way home to his siesta."

He took several puffs at his cigar in silence; then, in his best important manner, pronounced:

"The Spanish race, sir, is prolific of remarkable characters in every rank of life. . . . I propose we go now into the billiard-room, which is cool, for a quiet chat. There's never anybody there till after five. I could tell you episodes of the Separationist revolution that would astonish you. When the great heat's over, we'll take a turn on the Alameda."

The program went on relentlessly, like a law of Nature. The turn on the Alameda was taken with slow steps and stately remarks.

"All the great world of Sulaco here, sir." Captain Mitchell bowed right and left with no end of formality; then with animation, "Doña Emilia, Mrs. Gould's carriage. Look. Always white mules. The kindest, most gracious woman the sun ever shone upon. A great position, sir. A great position. First lady in Sulaco—far before the President's wife. And worthy of it." He took off his hat; then, with a studied change of tone, added, negligently, that the man in black by her side, with a high white collar and a scarred, snarly face, was Dr. Monygham, Inspector of State Hospitals, chief medical officer of the Consolidated San Tomé mines. "A familiar of the house. Everlastingly there. No wonder. The Goulds made him. Very clever man and all that, but I never liked him. Nobody does. I can recollect him limping about the streets in a check shirt and native sandals with a watermelon under his arm—all he would get to eat for the day. A big-wig now, sir, and as nasty as ever. However . . . There's no doubt he played his part fairly well at the time. He saved us all from the deadly incubus of Sotillo, where a more particular man might have failed—"

His arm went up.

"The equestrial statue that used to stand on the pedestal over there has been removed. It was an anachronism," Captain Mitchell commented, obscurely. "There is some talk of replacing it by a marble shaft commemorative of Separation, with angels of peace at the four corners, and bronze Justice holding an even balance, all gilt, on the top. Cavaliere Parrochetti was asked to make a design, which you can see framed under glass in the Municipal Sala. Names are to be engraved all round the base. Well! They could do no better than begin with the name of Nostromo. He has done for Separation as much as anybody else, and," added Captain Mitchell, "has got less than many others by it—when it comes to that." He dropped on to a stone seat under a tree, and tapped invitingly at the place by his side. "He carried to Barrios the letters from Sulaco which decided the General to abandon Cayta for a time, and come back to our help here by sea. The transports were still in harbor fortunately. Sir, I did not even know that my Capataz de Cargadores was alive. I had no idea. It was Dr. Monygham who came upon him, by chance, in the Custom House, evacuated an hour or two before by the wretched Sotillo. I was never told; never given a hint, nothing—as if I were unworthy of confidence. Monygham arranged it all. He went to the railway yards, and got admission to the engineer-in-chief, who, for the sake of the Goulds as much as for anything else, consented to let an engine make a dash down the line, one hundred and eighty miles, with Nostromo aboard. It was the only way to get him off. In the Construction Camp at the rail-head, he obtained a horse, arms, some clothing, and started alone on that marvelous ride—four hundred miles in six days, through a disturbed country, ending by the feat of passing through the Monterist lines outside Cayta. The history of that ride, sir, would make a most exciting book. He carried all our lives in his pocket. Devotion, courage, fidelity, intelligence were not enough. Of course, he was perfectly fearless and incorruptible. But a man was wanted that would know how to succeed. He was that man, sir. On the fifth of May, being practically a prisoner in the Harbor Office of my Company, I suddenly heard the whistle of an engine in the railway yards, a quarter of a mile away. I could not believe my ears. I made one jump on to the balcony, and beheld a locomotive under a great head of steam run out of the yard gates, screeching like mad, enveloped in a white cloud, and then, just abreast of old Viola's inn, check almost to a standstill. I made out, sir, a man —I couldn't tell who—dash out of the Albergo d'Italia Una, climb into the cab, and then, sir, that engine seemed positively to leap clear of the house, and was gone in the twinkling of an eye. As you blow a candle out, sir! There was a first-rate driver on the foot-plate, sir, I can tell you. They were fired heavily upon by the National Guards in Rincón and one other place. Fortunately the line had not been torn up. In four hours they reached the Construction Camp. Nostromo had his start. . . . The rest you know. You've got only to look round you. There are people on this Alameda that ride in their carriages, or even are alive at all today, because years ago I engaged a runaway Italian sailor for a foreman of our wharf simply on the strength of his looks. And that's a fact. You can't get over it, sir. On the seventeenth of May, just twelve days after I saw the man from the Casa Viola get on the engine, and wondered what it meant, Barrios's transports were entering this harbor, and the 'Treasure House of the

World,' as *The Times* man calls Sulaco in his book, was saved intact for civilization—
for a great future, sir. Pedrito, with Hernandez on the west, and the San Tomé miners
pressing on the land gate, was not able to oppose the landing. He had been sending
messages to Sotillo for a week to join him. Had Sotillo done so there would have been
massacres and proscription that would have left no man or woman of position alive.
But that's where Dr. Monygham comes in. Sotillo, blind and deaf to everything, stuck
on board his steamer watching the dragging for silver, which he believed to be sunk at
the bottom of the harbor. They say that for the last three days he was out of his mind
raving and foaming with disappointment at getting nothing, flying about the deck, and
yelling curses at the boats with the drags, ordering them in, and then suddenly
stamping his foot and crying out, 'And yet it is there! I see it! I feel it!'

"He was preparing to hang Dr. Monygham (whom he had on board) at the end of
the after-derrick, when the first of Barrios's transports, one of our own ships at that,
steamed right in, and ranging close alongside opened a small-arm fire without as much
preliminaries as a hail. It was the completest surprise in the world, sir. They were too
astounded at first to bolt below. Men were falling right and left like ninepins. It's a
miracle that Monygham, standing on the after-hatch with the rope already round his
neck, escaped being riddled through and through like a sieve. He told me since that he
had given himself up for lost, and kept on yelling with all the strength of his lungs:
'Hoist a white flag! Hoist a white flag!' Suddenly an old major of the Esmeralda
regiment, standing by, unsheathed his sword with a shriek: 'Die, perjured traitor!' and
ran Sotillo clean through the body, just before he fell himself shot through the head."

Captain Mitchell stopped for a while.

"Begad, sir! I could spin you a yarn for hours. But it's time we started off to
Rincón. It would not do for you to pass through Sulaco and not see the lights of the
San Tomé mine, a whole mountain ablaze like a lighted palace above the dark Campo.
It's a fashionable drive. . . . But let me tell you one little anecdote, sir; just to show
you. A fortnight or more later, when Barrios, declared Generalissimo, was gone in
pursuit of Pedrito away south, when the Provisional Junta, with Don Juste Lopez at its
head, had promulgated the new Constitution, and our Don Carlos Gould was packing
up his trunk bound on a mission to San Francisco and Washington (the United
States, sir, were the first great power to recognize the Occidental Republic)—a fortnight later, I say, when we were beginning to feel that our heads were safe on our
shoulders, if I may express myself so, a prominent man, a large shipper by our line,
came to see me on business, and, says he, the first thing: 'I say, Captain Mitchell, is
that fellow' (meaning Nostromo) 'still the Capataz of your *cargadores* or not?' 'What's
the matter?' says I. 'Because, if he is, then I don't mind; I send and receive a good lot
of cargo by your ships; but I have observed him several days loafing about the wharf,
and just now he stopped me as cool as you please with a request for a cigar. Now, you
know, my cigars are rather special, and I can't get them so easily as all that.' 'I hope
you stretched a point,' I said, very gently. 'Why, yes. But it's a confounded nuisance.
The fellow's everlastingly cadging for smokes.' Sir, I turned my eyes away, and then
asked, 'Weren't you one of the prisoners in the *cabildo?*' 'You know very well I was, and

in chains, too,' says he. 'And under a fine of fifteen thousand dollars?' He colored, sir, because it got about that he fainted from fright when they came to arrest him, and then behaved before Fuentes in a manner to make the very *policianos*, who had dragged him there by the hair of his head, smile at his cringing. 'Yes,' he says, in a sort of shy way. 'Why?' 'Oh, nothing. You stood to lose a tidy bit,' says I, 'even if you saved your life. . . . But what can I do for you?' He never even saw the point. Not he. And that's how the world wags, sir."

He rose a little stiffly, and the drive to Rincón would be taken with only one philosophical remark, uttered by the merciless *cicerone*, with his eyes fixed upon the lights of San Tomé, that seemed suspended in the dark night between earth and heaven.

"A great power, this, for good and evil, sir. A great power."

And the dinner of the Mirliflores would be eaten, excellent as to cooking, and leaving upon the traveler's mind an impression that there were in Sulaco many pleasant, able young men with salaries apparently too large for their discretion, and amongst them a few, mostly Anglo-Saxon, skilled in the art of, as the saying is, "taking a rise" out of his kind host.

With a rapid, jingling drive to the harbor in a two-wheeled machine (which Captain Mitchell called a curricle) behind a fleet and scraggy mule beaten all the time by an obviously Neapolitan driver, the cycle would be nearly closed before the lighted-up offices of the O.S.N. Company, remaining open so late because of the steamer. Nearly —but not quite.

"Ten o'clock. Your ship won't be ready to leave till half past twelve, if by then. Come in for a brandy-and-soda and one more cigar."

And in the superintendent's private room the privileged passenger by the *Ceres*, or *Juno*, or *Pallas*, stunned and as it were annihilated mentally by a sudden surfeit of sights, sounds, names, facts, and complicated information imperfectly apprehended, would listen like a tired child to a fairy tale; would hear a voice, familiar and surprising in its pompousness, tell him, as if from another world, how there was "in this very harbor" an international naval demonstration, which put an end to the Costaguana-Sulaco War. How the United States cruiser, *Powhattan*, was the first to salute the Occidental flag—white, with a wreath of green laurel in the middle encircling a yellow amarilla flower. Would hear how General Montero, in less than a month after proclaiming himself Emperor of Costaguana, was shot dead (during a solemn and public distribution of orders and crosses) by a young artillery officer, the brother of his then mistress.

"The abominable Pedrito, sir, fled the country," the voice would say. And it would continue: "A captain of one of our ships told me lately that he recognized Pedrito the Guerrillero, arrayed in purple slippers and a velvet smoking-cap with a gold tassel, keeping a disorderly house in one of the southern ports."

"Abominable Pedrito! Who the devil was he?" would wonder the distinguished bird of passage hovering on the confines of waking and sleep with resolutely open eyes and a faint but amiable curl upon his lips, from between which stuck out the eighteenth or twentieth cigar of that memorable day.

"He appeared to me in this very room like a haunting ghost, sir"—Captain Mitchell was talking of his Nostromo with true warmth of feeling and a touch of wistful pride. "You may imagine, sir, what an effect it produced on me. He had come round by sea with Barrios, of course. And the first thing he told me after I became fit to hear him was that he had picked up the lighter's boat floating in the gulf! He seemed quite overcome by the circumstance. And a remarkable enough circumstance it was, when you remember that it was then sixteen days since the sinking of the silver. At once I could see he was another man. He stared at the wall, sir, as if there had been a spider or something running about there. The loss of the silver preyed on his mind. The first thing he asked me about was whether Doña Antonia had heard yet of Decoud's death. His voice trembled. I had to tell him that Doña Antonia, as a matter of fact, was not then back in town yet. Poor girl! And just as I was making ready to ask him a thousand questions, with a sudden, 'Pardon me, *señor*,' he cleared out of the office altogether. I did not see him again for three days. I was terribly busy, you know. It seems that he wandered about in and out of the town, and on two nights he turned up to sleep in the baracoons of the railway people. He seemed absolutely indifferent to what went on. I asked him on the wharf, 'When are you going to take hold again, Nostromo? There will be plenty of work for the *cargadores* presently.'

" '*Señor*,' says he, looking at me in a slow, inquisitive manner, 'would it surprise you to hear that I am too tired to work just yet? And what work could I do now? How can I look my *cargadores* in the face after losing a lighter?'

"I begged him not to think any more about the silver, and he smiled. A smile that went to my heart, sir. 'It was no mistake,' I told him. 'It was a fatality. A thing that could not be helped.' '*Sí, sí!*' he said, and turned away. I thought it best to leave him alone for a bit to get over it. Sir, it took him years really, to get over it. I was present at his interview with Don Carlos. I must say that Gould is rather a cold man. He had to keep a tight hand on his feelings, dealing with thieves and rascals, in constant danger of ruin for himself and wife for so many years, that it had become a second nature. They looked at each other for a long time. Don Carlos asked what he could do for him, in his quiet, reserved way.

" 'My name is known from one end of Sulaco to the other,' he said, as quiet as the other. 'What more can you do for me?' That was all that passed on that occasion. Later, however, there was a very fine coasting schooner for sale, and Mrs. Gould and I put our heads together to get her bought and presented to him. It was done, but he paid all the price back within the next three years. Business was booming all along this seaboard, sir. Moreover, that man always succeeded in everything except in saving the silver. Poor Doña Antonia, fresh from her terrible experiences in the woods of Los Hatos, had an interview with him, too. Wanted to hear about Decoud: what they said, what they did, what they thought up to the last on that fatal night. Mrs. Gould told me his manner was perfect for quietness and sympathy. Miss Avellanos burst into tears only when he told her how Decoud had happened to say that his plan would be a glorious success . . . And there's no doubt, sir, that it is. It is a success."

The cycle was about to close at last. And while the privileged passenger, shivering with the pleasant anticipations of his berth, forgot to ask himself what on earth Decoud's plan could be, Captain Mitchell was saying, "Sorry we must part so soon. Your intelligent interest made this a pleasant day to me. I shall see you now on board. You had a glimpse of the 'Treasure House of the World.' A very good name that." And the coxwain's voice at the door, announcing that the gig was ready, closed the cycle.

Nostromo had, indeed, found the lighter's boat, which he had left on the Great Isabel with Decoud, floating empty far out in the gulf. He was then on the bridge of the first of Barrios's transports, and within an hour's steaming from Sulaco. Barrios, always delighted with a feat of daring and a good judge of courage, had taken a great liking to the Capataz. During the passage round the coast the General kept Nostromo near his person, addressing him frequently in that abrupt and boisterous manner which was the sign of his high favor.

Nostromo's eyes were the first to catch, broad on the bow, the tiny, elusive dark speck, which, alone with the forms of the Three Isabels right ahead, appeared on the flat, shimmering emptiness of the gulf. There are times when no fact should be neglected as insignificant; a small boat so far from the land might have had some meaning worth finding out. At a nod of consent from Barrios the transport swept out of her course, passing near enough to ascertain that no one manned the little cockle-shell. It was merely a common small boat gone adrift with her oars in her. But Nostromo, to whose mind Decoud had been insistently present for days, had long before recognized with excitement the dinghy of the lighter.

There could be no question of stopping to pick up that thing. Every minute of time was momentous with the lives and futures of a whole town. The head of the leading ship, with the General on board, fell off to her course. Behind her, the fleet of transports, scattered haphazard over a mile or so in the offing, like the finish of an ocean race, pressed on, all black and smoking on the western sky.

"Mi *General*," Nostromo's voice rang out loud, but quiet, from behind a group of officers. "I should like to save that little boat. *Por Dios*, I know her. She belongs to my Company."

"And, *por Dios*," guffawed Barrios, in a noisy, good-humored voice, "you belong to me. I am going to make you a captain of cavalry directly we get within sight of a horse again."

"I can swim far better than I can ride, *mi General*," cried Nostromo, pushing through to the rail with a set stare in his eyes. "Let me—"

"Let you? What a conceited fellow that is," bantered the General, jovially, without even looking at him. "Let him go! Ha! ha! ha! He wants me to admit that we cannot take Sulaco without him! Ha! ha! ha! Would you like to swim off to her, my son?"

A tremendous shout from one end of the ship to the other stopped his guffaw. Nostromo had leaped overboard; and his black head bobbed up far away already from the ship. The General muttered an appalled "*Cielo!* Sinner that I am!" in a thunder-struck tone. One anxious glance was enough to show him that Nostromo was swimming with perfect ease; and then he thundered terribly, "No! no! We shall not stop to pick up this impertinent fellow. Let him drown—that mad Capataz."

Nothing short of main force would have kept Nostromo from leaping overboard. That empty boat, coming out to meet him mysteriously, as if rowed by an invisible specter, exercised the fascination of some sign, of some warning, seemed to answer in a startling and enigmatic way the persistent thought of a treasure and of a man's fate. He would have leaped if there had been death in that half mile of water. It was as smooth as a pond, and for some reason sharks are unknown in the Placid Gulf, though on the other side of the Punta Mala the coastline swarms with them.

The Capataz seized hold of the stern and blew with force. A queer, faint feeling had come over him while he swam. He had got rid of his boots and coat in the water. He hung on for a time, regaining his breath. In the distance the transports, more in a bunch now, held on straight for Sulaco, with their air of friendly contest, of nautical sport, of a regatta; and the united smoke of their funnels drove like a thin, sulphurous fogbank right over his head. It was his daring, his courage, his act that had set these ships in motion upon the sea, hurrying on to save the lives and fortunes of the Blancos, the taskmasters of the people; to save the San Tomé mine; to save the children.

With a vigorous and skillful effort he clambered over the stern. The very boat! No doubt of it; no doubt whatever. It was the dinghy of the lighter No. 3—the dinghy left with Martin Decoud on the Great Isabel so that he should have some means to help himself if nothing could be done for him from the shore. And here she had come out to meet him empty and inexplicable. What had become of Decoud? The Capataz made a minute examination. He looked for some scratch, for some mark, for some sign. All he discovered was a brown stain on the gunwale abreast of the thwart. He bent his face over it and rubbed hard with his finger. Then he sat down in the stern sheets, passive, with his knees close together and legs aslant.

Streaming from head to foot, with his hair and whiskers hanging lank and dripping and a lusterless stare fixed upon the bottom boards, the Capataz of the Sulaco Cargadores resembled a drowned corpse come up from the bottom to idle away the sunset hour in a small boat. The excitement of his adventurous ride, the excitement of the return in time, of achievement, of success, all these excitements centered round the associated ideas of the great treasure and of the only other man who knew of its existence, had departed from him. To the very last moment he had been cudgeling his brains as to how he could manage to visit the Great Isabel without loss of time and undetected. For the idea of secrecy had come to be connected with the treasure so closely that even to Barrios himself he had refrained from mentioning the existence of Decoud and of the silver on the island. The letters he carried to the General, however, made brief mention of the loss of the lighter, as having its bearing upon the situation in Sulaco. In the circumstances, the one-eyed tiger-slayer, scenting battle from afar, had not wasted his time in making inquiries from the messenger. In fact, Barrios, talking with Nostromo, assumed that both Don Martin Decoud and the ingots of San Tomé were lost together, and Nostromo, not questioned directly, had kept silent, under the influence of some indefinable form of resentment and distrust. Let Don Martin speak of everything with his own lips—was what he told himself mentally.

And now, with the means of gaining the Great Isabel thrown thus in his way at the earliest possible moment, his excitement had departed, as when the soul takes flight leaving the body inert upon an earth it knows no more. Nostromo did not seem to know the gulf. For a long time even his eyelids did not flutter once upon the glazed emptiness of his stare. Then slowly, without a limb having stirred, without a twitch of muscle or quiver of an eyelash, an expression, a living expression came upon the still features, deep thought crept into the empty stare—as if an outcast soul, a quiet, brooding soul, finding that untenanted body in its way, had come in stealthily to take possession.

The Capataz frowned: and in the immense stillness of sea, islands, and coast, of cloud-forms on the sky and trails of light upon the water, the knitting of that brow had the emphasis of a powerful gesture. Nothing else budged for a long time; then the Capataz shook his head and again surrendered himself to the universal repose of all visible things. Suddenly he seized the oars, and with one movement made the dinghy spin round, head-on to the Great Isabel. But before he began to pull he bent once more over the brown stain on the gunwale.

"I know that thing," he muttered to himself, with a sagacious jerk of the head. "That's blood."

His stroke was long, vigorous, and steady. Now and then he looked over his shoulder at the Great Isabel, presenting its low cliff to his anxious gaze like an impenetrable face. At last the stem touched the strand. He flung rather than dragged the boat up the little beach. At once, turning his back upon the sunset, he plunged with long strides into the ravine, making the water of the stream spurt and fly upwards at every step, as if spurning its shallow, clear, murmuring spirit with his feet. He wanted to save every moment of daylight.

A mass of earth, grass, and smashed bushes had fallen down very naturally from above upon the cavity under the leaning tree. Decoud had attended to the concealment of the silver as instructed, using the spade with some intelligence. But Nostromo's half-smile of approval changed into a scornful curl of the lip by the sight of the spade itself flung there in full view, as if in utter carelessness or sudden panic, giving away the whole thing. Ah! They were all alike in their folly, these *hombres finos* that invented laws and governments and barren tasks for the people.

The Capataz picked up the spade, and with the feel of the handle in his palm the desire to have a look at the horse-hide boxes of treasure came upon him suddenly. In a very few strokes he uncovered the edges and corners of several; then, clearing away more earth, became aware that one of them had been slashed with a knife.

He exclaimed at that discovery in a stifled voice, and dropped on his knees with a look of irrational apprehension over one shoulder, then over the other. The stiff hide had closed, and he hesitated before he pushed his hand through the long slit and felt the ingots inside. There they were. One, two, three. Yes, four gone. Taken away. Four ingots. But who? Decoud? Nobody else. And why? For what purpose? For what cursed fancy? Let him explain. Four ingots carried off in a boat, and—blood!

In the face of the open gulf, the sun, clear, unclouded, unaltered, plunged into the waters in a grave and untroubled mystery of self-immolation consummated far from all mortal eyes, with an infinite majesty of silence and peace. Four ingots short!—and blood!

The Capataz got up slowly.

"He might simply have cut his hand," he muttered. "But, then—"

He sat down on the soft earth, unresisting, as if he had been chained to the treasure, his drawn-up legs clasped in his hands with an air of hopeless submission, like a slave set on guard. Once only he lifted his head smartly: the rattle of hot musketry fire had reached his ears, like pouring from on high a stream of dry peas upon a drum. After listening for a while, he said, half aloud:

"He will never come back to explain."

And he lowered his head again.

"Impossible!" he muttered gloomily.

The sounds of firing died out. The loom of a great conflagration in Sulaco flashed up red above the coast, played on the clouds at the head of the gulf, seemed to touch with a ruddy and sinister reflection the forms of the Three Isabels. He never saw it, though he raised his head.

"But, then, I cannot know," he pronounced, distinctly, and remained silent and staring for hours.

He could not know. Nobody was to know. As might have been supposed, the end of Don Martin Decoud never became a subject of speculation for anyone except Nostromo. Had the truth of the facts been known, there would always have remained the question, Why? Whereas the version of his death at the sinking of the lighter had no uncertainty of motive. The young apostle of Separation had died striving for his idea by an ever-lamented accident. But the truth was that he died from solitude, the enemy known but to few on this earth, and whom only the simplest of us are fit to withstand. The brilliant Costaguanero of the boulevards had died from solitude and want of faith in himself and others.

For some good and valid reasons beyond mere human comprehension, the sea-birds of the gulf shun the Isabels. The rocky head of Azuera is their haunt, whose stony levels and chasms resound with their wild and tumultuous clamor as if they were for ever quarreling over the legendary treasure.

At the end of his first day on the Great Isabel, Decoud, turning in his lair of coarse grass, under the shade of a tree, said to himself:

"I have not seen as much as one single bird all day."

And he had not heard a sound, either, all day but that one now of his own muttering voice. It had been a day of absolute silence—the first he had known in his life. And he had not slept a wink. Not for all these wakeful nights and the days of fighting, planning, talking; not for all that last night of danger and hard physical toil upon the gulf, had he been able to close his eyes for a moment. And yet from sunrise to sunset he had been lying prone on the ground, either on his back or on his face.

He stretched himself, and with slow steps descended into the gully to spend the night by the side of the silver. If Nostromo returned—as he might have done at any moment—it was there that he would look first; and night would, of course, be the proper time for an attempt to communicate. He remembered with profound indifference that he had not eaten anything yet since he had been left alone on the island.

He spent the night open-eyed, and when the day broke he ate something with the same indifference. The brilliant "Son Decoud," the spoiled darling of the family, the lover of Antonia and journalist of Sulaco, was not fit to grapple with himself single-handed. Solitude from mere outward condition of existence becomes very swiftly a state of soul in which the affectations of irony and skepticism have no place. It takes possession of the mind, and drives forth the thought into the exile of utter unbelief. After three days of waiting for the sight of some human face, Decoud caught himself entertaining a doubt of his own individuality. It had merged into the world of cloud and water, of natural forces and forms of nature. In our activity alone do we find the sustaining illusion of an independent existence as against the whole scheme of things of which we form a helpless part. Decoud lost all belief in the reality of his action past and to come. On the fifth day an immense melancholy descended upon him palpably. He resolved not to give himself up to these people in Sulaco, who had beset him, unreal and terrible, like jibbering and obscene specters. He saw himself struggling feebly in their midst, and Antonia, gigantic and lovely like an allegorical statue, looking on with scornful eyes at his weakness.

Not a living being, not a speck of distant sail, appeared within the range of his vision; and, as if to escape from this solitude, he absorbed himself in his melancholy. The vague consciousness of a misdirected life given up to impulses whose memory left a bitter taste in his mouth was the first moral sentiment of his manhood. But at the same time he felt no remorse. What should he regret? He had recognized no other virtue than intelligence, and had erected passions into duties. Both his intelligence and his passion were swallowed up easily in this great unbroken solitude of waiting without faith. Sleeplessness had robbed his will of all energy, for he had not slept seven hours in the seven days. His sadness was the sadness of a skeptical mind. He beheld the universe as a succession of incomprehensible images. Nostromo was dead. Everything had failed ignominiously. He no longer dared to think of Antonia. She had not survived. But if she survived he could not face her. And all exertion seemed senseless.

On the tenth day, after a night spent without even dozing off once (it had occurred to him that Antonia could not possibly have ever loved a being so impalpable as himself), the solitude appeared like a great void, and the silence of the gulf like a tense, thin cord to which he hung suspended by both hands, without fear, without surprise, without any sort of emotion whatever. Only towards the evening, in the comparative relief of coolness, he began to wish that this cord would snap. He imagined it snapping with a report as of a pistol—a sharp, full crack. And that would be the end of him. He contemplated that eventuality with pleasure, because he dreaded the sleepless nights in which the silence, remaining unbroken in the shape of a cord to which he hung with both hands, vibrated with senseless phrases, always the same but utterly incomprehensible, about Nostromo, Antonia, Barrios, and proclamations mingled into an ironical and senseless buzzing. In the daytime he could look at the silence like a still cord stretched to breaking-point, with his life, his vain life, suspended from it like a weight.

"I wonder whether I would hear it snap before I fell," he asked himself.

The sun was two hours above the horizon when he got up, gaunt, dirty, white-faced, and looked at it with his red-rimmed eyes. His limbs obeyed him slowly, as if full of lead, yet without tremor; and the effect of that physical condition gave to his movements an unhesitating, deliberate dignity. He acted as if accomplishing some sort of rite. He descended into the gully; for the fascination of all that silver, with its potential power, survived alone outside of himself. He picked up the belt with the revolver, that was lying there, and buckled it round his waist. The cord of silence could never snap on the island. It must let him fall and sink into the sea, he thought. And sink! He was looking at the loose earth covering the treasure. In the sea! His aspect was that of a somnambulist. He lowered himself down on his knees slowly and went on grubbing with his fingers with industrious patience till he uncovered one of the boxes. Without a pause, as if doing some work done many times before, he slit it open and took four ingots, which he put in his pockets. He covered up the exposed box again and step by step came out of the gully. The bushes closed after him with a swish.

It was on the third day of his solitude that he had dragged the dinghy near the water with an idea of rowing away somewhere, but had desisted partly at the whisper of lingering hope that Nostromo would return, partly from conviction of utter use-lessness of all effort. Now she wanted only a slight shove to be set afloat. He had eaten a little every day after the first, and had some muscular strength left yet. Taking up the oars slowly, he pulled away from the cliff of the Great Isabel, that stood behind him warm with sunshine, as if with the heat of life bathed in a rich light from head to foot as if in a radiance of hope and joy. He pulled straight towards the setting sun. When the gulf had grown dark, he ceased rowing and flung the sculls in. The hollow clatter they made in falling was the loudest noise he had ever heard in his life. It was a revelation. It seemed to recall him from far away. Actually the thought, "Perhaps I may sleep tonight," passed through his mind. But he did not believe it. He believed in nothing; and he remained sitting on the thwart.

The dawn from behind the mountains put a gleam into his unwinking eyes. After a clear daybreak the sun appeared splendidly above the peaks of the range. The great gulf burst into a glitter all around the boat; and in this glory of merciless solitude the silence appeared again before him, stretched taut like a dark, thin string.

His eyes looked at it while, without haste, he shifted his seat from the thwart to the gunwhale. They looked at it fixedly, while his hand, feeling about his waist, unbut-toned the flap of the leather case, drew the revolver, cocked it, brought it forward pointing at his breast, pulled the trigger, and, with convulsive force, sent the still-smoking weapon hurtling through the air. His eyes looked at it while he fell forward and hung with his breast on the gunwhale and the fingers of his right hand hooked under the thwart. They looked—

"It is done," he stammered out, in a sudden flow of blood. His last thought was: "I wonder how that Capataz died." The stiffness of the fingers relaxed, and the lover of Antonia Avellanos rolled overboard without having heard the cord of silence snap in the solitude of the Placid Gulf, whose glittering surface remained untroubled by the fall of his body.

A victim of the disillusioned weariness which is the retribution meted out to intellectual audacity, the brilliant Don Martin Decoud, weighted by the bars of San Tomé silver, disappeared without a trace, swallowed up in the immense indifference of things. His sleepless, crouching figure was gone from the side of the San Tomé silver; and for a time the spirits of good and evil that hover near every concealed treasure of the earth might have thought that this one had been forgotten by all mankind. Then, after a few days, another form appeared striding away from the setting sun to sit motionless and awake in the narrow black gully all through the night, in nearly the same pose, in the same place in which had sat that other sleepless man who had gone away for ever so quietly in a small boat, about the time of sunset. And the spirits of good and evil that hover about a forbidden treasure understood well that the silver of San Tomé was provided now with a faithful and lifelong slave.

The magnificent Capataz de Cargadores, victim of the disenchanted vanity which is the reward of audacious action, sat in the weary pose of a hunted outcast through a night of sleeplessness as tormenting as any known to Decoud, his companion in the most desperate affair of his life. And he wondered how Decoud had died. But he knew the part he had played himself. First a woman, then a man, abandoned each in their last extremity, for the sake of this accursed treasure. It was paid for by a soul lost and by a vanished life. The blank stillness of awe was succeeded by a gust of immense pride. There was no one in the world but Gian' Battista Fidanza, Capataz de Cargadores, the incorruptible and faithful Nostromo, to pay such a price.

He had made up his mind that nothing should be allowed now to rob him of his bargain. Nothing. Decoud had died. But how? That he was dead he had not a shadow of a doubt. But four ingots? . . . What for? Did he mean to come for more—some other time?

The treasure was putting forth its latent power. It troubled the clear mind of the man who had paid the price. He was sure that Decoud was dead. The island seemed full of that whisper. Dead? Gone! And he caught himself listening for the swish of bushes and the splash of footfalls in the bed of the brook. Dead! The talker, the *novio* of Doña Antonia!

"Ha!" he murmured, with his head on his knees, under the livid clouded dawn breaking over the liberated Sulaco and upon the gulf as gray as ashes. "It is to her that he will fly. To her that he will fly!"

And four ingots! Did he take them in revenge, to cast a spell, like the angry woman who had prophesied remorse and failure, and yet had laid upon him the task of saving the children? Well, he had saved the children. He had defeated the spell of poverty and starvation. He had done it all alone—or perhaps helped by the devil. Who cared? He had done it, betrayed as he was, and saving by the same stroke the San Tomé mine, which appeared to him hateful and immense, lording it by its vast wealth over the valor, the toil, the fidelity of the poor, over war and peace, over the labors of the town, the sea, and the Campo.

The sun lit up the sky behind the peaks of the Cordillera. The Capataz looked down for a time upon the fall of loose earth, stones, and smashed bushes, concealing the hiding-place of the silver.

"I must grow rich very slowly," he meditated, aloud.

XI

Sulaco outstripped Nostromo's prudence, growing rich swiftly on the hidden treasures of the earth, hovered over by the anxious spirits of good and evil, torn out by the laboring hands of the people. It was like a second youth, like a new life, full of promise, of unrest, of toil, scattering lavishly its wealth to the four corners of an excited world. Material changes swept along in the train of material interests. And other changes more subtle, outwardly unmarked, affected the minds and hearts of the workers. Captain Mitchell had gone home to live on his savings invested in the San Tomé mine; and Dr. Monygham had grown older, with his head steel-gray and the unchanged expression of his face, living on the inexhaustible treasure of his devotion drawn upon in the secret of his heart like a store of unlawful wealth.

The Inspector-General of State Hospitals (whose maintenance is a charge upon the Gould Concession), Official Adviser on Sanitation to the Municipality, Chief Medical Officer of the San Tomé Consolidated Mines (whose territory, containing gold, silver, copper, lead, cobalt, extends for miles along the foothills of the Cordillera), had felt poverty-stricken, miserable, and starved during the prolonged, second visit the Goulds paid to Europe and the United States of America. Intimate of the *casa*, proved friend, a bachelor without ties and without establishment (except of the professional sort), he had been asked to take up his quarters in the Gould house. In the eleven months of their absence the familiar rooms, recalling at every glance the woman to whom he had given all his loyalty, had grown intolerable. As the day approached for the arrival of the mail boat *Hermes* (the latest addition to the O.S.N. Company's splendid fleet), the doctor hobbled about more vivaciously, snapped more sardonically at simple and gentle out of sheer nervousness.

He packed up his modest trunk with speed, with fury, with enthusiasm, and saw it carried out past the old porter at the gate of the Casa Gould with delight, with intoxication; then, as the hour approached, sitting alone in the great landau behind the white mules, a little sideways, his drawn-in face positively venomous with effort of self-control, and holding a pair of new gloves in his left hand, he drove to the harbor.

His heart dilated within him so, when he saw the Goulds on the deck of the *Hermes*, that his greetings were reduced to a casual mutter. Driving back to town, all three were silent. And in the patio the doctor, in a more natural manner, said:

"I'll leave you now to yourselves. I'll call tomorrow if I may?"

"Come to lunch, dear Dr. Monygham, and come early," said Mrs. Gould, in her traveling dress and her veil down, turning to look at him at the foot of the stairs; while at the top of the flight the Madonna, in blue robes and the Child on her arm, seemed to welcome her with an aspect of pitying tenderness.

"Don't expect to find me at home," Charles Gould warned him. "I'll be off early to the mine."

After lunch, Doña Emilia and the Señor Doctor came slowly through the inner gateway of the patio. The large gardens of the Casa Gould, surrounded by high walls, and the red-tile slopes of neighboring roofs, lay open before them, with masses of shade under the trees and level surfaces of sunlight upon the lawns. A triple row of old orange trees surrounded the whole. Barefooted, brown gardeners, in snowy white shirts and wide *calzoneras*, dotted the grounds, squatting over flowerbeds, passing between the trees, dragging slender india-rubber tubes across the gravel of the paths; and the fine jets of water crossed each other in graceful curves, sparkling in the sunshine with a slight pattering noise upon the bushes, and an effect of showered diamonds upon the grass.

Doña Emilia, holding up the train of a clear dress, walked by the side of Dr. Monygham, in a longish black coat and severe black bow on an immaculate shirt-front. Under a shady clump of trees, where stood scattered little tables and wicker easy-chairs, Mrs. Gould sat down in a low and ample seat.

"Don't go yet," she said to Dr. Monygham, who was unable to tear himself away from the spot. His chin nestling within the points of his collar, he devoured her stealthily with his eyes, which, luckily, were round and hard like clouded marbles, and incapable of disclosing his sentiments. His pitying emotion at the marks of time upon the face of that woman, the air of frailty and weary fatigue that had settled upon the eyes and temples of the "Never-tired Señora" (as Don Pepe years ago used to call her with admiration), touched him almost to tears. "Don't go yet. Today is all my own," Mrs. Gould urged, gently. "We are not back yet officially. No one will come. It's only tomorrow that the windows of the Casa Gould are to be lit up for a reception."

The doctor dropped into a chair.

"Giving a *tertulia?*" he said, with a detached air.

"A simple greeting for all the kind friends who care to come."

"And only tomorrow?"

"Yes. Charles would be tired out after a day at the mine, and so I—It would be good to have him to myself for one evening on our return to this house I love. It has seen all my life."

"Ah, yes!" snarled the doctor, suddenly. "Women count time from the marriage feast. Didn't you live a little before?"

"Yes; but what is there to remember? There were no cares."

Mrs. Gould sighed. And as two friends, after a long separation, will revert to the most agitated period of their lives, they began to talk of the Sulaco Revolution. It seemed strange to Mrs. Gould that people who had taken part in it seemed to forget its memory and its lesson.

"And yet," struck in the doctor, "we who played our part in it had our reward. Don Pepe, though superannuated, still can sit a horse. Barrios is drinking himself to death in jovial company away somewhere on his *fundación* beyond the Bolson de Tonoro. And the heroic Father Román—I imagine the old padre blowing up systematically the San Tomé mine, uttering a pious exclamation at every bang, and taking handfuls of snuff between the explosions—the heroic Padre Román says that he is not afraid of the harm Holroyd's missionaries can do to his flock, as long as *he* is alive."

Mrs. Gould shuddered a little at the allusion to the destruction that had come so near to the San Tomé mine.

"Ah, but you, dear friend?"

"I did the work I was fit for."

"You faced the most cruel dangers of all. Something more than death."

"No, Mrs. Gould! Only death—by hanging. And I am rewarded beyond my deserts."

Noticing Mrs. Gould's gaze fixed upon him, he dropped his eyes.

"I've made my career—as you see," said the Inspector-General of State Hospitals, taking up lightly the lapels of his superfine black coat. The doctor's self-respect, marked inwardly by the almost complete disappearance from his dreams of Father Berón, appeared visibly in what, by contrast with former carelessness, seemed an immoderate cult of personal appearance. Carried out within severe limits of form and color, and in perpetual freshness, this change of apparel gave to Dr. Monygham an air at the same time professional and festive; while his gait and the unchanged crabbed character of his face acquired from it a startling force of incongruity.

"Yes," he went on. "We all had our rewards—the engineer-in-chief, Captain Mitchell—"

"We saw him," interrupted Mrs. Gould, in her charming voice. "The poor dear man came up from the country on purpose to call on us in our hotel in London. He comported himself with great dignity, but I fancy he regrets Sulaco. He rambled feebly about 'historical events' till I felt I could have a cry."

"H'm," grunted the doctor; "getting old, I suppose. Even Nostromo is getting older—though he is not changed. And, speaking of that fellow, I wanted to tell you something—"

For some time the house had been full of murmurs, of agitation. Suddenly the two gardeners, busy with rose trees at the side of the garden arch, fell upon their knees with bowed heads on the passage of Antonia Avellanos, who appeared walking beside her uncle.

Invested with the red hat after a short visit to Rome, where he had been invited by the Propaganda, Father Corbelán, missionary to the wild Indians, conspirator, friend and patron of Hernandez the robber, advanced with big, slow strides, gaunt and leaning forward, with his powerful hands clasped behind his back. The first Cardinal-Archbishop of Sulaco had preserved his fanatical and morose air; the aspect of a chaplain of bandits. It was believed that his unexpected elevation to the purple was a counter-move to the Protestant invasion of Sulaco organized by the Holroyd Missionary Fund. Antonia, the beauty of her face as if a little blurred, her figure slightly fuller, advanced with her light walk and her high serenity, smiling from a distance at Mrs. Gould. She had brought her uncle over to see dear Emilia, without ceremony, just for a moment before the siesta.

When all were seated again, Dr. Monygham, who had come to dislike heartily everybody who approached Mrs. Gould with any intimacy, kept aside, pretending to be lost in profound meditation. A louder phrase of Antonia made him lift his head.

"How can we abandon, groaning under oppression, those who have been our countrymen only a few years ago, who *are* our countrymen now?" Miss Avellanos was saying. "How can we remain blind, and deaf without pity to the cruel wrongs suffered by our brothers? There is a remedy."

"Annex the rest of Costaguana to the order and prosperity of Sulaco," snapped the doctor. "There is no other remedy."

"I am convinced, Señor Doctor," Antonia said, with the earnest calm of invincible resolution, "that this was from the first poor Martin's intention."

"Yes, but the material interests will not let you jeopardize their development for a mere idea of pity and justice," the doctor muttered, grumpily. "And it is just as well perhaps."

The Cardinal-Archbishop straightened up his gaunt, bony frame.

"We have worked for them; we have made them, these material interests of the foreigners," the last of the Corbeláns uttered in a deep, denunciatory tone.

"And without them you are nothing," cried the doctor from the distance. "They will not let you."

"Let them beware, then, lest the people, prevented from their aspirations, should rise and claim their share of the wealth and their share of the power," the popular Cardinal-Archbishop of Sulaco declared, significantly, menacingly.

A silence ensued, during which his Eminence stared, frowning at the ground, and Antonia, graceful and rigid in her chair, breathed calmly in the strength of her convictions. Then the conversation took a social turn, touching on the visit of the Goulds to Europe. The Cardinal-Archbishop, when in Rome, had suffered from neuralgia in the head all the time. It was the climate—the bad air.

When uncle and niece had gone away, with the servants again falling on their knees, and the old porter, who had known Henry Gould, almost totally blind and impotent now, creeping up to kiss his Eminence's extended hand, Dr. Monygham, looking after them, pronounced the one word:

"Incorrigible!"

Mrs. Gould, with a look upwards, dropped wearily on her lap her white hands flashing with the gold and stones of many rings.

"Conspiring. Yes!" said the doctor. "The last of the Avellanos and the last of the Corbeláns are conspiring with the refugees from Sta Marta that flock here after every revolution. The Café Lambroso at the corner of the Plaza is full of them; you can hear their chatter across the street like the noise of a parrot-house. They are conspiring for the invasion of Costaguana. And do you know where they go for strength, for the necessary force? To the secret societies amongst immigrants and natives, where Nostromo—I should say Captain Fidanza—is the great man. What gives him that position? Who can say? Genius? He has genius. He is greater with the populace than ever he was before. It was as if he had some secret power; some mysterious means to keep up his influence. He holds conferences with the Archbishop, as in those old days which you and I remember. Barrios is useless. But for a military head they have the pious Hernandez. And they may raise the country with the new cry of wealth for the people."

"Will there be never any peace? Will there be no rest?" Mrs. Gould whispered. "I thought that we—"

"No!" interrupted the doctor. "There is no peace and no rest in the development of material interests. They have their law, and their justice. But it is founded on expediency, and is inhuman; it is without rectitude, without the continuity and the force that can be found only in a moral principle. Mrs. Gould, the time approaches when all that the Gould Concession stands for shall weigh as heavily upon the people as the barbarism, cruelty, and misrule of a few years back."

"How can you say that, Dr. Monygham?" she cried out, as if hurt in the most sensitive place of her soul.

"I can say that is true," the doctor insisted, obstinately. "It'll weigh as heavily, and provoke resentment, bloodshed, and vengeance, because the men have grown different. Do you think that now the mine would march upon the town to save their Señor Administrador? Do you think that?"

She pressed the backs of her entwined hands on her eyes and murmured hopelessly: "Is it this we have worked for, then?"

The doctor lowered his head. He could follow her silent thought. Was it for this that her life had been robbed of all the intimate felicities of daily affection which her tenderness needed as the human body needs air to breathe? And the doctor, indignant with Charles Gould's blindness, hastened to change the conversation.

"It is about Nostromo that I wanted to talk to you. Ah! that fellow has some continuity and force. Nothing will put an end to him. But never mind that. There's something inexplicable going on—or perhaps only too easy to explain. You know, Linda is practically the lighthouse keeper of the Great Isabel light. The Garibaldino is too old now. His part is to clean the lamps and to cook in the house; but he can't get up the stairs any longer. The black-eyed Linda sleeps all day and watches the light all night. Not all day, though. She is up towards five in the afternoon, when our Nostromo, whenever he is in harbor with his schooner, comes out on his courting visit, pulling in a small boat."

"Aren't they married yet?" Mrs. Gould asked. "The mother wished it, as far as I can understand, while Linda was yet quite a child. When I had the girls with me for a year or so during the War of Separation, that extraordinary Linda used to declare quite simply that she was going to be Gian' Battista's wife."

"They are not married yet," said the doctor, curtly. "I have looked after them a little."

"Thank you, dear Dr. Monygham," said Mrs. Gould; and under the shade of the big trees her little, even teeth gleamed in a youthful smile of her gentle malice. "People don't know how really good you are. You will not let them know, as if on purpose to annoy me, who have put my faith in your good heart long ago."

The doctor, with a lifting up of his upper lip, as though he were longing to bite, bowed stiffly in his chair. With the utter absorption of a man to whom love comes late, not as the most splendid of illusions, but like an enlightening and priceless misfortune, the sight of that woman (of whom he had been deprived for nearly a year) suggested ideas of adoration, of kissing the hem of her robe. And this excess of feeling translated itself naturally into an augmented grimness of speech.

"I am afraid of being overwhelmed by too much gratitude. However, these people interest me. I went out several times to the Great Isabel light to look after old Giorgio."

He did not tell Mrs. Gould that it was because he found there, in her absence, the relief of an atmosphere of congenial sentiment in old Giorgio's austere admiration for the "English signora—the benefactress"; in black-eyed Linda's voluble, torrential, passionate affection for "our Doña Emilia—that angel"; in the white-throated, fair Giselle's adoring upward turn of the eyes, which then glided towards him with a sidelong, half-arch, half-candid glance, which made the doctor exclaim to himself mentally, "If I weren't what I am, old and ugly, I would think the minx is making eyes at me. And perhaps she is. I dare say she would make eyes at anybody." Dr. Monygham said nothing of this to Mrs. Gould, the providence of the Viola family, but reverted to what he called "our great Nostromo."

"What I wanted to tell you is this: Our great Nostromo did not take much notice of the old man and the children for some years. It's true, too, that he was away on his coasting voyages certainly ten months out of the twelve. He was making his fortune, as he told Captain Mitchell once. He seems to have done uncommonly well. It was only to be expected. He is a man full of resource, full of confidence in himself, ready to take chances and risks of every sort. I remember being in Mitchell's office one day, when he came in with that calm, grave air he always carries everywhere. He had been away trading in the Gulf of California, he said, looking straight past us at the wall, as his manner is, and was glad to see on his return that a lighthouse was being built on the cliff of the Great Isabel. Very glad, he repeated. Mitchell explained that it was the O.S.N. Company who were building it, for the convenience of the mail service, on his own advice. Captain Fidanza was good enough to say that it was excellent advice. I remember him twisting up his moustaches and looking all round the cornice of the room before he proposed that old Giorgio should be made the keeper of that light."

"I heard of this. I was consulted at the time," Mrs. Gould said. "I doubted whether it would be good for these girls to be shut up on that island as if in a prison."

"The proposal fell in with the Garibaldino's humor. As to Linda, any place was lovely and delightful enough for her as long as it was Nostromo's suggestion. She could wait for her Gian' Battista's good pleasure there as well as anywhere else. My opinion is that she was always in love with that incorruptible Capataz. Moreover, both father and sister were anxious to get Giselle away from the attentions of a certain Ramirez."

"Ah!" said Mrs. Gould, interested. "Ramirez? What sort of man is that?"

"Just a *mozo* of the town. His father was a *cargador*. As a lanky boy he ran about the wharf in rags, till Nostromo took him up and made a man of him. When he got a little older, he put him into a lighter and very soon gave him charge of the No. 3 boat —the boat which took the silver away, Mrs. Gould. Nostromo selected that lighter for the work because she was the best sailing and the strongest boat of all the Company's fleet. Young Ramirez was one of the five *cargadores* entrusted with the removal of the treasure from the Custom House on that famous night. As the boat he had charge of was sunk, Nostromo, on leaving the Company's service, recommended him to Captain Mitchell for his successor. He had trained him in the routine of work perfectly, and thus Mr. Ramirez, from a starving waif, becomes a man and the Capataz of the Sulaco *cargadores.*"

"Thanks to Nostromo," said Mrs. Gould, with warm approval.

"Thanks to Nostromo," repeated Dr. Monygham. "Upon my word, the fellow's power frightens me when I think of it. That our poor old Mitchell was only too glad to appoint somebody trained to work, who saved him trouble, is not surprising. What is wonderful is the fact that the Sulaco *cargadores* accepted Ramirez for their chief, simply because such was Nostromo's good pleasure. Of course, he is not a second Nostromo, as he fondly imagined he would be; but still, the position was brilliant enough. It emboldened him to make up to Giselle Viola, who, you know, is the recognized beauty of the town. The old Garibaldino, however, took a violent dislike to him. I don't know why. Perhaps because he was not a model of perfection like his Gian' Battista, the incarnation of the courage, the fidelity, the honor of 'the people.' Signor Viola does not think much of Sulaco natives. Both of them, the old Spartan and that white-faced Linda, with her red mouth and coal-black eyes, were looking rather fiercely after the fair one. Ramirez was warned off. Father Viola, I am told, threatened him with his gun once."

"But what of Giselle herself?" asked Mrs. Gould.

"She's a bit of a flirt, I believe," said the doctor. "I don't think she cared much one way or another. Of course she likes men's attentions. Ramirez was not the only one, let me tell you, Mrs. Gould. There was one engineer, at least, on the railway staff who got warned off with a gun, too. Old Viola does not allow any trifling with his honor. He has grown uneasy and suspicious since his wife died. He was very pleased to remove his youngest girl away from the town. But look what happens, Mrs. Gould. Ramirez, the honest, lovelorn swain, is forbidden the island. Very well. He respects the prohibition, but naturally turns his eyes frequently towards the Great Isabel. It seems as though he had been in the habit of gazing late at night upon the light. And during these sentimental vigils he discovers that Nostromo, Captain Fidanza that is, returns very late from his visits to the Violas. As late as midnight at times."

The doctor paused and stared meaningly at Mrs. Gould.

"Yes. But I don't understand," she began, looking puzzled.

"Now comes the strange part," went on Dr. Monygham. "Viola, who is king on his island, will allow no visitor on it after dark. Even Captain Fidanza has got to leave after sunset, when Linda has gone up to tend the light. And Nostromo goes away obediently. But what happens afterwards? What does he do in the gulf between half past six and midnight? He has been seen more than once at that late hour pulling quietly into the harbor. Ramirez is devoured by jealousy. He dare not approach old Viola; but he plucked up courage to rail Linda about it on Sunday morning as she came on the mainland to hear Mass and visit her mother's grave. There was a scene on the wharf, which, as a matter of fact, I witnessed. It was early morning. He must have been waiting for her on purpose. I was there by the merest chance, having been called to an urgent consultation by the doctor of the German gunboat in the harbor. She poured wrath, scorn, and flame upon Ramirez, who seemed out of his mind. It was a strange sight. Mrs. Gould: the long jetty, with this raving *cargador* in his crimson sash and the girl all in black, at the end; the early Sunday-morning quiet of the harbor in the shade of the mountains; nothing but a canoe or two moving between the ships at anchor, and the German gunboat's gig coming to take me off. Linda passed me within a foot. I noticed her wild eyes. I called out to her. She never heard me. She never saw me. But I looked at her face. It was awful in its anger and wretchedness."

Mrs. Gould sat up, opening her eyes wide.

"What do you mean, Dr. Monygham? Do you mean to say that you suspect the younger sister?"

"*Quién sabe!* Who can tell?" said the doctor, shrugging his shoulders like a born Costaguanero. "Ramirez came up to me on the wharf. He reeled—he looked insane. He took his head into his hands. He had to talk to someone—simply had to. Of course for all his mad state he recognized me. People know me well here. I have lived too long amongst them to be anything else but the evil-eyed doctor, who can cure all the ills of the flesh, and bring bad luck by a glance. He came up to me. He tried to be calm. He tried to make it out that he wanted merely to warn me against Nostromo. It seems that Captain Fidanza at some secret meeting or other had mentioned me as the worst despiser of all the poor—of the people. It's very possible. He honors me with his undying dislike. And a word from the great Fidanza may be quite enough to send some fool's knife into my back. The Sanitary Commission I preside over is not in favor with the populace. 'Beware of him, Señor Doctor. Destroy him, Señor Doctor,' Ramirez hissed right into my face. And then he broke out. 'That man,' he spluttered, 'has cast a spell upon both these girls.' As to himself, he had said too much. He must run away now—run away and hide somewhere. He moaned tenderly about Giselle, and then called her names that cannot be repeated. If he thought she could be made to love him by any means, he would carry her off from the island. Off into the woods. But it was no good . . . He strode away, flourishing his arms above his head. Then I noticed an old Negro, who had been sitting behind a pile of cases, fishing from the wharf. He wound up his lines and slunk away at once. But he must have heard something, and must have talked, too, because some of the old Garibaldino's railway friends, I suppose, warned him against Ramirez. At any rate, the father had been warned. But Ramirez has disappeared from the town."

"I feel I have a duty towards these girls," said Mrs. Gould, uneasily. "Is Nostromo in Sulaco now?"

"He is, since last Sunday."

"He ought to be spoken to—at once."

"Who will dare speak to him? Even the love-mad Ramirez runs away from the mere shadow of Captain Fidanza."

"I can. I will," Mrs. Gould declared. "A word will be enough for a man like Nostromo."

The doctor smiled sourly.

"He must end this situation which lends itself to—I can't believe it of that child," pursued Mrs. Gould.

"He's very attractive," muttered the doctor, gloomily.

"He'll see it, I am sure. He must put an end to all this by marrying Linda at once," pronounced the first lady of Sulaco with immense decision.

Through the garden gate emerged Basilio, grown fat and sleek, with an elderly hairless face, wrinkles at the corners of his eyes, and his jet-black, coarse hair plastered down smoothly. Stooping carefully behind an ornamental clump of bushes, he put down with precaution a small child he had been carrying on his shoulder—his own and Leonarda's last born. The pouting, spoiled *camerista* and the head *mozo* of the Casa Gould had been married for some years now.

He remained squatting on his heels for a time, gazing fondly at his offspring, which returned his stare with imperturbable gravity; then, solemn and respectable, walked down the path.

"What is it, Basilio?" asked Mrs. Gould.

"A telephone call came through from the office of the mine. The master remains to sleep at the mountain tonight."

Dr. Monygham had got up and stood looking away. A profound silence reigned for a time under the shade of the biggest trees in the lovely gardens of the Casa Gould.

"Very well, Basilio," said Mrs. Gould. She watched him walk away along the path, step aside behind the flowering bush, and reappear with the child seated on his shoulder. He passed through the gateway between the garden and the patio with measured steps, careful of his light burden.

The doctor, with his back to Mrs. Gould, contemplated a flower-bed away in the sunshine. People believed him scornful and soured. The truth of his nature consisted in his capacity for passion and in the sensitiveness of his temperament. What he lacked was the polished callousness of men of the world, the callousness from which springs an easy tolerance for oneself and others; the tolerance wide as poles asunder from true sympathy and human compassion. This want of callousness accounted for his sardonic turn of mind and his biting speeches.

In profound silence, and glaring viciously at the brilliant flowerbed, Dr. Monygham poured mental imprecations on Charles Gould's head. Behind him the immobility of Mrs. Gould added to the grace of her seated figure the charm of art, of an attitude caught and interpreted for ever. Turning abruptly, the doctor took his leave.

Mrs. Gould leaned back in the shade of the big trees planted in a circle. She leaned back with her eyes closed and her white hands lying idle on the arms of her seat. The half-light under the thick mass of leaves brought out the youthful prettiness of her face; made the clear, light fabrics and white lace of her dress appear luminous. Small and dainty, as if radiating a light of her own in the deep shade of the interlaced boughs, she resembled a good fairy, weary with a long career of well-doing, touched by the withering suspicion of the uselessness of her labors, the powerlessness of her magic.

Had anybody asked her of what she was thinking, alone in the garden of the *casa*, with her husband at the mine and the house closed to the street like an empty dwelling, her frankness would have had to evade the question. It had come into her mind that for life to be large and full, it must contain the care of the past and of the future in every passing moment of the present. Our daily work must be done to the glory of the dead, and for the good of those who come after. She thought that, and sighed without opening her eyes—without moving at all. Mrs. Gould's face became set and rigid for a second, as if to receive, without flinching, a great wave of loneliness that swept over her head. And it came into her mind, too, that no one would ever ask her with solicitude what she was thinking of. No one. No one, but perhaps the man who had just gone away. No; no one who could be answered with careless sincerity in the ideal perfection of confidence.

The word "incorrigible"—a word lately pronounced by Dr. Monygham—floated into her still and sad immobility. Incorrigible in his devotion to the great silver mine was the Señor Administrador! Incorrigible in his hard, determined service of the material interests to which he had pinned his faith in the triumph of order and justice. Poor boy! She had a clear vision of the great hairs on his temples. He was perfect— perfect. What more could she have expected? It was a colossal and lasting success; and love was only a short moment of forgetfulness, a short intoxication, whose delight one remembered with a sense of sadness, as if it had been a deep grief lived through. There was something inherent in the necessities of successful action which carried with it the moral degradation of the idea. She saw the San Tomé mountain hanging over the Campo, over the whole land, feared, hated, wealthy; more soulless than any tyrant, more pitiless and autocratic than the worst Government; ready to crush innumerable lives in the expansion of its greatness. He did not see it. He could not see it. It was not his fault. He was perfect, perfect; but she would never have him to herself. Never; not for one short hour altogether to herself in this old Spanish house she loved so well! Incorrigible, the last of the Corbeláns, the last of the Avellanos, the doctor had said; but she saw clearly the San Tomé mine possessing, consuming, burning up the life of the last of the Costaguana Goulds; mastering the energetic spirit of the son as it had mastered the lamentable weakness of the father. A terrible success for the last of the Goulds. The last! She had hoped for a long, long time that perhaps—But no! There were to be no more. An immense desolation, the dread of her own continued life, descended upon the first lady of Sulaco. With a prophetic vision she saw herself surviving alone the degradation of her young ideal life, of love, of work—all alone in the Treasure House of the World. The profound, blind, suffering expression of a painful dream settled on her face with its closed eyes. In the indistinct voice of an unlucky sleeper, lying passive in the grip of a merciless nightmare, she stammered out aimlessly the words:

"Material interest."

XII

Nostromo had been growing rich very slowly. It was an effect of his prudence. He could command himself even when thrown off his balance. And to become the slave of a treasure with full self-knowledge is an occurrence rare and mentally disturbing. But it was also in a great part because of the difficulty of converting it into a form in which it could become available. The mere act of getting it away from the island piecemeal, little by little, was surrounded by difficulties, by the dangers of imminent detection. He had to visit the Great Isabel in secret, between his voyages along the coast, which were the ostensible source of his fortune. The crew of his own schooner were to be feared as if they had been spies upon their dreaded captain. He did not dare stay too long in port. When his coaster was unloaded, he hurried away on another trip, for he feared arousing suspicion even by a day's delay. Sometimes during a week's stay, or more, he could only manage one visit to the treasure. And that was all. A couple of ingots. He suffered through his fears as much as through his prudence. To do things by stealth humiliated him. And he suffered most from the concentration of his thought upon the treasure.

A transgression, a crime, entering a man's existence, eats it up like a malignant growth, consumes it like a fever. Nostromo had lost his peace; the genuineness of all his qualities was destroyed. He felt it himself, and often cursed the silver of San Tomé. His courage, his magnificence, his leisure, his work, everything was as before, only everything was a sham. But the treasure was real. He clung to it with a more tenacious, mental grip. But he hated the feel of the ingots. Sometimes, after putting away a couple of them in his cabin—the fruit of a secret night expedition to the Great Isabel —he would look fixedly at his fingers, as if surprised they had left no stain on his skin.

He had found means of disposing of the silver bars in distant ports. The necessity to go far afield made his coasting voyages long, and caused his visits to the Viola household to be rare and far between. He was fated to have his wife from there. He had said so once to Giorgio himself. But the Garibaldino had put the subject aside with a majestic wave of his hand, clutching a smoldering black briar-root pipe. There was plenty of time; he was not the man to force his girls upon anybody.

As time went on, Nostromo discovered his preference for the younger of the two. They had some profound similarities of nature, which must exist for complete confidence and understanding, no matter what outward differences of temperament there may be to exercise their own fascination of contrast. His wife would have to know his secret or else life would be impossible. He was attracted by Giselle, with her candid gaze and white throat, pliable, silent, fond of excitement under her quiet indolence; whereas Linda, with her intense, passionately pale face, energetic, all fire and words, touched with gloom and scorn, a chip off the old block, true daughter of the austere republican, but with Teresa's voice, inspired him with a deep-seated mistrust. Moreover, the poor girl could not conceal her love for Gian' Battista. He could see it would be violent, exacting, suspicious, uncompromising—like her soul. Giselle, by her fair but warm beauty, by the surface placidity of her nature holding a promise of submissiveness, by the charm of her girlish mysteriousness, excited his passion and allayed his fears as to the future.

His absences from Sulaco were long. On returning from the longest of them, he made out lighters loaded with blocks of stone lying under the cliff of the Great Isabel; cranes and scaffolding above; workmen's figures moving about, and a small lighthouse already rising from its foundations on the edge of the cliff.

At this unexpected, undreamt-of, startling sight, he thought himself lost irretrievably. What could save him from detection now? Nothing! He was struck with amazed dread at this turn of chance, that would kindle a far-reaching light upon the only secret spot of his life; that life whose very essence, value, reality, consisted in its reflection from the admiring eyes of men. All of it but that thing which was beyond common comprehension; which stood between him and the power that hears and gives effect to the evil intention of curses. It was dark. Not every man had such a darkness. And they were going to put a light there. A light! He saw it shining upon disgrace, poverty, contempt. Somebody was sure to . . . Perhaps somebody had already . . .

The incomparable Nostromo, the Capataz, the respected and feared Captain Fidanza, the unquestioned patron of secret societies, a republican like old Giorgio, and a revolutionist at heart (but in another manner), was on the point of jumping overboard from the deck of his own schooner. That man, subjective almost to insanity, looked suicide deliberately in the face. But he never lost his head. He was checked by the thought that this was no escape. He imagined himself dead, and the disgrace, the shame going on. Or, rather, properly speaking, he could not imagine himself dead. He was possessed too strongly by the sense of his own existence, a thing of infinite duration in its changes, to grasp the notion of finality. The earth goes on for ever.

And he was courageous. It was a corrupt courage, but it was as good for his purposes as the other kind. He sailed close to the cliff of the Great Isabel, throwing a penetrating glance from the deck at the mouth of the ravine, tangled in an undisturbed growth of bushes. He sailed close enough to exchange hails with the workmen, shading their eyes on the edge of the sheer drop of the cliff overhung by the jib-head of a powerful crane. He perceived that none of them had any occasion even to approach the ravine where the silver lay hidden; let alone to enter it. In the harbor he learned that no one slept on the island. The laboring gangs returned to port every evening, singing chorus songs in the empty lighters towed by a harbor tug. For the moment he had nothing to fear.

But afterwards? he asked himself. Later, when a keeper came to live in the cottage that was being built some hundred and fifty yards back from the low light-tower, and four hundred or so from the dark, shaded, jungly ravine, containing the secret of his safety, of his influence, of his magnificence, of his power over the future, of his defiance of ill-luck, of every possible betrayal from rich and poor alike—what then? He could never shake off the treasure. His audacity, greater than that of other men, had welded that vein of silver into his life. And the feeling of fearful and ardent subjection, the feeling of his slavery—so irremediable and profound that often, in his thoughts, he compared himself to the legendary *gringos*, neither dead nor alive, bound down to their conquest of unlawful wealth on Azuera—weighted heavily on the independent Captain Fidanza, owner and master of a coasting schooner, whose smart appearance (and fabulous good luck in trading) were so well known along the western seaboard of a vast continent.

Fiercely whiskered and grave, a shade less supple in his walk, the vigor and symmetry of his powerful limbs lost in the vulgarity of a brown tweed suit, made by Jews in the slums of London, and sold by the clothing department of the Compañía Anzani, Captain Fidanza was seen in the streets of Sulaco attending to his business, as usual, that trip. And, as usual, he allowed it to get about that he had made a great profit on his cargo. It was a cargo of salt fish, and Lent was approaching. He was seen in tramcars going to and fro between the town and the harbor; he talked with people in a café or two in his measured, steady voice. Captain Fidanza was *seen*. The generation that would know nothing of the famous ride to Cayta was not born yet.

Nostromo, the miscalled Capataz de Cargadores, had made for himself, under his rightful name, another public existence, but modified by the new conditions, less picturesque, more difficult to keep up in the increased size and varied population of Sulaco, the progressive capital of the Occidental Republic.

Captain Fidanza, unpicturesque, but always a little mysterious, was recognized quite sufficiently under the lofty glass and iron roof of the Sulaco railway station. He took a local train, and got out in Rincón, where he visited the widow of the *cargador* who had died of his wounds (at the dawn of the New Era, like Don José Avellanos) in the patio of the Casa Gould. He consented to sit down and drink a glass of cool lemonade in the hut, while the woman, standing up, poured a perfect torrent of words to which he did not listen. He left some money with her, as usual. The orphaned children, growing up and well schooled, calling him uncle, clamored for his blessing. He gave that, too; and in the doorway paused for a moment to look at the flat face of the San Tomé mountain with a faint frown. This slight contraction of his bronzed brow casting a marked tinge of severity upon his usual unbending expression, was observed at the Lodge which he attended—but went away before the banquet. He wore it at the meeting of some good comrades, Italians and Occidentals, assembled in his honor under the presidency of an indigent, sickly, somewhat hunchbacked little photographer, with a white face and a magnanimous soul dyed crimson by a bloodthirsty hate of all capitalists, oppressors of the two hemispheres. The heroic Giorgio Viola, old revolutionist, would have understood nothing of his opening speech; and Captain Fidanza, lavishly generous as usual to some poor comrades, made no speech at all. He had listened, frowning with his mind far away, and walked off unapproachable, silent, like a man full of cares.

His frown deepened as, in the early morning, he watched the stone-masons go off to the Great Isabel, in lighters loaded with squared blocks of stone, enough to add another course to the squat light-tower. That was the rate of the work. One course per day.

And Captain Fidanza meditated. The presence of strangers on the island would cut him off completely from the treasure. It had been difficult and dangerous enough before. He was afraid, and he was angry. He thought with the resolution of a master and the cunning of a cowed slave. Then he went ashore.

He was a man of resource and ingenuity; and, as usual, the expedient he found at a critical moment was effective enough to alter the situation radically. He had the gift of evolving safety out of the very danger, this incomparable Nostromo, this "fellow in a thousand." With Giorgio established on the Great Isabel, there would be no need for concealment. He would be able to go openly, in daylight, to see his daughters—one of his daughters—and stay late talking to the old Garibaldino. Then in the dark . . . Night after night . . . He would dare to grow rich quicker now. He yearned to clasp, embrace, absorb, subjugate in unquestioned possession this treasure, whose tyranny had weighed upon his mind, his actions, his very sleep.

He went to see his friend Captain Mitchell—and the thing was done as Dr. Monygham had related to Mrs. Gould. When the project was mooted to the Garibaldino, something like the faint reflection, the dim ghost of a very ancient smile, stole under the white and enormous moustaches of the old hater of kings and ministers. His daughters were the object of his anxious care. The younger, especially. Linda, with her mother's voice, had taken more her mother's place. Her deep, vibrating "Eh, Padre?" seemed, but for the change of the word, the very echo of the impassioned, remonstrating "Eh, Giorgio?" of poor Signora Teresa. It was his fixed opinion that the town was no proper place for his girls. The infatuated but guileless Ramirez was the object of his profound aversion, as resuming the sins of the country whose people were blind, vile *esclavos*.

On his return from his next voyage, Captain Fidanza found the Violas settled in the light-keeper's cottage. His knowledge of Giorgio's idiosyncrasies had not played him false. The Garibaldino had refused to entertain the idea of any companion whatever, except his girls. And Captain Mitchell, anxious to please his poor Nostromo, with that felicity of inspiration which only true affection can give, had formally appointed Linda Viola as under-keeper of Isabel's Light.

"The light is private property," he used to explain. "It belongs to my Company. I've the power to nominate whom I like, and Viola it shall be. It's about the only thing Nostromo—a man worth his weight in gold, mind you—has ever asked me to do for him."

Directly his schooner was anchored opposite the New Custom House, with its sham air of a Greek temple, flat-roofed, with a colonnade, Captain Fidanza went pulling his small boat out of the harbor, bound for the Great Isabel, openly in the light of a declining day, before all men's eyes, with a sense of having mastered the fates. He must establish a regular position. He would ask him for his daughter now. He thought of Giselle as he pulled. Linda loved him, perhaps, but the old man would be glad to keep the eldest, who had his wife's voice.

He did not pull for the narrow strand where he had landed with Decoud, and afterwards alone on his first visit to the treasure. He made for the beach at the other end, and walked up the regular and gentle slope of the wedge-shaped island. Giorgio Viola, whom he saw from afar, sitting on a bench under the front wall of the cottage, lifted his arm slightly to his loud hail. He walked up. Neither of the girls appeared.

"It is good here," said the old man, in his austere, far-away manner.

Nostromo nodded; then, after a short silence:

"You saw my schooner pass in not two hours ago? Do you know why I am here before, so to speak, my anchor has fairly bitten into the ground of this port of Sulaco?"

"You are welcome like a son," the old man declared, quietly, staring away upon the sea.

"Ah! thy son. I know. I am what thy son would have been. It is well, *viejo*. It is a very good welcome. Listen, I have come to ask you for—"

A sudden dread came upon the fearless and incorruptible Nostromo. He dared not utter the name in his mind. The slight pause only imparted a marked weight and solemnity to the changed end of the phrase.

"For my wife!" . . . His heart was beating fast. "It is time you—"

The Garibaldino arrested him with an extended arm. "That was left for you to judge."

He got up slowly. His beard, unclipped since Teresa's death, thick, snow-white, covered his powerful chest. He turned his head to the door, and called out in his strong voice:

"Linda."

Her answer came sharp and faint from within; and the appalled Nostromo stood up, too, but remained mute, gazing at the door. He was afraid. He was not afraid of being refused the girl he loved—no mere refusal could stand between him and a woman he desired—but the shining specter of the treasure rose before him, claiming his allegiance in a silence that could not be gain-said. He was afraid, because, neither dead nor alive, like the *gringos* on Azuera, he belonged body and soul to the unlawfulness of his audacity. He was afraid of being forbidden the island. He was afraid, and said nothing.

Seeing the two men standing up side by side to await her, Linda stopped in the doorway. Nothing could alter the passionate dead whiteness of her face; but the black eyes seemed to catch and concentrate all the light of the low sun in a flaming spark within the black depths, covered at once by the slow descent of heavy eyelids.

"Behold thy husband, master, and benefactor." Old Viola's voice resounded with a force that seemed to fill the whole gulf.

She stepped forward with her eyes nearly closed, like a sleepwalker in a beatific dream.

Nostromo made a superhuman effort. "It is time, Linda, we two were betrothed," he said, steadily, in his level, careless, unbending tone.

She put her hand into his offered palm, lowering her head, dark with bronze glints, upon which her father's hand rested for a moment.

"And so the soul of the dead is satisfied."

This came from Giorgio Viola, who went on talking for a while of his dead wife; while the two, sitting side by side, never looked at each other. Then the old man ceased; and Linda, motionless, began to speak.

"Ever since I felt I lived in the world, I have lived for you alone, Gian' Battista. And that you knew! You knew it . . . Battistino."

She pronounced the name exactly with her mother's intonation. A gloom as of the grave covered Nostromo's heart.

"Yes. I knew," he said.

The heroic Garibaldino sat on the same bench bowing his hoary head, his old soul dwelling alone with its memories, tender and violent, terrible and dreary—solitary on the earth full of men.

And Linda, his best-loved daughter, was saying, "I was yours ever since I can remember. I had only to think of you for the earth to become empty to my eyes. When you were there, I could see no one else. I was yours. Nothing is changed. The world belongs to you, and you let me live in it. . . ." She dropped her low, vibrating voice to a still lower note, and found other things to say—torturing for the man at her side. Her murmur ran on ardent and voluble. She did not seem to see her sister, who came out with an altar-cloth she was embroidering in her hands, and passed in front of them, silent, fresh, fair, with a quick glance and a faint smile, to sit a little away on the other side of Nostromo.

The evening was still. The sun sank almost to the edge of a purple ocean; and the white lighthouse, livid against the background of clouds filling the head of the gulf, bore the lantern red and glowing, like a live ember kindled by the fire of the sky. Giselle, indolent and demure, raised the altar-cloth from time to time to hide nervous yawns, as of a young panther.

Suddenly Linda rushed at her sister, and, seizing her head, covered her face with kisses. Nostromo's brain reeled. When she left her, as if stunned by the violent caresses, with her hands lying in her lap, the slave of the treasure felt as if he could shoot that woman. Old Giorgio lifted his leonine head.

"Where are you going, Linda?"

"To the light, *padre mio.*"

"*Sí, sí*—to your duty."

He got up, too, looked after his eldest daughter; then, in a tone whose festive note seemed the echo of a mood lost in the night of ages:

"I am going in to cook something. Aha! Son! The old man knows where to find a bottle of wine, too."

He turned to Giselle, with a change to austere tenderness.

"And you, little one, pray not to the God of priests and slaves, but to the God of orphans, of the oppressed, of the poor, of little children, to give thee a man like this one for a husband."

His hand rested heavily for a moment on Nostromo's shoulder; then he went in. The hopeless slave of the San Tomé silver felt at these words the venomous fangs of jealousy biting deep into his heart. He was appalled by the novelty of the experience, by its force, by its physical intimacy. A husband! A husband for her! And yet it was natural that Giselle should have a husband at some time or other. He had never realized that before. In discovering that her beauty could belong to another he felt as though he could kill this one of old Giorgio's daughters also. He muttered moodily:

"They say you love Ramirez."

She shook her head without looking at him. Coppery glints rippled to and fro on the wealth of her gold hair. Her smooth forehead had the soft, pure sheen of a priceless pearl in the splendor of the sunset, mingling the gloom of starry spaces, the purple of the sea, and the crimson of the sky in a magnificent stillness.

"No," she said, slowly. "I never loved him. I think I never. . . . He loves me— perhaps."

The seduction of her slow voice died out of the air, and her raised eyes remained fixed on nothing, as if indifferent and without thought.

"Ramirez told you he loved you?" asked Nostromo, restraining himself.

"Ah! once—one evening . . ."

"The miserable . . . Ha!"

He had jumped up as if stung by a gad-fly, and stood before her mute with anger.

"*Misericordia Divina!* You, too, Gian' Battista! Poor wretch that I am!" she lamented in ingenuous tones. "I told Linda, and she scolded—she scolded. Am I to live blind, dumb, and deaf in this world? And she told father, who took down his gun and cleaned it. Poor Ramirez! Then you came, and she told you."

He looked at her. He fastened his eyes upon the hollow of her white throat, which had the invincible charm of things young, palpitating, delicate, and alive. Was this the child he had known? Was it possible? It dawned upon him that in these last years he had really seen very little—nothing—of her. Nothing. She had come into the world like a thing unknown. She had come upon him unawares. She was a danger. A frightful danger. The instinctive mood of fierce determination that had never failed him before the perils of this life added its steady force to the violence of his passion. She, in a voice that recalled to him the song of running water, the tinkling of a silver bell, continued:

"And between you three you have brought me here into this captivity to the sky and water. Nothing else. Sky and water. Oh, *Santissima Madre*. My hair shall turn gray on this tedious island. I could hate you, Gian' Battista!"

He laughed loudly. Her voice enveloped him like a caress. She bemoaned her fate, spreading unconsciously, like a flower its perfume in the coolness of the evening, the indefinable seduction of her person. Was it her fault that nobody ever had admired

Linda? Even when they were little, going out with their mother to Mass, she remembered that people took no notice of Linda, who was fearless, and chose instead to frighten her, who was timid, with their attention. It was her hair like gold, she supposed.

He broke out:

"Your hair like gold, and your eyes like violets, and your lips like the rose; your round arms, your white throat . . ."

Imperturbable in the indolence of her pose, she blushed deeply all over to the roots of her hair. She was not conceited. She was no more self-conscious than a flower. But she was pleased. And perhaps even a flower loves to hear itself praised. He glanced down, and added, impetuously:

"Your little feet!"

Leaning back against the rough stone wall of the cottage, she seemed to bask languidly in the warmth of the rosy flush. Only her lowered eyes glanced at her little feet.

"And so you are going at last to marry our Linda. She is terrible. Ah! now she will understand better since you have told her you love her. She will not be so fierce."

"*Chica!*" said Nostromo, "I have not told her anything."

"Then make haste. Come tomorrow. Come and tell her, so that I may have some peace from her scolding and—perhaps—who knows. . . ."

"Be allowed to listen to your Ramirez, eh? Is that it? You . . ."

"Mercy of God! How violent you are, Giovanni," she said, unmoved. "Who is Ramirez . . . Ramirez . . . Who is he?" she repeated, dreamily, in the dusk and gloom of the clouded gulf, with a low red streak in the west like a hot bar of glowing iron laid across the entrance of a world sombre as a cavern, where the magnificent Capataz de Cargadores had hidden his conquests of love and wealth.

"Listen, Giselle," he said, in measured tones; "I will tell no word of love to your sister. Do you want to know why?"

"Alas! I could not understand perhaps, Giovanni. Father says you are not like other men; that no one has ever understood you properly; that the rich will be surprised yet . . . Oh! saints in heaven! I am weary."

She raised her embroidery to conceal the lower part of her face, then let it fall on her lap. The lantern was shaded on the land side, but slanting away from the dark column of the lighthouse they could see the long shaft of light, kindled by Linda, go out to strike the expiring glow in a horizon of purple and red.

Giselle Viola, with her head resting against the wall of the house, her eyes half closed, and her little feet, in white stockings and black slippers, crossed over each other, seemed to surrender herself, tranquil and fatal, to the gathering dusk. The charm of her body, the promising mysteriousness of her indolence, went out into the night of the Placid Gulf like a fresh and intoxicating fragrance spreading out in the shadows, impregnating the air. The incorruptible Nostromo breathed her ambient seduction in the tumultuous heaving of his breast. Before leaving the harbor he had thrown off the store clothing of Captain Fidanza, for greater ease in the long pull out to the islands. He stood before her in the red sash and check shirt as he used to appear on the Company's wharf—a Mediterranean sailor come ashore to try his luck in Costaguana. The dusk of purple and red enveloped him, too—close, soft, profound, as no more than fifty yards from that spot it had gathered evening after evening about the self-destructive passion of Don Martin Decoud's utter skepticism, flaming up to death in solitude.

"You have got to hear," he began at last, with perfect self-control. "I shall say no word of love to your sister, to whom I am betrothed from this evening, because it is you that I love. It is you! . . ."

The dusk let him see yet the tender and voluptuous smile that came instinctively upon her lips shaped for love and kisses, freeze hard in the drawn, haggard lines of terror. He could not restrain himself any longer. While she shrank from his approach, her arms went out to him, abandoned and regal in the dignity of her languid surrender. He held her head in his two hands, and showered rapid kisses upon the upturned face that gleamed in the purple dusk. Masterful and tender, he was entering slowly upon the fullness of his possession. And he perceived that she was crying. Then the incomparable Capataz, the man of careless loves, became gentle and caressing, like a woman to the grief of a child. He murmured to her fondly. He sat down by her and nursed her fair head on his breast. He called her his star and his little flower.

It had grown dark. From the living-room of the light-keeper's cottage, where Giorgio, one of the Immortal Thousand, was bending his leonine and heroic head over a charcoal fire, there came the sound of sizzling and the aroma of an artistic *frittura*.

In the obscure disarray of that thing, happening like a cataclysm, it was in her feminine head that some gleam of reason survived. He was lost to the world in their embraced stillness. But she said, whispering into his ear:

"God of mercy! What will become of me—here—now—between this sky and this water I hate? Linda, Linda—I see her! . . ." She tried to get out of his arms, suddenly relaxed at the sound of that name. But there was no one approaching their black shapes, enlaced and struggling on the white background of the wall. "Linda! Poor Linda! I tremble! I shall die of fear before my poor sister Linda, betrothed today to Giovanni—my lover! Giovanni, you must have been mad! I cannot understand you! You are not like other men! I will not give you up—never—only to God himself! But why have you done this blind, mad, cruel, frightful thing?"

Released, she hung her head, let fall her hands. The altar-cloth, as if tossed by a great wind, lay far away from them, gleaming white on the black ground.

"From fear of losing my hope of you," said Nostromo.

"You knew that you had my soul! You know everything! It was made for you! But what could stand between you and me? What? Tell me!" she repeated, without impatience, in superb assurance.

"Your dead mother," he said, very low.

"Ah! . . . Poor mother! She has always. . . . She is a saint in heaven now, and I cannot give you up to her. No, Giovanni. Only to God alone. You were mad—but it is done. Oh! what have you done? Giovanni, my beloved, my life, my master, do not leave me here in this grave of clouds. You cannot leave me now. You must take me away—at once—this instant—in the little boat. Giovanni, carry me off tonight, from my fear of Linda's eyes, before I have to look at her again."

She nestled closer to him. The slave of the San Tomé silver felt the weight as of chains upon his limbs, a pressure as of a cold hand upon his lips. He struggled against the spell.

"I cannot," he said. "Not yet. There is something that stands between us and the freedom of the world."

She pressed her form closer to his side with a subtle and naïve instinct of seduction.

"You rave, Giovanni—my lover!" she whispered, engagingly. "What can there be? Carry me off—in thy very hands—to Doña Emilia—away from here. I am not very heavy."

It seemed as though she expected him to lift her up at once in his two palms. She had lost the notion of all impossibility. Anything could happen on this night of wonder. As he made no movement, she almost cried aloud:

"I tell you I am afraid of Linda!" And still he did not move. She became quiet and wily. "What can there be?" she asked, coaxingly.

He felt her warm, breathing, alive, quivering in the hollow of his arm. In the exulting consciousness of his strength, and the triumphant excitement of his mind, he struck out for his freedom.

"A treasure," he said. All was still. She did not understand. "A treasure. A treasure of silver to buy a gold crown for thy brow."

"A treasure?" she repeated in a faint voice, as if from the depths of a dream. "What is it you say?"

She disengaged herself gently. He got up and looked down at her, aware of her face, of her hair, her lips, the dimples on her cheeks—seeing the fascination of her person in the night of the gulf as if in the blaze of noonday. Her nonchalant and seductive voice trembled with the excitement of admiring awe and ungovernable curiosity.

"A treasure of silver!" she stammered out. Then pressed on faster: "What? Where? How did you get it, Giovanni?"

He wrestled with the spell of captivity. It was as if striking a heroic blow that he burst out:

"Like a thief!"

The densest blackness of the Placid Gulf seemed to fall upon his head. He could not see her now. She had vanished into a long, obscure, abysmal silence, whence her voice came back to him after a time with a faint glimmer, which was her face.

"I love you! I love you!"

These words gave him an unwonted sense of freedom; they cast a spell stronger than the accursed spell of the treasure; they changed his weary subjection to that dead thing into an exulting conviction of his power. He would cherish her, he said, in a splendor as great as Doña Emilia's. The rich lived on wealth stolen from the people, but he had taken from the rich nothing—nothing that was not lost to them already by their folly and their betrayal. For he had been betrayed—he said—deceived, tempted. She believed him . . . He had kept the treasure for purposes of revenge; but now he cared nothing for it. He cared only for her. He would put her beauty in a palace on a hill crowned with olive trees—a white palace above a blue sea. He would keep her there like a jewel in a casket. He would get land for her—her own land fertile with vines and corn—to set her little feet upon. He kissed them . . . He had already paid for it all with the soul of a woman and the life of a man. . . . The Capataz de Cargadores tasted the supreme intoxication of his generosity. He flung the mastered treasure superbly at her feet in the impenetrable darkness of the gulf, in the darkness defying—as men said—the knowledge of God and the wit of the devil. But she must let him grow rich first—he warned her.

She listened as if in a trance. Her finger stirred in his hair. He got up from his knees reeling, weak, empty, as though he had flung his soul away.

"Make haste, then," she said. "Make haste, Giovanni, my lover, my master, for I will give thee up to no one but God. And I am afraid of Linda."

He guessed at her shudder, and swore to do his best. He trusted the courage of her love. She promised to be brave in order to be loved always—far away in a white palace upon a hill above a blue sea. Then with a timid, tentative eagerness she murmured:

"Where is it? Where? Tell me that, Giovanni."

He opened his mouth and remained silent—thunderstruck.

"Not that! Not that!" he gasped out, appalled at the spell of secrecy that had kept him dumb before so many people falling upon his lips again with unimpaired force. Not even to her. Not even to her. It was too dangerous. "I forbid thee to ask," he cried at her, deadening cautiously the anger of his voice.

He had not regained his freedom. The specter of the unlawful treasure arose, standing by her side like a figure of silver, pitiless and secret, with a finger on its pale lips. His soul died within him at the vision of himself creeping in presently along the ravine, with the smell of earth, of damp foliage in his nostrils—creeping in, determined in a purpose that numbed his breast, and creeping out again loaded with silver, with his ears alert to every sound. It must be done on this very night—that work of a craven slave!

He stooped low, pressed the hem of her skirt to his lips, with a muttered command:

"Tell him I would not stay," and was gone suddenly from her, silent, without as much as a footfall in the dark night.

She sat still, her head resting indolently against the wall, and her little feet in white stockings and black slippers crossed over each other. Old Giorgio, coming out, did not seem to be surprised at the intelligence as much as she had vaguely feared. For she was full of inexplicable fear now—fear of everything and everybody except of her Giovanni and his treasure. But that was incredible.

The heroic Garibaldino accepted Nostromo's abrupt departure with a sagacious indulgence. He remembered his own feelings, and exhibited a masculine penetration of the true state of the case.

"*Va bene.* Let him go. Ha! ha! No matter how fair the woman, it galls a little. Liberty, liberty. There's more than one kind! He has said the great word, and son Gian' Battista is not tame." He seemed to be instructing the motionless and scared Giselle . . . "A man should not be tame," he added, dogmatically out of the doorway. Her stillness and silence seemed to displease him. "Do not give way to the enviousness of your sister's lot," he admonished her, very grave, in his deep voice.

Presently he had to come to the door again to call in his younger daughter. It was late. He shouted her name three times before she even moved her head. Left alone, she had become the helpless prey of astonishment. She walked into the bedroom she shared with Linda like a person profoundly asleep. That aspect was so marked that even old Giorgio, spectacled, raising his eyes from the Bible, shook his head as she shut the door behind her.

She walked right across the room without looking at anything, and sat down at once by the open window. Linda, stealing down from the tower in the exuberance of her happiness, found her with a lighted candle at her back, facing the black night full of sighing gusts of wind and the sound of distant showers—a true night of the gulf, too dense for the eye of God and the wiles of the devil. She did not turn her head at the opening of the door.

There was something in that immobility which reached Linda in the depths of her paradise. The elder sister guessed angrily: the child is thinking of that wretched Ramirez. Linda longed to talk. She said in her arbitrary voice, "Giselle!" and was not answered by the slightest movement.

The girl that was going to live in a palace and walk on ground of her own was ready to die with terror. Not for anything in the world would she have turned her head to face her sister. Her heart was beating madly. She said with subdued haste:

"Do not speak to me. I am praying."

Linda, disappointed, went out quietly; and Giselle sat on, unbelieving, lost, dazed, patient, as if waiting for the confirmation of the incredible. The hopeless blackness of the clouds seemed part of a dream, too. She waited.

She did not wait in vain. The man whose soul was dead within him, creeping out of the ravine, weighted with silver, had seen the gleam of the lighted window, and could not help retracing his steps from the beach.

On that impenetrable background, obliterating the lofty mountains by the seaboard, she saw the slave of the San Tomé silver, as if by an extraordinary power of a miracle. She accepted his return as if henceforth the world could hold no surprise for all eternity.

She rose, compelled and rigid, and began to speak long before the light from within fell upon the face of the approaching man.

"You have come back to carry me off. It is well! Open thy arms, Giovanni, my lover. I am coming."

His prudent footsteps stopped, and with his eyes glistening wildly, he spoke in a harsh voice:

"Not yet. I must grow rich slowly." . . . A threatening note came into his tone. "Do not forget that you have a thief for your lover."

"Yes! Yes!" she whispered, hastily. "Come nearer! Listen! Do not give me up, Giovanni! Never, never! . . . I will be patient! . . ."

Her form drooped consolingly over the low casement towards the slave of the unlawful treasure. The light in the room went out, and weighted with silver, the magnificent Capataz clasped her round her white neck in the darkness of the gulf as a drowning man clutches at a straw.

<h1 style="text-align:center">XIII</h1>

On the day Mrs. Gould was going, in Dr. Monygham's words, to "give a *tertulia*," Captain Fidanza went down the side of his schooner lying in Sulaco harbor, calm, unbending, deliberate in the way he sat down in his dinghy and took up his sculls. He was later than usual. The afternoon was well advanced before he landed on the beach of the Great Isabel, and with a steady pace climbed the slope of the island.

From a distance he made out Giselle sitting in a chair tilted back against the end of the house, under the window of the girl's room. She had her embroidery in her hands, and held it well up to her eyes. The tranquillity of that girlish figure exasperated the feeling of perpetual struggle and strife he carried in his breast. He became angry. It seemed to him that she ought to hear the clanking of his fetters—his silver fetters, from afar. And while ashore that day, he had met the doctor with the evil eye, who had looked at him very hard.

The raising of her eyes mollified him. They smiled in their flower-like freshness straight upon his heart. Then she frowned. It was a warning to be cautious. He stopped some distance away, and in a loud, indifferent tone, said:

"Good day, Giselle. Is Linda up yet?"

"Yes. She is in the big room with father."

He approached then, and, looking through the window into the bedroom for fear of being detected by Linda returning there for some reason, he said, moving only his lips:

"You love me?"

"More than my life." She went on with her embroidery under his contemplating gaze and continued to speak, looking at her work, "Or I could not live. I could not, Giovanni. For this life is like death. Oh, Giovanni, I shall perish if you do not take me away."

He smiled carelessly. "I will come to the window when it's dark," he said.

"No, don't, Giovanni. Not tonight. Linda and father have been talking together for a long time today."

"What about?"

"Ramirez, I fancy I heard. I do not know. I am afraid. I am always afraid. It is like dying a thousand times a day. Your love is to me like your treasure to you. It is there, but I can never get enough of it."

He looked at her very still. She was beautiful. His desire had grown within him. He had two masters now. But she was incapable of sustained emotion. She was sincere in what she said, but she slept placidly at night. When she saw him she flamed up always. Then only an increased taciturnity marked the change in her. She was afraid of betraying herself. She was afraid of pain, of bodily harm, of sharp words, of facing anger, and witnessing violence. For her soul was light and tender with a pagan sincerity in its impulses. She murmured:

"Give up the palazzo, Giovanni, and the vineyards on the hills, for which we are starving our love."

She ceased, seeing Linda standing silent at the corner of the house.

Nostromo turned to his affianced wife with a greeting, and was amazed at her sunken eyes, at her hollow cheeks, at the air of illness and anguish in her face.

"Have you been ill?" he asked, trying to put some concern into this question.

Her black eyes blazed at him. "Am I thinner?" she asked.

"Yes—perhaps—a little."

"And older?"

"Every day counts—for all of us."

"I shall go gray, I fear, before the ring is on my finger," she said, slowly, keeping her gaze fastened upon him.

She waited for what he would say, rolling down her turned-up sleeves.

"No fear of that," he said, absently.

She turned away as if it had been something final, and busied herself with household cares while Nostromo talked with her father. Conversation with the old Garibaldino was not easy. Age had left his faculties unimpaired, only they seemed to have withdrawn somewhere deep within him. His answers were slow in coming, with an effect of august gravity. But that day he was more animated, quicker; there seemed to be more life in the old lion. He was uneasy for the integrity of his honor. He believed in Sidoni's warning as to Ramirez's designs upon his younger daughter. And he did not trust her. She was flighty. He said nothing of his cares to "Son Gian' Battista." It was a touch of senile vanity. He wanted to show that he was equal yet to the task of guarding alone the honor of his house.

Nostromo went away early. As soon as he had disappeared, walking towards the beach, Linda stepped over the threshold and, with a haggard smile, sat down by the side of her father.

Ever since that Sunday, when the infatuated and desperate Ramirez had waited for her on the wharf, she had no doubts whatever. The jealous ravings of that man were no revelation. They had only fixed with precision, as with a nail driven into her heart, that sense of unreality and deception which, instead of bliss and security, she had found in her intercourse with her promised husband. She had passed on, pouring indignation and scorn upon Ramirez; but, that Sunday, she nearly died of wretchedness and shame, lying on the carved and lettered stone of Teresa's grave, subscribed for by the engine-drivers and the fitters of the railway workshops, in sign of their respect for the hero of Italian Unity. Old Viola had not been able to carry out his desire of burying his wife in the sea; and Linda wept upon the stone.

The gratuitous outrage appalled her. If he wished to break her heart—well and good. Everything was permitted to Gian' Battista. But why trample upon the pieces; why seek to humiliate her spirit? Aha! He could not break that. She dried her tears. And Giselle! Giselle! The little one that, ever since she could toddle, had always clung to her skirt for protection. What duplicity! But she could not help it probably. When there was a man in the case the poor featherheaded wretch could not help herself.

Linda had a good share of the Viola stoicism. She resolved to say nothing. But woman-like she put passion into her stoicism. Giselle's short answers, prompted by fearful caution, drove her beside herself by their curtness that resembled disdain. One day she flung herself upon the chair in which her indolent sister was lying and impressed the mark of her teeth at the base of the whitest neck in Sulaco. Giselle cried out. But she had her share of the Viola heroism. Ready to faint with terror, she only said, in a lazy voice, *"Madre de Dios!* Are you going to eat me alive, Linda?" And this outburst passed off leaving no trace upon the situation. "She knows nothing. She cannot know anything," reflected Giselle. "Perhaps it is not true. It cannot be true," Linda tried to persuade herself.

But when she saw Captain Fidanza for the first time after her meeting with the distracted Ramirez, the certitude of her misfortune returned. She watched him from the doorway go away to his boat, asking herself stoically, "Will they meet tonight?" She made up her mind not to leave the tower for a second. When he had disappeared she came out and sat down by her father.

The venerable Garibaldino felt, in his own words, "a young man yet." In one way or another a good deal of talk about Ramirez had reached him of late; and his contempt and dislike of that man who obviously was not what his son would have been, had made him restless. He slept very little now; but for several nights past instead of reading—or only sitting, with Mrs. Gould's silver spectacles on his nose, before the open Bible—he had been prowling actively all about the island with his old gun, on watch over his honor.

Linda, laying her thin brown hand on his knee, tried to soothe his excitement. Ramirez was not in Sulaco. Nobody knew where he was. He was gone. His talk of what he would do meant nothing.

"No," the old man interrupted. "But son Gian' Battista told me—quite of himself —that the cowardly *esclavo* was drinking and gambling with the rascals of Zapiga, over there on the north side of the gulf. He may get some of the worst scoundrels of that scoundrelly town of Negroes to help him in his attempt upon the little one. . . . But I am not so old. No!"

She argued earnestly against the probability of any attempt being made; and at last the old man fell silent, chewing his white moustache. Women had their obstinate notions which must be humored—his poor wife was like that, and Linda resembled her mother. It was not seemly for a man to argue. "Maybe. Maybe," he mumbled.

She was by no means easy in her mind. She loved Nostromo. She turned her eyes upon Giselle, sitting at a distance, with something of maternal tenderness, and the jealous anguish of a rival outraged in her defeat. Then she rose and walked over to her.

"Listen—you," she said, roughly.

The invincible candor of the gaze, raised up all violet and dew, excited her rage and admiration. She had beautiful eyes—the *chica*—this vile thing of white flesh and black deception. She did not know whether she wanted to tear them out with shouts of vengeance or cover up their mysterious and shameless innocence with kisses of pity and love. And suddenly they became empty, gazing blankly at her, except for a little fear not quite buried deep enough with all the other emotions in Giselle's heart.

Linda said, "Ramirez is boasting in town that he will carry you off from the island."

"What folly!" answered the other, and in a perversity born of long restraint, she added: "He is not a man," in a jesting tone with a resembling audacity.

"No?" said Linda, through her clenched teeth. "Is he not? Well, then, look to it; because father has been walking about with a loaded gun at night."

"It is not good for him. You must tell him not to, Linda. He will not listen to me."

"I shall say nothing—never any more—to anybody," cried Linda, passionately.

This could not last, thought Giselle. Giovanni must take her away soon—the very next time he came. She would not suffer these terrors for ever so much silver. To speak with her sister made her ill. But she was not uneasy at her father's watchfulness. She had begged Nostromo not to come to the window that night. He had promised to keep away for this once. And she did not know, could not guess or imagine, that he had another reason for coming on the island.

Linda had gone straight to the tower. It was time to light up. She unlocked the little door, and went heavily up the spiral staircase, carrying her love for the magnificent Capataz de Cargadores like an ever-increasing load of shameful fetters. No; she could not throw it off. No; let Heaven dispose of these two. And moving about the lantern, filled with twilight and the sheen of the moon, with careful movements she lighted the lamp. Then her arms fell along her body.

"And with our mother looking on," she murmured. "My own sister—the *chica!*"

The whole refracting apparatus, with its brass fittings and rings of prisms, glittered and sparkled like a dome-shaped shrine of diamonds, containing not a lamp, but some sacred flame, dominating the sea. And Linda, the keeper, in black, with a pale face, drooped low in a wooden chair, alone with her jealousy, far above the shames and passions of the earth. A strange, dragging pain, as if somebody were pulling her about brutally by her dark hair with bronze glints, made her put her hands up to her temples. They would meet. They would meet. And she knew where, too. At the window. The sweat of torture fell in drops on her cheeks, while the moonlight in the offing closed as if with a colossal bar of silver the entrance of the Placid Gulf—the somber cavern of clouds and stillness in the surf-fretted seaboard.

Linda Viola stood up suddenly with a finger on her lip. He loved neither her nor her sister. The whole thing seemed so objectless as to frighten her, and also give her some hope. Why did he not carry her off? What prevented him? He was incomprehensible. What were they waiting for? For what end were these two lying and deceiving? Not for the ends of their love. There was no such thing. The hope of regaining him for herself made her break her vow of not leaving the tower that night. She must talk at once to her father, who was wise, and would understand. She ran down the spiral stairs. At the moment of opening the door at the bottom she heard the sound of the first shot ever fired on the Great Isabel.

She felt a shock, as though the bullet had struck her breast. She ran on without pausing. The cottage was dark. She cried at the door, "Giselle! Giselle!" then dashed round the corner and screamed her sister's name at the open window, without getting an answer; but as she was rushing, distracted, round the house, Giselle came out of the door, and darted past her, running silently, her hair loose, and her eyes staring straight ahead. She seemed to skim along the grass as if on tiptoe, and vanished.

Linda walked on slowly, with her arms stretched out before her. All was still on the island; she did not know where she was going. The tree under which Martin Decoud spent his last days, beholding a life like a succession of senseless images, threw a large blotch of black shade upon the grass. Suddenly she saw her father, standing quietly all alone in the moonlight.

The Garibaldino—big, erect, with his snow-white hair and beard—had a monumental repose in his immobility, leaning upon a rifle. She put her hand upon his arm lightly. He never stirred.

"What have you done?" she asked, in her ordinary voice.

"I have shot Ramirez—*infame!*" he answered, with his eyes directed to where the shade was blackest. "Like a thief he came, and like a thief he fell. The child had to be protected."

He did not offer to move an inch, to advance a single step. He stood there, rugged and unstirring, like a statue of an old man guarding the honor of his house. Linda removed her trembling hand from his arm, firm and steady like an arm of stone, and, without a word, entered the blackness of the shade. She saw a stir of formless shapes on the ground, and stopped short. A murmur of despair and tears grew louder to her strained hearing.

"I entreated you not to come tonight. Oh, my Giovanni! And you promised. Oh! Why—why did you come, Giovanni?"

It was her sister's voice. It broke on a heartrending sob. And the voice of the resourceful Capataz de Cargadores, master and slave of the San Tomé treasure, who had been caught unawares by old Giorgio while stealing across the open towards the ravine to get some more silver, answered careless and cool, but sounding startlingly weak from the ground.

"It seemed as though I could not live through the night without seeing thee once more—my star, my little flower."

The brilliant *tertulia* was just over, the last guests had departed, and the Señor Administrador had gone to his room already, when Dr. Monygham, who had been expected in the evening but had not turned up, arrived driving along the wood-block pavement under the electric-lamps of the deserted Calle de la Constitución, and found the great gateway of the *casa* still open.

He limped in, stumped up the stairs, and found the fat and sleek Basilio on the point of turning off the lights in the *sala*. The prosperous majordomo remained open-mouthed at this late invasion.

"Don't put out the lights," commanded the doctor. "I want to see the *señora*."

"The *señora* is in the Señora Administrador's *cancillaría*," said Basilio, in an unctuous voice. "The Señor Administrador starts for the mountain in an hour. There is some trouble with the workmen to be feared, it appears. A shameless people without reason and decency. And idle, *señor*. Idle."

"You are shamelessly lazy and imbecile yourself," said the doctor, with that faculty for exasperation which made him so generally beloved. "Don't put the lights out."

Basilio retired with dignity. Dr. Monygham, waiting in the brilliantly lighted *sala*, heard presently a door close at the farther end of the house. A jingle of spurs died out. The Señor Administrador was off to the mountain.

With a measured swish of her long train, flashing with jewels and the shimmer of silk, her delicate head bowed as if under the weight of a mass of fair hair, in which the silver threads were lost, the "first lady of Sulaco," as Captain Mitchell used to describe her, moved along the lighted corridor, wealthy beyond great dreams of wealth, considered, loved, respected, honored, and as solitary as any human being had ever been, perhaps, on this earth.

The doctor's "Mrs. Gould! One minute!" stopped her with a start at the door of the lighted and empty *sala*. From the similarity of mood and circumstance, the sight of the doctor, standing there all alone amongst the groups of furniture, recalled to her emotional memory her unexpected meeting with Martin Decoud; she seemed to hear in the silence the voice of that man, dead miserably so many years ago, pronounce the words, "Antonia left her fan here." But it was the doctor's voice that spoke, a little altered by his excitement. She remarked his shining eyes.

"Mrs. Gould, you are wanted. Do you know what has happened? You remember what I told you yesterday about Nostromo. Well, it seems that a *lancha*, a decked boat, coming from Zapiga, with four Negroes in her, passing close to the Great Isabel, was hailed from the cliff by a woman's voice—Linda's, as a matter of fact—commanding them (it's a moonlight night) to go round to the beach and take up a wounded man to the town. The *patron* (from whom I've heard all this), of course, did so at once. He told me that when they got round to the low side of the Great Isabel, they found Linda Viola waiting for them. They followed her: she led them under a tree not far from the cottage. There they found Nostromo lying on the ground with his head in the younger girl's lap, and father Viola standing some distance off leaning on his gun. Under Linda's direction they got a table out of the cottage for a stretcher, after breaking off the legs. They are here, Mrs. Gould. I mean Nostromo and—and Giselle. The Negroes brought him in to the first-aid hospital near the harbor. He made the attendant send for me. But it is not me he wanted to see—it was you, Mrs. Gould! It was you."

"Me?" whispered Mrs. Gould, shrinking a little.

"Yes, you!" the doctor burst out. "He begged me—his enemy, as he thinks—to bring you to him at once. It seems he has something to say to you alone."

"Impossible!" murmured Mrs. Gould.

"He said to me, 'Remind her that I have done something to keep a roof over her head.' . . . Mrs. Gould," the doctor pursued, in the greatest excitement. "Do you remember the silver? The silver in the lighter—that was lost!"

Mrs. Gould remembered. But she did not say she hated the mere mention of that silver. Frankness personified, she remembered with an exaggerated horror that for the first and last time of her life she had concealed the truth from her husband about that very silver. She had been corrupted by her fears at that time, and she had never forgiven herself. Moreover, that silver, which would never have come down if her husband had been made acquainted with the news brought by Decoud, had been in a roundabout way nearly the cause of Dr. Monygham's death. And these things appeared to her very dreadful.

"Was it lost, though?" the doctor exclaimed. "I've always felt that there was a mystery about our Nostromo ever since. I do believe he wants now, at the point of death—"

"The point of death," repeated Mrs. Gould.

"Yes. Yes . . . He wants perhaps to tell you something concerning that silver which—"

"Oh, no! No!" exclaimed Mrs. Gould, in a low voice. "Isn't it lost and done with? Isn't there enough treasure without it to make everybody in the world miserable?"

The doctor remained still, in a submissive, disappointed silence. At last he ventured, very low:

"And there is that Viola girl. Giselle. What are we to do? It looks as though father and sister had—"

Mrs. Gould admitted that she felt in duty bound to do her best for these girls.

"I have a *volante* here," the doctor said. "If you don't mind getting into that—"

He waited, all impatience, till Mrs. Gould reappeared, having thrown over her dress a gray cloak with a deep hood.

It was thus that, cloaked and monastically hooded over her evening costume, this woman, full of endurance and compassion, stood by the side of the bed on which the splendid Capataz de Cargadores lay stretched out motionless on his back. The whiteness of sheets and pillows gave a somber and energetic relief to his bronzed face, to the dark, nervous hands, so good on a tiller, upon a bridle, and on a trigger, lying open and idle upon a white coverlet.

"She is innocent," the Capataz was saying in a deep and level voice, as though afraid that a louder word would break the slender hold his spirit still kept upon his body. "She is innocent. It is I alone. But no matter. For these things I would answer to no man or woman alive."

He paused. Mrs. Gould's face, very white within the shadow of the hood, bent over him with an invincible and dreary sadness. And the low sobs of Giselle Viola, kneeling at the end of the bed, her gold hair with coppery gleams loose and scattered over the Capataz's feet, hardly troubled the silence of the room.

"Ha! Old Giorgio—the guardian of thine honor! Fancy the Vecchio coming upon me so light of foot, so steady of aim. I myself could have done no better. But the price of a charge of powder might have been saved. The honor was safe . . . *Señora*, she would have followed to the end of the world Nostromo the thief . . . I have said the word. The spell is broken!"

A low moan from the girl made him cast his eyes down.

"I cannot see her. . . . No matter," he went on, with the shadow of the old magnificent carelessness in his voice. "One kiss is enough, if there is no time for more. An airy soul, *señora!* Bright and warm, like sunshine—soon clouded, and soon serene. They would crush it there between them. *Señora*, cast on her the eye of your compassion, as famed from one end of the land to the other as the courage and daring of the man who speaks to you. She will console herself in time. And even Ramirez is not a bad fellow. I am not angry. No! It is not Ramirez who overcame the Capataz of the Sulaco Cargadores." He paused, made an effort, and in a louder voice, a little wildly, declared:

"I die betrayed—betrayed by—"

But he did not say by whom or by what he was dying betrayed.

"She would not have betrayed me," he began again, opening eyes very wide. "She was faithful. We were going very far—very soon. I could have torn myself away from that accursed treasure for her. For that child I would have left boxes and boxes of it— full. And Decoud took four. Four ingots. Why? *Picardia!* To betray me? How could I give back the treasure with four ingots missing? They would have said I had purloined them. The doctor would have said that. Alas! It holds me yet!"

Mrs. Gould bent low, fascinated—cold with apprehension.

"What became of Don Martin on that night, Nostromo?"

"Who knows! I wondered what would become of me. Now I know. Death was to come upon me unawares. He went away! He betrayed me. And you think I have killed him! You are all alike, you fine people. The silver has killed me. It has held me. It holds me yet. Nobody knows where it is. But you are the wife of Don Carlos, who put it into my hands and said, 'Save it on your life.' And when I returned, and you all thought it was lost, what do I hear? It was nothing of importance. Let it go. Up, Nostromo, the faithful, and ride away to save us, for dear life!"

"Nostromo!" Mrs. Gould whispered, bending very low. "I, too, have hated the idea of that silver from the bottom of my heart."

"Marvelous!—that one of you should hate the wealth that you know so well how to take from the hands of the poor. The world rests upon the poor, as old Giorgio says. You have been always good to the poor. But there is something accursed in wealth. *Señora*, shall I tell you where the treasure is? To you alone . . . Shining! Incorruptible!"

A pained, involuntary reluctance lingered in his tone, in his eyes, plain to the woman with the genius of sympathetic intuition. She averted her glance from the miserable subjection of the dying man, appalled, wishing to hear no more of the silver.

"No, Capataz," she said. "No one misses it now. Let it be lost for ever."

After hearing these words, Nostromo closed his eyes, uttered no word, made no movement. Outside the door of the sick-room Dr. Monygham, excited to the highest pitch, his eyes shining with eagerness, came up to the two women.

"Now, Mrs. Gould," he said, almost brutally in his impatience, "tell me, was I right? There is a mystery. You have got the word of it, have you not? He told you—"

"He told me nothing," said Mrs. Gould, steadily.

The light of his temperamental enmity to Nostromo went out of Dr. Monygham's eyes. He stepped back submissively. He did not believe Mrs. Gould. But her word was law. He accepted her denial like an inexplicable fatality affirming the victory of Nostromo's genius over his own. Even before that woman, whom he loved with secret devotion, he had been defeated by the magnificent Capataz de Cargadores, the man who had lived his own life on the assumption of unbroken fidelity, rectitude, and courage!

"Pray send at once somebody for my carriage," spoke Mrs. Gould from within her hood. Then, turning to Giselle Viola, "Come nearer me, child; come closer. We will wait here."

Giselle Viola, heartbroken and childlike, her face veiled in her falling hair, crept up to her side. Mrs. Gould slipped her hand through the arm of the unworthy daughter of old Viola, the immaculate republican, the hero without a stain. Slowly, gradually, as a withered flower droops, the head of the girl, who would have followed a thief to the end of the world, rested on the shoulder of Doña Emilia, the first lady of Sulaco, the wife of the Señor Administrador of the San Tomé mine. And Mrs. Gould, feeling her suppressed sobbing, nervous and excited, had the first and only moments of bitterness in her life. It was worthy of Dr. Monygham himself.

"Console yourself, child. Very soon he would have forgotten you for his treasure."

"*Señora*, he loved me. He loved me," Giselle whispered, despairingly. "He loved me as no one had ever been loved before."

"I have been loved, too," Mrs. Gould said in a severe tone.

Giselle clung to her convulsively. "Oh, *señora*, but you shall live adored to the end of your life," she sobbed out.

Mrs. Gould kept an unbroken silence till the carriage arrived. She helped in the half-fainting girl. After the doctor had shut the door of the landau, she leaned over to him.

"You can do nothing?" she whispered.

"No, Mrs. Gould. Moreover, he won't let us touch him. It does not matter. I just had one look . . . Useless."

But he promised to see old Viola and the other girl that very night. He could get the police-boat to take him off to the island. He remained in the street, looking after the landau rolling away slowly behind the white mules.

The rumor of some accident—an accident to Captain Fidanza—had been spreading along the new quays with their rows of lamps and the dark shapes of towering cranes. A knot of night-prowlers—the poorest of the poor—hung about the door of the first-aid hospital, whispering in the moonlight of the empty street.

There was no one with the wounded man but the pale photographer, small, frail, bloodthirsty, the hater of capitalists, perched on a high stool near the head of the bed with his knees up and his chin in his hands. He had been fetched by a comrade who, working late on the wharf, had heard from a Negro belonging to a *lancha* that Captain Fidanza had been brought ashore mortally wounded.

"Have you any dispositions to make, comrade?" he asked, anxiously. "Do not forget that we want money for our work. The rich must be fought with their own weapons."

Nostromo made no answer. The other did not insist, remaining huddled up on the stool, shock-headed, wildly hairy, like a hunchbacked monkey. Then, after a long silence:

"Comrade Fidanza," he began, solemnly, "you have refused all aid from that doctor. Is he really a dangerous enemy of the people?"

In the dimly lit room Nostromo rolled his head slowly on the pillow and opened his eyes, directing at the weird figure perched by his bedside a glance of enigmatic and profound inquiry. Then his head rolled back, his eyelids fell, and the Capataz de Cargadores died without a word or moan after an hour of immobility, broken by short shudders testifying to the most atrocious sufferings.

Dr. Monygham, going out in the police-galley to the islands, beheld the glitter of the moon upon the gulf and the high black shape of the Great Isabel sending a shaft of light afar, from under the canopy of clouds.

"Pull easy," he said, wondering what he would find there. He tried to imagine Linda and her father, and discovered a strange reluctance within himself. "Pull easy," he repeated.

From the moment he fired at the thief of his honor, Giorgio Viola had not stirred from the spot. He stood, his old gun grounded, his hand grasping the barrel near the muzzle. After the *lancha* carrying off Nostromo for ever from her had left the shore, Linda, coming up, stopped before him. He did not seem to be aware of her presence, but when, losing her forced calmness, she cried out: "Do you know whom you have killed?" he answered: "Ramirez the vagabond."

White, and staring insanely at her father, Linda laughed in his face. After a time he joined her faintly in a deep-toned and distant echo of her peals. Then she stopped, and the old man spoke as if startled:

"He cried out in son Gian' Battista's voice."

The gun fell from his opened hand, but the arm remained extended for a moment as if still supported. Linda seized it roughly.

"You are too old to understand. Come into the house."

He let her lead him. On the threshold he stumbled heavily, nearly coming to the ground together with his daughter. His excitement, his activity of the last few days, had been like the flare of a dying lamp. He caught the back of his chair.

"In son Gian' Battista's voice," he repeated in a severe tone. "I heard him—Ramirez —the miserable—"

Linda helped him into the chair, and, bending low, hissed into his ear:

"You have killed Gian' Battista."

The old man smiled under his thick moustache. Women had strange fancies.

"Where is the child?" he asked, surprised at the penetrating chilliness of the air and the unwonted dimness of the lamp by which he used to sit up half the night with the open Bible before him.

Linda hesitated a moment, then averted her eyes.

"She is asleep," she said. "We shall talk of her tomorrow."

She could not bear to look at him. He filled her with terror and with an almost unbearable feeling of pity. She had observed the change that came over him. He would never understand what he had done; and even to her the whole thing remained incomprehensible. He said with difficulty:

"Give me the book."

Linda laid on the table the closed volume in its worn leather cover, the Bible given him ages ago by an Englishman in Palermo.

"The child had to be protected," he said, in a strange, mournful voice.

Behind his chair Linda wrung her hands, crying without noise. Suddenly she started for the door. He heard her move.

"Where are you going?" he asked.

"To the light," she answered, turning round to look at him balefully.

"The light! Sí—duty."

Very upright, white-haired, leonine, heroic in his absorbed quietness, he felt in the pocket of his red shirt for the spectacles given him by Doña Emilia. He put them on. After a long period of immobility he opened the book, and from on high looked through the glasses at the small print in double columns. A rigid, stern expression settled upon his features with a slight frown, as if in response to some gloomy thought or unpleasant sensation. But he never detached his eyes from the book while he swayed forward, gently, gradually, till his snow-white head rested upon the open pages. A wooden clock ticked methodically on the white-washed wall, and growing slowly cold the Garibaldino lay alone, rugged, undecayed, like an old oak uprooted by a treacherous gust of wind.

The light of the Great Isabel burned unfailing above the lost treasure of the San Tomé mine. Into the bluish sheen of a night without stars the lantern sent out a yellow beam towards the far horizon. Like a black speck upon the shining panes, Linda, crouching in the outer gallery, rested her head on the rail. The moon, drooping in the western board, looked at her radiantly.

Below, at the foot of the cliff, the regular splash of oars from a passing boat ceased, and Dr. Monygham stood up in the stern sheets.

"Linda!" he shouted, throwing back his head. "Linda!"

Linda stood up. She had recognized the voice.

"Is he dead?" she cried, bending over.

"Yes, my poor girl. I am coming round," the doctor answered from below. "Pull to the beach," he said to the rowers.

Linda's black figure detached itself upright on the light of the lantern with her arms raised above her head as though she were going to throw herself over.

"It is I who loved you," she whispered, with a face as set and white as marble in the moonlight. "I! Only I! She will forget thee, killed miserably for her pretty face. I cannot understand. I cannot understand. But I shall never forget thee. Never!"

She stood silent and still, collecting her strength to throw all her fidelity, her pain, bewilderment, and despair into one great cry.

"Never! Gian' Battista!"

Dr. Monygham, pulling round in the police-galley, heard the name pass over his head. It was another of Nostromo's triumphs, the greatest, the most enviable, the most sinister of all. In that true cry of undying passion that seemed to ring aloud from Punta Mala to Azuera and away to the bright line of the horizon, overhung by a big white cloud shining like a mass of solid silver, the genius of the magnificent Capataz de Cargadores dominated the dark gulf containing his conquests of treasure and love.

AUTOBIOGRAPHICAL WRITINGS

Conrad left one autobiography, *A Personal Record* (also called *Some Reminiscences*), published in 1912, but it should not be taken as a precise account of his life. It is full of inaccuracies as far as names and dates are concerned, and, as in much of his fiction, the time sequence is not linear. It is better looked upon as a kind of spiritual autobiography, a series of vignettes that together show the development of the man and the artist. About half of the book is excerpted here, showing his early attempts at writing, memories of his career at sea, and how these experiences influenced what he wrote.

The story "Youth" is in fact a work of fiction, not strict autobiography, and is generally considered his greatest short story. The events it describes happened nearly exactly as written, but Conrad did change some of the names. "Youth" gives us a unique insight into a period and an adventure that shaped the adult Conrad. Though generally ignored by the public when it was published in 1902, it did receive critical acclaim.

A Personal Record

Some Reminiscences

I

ooks may be written in all sorts of places. Verbal inspiration may enter the berth of a mariner on board a ship frozen fast in a river in the middle of a town; and since saints are supposed to look benignantly on humble believers, I indulge in the pleasant fancy that the shade of old Flaubert—who imagined himself to be (amongst other things) a descendant of Vikings—might have hovered with amused interest over the decks of a 2,000-ton steamer called the *Adowa*, on board of which, gripped by the inclement winter alongside a quay in Rouen, the tenth chapter of *Almayer's Folly* was begun. With interest, I say, for was not the kind Norman giant with enormous moustaches and a thundering voice the last of the Romantics? Was he not, in his unworldly, almost ascetic, devotion to his art a sort of literary, saint-like hermit?

" 'It has set at last,' said Nina to her mother, pointing to the hills behind which the sun had sunk." . . . These words of Almayer's romantic daughter I remember tracing on the gray paper of a pad which rested on the blanket of my bed-place. They referred to a sunset in Malayan Isles, and shaped themselves in my mind, in a hallucinated vision of forests and rivers and seas, far removed from a commercial and yet romantic town of the northern hemisphere. But at that moment the mood of visions and words was cut short by the third officer, a cheerful and casual youth, coming in with a bang of the door and the exclamation: "You've made it jolly warm in here."

It was warm. I had turned on the steam-heater after placing a tin under the leaky water-cock—for perhaps you do not know that water will leak where steam will not. I am not aware of what my young friend had been doing on deck all that morning, but the hands he rubbed together vigorously were very red and imparted to me a chilly feeling by their mere aspect. He has remained the only banjoist of my acquaintance, and being also a younger son of a retired colonel, the poem of Mr. Kipling, by a strange aberration of associated ideas, always seems to me to have been written with an exclusive view to his person. When he did not play the banjo he loved to sit and look at it. He proceeded to this sentimental inspection, and after meditating a while over the strings under my silent scrutiny, inquired airily:

"What are you always scribbling there, if it's fair to ask?"

It was a fair enough question, but I did not answer him, and simply turned the pad over with a movement of instinctive secrecy: I could not have told him he had put to flight the psychology of Nina Almayer, her opening speech of the tenth chapter and the words of Mrs. Almayer's wisdom which were to follow in the ominous oncoming of a tropical night. I could not have told him that Nina had said: "It has set at last." He would have been extremely surprised and perhaps have dropped his precious banjo. Neither could I have told him that the sun of my sea-going was setting too, even as I wrote the words expressing the impatience of passionate youth bent on its desire. I did not know this myself, and it is safe to say he would not have cared, though he was an excellent young fellow and treated me with more deference than, in our relative positions, I was strictly entitled to.

He lowered a tender gaze on his banjo and I went on looking through the port-hole. The round opening framed in its brass rim a fragment of the quays, with a row of casks ranged on the frozen ground and the tail-end of a great cart. A red-nosed carter in a blouse and a woolen nightcap leaned against the wheel. An idle, strolling custom-house guard, belted over his blue *capote*, had the air of being depressed by exposure to the weather and the monotony of official existence. The background of grimy houses found a place in the picture framed by my port-hole, across a wide stretch of paved quay, brown with frozen mud. The coloring was sombre, and the most conspicuous feature was a little *café* with curtained windows and a shabby front of white woodwork, corresponding with the squalor of these poorer quarters bordering the river. We had been shifted down there from another berth in the neighborhood of the Opera House, where that same port-hole gave me a view of quite another sort of *café*—the best in the town, I believe, and the very one where the worthy Bovary and his wife, the romantic daughter of old Père Renault, had some refreshment after the memorable performance of an opera which was the tragic story of Lucia di Lammermoor in a setting of light music.

I could recall no more the hallucination of the Eastern Archipelago which I certainly hoped to see again. The story of *Almayer's Folly* got put away under the pillow for that day. I do not know that I had any occupation to keep me away from it; the truth of the matter is, that on board that ship we were leading just then a contemplative life. I will not say anything of my privileged position. I was there "just to oblige," as an actor of standing may take a small part in the benefit performance of a friend.

As far as my feelings were concerned, I did not wish to be in that steamer at that time and in those circumstances. And perhaps I was not even wanted there in the usual sense in which a ship "wants" an officer. It was the first and last instance in my sea life when I served ship-owners who have remained completely shadowy to my apprehension. I do not mean this for the well-known firm of London ship-brokers which had chartered the ship to the, I will not say short-lived, but ephemeral Franco-Canadian

Transport Company. A death leaves something behind, but there was never anything tangible left from the F.C.T.C. It flourished no longer than roses live, and unlike the roses, it blossomed in the dead of winter, emitted a sort of faint perfume of adventure, and died before spring set in. But indubitably it was a company, it had even a house-flag, all white with the letters F.C.T.C. artfully tangled up in a complicated mono-gram. We flew it at our main-mast head, and now I have come to the conclusion that it was the only flag of its kind in existence. All the same, we on board, for many days, had the impression of being a unit of a large fleet with fortnightly departures for Montreal and Quebec as advertised in pamphlets and prospectuses which came aboard in a large package in Victoria Dock, London, just before we started for Rouen, France. And in the shadowy life of the F.C.T.C. lies the secret of that, my last employment in my calling, which in a remote sense interrupted the rhythmical development of Nina Almayer's story.

The then secretary of the London Shipmasters' Society, with its modest rooms in Fenchurch Street, was a man of indefatigable activity and the greatest devotion to his task. He is responsible for what was my last association with a ship. I call it that because it can hardly be called a sea-going experience. Dear Captain Froud—it is impossible not to pay him the tribute of affectionate familiarity at this distance of years—had very sound views as to the advancement of knowledge and status for the whole body of the officers of the mercantile marine. He organized for us courses of professional lectures, St. John Ambulance classes, corresponded industriously with public bodies and members of Parliament on subjects touching the interests of the service; and as to the oncoming of some inquiry or commission relating to matters of the sea and to the work of seamen, it was a perfect godsend to his need of exerting himself on our corporate behalf. Together with this high sense of his official duties he had in him a vein of personal kindness, a strong disposition to do what good he could to the individual members of that craft of which in his time he had been a very excellent master. And what greater kindness can one do to a seaman than to put him in the way of employment? Captain Froud did not see why the Shipmasters' Society, besides its general guardianship of our interests, should not be unofficially an employ-ment agency of the very highest class.

"I am trying to persuade all our great ship-owning firms to come to us for their men. There is nothing of a trade-union spirit about our society and I really don't see why they should not," he said once to me. "I am always telling the captains, too, that all things being equal they ought to give preference to the members of the society. In my position I can generally find for them what they want amongst our members or our associate members."

In my wanderings about London from West to East and back again (I was very idle then), the two little rooms in Fenchurch Street were a sort of resting-place where my spirit, hankering after the sea, could feel itself nearer to the ships, the men, and the life of its choice—nearer there than any other spot of the solid earth. This resting-place used to be, at about five o'clock in the afternoon, full of men and tobacco smoke, but Captain Froud had the smaller room to himself, and there he granted private interviews, whose principal motive was to render service. Thus, one murky November afternoon, he beckoned me in with a crooked finger and that peculiar glance above his spectacles which is perhaps my strongest physical recollection of the man.

"I have had in here a shipmaster this morning," he said, getting back to his desk and motioning me to a chair, "who is in want of an officer. It's for a steamship. You know, nothing pleases me more than to be asked, but unfortunately I do not quite see my way. . . ."

As the outer room was full of men, I cast a wondering glance at the closed door, but he shook his head.

"Oh, yes, I should be only too glad to get that berth for one of them. But the fact of the matter is, the captain of that ship wants an officer who can speak French fluently, and that's not so easy to find. I do not know anybody myself but you. It's a second officer's berth, and, of course, you would not care . . . would you now? I know that it isn't what you are looking for."

It was not. I had given myself up to the idleness of a haunted man who looks for nothing but words wherein to capture his visions. But I admit that outwardly I resembled sufficiently a man who could make a second officer for a steamer chartered by a French company. I showed no sign of being haunted by the fate of Nina and by the murmurs of tropical forests; and even my intimate intercourse with Almayer (a person of weak character) had not put a visible mark upon my features. For many years he and the world of his story had been the companions of my imagination without, I hope, impairing my ability to deal with the realities of sea life. I had had the man and his surroundings with me ever since my return from the eastern waters, some four years before the day of which I speak.

It was in the front sitting-room of furnished apartments in a Pimlico square that they first began to live again with a vividness and poignancy quite foreign to our former real intercourse. I had been treating myself to a long stay on shore, and in the necessity of occupying my mornings, Almayer (that old acquaintance) came nobly to the rescue. Before long, as was only proper, his wife and daughter joined him round my table, and then the rest of that Pantai band came full of words and gestures. Unknown to my respectable landlady, it was my practice directly after my breakfast to hold animated receptions of Malays, Arabs and half-castes. They did not clamor aloud for my attention. They came with silent and irresistible appeal—and the appeal, I affirm here, was not to my self-love or my vanity. It seems now to have had a moral character, for why should the memory of these beings, seen in their obscure sun-bathed existence, demand to express itself in the shape of a novel, except on the ground of that mysterious fellowship which unites in a community of hopes and fears all the dwellers on this earth?

I did not receive my visitors with boisterous rapture as the bearers of any gifts of profit or fame. There was no vision of a printed book before me as I sat writing at that table, situated in a decayed part of Belgravia. After all these years, each leaving its evidence of slowly blackened pages, I can honestly say that it is a sentiment akin to piety which prompted me to render in words assembled with conscientious care the memory of things far distant and of men who had lived.

But, coming back to Captain Froud and his fixed idea of never disappointing ship-owners or ship-captains, it was not likely that I should fail him in his ambition—to satisfy at a few hours' notice the unusual demand for a French-speaking officer. He explained to me that the ship was chartered by a French company intending to establish a regular monthly line of sailings from Rouen, for the transport of French emigrants to Canada. But, frankly, this sort of thing did not interest me very much. I said gravely that if it were really a matter of keeping up the reputation of the Shipmas-ters' Society, I would consider it. But the consideration was just for form's sake. The next day I interviewed the Captain, and I believe we were impressed favorably with each other. He explained that his chief mate was an excellent man in every respect, and that he could not think of dismissing him so as to give me the higher position; but that if I consented to come as second officer I would be given certain special advan-tages—and so on.

I told him that if I came at all the rank really did not matter.

"I am sure," he insisted, "you will get on first rate with Mr. Paramor."

I promised faithfully to stay for two trips at least, and it was in those circumstances that what was to be my last connection with a ship began. And after all there was not even one single trip. It may be that it was simply the fulfillment of a fate, of that written word on my forehead which apparently forbade me, through all my sea wan-derings, ever to achieve the crossing of the Western Ocean—using the words in that special sense in which sailors speak of Western Ocean trade, of Western Ocean packets, of Western Ocean hard cases. The new life attended closely upon the old, and the nine chapters of *Almayer's Folly* went with me to the Victoria Dock, whence in a few days we started for Rouen. I won't go so far as saying that the engaging of a man fated never to cross the Western Ocean was the absolute cause of the Franco-Canadian Transport Company's failure to achieve even a single passage. It might have been that, of course; but the obvious, gross obstacle was clearly the want of money. Four hundred and sixty bunks for emigrants were put together in the 'tween decks by industrious carpenters while we lay in the Victoria Dock, but never an emigrant turned up in Rouen—of which, being a humane person, I confess I was glad. Some gentlemen from Paris—I think there were three of them, and one was said to be the Chairman—turned up indeed and went from end to end of the ship, knocking their silk hats cruelly against the deck-beams. I attended them personally, and I can vouch for it that the interest they took in things was intelligent enough, though obviously they had never seen anything of the sort before. Their faces as they went ashore wore a cheer-fully inconclusive expression. Notwithstanding that this inspecting ceremony was sup-posed to be a preliminary to immediate sailing, it was then, as they filed down our gangway, that I received the inward monition that no sailing within the meaning of our charter-party would ever take place.

It must be said that in less than three weeks a move took place. When we first arrived we had been taken up with much ceremony well towards the center of the town, and, all the street corners being placarded with the tricolor posters announcing the birth of our company, the *petit bourgeois* with his wife and family made a Sunday holiday from the inspection of the ship. I was always in evidence in my best uniform to give information as though I had been a Cook's tourists' interpreter, while our quarter-masters reaped a harvest of small change from personally conducted parties. But when the move was made—that move which carried us some mile and a half down the stream to be tied up to an altogether muddier and shabbier quay—then indeed the desolation of solitude became our lot. It was a complete and soundless stagnation; for, as we had the ship ready for sea to the smallest detail, as the frost was hard and the days short, we were absolutely idle—idle to the point of blushing with shame when the thought struck us that all the time our salaries went on. Young Cole was aggrieved because, as he said, we could not enjoy any sort of fun in the evening after loafing like this all day: even the banjo lost its charm since there was nothing to prevent his strumming on it all the time between the meals. The good Paramor—he was really a most excellent fellow—became unhappy as far as was possible to his cheery nature, till one dreary day I suggested, out of sheer mischief, that he should employ the dormant energies of the crew in hauling both cables up on deck and turning them end for end.

For a moment Mr. Paramor was radiant. "Excellent idea!" but directly his face fell. "Why . . . Yes! But we can't make that job last more than three days," he muttered discontentedly. I don't know how long he expected us to be stuck on the river-side outskirts of Rouen, but I know that the cables got hauled up and turned end for end according to my satanic suggestion, put down again, and their very existence utterly forgotten, I believe, before a French river pilot came on board to take our ship down, empty as she came, into the Havre roads. You may think that this state of forced idleness favored some advance in the fortunes of Almayer and his daughter. Yet it was not so. As if it were some sort of evil spell, my banjoist cabin-mate's interruption, as related above, had arrested them short at the point of that fateful sunset for many weeks together. It was always thus with this book, begun in '89 and finished in '94— with that shortest of all the novels which it was to be my lot to write. Between its opening exclamation calling Almayer to his dinner in his wife's voice and Abdullah's (his enemy) mental reference to the God of Islam—"The Merciful, the Compassionate"—which closes the book, there were to come several long sea passages, a visit (to use the elevated phraseology suitable to the occasion) to the scenes (some of them) of my childhood and the realization of childhood's vain words, expressing a light-hearted and romantic whim.

It was in 1868, when nine years old or thereabouts, that while looking at a map of Africa of the time and putting my finger on the blank space then representing the unsolved mystery of that continent, I said to myself with absolute assurance and an amazing audacity which are no longer in my character now:

"When I grow up I shall go *there.*"

And of course I thought no more about it till after a quarter of a century or so an opportunity offered to go there—as if the sin of childish audacity was to be visited on my mature head. Yes. I did go there: *there* being the region of Stanley Falls which in '68 was the blankest of blank spaces on the earth's figured surface. And the MS. of *Almayer's Folly*, carried about me as if it were a talisman or a treasure, went *there* too. That it ever came out of *there* seems a special dispensation of Providence; because a good many of my other properties, infinitely more valuable and useful to me, remained behind through unfortunate accidents of transportation. I call to mind, for instance, a specially awkward turn of the Congo between Kinchassa and Leopoldsville—more particularly when one had to take it at night in a big canoe with only half the proper number of paddlers. I failed in being the second white man on record drowned at that interesting spot through the upsetting of a canoe. The first was a young Belgian officer, but the accident happened some months before my time, and he, too, I believe, was going home; not perhaps quite so ill as myself—but still he was going home. I got round the turn more or less alive, though I was too sick to care whether I did or not, and, always with *Almayer's Folly* amongst my diminishing baggage, I arrived at that delectable capital Boma, where before the departure of the steamer which was to take me home I had the time to wish myself dead over and over again with perfect sincerity. At that date there were in existence only seven chapters of *Almayer's Folly*, but the chapter in my history which followed was that of a long, long illness and very dismal convalescence. Geneva, or more precisely the hydropathic establishment of Champel, is rendered for ever famous by the termination of the eighth chapter in the history of Almayer's decline and fall. The events of the ninth are inextricably mixed up with the details of the proper management of a waterside warehouse owned by a certain city firm whose name does not matter. But that work, undertaken to accustom myself again to the activities of a healthy existence, soon came to an end. The earth had nothing to hold me with for very long. And then that memorable story, like a cask of choice Madeira, got carried for three years to and fro upon the sea. Whether this treatment improved its flavor or not, of course I would not like to say. As far as appearance is concerned, it certainly did nothing of the kind. The whole MS. acquired a faded look and an ancient, yellowish complexion. It became at last unreasonable to suppose that anything in the world would ever happen to Almayer and Nina. And yet something most unlikely to happen on the high seas was to wake them up from their state of suspended animation.

What is it that Novalis says? "It is certain my conviction gains infinitely the moment another soul will believe in it." And what is a novel if not a conviction of our fellow-men's existence strong enough to take upon itself a form of imagined life clearer than reality and whose accumulated verisimilitude of selected episodes puts to shame the pride of documentary history? Providence which saved my MS. from the Congo rapids brought it to the knowledge of a helpful soul far out on the open sea. It would be on my part the greatest ingratitude ever to forget the sallow, sunken face and the deep-set, dark eyes of the young Cambridge man (he was a "passenger for his health" on board the good ship *Torrens* outward bound to Australia) who was the first reader of *Almayer's Folly*—the very first reader I ever had. "Would it bore you very much reading a MS. in a handwriting like mine?" I asked him one evening on a sudden impulse at the end of a longish conversation whose subject was Gibbon's History. Jacques (that was his name) was sitting in my cabin one stormy dog-watch below, after bringing me a book to read from his own traveling store.

"Not at all," he answered with his courteous intonation and a faint smile. As I pulled a drawer open his suddenly aroused curiosity gave him a watchful expression. I wonder what he expected to see. A poem, maybe. All that's beyond guessing now. He was not a cold, but a calm man, still more subdued by disease—a man of few words and of an unassuming modesty in general intercourse, but with something uncommon in the whole of his person which set him apart from the undistinguished lot of our sixty passengers. His eyes had a thoughtful introspective look. In his attractive, re-served manner, and in a veiled, sympathetic voice, he asked:

"What is this?" "It is a sort of tale," I answered with an effort. "It is not even finished yet. Nevertheless, I would like to know what you think of it." He put the MS. in the breast-pocket of his jacket; I remember perfectly his thin brown fingers folding it lengthwise. "I will read it to-morrow," he remarked, seizing the door-handle, and then, watching the roll of the ship for a propitious moment, he opened the door and was gone. In the moment of his exit I heard the sustained booming of the wind, the swish of the water on the decks of the *Torrens*, and the subdued, as if distant, roar of the rising sea. I noted the growing disquiet in the great restlessness of the ocean, and responded professionally to it with the thought that at eight o'clock, in another half-hour or so at the furthest, the top-gallant sails would have to come off the ship.

Next day, but this time in the first dog-watch, Jacques entered my cabin. He had a thick, woolen muffler round his throat and the MS. was in his hand. He tendered it to me with a steady look but without a word. I took it in silence. He sat down on the couch and still said nothing. I opened and shut a drawer under my desk, on which a filled-up log-slate lay wide open in its wooden frame waiting to be copied neatly into the sort of book I was accustomed to write with care, the ship's log-book. I turned my back squarely on the desk. And even then Jacques never offered a word. "Well, what do you say?" I asked at last. "Is it worth finishing?" This question expressed exactly the whole of my thoughts.

"Distinctly," he answered in his sedate veiled voice, and then coughed a little.

"Were you interested?" I inquired further, almost in a whisper.

"Very much!"

In a pause I went on meeting instinctively the heavy rolling of the ship, and Jacques put his feet upon the couch. The curtain of my bed-place swung to and fro as it were a punkah, the bulkhead lamp circled in its gimbals, and now and then the cabin door rattled slightly in the gusts of wind. It was in latitude 40 south, and nearly in the longitude of Greenwich, as far as I can remember, that these quiet rites of Almayer's and Nina's resurrection were taking place. In the prolonged silence it occurred to me that there was a good deal of retrospective writing in the story as far as it went. Was it intelligible in its action? I asked myself, as if already the story-teller were being born into the body of a seaman. But I heard on deck the whistle of the officer of the watch and remained on the alert to catch the order that was to follow this call to attention. It reached me as a faint, fierce shout to "Square the yards." "Aha!" I thought to myself, "a westerly blow coming on." Then I turned to my very first reader, who, alas! was not to live long enough to know the end of the tale.

"Now let me ask you one more thing: Is the story quite clear to you as it stands?" He raised his dark, gentle eyes to my face and seemed surprised.

"Yes! Perfectly."

This was all I was to hear from his lips concerning the merits of *Almayer's Folly*. We never spoke together of the book again. A long period of bad weather set in and I had no thoughts left but for my duties, whilst poor Jacques caught a fatal cold and had to keep close in his cabin. When we arrived at Adelaide the first reader of my prose went at once up-country, and died rather suddenly in the end, either in Australia or it may be on the passage while going home through the Suez Canal. I am not sure which it was now, and I do not think I ever heard precisely; though I made inquiries about him from some of our return passengers who, wandering about to "see the country" during the ship's stay in port, had come upon him here and there. At last we sailed, homeward bound, and still not one line was added to the careless scrawl of the many pages which poor Jacques had had the patience to read with the very shadows of Eternity gathering already in the hollows of his kind, steadfast eyes.

The purpose instilled into me by his simple and final "Distinctly" remained dormant, yet alive to await its opportunity. I dare say I am compelled, unconsciously compelled, now to write volume after volume, as in past years I was compelled to go to sea, voyage after voyage. Leaves must follow upon each other as leagues used to follow in the days gone by, on and on to the appointed end, which, being Truth itself, is One—one for all men and for all occupations.

I do not know which of the two impulses has appeared more mysterious and more wonderful to me. Still, in writing, as in going to sea, I had to wait my opportunity. Let me confess here that I was never one of those wonderful fellows that would go afloat in a wash-tub for the sake of the fun, and if I may pride myself upon my consistency it was ever just the same with my writing. Some men, I have heard, write in railway carriages, and could do it, perhaps, sitting cross-legged on a clothes-line; but I must confess that my sybaritic disposition will not consent to write without something at least resembling a chair. Line by line, rather than page by page, was the growth of *Almayer's Folly*.

And so it happened that I very nearly lost the MS., advanced now to the first words of the ninth chapter, in the Friedrichstrasse railway station (that's in Berlin, you know) on my way to Poland, or more precisely Ukraine. On an early, sleepy morning, changing trains in a hurry, I left my Gladstone bag in a refreshment-room. A worthy and intelligent *Kofferträger* rescued it. Yet in my anxiety I was not thinking of the MS. but of all the other things that were packed in the bag.

In Warsaw, where I spent two days, those wandering pages were never exposed to the light, except once, to candle-light, while the bag lay open on a chair. I was dressing hurriedly to dine at a sporting club. A friend of my childhood (he had been in the Diplomatic Service, but had turned to growing wheat on paternal acres, and we had not seen each other for over twenty years) was sitting on the hotel sofa waiting to carry me off there.

"You might tell me something of your life while you are dressing," he suggested kindly.

I do not think I told him much of my life-story either then or later. The talk of the select little party with which he made me dine was extremely animated and embraced most subjects under heaven, from big-game shooting in Africa to the last poem published in a very modernist review, edited by the very young and patronized by the highest society. But it never touched upon *Almayer's Folly,* and next morning, in uninterrupted obscurity, this inseparable companion went on rolling with me in the southeast direction towards the Government of Kiev.

At that time there was an eight-hours' drive, if not more, from the railway station to the country house which was my destination.

"Dear boy" (these words were always written in English)—so ran the last letter from that house received in London—"Get yourself driven to the only inn in the place, dine as well as you can, and some time in the evening my own confidential servant, factotum and major-domo, a Mr. V. S. (I warn you he is of noble extraction), will present himself before you, reporting the arrival of the small sledge which will take you here on the next day. I send with him my heaviest fur, which I suppose, with such overcoats as you may have with you, will keep you from freezing on the road."

Sure enough, as I was dining, served by a Hebrew waiter, in an enormous barn-like bedroom with a freshly painted floor, the door opened and, in a traveling costume of long boots, big sheep-skin cap and a short coat girt with a leather belt, the Mr. V. S. (of noble extraction), a man of about thirty-five, appeared with an air of perplexity on his open and moustachioed countenance. I got up from the table and greeted him in Polish, with, I hope, the right shade of consideration demanded by his noble blood and his confidential position. His face cleared up in a wonderful way. It appeared that, notwithstanding my uncle's earnest assurances, the good fellow had remained in doubt of our understanding each other. He imagined I would talk to him in some foreign language. I was told that his last words on getting into the sledge to come to meet me shaped an anxious exclamation:

"Well! Well! Here I am going, but God only knows how I am to make myself understood to our master's nephew."

We understood each other very well from the first. He took charge of me as if I were not quite of age. I had a delightful boyish feeling of coming home from school when he muffled me up next morning in an enormous bear-skin traveling-coat and took his seat protectively by my side. The sledge was a very small one and it looked utterly insignificant, almost like a toy behind the four big bays harnessed two and two. We three, counting the coachman, filled it completely. He was a young fellow with clear blue eyes; the high collar of his livery fur coat framed his cheery countenance and stood all round level with the top of his head.

"Now, Joseph," my companion addressed him, "do you think we shall manage to get home before six?" His answer was that we would surely, with God's help, and providing there were no heavy drifts in the long stretch between certain villages whose names came with an extremely familiar sound to my ears. He turned out an excellent coachman with an instinct for keeping the road amongst the snow-covered fields and a natural gift of getting the best out of the horses.

"He is the son of that Joseph that I suppose the Captain remembers. He who used to drive the Captain's late grandmother of holy memory," remarked V.S., busy tucking fur rugs about my feet.

I remembered perfectly the trusty Joseph who used to drive my grandmother. Why! he it was who let me hold the reins for the first time in my life and allowed me to play with the great four-in-hand whip outside the doors of the coach-house.

"What became of him?" I asked. "He is no longer serving, I suppose."

"He served our master," was the reply. "But he died of cholera ten years ago now—that great epidemic we had. And his wife died at the same time—the whole houseful of them, and this is the only boy that was left."

The MS. of *Almayer's Folly* was reposing in the bag under our feet.

I saw again the sun setting on the plains as I saw it in the travels of my childhood. It set, clear and red, dipping into the snow in full view as if it were setting on the sea. It was twenty-three years since I had seen the sun set over that land; and we drove on in the darkness which fell swiftly upon the livid expanse of snows till, out of the waste of a white earth joining a be-starred sky, surged up black shapes, the clumps of trees about a village of the Ukrainian plain. A cottage or two glided by, a low interminable wall and then, glimmering and winking through a screen of fir-trees, the lights of the master's house.

That very evening the wandering MS. of *Almayer's Folly* was unpacked and unostentatiously laid on the writing-table in my room, the guest-room which had been, I was informed in an affectedly careless tone, awaiting me for some fifteen years or so. It attracted no attention from the affectionate presence hovering round the son of the favorite sister.

"You won't have many hours to yourself while you are staying with me, brother," he said—this form of address borrowed from the speech of our peasants being the usual expression of the highest good humor in a moment of affectionate elation. "I shall be always coming in for a chat."

As a matter of fact we had the whole house to chat in and were everlastingly intruding upon each other. I invaded the retirement of his study, where the principal feature was a colossal silver inkstand presented to him on his fiftieth year by a subscription of all his wards then living. He had been guardian of many orphans of land-owning families from the three southern provinces—ever since the year 1860. Some of them had been my schoolfellows and playmates, but not one of them, girls or boys, that I know of, has ever written a novel. One or two were older than myself—considerably older, too. One of them, a visitor I remember in my early years, was the man who first put me on horseback, and his four-horse bachelor turn-out, his perfect horsemanship and general skill in manly exercises was one of my earliest admirations. I seem to remember my mother looking on from a colonnade in front of the dining-room windows as I was lifted upon the pony, held, for all I know, by the very Joseph —the groom attached specially to my grandmother's service—who died of cholera. It was certainly a young man in a dark blue, tail-less coat and huge Cossack trousers, that being the livery of the men about the stables. It must have been in 1864, but reckoning by another mode of calculating time, it was certainly in the year in which my mother obtained permission to travel south and visit her family, from the exile into which she had followed my father. For that, too, she had had to ask permission, and I know that one of the conditions of that favor was that she should be treated exactly as a condemned exile herself. Yet a couple of years later, in memory of her eldest brother who had served in the Guards and dying early left hosts of friends and a loved memory in the great world of St. Petersburg, some influential personages procured for her this permission—it was officially called the "Highest Grace"—of a three months' leave from exile.

This is also the year in which I first begin to remember my mother with more distinctness than a mere loving, wide-browed, silent, protecting presence, whose eyes had a sort of commanding sweetness; and I also remember the great gathering of all the relations from near and far, and the gray heads of the family friends paying her the homage of respect and love in the house of her favorite brother who, a few years later, was to take the place for me of both my parents.

I did not understand the tragic significance of it all at the time, though indeed I remember that doctors also came. There were no signs of invalidism about her—but I think that already they had pronounced her doom unless perhaps the change to a southern climate could re-establish her declining strength. For me it seems the very happiest period of my existence. There was my cousin, a delightful, quick-tempered little girl, some months younger than myself, whose life, lovingly watched over, as if she were a royal princess, came to an end with her fifteenth year. There were other children too, many of whom are dead now, and not a few whose very names I have forgotten. Over all this hung the oppressive shadow of the great Russian Empire—the shadow lowering with the darkness of a new-born national hatred fostered by the Moscow school of journalists against the Poles after the ill-omened rising of 1863.

This is a far cry back from the MS. of *Almayer's Folly*, but the public record of these formative impressions is not the whim of an uneasy egotism. These, too, are things human, already distant in their appeal. It is meet that something more should be left for the novelist's children than the colors and figures of his own hard-won creation. That which in their grown-up years may appear to the world about them as the most enigmatic side of their natures and perhaps must remain for ever obscure even to themselves, will be their unconscious response to the still voice of that inexorable past from which his work of fiction and their personalities are remotely derived.

Only in men's imagination does every truth find an effective and undeniable existence. Imagination, not invention, is the supreme master of art as of life. An imaginative and exact rendering of authentic memories may serve worthily that spirit of piety towards all things human which sanctions the conceptions of a writer of tales, and the emotions of the man reviewing his own experience.

IV

It must not be supposed that in setting forth the memories of this half-hour between the moment my uncle left my room till we met again at dinner, I am losing sight of *Almayer's Folly*. Having confessed that my first novel was begun in idleness—a holiday task—I think I have also given the impression that it was a much-delayed book. It was never dismissed from my mind, even when the hope of ever finishing it was very faint. Many things came in its way: daily duties, new impressions, old memories. It was not the outcome of a need—the famous need of self-expression which artists find in their search for motives. The necessity which impelled me was a hidden, obscure necessity, a completely masked and unaccountable phenomenon. Or perhaps some idle and frivolous magician (there must be magicians in London) had cast a spell over me through his parlor window as I explored the maze of streets east and west in solitary leisurely walks without chart and compass. Till I began to write that novel I had written nothing but letters, and not very many of these. I never made a note of a fact, of an impression or of an anecdote in my life. The conception of a planned book was entirely outside my mental range when I sat down to write; the ambition of being an author had never turned up amongst these gracious imaginary existences one creates fondly for oneself at times in the stillness and immobility of a day-dream: yet it stands clear as the sun at noonday that from the moment I had done blackening over the first manuscript page of *Almayer's Folly* (it contained about two hundred words and this proportion of words to a page has remained with me through the fifteen years of my writing life), from the moment I had, in the simplicity of my heart and the amazing ignorance of my mind, written that page the die was cast. Never had Rubicon been more blindly forded, without invocation to the gods, without fear of men.

That morning I got up from my breakfast, pushing the chair back, and rang the bell violently, or perhaps I should say resolutely, or perhaps I should say eagerly, I do not know. But manifestly it must have been a special ring of the bell, a common sound made impressive, like the ringing of a bell for the raising of the curtain upon a new scene. It was an unusual thing for me to do. Generally, I dawdled over my breakfast and I seldom took the trouble to ring the bell for the table to be cleared away; but on that morning for some reason hidden in the general mysteriousness of the event I did not dawdle. And yet I was not in a hurry. I pulled the cord casually, and while the faint tinkling somewhere down in the basement went on, I charged my pipe in the usual way and I looked for the matchbox with glances distraught indeed but exhibiting, I am ready to swear, no signs of a fine frenzy. I was composed enough to perceive after some considerable time the matchbox lying there on the mantelpiece right under my nose. And all this was beautifully and safely usual. Before I had thrown down the match my landlady's daughter appeared with her calm, pale face and an inquisitive look, in the doorway. Of late it was the landlady's daughter who answered my bell. I mention this little fact with pride, because it proves that during the thirty or forty days of my tenancy I had produced a favorable impression. For a fortnight past I had been spared the unattractive sight of the domestic slave. The girls in that Bessborough Gardens house were often changed, but whether short or long, fair or dark, they were always untidy and particularly bedraggled, as if in a sordid version of the fairy tale the ashbin cat had been changed into a maid. I was infinitely sensible of the privilege of being waited on by my landlady's daughter. She was neat if anaemic.

"Will you please clear away all this at once?" I addressed her in convulsive accents, being at the same time engaged in getting my pipe to draw. This, I admit, was an unusual request. Generally on getting up from breakfast I would sit down in the window with a book and let them clear the table when they liked; but if you think that on that morning I was in the least impatient, you are mistaken. I remember that I was perfectly calm. As a matter of fact I was not at all certain that I wanted to write, or that I meant to write, or that I had anything to write about. No, I was not impatient. I lounged between the mantelpiece and the window, not even consciously waiting for the table to be cleared. It was ten to one that before my landlady's daughter was done I would pick up a book and sit down with it all the morning in a spirit of enjoyable indolence. I affirm it with assurance, and I don't even know now what were the books then lying about the room. Whatever they were they were not the works of great masters, where the secret of clear thought and exact expression can be found. Since the age of five I have been a great reader, as is not perhaps wonderful in a child who was never aware of learning to read. At ten years of age I had read much of Victor Hugo and other romantics. I had read in Polish and in French, history, voyages, novels; I knew *Gil Blas* and *Don Quixote* in abridged editions; I had read in early boyhood Polish poets and some French poets, but I cannot say what I read on the evening before I began to write myself. I believe it was a novel, and it is quite possible that it was one of Anthony Trollope's novels. It is very likely. My acquaintance with him was then very recent. He is one of the English novelists whose works I read for the first time in English. With men of European reputation, with Dickens and Walter Scott and Thackeray, it was otherwise. My first introduction to English imaginative literature was *Nicholas Nickleby*. It is extraordinary how well Mrs. Nickleby could chatter disconnectedly in Polish and the sinister Ralph rage in that language. As to the Crummles family and the family of the learned Squeers, it seemed as natural to them as their native speech. It was, I have no doubt, an excellent translation. This must have been in the year '70. But I really believe that I am wrong. That book was not my first introduction to English literature. My first acquaintance was (or were) the *Two Gentlemen of Verona*, and that in the very MS. of my father's translation. It was during our exile in Russia, and it must have been less than a year after my mother's death because I remember myself in the black blouse with a white border of my heavy mourning. We were living together, quite alone, in a small house on the outskirts of the town of T——. That afternoon, instead of going out to play in the large yard which we shared with our landlord, I had lingered in the room in which my father generally wrote. What emboldened me to clamber into his chair I am sure I don't know, but a couple of hours afterwards he discovered me kneeling in it with my elbows on the table and my head held in both hands over the MS. of loose pages. I was greatly confused, expecting to get into trouble. He stood in the doorway looking at me with some surprise, but the only thing he said after a moment of silence was:

"Read the page aloud."

Luckily the page lying before me was not over blotted with erasures and corrections, and my father's handwriting was otherwise extremely legible. When I got to the end he nodded and I flew out of doors thinking myself lucky to have escaped reproof for that piece of impulsive audacity. I have tried to discover since the reason of this mildness, and I imagine that all unknown to myself I had earned, in my father's mind, the right to some latitude in my relations with his writing-table. It was only a month before, or perhaps it was only a week before that I had read to him aloud from beginning to end, and to his perfect satisfaction, as he lay on his bed, not being very well at the time, the proofs of his translation of Victor Hugo's *Toilers of the Sea.* Such was my title to consideration, I believe, and also my first introduction to the sea in literature. If I do not remember where, how and when I learned to read, I am not likely to forget the process of being trained in the art of reading aloud. My poor father, an admirable reader himself, was the most exacting of masters. I reflect proudly that I must have read that page of *Two Gentlemen of Verona* tolerably well at the age of eight. The next time I met them was in a five-shilling one-volume edition of the dramatic works of William Shakespeare, read in Falmouth, at odd moments of the day, to the noisy accompaniment of caulkers' mallets driving oakum into the deck-seams of a ship in dry dock. We had run in, in a sinking condition and with the crew refusing duty after a month of weary battling with the gales of the North Atlantic. Books are an integral part of one's life and my Shakespearean associations are with that first year of our bereavement, the last I spent with my father in exile (he sent me away to Poland to my mother's brother directly he could brace himself up for the separation), and with the year of hard gales, the year in which I came nearest to death at sea, first by water and then by fire.

Those things I remember, but what I was reading the day before my writing life began I have forgotten. I have only a vague notion that it might have been one of Trollope's political novels. And I remember, too, the character of the day. It was an autumn day with an opaline atmosphere, a veiled, semi-opaque, lustrous day, with fiery points and flashes of red sunlight on the roofs and windows opposite, while the trees of the square with all their leaves gone were like tracings of indian ink on a sheet of tissue paper. It was one of those London days that have the charm of mysterious amenity, of fascinating softness. The effect of opaline mist was often repeated at Bessborough Gardens on account of the nearness to the river.

There is no reason why I should remember that effect more on that day than on any other day, except that I stood for a long time looking out of the window after the landlady's daughter was gone with her spoil of cups and saucers. I heard her put the tray down in the passage and finally shut the door; and still I remained smoking with my back to the room. It is very clear that I was in no haste to take the plunge into my writing life, if as plunge this first attempt may be described. My whole being was steeped deep in the indolence of a sailor away from the sea, the scene of never-ending labor and of unceasing duty. For utter surrender to indolence you cannot beat a sailor ashore when that mood is on him, the mood of absolute irresponsibility tasted to the full. It seems to me that I thought of nothing whatever, but this is an impression which is hardly to be believed at this distance of years. What I am certain of is, that I was very far from thinking of writing a story, though it is possible and even likely that I was thinking of the man Almayer.

I had seen him for the first time some four years before from the bridge of a steamer moored to a rickety little wharf forty miles up, more or less, a Bornean river. It was very early morning, and a slight mist, an opaline mist as in Bessborough Gardens only without the fiery flicks on roof and chimney-pot from the rays of the red London sun, promised to turn presently into a woolly fog. Barring a small dug-out canoe on the river, there was nothing moving within sight. I had just come up yawning from my cabin. The serang and the Malay crew were overhauling the cargo chains and trying the winches; their voices sounded subdued on the deck below and their movements were languid. That tropical daybreak was chilly. The Malay quartermaster, coming up to get something from the lockers on the bridge, shivered visibly. The forests above and below and on the opposite bank looked black and dank; wet dripped from the rigging upon the tightly stretched deck awnings, and it was in the middle of a shuddering yawn that I caught sight of Almayer. He was moving across a patch of burnt grass, a blurred, shadowy shape with the blurred bulk of a house behind him, a low house of mats, bamboos and palm-leaves with a high-pitched roof of grass.

He stepped upon the jetty. He was clad simply in flapping pajamas of cretonne pattern (enormous flowers with yellow petals on a disagreeable blue ground) and a thin cotton singlet with short sleeves. His arms, bare to the elbow, were crossed on his chest. His black hair looked as if it had not been cut for a very long time and a curly wisp of it strayed across his forehead. I had heard of him at Singapore; I had heard of him on board; I had heard of him early in the morning and late at night; I had heard of him at tiffin and at dinner; I had heard of him in a place called Pulo Laut from a half-caste gentleman there, who described himself as the manager of a coal-mine; which sounded civilized and progressive till you heard that the mine could not be worked at present because it was haunted by some particularly atrocious ghosts. I had heard of him in a place called Dongola, in the Island of Celebes, when the Rajah of that little-known sea-port (you can get no anchorage there in less than fifteen fathom, which is extremely inconvenient) came on board in a friendly way with only two attendants, and drank bottle after bottle of soda-water on the after-skylight with my good friend and commander Captain C——. At least I heard his name distinctly pronounced several times in a lot of talk in Malay language. Oh, yes, I heard it quite distinctly—Almayer, Almayer—and saw Captain C—— smile while the fat, dingy Rajah laughed audibly. To hear a Malay Rajah laugh outright is a rare experience, I can assure you. And I overheard more of Almayer's name amongst our deck passengers (mostly wandering traders of good repute) as they sat all over the ship—each man fenced round with bundles and boxes—on mats, on pillows, on quilts, on billets of wood, conversing of Island affairs. Upon my word, I heard the mutter of Almayer's name faintly at midnight, while making my way aft from the bridge to look at the patent taffrail-log tinkling its quarter-miles in the great silence of the sea. I don't mean to say that our passengers dreamed aloud of Almayer, but it is indubitable that two of them at least, who could not sleep apparently and were trying to charm away the trouble of insomnia by a little whispered talk at that ghostly hour were referring in some way or other to Almayer. It was really impossible on board that ship to get away definitely from Almayer; and a very small pony tied up forward and whisking its tail inside the galley, to the great embarrassment of our Chinaman cook, was destined for Almayer. What he wanted with a pony goodness only knows, since I am perfectly certain he could not ride it; but here you have the man, ambitious, aiming at the grandiose, importing a pony, whereas in the whole settlement at which he used to shake daily his impotent fist, there was only one path that was practicable for a pony: a quarter of a mile at most, hedged in by hundreds of square leagues of virgin forest. But who knows? The importation of that Bali pony might have been part of some deep scheme, of some diplomatic plan, of some hopeful intrigue. With Almayer one could never tell. He governed his conduct by considerations removed from the obvious, by incredible assumptions, which rendered his logic impenetrable to any reasonable person. I learned all this later. That morning, seeing the figure in pajamas moving in the mist, I said to myself: "That's the man."

He came quite close to the ship's side and raised a harassed countenance, round and flat, with that curl of black hair over the forehead and a heavy, pained glance.

"Good morning."

"Good morning."

He looked hard at me: I was a new face, having just replaced the chief mate he was accustomed to see; and I think that this novelty inspired him, as things generally did, with deep-seated mistrust.

"Didn't expect you in till this evening," he remarked suspiciously.

I don't know why he should have been aggrieved, but he seemed to be. I took pains to explain to him that having picked up the beacon at the mouth of the river just before dark and the tide serving, Captain C—— was enabled to cross the bar and there was nothing to prevent him going up the river at night.

"Captain C—— knows this river like his own pocket," I concluded discursively, trying to get on terms.

"Better," said Almayer.

Leaning over the rail of the bridge I looked at Almayer, who looked down at the wharf in aggrieved thought. He shuffled his feet a little; he wore straw slippers with thick soles. The morning fog had thickened considerably. Everything round us dripped: the derricks, the rails, every single rope in the ship—as if a fit of crying had come upon the universe.

Almayer again raised his head and, in the accents of a man accustomed to the buffets of evil fortune, asked hardly audibly: "I suppose you haven't got such a thing as a pony on board?"

I told him almost in a whisper, for he attuned my communications to his minor key, that we had such a thing as a pony, and I hinted, as gently as I could, that he was confoundedly in the way too. I was very anxious to have him landed before I began to handle the cargo. Almayer remained looking up at me for a long while with incredulous and melancholy eyes as though it were not a safe thing to believe my statement. This pathetic mistrust in the favorable issue of any sort of affair touched me deeply, and I added:

"He doesn't seem a bit the worse for the passage. He's a nice pony, too."

Almayer was not to be cheered up; for all answer he cleared his throat and looked down again at his feet. I tried to close with him on another track.

"By Jove!" I said. "Aren't you afraid of catching pneumonia or bronchitis or something, walking about in a singlet in such a wet fog?"

He was not to be propitiated by a show of interest in his health. His answer was a sinister "No fear," as much as to say that even that way of escape from inclement fortune was closed to him.

"I just came down . . ." he mumbled after a while.

"Well, then, now you're here I will land that pony for you at once and you can lead him home. I really don't want him on deck. He's in the way."

Almayer seemed doubtful. I insisted:

"Why, I will just swing him out and land him on the wharf right in front of you. I'd much rather do it before the hatches are off. The little devil may jump down the hold or do some other deadly thing."

"There's a halter?" postulated Almayer.

"Yes, of course there's a halter." And without waiting any more I leaned over the bridge rail.

"Serang, land Tuan Almayer's pony."

The cook hastened to shut the door of the galley and a moment later a great scuffle began on deck. The pony kicked with extreme energy, the kalashes skipped out of the way, the serang issued many orders in a cracked voice. Suddenly the pony leaped upon the fore-hatch. His little hoofs thundered tremendously; he plunged and reared. He had tossed his mane and his forelock into a state of amazing wildness, he dilated his nostrils, bits of foam flecked his broad little chest, his eyes blazed. He was something under eleven hands; he was fierce, terrible, angry, warlike, he said ha! ha! distinctly, he raged and thumped—and sixteen able-bodied kalashes stood round him like disconcerted nurses round a spoilt and passionate child. He whisked his tail incessantly; he arched his pretty neck; he was perfectly delightful; he was charmingly naughty. There was not an atom of vice in that performance; no savage baring of teeth and laying back of ears. On the contrary, he pricked them forward in a comically aggressive manner. He was totally unmoral and lovable; I would have liked to give him bread, sugar, carrots. But life is a stern thing and the sense of duty the only safe guide. So I steeled my heart and from my elevated position on the bridge I ordered the men to fling themselves upon him in a body.

The elderly serang, emitting a strange inarticulate cry, gave the example. He was an excellent petty officer—very competent indeed, and a moderate opium smoker. The rest of them in one great rush smothered that pony. They hung on to his ears, to his mane, to his tail; they lay in piles across his back, seventeen in all. The carpenter, seizing the hook of the cargo-chain, flung himself on the top of them. A very satisfactory petty officer too, but he stuttered. Have you ever heard a light-yellow, lean, sad, earnest Chinaman stutter in pidgin-English? It's very weird indeed. He made the eighteenth. I could not see the pony at all: but from the swaying and heaving of that heap of men I knew that there was something alive inside.

From the wharf Almayer hailed in quavering tones:

"Oh, I say!"

Where he stood he could not see what was going on on deck unless perhaps the tops of the men's heads; he could only hear the scuffle, the mighty thuds as if the ship were being knocked to pieces. I looked over: "What is it?"

"Don't let them break his legs," he entreated me plaintively.

"Oh, nonsense! He's all right now. He can't move." By that time the cargo-chain had been hooked to the broad canvas belt round the pony's body, the kalashes sprang off simultaneously in all directions, rolling over each other, and the worthy serang, making a dash behind the winch, turned the steam on.

"Steady!" I yelled, in great apprehension of seeing the animal snatched up to the very head of the derrick.

On the wharf Almayer shuffled his straw slippers uneasily. The rattle of the winch stopped, and in a tense, impressive silence that pony began to swing across the deck.

How limp he was! Directly he felt himself in the air he relaxed every muscle in a most wonderful manner. His four hoofs knocked together in a bunch, his head hung down, and his tail remained pendent in a nerveless and absolute immobility. He reminded me vividly of the pathetic little sheep which hangs on the collar of the Order of the Golden Fleece. I had no idea that anything in the shape of a horse could be so limp as that, either living or dead. His wild mane hung down lumpily, a mere mass of inanimate horsehair; his aggressive ears had collapsed, but as he went swaying slowly across the front of the bridge I noticed an astute gleam in his dreamy, half-closed eye. A trustworthy quartermaster, his glance anxious and his mouth on the broad grin, was easing over the derrick watchfully. I superintended, greatly interested.

"So! That will do."

The derrick-head stopped. The kalashes lined the rail. The rope of the halter hung perpendicular and motionless like a bell-pull in front of Almayer. Everything was very still. I suggested amicably that he should catch hold of the rope and mind what he was about. He extended a provokingly casual and superior hand.

"Look out, then! Lower away!"

Almayer gathered in the rope intelligently enough, but when the pony's hoofs touched the wharf he gave way all at once to a most foolish optimism. Without pausing, without thinking, almost without looking, he disengaged the hook suddenly from the sling, and the cargo-chain, after hitting the pony's quarters, swung back against the ship's side with a noisy, rattling slap. I suppose I must have blinked. I know I missed something, because the next thing I saw was Almayer lying flat on his back on the jetty. He was alone.

Astonishment deprived me of speech long enough to give Almayer time to pick himself up in a leisurely and painful manner. The kalashes lining the rail had all their mouths open. The mist flew in the light breeze, and it had come over quite thick enough to hide the shore completely.

"How on earth did you manage to let him get away?" I asked scandalized.

Almayer looked into the smarting palm of his right hand, but did not answer my inquiry.

"Where do you think he will get to?" I cried. "Are there any fences anywhere in this fog? Can he bolt into the forest? What's to be done now?"

Almayer shrugged his shoulders.

"Some of my men are sure to be about. They will get hold of him sooner or later."

"Sooner or later! That's all very fine, but what about my canvas sling—he's carried it off. I want it now, at once, to land two Celebes cows."

Since Dongola we had on board a pair of the pretty little island cattle in addition to the pony. Tied up on the other side of the fore deck they had been whisking their tails into the other door of the galley. These cows were not for Almayer, however, they were invoiced to Abdullah bin Selim, his enemy. Almayer's disregard of my requirements was complete.

"If I were you I would try to find out where he's gone," I insisted. "Hadn't you better call your men together or something? He will throw himself down and cut his knees. He may even break a leg, you know."

But Almayer, plunged in abstracted thought, did not seem to want that pony any more. Amazed at this sudden indifference, I turned all hands out on shore to hunt for him on my own account, or, at any rate, to hunt for the canvas sling which he had round his body. The whole crew of the steamer, with the exception of firemen and engineers, rushed up the jetty past the thoughtful Almayer and vanished from my sight. The white fog swallowed them up; and again there was a deep silence that seemed to extend for miles up and down the stream. Still taciturn, Almayer started to climb on board, and I went down from the bridge to meet him on the after deck.

"Would you mind telling the captain that I want to see him very particularly?" he asked me in a low tone, letting his eyes stray all over the place.

"Very well. I will go and see."

With the door of his cabin wide open Captain C——, just back from the bathroom, big and broad-chested, was brushing his thick, damp, iron-grey hair with two large brushes.

"Mr. Almayer told me he wanted to see you very particularly, sir."

Saying these words I smiled. I don't know why I smiled except that it seemed absolutely impossible to mention Almayer's name without a smile of a sort. It had not to be necessarily a mirthful smile. Turning his head towards me Captain C—— smiled too, rather joylessly.

"The pony got away from him—eh?"

"Yes, sir. He did."

"Where is he?"

"Goodness only knows."

"No. I mean Almayer. Let him come along."

The captain's state-room opening straight on deck under the bridge, I had only to beckon from the doorway to Almayer, who had remained aft, with down-cast eyes, on the very spot where I had left him. He strolled up moodily, shook hands, and at once asked permission to shut the cabin door.

"I have a pretty story to tell you," were the last words I heard. The bitterness of tone was remarkable.

I went away from the door, of course. For the moment I had no crew on board; only the Chinaman carpenter, with a canvas bag hung round his neck and a hammer in his hand, roamed about the empty decks knocking out the wedges of the hatches and dropping them into the bag conscientiously. Having nothing to do, I joined our two engineers at the door of the engine-room. It was near breakfast-time.

"He's turned up early, hasn't he?" commented the second engineer, and smiled indifferently. He was an abstemious man with a good digestion and a placid, reasonable view of life even when hungry.

"Yes," I said. "Shut up with the old man. Some very particular business."

"He will spin him a damned endless yarn," observed the chief engineer.

He smiled rather sourly. He was dyspeptic and suffered from gnawing hunger in the morning. The second smiled broadly, a smile that made two vertical folds on his shaven cheeks. And I smiled too, but I was not exactly amused. In that man, whose name apparently could not be uttered anywhere in the Malay Archipelago without a smile, there was nothing amusing whatever. That morning he breakfasted with us silently, looking mostly into his cup. I informed him that my men came upon his pony capering in the fog on the very brink of the eight-foot-deep well in which he kept his store of guttah. The cover was off, with no one near by, and the whole of my crew just missed going heels over head into that beastly hole. Jurumudi Itam, our best quartermaster, deft at fine needlework, he who mended the ship's flags and sewed buttons on our coats, was disabled by a kick on the shoulder.

Both remorse and gratitude seemed foreign to Almayer's character. He mumbled: "Do you mean that pirate fellow?"

"What pirate fellow? The man has been in the ship eleven years," I said indignantly.

"It's his looks," Almayer muttered for all apology.

The sun had eaten up the fog. From where we sat under the after-awning we could see in the distance the pony tied up in front of Almayer's house, to a post of the verandah. We were silent for a long time. All at once Almayer, alluding evidently to the subject of his conversation in the captain's cabin, exclaimed anxiously across the table.

"I really don't know what I can do now!"

Captain C—— only raised his eyebrows at him, and got up from his chair. We dispersed to our duties, but Almayer, half-dressed as he was in his cretonne pajamas and the thin cotton singlet, remained on board, lingering near the gangway as though he could not make up his mind whether to go home or stay with us for good. Our

Chinamen boys gave him side glances as they went to and fro; and Ah Sing, our young chief steward, the handsomest and most sympathetic of Chinamen, catching my eye, nodded knowingly at his burly back. In the course of the morning I approached him for a moment.

"Well, Mr. Almayer," I addressed him easily, "you haven't started on your letters yet."

We had brought him his mail and he had held the bundle in his hand ever since we got up from breakfast. He glanced at it when I spoke and, for a moment, it looked as if he were on the point of opening his fingers and letting the whole lot fall overboard. I believe he was tempted to do so. I shall never forget that man afraid of his letters.

"Have you been long out from Europe?" he asked me.

"Not very. Not quite eight months," I told him. "I left a ship in Samarang with a hurt back and have been in the hospital in Singapore some weeks."

He sighed.

"Trade is very bad here."

"Indeed!"

"Hopeless! . . . See these geese?"

With the hand holding the letters he pointed out to me what resembled a patch of snow creeping and swaying across the distant part of his compound. It disappeared behind some bushes.

"The only geese on the East Coast," Almayer informed me in a perfunctory mutter without a spark of faith, hope or pride. Thereupon, with the same absence of any sort of sustaining spirit, he declared his intention to select a fat bird and send him on board for us not later than next day.

I had heard of these largesses before. He conferred a goose as if it were a sort of Court decoration given only to the tried friends of the house. I had expected more pomp in the ceremony. The gift had surely its special quality, multiple and rare. From the only flock on the East Coast! He did not make half enough of it. That man did not understand his opportunities. However, I thanked him at some length.

"You see," he interrupted abruptly in a very peculiar tone, "the worst of this country is that one is not able to realize . . . it's impossible to realize . . ." His voice sank into a languid mutter. "And when one has very large interests . . . very important interests . . ." he finished faintly . . . "up the river."

We looked at each other. He astonished me by giving a start and making a very queer grimace.

"Well, I must be off," he burst out hurriedly. "So long!"

At the moment of stepping over the gangway he checked himself, though, to give me a mumbled invitation to dine at his house that evening with my captain, an invitation which I accepted. I don't think it could have been possible for me to refuse.

I like the worthy folk who will talk to you of the exercise of free will "at any rate for practical purposes." Free, is it? For practical purposes! Bosh! How could I have refused to dine with that man? I did not refuse simply because I could not refuse. Curiosity, a healthy desire for a change of cooking, common civility, the talk and the smiles of the previous twenty days, every condition of my existence at that moment and place made irresistibly for acceptance; and, crowning all that, there was the ignorance, the ignorance, I say, the fatal want of foreknowledge to counter-balance these imperative conditions of the problem. A refusal would have appeared perverse and insane. Nobody unless a surly lunatic would have refused. But if I had not got to know Almayer pretty well it is almost certain there would never have been a line of mine in print.

I accepted then—and I am paying yet the price of my sanity. The possessor of the only flock of geese on the East Coast is responsible for the existence of some fourteen volumes, so far. The number of geese he had called into being under adverse climatic conditions was considerably more than fourteen. The tale of volumes will never overtake the counting of heads, I am safe to say; but my ambitions point not exactly that way, and whatever the pangs the toil of writing has cost me I have always thought kindly of Almayer.

I wonder, had he known anything of it, what his attitude would have been? This is something not to be discovered in this world. But if we ever meet in the Elysian Fields —where I cannot depict him to myself otherwise than attended in the distance by his flock of geese (birds sacred to Jupiter)—and he addresses me in the stillness of that passionless region, neither light nor darkness, neither sound nor silence, and heaving endlessly with billowy mists from the impalpable multitudes of the swarming dead, I think I know what answer to make.

I would say, after listening courteously to the unvibrating tone of his measured remonstrances, which should not disturb, of course, the solemn eternity of stillness in the least—I would say something like this:

"It is true, Almayer, that in the world below I have converted your name to my own uses. But that is a very small larceny. What's in a name, O Shade? If so much of your old mortal weakness clings to you yet as to make you feel aggrieved (it was the note of your earthly voice, Almayer), then, I entreat you, seek speech without delay with our sublime fellow-Shade—with him who, in his transient existence as a poet, commented upon the smell of the rose. He will comfort you. You came to me stripped of all prestige by men's queer smiles and the disrespectful chatter of every vagrant trader in the Islands. Your name was the common property of the winds: it, as it were, floated naked over the waters about the Equator. I wrapped round its unhonored form the royal mantle of the tropics and have essayed to put into the hollow sound the very anguish of paternity—feats which you did not demand from me—but remember that all the toil and all the pain were mine. In your earthly life you haunted me, Almayer. Consider that this was taking a great liberty. Since you were always complaining of being lost to the world, you should remember that if I had not believed enough in your existence to let you haunt my rooms in Bessborough Gardens you would have been much more lost. You affirm that had I been capable of looking at you with a more perfect detachment and a greater simplicity, I might have perceived better the inward marvelousness which, you insist, attended your career upon that tiny pin-point of light, hardly visible, far, far below us, where both our graves lie. No doubt! But reflect, O complaining Shade! that this was not so much my fault as your crowning misfortune. I believed in you in the only way it was possible for me to believe. It was not worthy of your merits? So be it. But you were always an unlucky man, Almayer. Nothing was ever quite worthy of you. What made you so real to me was that you held this lofty theory with some force of conviction and with an admirable consistency."

It is with some such words translated into the proper shadowy expressions that I am prepared to placate Almayer in the Elysian Abode of Shades, since it has come to pass that having parted many years ago, we are never to meet again in this world.

VI

In the retrospect of a life which had, besides its preliminary stages of childhood and early youth, two distinct developments, and even two distinct elements, such as earth and water, for its successive scenes, a certain amount of naïveness is unavoidable. I am conscious of it in these pages. This remark is put forward in no apologetic spirit. As years go by and the number of pages grows steadily, the feeling grows upon one too that one can write only for friends. Then why should one put them to the necessity of protesting (as a friend would do) that no apology is necessary, or put, perchance, into their heads the doubt of one's discretion? So much as to the care due to those friends whom a word here, a line there, a fortunate page of just feeling in the right place, some happy simplicity, or even some lucky subtlety, has drawn from the great multitude of fellow-beings even as a fish is drawn from the depths of the sea. Fishing is notoriously (I am talking now of the deep sea) a matter of luck. As to one's enemies, those will take care of themselves.

There is a gentleman, for instance, who, metaphorically speaking, jumps upon me with both feet. This image has no grace, but it is exceedingly apt to the occasion—to the several occasions. I don't know precisely how long he had been indulging in that intermittent exercise, whose seasons are ruled by the custom of the publishing trade. Somebody pointed him out (in printed shape, of course) to my attention some time ago, and straightway I experienced a sort of reluctant affection for that robust man. He leaves not a shred of my substance untrodden: for the writer's substance is his writing; the rest of him is but a vain shadow, cherished or hated on uncritical grounds. Not a shred! Yet the sentiment owned to is not a freak of affectation or perversity. It has a deeper, and, I venture to think, a more estimable origin than the caprice of emotional lawlessness. It is, indeed, lawful in so much that it is given (reluctantly) for a consideration, for several considerations. There is that robustness, for instance, so often the sign of good moral balance. That's a consideration. It is not, indeed, pleasant to be stamped upon, but the very thoroughness of the operation, implying not only a careful reading, but some real insight into work whose qualities and defects, whatever they may be, are not so much on the surface, is something to be thankful for in view of the fact that it may happen to one's work to be condemned without being read at all. This is the most fatuous adventure that can well happen to a writer venturing his soul amongst criticisms. It can do one no harm, of course, but it is disagreeable. It is disagreeable in the same way as discovering a three-card trick man amongst a decent lot of folk in a third-class compartment. The open impudence of the whole transaction, appealing insidiously to the folly and credulity of mankind, the brazen, shameless patter, proclaiming the fraud openly while insisting on the fairness of the game, give one a feeling of sickening disgust. The honest violence of a plain man playing a fair game fairly—even if he means to knock you over—may appear shocking, but it remains within the pale of decency. Damaging as it may be, it is in no sense offensive. One may well feel some regard for honesty, even if practiced upon one's own vile body. But it is very obvious that an enemy of that sort will not be stayed by explanations or placated by apologies. Were I to advance the plea of youth in excuse of the naïveness to be found in these pages, he would be likely to say "Bosh!" in a column and a half of fierce print. Yet a writer is no older than his first published book, and, notwithstanding the vain appearances of decay which attend us in this transitory life, I stand here with the wreath of only fifteen short summers on my brow.

With the remark, then, that at such tender age, some naïveness of feeling and expression is excusable, I proceed to admit that, upon the whole, my previous state of existence was not a good equipment for a literary life. Perhaps I should not have used the word literary. That word pre-supposes an intimacy of acquaintance with letters, a turn of mind and a manner of feeling to which I dare lay no claim. I only love letters; but the love of letters does not make a literary man, any more than the love of the sea makes a seaman. And it is very possible too, that I love the letters in the same way a literary man may love the sea he looks at from the shore—a scene of great endeavor and of great achievements changing the face of the world, the great open way to all sorts of undiscovered countries. No, perhaps I had better say that the life at sea—and I don't mean a mere taste of it, but a good broad span of years, something that really counts as real service—is not, upon the whole, a good equipment for a writing life. God forbid, though, that I should be thought of as denying my masters of the quarter-deck. I am not capable of that sort of apostasy. I have confessed my attitude of piety towards their shades in three or four tales, and if any man on earth more than another needs to be true to himself as he hopes to be saved, it is certainly the writer of fiction.

What I mean to say, simply, is that the quarter-deck training does not prepare one sufficiently for the reception of literary criticism. Only that, and no more. But this defect is not without gravity. If it be permissible to twist, invert, adapt (and spoil) M. Anatole France's definition of a good critic, then let us say that the good author is he who contemplates without marked joy or excessive sorrow the adventures of his soul amongst criticisms. Far be from me the intention to mislead an attentive public into the belief that there is no criticism at sea. That would be dishonest, and even impolite. Everything can be found at sea, according to the spirit of your quest—strife, peace, romance, naturalism of the most pronounced kind, ideals, boredom, disgust, inspiration—and every conceivable opportunity, including the opportunity to make a fool of yourself—exactly as in the pursuit of literature. But the quarter-deck criticism is somewhat different from literary criticism. This much they have in common, that before the one and the other the answering back, as a general rule, does not pay.

Yes, you find criticism at sea, and even appreciation—I tell you everything is to be found on salt water—criticism generally impromptu, and always *viva voce,* which is the outward, obvious difference from the literary operation of that kind, with consequent freshness and vigor which may be lacking in the printed word. With appreciation, which comes at the end, when the critic and the criticized are about to part, it is otherwise. The sea appreciation of one's humble talents has the permanency of the written word, seldom the charm of variety, is formal in its phrasing. There the literary master has the superiority, though he, too, can in effect but say—and often says it in the very phrase—"I can highly recommend." Only usually he uses the word "We," there being some occult virtue in the first person plural, which makes it specially fit for critical and royal declarations. I have a small handful of these sea appreciations; signed by various masters, yellowing slowly in my writing-table's left-hand drawer, rustling under my reverent touch, like a handful of dry leaves plucked for a tender memento from the tree of knowledge. Strange! It seems that it is for these few bits of paper, headed by the names of a few ships and signed by the names of a few Scots and English shipmasters, that I have faced the astonished indignations, the mockeries and the reproaches of a sort hard to bear for a boy of fifteen; that I have been charged with the want of patriotism, the want of sense, and the want of heart too; that I went through agonies of self-conflict and shed secret tears not a few, and had the beauties of the Furca Pass spoiled for me, and have been called an "incorrigible Don Quixote," in allusion to the book-born madness of the knight. For that spoil! They rustle, those bits of paper—some dozens of them in all. In that faint, ghostly sound there live the memories of twenty years, the voices of rough men now no more, the strong voice of the everlasting winds, and the whisper of a mysterious spell, the murmur of the great sea, which must have somehow reached my inland cradle and entered my unconscious ear, like that formula of Mohammedan faith the Mussulman father whispers into the ear of his new-born infant, making him one of the faithful almost with his first breath. I do not know whether I have been a good seaman, but I know I have been a very faithful one. And after all there is that handful of "characters" from various ships to prove that all these years have not been altogether a dream. There they are, brief, and monotonous in tone, but as suggestive bits of writing to me as any inspired page to be found in literature. But then, you see, I have been called romantic. Well, that can't be helped. But stay. I seem to remember that I have been called a realist also. And as that charge too can be made out, let us try to live up to it, at whatever cost, for a change. With this end in view, I will confide to you coyly, and only because there is no one about to see my blushes by the light of the midnight lamp, that these suggestive bits of quarter-deck appreciation one and all contain the words "strictly sober."

Did I overhear a civil murmur, "That's very gratifying to be sure"? Well, yes, it is gratifying—thank you. It is at least as gratifying to be certified sober as to be certified romantic, though such certificates would not qualify one for the secretaryship of a temperance association or for the post of official troubadour to some lordly demo-cratic institution such as the London County Council, for instance. The above prosaic reflection is put down here only in order to prove the general sobriety of my judgment in mundane affairs. I make a point of it because a couple of years ago, a certain short story of mine being published in a French translation, a Parisian critic—I am almost certain it was M. Gustave Kahn, in the *Gil-Blas*—giving me a short notice, summed up his rapid impression of the writer's quality in the words *un puissant rêveur*. So be it! Who would cavil at the words of a friendly reader? Yet perhaps not such an unconditional dreamer as all that. I will make bold to say that neither at sea nor ashore have I ever lost the sense of responsibility. There is more than one sort of intoxication. Even before the most seductive reveries I have remained mindful of that sobriety of interior life, that asceticism of sentiment, in which alone the naked form of truth, such as one conceives it, such as one feels it, can be rendered without shame. It is but a maudlin and indecent verity that comes out through the strength of wine. I have tried to be a sober worker all my life—all my two lives. I did so from taste, no doubt, having an instinctive horror of losing my sense of full self-possession, but also from artistic conviction. Yet there are so many pitfalls on each side of the true path that, having gone some way, and feeling a little battered and weary, as a middle-aged traveler will from the mere daily difficulties of the march, I ask myself whether I have kept always, always faithful to that sobriety wherein there is power, and truth, and peace.

As to my sea-sobriety, that is quite properly certified under the sign-manual of several trustworthy shipmasters of some standing in their time. I seem to hear your polite murmur that "Surely this might have been taken for granted." Well, no. It might not have been. That august academical body of the Marine Department of the Board of Trade takes nothing for granted in the granting of its learned degrees. By its regulations issued under the first Merchant Shipping Act, the very word SOBER must be written, or a whole sackful, a ton, a mountain of the most enthusiastic appreciation will avail you nothing. The door of the examination rooms shall remain closed to your tears and entreaties. The most fanatical advocate of temperance could not be more pitilessly fierce in his rectitude than the Marine Department of the Board of Trade. As I have been face to face at various times with all the examiners of the Port of London in my generation, there can be no doubt as to the force and the continuity of my abstemiousness. Three of them were examiners in seamanship, and it was my fate to be delivered into the hands of each of them at proper intervals of sea service. The first of all, tall, spare, with a perfectly white head and mustache, a quiet, kindly manner, and an air of benign intelligence, must, I am forced to conclude, have been unfavorably impressed by something in my appearance. His old thin hands loosely clasped resting on his crossed legs, he began by an elementary question in a mild voice, and went on, went on . . . It lasted for hours, for hours. Had I been a strange microbe with potentialities of deadly mischief to the Merchant Service I could not have been submitted to a more microscopic examination. Greatly reassured by his apparent benevolence, I had been at first very alert in my answers. But at length the feeling of my brain getting addled crept upon me. And still the passionless process went on, with a sense of untold ages having been spent already on mere preliminaries. Then I got frightened. I was not frightened of being plucked; that eventuality did not even present itself to my mind. It was something much more serious, and weird. "This ancient person," I said to myself, terrified, "is so near his grave that he must have lost all notion of time. He is considering this examination in terms of unity. It is all very well for him. His race is run. But I may find myself coming out of this room into the world of men a stranger, friendless, forgotten by my very landlady, even were I able after this endless experience to remember the way to my hired home." This statement is not so much of a verbal exaggeration as may be supposed. Some very queer thoughts passed through my head while I was considering my answers; thoughts which had nothing to do with seamanship, nor yet with anything reasonable known to this earth. I verily believe that at times I was lightheaded in a sort of languid way. At last there fell a silence, and that too, seemed to last for ages, while, bending over his desk, the examiner wrote out my pass-slip slowly with a noiseless pen. He extended the scrap of paper to me and without a word inclined his white head gravely to my parting bow . . .

When I got out of the room I felt limply flat, like a squeezed lemon, and the doorkeeper in his glass cage, where I stopped to get my hat and tip him a shilling, said:

"Well! I thought you were never coming out."

"How long have I been in there?" I asked faintly.

He pulled out his watch.

"He kept you, sir, just under three hours. I don't think this ever happened with any of the gentlemen before."

It was only when I got out of the building that I began to walk on air. And the human animal being averse from change and timid before the unknown, I said to myself that I would not mind really being examined by the same man on a future occasion. But when the time of ordeal came round again the doorkeeper let me into another room, with the now familiar paraphernalia of models of ships and tackle, a board for signals on the wall, a big long table covered with official forms, and having an unrigged mast fixed to the edge. The solitary tenant was unknown to me by sight, though not by reputation, which was simply execrable. Short and sturdy as far as I could judge, clad in an old, brown, morning suit, he sat leaning on his elbow, his hand shading his eyes, and half averted from the chair I was to occupy on the other side of the table. He was motionless, mysterious, remote, enigmatical, with something mournful too in the pose, like that statue of Giuliano (I think) de Medici shading his face on the tomb by Michael Angelo, though, of course, he was far, far from being beautiful. He began by trying to make me talk nonsense. But I had been warned of that fiendish trait, and contradicted him with great assurance. After a while he left off. So far, good. But his immobility, the thick elbow on the table, the abrupt, unhappy voice, the shaded and averted face grew more and more impressive. He kept inscrutably silent for a moment, and then, placing me in a ship of a certain size at sea, under certain conditions of weather, season, locality, etc., etc.—all very clear and precise—ordered me to execute a certain maneuver. Before I was half through with it he did some material damage to the ship. Directly I had grappled with the difficulty he caused another to present itself, and when that too was met he stuck another ship before me, creating a very dangerous situation. I felt slightly outraged by this ingenuity in piling up trouble upon a man.

"I wouldn't have got into that mess," I suggested mildly. "I could have seen that ship before."

He never stirred the least bit.

"No, you couldn't. The weather's thick."

"Oh! I didn't know," I apologized blankly. I suppose that after all I managed to stave off the smash with sufficient approach to verisimilitude, and the ghastly business went on. You must understand that the scheme of the test he was applying to me was, I gathered, a homeward passage—the sort of passage I would not wish to my bitterest enemy. That imaginary ship seemed to labor under a most comprehensive curse. It's no use enlarging on these never-ending misfortunes; suffice it to say that long before the end I would have welcomed with gratitude an opportunity to exchange into the *Flying Dutchman*. Finally he shoved me into the North Sea (I suppose) and provided me with a leeshore with outlying sandbanks—the Dutch coast presumably. Distance, eight miles. The evidence of such implacable animosity deprived me of speech for quite half a minute.

"Well," he said—for our pace had been very smart indeed till then.

"I will have to think a little, sir."

"Doesn't look as if there were much time to think," he muttered sardonically from under his hand.

"No, sir," I said with some warmth. "Not on board a ship I could see. But so many accidents have happened that I really can't remember what there's left for me to work with."

Still half averted, and with his eyes concealed, he made unexpectedly a grunting remark.

"You've done very well."

"Have I the two anchors at the bow, sir?" I asked.

"Yes."

I prepared myself then, as a last hope for the ship, to let them both go in the most effectual manner, when his infernal system of testing resourcefulness came into play again.

"But there's only one cable. You've lost the other."

It was exasperating.

"Then I would back them, if I could, and tail the heaviest hawser on board on the end of the chain before letting go, and if she parted from that, which is quite likely, I would just do nothing. She would have to go."

"Nothing more to do, eh?"

"No, sir. I could do no more."

He gave a bitter half-laugh.

"You could always say your prayers."

He got up, stretched himself, and yawned slightly. It was a sallow, strong, unamiable face. He put me in a surly, bored fashion through the usual questions as to lights and signals, and I escaped from the room thankfully—passed! Forty minutes! And again I walked on air along Tower Hill, where so many good men had lost their heads, because, I suppose, they were not resourceful enough to save them. And in my heart of hearts I had no objection to meeting that examiner once more when the third and last ordeal became due in another year or so. I even hoped I should. I knew the worst of him now, and forty minutes is not an unreasonable time. Yes, I distinctly hoped . . .

But not a bit of it. When I presented myself to be examined for Master, the examiner who received me was short, plump, with a round soft face in gray, fluffy whiskers, and fresh, loquacious lips.

He commenced operations with an easy-going "Let's see. H'm. Suppose you tell me all you know of charter-parties." He kept it up in that style all through, wandering off in the shape of comment into bits out of his own life, then pulling himself up short and returning to the business in hand. It was very interesting. "What's your idea of a jury-rudder now?" he queried suddenly, at the end of an instructive anecdote bearing upon a point of stowage.

I warned him that I had no experience of a lost rudder at sea, and gave him two classical examples of makeshifts out of a text-book. In exchange he described to me a jury-rudder he had invented himself years before, when in command of a 3,000-ton steamer. It was, I declare, the cleverest contrivance imaginable. "May be of use to you some day," he concluded. "You will go into steam presently. Everybody goes into steam."

There he was wrong. I never went into steam—not really. If I only live long enough I shall become a bizarre relic of a dead barbarism, a sort of monstrous antiquity, the only seaman of the dark ages who had never gone into steam—not really.

Before the examination was over he imparted to me a few interesting details of the transport service in the time of the Crimean War.

"The use of wire rigging became general about that time too," he observed. "I was a very young master then. That was before you were born."

"Yes, sir. I am of the year 1857."

"The Mutiny year," he commented, as if to himself adding in a louder tone that his ship happened then to be in the Gulf of Bengal, employed under a Government charter.

Clearly the transport service had been the making of this examiner, who so unexpectedly had given me an insight into his existence, awakening in me the sense of the continuity of that sea-life into which I had stepped from outside; giving a touch of human intimacy to the machinery of official relations. I felt adopted. His experience was for me, too, as though he had been an ancestor.

Writing my long name (it has twelve letters) with laborious care on the slip of blue paper, he remarked:

"You are of Polish extraction."

"Born there, sir."

He laid down the pen and leaned back to look at me as it were for the first time. "Not many of your nationality in our service, I should think. I never remember meeting one either before or after I left the sea. Don't remember ever hearing of one. An inland people, aren't you?"

I said yes—very much so. We were remote from the sea not only by situation, but also from a complete absence of indirect association, not being a commercial nation at all, but purely agricultural. He made then the quaint reflection that it was "a long way for me to come out to begin a sea-life"; as if sea-life were not precisely a life in which one goes a long way from home.

I told him, smiling, that no doubt I could have found a ship much nearer my native place, but I had thought to myself that if I was to be a seaman then I would be a British seaman and no other. It was a matter of deliberate choice.

He nodded slightly at that; and as he kept on looking at me interrogatively, I enlarged a little, confessing that I had spent a little time on the way in the Mediterranean and in the West Indies. I did not want to present myself to the British Merchant Service in an altogether green state. It was no use telling him that my mysterious vocation was so strong that my very wild oats had to be sown at sea. It was the exact truth, but he would not have understood the somewhat exceptional psychology of my sea-going, I fear.

"I suppose you've never come across one of your countrymen at sea. Have you now?"

I admitted I never had. The examiner had given himself up to the spirit of gossiping idleness. For myself, I was in no haste to leave that room. Not in the least. The era of examinations was over. I would never again see that friendly man who was a professional ancestor, a sort of grandfather in the craft. Moreover, I had to wait till he dismissed me, and of that there was no sign. As he remained silent, looking at me, I added:

"But I have heard of one, some years ago. He seems to have been a boy serving his time on board a Liverpool ship, if I am not mistaken."

"What was his name?"

I told him.

"How did you say that?" he asked, puckering up his eyes at the uncouth sound.

I repeated the name very distinctly.

"How do you spell it?"

I told him. He moved his head at the impracticable nature of that name, and observed:

"It's quite as long as your own—isn't it?"

There was no hurry. I had passed for Master, and I had all the rest of my life before me to make the best of it. That seemed a long time. I went leisurely through a small mental calculation, and said:

"Not quite. Shorter by two letters, sir."

"Is it?" The examiner pushed the signed blue slip across the table to me, and rose from his chair. Somehow this seemed a very abrupt ending of our relations, and I felt almost sorry to part from that excellent man, who was master of a ship before the whisper of the sea had reached my cradle. He offered me his hand and wished me well.

He even made a few steps towards the door with me, and ended with good-natured advice.

"I don't know what may be your plans but you ought to go into steam. When a man has got his master's certificate it's the proper time. If I were you I would go into steam."

I thanked him, and shut the door behind me definitely on the era of examinations. But that time I did not walk on air, as on the first two occasions. I walked across the Hill of many beheadings with measured steps. It was a fact, I said to myself, that I was now a British master mariner beyond a doubt. It was not that I had an exaggerated sense of that very modest achievement, with which, however, luck, opportunity, or any extraneous influence could have had nothing to do. That fact, satisfactory and obscure in itself, had for me a certain ideal significance. It was an answer to certain outspoken skepticism, and even to some not very kind aspersions. I had vindicated myself from what had been cried upon as a stupid obstinacy or a fantastic caprice. I don't mean to say that a whole country had been convulsed by my desire to go to sea. But for a boy between fifteen and sixteen, sensitive enough, in all conscience, the commotion of his little world had seemed a very considerable thing indeed. So considerable that, absurdly enough, the echoes of it linger to this day. I catch myself in hours of solitude and retrospect meeting arguments and charges made thirty-five years ago by voices now for ever still; finding things to say that an assailed boy could not have found, simply because of the mysteriousness of his impulses to himself. I understood no more than the people who called upon me to explain myself. There was no precedent. I verily believe mine was the only case of a boy of my nationality and antecedents taking a, so to speak, standing jump out of his racial surroundings and associations. For you must understand that there was no idea of any sort of "career" in my call. Of Russia or Germany there could be no question. The nationality, the antecedents, made it impossible. The feeling against the Austrian service was not so strong, and I dare say there would have been no difficulty in finding my way into the Naval School at Pola. It would have meant six months' extra grinding at German, perhaps, but I was not past the age of admission, and in other respects I was well qualified. This expedient to palliate my folly was thought of—but not by me. I must admit that in that respect my negative was accepted at once. That order of feeling was comprehensible enough to the most inimical of my critics. I was not called upon to offer explanations; the truth is that what I had in view was not a naval career, but the sea. There seemed no way open to it but through France. I had the language at any rate, and of all the countries in Europe it is with France that Poland has most connection. There were some facilities for having me a little looked after, at first. Letters were being written, answers were being received, arrangements were being made for my departure for Marseilles, where an excellent fellow called Solary, got at in a roundabout fashion through various French channels, had promised good-naturedly to put *le jeune homme* in the way of getting a decent ship for his first start if he really wanted a taste of *ce métier de chien.*

I watched all these preparations gratefully, and kept my own counsel. But what I told the last of my examiners was perfectly true. Already the determined resolve, that "if a seaman, then an English seaman," was formulated in my head though, of course, in the Polish language. I did not know six words of English, and I was astute enough to understand that it was much better to say nothing of my purpose. As it was I was already looked upon as partly insane, at least by the more distant acquaintances. The principal thing was to get away. I put my trust in the good-natured Solary's very civil letter to my uncle, though I was shocked a little by the phrase about the *métier de chien.*

This Solary (Baptistin), when I beheld him in the flesh, turned out a quite young man, very good-looking, with a fine black, short beard, a fresh complexion, and soft, merry black eyes. He was as jovial and good-natured as any boy could desire. I was still asleep in my room in a modest hotel near the quays of the old port, after the fatigues of the journey *via* Vienna, Zurich, Lyons, when he burst in, flinging the shutters open to the sun of Provence and chiding me boisterously for lying abed. How pleasantly he startled me by his noisy objurgations to be up and off instantly for a "three years' campaign in the South Seas." O magic words! *"Une campagne de trois ans dans les mers du sud"*—that is the French for a three years' deep-water voyage.

He gave me a delightful waking, and his friendliness was unwearied; but I fear he did not enter upon the quest for a ship for me in a very solemn spirit. He had been at sea himself, but had left off at the age of twenty-five, finding he could earn his living on shore in a much more agreeable manner. He was related to an incredible number of Marseilles well-to-do families of a certain class. One of his uncles was a ship-broker of good standing, with a large connection amongst English ships; other relatives of his dealt in ships' stores, owned sail-lofts, sold chains and anchors, were master-stevedores, caulkers, ship-wrights. His grandfather (I think) was a dignitary of a kind, the Syndic of the Pilots. I made acquaintances amongst these people, but mainly amongst the pilots. The very first whole day I ever spent on salt water was by invitation, in a big half-decked pilot-boat, cruising under close reefs on the lookout, in misty, blowing weather, for the sails of ships and the smoke of steamers rising out there, beyond the slim and tall Planier lighthouse cutting the line of the wind-swept horizon with a white perpendicular stroke. They were hospitable souls, these sturdy Provençal seamen. Under the general designation of *le petit ami de Baptistin* I was made the guest of the Corporation of Pilots, and had the freedom of their boats night or day. And many a day and a night too did I spend cruising with these rough, kindly men, under whose auspices my intimacy with the sea began. Many a time "the little friend of Baptistin" had the hooded cloak of the Mediterranean sailor thrown over him by their honest hands while dodging at night under the lee of Château d'If on the watch for the lights of ships. Their sea-tanned faces, whiskered or shaved, lean or full, with the intent wrinkled sea-eyes of the pilot-breed, and here and there a thin gold loop at the lobe of a hairy ear, bent over my sea-infancy. The first operation of seamanship I had an opportunity of observing was the boarding of ships at sea, at all times, in all states of the weather. They gave it to me to the full. And I have been invited to sit in more than one tall, dark house of the old town at their hospitable board, had the *bouillabaisse* ladled out into a thick plate by their high-voiced, broad-browed wives, talked to their daughters—thick-set girls, with pure profiles, glorious masses of black hair arranged with complicated art, dark eyes, and dazzlingly white teeth.

I had also other acquaintances of quite a different sort. One of them, Madame Delestang, an imperious, handsome lady in a statuesque style, would carry me off now and then on the front seat of her carriage to the Prado, at the hour of fashionable airing. She belonged to one of the old aristocratic families in the south. In her haughty weariness she used to make me think of Lady Dedlock in Dickens's *Bleak House,* a work of the master for which I have such an admiration, or rather such an intense and unreasoning affection, dating from the days of my childhood, that its very weaknesses are more precious to me than the strength of other men's work. I have read it innumerable times, both in Polish and in English; I read it only the other day, and, by a not very surprising inversion, the Lady Dedlock of the book reminded me strongly of the *belle Madame Delestang.*

Her husband (as I sat facing them both), with his thin bony nose, and a perfectly bloodless, narrow physiognomy clamped together as it were by short formal side-whiskers, had nothing of Sir Leicester Dedlock's "grand air" and courtly solemnity. He belonged to the *haute bourgeoisie* only, and was a banker, with whom a modest credit had been opened for my needs. He was such an ardent—no, such a frozen-up, mummified Royalist that he used in current conversation turns of speech contempo-rary, I should say, with the good Henri Quatre; and when talking of money matters reckoned not in francs, like the common, godless herd of post-Revolutionary French-men, but in obsolete and forgotten *écus*—*écus* of all money units in the world!—as though Louis Quatorze were still promenading in royal splendor the gardens of Ver-sailles, and Monsieur de Colbert busy with the direction of maritime affairs. You must admit that in a banker of the nineteenth century it was a quaint idiosyncrasy. Luckily in the counting-house (it occupied part of the ground floor of the Delestang town residence, in a silent, shady street) the accounts were kept in modern money so that I never had any difficulty in making my wants known to the grave, low-voiced decorous, Legitimist (I suppose) clerks, sitting in the perpetual gloom of heavily-barred windows behind the somber, ancient counters, beneath lofty ceilings with heavily-molded cor-nices. I always felt on going out as though I had been in the temple of some very dignified but completely temporal religion. And it was generally on these occasions that under the great carriage gateway Lady Ded—I mean Madame Delestang, catching sight of my raised hat, would beckon me with an amiable imperiousness to the side of the carriage, and suggest with an air of amused nonchalance, *"Venez donc faire un tour avec nous,"* to which the husband would add an encouraging *"C'est ça. Allons, montez, jeune homme."* He questioned me sometimes, significantly but with perfect tact and delicacy, as to the way I employed my time, and never failed to express the hope that I wrote regularly to my "honored uncle." I made no secret of the way I employed my time, and I rather fancy that my artless tales of the pilots and so on entertained Madame Delestang, so far as that ineffable woman could be entertained by the prattle of a youngster very full of his new experience amongst strange men and strange sensations. She expressed no opinions, and talked to me very little; yet her portrait hangs in the gallery of my intimate memories, fixed there by a short and fleeting episode. One day, after putting me down at the corner of a street, she offered me her hand, and detained me by a slight pressure, for a moment. While the husband sat motionless and looking straight before him, she leaned forward in the carriage to say, with just a shade of warning in her leisurely tone: *"Il faut, cependant, faire attention à ne pas gâter sa vie."* I had never seen her face so close to mine before. She made my heart beat, and caused me to remain thoughtful for a whole evening. Certainly one must, after all, take care not to spoil one's life. But she did not know—nobody could know—how impossible that danger seemed to me.

VII

Can the transports of first love be calmed, checked, turned to a cold suspicion of the future by a grave quotation from a work on Political Economy? I ask—is it conceivable? Is it possible? Would it be right? With my feet on the very shores of the sea and about to embrace my blue-eyed dream, what could a good-natured warning as to spoiling one's life mean to my youthful passion? It was the most unexpected and the last, too, of the many warnings I had received. It sounded to me very *bizarre*—and, uttered as it was in the very presence of my enchantress, like the voice of folly, the voice of ignorance. But I was not so callous or so stupid as not to recognize there also the voice of kindness. And then the vagueness of the warning—because what can be the meaning of the phrase: to spoil one's life?—arrested one's attention by its air of wise profundity. At any rate, as I have said before, the words of *la belle Madame Delestang* made me thoughtful for a whole evening. I tried to understand and tried in vain, not having any notion of life as an enterprise that could be mismanaged. But I left off being thoughtful shortly before midnight, at which hour, haunted by no ghosts of the past and by no visions of the future, I walked down the quay of the *Vieux Port* to join the pilot-boat of my friends. I knew where she would be waiting for her crew, in the little bit of a canal behind the Fort at the entrance of the harbor. The deserted quays looked very white and dry in the moonlight and as if frost-bound in the sharp air of that December night. A prowler or two slunk by noiselessly; a custom-house guard, soldier-like, a sword by his side, paced close under the bow-sprits of the long row of ships moored bows on opposite the long, slightly curved, continuous flat wall of the tall houses that seemed to be one immense abandoned building with innumerable windows shuttered closely. Only here and there a small dingy *café* for sailors cast a yellow gleam on the bluish sheen of the flagstone. Passing by, one heard a deep murmur of voices inside—nothing more. How quiet everything was at the end of the quays on the last night on which I went out for a service cruise as a guest of the Marseilles pilots! Not a footstep, except my own, not a sigh, not a whispering echo of the usual revelry going on in the narrow, unspeakable lanes of the Old Town reached my ear—and suddenly, with a terrific jingling rattle of iron and glass, the omnibus of the Jolliette on its last journey swung round the corner of the dead wall which faces across the paved road the characteristic angular mass of the Fort St. Jean. Three horses trotted abreast with the clatter of hoofs on the granite setts, and the yellow, uproarious machine jolted violently behind them, fantastic, lighted up, perfectly empty and with the driver apparently asleep on his swaying perch above that amazing racket. I flattened myself against the wall and gasped. It was a stunning experience. Then after staggering on a few paces in the shadow of the Fort casting a darkness more intense than that of a clouded night upon the canal, I saw the tiny light of a lantern standing on the quay, and became aware of muffled figures making towards it from various directions— Pilots of the Third Company hastening to embark. Too sleepy to be talkative, they step on board in silence. But a few low grunts and an enormous yawn are heard. Somebody even ejaculates: *"Ah! Coquin de sort!"* and sighs wearily at his hard fate.

The *patron* of the Third Company (there were five companies of pilots at that time, I believe) is the brother-in-law of my friend Solary (Baptistin), a broad-shouldered, deep-chested man of forty, with a keen, frank glance which always seeks your eyes. He greets me by a low, hearty *"Hé, l'ami. Comment va?"* With his clipped mustache and massive open face, energetic and at the same time placid in expression, he is a fine specimen of the southerner of the calm type. For there is such a type in which the volatile southern passion is transmuted into solid force. He is fair, but no one could mistake him for a man of the north even by the dim gleam of the lantern standing on the quay. He is worth a dozen of your ordinary Normans or Bretons, but then, in the whole immense sweep of the Mediterranean shores, you could not find half a dozen men of his stamp.

Standing by the tiller, he pulls out his watch from under a thick jacket and bends his head over it in the light cast into the boat. Time's up. His pleasant voice commands in a quiet undertone, *"Larguez."* A suddenly projected arm snatches the lantern off the quay—and, warped along by a line at first, then with the regular tug of four heavy sweeps in the bow, the big half-decked boat full of men glides out of the black, breathless shadow of the Fort. The open water of the *avant-port* glitters under the moon as if sown over with millions of sequins, and the long white breakwater shines like a thick bar of solid silver. With a quick rattle of blocks and one single silky swish, the sail is filled by a little breeze keen enough to have come straight down from the frozen moon, and the boat, after the clatter of the hauled-in sweeps, seems to stand at rest, surrounded by a mysterious whispering so faint and unearthly that it may be the rustling of the brilliant, overpowering moonrays breaking like a shower upon the hard, smooth, shadowless sea.

I may well remember that last night spent with the pilots of the Third Company. I have known the spell of moonlight since, on various seas and coasts—coasts of forests, of rocks, of sand dunes—but no magic so perfect in its revelation of unsuspected character, as though one were allowed to look upon the mystic nature of material things. For hours I suppose no word was spoken in that boat. The pilots seated in two rows facing each other dozed with their arms folded and their chins resting upon their breasts. They displayed a great variety of caps: cloth, wool, leather, earflaps, tassels, with a picturesque round béret or two pulled down over the brows; and one grandfather, with a shaved, bony face and a great beak of a nose, had a cloak with a hood which made him look in our midst like a cowled monk being carried off goodness knows where by that silent company of seamen—quite enough to be dead.

My fingers itched for the tiller, and in due course my friend, the *patron*, surrendered it to me in the same spirit in which the family coachman lets a boy hold the reins on an easy bit of road. There was a great solitude around us; the islets ahead, Monte Cristo and the Château d'If in full light, seemed to float towards us—so steady, so imperceptible was the progress of our boat. "Keep her in the furrow of the moon," the *patron* directed me in a quiet murmur, sitting down ponderously in the stern-sheets and reaching for his pipe.

The pilot station in weather like this was only a mile or two to the westward of the islets; and presently, as we approached the spot, the boat we were going to relieve swam into our view suddenly, on her way home, cutting black and sinister into the wake of the moon under a sable wing, while to them our sail must have been a vision of white and dazzling radiance. Without altering the course a hair's-breadth, we slipped by each other within an oar's length. A drawling sardonic hail came out of her. Instantly, as if by magic, our dozing pilots got on their feet in a body. An incredible babel of bantering shouts burst out, a jocular, passionate, voluble chatter, which lasted till the boats were stern to stern, theirs all bright now and with a shining sail to our eye, we turned all black to their vision, and drawing away from them under a sable wing. That extraordinary uproar died away almost as suddenly as it had begun; first one had enough of it and sat down, then another, then three or four together, and when all had left off with mutters and growling half-laughs the sound of hearty chuckling became audible, persistent, unnoticed. The cowled grandfather was very much entertained somewhere within his hood.

He had not joined in the shouting of jokes, neither had he moved the least bit. He had remained quietly in his place against the foot of the mast. I had been given to understand long before that he had the rating of a second-class able seaman (*matelot léger*) in the fleet which sailed from Toulon for the conquest of Algeria in the year of grace 1830. And, indeed, I had seen and examined one of the buttons of his old brown patched coat, the only brass button of the miscellaneous lot, flat and thin, with the words *Equipages de ligne* engraved on it. That sort of button, I believe, went out with the last of the French Bourbons. "I preserved it from the time of my Navy Service," he explained, nodding rapidly his frail, vulture-like head. It was not very likely that he had picked up that relic in the street. He looked certainly old enough to have fought at Trafalgar—or at any rate to have played his little part there as a powder-monkey. Shortly after we had been introduced he had informed me in a Franco-Provençal jargon, mumbling tremulously with his toothless jaws, that when he was a "shaver no higher than that" he had seen the Emperor Napoleon returning from Elba. It was at night, he narrated vaguely, without animation, at a spot between Fréjus and Antibes in the open country. A big fire had been lit at the side of the crossroads. The population from several villages had collected there, old and young—down to the very children in arms because the women had refused to stay at home. Tall soldiers, wearing high, hairy caps, stood in a circle facing the people silently, and their stern eyes and big mustaches were enough to make everybody keep at a distance. He, "being an impudent little shaver," wriggled out of the crowd, creeping on his hands and knees as near as he dared to the grenadiers' legs, and peeping through discovered standing perfectly still in the light of the fire "a little fat fellow in a three-cornered hat, buttoned up in a long straight coat, with a big pale face, inclined on one shoulder, looking something like a priest. His hands were clasped behind his back . . . It appears that this was the Emperor," the Ancient commented with a faint sigh. He was staring from the ground with all his might, when "my poor father," who had been searching for his boy frantically everywhere, pounced upon him and hauled him away by the ear.

The tale seems an authentic recollection. He related it to me many times, using the very same words. The grandfather honored me by a special and somewhat embarrassing predilection. Extremes touch. He was the oldest member by a long way in that Company, and I was, if I may say so, its temporarily adopted baby. He had been a pilot longer than any man in the boat could remember: thirty—forty years. He did not seem certain himself, but it could be found out, he suggested, in the archives of the Pilot Office. He had been pensioned off years before, but he went out from force of habit; and, as my friend the *patron* of the Company once confided to me in a whisper, "the old chap did no harm. He was not in the way." They treated him with rough deference. One and another would address some insignificant remark to him now and again, but nobody really took any notice of what he had to say. He had survived his strength, his usefulness, his very wisdom. He wore long, green, worsted stockings, pulled up above the knee over his trousers, a sort of woolen nightcap on his hairless cranium, and wooden clogs on his feet. Without his hooded cloak he looked like a peasant. Half a dozen hands would be extended to help him on board, but afterwards he was left pretty much to his own thoughts. Of course he never did any work, except, perhaps, to cast off some rope when hailed: *"Hé, l'Ancien!* let go the halyards there, at your hand"—or some such request of an easy kind.

No one took notice in any way of the chuckling within the shadow of the hood. He kept it up for a long time with intense enjoyment. Obviously he had preserved intact the innocence of mind which is easily amused. But when his hilarity had exhausted itself, he made a professional remark in a self-assertive but quavering voice:

"Can't expect much work on a night like this."

No one took it up. It was a mere truism. Nothing under canvas could be expected to make a port on such an idle night of dreamy splendor and spiritual stillness. We would have to glide idly to and fro, keeping our station within the appointed bearings, and, unless a fresh breeze sprang up with the dawn, we would land before sunrise on a small islet that, within two miles of us, shone like a lump of frozen moonlight, to "break a crust and take a pull at the wine bottle." I was familiar with the procedure. The stout boat emptied of her crowd would nestle her buoyant, capable side against the very rock—such is the perfectly smooth amenity of the classic sea when in a gentle mood. The crust broken, and the mouthful of wine swallowed—it was literally no

more than that with this abstemious race—the pilots would pass the time stamping
their feet on the slabs of sea-salted stone and blowing into their nipped fingers. One or
two misanthropists would sit apart perched on boulders like man-like sea-fowl of
solitary habits; the sociably disposed would gossip scandalously in little gesticulating
knots; and there would be perpetually one or another of my hosts taking aim at the
empty horizon with the long, brass tube of the telescope, a heavy, murderous-looking
piece of collective property, everlastingly changing hands with brandishing and leveling
movements. Then about noon (it was a short turn of duty—the long turn lasted
twenty-four hours) another boatful of pilots would relieve us—and we would steer for
the old Phoenician port, dominated, watched over from the ridge of a dust-grey arid
hill by the red-and-white striped pile of the Notre Dame de la Garde.

All this came to pass as I had foreseen in the fullness of my very recent experience.
But also something not foreseen by me did happen, something which causes me to
remember my last outing with the pilots. It was on this occasion that my hand
touched, for the first time, the side of an English ship.

No fresh breeze had come with the dawn, only the steady little draught got a more
keen edge on it as the eastern sky became bright and glassy with a clean, colorless
light. It was while we were all ashore on the islet that a steamer was picked up by the
telescope, a black speck like an insect posed on the hard edge of the offing. She
emerged rapidly to her water-line and came on steadily, a slim hull with a long streak
of smoke slanting away from the rising sun. We embarked in a hurry, and headed the
boat out for our prey, but we hardly moved three miles an hour.

She was a big, high-class cargo-steamer of a type that is to be met on the sea no
more, black hull, with low, white superstructures, powerfully rigged with three masts
and a lot of yards on the fore; two hands at her enormous wheel—steam steering gear
was not a matter of course in these days—and with them on the bridge three others,
bulky in thick blue jackets, ruddy-faced, muffled up with peaked caps—I suppose all
her officers. There are ships I have met more than once and known well by sight whose
names I have forgotten; but the name of that ship seen once so many years ago in the
clear flush of a cold pale sunrise I have not forgotten. How could I—the first English
ship on whose side I ever laid my hand! The name—I read it letter by letter on the
bow—was "James Westoll." Not very romantic you will say. The name of a very
considerable, well-known and universally respected North-country ship-owner, I believe. James Westoll! What better name could an honorable hard-working ship have?
To me the very grouping of the letters is alive with the romantic feeling of her reality
as I saw her floating motionless, and borrowing an ideal grace from the austere purity
of the light.

We were then very near her, and, on a sudden impulse, I volunteered to pull bow in
the dinghy which shoved off at once to put the pilot on board while our boat, fanned
by the faint air which had attended us all through the night, went on gliding gently
past the black glistening length of the ship. A few strokes brought us alongside, and it
was then that, for the very first time in my life, I heard myself addressed in English—

the speech of my secret choice, of my future, of long friendships, of the deepest affections, of hours of toil and hours of ease, and of solitary hours too, of books read, of thoughts pursued, of remembered emotions—of my very dreams! And if (after being thus fashioned by it in that part of me which cannot decay) I dare not claim it aloud as my own, then, at any rate the speech of my children. Thus small events grow memorable by the passage of time. As to the quality of the address itself I cannot say it was very striking. Too short for eloquence and devoid of all charm of tone, it consisted precisely of the three words "Look out there," growled out huskily above my head.

It proceeded from a big fat fellow—he had an obtrusive, hairy double chin—in a blue woolen shirt and roomy breeches pulled up very high, even to the level of his breast-bone, by a pair of braces quite exposed to public view. As where he stood there was no bulwark but only a rail and stanchions, I was able to take in at a glance the whole of his voluminous person from his feet to the high crown of his soft black hat, which sat like an absurd flanged cone on his big head. The grotesque and massive aspect of that deck hand (I suppose he was that—very likely the lamp-trimmer) surprised me very much. My course of reading, of dreaming and longing for the sea had not prepared me for a sea-brother of that sort. I never met again a figure in the least like his except in the illustrations to Mr. W. W. Jacobs's most entertaining tales of barges and coasters; but the inspired talent of Mr. Jacobs for poking endless fun at poor, innocent sailors in a prose which, however extravagant in its felicitous invention, is always artistically adjusted to observed truth, was not yet. Perhaps Mr. Jacobs himself was not yet. I fancy that, at most, if he had made his nurse laugh it was about all he had achieved at that early date.

Therefore, I repeat, other disabilities apart, I could not have been prepared for the sight of that husky old porpoise. The object of his concise address was to call my attention to a rope which he incontinently flung down for me to catch. I caught it, though it was not really necessary, the ship having no way on her by that time. Then everything went on very swiftly. The dinghy came with a slight bump against the steamer's side, the pilot, grabbing the rope ladder, had scrambled halfway up before I knew that our task of boarding was done; the harsh, muffled clanging of the engine-room telegraph struck my ear through the iron plate; my companion in the dinghy was urging me to "shove off—push hard"; and when I bore against the smooth flank of the first English ship I ever touched in my life, I felt it already throbbing under my open palm.

Her head swung a little to the west, pointing towards the miniature lighthouse of the Jolliette breakwater, far away there, hardly distinguishable against the land. The dinghy danced a squashy, splashy jig in the wash of the wake and turning in my seat I followed the "James Westoll" with my eyes. Before she had gone in a quarter of a mile she hoisted her flag as the harbor regulations prescribe for arriving and departing ships. I saw it suddenly flicker and stream out on the flagstaff. The Red Ensign! In the pellucid, colorless atmosphere bathing the drab and gray masses of that southern land, the livid islets, the sea of pale glassy blue under the pale glassy sky of that cold sunrise, it was as far as the eye could reach the only spot of ardent color—flame-like, intense, and presently as minute as the tiny red spark the concentrated reflection of a great fire kindles in the clear heart of a globe of crystal. The Red Ensign—the symbolic, protecting warm bit of bunting flung wide upon the seas, and destined for so many years to be the only roof over my head.

YOUTH

A NARRATIVE

his could have occurred nowhere but in England, where men and sea interpenetrate, so to speak—the sea entering into the life of most men, and the men knowing something or everything about the sea, in the way of amusement, of travel, or of breadwinning.

We were sitting round a mahogany table that reflected the bottle, the claret glasses, and our faces as we leaned on our elbows. There was a director of companies, an accountant, a lawyer, Marlow, and myself. The director had been a *Conway* boy, the accountant had served four years at sea, the lawyer—a fine crusted Tory, High Churchman, the best of old fellows, the soul of honor—had been chief officer in the P. & O. service in the good old days when mailboats were square-rigged at least on two masts, and used to come down the China Sea before a fair monsoon with stun'sails set alow and aloft. We all began life in the merchant service. Between the five of us there was the strong bond of the sea, and also the fellowship of the craft, which no amount of enthusiasm for yachting, cruising, and so on can give, since one is only the amusement of life and the other is life itself.

Marlow (at least I think that is how he spelled his name) told the story, or rather the chronicle, of a voyage:

"Yes, I have seen a little of the Eastern seas; but what I remember best is my first voyage there. You fellows know there are those voyages that seem ordered for the illustration of life, that might stand for a symbol of existence. You fight, work, sweat, nearly kill yourself, sometimes do kill yourself, trying to accomplish something—and you can't. Not from any fault of yours. You simply can do nothing, neither great nor little—not a thing in the world—not even marry an old maid, or get a wretched 600-ton cargo of coal to its port of destination.

"It was altogether a memorable affair. It was my first voyage to the East, and my first voyage as second mate; it was also my skipper's first command. You'll admit it was time. He was sixty if a day; a little man, with a broad, not very straight back, with bowed shoulders and one leg more bandy than the other, he had that queer twisted-about appearance you see so often in men who work in the fields. He had a nutcracker face—chin and nose trying to come together over a sunken mouth—and it was framed in iron-gray fluffy hair, that looked like a chinstrap of cotton-wool sprinkled with coaldust. And he had blue eyes in that old face of his, which were amazingly like a boy's, with that candid expression some quite common men preserve to the end of their days by a rare internal gift of simplicity of heart and rectitude of soul. What induced him to accept me was a wonder. I had come out of a crack Australian clipper, where I had been third officer, and he seemed to have a prejudice against crack clippers as aristocratic and high-toned. He said to me, 'You know, in this ship you will have to work.' I said I had to work in every ship I had ever been in. 'Ah, but this is different, and you gentlemen out of them big ships; . . . but there! I dare say you will do. Join tomorrow.'

"I joined tomorrow. It was twenty-two years ago; and I was just twenty. How time passes! It was one of the happiest days of my life. Fancy! Second mate for the first time —a really responsible officer! I wouldn't have thrown up my new billet for a fortune. The mate looked me over carefully. He was also an old chap, but of another stamp. He had a Roman nose, a snow-white, long beard, and his name was Mahon, but he insisted that it should be pronounced Mann. He was well connected; yet there was something wrong with his luck, and he had never got on.

"As to the captain, he had been for years in coasters, then in the Mediterranean, and last in the West Indian trade. He had never been round the Capes. He could just write a kind of sketchy hand, and didn't care for writing at all. Both were thorough good seamen of course, and between those two old chaps I felt like a small boy between two grandfathers.

"The ship also was old. Her name was the *Judea*. Queer name, isn't it? She belonged to a man Wilmer, Wilcox—some name like that; but he has been bankrupt and dead these twenty years or more, and his name don't matter. She had been laid up in Shadwell basin for ever so long. You may imagine her state. She was all rust, dust, grime—soot aloft, dirt on deck. To me it was like coming out of a palace into a ruined cottage. She was about 400 tons, had a primitive windlass, wooden latches to the doors, not a bit of brass about her, and a big square stern. There was on it, below her name in big letters, a lot of scrollwork, with the gilt off, and some sort of a coat of arms, with the motto 'Do or Die' underneath. I remember it took my fancy immensely. There was a touch of romance in it, something that made me love the old thing—something that appealed to my youth!

"We left London in ballast—sand ballast—to load a cargo of coal in a northern port for Bangkok. Bangkok! I thrilled. I had been six years at sea, but had only seen Melbourne and Sydney, very good places, charming places in their way—but Bangkok!

"We worked out of the Thames under canvas, with a North Sea pilot on board. His name was Jermyn, and he dodged all day long about the galley drying his handkerchief before the stove. Apparently he never slept. He was a dismal man, with a perpetual tear sparkling at the end of his nose, who either had been in trouble, or was in trouble, or expected to be in trouble—couldn't be happy unless something went wrong. He mistrusted my youth, my common sense, and my seamanship, and made a point of showing it in a hundred little ways. I dare say he was right. It seems to me I knew very little then, and I know not much more now; but I cherish a hate for that Jermyn to this day.

"We were a week working up as far as Yarmouth Roads, and then we got into a gale —the famous October gale of twenty-two years ago. It was wind, lightning, sleet, snow, and a terrific sea. We were flying light, and you may imagine how bad it was when I tell you we had smashed bulwarks and a flooded deck. On the second night she shifted her ballast into the lee bow, and by that time we had been blown off some- where on the Dogger Bank. There was nothing for it but go below with shovels and try to right her, and there we were in that vast hold, gloomy like a cavern, the tallow dips stuck and flickering on the beams, the gale howling above, the ship tossing about like mad on her side; there we all were, Jermyn, the captain, everyone, hardly able to keep our feet, engaged on that gravedigger's work, and trying to toss shovelfuls of wet sand up to windward. At every tumble of the ship you could see vaguely in the dim light men falling down with a great flourish of shovels. One of the ship's boys (we had two), impressed by the weirdness of the scene, wept as if his heart would break. We could hear him blubbering somewhere in the shadows.

"On the third day the gale died out, and by and by a north-country tug picked us up. We took sixteen days in all to get from London to the Tyne! When we got into dock we had lost our turn for loading, and they hauled us off to a pier where we remained for a month. Mrs. Beard (the captain's name was Beard) came from Colchester to see the old man. She lived on board. The crew of runners had left, and there remained only the officers, one boy and the steward, a mulatto who answered to the name of Abraham. Mrs. Beard was an old woman, with a face all wrinkled and ruddy like a winter apple, and the figure of a young girl. She caught sight of me once, sewing on a button, and insisted on having my shirts to repair. This was something different from the captains' wives I had known on board crack clippers. When I brought her the shirts, she said: 'And the socks? They want mending, I am sure, and John's—Captain Beard's—things are all in order now. I would be glad of something to do.' Bless the old woman. She overhauled my outfit for me, and meantime I read for the first time *Sartor Resartus* and Burnaby's *Ride to Khiva*. I didn't understand much of the first then; but I remember I preferred the soldier to the philosopher at the time; a preference which life has only confirmed. One was a man, and the other was either more—or less. However, they are both dead and Mrs. Beard is dead, and youth, strength, genius, thoughts, achievements, simple hearts—all dies. . . . No matter.

"They loaded us at last. We shipped a crew. Eight able seamen and two boys. We hauled off one evening to the buoys at the dock gates, ready to go out, and with a fair prospect of beginning the voyage next day. Mrs. Beard was to start for home by a late train. When the ship was fast we went to tea. We sat rather silent through the meal— Mahon, the old couple, and I. I finished first, and slipped away for a smoke, my cabin being in a deckhouse just against the poop. It was high water, blowing fresh with a drizzle; the double dock gates were opened, and the steam colliers were going in and out in the darkness with their lights burning bright, a great plashing of propellers, rattling of winches, and a lot of hailing on the pierheads. I watched the procession of headlights gliding high and of green lights gliding low in the night, when suddenly a red gleam flashed at me, vanished, came into view again, and remained. The fore end of a steamer loomed up close. I shouted down the cabin, 'Come up, quick!' and then heard a startled voice saying afar in the dark, 'Stop her, sir.' A bell jingled. Another voice cried warningly. 'We are going right into that bark, sir.' The answer to this was a gruff 'All right,' and the next thing was a heavy crash as the steamer struck a glancing blow with the bluff of her bow about our forerigging. There was a moment of confusion, yelling, and running about. Steam roared. Then somebody was heard saying, 'All clear, sir.' . . . 'Are you all right?' asked the gruff voice. I had jumped forward to see the damage, and hailed back, 'I think so.' 'Easy astern,' said the gruff voice. A bell jingled. 'What steamer is that?' screamed Mahon. By that time she was no more to us than a bulky shadow maneuvering a little way off. They shouted at us some name—a woman's name, Miranda or Melissa—or some such thing. 'This means another month in this beastly hole,' said Mahon to me, as we peered with lamps about the splintered bulwarks and broken braces. 'But where's the captain?'

"We had not heard or seen anything of him all that time. We went aft to look. A doleful voice arose hailing somewhere in the middle of the dock, '*Judea* ahoy!' . . . How the devil did he get there? . . . 'Hallo!' we shouted. 'I am adrift in our boat without oars,' he cried. A belated water-man offered his services, and Mahon struck a bargain with him for a half crown to tow our skipper alongside; but it was Mrs. Beard that came up the ladder first. They had been floating about the dock in that mizzly cold rain for nearly an hour. I was never so surprised in my life.

"It appears that when he heard my shout 'Come up' he understood at once what was the matter, caught up his wife, ran on deck, and across, and down into our boat, which was fast to the ladder. Not bad for a sixty-year-old. Just imagine that old fellow saving heroically in his arms that old woman—the woman of his life. He set her down on a thwart, and was ready to climb back on board when the painter came adrift somehow, and away they went together. Of course in the confusion we did not hear him shouting. He looked abashed. She said cheerfully, 'I suppose it does not matter my losing the train now?' 'No, Jenny—you go below and get warm,' he growled. Then to us: 'A sailor has no business with a wife—I say. There I was, out of the ship. Well, no harm done this time. Let's go and look at what that fool of a steamer smashed.'

"It wasn't much, but it delayed us three weeks. At the end of that time, the captain being engaged with his agents, I carried Mrs. Beard's bag to the railway station and put her all comfy into a third-class carriage. She lowered the window to say, 'You are a good young man. If you see John—Captain Beard—without his muffler at night, just remind him from me to keep his throat well wrapped up.' 'Certainly, Mrs. Beard,' I said. 'You are a good young man; I noticed how attentive you are to John—to

Captain———' The train pulled out suddenly; I took my cap off to the old woman: I never saw her again. . . . Pass the bottle.

"We went to sea next day. When we made that start for Bangkok we had been already three months out of London. We had expected to be a fortnight or so—at the outside.

"It was January, and the weather was beautiful—the beautiful sunny winter weather that has more charm than in the summertime, because it is unexpected, and crisp, and you know it won't, it can't, last long. It's like a windfall, like a godsend, like an unexpected piece of luck.

"It lasted all down the North Sea, all down Channel; and it lasted till we were three hundred miles or so to the westward of the Lizards; then the wind went round to the sou'west and began to pipe up. In two days it blew a gale. The *Judea*, hove to, wallowed on the Atlantic like an old candle-box. It blew day after day: it blew with spite, without interval, without mercy, without rest. The world was nothing but an immensity of great foaming waves rushing at us, under a sky low enough to touch with the hand and dirty like a smoked ceiling. In the stormy space surrounding us there was as much flying spray as air. Day after day and night after night there was nothing round the ship but the howl of the wind, the tumult of the sea, the noise of water pouring over her deck. There was no rest for her and no rest for us. She tossed, she pitched, she stood on her head, she sat on her tail, she rolled, she groaned, and we had to hold on while on deck and cling to our bunks when below, in a constant effort of body and worry of mind.

"One night Mahon spoke through the small window of my berth. It opened right into my very bed, and I was lying there sleepless, in my boots, feeling as though I had not slept for years, and could not if I tried. He said excitedly:

" 'You got the sounding rod in here, Marlow? I can't get the pumps to suck. By God! It's no child's play.'

"I gave him the sounding rod and lay down again, trying to think of various things —but I thought only of the pumps. When I came on deck they were still at it, and my watch relieved at the pumps. By the light of the lantern brought on deck to examine the sounding rod I caught a glimpse of their weary, serious faces. We pumped all the four hours. We pumped all night, all day, all the week—watch and watch. She was working herself loose, and leaked badly—not enough to drown us at once, but enough to kill us with the work at the pumps. And while we pumped the ship was going from us piecemeal: the bulwarks went, the stanchions were torn out, the ventilators smashed, the cabin door burst in. There was not a dry spot in the ship. She was being gutted bit by bit. The longboat changed, as if by magic, into matchwood where she stood in her gripes. I had lashed her myself, and was rather proud of my handiwork, which had withstood so long the malice of the sea. And we pumped. And there was no break in the weather. The sea was white like a sheet of foam, like a caldron of boiling milk; there was not a break in the clouds, no—not the size of a man's hand—no, not for so much as ten seconds. There was for us no sky, there were for us no stars, no sun, no universe—nothing but angry clouds and an infuriated sea. We pumped watch and watch, for dear life; and it seemed to last for months, for years, for all eternity, as though we had been dead and gone to a hell for sailors. We forgot the day of the week, the name of the month, what year it was, and whether we had ever been ashore. The sails blew away, she lay broadside on under a weather cloth, the ocean poured over her, and we did not care. We turned those handles, and had the eyes of idiots. As soon as we had crawled on deck I used to take a round turn with a rope about the men, the pumps, and the mainmast, and we turned, we turned incessantly, with the water to our waists, to our necks, over our heads. It was all one. We had forgotten how it felt to be dry.

"And there was somewhere in me the thought: By Jove! This is the deuce of an adventure—something you read about; and it is my first voyage as second mate—and I am only twenty—and here I am lasting it out as well as any of these men, and keeping my chaps up to the mark. I was pleased. I would not have given up the experience for worlds. I had moments of exultation. Whenever the old dismantled craft pitched heavily with her counter high in the air, she seemed to me to throw up, like an appeal, like a defiance, like a cry to the clouds without mercy, the words written on her stern: 'Judea, London. Do or Die.'

"O youth! The strength of it, the faith of it, the imagination of it! To me she was not an old rattletrap carting about the world a lot of coal for a freight—to me she was the endeavor, the test, the trial of life. I think of her with pleasure, with affection, with regret—as you would think of someone dead you have loved. I shall never forget her. . . . Pass the bottle.

"One night when tied to the mast, as I explained, we were pumping on, deafened with the wind, and without spirit enough in us to wish ourselves dead, a heavy sea crashed aboard and swept clean over us. As soon as I got my breath I shouted, as in duty bound, 'Keep on, boys!' when suddenly I felt something hard floating on deck strike the calf of my leg. I made a grab at it and missed. It was so dark we could not see each other's faces within a foot—you understand.

"After that thump the ship kept quiet for a while, and the thing, whatever it was, struck my leg again. This time I caught it—and it was a saucepan. At first, being stupid with fatigue and thinking of nothing but the pumps, I did not understand what I had in my hand. Suddenly it dawned upon me, and I shouted, 'Boys, the house on deck is gone. Leave this, and let's look for the cook.'

"There was a deckhouse forward, which contained the galley, the cook's berth, and the quarters of the crew. As we had expected for days to see it swept away, the hands had been ordered to sleep in the cabin—the only safe place in the ship. The steward, Abraham, however, persisted in clinging to his berth, stupidly, like a mule—from sheer fright I believe, like an animal that won't leave a stable falling in an earthquake. So we went to look for him. It was chancing death, since once out of our lashings we were as exposed as if on a raft. But we went. The house was shattered as if a shell had exploded inside. Most of it had gone overboard—stove, men's quarters, and their property, all was gone; but two posts, holding a portion of the bulkhead to which Abraham's bunk was attached, remained as if by a miracle. We groped in the ruins and came upon this, and there he was, sitting in his bunk, surrounded by foam and wreckage, jabbering cheerfully to himself. He was out of his mind; completely and forever mad, with this sudden shock coming upon the fag-end of his endurance. We snatched him up, lugged him aft, and pitched him headfirst down the cabin companion. You understand there was no time to carry him down with infinite precautions and wait to see how he got on. Those below would pick him up at the bottom of the stairs all right. We were in a hurry to go back to the pumps. That business could not wait. A bad leak is an inhuman thing.

"One would think that the sole purpose of that fiendish gale had been to make a lunatic of that poor devil of a mulatto. It eased before morning, and next day the sky cleared, and as the sea went down the leak took up. When it came to bending a fresh set of sails the crew demanded to put back—and really there was nothing else to do. Boats gone, decks swept clean, cabin gutted, men without a stitch but what they stood in, stores spoiled, ship strained. We put her head for home, and—would you believe it? The wind came east right in our teeth. It blew fresh, it blew continuously. We had to beat up every inch of the way, but she did not leak so badly, the water keeping comparatively smooth. Two hours' pumping in every four is no joke—but it kept her afloat as far as Falmouth.

"The good people there live on casualties of the sea, and no doubt were glad to see us. A hungry crowd of shipwrights sharpened their chisels at the sight of that carcass of a ship. And, by Jove! they had pretty pickings off us before they were done. I fancy the owner was already in a tight place. There were delays. Then it was decided to take part of the cargo out and calk her topsides. This was done, the repairs finished, cargo reshipped; a new crew came on board, and we went out—for Bangkok. At the end of a week we were back again. The crew said they weren't going to Bangkok—a hundred and fifty days' passage—in a something hooker that wanted pumping eight hours out of the twenty-four; and the nautical papers inserted again the little paragraph: 'Judea. Bark. Tyne to Bangkok; coals; put back to Falmouth leaky and with crew refusing duty.'

"There were more delays—more tinkering. The owner came down for a day, and said she was as right as a little fiddle. Poor old Captain Beard looked like the ghost of a Geordie skipper—through the worry and humiliation of it. Remember he was sixty, and it was his first command. Mahon said it was a foolish business, and would end badly. I loved the ship more than ever, and wanted awfully to get to Bangkok. To Bangkok! Magic name, blessed name. Mesopotamia wasn't a patch on it. Remember I was twenty, and it was my first second-mate's billet, and the East was waiting for me.

"We went out and anchored in the outer roads with a fresh crew—the third. She leaked worse than ever. It was as if those confounded shipwrights had actually made a hole in her. This time we did not even go outside. The crew simply refused to man the windlass.

"They towed us back to the inner harbor, and we became a fixture, a feature, an institution of the place. People pointed us out to visitors as 'That 'ere bark that's going to Bangkok—has been here six months—put back three times.' On holidays the small boys pulling about in boats would hail, *Judea*, ahoy!' and if a head showed above the rail shouted, 'Where you bound to?—Bangkok?' and jeered. We were only three on board. The poor old skipper mooned in the cabin. Mahon undertook the cooking, and unexpectedly developed all a Frenchman's genius for preparing nice little messes. I looked languidly after the rigging. We became citizens of Falmouth. Every shopkeeper knew us. At the barber's or tobacconist's they asked familiarly, 'Do you think you will ever get to Bangkok?' Meantime the owner, the underwriters, and the charterers squabbled amongst themselves in London, and our pay went on. . . . Pass the bottle.

"It was horrid. Morally it was worse than pumping for life. It seemed as though we had been forgotten by the world, belonged to nobody, would get nowhere; it seemed that, as if bewitched, we would have to live for ever and ever in that inner harbor, a derision and a by-word to generations of longshore loafers and dishonest boatmen. I obtained three months' pay and a five days' leave, and made a rush for London. It took me a day to get there and pretty well another to come back—but three months' pay went all the same. I don't know what I did with it. I went to a music hall, I believe, lunched, dined, and supped in a swell place in Regent Street, and was back on time, with nothing but a complete set of Byron's works and a new railway rug to show for three months' work. The boatman who pulled me off to the ship said: 'Hallo! I thought you had left the old thing. *She* will never get to Bangkok.' 'That's all *you* know about it,' I said, scornfully—but I didn't like that prophecy at all.

"Suddenly a man, some kind of agent to somebody, appeared with full powers. He had grog-blossoms all over his face, an indomitable energy, and was a jolly soul. We leaped into life again. A hulk came alongside, took our cargo, and then we went into dry dock to get our copper stripped. No wonder she leaked. The poor thing, strained beyond endurance by the gale, had, as if in disgust, spat out all the oakum of her lower seams. She was recalked, new-coppered, and made as tight as a bottle. We went back to the hulk and reshipped our cargo.

"Then, on a fine moonlight night, all the rats left the ship.

"We had been infested with them. They had destroyed our sails, consumed more stores than the crew, affably shared our beds and our dangers, and now, when the ship was made seaworthy, concluded to clear out. I called Mahon to enjoy the spectacle. Rat after rat appeared on our rail, took a last look over his shoulder, and leaped with a hollow thud into the empty hulk. We tried to count them, but soon lost the tale. Mahon said: 'Well, well! don't talk to me about the intelligence of rats. They ought to have left before, when we had that narrow squeak from foundering. There you have the proof how silly is the superstition about them. They leave a good ship for an old rotten hulk, where there is nothing to eat, too, the fools! . . . I don't believe they know what is safe or what is good for them, any more than you or I.'

"And after some more talk we agreed that the wisdom of rats had been grossly overrated, being in fact no greater than that of men.

"The story of the ship was known, by this, all up the Channel from Land's End to the Forelands, and we could get no crew on the south coast. They sent us one all complete from Liverpool, and we left once more—for Bangkok.

"We had fair breezes, smooth water right into the tropics, and the old *Judea* lumbered along in the sunshine. When she went eight knots everything cracked aloft, and we tied our caps to our heads; but mostly she strolled on at the rate of three miles an hour. What could you expect? She was tired—that old ship. Her youth was where mine is—where yours is—you fellows who listen to this yarn; and what friend would throw your years and your weariness in your face? We didn't grumble at her. To us aft, at least, it seemed as though we had been born in her, reared in her, had lived in her for ages, had never known any other ship. I would just as soon have abused the old village church at home for not being a cathedral.

"And for me there was also my youth to make me patient. There was all the East before me, and all life, and the thought that I had been tried in that ship and had come out pretty well. And I thought of men of old who, centuries ago, went that road in ships that sailed no better, to the land of palms, and spices, and yellow sands, and of brown nations ruled by kings more cruel than Nero the Roman, and more splendid than Solomon the Jew. The old bark lumbered on, heavy with her age and the burden of her cargo, while I lived the life of youth in ignorance and hope. She lumbered on through an interminable procession of days; and the fresh gilding flashed back at the setting sun, seemed to cry out over the darkening sea the words painted on her stern, *Judea*, London. Do or Die.'

"Then we entered the Indian Ocean and steered northerly for Java Head. The winds were light. Weeks slipped by. She crawled on, do or die, and people at home began to think of posting us as overdue.

"One Saturday evening, I being off duty, the men asked me to give them an extra bucket of water or so—for washing clothes. As I did not wish to screw on the fresh-water pump so late, I went forward whistling, and with a key in my hand to unlock the forepeak scuttle, intending to serve the water out of a spare tank we kept there.

"The smell down below was as unexpected as it was frightful. One would have thought hundreds of paraffin lamps had been flaring and smoking in that hole for days. I was glad to get out. The man with me coughed and said, 'Funny smell, sir.' I answered negligently, 'It's good for the health, they say,' and walked aft.

"The first thing I did was to put my head down the square of the midship ventilator. As I lifted the lid a visible breath, something like a thin fog, a puff of faint haze, rose from the opening. The ascending air was hot, and had a heavy, sooty, paraffiny smell. I gave one sniff, and put down the lid gently. It was no use choking myself. The cargo was on fire.

"Next day she began to smoke in earnest. You see it was to be expected, for though the coal was of a safe kind, that cargo had been so handled, so broken up with handling, that it looked more like smithy coal than anything else. Then it had been wetted—more than once. It rained all the time we were taking it back from the hulk, and now with this long passage it got heated, and there was another case of spontaneous combustion.

"The captain called us into the cabin. He had a chart spread on the table, and looked unhappy. He said, 'The coast of West Australia is near, but I mean to proceed to our destination. It is the hurricane month, too; but we will just keep her head for Bangkok, and fight the fire. No more putting back anywhere, if we all get roasted. We will try first to stifle this 'ere damned combustion by want of air.'

"We tried. We battened down everything, and still she smoked. The smoke kept coming out through imperceptible crevices; it forced itself through bulkheads and covers; it oozed here and there and everywhere in slender threads, in an invisible film, in an incomprehensible manner. It made its way into the cabin, into the forecastle; it poisoned the sheltered places on the deck; it could be sniffed as high as the mainyard. It was clear that if the smoke came out the air came in. This was disheartening. This combustion refused to be stifled.

"We resolved to try water, and took the hatches off. Enormous volumes of smoke, whitish, yellowish, thick, greasy, misty, choking, ascended as high as the trucks. All hands cleared out aft. Then the poisonous cloud blew away, and we went back to work in a smoke that was no thicker now than that of an ordinary factory chimney.

"We rigged the force pump, got the hose along, and by and by it burst. Well, it was as old as the ship—a prehistoric hose, and past repair. Then we pumped with the feeble head pump, drew water with buckets, and in this way managed in time to pour lots of Indian Ocean into the main hatch. The bright stream flashed in sunshine, fell into a layer of white crawling smoke, and vanished on the black surface of coal. Steam ascended mingling with the smoke. We poured salt water as into a barrel without a bottom. It was our fate to pump in that ship, to pump out of her, to pump into her; and after keeping water out of her to save ourselves from being drowned, we frantically poured water into her to save ourselves from being burnt.

"And she crawled on, do or die, in the serene weather. The sky was a miracle of purity, a miracle of azure. The sea was polished, was blue, was pellucid, was sparkling like a precious stone, extending on all sides, all round to the horizon—as if the whole terrestrial globe had been one jewel, one colossal sapphire, a single gem fashioned into a planet. And on the luster of the great calm waters the *Judea* glided imperceptibly, enveloped in languid and unclean vapors, in a lazy cloud that drifted to leeward, light and slow; a pestiferous cloud defiling the splendor of sea and sky.

"All this time of course we saw no fire. The cargo smoldered at the bottom somewhere. Once Mahon, as we were working side by side, said to me with a queer smile: 'Now, if she only would spring a tidy leak—like that time when we first left the Channel—it would put a stopper on this fire. Wouldn't it?' I remarked irrelevantly, 'Do you remember the rats?'

"We fought the fire and sailed the ship too as carefully as though nothing had been the matter. The steward cooked and attended on us. Of the other twelve men, eight worked while four rested. Everyone took his turn, captain included. There was equality, and if not exactly fraternity, then a deal of good feeling. Sometimes a man, as he dashed a bucketful of water down the hatchway, would yell out, 'Hurrah for Bangkok!' and the rest laughed. But generally we were taciturn and serious—and thirsty. Oh! how thirsty! And we had to be careful with the water. Strict allowance. The ship smoked, the sun blazed. . . . Pass the bottle.

"We tried everything. We even made an attempt to dig down to the fire. No good, of course. No man could remain more than a minute below. Mahon, who went first, fainted there, and the man who went to fetch him out did likewise. We lugged them out on deck. Then I leaped down to show how easily it could be done. They had learned wisdom by that time, and contented themselves by fishing for me with a chainhook tied to a broom handle, I believe. I did not offer to go and fetch up my shovel, which was left down below.

"Things began to look bad. We put the longboat into the water. The second boat was ready to swing out. We had also another, a fourteen-foot thing, on davits aft, where it was quite safe.

"Then, behold, the smoke suddenly decreased. We redoubled our efforts to flood the bottom of the ship. In two days there was no smoke at all. Everybody was on the broad grin. This was on a Friday. On Saturday no work, but sailing the ship of course, was done. The men washed their clothes and their faces for the first time in a fortnight, and had a special dinner given them. They spoke of spontaneous combustion with contempt, and implied *they* were the boys to put out combustions. Somehow we all felt as though we each had inherited a large fortune. But a beastly smell of burning hung about the ship. Captain Beard had hollow eyes and sunken cheeks. I had never noticed so much before how twisted and bowed he was. He and Mahon prowled soberly about hatches and ventilators, sniffing. It struck me suddenly poor Mahon was a very, very old chap. As to me, I was pleased and proud as though I had helped to win a great naval battle. O youth!

"The night was fine. In the morning a homeward-bound ship passed us hull down —the first we had seen for months; but we were nearing the land at last, Java Head being about 190 miles off, and nearly due north.

"Next day it was my watch on deck from eight to twelve. At breakfast the captain observed, 'It's wonderful how that smell hangs about the cabin.' About ten, the mate being on the poop, I stepped down on the main deck for a moment. The carpenter's bench stood abaft the mainmast: I leaned against it sucking at my pipe, and the carpenter, a young chap, came to talk to me. He remarked, 'I think we have done very well, haven't we?' and then I perceived with annoyance the fool was trying to tilt the bench. I said curtly, 'Don't, Chips,' and immediately became aware of a queer sensation, of an absurd delusion—I seemed somehow to be in the air. I heard all round me like a pent-up breath released—as if a thousand giants simultaneously had said Phoo! —and felt a dull concussion which made my ribs ache suddenly. No doubt about it— I was in the air, and my body was describing a short parabola. But short as it was, I had the time to think several thoughts in, as far as I can remember, the following order: 'This can't be the carpenter—What is it?—Some accident—Submarine volcano?—Coals, gas!—By Jove! We are being blown up—Everybody's dead—I am falling into the afterhatch—I see fire in it.'

"The coaldust suspended in the air of the hold had glowed dull-red at the moment of the explosion. In the twinkling of an eye, in an infinitesimal fraction of a second since the first tilt of the bench, I was sprawling full length on the cargo. I picked

myself up and scrambled out. It was quick like a rebound. The deck was a wilderness
of smashed timber, lying crosswise like trees in a wood after a hurricane; an immense
curtain of solid rags waved gently before me—it was the mainsail blown to strips. I
thought: the masts will be toppling over directly; and to get out of the way bolted on
all fours towards the poop ladder. The first person I saw was Mahon, with eyes like
saucers, his mouth open, and the long white hair standing straight on end round his
head like a silver halo. He was just about to go down when the sight of the main deck
stirring, heaving up, and changing into splinters before his eyes, petrified him on the
top step. I stared at him in unbelief, and he stared at me with a queer kind of shocked
curiosity. I did not know that I had no hair, no eyebrows, no eyelashes, that my young
mustache was burnt off, that my face was black, one cheek laid open, my nose cut, and
my chin bleeding. I had lost my cap, one of my slippers, and my shirt was torn to rags.
Of all this I was not aware. I was amazed to see the ship still afloat, the poop deck
whole—and, most of all, to see anybody alive. Also the peace of the sky and the
serenity of the sea were distinctly surprising. I suppose I expected to see them
convulsed with horror. . . . Pass the bottle.

"There was a voice hailing the ship from somewhere—in the air, in the sky—I
couldn't tell. Presently I saw the captain—and he was mad. He asked me eagerly,
'Where's the cabin table?' and to hear such a question was a frightful shock. I had just
been blown up, you understand, and vibrated with that experience—I wasn't quite sure
whether I was alive. Mahon began to stamp with both feet and yelled at him, 'Good
God! don't you see the deck's blown out of her?' I found my voice, and stammered out
as if conscious of some gross neglect of duty, 'I don't know where the cabin table is.' It
was like an absurd dream.

"Do you know what he wanted next? Well, he wanted to trim the yards. Very
placidly, and as if lost in thought, he insisted on having the foreyard squared. 'I don't
know if there's anybody alive,' said Mahon, almost tearfully. 'Surely,' he said, gently,
'there will be enough left to square the foreyard.'

"The old chap, it seems, was in his own berth winding up the chronometers, when
the shock sent him spinning. Immediately it occurred to him—as he said afterwards—
that the ship had struck something, and ran out into the cabin. There, he saw, the
cabin table had vanished somewhere. The deck being blown up, it had fallen down
into the lazarette of course. Where we had our breakfast that morning he saw only a
great hole in the floor. This appeared to him so awfully mysterious, and impressed
him so immensely, that what he saw and heard after he got on deck were mere trifles in
comparison. And, mark, he noticed directly the wheel deserted and his bark off her
course—and his only thought was to get that miserable, stripped, undecked, smoldering shell of a ship back again with her head pointing at her port of destination.
Bangkok! That's what he was after. I tell you this quiet, bowed, bandy-legged, almost
deformed little man was immense in the singleness of his idea and in his placid
ignorance of our agitation. He motioned us forward with a commanding gesture, and
went to take the wheel himself.

"Yes; that was the first thing we did—trim the yards of that wreck! No one was killed, or even disabled, but everyone was more or less hurt. You should have seen them! Some were in rags, with black faces, like coal heavers, like sweeps, and had bullet heads that seemed closely cropped, but were in fact singed to the skin. Others, of the watch below, awakened by being shot out from their collapsing bunks, shivered incessantly, and kept on groaning even as we went about our work. But they all worked. That crew of Liverpool hard cases had in them the right stuff. It's my experience they always have. It is the sea that gives it—the vastness, the loneliness surrounding their dark stolid souls. Ah! Well! We stumbled, we crept, we fell, we barked our shins on the wreckage, we hauled. The masts stood, but we did not know how much they might be charred down below. It was nearly calm, but a long swell ran from the west and made her roll. They might go at any moment. We looked at them with apprehension. One could not foresee which way they would fall.

"Then we retreated aft and looked about us. The deck was a tangle of planks on edge, of planks on end, of splinters, of ruined woodwork. The masts rose from that chaos like big trees above a matted undergrowth. The interstices of that mass of wreckage were full of something whitish, sluggish, stirring—of something that was like a greasy fog. The smoke of the invisible fire was coming up again, was trailing, like a poisonous thick mist in some valley choked with dead wood. Already lazy wisps were beginning to curl upwards amongst the mass of splinters. Here and there a piece of timber, stuck upright, resembled a post. Half of a fife rail had been shot through the foresail, and the sky made a patch of glorious blue in the ignobly soiled canvas. A portion of several boards holding together had fallen across the rail, and one end protruded overboard, like a gangway leading upon nothing, like a gangway leading over the deep sea, leading to death—as if inviting us to walk the plank at once and be done with our ridiculous troubles. And still the air, the sky—a ghost, something invisible was hailing the ship.

"Someone had the sense to look over, and there was the helmsman, who had impulsively jumped overboard, anxious to come back. He yelled and swam lustily like a merman, keeping up with the ship. We threw him a rope, and presently he stood amongst us streaming with water and very crestfallen. The captain had surrendered the wheel, and apart, elbow on rail and chin in hand, gazed at the sea wistfully. We asked ourselves, What next? I thought, Now, this is something like. This is great. I wonder what will happen. O youth!

"Suddenly Mahon sighted a steamer far astern. Captain Beard said, 'We may do something with her yet.' We hoisted two flags, which said in the international language of the sea, 'On fire. Want immediate assistance.' The steamer grew bigger rapidly, and by and by spoke with two flags on her foremast, 'I am coming to your assistance.'

"In half an hour she was abreast, to windward, within hail, and rolling slightly, with her engines stopped. We lost our composure, and yelled all together with excitement, 'We've been blown up.' A man in a white helmet, on the bridge, cried, 'Yes! All right! all right!' and he nodded his head, and smiled, and made soothing motions with his hand as though at a lot of frightened children. One of the boats dropped in the water, and walked towards us upon the sea with her long oars. Four Calashes pulled a swinging stroke. This was my first sight of Malay seamen. I've known them since, but what struck me then was their unconcern: they came alongside, and even the bowman standing up and holding to our main chains with the boathook did not deign to lift his head for a glance. I thought people who had been blown up deserved more attention.

"A little man, dry like a chip and agile like a monkey, clambered up. It was the mate of the steamer. He gave one look, and cried, 'O boys—you had better quit!'

"We were silent. He talked apart with the captain for a time—seemed to argue with him. Then they went away together to the steamer.

"When our skipper came back we learned that the steamer was the *Somerville*, Captain Nash, from West Australia to Singapore via Batavia with mails, and that the agreement was she should tow us to Anjer or Batavia, if possible, where we could extinguish the fire by scuttling, and then proceed on our voyage—to Bangkok! The old man seemed excited. 'We will do it yet,' he said to Mahon, fiercely. He shook his fist at the sky. Nobody else said a word.

"At noon the steamer began to tow. She went ahead slim and high, and what was left of the *Judea* followed at the end of seventy fathom of towrope—followed her swiftly like a cloud of smoke with mastheads protruding above. We went aloft to furl the sails. We coughed on the yards, and were careful about the bunts. Do you see the lot of us there, putting a neat furl on the sails of that ship doomed to arrive nowhere? There was not a man who didn't think that at any moment the masts would topple over. From aloft we could not see the ship for smoke, and they worked carefully, passing the gaskets with even turns. 'Harbor furl—aloft there!' cried Mahon from below.

"You understand this? I don't think one of those chaps expected to get down in the usual way. When we did I heard them saying to each other, 'Well, I thought we would come down overboard, in a lump—sticks and all —blame me if I didn't.' 'That's what I was thinking to myself,' would answer wearily another battered and bandaged scarecrow. And, mind, these were men without the drilled-in habit of obedience. To an onlooker they would be a lot of profane scallywags without a redeeming point. What made them do it—what made them obey me when I, thinking consciously how fine it was, made them drop the bunt of the foresail twice to try and do it better? What? They had no professional reputation—no examples, no praise. It wasn't a sense of duty; they all knew well enough how to shirk, and laze, and dodge—when they had a mind to it—and mostly they had. Was it the two pounds ten a month that sent them there? They didn't think their pay half good enough. No; it was something in them, something inborn and subtle and everlasting. I don't say positively that the crew of a French or German merchantman wouldn't have done it, but I doubt whether it would have been done in the same way. There was a completeness in it, something solid like a principle, and masterful like an instinct—a disclosure of something secret—of that hidden something, that gift of good or evil that makes racial difference, that shapes the fate of nations.

"It was that night at ten that, for the first time since we had been fighting it, we saw the fire. The speed of the towing had fanned the smoldering destruction. A blue gleam appeared forward, shining below the wreck of the deck. It wavered in patches, it seemed to stir and creep like the light of a glowworm. I saw it first, and told Mahon. 'Then the game's up,' he said. 'We had better stop this towing, or she will burst out suddenly fore and aft before we can clear out.' We set up a yell; rang bells to attract their attention; they towed on. At last Mahon and I had to crawl forward and cut the rope with an axe. There was no time to cast off the lashings. Red tongues could be seen licking the wilderness of splinters under our feet as we made our way back to the poop.

"Of course they very soon found out in the steamer that the rope was gone. She gave a loud blast of her whistle, her lights were seen sweeping in a wide circle, she came up ranging close alongside, and stopped. We were all in a tight group on the poop looking at her. Every man had saved a little bundle or a bag. Suddenly a conical flame with a twisted top shot up forward and threw upon the black sea a circle of light, with the two vessels side by side and heaving gently in its center. Captain Beard had been sitting on the gratings still and mute for hours, but now he rose slowly and advanced in front of us, to the mizzen-shrouds. Captain Nash hailed: 'Come along! Look sharp. I have mailbags on board. I will take you and your boats to Singapore.'

" 'Thank you! No!' said our skipper. 'We must see the last of the ship.'

" 'I can't stand by any longer,' shouted the other. 'Mails—you know.'

" 'Ay! ay! We are all right.'

" 'Very well! I'll report you in Singapore. . . . Good-by!'

"He waved his hand. Our men dropped their bundles quietly. The steamer moved ahead, and passing out of the circle of light, vanished at once from our sight, dazzled by the fire which burned fiercely. And then I knew that I would see the East first as commander of a small boat. I thought it fine; and the fidelity to the old ship was fine. We should see the last of her. Oh, the glamour of youth! Oh, the fire of it, more dazzling than the flames of the burning ship, throwing a magic light on the wide earth, leaping audaciously to the sky, presently to be quenched by time, more cruel, more pitiless, more bitter than the sea—and like the flames of the burning ship surrounded by an impenetrable night.

"The old man warned us in his gentle and inflexible way that it was part of our duty to save for the underwriters as much as we could of the ship's gear. Accordingly we went to work aft, while she blazed forward to give us plenty of light. We lugged out a lot of rubbish. What didn't we save? An old barometer fixed with an absurd quantity of screws nearly cost me my life: a sudden rush of smoke came upon me, and I just got away in time. There were various stores, bolts of canvas, coils of rope; the poop looked like a marine bazaar, and the boats were lumbered to the gunwales. One would have thought the old man wanted to take as much as he could of his first command with him. He was very, very quiet, but off his balance evidently. Would you believe it? He wanted to take a length of old stream-cable and a kedge anchor with him in the longboat. We said, 'Ay, ay, sir,' deferentially, and on the quiet let the things slip overboard. The heavy medicine chest went that way, two bags of green coffee, tins of paint—fancy, paint!—a whole lot of things. Then I was ordered with two hands into the boats to make a stowage and get them ready against the time it would be proper for us to leave the ship.

"We put everything straight, stepped the longboat's mast for our skipper, who was to take charge of her, and I was not sorry to sit down for a moment. My face felt raw, every limb ached as if broken, I was aware of all my ribs, and would have sworn to a twist in the backbone. The boats, fast astern, lay in a deep shadow, and all around I could see the circle of the sea lighted by the fire. A gigantic flame arose forward straight and clear. It flared fierce, with noises like the whirr of wings, with rumbles as of thunder. There were cracks, detonations, and from the cone of flame the sparks flew upwards, as man is born to trouble, to leaky ships, and to ships that burn.

"What bothered me was that the ship, lying broadside to the swell and to such wind as there was—a mere breath—the boats would not keep astern where they were safe, but persisted, in a pigheaded way boats have, in getting under the counter and then swinging alongside. They were knocking about dangerously and coming near the flame, while the ship rolled on them, and, of course, there was always the danger of the masts going over the side at any moment. I and my two boatkeepers kept them off as best we could, with oars and boathooks; but to be constantly at it became exasperating, since there was no reason why we should not leave at once. We could not see those on board, nor could we imagine what caused the delay. The boatkeepers were swearing feebly, and I had not only my share of the work but also had to keep at it two men who showed a constant inclination to lay themselves down and let things slide.

"At last I hailed, 'On deck there,' and someone looked over. 'We're ready here,' I said. The head disappeared, and very soon popped up again. 'The captain says, All right, sir, and to keep the boats well clear of the ship.'

"Half an hour passed. Suddenly there was a frightful racket, rattle, clanking of chain, hiss of water, and millions of sparks flew up into the shivering column of smoke that stood leaning slightly above the ship. The catheads had burned away, and the two red-hot anchors had gone to the bottom, tearing out after them two hundred fathom of red-hot chain. The ship trembled, the mass of flame swayed as if ready to collapse, and the fore-topgallant mast fell. It darted down like an arrow of fire, shot under, and instantly leaping up within an oar's length of the boats, floated quietly, very black on the luminous sea. I hailed the deck again. After some time a man in an unexpectedly cheerful but also muffled tone, as though he had been trying to speak with his mouth shut, informed me, 'Coming directly, sir,' and vanished. For a long time I heard nothing but the whirr and roar of the fire. There were also whistling sounds. The boats jumped, tugged at the painters, ran at each other playfully, knocked their sides together, or, do what we would, swung in a bunch against the ship's side. I couldn't stand it any longer, and swarming up a rope, clambered aboard over the stern.

"It was as bright as day. Coming up like this, the sheet of fire facing me was a terrifying sight, and the heat seemed hardly bearable at first. On a settee cushion dragged out of the cabin Captain Beard, his legs drawn up and one arm under his head, slept with the light playing on him. Do you know what the rest were busy about? They were sitting on deck right aft, round an open case, eating bread and cheese and drinking bottled stout.

"On the background of flames twisting in fierce tongues above their heads they seemed at home like salamanders, and looked like a band of desperate pirates. The fire sparkled in the whites of their eyes, gleamed on patches of white skin seen through the torn shirts. Each had the marks as of a battle about him—bandaged heads, tied-up arms, a strip of dirty rag round a knee—and each man had a bottle between his legs and a chunk of cheese in his hand. Mahon got up. With his handsome and disreputable head, his hooked profile, his long white beard, and with an uncorked bottle in his hand, he resembled one of those reckless sea robbers of old making merry amidst violence and disaster. 'The last meal on board,' he explained solemnly. 'We had nothing to eat all day, and it was no use leaving all this.' He flourished the bottle and indicated the sleeping skipper. 'He said he couldn't swallow anything, so I got him to lie down,' he went on; and as I stared, 'I don't know whether you are aware, young fellow, the man had no sleep to speak of for days—and there will be dam' little sleep in the boats.' 'There will be no boats by and by if you fool about much longer,' I said, indignantly. I walked up to the skipper and shook him by the shoulder. At last he opened his eyes, but did not move. 'Time to leave her, sir,' I said quietly.

"He got up painfully, looked at the flames, at the sea sparkling round the ship, and black, black as ink farther away; he looked at the stars shining dim through a thin veil of smoke in a sky black, black as Erebus.

" 'Youngest first,' he said.

"And the ordinary seaman, wiping his mouth with the back of his hand, got up, clambered over the taffrail, and vanished. Others followed. One, on the point of going over, stopped short to drain his bottle, and with a great swing of his arm flung it at the fire. 'Take this!' he cried.

"The skipper lingered disconsolately, and we left him to commune alone for a while with his first command. Then I went up again and brought him away at last. It was time. The ironwork on the poop was hot to the touch.

"Then the painter of the longboat was cut, and the three boats, tied together, drifted clear of the ship. It was just sixteen hours after the explosion when we abandoned her. Mahon had charge of the second boat, and I had the smallest—the fourteen-foot thing. The longboat would have taken the lot of us; but the skipper said we must save as much property as we could—for the underwriters—and so I got my first command. I had two men with me, a bag of biscuits, a few tins of meat, and a breaker of water. I was ordered to keep close to the longboat, that in case of bad weather we might be taken into her.

"And do you know what I thought? I thought I would part company as soon as I could. I wanted to have my first command all to myself. I wasn't going to sail in a squadron if there were a chance for independent cruising. I would make land by myself. I would beat the other boats. Youth! All youth! The silly, charming, beautiful youth.

"But we did not make a start at once. We must see the last of the ship. And so the boats drifted about that night, heaving and setting on the swell. The men dozed, waked, sighed, groaned. I looked at the burning ship.

"Between the darkness of earth and heaven she was burning fiercely upon a disc of purple sea shot by the blood-red play of gleams; upon a disc of water glittering and sinister. A high, clear flame, an immense and lonely flame, ascended from the ocean, and from its summit the black smoke poured continuously at the sky. She burned furiously; mournful and imposing like a funeral pile kindled in the night, surrounded by the sea, watched over by the stars. A magnificent death had come like a grace, like a gift, like a reward to that old ship at the end of her laborious days. The surrender of her weary ghost to the keeping of stars and sea was stirring like the sight of a glorious triumph. The masts fell just before daybreak, and for a moment there was a burst and turmoil of sparks that seemed to fill with flying fire the night patient and watchful, the vast night lying silent upon the sea. At daylight she was only a charred shell, floating still under a cloud of smoke and bearing a glowing mass of coal within.

"Then the oars were got out, and the boats forming in a line moved round her remains as if in procession—the longboat leading. As we pulled across her stern a slim dart of fire shot out viciously at us, and suddenly she went down, head first, in a great hiss of steam. The unconsumed stern was the last to sink; but the paint had gone, had cracked, had peeled off, and there were no letters, there was no word, no stubborn device that was like her soul, to flash at the rising sun her creed and her name.

"We made our way north. A breeze sprang up, and about noon all the boats came together for the last time. I had no mast or sail in mine, but I made a mast out of a spare oar and hoisted a boat-awning for a sail, with a boathook for a yard. She was certainly over-masted, but I had the satisfaction of knowing that with the wind aft I could beat the other two. I had to wait for them. Then we all had a look at the captain's chart, and, after a sociable meal of hard bread and water, got our last instructions. These were simple: steer north, and keep together as much as possible. 'Be careful with that jury-rig, Marlow,' said the captain; and Mahon, as I sailed proudly past his boat, wrinkled his curved nose and hailed, 'You will sail that ship of yours under water, if you don't look out, young fellow.' He was a malicious old man— and may the deep sea where he sleeps now rock him gently, rock him tenderly to the end of time!

"Before sunset a thick rain-squall passed over the two boats, which were far astern, and that was the last I saw of them for a time. Next day I sat steering my cockleshell —my first command—with nothing but water and sky round me. I did sight in the afternoon the upper sails of a ship far away, but said nothing, and my men did not notice her. You see I was afraid she might be homeward bound, and I had no mind to turn back from the portals of the East. I was steering for Java—another blessed name —like Bangkok, you know. I steered many days.

"I need not tell you what it is to be knocking about in an open boat. I remember nights and days of calm, when we pulled, we pulled, and the boat seemed to stand still, as if bewitched within the circle of the sea horizon. I remember the heat, the deluge of rain-squalls that kept us baling for dear life (but filled our water cask), and I remember sixteen hours on end with a mouth dry as a cinder and a steering oar over the stern to keep my first command head on to a breaking sea. I did not know how good a man I was till then. I remember the drawn faces, the dejected figures of my two men, and I remember my youth and the feeling that will never come back any more—the feeling that I could last forever, outlast the sea, the earth, and all men; the deceitful feeling that lures us on to joys, to perils, to love, to vain effort—to death; the triumphant conviction of strength, the heat of life in the handful of dust, the glow in the heart that with every year grows dim, grows cold, grows small, and expires—and expires, too soon, too soon—before life itself.

"And this is how I see the East. I have seen its secret places and have looked into its very soul; but now I see it always from a small boat, a high outline of mountains, blue and afar in the morning; like faint mist at noon; a jagged wall of purple at sunset. I have the feel of the oar in my hand, the vision of a scorching blue sea in my eyes. And I see a bay, a wide bay, smooth as glass and polished like ice, shimmering in the dark. A red light burns far off upon the gloom of the land, and the night is soft and warm. We drag at the oars with aching arms, and suddenly a puff of wind, a puff faint and tepid and laden with strange odors of blossoms, of aromatic wood, comes out of the still night—the first sigh of the East on my face. That I can never forget. It was impalpable and enslaving, like a charm, like a whispered promise of mysterious delight.

"We had been pulling this finishing spell for eleven hours. Two pulled, and he whose turn it was to rest sat at the tiller. We had made out the red light in that bay and steered for it, guessing it must mark some small coasting port. We passed two vessels, outlandish and high-sterned, sleeping at anchor, and, approaching the light, now very dim, ran the boat's nose against the end of a jutting wharf. We were blind with fatigue. My men dropped the oars and fell off the thwarts as if dead. I made fast to a pile. A current rippled softly. The scented obscurity of the shore was grouped into vast masses, a density of colossal clumps of vegetation, probably—mute and fantastic shapes. And at their foot the semicircle of a beach gleamed faintly, like an illusion. There was not a light, not a stir, not a sound. The mysterious East faced me, perfumed like a flower, silent like death, dark like a grave.

"And I sat weary beyond expression, exulting like a conqueror, sleepless and entranced as if before a profound, a fateful enigma.

"A splashing of oars, a measured dip reverberating on the level of water, intensified by the silence of the shore into loud claps, made me jump up. A boat, a European boat, was coming in. I invoked the name of the dead; I hailed: 'Judea ahoy!' A thin shout answered.

"It was the captain. I had beaten the flagship by three hours, and I was glad to hear the old man's voice again, tremulous and tired. 'Is it you, Marlow?' 'Mind the end of that jetty, sir,' I cried.

"He approached cautiously, and brought up with the deep-sea lead line which we had saved—for the underwriters. I eased my painter and fell alongside. He sat, a broken figure at the stern, wet with dew, his hands clasped in his lap. His men were asleep already. 'I had a terrible time of it,' he murmured. 'Mahon is behind—not very far.' We conversed in whispers, in low whispers, as if afraid to wake up the land. Guns, thunder, earthquakes would not have awakened the men just then.

"Looking round as we talked, I saw away at sea a bright light traveling in the night. 'There's a steamer passing the bay,' I said. She was not passing, she was entering, and she even came close and anchored. 'I wish,' said the old man, 'you would find out whether she is English. Perhaps they could give us a passage somewhere.' He seemed nervously anxious. So by dint of punching and kicking I started one of my men into a state of somnambulism, and giving him an oar, took another and pulled towards the lights of the steamer.

"There was a murmur of voices in her, metallic hollow clangs of the engine room, footsteps on the deck. Her ports shone, round like dilated eyes. Shapes moved about, and there was a shadowy man high up on the bridge. He heard my oars.

"And then, before I could open my lips, the East spoke to me, but it was in a Western voice. A torrent of words was poured into the enigmatical, the fateful silence; outlandish, angry words, mixed with words and even whole sentences of good English, less strange but even more surprising. The voice swore and cursed violently; it riddled the solemn peace of the bay by a volley of abuse. It began by calling me Pig, and from that went crescendo into unmentionable adjectives—in English. The man up there raged aloud in two languages, and with a sincerity in his fury that almost convinced me I had, in some way, sinned against the harmony of the universe. I could hardly see him, but began to think he would work himself into a fit.

"Suddenly he ceased, and I could hear him snorting and blowing like a porpoise. I said:

" 'What steamer is this, pray?'

" 'Eh? What's this? And who are you?'

" 'Castaway crew of an English bark burnt at sea. We came here tonight. I am the second mate. The captain is in the longboat, and wishes to know if you would give us a passage somewhere.'

" 'Oh, my goodness! I say. . . . This is the *Celestial* from Singapore on her return trip. I'll arrange with your captain in the morning, . . . and, . . . I say, . . . did you hear me just now?'

" 'I should think the whole bay heard you.'

" 'I thought you were a shoreboat. Now, look here—this infernal lazy scoundrel of a caretaker has gone to sleep again—curse him. The light is out, and I nearly ran foul of the end of this damned jetty. This is the third time he plays me this trick. Now, I ask you, can anybody stand this kind of thing? It's enough to drive a man out of his mind. I'll report him. . . . I'll get the Assistant Resident to give him the sack, by—! See—there's no light. It's out, isn't it? I take you to witness the light's out. There should be a light, you know. A red light on the—'

" 'There was a light,' I said, mildly.

" 'But it's out, man! What's the use of talking like this? You can see for yourself it's out—don't you? If you had to take a valuable steamer along this Godforsaken coast you would want a light, too. I'll kick him from end to end of his miserable wharf. You'll see if I don't. I will—'

" 'So I may tell my captain you'll take us?' I broke in.

" 'Yes, I'll take you. Good night,' he said, brusquely.

"I pulled back, made fast again to the jetty, and then went to sleep at last. I had faced the silence of the East. I had heard some of its language. But when I opened my eyes again the silence was as complete as though it had never been broken. I was lying in a flood of light, and the sky had never looked so far, so high, before. I opened my eyes and lay without moving.

"And then I saw the men of the East—they were looking at me. The whole length of the jetty was full of people. I saw brown, bronze, yellow faces, the black eyes, the glitter, the color of an Eastern crowd. And all these beings stared without a murmur, without a sigh, without a movement. They stared down at the boats, at the sleeping men who at night had come to them from the sea. Nothing moved. The fronds of palms stood still against the sky. Not a branch stirred along the shore, and the brown roofs of hidden houses peeped through the green foliage, through the big leaves that hung shining and still like leaves forged of heavy metal. This was the East of the ancient navigators, so old, so mysterious, resplendent and somber, living and unchanged, full of danger and promise. And these were the men. I sat up suddenly. A wave of movement passed through the crowd from end to end, passed along the heads, swayed the bodies, ran along the jetty like a ripple on the water, like a breath of wind on a field—and all was still again. I see it now—the wide sweep of the bay, the glittering sands, the wealth of green infinite and varied, the sea blue like the sea of a dream, the crowd of attentive faces, the blaze of vivid color—the water reflecting it all, the curve of the shore, the jetty, the high-sterned outlandish craft floating still, and the three boats with the tired men from the West sleeping, unconscious of the land and the people and of the violence of sunshine. They slept thrown across the thwarts, curled on bottom-boards, in the careless attitudes of death. The head of the old skipper, leaning back in the stern of the longboat, had fallen on his breast, and he looked as though he would never wake. Farther out old Mahon's face was upturned to the sky, with the long white beard spread out on his breast, as though he had been shot where he sat at the tiller; and a man, all in a heap in the bows of the boat, slept with both arms embracing the stemhead and with his cheek laid on the gunwale. The East looked at them without a sound.

"I have known its fascination since; I have seen the mysterious shores, the still water, the lands of brown nations, where a stealthy Nemesis lies in wait, pursues, overtakes so many of the conquering race, who are proud of their wisdom, of their knowledge, of their strength. But for me all the East is contained in that vision of my youth. It is all in that moment when I opened my young eyes on it. I came upon it from a tussle with the sea—and I was young—and I saw it looking at me. And this is all that is left of it! Only a moment; a moment of strength, of romance, of glamour— of youth! . . . A flick of sunshine upon a strange shore, the time to remember, the time for a sigh, and—good-by!—Night—Good-by . . . !"

He drank.

"Ah! The good old time—the good old time. Youth and the sea. Glamour and the sea! The good, strong sea, the salt, bitter sea, that could whisper to you and roar at you and knock your breath out of you."

He drank again.

"By all that's wonderful it is the sea, I believe, the sea itself—or is it youth alone? Who can tell? But you here—you all had something out of life: money, love— whatever one gets on shore—and, tell me, wasn't that the best time, that time when we were young at sea; young and had nothing, on the sea that gives nothing, except hard knocks—and sometimes a chance to feel your strength—that only—that you all regret?"

And we all nodded at him: the man of finance, the man of accounts, the man of law, we all nodded at him over the polished table that like a still sheet of brown water reflected our faces, lined, wrinkled; our faces marked by toil, by deceptions, by success, by love; our weary eyes looking still, looking always, looking anxiously for something out of life, that while it is expected is already gone—has passed unseen, in a sigh, in a flash—together with the youth, with the strength, with the romance of illusions.